Archaeologist and anthropologist **Steven Erikson** is the bestselling author of the genre-defining The Malazan Book of the Fallen, a multi-volume epic fantasy that has been hailed a masterwork of the imagination and one of the top ten fantasy series of all time. The first novel in the series, *Gardens of the Moon*, was shortlisted for the World Fantasy Award. He has also written several novellas set in the same world. *Forge of Darkness* is the first Kharkanas novel and takes readers back to the origins of the Malazan world. *Fall of Light* continues this epic tale. A lifelong science fiction reader, he has also written fiction affectionately parodying a long-running SF television series and *Rejoice*, a novel of first contact. *The God is Not Willing* is the opening chapter in a new sequence – The Tales of Witness – and is set in the world of the Malazan Empire, ten years after the events recounted in *The Crippled God*.

Steven Erikson lives in Victoria, Canada. To find out more, visit www.steven-erikson.org – and you can also find him on Facebook: Steven Erikson – Author

www.penguin.co.uk

Acclaim for Steven Erikson's
THE MALAZAN BOOK OF THE FALLEN

'Erikson is an extraordinary writer . . . my advice to anyone
who might listen to me is: treat yourself'
STEPHEN R. DONALDSON

'Give me the evocation of a rich, complex and yet ultimately
unknowable other world, with a compelling suggestion of intricate
history and mythology and lore. Give me mystery amid the grand
narrative . . . Give me a world in which every sea hides a crumbled
Atlantis, every ruin has a tale to tell, every broken blade is a silent
legacy of struggles unknown. Give me, in other words, the fantasy
work of Steven Erikson . . . a master of lost and forgotten
epochs, a weaver of ancient epics'
SALON.COM

'I stand slack-jawed in awe of *The Malazan Book of the Fallen*.
This masterwork of the imagination may be the high
watermark of epic fantasy'
GLEN COOK

'The most masterful piece of fiction I have ever read. It has
single-handedly changed everything we thought we knew about
fantasy literature and redefined what is possible'
SF SITE

'Rare is the writer who so fluidly combines a sense of mythic power
and depth of world with fully realized characters and thrilling action,
but Steven Erikson manages it spectacularly'
MICHAEL A. STACKPOLE

'Erikson's magnum opus, *The Malazan Book of the Fallen*,
sits in pole position as the very best and most ambitious
epic fantasy saga ever written'
PAT'S FANTASY HOTLIST

'This is true myth in the making, a drawing upon fantasy to recreate
histories and legends as rich as any found within our culture'
INTERZONE

'Arguably the best fantasy series ever written. This is of course
subject to personal opinion . . . but few can deny that the quality
and ambition of the ten books that make up *The Malazan
Book of the Fallen* are unmatched within the genre'
FANTASY BOOK REVIEW

'Erikson is almost in a league of his own in genre fiction terms – by turns lyrical, bawdy, introspective, poetical and blood-soaked . . . an incredible journey'
BOOK GEEKS

'Erikson . . . is able to create a world that is both absorbing on a human level and full of magical sublimity . . . A wonderfully grand conception . . . splendidly written . . . fiendishly readable'
ADAM ROBERTS

'It's not just the vast imaginative sweep but the quality of prose that lifts this Malazan sequence above the usual run of heroic fantasy. Our author makes you work hard for the rewards of his narrative . . . it's well worth it though'
SFX

'One of the most promising new writers of the past few years, he has more than proved his right to A-list status'
BOOKSELLER

'Erikson's strengths are his grown-up characters and his ability to create a world every bit as intricate and messy as our own'
J. V. JONES

'An author who never disappoints on delivering stunning and hard-edged fantasy is Steven Erikson . . . a master of modern fantasy'
WBQ

'Wondrous voyages, demons and gods abound . . . dense and complex . . . ultimately rewarding'
LOCUS

'Hood's Breath! What a ride!'
KING OF NERDS

'A multi-layered tale of magic and war, loyalty and betrayal. Complexly drawn characters occupy a richly detailed world in this panoramic saga'
LIBRARY JOURNAL

'Gripping, fast-moving, delightfully dark . . . Erikson brings a punchy, mesmerizing writing style into the genre of epic fantasy, making an indelible impression. Utterly engrossing'
ELIZABETH HAYDEN

'Nobody does it better than Erikson . . . a fantastic addition to the best fantasy series around'
SFFWORLD

By Steven Erikson

The Malazan Book of the Fallen
GARDENS OF THE MOON
DEADHOUSE GATES
MEMORIES OF ICE
HOUSE OF CHAINS
MIDNIGHT TIDES
THE BONEHUNTERS
REAPER'S GALE
TOLL THE HOUNDS
DUST OF DREAMS
THE CRIPPLED GOD

THE FIRST COLLECTED TALES OF
BAUCHELAIN AND KORBAL BROACH
THE SECOND COLLECTED TALES OF
BAUCHELAIN AND KORBAL BROACH

The Kharkanas Trilogy
FORGE OF DARKNESS
FALL OF LIGHT

The Tales of Witness
THE GOD IS NOT WILLING

Other fiction
THIS RIVER AWAKENS
THE DEVIL DELIVERED AND OTHER
TALES
WILLFUL CHILD

For more information on Steven Erikson and his books,
see his website at www.steven-erikson.org

Memories of Ice
A Tale of the
Malazan Book of the Fallen

STEVEN ERIKSON

PENGUIN BOOKS

TRANSWORLD PUBLISHERS
Penguin Random House, One Embassy Gardens,
8 Viaduct Gardens, London SW11 7BW
www.penguin.co.uk

Transworld is part of the Penguin Random House group of companies
whose addresses can be found at global.penguinrandomhouse.com

Penguin
Random House
UK

First published in Great Britain in 2001 by Bantam Press
an imprint of Transworld Publishers
Bantam edition published 2002
Penguin paperback edition published 2024

Copyright © Steven Erikson 2001

Maps copyright © Neil Gower

Steven Erikson has asserted his right under the Copyright,
Designs and Patents Act 1988 to be identified as the author of this work.

This book is a work of fiction and, except in the case of historical fact, any
resemblance to actual persons, living or dead, is purely coincidental.

Every effort has been made to obtain the necessary permissions with
reference to copyright material, both illustrative and quoted. We apologize for
any omissions in this respect and will be pleased to make the appropriate
acknowledgements in any future edition.

A CIP catalogue record for this book
is available from the British Library.

ISBN
9781804995532 (B format)

Typeset in Goudy by Falcon Oast Graphic Art Ltd.
Printed and bound in Great Britain by Clays Ltd, Elcograf S.p.A.

The authorized representative in the EEA is Penguin Random House Ireland,
Morrison Chambers, 32 Nassau Street, Dublin D02 YH68.

Penguin Random House is committed to a sustainable
future for our business, our readers and our planet. This book is made from
Forest Stewardship Council® certified paper.

MIX
Paper | Supporting
responsible forestry
FSC® C018179

To R. S. Lundin

Acknowledgements

I extend my gratitude to the following for their support and friendship: Clare, Bowen, Mark, David, Chris, Rick, Cam, Courtney; Susan and Peter, David Thomas Sr and Jr, Harriet and Chris and Lily and Mina and Smudge; Patrick Walsh and Simon and Jane. Thanks also to Dave Holden and his friendly staff (Tricia, Cindy, Liz, Tanis, Barbara, Joan, Nadia, Amanda, Tony, Andi and Jody) of the Pizza Place, for the table and the refills. And thanks to John Meaney for the disgusting details on dead seeds.

Contents

Contents

GENABACKIS
The Pannion War ca. 1160 Burns Sleep

- PANNION DOMIN
- MALAZAN OCCUPATION
- ✗ BATTLES

SCALE
0   30   100 leagues

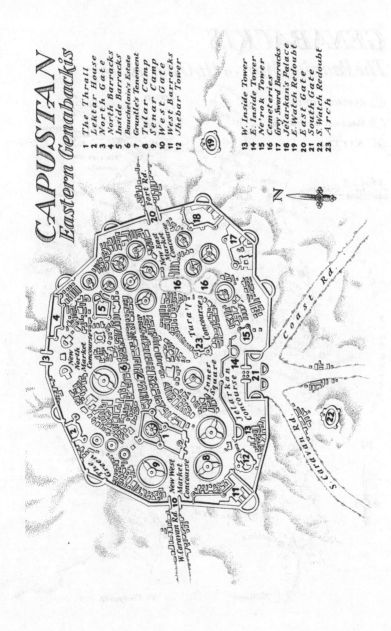

CAPUSTAN
Eastern Genabackis

1 The Thrall
2 Lektar House
3 North Gate
4 North Barracks
5 Inside Barracks
6 Bauchelain's Estate
7 Gruntle's Tenement
8 Tutar Camp
9 Senan Camp
10 West Gate
11 West Barracks
12 Jhebar Tower
13 W. Inside Tower
14 E. Inside Tower
15 Ne'rok Tower
16 Cemeteries
17 Grey Sword Barracks
18 Jelarkan's Palace
19 E. Watch Redoubt
20 East Gate
21 South Gate
22 S. Watch Redoubt
23 Arch

N

DRAMATIS PERSONAE

THE CARAVANSERAI

Gruntle, a caravan guard
Stonny Menackis, a caravan guard
Harllo, a caravan guard
Buke, a caravan guard
Bauchelain, an explorer
Korbal Broach, his silent partner
Emancipor Reese, a manservant
Keruli, a trader
Marble, a sorceror

In Capustan

Brukhalian, Mortal Sword of Fener's Reve (the Grey Swords)
Itkovian, Shield Anvil of Fener's Reve (the Grey Swords)
Karnadas, Destriant of Fener's Reve (the Grey Swords)
Recruit Velbara (the Grey Swords)
Master Sergeant Norul (the Grey Swords)
Farakalian (the Grey Swords)
Nakalian (the Grey Swords)
Torun (the Grey Swords)
Sidlis (the Grey Swords)
Nilbanas (the Grey Swords)
Jelarkan, prince and ruler of Capustan
Arard, prince and ruler in absentia of Coral
Rath'Fener (Priest of the Mask Council)
Rath'Shadowthrone (Priest of the Mask Council)
Rath'Queen of Dreams (Priestess of the Mask Council)
Rath'Hood (Priest of the Mask Council)
Rath'D'rek (Priest of the Mask Council)

Rath'Trake (Priest of the Mask Council)
Rath'Burn (Priestess of the Mask Council)
Rath'Togg (Priest of the Mask Council)
Rath'Fanderay (Priestess of the Mask Council)
Rath'Dessembrae (Priestess of the Mask Council)
Rath'Oponn (Priest of the Mask Council)
Rath'Beru (Priest of the Mask Council)

ONEARM'S HOST

Dujek Onearm, commander of renegade Malazan army
Whiskeyjack, second-in-command of renegade Malazan army
Twist, commander of the Black Moranth
Artanthos, standard-bearer of renegade Malazan army
Barack, a liaison officer
Hareb, a noble-born captain
Ganoes Paran, Captain, Bridgeburners
Antsy, sergeant, 7th Squad, Bridgeburners
Picker, corporal, 7th Squad, Bridgeburners
Detoran, soldier, 7th Squad
Spindle, mage and sapper, 7th Squad
Blend, soldier, 7th Squad
Mallet, healer, 9th Squad
Hedge, sapper, 9th Squad
Trotts, soldier, 9th Squad
Quick Ben, mage, 9th Squad
Aimless (Bridgeburner corporal)
Bucklund (Bridgeburner sergeant)
Runter (Bridgeburner sapper)
Mulch (Bridgeburner healer)
Bluepearl (Bridgeburner mage)
Shank (Bridgeburner mage)
Toes (Bridgeburner mage)

Brood's Host

Caladan Brood, warlord of liberation army on Genabackis
Anomander Rake, Lord of Moon's Spawn
Kallor, the High King, Brood's second-in-command
The Mhybe, matron of the Rhivi Tribes
Silverfox, the Rhivi Reborn
Korlat, a Tiste Andii Soletaken
Orfantal, Korlat's brother
Hurlochel, an outrider in the liberation army
Crone, a Great Raven and companion to Anomander Rake

The Barghast

Humbrall Taur, warchief of the White Face Clan
Hetan, his daughter
Cafal, his first son
Netok, his second son

Darujhistan Envoys

Coll, an ambassador
Estraysian D'Arle, a councilman
Baruk, an alchemist
Kruppe, a citizen
Murillio, a citizen

The T'lan Imass

Kron, ruler of the Kron T'lan Imass
Cannig Tol, clan chief
Bek Okhan, a Bonecaster
Pran Chole, a Bonecaster
Okral Lom, a Bonecaster
Bendal Home, a Bonecaster

Ay Estos, a Bonecaster
Olar Ethil, the First Bonecaster and First Soletaken
Tool, the Shorn, once First Sword
Kilava, a renegade Bonecaster
Lanas Tog, of Kerluhm T'lan Imass

THE PANNION DOMIN

The Seer, priest-king of the Domin
Ultentha, Septarch of Coral
Kulpath, Septarch of the besieging army
Inal, Septarch of Lest
Anaster, a Tenescowri Child of the Dead Seed
Seerdomin Kahlt

OTHERS

K'rul, an Elder God
Draconus, an Elder God
Sister of Cold Nights, an Elder Goddess
Lady Envy, a resident of Morn
Gethol, a Herald
Treach, a First Hero (the Tiger of Summer)
Toc the Younger, Aral Fayle, a Malazan scout
Garath, a large dog
Baaljagg, a larger wolf
Mok, a Seguleh
Thurule, a Seguleh
Senu, a Seguleh
The Chained One, an unknown ascendant (also known
   as the Crippled God)
The Witch of Tennes
Munug, a Daru artisan
Talamandas, a Barghast sticksnare
Ormulogun, artist in Onearm's Host

Gumble, his critic

Haradas, a Trygalle Trade Guild caravan master

Azra Jael, a marine in Onearm's Host

Straw, a Mott Irregular

Sty, a Mott Irregular

Stump, a Mott Irregular

Job Bole, a Mott Irregular

PROLOGUE

The ancient wars of the T'lan Imass and the Jaghut
saw the world torn asunder. Vast armies contended
on the ravaged lands, the dead piled high, their bone
the bones of hills, their spilled blood the blood of seas.
Sorceries raged until the sky itself was fire . . .

Ancient Histories, Vol. I
Kinicik Karbar'n

Maeth'ki Im (Pogrom of the Rotted Flower), the 33rd Jaghut War
298,665 years before Burn's Sleep

Swallows darted through the clouds of midges dancing over the mudflats. The sky above the marsh remained grey, but it had lost its mercurial wintry gleam, and the warm wind sighing through the air above the ravaged land held the scent of healing.

What had once been the inland freshwater sea the Imass called Jaghra Til – born from the shattering of the Jaghut ice-fields – was now in its own death-throes. The pallid overcast was reflected in dwindling pools and stretches of knee-deep water for as far south as the eye could scan, but none the less, newly birthed land dominated the vista.

The breaking of the sorcery that had raised the glacial age returned to the region the old, natural seasons, but the memories of mountain-high ice lingered. The exposed bedrock to the north was gouged and scraped, its basins filled with boulders. The heavy silts that had been the floor of the inland sea still bubbled with escaping gases, as the land, freed of the enormous weight with the glaciers' passing eight years past, continued its slow ascent.

Jaghra Til's life had been short, yet the silts that had settled on its bottom were thick. And treacherous.

Pran Chole, Bonecaster of Cannig Tol's clan among the Kron Imass, sat motionless atop a mostly buried boulder along an ancient beach ridge. The descent before him was snarled in low, wiry grasses and withered driftwood. Twelve paces beyond, the land dropped slightly, then stretched out into a broad basin of mud.

Three ranag had become trapped in a boggy sinkhole twenty paces into the basin. A bull male, his mate and their calf, ranged in a pathetic defensive circle. Mired and vulnerable, they must have seemed easy kills for the pack of ay that found them.

But the land was treacherous indeed. The large tundra wolves had succumbed to the same fate as the ranag. Pran Chole counted six ay, including a yearling. Tracks indicated that another yearling had circled the sinkhole dozens of times before wandering westward, doomed no doubt to die in solitude.

How long ago had this drama occurred? There was no way to tell. The mud had hardened on ranag and ay alike, forming cloaks of clay latticed with cracks. Spots of bright green showed where windborn seeds had germinated, and the Bonecaster was reminded of his visions when spirit-walking – a host of mundane details twisted into something unreal. For the beasts, the struggle had become eternal, hunter and hunted locked together for all time.

Someone padded to his side, crouched down beside him.

Pran Chole's tawny eyes remained fixed on the frozen tableau. The rhythm of footsteps told the Bonecaster the identity of his companion, and now came the warm-blooded smells that were as much a signature as resting eyes upon the man's face.

Cannig Tol spoke. 'What lies beneath the clay, Bonecaster?'

'Only that which has shaped the clay itself, Clan Leader.'

'You see no omen in these beasts?'

Pran Chole smiled. 'Do you?'

Cannig Tol considered for a time, then said, 'Ranag are gone from these lands. So too the ay. We see before us an ancient battle. These statements have depth, for they stir my soul.'

'Mine as well,' the Bonecaster conceded.

'We hunted the ranag until they were no more, and this brought starvation to the ay, for we had also hunted the tenag until they were no more as well. The agkor who walk with the bhederin would not share with the ay, and now

22

the tundra is empty. From this, I conclude that we were wasteful and thoughtless in our hunting.'

'Yet the need to feed our own young . . .'

'The need for more young was great.'

'It remains so, Clan Leader.'

Cannig Tol grunted. 'The Jaghut were powerful in these lands, Bonecaster. They did not flee – not at first. You know the cost in Imass blood.'

'And the land yields its bounty to answer that cost.'

'To serve our war.'

'Thus, the depths are stirred.'

The Clan Leader nodded and was silent.

Pran Chole waited. In their shared words they still tracked the skin of things. Revelation of the muscle and bone was yet to come. But Cannig Tol was no fool, and the wait was not long.

'We are as those beasts.'

The Bonecaster's eyes shifted to the south horizon, tightened.

Cannig Tol continued, 'We are the clay, and our endless war against the Jaghut is the struggling beast beneath. The surface is shaped by what lies beneath.' He gestured with one hand. 'And before us now, in these creatures slowly turning to stone, is the curse of eternity.'

There was still more. Pran Chole said nothing.

'Ranag and ay,' Cannig Tol resumed. 'Almost gone from the mortal realm. Hunter and hunted both.'

'To the very bones,' the Bonecaster whispered.

'Would that you had seen an omen,' the Clan Leader muttered, rising.

Pran Chole also straightened. 'Would that I had,' he agreed in a tone that only faintly echoed Cannig Tol's wry, sardonic utterance.

'Are we close, Bonecaster?'

Pran Chole glanced down at his shadow, studied the antlered silhouette, the figure hinted within furred cape, ragged hides and headdress. The sun's angle made him seem tall – almost as tall as a Jaghut. 'Tomorrow,' he said. 'They are weakening. A night of travel will weaken them yet more.'

'Good. Then the clan shall camp here tonight.'

The Bonecaster listened as Cannig Tol made his way back down to where the others waited. With darkness, Pran Chole would spiritwalk. Into the whispering earth, seeking those of his own kind. While their quarry was weakening, Cannig Tol's clan was yet weaker. Less than a dozen adults remained. When pursuing Jaghut, the distinction of hunter and hunted had little meaning.

He lifted his head and sniffed the crepuscular air. Another Bonecaster wandered this land. The taint was unmistakable. He wondered who it was, wondered why it travelled alone, bereft of clan and kin. And, knowing that even as he had sensed its presence so it in turn had sensed his, he wondered why it had not yet sought them out.

She pulled herself clear of the mud and dropped down onto the sandy bank, her breath coming in harsh, laboured gasps. Her son and daughter squirmed free of her leaden arms, crawled further onto the island's modest hump.

The Jaghut mother lowered her head until her brow rested against the cool, damp sand. Grit pressed into the skin of her forehead with raw insistence. The burns there were too recent to have healed, nor were they likely to – she was defeated, and death had only to await the arrival of her hunters.

They were mercifully competent, at least. These Imass cared nothing for torture. A swift killing blow. For her, then for her children. And with them – with this meagre, tattered family – the last of the Jaghut would vanish from this continent. Mercy arrived in many guises. Had they not joined in chaining Raest, they would all – Imass and Jaghut both – have found themselves kneeling before that Tyrant. A temporary truce of expedience. She'd known enough to flee once the chaining was done; she'd known, even then, that the Imass clan would resume the pursuit.

24

The mother felt no bitterness, but that made her no less desperate.

Sensing a new presence on the small island, her head snapped up. Her children had frozen in place, staring up in terror at the Imass woman who now stood before them. The mother's grey eyes narrowed. 'Clever, Bonecaster. My senses were tuned only to those behind us. Very well, be done with it.'

The young, black-haired woman smiled. 'No bargains, Jaghut? You always seek bargains to spare the lives of your children. Have you broken the kin-threads with these two, then? They seem young for that.'

'Bargains are pointless. Your kind never agree to them.'

'No, yet still *your* kind try.'

'I shall not. Kill us, then. Swiftly.'

The Imass was wearing the skin of a panther. Her eyes were as black and seemed to match its shimmer in the dying light. She looked well fed, her large, swollen breasts indicating she had recently birthed.

The Jaghut mother could not read the woman's expression, only that it lacked the typical grim certainty she usually associated with the strange, rounded faces of the Imass.

The Bonecaster spoke. 'I have enough Jaghut blood on my hands. I leave you to the Kron clan that will find you tomorrow.'

'To me,' the mother growled, 'it matters naught which of you kills us, only that you kill us.'

The woman's broad mouth quirked. 'I can see your point.'

Weariness threatened to overwhelm the Jaghut mother, but she managed to pull herself into a sitting position. 'What,' she asked between gasps, 'do you want?'

'To offer you a bargain.'

Breath catching, the Jaghut mother stared into the Bonecaster's dark eyes, and saw nothing of mockery. Her gaze then dropped, for the briefest of moments, on her son and daughter, then back up to hold steady on the woman's own.

The Imass slowly nodded.

The earth had cracked some time in the past, a wound of such depth as to birth a molten river wide enough to stretch from horizon to horizon. Vast and black, the river of stone and ash reached southwestward, down to the distant sea. Only the smallest of plants had managed to find purchase, and the Bonecaster's passage – a Jaghut child in the crook of each arm – raised sultry clouds of dust that hung motionless in her wake.

She judged the boy at perhaps five years of age; his sister perhaps four. Neither seemed entirely aware, and clearly neither had understood their mother when she'd hugged them goodbye. The long flight down the L'amath and across the Jagra Til had driven them both into shock. No doubt witnessing the ghastly death of their father had not helped matters.

They clung to her with their small, grubby hands, grim reminders of the child she had but recently lost. Before long, both began suckling at her breasts, evincing desperate hunger. Some time later, the children slept.

The lava flow thinned as she approached the coast. A range of hills rose into distant mountains on her right. A level plain stretched directly before her, ending at a ridge half a league distant. Though she could not see it, she knew that just the other side of the ridge, the land slumped down to the sea. The plain itself was marked by regular humps, and the Bonecaster paused to study them. The mounds were arrayed in concentric circles, and at the centre was a larger dome – all covered in a mantle of lava and ash. The rotted tooth of a ruined tower rose from the plain's edge, at the base of the first line of hills. Those hills, as she had noted the first time she had visited this place, were themselves far too evenly spaced to be natural.

The Bonecaster lifted her head. The mingled scents were

unmistakable, one ancient and dead, the other . . . less so. The boy stirred in her clasp, but remained asleep.

'Ah,' she murmured, 'you sense it as well.'

Skirting the plain, she walked towards the blackened tower.

The warren's gate was just beyond the ragged edifice, suspended in the air at about six times her height. She saw it as a red welt, a thing damaged, but no longer bleeding. She could not recognize the warren – the old damage obscured the portal's characteristics. Unease rippled faintly through her.

The Bonecaster set the children down by the tower, then sat on a block of tumbled masonry. Her gaze fell to the two young Jaghut, still curled in sleep, lying on their beds of ash. 'What choice?' she whispered. 'It must be Omtose Phellack. It certainly isn't Tellann. Starvald Demelain? Unlikely.' Her eyes were pulled to the plain, narrowing on the mound rings. 'Who dwelt here? Who else was in the habit of building in stone?' She fell silent for a long moment, then swung her attention back to the ruin. 'This tower is the final proof, for it is naught else but Jaghut, and such a structure would not be raised this close to an inimical warren. No, the gate is Omtose Phellack. It must be so.'

Still, there were additional risks. An adult Jaghut in the warren beyond, coming upon two children not of its own blood, might as easily kill them as adopt them. 'Then their deaths stain another's hands, a Jaghut's.' Scant comfort, that distinction. *It matters naught which of you kills us, only that you kill us.* The breath hissed between the woman's teeth. 'What choice?' she asked again.

She would let them sleep a little longer. Then, she would send them through the gate. A word to the boy – *take care of your sister. The journey will not be long.* And to them both – *your mother waits beyond.* A lie, but they would need courage. *If she cannot find you, then one of her kin will. Go then, to safety, to salvation.*

After all, what could be worse than death?

She rose as they approached. Pran Chole tested the air, frowned. The Jaghut had not unveiled her warren. Even more disconcerting, where were her children?

'She greets us with calm,' Cannig Tol muttered.

'She does,' the Bonecaster agreed.

'I've no trust in that – we should kill her immediately.'

'She would speak with us,' Pran Chole said.

'A deadly risk, to appease her desire.'

'I cannot disagree, Clan Leader. Yet ... what has she done with her children?'

'Can you not sense them?'

Pran Chole shook his head. 'Prepare your spearmen,' he said, stepping forward.

There was peace in her eyes, so clear an acceptance of her own imminent death that the Bonecaster was shaken. Pran Chole walked through shin-deep water, then stepped onto the island's sandy bank to stand face to face with the Jaghut. 'What have you done with them?' he demanded.

The mother smiled, lips peeling back to reveal her tusks. 'Gone.'

'Where?'

'Beyond your reach, Bonecaster.'

Pran Chole's frown deepened. 'These are our lands. There is no place here that is beyond our reach. Have you slain them with your own hands, then?'

The Jaghut cocked her head, studied the Imass. 'I had always believed you were united in your hatred for our kind. I had always believed that such concepts as compassion and mercy were alien to your natures.'

The Bonecaster stared at the woman for a long moment, then his gaze dropped away, past her, and scanned the soft clay ground. 'An Imass has been here,' he said. 'A woman. The Bonecaster—' *the one I could not find in my spiritwalk. The one who chose not to be found.* 'What has she done?'

28

'She has explored this land,' the Jaghut replied. 'She has found a gate far to the south. It is Omtose Phellack.'

'I am glad,' Pran Chole said, 'I am not a mother.' *And you, woman, should be glad I am not cruel.* He gestured. Heavy spears flashed past the Bonecaster. Six long, fluted heads of flint punched through the skin covering the Jaghut's chest. She staggered, then folded to the ground in a clatter of shafts.

Thus ended the thirty-third Jaghut War.

Pran Chole whirled. 'We've no time for a pyre. We must strike southward. Quickly.'

Cannig Tol stepped forward as his warriors went to retrieve their weapons. The Clan Leader's eyes narrowed on the Bonecaster. 'What distresses you?'

'A renegade Bonecaster has taken the children.'

'South?'

'To Morn.'

The Clan Leader's brows knitted.

'The renegade would save this woman's children. The renegade believes the Rent to be Omtose Phellack.'

Pran Chole watched the blood leave Cannig Tol's face. 'Go to Morn, Bonecaster,' the Clan Leader whispered. 'We are not cruel. Go now.'

Pran Chole bowed. The Tellann warren engulfed him.

The faintest release of her power sent the two Jaghut children upward, into the gate's maw. The girl cried out a moment before reaching it, a longing wail for her mother, who she imagined waited beyond. Then the two small figures vanished within.

The Bonecaster sighed and continued to stare upward, seeking any evidence that the passage had gone awry. It seemed, however, that no wounds had reopened, no gush of wild power bled from the portal. Did it look different? She could not be sure. This was new land for her; she had nothing of the bone-bred sensitivity that she had known all her life among the lands of the Tarad clan, in the heart of the First Empire.

The Tellann warren opened behind her. The woman spun round, moments from veering into her Soletaken form.

An arctic fox bounded into view, slowed upon seeing her, then sembled back into its Imass form. She saw before her a young man, wearing the skin of his totem animal across his shoulders, and a battered antler headdress. His expression was twisted with fear, his eyes not on her, but on the portal beyond.

The woman smiled. 'I greet you, fellow Bonecaster. Yes, I have sent them through. They are beyond the reach of your vengeance, and this pleases me.'

His tawny eyes fixed on her. 'Who are you? What clan?'

'I have left my clan, but I was once counted among the Logros. I am named Kilava.'

'You should have let me find you last night,' Pran Chole said. 'I would then have been able to convince you that a swift death was the greater mercy for those children than what you have done here, Kilava.'

'They are young enough to be adopted—'

'You have come to the place called Morn,' Pran Chole interjected, his voice cold. 'To the ruins of an ancient city—'

'Jaghut—'

'Not Jaghut! This tower, yes, but it was built long afterward, in the time between the city's destruction and the T'ol Ara'd – this flow of lava which but buried something already dead.' He raised a hand, pointed towards the suspended gate. 'It was this – this wounding – that destroyed the city, Kilava. The warren beyond – do you not understand? It is *not* Omtose Phellack! Tell me this – how are such wounds sealed? You know the answer, Bonecaster!'

The woman slowly turned, studied the Rent. 'If a soul sealed that wound, then it should have been freed . . . when the children arrived—'

'Freed,' Pran Chole hissed, '*in exchange!*'

Trembling, Kilava faced him again. 'Then where is it? Why has it not appeared?'

Pran Chole turned to study the central mound on the plain. 'Oh,' he whispered, 'but it has.' He glanced back at his fellow Bonecaster. 'Tell me, will you in turn give up your life for those children? They are trapped now, in an eternal nightmare of pain. Does your compassion extend to sacrificing yourself in yet another exchange?' He studied her, then sighed. 'I thought not, so wipe away those tears, Kilava. Hypocrisy ill suits a Bonecaster.'

'What . . .' the woman managed after a time, 'what has been freed?'

Pran Chole shook his head. He studied the central mound again. 'I am not sure, but we shall have to do something about it, sooner or later. I suspect we have plenty of time. The creature must now free itself of its tomb, and that has been thoroughly warded. More, there is the T'ol Ara'd's mantle of stone still clothing the barrow.' After a moment, he added. 'But time we shall have.'

'What do you mean?'

'The Gathering has been called. The Ritual of Tellann awaits us, Bonecaster.'

She spat. 'You are all insane. To choose immortality for the sake of a war – madness. I shall defy the call, Bonecaster.'

He nodded. 'Yet the Ritual shall be done. I have spirit-walked into the future, Kilava. I have seen my withered face of two hundred thousand and more years hence. We shall have our eternal war.'

Bitterness filled Kilava's voice. 'My brother will be pleased.'

'Who is your brother?'

'Onos T'oolan, the First Sword.'

Pran Chole turned at this. 'You are the Defier. You slaughtered your clan – your kin—'

'To break the link and thus achieve freedom, yes. Alas,

31

my eldest brother's skills more than matched mine. Yet now we are *both* free, though what I celebrate, Onos T'oolan curses.' She wrapped her arms around herself, and Pran Chole saw upon her layers and layers of pain. Hers was a freedom he did not envy. She spoke again. 'This city, then. Who built it.'

'K'Chain Che'Malle.'

'I know the name, but little else of them.'

Pran Chole nodded. 'We shall, I expect, learn.'

II

Continents of Korelri and Jacuruku, in the Time of Dying
119,736 years before Burn's Sleep (three years after the Fall of
the Crippled God)

The Fall had shattered a continent. Forests had burned, the firestorms lighting the horizons in every direction, bathing crimson the heaving ash-filled clouds blanketing the sky. The conflagration had seemed unending, world-devouring, weeks into months, and through it all could be heard the screams of a god.

Pain gave birth to rage. Rage, to poison, an infection sparing no-one.

Scattered survivors remained, reduced to savagery, wandering a landscape pocked with huge craters now filled with murky, lifeless water, the sky churning endlessly above them. Kinship had been dismembered, love had proved a burden too costly to carry. They ate what they could, often each other, and scanned the ravaged world around them with rapacious intent.

One figure walked this landscape alone. Wrapped in rotting rags, he was of average height, his features blunt and unprepossessing. There was a dark cast to his face, a heavy inflexibility in his eyes. He walked as if gathering suffering unto himself, unmindful of its vast weight; walked as if incapable of yielding, of denying the gifts of his own spirit.

In the distance, ragged bands eyed the figure as he strode, step by step, across what was left of the continent that would one day be called Korelri. Hunger might have driven them closer, but there were no fools left among the survivors of the Fall, and so they maintained a watchful distance, curiosity dulled by fear. For the man was an ancient god, and he walked among them.

Beyond the suffering he absorbed, K'rul would have will-ingly embraced their broken souls, yet he had fed – was feeding – on the blood spilled onto this land, and the truth was this: the power born of that would be needed.

In K'rul's wake, men and women killed men, killed women, killed children. Dark slaughter was the river the Elder God rode.

Elder Gods embodied a host of harsh unpleasantries.

The foreign god had been torn apart in his descent to earth. He had come down in pieces, in streaks of flame. His pain was fire, screams and thunder, a voice that had been heard by half the world. Pain, and outrage. And, K'rul reflected, grief. It would be a long time before the foreign god could begin to reclaim the remaining fragments of its life, and so begin to unveil its nature. K'rul feared that day's arrival. From such a shattering could only come madness.

The summoners were dead. Destroyed by what they had called down upon them. There was no point in hating them, no need to conjure up images of what they in truth deserved by way of punishment. They had, after all, been desperate. Desperate enough to part the fabric of chaos, to open a way into an alien, remote realm; to then lure a curious god of that realm closer, ever closer to the trap they had prepared. The summoners sought power.

All to destroy one man.

The Elder God had crossed the ruined continent, had looked upon the still-living flesh of the Fallen God, had seen the unearthly maggots that crawled forth from that rotting, endlessly pulsing meat and broken bone. Had seen what those maggots flowered into. Even now, as he reached the battered shoreline of Jacuruku, the ancient sister continent to Korelri, they wheeled above him on their broad, black wings. Sensing the power within him, they were hungry for its taste.

But a strong god could ignore the scavengers that trailed in his wake, and K'rul was a strong god. Temples had been raised in his name. Blood had for generations soaked count-less altars in worship of him. The nascent cities were wreathed in the smoke of forges, pyres, the red glow of humanity's dawn. The First Empire had risen, on a continent half a world away from where K'rul now walked. An empire of humans, born from the legacy of the T'lan Imass, from whom it took its name.

But it had not been alone for long. Here, on Jacuruku, in the shadow of long-dead K'Chain Che'Malle ruins, another empire had emerged. Brutal, a devourer of souls, its ruler was a warrior without equal.

K'rul had come to destroy him, had come to snap the chains of twelve million slaves – even the Jaghut Tyrants had not commanded such heartless mastery over their subjects. No, it took a mortal human to achieve this level of tyranny over his kin.

Two other Elder Gods were converging on the Kallorian Empire. The decision had been made. The three – last of the Elder – would bring to a close the High King's despotic rule. K'rul could sense his companions. Both were close; both had been comrades once, but they all – K'rul included – had changed, had drifted far apart. This would mark the first conjoining in millennia.

He could sense a fourth presence as well, a savage, ancient beast following his spoor. A beast of the earth, of winter's frozen breath, a beast with white fur bloodied, wounded almost unto death by the Fall. A beast with but one surviving eye to look upon the destroyed land that had once been its home – long before the empire's rise. Trailing, but coming no closer. And, K'rul well knew, it would remain a distant observer of all that was about to occur. The Elder god could spare it no sorrow, yet was not indifferent to its pain.

We each survive as we must, and when time comes to die, we find our places of solitude . . .

The Kallorian Empire had spread to every shoreline of Jacuruku, yet K'rul saw no-one as he took his first steps inland. Lifeless wastes stretched on all sides. The air was grey with ash and dust, the skies overhead churning like lead in a smith's cauldron. The Elder God experienced the first breath of unease, sidling chill across his soul.

Above him the god-spawned scavengers cackled as they wheeled.

A familiar voice spoke in K'rul's mind. *Brother, I am upon the north shore.*

'And I the west.'

Are you troubled?

'I am. All is . . . dead.'

Incinerated. The heat remains deep beneath the beds of ash. Ash . . . and bone.

A third voice spoke. *Brothers, I am come from the south, where once dwelt the cities. All destroyed. The echoes of a continent's death-cry still linger. Are we deceived? Is this illusion?*

K'rul addressed the first Elder who had spoken in his mind. 'Draconus, I too feel that death-cry. Such pain . . . indeed, more dreadful in its aspect than that of the Fallen One. If not a deception as our sister suggests, what has he done?'

We have stepped onto this land, and so all share what you sense, K'rul, Draconus replied. *I, too, am not certain of its truth. Sister, do you approach the High King's abode?*

The third voice replied, *I do, brother Draconus. Would you and brother K'rul join me now, that we may confront this mortal as one?*

'We shall.'

Warrens opened, one to the far north, the other directly before K'rul.

The two Elder Gods joined their sister upon a ragged hilltop where wind swirled through the ashes, spinning funereal wreaths skyward. Directly before them, on a heap of burnt bones, was a throne.

The man seated upon it was smiling. 'As you can see,' he rasped after a moment of scornful regard, 'I have . . . prepared for your arrival. Oh yes, I knew you were coming. Draconus, of Tiam's kin. K'rul, Opener of the Paths.' His grey eyes swung to the third Elder. 'And *you*. My dear, I was under the impression that you had abandoned your . . . old self. Walking among the mortals, playing the role of middling sorceress – such a deadly risk, though perhaps this is what entices you so to the mortal game. You've stood on fields of battles, woman. One stray arrow . . .' He slowly shook his head.

'We have come,' K'rul said, 'to end your reign of terror.'

Kallor's brows rose. 'You would take from me all that I have worked so hard to achieve? Fifty years, dear rivals, to conquer an entire continent. Oh, perhaps Ardatha still held out – always late in sending me my rightful tribute – but I ignored such petty gestures. She has fled, did you know? The bitch. Do you imagine yourselves the first to challenge me? The Circle brought down a foreign god. Aye, the effort went . . . awry, thus sparing me the task of killing the fools with my own hand. And the Fallen One? Well, he'll not recover for some time, and even then, do you truly imagine he will accede to anyone's bidding? I would have—'

'Enough,' Draconus growled. 'Your prattling grows wearisome, Kallor.'

'Very well,' the High King sighed. He leaned forward. 'You've come to liberate my people from my tyrannical rule. Alas, I am not one to relinquish such things. Not to you, not to anyone.' He settled back, waved a languid hand. 'Thus, what you would refuse me, I now refuse you.'

36

Though the truth was before K'rul's eyes, he could not believe it. 'What have—'

'*Are you blind?*' Kallor shrieked, clutching at the arms of his throne. 'It is gone! *They* are gone! Break the chains, will you? Go ahead – no, I surrender them! Here, all about you, is *now free*! Dust! Bones! All free!'

'You have in truth incinerated an entire continent?' the sister Elder whispered. 'Jacuruku—'

'Is no more, and never again shall be. What I have unleashed will never heal. Do you understand me? Never. And it is all your fault. Yours. Paved in bone and ash, this noble road you chose to walk. *Your* road.'

'We cannot allow this—'

'It has already happened, you foolish woman!'

K'rul spoke within the minds of his kin. *It must be done. I will fashion a . . . a place for this. Within myself.*

A warren to hold all this? Draconus asked in horror. *My brother—*

No, it must be done. Join with me now, this shaping will not be easy—

It will break you, K'rul, his sister said. *There must be another way.*

None. To leave this continent as it is . . . no, this world is young. To carry such a scar . . .

What of Kallor? Draconus enquired. *What of this . . . this creature?*

We mark him, K'rul replied. *We know his deepest desire, do we not?*

And the span of his life?

Long, my friends.

Agreed.

K'rul blinked, fixed his dark, heavy eyes on the High King. 'For this crime, Kallor, we deliver appropriate punishment. Know this: you, Kallor Eiderann Tes'thesula, shall know mortal life unending. Mortal, in the ravages of age, in the pain of wounds and the anguish of despair. In dreams brought to ruin. In love withered. In the shadow of Death's

37

spectre, ever a threat to end what you will not relinquish.'

Draconus spoke, 'Kallor Eiderann Tes'thesula, you shall never *ascend*.'

Their sister said, 'Kallor Eiderann Tes'thesula, each time you rise, you shall then fall. All that you achieve shall turn to dust in your hands. As you have wilfully done here, so it shall be in turn visited upon all that you do.'

'Three voices curse you,' K'rul intoned. 'It is done.'

The man on the throne trembled. His lips drew back in a rictus snarl. 'I shall break you. Each of you. I swear this upon the bones of seven million sacrifices. K'rul, you shall fade from the world, you shall be forgotten. Draconus, what you create shall be turned upon you. And as for you, woman, unhuman hands shall tear your body into pieces, upon a field of battle, yet you shall know no respite – thus, my curse upon you, Sister of Cold Nights. Kallor Eiderann Tes'thesula, one voice, has spoken three curses. Thus.'

They left Kallor upon his throne, upon its heap of bones. They merged their power to draw chains around a continent of slaughter, then pulled it into a warren created for that sole purpose, leaving the land itself bared. To heal.

The effort left K'rul broken, bearing wounds he knew he would carry for all his existence. More, he could already feel the twilight of his worship, the blight of Kallor's curse. To his surprise, the loss pained him less than he would have imagined.

The three stood at the portal of the nascent, lifeless realm, and looked long upon their handiwork.

Then Draconus spoke, 'Since the time of All Darkness, I have been forging a sword.'

Both K'rul and the Sister of Cold Nights turned at this, for they had known nothing of it.

Draconus continued. 'The forging has taken . . . a long time, but I am now nearing completion. The power invested within the sword possesses a . . . a finality.'

38

'Then,' K'rul whispered after a moment's consideration, 'you must make alterations in the final shaping.'

'So it seems. I shall need to think long on this.'

After a long moment, K'rul and his brother turned to their sister.

She shrugged. 'I shall endeavour to guard myself. When my destruction comes, it will be through betrayal and naught else. There can be no precaution against such a thing, lest my life become its own nightmare of suspicion and mistrust. To this, I shall not surrender. Until that moment, I shall continue to play the mortal game.'

'Careful, then,' K'rul murmured, 'whom you choose to fight for.'

'Find a companion,' Draconus advised. 'A worthy one.'

'Wise words from you both. I thank you.'

There was nothing more to be said. The three had come together, with an intent they had now achieved. Perhaps not in the manner they would have wished, but it was done. And the price had been paid. Willingly. Three lives and one, each destroyed. For the one, the beginning of eternal hatred. For the three, a fair exchange.

Elder Gods, it has been said, embodied a host of unpleasantries.

In the distance, the beast watched the three figures part ways. Riven with pain, white fur stained and dripping blood, the gouged pit of its lost eye glittering wet, it held its hulking mass on trembling legs. It longed for death, but death would not come. It longed for vengeance, but those who had wounded it were dead. There but remained the man seated on the throne, who had laid waste to the beast's home.

Time enough would come for the settling of that score.

A final longing filled the creature's ravaged soul. Somewhere, amidst the conflagration of the Fall and the chaos that followed, it had lost its mate, and was now alone. Perhaps she still lived. Perhaps she wandered, wounded as he was, searching the broken wastes for sign of him.

Or perhaps she had fled, in pain and terror, to the warren that had given fire to her spirit.

Wherever she had gone – assuming she still lived – he would find her.

The three distant figures unveiled warrens, each vanishing into their Elder realms.

The beast elected to follow none of them. They were young entities as far as he and his mate were concerned, and the warren she might have fled to was, in comparison to those of the Elder Gods, ancient.

The path that awaited him was perilous, and he knew fear in his labouring heart.

The portal that opened before him revealed a grey-streaked, swirling storm of power. The beast hesitated, then strode into it.

And was gone.

BOOK ONE

THE SPARK AND THE ASHES

Five mages, an Adjunct, countless Imperial
Demons, and the debacle that was Darujhistan,
all served to publicly justify the outlawry proclaimed by
the Empress on Dujek Onearm and his battered legions.
That this freed Onearm and his Host to launch a new
campaign, this time as an independent military
force, to fashion his own unholy alliances which
were destined to result in a continuation of the
dreadful Sorcery Enfilade on Genabackis, is,
one might argue, incidental. Granted, the countless
victims of that devastating time might, should Hood
grant them the privilege, voice an entirely different
opinion. Perhaps the most poetic detail of what
would come to be called the Pannion Wars was
in fact a precursor to the entire campaign: the casual,
indifferent destruction of a lone, stone bridge,
by the Jaghut Tyrant on his ill-fated march to
Darujhistan . . .

Imperial Campaigns (The Pannion War)
1194–1195, Volume IV, Genabackis
Imrygyn Tallobant (b. 1151)

CHAPTER ONE

Memories are woven tapestries hiding hard walls—
tell me, my friends, what hue your favoured thread,
and I in turn, will tell the cast of your soul . . .

Life of Dreams
Ilbares the Hag

1164th Year of Burn's Sleep (two months after the Darujhistan Fete)
4th Year of the Pannion Domin
Tellann Year of the Second Gathering

The bridge's Gadrobi limestone blocks lay scattered, scorched and broken in the bank's churned mud, as if a god's hand had swept down to shatter the stone span in a single, petty gesture of contempt. And that, Gruntle suspected, was but a half-step from the truth.

The news had trickled back into Darujhistan less than a week after the destruction, as the first eastward-bound caravans this side of the river reached the crossing, to find that where once stood a serviceable bridge was now nothing but rubble. Rumours whispered of an ancient demon, unleashed by agents of the Malazan Empire, striding down out of the Gadrobi Hills bent on the annihilation of Darujhistan itself.

Gruntle spat into the blackened grasses beside the carriage. He had his doubts about that tale. Granted, there'd been strange goings on the night of the city's Fete two months back – not that he'd been sober enough to notice much of anything – and sufficient witnesses to give credence to the sightings of dragons, demons and the terrifying descent of Moon's Spawn, but any conjuring with the power to lay waste to an entire countryside would have reached Darujhistan. And, since the city was not a smouldering heap – or no more than was usual after a city-wide celebration – clearly nothing did.

No, far more likely a god's hand, or possibly an earthquake – though the Gadrobi Hills were not known to be restless. Perhaps Burn had shifted uneasy in her eternal sleep.

In any case, the truth of things now stood before him. Or, rather, did not stand, but lay scattered to Hood's gate and beyond. And the fact remained, whatever games the gods played, it was hard-working dirt-poor bastards like him who suffered for it.

The old ford was back in use, thirty paces upriver from where the bridge had been built. It hadn't seen traffic in centuries, and with a week of unseasonal rains both banks had become a morass. Caravan trains crowded the crossing, the ones on what used to be ramps and the ones out in the swollen river hopelessly mired down; while dozens more waited on the trails, with the tempers of merchants, guards and beasts climbing by the hour.

Two days now, waiting to cross, and Gruntle was pleased with his meagre troop. Islands of calm, they were. Harllo had waded out to a remnant of the bridge's nearside pile, and now sat atop it, fishing pole in hand. Stonny Menackis had led a ragged band of fellow caravan guards to Storby's wagon, and Storby wasn't too displeased to be selling Gredfallan ale by the mug at exorbitant prices. That the ale casks were destined for a wayside inn outside Saltoan was just too bad for the expectant innkeeper. If things continued as they did, there'd be a market growing up here, then a Hood-damned town. Eventually, some officious planner in Darujhistan would conclude that it'd be a good thing to rebuild the bridge, and in ten or so years it would finally get done. Unless, of course, the town had become a going concern, in which case they'd send a tax collector.

Gruntle was equally pleased with his employer's equanimity at the delay. News was, the merchant Manqui on the other side of the river had burst a blood vessel in his head and promptly died, which was more typical of the breed. No, their master Keruli ran against the grain, enough to threaten Gruntle's cherished disgust for merchants in general. Then again, Keruli's list of peculiar traits had led the guard captain to suspect that the man wasn't a merchant at all.

Not that it mattered. Coin was coin, and Keruli's rates were good. Better than average, in fact. The man might be Prince Arard in disguise, for all Gruntle cared.

'You there, sir!'

Gruntle pulled his gaze from Harllo's fruitless fishing. A grizzled old man stood beside the carriage, squinting up at him. 'Damned imperious of you, that tone,' the caravan captain growled, 'since by the rags you're wearing you're either the world's worst merchant or a poor man's servant.'

'Manservant, to be precise. My name is Emancipor Reese. As for my masters' being poor, to the contrary. We have, however, been on the road for a long time.'

'I'll accept that,' Gruntle said, 'since your accent is unrecognizable, and coming from me that's saying a lot. What do you want, Reese?'

The manservant scratched the silvery stubble on his lined jaw. 'Careful questioning among this mob had gleaned a consensus that, as far as caravan guards go, you're a man who's earned respect.'

'As far as caravan guards go, I might well have at that,' Gruntle said drily. 'Your point?'

'My masters wish to speak with you, sir. If you're not too busy – we have camped not far from here.'

45

Leaning back on the bench, Gruntle studied Reese for a moment, then grunted. 'I'd have to clear with my employer any meetings with other merchants.'

'By all means, sir. And you may assure him that my masters have no wish to entice you away or otherwise compromise your contract.'

'Is that a fact? All right, wait there.' Gruntle swung himself down from the buckboard on the side opposite Reese. He stepped up to the small, ornately framed door and knocked once. It opened softly and from the relative darkness within the carriage's confines loomed Keruli's round, expressionless face.

'Yes, Captain, by all means go. I admit as to some curiosity about this man's two masters. Be most studious in noting details of your impending encounter. And, if you can, determine what precisely they have been up to since yesterday.'

The captain grunted to disguise his surprise at Keruli's clearly unnatural depth of knowledge – the man had yet to leave the carriage – then said, 'As you wish, sir.'

'Oh, and retrieve Stonny on your way back. She has had far too much to drink and has become most argumentative.'

'Maybe I should collect her now, then. She's liable to poke someone full of holes with that rapier of hers. I know her moods.'

'Ah, well. Send Harllo, then.'

'Uh, he's liable to join in, sir.'

'Yet you speak highly of them.'

'I do,' Gruntle replied. 'Not to be too immodest, sir, the three of us working the same contract are as good as twice that number, when it comes to protecting a master and his merchandise. That's why we're so expensive.'

'Your rates were high? I see. Hmm. Inform your two companions, then, that an aversion to trouble will yield substantial bonuses to their pay.'

Gruntle managed to avoid gaping. 'Uh, that should solve the problem, sir.'

'Excellent. Inform Harllo thus, then, and send him on his way.'

'Yes, sir.'

The door swung shut.

As it turned out, Harllo was already returning to the carriage, fishing pole in one massive hand, a sad sandal-sole of a fish clutched in the other. The man's bright blue eyes danced with excitement.

'Look, you sour excuse for a man – I've caught supper!'

'Supper for a monastic rat, you mean. I could inhale that damned thing up one nostril.'

Harllo scowled. 'Fish soup. Flavour—'

'That's just great. I love mud-flavoured soup. Look, the thing's not even breathing – it was probably dead when you caught it.'

'I banged a rock between its eyes, Gruntle—'

'Must have been a small rock.'

'For that you don't get any—'

'For that I bless you. Now listen. Stonny's getting drunk—'

'Funny, I don't hear no brawl—'

'Bonuses from Keruli if there isn't one. Understood?'

Harllo glanced at the carriage door, then nodded. 'I'll let her know.'

'Better hurry.'

'Right.'

Gruntle watched him scurry off, still carrying his pole and prize. The man's arms were enormous, too long and too muscled for the rest of his scrawny frame. His weapon of choice was a two-handed sword, purchased from a weapon-smith in Deadman's Story. As far as those apish arms were concerned, it might be made of bamboo. Harllo's shock of pale blond hair rode his pate like a tangled bundle of fishing thread. Strangers laughed upon seeing him for the first time, but Harllo used the flat of a blade to stifle that response. Succinctly.

47

Sighing, Gruntle returned to where Emancipor Reese stood waiting. 'Lead on,' he said.

Reese's head bobbed. 'Excellent.'

The carriage was massive, a house perched on high, spoked wheels. Ornate carvings crowded the strangely arched frame, tiny painted figures capering and climbing with leering expressions. The driver's perch was canopied in sun-faded canvas. Four oxen lumbered freely in a makeshift corral ten paces downwind from the camp.

Privacy obviously mattered to the manservant's masters, since they'd parked well away from both the road and the other merchants, affording them a clear view of the hummocks rising on the south side of the road, and, beyond it, the broad sweep of the plain.

A mangy cat lying on the buckboard watched Reese and Gruntle approach.

'That your cat?' the captain asked.

Reese squinted at it, then sighed. 'Aye, sir. Her name's Squirrel.'

'Any alchemist or wax-witch could treat that mange.'

The manservant seemed uncomfortable. 'I'll be sure to look into it when we get to Saltoan,' he muttered. 'Ah,' he nodded towards the hills beyond the road, 'here comes Master Bauchelain.'

Gruntle turned and studied the tall, angular man who'd reached the road and now strode casually towards them. Expensive, ankle-length cloak of black leather, high riding boots of the same over grey leggings, and, beneath a loose silk shirt – also black – the glint of fine blackened chain armour.

'Black,' the captain said to Reese, 'was last year's shade in Darujhistan.'

'Black is Bauchelain's eternal shade, sir.'

The master's face was pale, shaped much like a triangle, an impression further accented by a neatly trimmed beard. His hair, slick with oil, was swept back from his high brow.

His eyes were flat grey – as colourless as the rest of him – and upon meeting them Gruntle felt a surge of visceral alarm.

'Captain Gruntle,' Bauchelain spoke in a soft, cultured voice, 'your employer's prying is none too subtle. But while we are not ones to generally reward such curiosity regarding our activities, this time we shall make an exception. You shall accompany me.' He glanced at Reese. 'Your cat seems to be suffering palpitations. I suggest you comfort the creature.'

'At once, master.'

Gruntle rested his hands on the pommels of his cutlasses, eyes narrowed on Bauchelain. The carriage springs squeaked as the manservant clambered up to the buckboard.

'Well, Captain?'

Gruntle made no move.

Bauchelain raised one thin eyebrow. 'I assure you, your employer is eager that you comply with my request. If, however, you are afraid to do so, you might be able to convince him to hold your hand for the duration of this enterprise. Though I warn you, levering him into the open may prove something of a challenge, even for a man of your bulk.'

'Ever done any fishing?' Gruntle asked.

'Fishing?'

'The ones that rise to any old bait are young and they don't get any older. I've been working caravans for more than twenty years, sir. I ain't young. You want a rise, fish elsewhere.'

Bauchelain's smile was dry. 'You reassure me, Captain. Shall we proceed?'

'Lead on.'

They crossed the road. An old goat trail led them into the hills. The caravan camp this side of the river was quickly lost to sight. The scorched grass of the conflagration that had struck this land marred every slope and summit, although new green shoots had begun to appear.

'Fire,' Bauchelain noted as they walked on, 'is essential for the health of these prairie grasses. As is the passage of bhederin, the hooves in their hundreds of thousands compacting the thin soil. Alas, the presence of goats will spell the end of verdancy for these ancient hills. But I began with the subject of fire, did I not? Violence and destruction, both vital for life. Do you find that odd, Captain?'

'What I find odd, sir, is this feeling that I've left my wax-tablet behind.'

'You have had schooling, then. How interesting. You're a swordsman, are you not? What need you for letters and numbers?'

'And you're a man of letters and numbers – what need you for that well-worn broadsword at your hip and that fancy mail hauberk?'

'An unfortunate side effect of education among the masses is lack of respect.'

'Healthy scepticism, you mean.'

'Disdain for authority, actually. You may have noted, to answer your question, that we have but a single, rather elderly manservant. No hired guards. The need to protect oneself is vital in our profession—'

'And what profession is that?'

They'd descended onto a well-trodden path winding between the hills. Bauchelain paused, smiling as he regarded Gruntle. 'You entertain me, Captain. I understand now why you are well spoken of among the caravanserai, since you are unique among them in possessing a functioning brain. Come, we are almost there.'

They rounded a battered hillside and came to the edge of a fresh crater. The earth at its base was a swath of churned mud studded with broken blocks of stone. Gruntle judged the crater to be forty paces across and four or five arm-lengths in depth. A man sat nearby on the edge of the rim, also dressed in black leather, his bald pate the colour of bleached parchment. He rose silently, for all his considerable size, and turned to them with fluid grace.

'Korbal Broach, Captain. My ... partner. Korbal, we have here Gruntle, a name that is most certainly a slanting hint to his personality.'

If Bauchelain had triggered unease in the captain, then this man – his broad, round face, his eyes buried in puffed flesh and wide full-lipped mouth set slightly downturned at the corners, a face both childlike and ineffably monstrous – sent ripples of fear through Gruntle. Once again, the sensation was wholly instinctive, as if Bauchelain and his partner exuded an aura somehow tainted.

'No wonder the cat had palpitations,' the captain muttered under his breath. He pulled his gaze from Korbal Broach and studied the crater.

Bauchelain moved to stand beside him. 'Do you understand what you are seeing, Captain?'

'Aye, I'm no fool. It's a hole in the ground.'

'Amusing. A barrow once stood here. Within it was chained a Jaghut Tyrant.'

'Was.'

'Indeed. A distant empire meddled, or so I gather. And, in league with a T'lan Imass, they succeeded in freeing the creature.'

'You give credence to the tales, then,' Gruntle said. 'If such an event occurred, then what in Hood's name happened to it?'

'We wondered the same, Captain. We are strangers to this continent. Until recently, we'd never heard of the Malazan Empire, nor the wondrous city called Darujhistan. During our all too brief stay there, however, we heard stories of events just past. Demons, dragons, assassins. And the Azath house named Finnest, which cannot be entered yet, seems to be occupied none the less – we paid that a visit, of course. More, we'd heard tales of a floating fortress, called Moon's Spawn, that once hovered over the city—'

'Aye, I'd seen that with my own eyes. It left a day before I did.'

Bauchelain sighed. 'Alas, it appears we have come too late to witness for ourselves these dire wonders. A Tiste Andii lord rules Moon's Spawn, I gather.'

Gruntle shrugged. 'If you say so. Personally, I dislike gossip.'

Finally, the man's eyes hardened.

The captain smiled inwardly.

'Gossip. Indeed.'

'This is what you wanted to show me, then? This ... hole?'

Bauchelain raised an eyebrow. 'Not precisely. This *hole* is but the entrance. We intend to visit the Jaghut tomb that lies below it.'

'Oponn's blessing to you, then,' Gruntle said, turning away.

'I imagine,' the man said behind him, 'that your master would urge you to accompany us.'

'He can urge all he likes,' the captain replied. 'I wasn't contracted to sink in a pool of mud.'

'We've no intention of getting covered in mud.'

Gruntle glanced back at him, crooked a wry grin. 'A figure of speech, Bauchelain. Apologies if you misunderstood.' He swung round again and made his way towards the trail. Then he stopped. 'You wanted to see Moon's Spawn, sirs?' He pointed.

Like a towering black cloud, the basalt fortress stood just above the south horizon.

Boots crunched on the ragged gravel, and Gruntle found himself standing between the two men, both of whom studied the distant floating mountain.

'Scale,' Bauchelain muttered, 'is difficult to determine. How far away is it?'

'I'd guess a league, maybe more. Trust me, sirs, it's close enough for my tastes. I've walked its shadow in Darujhistan – hard not to for a while there – and believe me, it's not a comforting feeling.'

'I imagine not. What is it doing here?'

Gruntle shrugged. 'Seems to be heading southeast—'

'Hence the tilt.'

'No. It was damaged over Pale. By mages of the Malazan Empire.'

'Impressive effort, these mages.'

'They died for it. Most of them, anyway. So I heard. Besides, while they managed to damage Moon's Spawn, its lord remains hale. If you want to call kicking a hole in a fence before getting obliterated by the man who owns the house "impressive", go right ahead.'

Korbal Broach finally spoke, his voice reedy and high-pitched. 'Bauchelain, does he sense us?'

His companion frowned, eyes still on Moon's Spawn, then shook his head. 'I detect no such attention accorded us, friend. But that is a discussion that should await a more private moment.'

'Very well. You don't want me to kill this caravan guard, then?'

Gruntle stepped away in alarm, half drawing his cutlasses. 'You'll regret the attempt,' he growled.

'Be calmed, Captain.' Bauchelain smiled. 'My partner has simple notions—'

'Simple as an adder's, you mean.'

'Perhaps. None the less, I assure you, you are perfectly safe.'

Scowling, Gruntle backed away down the trail. 'Master Keruli,' he whispered, 'if you're watching all this – and I think you are – I trust my bonus will be appropriately generous. And, if my advice is worth anything, I suggest we stride clear and wide of these two.'

Moments before he moved beyond sight of the crater, he saw Bauchelain and Korbal Broach turn their backs on him – and Moon's Spawn. They stared down into the hole for a brief span, then began the descent, disappearing from view.

Sighing, Gruntle swung about and made his way back to the camp, rolling his shoulders to release the tension that gripped him.

As he reached the road his gaze lifted once more, south-ward to find Moon's Spawn, hazy now with distance. 'You there, lord, I wish you *had* caught the scent of Bauchelain and Korbal Broach, so you'd do to them what you did to the Jaghut Tyrant – assuming you had a hand in that. Preventative medicine, the cutters call it. I only pray we don't all one day come to regret your disinterest.'

Walking down the road, he glanced over to see Emancipor Reese, sitting atop the carriage, one hand stroking the ragged cat in his lap. Mange? Gruntle considered. *Probably not.*

The huge wolf circled the body, head low and turned inward to keep the unconscious mortal within sight of its lone eye.

The Warren of Chaos had few visitors. Among those few, mortal humans were rarest of all. The wolf had wandered this violent landscape for a time that was, to it, immeasurable. Alone and lost for so long, its mind had found new shapes born of solitude; the tracks of its thoughts twisted on seemingly random routes. Few would recognize awareness or intelligence in the feral gleam of its eye, yet they existed none the less.

The wolf circled, massive muscles rippling beneath the dull white fur. Head low and turned inward. Lone eye fixed on the prone human.

The fierce concentration was efficacious, holding the object of its attention in a state that was timeless – an accidental consequence of the powers the wolf had absorbed within this warren.

The wolf recalled little of the other worlds that existed beyond Chaos. It knew nothing of the mortals who worshipped it as they would a god. Yet a certain knowledge had come to it, an instinctive sensitivity that told it of . . . possibilities. Of potentials. Of choices now available to the wolf, with the discovery of this frail mortal.

Even so, the creature hesitated.

There were risks. And the decision that now gnawed its way to the forefront had the wolf trembling.

Its circling spiralled inward, closer, ever closer to the unconscious figure. Lone eye fixing finally on the man's face.

The gift, the creature saw at last, was a true one. Nothing else could explain what it discovered in the mortal man's face. A mirrored spirit, in every detail. This was an opportunity that could not be refused.

Still the wolf hesitated.

Until an ancient memory rose before its mind's eye. An image, frozen, faded with the erosion of time.

Sufficient to close the spiral.

And then it was done.

His single functioning eye blinked open to a pale blue, cloudless sky. The scar tissue covering what was left of his other eye tingled with a maddening itch, as if insects crawled under the skin. He was wearing a helm, the visor raised. Beneath him, hard sharp rocks dug into his flesh.

He lay unmoving, trying to remember what had happened. The vision of a dark tear opening before him – he'd plunged into it, was flung into it. A horse vanishing beneath him, the thrum of his bowstring. A sense of unease, which he'd shared with his companion. A friend who rode at his side. Captain Paran.

Toc the Younger groaned. *Hairlock. That mad puppet. We were ambushed.* The fragments coalesced, memory returning with a surge of fear. He rolled onto his side, every muscle protesting. *Hood's breath, this isn't the Rhivi Plain.*

A field of broken black glass stretched away on all sides. Grey dust hung in motionless clouds an arm's span above it. Off to his left, perhaps two hundred paces away, a low mound rose to break the flat monotony of the landscape.

His throat felt raw. His eye stung. The sun was blistering overhead. Coughing, Toc sat up, the obsidian crunching beneath him. He saw his recurved horn bow lying beside him and reached for it. The quiver had been strapped onto the saddle of his horse. Wherever he'd gone, his faithful Wickan mount had not followed. Apart from the knife at his hip and the momentarily useless bow in his hand, then, he possessed nothing. No water, no food. A closer examination of his bow deepened his scowl. The gut string had stretched.

Badly. Meaning I've been . . . away . . . for some time. Away. Where? Hairlock had thrown him into a warren. Somehow, time had been lost within it. He was not overly thirsty, nor particularly hungry. But, even if he had arrows, the bow's pull was gone. Worse, the string had dried, the wax absorbing obsidian dust. It wouldn't survive retightening. That suggested days, if not weeks, had passed, though his body told him otherwise.

He climbed to his feet. The chain armour beneath his tunic protested the movement, shedding glittering dust.

Am I within a warren? Or has it spat me back out? Either way, he needed to find an end to this lifeless plain of volcanic glass. Assuming one existed . . .

He began walking towards the mound. Though it wasn't especially high, he would take any vantage point that was available. As he approached, he saw others like it beyond, regularly spaced. *Barrows. Great, I just love barrows.* And then a central one, larger than the rest.

Toc skirted the first mound, noting in passing that it had been holed, likely by looters. After a moment he paused, turned and walked closer. He squatted beside the excavated shaft, peered down into the slanting tunnel. As far as he could see – over a man's height in depth – the mantle of obsidian continued down. For the mounds to have showed at all, they must be huge, more like domes than beehive tombs. 'Whatever,' he muttered. 'I don't like it.'

He paused, considering, running through in his mind the events that had led him to this . . . unfortunate situation. The deathly rain of Moon's Spawn seemed to mark some kind of beginning. Fire and pain, the death of an eye, the kiss that left a savagely disfiguring scar on what had been a young, reputedly handsome face.

A ride north onto the plain to retrieve Adjunct Lorn, a

skirmish with Ilgres Barghast. Back in Pale, still more trouble. Lorn had drawn his reins, reviving his old role as a Claw courier. *Courier? Let's speak plain, Toc, especially to yourself. You were a spy. But you had been turned. You were a scout in Onearm's Host. That and nothing more, until the Adjunct showed up.* There'd been trouble in Pale. Tattersail, then Captain Paran. Flight and pursuit. 'What a mess,' he muttered.

Hairlock's ambush had swatted him like a fly, into some kind of malign warren. *Where I . . . lingered. I think. Hood take me, time's come to start thinking like a soldier again. Get your bearings. Do nothing precipitous. Think about survival, here in this strange, unwelcome place . . .*

He resumed his trek to the central barrow. Though gently sloped, it was at least thrice the height of a man. His cough worsened as he scrambled up its side.

The effort was rewarded. On the summit, he found himself standing at the hub of a ring of lesser tombs. Directly ahead, three hundred paces beyond the ring's edge yet almost invisible through the haze, rose the bony shoulders of grey-cloaked hills. Closer and to his left were the ruins of a stone tower. The sky behind it glowed a sickly red colour.

Toc glanced up at the sun. When he'd awoken, it had been at little more than three-quarters of the wheel; now it stood directly above him. He was able to orientate himself. The hill lay to the northwest, the tower a few points north of due west.

His gaze was pulled back to the reddish welt in the sky beyond the tower. Yes, it pulsed, as regular as a heart. He scratched at the scar tissue covering his left eye-socket, winced at the answering bloom of colours flooding his mind. *That's sorcery over there. Gods, I'm acquiring a deep hatred of sorcery.*

A moment later, more immediate details drew his attention. The north slope of the central barrow was marred by a deep pit, its edges ragged and glistening. A tumble of cut stone – still showing the stains of red paint –

crowded the base. The crater, he slowly realized, was not the work of looters. Whatever had made it had pushed up from the tomb, violently. *In this place, it seems that even the dead do not sleep eternal.* A moment of nervousness shook him, then he shrugged it off with a soft curse. *You've known worse, soldier. Remember that T'lan Imass who'd joined up with the Adjunct. Laconic desiccation on two legs, Beru fend us all. Hooded eye-sockets with not a glimmer or gleam of mercy. That thing had spitted a Barghast like a Rhivi a plains boar.*

Eye still studying the crater in the mound's flank, his thoughts remained on Lorn and her undead companion. They'd sought to free such a restless creature, to loose a wild, vicious power upon the land. He wondered if they'd succeeded. The prisoner of the tomb he now stood upon had faced a dreadful task, without question – wards, solid walls, and armspan after armspan of compacted, crushed glass. *Well, given the alternatives, I imagine I would have been as desperate and as determined. How long did it take? How malignly twisted the mind once freed?*

He shivered, the motion triggering another harsh cough. There were mysteries in the world, few of them pleasant.

He skirted the pit on his descent and made his way towards the ruined tower. He thought it unlikely that the occupant of the tomb would have lingered long in the area. *I would have wanted to get as far away from here and as fast as was humanly possible.* There was no telling how much time had passed since the creature's escape, but Toc's gut told him it was years, if not decades. He felt strangely unafraid in any case, despite the inhospitable surroundings and all the secrets beneath the land's ravaged surface. Whatever threat this place had held seemed to be long gone.

Forty paces from the tower he almost stumbled over a corpse. A fine layer of dust had thoroughly disguised its presence, and that dust, now disturbed by Toc's efforts to step clear, rose in a cloud. Cursing, the Malazan spat grit from his mouth.

Through the swirling, glittering haze, he saw that the

bones belonged to a human. Granted, a squat, heavy-boned one. Sinews had dried nut-brown, and the furs and skins partially clothing it had rotted to mere strips. A bone helm sat on the corpse's head, fashioned from the frontal cap of a horned beast. One horn had snapped off some time in the distant past. A dust-sheathed two-handed sword lay nearby. *Speaking of Hood's skull . . .*

Toc the Younger scowled down at the figure. 'What are *you* doing here?' he demanded.

'Waiting,' the T'lan Imass replied in a leather-rasp voice.

Toc searched his memory for the name of this undead warrior. 'Onos T'oolan,' he said, pleased with himself. 'Of the Tarad Clan—'

'I am now named Tool. Clanless. Free.'

Free? Free to do precisely what, you sack of bones? Lie around in wastelands?

'What's happened to the Adjunct? Where are we?'

'Lost.'

'Which question is that an answer to, Tool?'

'Both.'

Toc gritted his teeth, resisting the temptation to kick the T'lan Imass. 'Can you be more specific?'

'Perhaps.'

'Well?'

'Adjunct Lorn died in Darujhistan two months ago. We are in the ancient place called Morn, two hundred leagues to the south. It is just past midday.'

'Just past midday, you said. Thank you for the enlightenment.' He found little pleasure in conversing with a creature that had existed for hundreds of thousands of years, and that discomfort unleashed his sarcasm – a precarious presumption indeed. *Get back to seriousness, idiot. That flint sword ain't just for show.* 'Did you two free the Jaghut Tyrant?'

'Briefly. Imperial efforts to conquer Darujhistan failed.'

Scowling, Toc crossed his arms. 'You said you were waiting. Waiting for what?'

'She has been away for some time. Now she returns.'

'Who?'

'She who has taken occupation of the tower, soldier.'

'Can you at least stand up when you're talking to me.' *Before I give in to temptation.*

The T'lan Imass rose with an array of creaking complaints, dust cascading from its broad, bestial form. Something glittered for the briefest of moments in the depths of its eye-sockets as it stared at Toc, then Tool turned and retrieved the flint sword.

Gods, better I'd insisted he just stay lying down. Parched leather skin, taut muscle and heavy bone . . . all moving about like something alive. Oh, how the Emperor loved them. An army he never had to feed, he never had to transport, an army that could go anywhere and do damn near anything. And no desertions – except for the one standing in front of me right now.

How do you punish a T'lan Imass deserter anyway?

'I need water,' Toc said after a long moment in which they simply stared at each other. 'And food. And I need to find some arrows. And bowstring.' He unstrapped his helmet and pulled it clear. The leather cap beneath it was soaked through with sweat. 'Can't we wait in the tower? This heat is baking my brain.' *And why am I talking as if I expect you to help me, Tool?*

'The coast lies a thousand paces to the southwest,' Tool said. 'Food is available there, and a certain seagrass that will suffice as bowstring until some gut can be found. I do not, alas, smell fresh water. Perhaps the tower's occupant will be generous, though she is less likely to be so if she arrives to find you within it. Arrows can be made. There is a salt-marsh nearby, where we can find bone-reed. Snares for coast birds will offer us fletching. Arrowheads . . .' Tool turned to survey the obsidian plain. 'I foresee no shortage of raw material.'

All right, so help me you will. Thank Hood for that. 'Well, I hope you can still chip stone and weave seagrass, T'lan Imass, not to mention work bone-reed – whatever that is –

into true shafts, because I certainly don't know how. When I need arrows, I requisition them, and when they arrive they're iron-headed and straight as a plumb-line.'

'I have not lost the skills, soldier—'

'Since the Adjunct never properly introduced us, I am named Toc the Younger, and I am not a soldier, but a scout—'

'You were in the employ of the Claw.'

'With none of the assassin training, nor the magery. Besides which, I have more or less renounced that role. All I seek to do now is to return to Onearm's Host.'

'A long journey.'

'So I gathered. The sooner I start the better, then. Tell me, how far does this glass wasteland stretch?'

'Seven leagues. Beyond it you will find the Lamatath Plain. When you have reached it, set a course north by northeast—'

'Where will that take me? Darujhistan? Has Dujek besieged the city?'

'No.' The T'lan Imass swung its head round. 'She comes.'

Toc followed Tool's gaze. Three figures had appeared from the south, approaching the edge of the ring of barrows. Of the three, only the one in the middle walked upright. She was tall, slim, wearing a flowing white telaba such as were worn by highborn women of Seven Cities. Her black hair was long and straight. Flanking her were two dogs, the one on her left as big as a hill-pony, shaggy, wolf-like, the other short-haired, dun-coloured and heavily muscled.

Since Tool and Toc stood in the open, it was impossible that they had not been seen, yet the three displayed no perturbation or change of pace as they strode nearer. At a dozen paces the wolfish dog loped forward, tail wagging as it came up to the T'lan Imass.

Musing on the scene, Toc scratched his jaw. 'An old friend, Tool? Or does the beast want you to toss it one of your bones?'

The undead warrior regarded him in silence.

'Humour,' Toc said, shrugging. 'Or a poor imitation. I didn't think T'lan Imass could take offence.' *Or, rather, I'm hoping that's the case. Gods, my big mouth . . .*

'I was considering,' Tool replied slowly. 'This beast is an ay, and thus has little interest in bones. Ay prefer flesh, still warm if possible.'

Toc grunted. 'I see.'

'Humour,' Tool said after a moment.

'Right.' *Oh. Maybe this won't be so bad after all. Surprises never cease.*

The T'lan Imass reached out to rest the tips of its bony fingers on the ay's broad head. The animal went perfectly still. 'An old friend? Yes, we adopted such animals into our tribes. It was that or see them starve. We were, you see, responsible for that starvation.'

'Responsible? As in overhunting? I'd have thought your kind was one with nature. All those spirits, all those rituals of propitiation—'

'Toc the Younger,' Tool interrupted, 'do you mock me, or your own ignorance? Not even the lichen of the tundra is at peace. All is struggle, all is war for dominance. Those who lose, vanish.'

'And we're no different, you're saying—'

'We are, soldier. We possess the privilege of choice. The gift of foresight. Though often we come too late in acknowledging those responsibilities . . .' The T'lan Imass's head tilted as he studied the ay before him, and, it seemed, his own skeletal hand where it rested upon the beast's head.

'Baaljagg awaits your command, dear undead warrior,' the woman said upon arriving, her voice a lilting melody. 'How sweet. Garath, go join your brother in greeting our desiccated guest.' She met Toc's gaze and smiled. 'Garath, of course, might decide your companion's worth burying – wouldn't that be fun?'

'Momentarily,' Toc agreed. 'You speak Daru, yet wear the telaba of Seven Cities . . .'

Her brows arched. 'Do I? Oh, such confusion! Mind you, sir, you speak Daru yet you are from that repressed woman's empire – what was her name again?'

'Empress Laseen. The Malazan empire.' *And how did you know that? I'm not in uniform . . .*

She smiled. 'Indeed.'

'I am Toc the Younger, and the T'lan Imass is named Tool.'

'How apt. My, it is hot out here, don't you think? Let us retire within the Jaghut tower. Garath, cease sniffing the T'lan Imass and awaken the servants.'

Toc watched the burly dog trot towards the tower. The entrance, the scout now saw, was in fact via a balcony, probably the first floor – yet another indication of the depth of the crushed glass. 'That place doesn't appear very habitable,' he observed.

'Appearances deceive,' she murmured, once again flashing him a heart-stuttering smile.

'Have you a name?' Toc asked her as they began walking.

'She is Lady Envy,' Tool said. 'Daughter of Draconus – he who forged the sword Dragnipur, and was slain by its present wielder, Anomander Rake, lord of Moon's Spawn, with that selfsame sword. Draconus had two daughters, it is believed, whom he named Envy and Spite—'

'Hood's breath, you can't be serious,' Toc muttered.

'The names no doubt amused him, as well,' the T'lan Imass continued.

'Really,' Lady Envy sighed, 'now you've gone and ruined all my fun. Have we met before?'

'No. None the less, you are known to me.'

'So it seems! It was, I admit, over-modest of me to assume that I would not be recognized. After all, I've crossed paths with the T'lan Imass more than once. At least twice, that is.'

Tool regarded her with his depthless gaze. 'Knowing who you are does not answer the mystery of your present residency here in Morn, should you look to pursue coyness, Lady. I would know what you seek in this place.'

'Whatever do you mean?' she asked mockingly.

As they approached the tower's entrance a leather-armoured masked figure appeared in the gaping doorway. Toc stopped in his tracks. 'That's a Seguleh!' He spun to Lady Envy. 'Your servant's a Seguleh!'

'Is that what they're called?' Her brow wrinkled. 'A familiar name, though its context escapes me. Ah well. I have gleaned their personal names, but little else. They happened by and chanced to see me – this one, who is called Senu, and two others. They concluded that killing me would break the monotony of their journey.' She sighed. 'Alas, now they serve me.' She addressed the Seguleh. 'Senu, have your brothers fully awakened?'

The short, lithe man tilted his head, his dark eyes flat within the slits of his ornate mask.

'I've gathered,' Lady Envy said to Toc, 'that gesture indicates acquiescence. They are not a loquacious lot, I have found.'

Toc shook his head, his eyes on the twin broadswords slung under Senu's arms. 'Is he the only one of the three to acknowledge you directly, Lady?'

'Now that you mention it . . . Is that significant?'

'Means he's on the bottom rung in the hierarchy. The other two are above conversing with non-Seguleh.'

'How presumptuous of them!'

The scout grinned. 'I've never seen one before – but I've heard plenty. Their homeland is an island south of here, and they're said to be a private lot, disinclined to travel. But they are known of as far north as Nathilog.' *And Hood take me, aren't they known.*

'Hmm, I did sense a certain arrogance that has proved entertaining. Lead us within, dear Senu.'

The Seguleh made no move. His eyes had found Tool and now held steady on the T'lan Imass.

Hackles rising, the ay stepped to one side to clear a space between the two figures.

'Senu?' Lady Envy enquired with honeyed politeness.

'I think,' Toc whispered, 'he's challenging Tool.'

'Ridiculous! Why would he do that?'

'For the Seguleh, rank is everything. If the hierarchy's in doubt, challenge it. They don't waste time.'

Lady Envy scowled at Senu. 'Behave yourself, young man!' She waved him into the room beyond.

Senu seemed to flinch at the gesture.

An itch spasmed across Toc's scar. He scratched it vigorously, breathing a soft curse.

The Seguleh backed into the small room, then hesitated a moment before turning and leading the others to the doorway opposite. A curved hallway brought them to a central chamber in which a tightly wound staircase rose from the centre. The walls were unadorned, roughly pitted pumice. Three limestone sarcophagi crowded the far end of the room, their lids leaning in a neatly arranged row against the wall behind them. The dog Lady Envy had sent in ahead sat nearby. Just within the entrance was a round wooden table, crowded with fresh fruit, meats, cheese and bread, as well as a beaded clay jug and a collection of cups.

Senu's two companions stood motionless over the table, as if standing guard and fully prepared to give their lives in its defence. Both were a match to their companion's height and build, and similarly armed; the difference between each was evident only in their masks. Where Senu's enamelled face-covering was crowded with dark-stained patterns, such decoration diminished successively in the other two examples. One was only slightly less marked than Senu's, but the third mask bore naught but twin slashes, one on each gleaming white cheek. The eyes that stared out from the slits of this mask were like chips of obsidian.

The twin-scarred Seguleh stiffened upon seeing the T'lan Imass, took one step forward.

'Oh really!' Lady Envy hissed. 'Challenges are forbidden! Any more of this nonsense and I shall lose my temper—'

All three Seguleh flinched back a step.

'There,' the woman said, 'that's much better.' She swung

to Toc. 'Assuage your needs, young man. The jug contains Saltoan white wine, suitably chilled.'

Toc found himself unable to look away from the Seguleh wearing the twin-scarred mask.

'If a fixed stare represents a challenge,' Lady Envy said quietly, 'I suggest, for the sake of peace – not to mention your life – that you refrain from your present engagement, Toc the Younger.'

He grunted in sudden alarm, tore his gaze from the man. 'Good point, Lady. It's only that I've never heard of . . . well, never mind. Doesn't matter.' He approached the table, reached for the jug.

Movement exploded behind him, followed by the sound of a body skidding across the room, striking the wall with a sickly thud. Toc spun round to see Tool, sword upraised, facing the two remaining Seguleh. Senu lay crumpled ten paces away, either unconscious or dead. His two swords were both halfway out of their sheaths.

Standing beside Tool, the ay named Baaljagg was staring at the body, tail wagging.

Lady Envy regarded the other Seguleh with eyes of ice. 'Given that my commands have proved insufficient, I now leave future encounters in the T'lan Imass's obviously capable hands.' She swung to Tool. 'Is Senu dead?'

'No. I used the flat of my blade, Lady, having no desire to slay one of your servants.'

'Considerate of you, given the circumstances.'

Toc closed one shaky hand on the jug's handle. 'Shall I pour one for you as well, Lady Envy?'

She glanced at him, raised one eyebrow, then smiled. 'A splendid idea, Toc the Younger. Clearly, it falls to you and me to establish civility.'

'What have you learned,' Tool said, addressing her, 'of the Rent?'

Cup in hand, she faced him. 'Ah, you cut to the quick in all matters, I see. It has been bridged. By a mortal soul. As I am sure you are aware. The focus of my studies, however,

66

has been on the identity of the warren itself. It is unlike any other. The portal seems almost . . . mechanical.'

Rent? That would be the red welt in the air. Uh.

'You have examined the K'Chain Che'Malle tombs, Lady?'

She wrinkled her nose. 'Briefly. They are all empty, and have been for some time. Decades.'

Tool's head tilted with a soft creak. 'Only decades?'

'Unpleasant detail, indeed. I believe the Matron experienced considerable difficulty in extricating herself, then spent still further time in recovering from her ordeal, before releasing her children. She and her brood made further efforts in the buried city to the northwest, though incomplete, as if the results proved unsatisfactory. They then appear to have departed the area entirely.' She paused, then added, 'It may be relevant that the Matron was the original soul sealing the Rent. Another hapless creature resides there now, we must presume.'

The T'lan Imass nodded.

During the exchange Toc had been busy eating, and was on his second cup of the crisp, cold wine. Trying to make sense of the conversation thus far was giving him a headache – he'd mull on it later. 'I need to head north,' he said round a mouthful of grainy bread. 'Is there any chance, Lady, that you can furnish me with suitable supplies? I would be in your debt . . .' His words trailed away at seeing the avid flash in her eyes.

'Careful what you offer, young man—'

'No offence, but why do you call me "young man"? You look not a day over twenty-five.'

'How flattering. Thus, despite Tool's success in identifying me – and I admit that I find the depth of his knowledge most disconcerting – the names the T'lan Imass revealed meant little to you.'

Toc shrugged. 'Anomander Rake I've heard, of course. I didn't know he took a sword from someone else – nor when that event occurred. It strikes me, however, that you may well be justified in feeling some animosity towards him, since he killed your father – what was his name? Draconus. The Malazan Empire shares that dislike. So, in sharing enemies—'

'We are perforce allies. A reasonable surmise. Unfortunately wrong. Regardless, I would be pleased to provide what food and drink you are able to carry, though I have nothing in the way of weapons, I'm afraid. In return, I may some day ask of you a favour – nothing grand, of course. Something small and relatively painless. Is this acceptable?'

Toc felt his appetite draining away. He glanced at Tool, got no help from the undead warrior's expressionless face. The Malazan scowled. 'You have me at a disadvantage, Lady Envy.'

She smiled.

And here I was hoping we'd get past the polite civility to something more . . . intimate. Here you go again, Toc, thinking with the wrong brain—

Her smile broadened.

Flushing, he reached for his cup. 'Very well, I agree to your proposal.'

'Your equanimity is a delight, Toc the Younger.'

He almost choked on his wine. *If I wasn't a sword-kissed one-eyed bastard, I'd be tempted to call that a flirt.*

Tool spoke. 'Lady Envy, if you seek further knowledge of this Rent, you will not find it here.'

Toc was pleased to see the mild shock on her face as she swung to the T'lan Imass. 'Indeed? It appears I am not alone in enjoying a certain coyness. Can you explain?'

Anticipating the response to that, Toc the Younger grunted, then ducked as she flashed him a dark look.

'Perhaps,' Tool predictably replied.

Hah, I knew it.

An edge came into her tone. 'Please do so, then.'

'I follow an ancient trail, Lady Envy. Morn was but one stop on that trail. It now leads northward. You would find your answers among those I seek.'

'You wish me to accompany you.'

'I care not either way,' Tool said in his uninflected rasp. 'Should you choose to stay here, however, I must warn you. Meddling with the Rent has its risks – even for one such as you.'

She crossed her arms. 'You think I lack suitable caution?'

'Even now you have reached an impasse, and your frustration mounts. I add one more incentive, Lady Envy. Your old travelling companions are converging on the very same destination – the Pannion Domin. Both Anomander Rake and Caladan Brood prepare to wage war against the Domin. A grave decision – does that not make you curious?'

'You are no simple T'lan Imass,' she accused.

Tool made no reply to that.

'He has you at a disadvantage, it seems,' Toc said, barely restraining his amusement.

'I find impertinence disgustingly unattractive,' she snapped. 'Whatever happened to your affable equanimity, Toc the Younger?'

He wondered at his sudden impulse to fling himself down at her feet, begging forgiveness. Shrugging the absurd notion off, he said, 'Badly stung, I think.'

Her expression softened to something doe-like.

The irrational desire returned. Toc scratched his scar, looked away.

'I did not intend to sting you—'

Right, and the Queen of Dreams has chicken feet.

'—and I sincerely apologize.' She faced Tool again. 'Very well, we shall all of us undertake a journey. How exciting!' She gestured to her Seguleh servants. 'Begin preparations at once!'

Tool said to Toc, 'I shall collect materials for your bow and arrows now. We can complete them on the way.'

The scout nodded, then added, 'I wouldn't mind watching you make them, Tool. Could be useful knowledge . . .'

The T'lan Imass seemed to consider, then tilted his head. 'We found it so.'

They all turned at a loud grunt from where Senu lay against the wall. He had regained consciousness, to find the ay standing over him, the beast licking with obvious pleasure the painted patterns on his mask.

'The medium,' Tool explained in his usual deadpan tone, 'appears to be a mixture of charcoal, saliva and human blood.'

'Now that,' Toc muttered, 'is what I call a rude awakening.'

Lady Envy brushed close to him as she moved towards the doorway, and cast him a glance as she passed. 'Oh, I *am* looking forward to this outing!'

The anything but casual contact slipped a nest of serpents into Toc's gut. Despite his thudding heart, the Malazan was not sure if he should be pleased, or terrified.

CHAPTER TWO

Onearm's Host bled from countless wounds. An
endless campaign, successive defeats followed by
even costlier victories. But of all the wounds
borne by the army of Dujek Onearm, those to
its soul were the gravest . . .

Silverfox
Outrider Hurlochel

Nestled amidst the rocks and tumbled boulders of
the hillside, Corporal Picker watched the old man
make his laborious way up the trail. His shadow
slipped over Blend's position, yet the man who cast it knew
nothing of the soldier's proximity. Blend rose in silence
behind him, dust sloughing down, and made a series of
hand gestures intended for Picker.

The old man continued on unawares. When he was but
a half-dozen paces away, Picker straightened, the grey cloak
left by the morning's dust-storm cascading away as she
levelled her crossbow. 'Far enough, traveller,' she growled.

His surprise sent the old man stumbling back a step. A
stone turned underfoot and he pitched to the ground, crying out yet managing to twist to avoid landing atop the
leather pack strapped to his back. He skidded another pace
down the trail, and found himself almost at Blend's feet.

Picker smiled, stepped forward. 'That'll do,' she said.
'You don't look dangerous, old fella, but just in case, there's

five other crossbows trained on you right now. So, how about you tell me what in Hood's name you're doing here?'

Sweat and dust stained the old man's threadbare tunic. His sunburned forehead was broad over a narrow set of features, vanishing into an almost chinless jaw. His snaggled, crooked teeth jutted out in all directions, making his smile an argumentative parody. He pulled his thin, leather-wrapped legs under himself and slowly levered upright. 'A thousand apologies,' he gasped, glancing over a shoulder at Blend. He flinched at what he saw in her eyes, swung hastily back to face Picker. 'I'd thought this trail untenanted – even by thieves. You see, my life's savings are invested in what I carry – I could not afford a guard, nor even a mule—'

'You're a trader, then,' Picker drawled. 'Bound where?'

'Pale. I am from Darujhistan—'

'That's obvious enough,' Picker snapped. 'Thing is, Pale is now in imperial hands . . . as are these hills.'

'I did not know – about these hills, that is. Of course I am aware that Pale has entered the Malazan embrace—'

Picker grinned at Blend. 'Hear that? An *embrace*. That's a good one, old man. A motherly hug, right? What's in the sack, then?'

'I am an artisan,' the old man said, ducking his head. 'Uh, a carver of small trinkets. Bone, ivory, jade, serpentine—'

'Anything invested – spells and the like?' the corporal asked. 'Anything blessed?'

'Only by my talents, to answer your first query. I am no mage, and I work alone. I was fortunate, however, in acquiring a priest's blessings on a set of three ivory torcs—'

'What god?'

'Treach, the Tiger of Summer.'

Picker sneered. 'That's not a god, you fool. Treach is a First Hero, a demigod, a Soletaken ascendant—'

'A new temple has been sanctified in his name,' the old man interrupted. 'On the Street of the Hairless Ape, in the

72

Gadrobi Quarter – I myself was hired to punch the leather binding for the Book of Prayers and Rituals.'

Picker rolled her eyes and lowered the crossbow. 'All right, let's see these torcs, then.'

With an eager nod, the old man unslung his pack and set it down before him. He released the lone strap.

'Remember,' Picker grunted, 'if you pull out anything awry you'll get a dozen quarrels airing your skull.'

'This is a pack, not my breeches,' the trader murmured. 'Besides, I thought it was five.'

The corporal scowled.

'Our audience,' Blend said quietly, 'has grown.'

'That's right,' Picker added hastily. 'Two whole squads, hiding, watching your every move.'

With exaggerated caution, the old man drew forth a small packet of twine-wrapped doeskin. 'The ivory is said to be ancient,' he said in a reverent tone. 'From a furred, tusked monster that was once Treach's favoured prey. The beast's corpse was found in frozen mud in distant Elingarth—'

'Never mind all that,' Picker snapped. 'Let's see the damned things.'

The trader's white, wiry eyebrows rose in alarm. 'Damned! No! Not ever! You think I would sell cursed items?'

'Be quiet, it was just a damned expression. Hurry up, we haven't got all damned day.'

Blend made a sound, quickly silenced by a glare from her corporal.

The old man unwrapped the packet, revealing three upper-arm rings, each of one piece and undecorated, polished to a gleaming, pale lustre.

'Where's the blessing marks?'

'None. They were each in turn wrapped within a cloth woven from Treach's own moult-hair – for nine days and ten nights—'

Blend snorted.

'Moult-hair?' The corporal's face twisted. 'What a disgusting thought.'

'Spindle wouldn't think so,' Blend murmured.

'A set of three arm torcs,' Picker mused. 'Right arm, left arm ... then where? And watch your mouth – we're delicate flowers, Blend and me.'

'All for one arm. They are solid, yet they interlock – such was the instruction of the blessing.'

'Interlocking yet seamless – this I have to see.'

'I cannot, alas, demonstrate this sorcery, for it will occur but once, when the purchaser has threaded them onto his – or her – weapon arm.'

'Now that has swindle written all over it.'

'Well, we got him right here,' Blend said. 'Cheats only work if you can make a clean getaway.'

'Like in Pale's crowded markets. Well indeed,' Picker grinned down at the old man, 'we're not in a crowded market, are we? How much?'

The trader squirmed. 'You have selected my most valued work – I'd intended an auction for these—'

'How much, old man?'

'Th-three hundred g-gold councils.'

'Councils. That's Darujhistan's new coinage, isn't it?'

'Pale's adopted the Malazan jakata as standard weight,' Blend said. 'What's the exchange?'

'Damned if I know,' Picker muttered.

'If you please,' the trader ventured, 'the exchange in Darujhistan is two and one-third jakatas to one council. Broker's fees comprise at least one jakata. Thus, strictly speaking, one and a third.'

Blend shifted her weight, leaned forward for a closer look at the torcs. 'Three hundred councils would keep a family comfortable for a couple of years at least . . .'

'Such was my goal,' the old man said. 'Although, as I live alone and modestly, I anticipated four or more years, including materials for my craft. Anything less than three hundred councils and I would be ruined.'

'My heart weeps,' Picker said. She glanced over at Blend. 'Who'll miss it?'

The soldier shrugged.

'Rustle up three columns, then.'

'At once, Corporal.' Blend stepped past the old man, moved silently up the trail, then out of sight.

'I beg you,' the trader whined. 'Do not pay me in jakatas—'

'Calm down,' Picker said. 'Oponn's smiling on you today. Now, step away from the pack. I'm obliged to search it.'

Bowing, the old man backed up. 'The rest is of lesser value, I admit. Indeed, somewhat rushed—'

'I'm not looking to buy anything else,' Picker said, rummaging with one hand through the pack. 'This is official, now.'

'Ah, I see. Are some trade items now forbidden in Pale?'

'Counterfeit jakatas, for one. Local economy's taking a beating, and Darujhistan councils aren't much welcome, either. We've had quite a haul this past week.'

The trader's eyes widened. 'You will pay me in counterfeited coin?'

'Tempting, but no. Like I said, Oponn's winked your way.' Finished with her search, Picker stepped back, and pulled out a small wax tablet from her belt-pouch. 'I need to record your name, trader. It's mostly smugglers using these trails, trying to avoid the post at the plains track through the Divide – you're one of the few honest ones, it seems. Those clever smugglers end up paying for their cleverness tenfold on these here trails, when the truth is they'd have a better chance slipping through the chaos at the post.'

'I am named Munug.'

Picker glanced up. 'You poor bastard.'

Blend returned down the trail, three wrapped columns of coins cradled in her arms.

The trader shrugged sheepishly, his eyes on the wrapped coin stacks. 'Those are councils!'

'Aye,' Picker muttered. 'In hundred-columns – you'll probably throw your back lugging them to Pale, not to mention back again. In fact, you needn't bother making the trip at all, now, right?' She fixed him with her eyes as she put the tablet back into the pouch.

'You have a valid point,' Munug conceded, rewrapping the torcs and passing the packet to Blend. 'I shall journey to Pale none the less – to deal the rest of my work.' Eyes shifting nervously, he bared his crooked teeth in a weak smile. 'If Oponn's luck holds, I might well double my take.'

Picker studied the man a moment longer, then shook her head. 'Greed never pays, Munug. I'd lay a wager that in a month's time you'll come wending back down this trail with nothing but dust in your pockets. What say you? Ten councils.'

'If I lose, you'd have me ten in debt to you.'

'Ah well, I'd consider a trinket or three instead – you've skilled hands, old man, no question of that.'

'Thank you, but I respectfully decline the wager.'

Picker shrugged. 'Too bad. You've another bell of daylight. There's a wayside camp up near the summit – if you're determined enough you might reach it before sunset.'

'I shall make the endeavour.' He slung his arms through the pack's straps, grunted upright, then, with a hesitant nod, moved past the corporal.

'Hold on there,' Picker commanded.

Munug's knees seemed to weaken and the old man almost collapsed. 'Y-yes?' he managed.

Picker took the torcs from Blend. 'I've got to put these on, first. Interlocking, you claimed. But seamless.'

'Oh! Yes, of course. By all means, proceed.'

The corporal rolled back the sleeve of her dusty shirt, revealing, in the heavy wool's underside, its burgundy dye.

Munug's gasp was audible.

Picker smiled. 'That's right, we're Bridgeburners. Amazing what dust disguises, hey?' She worked the ivory rings up her scarred, muscled arm. Between her biceps and

76

shoulder there was a soft click. Frowning, Picker studied the three torcs, then hissed in surprise. 'I'll be damned.'

Munug's smile broadened for the briefest of moments, then he bowed slightly. 'May I now resume my journey?'

'Go on,' she replied, barely paying him any further attention, her eyes studying the gleaming torcs on her arm.

Blend stared after the man for a full minute, a faint frown wrinkling her dusty brow.

Munug found the side-cut in the path a short while later. Glancing back down the trail to confirm for at least the tenth time that he was not followed, he quickly slipped between the two tilting stones that framed the hidden entrance.

The gloomy passage ended after a half-dozen paces, opening out onto a track winding through a high-walled fissure. Shadows swallowed the trader as he scurried down it. Sunset was less than a hundred heartbeats away, he judged – the delay with the Bridgeburners could prove fatal, if he failed to make the appointment.

'After all,' he whispered, 'gods are not known for forgiving natures . . .'

The coins were heavy. His heart thumped hard in his chest. He wasn't used to such strenuous efforts. He was an artisan, after all. Down on his luck of late, perhaps, weakened by the tumours between his legs, no doubt, but his talent and vision had if anything grown sharper for all the grief and pain he'd suffered. *I have chosen you for those very flaws, Munug. That, and your skills, of course. Oh yes, I have great need of your skills . . .*

A god's blessing would surely take care of those tumours. And, if not, then three hundred councils would come close to paying for a Denul healer's treatment back in Darujhistan. After all, it wasn't wise to trust solely in a god's payment for services. Munug's tale to the Bridgeburners about an auction in Pale was true enough – it paid to fashion options, to map out fall-back plans – and while sculpting and carving were his lesser skills, he was not so modest as to deny the high quality of his work. Of course, they were as nothing compared to his painting. As *nothing, nothing at all.*

He hastened along the track, ignoring the preternatural mists that closed in around him. Ten paces later, as he passed through the warren's gate, the clefts and crags of the East Tahlyn Hills disappeared entirely, the mists thinning to reveal a featureless, stony plain beneath a sickly sky. Further out on the plain sat a ragged hide tent, smoke hanging over it in a sea-blue haze. Munug hurried towards it.

Chest labouring, the artisan crouched down before the entrance and scratched on the flap covering it.

A ragged cough sounded from within, then a voice rasped, 'Enter, mortal.'

Munug crawled in. Thick, acrid smoke assaulted his eyes, nostrils and throat, but after his first breath a cool numbness spread out from his lungs. Keeping his head lowered and eyes averted, Munug stopped just within the entrance, and waited.

'You are late,' the god said, wheezing with each breath.

'Soldiers on the trail, master—'

'Did they discover it?'

The artisan smiled down at the dirty rushes of the tent floor. 'No. They searched my pack, as I knew they would, but not my person.'

The god coughed again, and Munug heard a scrape as the brazier was drawn across the floor. Seeds popped on its coals, and the smoke thickened. 'Show me.'

The artisan reached into the folds of his threadbare tunic and drew forth a thick, book-sized package. He unwrapped it to reveal a stack of wooden cards. Head still lowered and working blind, Munug pushed the cards towards the god, splaying them out as he did so.

He heard the god's breath catch, then a soft rustle. When it spoke again the voice was closer. 'Flaws?'

78

'Aye, master. One for each card, as you instructed.'

'Ah, this pleases me. Mortal, your skill is unsurpassed. Truly, these are images of pain and imperfection. They are tortured, fraught with anguish. They assault the eye and bleed the heart. More, I see chronic loneliness in such faces as you have fashioned within the scenes.' Dry amusement entered its tone. 'You have painted your own soul, mortal.'

'I have known little happiness, mast—'

The god hissed. 'Nor should you expect it! Not in this life, not in the thousand others you are doomed to endure before you attain salvation – assuming you have suffered enough to have earned it!'

'I beg that there be no release in my suffering, master,' Munug mumbled.

'Lies. You dream of comfort and contentment. You carry the gold that you believe will achieve it, and you mean to prostitute your talent to achieve yet more – do not deny this, mortal. I know your soul – I see its avidness and yearning here in these images. Fear not, such emotions amuse me, for they are the paths to despair.'

'Yes, master.'

'Now, Munug of Darujhistan, your payment . . .'

The old man screamed as fire blossomed within the tumours between his legs. Twisting with agony, he curled up tight on the filthy rushes.

The god laughed, the horrible sound breaking into lung-ravaging coughs that were long in passing.

The pain, Munug realized after a while, was fading.

'You are healed, mortal. You are granted more years of your miserable life. Alas, as perfection is anathema to me, so it must be among my cherished children.'

'M-master, I cannot feel my legs!'

'They are dead, I am afraid. Such was the price of curing. It seems, artisan, that you will have a long, wearying crawl to wherever it is you seek to go. Bear in mind, child, that the value lies in the journey, not in the goal achieved.' The god laughed again, triggering yet another fit of coughing.

Knowing he was dismissed, Munug pulled himself around, dragged the dead weight of his lower limbs through the tent entrance, then lay gasping. The pain he now felt came from his own soul. He pulled his pack up alongside him, rested his head on it. The columns of stacked coins were hard against his sweat-runnelled forehead. 'My rewards,' he whispered. 'Blessed is the touch of the Fallen One. Lead me, dear master, down the paths of despair, for I deserve this world's pain in unending bounty . . .'

From the tent behind him, the Crippled God's laughter hacked the air. 'Cherish this moment, dear Munug! By your hand, the new game is begun. By your hand, the world shall tremble!'

Munug closed his eyes. 'My rewards . . .'

Blend continued staring up the trail long after the trader had disappeared from view. 'He was not,' she muttered, 'as he seemed.'

'None of them are,' Picker agreed, tugging at the torcs on her arm. 'These things are damned tight.'

'Your arm will probably rot and fall off, Corporal.'

She looked up with wide eyes. 'You think they're cursed?'

Blend shrugged. 'If it was me I'd have Quick Ben take a good long peer at them, and sooner not later.'

'Togg's balls, if you'd a suspicion—'

'Didn't say I did, Corporal – it was you complaining they were tight. Can you get them off?'

She scowled. 'No, damn you.'

'Oh.' Blend looked away.

Picker contemplated giving the woman a good, hard cuff, but it was a thought she entertained at least ten times a day since they'd paired up for this posting, and once again she resisted it. 'Three hundred councils to buy my arm falling off. Wonderful.'

'Think positive, Corporal. It'll give you something to talk about with Dujek.'

'I really do hate you, Blend.'

She offered Picker a bland smile. 'So, did you drop a pebble in that old man's pack, then?'

'Aye, he was fidgety enough to warrant it. He damn near fainted when I called him back, didn't he?'

Blend nodded.

'So,' Picker said, unrolling her sleeve, 'Quick Ben tracks him—'

'Unless he cleans out his pack—'

The corporal grunted. 'He cared less about what was in it than I did. No, whatever serious booty he carried was under his shirt, no doubt about it. Anyway, he'll be sure to put out the word when he gets to Pale – the traffic of smugglers through these hills will drop right off, mark my words and I'll lay coin on that wager – and I threw him the line about better chances at the Divide when you was off collecting the councils.'

Blend's smile broadened. '"Chaos at the crossroads", eh? The only chaos Paran's crew has over there is what to do with all the takings.'

'Let's fix some food – the Moranth will likely be as punctual as usual.'

The two Bridgeburners made their way back up the trail.

An hour after sunset the flight of Black Moranth arrived, descending on their quorls in a slithering flutter of wings to the circle of lanterns Picker and Blend had set out. One of them carried a passenger who clambered off as soon as his quorl's six legs alighted on the stony ground.

Picker grinned at the cursing man. 'Over here, Quick—'

He spun to face her. 'What in Hood's name have you been up to, Corporal?'

Her grin fell away. 'Not much, Wizard. Why?'

The thin, dusk-skinned man glanced over a shoulder at the Black Moranth, then hastened to the position where Picker and Blend waited. He lowered his voice. 'We need to keep things simple, damn it. Coming over the hills I almost fell out of that knobby saddle – there's warrens

swirling around down here, power bleeding from everywhere—' He stopped, stepped closer, eyes glittering. 'From
you, too, Picker . . .'

'Cursed after all,' Blend muttered.

Picker glared at her companion and threw as much
sarcasm into her tone as she could muster, 'Just like you suspected all along, right, Blend? You lying—'

'You've acquired the blessing of an ascendant!' Quick
Ben accused in a hiss. 'You idiot! Which one, Picker?'

She struggled to swallow with a suddenly dry throat. 'Uh,
Treach?'

'Oh, that's just great.'

The corporal scowled. 'What's wrong with Treach?
Perfect for a soldier – the Tiger of Summer, the Lord of
Battle—'

'Five centuries ago, maybe! Treach veered into his
Soletaken form hundreds of years ago – the beast hasn't had
a human thought since! It's not just mindless – it's insane,
Picker!'

Blend snickered.

The wizard whirled on her. 'What are you laughing at?'

'Nothing. Sorry.'

Picker rolled up her sleeve to reveal the torcs. 'It's these,
Quick Ben,' she explained hastily. 'Can you get them off
me?'

He recoiled upon seeing the ivory bands, then shook his
head. 'If it was a sane, reasonable ascendant, maybe some
. . . negotiation might be possible. In any case, never
mind—'

'Never mind?' Picker reached out and gripped handfuls
of raincape. She shook the wizard. 'Never mind? You
snivelling worm—' She stopped suddenly, eyes widening.

Quick Ben regarded her with a raised eyebrow. 'What are
you doing, Corporal?' he asked softly.

'Uh, sorry, Wizard.' She released him.

Sighing, Quick Ben adjusted his cape. 'Blend, lead the
Moranth to the cache.'

'Sure,' she said, ambling towards the waiting warriors.

'Who made the delivery, Corporal?'

'The torcs?'

'Forget the torcs – you're stuck with them. The councils from Darujhistan. Who delivered them?'

'Odd thing, that,' Picker said, shrugging. 'A huge carriage showed up, as if from nowhere. One moment the trail's empty, the next there's six stamping horses and a carriage – Wizard, this trail up here can't manage a two-wheeled cart, much less a carriage. The guards were armed to the teeth, too, and jumpy – I suppose that makes sense, since they were carrying ten thousand councils.'

'Trygalle,' Quick Ben muttered. 'Those people make me nervous . . .' After a moment he shook his head. 'Now, my last question. The last tracker you sent off – where is it?'

Picker frowned. 'Don't you know? They're *your* pebbles, Wizard!'

'Who did you give it to?'

'A carver of trinkets—'

'Trinkets like the one you're wearing on your arm, Corporal?'

'Well, yes, but that was his lone prize – I looked at all the rest and it was good but nothing special.'

Quick Ben glanced over to where the black-armoured Moranth were loading wrapped columns of coin onto their quorls under Blend's smirking gaze. 'Well, I don't think it's gone far. I guess I'll just have to go and find it. Shouldn't take long . . .'

She watched him walk off a short distance, then sit cross-legged on the ground.

The night air was growing cold, a west wind arriving from the Tahlyn Mountains. The span of stars overhead had become sharp and crisp. Picker turned and watched the loading. 'Blend,' she called, 'make sure there's two spare saddles besides the wizard's.'

'Of course,' she replied.

The city of Pale wasn't much, but at least the nights were

83

warm. Picker was getting too old to be camping out night after night, sleeping on cold, hard ground. The past week waiting for the delivery had settled a dull ache into her bones. At least, with Darujhistan's generous contribution, Dujek would be able to complete the army's resupply.

With Oponn's luck, they'd be on the march within a week. *Off to another Hood-kissed war, as if we ain't weary enough. Fener's hoof, who or what is the Pannion Domin, anyway?*

Since leaving Darujhistan eight weeks past, Quick Ben had been attached to Second-in-Command Whiskeyjack's staff, with the task of assisting in the consolidation of Dujek's rebel army. Bureaucracy and minor sorceries seemed strangely well suited to one another. The wizard had been busy weaving a network of communications through Pale and its outlying approaches. Tithes and tariffs, in answer to the army's financial needs, and the imposition of control, easing the transition from occupation to possession. *At least for the moment.* Onearm's Host and the Malazan Empire had parted ways, after all, yet the wizard had wondered, more than once, at the curiously imperial responsibilities he had been tasked to complete.

Outlaws, are we? Indeed, and Hood dreams of sheep gambolling in green pastures, too.

Dujek was . . . waiting. Caladan Brood's army had taken its time coming south, and had only the day before reached the plain north of Pale – Tiste Andii at its heart with mercenaries and Ilgres Barghast on one flank and the Rhivi and their massive bhederin herds on the other.

But there would be no war. Not this time.

No, by the Abyss, we've all decided to fight a new enemy, assuming the parley goes smoothly – and given that Darujhistan's rulers are already negotiating with us, that seems likely. A new enemy. Some theocratic empire devouring city after city in a seemingly unstoppable wave of fanatic ferocity. The Pannion Domin – why do I have a bad feeling about this? Never mind, it's time to find my wayward tracker . . .

Eyes closing, Quick Ben loosed his soul's chains and slipped away from his body. For the moment, he could sense nothing of the innocuous waterworn pebble he'd dipped into his particular host of sorceries, so he had little choice but to fashion his search into an outward spiral, trusting in proximity to brush his senses sooner or later.

It meant proceeding blind, and if there was one thing the wizard hated—

Ah, found you!

Surprisingly close, as if he'd crossed some kind of hidden barrier. His vision showed him nothing but darkness – not a single star visible overhead – but beneath him the ground had levelled out. *I'm into a warren, all right. What's alarming is, I don't quite recognize it. Familiar, but wrong.*

He discerned a faint reddish glow ahead, rising from the ground. It coincided with the location of his tracker. The smell of sweet smoke was in the tepid air. Quick Ben's unease deepened, but he approached the glow none the less.

The red light bled from a ragged tent, he now saw. A hide flap covered the entrance, but it hung untied. The wizard sensed nothing of what lay within.

He reached the tent, crouched down, then hesitated. *Curiosity is my greatest curse, but simple acknowledgement of a flaw does not correct it. Alas.* He drew the flap aside and looked inside.

A blanket-wrapped figure sat huddled against the tent's far wall, less than three paces away, leaning over a brazier from which smoke rose in sinuous coils. Its breathing was loud, laboured. A hand that appeared to have had every one of its bones broken lifted into view and gestured. A voice rasped from beneath the hooded blanket. 'Enter, mage. I believe I have something of yours . . .'

Quick Ben accessed his warrens – he could only manage seven at any one time though he possessed more. Power rippled through him in waves. He did so with reluctance –

to unveil simultaneously nearly all he possessed filled him with a delicious whisper of omnipotence. Yet he knew that sensation for the dangerous, potentially fatal illusion it was.

'You realize now,' the figure continued between wheezing gasps, 'that you must retrieve it. For one such as myself to hold such a link to your admirable powers, mortal—'

'Who are you?' the wizard asked.

'Broken. Shattered. Chained to this fevered corpse beneath us. I did not ask for such a fate. I was not always a thing of pain . . .'

Quick Ben pressed a hand to the earth outside the tent, quested with his powers. After a long moment, his eyes widened, then slowly closed. 'You have infected her.'

'In this realm,' the figure said, 'I am as a cancer. And, with each passing of light, I grow yet more virulent. She cannot awaken, whilst I burgeon in her flesh.' He shifted slightly, and from beneath the folds of filthy blanket came the rustle of heavy chain. 'Your gods have bound me, mortal, and think the task complete.'

'You wish a service in exchange for my tracker,' Quick Ben said.

'Indeed. If I must suffer, then so too must the gods and their world—'

The wizard unleashed his host of warrens. Power ripped through the tent. The figure shrieked, jerking backward. The blanket burst into flame, as did the creature's long, tangled hair. Quick Ben darted into the tent behind the last wave of his sorcery. One hand flashed out, angled down at the wrist, palm up. His fingertips jabbed into the figure's eye-sockets, his palm slamming into its forehead, snapping the head back. Quick Ben's other hand reached out and unerringly scooped up the pebble as it rolled amidst the rushes.

The power of the warrens winked out. Even as the wizard pulled back, pivoted and dived for the entrance, the chained creature bellowed with rage. Quick Ben scrambled to his feet and ran.

The wave struck him from behind, sent him sprawling onto the hot, steaming ground. Screaming, the wizard writhed beneath the sorcerous onslaught. He tried to pull himself further away, but the power was too great. It began dragging him back. He clawed at the ground, stared at the furrows his fingers gouged in the earth, saw the dark blood welling from them.

Oh, Burn, forgive me.

The invisible, implacable grip pulled him closer to the tent entrance. Hunger and rage radiated from the figure within, as well as a certainty that such desires were moments from deliverance.

Quick Ben was helpless.

'You will know such pain!' the god roared.

Something reached up through the earth, then. A massive hand closed about the wizard, like a giant child snatching at a doll. Quick Ben screamed again as it pulled him down into the churning, steaming soil. His mouth filled with bitter earth.

A bellow of fury echoed dimly from above.

Jagged rocks ripped along the wizard's body as he was pulled further down through the flesh of the Sleeping Goddess. Starved of air, darkness slowly closed around his mind.

Then he was coughing, spitting up mouthfuls of gritty mud. Warm, sweet air filled his lungs. He clawed dirt from his eyes, rolled onto his side. Echoing groans buffeted him, the flat, hard ground beneath him slowly buckling and shifting. Quick Ben rose to his hands and knees. Blood dripped from his soul's torn flesh – his clothes were naught but strips – but he was alive. He looked up.

And almost cried out.

A vaguely human-shaped figure towered over him, easily fifteen times the wizard's own height, its bulk nearly reaching the cavern's domed ceiling. Dark flesh of clay studded with rough diamonds gleamed and glittered as the apparition shifted slightly. It seemed to be ignoring Quick

Ben – though the wizard knew that it had been this beast that had saved him from the Crippled God. Its arms were raised to the ceiling directly above it, hands disappearing into the murky, red-stained roof. Vast arcs of dull white gleamed in that ceiling, evenly spaced like an endless succession of ribs. The hands appeared to be gripping or possibly were fused to two such ribs.

Just visible beyond the creature, perhaps a thousand paces down the cavern's length, squatted another such apparition, its arms upraised as well.

Twisting, Quick Ben's gaze travelled the opposite length of the cavern. More servants – the wizard saw four, possibly five of them – each one reaching up to the ceiling. The cavern was in fact a vast tunnel, curving in the distance.

I am indeed within Burn, the Sleeping Goddess. A living warren. Flesh, and bone. And these . . . servants . . .

'You have my gratitude!' he called up to the creature looming above him.

A flattened, misshapen head tilted down. Diamond eyes stared like descending stars. 'Help us.'

The voice was childlike, filled with despair.

Quick Ben gaped. *Help?*

'She weakens,' the creature moaned. 'Mother weakens. We die. Help us.'

'How?'

'Help us, please.'

'I-I don't know how.'

'Help.'

Quick Ben staggered upright. The clay flesh, he now saw, was melting, running in wet streams down the giant's thick arms. Chunks of diamond fell away. *The Crippled God's killing them, poisoning Burn's flesh.* The wizard's thoughts raced. 'Servant, child of Burn! How much time? Until it is too late?'

'Not long,' the creature replied. 'It nears. The moment nears.'

Panic gripped Quick Ben. 'How close? Can you be more

88

specific? I need to know what I can work with, friend. Please try!'

'Very soon. Tens. Tens of years, no more. The moment nears. Help us.'

The wizard sighed. For such powers, it seemed, centuries were as but days. Even so, the enormity of the servant's plea threatened to overwhelm him. As did the threat. *What would happen if Burn dies? Beru fend, I don't think I want to find out. All right, then, it's my war, now.* He glanced down at the mud-strewn ground around him, questing with his senses. He quickly found the tracker. 'Servant! I will leave something here, so that I may find you again. I will find help – I promise – and I will come back to you—'

'Not me,' the giant said. 'I die. Another will come. Perhaps.' The creature's arms had thinned, were now almost devoid of their diamond armour. 'I die now.' It began to sag. The red stain in the ceiling had spread to the ribs it held, and cracks had begun to show.

'I will find an answer,' Quick Ben whispered. 'I swear it.' He gestured and a warren opened. Without a last glance – lest the vision break his heart – he stepped within, and was gone.

A hand shook his shoulder incessantly. Quick Ben opened his eyes.

'Damn you, mage,' Picker hissed. 'It's almost dawn – we have to fly.'

Groaning, the wizard unfolded his legs, wincing with every move, then let the corporal help him upright.

'Did you get it back?' she demanded as she half carried him to the waiting quorl.

'Get what back?'

'That pebble.'

'No. We're in trouble, Picker—'

'We're always in trouble—'

'No, I mean all of us.' He dug in his heels, stared at her. '*All of us.*'

Whatever she saw in his expression left her shaken. 'All right. But right now we've got to get moving.'

'Aye. You'd better strap me in – I won't be able to stay awake.'

They came to the quorl. The Moranth seated in the forward chitinous saddle swung its helmed head to regard them in silence.

'Queen of Dreams,' Picker muttered as she wrapped the leather harness around Quick Ben's limbs. 'I ain't never seen you this scared, Wizard. You got me ready to piss icecubes.'

They were the last words of the night that Quick Ben remembered, but remember them he did.

Ganoes Paran was plagued by images of drowning, but not in water. Drowning in darkness. Disorientated, thrashing in panic in an unknown and unknowable place. Whenever he closed his eyes, vertigo seized him, knots tightening in his gut, and it was as if he'd been stripped down to a child once again. Terrified, uncomprehending, his soul twisting with pain.

The captain left the barricade at the Divide, where the day's last traders were still struggling through the press of Malazan guards, soldiers and clerics. He'd done as Dujek had commanded, setting up his encampment across the throat of the pass. Taxation and wagon searches had yielded a substantial haul, although, as the news spread, the takings were diminishing. It was a fine balance, keeping the tax at a level that the merchants could stomach, and allowing enough contraband through lest the chokehold turn to strangulation and travel between Darujhistan and Pale dried up entirely. Paran was managing, but just barely. Yet it was the least of his difficulties.

Since the debacle at Darujhistan, the captain had been feeling adrift, tossed this way and that by the chaotic transformation of Dujek and his renegade army. The Malazans' anchor had been cut away. Support structures had collapsed. The burden upon the officer corps had grown overwhelming. Almost ten thousand soldiers had suddenly acquired an almost childlike need for reassurance.

And reassurance was something Paran was unable to give. If anything, the turmoil within him had deepened. Threads of bestial blood coursed his veins. Fragmented memories – few of them his own – and strange, unearthly visions plagued his nights. Daylight hours passed in a confused haze. Endless problems of matériel and logistics to deal with, the turgid needs of management pushed again and again through the rising flood of physical maladies now besetting him.

He'd been feeling ill for weeks, and Paran had his suspicions as to the source. *The blood of the Hound of Shadow. A creature that plunged into Dark's own realm . . . yet can I be sure of this? The emotions frothing this crest . . . more like a child's. A child's . . .*

He pushed the thought away once more, knowing full well it would soon return – even as the pain in his stomach flared once again – and, with another glance up to where Trotts held sentinel position, continued making his way up the hillside.

The pain of illness had changed him – he could see that within himself, conjured as an image, a scene both peculiar and poignant. He felt as if his own soul had been reduced into something piteous – a bedraggled, sweat-smeared rat, trapped within a rock-fall, twisting and squirming through cracks in a desperate search for a place where the pressure – the vast, shifting weight – relented. *A space in which to breathe. And the pain all around me, those sharp stones, are settling, still settling, the spaces between them vanishing . . . darkness rising like water . . .*

Whatever triumphs had been achieved in Darujhistan now seemed trivial to Paran. Saving a city, saving the lives of Whiskeyjack and his squad, the shattering of Laseen's plans, they had one and all crumbled into ash in the captain's mind.

91

He was not as he had been, and this new shaping was not to his liking.

Pain darkened the world. Pain dislocated. Turned one's own flesh and bones into a stranger's house, from which no escape seemed possible.

Bestial blood . . . it whispers of freedom. Whispers of a way out – but not from the darkness. No. Into that darkness, where the Hounds went, deep into the heart of Anomander Rake's cursed sword – the secret heart of Dragnipur.

He almost cursed aloud at that thought, as he worked his way along the hillside trail overlooking the Divide. Day's light was fading. The wind combing the grasses had begun to fall away, the rasping voice retreating to a murmur.

The blood's whisper was but one of many, each demanding his attention, each offering contradictory invitations – disparate paths of escape. *But always escape. Flight. This cowering creature can think of nothing else . . . even as the burdens settle . . . and settle.*

Dislocation. *All I see around me . . . feels like someone else's memories. Grass woven on low hills, outcrops of bedrock studding the summits, and when the sun sets and the wind cools, the sweat on my face dries, and darkness comes – and I drink its air as if it was the sweetest water. Gods, what does that mean?*

The confusion within him would not settle. *I escaped the world of that sword, yet I feel its chains about me none the less, drawing ever tighter.* And within that tension, there was an expectation. Of surrender, of yielding . . . an expectation to become . . . *what? Become what?*

The Barghast sat amidst high, tawny grasses on a summit overlooking the Divide. The day's flow of traders had begun to ebb on both sides of the barricade, the clouds of dust fading over the rutted road. Others were setting up camps – the throat of the pass was turning into an unofficial wayside. If the situation remained as it was, the wayside would take root, become a hamlet, then a village.

But it won't happen. We're too restless for that. Dujek's mapped out our immediate future, shrouded in the dust of an army on the march. Even worse, there're creases in that map, and it's starting to look like the Bridgeburners are about to fall into one. A deep one.

Breathless and fighting yet more twinges, Captain Paran moved to crouch down beside the half-naked, tattooed warrior. 'You've been strutting like a bull bhederin since this morning, Trotts,' he said. 'What have you and Whiskeyjack brewed up, soldier?'

The Barghast's thin, wide mouth twisted into something like a smile, his dark eyes remaining fixed on the scene down in the valley. 'The cold darkness ends,' he growled.

'To Hood it does – the sun's moments from setting, you grease-smeared fool.'

'Cold and frozen,' Trotts continued. 'Blind to the world. I am the Tale, and the Tale has been unspoken for too long. But no longer. I am a sword about to leave its scabbard. I am iron, and in the day's light I shall blind you all. Hah.'

Paran spat into the grasses. 'Mallet mentioned your sudden . . . loquaciousness. He also mentioned that it hasn't done anyone else any good, since with its arrival you've lost what little sense you showed before then.'

The Barghast thumped his chest, the sound reverberating like a drumbeat. 'I am the Tale, and soon it shall be told. You will see, Malazan. You all will.'

'The sun's withered your brain, Trotts. Well, we're heading back to Pale tonight – though I'd imagine Whiskeyjack's already told you that. Here comes Hedge to relieve you as lookout.' Paran straightened, disguising the wince that came with the movement. 'I'll just finish my rounds, then.'

He trudged off.

Damn you, Whiskeyjack, what have you and Dujek cooked up? The Pannion Domin . . . why are we sparing a mole's ass for some upstart zealots? These things burn out. Every time. They implode. The scroll scribblers take over – they always do – and start arguing obscure details of the faith. Sects form. Civil war erupts, and there it is, just one more dead flower trampled on history's endless road.

Aye, it's all so bright and flushed right now. Only, colours fade. They always do.

One day, the Malazan Empire will come face to face with its own mortality. One day, dusk will fall on the empire.

He bent over as yet another knot of burning pain seized his stomach. *No, think not of the empire! Think not of Laseen's cull! Trust in Tavore, Ganoes Paran – your sister will salvage the House. Better than you might have managed. Far better. Trust in your sister . . .* The pain eased slightly. Drawing a deep breath, the captain resumed making his way down to the crossing.

Drowning. By the Abyss, I am drowning.

Clambering like a rock ape, Hedge reached the summit. His bandy legs carried him to the Barghast's side. As he passed behind Trotts he reached out and gave the warrior's single knotted braid a sharp tug. 'Hah,' he said, moving to settle down beside the warrior, 'I love the way your eyes bug out when I do that.'

'You, sapper,' the Barghast said, 'are the scum beneath a pebble in a stream running through a field of sickly pigs.'

'Good one, though a tad longwinded. Got the captain's head spinning, have ya?'

Trotts said nothing, his gaze now on the distant Tahlyn Mountains.

Hedge pulled his scorched leather cap from his head, scratched vigorously through the few remaining wisps of hair on his pate, studied his companion for a long moment. 'Not bad,' he judged. 'Noble and mysterious. I'm impressed.'

'You should be. Such poses are not easy to hold, you know.'

'You're a natural. So why are you twisting Paran around?'

Trotts grinned, revealing a blue-stained row of filed teeth. 'It is fun. Besides, it's up to Whiskeyjack to explain things—'

'Only he ain't done any explaining yet. Dujek wants us

back in Pale, gathering up what's left of the Bridgeburners. Paran should be happy he's getting a company to command again, instead of just a couple of beat-up squads. Did Whiskeyjack say anything about the upcoming parley with Brood?'

Trotts slowly nodded.

Hedge scowled. 'Well, what?'

'It is coming up.'

'Oh, thanks for that. By the way, you're officially relieved of this post, soldier. They're cooking up a bhederin carcass for you down there. I had the cook stuff it with dung since that's how you like it.'

Trotts rose. 'One day I may cook and eat you, sapper.'

'And choke to death on my lucky bone.'

The Barghast frowned. 'My offer was true, Hedge. To honour you, my friend.'

The sapper squinted up at Trotts, then grinned. 'Bastard! You almost had me there!'

Sniffing, Trotts turned away. '"Almost", he said. Hah hah.'

Whiskeyjack was waiting when Paran returned to the trader post and its makeshift barricade. Once sergeant, now Dujek Onearm's second-in-command, the grizzled veteran had come in with the last flight of Moranth. He stood with his old squad's healer, Mallet, the two of them watching a score of soldiers from the 2nd Army loading the past week's toll onto the quorls. Paran approached, walking cautiously so as to hide the pain within him.

'How fares the leg, Commander?' he asked.

Whiskeyjack shrugged.

'We were just discussing that,' Mallet said, his round face flushed. 'It's healed badly. Needs serious attention—'

'Later,' the bearded commander growled. 'Captain Paran, have the squads assembled in two bells – have you decided what to do with what's left of the Ninth?'

'Aye, they'll join what's left of Sergeant Antsy's squad.'

Whiskeyjack frowned. 'Give me some names.'

'Antsy's got Corporal Picker, and . . . let's see . . . Spindle, Blend, Detoran. So, with Mallet here, and Hedge, Trotts and Quick Ben—'

'Quick Ben and Spindle are now cadre mages, Captain. But you'll have them with your company in any case. Otherwise, I'd guess Antsy will be happy enough—'

Mallet snorted. 'Happy? Antsy don't know the meaning of the word.'

Paran's eyes narrowed. 'I take it, then, that the Bridgeburners won't be marching with the rest of the Host.'

'No, you won't be – we'll go into that back at Pale, though.' Whiskeyjack's flat grey eyes studied the captain for a moment, then slid away. 'There's thirty-eight Bridgeburners left – not much of a company. If you prefer, Captain, you can decline the position. There's a few companies of elite marines short on officers, and they're used to nobleborns commanding them . . .'

There was silence.

Paran turned away. Dusk was coming, the valley's shadow rising up the slopes of the surrounding hillsides, a spatter of dim stars emerging from the sky's dome. *I might take a knife in the back, is what he's telling me. Bridgeburners have an abiding dislike for nobleborn officers.* A year ago he would have spoken those words out loud, in the belief that baring ugly truths was a good thing to do. *The misguided notion that it was the soldier's way . . . when in fact it's the opposite that is a soldier's way. In a world full of pitfalls and sinkholes, you dance the edges. Only fools jump feet first, and fools don't live long besides.* He'd felt knives enter his body once. Wounds that should have been fatal. The memory sheathed him in sweat. The threat was not something he could simply shrug off in a display of youthful, ignorant bravado. He knew that, and the two men facing him knew it as well. 'I still,' Paran said, eyes on the darkness devouring the south road, 'would consider it an honour to command the Bridgeburners, sir. Perhaps, in time, I might have the opportunity to prove myself worthy of such soldiers.'

Whiskeyjack grunted. 'As you like, Captain. The offer remains open if you change your mind.'

Paran faced him.

The commander grinned. 'For a little while longer, anyway.'

A huge, dark-skinned figure emerged from the gloom, her weapons and armour softly clinking. Seeing both Whiskeyjack and Paran, the woman hesitated, then, fixing her gaze on the commander, she said, 'The watch is being turned over, sir. We're all coming in, as ordered.'

'Why are you telling me, soldier?' Whiskeyjack rumbled. 'You talk to your immediate superior.'

The woman scowled, pivoted to face Paran. 'The watch—'

'I heard, Detoran. Have the Bridgeburners get their gear and assemble in the compound.'

'It's still a bell and a half before we leave—'

'I'm aware of that, soldier.'

'Yes, sir. At once, sir.'

The woman ambled off.

Whiskeyjack sighed. 'About that offer—'

'My tutor was Napan,' Paran said. 'I've yet to meet a Napan who knows the meaning of respect, and Detoran's no exception. I'm also aware,' he continued, 'that she's no exception as far as Bridgeburners go, either.'

'It seems your tutor taught you well,' Whiskeyjack muttered.

Paran frowned. 'What do you mean?'

'His disrespect for authority's rubbed off, Captain. You just interrupted your commander.'

'Uh, my apologies. I keep forgetting you're not a sergeant any more.'

'So do I, which is why I need people like you to get it right.' The veteran turned to Mallet. 'Remember what I said, Healer.'

'Aye, sir.'

Whiskeyjack glanced once more at Paran. 'The hurry up and wait was a good touch, Captain. Soldiers love to stew.'

Paran watched the man head off towards the gatehouse, then said to Mallet, 'Your private discussion with the commander, Healer. Anything I should know?'

Mallet's blink was sleepy. 'No, sir.'

'Very well. You may rejoin your squad.'

'Yes, sir.'

When he was alone, Paran sighed. *Thirty-eight bitter, resentful veterans, already twice betrayed. I wasn't part of the treachery at the siege of Pale, and Laseen's proclamation of outlawry embraced me as much as it did them. Neither event can be laid at my feet, yet they're doing it anyway.*

He rubbed at his eyes. Sleep had become an ... unwelcome thing. Night after night, ever since their flight from Darujhistan ... *pain – and dreams, no, nightmares. Gods below* ... He spent the dark hours twisted beneath his blankets, his blood racing through him, acids bubbling in his stomach, and when consciousness finally slipped from him, his sleep was fitful, racked with dreams of running. *Running on all fours. Then drowning.*

It's the blood of the Hound, coursing undiminished within me. It must be.

He had tried to tell himself more than once that the Shadow Hound's blood was also the source of his paranoia. The thought elicited a sour grin. *Untrue. What I fear is all too real. Worse, this vast sense of loss ... without the ability to trust – anyone. Without that, what do I see in the life awaiting me? Naught but solitude, and thus, nothing of value. And now, all these voices ... whispering of escape. Escape.*

He shook himself, spat to clear the sour phlegm in his throat. *Think of that other thing, that other scene. Solitary. Baffling. Remember, Paran, the voice you heard. It was Tattersail's – you did not doubt it then, why do so now? She lives. Somehow, some way, the sorceress lives ...*

Ahh, the pain! A child screaming in darkness, a Hound

*howling lost in sorrow. A soul nailed to the heart of a wound
. . . and I think myself alone! Gods, I wish I were!*

Whiskeyjack entered the gatehouse, closed the door
behind him and strode over to the scribe's table. He leaned
against it, stretched out his aching leg. His sigh was like the
easing of endless knots, and when it was done he was
trembling.

After a moment the door opened.

Straightening, Whiskeyjack scowled at Mallet. 'I
thought your captain'd called for an assembly, Healer—'

'Paran's in worse shape than even you, sir.'

'We've covered this. Guard the lad's back – you having
second thoughts, Mallet?'

'You misunderstand. I just quested in his direction – my
Denul warren recoiled, Commander.'

Whiskeyjack only now noted the pallid cast of the
healer's round face. 'Recoiled?'

'Aye. That's never happened before. The captain's *sick*.'

'Tumours? Cancers? Be specific, damn it!'

'Nothing like that, sir. Not yet, but they'll come. He's
eaten a hole in his own gut. All that he's holding in, I guess.
But there's more – we need Quick Ben. Paran's got sorceries
running through him like fireweed roots.'

'Oponn—'

'No, the Twin Jesters are long gone. Paran's journey to
Darujhistan – something happened to him on the way. No,
not something. *Lots* of things. Anyway, he's fighting those
sorceries, and that's what's killing him. I could be wrong in
that, sir. We need Quick Ben—'

'I hear you. Get him on it when we get to Pale. But make
sure he's subtle. No point in adding to the captain's unease.'

Mallet's frown deepened. 'Sir, it's just . . . Is he in any
shape to take command of the Bridgeburners?'

'You're asking me? If you want to talk to Dujek about
your concerns, that's your prerogative, Healer. If you think
Paran's unfit for duty – do you, Mallet?'

After a long moment, the man sighed. 'Not yet, I suppose. He's as stubborn as you are . . . sir. Hood, you sure you two aren't related?'

'Damned sure,' Whiskeyjack growled. 'Your average camp dog has purer blood than what's in my family line. Let it rest for now, then. Talk to Quick and Spindle. See what you can find out about those hidden sorceries – if gods are plucking Paran's strings again, I want to know who, and then we can mull on why.'

Mallet's eyes thinned as he studied the commander. 'Sir, what are we heading into?'

'I'm not sure, Healer,' Whiskeyjack admitted with a grimace. Grunting, he shifted weight off his bad leg. 'With Oponn's luck I won't have to pull a sword – commanders usually don't, do they?'

'If you gave me the time, sir—'

'Later, Mallet. Right now I've got a parley to think about. Brood and his army's arrived outside Pale.'

'Aye.'

'And your captain's probably wondering where in Hood's name you've disappeared to. Get out of here, Mallet. I'll see you again after the parley.'

'Yes, sir.'

CHAPTER THREE

Dujek Onearm and his army awaited the arrival of
Caladan Brood and his allies: the fell Tiste Andii,
Barghast clans from the far north, a half-score
mercenary contingents, and the plains-dwelling Rhivi.
There, on the still raw killing ground outside the
city of Pale, the two forces would meet. Not to
wage war, but to carve from bitter history, peace.
Neither Dujek nor Brood, nor anyone else among
their legendary company, could have anticipated
the ensuing clash – not of swords, but of worlds . . .

Confessions of Artanthos

S hallow ridges ribboned the hillsides a league north of
Pale, barely healed scars of a time when the city's pre-
sumptions reached out to devour the steppes
bordering the Rhivi Plain. Since memories began the hills
had been sacred to the Rhivi. Pale's farmers had paid for
their temerity with blood.

Yet the land was slow to heal; few of the ancient
menhirs, boulder rings and flat-stone crypts remained in
place. The stones were now haphazardly piled into meaningless cairns alongside what used to be terraced fields of
maize. All that was sacred in these hills was held so only
within the minds of the Rhivi.

As in faith, so we are in truth. The Mhybe drew the
antelope hide closer about her thin, bony shoulders. A new

101

array of pains and aches mapped her frame this morning, evidence that the child had drawn more from her in the night just past. The old woman told herself she felt no resentment – such needs could not be circumvented, and there was little in the child that was natural in any case. Vast, cold-hearted spirits and the blind spells of sorcery had conspired to carve into being something new, unique.

And time was growing short, so very short.

The Mhybe's dark eyes glittered within their nests of wrinkles as she watched the child scampering over the weathered terraces. A mother's instincts ever abided. It was not right to curse them, to lash out at the bindings of love that came in the division of flesh. For all the flaws raging within her, and for all the twisted demands woven into her daughter, the Mhybe could not – would not – spin webs of hate.

None the less, the withering of her body weakened the gifts of the heart to which she so desperately clung. Less than a season past, the Mhybe had been a young woman, not yet wedded. She had been proud, unwilling to accept the half-braids of grass that numerous young, virile men had set down before the entrance to her tent – not yet ready to entwine her own braid and thus bind herself to marriage.

The Rhivi were a damaged people – how could one think of husband and family in this time of endless, devastating war? She was not as blind as her sister-kin; she did not embrace the supposed spirit-blessed duty to produce sons to feed into the ground before the Reaper's Plough. Her mother had been a reader of bones, gifted with the ability to hold the people's entire repository of memories – every lineage, reaching back to the Dying Spirit's Tear. And her father had held the Spear of War, first against the White Face Barghast, then against the Malazan Empire.

She missed them both, deeply, yet understood how their deaths, and her own defiance of accepting a man's touch,

102

had together conspired to make her the ideal choice in the eyes of the host of spirits. An untethered vessel, a vessel in which to place two shattered souls – one beyond death and the other held back from death through ancient sorceries, two identities braided together – a vessel that would be used to feed the unnatural child thus created.

Among the Rhivi, who travelled with the herds and raised no walls of stone or brick, such a container, intended for a singular use after which it would be discarded, was called a *mhybe*, and so she had found herself a new name, and now every truth of her life was held within it.

Old without wisdom, weathered without the gift of years, yet I am expected to guide this child – this creature – who gains a season with every one I lose, for whom weaning will mean my death. Look at her now, playing the games a child would play; she smiles all unknowing of the price her existence, her growth, demands of me.

The Mhybe heard footsteps behind her, and a moment later a tall, black-skinned woman arrived to stand beside the Rhivi. The newcomer's angled eyes held on the child playing on the hillside. The prairie wind sent strands of long black hair over her face. Fine, scaled armour glinted from beneath her black-dyed, rawhide shirt.

'Deceptive,' the Tiste Andii woman murmured, 'is she not?'

The Mhybe sighed, then nodded.

'Hardly a thing to generate fear,' the midnight-skinned woman continued, 'or be the focus of searing arguments . . .'

'There have been more, then?'

'Aye. Kallor renews his assault.'

The Mhybe stiffened. She looked up at the Tiste Andii. 'And? Has there been a change, Korlat?'

'Brood remains steadfast,' Korlat replied after a moment. She shrugged. 'If he has doubts, he hides them well.'

'He has,' the Mhybe said. 'Yet his need for the Rhivi and our herds outweighs them still. This is calculation, not

103

faith. Will such need remain, once an alliance with the one-armed Malazan is fashioned?'

'It is hoped,' Korlat ventured, 'that the Malazans will possess more knowledge of the child's origins—'

'Enough to alleviate the potential threat? You must make Brood understand, Korlat, that what the two souls once were is nothing to what they have become.' Her eyes on the playing child, the Mhybe continued, 'She was created within the influence of a T'lan Imass – its timeless warren became the binding threads, and were so woven by an Imass bonecaster – a bonecaster of flesh and blood, Korlat. This child belongs to the T'lan Imass. She may well be clothed in the flesh of a Rhivi, and she may well contain the souls of two Malazan mages, but she is now a Soletaken, and more – a Bonecaster. And even these truths but brush the edges of what she will become. Tell me, what need have the immortal T'lan Imass for a flesh and blood Bonecaster?'

Korlat's grimace was wry. 'I am not the person to ask.'

'Nor are the Malazans.'

'Are you certain of that? Did not the T'lan Imass march under Malazan banners?'

'Yet they do so no longer, Korlat. What hidden breach exists between them now? What secret motives might lie beneath all that the Malazans advise? We have no way of guessing, have we?'

'I imagine Caladan Brood is aware of such possibilities,' the Tiste Andii said drily. 'In any case, you may witness and partake in these matters, Mhybe. The Malazan contingent approaches, and the Warlord seeks your presence at the parley.'

The Mhybe turned about. Caladan Brood's encampment stretched out before her, precisely organized as usual. Mercenary elements to the west, the Tiste Andii holding the centre, and her own Rhivi camps and the bhederin herds to the east. The march had been a long one, from the Old King Plateau, through the cities of Cat and then Patch, and finally onto the south-wending old Rhivi Trail crossing the plain that was the Rhivi's traditional home. *A home torn apart by years of war, of marching armies and the incendiaries of the Moranth falling from the sky . . . quorls whirling in black-specked silence, horror descending on our camps . . . our sacred herds.*

Yet now, we are to clasp wrists with our enemy. With the Malazan invaders and the cold-blooded Moranth, we are to weave braids of marriage – our two armies – jaws locked on one another's throats for so long, but a marriage not in the name of peace. No, these warriors now seek another enemy, a new enemy . . .

Beyond Brood's army to the south rose the recently mended walls of Pale, the stains of violence a chilling reminder of Malazan sorceries. A knot of riders had just departed from the city's north gate, an unmarked grey banner announcing their outlawry for all to see as they slowly rode across the bare killing ground towards Brood's encampment.

The Mhybe's gaze narrowed suspiciously on that pennant. *Old woman, your fears are a curse. Think not of mistrust, think not of the horrors visited upon us by these once-invaders. Dujek Onearm and his Host have been outlawed by the hated Empress. One campaign has ended. A new one begins. Spirits below, shall we ever see an end to war?*

The child joined the two women. The Mhybe glanced down at her, saw within the steady, unwavering eyes of the girl a knowledge and wisdom that seemed born of millennia – and perhaps it was indeed so. *Here we three stand, for all to see – a child of ten or eleven years, a woman of youthful visage with unhuman eyes, and a bent old woman – and it is, in every detail, an illusion, for what lies within us is reversed. I am the child. The Tiste Andii has known thousands of years of life, and the girl . . . hundreds of thousands.*

Korlat had also looked down at the child. The Tiste Andii smiled. 'Did you enjoy your play, Silverfox?'

'For a time,' the girl replied in a voice surprisingly low. 'But I grew sad.'

Korlat's brows rose. 'And why is that?'

'There was once a sacred trust here – between these hills and spirits of the Rhivi. It is now broken. The spirits were naught but untethered vessels of loss and pain. The hills will not heal.'

The Mhybe felt her blood turn to ice. Increasingly, the child was revealing a sensitivity to rival the wisest shoulderwoman among the tribes. Yet there was a certain coolness to that sensitivity, as if a hidden intent lay behind every compassionate word. 'Can nothing be done, daughter?'

Silverfox shrugged. 'It is no longer necessary.'

Such as now. 'What do you mean?'

The round-faced girl smiled up at the Mhybe. 'If we are to witness the parley, Mother, we'd best hurry.'

The place of meeting was thirty paces beyond the outermost pickets, situated on a low rise. The recent barrows that had been raised to dispose of the dead after the fall of Pale were visible to the west. The Mhybe wondered if those countless victims now watched from afar the scene unfolding before her. *Spirits are born of spilled blood, after all. And without propitiation, they often twist into inimical forces, plagued by nightmare visions and filled with spite. Is it only the Rhivi who know these truths?*

From war to alliance – how would such ghosts look upon this?

'They feel betrayed,' Silverfox said beside her. 'I will answer them, Mother.' She reached out to take the Mhybe's hand as they walked. 'This is a time for memories. Ancient memories, and recent memories . . .'

'And you, daughter,' the Mhybe asked in a low, febrile tone, 'are you the bridge between the two?'

'You *are* wise, Mother, despite your own lack of faith in yourself. The hidden is slowly revealed. Look on these once-enemies. You fight in your mind, raising up all the differences between us, you struggle to hold on to your dislike, your hatred of them, for that is what is familiar.

Memories are the foundations of such hatred. But, Mother, memories hold another truth, a secret one, and that is all that we have experienced, yes?'

The Mhybe nodded. 'So our elders tell us, daughter,' she said, biting back a faint irritation.

'Experiences. They are what we share. From opposite sides, perhaps, but they are the same. The same.'

'I know this, Silverfox. Blame is meaningless. We are all pulled, as tides are pulled by an unseen, implacable will—'

The girl's hand tightened in the Mhybe's hand. 'Then ask Korlat, Mother, what her memories tell her.'

Glancing over at the Tiste Andii, the Rhivi woman raised her brows and said, 'You have been listening, yet saying nothing. What reply does my daughter expect from you?'

Korlat's smile was wistful. 'Experiences are the same. Between your two armies, indeed. But also . . . across the breadth of time. Among all who possess memories, whether an individual or a people, life's lessons are ever the same lessons.' The Tiste Andii's now-violet eyes rested on Silverfox. 'Even among the T'lan Imass – is this what you are telling us, child?'

She shrugged. 'In all that is to come, think on forgiveness. Hold to it, but know too that it must not always be freely given.' Silverfox swung her sleepy gaze to Korlat and the dark eyes suddenly hardened. 'Sometimes forgiveness *must be denied.*'

Silence followed. *Dear spirits, guide us. This child frightens me. Indeed, I can understand Kallor . . . and that is more worrying than anything else.*

They came to a halt far to one side of the place of parley just beyond the pickets of Brood's encampment.

Moments later, the Malazans reached the rise. There were four of them. The Mhybe had no difficulty in recognizing Dujek, the now-renegade High Fist. The one-armed man was older than she had expected, however, and he sat in the saddle of his roan gelding as would a man pained with old aches and stiff bones. He was thin, of average height, wearing plain armour and an undecorated standard-issue shortsword strapped to his belt. His narrow, hatchet face was beardless, displaying a lifetime of battle scars. He wore no helmet, the only indication of rank being his long grey cape and its silver-wrought fastening.

At Dujek's left side rode another officer, grey-bearded and solidly built. A visored helm with a chain camail disguised much of his features, but the Mhybe sensed in him an immeasurable strength of will. He sat straight in his saddle, though she noted that his left leg was held awkwardly, the boot not in the stirrup. The chain of his calf-length hauberk was battered and ribboned with leather stitches. That he sat on Dujek's unprotected left side was not lost on the Mhybe.

To the renegade High Fist's right sat a young man, evidently an aide of some sort. He was nondescript, yet she saw that his eyes roved ceaselessly, taking in details of all that he saw. It was this man who held the outlawry pennon in one leather-gloved hand.

The fourth rider was a Black Moranth, entirely encased in chitinous armour, and that armour was badly damaged. The warrior had lost all four fingers of his right hand, yet he continued to wear what was left of its gauntlet. Countless sword-slashes marred the gleaming black armour.

Korlat grunted softly beside her. 'That's a hard-bitten lot, wouldn't you say?'

The Mhybe nodded. 'Who is that on Dujek Onearm's left?'

'Whiskeyjack, I would imagine,' the Tiste Andii replied with a wry smile. 'Cuts quite a figure, doesn't he?'

For a moment the Mhybe felt like the young woman that she was in truth. She wrinkled her nose. 'Rhivi aren't that hairy, thank the spirits.'

'Even so . . .'

'Aye, even so.'

Silverfox spoke. 'I would like him for an uncle.'

The two women looked down at her in surprise.

'An uncle?' the Mhybe asked.

The girl nodded. 'You can trust him. While the one-armed old man is hiding something – well, no, they both are and it's the same secret, yet I trust the bearded one anyway. The Moranth – he laughs inside. Always laughs, and no-one knows this. Not a cruel laugh, but one filled with sorrow. And the one with the banner . . .' Silverfox frowned. 'I am uncertain of him. I think I always have been . . .'

The Mhybe met Korlat's eyes over the girl's head.

'I suggest,' the Tiste Andii said, 'we move closer.'

As they approached the rise two figures emerged from the picket line, followed by an outrider bearing a pennon-less standard, all on foot. Seeing them, the Mhybe wondered what the Malazans would make of the two warriors in the lead. There was Barghast blood in Caladan Brood, reflected in his tall, hulking form and his wide, flat face; and something else besides, something not quite human. The man was huge, well matched to the iron hammer strapped to his back. He and Dujek had been duelling on this continent for over twelve years, a clash of wills that had seen more than a score pitched battles and as many sieges. Both soldiers had faced dire odds more than once, yet had come through, bloodied but alive. They had long since taken the measure of the other on fields of battle, but now, finally, they were about to come face to face.

At Brood's side strode Kallor, tall, gaunt and grey. His full-length surcoat of chain glittered in the morning's diffuse light. A plain bastard sword hung from the iron rings of his harness, swinging in time with his heavy steps. If any player in this deadly game had remained a mystery to the Mhybe, it was the self-named High King. Indeed, all the Rhivi woman could be certain of was Kallor's hatred for Silverfox, a hatred bred of fear, and perhaps a knowledge that the man alone possessed – a knowledge he was unwilling to share with anyone. Kallor claimed to have lived through millennia, claimed to have once ruled an empire that he himself had finally destroyed, for reasons he would not reveal. Yet he was not an ascendant – his longevity probably came from alchemies, and was anything but perfect, for his face and body were as ravaged as those of a mortal man who was nearing a century of life.

Brood made use of Kallor's knowledge of tactics, what seemed an instinctive mastery of the sweep and shift of vast campaigns, but for the High King it was clear to all that such contests were but passing games, attended to with distraction and barely veiled disinterest. Kallor commanded no loyalty among the soldiers. Grudging respect was all the man achieved, and, the Mhybe suspected, all he ever had achieved, or ever would.

His expression now, as he and Brood reached the rise, revealed disdain and contempt as he regarded Dujek, Whiskeyjack, and the Moranth commander. It would be a struggle not to take offence, yet all three Malazans seemed to be ignoring the High King as they dismounted, their attention fixed unwaveringly on Caladan Brood.

Dujek Onearm stepped forward. 'Greetings, Warlord. Permit me to introduce my modest contingent. Second-in-command Whiskeyjack. Artanthos, my present standard-bearer. And the leader of the Black Moranth, whose title translates into something like Achievant, and whose name is entirely unpronounceable.' The renegade High Fist grinned over at the armoured figure. 'Since he shook hands with a Rhivi spirit up in Blackdog Forest, we've taken to calling him Twist.'

'Artanthos . . .' Silverfox quietly murmured. 'He's not used that name in a long time. Nor is he as he appears.'

'If an illusion,' Korlat whispered, 'then it is masterful. I sense nothing untowards.'

The child nodded. 'The prairie air's . . . rejuvenated him.'

'Who is he, daughter?' the Mhybe asked.

'A chimera, in truth.'

Following Dujek's words, Brood grunted and said, 'At my side is Kallor, my second-in-command. On behalf of the Tiste Andii is Korlat. Of the Rhivi, the Mhybe and her young charge. Bearing what's left of my standard is Outrider Hurlochel.'

Dujek was frowning. 'Where is the Crimson Guard?'

'Prince K'azz D'Avore and his forces are attending to internal matters, for the moment, High Fist. They will not be joining our efforts against the Pannion Domin.'

'Too bad,' Dujek muttered.

Brood shrugged. 'Auxiliary units have been assembled to replace them. A Saltoan Horse Regiment, four clans of the Barghast, a mercenary company from One Eye Cat, and another from Mott—'

Whiskeyjack seemed to choke. He coughed, then shook his head. 'That wouldn't be the Mott Irregulars, Warlord, would it?'

Brood's smile revealed filed teeth. 'Aye, you've some experience with them, haven't you, Commander? When you soldiered among the Bridgeburners.'

'They were a handful,' Whiskeyjack agreed, 'though not just in a fight – they spent most of their time stealing our supplies then running away, as I recall.'

'A talent for logistics, we called it,' Kallor commented.

'I trust,' Brood said to Dujek, 'that the arrangements with Darujhistan's Council have proved satisfactory.'

'They have, Warlord. Their ... donations ... have allowed us to fulfil our resupply needs.'

'I believe a delegation is on its way from Darujhistan and should be here in a short while,' Brood added. 'Should you require additional assistance ...'

'Generous of them,' the High Fist said, nodding.

'The command tent awaits us,' the warlord said. 'There are details that need to be discussed.'

'As you say,' Dujek agreed. 'Warlord, we have battled one another for a long time – I look forward to fighting side by side for a change. Let us hope the Pannion Domin proves a worthy foe.'

Brood grimaced. 'But not too worthy.'

'Granted,' Dujek said, grinning.

Still standing slightly apart with the Tistë Andii and the Mhybe, Silverfox smiled and spoke quietly. 'So we have it. They have locked gazes. Taken the measure of the other . . . and both are pleased.'

'A remarkable alliance, this,' Korlat muttered with a faint shake of her head. 'To so easily relinquish so much . . .'

'Pragmatic soldiers,' the Mhybe said, 'are the most frightening among the people whom I have known in my short life.'

Silverfox laughed low in her throat. 'And you doubt your own wisdom, Mother . . .'

Caladan Brood's command tent was situated in the centre of the Tistë Andii encampment. Though she had visited it many times and had acquired some familiarity with the Tistë Andii, the Mhybe was once again struck by the sense of strangeness as she strode with the others into their midst. Antiquity and pathos were twin breaths filling the aisles and pathways between the high-peaked narrow tents. There was little in the way of conversation among the few tall, dark-clothed figures they passed, nor was any particular attention accorded Brood and his entourage – even Korlat, Anomander Rake's second-in-command, received but scant notice.

It was difficult for the Mhybe to understand – a people plagued by indifference, an apathy that made even the efforts of civil discourse too much to contemplate. There were secret tragedies in the long, tortured past of the Tistë Andii. Wounds that would never heal. Even suffering, the Rhivi had come to realize, was capable of becoming a way of life. To then extend such an existence from decades into centuries, then into millennia, still brought home to the Mhybe a dull shock of horror.

These narrow, arcane tents might be home to ghosts, a restless, roving necropolis haunted with lost spirits. The strangely stained, ragged ribbons tied to the iron tent poles added a votive touch to the scene, as did the gaunt, spectral figures of the Tiste Andii themselves. They seemed to be waiting, an eternal expectation that never failed to send shivers through the Mhybe. And worse, she knew their capabilities – she had seen them draw blades in anger, then wield them with appalling efficiency. And she had seen their sorcery.

Among humans, cold indifference was often manifested in acts of brutal cruelty, was often the true visage of evil – if such a thing existed – but the Tiste Andii had yet to reveal such wanton acts. They fought at Brood's command, for a cause not their own, and those few of them who were killed on such occasions were simply left on the ground. It had fallen to the Rhivi to retrieve those bodies, to treat them in the Rhivi way and to mourn their passing. The Tiste Andii looked upon such efforts without expression, as if bemused by the attention accorded to a mere corpse.

The command tent waited directly ahead, octagonal and wood-framed, the canvas a much-mended sun-faded orange that had once been red. It had once belonged to the Crimson Guard, and had been left on a rubbish heap before Outrider Hurlochel had come to rescue it for the warlord. As with the standard, Brood wasn't much for proud accoutrements.

The large flap at the entrance had been tied back. Atop the front support pole sat a Great Raven, head cocked towards the group, beak open as if in silent laughter. The Mhybe's thin lips quirked into a half-smile upon seeing Crone. Anomander Rake's favoured servant had taken to hounding Caladan Brood, offering incessant advice like a conscience twisted awry. The Great Raven had tested the warlord's patience more than once – *yet Brood tolerates her in the same way he tolerates Anomander Rake himself. Uneasy allies . . . the tales all agree that Brood and Rake have worked side by side for a long, long time, yet is there trust between them? That particular relationship is a hard one to understand, with layers upon layers of complexity and ambiguity, all the more confusing for Crone's dubious role in providing the bridge between the two warriors.*

'Dujek Onearm!' Crone screamed, the outburst followed by a mad cackle. 'Whiskeyjack! I bring you greetings from one Baruk, an alchemist in Darujhistan. And, from my master, Anomander Rake, Lord of Moon's Spawn, Knight of High House Darkness, son of Mother Dark herself, I convey to you his . . . no, not greeting as such . . . not greeting . . . but amusement. Yes, amusement!'

Dujek frowned. 'And what so amuses your master, bird?'

'Bird?' the Great Raven shrieked. 'I am Crone, the unchallenged matriarch of Moon's Spawn's cacophonous, vast murder of kin!'

Whiskeyjack grunted. 'Matriarch to the Great Ravens? You speak for them all, do you? I'd accept that – Hood knows you're loud enough.'

'Upstart! Dujek Onearm, my master's amusement is beyond explanation—'

'Meaning you don't know,' the renegade High Fist interjected.

'Outrageous audacity – show respect, mortal, else I choose your carcass to feed on when the day comes!'

'You'd likely break your beak on my hide, Crone, but you're welcome to it when that moment arrives.'

Brood growled, 'Do you still have that beak-strap, Hurlochel?'

'I do, sir.'

The Great Raven hissed, ducking her head and half raising her vast wings. 'Don't you dare, ox! Repeat that affront at your peril!'

'Then hold your tongue.' Brood faced the others and waved them to the entrance. Crone, perched over everyone, bobbed her head as each soldier strode beneath her.

When it was the Mhybe's turn the Great Raven chuckled. 'The child in your hand is about to surprise us all, old woman.'

The Rhivi paused. 'What do you sense, old crow?'

Crone laughed in silence before replying, 'Immanence, dearest clay pot, and naught else. Greetings, child Silverfox.'

The girl studied the Great Raven for a moment, then said, 'Hello, Crone. I had not before realized that your kind were born in the rotting flesh of a—'

'Silence!' Crone shrieked. 'Such knowledge should never be spoken! You must learn to remain silent, child – for your own safety—'

'For yours, you mean,' Silverfox said, smiling.

'In this instance, aye, I'll not deny it. Yet listen to this wise old creature before stepping into this tent, child. There are those waiting within who will view the extent of your awareness – should you be foolish enough to reveal it – as the deadliest threat. Revelations could mean your death. And know this: you are not yet able to protect yourself. Nor can the Mhybe, whom I cherish and love, hope to defend you – hers is not a violent power. You will both need protectors, do you understand?'

Her smile unperturbed, Silverfox nodded.

The Mhybe's hand tightened instinctively around her daughter's, even as a tumult of emotions assailed her. She was not blind to the threats to Silverfox and herself, nor was she unaware of the powers burgeoning within the child. *But I sense no power within me, violent or otherwise. Though spoken with affection, Crone named me 'clay pot' in truth, and all that it once protected is no longer within me, but standing here, exposed and vulnerable, at my side.* She glanced up at the Great Raven one last time as Silverfox led her inside. She met Crone's black, glittering eyes. *Love and cherish me, do you, crow? Bless you for that.*

The command tent's central chamber was dominated by a large map table of rough-hewn wood, warped and misshapen as if cobbled together by a drunken carpenter. As the Mhybe and Silverfox entered, the veteran Whiskeyjack – helmet unstrapped and under one arm – was laughing, his eyes fixed upon the table.

'You bastard, Warlord,' he said, shaking his head.

Brood was frowning at the object of Whiskeyjack's attention. 'Aye, I'll grant you it's not pretty—'

'That's because Fiddler and Hedge made the damned thing,' the Malazan said. 'In Mott Wood—'

'Who are Fiddler and Hedge?'

'My two sappers, when I was commanding the Ninth Squad. They'd organized one of their notorious card games, using the Deck of Dragons, and needed a surface on which to play it. A hundred fellow Bridgeburners had gathered the game, despite the fact that we were under constant attack, not to mention bogged down in the middle of a swamp. The game was interrupted by a pitched battle – we were overrun, then driven back, then we retook the position, all of which consumed maybe a bell – and lo, someone had walked off with a two hundred pound table in the meantime! You should have heard the sappers cursing . . .'

Caladan Brood crossed his arms, still frowning at the table. After a few moments he grunted. 'A donation from the Mott Irregulars. It has served me well – my, uh, compliments to your sappers. I can have it returned—'

'No need, Warlord . . .' It seemed the Malazan was about to say something more, something important, but then he simply shook his head.

A soft gasp from Silverfox startled the Mhybe. She looked down, brows raised questioningly, but the girl's attention was swinging from the table to Whiskeyjack, then back again, a small smile on her lips. 'Uncle Whiskeyjack,' she said suddenly.

All eyes turned to Silverfox, who blithely continued, 'Those sappers and their games – they cheat, don't they?'

The bearded Malazan scowled. 'Not an accusation I'd

116

recommend you repeat, especially if there's any Bridgeburners around, lass. A lot of coin's gone one way and one way only in those games. Did Fid and Hedge cheat? They made their rules so complicated no-one could tell one way or the other. So, to answer you, I don't know.' His scowl was deepening as he studied Silverfox, as if the man was growing troubled by something.

Something . . . like a sense of familiarity . . . Realization dawned within the Mhybe. *Of course, he knows nothing about her – about what she is, what she was. It's their first meeting, as far as he's concerned, yet she called him uncle, and more, there's that voice – throaty, knowing . . . He knows not the child, but the woman she once was.*

Everyone waited for Silverfox to say more, to offer explanation. Instead she simply walked up to the table and slowly ran her hand across its battered surface. A fleeting smile crossed her features. Then she pulled close one of the mismatched chairs and sat down.

Brood sighed, gestured to Hurlochel. 'Find us that map of the Pannion Domin territories.'

With the large map laid out, the others slowly gathered round the table. After a moment, Dujek grunted. 'None of our own maps are this detailed,' he said. 'You've noted the locations of various Pannion armies – how recent is this?'

'Three days,' Brood said. 'Crone's cousins are there, tracking movements. The notes referring to the Pannions' means of organization and past tactics have been culled from various sources. As you can see, they're poised to take the city of Capustan. Maurik, Setta and Lest have all fallen within the past four months. The Pannion's forces are still on the south side of the Catlin River, but preparations for the crossing have begun—'

'The Capustan army won't contest that crossing?' Dujek asked. 'If not, then they're virtually inviting a siege. I take it no-one expects Capustan to put up much of a fight.'

'The situation in Capustan is a bit confused,' the warlord explained. 'The city's ruled by a prince and a coalition of

High Priests, and the two factions are ever at odds with each other. Problems have been compounded by the prince's hiring a mercenary company to augment his own minimal forces—'

'What company?' Whiskeyjack asked.

'The Grey Swords. Have you heard of them, Commander?'

'No.'

'Nor have I,' Brood said. 'It's said they're up from Elingarth – a decent complement: over seven thousand. Whether they'll prove worthy of the usurious fees they've carved from the prince remains to be seen. Hood knows, their so-called standard contract is almost twice the coin of what the Crimson Guard demands.'

'Their commander read the situation,' Kallor commented, his tone suggesting vast weariness, if not outright boredom. 'Prince Jelarkan has more coin than soldiers, and the Pannions won't be bought off – it's a holy war as far as the Seer's concerned, after all. To worsen matters, the council of High Priests has the backing of each temple's private company of highly trained, well-equipped soldiers. That's almost three thousand of the city's most able fighters, whilst the prince himself has been left with dregs for his own Capanthall – which he's prevented from expanding beyond two thousand by law. For years the Mask Council – the coalition of temples – has been using the Capanthall as a recruiting ground for their own companies, bribing away the best—'

Clearly the Mhybe wasn't alone in suspecting that, given the opportunity, Kallor would have gone on all afternoon, for Whiskeyjack interrupted the man as he drew breath.

'So this Prince Jelarkan circumvented the law by hiring mercenaries.'

'Correct,' was Brood's swift reply. 'In any case, the Mask Council has managed to invoke yet another law, preventing the Grey Swords from active engagement beyond the city walls, so the crossing will not be contested—'

'Idiots,' Dujek growled. 'Given this is a holy war, you'd think the temples would do all they could to effect a united front against the Pannions.'

'I imagine they believe they are,' Kallor answered with a sneer that could have been meant for Dujek or the priests in Capustan, or both. 'While at the same time ensuring that the prince's power remains held in check.'

'It's more complicated than that,' Brood countered. 'The ruler of Maurik capitulated with little bloodshed by arresting all the priests in her city and handing them over to the Pannions' Tenescowri. In one move, she saved her city and its citizens, topped up her royal coffers with booty from the temples and got rid of an eternal thorn in her side. The Pannion Seer granted her a governorship which is better than being torn apart and devoured by the Tenescowri – which is what happened to the priests.'

The Mhybe hissed. 'Torn apart and *devoured?*'

'Aye,' the warlord said. 'The Tenescowri are the Seer's peasant army – they're fanatics that the Seer doesn't bother supplying. Indeed, he's given them his holy blessing to do whatever is necessary to feed and arm themselves. If certain other rumours are true, then cannibalism is the least of the horrors—'

'We've heard similar rumours,' Dujek muttered. 'So, Warlord, the question before us is, do we seek to save Capustan or let it fall? The Seer must know we're coming – his followers have spread the cult far beyond his borders, in Darujhistan, in Pale, in Saltoan – meaning he knows we will be crossing Catlin River somewhere, somewhen. If he takes Capustan, then the river's widest ford is in his hands. Which leaves us with naught but the old ford west of Saltoan where the stone bridge used to be. Granted, our engineers could float us a bridge there, provided we bring the wood with us. That's the overland option, in any case. We've two others, of course . . .'

Crone, perched on one end of the table, cackled. 'Listen to him!'

The Mhybe nodded, understanding the Great Raven and experiencing her own amused disbelief.

Dujek scowled down the length of the table at Crone. 'You have a problem, bird?'

'You are the warlord's match indeed! Word for word, you think aloud as he does! Oh, how can one not see the honed edge of poetry in your mutual war of the past twelve years?'

'Be quiet, Crone,' Brood commanded. 'Capustan will be besieged. The Pannions' forces are formidable – we've learned that Septarch Kulpath is commanding the expedition, and he's the ablest of all the Seer's septarchs. He has half the total number of Beklites with him – that's fifty thousand regular infantry – and a division of Urdomen besides the usual support attachments and auxiliary units. Capustan is a small city, but the prince has worked hard on the walls, and the city's layout itself is peculiarly suited to district by district defence. If the Grey Swords don't pull out with the first skirmish, Capustan might hold for a time. None the less . . .'

'My Black Moranth could land a few companies in the city,' Dujek said, glancing over at the silent Twist, 'but without an explicit invitation to do so, tension could prove problematic.'

Kallor snorted. 'Now that is an understatement. What city on Genabackis would welcome Malazan legions into their midst? More, you'd have to bring your own food – you can be sure of that, High Fist – not to mention face outright hostility if not actual betrayal from the Capan people.'

'It's clear,' Whiskeyjack ventured, 'that we need to establish preliminary contact with Capustan's prince.'

Silverfox giggled, startling everyone. 'All this orchestration, Uncle! You've already set in motion a plan to do so. You and the onearmed soldier have schemed this to the last detail. You plan on liberating Capustan, though of course not directly – you two never do anything directly, do you? You want to remain hidden behind the events, a classic Malazan tactic if ever there was one.'

Like the master gamblers they were, the two men showed no expression at her words.

Kallor's chuckle was a soft rattle of bones.

The Mhybe studied Whiskeyjack. *The child's so very alarming, isn't she? By the spirits, she alarms even me, and I know so much more than you do, sir.*

'Well,' Brood rumbled after a moment, 'I'm delighted to hear we're in agreement – Capustan mustn't fall if we can help it, and an indirect means of relief is probably the best option, all things considered. On the surface, we must be seen – the majority of your forces as well as mine, Onearm – to be marching overland, at a predictable pace. That will establish Septarch Kulpath's timetable for the siege, for both him and us. I take it we're also agreed that Capustan must not be our sole focus.'

Dujek slowly nodded. 'It may still fall, despite our efforts. If we're to defeat the Pannion Domin, we must strike for its heart.'

'Agreed. Tell me, Onearm, which city have you targeted for this first season of the campaign?'

'Coral,' Whiskeyjack replied immediately.

All eyes returned to the map. Brood was grinning. 'It seems we do indeed think alike. Once we reach the north border of the Domin, we drive like a spear southward, a swift succession of liberated cities . . . Setta, Lest, Maurik – won't the governess be pleased – then to Coral itself. We undo in a single season the Seer's gains over the past four years. I want that cult reeling, I want cracks sent right through the damned thing.'

'Aye, Warlord. So we march overland, yes? No boats – that would hasten Kulpath's hand, after all. There's one more issue to clarify, however,' Whiskeyjack continued, his grey eyes swinging to the one representative – apart from the Black Moranth commander – who'd yet to speak, 'and that is, what can we expect from Anomander Rake? Korlat? Will the Tiste Andii be with us?'

The woman simply smiled.

121

Brood cleared his throat. 'Like you,' he said, 'we have initiated some moves of our own. As we speak, Moon's Spawn travels towards the Domin. Before it reaches the Seer's territory, it will . . . disappear.'

Dujek raised his brows. 'An impressive feat.'

Crone cackled.

'We know little of the sorcery behind the Seer's power,' the warlord said, 'only that it exists. Like your Black Moranth, Moon's Spawn represents tactical opportunities we'd be fools not to exploit.' Brood's grin broadened. 'Like you, High Fist, we seek to avoid predictability.' He nodded towards Korlat. 'The Tiste Andii possess formidable sorceries—'

'Not enough,' Silverfox cut in.

The Tiste Andii woman frowned down at the girl. 'That is quite an assertion, child.'

Kallor hissed. 'Trust nothing of what she says. Indeed, as Brood well knows, I consider her presence at this meeting foolish – she is no ally of ours. She will betray us all, mark my words. Betrayal, it is her oldest friend. Hear me, all of you. This creature is an abomination.'

'Oh, Kallor,' Silverfox sighed, 'must you always go on like that?'

Dujek turned to Caladan Brood. 'Warlord, I admit to some confusion over the girl's presence – who in Hood's name is she? She seems in possession of preternatural knowledge. For what seems a ten-year-old child—'

'She is far more than that,' Kallor snapped, staring at Silverfox with hard, hate-filled eyes. 'Look at the hag beside her,' the High King growled. 'She's barely seen twenty summers, High Fist, and this *child* was torn from her womb not six months ago. The abomination feeds on the life force of her mother – no, not mother, the unfortunate vessel that once hosted the child – you all shivered at the cannibalism of the Tenescowri, what think you of a creature that so devours the life-soul of the one who birthed it? And there is more—' He stopped, visibly bit

122

back what he was about to say, and sat back. 'She should be killed. Now. Before her power surpasses us all.'

There was silence within the tent.

Damn you, Kallor. Is this what you want to show our new-found allies? A camp divided. And . . . spirits below . . . damn you a second time, for she never knew. She never knew . . .

Trembling, the Mhybe looked down at Silverfox. The girl's eyes were wide, even now filling with tears as she stared up at her mother. 'Do I?' she whispered. 'Do I *feed* on you?'

The Mhybe closed her eyes, wishing she could hide the truth from Silverfox once again, and for ever more. Instead, she said, 'Not your choice, daughter – it is simply part of what you are, and I accept this' – *and yet rage at the foul cruelty of it* – 'as must you. There is an urgency within you, Silverfox, a force ancient and undeniable – you know it as well, feel it—'

'Ancient and undeniable?' Kallor rasped. 'You don't know the half of it, woman.' He jolted forward across the table and grasped Silverfox's tunic, pulled her close. Their faces inches apart, the High King bared his teeth. 'You're in there, aren't you? I know it. I feel it. Come out, bitch—'

'Release her,' Brood commanded in a low, soft voice.

The High King's sneer broadened. He relented his grip on the girl's tunic, slowly leaned back.

Heart pounding, the Mhybe raised a trembling hand to her face. Terror had ripped through her when Kallor had grasped her daughter, an icy flood that left her limbs without strength – vanquishing with ease her maternal instinct to defend – revealing to herself, and to everyone present, her own cowardice. She felt tears of shame well in her eyes, trickle down her lined cheeks.

'Touch her again,' the warlord continued, 'and I will beat you senseless, Kallor.'

'As you like,' the ancient warrior replied.

Armour rustled as Whiskeyjack turned to Caladan Brood. The commander's face was dark, his expression

123

harsh. 'Had you not done so, Warlord, I would have voiced my own threat.' He fixed iron eyes on the High King. 'Harm a child? I would not beat you senseless, Kallor, I would rip your heart out.'

The High King grinned. 'Indeed. I shake with fear.'

'That will do,' Whiskeyjack murmured. His gauntleted left hand lashed out in a backhanded slap, striking Kallor's face. Blood sprayed across the table as the High King's head snapped back. The force of the blow staggered him. The handle of his bastard sword was suddenly in his hands, the sword hissing – then halting, half drawn.

Kallor could not move his arms further, for Caladan Brood now gripped both wrists. The High King strained, blood vessels swelling on his neck and temple, achieving nothing. Brood must have tightened his huge hands then, for he gasped, the sword's handle dropping from his grasp, the weapon thunking back into the scabbard. Brood stepped closer, but the Mhybe heard his soft words none the less. 'Accept what you have earned, Kallor. I have had quite enough of your contempt at this gathering. Any further test of my temper and it shall be my hammer striking your face. Understood?'

After a long moment, the High King grunted.

Brood released him.

Silence filled the tent, no-one moving, all eyes on Kallor's bleeding face.

Dujek withdrew a cloth from his belt – crusted with dried shaving soap – and tossed it at the High King. 'Keep it,' he growled.

The Mhybe moved up behind a pale, wide-eyed Silverfox, and laid her hands on her daughter's shoulders. 'No more,' she whispered. 'Please.'

Whiskeyjack faced Brood once again, ignoring Kallor as if the man had ceased to exist. 'Explain please, Warlord,' he said in a calm voice. 'What in Hood's name is this child?'

Shrugging her mother's hands from her shoulders, Silverfox stood, poised as if about to flee. Then she shook her head, wiped her eyes and drew a shuddering breath. 'No,' she said, 'let none answer but me.' She looked up at her mother – the briefest meeting of gazes – then surveyed the others once more. 'In all things,' she whispered, 'let none answer but me.'

The Mhybe reached out a hand, but could not touch. 'You must accept it, daughter,' she said, hearing the brittleness of her own conviction, and knowing – with a renewed surge of shame – that the others heard it as well. *You must forgive . . . forgive yourself. Oh, spirits below, I dare not speak such words – I have lost that right, I have surely lost it now . . .*

Silverfox turned to Whiskeyjack. 'The truth, now, Uncle. I am born of two souls, one of whom you knew very well. The woman Tattersail. The other soul belonged to the discorporate, ravaged remnants of a High Mage named Nightchill – in truth, little more than her charred flesh and bones, though other fragments of her were preserved as a consequence of a sealing spell. Tattersail's . . . death . . . occurred within the sphere of the Tellann warren – as projected by a T'lan Imass—'

The Mhybe alone saw the standard-bearer Artanthos flinch. *And what, sir, do you know of this?* The question flitted briefly through her mind – conjecture and consideration were tasks too demanding to exercise.

'Within that influence, Uncle,' Silverfox continued, 'something happened. Something unexpected. A Bonecaster from the distant past appeared, as did an Elder God, and a mortal soul—'

Cloth held to his face, Kallor's snort was muffled. '"*Nightchill*",' he murmured. 'Such a lack of imagination . . . Did K'rul even know? Ah, what irony . . .'

Silverfox resumed. 'It was these three who gathered to help my mother, this Rhivi woman who found herself with an impossible child. I was born in two places at once – among the Rhivi in this world, and into the hands of the Bonecaster in the Tellann warren.' She hesitated, shuddering as if suddenly spent. 'My future,' she whispered after a moment, her arms drawing around herself, 'belongs to the T'lan Imass.' She spun suddenly to Korlat. 'They are gathering, and you will need their power in the war to come.'

'Unholy conjoining,' Kallor rasped, hand and cloth falling away, eyes narrowed, his face white as parchment behind the smeared blood. 'As I had feared – oh, you fools. Every one of you. Fools—'

'Gathering,' the Tiste Andii repeated, also ignoring the High King. 'Why? To what end, Silverfox?'

'That is for me to decide, for I exist to command them. To command them all. My birth proclaimed the Gathering – a demand that every T'lan Imass on this world has heard. And now, those who are able, are coming. They are *coming.*'

In his mind, Whiskeyjack was reeling. Fissures in Brood's contingent was alarming enough, but the child's revelations . . . his thoughts spun, spiralled down . . . then arose in a new place. The command tent and its confines slipped away, and he found himself in a world of twisted schemes, dark betrayals and their fierce, unexpected consequences – a world he hated with a passion.

Memories rose like spectres. The Enfilade at Pale, the decimation of the Bridgeburners, the assault on Moon's Spawn. A plague of suspicions, a maelstrom of desperate schemes . . .

A'Karonys, Bellurdan, Nightchill, Tattersail . . . The list of mages whose deaths could be laid at High Mage Tayschrenn's sandalled feet was written in the blood of senseless paranoia. Whiskeyjack had not been sorry to see the High Mage take his leave, though the commander suspected he was not as far off as it seemed. *Outlawry, Laseen's proclamation cut us loose . . . but it's all a lie.* Only he and Dujek knew the truth of that – the remainder of the Host believed they had indeed been outlawed by the Empress. Their loyalty was to Dujek Onearm, *and, perhaps, to me as well. And Hood knows, we'll test that loyalty before we're done . . .*

Yet she knows. The girl knows. He had no doubt that she was Tattersail reborn – the sorceress was there, in the cast of the child's features, in the way she stood and moved, in that sleepy, knowing gaze. The repercussions that tumbled from that truth overwhelmed Whiskeyjack – he needed time, time to think . . .

Tattersail reborn . . . damn you to Hood, Tayschrenn – inadvertent or not – what have you done?

Whiskeyjack had not known Nightchill – they'd never spoken and the breadth of his knowledge was based solely on the tales he'd heard. Mate to the Thelomen, Bellurdan, and a practitioner of High Rashan sorcery, she had been among the Emperor's chosen. Ultimately betrayed, just as the Bridgeburners had been . . .

There had been an edge to her, it was said, a hint of jagged bloodstained iron. And, he could see, what remained of that woman had cast a shadow over the child – the soft gleam in Tattersail's sleepy eyes had darkened, somehow, and seeing it frayed the commander's already rattled nerves.

Oh, Hood. One of those repercussions had just settled in his mind with a thunderous clang. *Oh, the gods forgive us our foolish games . . .*

Back in Pale waited Ganoes Paran. *Tattersail's lover. What will he make of Silverfox?* From woman to a newborn babe in an instant, then from that newborn to a ten-year-old child in six months. *And six months from now? A twenty-year-old woman? Paran . . . lad . . . is it grief that is burning holes in your gut? If so, then what will its answering do to you?*

As he struggled to comprehend the young girl's words, and all that he saw in her face, his thoughts turned to the Mhybe standing beside Silverfox. Sorrow flooded him. The gods were cruel indeed. The old woman would likely be dead within the year, a brutal sacrifice to the child's needs. *A malign, nightmarish twist to the role of motherhood.*

The girl's final words jarred the commander yet again. *'They are coming.' The T'lan Imass – Hood's breath, as if matters weren't complicated enough. Where do I place my faith in all this? Kallor – a cold, uncanny bastard himself – calls her an abomination – he would kill her if he could. That much is plain. I'll not abide harming a child . . . but is she a child?*

Yet . . . Hood's breath! She's Tattersail reborn, a woman of courage and integrity. And Nightchill, a High Mage who served the Emperor. And, now, strangest, most alarming fact of all, she is the new ruler of the T'lan Imass . . .

Whiskeyjack blinked, the tent and its occupants coming into focus once again. Silence writhing with tumultuous thoughts. His gaze swung back to Silverfox – saw the paleness of her young, round face, noted with a pang of empathy the tremble in the child's hands – then away again. The Tiste Andii, Korlat, was watching him. Their eyes locked. *Such extraordinary beauty . . . while Dujek is dog-face ugly, further proof I chose the wrong side all those years back. She's hardly interested in me that way, no, she's trying to say something else entirely . . .* After a long moment, he nodded. *Silverfox . . . she's still a child, aye.* A clay tablet scarcely etched. *Aye, Tiste Andii, I understand you.*

Those who chose to stand close to Silverfox might well be able to influence what she was to become. Korlat sought a private conversation with him, and he'd just accepted the invitation. Whiskeyjack wished he had Quick Ben at his side right now – the Seven Cities mage was sharp when it came to situations like these. The commander already felt out of his depth. *Paran, you poor bastard. What do I tell you? Should I arrange a meeting between you and Silverfox? Will I be able to prevent one once you're told? Is it even any of my business?*

Crone's beak gaped, but not in soundless laughter this time. Instead, unfamiliar terror raced through her. *T'lan Imass! And K'rul, the Elder God! Holders of the truth of the Great Ravens, a truth no-one else knows – except for Silverfox, by the*

128

Abyss . . . Silverfox, who looked upon my soul and read all within it.

Careless, careless child! Would you force us to defend ourselves from you? From those whom you claim to command? We Great Ravens have never fought our own wars – would you see us unleashed by your unmindful revelations?

Should Rake learn . . . protestations of innocence will avail us naught. We were there at the Chaining, were we not? Yet . . . aye, we were there at Fall itself! The Great Ravens were born like maggots in the flesh of the Fallen One and that, oh, that will damn us! But wait! Have we not been honourable guardians of the Crippled God's magic? And were we not the ones who delivered to one and all the news of the Pannion Domin, the threat it represents?

A magic we can unleash, if forced to. Ah, child, you threaten so much with your careless words . . .

Her black, glittering eyes sought out and fixed on Caladan Brood. Whatever thoughts the warlord possessed remained hidden behind the flat, bestial mask that was his face.

Rein in your panic, old hag. Return to the concerns before us. Think!

The Malazan Empire had made use of the T'lan Imass in the Emperor's time. The conquest of Seven Cities had been the result. Then, with Kellanved's death, the alliance had dissolved, and so Genabackis was spared the devastating implacability of tens of thousands of undead warriors who could travel as dust in the wind. This alone had allowed Caladan Brood to meet the Malazan threat on an equal footing . . . *ah, perhaps it only seemed that way. Has he ever truly unleashed the Tiste Andii? Has he ever let loose Anomander Rake? Has he ever shown his own true power? Brood's an ascendant – one forgets that, in careless times. His warren is Tennes – the power of the land itself, the earth that is home to the eternal sleeping goddess, Burn. Caladan Brood has the power – there in his arms and in that formidable hammer on his back – to shatter mountains. An exaggeration? A low flight*

*over the broken peaks east of the Laederon Plateau is proof
enough of his younger, more precipitous days . . . Grandmother
Crone, you should know better! Power draws power. It has
always been thus, and now have come the T'lan Imass, and
once again the balance shifts.*

*My children spy upon the Pannion Domin – they can smell
the power rising from those lands so thoroughly sanctified in
blood, yet it remains faceless, as if hidden beneath layer after
deceiving layer. What hides at the core of that empire of
fanatics?*

*The horrific child knows – I'd swear on the god's bed of
broken flesh to that, oh yes. And she will lead the T'lan Imass
. . . to that very heart.*

*Do you grasp this, Caladan Brood? I think you do. And,
even as that hoary old tyrant Kallor utters his warnings with a
bloodless will . . . even as you are rocked by the imminent
arrival of undead allies, so you are jolted even more by the fact
that they will be needed. Against what have we proclaimed war?
What will be left of us when we are done?*

*And, by the Abyss, what secret truth about Silverfox does
Kallor possess?*

Defying her own overwhelming self-disgust, the Mhybe
forced brutal clarity into her thoughts, listening to all that
Silverfox said, to each word, to what lay between each
word. She hugged herself beneath the barrage of her
daughter's pronouncements. The laying bare of secrets
assailed her every instinct – such exposure was fraught with
risks. Yet she finally understood something of the position
in which Silverfox had found herself – the confessions were
a call for help.

*She needs allies. She knows I am not enough – spirits below,
she has been shown that here. More, she knows that these two
camps – enemies for so long – need to be bridged. Born in one,
she reaches out to the other. All that was Tattersail and
Nightchill cries out to old comrades. Will they answer?*

She could discern nothing of Whiskeyjack's emotions.

130

His thoughts might well be echoing Kallor's position. *An abomination.* She saw him meet Korlat's eyes and wondered at what passed between them.

Think! It is the nature of everyone here to treat every situation tactically, to push away personal feelings, to gauge, to weigh and balance. Silverfox has stepped to the fore; she has claimed a position of power to rival Brood, Anomander Rake and Kallor. Does Dujek Onearm now wonder with whom he should be dealing? Does he realize that we were all united because of him – that, for twelve years, the clans of Barghast and Rhivi, the disparate companies from a score or more cities, the Tiste Andii, the presence of Rake, Brood and Kallor, not to mention the Crimson Guard – all of us, we stood shoulder to shoulder because of the Malazan Empire? Because of the High Fist himself.

But we have a new enemy now, and much of its nature remains unknown, and it has engendered a kind of fragility among us – oh, what an understatement – that Dujek Onearm now sees.

Silverfox states that we shall have need of the T'lan Imass. Only the vicious old Emperor could have been comfortable with such creatures as allies – even Kallor recoils from what is being forced upon us. The fragile alliance now creaks and totters. You are too wise a man, High Fist, to not now possess grave doubts.

The one-armed old man was the first to speak after Silverfox's statement, and he addressed the child with slow, carefully measured words. 'The T'lan Imass with whom the Malazan Empire is familiar is the army commanded by Logros. By your words we must assume there are other armies, yet no knowledge of them has ever reached us. Why is that, child?'

'The last Gathering,' Silverfox replied, 'was hundreds of thousands of years ago, at which was invoked the Ritual of Tellann – the binding of the Tellann warren to each and every Imass. The ritual made them immortal, High Fist. The life force of an entire people was bound in the name of a holy war destined to last for millennia—'

131

'Against the Jaghut,' Kallor rasped. His narrow, withered face twisted into a sneer behind the already-drying blood. 'Apart from a handful of Tyrants, the Jaghut were pacifists. Their only crime was to exist—'

Silverfox rounded on the warrior. 'Do not hint at injustices, High King! I possess enough of Nightchill's memories to recall the Imperial Warren – the place you once ruled, Kallor, before the Malazans made claim to it. You laid waste an entire realm – you stripped the life from it, left nothing but ash and charred bones. *An entire realm!*'

The tall warrior's blood-smeared grin was ghastly. 'Ah, you *are* there, aren't you. But hiding, I think, twisting the truth into false memories. Hiding, you pathetic, cursed woman!' His smile hardened. 'Then you should know not to test my temper, Bonecaster. Tattersail. *Nightchill . . . dear child . . .*'

The Mhybe saw her daughter pale. *Between these two . . . the feel of a long enmity – why had I not seen that before? There are old memories here, a link between them. Between my daughter and Kallor – no, between Kallor and one of the souls within her . . .*

After a moment, Silverfox returned her attention to Dujek. 'To answer you, Logros and the clans under his command were entrusted with the task of defending the First Throne. The other armies departed to hunt down the last Jaghut strongholds – the Jaghut had raised barriers of ice. Omtose Phellack is a warren of ice, High Fist, a place deathly cold and almost lifeless. Jaghut sorceries threatened the world . . . sea levels dropped, whole species died out – every mountain range was a barrier. Ice flowed in white rivers down from the slopes. Ice formed a league deep in places. As mortals, the Imass were scattered, their unity lost. They could not cross such barriers. There was starvation—'

'The war against the Jaghut had begun long before then,' Kallor snapped. 'They sought to defend themselves, and who would not?'

Silverfox simply shrugged. 'As Tellann undead, our armies could cross such barriers. The efforts at eradication proved ... costly. You have heard no whispers of those armies because many have been decimated, whilst others perhaps continue the war in distant, inhospitable places.'

There was a pained expression on the High Fist's face. 'The Logros themselves left the empire and disappeared into the Jhag Odhan for a time, and when they returned they were much diminished.'

She nodded.

'Have the Logros answered your call?'

Frowning, the girl said, 'I cannot be certain of that – of any of them. They have *heard*. All will come if they are able, and I sense the nearness of one army – at least I think I do.'

There is so much you are not telling us, daughter. I can see it in your eyes. You fear your call for help will go unanswered if you reveal too much.

Dujek sighed and faced the warlord. 'Caladan Brood, shall we resume our discussion of strategy?'

The soldiers once again leaned over the map table, joined by a softly cackling Crone. After a moment, the Mhybe collected her daughter's hand and guided her towards the entrance. Korlat joined them as they made their way out. To the Mhybe's surprise, Whiskeyjack followed.

The cool afternoon breeze was welcome after the close confines of the command tent. Without a word, the small group walked a short distance to a clearing between the Tiste Andii and Barghast encampments. Once they halted, the commander fixed his grey eyes on Silverfox.

'I see much of Tattersail in you, lass – how much of her life, her memories, do you recall?'

'Faces,' she answered, with a tentative smile. 'And the feelings attached to them, Commander. You and I were allies for a time. We were, I think, friends . . .'

His nod was grave. 'Aye, we were. Do you remember

Quick Ben? The rest of my squad? What of Hairlock? Tayschrenn? Do you recall Captain Paran?'

'Quick Ben,' she whispered uncertainly. 'A mage? Seven Cities . . . a man of secrets . . . yes,' she smiled again, 'Quick Ben. Hairlock – not a friend, a threat – he caused me pain . . .'

'He's dead, now.'

'I am relieved. Tayschrenn is a name I've heard recently – Laseen's favoured High Mage – we sparred, he and I, when I was Tattersail, and, indeed, when I was Nightchill. No sense of loyalty, no sense of trust – thoughts of him confuse me.'

'And the captain?'

Something in the commander's tone brought the Mhybe alert.

Silverfox glanced away from Whiskeyjack's eyes. 'I look forward to seeing him again.'

The commander cleared his throat. 'He's in Pale right now. While it's not my business, lass, you might want to consider the consequences of meeting him, of, uh, his finding out . . .' His words trailed away in evident discomfort.

Spirits below! This Captain Paran was Tattersail's lover – I should have anticipated something like this. The souls of two grown women . . . 'Silverfox – daughter—'

'We have met him, Mother,' she said. 'When driving the bhederin north – do you recall? The soldier who defied our lances? I knew then – I knew him, who he was.' She faced the commander again. 'Paran knows. Send him word that I am here. Please.'

'Very well, lass.' Whiskeyjack raised his head and studied the Barghast encampment. 'The Bridgeburners will be . . . visiting . . . in any case. The captain now commands them. I am sure that Quick Ben and Mallet will be pleased to make your reacquaintance—'

'You wish them to examine me, you mean,' Silverfox said, 'to help you decide whether I am worthy of your support. Fear not, Commander, the prospect does not

134

concern me – in many ways I remain a mystery to myself, as well, and so I am curious as to what they will discover.'

Whiskeyjack smiled wryly. 'You've the sorceress's blunt honesty, lass – if not her occasional tact.'

Korlat spoke. 'Commander Whiskeyjack, I believe we have things to discuss, you and I.'

'Aye,' he said.

The Tiste Andii turned to the Mhybe and Silverfox. 'We shall take our leave of you two, now.'

'Of course,' the old woman replied, struggling to master her emotions. *The soldier who defied our lances – oh yes, I recall, child. Old questions . . . finally answered . . . and a thousand more to plague this old woman . . .* 'Come along, Silverfox, it's time to resume your schooling in the ways of the Rhivi.'

'Yes, Mother.'

Whiskeyjack watched the two Rhivi walk away. 'She revealed far too much,' he said after a moment. 'The parley was working, drawing the bindings closer . . . then the child spoke . . .'

'Yes,' Korlat murmured. 'She is in possession of secret knowledge – the knowledge of the T'lan Imass. Memories spanning millennia on this world. So much that those people witnessed . . . the Fall of the Crippled God, the arrival of the Tiste Andii, the last flight of the Dragons into Starvald Demelain . . .' She fell silent, a veil descending over her eyes.

Whiskeyjack studied her, then said, 'I've never seen a Great Raven become so obviously . . . flustered.'

Korlat smiled. 'Crone believes the secret of her kind's birth is not known to us. It is the shame of their origins, you see – or so they themselves view it. Rake is indifferent to its . . . moral context, as we all are.'

'What is so shameful?'

'The Great Ravens are unnatural creatures. The bringing down of the alien being who would come to be called the

135

Crippled God was a . . . violent event. Parts of him were torn away, falling like balls of fire to shatter entire lands. Pieces of his flesh and bone lay rotting yet clinging to a kind of life in their massive craters. From that flesh the Great Ravens were born, carrying with them fragments of the Crippled God's power. You have seen Crone and her kin – they devour sorcery, it is their true sustenance. To attack a Great Raven with magic serves only to make the creature stronger, to bolster its immunity. Crone is the First Born. Rake believes the potential within her is . . . appalling, and so he keeps her and ilk close.'

She paused, then faced him. 'Commander Whiskeyjack, in Darujhistan, we clashed with a mage of yours . . .'

'Aye. Quick Ben. He'll be here shortly, and I will have his thoughts on all this.'

'The man you mentioned earlier to the child.' She nodded. 'I admit to a certain admiration for the wizard and so look forward to meeting him.' Their gazes locked. 'And I am pleased to have met you as well. Silverfox spoke true words when she said she trusted you. And I believe I do as well.'

He shifted uncomfortably. 'There has been scant contact between us that would earn such trust, Korlat. None the less, I will endeavour to earn it.'

'The child has Tattersail within her, a woman who knew you well. Though I never met the sorceress, I find that the woman she was – emerging further with each day in Silverfox – possessed admirable qualities.'

Whiskeyjack slowly nodded. 'She was . . . a friend.'

'How much do you know of the events leading to this . . . rebirth?'

'Not enough, I am afraid,' he replied. 'We learned of Tattersail's death from Paran, who came upon her . . . remains. She died in the embrace of a Thelomen High Mage, Bellurdan, who had travelled out onto the plain with the corpse of his mate, Nightchill, presumably intending to bury the woman. Tattersail was already a fugitive, and it's

136

likely Bellurdan was instructed to retrieve her. It is as Silverfox says, as far as I can tell.'

Korlat looked away and said nothing for a long time. When she finally did, her question, so simple and logical, left Whiskeyjack with a pounding heart: 'Commander, we sense Tattersail and Nightchill within the child – and she herself admits to these two – but now I wonder, where then is this Thelomen, Bellurdan?'

He could only draw a deep breath and shake his head. *Gods, I don't know . . .*

CHAPTER FOUR

Mark these three, they are all that give shape,
all that lie beneath the surface of the world,
these three, they are the bones of history.
Sister of Cold Nights! Betrayal greets your dawn!
You chose to trust the knife, even as it found your heart.
Draconus, Blood of Tiam! Darkness was made
to embrace your soul, and these chains that now
hold you, they are of your own fashioning.
K'rul, yours was the path the Sleeping Goddess chose,
a thousand and more years ago, and she sleeps still,
even as you awaken – the time has come, Ancient One,
to once more walk among the mortals,
and make of your grief, the sweetest gift.

Anomandaris
Fisher Kel Tath

Covered from head to toe in mud, Harllo and Stonny
Menackis emerged from behind the carriage as it
rocked its way up the slope. Grinning at the sight,
Gruntle leaned against the buckboard.

'Serves us right to lay wagers with you,' Harllo muttered.
'You always win, you bastard.'

Stonny was looking down at her smeared clothing
with dismay. 'Callows leathers. They'll never recover.'
She fixed hard blue eyes on Gruntle. 'Damn you – you're
the biggest of us all. Should have been you pushing,

not sitting up there, and never mind winning any bet.'

'Hard lessons, that's me,' the man said, his grin broadening. Stonny's fine green and black attire was covered in brown slime. Her thick black hair hung down over her face, dripping milky water. 'Anyway, we're done for the day, so let's pull this thing off to the side – looks like you two could do with a swim.'

'Hood take you,' Harllo snapped, 'what do you think we was doing?'

'From the sounds, I'd say drowning. The clean water's upstream, by the way.' Gruntle gathered the tresses again. The crossing had left the horses exhausted, reluctant to move, and it took some cajoling on the captain's part to get them moving again. He halted the carriage a short distance off to one side of the ford. Other merchants had camped nearby, some having just managed the crossing and others preparing to do so on their way to Darujhistan. In the past few days, the situation had, if anything, become even more chaotic. Whatever had remained of the ford's laid cobbles in the river bed had been pushed either askew or deeper into the mud.

It had taken four bells to manage the crossing, and for a time there Gruntle had wondered if they would ever succeed. He climbed down and turned his attention to the horses. Harllo and Stonny, now bickering with each other, set off upstream.

Gruntle threw an uneasy glance towards the massive carriage that had gone before them on the ford, now parked fifty paces away. It had been an unfair bet. *The best kind.* His two companions had been convinced that this day wouldn't see the crossing of their master Keruli's carriage. They'd been certain that the monstrous vehicle ahead of them would bog down, that it'd be days sitting there in midstream before other merchants got impatient enough to add the muscle of their own crews to moving it out of the way.

Gruntle had suspected otherwise. Bauchelain and Korbal

Broach were not the kind of people to stomach in-convenience. *They're damned sorcerors, anyway.* Their servant, Emancipor Reese, had not even bothered to get down from the driver's bench, and simple twitches of the tresses had led the train of oxen onwards. The huge contrivance seemed to glide across the ford, not even jolting as the wheels moved over what Gruntle knew to be churned, uneven footing. *Unfair bet, aye. At least I'm dry and clean.*

There had been enough witnesses to the unnatural event to accord a certain privacy to the mages' present encamp-ment, so it was with considerable curiosity that Gruntle watched a caravan guard stride towards it. He knew the man well. A Daru, Buke worked the smaller caravanserai, signing with merchants just scraping by. He preferred work-ing alone, and Gruntle knew why.

Buke's master had tried the crossing earlier in the day. The dilapidated wagon had fallen to pieces in midstream, bits of wood and precious bundles of produce floating away as the master wallowed helplessly. Buke had managed to save the merchant, but with the loss of goods the contract had ceased to exist. After making arrangements for the master to accompany a train back to Darujhistan, Buke was, with scant gratitude for his efforts, cut loose by the merchant.

Gruntle had expected him to make his own way back to the city. Buke had a fine, healthy and well-equipped horse. A three days' journey at the most.

Yet here he was, his tall, lean figure fully attired in a guard's accoutrements, scale hauberk freshly oiled, cross-bow strapped to back and longsword scabbarded at his hip, in quiet conversation with Emancipor Reese.

Though out of earshot, Gruntle could follow the course of the conversation by the shifting postures of the two men. After a brief exchange, he saw Buke's shoulders drop fractionally. The grey-bearded guard glanced away. Emancipor Reese shrugged and half turned in dismissal.

Both men then swung about to face the carriage, and a moment later Bauchelain emerged, drawing his black leather cape around his broad shoulders. Buke straightened under the sorcerer's attention, answered a few terse questions with equally terse replies, then gave a respectful nod. Bauchelain laid a hand on his servant's shoulder and the old man came close to buckling under that light touch.

Gruntle clucked softly in sympathy. *Aye, that mage's touch could fill an average man's breeches, Queen knows . . . Beru fend, Buke's just been hired. Pray he doesn't come to regret it.*

Tenement fires were deadly in Darujhistan, especially when gas was involved. The conflagration that had killed Buke's wife, mother and four children had been particularly ugly. That Buke himself had been lying drunk and dead to the world in an alley not a hundred paces from the house hadn't helped in the man's recovery. Like many of his fellow guards, Gruntle had assumed that Buke would turn to the bottle with serious intent after that. Instead, he'd done the opposite. Taking solitary contracts with poor, vulnerable merchants obviously offered to Buke a greater appeal than the wasting descent of a permanent drunk. Poor merchants were robbed far more often than rich ones. *The man wants to die, all right. But swiftly, even honourably. He wants to go down fighting, as did his family, by all accounts. Alas, when sober – as he's been ever since that night – Buke fights extremely well, and the ghosts of at least a dozen highwaymen would bitterly attest to that.*

The chill dread that seemed to infuse the air around Bauchelain and, especially, around Korbal Broach, would have deterred any sane guard. But a man eager to embrace death would see it differently, wouldn't he?

Ah, friend Buke, I hope you do not come to regret your choice. No doubt violence and horror swirls around your two new masters, but you're more likely to be a witness to it than a victim yourself. Haven't you been in suffering's embrace long enough?

141

Buke set off to collect his horse and gear. Gruntle had begun a cookfire by the time the old man returned. He watched Buke stow his equipment and exchange a few more words with Emancipor Reese, who had begun cooking a meal of their own, then the man glanced over and met Gruntle's gaze.

Buke strode over.

'A day of changes, friend Buke,' Gruntle said from where he squatted beside the hearth. 'I'm brewing some tea for Harllo and Stonny who should be back any moment – care to join us in a mug?'

'That is kind of you, Gruntle. I will accept your offer.' He approached the captain.

'Unfortunate, what happened to Murk's wagon.'

'I warned him against the attempt. Alas, he did not appreciate my advice.'

'Even after you pulled him from the river and pumped the water out of his lungs?'

Buke shrugged. 'Hood brushing his lips put him in bad mood, I would imagine.' He glanced over at his new masters' carriage, lines crinkling the corners of his sad eyes. 'You have had discourse with them, have you not?'

Gruntle spat into the fire. 'Aye. Better had you sought my advice before taking the contract.'

'I respect your advice and always have, Gruntle, but you would not have swayed me.'

'I know that, so I'll say no more of them.'

'The other one,' Buke said, accepting a tin mug from Gruntle and cradling it in both hands as he blew on the steaming liquid. 'I caught a glimpse of him earlier.'

'Korbal Broach.'

'As you say. He's the killer, you realize.'

'Between the two, I don't see much difference, to be honest.'

Buke was shaking his head. 'No, you misunderstand. In Darujhistan, recall? For two weeks running, horribly mangled bodies were found in the Gadrobi District, every

142

night. Then the investigators called in a mage to help, and it was as if someone had kicked a hornet's nest – that mage discovered something, and that knowledge had him terrified. It was quiet, grant you, but I chanced on the details that followed. Vorcan's guild was enlisted. The Council itself set forth the contract to the assassins. Find the killer, they said, using every method at your disposal, legal or otherwise. Then the murders stopped—'

'I vaguely recall a fuss,' Gruntle said, frowning.

'You were in Quip's, weren't you? Blind for days on end.'

Gruntle winced. 'Had my eye on Lethro, you know – went out on a contract and came back to find—'

'She'd gone and married someone else,' Buke finished, nodding.

'Not just someone else.' Gruntle scowled. 'That bloated crook, Parsemo—'

'An old master of yours, I seem to recall. Anyway. Who was the killer and why did the killings stop? Vorcan's guild did not step forward to claim the Council's coin. The murders stopped because the murderer had left the city.' Buke nodded towards the massive carriage. 'He's the one. Korbal Broach. The man with the round face and fat lips.'

'What makes you so certain, Buke?' The air had gone cold. Gruntle poured himself a second cup.

The man shrugged, eyes on the fire. 'I just know. Who can abide the murder of innocents?'

Hood's breath, Buke, I see both edges to that question well enough – do you? You mean to kill him, or at least die trying. 'Listen to me, friend. We may be out of the city's jurisdiction, but if Darujhistan's mages were in truth so thoroughly alarmed – and given that Vorcan's guild might still have an interest – issues of jurisdiction are meaningless. We could send word back – assuming you're right and you've proof of your certainty, Buke – and in the meantime you just keep your eye on the man. Nothing else. He's a sorceror – mark my words. You won't stand a chance. Leave the execution to the assassins and mages.'

143

Buke glanced up at the arrival of Harllo and Stonny Menackis. The two had come up quietly, each wrapped in blankets, with their clothing washed and bundled in their arms. Their troubled expressions told Gruntle they'd heard at the very least his last statement.

'Thought you'd be halfway back to Darujhistan,' Harllo said.

Buke studied the guard over the rim of the mug. 'You are so clean I barely recognize you, friend.'

'Ha ha.'

'I have found myself a new contract, to answer you, Harllo.'

'You idiot,' Stonny snapped. 'When are you going to get some sense back into your head, Buke? It's been years and years since you last cracked a smile or let any light into your eyes. How many bear traps are you going to stick your head in, man?'

'Until one snaps,' Buke said, meeting Stonny's dark, angry eyes. He rose, tossing to one side the dregs from the mug. 'Thank you for the tea ... and advice, friend Gruntle.' With a nod to Harllo, then Stonny, he headed back to Bauchelain's carriage.

Gruntle stared up at Stonny. 'Impressive tact, my dear.'

She hissed. 'The man's a fool. He needs a woman's hand on his sword-grip, if you ask me. Needs it bad.'

Harllo grunted. 'You volunteering?'

Stonny Menackis shrugged. 'It's not his appearance that one balks at, it's his attitude. The very opposite of you, ape.'

'Sweet on my personality, are you?' Harllo grinned over at Gruntle. 'Hey, you could break my nose again – then we could straighten it and I'd be good as new. What say you, Stonny? Would the iron petals of your heart unfold for me?'

She sneered. 'Everyone knows that two-handed sword of yours is nothing but a pathetic attempt at compensation, Harllo.'

'He's a nice turn at the poetic, though,' Gruntle pointed out. 'Iron petals – you couldn't get more precise than that.'

'There's no such thing as iron petals,' Stonny snorted. 'You don't get iron flowers. And hearts aren't flowers, they're big red, messy things in your chest. What's poetic about not making sense? You're as big an idiot as Buke and Harllo, Gruntle. I'm surrounded by thick-skulled witless fools.'

'It's your lot in life, alas,' Gruntle said. 'Here, have some tea – you could do with . . . the warmth.'

She accepted the mug, while Gruntle and Harllo avoided meeting each other's eyes.

After a few moments, Stonny cleared her throat. 'What was all that about leaving the execution to assassins, Gruntle? What kind of mess has Buke got himself into now?'

Oh, Mowri, she truly cares for the man. He frowned into the fire and tossed in a few more lumps of dung before replying, 'He has some . . . suspicions. We were, uh, speaking hypothetically—'

'Togg's tongue you were, ox-face. Out with it.'

'Buke chose to speak with me, not you, Stonny,' Gruntle growled, irritated. 'If you've questions, ask them of him and leave me out of it.'

'I will, damn you.'

'I doubt you'll get anywhere,' Harllo threw in, somewhat unwisely, 'even if you do bat your eyes and pout those rosy lips of yours—'

'Those are the last things you'll see when I push my knife through that tin tuber in your chest. Oh, and I'll blow a kiss, too.'

Harllo's bushy brows rose. 'Tin tuber! Stonny, my dear – did I hear you right?'

'Shut up, I'm not in the mood.'

'You're *never* in the mood, Stonny!'

She answered him with a contemptuous smile.

'Don't bother saying it, dear,' Gruntle sighed.

The shack leaned drunkenly against the city of Pale's inner

wall, a confused collection of wooden planks, stretched hides and wicker, its yard a threshold of white dust, gourd husks, bits of broken crockery and wood shavings. Fragments of lacquered wooden cards hung from twine above the narrow door, slowly twisting in the humid heat.

Quick Ben paused, glanced up and down the littered alleyway, then stepped into the yard. A cackle sounded from within. The wizard rolled his eyes and, muttering under his breath, reached for the leather loop nailed to the door.

'Don't push!' a voice shrieked behind it. 'Pull, you snake of the desert!'

Shrugging, Quick Ben tugged the door towards him.

'Only fools push!' hissed the old woman from her cross-legged perch on a reed mat just within. 'Scrapes my knee! Bruises and worse plague me when fools come to visit. Ah, I sniffed Raraku, didn't I?'

The wizard peered into the shack's interior. 'Hood's breath, there's only room for you in there!' Vague objects cluttered the walls, dangled from the low ceiling. Shadows swallowed every corner, and the air still held the chill of the night just past.

'Just me!' the woman cackled. Her face was little more than skin over bones, her pate hairless and blotched with moles. 'Show what you have, many-headed snake, the breaking of curses is my gift!' She withdrew from the tattered folds of her robes a wooden card, held it up in trembling hands. 'Send your words into my warren and their shape shall be carved hereupon, burned true—'

'No curses, woman,' Quick Ben said, crouching down until his eyes were level with hers. 'Only questions.'

The card slipped beneath her robes. Scowling, the witch said, 'Answers cost plenty. Answers are worth more than the breaking of curses. Answers are not easily found—'

'All right all right, how much?'

'Colour the coin of your questions, twelve-souls.'

'Gold.'

146

'Then gold councils, one for each—'

'Provided you give worthy answer.'

'Agreed.'

'Burn's Sleep.'

'What of it?'

'Why?'

The old woman gaped toothlessly.

'Why does the goddess sleep, witch? Does anyone know? Do you?'

'You are a learned scoundrel—'

'All I've read has been speculation. No-one knows. Scholars don't have the answer, but this world's oldest witch of Tennes just might. Tell me, why does Burn sleep?'

'Some answers must be danced around. Give me another question, child of Raraku.'

Sighing, Quick Ben lowered his head, studied the ground for a moment, then said, 'It's said the earth shakes and molten rock pours out like blood when Burn stirs towards wakefulness.'

'So it is said.'

'And that destruction would be visited upon all life were she to awaken.'

'So it is said.'

'Well?'

'Well nothing. The land shakes, mountains explode, hot rivers flow. These are natural things of a world whose soul is white hot. Bound to their own laws of cause and effect. The world is shaped like a beetle's ball of dung, and it travels through a chilling void around the sun. The surface floats in pieces, on a sea of molten rock. Sometimes the pieces grind together. Sometimes they pull apart. Pulled and pushed by tides as the seas are pulled and pushed.'

'And where is the goddess in such a scheme?'

'She was the egg within the dung. Hatched long ago. Her mind rides the hidden rivers beneath our feet. She is the pain of existence. The queen of the hive and we her workers and soldiers. And every now and then . . . we *swarm*.'

147

'Into the warrens?'

The old woman shrugged. 'By whatever paths we find.'

'Burn is sick.'

'Aye.'

Quick Ben saw a sudden intensity light the witch's dark eyes. He thought for a long moment, then said, 'Why does Burn sleep?'

'It's not yet time for that. Ask another question.'

The wizard frowned, looked away. 'Workers and soldiers . . . you make us sound like slaves.'

'She demands nothing, what you do you do for yourselves. You work to earn sustenance. You fight to protect it or to gain more. You work to confound rivals. You fight from fear and hatred and spite and honour and loyalty and whatever other causes you might fashion. Yet, all that you do serves her . . . no matter what you do. Not simply benign, Adaephon Delat, but amoral. We can thrive, or we can destroy ourselves, it matters not to her – she will simply birth another brood and it begins again.'

'You speak of the world as a physical thing, subject to natural laws. Is that all it is?'

'No, in the end the minds and senses of all that is alive define what is real – real for us, that is.'

'That's a tautology.'

'So it is.'

'Is Burn the cause to our effect?'

'Ah, you wind sideways like the desert snake you are in truth! Ask your question!'

'Why does Burn sleep?'

'She sleeps . . . *to dream*.'

Quick Ben said nothing for a long time. When he finally looked into the old woman's eyes he saw confirmation of his greatest fears. 'She is sick,' he said.

The witch nodded. 'Fevered.'

'And her dreams . . .'

'Delirium descends, lad. Dreams become nightmares.'

'I need to think of a way to excise that infection, because

I don't think Burn's fever will be enough. If anything, that heat that's meant to cleanse is achieving the opposite effect.'

'Think on it, then, dearest worker.'

'I may need help.'

The witch held out a withered hand, palm up.

Quick Ben fished beneath his shirt and withdrew a waterworn pebble. He dropped it into her hand.

'When the time comes, Adaephon Delat, call upon me.'

'I shall. Thank you, mistress.' He set a small leather bag filled with gold councils on the ground between them. The witch cackled. Quick Ben backed away.

'Now shut that door – I prefer the cold!'

As the wizard strode down the alley, his thoughts wandered loose, darted and whipped on gusts – most of the currents false and without significance. One, however, snagged in his mind and stayed with him, at first meaningless, a curiosity and nothing more: *she prefers the cold. Strange. Most old people like heat and plenty of it . . .*

Captain Paran saw Quick Ben leaning against the pitted wall beside the headquarters entrance, arms wrapped tightly about himself and looking ill-tempered. The four soldiers stationed as guards were all gathered ten paces away from the mage, showing obvious unease.

Paran led his horse forward by the reins, handed them to a stabler who appeared from the compound gateway, then strode towards Quick Ben.

'You look miserable, mage – and that makes me nervous.'

The Seven Cities native scowled. 'You don't want to know, Captain. Trust me in this.'

'If it concerns the Bridgeburners, I'd better hear it, Quick Ben.'

'The Bridgeburners?' He barked a humourless laugh. 'This goes far beyond a handful of bellyaching soldiers, sir. At the moment, though, I haven't worked out any possible solutions. When I do, I'll lay it all out for you. In the meantime, you might want to requisition a fresh mount – we're to join Dujek and Whiskeyjack at Brood's camp. Immediately.'

'The whole company? I just got them settled!'

'No, sir. You, me, Mallet and Spindle. There've been some . . . unusual developments, I gather, but don't ask me what because I don't know.'

Paran grimaced.

'I've sent for the other two already, sir.'

'Very well. I'll go find myself another horse, then.' The captain swung about and headed towards the compound, trying to ignore the fiery pain in his stomach. Everything was taking too long – the army had been sitting here in Pale for months now, and the city didn't want it. With the outlawing, none of the expected imperial support had arrived, and without that administrative infrastructure, there had been no relief from the tense, unpleasant role of occupiers.

The Malazan system of conquest followed a set of rules that was systematic and effective. The victorious army was never meant to remain in place beyond the peacekeeping transition and handover to a firmly entrenched and fully functioning civil government in the Malazan style. Civic control was not a burden the army had been trained for – it was best achieved through bureaucratic manipulation of the conquered city's economy. *'Hold those strings and the people will dance for you,'* had been the core belief of the Emperor, and he'd proved the truth of it again and again – nor did the Empress venture any alterations to the method. Acquiring that control involved both the imposition of legal authority and a thorough infiltration of whatever black market happened to be operating at the time. *'Since you can never crush a black market the next best thing is to run it.'* And that task belonged to the Claw.

But there are no Claw agents, are there? No scroll scribblers, either. We don't control the black market. We can't even manage the above-board economy, much less run a civil

150

administration. Yet we continue to proceed as if imperial support is imminent, when it most decidedly is not. I don't understand this at all.

Without the Darujhistan gold, Dujek's army would be starving right now. Desertions would have begun, as soldier after soldier left with the hope of returning to the imperial embrace, or seeking to join mercenary companies or caravanserai. Onearm's army would vanish before his very eyes. *Loyalty never survives a pinched stomach.*

After some confusion, the stablers found Paran another mount. He wearily swung himself into the saddle and guided the animal out of the compound. The afternoon sun had begun to throw cooling shadows onto the city's bleached streets. Pale's denizens began emerging, though few lingered anywhere near the Malazan headquarters. The guards held a finely honed sense of suspicion for anyone who hovered overlong, and the assault-issue heavy cross-bows cradled in their arms were kept locked back.

Blood had been spilled at the headquarters entrance, and within the building itself. A Hound of Shadow had attacked, not so long ago, leaving a score dead. Paran's memories of that event were still fragmentary. The beast had been driven off by Tattersail . . . and the captain himself. For the soldiers on guard at the headquarters, however, a peaceful posting had turned into a nightmare. They'd been caught woefully unprepared, a carelessness that would not be repeated. Such a Hound would still scythe through them almost effortlessly, but at least they would go down fighting, not staring slack-jawed.

Paran found Quick Ben, Mallet and Spindle awaiting him astride their own horses. Of the three, the captain knew Spindle the least. The short, bald man's skills ranged from sorcery to sapping, or so he'd been told. His eternally sour disposition did not invite conversation, nor did the foul-smelling thigh-length black and grey hairshirt he wore – woven from his dead mother's hair, if the rumour held any truth. As Paran pulled in alongside the man, he glanced at that shirt. *Hood's breath, that could be an old woman's hair!* The realization made him even more nauseous.

'Take point, Spindle.'

'Aye, Captain – we'll have a real crush to push through when we hit North Market Round.'

'So find us a way round the place.'

'Them alleys ain't safe, sir—'

'Access your warren, then, and let it bleed enough to make hairs stand on end. You can do that, can't you?'

Spindle glanced at Quick Ben. 'Uh, sir, my warren . . . triggers things.'

'Serious things?'

'Well, not really—'

'Proceed, soldier.'

'Aye, Captain.'

Expressionless, Quick Ben took rear position, whilst an equally silent Mallet rode alongside Paran.

'Any idea what's going on at Brood's camp, Healer?' the captain asked.

'Not specifically, sir,' Mallet replied. 'Just . . . sensations.' He continued after an enquiring glance from Paran. 'A real brew of powers over there, sir. Not just Brood and the Tiste Andii – I'm familiar with those. And Kallor's, too, for that matter. No, there's something else. Another presence. Old, yet new. Hints of T'lan Imass, maybe . . .'

'T'lan Imass?'

'Maybe – I'm just not sure, truth to tell, Captain. It's overpowering everyone else, though.'

Paran's head turned at that.

A cat yowled nearby, followed by a flash of grey as the creature darted along a garden wall then vanished from sight. More yowls sounded, this time from the other side of the narrow street.

A shiver danced up Paran's spine. He shook himself. 'The last thing we need is a new player. The situation's tense enough as it is—'

Two dogs locked in a vicious fight tumbled from an alley

mouth just ahead. A panicked cat zigzagged around the snarling, snapping beasts. As one, the horses shied, ears flattening. In the drain gutter to their right the captain saw – with widening eyes – a score of rats scampering parallel to them.

'What in Hood's name—'

'Spindle!' Quick Ben called from behind them. The lead sorceror twisted in his saddle, a miserable expression on his weathered face.

'Ease off some,' Quick Ben instructed, not unkindly.

Spindle nodded, turned back.

Paran waved buzzing flies from his face. 'Mallet, what warren does Spindle call upon?' he asked quietly.

'It's not his warren that's the problem, sir, it's how he channels it. This has been mild so far, all things considered.'

'Must be a nightmare for our cavalry—'

'We're foot soldiers, sir,' Mallet pointed out, with a dry grin. 'In any case, I've seen him break up an enemy charge all by himself. Needless to say, he's useful to have around . . .'

Paran had never before seen a cat run head first into a wall. The dull thud was followed by a crazed scraping of claws as the animal bounced away in stunned surprise. Its antics were enough to attract the attention of the two dogs. A moment later they set off after the cat. All three vanished down another alley.

The captain's own nerves were jittering, adding to the discomfort in his belly. *I could call Quick Ben to point and have him take over, but his is a power that would get noticed – sensed from afar, in fact – and I'd rather not risk that. Nor, I suspect, would he.*

Each neighbourhood they passed through rose in cacophony – the spitting of cats, the howling and barking of dogs and the braying of mules. Rats raced round the group on all sides, as mindless as lemmings.

When Paran judged that they had circumvented the

market round, he called forward to Spindle to yield his warren. The man did so with a sheepish nod.

A short while later they reached North Gate and rode out onto what had once been a killing field. Vestiges of that siege remained, if one looked carefully amidst the tawny grasses. Rotting pieces of clothing, the glint of rivets and the bleached white of splintered bones. Midsummer flowers cloaked the flanks of the recent barrows two hundred paces to their left in swathes of brittle blue, the hue deepening as the sun sank lower behind the mounds.

Paran was glad for the relative quiet of the plain, despite the heavy, turgid air of restless death that he felt seeping into his marrow as they crossed the scarred killing field. *It seems I am ever riding through such places. Since that fated day in Itko Kan, with angry wasps stinging me for disturbing their blood-drenched feast, I have been stumbling along in Hood's wake. I feel as if I've known naught but war and death all my life, though in truth it's been but a scant few years. Queen of Dreams, it makes me feel old . . .* He scowled. Self-pity could easily become a well-worn path in his thoughts, unless he remained mindful of its insipid allure.

Habits inherited from my father and mother, alas. And whatever portion sister Tavore received she must have somehow shunted onto me. Cold and canny as a child, even more so as an adult. If anyone can protect our House during Laseen's latest purge of the nobility, it will be her. No doubt I'd recoil from using whatever tactics she's chosen, but she's not the type to accept defeat. Thus, better her than me. None the less, unease continued to gnaw Paran's thoughts. Since the outlawing, they'd heard virtually nothing of events occurring elsewhere in the empire. Rumours of a pending rebellion in Seven Cities persisted, though that was a promise oft whispered but yet to be unleashed. Paran had his doubts.

No matter what, Tavore will take care of Felisin. That, at least, I can take comfort from . . .

Mallet interrupted his thoughts. 'I believe Brood's

154

command tent is in the Tiste Andii camp, Captain. Straight ahead.'

'Spindle agrees with you,' Paran observed. The mage was leading them unerringly to that strange – even from a distance – and eerie encampment. No-one was visible maintaining vigil at the pickets. In fact, the captain saw no-one at all.

'Looks like the parley went off as planned,' the healer commented. 'We haven't been cut down by a sleet of quarrels yet.'

'I too take that as promising,' Paran said.

Spindle led them into a kind of main avenue between the tall, sombre tents of the Tiste Andii. Dusk had begun to fall; the tattered strips of cloth tied to the tent poles were losing their already-faded colours. A few shadowy, spectral figures appeared from the various side trackways, paying the group little heed.

'A place to drag the spirit low,' Mallet muttered under his breath.

The captain nodded. *Like travelling a dark dream . . .*

'That must be Brood's tent up ahead,' the healer continued.

Two figures waited outside the utilitarian command tent, their attention on Paran and his soldiers. Even in the gloom the captain had no trouble identifying them.

The visitors drew their horses to a halt then dismounted and approached.

Whiskeyjack wasted little time. 'Captain, I need to speak with your soldiers. Commander Dujek wishes to do the same with you. Perhaps we can all gather afterwards, if you're so inclined.'

The heightened propriety of Whiskeyjack's words put Paran's nerves on edge. He simply nodded in reply, then, as the bearded second-in-command marched off with Mallet, Quick Ben and Spindle following, the captain fixed his attention on Dujek.

The veteran studied Paran's face for a moment, then

sighed. 'We've received news from the empire, Captain.'

'How, sir?'

Dujek shrugged. 'Nothing direct, of course, but our sources are reliable. Laseen's cull of the nobility proved . . . efficient.' He hesitated, then said, 'The Empress has a new Adjunct . . .'

Paran slowly nodded. There was nothing surprising in that. Lorn was dead. The position needed to be filled. 'Have you news of my family, sir?'

'Your sister Tavore salvaged what she could, lad. The Paran holdings in Unta, the outlying estates . . . most of the trade agreements. Even so . . . your father passed away, and, a short while later, your mother elected . . . to join him on the other side of Hood's Gate. I am sorry, Ganoes . . .'

Yes, she would do that, wouldn't she? Sorry? Aye, as am I. 'Thank you, sir. To be honest, I'm less shocked by that news than you might think.'

'There's more, I'm afraid. Your, uh, outlawry left your House exposed. I don't think your sister saw much in the way of options. The cull promised to be savage. Clearly, Tavore had been planning things for some time. She well knew what was coming. Nobleborn children were being . . . raped. Then murdered. The order to have every nobleborn child under marrying age slain was never made official, perhaps indeed Laseen was unaware of what was going on—'

'I beg you sir, if Felisin is dead, tell me so and leave out the details.'

Dujek shook his head. 'No, she was spared that, Captain. That is what I am trying to tell you.'

'And what did Tavore sell to achieve that . . . sir?'

'Even as the new Adjunct, Tavore's powers were limited. She could not be seen to reveal any particular . . . favouritism – or so I choose to read her intentions . . .'

Paran closed his eyes. *Adjunct Tavore. Well, sister, you knew your own ambition.* 'Felisin?'

'The Otataral Mines, Captain. Not a life sentence, you

156

can be sure of that. Once the fires cool in Unta, she will no doubt be quietly retrieved—'

'Only if Tavore judges it to be without risk to her reputation—'

Dujek's eyes widened. 'Her rep—'

'I don't mean among the nobility – they can call her a monster all they want, as I'm sure they are doing right now – she does not care. Never did. I mean her professional reputation, Commander. In the eyes of the Empress and her court. For Tavore, nothing else will matter. Thus, she is well suited to be the new Adjunct.' Paran's voice was toneless, the words measured and even. 'In any case, as you said, she was forced to make do with the situation, and as to that situation . . . I am to blame for all that's happened, sir. The cull – the rapes, the murders, the deaths of my parents, and all that Felisin must now endure.'

'Captain—'

'It is all right, sir.' Paran smiled. 'The children of my parents are, one and all, capable of virtually anything. We can survive the consequences. Perhaps we lack normal conscience, perhaps we are monsters in truth. Thank you for the news, Commander. How went the parley?' Paran did all he could to ignore the quiet grief in Dujek's eyes.

'It went well, Captain,' the old man whispered. 'You will depart in two days, barring Quick Ben who will catch up later. No doubt your soldiers are ready for—'

'Yes, sir, they are.'

'Very good. That is all, Captain.'

'Sir.'

Like the laying of a silent shroud, darkness arrived. Paran stood atop the vast barrow, his face caressed by the mildest of winds. He had managed to leave the encampment without running into Whiskeyjack and the Bridgeburners. Night had a way of inviting solitude, and he felt welcome on this mass grave with all its echoing memories of pain, anguish and despair. *Among the dead beneath me, how many adult voices cried out for their mothers?*

Death and dying makes us into children once again, in truth, one last time, there in our final wailing cries. More than one philosopher has claimed that we ever remain children, far beneath the indurated layers that make up the armour of adulthood.

Armour encumbers, restricts the body and soul within it. But it also protects. Blows are blunted. Feelings lose their edge, leaving us to suffer naught but a plague of bruises, and, after a time, bruises fade.

Tilting his head back triggered sharp protests from the muscles of his neck and shoulders. He stared skyward, blinking against the pain, the tautness of his flesh wrapped around bones like a prisoner's bindings.

But there's no escape, is there? Memories and revelations settle in like poisons, never to be expunged. He drew the cooling air deep into his lungs, as if seeking to capture in the breath of the stars their coldness of regard, their indifferent harshness. *There are no gifts in suffering. Witness the Tiste Andii.*

Well, at least the stomach's gone quiet . . . building, I suspect, for another eye-watering bout . . .

Bats flitted through the darkness overhead, wheeling and darting as they fed on the wing. The city of Pale flickered to the south, like a dying hearth. Far to the west rose the hulking peaks of the Moranth Mountains. Paran slowly realized that his folded arms now gripped his sides, struggling to hold all within. He was not a man of tears, nor did he rail at all about him. He'd been born to a carefully sculpted, cool detachment, an education his soldier's training only enhanced. *If such things are qualities, then she has humbled me. Tavore, you are indeed the master of such schooling. Oh, dearest Felisin, what life have you now found for yourself? Not the protective embrace of the nobility, that's for certain.*

Boots sounded behind him.

Paran closed his eyes. *No more news, please. No more revelations.*

'Captain.' Whiskeyjack settled a hand on Paran's shoulder.

'A quiet night,' the captain observed.

'We looked for you, Paran, after your words with Dujek. It was Silverfox who quested outward, found you.' The hand withdrew. Whiskeyjack stood alongside him, also studying the stars.

'Who is Silverfox?'

'I think,' the bearded veteran rumbled, 'that's for you to decide.'

Frowning, Paran faced the commander. 'I've little patience for riddles at the moment, sir.'

Whiskeyjack nodded, eyes still on the glittering sweep of the night sky. 'You will just have to suffer the indulgence, Captain. I can lead you forward a step at a time, or with a single shove from behind. There may be a time when you look back on this moment and come to appreciate which of the two I chose.'

Paran bit back a retort, said nothing.

'They await us at the base of the barrow,' Whiskeyjack continued. 'As private an occasion as I could manage. Just Mallet, Quick Ben, the Mhybe and Silverfox. Your squad members are here in case you have ... doubts. They've both exhausted their warrens this night – to assure the veracity of what has occurred—'

'*What,*' Paran snapped, '*are you trying to say, sir?*'

Whiskeyjack met the captain's eyes. 'The Rhivi child, Silverfox. She is Tattersail reborn.'

Paran slowly turned, gaze travelling down to the foot of the barrow, where four figures waited in the darkness. And there stood the Rhivi child, a sunrise aura about her person, a penumbra of power that stirred the wilder blood that coursed within him. *Yes. She is the one. Older now, revealing what she will become. Dammit, woman, you never could keep things simple.* All that was trapped within him seemed to

159

wash through his limbs, leaving him weak and suddenly shivering. He stared down at Silverfox. 'She is a child.' *But I knew that, didn't I? I've known that for a while, I just didn't want to think about it . . . And now, no choice.*

Whiskeyjack grunted. 'She grows swiftly – there are eager, impatient forces within her, too powerful for a child's body to contain. You'll not have long—'

'Before propriety arrives,' Paran finished drily, not noticing Whiskeyjack's start. 'Fine for then, what of now? Who will naught but see me as a monster should we even so much as hold hands? What can I say to her? What can I possibly say?' He spun to Whiskeyjack. 'This is impossible – *she is a child!*'

'And within her is Tattersail. And Nightchill—'

'*Nightchill!* Hood's breath! What has happened – *how?*'

'Questions not easily answered, lad. You'd do better to ask them of Mallet and Quick Ben – and of Silverfox herself.'

Paran involuntarily took a step back. 'Speak with her? No. I cannot—'

'She wishes it, Paran. She awaits you now.'

'No.' His eyes were once again pulled downslope. 'I see Tattersail, yes. But there's more – not just this Nightchill woman – she's a Soletaken, now, Whiskeyjack. The creature that gave her her Rhivi name – the power to change . . .'

The commander's eyes narrowed. 'How do you know, Captain?'

'I just know—'

'Not good enough. It wasn't easy for Quick Ben to glean that truth. Yet you *know*. How, Paran?'

The captain grimaced. 'I've felt Quick Ben's probings in my direction – when he thinks my attention is elsewhere. I've seen the wariness in his eyes. What has he found, Commander?'

'Oponn's abandoned you, but something else has taken

its place. Something savage. His hackles rise whenever you're close—'

'Hackles.' Paran smiled. 'An apt choice of word. Anomander Rake killed two Hounds of Shadow – I was there. I saw it. I felt the stain of a dying Hound's blood – on my flesh, Whiskeyjack. Something of that blood now runs in my veins.'

The commander's voice was deadpan. 'What else?'

'There has to be something else, sir?'

'Yes. Quick Ben caught hints – there's much more than simply an ascendant's blood to what you've become.' Whiskeyjack hesitated, then said, 'Silverfox has fashioned for you a Rhivi name. Jen'isand Rul.'

'Jen'isand Rul.'

'It translates as "the Wanderer within the Sword". It means, she says, that you have done something no other creature has ever done – mortal or ascendant – and that something has set you apart. You have been marked, Ganoes Paran – yet no-one, not even Silverfox, knows what it portends. Tell me what happened.'

Paran shrugged. 'Rake used that black sword of his. When he killed the Hounds. I followed them . . . into that sword. The spirits of the Hounds were trapped, chained with all the . . . all the others. I think I freed them, sir. I can't be sure of that – all I know is that they ended up somewhere else. No longer chained.'

'And have they returned to this world?'

'I don't know. Jen'isand Rul . . . why should there be any significance to my having wandered within that sword?'

Whiskeyjack grunted. 'You're asking the wrong man, Captain. I'm only repeating what Silverfox has said. One thing, though, that has just occurred to me.' He stepped closer. 'Not a word to the Tiste Andii – not Korlat, not Anomander Rake. The Son of Darkness is an unpredictable bastard, by all accounts. And if the legend of Dragnipur is true, the curse of that sword of his is that no-one escapes its nightmare prison – their souls are chained . . . for ever.

You've cheated that, and perhaps the Hounds have as well. You've set an alarming . . . precedent.'

Paran smiled bitterly in the darkness. 'Cheated. Yes, I have cheated many things, even death.' *But not pain. No, that escape still eludes me.* 'You think Rake takes much comfort in the belief of his sword's . . . finality.'

'Seems likely, Ganoes Paran, does it not?'

The captain sighed. 'Aye.'

'Now, let us go down to meet Silverfox.'

'No.'

'Damn you, Paran,' Whiskeyjack growled. 'This is about more than just you and her all starry-eyed. That child possesses power, and it's vast and . . . and unknown. Kallor has murder in his eyes when he looks at her. Silverfox is in danger. The question is, do we protect her or stand aside? The High King calls her an abomination, Captain. Should Caladan Brood turn his back at the wrong moment—'

'He'll kill her? Why?'

'He fears, I gather, the power within her.'

'Hood's breath, she's just a—' He stopped, realizing the venality of the assertion. *Just a child? Hardly.* 'Protect her against Kallor, you said. That's a risky position to assume, Commander. Who stands with us?'

'Korlat, and by extension, all of the Tiste Andii.'

'Anomander Rake?'

'That we don't yet know. Korlat's mistrust of Kallor, coupled with a friendship with the Mhybe, has guided her to her decision. She says she will speak with her master when he arrives—'

'Arrives?'

'Aye. Tomorrow, possibly early, and if so you'd best avoid him, if at all possible.'

Paran nodded. *One meeting was enough.* 'And the warlord?'

'Undecided, we think. But Brood needs the Rhivi and their bhederin herds. For the moment, at least, he remains the girl's chief protector.'

'And what does Dujek think of all this?' the captain asked.

'He awaits your decision.'

'Mine? Beru fend, Commander – I'm no mage or priest. Nor can I glean the child's future.'

'Tattersail resides within Silverfox, Paran. She must be drawn forth . . . to the fore.'

'Because Tattersail would never betray us. Yes, now I see.'

'You needn't sound so miserable about it, Paran.'

No? And if you stood in my place, Whiskeyjack? 'Very well, lead on.'

'It seems,' Whiskeyjack said, striding to the edge of the barrow's summit, 'we will have to promote you to a rank equal to mine, Captain, if only to circumvent your confusion as to who commands who around here.'

Their arrival was a quiet, stealthy affair, leading their mounts into the encampment with the minimum of fuss. Few Tiste Andii remained outside their tents to take note. Sergeant Antsy led the main group of Bridgeburners towards the kraal to settle in the horses, whilst Corporal Picker, Detoran, Blend, Trotts and Hedge slipped away to find Brood's command tent. Spindle awaited them at its entrance.

Picker gave him a nod and the mage, wrapped in his foul-smelling hairshirt with its equally foul hood thrown over his head, turned to face the tied-down entrance flap. He made a series of hand gestures, paused, then spat at the canvas. There was no sound as the spit struck the flap. He swung a grin to Picker, then bowed before the entrance in invitation.

Hedge nudged the corporal and rolled his eyes.

There were two rooms within, she knew, and the warlord was sleeping in the back one. *Hopefully.* Picker looked around for Blend – *damn, where is she? Here a moment ago—*

Two fingers brushed her arm and she nearly leapt out of her leathers. Beside her, Blend smiled. Picker mouthed a

163

silent stream of curses. Blend's smile broadened, then she stepped past, up to the tent entrance, where she crouched down to untie the fastenings.

Picker glanced over a shoulder. Detoran and Trotts stood side by side a few paces back, both hulking and monstrous.

At the corporal's side Hedge nudged her again, and she turned to see that Blend had drawn back the flap.

All right, let's get this done.

Blend led the way, followed by Spindle, then Hedge. Picker waved the Napan and the Barghast forward, then followed them into the tent's dark confines.

Even with Trotts at one end and Detoran at the other, with Spindle and Hedge at the sides, the table had them staggering before they'd gone three paces. Blend moved ahead of them to pull the flap back as far as she could. Within the sorcerous silence, the four soldiers managed to manoeuvre the massive table outside. Picker watched, glancing back at the divider every few moments – but the warlord made no appearance. *So far so good.*

The corporal and Blend added their muscles in carrying the table, and the six of them managed to take it fifty paces before exhaustion forced them to halt.

'Not much further,' Spindle whispered.

Detoran sniffed. 'They'll find it.'

'That's a wager I'll call you on,' Picker said. 'But first, let's get it there.'

'Can't you make this thing any lighter?' Hedge whined at Spindle. 'What kind of mage are you, anyway?'

Spindle scowled. 'A weak one, what of it? Look at you – you're not even sweating!'

'Quiet, you two,' Picker hissed. 'Come on, heave her up, now.'

'Speaking of heaving,' Hedge muttered as, amid a chorus of grunts, the table once again rose from the ground, 'when are you gonna wash that disgusting shirt of yours, Spindle?'

'Wash it? Mother never washed her hair when she was alive – why should I start now? It'll lose its lustre—'

164

'Lustre? Oh, you mean fifty years of sweat and rancid lard—'

'Wasn't rancid when she was alive, though, was it?'

'Thank Hood I don't know—'

'Will you two save your foul breath? Which way now, Spindle?'

'Right. Down that alley. Then left – the hide tent at the end—'

'Bet someone's living in it,' Detoran muttered.

'You're on with that one, too,' Picker said. 'It's the one the Rhivi use to lay out Tiste Andii corpses before cremation. Ain't been a killed Tiste since Darujhistan.'

'How'd you find it anyway?' Hedge asked.

'Spindle sniffed it out—'

'Surprised he can sniff anything—'

'All right, set her down. Blend – the flap.'

The table filled the entire room within, with only an arm's length of space around it on all sides. The low cots that had been used for the corpses went beneath, folded and stacked. A shuttered lantern was lit and hung from the centre-pole hook. Picker watched Hedge crouch down, his eyes inches from the table's scarred, pitted surface, and run his blunt, battered fingers lovingly along the wood's grain. 'Beautiful,' he whispered. He glanced up, met Picker's eyes. 'Call in the crew, Corporal, the game's about to start.'

Grinning, Picker nodded. 'Go get 'em, Blend.'

'Even cuts,' Hedge said, glaring at everyone. 'We're a squad now—'

'Meaning you let us in on the secret,' Spindle said, scowling. 'If we'd known you was cheating all that time—'

'Yeah, well, your fortunes are about to turn, ain't they? So quit the complaining.'

'Aren't you two a perfect match,' Picker observed. 'So tell us, Hedge, how does this work?'

'Oppositions, Corporal. Both Decks are the real thing, you see. Fiddler had the better sensitivity, but Spindle

165

should be able to pull it off.' He faced the mage. 'You've done readings before, haven't you? You said—'

'Yeah yeah, squirt – no problem, I got the touch—'

'You'd better,' the sapper warned. He caressed the table-top again. 'Two layers, you see, with the fixed Deck in between 'em. Lay a card down and there's a tension formed, and it tells ya which one the face-down one is. Never fails. Dealer knows every hand he plays out. Fiddler—'

'Ain't here,' Trotts growled, his arms crossed. He bared his teeth at Spindle.

The mage sputtered. 'I can do it, you horse-brained savage! Watch me!'

'Shut up,' Picker snapped. 'They're coming.'

It was near dawn when the other squads began filing back out of the tent, laughing and back-slapping as they jingled bulging purses. When the last of them had left, voices trailing away, Picker slumped wearily down on the table. Spindle, sweat dripping from his gleaming hairshirt, groaned and dropped his head, thumping against the thick wood.

Stepping up behind him, Hedge raised a hand.

'At ease, soldier,' Picker warned. 'Obviously, the whole damn thing's been corrupted – probably never worked to start with—'

'It did! Me and Fid made damned sure—'

'But it was stolen before you could try it out for real, wasn't it?'

'That doesn't matter – I tell you—'

'Everybody shut up,' Spindle said, slowly raising his head, his narrow forehead wrinkled in a frown as he scanned the tabletop. 'Corrupted. You may have something there, Picker.' He sniffed the air as if seeking a scent, then crouched down. 'Yeah. Give me a hand, someone, with these here cots.'

No-one moved.

'Help him, Hedge,' Picker ordered.

'Help him crawl under the table? It's too late to hide—'

'That's an order, soldier.'

Grumbling, the sapper lowered himself down. Together, the two men dragged the cots clear. Then Spindle edged beneath the table. A faint glow of sorcerous light slowly blossomed, then the mage hissed. 'It's the underside all right!'

'Brilliant observation, Spindle. Bet there's legs, too.'

'No, you fool. There's an image painted onto the underside . . . one big card, it looks like – only I don't recognize it.'

Scowling, Hedge joined the mage. 'What are you talking about? We didn't paint no image underneath – Hood's mouldering moccasins, what is *that*?'

'Red ochre, is my guess. Like something a Barghast would paint—'

'Or a Rhivi,' Hedge muttered. 'Who's that figure in the middle – the one with the dog-head on his chest?'

'How should I know? Anyway, I'd say the whole thing is pretty fresh. Recent, I mean.'

'Well, rub it off, dammit.'

Spindle crawled back out. 'Not a chance – the thing's webbed with wards, and a whole lot else besides.' He straightened, met Picker's eyes, then shrugged. 'It's a new card. Unaligned, without an aspect. I'd like to make a copy of it, Deck-sized, then try it out with a reading—'

'Whatever,' Picker said.

Hedge reappeared, suddenly energized. 'Good idea, Spin – you could charge for the readings, too. If this new Unaligned plays true, then you could work out the new tensions, the new relationships, and once you know them—'

Spindle grinned. 'We could run another game. Yeah—'

Detoran groaned. 'I have lost all my money.'

'We all have,' Picker snapped, glaring at the two sappers. 'It'll work next time,' Hedge said. 'You'll see.'

Spindle was nodding vigorously.

'Sorry if we seem to lack enthusiasm,' Blend drawled.

Picker swung to the Barghast. 'Trotts, take a look at that drawing.'

The warrior sniffed, then sank down to his hands and knees. Grunting, he made his way under the table. 'It's gone dark,' he said.

Hedge turned to Spindle. 'Do that light trick again, you idiot.'

The mage sneered at the sapper, then gestured. The glow beneath the table returned.

Trotts was silent for a few moments, then he crawled back out and climbed upright.

'Well?' Picker asked.

The Barghast shook his head. 'Rhivi.'

'Rhivi don't play with Decks,' Spindle said.

Trotts bared his teeth. 'Neither do Barghast.'

'I need some wood,' Spindle said, scratching the stubble lining his narrow jaw. 'And a stylus,' he went on, ignoring everyone else. 'And paints, and a brush . . .'

They watched as he wandered out of the tent. Picker sighed, glared one last time at Hedge. 'Hardly an auspicious entry into the Seventh Squad, sapper. Antsy's heart damn near stopped when he lost his whole column. Your sergeant is probably gutting black-livered wood pigeons and whispering your name right now – who knows, your luck might change and a demon *won't* hear him.'

Hedge scowled. 'Ha ha.'

'I don't think she's kidding,' Detoran said.

'Fine,' Hedge snapped. 'I got a cusser waiting for it, and damned if I won't make sure I take you all with me.'

'Team spirit,' Trotts said, his smile broadening.

Picker grunted. 'All right, soldiers, let's get out of here.'

Paran and Silverfox stood apart from the others, watching the eastern sky grow light with streaks of copper and bronze. The last of the stars were withdrawing overhead, a cold, indifferent scatter surrendering to the warmth of a blue, cloudless day.

Through the awkwardness of the hours just past, stretching interminable as a succession of pain and discomfort in Paran's mind, emotional exhaustion had arrived, and with it a febrile calm. He had fallen silent, fearful of shattering that inner peace, knowing it to be nothing but an illusion, a pensively drawn breath within a storm.

'Tattersail must be drawn forth.' He had indeed done that. The first meeting of their eyes had unlocked every shared memory, and that unlocking was an explosive curse for Paran. *A child. I face a child, and so recoil at the thought of intimacy – even if it had once been with a grown woman. The woman is no more. This is a child.* But there was yet more to the anguish that boiled within the man. Another presence, entwined like wires of black iron through all that was Tattersail. Nightchill, the sorceress, once lover to Bellurdan – where she had led, the Thelomen had followed. Anything but an equal relationship, and now, with Nightchill, had come a bitter, demanding presence. *Bitter, indeed. With Tayschrenn . . . with the Empress and the Malazan Empire and Hood knows what or who else. She knows she was betrayed at the Enfilade at Pale. Both her and, out there on the plain, Bellurdan. Her mate.*

Silverfox spoke. 'You need not fear the T'lan Imass.'

He blinked, shook himself. 'So you have explained. Since you command them. We are all wondering, however, precisely what you plan with that undead army? What's the significance of this Gathering?'

She sighed. 'It is very simple, really. They gather for benediction. Mine.'

He faced her. 'Why?'

'I am a flesh and blood Bonecaster – the first such in hundreds of thousands of years.' Then her face hardened. 'But we shall need them first. In their fullest power. There are horrors awaiting us all . . . in the Pannion Domin.'

'The others must know of this, this benediction – what

169

it means, Silverfox – and more of the threat that awaits us in the Pannion Domin. Brood, Kallor—'

She shook her head. 'My blessing is not their concern. Indeed, it is no-one's concern but mine. And the T'lan Imass themselves. As for the Pannion ... I myself must learn more before I dare speak. Paran, I have told you these things for what we were, and for what you – we – have become.'

And what have we become? No, not a question for now. 'Jen'isand Rul.'

She frowned. 'That is a side of you that I do not understand. But there is more, Paran.' She hesitated, then said, 'Tell me, what do you know of the Deck of Dragons?'

'Almost nothing.' But he smiled, for he heard Tattersail now, more clearly than at any other time since they'd first met.

Silverfox drew a deep breath, held it a moment, then slowly released it, her veiled eyes once again on the rising sun. 'The Deck of Dragons. A kind of structure, imposed on power itself. Who created it? No-one knows. My belief – Tattersail's belief – is that each card is a gate into a warren, and there were once many more cards than there are now. There may have been other Decks – there may well be other Decks . . .'

He studied her. 'You have another suspicion, don't you?'

'Yes. I said no-one knows who created the Deck of Dragons. Yet there is another entity equally mysterious, also a kind of structure, focused upon power itself. Think of the terminology used with the Deck of Dragons. Houses . . . Houses of Dark, of Light, of Life and Death . . .' She slowly faced him. 'Think of the word "Finnest". Its meaning, as the T'lan Imass know it, is "Hold of Ice". Long ago, among the Elder races, a Hold was synonymous with a House in its meaning and common usage, and indeed, synonymous with Warren. Where resides a Jaghut's wellspring of power? In a Finnest.' She paused again, searching Paran's eyes. 'Tremorlor is Trellish for "House of Life".'

170

Finnest . . . as in Finnest House, in Darujhistan . . . a House of the Azath. 'I've never heard of Tremorlor.'

'It is an Azath House in Seven Cities. In Malaz City in your own empire, there is the Deadhouse – the House of Death . . .'

'You believe the Houses of the Azath and the Houses of the Deck are one and the same.'

'Yes. Or linked, somehow. Think on it!'

Paran was doing just that. He had little knowledge of either, and could not think of any possible way in which he might be connected with them. His unease deepened, followed by a painful roil in his stomach. The captain scowled. He was too tired to think, yet think he must. 'It's said that the old emperor, Kellanved, and Dancer found a way into Deadhouse . . .'

'Kellanved and Dancer have since ascended and now hold the House of Shadow. Kellanved is Shadowthrone, and Dancer is Cotillion, the Rope, Patron of Assassins.'

The captain stared at her. 'What?'

Silverfox grinned. 'It's obvious when you consider it, isn't it? Who among the ascendants went after Laseen . . . with the aim of destroying her? Shadowthrone and Cotillion. Why would any ascendant care one way or another about a mortal woman? Unless they thirsted for vengeance.'

Paran's mind raced back, to a road on the coast of Itko Kan, to a dreadful slaughter, wounds made by huge, bestial jaws – *Hounds. Hounds of Shadow – Shadowthrone's pups . . .* From that day, the captain had begun a new path. On the trail of the young woman Cotillion had possessed. From that day, his life had begun its fated unravelling. 'Wait! Kellanved and Dancer went into *Deadhouse* – why didn't they take that aspect – the aspect of the House of Death?'

'I've thought about that myself, and have arrived at one possibility. The realm of Death was already occupied, Paran. The King of High House Death is Hood. I believe now that each Azath is home to every gate, a way into

171

every warren. Gain entry to the House, and you may . . . *choose*. Kellanved and Dancer found an empty House, an empty throne, and upon taking their places as Shadow's rulers, the House of Shadow appeared, and became part of the Deck of Dragons. Do you see?'

Paran slowly nodded, struggling to take it all in. Tremors of pain twisted his stomach – he pushed them away. *But what has this to do with me?*

'The House of Shadow was once a Hold,' Silverfox went on. 'You can tell – it doesn't share the hierarchical structure of the other Houses. It is bestial, a wilder place, and apart from the Hounds it knew no ruler for a long, long time.'

'What of the Deck's Unaligned?'

She shrugged. 'Failed aspects? The imposition of chance, of random forces? The Azath and the Deck are both impositions of order, but even order needs freedom, lest it solidify and become fragile.'

'And where do you think I fit in? I'm nothing, Silverfox. A stumble-footed mortal.' *Gods, leave me out of all this – all that you seem to be leading up to. Please.*

'I have thought long and hard on this, Paran. Anomander Rake is Knight of the House of Dark,' she said, 'yet where is the House itself? Before all else there was Dark, the Mother who birthed all. So it must be an ancient place, a Hold, or perhaps something that came before Holds themselves. A focus for the gate into Kurald Galain . . . undiscovered, hidden, the First Wound, with a soul trapped in its maw, thus sealing it.'

'A soul,' Paran murmured, a chill clambering up his spine, 'or a legion of souls . . .'

The breath hissed from Silverfox.

'Before Houses there were Holds,' Paran continued with remorseless logic. 'Both fixed, both stationary. Settled. Before settlement . . . there was *wandering*. House from Hold, Hold from . . . a gate in motion, ceaseless motion . . .' He squeezed shut his eyes. 'A wagon, burdened beneath the countless souls sealing the gate into Dark . . .' *And I sent two Hounds through that wound, I saw the seal punctured . . . by the Abyss . . .*

'Paran, something has happened – to the Deck of Dragons. A new card has arrived. Unaligned, yet, I think, dominant. The Deck has never possessed a . . . master.' She faced him. 'I now believe it has one. You.'

His eyes snapped open; he stared at her in disbelief, then scorn. 'Nonsense, Tatter— Silverfox. Not me. You are wrong. You must be—'

'I am not. My hand was guided in fashioning the card that is you—'

'What card?'

She did not answer, continued as if she had not heard him. 'Was it the Azath that guided me? Or some other unknown force? I do not know. *Jen'isand Rul*, the Wanderer within the Sword.' She met his eyes. 'You are a new Unaligned, Ganoes Paran. Birthed by accident or by some purpose the need of which only the Azath know. You must find the answer for your own creation, you must find the purpose behind what you have become.'

His brows rose mockingly. 'You set for me a quest? Really, Silverfox. Aimless, purposeless men do not undertake quests. That's for wall-eyed heroes in epic poems. I don't believe in goals – not any more. They're naught but self-delusions. You set for me this task and you shall be gravely disappointed. As shall the Azath.'

'An unseen war has begun, Paran. The warrens themselves are under assault – I can feel the pressure within the Deck of Dragons, though I have yet to rest a hand upon one. An army is being . . . assembled, perhaps, and you – a soldier – are part of that army.'

Oh yes, so speaks Tattersail. 'I have enough wars to fight, Silverfox . . .'

Her eyes glistened as she looked up at him. 'Perhaps, Ganoes Paran, they are all one war.'

'I'm no Dujek, or Brood – I can't manage all these . . . campaigns. It's – it's tearing me apart.'

'I know. You cannot hide your pain from me – I see it in your face, and it breaks my heart.'

He looked away. 'I have dreams as well . . . a child within a wound. Screaming.'

'Do you run from that child?'

'Aye,' he admitted shakily. 'Those screams are . . . terrible.'

'You must run towards the child, my love. Flight will close your heart.'

He turned to her. '*My love*' – *words to manipulate my heart?* 'Who is that child?'

She shook her head. 'I don't know. A victim in the unseen war, perhaps.' She attempted a smile. 'Your courage has been tested before, Paran, and it did not fail.'

Grimacing, he muttered, 'There's always a first time.'

'You are the Wanderer within the Sword. The card exists.'

'I don't care.'

'Nor does it,' she retorted. 'You don't have any choice—'

He rounded on her. 'Nothing new in that! Now ask Oponn how well I performed!' His laugh was savage. 'I doubt the Twins will ever recover. The wrong choice, Tattersail, I am *ever the wrong choice!*'

She stared up at him, then, infuriatingly, simply shrugged.

Suddenly deflated, Paran turned away. His gaze fell on the Mhybe, Whiskeyjack, Mallet and Quick Ben. The four had not moved in all this time. Their patience – *dammit, their faith* – made the captain want to scream. *You choose wrongly. Every damned one of you.* But he knew they would not listen. 'I know nothing of the Deck of Dragons,' he said dully.

'If we've the time, I will teach you. If not, you will find your own way.'

Paran closed his eyes. The pain in his stomach was returning, rising, a slowly building wave he could no longer push back. *Yes, of course. Tattersail could do no less than she has done. There you have it then, Whiskeyjack. She now leads, and the others follow. A good soldier, is Captain Ganoes Paran . . .*

In his mind he returned to that fraught, nightmarish realm within the sword Dragnipur, the legions of chained souls ceaselessly dragging their impossible burden . . . and at the heart of the wagon, a cold, dark void, from whence came the chains. *The wagon carries the gate, the gate into Kurald Galain, the warren of Darkness. The sword gathers souls to seal it . . . such a wound it must be, to demand so many souls . . .* He grunted at a wave of pain. Silverfox's small hand reached up to touch his arm.

He almost flinched at the contact.

I will fail you all.

CHAPTER FIVE

He rises bloodless from dust,
with dead eyes that are pits
twin reaches to eternal pain.

He is the lodestone
to the gathering clan,
made anew and dream-racked.

The standard a rotted hide,
the throne a bone cage, the king
a ghost from dark fields of battle.

And now the horn moans
on this grey clad dawn
drawing the disparate host

To war, to war,
and the charging frenzy
of unbidden memories of ice.

Lay of the First Sword
Irig Thann Delusa (b. 1091)

Two days and seven leagues of black, clinging clouds of ash, and Lady Envy's telaba showed not a single stain. Grumbling, Toc the Younger pulled the caked cloth from his face and slowly lowered his heavy leather pack to the ground. He never thought he'd bless the sight of a sweeping, featureless grassy plain, but, after the volcanic ash, the undulating vista stretching northward beckoned like paradise.

'Will this hill suffice for a camp?' Lady Envy asked, striding over to stand close to him. 'It seems frightfully exposed. What if there are marauders on this plain?'

'Granted, marauders aren't usually clever,' Toc replied, 'but even the stupidest bandit would hesitate before trying three Seguleh. The wind you're feeling up here will keep the biting insects away come night, Lady. I wouldn't recommend low ground – on any prairie.'

'I bow to your wisdom, Scout.'

He coughed, straightening to scan the area. 'Can't see your four-legged friends anywhere.'

'Nor your bony companion.' She turned wide eyes on him. 'Do you believe they have stumbled into mischief?'

He studied her, bemused, and said nothing.

She raised an eyebrow, then smiled.

Toc swiftly turned his attention back to his pack. 'I'd best pitch the tents,' he muttered.

'As I assured you last night, Toc, my servants are quite capable of managing such mundane activities. I'd much rather you assumed for yourself a higher rank than mere menial labourer for the duration of this great adventure.'

He paused. 'You wish me to strike heroic poses against the sunset, Lady Envy?'

'Indeed!'

'I wasn't aware I existed for your entertainment.'

'Oh, now you're cross again.' She stepped closer, rested a sparrow-light hand on his shoulder. 'Please don't be angry with me. I can hardly hold interesting conversations with my servants, can I? Nor is your friend Tool a social blossom flushed with enlivening vigour. And while my two pups are near-perfect companions in always listening and never interrupting, one yearns for the spice of witty exchanges.

You and I, Toc, we have only each other for this journey, so let us fashion the bonds of friendship.'

Staring down at the bundled tents, Toc the Younger was silent for a long moment, then he sighed. 'I'm a poor excuse for witty exchanges, Lady, alas. I am a soldier and scant else.' *More, I've a soldier's scars – who can naught but flinch upon seeing me?*

'Not modesty, but deception, Toc.'

He winced at the edge to her tone.

'You have been educated, far beyond what is common for a professional soldier. And I have heard enough of your sharp exchanges with the T'lan Imass to value your wit. What is this sudden shyness? Why the growing discomfort?'

Her hand had not moved from his shoulder. 'You are a sorceress, Lady Envy. And sorcery makes me nervous.'

The hand withdrew. 'I see. Or, rather, I do not. Your T'lan Imass was forged by a ritual of such power as this world has not seen in a long time, Toc the Younger. His stone sword alone is invested to an appalling degree – it cannot be broken, not even chipped, and it will cut through wards effortlessly. No warren can defend against it. I would not wager on any blade against it when in Tool's hands. And the creature himself. He is a champion of sorts, isn't he? Among the T'lan Imass, Tool is something unique. You have no idea of the power – the *strength* – he possesses. Does Tool make you nervous, soldier? I've seen no sign of that.'

'Well,' Toc snapped, 'he's shrunken hide and bones, isn't he? Tool doesn't brush against me at every chance. He doesn't throw smiles at me like lances into my heart, does he? He doesn't mock that I once had a face that didn't make people turn away, does he?'

Her eyes were wide. 'I do not mock your scars,' she said quietly.

He glared over to the three motionless, masked Seguleh. *Oh, Hood, I've made a mess of things here, haven't I? Are you laughing behind those face-shields, warriors?* 'My apologies, Lady,' he managed. 'I regret my words—'

178

'Yet hold to them none the less. Very well, it seems I must accept the challenge, then.'

He looked up at her. 'Challenge?'

She smiled. 'Indeed. Clearly, you think my affection for you is not genuine. I must endeavour to prove otherwise.'

'Lady—'

'And in your efforts to push me away, you'll soon discover that I am not easily pushed.'

'To what end, Lady Envy?' *All my defences broken down . . . for your amusement?*

Her eyes flashed and Toc knew, with certainty, the truth of his thoughts. Pain stole through him like cold iron. He began unfolding the first tent.

Garath and Baaljagg arrived, bounding up to circle around Lady Envy. A moment later a swirl of dust rose from the ochre grasses a few paces from where Toc crouched. Tool appeared, carrying across his shoulders the carcass of a pronghorn antelope, which he shrugged off to thump on the ground.

Toc saw no wounds on the animal. *Probably scared it to death.*

'Oh, wonderful!' Lady Envy cried. 'We shall dine like nobles tonight!' She swung to her servants. 'Come, Senu, you have some butchering to do.'

Won't be the first time, either.

'And you other two, uhm, what shall we devise for you? Idle hands just won't do. Mok, you shall assemble the hide bath-tub. Set it on that hill over there. You needn't worry about water or perfumed oils – I shall take care of all that. Thurule, unpack my combs and robe, there's a good lad.'

Toc glanced over to see Tool facing him. The scout grimaced wryly.

The T'lan Imass strode over. 'We can begin our arrow-making efforts, soldier.'

'Aye, once I'm done with the tents.'

'Very well. I shall assemble the raw material we have collected. We must fashion a tool kit.'

179

Toc had put up enough tents in his soldiering days to allow him to maintain fair attention on Tool's preparations while he worked. The T'lan Imass knelt beside the antelope and, with no apparent effort, broke off both antlers down near the base. He then moved to one side and unslung the hide bag he carried, loosening the drawstring so that it unfolded onto the ground, revealing a half-dozen large obsidian cobbles collected on their passage across the old lava flow, and an assortment of different kinds of stones which had come from the shoreline beyond the Jaghut tower, along with bone-reeds and a brace of dead seagulls, both of which were still strapped to Toc's pack.

It was always a wonder – and something of a shock – to watch the deftness of the undead warrior's withered, almost fleshless hands, as he worked. *An artist's hands*. Selecting one of the obsidian cobbles, the T'lan Imass picked up one of the larger beach stones and with three swift blows detached three long, thin blades of the volcanic glass. A few more concussive strikes created a series of flakes that varied in size and thickness.

Tool set down the hammerstone and the obsidian core. Sorting through the flakes, he chose one, gripping it in his left hand, then, with his right, he reached for one of the antlers. Using the tip of the foremost tine of the antler, the T'lan Imass began punching minute flakes from the edge of the larger flake.

Beside Toc the Younger, Lady Envy sighed. 'Such extraordinary skill. Do you think, in the time before we began to work metal, we all possessed such abilities?'

The scout shrugged. 'Seems likely. According to some Malazan scholars, the discovery of iron occurred only half a thousand years ago – for the peoples of the Quon Tali continent, in any case. Before that, everyone used bronze. And before bronze we used unalloyed copper and tin. Before those, why not stone?'

'Ah, I knew you had been educated, Toc the Younger. Human scholars, alas, tend to think solely in terms of human accomplishments. Among the Elder Races, the forging of metals was quite sophisticated. Improvements on iron itself were known. My father's sword, for example.'

He grunted. 'Sorcery. Investment. It replaces technological advancement – it's often a means of supplanting the progress of mundane knowledge.'

'Why, soldier, you certainly do have particular views when it comes to sorcery. However, did I detect something of rote in your words? Which bitter scholar – some failed sorceror no doubt – has espoused such views?'

Despite himself, Toc grinned. 'Aye, fair enough. Not a scholar, in fact, but a High Priest.'

'Ah, well, cults see *any* advancement – sorcerous or, indeed, mundane – as potential threats. You must dismantle your sources, Toc the Younger, lest you do nothing but ape the prejudices of others.'

'You sound just like my father.'

'You should have heeded his wisdom.'

I should have. But I never did. Leave the Empire, he said. Find someplace beyond the reach of the court, beyond the commanders and the Claw. Keep your head low, son . . .

Finished with the last of the three tents, Toc made his way to Tool's side. Seventy paces away, on the summit of a nearby hill, Mok had assembled the wood-framed hide-lined bath-tub. Lady Envy, Thurule marching at her side with folded robe and bath-kit in his arms, made her way towards it. The wolf and dog sat close to Senu where he worked on the antelope. The Seguleh flung spare bits of meat to the animals every now and then.

Tool had completed four small stone tools – a backed blade; some kind of scraper, thumbnail-sized; a crescent-bladed piece with its inside edge finely worked; and a drill or punch. He now turned to the original three large flakes of obsidian.

Crouching down beside the T'lan Imass, Toc examined the finished items. 'All right,' he said after a few moments' examination, 'I'm starting to understand this. These ones are for working the shaft and the fletching, yes?'

Tool nodded. 'The antelope will provide us with the raw material. We need gut string for binding. Hide for the quiver and its straps.'

'What about this crescent-shaped one?'

'The bone-reed shafts must be trued.'

'Ah, yes, I see. Won't we need some kind of glue or pitch?'

'Ideally, yes. Since this is a treeless plain, however, we shall make do with what we possess. The fletching will be tied on with gut.'

'You make the fashioning of arrowheads look easy, Tool, but something tells me it isn't.'

'Some stone is sand, some is water. Edged tools can be made of the stone that is water. Crushing tools are made of the stone that is sand, but only the hardest of those.'

'And here I've gone through life thinking stone is stone.'

'In our language, we possess many names for stone. Names that tell of its nature, names that describe its function, names for what has happened to it and what will happen to it, names for the spirit residing within it, names—'

'All right, all right! I see your point. Why don't we talk about something else?'

'Such as?'

Toc glanced over at the other hill. Only Lady Envy's head and knees were visible above the tub's framework. The sunset blazed behind her. The two Seguleh, Mok and Thurule, stood guard over her, facing outward. 'Her.'

'Of Lady Envy, I know little more than what I have already said.'

'She was a . . . companion of Anomander Rake's?'

Tool resumed removing thin, translucent flakes of obsidian from what was quickly assuming the shape of a lanceolate arrowhead. 'At first, there were three others, who wandered together, for a time. Anomander Rake,

182

Caladan Brood, and a sorceress who eventually ascended to become the Queen of Dreams. Following that event, dramas ensued – or so it is told. The Son of Darkness was joined by Lady Envy, and the Soletaken known as Osric. Another three who wandered together. Caladan Brood chose a solitary path at the time, and was not seen on this world for score centuries. When he finally returned – perhaps a thousand years ago – he carried the hammer he still carries: a weapon of the Sleeping Goddess.'

'And Rake, Envy and this Osric – what were they up to?'

The T'lan Imass shrugged. 'Of that, only they could tell you. There was a falling out. Osric is gone – where, no-one knows. Anomander Rake and Lady Envy remained companions. It is said they parted – argumentatively – in the days before the ascendants gathered to chain the Fallen One. Rake joined in that effort. The lady did not. Of her, this is the sum of my knowledge, soldier.'

'She's a mage.'

'The answer to that is before you.'

'The hot bathwater appearing from nowhere, you mean.'

Tool set the finished arrowhead down and reached for another blank. 'I meant the Seguleh, Toc the Younger.'

The scout grunted. 'Ensorcelled – forced to serve her – Hood's breath, she's made them slaves!'

The T'lan Imass paused to regard him. 'This bothers you? Are there not slaves in the Malazan Empire?'

'Aye. Debtors, petty criminals, spoils of war. But, Tool, these are *Seguleh*! The most feared warriors on this continent. Especially the way they attack without the slightest warning, for reasons only they know—'

'Their communication,' Tool said, 'is mostly non-verbal. They assert dominance with posture, faint gestures, direction of stance and tilt of head.'

Toc blinked. 'They do? Oh. Then why haven't I, in my ignorance, been cut down long ago?'

'Your unease in their presence conveys submission,' the T'lan Imass replied.

'A natural coward, that's me. I take it, then, that you show no . . . unease.'

'I yield to no-one, Toc the Younger.'

The Malazan was silent, thinking on Tool's words. Then he said, 'That oldest brother – Mok – his mask bears but twin scars. I think I know what that means, and if I'm right . . .' He slowly shook his head.

The undead warrior glanced up, shadowed gaze not wavering from the scout's face. 'The young one who challenged me – Senu – was . . . good. Had I not antici- pated him, had I not prevented him from fully drawing his swords, our duel might well have been a long one.'

Toc scowled. 'How could you tell how good he was when he didn't even get his swords clear of their scabbards?'

'He parried my attacks with them none the less.'

Toc's lone eye slowly widened. 'He parried you with *half- drawn* blades?'

'The first two attacks, yes, but not the third. I need only to study the eldest's movements, the lightness of his steps on the earth – his grace – to sense the full measure of his skill. Senu and Thurule both acknowledge him as their master. Clearly you believe, by virtue of his mask, that he is highly ranked among his own kind.'

'Third, I think. Third highest. There's supposed to be a legendary Seguleh with an unmarked mask. White porcelain. Not that anyone has ever seen him, except the Seguleh themselves, I suppose. They are a warrior caste. Ruled by the champion.' Toc turned to study the two distant warriors, then glanced over a shoulder at Senu, who still knelt over the antelope not ten paces away. 'So what has brought them to the mainland, I wonder?'

'You might ask the youngest, Toc.'

The scout grinned at Tool. 'Meaning you're as curious as I am. Well, I am afraid I can't do your dirty work for you, since I rank below him. He may choose to speak with me, but I cannot initiate. If you want answers, it is up to you to ask the questions.'

Tool set down the antler and blank, then rose to his feet in a muted clack of bones. He strode towards Senu. Toc followed.

'Warrior,' the T'lan Imass said.

The Seguleh paused in his butchering, dipped his head slightly.

'What has driven you to leave your homeland? What has brought you and your brothers to this place?'

Senu's reply was a dialect of Daru, slightly archaic to Toc's ears. 'Master Stoneblade, we are the punitive army of the Seguleh.'

Had anyone other than a Seguleh made such a claim, Toc would have laughed outright. As it was, he clamped his jaw tight.

Tool seemed as taken aback as was the scout, for it was a long moment before he spoke again. 'Punitive. Whom does the Seguleh seek to punish?'

'Invaders to our island. We kill all that come, yet the flow does not cease. The task is left to our Blackmasks – the First Level Initiates in the schooling of weapons – for the enemy comes unarmed and so are not worthy of duelling. But such slaughter disrupts the discipline of training, stains the mind and so damages the rigours of mindfulness. It was decided to travel to the homeland of these invaders, to slay the one who sends his people to our island. I have given you answer, Master Stoneblade.'

'Do you know the name of these people? The name by which they call themselves?'

'Priests of Pannion. They come seeking to convert. We are not interested. They do not listen. And now they warn of sending an army to our island. To show our eagerness for such an event, we sent them many gifts. They chose to be insulted by our invitation to war. We admit we do not understand, and have therefore grown weary of discourse with these Pannions. From now on, only our blades will speak for the Seguleh.'

'Yet Lady Envy has ensnared you with her charms.'

Toc's breath caught.

Senu dipped his head again, said nothing.

'Fortunately,' Tool continued in his dry, uninflected tone, 'we are now travelling towards the Pannion Domin.'

'The decision pleased us,' Senu grated.

'How many years since your birth, Senu?' the T'lan Imass asked.

'Fourteen, Master Stoneblade. I am Eleventh Level Initiate.'

Square-cut pieces of meat on skewers dripped sizzling fat into the flames. Lady Envy appeared from the gloom with her entourage in tow. She was dressed in a thick, midnight blue robe that hung down to brush the dew-laden grasses. Her hair was tied back into a single braid.

'A delicious aroma – I am famished!'

Toc caught Thurule's casual turn, gloved hands lifting. The unsheathing of his two swords was faster than the scout's eye could track, as was the whirling attack. Sparks flashed as bright steel struck flint. Tool was driven back a half-dozen paces as blow after blow rained down on his own blurred weapon. The two warriors vanished into the darkness beyond the hearth's lurid glow.

Wolf and dog barked, plunging after them.

'This is infuriating!' Lady Envy snapped.

Sparks exploded ten paces away, insufficient light for Toc to discern anything more than the vague twisting of arms and shoulders. He shot a glance at Mok and Senu. The latter still crouched at the hearth, studiously tending to the supper. The twin-scarred eldest stood motionless, watching the duel – though it seemed unlikely he could see any better than Toc could. *Maybe he doesn't need to . . .*

More sparks rained through the night.

Lady Envy stifled a giggle, one hand to her mouth.

'I take it you can see in the dark, Lady,' Toc murmured.

'Oh yes. This is an extraordinary duel – I have never . . . no, it's more complicated. An old memory, dredged free

186

when you first identified these as Seguleh. Anomander Rake once crossed blades with a score of Seguleh, one after the other. He'd paid an unannounced visit to the island – knowing nothing of the inhabitants. Taking human form and fashioning a mask for himself, he elected to walk down the city's main thoroughfare. Being naturally arrogant, he showed no deference to any who crossed his path . . .'

Another clash lit up the night, the exchange followed by a loud, solid grunt. Then the blades collided once again.

'Two bells. That was the full duration of Rake's visit to the island and its people. He described the ferocity of that short time, and his dismay and exhaustion which led him to withdraw into his warren if only to slow the hammering of his heart.'

A new voice, rasping and cold, now spoke. 'Blacksword.'

They turned to see Mok facing them.

'That was centuries ago,' Lady Envy said.

'The memory of worthy opponents does not fade among the Seguleh, mistress.'

'Rake said the last swordsman he faced wore a mask with seven symbols.'

Mok tilted his head. 'That mask still awaits him. Blacksword holds the Seventh position. Mistress, we would have him claim it.'

She smiled. 'Perhaps soon you can extend to him the invitation in person.'

'It is not an invitation, mistress. It is a demand.'

Her laugh was sweet and full-throated. 'Dear servant, there is *no-one* whom the Lord of Darkness will not meet with a steady, unwavering eye. Consider that a warning.'

'Then shall our swords cross, mistress. He is the Seventh. I am the Third.'

She turned on him, arms folded. 'Oh, really! Do you know where that score of Seguleh souls ended up when he killed them . . . *including* the Seventh? Chained within the sword Dragnipur, that's where. For eternity. Do you truly wish to join them, Mok?'

There was another loud thud from the darkness beyond the firelight, then silence.

'Seguleh who die, fail,' Mok said. 'We spare no thoughts for the failed among us.'

'Does that,' Toc softly enquired, 'include your brother?'

Tool had reappeared, his flint sword in his left hand, dragging Thurule's body by the collar with his right. The Seguleh's head lolled. Dog and wolf trailed the two, tails wagging.

'Have you killed my servant, T'lan Imass?' Lady Envy asked.

'I have not,' Tool replied. 'Broken wrist, broken ribs, a half-dozen blows to the head. I believe he will recover. Eventually.'

'Well, that won't do at all, I'm afraid. Bring him here, please. To me.'

'He is not to be healed magically,' Mok said.

The Lady's temper snapped then. She spun, a wave of argent power surging out from her. It struck Mok, threw him back through the air. He landed with a heavy thud. The coruscating glare vanished. 'Servants do not make demands of me! I remind you of your place, Mok. I trust once is enough.' She swung her attention back to Thurule. 'Heal him I shall. After all,' she continued in a milder tone, 'as any lady of culture knows, three is the absolute minimum when it comes to servants.' She laid a hand on the Seguleh's chest.

Thurule groaned.

Toc glanced at Tool. 'Hood's breath, you're all chopped up!'

'It has been a long time since I last faced such a worthy opponent,' Tool said. 'All the more challenging for using the flat of my blade.'

Mok was slowly climbing to his feet. At the T'lan Imass's last words, he went still, then slowly faced the undead warrior.

I'll be damned, Tool, you gave the Third pause.

'There will be no more duels this night,' Lady Envy said in a stern voice. 'I'll not constrain my wrath the next time.'

Mok casually slid his attention away from the T'lan Imass.

Straightening, Lady Envy sighed. 'Thurule is mended. I am almost weary! Senu, dear, get out the plates and utensils. And the Elin Red. A nice quiet meal is called for, I should say.' She flashed Toc a smile. 'And witty discourse, yes?'

It was now Toc's turn to groan.

The three horsemen drew rein to halt on the low hill's summit. Pulling his mount around to face the city of Pale, Whiskeyjack stared for a time, jaw muscles bunching.

Quick Ben said nothing, watching the grey-bearded commander, his old friend, with fullest understanding. *Upon this hill, we came to retrieve Hairlock. Amidst piles of empty armour – gods, they're still here, rotting in the grasses – and the sorceress Tattersail, the last left standing of the cadre. We'd just crawled out of the collapsed tunnels, leaving hundreds of brothers and sisters buried behind us. We burned with rage . . . we burned with the knowledge of betrayal.*

Here . . . on this sorcery-blasted hill, we were ready to commit murder. With cold, cold hands . . . The wizard glanced over at Mallet. The healer's small eyes were narrowed on Whiskeyjack, and Quick Ben knew that he too was reliving bitter memories.

There is no burying the history of our lives. Yellow nails and fingers of bone claw up from the ground at our feet, and hold us fast.

'Summarize,' Whiskeyjack growled, his grey eyes on the empty sky above the city.

Mallet cleared his throat. 'Who starts?'

The commander swung his head to the healer.

'Right,' Mallet said. 'Paran's . . . affliction. His mortal flesh has the taint of ascendant blood . . . and ascendant places . . . but as Quick will tell you, neither one should be manifesting as illness. No, that blood, and those places, are like shoves down a corridor.'

'And he keeps crawling back,' Quick Ben added. 'Trying to escape. And the more he tries—'

'The sicker he gets,' Mallet finished.

Whiskeyjack, eyes once again on Pale, grimaced wryly. 'The last time I stood on this hill I had to listen to Quick and Kalam finishing each other's sentences. Turns out less has changed than I'd thought. Is the captain himself ascendant?'

'As near as,' the wizard admitted. *And, needless to say, that's worrying. But it'd be even more worrying if Paran . . . wanted it. Then again, who knows what ambitions lie hidden beneath that reluctant visage?*

'What do you two make of his tale of the Hounds and Rake's sword?'

'Troubling,' Mallet replied.

'That's an understatement,' Quick Ben said. 'Damned scary.'

Whiskeyjack scowled at him. 'Why?'

'Dragnipur's not Rake's sword – he didn't forge it. How much does the bastard know about it? How much *should* he know? And where in Hood's name did those Hounds go? Wherever it is, Paran's linked by blood with one of them—'

'And that makes him . . . unpredictable,' Mallet interjected.

'What's at the end of this corridor you described?'

'I don't know.'

'Me neither,' Quick Ben said regretfully. 'But I think we should add a few shoves of our own. If only to save Paran from himself.'

'And how do you propose we do that?'

The wizard grinned. 'It's already started, Commander. Connecting him to Silverfox. She reads him like Tattersail did a Deck of Dragons, sees more every time she rests eyes on him.'

'Maybe that's just Tattersail's memories . . . undressing him,' Mallet commented.

'Very funny,' Whiskeyjack drawled. 'So Silverfox dips into his soul – no guarantee she'll be sharing her discoveries with us, is there?'

'If Tattersail and Nightchill's personae come to dominate . . .'

'The sorceress is well enough, but Nightchill . . .' Whiskeyjack shook his head.

'She was a nasty piece of work,' Quick Ben agreed. 'Something of a mystery there. Still, a Malazan . . .'

'Of whom we know very little,' the commander growled. 'Remote. Cold.'

Mallet asked, 'What was her warren?'

'Rashan, as far as I could tell,' Quick Ben said sourly. 'Darkness.'

'That's knowledge that Silverfox can draw on, then,' the healer said after a moment.

'Probably instinctively, in fragments – not much of Nightchill survived, I gather.'

'Are you sure of that, wizard?' Whiskeyjack asked.

'No.' *About Nightchill, I'm less sure than I'm implying. There have been other Nightchills . . . long before the Malazan Empire. The First Age of the Nathilog Wars. The Liberation of Karakarang on Seven Cities, nine centuries back. The Seti and their expulsion from Fenn, on Quon Tali, almost two thousand years ago. A woman, a sorceress, named Nightchill, again and again. If she's the same one . . .*

The commander leaned in his saddle and spat to the ground. 'I'm not happy.'

Wizard and healer said nothing.

I'd tell him about Burn . . . but if he ain't happy now what'll the news of the world's impending death do to him? No, deal with that one on your own, Quick, and be ready to jump when the time comes . . . The Crippled God's declared war on the gods, on the warrens, on the whole damned thing and every one of us in it. Fine, O Fallen One, but that means you'll have to outwit me. Forget the gods and their clumsy games, I'll have you crawling in circles before long . . .

191

Moments passed, the horses motionless under the riders except for the flicking of tails and the twitching of coats and ears to ward off biting flies.

'Keep facing Paran in the right direction,' Whiskeyjack finally said. 'Shove when the opportunity arises. Quick Ben, find out all you can about Nightchill – through any and every source available. Mallet, explain about Paran to Spindle – I want all three of you close enough to the captain to count nose hairs.' He gathered the reins and swung his mount round. 'The Darujhistan contingent's due to arrive at Brood's any time now – let's head back.'

They rode down from the hill and its ruinous vestiges at a canter, leaving the flies buzzing aimlessly above the summit.

Whiskeyjack reined in before the tent that had been provided for Dujek Onearm, his horse breathing hard from the extended ride, through the Bridgeburners' encampment where he'd left Quick Ben and Mallet, and into Brood's sprawled camp. He swung from the saddle, wincing as he stepped down on his bad leg.

The standard-bearer Artanthos appeared. 'I'll take the reins, Commander,' the young man said. 'The beast needs rubbing down—'

'He ain't the only one,' Whiskeyjack muttered. 'Onearm's within?'

'Aye. He has been expecting you.'

Without another word the commander entered the tent.

'Damned about time,' Dujek growled from his cot, grunting as as he sat up. 'Pour us some ale, there, on the table. Find a chair. You hungry?'

'No.'

'Me neither. Let's drink.'

Neither spoke until Whiskeyjack had finished repositioning furniture and pouring ale. The silence continued until they'd both finished the first tankards and the commander refilled them from the jug.

192

'Moon's Spawn,' Dujek said after wiping his mouth then reaching for the tankard once again. 'If we're lucky, we'll see it again, but not till Coral, or even later. So, Anomander Rake's agreed to throw his – and the Moon's – weight against this Pannion Domin. Reasons? Unknown. Maybe he just likes a fight.'

Whiskeyjack frowned. 'At Pale, he struck me as a reluctant combatant, Dujek.'

'Only because his Tiste Andii were busy elsewhere. Good thing, too, or we would have been annihilated.'

'You might be right. Seems we're mustering a whole lot to take on a middling-sized empire of zealots, Dujek. I know, the Domin's smelled foul from the start, and something's building. Even so . . .'

'Aye.' After a moment, Dujek shrugged. 'We'll see what we see. Did you speak with Twist?'

Whiskeyjack nodded. 'He agrees that his flights should remain unseen – no supplying of our forces on the march if at all possible. He has scouts seeking a strategic place to hold up close to the Pannion border – hidden but close enough to strike when the time comes.'

'Good. And is our army ready to leave Pale?'

'As ready as it'll ever be. The question of supply on the march remains.'

'We'll cover that when the emissaries from Darujhistan get here. Now. Silverfox . . .'

'Hard to say, Dujek. This gathering of T'lan Imass is worrying, especially when she asserts that we'll all need those undead warriors when we take on the Pannion Domin. High Fist, we don't know enough about our enemy—'

'That will change – have you instructed Quick Ben on initiating contact with that mercenary company in Capustan?'

'He's worked something out. We'll see if they take the bait.'

'Back to Silverfox, Whiskeyjack. Tattersail was a solid ally – a friend—'

'She's there, in this Rhivi child. Paran and she have . . . spoken.' He fell silent for a moment, then sighed, his eyes on the tankard in his hands. 'Things have yet to unfold, so we'll just have to wait and see.'

'Any creature that so devours its parent . . .'

'Aye, but then again, whenever have the T'lan Imass shown a speck of compassion? They're undead, soulless and let's face it, once-allies or not, damned horrific. They were on the Emperor's leash and no-one else's. Fighting alongside them back in Seven Cities was not a comforting experience – we both know that, Dujek.'

'Expedience always comes arm-in-arm with discomfort,' the High Fist muttered. 'And now they're back, only this time they're on a child's leash . . .'

Whiskeyjack grunted. 'That's a curious observation, but I see what you mean. Kellanved showed . . . restraint with the T'lan Imass, discounting that mess at Aren. Whereas a child, born of ravaged souls within the warren of Tellann, acquiring such power . . .'

'And how many children have you met capable of showing restraint? Tattersail's wisdom needs to come to the fore, and soon.'

'We'll do all we can, Dujek.'

The old man sighed, then nodded. 'Now, your sense of our newfound allies?'

'The departure of the Crimson Guard is a blow,' Whiskeyjack said. 'A disparate collection of dubious mercenaries and hangers-on in their place signifies a drop in quality. The Mott Irregulars are the best of the bunch, but that's not saying a whole lot. The Rhivi and Barghast are solid enough, as we both know, and the Tiste Andii are unequalled. Still, Brood needs us. Badly.'

'Perhaps more than we need him and his forces, aye,' Dujek said. 'In a normal kind of war, that is.'

'Rake and Moon's Spawn are Brood's true shaved knuckles in the hole. High Fist, with the T'lan Imass joined to our cause, I cannot see any force on this continent or any other that could match us. God knows, we could annex half the continent—'

'Could we now?' Dujek grinned sourly. 'Stow that thought, old friend, stow it deep so it never again sees the light of day. We're about to march off and sword-kiss a tyrant – what happens afterwards is a discussion that will have to await another time. Right now, we're both edging around a deadly pit—'

'Aye, we are. Kallor.'

'Kallor.'

'He will try to kill the child,' Whiskeyjack said.

'He won't,' Dujek countered. 'If he tries, Brood will go for him.' The one-armed man leaned forward with his tankard and Whiskeyjack refilled it. Settling back, the High Fist studied the commander, then said, 'Caladan Brood is the *real* shaved knuckle in the hole, old friend. I've read of his times up around Laederon, in the Nathilog Histories. Hood's breath, you don't want to get him riled – whether you're an ally or an enemy makes no difference to Brood when his rage is unleashed. At least with Anomander Rake, it's a cold, taut power. Not so with the warlord. That hammer of his . . . it's said that it's the only thing that can awaken Burn. Swing it against the ground, hard enough, and the goddess will open her eyes. And the truth is, if Brood didn't have the strength to do so, he wouldn't be carrying the hammer in the first place.'

Whiskeyjack mused on this for a while, then said, 'We have to hope that Brood remains as the child's protector.'

'Kallor will work to sway the warlord,' Dujek asserted, 'with argument rather than with his sword. He may well seek Rake's support, as well . . .'

The commander eyed the High Fist. 'Kallor's paid you a visit.'

'Aye, and he's a persuasive bastard. Even to the point of dispelling his enmity towards you – he's not been physically struck in centuries, or so he said. He also said he deserved it.'

'Generous of him,' Whiskeyjack drawled. *When it's politically expedient.* 'I'll not stand to one side in the butchering of a child,' the commander added in a cold voice. 'No matter what power or potential is within her.'

Dujek glanced up. 'In defiance of my command, should I give it?'

'We've known each other a long time, Dujek.'

'Aye, we have. Stubborn.'

'When it matters.'

The two men said nothing for a time, then the High Fist looked away and sighed. 'I should bust you back down to sergeant.'

Whiskeyjack laughed.

'Pour me another,' Dujek growled. 'We've got an emissary from Darujhistan on the way and I want to be properly cheerful when he arrives.'

'What if Kallor's right?'

The Mhybe's eyes narrowed. 'Then, Warlord, you had best give him leave to cut me down the same time he kills my daughter.'

Caladan Brood's wide, flat brow furrowed as he scowled down at her. 'I remember you, you know. Among the tribes when we campaigned in the north. Young, fiery, beautiful. Seeing you – seeing what the child has done to you – causes pain within me, woman.'

'Mine is greater, I assure you, Warlord, yet I choose to accept it—'

'Your daughter is killing you – why?'

The Mhybe glanced across at Korlat. The Tiste Andii's expression was distraught. The air within the tent was sweltering, the currents around the three of them damp and turgid. After a moment, the old woman returned her gaze to Caladan Brood. 'Silverfox is of Tellann, of the T'lan Imass, Warlord. They have no life-force to give her. They are kin, yet can offer no sustenance, for they are undead, whilst their new child is flesh and blood. Tattersail too is

196

dead. As was Nightchill. Kinship is more important than you might think. Blood-bound lives are the web that carries each of us; they make up that which a life climbs, from newborn to child, then child to adulthood. Without such life-forces, one withers and dies. To be alone is to be ill, Warlord, not just spiritually, but physically as well. I am my daughter's web, and I am alone in that—'

Brood was shaking his head. 'Your explanation does not answer her . . . impatience, Mhybe. She claims she will command the T'lan Imass. She claims they have heard her summons. Does this not in turn mean that the undead armies have already accepted her?'

Korlat spoke up. 'Warlord, you believe Silverfox seeks to hasten her own growth in order to confirm her authority when she comes face to face with the T'lan Imass? The undead armies will reject a child summoner – is this your belief?'

'I am seeking the reason for what she's doing to her mother, Korlat,' Brood said, with a pained expression.

'You might well be correct, Warlord,' the Mhybe said. 'Bone and flesh can hold only so much power – the limit is always finite. For such beings as you and Anomander Rake – and you, too, Korlat – you possess the centuries of living necessary to contain what you command. Silverfox does not, or, rather, her memories tell her she does, yet her child's body denies those memories. Thus, vast power awaits her, and to fully command it she must be a grown woman – and even then . . .'

'Ascendancy is born of experience,' Korlat said. 'An interesting notion, Mhybe.'

'And experience . . . tempers,' the Rhivi woman nodded.

'Thus, Kallor's fear,' Brood rumbled, rising from his chair with a restless sigh. 'Untempered power.'

'It may be,' Korlat said in a low voice, 'that Kallor himself is the cause of the child's impatience – she seeks to become a woman in order to alleviate his fears.'

'I'd doubt he'd appreciate the irony,' the warlord

muttered. 'Alleviate, you said? Thinking on it, more likely she knows she'll have to defend herself against him sooner or later—'

'A secret hovers between them,' Korlat murmured.

There was silence. All knew the truth of that, and all were troubled. One of the souls within Silverfox had crossed paths with Kallor before. Tattersail, Bellurdan or Nightchill.

After a long moment, Brood cleared his throat. 'Life experiences . . . the child possesses those, does she not, Mhybe? The three Malazan mages . . .'

The Mhybe smiled wearily. 'A Thelomen, two women, and myself – one father and three reluctant mothers to the same child. The father's presence seems so faint that I have begun to suspect it exists only as Nightchill's memory. As for the two women, I am seeking to discover who they were, and what I have learned thus far – of Tattersail – comforts me.'

'And Nightchill?' Korlat asked.

Brood interjected, 'Did not Rake kill her here at Pale?'

'No, Nightchill was ambushed – betrayed – by the High Mage Tayschrenn,' the Tiste Andii replied. 'We have been informed,' she added drily, 'that Tayschrenn has since fled back to the Empress.' Korlat faced the Mhybe again. 'What have you learned of her?'

'I have seen flashes of darkness within Silverfox,' the Rhivi woman replied reluctantly, 'which I would attribute to Nightchill. A seething anger, a hunger for vengeance, possibly against Tayschrenn. At some time, perhaps soon, there will be a clash between Tattersail and Nightchill – the victor will come to dominate my daughter's nature.'

Brood was silent for a half-dozen breaths, then said, 'What can we do to aid this Tattersail?'

'The Malazans are seeking to do that very thing, Warlord. Much rests on their efforts. We must have faith in them. In Whiskeyjack, and in Captain Paran – the man who was once Tattersail's lover.'

'I have spoken with Whiskeyjack,' Korlat said. 'He possesses an unshakeable integrity, Warlord. An honourable man.'

'I hear your heart in your words,' Brood observed.

Korlat shrugged. 'Less cause to doubt me, then, Caladan. I am not careless in such matters.'

The warlord grunted. 'I dare not take another step in that direction,' he said wryly. 'Mhybe, hold close to your daughter. Should you begin to see the spirit of Nightchill rising and that of Tattersail setting, inform me at once.'

And should that occur, my telling you will see my daughter killed.

'My thoughts,' Brood continued, his thin eyes fixed on her, 'are not settled on that matter. Rather, such an event may well lead to my more directly supporting the Malazans in their efforts on Tattersail's behalf.'

The Mhybe raised her brows. 'Precisely how, Warlord?'

'Have faith in me,' Brood said.

The Rhivi woman sighed, then nodded. 'Very well, I shall so inform you.'

The tent flap was drawn back and Hurlochel, Brood's standard-bearer, entered. 'Warlord,' he said, 'the Darujhistan contingent approach our camp.'

'Let us go to meet them, then.'

Since arriving, the hooded driver seemed to have fallen asleep. The huge, ornate carriage's double doors opened from within and a regent-blue slippered foot emerged. Arrayed before the carriage and its train of six jewel-decked horses, in a crescent, were the representatives of the two allied armies: Dujek, Whiskeyjack, Twist and Captain Paran to the left, and Caladan Brood, Kallor, Korlat, Silverfox and the Mhybe to the right.

The Rhivi matron had been left exhausted by the events of the night just past, and her meeting with Brood had added yet more layers of weariness – the holding back on so much in the face of the warlord's hard questions had been difficult, yet, she felt, necessary. Her daughter's meeting with Paran had been far more strained and uncertain than the Mhybe had suggested to Brood. Nor had the intervening hours since then diminished the awkwardness of the situation. Worse, the reunion may have triggered something within Silverfox – the child had drawn heavily on the Mhybe since then, stripping away year after year from her mother's failing life. *Is it Tattersail behind the fevered demand on my life-spirit? Or Nightchill?*

This will end soon. I yearn for the release of the Hooded One's embrace. Silverfox has allies, now. They will do what is necessary, I am certain of it – please, Spirits of the Rhivi, make me certain of it. The time for me is surely past, yet those around me continue to make demands of me. No, I cannot go on . . .

The slippered foot probed daintily downward, wavering until it touched ground. A rather plump calf, knee and thigh followed. The short, round man who emerged was wearing silks of every colour, the effect one of clashing discord. A shimmering, crimson handkerchief was clutched in one pudgy hand, rising to dab a glittering forehead. Both feet finally on the ground, the Daru loosed a loud sigh. 'Burn's fiery heart, but it's hot!'

Caladan Brood stepped forward. 'Welcome, representative of the City of Darujhistan, to the armies of liberation. I am Caladan Brood, and this is Dujek Onearm . . .'

The short, round man blinked myopically, mopped his brow once again, then beamed a smile. 'Representative of the City of Darujhistan? Indeed! None better, Kruppe says, though he be a lowly citizen, a curious commoner come to cast kindly eyes upon this momentous occasion! Kruppe is suitably honoured by your formal, nay, respectful welcome – what vast display, Kruppe wonders, will you formidable warriors unveil when greeting the Council of Darujhistan's *official* representatives? The sheer escalation now imminent has Kruppe's heart all apatter with anticipation! Look on, to the south – the councillors' carriage even now approaches!'

A Great Raven's cackle spilled into the silence following the man's pronouncements.

Despite her fraught, worn emotions, the Mhybe smiled. *Oh yes, of course. I know this man.* She stepped forward, unable to resist herself as she said, 'I have been in your dreams, sir.'

Kruppe's eyes fixed on her and widened in alarm. He mopped his brow. 'My dear, while all things are possible . . .'

Crone cackled a second time.

'I was younger then,' the Mhybe added. 'And with child. We were in the company of a Bonecaster . . . and an Elder God.'

Recognition lit his round, flushed face, followed swiftly by dismay. For once he seemed at a loss for words. His gaze held on hers a moment longer, then dropped to the child at her side. She noted his narrowing eyes. *He senses the way of things between us. Instantly. How? And why is it I know the truth of my conviction? How profound is this link?*

Caladan Brood cleared his throat. 'Welcome, citizen Kruppe. We are now aware of the events surrounding the birth of the child, Silverfox. You, then, are the mortal involved. The identity of this Elder God, however, remains unknown to us. Which one? The answer to that question may well do much to determine our . . . relationship with the girl.'

Kruppe blinked up at the warlord. He patted the soft flesh beneath his chin with the silk cloth. 'Kruppe understands. Indeed he does. A sudden tension permeates this prestigious gathering, yes? The god in question. Yes, hmm. Ambivalence, uncertainty, all anathema to Kruppe of Darujhistan . . . possibly, then again possibly not.' He glanced over a shoulder as the official delegation's carriage approached, mopped his brow again. 'Swift answers may well mislead, nay, give the wrong impression entirely. Oh my, what to do?'

'Damn you!' The cry came from the other carriage driver as the ornate contrivance arrived. 'Kruppe! What in Hood's name are you doing here?'

The silk-clad man pivoted and attempted a sweeping bow which, despite its meagre success, nevertheless managed to seem elegant. 'Dear friend Murillio. Have you climbed in the world with this new profession, or perhaps sidled sideways? Kruppe was unaware of your obvious talents in leading mules—'

The driver scowled. 'Seems the Council's select train of horses inexplicably vanished moments before our departure. Horses decidedly similar to ones you and Meese seem to have acquired, might I add.'

'Extraordinary coincidence, friend Murillio.'

The carriage doors opened and out climbed a broad-shouldered, balding man. His blunt-featured face was dark with anger as he strode towards Kruppe.

The small round citizen spread his arms wide even as he involuntarily stepped back. 'Dearest friend and lifelong companion. Welcome, Councillor Coll. And who is that behind you? Why, none other than Councillor Estraysian D'Arle! In such fashion all the truly vital representatives of fair Darujhistan are thus gathered!'

'Excluding you, Kruppe,' Coll growled, still advancing on the man who was now back-pedalling to his own carriage.

'Untrue, friend Coll! I am here as representative of Master Baruk—'

Coll halted. He crossed his burly arms. 'Oh, indeed? The alchemist sent you on his behalf, did he?'

'Well, not in so many words, of course. Baruk and I are of such closeness in friendship that words are often unnecessary—'

'Enough, Kruppe.' Coll turned to Caladan Brood. 'My deepest apologies, Warlord. I am Coll, and this gentleman at my side is Estraysian D'Arle. We are here on behalf of the Ruling Council of Darujhistan. The presence of this . . . this Kruppe . . . was unintended, and indeed is unwelcome. If you can spare me a moment I will send him on his way.'

'Alas, it seems we have need of him,' Brood replied. 'Rest

202

assured I will explain. For now, however, perhaps we should reconvene in my command tent.'

Coll swung a glare on Kruppe. 'What outrageous lies have you uttered now?'

The round man looked offended. 'Kruppe and the truth are lifelong partners, friend Coll! Indeed, wedded bliss – we only yesterday celebrated out fortieth anniversary, the mistress of veracity and I. Kruppe is most certainly of need – in all things, at all times and in all places! It is a duty Kruppe must accept, howsoever humbly—'

With a low growl Coll raised a hand to cuff the man.

Estraysian D'Arle stepped forward and laid a hand on Coll's shoulder. 'Be at ease,' the councillor murmured. 'It appears to be obvious to all that Kruppe does not speak for anyone but Kruppe. We are not responsible for him. If in truth he is to prove useful, the task of impressing us falls upon him and him alone.'

'And impress I shall!' Kruppe cried, suddenly beaming again.

Crone bounded down to hop towards Kruppe. 'You, sir, should have been a Great Raven!'

'And you a dog!' he shouted back.

Crone halted, teetered a moment, wings half spreading. She cocked her head, whispered, 'A dog?'

'Only so that I might ruffle you behind the ears, my dear!'

'Ruffle? *Ruffle!*'

'Very well, not a dog, then. A parrot?'

'A parrot!'

'Perfect!'

'Enough!' Brood roared. 'All of you, follow me!' He whirled and stomped towards the Tiste Andii encampment.

It took only a glance from the Mhybe to start Whiskeyjack laughing. Dujek joined him a moment later, then the others.

Silverfox squeezed her hand. 'Kruppe has already revealed his value,' she said in low voice, 'don't you think?'

'Aye, child, that he has. Come, we'd best lead the way in catching up with the warlord.'

As soon as all were within the command tent and the removal of cloaks and weapons had begun, Paran strode over to Councillor Coll. 'It is good to see you again,' the captain said, 'though,' he added in a low tone, 'you wore a soldier's armour with more ease, I think, than those robes.'

Coll grimaced. 'You're right enough in that. Do you know I at times think back on that night camped in the Gadrobi Hills with something like nostalgia. We weren't anything but ourselves, then.' He met Paran's eyes with a flicker of worry at what he saw. They gripped hands. 'Simpler times . . .'

'An unlikely toast,' a voice said and they turned as Whiskeyjack joined them, an earthenware jug in one hand. 'There's tankards there behind you, Councillor, on what passes for a table. Brood has no servants as such so I've elected myself to that worthy task.'

Pulling three tankards close, Paran frowned at the table. 'This is the bed of a wagon – you can still see the straw.'

'Which also explains this place smelling like a stable,' the commander added, pouring the tankards full of Gredfallan ale. 'Brood's map table went missing last night.'

Coll raised an eyebrow. 'Someone stole a *table*?'

'Not someone,' Whiskeyjack replied, glancing at Paran. 'Your Bridgeburners, Captain. I'd lay a column on it.'

'What in Hood's name for?'

'That's something you'll have to find out. Fortunately, the warlord's only complaint was at the inconvenience.'

Caladan Brood's deep voice rose then. 'If one and all will find seats, we can get to the business of supply and matériel.'

Kruppe was the first to lower himself into a chair – at the head of the makeshift table. He held a tankard and a handful of Rhivi sweetcakes. 'Such rustic environs!' he sighed, round face flushed with pleasure. 'And traditional pastries of the plains to lure the palate. More, this ale is most delicious, perfectly cooled—'

'Be quiet, damn you,' Coll growled. 'And what are you doing in that chair?'

'Why, sitting, friend Coll. Our mutual friend the alchemist—'

'Would skin you alive if he knew you were here, claiming to represent him.'

Kruppe's brows rose and he nearly choked on a mouthful of sweetcake, spraying crumbs as he coughed. He quickly drank down his ale, then belched. 'By the Abyss, what a distasteful notion. And entirely in error, Kruppe assures everyone. Baruk has a keen interest in the smooth conduct of this prestigious gathering of legendary persons. The success of the venture impending is uppermost in his mind, and he pledges to do all that is within his – and his servant Kruppe's – formidable abilities.'

'Has your master specific suggestions?' Brood asked.

'Innumerable suggestions of a specific nature, sir Warlord. So many that, when combined, they can only be seen or understood in the most general terms!' He then lowered his tone. 'Vague and seemingly vacuous generalities are proof of Master Baruk's all-embracing endeavours, Kruppe sagely points out.' He offered everyone a broad, crumb-flecked smile. 'But please, let us get under way lest this meeting stretch on, forcing the delivery of a sumptuous supper replete with the dryest of wines to whet the gullet and such a selection of sweets as to leave Kruppe groaning in fullest pleasure!'

'Gods forbid,' Coll muttered.

Estraysian D'Arle cleared his throat. 'We are faced with only minor difficulties in maintaining a supply route to your combined armies, Warlord and Dujek Onearm. The most pressing of these centres on the destroyed bridge west of Darujhistan. There are but few manageable crossings on the Catlin River, and the destruction of that stone bridge by the Jaghut Tyrant has created an inordinate amount of difficulty—'

'Ah,' Kruppe interjected, raising a pudgy finger, 'but are not bridges naught but a means of travelling from one side of a river to another? Does this not assume certain pre-requisites regarding the projected plans of movement as directed by the leaders of the armies? Kruppe is left wondering . . .' He reached for another sweetcake.

'As are we all,' D'Arle drawled after a moment.

Dujek, his eyes narrowed on Kruppe, cleared his throat. 'Well, much as I hate to admit it, there's something in that.' He swung his gaze to Estraysian. 'Catlin River only presents a problem if we look to employing the south routes. And we'd only want those if the armies seek to cross early in the march.'

Both councillors frowned.

'It is our intent,' Brood explained, 'to remain north of the river, to march directly towards Capustan. Our route will take us north of Saltoan . . . well north. Then proceed in a southeast direction.'

Coll spoke. 'You describe a direct route to Capustan, sir, for your forces. Such a route will, however, strain our efforts at maintaining supply. We will not be able to deliver via the river. An overland train of such magnitude will sorely test our capabilities.'

'It must be understood,' Estraysian D'Arle added, 'that the Council must needs deal with private enterprises in fulfilling your supply needs.'

'Such delicacy!' Kruppe cried. 'The issues, martial comrades, are these. The Council of Darujhistan consists of various noble houses, of which virtually one and all possess interests in mercantile endeavours. Discounting the potentially confusing reality of the Council's providing vast loans to your armies with which you will in turn purchase supplies from the Council, the particular *nature* of the redistribution of said wealth is paramount to specific members of the Council. The vying, the back-chamber deals and conniving – well! One would be hard-pressed to imagine such a nightmarish tangle of weights, measures, wefts and webs, dare Kruppe say! The instructions delivered to these two worthy representatives are no doubt manifest, not to mention a veritable skein of conflicting commands. The councillors here before you are thus constrained by a knot that not even the gods could disentangle! It falls to Kruppe, lowly but worthy citizen of fair Darujhistan, to propose his and Master Baruk's solution.'

Coll leaned forward and rubbed his eyes. 'Let's hear it, then, Kruppe.'

'An impartial and exquisitely competent manager of said supply is required, of course. Not on the Council and therefore possessing nothing of the internal pressures so afflicting its honourable members. Skilled, as well, in mercantile matters. A vast capacity for organizing. In all, a superior—'

Coll's fist thumped down on the table, startling everyone. He rounded on Kruppe. 'If you imagine yourself in such a role – you, a middling fence to middling pickpockets and warehouse thieves—'

But the small, round man raised his hands and leaned back. 'Dear friend Coll! You flatter me with such an offer! However, poor Kruppe is far too busy with his own middling affairs to tackle such an endeavour. Nay, in close consultation with his loyal and wise servant Kruppe, Master Baruk proposes a different agent entirely—'

'What is all this?' Coll hissed dangerously. 'Baruk doesn't even know you're here!'

'A minor breakdown in communication, nothing more. The alchemist's *desire* was plain to Kruppe, he assures you one and all! Whilst Kruppe may well and with some justification claim sole credit for the impending proposal, alas, he must bow to the virtue of truthfulness and therefore acknowledge Master Baruk's minor – yet vital – contribution. Why, it was only yesterday that he mused on the peculiar talents of the agent in question, and if this was not a hint as to his desires, then what, dear Coll, could it have been?'

'Get on with it, sir,' Estraysian D'Arle grated.

'Kruppe delights in doing so, friend Councillor – and by the way, how fares your daughter, Challice? Has she indeed partaken of marriage nuptials with that hero of the fete? Kruppe so regrets his missing that no doubt sumptuous event—'

'Which has yet to occur,' D'Arle snapped. 'She is well, sir. My patience with you is growing very thin, Kruppe—'

'Alas, I can only *dream* of thin. Very well, the agent in question is none other than the newly arrived mercantile enterprise known as the Trygalle Trade Guild.' Beaming, he sat back, lacing his fingers together over his belly.

Brood turned to Coll. 'An enterprise I have never heard of . . .'

The councillor was frowning. 'As Kruppe said, newly arrived in Darujhistan. From the south – Elingarth, I believe. We used them but once – a singularly difficult delivery of funds to Dujek Onearm.' He looked to Estraysian D'Arle, who shrugged, then spoke.

'They have made no bids regarding the contracts to supply the combined armies. Indeed, they have sent no representative to the meetings – that single use of them Coll mentioned was a sub-contract, I believe.' He swung a scowl on Kruppe. 'Given their obvious lack of interest, why would you – or, rather, Master Baruk – believe that this Trygalle Trade Guild is amenable to participating, much less acting as mitigator?'

Kruppe poured himself another tankard of ale, sipped, then smacked his lips appreciatively. 'The Trygalle Trade Guild does not offer bids, for every other enterprise would be sure to greatly underbid them without even trying. In other words, they are not cheap. More exactly, their services demand a king's ransom generally. One thing you can be sure of, however, is that they will do precisely what they have been hired to do, no matter how . . . uh, night-marish . . . the logistics.'

'You've invested in them, haven't you, Kruppe?' Coll's face had darkened. 'So much for *impartial* advice – and Baruk has absolutely nothing to do with you being here. You're acting on behalf of this Trygalle Trade Guild, aren't you?'

'Kruppe assures, the conflict of interest is a matter of appearance only, friend Coll! The truth is more precisely a convergence. The needs are evident here before us all, and so too is the means of answering them! Happy coincidence! Now, Kruppe would partake of more of these delicious Rhivi cakes, whilst you discuss the merits of said proposal and no doubt reach the propitious, inevitable conclusion.'

Crone could smell sorcery in the air. *And it doesn't belong. No, not Tiste Andii, not the Rhivi spirits awakened either . . .* She circled over the encampment, questing with all her senses. The afternoon had drawn into dusk, then night, as the meeting within Caladan Brood's command tent stretched on, and on. The Great Raven was quickly bored by interminable discussions of caravan routes and how many tons of this and that were required on a weekly basis to keep two armies fed and content on the march. Granted, that repugnant creature Kruppe was amusing enough, in the manner that an obese rat trying to cross a rope bridge was worth a cackle or three. A finely honed mind dwelt beneath the smeared, grotesque affectations, she well knew, and his ability at earning his seat at the head of the table and of confounding the flailing councillors of Darujhistan was most certainly an entertaining enough display of deftness . . . until Crone had sensed the stirrings of magic somewhere in the camp.

There, that large tent directly below . . . . I know it. The place where the Rhivi dress the Tiste Andii dead. Crooking her wings, she dropped in a tight spiral.

She landed a few paces from the entrance. The flap was

drawn shut, tightly tied, but the leather thongs and their knots were poor obstacles for Crone's sharp beak. In moments she was within, hopping silently and unseen beneath the huge table – a table she recognized with a silent chuckle – and among a few scattered folded cots in the darkness.

Four figures leaned on the table above her, whispering and muttering. The muted clatter of wooden cards echoed through to Crone, and she cocked her head.

'There it is again,' a gravelly-voiced woman said. 'You sure you shuffled the damned things, Spin?'

'Will you – of course I did, Corporal. Stop asking me. Look, four times now, different laying of the fields every one, and it's simple. Obelisk dominates – the dolmen of time is the core. It's active, plain as day – the first time in decades . . .'

'Could still be that untoward skew,' another voice interjected. 'You ain't got Fid's natural hand, Spin—'

'Enough of that, Hedge,' the corporal snapped. 'Spindle's done enough readings to be the real thing, trust me.'

'Didn't you just—'

'Shut up.'

'Besides,' Spindle muttered, 'I told you already, the new card's got a fixed influence – it's the glue holding everything together, and once you see that it all makes sense.'

'The glue, you said,' the fourth and final voice – also a woman's – mused. 'Linked to a new ascendant, you think?'

'Beats me, Blend,' Spindle sighed. 'I said a fixed influence, but I didn't say I knew the aspect of that influence. I don't know, and not because I'm not good enough. It's like it hasn't . . . woken up yet. A passive presence, for the moment. Nothing more than that. When it does awaken . . . well, things should heat up nicely, is my guess.'

'So,' the corporal said, 'what are we looking at here, mage?'

'Same as before. Soldier of High House Death's right-hand to Obelisk. Magi of Shadow's here – first time for that one, too – a grand deception's at work, is my guess. The Captain of High House Light holds out some hope, but it's shaded by Hood's Herald – though not directly, there's a distance there, I think. The Assassin of High House Shadow seems to have acquired a new face, I'm getting hints of it . . . bloody familiar, that face.'

The one named Hedge grunted. 'Should bring Quick Ben in on this—'

'That's it!' Spindle hissed. 'The Assassin's face – it's Kalam!'

'Bastard!' Hedge growled. 'I'd suspected as much – him and Fid paddling off the way they did – you know what this means, don't you . . .'

'We can guess,' the corporal said, sounding unhappy. 'But the other thing's clear, Spin, isn't it?'

'Aye. Seven Cities is about to rise – may have already. The Whirlwind . . . Hood must be smiling right now. Smiling something fierce.'

'I got some questions for Quick Ben,' Hedge muttered. 'Don't I just.'

'You should ask him about the new card, too,' Spindle said. 'If he don't mind crawling, let him take a look.'

'Aye . . .'

A new card of the Deck of Dragons? Crone cocked her head up farther, thinking furiously. New cards were trouble, especially ones with power. The House of Shadow was proof enough of that . . . Her eyes – one, then, as she further cocked her head, the other – slowly focused, her mind dragged back from its abstracted realm, fixing at last on the underside of the table.

To find a pair of human eyes, the paint glittering as if alive, staring back down at her.

The Mhybe stepped out of the tent, her mind befuddled with exhaustion. Silverfox had fallen asleep in her chair, during one of Kruppe's rambling accounts describing yet another peculiarity of the Trygalle Trade Guild's Rules of

Contract, and the Mhybe had decided to let the child be.

In truth, she longed for some time away from her daughter. A pressure was building around Silverfox, an incessant need that, moment by moment, was taking ever more of the Mhybe's life-spirit. Of course, this feeble attempt at escape was meaningless. The demand was boundless, and no conceivable distance could effect a change. Her flight from the tent, from her daughter's presence, held naught but symbolic meaning.

Her bones were a rack of dull, incessant pains, an ebb and flow of twinges that only the deepest of sleep could temporarily evade – the kind of sleep that had begun to elude her.

Paran emerged from the tent and approached. 'I would ask you something, Mhybe, then I shall leave you in peace.'

Oh, you poor, savaged man. What would you have me answer? 'What do you wish to know, Captain?'

Paran stared out at the sleeping camp. 'If someone wished to hide a table . . .'

She blinked, then smiled. 'You will find them in the tent of the Shrouds – it is unfrequented for the moment. Come, I shall take you there.'

'Directions will suffice—'

'Walking eases the aches, Captain. This way.' She made her way between the first of the tent rows. 'You have stirred Tattersail awake,' she observed after a few moments. 'As a dominant personality for my daughter, I think I am pleased by the development.'

'I am glad for that, Mhybe.'

'What was the sorceress like, Captain?'

'Generous . . . perhaps to a fault. A highly respected and indeed well-liked cadre mage.'

Oh, sir, you hold so much within yourself, chained and in darkness. Detachment is a flaw, not a virtue – don't you realize that?

He went on, 'You might well have viewed, from your Rhivi perspective, the Malazan forces on this continent as

212

some kind of unstoppable, relentless monster, devouring city after city. But it was never like that. Poorly supplied, often outnumbered, in territories they had no familiarity with – by all accounts, Onearm's Host was being chewed to pieces. The arrival of Brood, the Tiste Andii, and the Crimson Guard stopped the campaign in its tracks. The cadre mages were often all that stood between the Host and annihilation.'

'Yet they had the Moranth . . .'

'Aye, though not as reliable as you might think. None the less, their alchemical munitions have changed the nature of warfare, not to mention the mobility of their quorls. The Host has come to rely heavily on both.'

'Ah, I see faint lantern-glow coming from the Shroud – there, directly ahead. There have been rumours that all was not well with the Moranth . . .'

Paran shot her a glance, then shrugged. 'A schism has occurred, triggered by a succession of defeats weathered by their elite forces, the Gold. At the moment, we have the Black at our side, and none other, though the Blue continue on the sea-lanes to Seven Cities.'

They were startled by the staggering appearance of a Great Raven from the Shroud's flap. She reeled drunkenly, flopped onto her chest but three paces from the Mhybe and the Malazan. Crone's head jerked up, one eye fixing on Paran.

'You!' she hissed, then, spreading her vast wings, she sprang into the air. Heavy, savage thuds of her wings lifted her up into the darkness. A moment later she was gone.

The Mhybe glanced at the captain. The man was frowning.

'Crone showed no sign of fearing you before,' she murmured.

Paran shrugged.

Voices sounded from the Shroud, and a moment later figures began filing out, the lead one carrying a hooded lantern.

'Far enough,' the captain growled.

The woman with the lantern flinched, then thumped a wrong-handed salute. 'Sir. We have just made a discovery – in this tent, sir. The purloined table has been found.'

'Indeed,' Paran drawled. 'Well done, Corporal. You and your fellow soldiers have shown admirable diligence.'

'Thank you, sir.'

The captain strode towards the tent. 'It is within, you said?'

'Yes sir.'

'Well, military decorum insists we return it to the warlord at once, wouldn't you agree, Picker?'

'Absolutely, sir.'

Paran paused and surveyed the soldiers. 'Hedge, Spindle, Blend. Four in all. I trust you will be able to manage.'

Corporal Picker blinked. 'Sir?'

'Carrying the table, of course.'

'Uh, might I suggest we find a few more soldiers—'

'I think not. We are departing in the morning, and I want the company well rested, so best not disturb their sleep. It shouldn't take the four of you more than an hour, I would judge, which will give you a few moments to spare readying your kits. Well, best not delay, Corporal, hmm?'

'Yes, sir.' Picker glumly swung to her soldiers. 'Dust up your hands, we've work to do. Spindle, you got a problem?'

The man in question was staring slack-jawed at Paran. 'Spindle?'

'Idiot,' the mage whispered.

'Soldier!'

'How could I have missed it? It's *him*. As plain as can be . . .'

Picker stepped up and cuffed the mage. 'Snap out of it, damn you!'

Spindle stared at her, then scowled. 'Don't hit me again, or you'll regret it till the end of your days.'

The corporal stood firm. 'The next time I hit you,

214

soldier, you won't be getting up. Any more threats from you will be your last, am I clear?'

The mage shook himself, eyes straying once more to Paran. 'Everything will change,' he whispered. 'Can't happen yet. I need to think. Quick Ben . . .'

'*Spindle!*'

He flinched, then gave his corporal a sharp nod. 'Pick up the table, aye. Let's get to it, aye, right away. Come on, Hedge. Blend.'

The Mhybe watched the four soldiers re-enter the Shroud, then turned to Paran. 'What was all that about, Captain?'

'I have no idea,' he replied levelly.

'That table needs more than four pairs of hands.'

'I imagine it does.'

'Yet you won't provide them.'

He glanced at her. 'Hood no. They stole the damned thing in the first place.'

A bell remained before the sun's rise. Leaving Picker and her hapless crew to their task, and departing as well from the Mhybe's presence, Paran made his way to the Bridgeburner encampment situated at the southwest edge of Brood's main camp. A handful of soldiers stood at sentry duty at the pickets, offering ragged salutes as the captain passed them.

He was surprised to find Whiskeyjack near the centre hearth, the commander busy saddling a tall chestnut gelding.

Paran approached. 'Has the meeting concluded, sir?' he asked.

The commander's glance was wry. 'I am beginning to suspect it will never end, if Kruppe has his way.'

'This trade guild of his has not gone down well, then.'

'To the contrary, it has been fully endorsed, though they'll cost the Council a king's ransom in truth. We have guarantees, now, ensuring the overland supply lines. Precisely what we required.'

'Why then does the meeting continue, sir?'

'Well, it seems that we'll have some envoys attached to our army.'

'Not Kruppe—'

'Indeed, the worthy Kruppe. And Coll – I suspect he's eager to get out of those fancy robes and back into armour.'

'Aye, he would be.'

Whiskeyjack cinched the girth strap one last time, then faced Paran. He seemed about to say one thing, then he hesitated, and chose another. 'The Black Moranth will take you and the Bridgeburners to the foot of the Barghast Range.'

The captain's eyes widened. 'That's quite a journey. And once there?'

'Once there, Trotts detaches from your command. He's to initiate contact with the White Face Barghast, by whatever means he deems proper. You and your company are to provide his escort, but you will not become otherwise entangled in the negotiations. We need the White Face clan – the entire clan.'

'And Trotts will do the negotiating? Beru fend.'

'He's capable of surprising you, Captain.'

'I see. Assuming he manages to succeed, we are then to proceed south?'

Whiskeyjack nodded. 'To the relief of Capustan, aye.' The commander set a boot within the stirrup and, with a wince, pulled himself up into the saddle. He gathered the reins, looking down on the captain. 'Any questions?'

Paran glanced around, studying the sleeping camp, then shook his head.

'I'd offer you Oponn's luck—'

'No, thank you, sir.'

Whiskeyjack nodded.

The gelding shied under the commander suddenly, pitching to one side with a squeal of terror. Wind buffeted the camp, ripping the small tents from their shallow moorings. Voices shouted in alarm. Paran stared upward as a vast black shape swept towards the Tiste Andii encampment. A faint aura outlined the enormous draconian form to the captain's eyes, silvery-white and flickering. Paran's stomach flared with pain, intense but mercifully brief, leaving him trembling.

'Hood's breath,' Whiskeyjack cursed, struggling to calm his horse as he looked around. 'What was that?'

He could not see as I saw – he has not the blood for that. 'Anomander Rake has arrived, sir. He descends among his Tiste Andii.' Paran studied the chaos that had been the slumbering Bridgeburners' camp, then sighed. 'Well, it's a little early, but now's as good a time as any.' He strode forward, raised his voice. 'Everyone up! Break camp! Sergeant Antsy – rouse the cooks, will you?'

'Uh, aye, sir! What woke us?'

'A gust of wind, Sergeant. Now get moving.'

'Aye, sir!'

'Captain.'

Paran turned to Whiskeyjack. 'Sir?'

'I believe you will find yourself busy for the next few bells. I return to Brood's tent – would you like me to send Silverfox to you for a final goodbye?'

The captain hesitated, then shook his head. 'No, thank you, sir.' *Distance no longer presents a barrier to us – a private, personal link, too fraught to be unveiled to anyone. Her presence in my head is torture enough.* 'Fare you well, Commander.'

Whiskeyjack studied him a moment longer, then nodded. He wheeled his horse around and nudged the gelding into a trot.

The Tiste Andii had gathered into a silent ring around the central clearing, awaiting the arrival of their master.

The black, silver-maned dragon emerged from the darkness overhead like a piece of night torn loose, flowing down to settle with a soft crunch of talons in the plain's stony soil. The huge, terrible beast blurred even as it landed, with a warm flow of spice-laden air swirling out to all sides as the sembling drew the dragon's shape inward. A moment later the Son of Darkness stood, cloaked, framed by the gouged tracks of the dragon's front talons, his slightly epicanthic eyes glimmering dull bronze as he surveyed his kin.

The Mhybe watched as Korlat strode to meet her master. She had seen Anomander Rake but once before, just south of Blackdog Forest, and then from a distance as the Son of Darkness spoke with Caladan Brood. She remembered Moon's Spawn, filling the sky above the Rhivi Plain. Rake had been about to ascend to that floating fortress. A pact with the wizards of Pale had been achieved, and the city was about to be besieged by Onearm's Host. He had stood then as he did now: tall, implacable, a sword emanating sheer terror hanging down the length of his back, his long, silver hair drifting in the breeze.

A slight turn of his head was his only acknowledgement of Korlat's approach.

Off to their right appeared Caladan Brood, Kallor, Dujek and the others.

Tension bristled in the air, yet one that the Mhybe recalled as being present at that last meeting, years before. Anomander Rake was an ascendant as unlike Caladan Brood as to make them seem the opposite ends of power's vast spectrum. Rake was an atmosphere, a heart-thudding, terror-threaded presence no-one could ignore, much less escape. Violence, antiquity, sombre pathos, and darkest horror – the Son of Darkness was a gelid eddy in immortality's current, and the Mhybe could feel, crawling beneath her very skin, every Rhivi spirit awakened in desperation.

The sword, yet more than the sword. Dragnipur in the hands of cold justice, cold and unhuman. Anomander Rake, the only one among us whose presence sparks fear in Kallor's eyes . . . the only one . . . except, it seems, for Silverfox – for my daughter. What might Kallor fear most, if not an alliance between the Son of Darkness and Silverfox?

All traces of exhaustion torn away by the thought, the Mhybe stepped forward.

Kallor's voice boomed. 'Anomander Rake! I seek your clearest vision – I seek the justice of your sword – allow none to sway you with sentiment, and that includes Korlat, who would now whisper urgent in your ear!'

The Son of Darkness, a lone brow raised, slowly turned to regard the High King. 'What else, Kallor,' he said in a low, calm voice, 'keeps my blade from your black heart . . . if not *sentiment*?'

With the light of the dawn finally stealing into the sky, the ancient warrior's weathered, lean face assumed a paler shade. 'I speak of a child,' he rumbled. 'No doubt you sense her power, the foulest of blossoms—'

'Power? It abounds in this place, Kallor. This camp has become a lodestone. You are right to fear.' His gaze swung to the Mhybe, who had stopped but a few paces from him.

Her steps ceased. His attention was a fierce pressure, power and threat, enough to make her softly gasp, her limbs weakening.

'Forces of nature, Mother,' he said, 'are indifferent to justice, would you not agree?'

It was a struggle to reply. 'I would, Lord of Moon's Spawn.'

'Thus it falls to us sentient beings, no matter how unworthy, to impose the moral divide.'

Her eyes flashed. 'Does it now?'

'She has spawned the abomination, Rake,' Kallor said, striding closer, his expression twisted with anger as he glared at the Mhybe. 'Her vision is stained. Understandably, granted, but even that does not exculpate.'

'Kallor,' the Son of Darkness murmured, his eyes still on the Mhybe, 'approach further at your peril.'

The High King halted.

'It would appear,' Rake continued, 'that my arrival has been anticipated, with the collective desire that I adjudicate what is clearly a complex situation—'

'Appearances deceive,' Caladan Brood said from where he stood outside the command tent – and the Mhybe now saw that Silverfox was at the warlord's side. 'Decide what you will, Rake, but I will not countenance Dragnipur's unsheathing in my camp.'

There was silence, as explosive as any the Rhivi woman had ever felt. *By the Abyss, this could go very, very wrong . . .* She glanced over at the Malazans. Dujek had drawn his soldier's expressionless mask over his features, but his taut stance revealed his alarm. The standard-bearer Artanthos was a step behind and slightly to the right of Onearm, a marine's rain cape drawn about him, hiding his hands. The young man's eyes glittered. *Is that power swirling from the man? No, I am mistaken – I see nothing now . . .*

Anomander Rake slowly faced the warlord. 'I see that the lines have been drawn,' he said quietly. 'Korlat?'

'I side with Caladan Brood in this, Master.'

Rake eyed Kallor. 'It seems you stand alone.'

'It was ever thus.'

Oh, a sharp reply, that.

Anomander Rake's expression tightened momentarily. 'I am not unfamiliar with that position, High King.'

Kallor simply nodded.

Horse hooves sounded then, and the Tiste Andii lining the southeast side of the ring parted. Whiskeyjack rode into the clearing, slowing his mount to a walk, then to a perfect square-stanced halt. It was unclear what the commander had heard, yet he acted none the less. Dismounting, he strode towards Silverfox, stopping directly before her. His sword slid smoothly from its scabbard. Whiskeyjack faced Rake, Kallor and the others in the centre of the clearing, then planted his sword in the ground before him.

Caladan Brood stepped to the Malazan's side. 'With what you might face, Whiskeyjack, it would be best if you—'

'I stand here,' the commander growled.

Sorcery flowed from Anomander Rake, grainy grey, rolling in a slow wave across the clearing, passing through Whiskeyjack effortlessly, then swallowing Silverfox in an opaque, swirling embrace.

The Mhybe cried out, lurched forward, but Korlat's hand closed on her arm. 'Fear not,' she said, 'he but seeks to understand her – understand what she is . . .'

The sorcery frayed suddenly, flung away in tattered fragments to all sides. The Mhybe hissed. She knew enough of her daughter to see, in her reappearance, that she was furious. Power, twisting like taut ropes, rose around her, knotting, bunching.

Oh, spirits below, I see Nightchill and Tattersail both . . . a shared rage. And, by the Abyss, another! A stolid will, a sentience slow to anger . . . so much like Brood – who? Is this – oh! – is this Bellurdan? Gods! We are moments from tearing ourselves apart. Please . . .

'Well,' Rake drawled, 'I have never before had my hand slapped in such a fashion. Impressive, though perilously impertinent. What is it, then, that the child does not wish me to discover?' He reached over his left shoulder for Dragnipur's leather-wrapped handle.

Grunting a savage curse, Brood unlimbered his hammer.

Whiskeyjack shifted his stance, raising his own blade.

Gods no, this is wrong—

'Rake,' Kallor rasped, 'do you wish me on your left or right?'

Snapping tent poles startled everyone. A loud yelp from the command tent was followed by a massive, awkward, flying shape exploding out from the tent's entrance. Cavorting, spinning wildly in the air, the huge wooden table the Mhybe had last seen emerging from the Shroud now rose above the clearing, and from one leg dangled Kruppe, sweetcakes fluttering away from him. He yelped again, kicking the air with his slippered feet. 'Aai! Help! Kruppe hates flying!'

* * *

As the Bridgeburners completed assembling their gear, the sentries positioned to the east shouting out the news that the Black Moranth had been seen and now approached on their winged quorls, Captain Paran, plagued by a growing unease, strode among the gathered soldiers.

Off to one side, an exhausted Picker sat watching him, her expression a strange mixture of dismay and admiration, and thus she was the only one to see him taking yet another forward step, then simply vanishing.

The corporal bolted to her feet. 'Oh, Hood's balls! Spindle! Get Quick Ben!'

A few paces away, the hairshirted mage glanced up. 'Why?'

'Someone's just snatched Paran – find Quick Ben, damn you!'

The vision of busy soldiers vanished before the captain's eyes, and from a blurred veil that swiftly parted Paran found himself facing Anomander Rake and Kallor – both with weapons drawn – and behind them the Mhybe and Korlat, with a ring of alert Tiste Andii just beyond.

Countless eyes fixed on him, then darted up over his right shoulder, then back down. No-one moved, and Paran realized he was not alone in his shock.

'Help!'

The captain spun at that plaintive cry, then looked up. An enormous wooden table twisted silently in the air, Kruppe's round, silk-flowing form hanging beneath it. On the underside of the table, painted in bright, now glowing colours, was the image of a man. Slowly blinking in and out of Paran's view, it was a few moments before he recognized the figure's face. *That's me* . . .

Pain ripped into him, a black surge that swallowed him whole.

The Mhybe saw the young captain buckle, drop to his knees, as if drawing tight around an overwhelming agony.

Her attention darted to her daughter, in time to see those bound coils of power snake outward from Silverfox, slipping round and past the motionless forms of Brood and Whiskeyjack, then upward to touch the table.

The four legs snapped. With a shriek Kruppe plunged earthward, to land in a flailing of limbs and silk among a crowd of Tiste Andii. Cries and grunts of pain and surprise followed. The table now steadied, the underside facing Rake and Kallor, the image of Paran coruscating with sorcery. Wisps of it reached down to clothe the hunched, kneeling captain in glittering, silver chains.

'Well,' a slightly breathless voice said beside her, 'that's the largest card of the Deck I've ever seen.'

She pulled her gaze away, stared wide-eyed at the lithe, dark-skinned mage standing beside her. 'Quick Ben . . .'

The Bridgeburner stepped forward then, raising his hands. 'Please excuse my interruption, everyone! Whilst it seems that a confrontation is desired by many of you here, might I suggest the absence of . . . uh, wisdom . . . in inviting violence here and now, when it is clear that the significance of all that seems to be occurring is as yet undetermined. The risks of precipitate action right now . . . Well, I trust you see what I mean.'

Anomander Rake stared at the mage a moment, then, with a faint smile, he sheathed his sword. 'Cautious words, but wise ones. Who might you be, sir?'

'Just a soldier, Son of Darkness, come to retrieve my captain.'

At that moment Kruppe emerged from the muttering, no doubt bruised crowd that had cushioned his fall. Brushing dust from his silks, he strode seemingly unaware to halt directly between the kneeling Paran and Anomander Rake. He looked up then, blinking owlishly. 'What an unseemly conclusion to Kruppe's post-breakfast repast! Has the meeting adjourned?'

Captain Paran was insensate to the power bleeding into

223

him. In his mind he was falling, falling. Then striking hard, rough flagstones, the clash of his armour echoing. The pain was gone. Gasping, shivering uncontrollably, he raised his head.

In the dim light of reflected lanterns, he saw that he was sprawled in a narrow, low-ceilinged hallway. Heavy twin doors divided the strangely uneven wall on his right; on his left, opposite the doors, was a wide entrance, with niches set in its flanking walls. On all sides, the stone appeared rough, undressed, resembling the bark of trees. A heavier door of sheeted bronze – black and pitted – was at the far end, eight or so paces distant. Two shapeless humps lay at the inner threshold.

Where? What?

Paran pushed himself upright, using one wall for support. His gaze was drawn once again to the shapes at the foot of the bronze door. He staggered closer.

A man, swathed in the tightly bound clothes of an assassin, his narrow, smooth-shaven face set in a peaceful expression, his long black braids still glistening with oil. An old-fashioned crossbow lay beside him.

Lying at his side, a woman, her cloak stretched and twisted as if the man had dragged her across the threshold. A nasty head wound glittered wetly on her brow, and, from the blood-smears on the flagstones, she was the bearer of other wounds as well.

They're both Daru . . . wait, I have seen the man before. At Simtal's Fete . . . and the woman! She's the Guild Master . . .

Rallick Nom and Vorcan, both of whom vanished that night of the ill-fated fete. *I am in Darujhistan, then. I must be.*

Silverfox's words returned to him, resounding now with veracity. He scowled. *The table – the card, with my image painted upon it. Jen'isand Rul, the Unaligned newly come to the Deck of Dragons . . . powers unknown. I have walked within a sword. It seems now that I can walk . . . anywhere.*

And this place, this place . . . I am in the Finnest House. Gods, I am in a House of the Azath!

He heard a sound, a shuffling motion approaching the twin doors opposite, and slowly turned, reaching for the sword belted at his hip.

The wooden portals swung wide.

Hissing, Paran backed up a step, his blade sliding from its scabbard.

The Jaghut standing before him was almost fleshless, ribs snapped and jutting, strips of flayed skin and muscle hanging in ghastly ribbons from his arms. His gaunt, ravaged face twisted as he bared his tusks. 'Welcome,' he rumbled. 'I am Raest. Guardian, prisoner, damned. The Azath greets you, as much as sweating stone is able. I see that, unlike the two sleeping in the threshold, you have no need for doors. So be it.' He lurched a step closer, then cocked his head. 'Ah, you are not here in truth. Only your spirit.'

'If you say so.' His thoughts travelled back to that last night of the fete. The debacle in the estate's garden. Memories of sorcery, detonations, and Paran's unexpected journey into the realm of Shadow, the Hounds and Cotillion. *A journey such as this one* . . . He studied the Jaghut standing before him. *Hood take me, this creature is the Jaghut Tyrant – the one freed by Lorn and the T'lan Imass – or, rather, what's left of him.* 'Why am I here?'

The grin broadened. 'Follow me.'

Raest stepped into the corridor and turned to his right, each bared foot dragging, grinding as if the bones beneath the skin were all broken. Seven paces along, the hallway ended with a door on the left and another directly in front. The Jaghut opened the one on the left, revealing a circular chamber beyond, surrounding spiral stairs of root-bound wood. There was no light, yet Paran found he could see well enough.

They went down, the steps beneath them like flattened branches spoking out from the central trunk. The air warmed, grew moist and sweet with the smell of humus.

'Raest,' Paran said as they continued to descend, 'the

assassin and the Guild Master . . . you said they were asleep – how long have they been lying there?'

'I measure no days within the House, mortal. The Azath took me. Since that event, a few outsiders have sought entry, have probed with sorceries, have indeed walked the yard, but the House has denied them all. The two within the threshold were there when I awoke, and have not moved since. It follows, then, that the House has already chosen.'

As the Deadhouse did Kellanved and Dancer. 'All very well, but can't you awaken them?'

'I have not tried.'

'Why not?'

The Jaghut paused, glanced back up at the captain. 'There has been no need.'

'Are they guardians as well?' Paran asked as they resumed the descent.

'Not directly. I suffice, mortal. Unwitting servants, perhaps. *Your* servants.'

'Mine? I don't need servants – I don't *want* servants. Furthermore, I don't care what the Azath expects of me. The House is mistaken in its faith, Raest, and you can tell it that for me. Tell it to find another . . . another whatever I am supposed to be.'

'You are the Master of the Deck. Such things cannot be undone.'

'The what? Hood's breath, the Azath had better find a way of undoing *that* choice, Jaghut,' Paran growled.

'It cannot be undone, as I've already told you. A Master is needed, so here you are.'

'I don't want it!'

'I weep a river of tears for your plight, mortal. Ah, we have arrived.'

They stood on a landing. Paran judged that they had gone down six, perhaps seven levels into the bowels of the earth. The stone walls had disappeared, leaving only gloom, the ground underfoot a mat of snaking roots.

'I can go no further, Master of the Deck,' Raest said. 'Walk into the darkness.'

'And if I refuse?'

'Then I kill you.'

'Unforgiving bastard, this Azath,' Paran muttered.

'I kill you, not for the Azath, but for the wasted effort of this journey. Mortal, you've no sense of humour.'

'And you think you do?' the captain retorted.

'If you refuse to go further, then . . . nothing. Apart from irritating me, that is. The Azath is patient. You will make the journey eventually, though the privilege of my escort occurs but once, and that once is now.'

'Meaning I won't have your cheery company next time? How will I cope?'

'Miserably, if there was justice in the world.'

Paran faced the darkness. 'And is there?'

'You ask that of a Jaghut? Now, do we stand here for ever?'

'All right, all right,' the captain sighed. 'Pick any direction?'

Raest shrugged. 'They are all one to me.'

Grinning in spite of himself, Paran strode forward. Then he paused and half turned. 'Raest, you said the Azath has *need* for a Master of the Deck. Why? What's happened?'

The Jaghut bared his tusks. 'A war has begun.'

Paran fought back a sudden shiver. 'A war? Involving the Houses of the Azath?'

'No entity will be spared, mortal. Not the Houses, not the gods. Not you, human, nor a single one of your short-lived, insignificant comrades.'

Paran grimaced. 'I've enough wars to deal with as it is, Raest.'

'They are all one.'

'I don't want to think about any of this.'

'Then don't.'

After a moment, Paran realized his glare was wasted on the Jaghut. He swung about and resumed his journey. With

227

his third step his boot struck flagstone instead of root, and the darkness around him dissolved, revealing, in a faint, dull yellow light, a vast concourse. Its edges, visible a hundred paces or more in every direction, seemed to drift back into gloom. Of Raest and the wooden stairs there was no sign. Paran's attention was drawn to the flagstones beneath him.

Carved into their bleached surfaces were cards of the Deck of Dragons. *No, more than just the Deck of Dragons – there's cards here I don't recognize. Lost Houses, and countless forgotten Unaligned. Houses, and . . .* The captain stepped forward, crouched down to study one image. As he focused his attention on it the world around him faded, and he felt himself moving into the carved scene.

A chill wind slid across his face, the air smelling of mud and wet fur. He could feel the earth beneath his boots, chill and yielding. Somewhere in the distance crows cackled. The strange hut he had seen in the carving now stood before him, long and humped, the huge bones and long tusks comprising its framework visible between gaps in the thick, umber fur-skins clothing it. *Houses . . . and Holds, the first efforts at building. People once dwelt within such structures, like living inside the rib-cage of a dragon. Gods, those tusks are huge – whatever beast these bones came from must have been massive . . .*

I can travel at will, it seems. Into each and every card, of every Deck that ever existed. Amidst the surge of wonder and excitement he felt ran an undercurrent of terror. The Deck possessed a host of unpleasant places.

And this one?

A small stone-lined hearth smouldered before the hut's entrance. Wreathed in the smoke was a rack made of branches, on which hung strips of meat. The clearing, Paran now saw, was ringed with weathered skulls – doubtless from the beasts whose bones formed the framework of the hut itself. The skulls faced inward, and he could see by the long, yellowed molars in the jaws that the animals had been eaters of plants, not flesh.

Paran approached the hut's entrance. The skulls of carnivores hung down from the doorway's ivory frame, forcing him to duck as he entered.

Swiftly abandoned, from the looks of it. As if the dwellers just left but moments ago . . . At the far end sat twin thrones, squat and robust, made entirely of bones, on a raised dais of ochre-stained human skulls – *well, close enough to human in any case. More like T'lan Imass . . .*

Knowledge blossomed in his mind. He knew the name of this place, knew it deep in his soul. *The Hold of the Beasts . . . long before the First Throne . . . this was the heart of the T'lan Imass's power – their spirit world, when they were still flesh and blood, when they still possessed spirits to be worshipped and revered. Long before they initiated the Ritual of Tellann . . . and so came to outlast their own pantheon . . .*

A realm, then, abandoned. Lost to its makers. *What then, is the Warren of Tellann that the T'lan Imass now use? Ah, that warren must have been born from the Ritual itself, a physical manifestation of their Vow of Immortality, perhaps. Aspected, not of life, nor even death. Aspected . . . of dust.*

He stood unmoving for a time, struggling to comprehend the seemingly depthless layers of tragedy that were the burden of the T'lan Imass.

Oh my, they've outlasted their own gods. They exist in a world of dust in truth – memories untethered, an eternal existence . . . no end in sight. Sorrow flooded him in a profound, heart-rending wave. *Beru fend . . . so alone, now. So alone for so long . . . yet now they are gathering, coming to the child seeking benediction . . . and something more . . .*

Paran stepped back – and stood on the flagstones once again. With an effort he pulled his eyes from the carved Hold of Beasts – *but why were there two thrones and not just one?* – as he now knew the card was called. Another etched stone, a dozen paces to his left, caught his attention. A throbbing, crimson glow suffused the air directly above it.

He walked to it, looked down.

The image of a sleeping woman, as seen from above,

dominated the flagstone. Her flesh seemed to spin and swirl. Paran slowly lowered himself into a crouch, his eyes narrowing. Her skin was depthless, revealing ever more detail as the captain's vision was drawn ever closer. *Skin, not skin. Forests, sweeps of bedrock, the seething floor of the oceans, fissures in the flesh of the world – she is Burn! She is the Sleeping Goddess.*

Then he saw the flaw, the marring a dark, suppurating welt. Waves of nausea swept through Paran, yet he would not look away. There, at the wound's heart, a humped, kneeling, broken figure. Chained. Chained to Burn's own flesh. From the figure, down the length of the chains, poison flowed into the Sleeping Goddess.

She sensed the sickness coming, sinking claws into her. Sensed . . . and chose to sleep. Less than two thousand years ago, she chose to sleep. She sought to escape the prison of her own flesh, in order to do battle with the one who was killing that flesh. She – oh gods above and below! She made of herself a weapon! Her entire spirit, all its power, into a single forging . . . a hammer, a hammer capable of breaking . . . breaking anything. And Burn then found a man to wield it . . .

Caladan Brood.

But breaking the chains meant freeing the Crippled God. And an unchained Crippled God meant an unleashing of vengeance – enough to sweep all life from the surface of this world. And yet Burn, the Sleeping Goddess, was indifferent to that. She would simply begin again.

Now he saw it, saw the truth – *he refuses! The bastard refuses! To defy the Crippled God's unleashing of a deadly will, that would see us all destroyed, Caladan Brood refuses her!*

Gasping, Paran pulled himself away, pushed himself upright, staggering back – and was at Raest's side once again.

The Jaghut's tusks glimmered. 'Have you found knowledge a gift, or a curse?'

Too prescient a question . . . 'Both, Raest.'

'And which do you choose to embrace?'

230

'I don't know what you mean.'

'You are weeping, mortal. In joy or sorrow?'

Paran grimaced, wiped at his face. 'I want to leave, Raest,' he said gruffly. 'I want to return—'

His eyes blinked open, and he found himself on his knees, facing, with an interval of but a half-dozen paces, a bemused Son of Darkness. Paran sensed that but moments had passed since his sudden arrival, yet something of the tension he had first picked up had eased in the interval.

A hand rested on his shoulder and he looked up to find Silverfox standing beside him, the Mhybe hovering un-certainly a step behind. The Daru, Kruppe, stood nearby, carefully adjusting his silk clothing and humming softly, while Quick Ben took a step closer to the captain – though the wizard's eyes held on the Knight of Darkness.

The captain closed his eyes. His mind was spinning. He felt uprooted by all that he had discovered – *starting with myself. Master of the Deck. Latest recruit to a war I know nothing about. And now . . . this.* 'What,' Paran growled, 'in Hood's name is going on here?'

'I drew on power,' Silverfox replied, her eyes slightly wild.

Paran drew a deep breath. *Power, oh yes, I am coming to know that feeling. Jen'isand Rul. We each have begun our own journey, yet you and I, Silverfox, are destined to arrive at the same place. The Second Gathering. Who, I wonder, will ascend to those two ancient, long-forgotten thrones? Where, dear child, will you lead the T'lan Imass?*

Anomander Rake spoke. 'I had not anticipated such a . . . taut reunion, Caladan—'

Paran's head snapped around, found the warlord. And the hammer held so lightly in his massive arms. *I know you now, Warlord. Not that I'll reveal your dark secret – what would be the point in that? The choice is yours and yours alone. Kill us all, or the goddess you serve. Brood, I do not envy the curse of your privilege to choose. Oh, I do*

231

not, you poor bastard. Still, what is the price of a broken vow?

The Son of Darkness continued. 'My apologies to one and all. As this man,' Rake gestured towards Quick Ben, 'has wisely noted, to act now – knowing so little of the nature of the powers revealed here – would indeed be precipitous.'

'It may already be too late,' Kallor said, his flat, ancient eyes fixed on Silverfox. 'The child's sorcery was Tellann, and it has been a long time since it has been so thoroughly awakened. We are now all of us in peril. A combined effort, begun immediately, might succeed in cutting down this creature – we may never again possess such an opportunity.'

'And should we fail, Kallor?' Anomander Rake asked. 'What enemy will we have made for ourselves? At the moment this child has acted to defend herself, nothing more. Not an inimical stance, is it? You risk too much in a single cast, High King.'

'Finally,' boomed Caladan Brood, returning the dreaded, all-breaking hammer to its harness, 'the notion of *strategy* arrives.' The anger remained in his voice, as if he was furious at having to state what to him had been obvious all along. 'Neutrality remains the soundest course open to us, until the nature of Silverfox's power reveals itself. We've enough enemies on our plate as it is. Now, enough of the drama, if you please. Welcome back, Rake. No doubt you've information to impart regarding the status of Moon's Spawn, among other details of note.' He faced Paran with sudden exasperation. 'Captain, can you not do something about that damned floating table!'

Flinching at the attention, Paran stared up at it. 'Well,' he managed, 'nothing immediately comes to mind, Warlord. Uh, I'm no mage—'

Brood grunted, swung away. 'Never mind, then. We'll consider it a crass ornament.'

Quick Ben cleared his throat. 'I might be able to manage something, Warlord, in time . . .'

Caladan glanced at Dujek, who grinned and nodded his permission to Quick Ben.

'Not simply a soldier, I see,' Anomander Rake said.

The Seven Cities mage shrugged. 'I appreciate challenges, Lord. No guarantee that I'll have any success, mind you – no, do not quest towards me, Son of Darkness. I value my privacy.'

'As you wish,' Rake said, turning away.

'Is anyone else hungry?'

All eyes turned to Kruppe.

With everyone's attention elsewhere, the Mhybe edged away from the clearing, between two rows of peaked Tiste Andii tents, then she spun and tried to run. Bone and muscle protested, even as her veins burned with panic and terror.

She hobbled on, half blinded by tears, her breath harsh, rattling gasps broken by soft whimpers. *Oh . . . dear spirits . . . look upon me. Show me mercy, I beg you. Look at me stumble and totter – look! Pity me, spirits below! I demand it! Take my soul, you cruel ancestors, I beg you!*

The copper on her wrists and ankles – minor tribal wards against the aches in her bones – felt cold as ice against her withered skin, cold as a rapist's touch, disdainful of her frailty, contemptuous of her labouring heart.

The Rhivi spirits refused her, mocking, laughing.

The old woman cried out, staggered, fell hard to her knees. The jolt of the impact drove the air from her lungs. Twisting, she sagged to the ground, bedraggled, alone in an alley of dirt.

'"Flesh,"' a voice murmured above her, '"which is the life within." These, cherished friend, are the words of birth, given in so many forms, in countless languages. They are joy and pain, loss and sacrifice, they give voice to the binds of motherhood . . . and more, they are the binds of life itself.'

Grey hair dangling, the Mhybe raised her head.

Crone sat atop a tent's ridgepole, wings hunched, eyes glittering wet. 'I am not immune to grief, you see, my dear

– tell no-one you have seen me so weakened by love. How can I comfort you?'

The Mhybe shook her head, croaked, 'You cannot.'

'She is you more than the others – more than the woman Tattersail, and Nightchill, more than the T'lan Imass—'

'Do you see me, Crone? Do you truly see me?' The Mhybe pushed herself to her hands and knees, then sat back and glared up at the Great Raven. 'I am naught but bones and leather skin, I am naught but endless aches. Dried brittle – spirits below, each moment of this life, this terrible existence, and I edge closer to . . . to . . .' her head drooped, 'to hatred,' she finished in a ragged whisper. A sob racked her.

'And so you would die now,' Crone said. 'Yes, I understand. A mother must not be led to hate the child she has birthed . . . yet you demand too much of yourself.'

'*She has stolen my life!*' the Mhybe screamed, gnarled hands closing to fists from which the blood within them fled. The Rhivi woman stared at those fists, eyes wide as if they were seeing a stranger's hands, skeletal and dead, there at the end of her thin arms. 'Oh, Crone,' she cried softly. 'She has stolen my life . . .'

The Great Raven spread her wings, tilted forward on the pole, then dropped in a smooth curve to thud on the ground before the Mhybe. 'You must speak with her.'

'I cannot!'

'She must be made to understand—'

'She knows, Crone, she knows. What would you have me do – ask my daughter to stop growing? This river flows unceasing, unceasing . . .'

'Rivers can be dammed. Rivers can be . . . diverted.'

'Not this one, Crone.'

'I do not accept your words, my love. And I shall find a way. This I swear.'

'There is no solution – do not waste your time, my friend. My youth is gone, and it cannot be returned, not by alchemy and not by sorcery – Tellann is an unassailable warren, Crone. What it demands cannot be undone. And should you somehow succeed in stopping this flow, what then? You would have me an old woman for decades to come? Year after year, trapped within this cage? There is no mercy in that – no, it would be a curse unending. No, leave me be, please . . .'

Footsteps approached from behind. A moment later Korlat lowered herself to the Mhybe's side, laid a protective arm around her and held her close. 'Come,' the Tiste Andii murmured. 'Come with me.'

The Mhybe let Korlat help her to her feet. She felt ashamed at her own weakness, but all her defences had crumbled, her pride was in tatters, and she felt in her soul nothing but helplessness. *I was a young woman once. What point in raging at the loss? My seasons have tumbled, it is done. And the life within fades, whilst the life beyond flowers. This is a battle no mortal can win, but where, dear spirits, is the gift of death? Why do you forbid me an end?*

She straightened slightly in Korlat's arms. *Very well, then. Since you have already so cursed my soul, the taking of my own life can cause me no greater pain. Very well, dear spirits, I shall give you my answer. I shall defy your plans.* 'Take me to my tent,' she said.

'No,' Korlat said.

The Mhybe twisted round, glared up at the Tiste Andii. 'I said—'

'I heard you, Mhybe, indeed, more than you intended me to hear. The answer is no. I shall remain at your side, and I am not alone in my faith—'

The Rhivi woman snorted. 'Faith? You are Tiste Andii! Do you take me for a fool with your claims to faith?'

Korlat's expression tightened and she looked away. 'Perhaps you are right.'

Oh, Korlat, I am sorry for that – I would take it back, I swear—

'None the less,' the Tiste Andii continued, 'I shall not abandon you to despair.'

235

'I am familiar with being a prisoner,' the Mhybe said, angry once again. 'But I warn you, Korlat – I warn you all, hatred is finding fertile soil within me. And in your compassion, in your every good intention, you nurture it. I beg you, let me end this.'

'No, and you underestimate our resilience, Mhybe. You'll not succeed in turning us away.'

'Then you shall indeed drag me into hatred, and the price will be all I hold dear within me, all that you might have once valued.'

'You would make our efforts worthless?'

'Not by choice, Korlat – and this is what I am telling you – I have lost all choice. To my daughter. And now, to you. You will create of me a thing of spite, and I beg you again – if you care for me at all – to let me cease this terrible journey.'

'I'll not give you permission to kill yourself, Mhybe. If it must be hate that fuels you, so be it. You are under the care – the guardianship – of the Tiste Andii, now.'

The Rhivi woman sagged, defeated. She struggled to fashion words for the feelings within her, and what came to her left her cold.

Self-pity. To this I have fallen . . .

All right, Korlat, you've won for now.

'Burn is dying.'

Caladan Brood and Anomander Rake stood alone in the tent, the remnants of tension still swirling around them. From the sounds in the clearing outside the mage Quick Ben seemed to have succeeded in pulling the massive wooden card back to the ground, and a discussion was under way as to what to do with it.

The Son of Darkness removed his gauntlets, letting them drop to the tabletop before facing the warlord. 'Barring the one thing you must not do, can you do nothing else?'

Brood shook his head. 'Old choices, friend – only the one possibility remains, as it always has. I am Tennes –

the goddess's own warren – and what assails her assails me as well. Aye, I could shatter the one who has so infected her—'

'The Crippled God,' Rake murmured, going perfectly still. 'He has spent an eternity nurturing his spite – he will be without mercy, Brood. This is an old tale. We agreed – you, I, the Queen of Dreams, Hood – we all agreed . . .'

The warlord's broad face seemed on the verge of crumpling. Then he shook himself as would a bear, turned away. 'Almost twelve hundred years, this burden—'

'And if she dies?'

He shook his head. 'I do not know. Her warren dies, surely, that at the least, even as it becomes the Crippled God's pathway into every other warren . . . then they *all* die.'

'And with that, all sorcery.'

The warlord nodded, then drew a deep breath and straightened. 'Would that be so bad a thing, do you think?'

Rake snorted. 'You assume the destruction would end with that. It seems that, no matter which of the two choices is made, the Crippled God wins.'

'So it seems.'

'Yet, having *made* your choice, you gift this world, and everyone on it, with a few more generations of living—'

'Living, and dying, waging wars and unleashing slaughter. Of dreams, hopes and tragic ends—'

'Not a worthy track, these thoughts of yours, Caladan.' Rake stepped closer. 'You have done, you continue to do, all that could be asked of you. We were there to share your burden, back then, but it seems we are – each of us – ever drawn away, into our own interests . . . abandoning you . . .'

'Leave this path, Anomander. It avails us nothing. There are more immediate concerns to occupy this rare opportunity to speak in private.'

Rake's broad mouth found a thin smile. 'True enough.' He glanced over to the tent's entrance. 'Out there . . .' He faced Brood again, 'Given the infection of Tennes, was your challenge a bluff?'

The warlord bared his filed teeth. 'Somewhat, but not entirely. The question is not my ability to unleash power, it is the nature of that power. Wrought through with poison, rife with chaos—'

'Meaning it might well be wilder than your usual maelstrom? That is alarming indeed, Brood. Is Kallor aware of this?'

'No.'

Rake grunted. 'Best keep it that way.'

'Aye,' the warlord growled. 'So practise some restraint of your own, next time, Rake.'

The Tiste Andii walked over to pour himself some wine. 'Odd, I could have sworn I'd just done that.'

'We must now speak of the Pannion Domin.'

'A true mystery indeed, Caladan. Far more insidious than we had surmised. Layers of power, one hidden beneath another, then another. The Warren of Chaos lies at its heart, I suspect – and the Great Ravens concur.'

'This strides too close a path to the Crippled God for it to be accidental, Rake. The Chained One's poison is that of Chaos, after all.'

'Aye,' Rake smiled. 'Curious, isn't it? I think there can be no question of who is using whom—'

'Maybe.'

'Dealing with the Pannion Domin will present us with formidable challenges.'

Brood grimaced, 'As the child insisted, *we will need help.*'

The Son of Darkness frowned. 'Explain, please.'

'The T'lan Imass, friend. The undead armies are coming.'

The Tiste Andii's face darkened. 'Is this Dujek Onearm's contribution, then?'

'No, the child. Silverfox. She is a flesh and blood Bonecaster, the first in a long, long time.'

'Tell me of her.'

The warlord did, at length, and when he was done there was silence in the tent.

Studying Paran with hooded eyes, Whiskeyjack strode over. The young captain was trembling, as if gripped by fever, his face bone-white and slick with sweat. Quick Ben had somehow managed to lower the tabletop to the ground; sorcery still wreathed it with dancing lightning that seemed reluctant to fade. The wizard had crouched down beside it and Whiskeyjack recognized by his flat expression that the man was in a sorcerous trance. Questing, probing . . .

'You are a fool.'

The commander turned at the rasping words. 'None the less, Kallor.'

The tall, grey-haired man smiled coldly. 'You will come to regret your vow to protect the child.'

Shrugging, Whiskeyjack turned to resume his walk.

'I am not done with you!' Kallor hissed.

'But I am with you,' the Malazan calmly replied, continuing on.

Paran was facing him now. The captain's eyes were wide, uncomprehending. Behind him, the Tiste Andii had begun to drift away, spectral and seemingly indifferent now that their lord had retired within the command tent with Caladan Brood. Whiskeyjack looked for Korlat but didn't see her; nor, he realized after a moment, was the Mhybe anywhere in sight. The child Silverfox stood a dozen paces from Paran, watching the captain with Tattersail's eyes.

'No questions,' Paran growled as Whiskeyjack halted before him. 'I have no answers for you – not for what's happened here, not for what I've become. Perhaps it would be best if you placed someone else in command of the Bridgeburners—'

'No reason for that,' Whiskeyjack said. 'Besides, I hate changing my mind on anything, Captain.'

Quick Ben joined them. He grinned. 'That was close, wasn't it?'

'What is that thing?' Whiskeyjack asked him, nodding towards the tabletop.

'Just what it appears to be. A new Unaligned card in the Deck of Dragons. Well, it's the Unaligned of all Unaligneds. The table holds the entire Deck, remember.' The wizard glanced over at Paran. 'The captain here's on the threshold of ascendancy, as we suspected. And that means that what he does – or chooses not to do – could have profound effects. On all of us. The Deck of Dragons seems to have acquired a Master. Jen'isand Rul.'

Paran turned away, clearly not wanting to be part of this conversation.

Whiskeyjack frowned at the wizard. 'Jen'isand Rul. I thought that was a name referring to his . . . escapades within a certain weapon.'

'It is, but since that name is on the card it seems the two are linked . . . somehow. If the captain's in the dark as much as the rest of us, then I'll have to do some hard thinking on what that linkage signifies. Of course,' he added, 'the captain might well know enough to help me along in this, provided he's willing.'

Paran opened his mouth for a reply but Whiskeyjack spoke first. 'He's got no answers for us . . . right now. I take it we're carrying that ridiculous tabletop along with us on the march?'

Quick Ben slowly nodded. 'It would be best, at least for a while, so I can study it some more. Still, I would advise we unload it before we cross into Pannion territory. The Trygalle Trade Guild can deliver it to the alchemist in Darujhistan for safekeeping.'

A new voice cut in, 'The card does not leave us.'

The three men turned to find Silverfox standing close. Behind her, a dozen Rhivi warriors were lifting the tabletop.

Watching the dark-skinned, lithe men carrying the tabletop away, Quick Ben frowned. 'Risky, taking an object of such power into battle, lass.'

'We must accept that risk, Wizard.'

Whiskeyjack grunted. 'Why?'

'Because the card belongs to Paran, and he will have need of it.'

'Can you explain that?'

'We struggle against more than one enemy, as shall be seen.'

'I don't want that card,' Paran snapped. 'You'd better paint a new face on that thing. I have the blood of a Hound of Shadow within me. I am a liability – when will you all see that? Hood knows, I do!'

The rustle of armour alerted them to Kallor's approach.

Whiskeyjack scowled. 'You are not part of this conversation.'

Kallor smiled wryly. 'Never part of, but often the subject of—'

'Not this time.'

The High King's flat, grey eyes fixed on Quick Ben. 'You, wizard, are a hoarder of souls . . . I am a man who *releases* souls – shall I break the chains within you? An easy thing, to leave you helpless.'

'Even easier,' Quick Ben replied, 'to make a hole in the ground.'

Kallor dropped from sight, the earth gone from beneath him. Armour clattered, followed by a bellow of rage.

Silverfox gasped, eyes widening on Quick Ben.

The wizard shrugged. 'You're right, I don't care who, or what, Kallor is.'

Whiskeyjack stepped to the edge of the pit, glanced down. 'He's climbing out . . . not bad for an old man.'

'But since I'm not stupid,' Quick Ben said hastily, 'I'll take leave, now.' The wizard gestured and seemed to blur a moment before vanishing altogether.

Turning his back on the grunting, cursing Kallor – whose gauntleted hands were now visible scrabbling at the crumbly edge of the pit – Whiskeyjack said to Paran, 'Return to the Bridgeburners, Captain. If all goes well, we'll meet again at Capustan.'

241

'Yes, sir.' Somewhat unsteadily, Paran strode away.

'I suggest,' Silverfox said, eyes fixed on Kallor's efforts to extricate himself, 'we too should depart this particular place.'

'Agreed, lass.'

Slumped in his saddle, Whiskeyjack watched the columns of Onearm's Host marching out from the city of Pale. The day was hot, the hint of thunderstorms in the humid air. Quorl-mounted Black Moranth circled high above the two de-camped armies, fewer in number than was usual – their Achievant, Twist, had departed with Captain Paran and the Bridgeburners four days ago, and eight of the eleven Flights had left in the night just past, on their way to the Vision Mountains on the northwest border of the Domin.

The commander was exhausted. The ache in his leg was robbing him of sleep, and each day was filled with the demands of supply, details on the planned deployment on the march, and the ceaseless swarm of messengers delivering reports and orders then hurrying off with the same. He was restless to begin the journey across half a continent, if only to answer the thousand questions of what awaited them.

Quick Ben sat in silence beside Whiskeyjack, the mage's horse shifting nervously beneath him.

'Your mount's picked up on your state of mind, Quick,' the commander said.

'Aye.'

'You're wondering when I'll cut you loose so you can chase after and catch up with Paran and the Bridgeburners, and put some distance between you and Kallor. You're also eager to get as far away from Silverfox as you can.'

Quick Ben started at this last observation, then he sighed. 'Aye. I imagine I haven't managed to hide my unease – at least not from you, it's clear. The child's grown five years or more since we arrived, Whiskeyjack – I looked in on the Mhybe this morning. Korlat's doing what she can,

242

as are the Rhivi shoulderwomen, but Silverfox has taken from that old woman almost her entire life-force – Hood knows what's keeping her alive. The thought of converging T'lan Imass ain't making me happy, either. And then there's Anomander Rake – he wants to know all about me—'

'Has he attempted any further probing?'

'Not yet, but why tempt him?'

'I need you for a while longer,' Whiskeyjack said. 'Ride with my entourage – we'll keep our distance from the Son of Darkness, as best we can. Have those mercenaries in Capustan taken your bait yet?'

'They're playing with it.'

'We'll wait another week, then. If nothing, then off you go.'

'Yes, sir.'

'Now,' Whiskeyjack drawled, 'why don't you tell me what else you've got going, Quick Ben?'

The mage blinked innocently. 'Sir?'

'You've visited every temple and every seer in Pale, mage. You've spent a small fortune on readers of the Deck. Hood, I've had a report of you sacrificing a goat at dawn atop a barrow – what in the Abyss were you up to with that, Quick?'

'All right,' the man muttered, 'the goat thing stinks of desperation. I admit it. I got carried away.'

'And what did the lost spirits in the barrow tell you?'

'Nothing. There, uh, there weren't any.'

Whiskeyjack's eyes narrowed. 'There weren't any? It was a Rhivi barrow, was it not?'

'One of the few still remaining in the area, aye. It was, uh, cleaned out. Recently.'

'*Cleaned out?*'

'Someone or something gathered them up, sir. Never known *that* to happen before. It's the strangest thing. Not a single soul remains within those barrows. I mean, *where are they?*'

'You're changing the subject, Quick Ben. Nice try.'

The mage scowled. 'I'm doing some investigating. Nothing I can't handle, and it won't interfere with anything else. Besides, we're now officially on the march, right? Not much I can do out in the middle of nowhere, is there? Besides, I *have* been sidetracked, sir. Those snatched spirits . . . *someone* took them, and it's got me curious.'

'When you figure it out you'll let me know, right?'

'Of course, sir.'

Whiskeyjack gritted his teeth and said no more. *I've known you too long, Quick Ben. You've stumbled onto something, and it's got you scampering like a stoat with its tail between its legs.*

Sacrificing a goat, for Hood's sake!

On the road from Pale, Onearm's Host – almost ten thousand veterans of the Genabackan Campaign – moved to join the ranks of Caladan Brood's vast army. The march had begun, onward to war, against an enemy they had never seen and of whom they knew almost nothing.

244

CHAPTER SIX

Where they tread, blood follows . . .

Kulburat's Vision
Horal Thume (b.1134)

Saltoan's sunset gate was reached by a broad, arching causeway over the canal. Both the bridge and the canal itself were in serious need of repair, the mortar crumbling and webbed in wide, grass-tufted cracks where the foundations had settled. One of the Vision Plain's oldest cities, Saltoan had once stood alongside the river Catlin, growing rich on the cross-continent trade, until the river changed its course in the span of a single, rain-drenched spring. Korselan's Canal was built in an effort to re-establish the lucrative link with the river trade, as well as four deep lakes – two within the old river bed itself – for moorage and berths. The effort had seen only marginal success, and the four hundred years since that time had witnessed a slow, inexorable decline.

Gruntle's scowl as he guided his horse onto the causeway deepened upon seeing Saltoan's low, thick walls ahead. Brown stains ran in streaks down their sloped sides. The caravan captain could already smell the raw sewage. There were plenty of figures lining the battlements, but few if any of them actual constabulary or soldiers. The city had sent its vaunted Horse Guard north to join Caladan Brood's forces in the war against the Malazan Empire. What remained of its army wasn't worth the polish on their boots.

He glanced back as his master's carriage clattered onto the causeway. Sitting on the driver's bench, Harllo waved. At his side, Stonny held the traces and Gruntle could see her lips moving to a stream of curses and complaints. Harllo's wave wilted after a moment.

Gruntle returned his attention to Sunset Gate. There were no guards in sight, and little in the way of traffic. The two huge wooden doors hung ajar and looked not to have been closed in a long time. The captain's mood soured even further. He slowed his horse until the carriage drew along-side him.

'We're passing right through, right?' Stonny asked. 'Straight through to Sunrise Gate, right?'

'So I have advised,' Gruntle said.

'What's the point of our long experience if the master won't heed our advice? Answer me that, Gruntle!'

The captain simply shrugged. No doubt Keruli could hear every word, and no doubt Stonny knew that.

They approached the arched entrance. The avenue within quickly narrowed to a tortuous alley buried beneath the gloom of the flanking buildings' upper levels, which projected outward until they almost touched overhead. Gruntle moved ahead of the carriage again. Mangy chickens scattered from their path, but the fat, black rats in the gutters only momentarily paused in their feasting on rotting rubbish to watch the carriage wheels slip past.

'We'll be scraping sides in a moment,' Harllo said.

'If we can manage Twistface Passage, we'll be all right.'

'Aye, but that's a big if, Gruntle. Mind you, there's enough that passes for grease on these walls . . .'

The alley narrowed ahead to the chokepoint known as Twistface Passage. Countless trader wagons had gouged deep grooves in both walls. Broken spokes and torn fittings littered the cobbles. The neighbourhood had a wreckers' mentality, Gruntle well knew. Any carriage trapped in the Passage was free salvage, and the locals weren't averse to swinging swords if their claims were contested. Gruntle had only spilled blood here once, six, seven years back. A messy night, he recalled. He and his guards had depopulated half a tenement block of cut-throats and thugs in those dark, nightmarish hours before they'd managed to back the wagon out of the passage, remove the wheels, lay rollers and manhandle their way through.

He did not want a repetition.

The hubs scraped a few times as they passed through the chokepoint, but then, with a swearing Stonny and a grinning Harllo ducking beneath sodden clothes hanging from a line, they were clear and into the square beyond.

No deliberate intent created Wu's Closet Square. The open space was born of the happenstance convergence of thirteen streets and alleys of various breadth. The inn to which they all once led no longer existed, having burned down a century or so ago, leaving a broad, uneven expanse of flagstones and cobbles that had, unaccountably, acquired the name of Wu's Closet.

'Take Mucosin Street, Stonny,' Gruntle directed, gesturing towards the wide avenue on the east side of the square.

'I remember well enough,' she growled. 'Gods, the stink!'

A score of urchins had discovered their arrival, and now trailed the carriage like flightless vultures, their dirty, pocked faces closed and all too serious. None spoke.

Still in the lead, Gruntle walked his horse into Mucosin Street. He saw a few faces peer out from grimy windows, but there was no other traffic. *Not here . . . not ahead. This isn't good.*

'Captain,' Harllo called.

Gruntle did not turn. 'Aye?'

'Them kids . . . they've just vanished.'

'Right.' He loosened his Gadrobi cutlasses. 'Load your crossbow, Harllo.'

'Already done.'

I know, but why not announce it anyway.

Twenty paces ahead three figures stepped into the street.

247

Gruntle squinted. He recognized the tall woman in the middle. 'Hello, Nektara. I see you've expanded your holdings.'

The scar-faced woman smiled. 'Why, it's Gruntle. And Harllo. And who else? Oh, would that be Stonny Menackis? No doubt as unpleasant as ever, my dear, though I still lay down my heart at your feet.'

'Unwise,' Stonny drawled. 'I never step lightly.'

Nektara's smile broadened. 'And you do make that heart race, love. Every time.'

'What's the toll?' Gruntle asked, drawing his mount to a halt ten paces from the woman and her two silent bodyguards.

Nektara's plucked brows rose. 'Toll? Not this time, Gruntle. We're still in Garno's holdings – we've been granted passage. We're simply here by way of escort.'

'Escort?'

The sound of the carriage's shutters clattering open made the captain turn. He saw his master's hand appear, then languidly wave him over.

Gruntle dismounted. He reached the carriage's side door, peered in to see Keruli's round, pale face.

'Captain, we are to meet with this city's . . . rulers.'

'The king and his Council? Why—'

A soft laugh interrupted him. 'No, no. Saltoan's *true* rulers. At great expense, and through extraordinary negotiation, a gathering of all the hold-masters and mistresses has been convened, to whom I shall make address this night. You have leave to permit the escort just offered. I assure you, all is well.'

'Why didn't you explain all this earlier?'

'I was not certain that the negotiations were successful. The matter is complex, for it is the masters and mistresses who have asked for . . . assistance. I, in turn, must endeavour to earn their confidence, to the effect that I represent the most efficacious agent to provide said assistance.'

You? Then who in Hood's name are you? 'I see. All right, then, trust these criminals if you like, but I'm afraid we'll not be sharing your faith.'

'Understood, Captain.'

Gruntle returned to his horse. Collecting the reins he faced Nektara. 'Lead on.'

Saltoan was a city with two hearts, their chambers holding different hues of blood but both equally vile and corrupt. Seated with his back to the wall of the low-ceilinged, crowded tavern, Gruntle looked out with narrowed eyes on a motley collection of murderers, extortionists and thugs whose claim to power was measured in fear.

Stonny leaned against the wall to the captain's left, Harllo sharing the bench on his right. Nektara had dragged her chair and a small, round table close to Stonny. Thick coils of smoke rose from the hookah before the hold-mistress, wreathing her knife-kissed features in the cloying, tarry fumes. With the hookah's mouthpiece in her left hand, her other hand was on Stonny's leather-clad thigh.

Keruli stood in the centre of the room, facing the majority of the crimelords and ladies. The short man's hands were clasped above his plain grey silk belt, his cloak of black silk shimmering like molten obsidian. A strange, close-fitting cap covered his hairless pate, its style reminiscent of that worn by figures found among Darujhistan's oldest sculptures and in equally ancient tapestries.

He had begun his speech in a voice soft and perfectly modulated. 'I am pleased to be present at this auspicious gathering. Every city has its secret veils, and I am honoured by this one's select parting. Of course I realize that many of you might see me as cut from the same cloth as your avowed enemy, but I assure you this is not the case. You have expressed your concern as regards the influx of priests of the Pannion Domin into Saltoan. They speak of cities newly come under the divine protection of the Pannion Seer's cult, and offer to the common people tales of laws applied impartially to all citizens, of rights and enscripted privileges, of the welcome imposition of order in defiance of local traditions and manners. They sow seeds of discord among your subjects – a dangerous precedent, indeed.'

Murmurs of agreement followed from the masters and mistresses. Gruntle almost smiled at the mannered decorum among these street-bred killers. Glancing over, he saw, his brows rising, Nektara's hand plunged beneath the leather folds of Stonny's leggings at the crotch. Stonny's face was flushed, a faint smile on her lips, her eyes almost closed. *Queen of Dreams, no wonder nine-tenths of the men in this room are panting, not to mention drinking deep from their cups of wine.* He himself reached for his tankard.

'A wholesale slaughter,' one of the mistresses growled. 'Every damned one of them priests should be belly-smiling, that's the only way to deal with this, I say.'

'Martyrs to the faith,' Keruli responded. 'Such a direct attack is doomed to fail, as it has in other cities. This conflict is one of information, lords and ladies, or, rather, misinformation. The priests are conducting a campaign of deception. The Pannion Domin, for all its imposition of law and order, is a tyranny, characterized by extraordinary levels of cruelty to its people. No doubt you have heard tales of the Tenescowri, the Seer's army of the dispossessed and the abandoned – all that you may have heard is without exaggeration. Cannibals, rapers of the dead—'

'Children of the Dead Seed.' One man spoke up, leaning forward. 'It is true? Is it even possible? That women should descend onto battlefields and soldiers whose corpses are not yet cold . . .'

Keruli's nod was sombre. 'Among the Tenescowri's youngest generation of followers . . . aye, there are the Children of the Dead Seed. Singular proof of what is possible.' He paused, then continued, 'The Domin possesses its sanctified faithful, the citizens of the original Pannion cities, to whom all the rights and privileges the priests speak of applies. No-one else can acquire that citizenship. Non-citizens are less than slaves, for they are the subjects – the *objects* – of every cruelty conceivable, without recourse to mercy or justice. The Tenescowri offers their only escape, the chance to match the inhumanity inflicted on them. The citizens of Saltoan, should the Domin subjugate this city, will be one and all cast from their homes, stripped of all possessions, denied food, denied clean water. Savagery will be their only possible path, as followers sworn into the Tenescowri.

'Masters and mistresses, we must fight this war with the weapon of truth, the laying bare of the lies of the Pannion priests. This demands a very specific kind of organization, of dissemination, of crafted rumours and counter-intelligence. Tasks at which you all excel, my friends. The city's commonalty must themselves drive the priests from Saltoan. They must be guided to that decision, to that cause, not with fists and knouts, but with words.'

'What makes you so sure that will work?' a master demanded.

'You have no choice but to make it work,' Keruli replied. 'To fail is to see Saltoan fall to the Pannions.'

Keruli continued, but Gruntle was no longer listening. His eyes, half shut, studied the man who had hired them. An intermediary had brokered the contract in Darujhistan. Gruntle's first sight of the master was the morning outside Worry Gate, at the rendezvous, arriving on foot, robed as he was now. The carriage was delivered scant moments after him, of local hire. Keruli had quickly entered it and from then on Gruntle had seen and spoken with his master but twice on this long, wearying journey.

A mage, I'd concluded. But now, I think, a priest. Kneeling before which god, I wonder? No obvious signs. That itself is telling enough, I suppose. There's nothing obvious about Keruli, except maybe the bottomless coin-chest backing his generosity. Any new temples in Darujhistan lately? Can't recall – oh, that one in Gadrobi District. Sanctified to Treach, though why anyone would be interested in worshipping the Tiger of Summer is beyond me—

'—killings.'

'Been quiet these two nights past, though.'

The masters and mistresses were speaking amongst themselves. Keruli's attention was nevertheless keen, though he said nothing.

Blinking, Gruntle eased slightly straighter on the bench. He leaned close to Harllo. 'What was that about killings?'

'Unexplained murders for four nights running, or something like that. A local problem, though I gather it's past.'

The captain grunted, then settled back once again, trying to ignore the cool sweat now prickling beneath his shirt. *They made good time, well ahead of us – that carriage moved with preternatural speed. But it would never have managed Saltoan's streets. Too wide, too high. Must have camped in Waytown. A score of paces from Sunrise Gate . . . Proof of your convictions, friend Buke?*

'I was bored out of my mind, what do you think?' Stonny poured herself another cup of wine. 'Nektara managed to alleviate that, and – if all those sweating hairy faces were any indication – not just for me. You're all pigs.'

'Wasn't us on such public display,' Gruntle said.

'So what? You didn't all have to watch, did you? What if it'd been a baby on my hip and my tit bared?'

'If that,' Harllo said, 'I would have positively *stared*.'

'You're disgusting.'

'You misunderstand me, dearest. Not your tit – though that would be a fine sight indeed – but you with a baby! Hah, a baby!'

Stonny threw him a sneer.

They were sitting in a back room in the tavern, the leavings of a meal on the table between them.

'In any case,' Gruntle said, sighing, 'that meeting will last the rest of the night, and come the morning our master will be the only one among us privileged to catch up on his sleep – in the comfy confines of his carriage. We've got rooms upstairs with almost-clean beds and I suggest we make use of them.'

'That would be to actually sleep, dearest Stonny,' Harllo explained.

'Rest assured I'll bar the door, runt.'

'Nektara has a secret knock, presumably.'

'Wipe that grin off your face or I'll do it for you, Harllo.'

'How come you get all the fun, anyway?'

She grinned. 'Breeding, mongrel. What I got and you ain't got.'

'Education, too, huh?'

'Precisely.'

A moment later, the door swung open and Keruli entered.

Gruntle leaned back in his chair and eyed the priest. 'So, have you succeeded in recruiting the city's thugs, murderers and extortionists to your cause?'

'More or less,' Keruli replied, striding over to pour himself some wine. 'War, alas,' he sighed, 'must be fought on more than one kind of battlefield. The campaign will be a long one, I fear.'

'Is that why we're headed to Capustan?'

The priest's gaze settled on Gruntle for a moment, then he turned away. 'I have other tasks awaiting me there, Captain. Our brief detour here in Saltoan is incidental, in the great scheme of things.'

And which great scheme is that, Priest? Gruntle wanted to ask, but didn't. His master was beginning to make him nervous, and he suspected that any answer to that question would only make matters worse. *No, Keruli, you keep your secrets.*

The archway beneath Sunrise Gate was as dark as a tomb, the air chill and damp. Waytown's shanty sprawl was visible just beyond, through a haze of smoke lit gold by the morning sun.

Grainy-eyed and itching with flea bites, Gruntle nudged his horse into an easy trot as soon as he rode into the sunlight. He'd remained in Saltoan, lingering around the Gate for two bells, whilst Harllo and Stonny had driven the carriage and its occupant out of the city a bell before dawn. They would be at least two leagues along the river road, he judged.

Most of the banditry on the first half of this stretch to Capustan was headquartered in Saltoan – the stretch's second half, in Capan territory, was infinitely safer. Spotters hung around Sunrise Gate to mark the caravans heading east, much as he'd seen their counterparts on the west wall at Sunset Gate keeping an eye out for caravans bound for Darujhistan. Gruntle had waited to see if any local packs had made plans for Keruli's party, but no-one had set out in pursuit, confirming the master's assertion that safe passage had been guaranteed. It wasn't in Gruntle's nature to take thieves at their word, however.

He worked his horse into a canter to escape Waytown's clouds of flies and, flanked by half-wild, barking dogs, rode clear of the shanty-town and onto the open, rocky river road. Vision Plain's gently rolling prairie reached out to the distant Barghast Range on his left. To his right was a rough bank of piled stones – mostly overgrown with grasses – and beyond it the reedy flats of the river's floodplain.

The dogs abandoned him a few hundred paces beyond Waytown and the captain found himself alone on the road. The trader track would fade before long, he recalled, the dyke on his right dwindling, the road itself becoming a sandy swath humped with ant nests, bone-white driftwood and yellow knots of grass, with floods wiping the ruts away every spring. There was no chance of getting lost, of course, so long as one kept Catlin River within sight to the south.

He came upon the corpses less than a league further on. The highwaymen had perfectly positioned their ambush, emerging from a deeply cut, seasonal stream bed and no doubt surrounding their victim's carriage in moments. The precise planning hadn't helped, it seemed. Two or three days old at the most, bloated and almost black under the sun, their bodies were scattered to both sides of the track. Swords, lance-heads, buckles and anything else that was metal had all melted under some ferocious heat, yet clothing and leather bindings were unmarked. A number of the bandits wore spurs, and indeed there would have been no way of getting out this far without horses, but of the beasts there was no sign.

Dismounted and wandering among the dead, Gruntle noted that the tracks of Keruli's carriage – they too had stopped to examine the scene – were overlying another set. A wider, heavier carriage, drawn by oxen.

There were no visible wounds on the corpses.

I doubt Buke had to even so much as draw his blade . . .

The captain climbed back into his saddle and resumed his journey.

He caught sight of his companions half a league further on, and rode up alongside the carriage a short while later.

Harllo gave him a nod. 'A fine day, wouldn't you say, Gruntle?'

'Not a cloud in the sky. Where's Stonny?'

'Took one of the horses ahead. Should be back soon.'

'Why did she do that?'

'Just wanted to make certain the wayside camp was . . . uh, unoccupied. Ah, here she comes.'

Gruntle greeted her with a scowl as she reined in before them. 'Damned stupid thing to do, woman.'

'This whole journey's stupid if you ask me. There's three Barghast at the wayside camp – and no, they ain't roasted any bandits lately. Anyway, Capustan's bare days away from a siege – maybe we make the walls in time, in which case we'll be stuck there with the whole Pannion army between us and the open road, or we don't make it in time and those damned Tenescowri have fun with us.'

Gruntle's scowl deepened. 'Where are those Barghast headed, then?'

'They came down from the north, but now they're travelling the same as us – they want to take a look at things closer to Capustan and don't ask me why – they're Barghast, ain't they? Brains the size of walnuts. We got to talk with the master, Gruntle.'

The carriage door swung open and Keruli climbed out. 'No need, Stonny Menackis, my hearing is fine. Three Barghast, you said. Which clan?'

'White Face, if the paint's any indication.'

'We shall invite them to travel with us, then.'

'Master—' Gruntle began, but Keruli cut him off.

'We shall arrive in Capustan well before the siege, I believe. The Septarch responsible for the Pannion forces is known for a methodical approach. Once I am delivered, your duties will be discharged and you will be free to leave immediately for Darujhistan.' His dark, uncanny eyes narrowed on Gruntle. 'You do not have a reputation for breaking contracts, else I would not have hired you.'

'No, sir, we've no intention of breaking our contract. None the less, it might be worth discussing our options – what if Capustan is besieged before we arrive?'

'Then I shall not see you lose your lives in any desperate venture, Captain. I need then only be dropped off outside the range of the enemy, and I shall make my own way into the city, and such subterfuge is best attempted alone.'

'You would attempt to pass through the Pannion cordon?'

Keruli smiled. 'I have relevant skills for such an undertaking.'

Do you now? 'What about these Barghast? What makes you think they can be trusted to travel in our company?'

'If untrustworthy, better they be in sight than out of it, wouldn't you agree, Captain?'

He grunted. 'You've a point there, master.' He faced Harllo and Stonny, slowly nodded.

Harllo offered him a resigned smile.

Stonny was, predictably, not so nearly laconic. 'This is

insanity!' Then she tossed up her hands. 'Fine, then! We ride into the dragon's maw, why not?' She spun her horse round. 'Let's go throw bones with the Barghast, shall we?'

Grimacing, Gruntle watched her ride off.

'She is a treasure, is she not?' Harllo murmured with a sigh.

'Never seen you so lovestruck before,' Gruntle said with a sidelong glance.

'It's the unattainable, friend, that's what's done for me. I long helplessly, morosely maundering over unrequited adoration. I dream of her and Nektara ... with me snug between 'em—'

'Please, Harllo, you're making me sick.'

'Uhm,' Keruli said, 'I believe I shall now return to the carriage.'

The three Barghast were clearly siblings, with the woman the eldest. White paint had been smeared on their faces, giving them a skull-like appearance. Braids stained with red ochre hung down to their shoulders, knotted with bone fetishes. All three wore hauberks of holed coins – the currency ranging from copper to silver and no doubt from some looted hoard, as most of them looked ancient and unfamiliar to Gruntle's eye. Coin-backed gauntlets covered their hands. A guardblock's worth of weapons accompanied the trio – bundled lances, throwing axes and copper-sheathed long-hafted fighting axes, hook-bladed swords and assorted knives and daggers.

They stood on the other side of a small stone-ringed firepit – burned down to faintly smouldering coals – with Stonny still seated on her horse to their left. A small heap of jackrabbit bones indicated a meal just completed.

Gruntle's gaze settled on the Barghast woman. 'Our master invites you to travel in our company. Do you accept?'

The woman's dark eyes flicked to the carriage as Harllo drove it to the camp's edge. 'Few traders still journey to Capustan,' she said after a moment. 'The trail has become ... perilous.'

Gruntle frowned. 'How so? Have the Pannions sent raid-ing parties across the river?'

'Not that we have heard. No, demons stalk the wild-lands. We have been sent to discover the truth of them.'

Demons? Hood's breath. 'When did you learn of these demons?'

She shrugged. 'Two, three months past.'

The captain sighed, slowly dismounted. 'Well, let us hope there's nothing to such tales.'

The woman grinned. 'We hope otherwise. I am Hetan, and these are my miserable brothers, Cafal and Netok. This is Netok's first hunt since his Deathnight.'

Gruntle glanced at the glowering, hulking youth. 'I can see his excitement.'

Hetan turned, gaze narrowing on her brother. 'You must have sharp eyes.'

By the Abyss, another humourless woman for company . . .

Looping a leg over her saddle, Stonny Menackis dropped to the ground, raising a puff of dust. 'Our captain's too obvious with his jokes, Hetan. They end up thudding like ox dung, and smelling just as foul. Pay him no mind, lass, unless you enjoy being confused.'

'I enjoy killing and riding men and little else,' Hetan growled, crossing her muscled arms.

Harllo quickly clambered down from the carriage and approached her with a broad smile. 'I am named Harllo and I am delighted to make your acquaintance, Hetan!'

'You can kill him any time you like,' Stonny drawled.

The two brothers were indeed miserable creatures, taciturn and, as far as Gruntle could determine, singularly thick. Harllo's futile efforts with Hetan proved amusing enough whilst they sat around the rekindled hearth beneath a star-spattered sky. Keruli made a brief appearance shortly before everyone began bedding down, but only to share a bowl of herbal tea before once again retiring to his carriage. It fell to Gruntle – he and Hetan the last two lingering at the firepit – to pry loose more information from the Barghast.

'These demons,' he began, 'how have they been described?'

She leaned forward and ritually spat into the fire. 'Fast on two legs. Talons like an eagle's, only much larger, at the ends of those legs. Their arms are blades—'

'Blades? What do you mean?'

She shrugged. 'Bladed. Blood-iron. Their eyes are hollow pits. They stink of urns in the dark circle. They make no sound, no sound at all.'

Urns in the dark circle? Cremation urns . . . in a chamber barrow. Ah, they smell of death, then. Their arms are blades . . . how? What in Hood's name does that mean? Blood-iron – that's iron quenched in snow-chilled blood . . . a Barghast practice when shamans invest weapons. Thus, the wielder and the weapon are linked. Merged . . . 'Has anyone in your clan seen one?'

'No, the demons have not journeyed north to our mountain fastnesses. They remain in these grasslands.'

'Who, then, delivered the tales?'

'Our shouldermen have seen them in their dreams. The spirits whisper to them and warn of the threat. The White Clan has chosen a warchief – our father – and await what is to come. But our father would know his enemy, so he has sent his children down onto the flatlands.'

Gruntle ruminated on this, his eyes watching the fire slowly ebb. 'Will your father the warchief of the White Faces lead the clans south? If Capustan is besieged, the Capan territories will be vulnerable to your raids, at least until the Pannions complete their conquest.'

'Our father has no plans to lead us south, Captain.' She spat a second time into the fire. 'The Pannion war will come to us, in time. So the shouldermen have read in bhederin blades. Then, there shall be war.'

'If these demons are advance elements of the Pannion forces . . .'

'Then, when they first appear in our fastnesses, we will know that the time has come.'

'Fighting,' Gruntle muttered. 'What you enjoy the most.'

'Yes, but for now, I would ride you.'

Ride? More like batter me senseless. Ah, well . . . 'What man would say no to such an elegant offer?'

Collecting her bedroll in both arms, Hetan rose. 'Follow me, and hurry.'

'Alas,' he replied, slowly gaining his feet, 'I never hurry, as you're about to discover.'

'Tomorrow night I shall ride your friend.'

'You're doing so tonight, dear, in his dreams.'

She nodded seriously. 'He has big hands.'

'Aye.'

'So do you.'

'I thought you were in a hurry, Hetan.'

'I am. Let's go.'

The Barghast Range crept down from the north as the day slowly passed, from distant mountains to worn, humped-back hills. Many of the hills edging the traders' track to Capustan were sacred sites, their summits displaying the inverted tree trunks that were the Barghast custom of anchoring spirits – or so Hetan explained as she walked alongside Gruntle, who was leading his horse by the reins. While the captain had little interest in things religious, he admitted to some curiosity as to why the Barghast would bury trees upside-down in hills.

'Mortal souls are savage things,' she explained, spitting to punctuate her words. 'Many must be held down to keep them from ill-wandering. Thus, the oaks are brought down from the north. The shouldermen carve magic into their trunks. The one to be buried is pinned beneath the tree. Spirits are drawn as well, as guardians, and other traps are placed along the edges of the dark circle. Even so, sometimes the souls escape – imprisoned by one of the traps, yet able to travel the land. Those who return to the clans where they once lived are quickly destroyed, so they have learned to stay away – here, in these lowlands. Sometimes, such a sticksnare retains a loyalty to its mortal kin, and will send dreams to our shouldermen, to tell us of danger.'

'A sticksnare, you called it. What does that mean?'

'You may well see for yourself,' she replied with a shrug.

'Was it one of these sticksnares that sent the dreams of demons?'

'Yes, and other spirits besides. That so many sought to reach us . . .'

Added veracity to the threat, aye, I understand. He scanned the empty land before them, wondering what was out there.

Stonny rode fifty paces ahead. At the moment, Gruntle could not see her, as the trail leaned round a boulder-studded hill and vanished from sight thirty paces on. She had a frustrating knack for ignoring his orders – he'd wanted her to remain in sight at all times. The two Barghast brothers ranged to the sides, flanking the carriage from a distance that varied with the demands of the ground they covered. Cafal had taken the inland side and was jogging up the same hill's rocky slope. Netok walked along the sandy bank of the river, surrounded by a cloud of midges that seemed to grow larger and thicker with every stride. Given the alarmingly thick and rancid greases with which the Barghast covered their bodies, Gruntle suspected those insects were suffering from frustration – drawn close by a warm body but unwilling or unable to alight.

That grease had been something of a challenge the night just past, Gruntle reflected, but he'd managed none the less, sporting a formidable collection of bruises, scratches and bites as proof. Hetan had been . . . energetic—

A shout from Cafal. At the same moment Stonny re-appeared. The slow canter at which she approached eased the captain's nerves somewhat, though it was clear that both she and the Barghast on the hill had spotted something ahead. He glanced over to see Cafal now crouched low, his attention fixed on something further up the trail, but he had not drawn his weapons.

Stonny reined in, her expression closed. 'Bauchelain's

carriage ahead. It's been . . . damaged. There's been a fight of some kind. Messy.'

'See anyone still standing?'

'No, just the oxen, looking placid enough. No bodies either.'

Hetan faced her brother on the hill and caught his eye. She made a half-dozen hand gestures, and, drawing forth a lance, Cafal padded forward, dropping down from view.

'All right,' Gruntle sighed. 'Weapons out – let's go for a look.'

'Want me to keep back?' Harllo asked from the driver's bench.

'No.'

Rounding the hill, they saw that the trail opened out again, the land flattening on both sides. Forty paces on was Bauchelain and Korbal Broach's massive carriage, on its side, the rear spoke torn entirely off and lying shattered nearby. The four oxen stood a few paces away, grazing on the prairie grasses. Swathes of burned ground stretched out from the carriage, the air reeking of sorcery. A low mound just beyond had been blasted open, the inverted tree it had contained torn up and shattered as if it had been struck by lightning. Smoke still drifted from the gaping pit where the burial chamber had once been. Cafal was even now cautiously approaching it, his left hand scribing warding gestures in the air, the lance poised for a cast in his right.

Netok jogged up from the river bank, a two-handed axe in his grip. He halted at his sister's side. 'Something is loose,' he growled, his small eyes darting.

'And still close,' Hetan nodded. 'Flank your brother.'

He padded off.

Gruntle strode up to her. 'That barrow . . . you're saying a spirit or ghost's broken free.'

'Aye.'

Drawing a hook-bladed sword, the Barghast woman walked slowly towards the carriage. The captain followed.

Stonny trotted her horse back to take a defensive position beside Keruli's contrivance.

A savage hole had been torn into the carriage's side, revealing on its jagged edges what looked to be sword-cuts, though larger than any blade Gruntle had ever seen. He clambered up to peer inside the compartment, half dreading what he might discover.

It was empty – no bodies. The leather-padded walls had been shredded, the ornate furnishings scattered. Two huge trunks, once bolted to the floorboards, had been ripped loose. Their lids were open, contents spilled out. 'Hood take us,' the captain whispered, his mouth suddenly dry. One of the trunks contained flat slabs of slate – now shattered – on which arcane symbols had been meticulously etched, but it was the other trunk whose contents had Gruntle close to gagging. A mass of blood-slick ... organs. Livers, lungs, hearts, all joined together to form a shape all the more horrifying for its familiarity. When alive – as he sensed it must have been until recently – it had been human-shaped, though no more than knee-high when perched on its boneless, pod-like appendages. Eyeless and, as far as Gruntle could see in the compartment's gloom, devoid of anything resembling a brain, the now-dead creature still leaked thin, watery blood.

Necromancy, but not the demonic kind. These are the arts of those who delve into mortality, into resurrection and undeath. Those organs ... they came from living people. People murdered by a madman. Damn you, Buke, why did you have to get involved with those bastards?

'Are they within?' Hetan asked from below.

He leaned back, shook his head. 'Just wreckage.'

Harllo called out from the driver's bench. 'Look uptrail, Gruntle! Party coming.'

Four figures, two leather-cloaked and in black, one short and bandy-legged, the last one tall, thin. *No losses, then. Still, something nasty hit them. Hard.* 'That's them,' he muttered.

Hetan squinted up at him. 'You know these men?'

'Aye, only one well, though. The guard – that grey-haired, tall one.'

'I don't like them,' the woman growled, her sword twitching as she adjusted her grip.

'Keep your distance,' Gruntle advised. 'Tell your brothers. You don't want to back-brush their hides – those cloaked two. Bauchelain – with the pointed beard – and Korbal Broach – the . . . the other one.'

Cafal and Netok rejoined their sister. The older brother was scowling. 'It was taken yesterday,' he said. 'The wards were unravelled. Slow. Before the hill was broken open.'

Gruntle, still perched on top of the carriage, narrowed his gaze on the approaching men. Buke and the servant, Emancipor Reese, both looked exhausted, deeply shaken, whilst the sorcerors might well have simply been out on a stroll for all the discomfort in their composure. Yet they were armed. All-metal crossbows, stained black, were cradled on their vambraced forearms, quarrels set and locked. Squat black quivers at their hips showed but a few quarrels remaining in each.

Climbing down from the carriage, Gruntle strode to meet them.

'Well met, Captain,' Bauchelain said with a faint smile. 'Fortunate for you that we made better time since the river. Since Saltoan our peregrination has been anything but peaceful.'

'So I've gathered, sir.' Gruntle's eyes strayed to Buke. His friend looked ten years older than when he'd last seen him. He would not meet the captain's eyes.

'I see your entourage has grown since we last met,' Bauchelain observed. 'Barghast, yes? Extraordinary, isn't it, that such people can be found on other continents as well, calling themselves by the same name and practising, it seems, virtually identical customs. What vast history lies buried and now lost in their ignorance, I wonder?'

'Generally,' Gruntle said quietly, 'that particular usage of the word "buried" is figurative. Yet you have taken it literally.'

The black-clad man shrugged. 'Plagued by curiosity, alas. We could not pass by the opportunity. We never can, in fact. As it turned out, the spirit we gathered into our embrace – though once a shaman of some power – could tell us nothing other than what we had already surmised. The Barghast are an ancient people indeed, and were once far more numerous. Accomplished seafarers as well.' His flat, grey eyes fixed on Hetan. A thin brow slowly lifted. 'Not a question of a fall from some civilized height into savagery, however. Simply an eternal ... stagnation. The belief system, with all its ancestor worship, is anathema to progress, or so I have concluded given the evidence.'

Hetan offered the sorceror a silent snarl.

Cafal spoke, his voice ragged with fury. 'What have you done with our soul-kin?'

'Very little, warrior. He had already eluded the inner bindings, yet had fallen prey to one of your shamanistic traps – a tied bundle of sticks, twine and cloth. Was it compassion that offered them the semblance of bodies with those traps? Misguided, if so—'

'Flesh,' Korbal Broach said in a reedy, thin voice, 'would far better suit them.'

Bauchelain smiled. 'My companion is skilled in such ... assemblages, a discipline of lesser interest to me.'

'What happened here?' Gruntle asked.

'That is plain,' Hetan snapped. 'They broke into a dark circle. Then a demon attacked them – a demon such as the one my brothers and I hunt. And these ... men ... fled and somehow eluded it.'

'Not quite, my dear,' Bauchelain said. 'Firstly, the creature that attacked us was not a demon – you can take my word on such matters for demons are entities I happen to know very well indeed. We were most viciously set upon, however, as you surmise. Whilst we were preoccupied with this barrow. Had not Buke alerted us, we might well have sustained even further damage to our accoutrements, not to mention our less capable companions.'

'So,' Gruntle cut in, 'if not a demon, then what was it?'

'Ah, a question not easily answered, Captain. Undead, most certainly. Commanded by a distant master, and formidable in the extreme. Korbal and I were perforce required to unleash the full host of our servants to fend the apparition off, nor did the subsequent pursuit yield us any profit. Indeed, the loss of a good many of those servants was incurred, upon the appearance of two more of the undead hunters. And while the trio have been driven off, the relief is but temporary. They will attack again, and if they have gathered in greater numbers, we might well – all of us – be sorely tested.'

'If I may,' Gruntle said, 'I would like to speak in private with my master, and with Hetan, here.'

Bauchelain tilted his head. 'By all means. Come, Korbal and companions, let us survey the full damage to our hapless carriage.'

Taking Hetan's arm, Gruntle led her to where Harllo and Stonny waited beside Keruli's carriage. Cafal and Netok followed.

'They have enslaved our soul-kin,' Hetan hissed, her eyes like fanned coals. 'I will kill them – kill them all!'

'And die before you close a single step,' Gruntle snapped. 'These are sorcerors, Hetan. Worse, they're necromancers. Korbal practises the art of the undead. Bauchelain's is demonic summoning. The two sides of the skull-faced coin. Hood-cursed and foul ... and *deadly*. Do you understand me? Don't even think of trying them.'

Keruli's voice emerged from the carriage, 'Even more poignantly, my friends, very soon, I fear, we will have *need* of those terrible men and their formidable powers.'

Gruntle turned with a scowl. The door's window shutter had been opened to a thin slit. 'What are these undead hunters, master? Do you know?'

There was a long pause before Keruli responded. 'I have

... suspicions. In any case, they are spinning threads of power across this land, like a web, from which they can sense any tremor. We cannot pass undetected—'

'Then let us turn round,' Stonny snapped. 'Now, before it's too late.'

'But it already is,' Keruli replied. 'These undead servants continue to cross the river from the southlands, all in service to the Pannion Seer. They range ever closer to Saltoan. Indeed, I believe there are now more of them behind us than between here and Capustan.'

Hood-damned convenient, Master Keruli.

'We must,' the man within the carriage continued, 'fashion a temporary alliance with these necromancers – until we reach Capustan.'

'Well,' Gruntle said, '*they* certainly view it as an obvious course to take.'

'They are practical men, for all their other . . . faults.'

'The Barghast will not travel with them,' Hetan snarled.

'I don't think we have any choice,' Gruntle sighed. 'And that includes you and your brothers, Hetan. What's the point of finding these undead hunters only to have them tear you to pieces?'

'You think we come unprepared for such battle? We stood long in the bone circle, Captain, whilst every shaman of the gathered clans danced the weft of power. Long in the bone circle.'

'Three days and three nights,' Cafal growled.

No wonder she damn near ripped my chest open last night.

Keruli spoke. 'It may prove insufficient, should your efforts draw the full attention of the Pannion Seer. Captain, how many days of travel before we reach Capustan?'

You know as well as I. 'Four, master.'

'Surely, Hetan, you and your brothers can achieve a certain stoicism for such a brief length of time? We well understand your outrage. The desecration of your sacred ancestors is an insult not easily accommodated. But, do not

267

your own kind bow to a certain pragmatism in this regard as well? The inscribed wards, the sticksnares? Consider this an extension of such necessity . . .'

Hetan spat, turned away. 'It is as you say,' she conceded after a moment. 'Necessary. Very well.'

Gruntle returned to Bauchelain and the others. The two sorcerors were crouched down with the shattered axle between them. The stench of melted iron wafted up.

'Our repairs, Captain,' Bauchelain murmured, 'will not take long.'

'Good. You said there's three of these creatures out there – how far away?'

'Our small shaman friend keeps pace with the hunters. Less than a league, and I assure you, they can – if they so will it – cover that distance in a matter of a few hundred heartbeats. We will have little warning, but enough to muster a defence, I believe.'

'Why are you travelling to Capustan?'

The sorceror glanced up, an eyebrow lifting. 'No particular reason. By nature, we wander. Upon arriving on the west coast of this continent, we set our sights eastward. Capustan is as far as we can travel east, yes?'

'Close enough, I suppose. The land juts further east to the south, beyond Elingarth, but the kingdoms and city states down there are little more than pirate and bandit holdings. Besides, you'd have to pass through the Pannion Domin to get there.'

'And I gather that would be trying.'

'You'd never make it.'

Bauchelain smiled, bent once more to concentrate on the axle.

Looking up, Gruntle finally caught Buke's eye. A slight head movement drew the man – reluctantly – off to one side.

'You're in trouble, friend,' the captain said in a low voice.

Buke scowled, said nothing – but the truth was evident in his eyes.

'When we reach Capustan, take the closing coin and don't look back. I know, Buke, you were right in your suspicions – I saw what was within the carriage. *I saw*. They'll do worse than kill you if you try anything. Do you understand? Worse.'

The man grinned wryly, squinted out to the east. 'You think we'll make it that far, do you, Gruntle? Well, surprise – we won't live to see the next dawn.' He fixed wild eyes on the captain. 'You wouldn't believe what my masters unleashed – such a nightmare menagerie of servants, guardians, spirit-slayers – and their own powers! Hood take us! Yet all of it barely managed to drive one of those beasts off, and when the other two arrived, we were the ones retreating. That menagerie is nothing but smouldering pieces scattered for leagues across the plain. Gruntle, I saw *demons* cut to shreds. Aye, these two look unshaken, but believe me, that's of no account. None at all.' He lowered his voice still further. 'They are insane, friend. Thoroughly, ice-blooded, lizard-eyed insane. And poor Mancy's been with them for three years now and counting – the stories he's told me . . .' The man shuddered.

'Mancy? Oh, Emancipor Reese. Where's the cat, by the way?'

Buke barked a laugh. 'Ran off – just like all our horses and we had an even dozen of them after those stupid bandits attacked us. Ran off, once I'd done prying its claws from Mancy's back, which was where it jumped when all the warrens broke loose.'

Repairs completed and carriage righted, the journey resumed. A league or two of daylight remained. Stonny once again rode to point, Cafal and Netok taking their places ranging on the flanks. Emancipor guided the carriage, the two sorcerors having retired within.

Buke and Gruntle walked a few paces ahead of Keruli's carriage, saying little for a long while, until the captain sighed heavily and glanced at his friend. 'For what it's worth, there's people who don't want to see you dead, Buke. They see you wasting away inside, and they care enough so that it pains them—'

'Guilt's a good weapon, Gruntle, or at least it has been for a long time. Doesn't cut any more, though. If you choose to care, then you better swallow the pain. I don't give a damn, myself.'

'Stonny—'

'Is worth more than messing herself up with me. I'm not interested in being saved, anyway. Tell her that.'

'You tell her, Buke, and when she puts her fist in your face just remember that I warned you here and now. You tell her – I won't deliver your messages of self-pity.'

'Back off, Gruntle. I'd hurt you bad before you finished using those cutlasses on me.'

'Oh, that's sweet – get one of your few remaining friends to kill you. Seems I was wrong, it's not just self-pity, is it? You're not obsessed with the tragic deaths of your family, you're obsessed with yourself, Buke. Your guilt's an endlessly rising tide, and that ego of yours is a levee and all you do is keep slapping fresh bricks on it. The wall gets higher and higher, and you're looking down on the world from a lofty height – with a Hood-damned sneer.'

Buke was pale and trembling. 'If that's the way you see it,' he rasped, 'then why call me friend at all?'

Beru knows, I'm beginning to wonder. He drew a deep breath, managed to calm himself down. 'We've known each other a long time. We've never crossed blades.' *And you were in the habit of getting drunk for days on end, a habit you broke . . . but one I haven't. Took the deaths of everyone you loved to do that, and I'm terrified it might take the same for me.*

Thank Hood the lass married that fat merchant.

'Doesn't sound like much, Gruntle.'

We're two of a kind, you bastard – cut past your own ego and you'd see that fast enough. But he said nothing.

'Sun's almost down,' Buke observed after a time. 'They'll attack when it's dark.'

270

'How do you defend against them?'

'You don't. Can't. Like chopping into wood, from what I've seen, and they're fast. Gods, *they're fast!* We're all dead, Gruntle. Bauchelain and Korbal Broach ain't got much left – did you see them sweat mending the carriage? They're wrung dry, those two.'

'Keruli is a mage as well,' Gruntle said. 'Well, more likely a priest.'

'Let's hope his god's cocked an eye on us, then.'

And what are the chances of that?

With the sun's light pooling crimson on the horizon behind them, they made camp. Stonny guided the horses and oxen into a makeshift, rope-lined kraal to one side of the carriages – a position that would give them a chance to flee inland if it came to that.

A kind of resignation descended within the growing gloom as a meal was prepared over a small fire, Harllo electing himself cook. Neither Keruli nor the two sorcerors emerged from their respective carriages to join the small group.

Moths gathered around the smokeless flames. Sipping mulled wine, Gruntle watched their fluttering, mindless plunges into oblivion with a faintly bitter amusement.

Darkness closed in, the scatter of stars overhead sharpening. With the supper done, Hetan rose. 'Harllo, come with me now. Quickly.'

'My lady?' the man enquired.

Gruntle sprayed a mouthful of wine. Choking, coughing, with Stonny pounding on his back, it was a while before he managed to recover. Through watering eyes, he grinned at Harllo. 'You heard the lady.'

He watched his friend's eyes slowly grow wide.

Impatient, Hetan stepped forward and gripped Harllo by one arm. She pulled him to his feet, then dragged him out into the darkness.

Staring after them, Stonny frowned. 'What's all that about?'

Not a single man spoke up.

She swung a glare on Gruntle. After a moment, she hissed with understanding. 'What an outrage!'

'My dear,' the captain laughed, 'after Saltoan, that's a little rich coming from you.'

'Don't you "dear" me, Gruntle! What are the rest of us supposed to do – sit here and listen to gross grunting and groaning from that hump of grasses over there? Disgusting!'

'Really, Stonny. In the circumstances, it makes perfect sense—'

'It's not *that*, you idiot! That woman chose *Harllo*! Gods, I'm going to be sick! Harllo! Look around this fire – there's you, and let's face it, a certain type of uncultured, trashy woman couldn't resist you. And Buke, tall and weathered with a tortured soul – surely worth a snakefight or three. But Harllo? That tangled-haired ape?'

'He's got big hands,' Gruntle murmured. 'So Hetan observed last . . . uh, last night.'

Stonny stared, then leaned forward. '*She had you last night!* Didn't she? That loose, grease-smeared savage had you! I can see the truth in your smug face, Gruntle, so don't deny it!'

'Well, you just heard her – how could any warm-blooded man resist?'

'Fine, then!' she snapped, rising. 'Buke, on your feet, damn you.'

He flinched back. 'No – I couldn't – I, uh, no, I'm sorry, Stonny—'

Snarling, she whirled on the two silent Barghast.

Cafal smiled. 'Choose Netok. He's yet—'

'Fine!' She gestured.

The youth rose unsteadily.

'Big hands,' Gruntle observed.

'Shut up, Gruntle.'

'Head in the other direction, please,' he continued. 'You wouldn't want to stumble over anything . . . unsightly.'

'Damn right in that. Let's go, Netok.'

They walked off, the Barghast trailing like a pup on a leash.

The captain swung to Buke. 'You fool.'

The man just shook his head, staring down at the fire.

Emancipor Reese reached for the tin pot holding the spiced wine. 'Two more nights,' he muttered. 'Typical.'

Gruntle stared at the old man for a moment, then grinned. 'We ain't dead yet – who knows, maybe Oponn's smiling down on you.'

'That'd make a change,' Reese grumbled.

'How in Hood's name did you get tied up with your two masters, anyway?'

'Long story,' he muttered, sipping at his wine. 'Too long to tell, really. My wife, you see . . . Well, the posting offered travel . . .'

'Are you suggesting you chose the lesser of two evils?'

'Heavens forfend, sir.'

'Ah, you've regrets now, then.'

'I didn't say that, neither.'

A sudden yowl from the darkness startled everyone.

'Which one made that sound, I wonder?' Gruntle mused.

'None,' Reese said. 'My cat's come back.'

A carriage door opened. Moments later Bauchelain's black-clad form appeared. 'Our sticksnare returns . . . hastily. I suggest you call in the others and prepare your weapons. Tactically, attempt to hamstring these hunters, and stay low when you close – they prefer horizontal cuts. Emancipor, if you would kindly join us. Captain Gruntle, perhaps you might inform your master, though no doubt he is already aware.'

Suddenly chilled, Gruntle rose. 'We'll be lucky to see anything, dammit.'

'That will not be an issue,' Bauchelain replied. 'Korbal, dear friend,' he called out behind him, 'a broad circle of light, if you please.'

The area was suddenly bathed in a soft, golden glow, reaching out thirty or more paces on all sides.

The cat yowled again and Gruntle caught sight of a tawny flash, darting back out into the darkness. Hetan and Harllo approached from one side, hastily tucking in clothing. Stonny and Netok arrived as well. The captain managed a strained grin. 'Not enough time, I take it,' he said to her.

Stonny grimaced. 'You should be more forgiving – it was the lad's first try.'

'Oh, right.'

'A damned shame, too,' she added, pulling on her duelling gloves. 'He had potental, despite the grease.'

The three Barghast had gathered now, Cafal jabbing a row of lances into the stony earth whilst Hetan busied herself tying a thick cord to join the three of them. Fetishes of feather and bone hung from knots in the cord, and Gruntle judged that the span between each warrior would be five or six arm-lengths. When the other two were done, Netok handed them double-bladed axes. All three set the weapons down at their feet and collected a lance each. Hetan leading, they began a soft, rumbling chant.

'Captain.'

Gruntle pulled his gaze from the Barghast and found Master Keruli at his side. The man's hands were folded on his lap, his silk cape shimmering like water. 'The protection I can offer is limited. Stay close to me, you and Harllo and Stonny. Do not allow yourselves to be drawn forward. Concentrate on defence.'

Unsheathing his cutlasses, Gruntle nodded. Harllo moved to the captain's left, his two-handed sword held steady before him. Stonny stood to Gruntle's right, rapier and sticker readied.

He feared for her the most. Her weapons were too light for what was coming – he recalled the chop-marks on Bauchelain's carriage. This would be brutal strength at play here, not finesse. 'Stay back a step, Stonny,' he said.

'Don't be stupid.'

'I'm not talking chivalry, Stonny. Poking wire-thin holes won't hurt an undead.'

'We'll just see, won't we?'

'Stay close to the master – guard him. That's an order, Stonny.'

'I hear you,' she growled.

Gruntle faced Keruli again. 'Sir, who is your god? If you call upon him or her, what should we expect?'

The round-faced man frowned slightly. 'Expect? I am afraid I have no idea, Captain. My – uh – god's powers are newly awakened from thousands of years of sleep. My god is *Elder*.'

Gruntle stared. *Elder? Weren't the Elder gods abandoned because of their ferocity? What might be unleashed here? Queen of Dreams defend us.*

He watched as Keruli drew forth a thin-bladed dagger and cut deep into his left palm. Blood dripped into the grass at his feet. The air suddenly smelled like a slaughterhouse.

A small, man-shaped collection of sticks and twigs and twine scurried into the circle of light, trailing sorcery like smoke. *The sticksnared shaman.*

Gruntle felt the earth shuddering to fast approaching steps, a low, relentless drumming like warhorses. *No, more like giants. Upright, five pairs, maybe more.* They were coming from the east.

Ghostly shapes loomed into sight, then faded again. The tremors in the earth slowed, scattered, as the creatures spread out.

The Barghast chant ended abruptly. Gruntle glanced in their direction. The three warriors faced east, lances ready. Coils of fog rose around their legs, thickening. In moments Hetan and her brothers would be completely enveloped.

Silence.

The familiar leather-bound grips of the heavy cutlasses felt slick in Gruntle's hands. He could feel the thud of his heart in his chest. Sweat gathered, dripped from chin and lips. He strained to see into the darkness beyond the sphere of light. Nothing. *The soldier's moment, now, before the battle begins – who would choose such a life? You stand with others, all facing the same threat, all feeling so very alone. In the cold embrace of fear, that sense that all that you are might end in moments. Gods, I've no envy for a soldier's life—*

Flat, wide, fang-bristling faces – sickly pale like snake bellies – emerged from the darkness. Eyes empty pits, the heads seemed to hover for a moment, as if suspended, at a height twice that of a man. Huge black-pocked iron swords slid into the light. The blades were fused to the creatures' wrists – no hands were visible – and Gruntle knew that a single blow from one of those swords could cut through a man's thigh effortlessly.

Reptilian, striding on hind legs like giant wingless birds and leaning forward with the counterweight of long, tapering tails, the undead apparitions wore strangely mottled armour: across the shoulders, on the chest to either side of the jutting sternum, and high on the hips. Skull-cap helmets, low and long, protected head and nape, with sweeping cheek-guards meeting over the snout to join and bend sharply to form a bridge-guard.

At Gruntle's side Keruli hissed. 'K'Chain Che'Malle. K'ell Hunters, these ones. Firstborn of every brood. The Matron's own children. Fading memories even to the Elder gods, this knowledge. Now, in my heart, I feel dismay.'

'What in Hood's name are they waiting for?' the captain growled.

'Uneasy – the swirling cloud that is Barghast sorcery. An unknown to their master.'

Disbelieving, the captain asked, 'The Pannion Seer commands these—'

The five hunters attacked. Heads darting forward, blades rising, they were a blur. Three struck for the Barghast, plunging towards that thick, twisting fog. The other two charged Bauchelain and Korbal Broach.

Moments before reaching the cloud, three lances flashed out, all striking the lead hunter. Sorcery ripped through the beast's withered, lifeless flesh with a sound like spikes driven into – then through – tree trunks. Dark grey muscle tissue, bronze-hued bone and swaths of burning hide flew in all directions. The hunter's head wobbled atop a shattered neck. The K'Chain Che'Malle staggered, then collapsed, even as its two kin swept round it and vanished into the sorcerous cloud. Iron on iron rang explosively from within.

Before Bauchelain and Korbal Broach, the other two hunters were engulfed in roiling, black waves of sorcery before they had taken two strides. The magic lacerated their bodies, splashed rotting, acidic stains that devoured their hides. The beasts drove through without pause, to be met by the two mages – both wearing ankle-length coats of black chain, both wielding hand-and-a-half swords that trailed streamers of smoke.

''Ware behind us!' Harllo suddenly screamed.

Gruntle spun.

To see a sixth hunter darting through screaming, bolting horses, charging directly for Keruli. Unlike the other K'Chain Che'Malle, this creature's hide was covered in intricate markings, and bore a dorsal ridge of steel spikes running down its spine.

Gruntle threw a shoulder against Keruli, sending the man sprawling. Ducking low, he threw up both cutlasses in time to catch a horizontal slash from one of the hunter's massive blades. The Gadrobi steel rang deafeningly, the impact bolting like shocks up the captain's arms. Gruntle heard more than felt his left wrist snap, the broken ends of the bones grinding and twisting impossibly before suddenly senseless hands released the cutlasses – wheeling, spinning away. The hunter's second blade should have cut him in half. Instead, it clashed against Harllo's two-handed sword. Both weapons shattered. Harllo lurched away, his chest and face spraying blood from a savage hail of iron shards.

A taloned, three-toed foot struck Gruntle on an upward track. Grunting, the captain was thrown into the air. Pain exploded in his skull as he collided with the hunter's jaw, snapping the creature's head up with a bone-breaking, crunching sound.

Stunned, the breath driven from his lungs, Gruntle fell to the ground in a heap. An enormous weight pinned him, talons puncturing armour to pierce flesh. The three toes clenched around his chest, snapping bones, and he felt himself dragged forward. The scales of his armour clicked and clattered, dropping away as he was pulled along through dust and gravel. Twisted buckles and clasps dug into the earth. Blind, limbs flopping, Gruntle felt the talons digging ever deeper. He coughed and his mouth filled with frothy blood. The world darkened.

He felt the talons shudder, as if resonating from some massive blow. Another followed, then another. The claws spasmed. Then he was lifted into the air again, sent flying. Striking the ground, rolling, crashing up against the shattered spokes of a carriage wheel.

He felt himself dying, knew himself dying. He forced his eyes open, desperate for one last look upon the world – something, anything to drive away this overwhelming sense of confused sadness. *Could it not have been sudden? Instant? Why this lingering, bemused draining away? Gods, even the pain is gone – why not awareness itself? Why torture me with the knowing of what I am about to surrender?*

Someone was shrieking, the sound one of dying, and Gruntle understood it at once. *Oh yes, scream your defiance, your terror and your rage – scream at that web even as it closes about you. Waves of sound out into the mortal world, one last time—* The shrieks fell away, and now there was silence, save for the stuttering heart in Gruntle's chest.

He knew his eyes were open, yet he could see nothing. Either Korbal Broach's spell of light had failed, or the captain had found his own darkness.

Stumbling, that heart. Slowing, fading like a pale horse riding away down a road. Farther, fainter, fainter . . .

278

BOOK TWO

HEARTHSTONE

Midnight comes often in the dusk of my life, when
I look back upon all that I have survived. The deaths
of so many for whom I cared and loved in my heart,
have expunged all sense of glory from my thoughts.
To have escaped those random fates has lost all
triumph.

I know you have seen me, friend, my lined face
and silent regard, the cold calcretions that slow
my embittered pace, as I walk down the last
years, clothed in darkness as are all old men,
haunted by memories . . .

The Road Before You
Jhorum of Capustan

CHAPTER SEVEN

And all who would walk the fields
when the Boar of Summer strides
in drum-beat hooves,
and the Iron Forest converges
to its fated, inevitable clash – all,
all are as children, as children once more.

Fener's Reve
Destriant Dellem (b?)

Born on a sea dark as spiced wine, the wind moaned its way across the seaside killing ground, over and around the East Watch on its low, brick-strewn hill, where faint torchlight glimmered from the fortress's battened shutters. The wind's voice rose in pitch as it rolled up against the city's mortarless walls, flinging salty spray against its rounded, weathered stone. Rising then, the night's breath reached the battlements and swept between the merlons and along the platforms, then down into Capustan's curving, undulating streets, where not a soul stirred.

From the corner tower parapet looming above the ancient barracks, Karnadas stood facing the storm, alone, his boar-maned cloak whipping in the savage gusts. Though the parapet's killing arc guarded the southeast approach, from his position he could just make out, five hundred paces to the north along the wall, the object of his fiercest attention.

The brooding, cliff-like palace of Prince Jelarkan was like no other building in Capustan. Windowless, the grey-stoned structure towered in a chaotic confusion of planes, angles, overhangs and seemingly pointless ledges. It rose well above the flanking coast-facing wall, and in his mind's eye the mercenary watched huge boulders arcing towards it from the killing field beyond, crashing into its sides, sending the whole edifice down into ruin.

Unworthy of you. Where resides the comforting knowledge of history's vast, cyclical sweep, the ebb and flow of wars and of peace? Peace is the time of waiting for war. A time of preparation, or a time of wilful ignorance, blind, blinkered and prattling behind secure walls.

Within the palace, the Mortal Sword Brukhalian was mired in yet another meeting with the prince and a half-dozen representatives of the Mask Council. The Grey Swords' commander forbore such tangled marathons with what seemed to Karnadas superhuman patience. *I would never have suffered this spider-bitten dance, not this long, not night after night, weeks on end. Still, it's remarkable what can be achieved even as the debates rage on, and on. How many of the Mortal Sword's – and Prince Jelarkan's – proposals have already been implemented, whilst the wrangling continues unending and those masked bastards utter their lists of objections in all ignorance. It's too late, you fools – we've already done what we could . . . to save your damned city.*

In his mind's eye rose the fur-painted, articulated mask of the one priest on the Council he and the company should have been able to count on as an ally. Rath'Fener spoke for the Boar of Summer – the Grey Swords' own patron god. *But political ambition consumes you, as it does your rivals in the Council. You kneel before summer's bloody tusk, yet . . . is it naught but a lie?*

The wind howled, the only answer to Karnadas's silent question. Lightning lit the clouds churning over the distant bay. Rath'Fener was a priest of the Sceptred Rank, a veteran of temple politics and thus at the pinnacle of what a mortal could achieve within Fener's sanctified walls. *But the Boar of Summer is not a civilized god. Ranks and orders and ivory-clasped gowns . . . secular pomp, petty plays of arrogance in the pursuit of mundane power. No, I must not impugn Rath'Fener with questions of his faith – he serves our god in his own way.*

The Boar of Summer was the voice of war. Dark and grisly, as ancient as humanity itself. The song of battle – the screams of the dying and the vengeful, the discordant, hacking music of iron weapons, of shields resounding to blows, of hissing arrows and quarrels . . . *And forgive us all, the voice grows to a roar. It is not the time to hide behind temple walls. Not the time for foolish politics. We serve Fener by striding the soaked, steaming earth, weapons bared in quicksilver promise. We are the clash and clangour, the bellows of rage, pain and terror . . .*

Rath'Fener was not the only priest of the Boar in this city to have achieved a Sceptred Rank. The difference was this: while Rath'Fener possessed such an ambition – to kneel before the boar cloak and humbly assume the ancient title of Destriant, vacant for so long – Karnadas had already achieved it.

Karnadas could put Rath'Fener in his place with a simple unveiling of his own position in the mortal hierarchy. *In his place? I could depose the bastard with a gesture.* But Brukhalian had forbidden him that sweet revelation. Nor could the Mortal Sword be swayed. The time for such a move was not propitious, he'd said, its yield as yet of too low a currency. *Patience, Karnadas, that time will come . . .*

Not an easy thing to accept . . .

'Is this a welcome night, Destriant?'

'Ah, Itkovian, I did not see you there in the gloom. 'Tis the Boar's storm, this night. So, how long have you stood there, Shield Anvil?' *How long, in your cold, closed-in fashion, have you stared upon your High Priest? Black-mannered Itkovian, will you ever unsheathe your true self?*

There was no way to read the man's expression in the darkness. 'Moments only, Destriant.'

'Does sleep elude you, sir?'

'Not when I seek it.'

Looking upon the Shield Anvil's blue chain surcoat beneath the grey rain-cape, the wrist-length cuffed gauntlets now slick and black with rain, Karnadas slowly nodded. 'I had not realized it was so close to dawn. Do you anticipate being gone for long?'

Itkovian shrugged. 'No, assuming they have indeed crossed in strength. I am restricted to leading but two wings in any case. Should we come upon little more than scouting parties, however, then the first blows against the Domin shall be made.'

'At last,' the Destriant said, grimacing as yet another gust of wind roiled over the battlement.

There was silence for a while.

Then Karnadas cleared his throat. 'What then, may I ask, has brought you up here, Shield Anvil?'

'The Mortal Sword has returned from the latest gathering. He wishes to speak with you.'

'And he has sat patiently waiting whilst we chatted?'

'I would imagine so, Destriant.'

The two Grey Swords turned to the tower's spiral stairs. They descended the slick, limned steps amidst streams trickling down the stone walls to either side. By the third tier down they could see their breaths. Until the arrival of the company, these barracks had been left virtually uninhabited for close to a century. The chill that had seeped into the thick-walled old fortress keep defied every effort to dispel it. Among the major structures in Capustan, it predated the Daru Keep – now re-named the Thrall and home to the Mask Council – and every other building with the exception of Prince Jelarkan's Palace. *And that palace was not raised by human hands, most certainly not. I'd swear that on Fener's bristly hump.*

Reaching ground level, Itkovian pushed open the

squealing door that led directly into the central Round Hall. Alone in the massive, barely furnished chamber stood the Mortal Sword Brukhalian, motionless before the hearth and almost spectral despite his formidable height and build. His back was to the two newcomers, his long, wavy black hair unbound and down to just above his belted hips.

'Rath'Trake believes,' the commander rumbled without turning, 'there are unwelcome intruders on the plains west of the city. Demonic apparitions.'

Karnadas unclasped his cloak and shook the water from it. 'Rath'Trake, you said. I admit I do not understand the Tiger's sudden claim to true godhood. That a cult of a First Hero should have succeeded in shouldering its way into a council of temples—'

Brukhalian slowly turned, his soft brown eyes fixing on the Destriant. 'An unworthy rivalry, sir. The Season of Summer is home to more than one voice of war, or would you now challenge the fierce spirits of the Barghast and the Rhivi as well?'

'First Heroes are not gods,' Karnadas growled, rubbing at his face as the cold, wind-blasted numbness faded. 'They're not even tribal spirits, sir. Have any of the other priests supported Rath'Trake's claim?'

'No.'

'I thought as—'

'Of course,' Brukhalian went on, 'they also are not convinced that the Pannion Domin intends to lay siege to Capustan.'

Karnadas clamped his mouth shut. *Point taken, Mortal Sword.*

Brukhalian's gaze flicked to Itkovian. 'Are your wings unfurled, Shield Anvil?'

'They are, sir.'

'It would be foolish, do you not think, sir,' the Mortal Sword said, 'to discard such warnings during your patrol?'

'I discard nothing, sir. We shall be vigilant.'

'As you always are, Shield Anvil. You may take charge

of your wings, now, sir. The Twin Tusks guard you.'

Itkovian bowed, then strode from the room.

'And now, dear priest,' Brukhalian said. 'Are you certain of this . . . invitation of yours?'

Karnadas shook his head. 'No, I am not. I can discern nothing of its sender's identity, nor even if its stance is true to ours or inimical.'

'Yet it awaits a reply still?'

'Yes, Mortal Sword, it does.'

'Then let us make one. Now.'

Karnadas's eyes widened slightly. 'Sir, perhaps then we should call in a Mane, in case we invite an enemy into our midst?'

'Destriant, you forget. I am Fener's own weapon.'

Aye, but will that be enough? 'As you say, sir.' Karnadas strode to a cleared space in the chamber. He folded back the sodden sleeves of his shirt, then made a slight gesture with his left hand. A small, pulsing orb of light took form in front of the priest. 'This fashioning is in our language,' he said, studying the manifestation again. 'The language of Fener's Reve, intimating a certain knowledge of our company and its immortal benefactor. There is a message intended in such knowing.'

'Which you have yet to ascertain.'

A scowl flickered for a moment in the Destriant's weathered face. 'I have narrowed the list of possibilities, Mortal Sword. Such knowledge suggests arrogance in the sender, or, indeed, it offers us a hint of brotherhood.'

'Release the invitation, sir.'

'As you command.' He gestured again. The orb brightened, then began growing, its light thinning, the sphere growing translucent. Karnadas stepped back to give it space, fighting down his alarm at the sheer power behind this communication. 'Sir, there are souls within this. Not two or three – a dozen, maybe more – yet they are bound within one. I have not seen its like before.'

A figure, sitting cross-legged, slowly took form within

286

the orb, dark-skinned, lean, wearing light leather armour. The man's face showed an expression of mild surprise. In the background, the two Grey Swords could see the interior walls of a small tent. A brazier sat before the man, giving his dark eyes a lurid glow.

'Address him,' Brukhalian commanded.

'In what language, sir? Our native Elin?'

The figure cocked his head at the quiet exchange. 'That's an awkward dialect,' he said in Daru, 'with Daru the obvious mother. Can you understand me?'

Karnadas nodded. 'Aye, close enough to Capan.'

The man straightened. 'Capan? I've reached through, then! You are in Capustan, excellent. Are you the city's rulers, then?'

The Destriant frowned. 'You do not know us? Your . . . communication suggested a certain knowledge of our Reve . . .'

'Ah, yes, well, that particular weaving of my warrens has a way of reflecting those who stumble on it – though only among priests, of course, the target it was intended to reach. I assume you are of Capustan's temple council? What's that title again – Mask Council, yes?'

'No,' Brukhalian rumbled, 'we are not.'

'Go on, please, I am truly intrigued now.'

'Pleased to hear it, sir,' the Mortal Sword replied, stepping forward. 'Your invitation has been answered by Destriant Karnadas – who stands beside me – at my request. I command the Grey Swords—'

'Mercenaries! Hood's breath! If I'd wanted to contact a bunch of over-priced sword-hackers—'

'Sir.' Brukhalian's voice was hard but low. 'We are an army of the Boar of Summer. Sworn to Fener. Each soldier among us has chosen this path. Schooled in the sacred scriptures, blessed by the Destriant's hand in the Tusked One's name. Aye, we are a company of . . . sword-hackers. We are also our own temple, our acolytes numbering well over seven thousand – and the number grows with each day.'

'All right, all right, sir, I understand now. Wait – you say you're growing? The city's given you leave to accept new followers?'

Brukhalian smiled. 'Capustan is but half armed, sir. Remnants of its tribal origins remain, and peculiar ones they are. Women are forbidden from the art of war. The Boar of Summer, however, acknowledges no such arbitrary exclusions—'

'And you're getting away with it?' the man laughed.

'Our new acolytes number but twelve hundred to date. Since many second and third born daughters are cast out onto the city's streets, none among the rulers have as yet noticed the diminishment of those numbers. Now, I have granted you enough in the way of introduction. Who, sir, are you?'

'How rude of me. I am Adaephon Ben Delat. To make things simpler, call me Quick Ben—'

'You are from Darujhistan?' Karnadas asked.

'Hood, no, I mean, no, I am not. I am with . . . uh, Caladan Brood.'

'We have heard that name since coming north,' Brukhalian said. 'A warlord who leads an army against an invading empire.'

'Well, that invading empire has . . . withdrawn its interests. In any case, we are seeking to get a message through to Capustan's rulers . . .'

'If only it were that simple,' Karnadas muttered.

The Mortal Sword was nodding. 'Then you must choose, sir. The Mask Council and the city's Prince Jelarkan are balanced upon the claim. There are countless factions among the council itself, and some discord has resulted. The Grey Swords answer to the prince. Our task is simple – to make the taking of Capustan by the Pannion Domin too costly. The Seer's expansion will stop at the city's walls and go no further. Thus, you can deliver your warlord's message to me and hence to the prince. Or you can resume your attempts to contact the Mask Council.'

'We suspected it'd get complicated,' Quick Ben sighed. 'We know next to nothing of your company. Or, rather, knew next to little. With this contact I am no longer so ignorant.' The man's eyes swung to Karnadas. 'Destriant. In Fener's Reve that means Arch-Priest, doesn't it? But only in the martial arena – the temple of hallowed ground that is the field of battle. Does Fener's representative in the Mask Council acknowledge that you outrank him or her, as a tiger does a cat?'

Karnadas grimaced. 'He does not know my true title, sir. There are reasons for that. I am impressed by your knowledge of Fener's priesthood. No, more than impressed. I am stunned.'

The man seemed to flinch. 'Well, yes. Thank you.' He turned to study Brukhalian. 'You're the god's Mortal Sword.' He paused then, and it was as if the full significance of that title only now struck home, for his eyes slowly widened. 'Uh, all right. I think the warlord would endorse my decision to deliver his message to you. In fact, I have no doubt at all. Good.' He drew a breath, then resumed. 'Caladan Brood leads an army to the relief of Capustan. The siege – as I'm sure you well understand – is not only inevitable, it is imminent. Now, our challenge is getting there in time—'

'Sir,' Brukhalian interrupted, frowning, 'how large is Caladan Brood's army? Understand, we will be facing perhaps sixty thousand Pannions – veterans one and all. Does he grasp the maelstrom he so generously wishes to enter on our behalf?'

'Well, we don't have the numbers to match. But we will be' – Quick Ben grinned – 'bringing a few surprises with us. Now, Destriant – we need to reconvene. I need to bring the warlord and his officers in on this. Can I suggest we resume this conversation in a bell's time?'

'Perhaps it would be best to postpone it until the dead of night, sir,' Brukhalian said. 'My daylight hours are rather full – and public. As are Prince Jelarkan's.'

Quick Ben nodded. 'Two bells before next dawn, then.' He glanced around all of a sudden. 'I'll need a bigger tent . . .'

A moment later he faded from view. The sphere contracted once more, then slowly vanished at a wave from Karnadas. The Destriant turned to Brukhalian. 'This was unexpected.'

The Mortal Sword grunted. 'We must be certain to condition the prince, sir. Perhaps this warlord's army can harry the besieging forces slightly, but it will probably achieve little else. We must keep Jelarkan's vision realistic . . . assuming we tell him.'

We'll not win this war. Aye. No false hopes here.

Brukhalian asked, 'What think you of this Quick Ben?'

'A man of many veils, sir. An ex-priest of Fener, perhaps. His knowledge was too precise.'

'Many souls, within one, you said.'

Karnadas shivered. 'I must have been mistaken,' he said. 'Perhaps the ritual required the assistance of other mages, and it was these that I sensed.'

Brukhalian studied his priest long and hard at that, but said nothing. He turned away after a moment. 'You look exhausted, sir. Get some sleep.'

Karnadas slowly bowed.

As the spell faded, Quick Ben sighed, glanced to his right. 'Well?'

Seated against the tent's wall on that side, Whiskeyjack leaned forward to refill their goblets with Gredfallan ale. 'They'll fight,' the bearded man said, 'for a while at least. That commander looks a tough sword-hacker, but it might be all show and no iron – he must be a shrewd enough man of business to know the value of appearances. What was that you called him?'

'Mortal Sword. Not likely – once, long ago, that title was for real. Long before the Deck of Dragons acknowledged the place of Knights of the High Houses, Fener's cult had its own. They've got the serious titles down with exactness. Destriant ... Hood's breath, there hasn't been a real Destriant in the cult for a thousand years. The titles are for show, Whiskeyjack—'

'Indeed,' the commander cut in, 'then why keep it a secret from the Fener priest on the Mask Council?'

'Uh. Well ... Oh, it's simple. That priest would know it for a lie, of course. There, easy answer to your question.'

'Easy answer, as you say. So, are easy answers always right answers, Quick?'

Ignoring the question, the wizard drained his goblet. 'In any case, I'd count the Grey Swords as best among the bunch over there, but that's not saying much.'

'Were they fooled by the "accidental" contact?'

'I think so. I'd shaped the spell to reflect the company's own nature – whether greedy and rapacious, or honourable or whatever. I admit, though, I didn't expect it to find pious faith. Still, the spell was intended to be malleable, and so it was.'

Whiskeyjack climbed to his feet, wincing as he put his weight down on his bad leg. 'I'd better track down Brood and Dujek, then.'

'At the head of the column, is my guess,' Quick Ben said.

'You're sharp tonight,' the commander noted as he made his way out.

A moment later, when Whiskeyjack's sarcasm finally seeped into Quick Ben's thoughts, he scowled.

On the other side of the street, opposite the barracks gate and behind an ancient bronze fence, was a cemetery that had once belonged to one of Capustan's founding tribes. The sun-fired columns of mud with their spiral incisions – each one containing an upright corpse – rose like the boles of a crowded forest in the cemetery's heart, surrounded on all sides by the more mundane Daru stone urns. The city's history was a tortured, bizarre tale, and it had been Itkovian's task among the company to glean its depths. The

Shield Anvil of the Grey Swords was a position that demanded both scholarly pursuits and military prowess. While many would hold the two disciplines as distinct, the truth was in fact the opposite.

From histories and philosophies and religions came an understanding of human motivation, and motivation lay at the heart of tactics and strategy. Just as people moved in patterns, so too did their thoughts. A Shield Anvil must predict, anticipate, and this applied to the potential actions of allies as well as enemies.

Before the arrival of Daru peoples from the west, the tribes that had founded Capustan had only a generation before been nomadic. *And their dead are left standing. Free to wander in their unseen spirit world.* That restless mobility resided still in the minds of the Capan, and since the Daru communities held to their own, it was scarcely diluted despite the now dozens of generations who had lived and died in this one place.

Yet much of Capustan's early history remained mysterious, and Itkovian found himself pondering what little he could piece together of those times, as he led the two wings of riders down the wide, cobbled street towards Jelarkan's Concourse, and beyond it to the south-facing Main Gate.

The rain was abating, the dawn's steel smear pushing through the heavy clouds to the east, the wind falling off into fitful gusts.

The districts making up the city were called Camps, and each Camp was a distinct, self-contained settlement, usually circular, with a private open ground at the central hub. The wide, uneven spaces between each Camp formed Capustan's streets. This pattern changed only in the area surrounding the old Daru Keep – now the Thrall and home to the Mask Council – called the Temple District, which represented the sole Daru-style imposition of a gridwork layout of streets.

The Camps, Itkovian suspected, had once been precisely that. Tribal encampments, tightly bound in ties of kinship.

292

Positioned on the banks of the Catlin River among sea-fearing peoples, this site had become a focus for trade, encouraging sedentary behaviour. The result was one of the oddest-looking cities Itkovian had ever seen. Wide, open concourses and avenues defined by curving walls; random clay stands of burial pillars; well pools surrounded by sand-pits; and, moving through Capustan's winding spaces, Daru and Capan citizens, the former holding to the disparate styles and ornamentation of their heritage – no two dressed alike – whilst the latter, kin-bound, wore the bright colours of their families, creating a flow in the streets that sharply contrasted with the plain, unpainted architecture. *The beauty of Capustan lies in its people, not in its buildings* . . . Even the Daru temples had bowed to the local, modest style of architecture. The effect was that of ceaseless move-ment, dominating its fixed, simple surroundings. The Capan tribes celebrated themselves, colours in a colourless world.

The only unknowns in Itkovian's scenario were the old keep that the Grey Swords now occupied, and Jelarkan's Palace. The old keep had been built before the coming of both the Capan and the Daru, by unknown hands, and it had been constructed almost in the shadow of the palace.

Jelarkan's fortress was a structure unlike anything Itkovian had ever seen before. It predated all else, its severe architecture throughly alien and strangely unwelcoming. No doubt the royal line of Capustan had chosen to occupy it for its imposing prominence rather than any particular notions of its defensive capacities. The stone walls were perilously thin, and its absence of windows or flat rooftops made those within it blind to all that occurred on the outside. Worse, there was but one entrance – the main approach, a wide ramp leading into a courtyard. Previous princes had raised guard houses to either side of the entrance, and a walkway along the courtyard's walls. Actual additions to the palace itself had a habit of falling down – the palace's stone facings refused to take mortar, for some reason, and the walls were not deemed strong enough to assume additional burdens of a substantial nature. In all, a curious edifice.

Passing out through the crowded Main Gate – harsh black iron and dark leather amidst streams of saturated colours – the troop swung right, rode a short distance down the south caravan road, then left it and its traffic as soon as they reached open plain, riding due west, past the few goat, cattle and sheep farms and their low stone walls breaking up the landscape, out onto unoccupied prairie.

As they moved further inland, the overcast above them began to clear, until by the midday break – fourteen leagues from Capustan – the sky above them was an unbroken blue. The meal was brief, conducted with few words among the thirty soldiers. They had crossed no-one's trail as yet, which, given it was nearing the height of caravan season, was unusual.

As the Grey Swords completed repacking their kits, the Shield Anvil addressed them for the first time since leaving the barracks. 'Raptor formation at slow canter. Outrider Sidlis twenty lengths to point. Everyone track-hunting.'

One soldier, a young woman acolyte and the only recruit in the company, asked, 'What kind of tracks are we looking for, sir?'

Ignoring the impropriety, Itkovian replied. 'Any kind, soldier. Wings mount up.'

He watched as the soldiers swung into their saddles in perfect unison, barring the recruit who struggled a moment before settling and closing up the reins.

Few words were offered at this early stage of training – the recruit either would quickly follow the example set by the experienced soldiers, or would not stay long in the company. She had been taught to ride, well enough not to fall off her horse at a canter, and was wearing her weapons and armour to get used to their weight. Schooling in the art of wielding those weapons would come later. If the wings found themselves in a skirmish, two veterans would guard the recruit at all times.

At the moment, the young woman's master was her horse. The chestnut gelding knew its place in the crooked wing shape of the raptor formation. If trouble came, it would also know enough to pull its rider away from danger.

It was enough that she had been chosen to accompany the patrol. *Train the soldier in the real world* was one of the company's tenets.

Spread out into the formation, with Itkovian as the raptor's head, the troop rode on at a slow canter. A league, then another as the heat slowly became oppressive.

The sudden slowing of the north wing pulled the others round as if invisible ropes bound every animal together. A trail had been found. Itkovian glanced ahead to see Outrider Sidlis slow her horse, wheel it round, confirming that both she and her mount had sensed the shift in motion behind them. She held position, watching.

The Shield Anvil slowed his horse as he approached his right-flanking riders.

'Report.'

'Recruit caught the trail first, sir,' the wing's spokesman said. 'The tip of a spiral. The pattern of discovery that followed suggests a northwest direction. Something upright, on two legs, sir. Large. Three-toed and taloned.'

'Just the one set?'

'Yes, sir.'

'How old?'

'Passed this way this morning, sir.'

A second glance at Sidlis brought her riding back towards the troop.

'Relieve the outrider, Nakalian. We'll pick up this trail and pursue.'

'Sir,' the spokesman acknowledged. He hesitated, then said, 'Shield Anvil, the span between the steps is . . . vast. The creature was moving with speed.'

Itkovian met the soldier's eyes. 'How fast, sir? A canter? Gallop?'

'Hard to know for certain. I'd judge twice a canter, sir.'

We have, it seems, found our demonic apparition. 'Archers on the tips. All others barring Torun, Farakalian and the recruit, lances to hand. Named soldiers, coils out.'

Nakalian now in the lead, the wings moved out once again, the riders at the very ends with arrows fitted to their short, recurved bows. Torun and Farakalian rode to either side of the Shield Anvil, lasso and rope coils in hand.

The sun crawled across the sky. Nakalian held them to the trail without much difficulty, the tracks now a straight, direct line northwest. Itkovian had opportunity to see the imprints in the hard earth himself. A huge animal indeed, to have driven such deep impressions. Given its obvious speed, the Shield Anvil suspected they would never catch up with the creature.

Unless, of course, Itkovian silently added as he watched Nakalian suddenly rein in at the top of a low rise ahead, *the beast decided to stop and wait for us.*

The troop slowed, all eyes on the soldier on point. Nakalian's attention remained fixed on something only he could see. He had drawn his lance but was not readying for a charge. His horse shied nervously beneath him, and as Itkovian and the others neared, the Shield Anvil could see the animal's fear.

They reached the rise.

A basin stretched out before them, the grasses trampled and scattered in a wide swathe – the recent passing of a herd of wild bhederin – cutting diagonally across the plain. Towards the centre, at a distance of at least two hundred paces, stood a grey-skinned creature, two-legged, long-tailed, its snout two rows of jagged fangs. Broad-bladed swords flashed from the ends of its arms. Motionless, its head, torso and tail almost horizontal as it balanced on its two legs, the creature was watching them.

Itkovian's eyes narrowed to slits.

'I judge,' Nakalian said at his side, 'five heartbeats to cover the distance between us, Shield Anvil.'

'Yet it makes no move.'

'With that speed, sir, it needn't bother.'

Until it elects to, at which point it will be upon us. We'd best test this apparition's abilities. 'Let us choose our own timing, sir,' Itkovian said. 'Lancers – hit the beast low and leave your weapons in, foul its stride if you can. Archers, go for the eyes and neck. One down the throat as well if the opportunity presents itself. A staggered pass, random evasion once you've planted your weapons, then draw swords. Torun and Farakalian' – he drew his longsword – 'you're with me. Very well, canter to gallop at fifty, sooner if the beast reacts.'

The wings rode forward, down the gentle slope, lances levelling.

The creature continued to watch them, unmoving. With a hundred paces remaining between them, it slowly raised its blades, head dropping enough for the riders to see its ridged shoulders behind what was clearly some kind of helmet.

At seventy paces the creature swung round to face them, swords out to the sides, tail twitching.

Out on the tips the archers rose high in their stirrups, drew taut on the strings of their squat, powerful bows, held them motionless for a long moment, then loosed.

The arrows converged on the creature's head. Barbed heads plunged into its black eye sockets. Seemingly in-different to the arrows buried deep, the beast took a step forward.

Fifty paces. Again the bowstrings thrummed. Shafts sprouted on either side of the neck. The archers angled their mounts away to maintain distance in their pass. The lancers' horses stretched their necks, and the closing charge had begun.

Blinded, yet not blind. I see no blood. Fener, reveal to me the nature of this demon. A command to evade—

The creature darted forward with unbelievable speed. At once, it was among the Grey Swords. Lances skewered it from all sides, then the huge blades flashed. Screams. Blood flying in gouts. Itkovian saw the rump of a horse plunge down in front of him, saw the soldier's right leg, foot still in the stirrup, falling outward. Without comprehension, he watched the rump – legs kicking spasmodically – twist round, revealing that the front half of the horse was gone. Severed spine, curved rows of rib stubs, intestines tumbling out, blood spraying from red flesh.

His own horse leapt high to clear the animal wreckage.

Crimson rain splashed the Shield Anvil's face as the creature's massive jaws – studded with arrows – snapped out at him. He leaned to his left, barely avoiding the meat-strewn fangs, and swung a wild backhand slash with his longsword as he rode past. The blade clashed against armour.

In mid-leap, his horse shrieked as something clipped it from behind. Plunging down on its forelimbs and still screaming, it managed a stagger forward before its rump sank down behind Itkovian. Knowing that something had gone desperately wrong with the beast's rocking, horrible stumble, he pulled free his heart-knife, leaned forward and opened the animal's jugular with a single slash. Then, kicking free of the stirrups, the Shield Anvil pitched forward and to the left even as he yanked the dying horse's head to the right.

They struck the ground, rolled apart.

Completing his tumble at a crouch, Itkovian spared a glance at his horse, to see the animal kicking in the air. The two hind legs ended just above the fetlocks. Both hooves had been sliced off. The dead animal quickly stilled.

The bodies of mounts and soldiers lay on both sides of the creature, which was now slowly turning to face Itkovian. Blood and gore painted its long, leathery arms. A woman's red-streaked brown hair had snagged in thick tufts between the beast's smeared fangs.

Then Itkovian saw the lassos. Both hung loose, one around the creature's neck, the other high on its right leg.

Earth thumped as the demon took a step towards the

Shield Anvil. Itkovian raised his longsword.

As it lifted a three-toed foot for another stride, the two ropes snapped taut, neck to the left, leg to the right. The creature was thrown upward by the savage, perfectly timed yanks to opposite sides. Leg tore away from hip in a dry, ripping snap, even as the head parted from the neck with an identical sickly sound.

Torso and head struck the earth with heavy, bone-breaking thumps.

No movement. The beast was dead.

Suddenly trembling, Itkovian slowly straightened.

Torun had taken three riders with him. Farakalian had done the same. Ropes wound around each saddlehorn, the force behind the sudden, explosive tightening – four warhorses to each side – had managed what weapons could not.

The pair of archers rode up to the Shield Anvil. One reached down an arm. 'Quickly, sir, the stirrup's clear.'

Unquestioningly, Itkovian clasped the wrist and swung himself up behind the rider. And saw what approached.

Four more demons, four hundred paces away and closing with the speed of boulders tumbling down a mountainside.

'We'll not outrun them.'

'Yes, sir.'

'So we split up,' Itkovian said.

The rider kicked his mount into a gallop. 'Yes, sir. We're the slowest – Torun and Farakalian will engage – give us time—'

The horse swerved suddenly beneath them. Caught unprepared, the Shield Anvil's head snapped back, and he tumbled from the saddle. He hit the hard-packed soil, the air bursting from his lungs, then rolled, stunned, to come to a stop against a pair of legs hard as iron.

Blinking, gasping, Itkovian found himself staring up at a squat, fur-clad corpse. The dark-brown, withered face beneath the antlered head-dress tilted downward. Shadowed sockets studied him.

Gods, what a day.

'Your soldiers approach,' the apparition rasped in Elin. 'From this engagement . . . you are relieved.'

The archer was still struggling with his startled horse, cursing, then he hissed in surprise.

The Shield Anvil frowned up at the undead figure. 'We are?'

'Against undead,' the corpse said, 'arises an army in kind.'

Distantly, Itkovian heard the sounds of battle – no screams, simply the clash of weapons, relentless, ever growing. With a groan, he rolled onto his side. A headache was building in the back of his skull, waves of nausea rippling through him. Gritting his teeth, he sat up.

'Ten survivors,' the figure above him mused. 'You did well . . . for mortals.'

Itkovian stared across the basin. An army of corpses identical to the one beside him surrounded the demons, of which only two remained standing. The battle around those two creatures was horrible to witness. Pieces of the undead warriors flew in all directions, but still they kept coming, huge flint swords chopping into the demons, carving them down where they stood. A half-dozen heart-beats later, the fight was over.

The Shield Anvil judged that at least sixty of the fur-clad warriors had been destroyed. The others continued chopping on the felled beasts, swinging ever lower as the remaining pieces grew ever smaller. Even as he watched, dust swirled from the hillsides in every direction – more of the undead warriors with their weapons of stone. An army, motionless beneath the sun.

'We did not know that K'Chain Che'Malle had returned to this land,' the hide-wrapped corpse said.

Itkovian's remaining soldiers approached, tense, driven into watchful silence by the conjurations rising on all sides.

'Who,' Itkovian asked dully, 'are you?'

'I am the Bonecaster Pran Chole, of the Kron T'lan

Imass. We are come to the Gathering. And, it seems, to a war. I think, mortal, you have need of us.'

The Shield Anvil looked upon his ten surviving soldiers. The recruit was among them, but not her two guardians. *Twenty. Soldiers and horses. Twenty . . . gone.* He scanned the faces now arrayed before him, and slowly nodded. 'Aye, Pran Chole, we have need.'

The recruit's face was the hue of bleached parchment. She sat on the ground, eyes unfocused, spattered with the blood of one or both of the soldiers who had given their lives protecting her.

Itkovian stood beside her, saying nothing. The brutality of the engagement may well have broken the Capan recruit, he suspected. Active service was intended to hone, not destroy. The Shield Anvil's underestimation of the enemy had made of this young woman's future a world of ashes. Two blindingly sudden deaths would haunt her for the rest of her days. And there was nothing Itkovian could do, or say, to ease the pain.

'Shield Anvil.'

He looked down at her, surprised that she would speak, wondering at the hardness of her voice. 'Recruit?'

She was looking round, eyes thinning as she studied the legions of undead warriors who stood in ragged ranks, unmoving, on all sides. 'There are thousands.'

Spectral figures, risen to stand above the plain's tawny grasses, row on row. As if the earth herself had thrust them clear of her flesh. 'Aye. I'd judge well over ten thousand. T'lan Imass. Tales of these warriors had reached us' – *tales I found hard to countenance* – 'but this represents our first encounter, and a timely one at that.'

'Do we return to Capustan now?'

Itkovian shook his head. 'Not all of us. Not immediately. There are more of these K'Chain Che'Malle on this plain. Pran Chole – the unarmed one, some kind of high priest or shaman – has suggested a joint exercise, and I have approved. I will lead eight of the troop west.'

'Bait.'

He raised a brow. 'Correct. The T'lan Imass travel unseen, and will therefore surround us at all times. Were they to remain visible in this hunt, the K'Chain Che'Malle would probably avoid them, at least until they have gathered in such numbers as to challenge the entire army. Better they were cut down in twos and threes. Recruit, I am attaching an escort of one soldier to you for an immediate return to Capustan. A report must needs be made to the Mortal Sword. Accompanying the two of you, unseen, will be a select squad of T'lan Imass. Emissaries. I have been assured that no K'Chain Che'Malle are present between here and the city.'

She slowly rose. 'Sir, a single rider would do as well. You return me to Capustan to spare me . . . from what? From seeing K'Chain Che'Malle cut to pieces by these T'lan Imass? Shield Anvil, there is no mercy or compassion in your decision.'

'It seems,' Itkovian said, staring out upon the vast army arrayed around them, 'you are not lost to us, after all. The Boar of Summer despises blind obedience. You will ride with us, sir.'

'Thank you, Shield Anvil.'

'Recruit, I trust you have not deluded yourself into believing that witnessing the destruction of more K'Chain Che'Malle will silence the cries within you. Soldiers are issued armour for their flesh and bones, but they must fashion their own for their souls. Piece by piece.'

She looked down at the blood spattered across her uniform. 'It has begun.'

Itkovian was silent for a moment, studying the recruit at his side. 'The Capan are a foolish people, to deny freedom to their women. The truth of that is before me.'

She shrugged. 'I am not unique.'

'Attend to your horse, soldier. And direct Sidlis to join me.'

'Sir.'

He watched her walk towards the waiting horses and the surviving soldiers of the wings, all of whom had gathered around their mounts to check girth straps, fittings and equipment. She joined their ranks, spoke with Sidlis, who nodded and approached the Shield Anvil.

Pran Chole strode up at the same time. 'Itkovian, our choices have been made. Kron's emissaries have been assembled and await your messenger.'

'Understood.'

Sidlis arrived. 'Capustan, Shield Anvil?' she asked.

'With an unseen escort. Report directly to the Mortal Sword and the Destriant. In private. The T'lan Imass emissaries are to speak with the Grey Swords and none other, for the moment at least.'

'Sir.'

'Mortals,' Pran Chole addressed them tonelessly, 'Kron has commanded that I inform you of certain details. These K'Chain Che'Malle are what was once known as K'ell Hunters. Chosen children of a matriarch, bred to battle. However, they are undead, and that which controls them hides well its identity – somewhere to the south, we believe. The K'ell Hunters were freed from tombs situated in the Place of the Rent, called Morn. We do not know if present maps of this land mass know the place by these ancient names—'

'Morn,' Itkovian nodded. 'South of the Lamatath Plain, on the west coast and directly north of the island wherein dwell the Seguleh. Our company is from Elingarth, which borders the Lamatath Plain to the east. While we know of no-one who has visited Morn, the name has been copied from the oldest maps and so remains. The general understanding is that nothing is there. Nothing at all.'

The Bonecaster shrugged. 'The barrows are much worn down, I would imagine. It has been a long time since we last visited the Rent. The K'ell Hunters may well be under the command of their matriarch, for we believe she has finally worked her way free from her own imprisonment. This, then, is the enemy you face.'

Frowning, the Shield Anvil shook his head and said, 'The threat from the south comes from an empire called the Pannion Domin, ruled by the Seer – a mortal man. The reports of these K'Chain Che'Malle are recent developments, whilst the expansion of the Pannion Domin has been under way for some years now.' He drew breath to say more, then fell silent, realizing that over ten thousand withered, undead faces were now turned towards him. His mouth dried to parchment, his heart suddenly pounding.

'Itkovian,' Pran Chole rasped, 'this word "Pannion". Has it a particular meaning among the natives?'

He shook his head, not trusting himself to speak.

'Pannion,' the Bonecaster said. 'A Jaghut word. A Jaghut name.'

As the afternoon waned, Toc the Younger sat by the fire, his lone eye studying the huge, sleeping wolf at his side. Baaljagg – *what had Tool called her? An ay* – had a face longer and narrower than the timber wolves the scout recalled seeing in Blackdog Forest, hundreds of leagues to the north. At the shoulder, the creature beside him had two, maybe three hands on those formidable northern wolves. Sloping brow, small ears, with canines to challenge those of a lion or a plains bear. Broadly muscled, the animal nevertheless had a build suggesting both speed and endurance. A swift kill or a league-devouring pursuit, Baaljagg looked capable of both.

The wolf opened one eye to look upon him.

'You're supposed to be extinct,' Toc murmured. 'Vanished from the world for a hundred thousand years. What are you doing here?'

The ay was the scout's only company, for the moment. Lady Envy had elected to make a detour through her warren, northwestward a hundred and twenty leagues to the city of Callows, to replenish her supplies. *Supplies of what? Bath oil?* He was unconvinced of the justification, but even his suspicious nature yielded him no clue as to her real reasons. She had taken the dog, Garath, with her, as well as Mok. *Safe enough to leave Senu and Thurule, I suppose. Tool dropped them both, after all. Still, what was important enough to make Envy break her own rule of a minimum of three servants?*

Tool had vanished into a dusty swirl a half-bell earlier, off on another hunt. The remaining two Seguleh weren't in a generous mood, not deigning to engage the unranked Malazan in conversation. They stood off to one side. *Watching the sunset? Relaxing at ramrod attention?*

He wondered what was happening far to the north. Dujek had chosen to march on the Pannion Domin. A new war, against an unknown foe. Onearm's Host was Toc's family, or at least what passed for family for a child born to an army. The only world he knew, after all. A family pursued by jackals of attrition. What kind of war were they heading into? Vast, sweeping battles, or the crawling pace of contested forests, jagged ranges and sieges? He fought back another surge of impatience, a tide that had been building within him day after day on this endless plain, building and threatening to escape the barriers he'd raised in his mind.

Damn you, Hairlock, for sending me so far away. All right, so that warren was chaotic – so was the puppet that used it on me. But why did it spit me out at Morn? And where did all those months go, anyway? He had begun to mistrust his belief in happenstance, and the crumbling of that belief left him feeling on shaky ground. *To Morn and its wounded warren . . . to Morn, where a renegade T'lan Imass lay in the black dust, waiting – not for me, he said, but for Lady Envy. Not any old renegade T'lan Imass, either. One I've met before. The only one I've met before. And then there's Lady Envy herself, and her damned Seguleh servants and four-legged companions – uh, don't go there, Toc . . .*

Anyway. Now we're travelling together. North, to where

305

each of us wants to be. What luck. What happy coincidence!

Toc disliked the notion of being used, of being manipulated. He'd seen what that had cost his friend, Captain Paran. *Paran was tougher than me – I saw that from the start. He'd take the hits, blink, then just keep going. He'd some kind of hidden armour, something inside him that kept him sane.*

Not me, alas. Things get tough, and I'm liable to curl up and start whimpering.

He glanced over at the two Seguleh. It seemed they were as loth to talk to each other as they were to anyone else. *Strong, silent types. I hate those. I didn't before. I do, now.*

So . . . here I am, in the middle of nowhere, and the only truly sane creature in my company is an extinct wolf. His gaze returned once more to Baaljagg. 'And where's your family, beastie?' he asked softly, meeting the ay's soft, brown gaze.

The answer came, a sudden explosion of swirling colours directly behind the socket of his lost eye – colours that settled into an image. Kin assailing three musk oxen, hunters and hunted mired deep in mud, trapped, doomed to die. The point of view was low, from just beyond the sink-hole, circling, ever circling. Whimpering filled Toc's mind. Desperate love unanswered. Panic, filling the cold air.

A pup's confusion.

Fleeing. Wandering mudflats and sandbanks, across a dying sea.

Hunger.

Then, standing before her, a figure. Cowled, swathed in roughly woven black wool, a hand – wrapped in leather straps, down to the very fingers – reaching out. Warmth. Welcome. A palpable compassion, a single touch to the creature's lowered forehead. The touch, Toc realized, of an Elder God. And a voice: *You are the last, now. The very last, and there will be need for you. In time . . .*

Thus, I promise that I shall bring to you . . . a lost spirit. Torn from its flesh. A suitable one, of course. For that reason, my search may be a long one. Patience, little one . . . and in the meantime, this gift . . .

306

The pup closed her eyes, sank into instant sleep – and found herself no longer alone. Loping across vast tundras, in the company of her own kind. An eternity of loving dreams, secured with joy, a gift made bitter only by waking hours, waking years, centuries, millennia spent . . . alone.

Baaljagg, unchallenged among the dreamworld's ay, ruling mother of countless children in a timeless land. No lack of quarry, no lean times. Upright figures on distant horizons, seen but rarely, and never approached. Cousins to come across every now and then. Forest-dwelling agkor, white bendal, yellow-haired ay'tog of the far south – names that had sunk their meaning into Baaljagg's immortal mind . . . eternal whisperings from those ay that had joined the T'lan Imass, there, then, at the time of the Gathering. A whole other kind of immortality . . .

Wakeful, solitary Baaljagg's eyes had seen more of the world than could be fathomed. Finally, however the gift had come, the torn soul delivered to her own, where they merged, eventually became one. And in this, yet another layer of loss and pain. The beast now sought . . . *something.* Something like . . . *redress . . .*

What do you ask of me, wolf? No, not of me – you ask not of me, do you? You ask of my companion, the undead warrior. Onos T'oolan. It was him you awaited, whilst you shared company with Lady Envy. And Garath? Ah, another mystery . . . for another time . . .

Toc blinked, his head jerking back as the link snapped. Baaljagg slept at his side. Dazed, trembling, he looked around in the gloom.

A dozen paces away, Tool stood facing him, a brace of hares dangling from one shoulder.

Oh, Beru fend. See? Soft inside. Far too soft for this world and its layered histories, its endless tragedies. 'What?' Toc asked, his voice rasping. 'What is it this wolf wants of you, T'lan Imass?'

The warrior cocked his head. 'An end to her loneliness, mortal.'

'Have you – have you given answer?'

Tool turned away, dropping the hares to the ground. His voice when he spoke shocked the scout with its raw mournfulness. 'I can do nothing for her.'

The cold, lifeless tone was gone, and for the first time Toc saw something of what hid behind that deathly, desiccated visage. 'I've never heard you speak in pain before, Tool. I didn't think—'

'You heard wrong,' the T'lan Imass said, his tone once again devoid of inflection. 'Have you completed the fletching for your arrows, Toc the Younger?'

'Aye, like you showed me. They're done, twelve of the ugliest-looking arrows I've ever had the pleasure of owning. Thank you, Tool. It's outrageous, but I am proud to own them.'

Tool shrugged. 'They will serve you well.'

'I hope you're right.' He rose with a grunt. 'I'll do the meal, then.'

'That is Senu's task.'

Toc squinted at the T'lan Imass. 'Not you, as well? They're Seguleh, Tool, not servants. While Lady Envy isn't here, I will treat them as travelling companions, and be honoured by their company.' He glanced over to find the two warriors staring at him. 'Even if they won't talk to me.'

He took the hares from the T'lan Imass, crouched down beside the hearth. 'Tell me, Tool,' he said as he began skinning the first of the creatures, 'when you're out there hunting . . . any sign of other travellers? Are we completely alone on this Lamatath Plain?'

'I have seen no evidence of traders or other humans, Toc the Younger. Bhederin herds, antelope, wolves, coyotes, fox, hares and the occasional plains bear. Birds of prey and birds that scavenge. Various snakes, lizards—'

'A veritable menagerie,' Toc muttered. 'Then how is it that every time I scan the horizons, I see nothing? Nothing. No beasts, no birds, even.'

'The plain is vast,' Tool replied. 'Also, there are the

effects of the Tellann warren which surrounds me – though that is much weakened at the moment. Someone has drawn on my life-force, almost to exhaustion. Ask me no questions regarding this. My Tellann powers none the less discourage mortal beasts. Creatures are given to avoidance when able. We are, however, being trailed by a pack of ay'-tog – yellow-haired wolves. But they yet remain shy. Curiosity may overcome that, eventually.'

Toc's gaze returned to Baaljagg. 'Ancient memories.'

'Memories of ice.' The T'lan Imass's cavern eyes were fixed on the Malazan. 'By this and your earlier words, I conclude that something has occurred – a binding of souls – between you and the ay. How?'

'I'm not aware of any binding of souls,' Toc answered, still staring at the sleeping wolf. 'I was granted . . . visions. We shared remembrances, I think. How? I don't know. There were emotions within it, Tool, enough to make one despair.' After a moment he returned to cleaning the scrawny creature beneath his hands.

'Every gift is edged.'

Toc grimaced as he gutted the animal. 'Edged. I suppose so. I'm beginning to suspect the truth of the legends – lose an eye to receive the gift of true vision.'

'How did you lose your eye, Toc the Younger?'

'A sizzling chunk from Moon's Spawn – that deathly rain when the Enfilade was in full swing.'

'Stone.'

Toc nodded. 'Stone.' Then he stopped, looked up.

'Obelisk,' Tool said. 'In the ancient Deck of Holds, it was known as Menhir. Touched by stone, mortal – *Chen're aral lich'fayle* – there, on your brow. I give you a new name. Aral Fayle.'

'I don't recall asking for a new name, Tool.'

'Names are not for the asking, mortal. Names are earned.'

'Huh, sounds like the Bridgeburners.'

'An ancient tradition, Aral Fayle.'

Hood's breath. 'Fine!' he snapped. 'Only I can't see that I've earned anything—'

'You were sent into a Warren of Chaos, mortal. You survived – in itself an unlikely event – and travelled the slow vortex towards the Rent. Then, when Morn's portal should have taken you, it instead cast you out. Stone has taken one of your eyes. And the ay here has chosen you in the sharing of her soul. Baaljagg has seen in you a rare worthiness, Aral Fayle—'

'I still don't want any new names! Hood's breath!' He was sweating beneath his worn, dust-caked armour. He searched desperately for a way to change the subject, to shift the conversation away from himself. 'What's yours mean, anyway? Onos T'oolan – what's that from?'

'*Onos* is "clanless man". *T'* is "broken". *Ool* is "veined" while *lan* is "flint" and in combination *T'oolan* is "flawed flint".'

Toc stared at the T'lan Imass for a long moment. 'Flawed flint.'

'There are layers of meaning.'

'I'd guessed.'

'From a single core are struck blades, each finding its own use. If veins or knots of crystal lie hidden within the heart of the core, the shaping of the blades cannot be predicted. Each blow to the core breaks off useless pieces – hinge-fractured, step-fractured. Useless. Thus it was with the family in which I was born. Struck wrong, each and all.'

'Tool, I see no flaws in you.'

'In pure flint all the sands are aligned. All face in the same direction. There is unity of purpose. The hand that shapes such flint can be confident. I was of Tarad's clan. Tarad's reliance in me was misplaced. Tarad's clan no longer exists. At the Gathering, Logros was chosen to command the clans native to the First Empire. He had the expectation that my sister, a Bonecaster, would be counted among his servants. She defied the ritual, and so the Logros T'lan Imass were weakened. The First Empire fell. My two brothers, T'ber Tendara and Han'ith Iath, led hunters to the north and never returned. They too failed. I was chosen First Sword, yet I have abandoned Logros T'lan Imass. I travel alone, Aral Fayle, and thus am committing the greatest crime known among my people.'

'Wait a moment,' Toc objected. 'You said you're heading to a second Gathering – you're *returning* to your people . . .'

The undead warrior did not respond, head slowly turning to gaze northward.

Baaljagg rose, stretched, then padded to Tool's side. The massive creature sat, matching the T'lan Imass's silent regard.

A sudden chill whispered through Toc the Younger. *Hood's breath, what are we headed into?* He glanced at Senu and Thurule. The Seguleh seemed to be watching him. 'Hungry, I gather. I see your bridling impatience. If you like, I could—'

Rage.

Cold, deadly.

Unhuman.

Toc was suddenly elsewhere, seeing through a beast's eyes – but not the ay, not this time. And not images from long ago, but from this moment; behind which tumbled a cascade of memories. A moment later, all sense of himself was swallowed, his identity swept away before the storm of another creature's thoughts.

It has been so long since life found shape . . . with words, with awareness.

And now, too late.

Muscles twitched, leaked blood from beneath his slashed, torn hide. So much blood, soaking the ground under his flesh, smearing the grasses in a crawling track up the hill's slope.

Crawling, a journey of return. To find oneself, now, at the very end. And memories awakened . . .

The final days – so long ago, now – had been chaotic.

311

The ritual had unravelled, unexpectedly, unpredictably. Madness gripped the Soletaken. Madness splintered the more powerful of his kin, broke one into many, the burgeoning power wild, blood-hungry, birthing the D'ivers. The Empire was tearing itself apart.

But that was long ago, so very long ago . . .

I am Treach – one of many names. Trake, the Tiger of Summer, the Talons of War. Silent Hunter. I was there at the end, one of the few survivors once the T'lan Imass were done with us. Brutal, merciful slaughter. They had no choice – I see that now, though none of us were prepared to forgive. Not then. The wounds were too fresh.

Gods, we tore a warren to pieces on that distant continent. Turned the eastlands into molten stone that cooled and became something that defied sorcery. The T'lan Imass sacrificed thousands to cut away the cancer we had become. It was the end, the end of all that promise, all that bright glory. The end of the First Empire. Hubris, to have claimed a name that rightly belonged to the T'lan Imass . . .

We fled, a handful of survivors. Ryllandaras, old friend – we fell out, clashed, then clashed again on another continent. He had gone the farthest, found a way to control the gifts – Soletaken and D'ivers both. White Jackal. Ay'tog. Agkor. And my other companion, Messremb – where has he gone? A kind soul, twisted by madness, yet so loyal, ever loyal . . .

Ascending. Fierce arrival – the First Heroes. Dark, savage.

I remember a vast sweep of grasses beneath a sky deepening to dusk. A wolf, its single eye like a smear of moonlight, on a distant ridgeline. This strangely singular memory, sharp as talons, returning to me now. Why?

I padded this earth for thousands of years, sunk deep into the beast, human memories fading, fading, gone. And yet . . . this vision of the wolf, awakening all within me . . .

I am Treach. Memories returning in full flood, even as my body grows cold, so very cold.

He'd tracked the mysterious beasts for days, driven by relentless curiosity. A scent unknown to him, a swirling wake of death and old blood. Fearless, he'd thought only of delivering destruction, as he had done without challenge for so long. The White Jackal had vanished into the mists centuries past, dead, or if not dead, then as good as. Treach had driven him from a ledge, sent him spinning and writhing down into the fathomless crevasse. No enemies worthy of the name since then. The tiger's arrogance was legendary – it had not been difficult, embracing such assurity.

The four K'Chain Che'Malle hunters had circled back, awaited him with cold intent.

I tore into them. Slashed flesh, shattered bones. I dragged one down, fangs deep in its lifeless neck. Another moment, another heartbeat, and there would have been but three.

So close a thing . . .

Treach lay dying from a dozen mortal wounds. Indeed, he should have been dead already, yet he clung on, with blind, bestial determination, fuelled by rage. The four K'Chain Che'Malle had left him, contemptuously, knowing he would not rise again and immune to mercy.

Prone on the grasses, the Tiger of Summer had watched with dulled eyes as the creatures padded away, noted with satisfaction as an arm on one of them, dangling from the thinnest strip of skin, finally parted and fell to the ground – to be left behind with utter indifference.

Then, as the undead hunters reached the crest of a nearby hill, his eyes had flashed. A sleek, long black shape flowed from the grasses, was among his slayers. Power flowed like black water. The first K'Chain Che'Malle withered beneath the onslaught.

The clash descended beyond the crest, beyond Treach's line of sight, yet, dimly heard past the deafening thunder of his waning life, the battle continued. He began dragging himself forward, inch by inch.

Within moments, all sounds from the other side of the hill fell away, yet Treach struggled on, his blood a slick trail behind him, his amber eyes fixed on the crest, his will to live reduced to something bestial, something that refused to recognize an end to its life.

I have seen this. Antelope. Bhederin. The wilful denial, the pointless struggle, efforts to escape, even as throat gushes blood to fill my mouth. Limbs kicking in the illusion of running, of fleeing, even as I begin feeding. I have seen this, and now understand it.

The tiger is humbled by memories of prey.

He forgot the reason for the struggle to reach the crest, knew only that he must achieve it, a final ascent, to see what lay beyond.

What lay beyond. Yes. A sun low on the horizon. The endless sweep of unbroken, untamed prairie. A final vision of wildness, before I slink through Hood's cursed gates.

She appeared before him, sleek and muscled and smooth-skinned. A woman, small yet not frail, the fur of a panther on her shoulders, her long black hair unkempt yet gleaming in the day's dying light. Almond-shaped eyes, amber like his own. Heart-shaped face, robustly featured.

Coarse queen, why does this sight of you break my heart?

She approached, settled down to lift his massive head, rest it against her lap. Small hands stroked the blood and dried froth from around his eyes. 'They are destroyed,' she said in the ancient language, the language of the First Empire. 'Not so difficult – you left them with little, Silent Hunter. Indeed, they veritably flew apart at my softest touch.'

Liar.

She smiled. 'I have crossed your wake before, Treach, yet would not approach – recalling your rage when we destroyed your empire, so long ago.'

It has long cooled, Imass. You did only what was necessary. You mended the wounds—

'The Imass cannot take credit for that. Others were involved in the task of repairing the shattered warren. We did nothing but slay your kind – those whom we could find, that is. It is our singular skill.'

Killing.

'Yes. Killing.'

I cannot return to my human form. I cannot find it within myself.

'It has been too long, Treach.'

Now, I die.

'Yes. I have no skills in healing.'

Within his mind, he smiled. *No, only killing.*

'Only killing.'

Then an end to my suffering, please.

'That is the man speaking. The beast would never ask such a thing. Where is your defiance, Treach? Where is your cunning?'

Do you mock me?

'No. I am here. As are you. Tell me, who then is this other presence?'

Other?

'Who has unchained your memories, Treach? Who has returned you to yourself? For centuries you were a beast, with a beast's mind. Once that place is reached, there is no return. Yet . . .'

Yet I am here.

'When your life fades from this world, Treach, I suspect you will find yourself, not before Hood's gates, but . . . else-where. I can offer nothing of certainty. But I have sensed the stirrings. An Elder God is active once again, perhaps the most ancient one of all. Subtle moves are being made. Select mortals have been chosen, and are being shaped. Why? What does this Elder God seek? I know not, but I believe it is in answer to a grave – and vast – threat. I believe the game that has begun will take a long time in its playing out.'

A new war?

'Are you not the Tiger of Summer? A war in which, this Elder God has judged, you *will be needed.*'

Wry amusement flooded Treach's mind. *I have never been needed, Imass.*

315

'Changes have come. Upon us all, it seems.'

Ah, then we shall meet again? I would wish it. I would see you, once more, as the midnight panther.

She laughed, low in her throat. 'And so the beast awakens. Farewell, Treach.'

She had, in that last moment, seen what he only now felt. Darkness closed around him, narrowed his world. Vision . . . from two eyes . . . to one.

One. Looking across a stretch of grasses as night fell, watching the massive Soletaken tiger pause warily above the dead bull ranag upon which it had been feeding. Seeing the twin flares of its cold, challenging glare. All . . . so long ago, now . . .

Then nothing.

A gloved hand slapped him hard. Groggily, Toc the Younger pried open his lone eye, found himself staring up at Senu's painted mask.

'Uh . . .'

'An odd time to fall asleep,' the Seguleh said tonelessly, then straightened and moved away.

The air was sweet with the smell of roasting meat. Groaning, Toc rolled over, then slowly sat up. Echoes rolled through him, ineffable sadness, half-formed regrets, and the long exhalation of a final breath. *Gods, no more visions. Please.* He struggled to clear his head, looked around. Tool and Baaljagg had not moved from their stance of before: both staring northward, motionless and – Toc eventually realized – taut with tension. And he thought he knew why.

'She's not far off,' he said. 'Coming fast.' *With the night, flowing as the sun flees. Deadly majesty; ancient, so very ancient, eyes.*

Tool turned. 'What have you seen, Aral Fayle? To where did you journey?'

The Malazan clambered weakly upright. 'Beru fend, I'm hungry. Hungry enough to eat that antelope raw.' He paused, drew a deep breath. 'What have I seen? I was

316

witness, T'lan Imass, to the death of Treach. Trake, as he's known round here, the Tiger of Summer. Where? North of here. Not far. And no, I don't know why.'

Tool was silent for a moment, then he simply nodded and said, '*Chen're aral lich'fayle*. The Menhir, heart of memory.' He swung round again as Baaljagg rose suddenly, hackles rising.

The panther that Toc knew was coming finally appeared, more than twice a man's height in length, eyes almost level with Toc's own, her sleek fur blue-black and shimmering. A scent of spice swept forward like an exhaled breath, and the creature began sembling, the shift an uncertain blurring, a folding in of darkness itself. Then a small woman stood before them, her eyes on Tool. 'Hello, brother.'

The T'lan Imass slowly nodded. 'Sister.'

'You've not aged well,' she noted, lithely stepping forward.

Baaljagg backed away.

'You have.'

Her smile transformed bold features into a thing of beauty. 'Generous of you, Onos. You have a mortal ay for a companion, I see.'

'As mortal as you, Kilava Onass.'

'Indeed? Predictably shy of my kind, of course. None the less, an admirable beast.' She held out a hand.

Baaljagg edged closer.

'Imass,' she murmured. 'Yes, but flesh and blood. Like you. Do you remember, now?'

The huge wolf ducked her head and padded up to Kilava, leaned a shoulder against that of the woman, who pressed her face into the animal's mane, drew deep the scent, then sighed. 'This is an unexpected gift,' she whispered.

'More than that,' Toc the Younger said.

He twisted inside as she looked up at him to reveal the raw sensuality in her eyes, a thing so clearly natural that he knew in an instant that he was no more the focus of it than anyone else upon whom she turned her gaze. *The Imass as*

317

they once were, before the Ritual. As they would have remained, if, like her, they had refused its power. A moment later, those eyes narrowed.

Toc nodded.

'I saw you,' she said, 'looking out from Treach's eyes—'

'Both eyes?'

She smiled. 'No. Only one – the one you no longer have, mortal. I would know what the Elder God has planned . . . for us.'

He shook his head. 'I don't know. I can't recall ever meeting him, alas. Not even a whisper in my ear.'

'Brother Onos, who is this mortal?'

'I have named him Aral Fayle, sister.'

'And you have given him weapons of stone.'

'I have. Unintended.'

'By you, perhaps . . .'

'I serve no god,' Tool growled.

Her eyes flashed. 'And I do? These steps are not our own, Onos! Who would dare manipulate us? An Imass Bonecaster and the First Sword of the T'lan Imass – prodded this way and that. He risks our wrath—'

'Enough,' Tool sighed. 'You and I are not of a kind, sister. We have never walked in step. I travel to the Second Gathering.'

Her sneer was decidedly unpleasant. 'Think you I did not hear the summons?'

'Made by whom? Do you know, Kilava?'

'No, nor do I care. I shall not attend.'

Tool cocked his head. 'Then why are you here?'

'That is my business.'

She seeks . . . redress. The realization flooded Toc's mind, and he knew that the knowledge was not his, but an Elder God's. Who now spoke directly, in a voice that trickled like sand into the Malazan's thoughts. *To right an old wrong, heal an old scar. You shall cross paths again. It is, however, of little consequence. It is the final meeting that concerns me, and that will be years away in all likelihood. Ah, but I reveal unworthy*

318

impatience. Mortal, the children of the Pannion Seer are suffer-
ing. You must find a way to release them. It is difficult – a risk
beyond imagining – but I must send you into the Seer's embrace.
I do not think you will forgive me.

Struggling, Toc pushed his question forward in his mind.
Release them. Why?

An odd question, mortal. I speak of compassion. There are
gifts unimagined in such efforts. A man who dreams has shown
me this, and indeed, you shall soon see for yourself. Such
gifts . . .

'Compassion,' Toc said, mentally jarred by the Elder
God's sudden departure. He blinked, saw that Tool and
Kilava were staring at him. The woman's face had paled.

'My sister,' the First Sword said, 'knows nothing of
compassion.'

Toc stared at the undead warrior, trying to retrieve what
had been spoken last – before the . . . visitation. He could
not recall.

'Brother Onos, you should have realized it by now,'
Kilava slowly said. 'All things change.' Studying Toc once
more, the woman smiled, but it was a smile of sorrow. 'I
leave now—'

'Kilava.' Tool stepped forward, a faint clash of bones and
skin. 'The ritual that sundered you from your kin, the
breaking of blood-ties – this Second Gathering,
perhaps . . .'

Her expression softened. 'Dear brother, the summoner
cares nothing for me. My ancient crime will not be undone.
Moreover, I suspect that what will await you at the Second
Gathering will not be as you imagine. But I . . . I thank you,
Onos T'oolan, for the kind thought.'

'I said . . . we do not . . . travel in step,' the undead
warrior whispered, struggling with each word. 'I was angry,
sister – but it is an old anger. Kilava—'

'Old anger, yes. But you were right, none the less. We
have never walked in step with each other. Our past ever
dogs our trail. Perhaps some day we will mend our shared

319

wounds, brother. This meeting has given me . . . hope.' She briefly laid a hand on Baaljagg's head, then turned away.

Toc watched her vanish into the dusk's shroud.

Another clattering of bones within leather skin made him swing round. To see Tool on his knees, head hung. There could be no tears from a corpse, yet . . .

Toc hesitated, then strode to the undead warrior. 'There was untruth in your words, Tool,' he said.

Swords hissed out and the Malazan spun to see Senu and Thurule advancing on him.

Tool snapped out a hand. 'Stop! Sheathe your weapons, Seguleh. I am immune to insults – even those delivered by one I would call a friend.'

'Not an insult,' Toc said levelly, turning back to the T'lan Imass. 'An observation. What did you call it? The breaking of blood-ties.' He laid a hand on Tool's shoulder. 'It's clear to me, for what that's worth, that the breaking failed. The blood-ties remain. Perhaps you could take heart in that, Onos T'oolan.'

The head tilted up, withered sockets revealed beneath the bone shelf of the helm.

Gods, I look and see nothing. He looks and sees . . . what? Toc the Younger struggled to think of what to do, what to say next. As the moment stretched, he shrugged, offered his hand.

To his amazement, Tool grasped it.

And was lifted upright, though the Malazan grunted with the effort, his every muscle protesting. *Hood take me, that's the heaviest sack of bones I've . . . never mind.*

Senu broke the silence, his tone firm. 'Stoneblade and Stonearrow, attend. The meal awaits us.'

Now, how in Hood's name did I earn all this? Onos T'oolan. And respect from a Seguleh, no less . . . In a night of wonders, that one surely takes the crown.

'I have truly known but two mortal humans,' Tool said at his side. 'Both underestimated themselves, the first one fatally so. This night, friend Aral Fayle, I shall

320

endeavour to tell you of the fall of Adjunct Lorn.'

'A moral to the tale, no doubt,' Toc commented wryly.

'Indeed.'

'And here I was planning to spend the night tossing bones with Senu and Thurule.'

Senu snapped, 'Come and eat, Stonearrow!'

Uh oh, I think I just overstepped the familiarity thing.

Blood had filled the gutters, not long past. Sun and absence of rain had preserved the turgid flow as dust-dulled black, deep enough to hide the hump of the cobbles lying underneath, the mortal river reaching down to the silty waters of the bay.

No-one in Callows had been spared. She had come upon the heaped pyres on her approach down the inland road, and judged the slaughter at perhaps thirty thousand.

Garath ranged ahead, slipping beneath the arch of the gate. She followed at a slower pace.

The city had been beautiful, once. Copper-sheathed domes, minarets, poetically winding streets overlooked by ornate balconies riotous with flowering plants. The lack of hands to nourish the precious plants had turned the gardens brown and grey. Leaves crackled underfoot as Lady Envy walked down the central avenue.

A trader city, a merchants' paradise. The masts of countless ships were visible in the harbour ahead, all motionless, indicating that the crafts had been holed and sat one and all in the mud of the bay.

Ten days, no more, since the slaughter. She could smell Hood's breath, a sigh at unexpected bounty, a faint ripple of unease at what it signified. *You are troubled, dear Hood. This bodes ill, indeed . . .*

Garath led her unerringly, as she knew he would. An ancient, almost forgotten alleyway, the cobbles heaved, cracked and covered in decades of rubbish. Into a small, sagging house, its foundation stones of a far sharper cut than those that rested upon them. Within, a single room with a reed-matted floor of thick, wooden boards. A desultory scatter of poorly made furniture, bronze cooking plate over a brick-housed hearth, rotting foodstuffs. A child's toy wagon off to one side.

The dog circled in the centre of the small room.

Lady Envy approached, kicked aside the reed mats. No trapdoor. The inhabitants had had no idea of what lay beneath their home. She unveiled her warren, passed a hand over the floorboards, watched them dissolve into dust, creating a circular hole. A damp, salty breath wafted from its darkness.

Garath padded to the edge, then dropped out of sight. She heard the clatter of claws some distance below.

With a sigh, Lady Envy followed.

No stairs, and the pavestones of the floor were a long time in halting her warren-slowed fall. Vision enhanced, she looked around, then sniffed. The temple was all of this one chamber, squalid, once low-ceilinged though the beams of that roof had long since vanished. There was no raised altarstone, but she knew that for this particular ascendant, the entire floor of cut stone served that sacred function. *Back in the days of blood . . .* 'I can imagine what awakened this place to you,' she said, eyes on Garath, who had lain down and was moments from sleep. 'All that blood, seeping down, dripping, dripping onto your altar. I admit, I prefer your abode in Darujhistan. Far grander, almost worthy of complementing my esteemed presence. But this . . .' Her nose wrinkled.

Garath, eyes closed, twitched.

Welcome, Lady Envy.

'Your summons was uncharacteristically distraught, K'rul. Is this the work of the Matron and her undead hunters? If so, then calling me here was unnecessary. I am well aware of their efficacy.'

Crippled and chained he may be, Lady Envy, but this particular god is never so obvious. His game displays a master's sleight of hand. Nothing is as he would have us believe, and his

*use of unwitting servants is as brutal as his treatment of
enemies. Consider, after all, the Pannion Seer. No, for
Callows, death came from the sea. A warren-twisted fleet.
Cold-eyed, unhuman killers. Seeking, ever seeking, they now
ply the world's oceans.*

'Seeking what, dare I ask?'

A worthy challenge, no less.

'And do these dreadful seaborne murderers have a
name?'

*One enemy at a time, Lady Envy. You must cultivate
patience.*

She crossed her arms. 'You sought me out, K'rul, and you
can be certain that I had not anticipated that you and I
would ever meet again. The Elder Gods are gone, and good
riddance, as far as I'm concerned – and that includes my
father, Draconus. Were we companions two hundred
thousand years ago, you and I? I think not, though the
memories are admittedly vague. Not enemies, true enough.
But friends? Allies? Most certainly not. Yet here you have
come. I have gathered your own *unwitting* servants, as you
asked. Have you any idea the demands on my energies to
hold those three Seguleh in check?'

Ah, yes, and where is the Third now?

'Stretched senseless half a league from the city. It was
vital to get him away from that T'lan Imass – the gods
know, I didn't drag him along for the company. You're missing my point, K'rul. The Seguleh *will not be controlled.*
Indeed, I wonder who humours whom when it comes to
those three frightful warriors. Mok will challenge Tool.
Mark my words, and while a part of me thrills at
the thought – to witness such a clash! None the less, the
destruction of one or the other will ill suit your plans, I
imagine. The First Sword was almost defeated by Thurule,
you know. Mok will chop him into kindling—'

K'rul's soft laughter filled her head. *Hopefully, not before
Mok and his brothers have carved their way into the Pannion
Seer's throne room. Besides, Onos T'oolan is far more subtle of*

thought than you might imagine, Lady Envy. Let them battle, if Mok so chooses. I suspect, however, that the Third may well surprise you with his . . . constraint.

'Constraint? Tell me, K'rul, did you think the Seguleh First would send someone as highly ranked as the Third to lead his punitive army?'

Admittedly, no. For this task, of splitting the Seer's forces into two fronts, I had expected perhaps three or four hundred Eleventh Level initiates. Sufficient to inconvenience the Seer enough to draw an army or two away from the approaching Malazans. Yet, with the Second missing, and with Mok's growing prowess, no doubt the First had his reasons.

'One final question, then. Why am I doing you these favours, anyway?'

As petulant as ever, I see. Very well. You chose to turn your back on the need, when last it arose. Disappointing, that, yet enough did indeed attend to manage the Chaining – although at a cost that your presence would have diminished. But, even chained, the Crippled God will not rest. He exists in endless, tormenting pain, shattered, broken within and without, yet he has turned that into a strength. The fuel for his rage, his hunger for vengeance—

'The fools who pulled him down are long dead, K'rul. Vengeance is just an excuse. The Crippled God is driven by ambition. Lust for power is the core of his rotten, shrivelled heart.'

Perhaps, perhaps not. Time will tell, as the mortals say. In any case, you defied the summons at the Chaining, Lady Envy. I will not brook your indifference a second time.

'You?' She sneered. 'Are you my master, K'rul? Since when—'

Visions flooded her mind, staggering her. Darkness. Then chaos, wild, unfocused power, a universe devoid of sense, of control, of meaning. Entities flung through the maelstrom. Lost, terrified by the birth of light. A sudden sharpening – pain as of wrists opened, the heat spilling forth – a savage imposition of order, the heart from which

324

blood flowed in even, steady streams. Twin chambers to that heart – Kurald Galain, the Warren of Mother Dark – and Starvald Demelain, the Warren of . . . Dragons. And the blood – the power – now sweeping in currents through veins, through arteries, branching out through all existence, and the thought that came to her then stole all warmth from her flesh. *Those veins, those arteries, they are the warrens.* 'Who created this? *Who?*'

Dear Lady, K'rul replied, *you have your answer, and I will be damned if I am going to countenance your impertinence. You are a sorceress. By Light's Wild Mane, your power feeds on the very blood of my eternal soul,* and I will have your obedience in this!

Lady Envy staggered another step, suddenly released by the visions, disorientated, her heart thudding in her chest. She drew in a sharp breath. 'Who knows the . . . the truth, K'rul?' *That, in striding through the warrens, we travel through your very flesh. That, when we draw upon the power of the warrens, we draw your very blood?* Who knows?'

She felt a casual shrug in his reply.

Anomander Rake, Draconus, Osric, a handful of others. And now you. Forgive me, Lady Envy, I have no wish to be a tyrant. My presence within the warrens has ever been passive – you are free to do as you choose, as is every other creature who swims my immortal blood. I have but one excuse, if you will. This Crippled God, this stranger from an unknown realm . . . Lady Envy, I am frightened.

A chill stole through her as the words sank into her mind.

K'rul continued after a moment. *We have lost allies in our foolishness. Dassem Ultor, who was broken by Hood's taking of his daughter at the Time of the Chaining – this was a devastating blow. Dassem Ultor, the First Sword reborn—*

'Do you think,' she asked slowly, 'that Hood would have taken her for the Chaining, had I answered the summons?' *Am I,* she wondered, *to blame for Dassem Ultor's loss?*

Hood alone could answer that question, Lady Envy. And

he'd likely lie, in any case. Dassem, his Champion —
Dessembrae — had grown to rival his power. There is little value
in worrying such questions, beyond the obvious lesson that in-
action is a deadly choice. Consider: from Dassem's fall, a mortal
empire now totters on the edge of chaos. From Dassem's fall, the
Shadow Throne found a new occupant. From Dassem's fall . . .
ah, well, the tumbling dominoes are almost countless. It is done.

'What is it you wish of me, now, K'rul?'

There was need. To show you the vastness of the threat. This
Pannion Domin is but a fragment of the whole, yet you must
lead my chosen into its very heart.

'And once there? Am I a match for the power that
resides there?'

Perhaps, but that is a path it may prove unwise to take, Lady
Envy. I shall trust in your judgement, and in that of others,
unwitting and otherwise. Indeed, you may well choose to cut the
knot that is at the heart of the Domin. Or, you may find a way
to loosen it, to free all that has been bound for three hundred
thousand years.

'Very well, we shall play it as it comes. What joy! I can
leave now? I so long to return to the others, to Toc the
Younger in particular. He's a darling, isn't he?'

Take great care of him, Lady. The scarred and the flawed are
what the Crippled God seeks in his servants. I shall endeavour to
keep Toc's soul from the Chained One's grasp, but, please, main-
tain your guard. Also . . . there is something else to that man,
something . . . wild. We shall have to await its awakening before
understanding comes to us, however. Oh, one last thing . . .

'Yes?'

Your party nears the Domin's territory. When you return to
them, you must not attempt your warren in an effort to hasten
your journey.

'Why?'

Within the Pannion Domin, Lady, my blood is poisoned. It is
a poison you can defeat, but Toc the Younger cannot.

Garath awoke, rose and stretched before her. K'rul was
gone.

'Oh my,' Lady Envy whispered, suddenly soaked in sweat. 'Poisoned. By the Abyss . . . I need a bath. Come, Garath, let us go collect the Third. Shall I awaken him with a kiss?'

The dog glanced over at her.

'Twin scars on his mask, and the imprint of painted lips! Would he be the Fourth, then, or the Fifth? How do they count lips, do you think? One upper, one lower, or both together? Let's find out.'

Dust and the dark swirl of sorcery rose beyond the hills directly ahead.

'Shield Anvil,' Farakalian said, 'have our allies already sprung a trap?'

Itkovian frowned. 'I do not know. No doubt we shall discover the truth when they elect to reappear and inform us.'

'Well,' the soldier muttered, 'that is a fight before us. An ugly one, by the looks of the magic unleashed.'

'I'll not argue that observation, sir,' the Shield Anvil replied. 'Riders, re-form as inverted crescent, hands to weapons. Slow trot to first line-of-sight.'

The decimated wing fell into formation, rode on.

They were close to the trader road, now, Itkovian judged. If a caravan had been hit by some of these K'Chain Che'Malle, the outcome was foregone. A caravan with an attendant mage or two might well make a fight of it, and from the brimstone stench that now wafted towards them, the latter circumstance seemed the likeliest.

As they approached a rise, a row of T'lan Imass emerged to stand along its crest, backs to Itkovian and his riders. The Shield Anvil counted a dozen. Perhaps the rest were busy with the battle – still beyond his line of sight. He saw the Bonecaster Pran Chole and angled his new horse in the undead shaman's direction.

They reached the rise. The sorcerous detonations had ceased, all sounds of battle fading away.

The trader road ran below. Two carriages had made up the caravan, one much larger than the other. Both had been destroyed, ripped apart. Splintered wood, plush padding and clothes lay strewn on all sides. On a low hill off to the right lay three figures, the ground blackened around them. None moved. Eight more bodies were visible around the wagons, only two conscious – black-chain-armoured men slowly regaining their feet.

These details registered only briefly on the Shield Anvil's senses. Wandering among the dismembered corpses of five K'Chain Che'Malle hunters were hundreds of huge, gaunt wolves – with pitted eyes that were a match to those of the T'lan Imass.

Studying the silent, terrifying creatures, Itkovian spoke to Pran Chole. 'Are these . . . yours, sir?'

The Bonecaster at his side shrugged. 'Gone from our company for a time. T'lan Ay often accompany us, but are not bound to us . . . beyond the Ritual itself.' He was silent for a long moment, then continued, 'We had thought them lost. But it seems that they too have heard the summons. Three thousand years since our eyes last rested upon the T'lan Ay.'

Itkovian finally looked down on the undead shaman. 'Is that a hint of pleasure in your voice, Pran Chole?'

'Yes. And sorrow.'

'Why sorrow? From the looks of it, these T'lan Ay took not a single loss against these K'Chain Che'Malle. Four, five hundred . . . against five. Swift destruction.'

The Bonecaster nodded. 'Their kind are skilled at defeating large beasts. My sorrow arises from a flawed mercy, mortal. At the First Gathering, our misplaced love for the ay – these few that remained – led us onto a cruel path. We chose to include them in the Ritual. Our selfish needs were a curse. All that made the flesh and blood ay honourable, proud creatures was taken away. Now, like us, they are husks, plagued by dead memories.'

'Even undead, they have majesty,' Itkovian acknowledged. 'As with you.'

328

'Majesty in the T'lan Ay, yes. Among the T'lan Imass? No, mortal. None.'

'We differ in opinion, then, Pran Chole.' Itkovian turned to address his soldiers. 'Check the fallen.'

The Shield Anvil rode down to the two chain-clad men, who now stood together beside the remnants of the larger of the two carriages. Their ringed armour was in tatters. Blood leaked from them, forming sodden pools at their feet. Something about the two men made Itkovian uneasy, but he pushed the emotion away.

The bearded one swung to face the Shield Anvil as he reined in before them. 'I bid you welcome, warrior,' he said, his accent strange to Itkovian's ears. 'Extraordinary events, just past.'

Despite his inner discipline, his unease deepened. None the less, he managed an even tone as he said, 'Indeed, sir. I am astonished, given the attention the K'ell Hunters evidently showed you two, that you are still standing.'

'We are resilient individuals, in truth.' His flat gaze scanned the ground beyond the Shield Anvil. 'Alas, our companions were found lacking in such resources.'

Farakalian, having conferred with the soldiers crouched among the fallen, now rode towards Itkovian.

'Shield Anvil. Of the three Barghast on the hill, one lies dead. The other two are injured, but will survive with proper ministration. Of the rest, only one breathes no more. An array of injuries to attend to. Two may yet die, sir. None of the survivors has yet regained consciousness. Indeed, each seems in unusually deep sleep.'

Itkovian glanced at the bearded man. 'Do you know more of this unnatural sleep, sir?'

'I am afraid not.' He faced Farakalian. 'Sir, among the survivors, can you include a tall, lean, somewhat elderly man, and a shorter, much older one?'

'I can. The former, however, hovers at the gates.'

'We'd not lose him, if at all possible.'

Itkovian spoke, 'Soldiers of the Grey Swords are skilled

in the art of healing, sir. They shall endeavour to the best of their abilities, and no more can be asked of them.'

'Of course. I am . . . distraught.'

'Understood.' The Shield Anvil addressed Farakalian: 'Draw on the Destriant's power if necessary.'

'Yes, sir.'

He watched the man ride off.

'Warrior,' the bearded man said, 'I am named Bauchelain, and my companion here is Korbal Broach. I must ask, these undead servants of yours – four-footed and otherwise—'

'Not servants, Bauchelain. Allies. These are T'lan Imass. The wolves, T'lan Ay.'

'T'lan Imass,' the one named Korbal Broach whispered in a reedy thin voice, his eyes suddenly bright as he stared at the figures on the ridge. 'Undead, born of the greatest necromantic ritual there has ever been! I would speak with them!' He swung to Bauchelain. 'May I? Please?'

'As you wish,' Bauchelain replied with an indifferent shrug.

'A moment,' Itkovian said. 'You both bear wounds that require attending to.'

'No need, Shield Anvil, though I thank you for your concern. We heal . . . swiftly. Please, concentrate on our companions. Now, that is odd – our beasts of burden and sundry horses are untouched – do you see? Fortunate indeed, once I complete my repairs to our carriage.'

Itkovian studied the wreckage to which Bauchelain now swung his attention.

Repairs? 'Sir, we return to Capustan immediately. There will be no time to spare effecting . . . repairs . . . to your carriage.'

'I shall not be long, I assure you.'

A shout from the ridge pulled the Shield Anvil round, in time to see Korbal Broach flying backwards from a back-handed blow – delivered by the Bonecaster Pran Chole. The man struck the slope, rolled down to its base.

Bauchelain sighed. 'He lacks manners, alas,' he said, eyes on his companion, who was slowly regaining his feet. 'The price of a sheltered, nay, isolated childhood. I hope the T'lan Imass are not too offended. Tell me, Shield Anvil, do these undead warriors hold grudges?'

Itkovian allowed himself a private smile. *You can ask that of the next Jaghut we happen across.* 'I wouldn't know, sir.'

From the ruins of the smaller carriage, three wide travois were cobbled together. The T'lan Imass fashioned leather harnesses for the undead ay chosen to pull them. The caravan's collection of horses went under the care of Farakalian and the recruit.

Itkovian watched Korbal Broach lead the oxen back to the rebuilt carriage. The Shield Anvil found his gaze avoiding the contraption; the details in the mending made his skin crawl. Bauchelain had elected to use the various bones of the dismembered K'Chain Che'Malle hunters in the reconstruction. Sorcerously melded into the carriage's frame, the bones formed a bizarre skeleton, which Bauchelain then covered with swathes of grey, pebbled skin. The effect was horrific.

Yet no more so than the carriage's owners, I suspect . . .

Pran Chole appeared at the Shield Anvil's side. 'Our preparations are complete, soldier.'

Itkovian nodded, then said in a low voice, 'Bonecaster, what do you make of these two sorcerors?'

'The unmanned one is insane, yet the other is the greater threat. They are not welcome company, Shield Anvil.'

'Unmanned?' Itkovian's eyes narrowed on Korbal Broach. 'A eunuch. Yes, of course. They are necromancers?'

'Yes. The unmanned one plies the chaos on the edge of Hood's realm. The other has more arcane interests – a summoner, of formidable power.'

'We cannot abandon them, none the less.'

'As you wish.' The Bonecaster hesitated, then said, 'Shield Anvil, the injured mortals are, one and all, dreaming.'

'Dreaming?'

'A familiar flavour,' the T'lan Imass said. 'They are being . . . protected. I look forward to their awakening, in particular the priest. Your soldiers displayed considerable skill in healing.'

'Our Destriant is High Denul – we are able to draw on his power in times of need, though I imagine his mood is dark at the moment. Exhausted, knowing that healing has occurred, but little else. Karnadas dislikes uncertainty. As does the Mortal Sword, Brukhalian.' He gathered his reins, straightened in the saddle. 'The eunuch has completed his task. We may now proceed. We shall ride through the night, sir, greeting the dawn at Capustan's gates.'

'And the presence of the T'lan Imass and T'lan Ay?' Pran Chole enquired.

'Hidden, if you please. Excepting those ay pulling the travois. They shall lead their charges through the city and into the compound in our barracks.'

'And you have reason for this, Shield Anvil?'

Itkovian nodded.

The sun low at their backs, the entourage set off.

Hands folded on his lap, the Destriant looked upon Prince Jelarkan with deep sympathy. No, more than that, given the man's obvious exhaustion . . . empathy. Karnadas's head pounded behind his eyes. His Denul warren felt hollow, coated with ash. Were he to have left his hands on the tabletop, their tremble would have been obvious.

Behind him, the Mortal Sword paced.

Itkovian and two wings rode the plain to the west, and something had happened. Concern echoed in every restless step at the Destriant's back.

The prince of Capustan's eyes were squeezed shut, fingers kneading his temples beneath the circlet of cold-hammered copper that was his crown. Twenty-two years old, his lined, drawn face could have belonged to a man of forty. His shaved pate revealed the scatter of moles that marked his royal line, as if he had been sprayed in blood that had since dried and grown dark. After a long sigh, the prince spoke. 'The Mask Council will not be swayed, Mortal Sword. They insist that their Gidrath occupy the outlying strongpoints.'

'Those fortifications will become isolated once the siege begins, Prince,' Brukhalian rumbled.

'I know. We both know. Isolated, dismantled, every soldier within slaughtered . . . then raped. The priests fancy themselves master strategists in warfare. A religious war, after all. The temples' own elite warriors must strike the first blows.'

'No doubt they will,' Brukhalian said. 'And little else.'

'And little else. Perhaps corridors, a series of sorties to effect a withdrawal—'

'Costing yet more lives, Prince, and likely to fail. My soldiers will not be party to suicide. And please, do not attempt to impose your will on me in this. We are contracted to hold the city. In our judgement, the best means of doing so are with maintaining the walls. The redoubts have always been a liability – they will serve the enemy better than they will serve us, as headquarters, defensible rallying positions. The Gidrath will be handing them fortifications in the killing ground. Once siege weapons are stationed there, we shall suffer ceaseless bombardment.'

'The Mask Council does not expect the strongpoints to fall, Mortal Sword. Nailed to that particular belief, all your stated fears are irrelevant, as far as they are concerned.'

There was silence, apart from Brukhalian's uncharacteristic pacing. The prince looked up finally, brown eyes following the Mortal Sword's catlike padding. Jelarkan frowned, then sighed and pushed himself to his feet. 'I need leverage, Mortal Sword. Find it for me, and quickly.' He swung about and strode to the chamber's doors, where waited his two bodyguards.

As soon as the massive doors closed behind the prince,

Brukhalian spun to Karnadas. 'Do they continue to draw on your powers, sir?'

The Destriant shook his head. 'Not for some time, now, since shortly after the prince's unexpected visit. In any case, sir, they have taken all I possess, and it will be days before I fully recover.'

Brukhalian released a long, slow breath. 'Well, the risk of a skirmish was recognized. From this, we must conclude that the Pannion has sent forces across the river. The question is, how many?'

'Sufficient to maul two wings, it seems.'

'Then Itkovian should have avoided engagement.'

Karnadas studied the Mortal Sword. 'Unworthy, sir. The Shield Anvil understands caution. If avoidance was possible, he would have done so.'

'Aye,' Brukhalian growled. 'I know.'

Voices at the compound's outer gates reached through to the two men. Hooves clapped on the cobbles.

Sudden tension filled the chamber, yet neither man spoke.

The doors swung open and they turned to see Itkovian's outrider, Sidlis. The soldier took two steps into the room, then halted and tilted her head. 'Mortal Sword. Destriant. I bring word from the Shield Anvil.'

'You have seen battle, sir,' Brukhalian murmured.

'We have. A moment, sirs.' Sidlis swung about and softly shut the doors. She faced the commander and priest. 'Demonic servants of the Pannion Seer are present on the plain,' she said. 'We came upon one and closed with it. The tactics employed should have sufficed, and the damage we delivered was severe and flawlessly executed. The beast, however, was undead – an animated corpse, and this discovery came too late for disengagement. It was virtually impervious to the wounds we delivered. Nevertheless, we succeeded in destroying the demon, though at great cost.'

'Outrider Sidlis,' Karnadas said, 'the battle you describe

must have occurred some time past – else you would not be here – yet the demands on my powers of healing have but just ended.'

Sidlis frowned. 'The survivors of the engagement did not require a drawing of your powers, sir. If I may, I will complete the tale, and perhaps further clarification will become . . . available.'

Raising an eyebrow at the awkward reply, Brukhalian rumbled, 'Proceed.'

'Upon the destruction of the demon, we regrouped, only to find that four additional demons had arrived.'

The Destriant winced. *How, then, are any of you left breathing?*

'At that moment, to our fortune,' Sidlis continued, 'unexpected allies arrived. The undead demons were one and all swiftly destroyed. The issue of said alliance of course needs formalization. For the moment, it is the recognition of a common enemy that yielded the combined efforts – which I believe continue at this moment, with the Shield Anvil and the troop riding in the company of our propitious companions, their intent to extend the hunt for more of these fell demons.'

'Given the Destriant's exhaustion,' the Mortal Sword said, 'they found them, it seems.'

Sidlis nodded.

'There is more, sir?' Karnadas asked.

'Sir. Accompanying me are emissaries from these potential allies. The Shield Anvil judged that such negotiation as may follow be solely between the Grey Swords and our guests; and that any decision of revelation, to the prince or to the Mask Council, should only follow considered counsel among yourselves, sirs.'

Brukhalian grunted his agreement. 'The emissaries await in the compound?'

The answer to his question rose in swirls of dust to the outrider's left. Three desiccated, fur-clad figures shimmered into being, rising up from the stone floor. Rotted furs and leathers, skin polished deep brown, massive shoulders and long, muscle-twisted arms.

The Destriant staggered back out of his chair, eyes wide.

Brukhalian had not moved. His eyes narrowed on the three apparitions.

The air suddenly smelled of thawed mud.

'They call themselves the Kron T'lan Imass,' Sidlis said calmly. 'The Shield Anvil judged their warriors to number perhaps fourteen thousand.'

'T'lan Imass,' Karnadas whispered. 'This is a most disturbing . . . convergence.'

'If I may make introductions,' Sidlis continued, 'these are Bonecasters – shamans. The one to the far left, upon whose shoulders is the fur of a snow bear, is Bek Okhan. Next to him, in the white wolf fur, is Bendal Home. The Bonecaster at my side, in the skin of a plains bear, is Okral Lom. I specify the nature of the furs as it relates directly to their . . . Soletaken forms. Or so they have informed me.'

The one named Bendal Home stepped forward. 'I bring greeting from Kron of Kron T'lan Imass, mortal,' he said in a soft, smooth whisper. 'Further, I have recent news from the clans escorting your Shield Anvil and his soldiers. Additional K'Chain Che'Malle K'ell Hunters were found, engaged in an attack on a cavaran. These hunters have been despatched. Your soldiers have administered to the wounds of the caravan survivors. All are now returning to Capustan. No further engagements are anticipated, and their arrival will coincide with the dawn.'

Trembling, Karnadas once more sat down in his chair. He struggled to speak past a suddenly parched throat. 'K'Chain Che'Malle? Animated?'

'Thank you, Sidlis,' Brukhalian said. 'You may now depart.' He faced Bendal Home. 'Do I understand correctly that Kron seeks an alliance against the Pannion Domin, and these . . . K'Chain Che'Malle?'

The Bonecaster cocked his head, his long, pale hair dangling loose from beneath the wolf-skull helmet. 'Such a battle is not our primary task. We have come to this land in answer to a summons. The presence of K'Chain Che'Malle was unexpected – and unacceptable. Further, we are curious as to the identity of the one named Pannion – we suspect he is not the mortal human you believe him to be. Kron has judged that our involvement in your conflict is required for the present. There is a caveat, however. The one who has summoned us approaches. With her arrival, the Second Gathering of the T'lan Imass will commence. At this time, our disposition will be for her to decide. Furthermore, it may well be that we become ... of less value to you ... upon completion of the Gathering.'

Brukhalian slowly turned to Karnadas. 'Sir? You have questions for the one named Bendal Home?'

'So many that I do not know where to begin, Mortal Sword. Bonecaster, what is this "Gathering" that you speak of?'

'That is a matter for the T'lan Imass, mortal.'

'I see. Well, that shuts the door on one line of inquiry, and its attendant multitude of questions. Regards the Pannion Seer – he is indeed a mortal human. I have seen him myself, and there is no scent of illusion to his flesh and bone. He is an old man, and nothing more.'

'And who stands in his shadow?' the Bonecaster named Bek Okhan rasped.

The Destriant blinked. 'No-one, as far as I can tell.'

The three T'lan Imass said nothing, yet Karnadas suspected a silent exchange among them, and perhaps with their distant kin as well.

'Mortal Sword,' the priest said in a low voice, 'do we inform the prince of this? What of the Mask Council?'

'Further counsel is indeed required before that decision can be made, sir,' Brukhalian replied. 'At the very least, we shall await the return of the Shield Anvil. Furthermore, there is the issue of additional communications this night, is there not?'

Fener's blessing, I'd forgotten. 'Indeed there is.' *Quick Ben*

. . . by the cloven hoof, we have allies stepping out of every closet . . .

Bendal Home spoke. 'Mortal Sword Brukhalian, your soldier Itkovian has decided that their public arrival into the city – with the company of the caravan's wounded – will include six of the T'lan Ay that now accompany our kin.'

'T'lan Ay?' Karnadas asked. 'Not a name I've heard before.'

'Wolves from the times of ice, long ago. Like us, undead.' Brukhalian smiled.

A moment later, Karnadas also smiled. 'The prince asked for . . . leverage, did he not, Mortal Sword?'

'He shall have it, sir.'

'So he shall.'

'If you have further need of us this evening,' Bendal Home said to Brukhalian, 'simply call upon us.'

'Thank you, sirs.'

The three T'lan Imass fell into clouds of dust.

'I take it,' the Destriant murmured, 'we need not offer our guests accommodation.'

'Evidently not. Walk with me, sir, we have much to discuss and scant time.'

Karnadas rose. 'No sleep this night.'

'None, alas.'

Two bells before dawn, Brukhalian stood alone in his private chamber. Exhaustion hung on him like a rain-sodden cloak, yet he would not yield to it. The Shield Anvil and his troop were soon to arrive, and the Mortal Sword was determined to await them – a commander could do no less.

A single lantern defied the gloom in the chamber, throwing lurid shadows before it. The centre hearth remained a grey smudge of dead coals and ashes. The air was bitter cold, and it was this alone that kept Brukhalian wakeful.

338

The sorcerous meeting with Quick Ben and Caladan Brood had proved, beneath its surface courtesies, strained – it was clear to both the Mortal Sword and Karnadas that their distant allies were holding back. The uncertainties plaguing their final intentions, and their guardedness, though understandable in the circumstances, left the two Grey Swords uncomfortable. Relief of Capustan was not, it seemed, their primary goal. An attempt would be made, but the Mortal Sword began to suspect it would be characterized by feints and minor skirmishes – late arriving at best – rather than a direct confrontation. This led Brukhalian to suspect that Caladan Brood's vaunted army, worn down by years of war with this Malazan Empire, had either lost the will to fight, or was so badly mauled that its combat effectiveness was virtually gone.

None the less, he could still think of ways in which to make these approaching allies useful. Often, the perception of threat was sufficient . . . *if we can hurt the Septarch badly enough to make him lose his nerve upon the imminent arrival of Brood's relieving army.* Or, if the defence crumbled, then an avenue of withdrawal for the Grey Swords was possible. The question then would be, at what point could the Mortal Sword honourably conclude that the contract's objectives no longer obtained? The death of Prince Jelarkan? Collapse of wall defences? Loss of a section of the city?

He sensed the air suddenly tear behind him, the sound like the faintest whisper as of parting fabric. A breath of lifeless wind flowed around him. The Mortal Sword slowly turned.

A tall, gauntly armoured figured was visible within the warren's grey-smeared portal. A face of pallid, lined skin over taut bones, eyes set deep within ridged sockets and brow, the glimmer of tusks protruding above the lower lip. The figure's mouth curved into a faint, mocking smile. 'Fener's Mortal Sword,' he said in the language of the Elin, his voice low and soft, 'I bring you greetings from Hood, Lord of Death.'

Brukhalian grunted, said nothing.

'Warrior,' the apparition continued after a moment, 'your reaction to my arrival seems almost . . . laconic. Are you truly as calm as you would have me believe?'

'I am Fener's Mortal Sword,' Brukhalian replied.

'Yes,' the Jaghut drawled, 'I know. I, on the other hand, am Hood's Herald, once known as Gethol. The tale that lies behind my present . . . servitude, is more than worthy of an epic poem. Or three. Are you not curious?'

'No.'

The face fell into exaggerated despondency, then the eyes flashed. 'How unimaginative of you, Mortal Sword. Very well, hear then, without comforting preamble, the words of my lord. While none would deny Hood's eternal hunger, and indeed his anticipation for the siege to come, certain complexities of the greater scheme lead my lord to venture an invitation to Fener's mortal soldiers—'

'Then you should be addressing the Tusked One himself, sir,' Brukhalian rumbled.

'Ah, alas, this has proved no longer posssible, Mortal Sword. Fener's attention is elsewhere. In fact, your lord has been drawn, with great reluctance, to the very edge of his realm.' The Herald's unhuman eyes narrowed. 'Fener is in great peril. The loss of your patron's power is imminent. The time has come, Hood has decided, for compassionate gestures, for expressions of the true brotherhood that exists between your lord and mine.'

'What does Hood propose, sir?'

'This city is doomed, Mortal Sword. Yet your formidable army need not join in the inevitable crush at Hood's gate. Such a sacrifice would be pointless, and indeed a great loss. The Pannion Domin is no more than a single, rather minor, element in a far vaster war – a war in which all the gods shall partake . . . *allied one and all* . . . against an enemy who seeks nothing less than the annihilation of all rivals. Thus, Hood offers you his warren, a means of extrication for you

340

and your soldiers. Yet you must choose quickly, for the warren's path here cannot survive the arrival of the Pannion's forces.'

'What you offer, sir, demands the breaking of our contract.'

The Herald's laugh was contemptuous. 'As I most vehemently told Hood, you humans are a truly pathetic lot. A contract? Scratchings on vellum? My lord's offer is not a thing to be negotiated.'

'And in accepting Hood's warren,' Brukhalian said quietly, 'the face of our patron changes, yes? Fener's . . . inaccessibility . . . has made him a liability. And so Hood acts quickly, eager to strip the Boar of Summer's mortal servants, preferably intact, to thereafter serve him and him alone.'

'Foolish man,' Gethol sneered. 'Fener shall be the first casualty in the war with the Crippled God. The Boar shall fall – and none can save him. The patronage of Hood is not casually offered, mortal, to just anyone. To be so honoured—'

'Honoured?' Brukhalian cut in, his voice the slide of iron on stone, his eyes flickering with a strange light. 'Allow me, on Fener's behalf,' he said in a low whisper, 'to comment on the question of honour.' The Mortal Sword's broadsword hissed in a blur from its scabbard, the blade cleaving upward to strike the Herald across the face. Bone snapped, dark blood sprayed.

Gethol reared back a step, withered hands rising to his shattered features.

Brukhalian lowered his weapon, his eyes burning with a deep rage. 'Come forward again, Herald, and I shall resume my commentary.'

'I do not,' Gethol rasped through torn lips, 'appreciate your . . . tone. It falls to me to answer in kind, not on Hood's behalf. Not any more. No, this reply shall be mine and mine alone.' A longsword appeared in each gauntleted hand, the blades shimmering like liquid gold. The Herald's eyes glittered like mirrors to the weapons. He took a step forward.

Then stopped, swords lifting into a defensive position.

A soft voice spoke behind Brukhalian. 'We greet you, Jaghut.'

The Mortal Sword turned to see the three T'lan Imass, each one strangely insubstantial, as if moments from assuming new forms, new shapes. Moments, Brukhalian realized, from veering into their Soletaken beasts. The air filled with a stale stench of spice.

'Not your concern, this fight,' Gethol hissed.

'The fight with this mortal?' Bek Okhan asked. 'No. However, Jaghut, you are.'

'I am Hood's Herald – do you dare challenge a servant of the lord of death?'

The T'lan Imass's desiccated lips peeled back. 'Why would we hesitate, Jaghut? Now ask of your lord, does he dare challenge us?'

Gethol grunted as something dragged him bodily back, the warren snapping shut, swallowing him. The air swirled briefly in the wake of the portal's sudden vanishing, then settled.

'Evidently not,' Bek Okhan said.

Sighing, Brukhalian sheathed his sword and faced the T'lan Imass Bonecasters. 'Your arrival has left me disappointed, sirs.'

'We understand this, Mortal Sword. You were doubtless well matched. Yet our hunt for this Jaghut demanded our . . . interruption. His talent for escaping us is undiminished, it seems, even to the point of bending a knee in the service of a god. Your defiance of Hood makes you a worthwhile companion.'

Brukhalian grimaced. 'If only to improve your chances of closing with this Jaghut, I take it.'

'Indeed.'

'So we are understood in this.'

'Yes. It seems we are.'

He stared at the three creatures for a moment, then

342

turned away. 'I think we can assume the Herald will not be returning to us this evening. Forgive my curtness, sirs, but I wish solitude once again.'

The T'lan Imass each bowed, then disappeared.

Brukhalian walked to the hearth, drawing his sword once more. He set the blunt end amongst the cold embers, slowly stirred the ashes. Flames licked into life, the coals burgeoning a glowing red. The spatters and streaks of Jaghut blood on the blade sizzled black, then burned away to nothing.

He stared down at the hearth for a long time, and despite the unveiled power of the sanctified sword, the Mortal Sword saw before him nothing but ashes.

Up from the darkness, a clawing, gasping struggle. Explosive blooms of pain, like a wall of fire rising behind his eyes, the shivering echoes of wounds, a tearing and puncturing of flesh – his own flesh.

A low groan escaped him, startled him into an awareness – he lay propped at an angle, taut skins stretched beneath him. There had been motion, a rocking and bumping and scraping, but that had ceased. He opened his eyes, found himself in shadow. A stone wall reared to his left, within reach. The air smelled of horses and dust and, much closer, blood and sweat.

Morning sunlight bathed the compound to his right, glimmered off the blurred figures moving about there. Soldiers, horses, impossibly huge, lean wolves.

Boots crunched on gravel and the shadow over him deepened. Blinking, Gruntle looked up.

Stonny's face was drawn, spattered with dried blood, her hair hanging in thick, snarled ropes. She laid a hand on his chest. 'We've reached Capustan,' she said in a ragged voice.

He managed a nod.

'Gruntle—'

Pain filled her eyes, and he felt a chill sweep over him.

'Gruntle . . . Harllo's dead. They – they left him, buried under rocks. They left him. And Netok – Netok, that dear boy . . . so wide-eyed, so innocent. I gave him his manhood, Gruntle, I did that, at least. Dead – we lost them both.' She reeled away then, out of the range of his vision, though he heard her rushed footsteps, dwindling.

Another face appeared, a stranger's, a young woman, helmed, her expression gentle. 'We are safe now, sir,' she said, her accent Capan. 'You have been force-healed. I grieve for your losses. We all do – the Grey Swords, that is. Rest assured, sir, you were avenged against the demons . . .'

Gruntle stopped listening, his eyes pulling away, fixing on the clear blue sky directly overhead. *I saw you, Harllo. You bastard. Throwing yourself in that creature's path, between us. I saw, damn you.*

A corpse beneath rocks, a face in the darkness, smeared in dust, that would never again smile.

A new voice. 'Captain.'

Gruntle turned his head, forced words through the clench of his throat. 'It's done, Keruli,' he said. 'You've been delivered. It's done. Damn you to Hood, get out of my sight.'

The priest bowed his head, withdrew through the haze of Gruntle's anger; withdrew, then was gone.

CHAPTER EIGHT

The harder the world, the fiercer the honour.
                                        Dancer

The bones formed hills, stretching out on all sides. Clattering, shifting beneath Gethol as the Jaghut struggled for purchase against the slope. The blood had slowed its flow down his ruined face, though the vision of one eye was still obscured – blocked by an upthrust shard that glimmered pink-white – and the pain had dulled to a pulsing throb.

'Vanity,' he mumbled through scabbed lips, 'is not *my* curse.' He gained his balance, straightened, tottering, on the hillside. 'No predicting mortal humans – no, not even Hood could have imagined such . . . insolence. But ah! The Herald's visage is now broken, and that which is broken must be discarded. Discarded . . .'

Gethol looked around. The endless hills, the formless sky, the cool, dead air. The bones. The Jaghut's undamaged eyebrow lifted. 'None the less, I appreciate the joke, Hood. Ha ha. Here you have tossed me. Ha ha. And now, I have leave to crawl free. Free from your service. So be it.'

The Jaghut opened his warren, stared into the portal that formed before him, his path into the cold, almost airless realm of Omtose Phellack. 'I know you, now, Hood. I know who – what – you are. Delicious irony, the mirror of your face. Do you in turn, I now wonder, know me?'

He strode into the warren. The familiar gelid embrace

eased his pain, the fire of his nerves. The steep, jagged walls of ice to either side bathed him in blue-green light. He paused, tested the air. No stench of Imass, no signs of intrusion, yet the power he sensed around him was weakened, damaged by millennia of breaches, the effrontery of T'lan. Like the Jaghut themselves, Omtose Phellack was dying. A slow, wasting death.

'Ah, my friend,' he whispered, 'we are almost done. You and I, spiralling down into . . . oblivion. A simple truth. Shall I unleash my rage? No. After all, my rage is not enough. It never was.'

He walked on, through the frozen memories that had begun to rot, there, within his reach, ever narrowing, ever closing in on the Jaghut.

The fissure was unexpected, a deep cleft slashing diagonally across his path. A soft, warm breath flowed from it, sweet with decay and disease. The ice lining its edges was bruised and pocked, riven with dark veins. Halting before it, Gethol quested with his senses. He hissed in recognition. 'You have not been idle, have you? What is this invitation you set before me? I am of this world, whilst you, stranger, are not.'

He moved to step past it, his torn lips twisting into a snarl. Then stopped, head slowly turning. 'I am no longer Hood's Herald,' he whispered. 'Dismissed. A flawed service. Unacceptable. What would you say to me, Chained One?'

There would be no answer, until the decision was made, until the journey's end.

Gethol entered the fissure.

The Crippled God had fashioned a small tent around his place of chaining, the Jaghut saw with some amusement. Broken, shattered, oozing with wounds that never healed, here then was the true face of vanity.

Gethol halted before the entrance. He raised his voice. 'Dispense with the shroud – I shall not crawl to you.'

The tent shimmered, then dissolved, revealing a robed,

hooded, shapeless figure sitting on damp clay. A brazier lifted veils of smoke between them, and a mangled hand reached out to fan the sweet tendrils into the hood-shadowed face. 'A most,' the Chained One said in a wheeze, 'a most devastating kiss. Your sudden lust for vengeance was ... felt, Jaghut. Your temper endangered Hood's meticulous plans, you see that, do you not? It was this that so ... disappointed the Lord of Death. His Herald must be obedient. His Herald must possess no personal desires, no ambitions. Not a worthy ... employer ... for one such as you.'

Gethol glanced around. 'There is heat beneath me. We chained you to Burn's flesh, anchored you to her bones – and you have poisoned her.'

'I have. A festering thorn in her side ... that shall one day kill her. And with Burn's death, this world shall die. Her heart cold, lifeless, will cease its life-giving bounty. These chains must be broken, Jaghut.'

Gethol laughed. 'All worlds die. I shall not prove the weak link, Crippled God. I was here for the Chaining, after all.'

'Ah,' the creature hissed, 'but you *are* the weak link. You ever were. You thought you could earn Hood's trust, and you failed. Not the first failure, either, as we both know. When your brother Gothos called upon you—'

'Enough! Who is the vulnerable one here?'

'We both are, Jaghut. We both are.' The god raised his hand again, waved it slowly between them. Lacquered, wooden cards appeared, suspended in the air, their painted images facing Gethol. 'Behold,' the Crippled God whispered, 'the House of Chains ...'

The Jaghut's lone functioning eye narrowed. 'What – what have you done?'

'No longer an outsider, Gethol. I would ... *join the game*. And look more carefully. The role of Herald is ... vacant.'

Gethol grunted. 'More than just the Herald ...'

'Indeed, these are early days. Who, I wonder, will earn

the right of King in my House? Unlike Hood, you see, I welcome personal ambition. Welcome independent thought. Even acts of vengeance.'

'The Deck of Dragons will resist you, Chained One. Your House will be . . . assailed.'

'It was ever thus. You speak of the Deck as an entity, but its maker is dust, as we both know. There is no-one who can control it. Witness the resurrection of the House of Shadows. A worthy precedent. Gethol, I have need of you. I embrace your . . . flaws. None among my House of Chains shall be whole, in flesh or in spirit. Look upon me, look upon this broken, shattered figure – my House reflects what you see before you. Now cast your gaze upon the world beyond, the nightmare of pain and failure that is the mortal realm. Very soon, Gethol, my followers shall be legion. Do you doubt that? Do you?'

The Jaghut was silent for a long time, then he growled, 'The House of Chains has found its Herald. What would you have me do?'

'I've lost my mind,' Murillio muttered, but he threw the bones none the less. The carved phalanges bounced and rolled, then came to a stop.

'The Lord's Push, dear friend, alas for you but not for worthy self!' Kruppe cried, reaching out to gather the bones. 'And now Kruppe doubles the bid on a clear skid – ah, exquisite rhyme exquisitely delivered – ho!' The bones bounced, settled with unmarked sides facing up. 'Ha! Riches tumble upon Kruppe's ample lap! Gather them up, formidable wizard!'

Shaking his head, Quick Ben collected the finger bones. 'I've seen every cheat possible – the bad and the superb – but Kruppe, you continue to evade my sharpest eye.'

'Cheat? Gods forbid! What hapless victims are witness to on this night of nights is naught but cosmic sympathy for worthy Kruppe!'

'Cosmic sympathy?' Murillio snorted. 'What in Hood's name is that?'

'Euphemism for cheating,' Coll grumbled. 'Make your call, Quick, I'm eager to lose still more of my hard-earned coin.'

'It's this table,' Murillio said. 'It skews everything, and somehow Kruppe's found the pattern – don't deny it, you block of cheesy lard.'

'Kruppe denies all things patently deniable, dearest companions. No pattern has yet formed, by way of sincerest assurance, for the principal in question has fled from his appointed role. Said flight naught but an illusion, of course, though the enforced delay in self-recognition may well have direst consequences. Fortunate for one and all, Kruppe is here with cogent regard—'

'Whatever,' Quick Ben cut in. 'Dark heart where it matters most and skull in the corner.'

'Bold wager, mysterious mage. Kruppe challenges treble with a true hand and not a nudge askew!'

The wizard snorted. 'Never seen one of those, ever. Not ever. Not once.' He sent the bones skidding across the table.

The polished finger bones came to a stop, arrayed in a spread hand, all the symbols and patterns revealing perfect alignment.

'And now, wondering wizard, you have! Kruppe's coffers overflow!'

Quick Ben stared at the skeletal hand on the table's battered surface.

'What's the point of this?' Coll sighed. 'Kruppe wins every cast. Not subtle, little man – a good cheat makes sure there's losses thrown in every now and then.'

'Thus Kruppe's true innocence is displayed! A cheat of successive victories would be madness indeed – no, this sympathy is true and well beyond Kruppe's control.'

'How did you do that?' Quick Ben whispered.

Kruppe removed a mottled silk handkerchief from his

sleeve and mopped his brow. 'Warrens suddenly abound, licking the air with invisible flames, aaii! Kruppe withers beneath such scrutiny – mercy, Kruppe begs you, malicious mage!'

Quick Ben leaned back, glanced over to where Whiskeyjack sat apart from the others, his back to the tent wall, his eyes half closed. 'There's something there – I swear it – but I can't pin him down. He's slippery – gods, he's slippery!'

Whiskeyjack grunted. 'Give it up,' he advised, grinning. 'You won't catch him, I suspect.'

The mage swung on Kruppe. 'You are not what you seem—'

'Oh but he is,' Coll interjected. 'Look at him. Greasy, slimy, slick like one giant hairy ball of buttered eel. Kruppe is precisely as he seems, trust me. Look at the sudden sweat on his brow, the boiled lobster face, the bugged-out eyes – look at him squirm! That's Kruppe, every inch of him!'

'Abashed, is Kruppe! Cruel scrutiny! Kruppe crumbles beneath such unwarranted attention!'

They watched as the man wrung out the handkerchief, their eyes widening at the torrent of oily water that poured from it to pool on the tabletop.

Whiskeyjack barked a laugh. 'He has you all in his belt-pouch, even now! Squirm, is it? Sweat? All an illusion.'

'Kruppe buckles under such perceptive observations! He wilts, melts, dissolves into a blubbering fool!' He paused, then leaned forward and gathered in his winnings. 'Kruppe is thirsty. Does any wine remain in that smudged jug, he wonders? Yet more than that, Kruppe wonders what has brought Korlat to the tent's entrance here in the dead of night, with one and all exhausted by yet another day of interminable marching?'

The flap was drawn back and the Tiste Andii woman stepped into the lantern light. Her violet eyes found Whiskeyjack. 'Commander, my lord requests the pleasure of your company.'

Whiskeyjack raised his brows. 'Now? Very well, I accept the invitation.' He rose slowly, favouring his bad leg.

'I'll figure you out yet,' Quick Ben said, glaring at Kruppe.

'Kruppe denies the existence of elusive complexity regarding self, worrisome wizard. Simplicity is Kruppe's mistress – in joyful conspiracy with his dear wife, Truth, of course. Long and loyal in allegiance, this happy threesome—'

He was still talking as Whiskeyjack left the tent and walked with Korlat towards the Tiste Andii encampment. After a few minutes, the commander glanced at the woman beside him. 'I would have thought your lord would have departed by now – he's not been seen for days.'

'He will remain in our company for a time,' Korlat said. 'Anomander Rake has little patience for staff meetings and the like. Crone keeps him informed of developments.'

'Then I am curious – what would he have of me?'

She smiled slightly. 'That is for my lord to reveal, Commander.'

Whiskeyjack fell silent.

The Knight of Dark's tent was indistinguishable from all the other tents of the Tiste Andii, unguarded and a little more than halfway down a row, weakly lit from within by a single lantern. Korlat halted before the flap. 'My escort is done. You may enter, Commander.'

He found Anomander Rake seated in a leather-backed folding camp chair, his long legs stretched out before him. An empty matching chair was opposite, and set to one side within reach of both was a small table on which sat a carafe of wine and two goblets.

'Thank you for coming,' the Knight of Dark said. 'Please, make yourself comfortable.'

Whiskeyjack settled into the chair.

Rake leaned forward and filled the two goblets, passed one over to the commander who accepted it gratefully. 'With the proper perspective,' the Tiste Andii said, 'even a mortal life can seem long. Fulfilling. What I contemplate at the moment is the nature of happenstance. Men and women who, for a time, find themselves walking in step, on parallel paths. Whose lives brush close, howsoever briefly, and are so changed by the chance contact.'

Whiskeyjack studied the man opposite him through half-closed eyes. 'I don't view change as particularly threatening, Lord.'

'Rake will suffice. To your point, I agree . . . more often than not. There is tension among the command, of which I am sure you are fully aware.'

The Malazan nodded.

Rake's veiled eyes sharpened on Whiskeyjack's for a moment, then casually slid away once more. 'Concerns. Long-bridled ambitions now straining. Rivalries old and new. The situation has the effect of . . . separating. Each and every one of us, from all the others. Yet, if we abide, the calm return of instinct makes itself heard once more, whispering of . . . hope.' The extraordinary eyes found the commander once again, a contact just as brief as the first.

Whiskeyjack drew a slow, silent breath. 'The nature of this hope?'

'My instincts – at the instant when lives brush close, no matter how momentary – inform me who is worthy of trust. Ganoes Paran, for example. We first met on this plain, not too far from where we are now camped. A tool of Oponn, moments from death within the jaws of Shadowthrone's Hounds. A mortal, his every loss written plain, there in his eyes. Living or dying, his fate meant nothing to me. Yet . . .'

'You liked him.'

Rake smiled, sipped wine. 'Aye, an accurate summation.'

There was silence, then, that stretched as the two men sat facing each other. After a long while, Whiskeyjack slowly straightened in his chair, a quiet realization stealing through him. 'I imagine,' he finally said, studying the wine in his goblet, 'Quick Ben has you curious.'

Anomander Rake cocked his head. 'Naturally,' he

replied, revealing faint surprise and questioning in his tone.

'I first met him in Seven Cities ... the Holy Desert Raraku, to be more precise,' Whiskeyjack said, leaning forward to refill both goblets, then settling back before continuing. 'It's something of a long tale, so I hope you can be patient.'

Rake half smiled his reply.

'Good. I think it will be worth it.' Whiskeyjack's gaze wandered, found the lantern hanging from a pole, settled on its dim, flaring gold flame. 'Quick Ben. Adaephon Delat, a middling wizard in the employ of one of the Seven Holy Protectors during an abortive rebellion that originated in Aren. Delat and eleven other mages made up the Protector's cadre. Our besieging army's own sorcerors were more than their match – Bellurdan, Nightchill, Tayschrenn, A'Karonys, Tesormalandis, Stumpy – a formidable gathering known for their brutal execution of the Emperor's will. Well, the city the Protector was holed up in was breached, the walls sundered, slaughter in the streets, the madness of battle gripped us all. Dassem struck down the Holy Protector – Dassem and his band of followers he called his First Sword – they chewed their way through the enemy ranks. The Protector's cadre, seeing the death of their master and the shattering of the army, fled. Dassem ordered my company in pursuit, out into the desert. Our guide was a local, a man recently recruited into our own Claw . . .'

Kalam Mekhar's broad, midnight face glistened with sweat. Whiskeyjack watched as the man twisted in the saddle, watched the wide shoulders shrug beneath the dusty, stained telaba.

'They remain together,' the guide rumbled. 'I would have thought they'd split . . . and force you to do the same. Or to choose among them, Commander. The trail leads out, sir, out into Raraku's heart.'

'How far ahead?' Whiskeyjack asked.

'Half a day, no more. And on foot.'

353

The commander squinted out into the desert's ochre haze. Seventy soldiers rode at his back, a cobbled-together collection of marines, engineers, infantry and cavalry; each from squads that had effectively ceased to exist. Three years of sieges, set battles and pursuits for most of them. They were what Dassem Ultor judged could be spared, and, if necessary, sacrificed.

'Sir,' Kalam said, cutting into his thoughts. 'Raraku is a holy desert. A place of power . . .'

'Lead on,' Whiskeyjack growled.

Dust-devils swirled random paths across the barren, wasted plain. The troop rode at a trot with brief intervals of walking. The sun climbed higher in the sky. Somewhere behind them, a city still burned, yet before them they saw an entire landscape that seemed lit by fire.

The first corpse was discovered early in the afternoon. Curled, a ragged, scorched telaba fluttering in the hot wind, and beneath it a withered figure, head tilted skyward, eye sockets hollowed pits. Kalam dismounted and was long in examining the body. Finally, he rose and faced Whiskeyjack. 'Kebharla, I think. She was more a scholar than a mage, a delver of mysteries. Sir, there's something odd—'

'Indeed?' the commander drawled. He leaned forward in his saddle, studied the corpse. 'Apart from the fact that she looks like she died a hundred years ago, what do you find odd, Kalam?'

The man's face twisted in a scowl.

A soldier chuckled behind Whiskeyjack.

'Will that funny man come forward, please,' the commander called out without turning.

A rider joined him. Thin, young, an ornate, oversized Seven Cities helmet on his head. 'Sir!' the soldier said.

Whiskeyjack stared at him. 'Gods, man, lose that helm – you'll cook your brains. And the fiddle – the damned thing's broken anyway.'

'The helmet's lined with cold-sand, sir.'

'With what?'

'Cold-sand. Looks like shaved filings, sir, but you could

354

throw a handful into a fire and it won't get hot. Strangest thing, sir.'

The commander's eyes narrowed on the helmet. 'By the Abyss, the Holy Protector wore that!'

The man nodded solemnly. 'And when Dassem's sword clipped it, it went flying, sir. Right into my arms.'

'And the fiddle followed?'

The soldier's eyes thinned suspiciously. 'No, sir. The fiddle's mine. Bought it in Malaz City, planned on learning how to play it.'

'So who put a fist through it, soldier?'

'That would be Hedge, sir – that man over there beside Picker.'

'He can't play the damn thing!' the soldier in question shouted over.

'Well I can't now, can I? It's broke. But once the war's done I'll get it fixed, won't I?'

Whiskeyjack sighed. 'Return to your position, sir Fiddler, and not another sound from you, understood?'

'One thing, sir. I got a bad feeling . . . about . . . about all of this.'

'You're not alone in that, soldier.'

'Well, uh, it's just that—'

'Commander!' the soldier named Hedge called out, nudging his mount forward. 'The lad's hunches, sir, they ain't missed yet. He told Sergeant Nubber not to drink from that jug, but Nubber did anyway, and now he's dead, sir.'

'Poisoned?'

'No, sir. A dead lizard. Got stuck in his throat. Nubber choked to death on a dead lizard! Hey, Fiddler – a good name, that. Fiddler. Hah!'

'Gods,' Whiskeyjack breathed. 'Enough.' He faced Kalam again. 'Ride on.'

The man nodded, climbed back in his saddle.

Eleven mages on foot, without supplies, fleeing across a lifeless desert, the hunt should have been completed quickly. Late in the afternoon they came upon another body, as shrivelled as the first one; then, with the sun spreading crimson on the west horizon, a third corpse was found on the trail. Directly ahead, half a league distant, rose the bleached, jagged teeth of limestone cliffs, tinted red with the sunset. The trail of the surviving wizards, Kalam informed the commander, led towards them.

The horses were exhausted, as were the soldiers. Water was becoming a concern. Whiskeyjack called a halt, and camp was prepared.

After the meal, and with soldiers stationed at pickets, the commander joined Kalam Mekhar at the hearth.

The assassin tossed another brick of dung onto the flames, then checked the water in the battered pot suspended by a tripod over the fire. 'The herbs in this tea will lessen the loss of water come the morrow,' the Seven Cities native rumbled. 'I'm lucky to have it – it's rare and getting rarer. Makes your piss thick as soup, but short. You'll still sweat, but you need that—'

'I know,' Whiskeyjack interjected. 'We've been on this damned continent long enough to learn a few things, Clawleader.'

The man glanced over at the settling soldiers. 'I keep forgetting that, Commander. You're all so . . . young.'

'As young as you, Kalam Mekhar.'

'And what have I seen of the world, sir? Scant little. Bodyguard to a Holy Falah in Aren—'

'Bodyguard? Why mince words? You were his private assassin.'

'My journey has just begun, is what I was trying to say, sir. You – your soldiers – what you've seen, what you've been through . . .' He shook his head. 'It's all there, in your eyes.'

Whiskeyjack studied the man, the silence stretching.

Kalam removed the pot and poured out two cups of the medicinal-smelling brew, handed one up to the commander. 'We'll catch up with them tomorrow.'

'Indeed. We've ridden steady the day through, twice the pace of a soldier's jog. How much distance have we closed with these damned mages? A bell's worth? Two? No more than two. They're using warrens . . .'

356

The assassin, frowning, slowly shook his head. 'Then I would have lost the trail, sir. Once they entered a warren, all signs of them would have vanished.'

'Yes. Yet the footprints lead on, unbroken. Why is that?'

Kalam squinted into the fire. 'I don't know, sir.'

Whiskeyjack drained the bitter tea, dropped the tin cup to the ground beside the assassin, then strode away.

Day followed day, the pursuit taking them through the battered ravines, gorges and arroyos of the hills. More bodies were discovered, desiccated figures that Kalam identified one after another: Renisha, a sorceror of High Meanas; Keluger, a Septime Priest of D'riss, the Worm of Autumn; Narkal, the warrior-mage, sworn to Fener and aspirant to the god's Mortal Sword; Ullan, the Soletaken priestess of Soliel.

Deprivation took its toll on the hunters. Horses died, were butchered and eaten. The surviving beasts thinned, grew gaunt. Had not the mages' trail led Kalam and the others unerringly to one hidden spring after another, everyone would have died, there in Raraku's relentless wasteland.

Set'alahd Crool, a Jhag half-blood who'd once driven Dassem Ultor back a half-dozen steps in furious counterattack, his sword ablaze with the blessing of some unknown ascendant; Etra, a mistress of the Rashan warren; Birith'erah, mage of the Serc warren who could pull storms down from the sky; Gellid, witch of the Tennes warren . . .

And now but one remained, ever ahead, elusive, his presence revealed only by the light footprints he left behind.

The hunters were embraced in silence, now. Raraku's silence. Tempered, honed, annealed under the sun. The horses beneath them were their match, lean and defiant, tireless and wild-eyed.

Whiskeyjack was slow to understand what he saw in Kalam's face when the assassin looked upon him and his soldiers, slow to grasp that the killer's narrowed eyes held disbelief, awe, and more than a little fear. Yet Kalam himself had changed. He'd not travelled far from the land he called home, yet an entire world had passed beneath him.

Raraku had taken them all.

Up a steep, rocky channel, through an eroded fissure, the limestone walls stained and pitted, and out into a natural amphitheatre, and there, seated cross-legged on a boulder on the clearing's opposite side, waited the last mage.

He wore little more than rags, was emaciated, his dark skin cracked and peeling, his eyes glittering hard and brittle as obsidian.

Kalam's reining in looked to be a tortured effort. He managed to turn his horse round, met Whiskeyjack's eyes. 'Adaephon Delat, a mage of Meanas,' he said in a bone-dry rasp, his split lips twisting into a grin. 'He was never much, sir. I doubt he'll be able to muster a defence.'

Whiskeyjack said nothing. He angled his mount past the assassin, approached the wizard.

'One question,' the wizard asked, his voice barely a whisper yet carrying clearly across the amphitheatre.

'What?'

'Who in Hood's name are you?'

Whiskeyjack raised a brow. 'Does it matter?'

'We have crossed Raraku entire,' the wizard said. 'Other side of these cliffs is the trail leading down to G'danisban. You chased me across the Holy Desert . . . gods, no man is worth that. Not even me!'

'There were eleven others in your company, wizard.'

Adaephon Delat shrugged. 'I was the youngest – the healthiest – by far. Yet now, finally, even my body has given up. I can go no further.' His dark eyes reached past Whiskeyjack. 'Commander, your soldiers . . .'

'What of them?'

'They are more . . . and less. No longer what they once were. Raraku, sir, has burned the bridges of their pasts, one and all – it's all gone.' He met Whiskeyjack's eyes in wonder. 'And they are yours. Heart and soul. They are yours.'

'More than you realize,' Whiskeyjack said. He raised his voice. 'Hedge, Fiddler, are we in place?'

'Aye!' two voices chorused.

Whiskeyjack saw the wizard's sudden tension. After a

moment, the commander twisted in his saddle. Kalam sat stiffly on his horse a dozen paces back, sweat streaming down his brow. Flanking him and slightly behind were Fiddler and Hedge, both with their crossbows trained on the assassin. Smiling, Whiskeyjack faced Adaephon Delat once again.

'You two have played an extraordinary game. Fiddler sniffed out the secret communications – the scuffed stone-faces, the postures of the bodies, the curled fingers – one, three, two, whatever was needed to complete the cipher – we could have cut this to a close a week past, but by then I'd grown . . . curious. Eleven mages. Once the first one revealed her arcane knowledge to you – knowledge she was unable to use – it was just a matter of bargaining. What choice did the others possess? Death by Raraku's hand, or mine. Or . . . a kind of salvation. But was it, after all? Do their souls clamour within you, now, Adaephon Delat? Screaming to escape their new prison? But I am left wondering, none the less. This game – you and Kalam – to what end?'

The illusion of deprivation slowly faded from the wizard, revealing a fit, hale young man. He managed a strained smile. 'The clamour has . . . subsided somewhat. Even the ghost of a life is better than Hood's embrace, Commander. We've achieved a . . . balance, you could say.'

'And you a host of powers unimagined.'

'Formidable, granted, but I've no desire to use them now. The game we played, Whiskeyjack? Only one of survival. At first. We didn't think you'd make it, to be perfectly honest. We thought Raraku would come to claim you – I suppose she did, in a way, though not in a way I would have anticipated. What you and your soldiers have become . . .' He shook his head.

'What we have become,' Whiskeyjack said, 'you have shared. You and Kalam.'

The wizard slowly nodded. 'Hence this fateful meeting. Sir, Kalam and I, we'll follow you, now. If you would have us.'

Whiskeyjack grunted. 'The Emperor will take you from me.'

'Only if you tell him, Commander.'

'And Kalam?' Whiskeyjack glanced back at the assassin.

'The Claw will be . . . displeased,' the man rumbled. Then he smiled. 'Too bad for Surly.'

Grimacing, Whiskeyjack twisted further to survey his soldiers. The array of faces could have been carved from stone. A company, culled from the army's cast-offs, now a bright, hard core. 'Gods,' he whispered under his breath, 'what have we made here?'

The first blood-letting engagement of the Bridgeburners was the retaking of G'danisban – a mage, an assassin, and seventy soldiers who swept into a rebel stronghold of four hundred desert warriors and crushed them in a single night.

The lantern's light had burned low, but the tent's walls revealed the dawn's gentle birth. The sounds of a camp awakening and preparing for the march slowly rose to fill the silence that followed Whiskeyjack's tale.

Anomander Rake sighed. 'Soul-shifting.'

'Aye.'

'I have heard of shifting one soul – sending it into a vessel prepared for it. But to shift eleven souls – eleven mages – into the already-occupied body of a twelfth . . .' He shook his head in disbelief. 'Brazen, indeed. I see now why Quick Ben requested I probe him no further.' His eyes lifted. 'Yet here, this night, you unveil him. I did not ask—'

'To have asked, Lord, would have been a presumption,' Whiskeyjack said.

'Then you understood me.'

'Instinct,' the Malazan smiled. 'I trust mine as well, Anomander Rake.'

The Tiste Andii rose from the chair.

Whiskeyjack followed suit.

'I was impressed,' Rake said, 'when you stood ready to defend the child Silverfox.'

'And I was in turn impressed when you reined yourself in.'

'Yes,' the Knight of Dark muttered, eyes suddenly averted and a faint frown marring his brow. 'The mystery of the cherub . . .'

360

'Excuse me?'

The Tiste Andii smiled. 'I was recalling my first meeting with the one named Kruppe.'

'I am afraid, Lord, that Kruppe is one mystery for whom I can offer nothing in way of revelation. Indeed, I think that effort will likely defeat us all.'

'You may be right in that, Whiskeyjack.'

'Quick Ben leaves this morning, to join Paran and the Bridgeburners.'

Rake nodded. 'I shall endeavour to keep my distance, lest he grow nervous.' After a moment, the Tiste Andii held out his hand.

They locked wrists.

'A welcome evening just past,' Rake said.

Whiskeyjack grimaced. 'I'm not much for spinning entertaining tales. I appreciate your patience.'

'Perhaps I can redress the balance some other evening – I've a few stories of my own.'

'I'm sure you have,' Whiskeyjack managed.

They released their grips and the commander turned to the entrance.

Behind him, Rake spoke, 'One last thing. Silverfox need have nothing to fear from me. More, I will instruct Kallor accordingly.'

Whiskeyjack looked down at the ground for a moment. 'I thank you, Lord,' he breathed, then made his way out.

Gods below, I have made a friend this night. When did I last stumble on such a gift? I cannot remember. Hood's breath, I cannot.

Standing at the tent entrance, Anomander Rake watched the old man limp away down the track.

A soft patter of taloned feet approached from behind. 'Master,' Crone muttered, 'was that wise?'

'What do you mean?' he asked distractedly.

'There is a price for making friends among such short-

361

lived mortals – as you well can attest from your own typically tragic memories.'

'Careful, hag.'

'Do you deny the truth of my words, Lord?'

'One can find precious value in brevity.'

The Great Raven cocked her head. 'Honest observation? Dangerous admonition? Twisted and all too unhappy wisdom? I doubt you'll elaborate. You won't, will you? You'll leave me wondering, pecking endlessly in fretful obsession! You pig!'

'Do you smell carrion on the wind, my dear? I swear I do. Why not go find it. Now. This instant. And once you have filled your belly, find Kallor and bring him to me.'

With a snarl the Great Raven leapt outside, wings spreading explosively, heaving the huge bird skyward.

'Korlat,' Rake murmured. 'Attend me, please.' He swung back to the tent's interior. Moments later Korlat arrived. Rake remained facing the back wall.

'Lord?'

'I shall depart for a short time. I feel the need for Silannah's comfort.'

'She will welcome your return, Lord.'

'A few days' absence, no more than that.'

'Understood.'

Rake faced her. 'Extend your protection to Silverfox.'

'I am pleased by the instruction.'

'Unseen watchers on Kallor as well. Should he err, call upon me instantly, but do not hesitate in commanding the full force of the Tiste Andii down upon him. At the very least, I can be witness to the gathering of his pieces.'

'The full force, Lord? We have not done so in a long, long time. Do you believe it will be necessary in destroying Kallor?'

'I cannot be sure, Korlat. Why risk otherwise?'

'Very well. I shall begin the preparation for our warrens' joining.'

'I see that it troubles you none the less.'

'There are eleven hundred Tiste Andii, Lord.'

'I am aware of that, Korlat.'

'At the Chaining, there were but forty of us, yet we destroyed the Crippled God's entire realm – granted, a nascent realm. None the less, Lord. Eleven hundred . . . we risk devastating this entire continent.'

Rake's eyes grew veiled. 'I would advise some restraint in the unleashing, Korlat, should it prove necessary to collectively release Kurald Galain. Brood would not be pleased. I suspect that Kallor will do nothing precipitous, in any case. These are all but precautions.'

'Understood.'

He turned back to the tent's interior. 'That will be all, Korlat.'

The Mhybe dreamed. Once more – after so long – she found herself wandering the tundra, the lichen and moss crunching underfoot as a dry wind swept over her, smelling of dead ice. She walked without aches, heard no rattle deep in her chest as she breathed the crisp air. She had returned, she realized, to the place of her daughter's birth.

Tellann's warren, a place not where, but when. The time of youth. For the world. For me.

She lifted her arms, saw their amber smoothness, the tendons and roped veins of her hands almost undiscernible beneath plump flesh.

I am young. I am as I should be.

Not a gift. No, this was torture. She knew she was dreaming; she knew what she would find when she awakened.

A small herd of some ancient, long-extinct beast rolled soft thunder through the hard earth beneath her moccasined feet, running parallel to the path she had chosen along a ridge, their humped backs appearing every now and then above the crest – a blurred flow of burnt umber. Something within her stirred, a quiet exultation to answer the majesty of those creatures.

Kin to the bhederin, only larger, with horns spreading out to the sides, massive, regal.

Glancing down, she paused in her steps. Footprints crossed her path. Hide-wrapped feet had punched through the brittle lichen. Eight, nine individuals.

Flesh and blood Imass? The Bonecaster Pran Chole and his companions? Who walks my dreamscape this time?

Her eyes blinked open to musty darkness. Dull pain wrapped her thinned bones. Gnarled hands drew the furs close to her chin against the chill. She felt her eyes fill with water, blinked up at the swimming, sloped ceiling of the hide tent, and released a slow, agonized breath.

'Spirits of the Rhivi,' she whispered, 'take me now, I beg you. An end to this life, please. Jaghan, Iruth, Mendalan, S'ren Tahl, Pahryd, Neprool, Manek, Ibindur – I name you all, take me, spirits of the Rhivi . . .'

The rattle of her breath, the stubborn beat of her heart . . . the spirits were deaf to her prayer. With a soft whimper, the Mhybe sat up, reached for her clothes.

She tottered out into misty light. The Rhivi camp was awakening around her. Off to one side she heard the low of the bhederin, felt the restless rumble through the ground, then the shouts of the tribe's youths returning from a night spent guarding the herd. Figures were emerging from the nearby tents, voices softly singing in ritual greeting of the dawn.

Iruth met inal barku sen netral . . . ah'rhitan! Iruth met inal . . .

The Mhybe did not sing. There was no joy within her for another day of life.

'Dear lass, I have just the thing for you.'

She turned at the voice. The Daru Kruppe was waddling down the path towards her, clutching a small wooden box in his pudgy hands.

She managed a wry smile. 'Forgive me if I hesitate at your gifts. Past experience . . .'

'Kruppe sees beyond the wrinkled veil, my dear. In all

364

things. Thus, his midnight mistress is Faith – a loyal aide whose loving touch Kruppe deeply appreciates. Mercantile interests,' he continued, arriving to stand before her, his eyes on the box, 'yield happy, if unexpected gifts. Within this modest container awaits a treasure, which I offer to you, dear.'

'I have no use for treasures, Kruppe, though I thank you.'

'A history worth recounting, Kruppe assures you. In extending the tunnel network leading to and from the famed caverns of gaseous bounty beneath fair Darujhistan, hewn chambers were found here and there, the walls revealing each blow of countless antler picks, and upon said rippling surfaces glorious scenes from the distant past were found. Painted in spit and charcoal and haematite and blood and snot and Hood knows what else, but there was more. More indeed. Pedestals, carved in the fashion of rude altars, and upon these altars – these!'

He flipped back the lid of the box.

At first, the Mhybe thought she was looking upon a collection of flint blades, resting on strangely wrought bangles seemingly of the same fractious material. Then her eyes narrowed.

'Aye,' Kruppe whispered. 'Fashioned *as if* they were indeed flint. But no, they are copper. Cold-hammered, the ore gouged raw from veins in rock, flattened beneath pounding stones. Layer upon layer. Shaped, worked, to mirror a heritage.' His small eyes lifted, met the Mhybe's. 'Kruppe sees the pain of your twisted bones, my dear, and he grieves. These copper objects are not tools, but ornaments, to be worn about the body – you will find the blades have clasps suitable for a hide thong. You will find wristlets and anklets, arm-torcs and . . . uh, necklets. There is efficacy in such items . . . to ease your aches. Copper, the first gift of the gods.'

Bemused at her own sentimentality, the Mhybe wiped the tears from her lined cheeks. 'I thank you, friend Kruppe. Our tribe retains the knowledge of copper's healing qualities. Alas, they are not proof against old age . . .'

The Daru's eyes flashed. 'Kruppe's story is not yet complete, lass. Scholars were brought down to those chambers, sharp minds devoted to the mysteries of antiquity. The altars, one for each each chamber . . . eight in all . . . individually aspected, the paintings displaying crude but undeniable images. Traditional representations. Eight caverns, each clearly identified. We know the hands that carved each of them – the artists identified themselves – and Darujhistan's finest seers confirmed the truth. We know, my dear, the names of those to whom these ornaments belonged.' He reached into the box and withdrew a blade. 'Jaghan.' He set it down and picked up an anklet. 'S'ren Tahl. And here, this small, childlike arrowhead . . . Manek, the Rhivi imp – a mocker, was he not? Kruppe feels an affinity with this trickster runt, Manek, oh yes. Manek, for all his games and deceits, has a vast heart, does he not? And here, this torc. Iruth, see its polish? The dawn's glow, captured here, in this beaten metal—'

'Impossible,' the Mhybe whispered. 'The spirits—'

'Were once flesh, my dear. Once mortal. That first band of Rhivi, perhaps? Faith,' he said with a wistful smile, 'is ever a welcoming mistress. Now, upon completing of morning ablutions, Kruppe expects to see said items adorning you. Through the days to come, through the nights yet to pass, Holy Vessel, hold fast to this faith.'

She could say nothing. Kruppe offered her the box. She took its weight in her hands.

How did you know? This morning of mornings, awakening in the ashes of abandonment. Bereft of lifelong beliefs. How, my dear, deceptive man, did you know?

The Daru stepped back with a sigh. 'The rigours of delivery have left Kruppe exhausted and famished! Said box trembled these all too civilized appendages.'

She smiled. 'Rigours of delivery, Kruppe? I could tell you a thing or two.'

'No doubt, but do not despair of ever receiving just

366

reward, lass.' He winked, then swung about and ambled off. A few paces away, Kruppe stopped and turned. 'Oh, Kruppe further informs that Faith has a twin, equally sweet, and that is Dreams. To discount such sweetness is to dismiss the truth of her gifts, lass.' He fluttered one hand in a wave then turned once more.

He walked on, and moments later was beyond her line of sight. *So like Manek, indeed. You buried something there, didn't you, Kruppe? Faith and dreams. The dreams of hope and desire? Or the dreams of sleep?*

Whose path did I cross last night?

Eighty-five leagues to the northeast, Picker leaned back against the grassy slope, squinting as she watched the last of the quorls – tiny specks against a sea-blue sky – dwindle westward.

'If I have to sit another heartbeat on one a those,' a voice growled beside her, 'someone kill me now and I'll bless 'em for the mercy.'

The corporal closed her eyes. 'If you're giving leave to wring your neck, Antsy, I'll lay odds one of us will take you up on it before the day's done.'

'What an awful thing to say, Picker! What's made me so unpopular? I ain't done nothing to no-one never how, have I?'

'Give me a moment to figure out what you just said and I'll answer you honestly.'

'I didn't not make any sense, woman, and you know it.' He lowered his voice. 'Captain's fault, anyhow—'

'No it ain't, Sergeant, and that kinda muttering's damn unfair and could end up spitting poison right back in your eye. This deal was cooked up by Whiskeyjack and Dujek. You feel like cursing someone, try them.'

'Curse Whiskeyjack and Onearm? Not a chance.'

'Then stop your grumbling.'

'Addressing your superior in that tone earns you the role of duffer today, Corporal. Maybe tomorrow, too, if I feel like it.'

'Gods,' she muttered, 'I do hate short men with big moustaches.'

'Gettin' all personal, are ya? Fine, y'can scrub the pots and plates tonight, too. And I got a real complicated meal in mind. Hare stuffed with figs—'

Picker sat up, eyes wide. 'You're not gonna make us eat Spindle's hairshirt? With figs?'

'Hare, you idiot! The four-legged things, live in holes, saw a brace of 'em in the foodpack. With figs, I said. Boiled. And rubyberry sauce, with freshwater oysters—'

Picker sat back with a groan. 'I'll take the hairshirt, thanks.'

The journey had been gruelling, with few and all too brief rest-stops. Nor were the Black Moranth much in the way of company. Virtually silent, aloof and grim – Picker had yet to see one of the warriors shed his or her armour. They wore it like a chitinous second skin. Their commander, Twist, and his quorl were all that remained of the flight that had transported them to the foot of the Barghast Range. Captain Paran was saddled with the task of communicating with the Black Moranth commander – *and Oponn's luck to him, too.*

The quorls had taken them high, flying through the night, and the air had been frigid. Picker ached in every muscle. Eyes closed once more, she sat listening to the other Bridgeburners preparing the gear and food supplies for the journey to come. At her side, Antsy muttered under his breath a seemingly endless list of complaints.

Heavy boots approached, unfortunately coming to a halt directly in front of her, blocking out the morning sun. After a moment, Picker pried open one eye.

Captain Paran's attention, however, was on Antsy. 'Sergeant.'

Antsy's muttering ceased abruptly. 'Sir?'

'It appears that Quick Ben's been delayed. He will have to catch up with us, and your squad will provide his escort. The rest of us, with Trotts, will move out.

Detoran's separated out the gear you'll need.'

'As you say, sir. We'll wait for the snake, then – how long should we give him afore we chase after you?'

'Spindle assures me the delay will be a short one. Expect Quick Ben some time today.'

'And if he don't show?'

'He'll show.'

'But if he don't?'

With a growl, Paran marched off.

Antsy swung a baffled expression on Picker. 'What if Quick Ben don't show?'

'You idiot, Antsy.'

'It's a legit question, dammit! What got him all huffy about it?'

'You got a brain in there somewhere, Sergeant, why not use it? If the mage don't show up, something's gone seriously wrong, and if that happens we're better off high-tailing it – anywhere, so long as it's away. From everything.'

Antsy's red face paled. 'Why won't he make it? What's gone wrong? Picker—'

'Ain't nothing's gone wrong, Antsy! Hood's breath! Quick Ben will get here today – as sure as that sun just rose and is even now baking your brain! Look at your new squad members, Sergeant – Mallet, there, and Hedge – you're embarrassing the rest of us!'

Antsy snarled and clambered to his feet. 'What're you toads staring at? Get to work! You, Mallet, give Detoran a hand – I want those hearth-stones level! If the pot tips because they weren't, you'll be sorry and I ain't exaggerating neither. And you, Hedge, go find Spindle—'

The sapper pointed up the hill. 'He's right there, Sergeant. Checking out that upside-down tree.'

Hands on hips, Antsy pivoted, then slowly nodded. 'And it's no wonder. What kinda trees grow upside-down, anyway? A smart man can't help but be curious.'

'If you're so curious,' Picker muttered, 'why not go and look for yourself?'

'Nah, what's the point? Go collect Spindle, then, Hedge. Double-time.'

'Double-time up a hill? Beru fend, Antsy, it's not like we're going anywhere!'

'You heard me, soldier.'

Scowling, the sapper began jogging up the slope. After a few strides, he slowed to a stagger. Picker grinned.

'Now where's Blend?' Antsy demanded.

'Right here beside you, sir.'

'Hood's breath! Stop doing that! Where you been skulking, anyway?'

'Nowhere,' she replied.

'Liar,' Picker said. 'Caught you sliding up outa the corner of my eye, Blend. You're mortal, after all.'

She shrugged. 'Heard an interesting conversation between Paran and Trotts. Turns out that Barghast bastard once had some kind of high rank in his own tribe. Something about all those tattoos. Anyway, turns out we're here to find the biggest local tribe – the White Faces – with the aim of enlisting their help. An alliance against the Pannion Domin.'

Picker snorted. 'Flown then dropped off at the foot of the Barghast Range, what else did you think we were up to?'

'Only there's a problem,' she continued laconically, examining her nails. 'Trotts will get us face to face without all of us getting skewered, but he might end up fighting a challenge or two. Personal combat. If he wins, we all live. If he gets himself killed . . .'

Antsy's mouth hung open, his moustache twitching as if independently alive.

Picker groaned.

The sergeant spun. 'Corporal – find Trotts! Sit 'im down with that fancy whetstone of yours and get 'im to sharpen his weapons real good—'

'Oh, really, Antsy!'

'We gotta do something!'

'About what?' a new voice asked.

Antsy whirled again. 'Spindle, thank the Queen! Trotts is going to get us all killed!'

The mage shrugged beneath his hairshirt. 'That explains all those agitated spirits in this hill, then. They can smell him, I guess—'

'Smell? Agitated? Hood's bones, we're all done for!'

Standing with the rest of the Bridgeburners, Paran's eyes narrowed on the squad at the foot of the barrow. 'What's got Antsy all lit up?' he wondered aloud.

Trotts bared his teeth. 'Blend was here,' he rumbled. 'Heard everything.'

'Oh, that's terrific news – why didn't you say anything?'

The Barghast shrugged his broad shoulders, was silent.

Grimacing, the captain strode over to the Black Moranth commander.

'Is that quorl of yours rested enough, Twist? I want you high over us. I want to know when we've been spotted—'

The chitinous black helm swung to face him. 'They are already aware, Nobleborn.'

'Captain will do, Twist. I don't need reminding of my precious blood. Aware, are they? How, and just as important, how do you know they know?'

'We stand on their land, Captain. The soul beneath us is the blood of their ancestors. Blood whispers. The Moranth hear.'

'Surprised you can hear anything inside that helm of yours,' Paran muttered, tired and irritated. 'Never mind. I want you over us anyway.'

The commander slowly nodded.

The captain turned and surveyed his company. Veteran soldiers – virtually every one of them. Silent, frighteningly professional. He wondered what it would be like to see out through the eyes of any one of them, through the layers of the soul's exhaustion that Paran had barely begun to find within himself. *Soldiers now and soldiers to the end of their days – none would dare leave to find peace. Solicitude and calm would unlock that safe prison of cold control – the only thing keeping them sane.*

Whiskeyjack had said to Paran that, once this war was done, the Bridgeburners would be retired. Forcibly if necessary.

Armies possessed traditions, and these had less to do with discipline than with the fraught truths of the human spirit. Rituals at the beginning, shared among each and every recruit. And rituals at the end, a formal closure that was recognition – recognition in every way imaginable. They were necessary. Their gift was a kind of sanity, a means of coping. A soldier cannot be sent away without guidance, cannot be abandoned and left lost in something unrecognizable and indifferent to their lives. *Remembrance and honouring the ineffable. Yet, when it's done, what is the once-soldier? What does he or she become? An entire future spent walking backward, eyes on the past – its horrors, its losses, its grief, its sheer heart-bursting living? The ritual is a turning round, a facing forward, a gentle and respectful hand like a guide on the shoulder.*

Sorrow was a steady, faint susurration within Paran, a tide that neither ebbed nor flowed, yet threatened to drown him none the less.

And when the White Faces find us . . . each and every man and woman here could end up with slit throats, and Queen help me, I begin to wonder if it would be a mercy. Queen help me . . .

A swift flutter of wings and the quorl was airborne, the Black Moranth commander perched on the moulded saddle.

Paran watched them rise for a moment longer, his stomach churning, then turned to his company. 'On your feet, Bridgeburners. Time to march.'

The dark, close air was filled with sickly mist. Quick Ben felt himself moving through it, his will struggling like a swimmer against a savage current. After a few more moments he withdrew his questing, slipped sideways into yet another warren.

It fared little better. Some kind of infection had seeped in from the physical world beyond, was corrupting every sorcerous path he attempted. Fighting nausea, he pushed himself forward.

This has the stench of the Crippled God . . . yet the enemy whose lands we approach is the Pannion Seer. Granted, an obvious means of self-defence, sufficient to explain the co-incidence. Then again, since when do I believe in coincidences? No, this comingling of scents hinted at a deeper truth. *That bastard ascendant may well be chained, his body broken, but I can feel his hand – even here – twitching at invisible threads.*

The faintest of smiles touched the wizard's lips. *A worthy challenge.*

He shifted warrens once again, and found himself on the trail of . . . something. A presence was ahead, leaving a cooled, strangely lifeless wake. *Well, perhaps no surprise – I'm striding the edge of Hood's own realm now, after all. None the less* . . . Unease pattered within him like sleet. He pushed his nervousness down. Hood's warren was resisting the poison better than many others Quick Ben had attempted.

The ground beneath him was clay, damp and clammy, the cold reaching through the wizard's moccasins. Faint, colourless light bled down from a formless sky that seemed no higher than a ceiling. The haze filling the air felt oily, thick enough on either side to make the path seem like a tunnel.

Quick Ben's steps slowed. The clay ground was no longer smooth. Deep incisions crossed it, glyphs in columns and panels. Primitive writing, the wizard suspected, yet . . . He crouched and reached down. 'Freshly cut . . . or timeless.' At a faint tingle from the contact he withdrew his hand. 'Wards, maybe. Bindings.'

Stepping carefully to avoid the glyphs, Quick Ben padded forward.

373

He skirted a broad sinkhole filled with painted pebbles – offerings to Hood from some holy temple, no doubt – benedictions and prayers in a thousand languages from countless supplicants. *And there they lie. Unnoticed, ignored or forgotten. Even clerks die, Hood – why not put them to good use cleaning all this up? Of all our traits to survive the passage of death, surely obsessiveness must be counted high among them.*

The incisions grew thicker, more crowded, forcing the wizard to slow his pace yet further. It was becoming difficult to find a clear space on the clay for his feet. Binding sorceries – the whispered skeins of power made manifest, here on the floor of Hood's realm.

A dozen paces ahead was a small, bedraggled object, surrounded in glyphs. Quick Ben's frown deepened as he edged closer. Like the makings of fire . . . sticks and twisted grasses on a round, pale hearthstone.

Then he saw it tremble.

Ah, these binding spells belong to you, little one. Your soul, trapped. As I once did to that mage, Hairlock, someone's done to you. Curious indeed. He moved as close as he could, then slowly crouched.

'You're looking a little worse for wear, friend,' the wizard said.

The minuscule acorn head swivelled slightly, then flinched back. 'Mortal!' the creature hissed in the language of the Barghast. 'The clans must be told! I can go no further – look, the wards pursued, the wards closed the web – I am trapped!'

'So I see. You were of the White Faces, shaman?'

'*And so I remain!*'

'Yet you escaped your barrow – you eluded the binding spells of your kin, for a while at least, in any case. Do you truly believe they will welcome your return, Old One?'

'I was *dragged* from my barrow, fool! You are journeying to the clans – I see the truth of that in your eyes. I shall tell you my tale, mortal, and so they know the truth of all that you tell them, I shall give you my true name—'

'A bold offer, Old One. What's to prevent me from twisting you to my will?'

The creature twitched, a snarl in its tone as it replied, 'You could be no worse than my last masters. I am Talamandas, born of the First Hearth in the Knotted Clan. The first child birthed on this land – do you know the significance of that, mortal?'

'I am afraid not, Talamandas.'

'My previous masters – those damned necromancers – had worked through, mortal, were mere moments from discovering my true name – worked through, I tell you, with brutal claws indifferent to pain. With my name they would have learned secrets that even my own people have long forgotten. Do you know the significance of the trees on our barrows? No, you do not. Indeed they hold the soul, keep it from wandering, but *why*?

'We came to this land from the seas, plying the vast waters in dugouts – the world was young, then, our blood thick with the secret truths of our past. Look upon the faces of the Barghast, mortal – no, look upon a Barghast skull stripped of skin and muscle . . .'

'I've seen . . . Barghast skulls,' Quick Ben said slowly.

'Ah, and have you seen their like . . . *animate?*'

The wizard scowled. 'No, but something similar, squatter – the features slightly more pronounced—'

'Slightly, aye, slightly. Squatter? No surprise, we never went hungry, for the sea provided. Yet more, Tartheno Toblakai were among us . . .'

'You were T'lan Imass! Hood's breath! Then . . . you and your kin must have defied the Ritual—'

'Defied? No. We simply failed to arrive in time – our pursuit of the Jaghut had forced us to venture onto the seas, to dwell among iceflows and on treeless islands. And in our isolation from kin, among the elder peoples – the Tartheno – we changed . . . when our distant kin did not. Mortal, wherever land proved generous enough to grant us a birth, we buried our dugouts – for ever. From this was born the custom of the trees on our barrows – though none among my kind remembers. It has been so long . . .'

'Tell me your tale, Talamandas. But first, answer me this. What would you do . . . if I freed you of these bindings?'

'You cannot.'

'Not an answer.'

'Very well, though it be pointless. I would seek to set free the First Families – aye, we are spirits, and now worshipped by the living clans. But the ancient bindings have kept us as children in so many ways. Well meant, yet a curse none the less. We must be freed. To grow into true power—'

'To ascend into true gods,' Quick Ben whispered, his eyes wide as he stared down at the ragged figure of grasses and twigs.

'The Barghast refuse to change, the living think now as the living always did. Generation after generation. Our kind are dying out, mortal. We rot from within. For the ancestors are prevented from giving true guidance, prevented from maturing into their power – *our* power. To answer your question, mortal, I would save the living Barghast, if I could.'

'Tell me, Talamandas,' Quick Ben asked with veiled eyes, 'is survival a right, or a privilege?'

'The latter, mortal. The latter. And it must be earned. I wish for the chance. For all my people, I wish for the chance.'

The wizard slowly nodded. 'A worthy wish, Old One.' He held out his hand, palm up, stared down at it. 'There's salt in this clay, is there not? I smell it. Clay is usually airless, lifeless. Defiant of the tireless servants of the soil. But the salt, well . . .' A writhing clump took shape on Quick Ben's palm. 'Sometimes,' he went on, 'the simplest of creatures can defeat the mightiest sorceries, in the simplest way imaginable.' The worms – red like blood, thin, long and ridged with leg-like cilia along their lengths – twisted and heaved, fell in clumps to the glyph-strewn ground. 'These are native to a distant continent. They feed on salt, or so it seems – the mines on the dry sea beds of Setta are thick with these things, especially in the dry season. They can turn the hardest pan of clay into sand. To put it another way, they bring air to the airless.' He dropped the clump onto the ground, watched as the worms spread out, began burrowing. 'And they breed faster than maggots. Ah, see those glyphs – there, on the edges? Their binding's crumbling – can you feel the loosening?'

'Mortal, who are you?'

'In the eyes of the gods, Talamandas? Just a lowly salt-worm. I'll hear your tale now, Old One . . .'

CHAPTER NINE

On the subcontinent of Stratem, beyond Korelri's
south range, can be found a vast peninsula where
even the gods do not tread. Reaching to each coast,
encompassing an area of thousands of square leagues,
stretches a vast *plaza*. Aye, dear readers, there is
no other word for it. Fashion this in your mind:
near-seamless flagstones, unmarred by age and
of grey, almost black, stone. Rippled lines of
dark dust, minuscule dunes heaped by the moaning
winds, these are all that break the breathless
monotony. Who laid such stones?

Should we give credence to Gothos's hoary
tome, his glorious 'Folly'? Should we attach
a dread name to the makers of this plaza? If
we must, then that name is K'Chain Che'Malle.
Who, then, were the K'Chain Che'Malle? An
Elder Race, or so Gothos tells. Extinct even before
the rise of the Jaghut, the T'lan Imass, the Forkrul
Assail.

Truth? Ah, if so, then these stones were
laid down half a million – perhaps more – years
ago. In the opinion of this chronicler, what utter
nonsense.

My Endless Travels
Esslee Monot (the Dubious)

'How do you measure a life, Toc the Younger? Please, darling, I would hear your thoughts. Deeds are the crudest measure of all, wouldn't you say?'

He cast her a glower as they walked. 'You suggesting that good intentions are enough, Lady?'

Envy shrugged. 'Can no value be found in good intentions?'

'What, precisely, are you trying to justify? And to me, or yourself?'

She glared, then quickened her pace. 'You're no fun at all,' she sniffed as she pulled ahead, 'and presumptuous as well. I'm going to talk with Tool – *his* moods don't swing!'

No, they just hang there, twisting in the wind.

Not entirely true, he realized after a moment. The T'lan Imass had showed the fullest measure of his emotions a week past. With his sister's departure. *None of us are immune to tortured hearts, I guess.* He rested a hand on Baaljagg's shoulder, squinted towards the distant ridgeline to the northeast, and the washed-out mountains beyond.

The ridge marked the borders of the Pannion Domin. There was a city at the foot of those mountains, or so the Lady had assured him. Bastion. An ominous name. *And strangers aren't welcome . . . So why in Hood's name are we heading there?*

Onearm's Host had effectively declared war on the theocratic empire. Tool's knowledge of the details had Toc wondering, but not doubting. Every description of the Pannion Domin simply added fuel to the likelihood of Dujek taking . . . umbrage. The old High Fist despised tyranny. *Which is ironic, since the Emperor was a tyrant . . . I think. Then again, maybe not. Despotic, sure, and monomaniacal, even slightly insane . . .* He scowled, glanced back to the three Seguleh trailing him. Glittering eyes within hard masks. Toc resumed his study of the ridge ahead, shivering.

Something's awry, somewhere. Maybe right here. Since her

return from Callows, with Mok in tow and his mask sporting a crimson, thickly planted kiss – Hood's breath, does the man even know? If I was Senu or Thurule, would I dare tell him? Since her return, yes, there's been a change. A skittery look in her eyes – just the occasional flash, but I'm not mistaken. The stakes have been raised, and I'm in a game I don't even know. I don't know the players ranged against me, either.

He blinked suddenly, finding Lady Envy walking alongside him once again. 'Tool say the wrong thing?' he asked.

Her nose wrinkled in distaste. 'Haven't you ever wondered what the undead think about, Toc the Younger?'

'No. That is, I don't ever recall musing on the subject, Lady.'

'They had gods, once, you know.'

He shot her a glance. 'Oh?'

'Well. Spirits, then. Earth and rock and tree and beast and sun and stars and antler and bone and blood—'

'Yes, yes, Lady, I grasp the theme.'

'Your interruptions are most rude, young man – are you typical of your generation? If so, then the world is indeed on a downward spiral into the Abyss. Spirits, I was saying. All extinct now. All nothing more than dust. The Imass have outlasted their own deities. Difficult to imagine, but they are godless in every sense, Toc the Younger. Faith . . . now ashes. Answer me this, my dear, do you envisage your afterlife?'

He grunted. 'Hood's gate? In truth, I avoid thinking about it, Lady. What's the point? We die and our soul passes through. I suppose it's up to Hood or one of his minions to decide what to do with it, if anything.'

Her eyes flashed. 'If anything. Yes.'

A chill prickled Toc's skin.

'What would you do,' Lady Envy asked, 'with the knowledge that Hood does *nothing* with your soul? That it's left to wander, eternally lost, purposeless? That it exists without hope, without dreams?'

'Do you speak the truth, Lady? Is this knowledge you possess? Or are you simply baiting me?'

'I am baiting you, of course, my young love. How would I know anything of Hood's hoary realm? Then again, think of the physical manifestations of that warren – the cemeteries in your cities, the forlorn and forgotten barrows – not places conducive to festive occasions, yes? Think of all of Hood's host of holidays and celebrations. Swarming flies, blood-covered acolytes, cackling crows and faces stained with the ash from cremations – I don't know about you, but I don't see much fun going on, do you?'

'Can't we be having some other kind of conversation, Lady Envy? This one's hardly cheering me up.'

'I was simply musing on the T'lan Imass.'

You were? Oh . . . right. He sighed. 'They war with the Jaghut, Lady. That is their purpose, and it certainly seems sufficient to sustain them. I'd imagine they've little need for spirits or gods or faith, even. They exist to wage their war, and so long as a single Jaghut's still breathing on this world . . .'

'And are any? Still breathing, that is?'

'How should I know? Ask Tool.'

'I did.'

'And?'

'And . . . he doesn't know.'

Toc stumbled a step, slowed, staring at her, then at the T'lan Imass striding ahead. *'He doesn't know?'*

'Indeed, Toc the Younger. Now, what do you make of that?'

He could manage no reply.

'What if the war's ended? What next, for the T'lan Imass?'

He considered, then slowly said, 'A second Ritual of Gathering?'

'Mhmm . . .'

'An end? An *end* to the T'lan Imass? Hood's breath!'

'And not a single spirit waiting to embrace all those weary, so very weary souls . . .'

An end, an end. Gods, she might be right. He stared at Tool's fur-clad back, and was almost overcome with a sense of loss. Vast, ineffable loss. 'You might be wrong, Lady.'

'I might,' she agreed affably. 'Do you hope that I am, Toc the Younger?'

He nodded.

'Why?' she asked.

Why? Unhuman creatures sworn to genocide. Brutal, deadly, implacable. Relentless beyond all reason. Toc nodded towards the T'lan Imass ahead of them. 'Because he's my friend, Lady Envy.'

They had not been speaking in low tones. At Toc's words, Tool's head turned, the shelf of the brow hiding the pits of eyes that seemed to fix on the Malazan for a moment. Then the head swung forward once more.

'The summoner of the Gathering,' Lady Envy slowly spoke, 'is among your Malazan punitive army, Toc the Younger. We shall converge within the Pannion Domin. Us, them, and the surviving clans of the T'lan Imass. There will be, without doubt, battles aplenty. The crushing of an empire is never easy. I should know, having crushed a few in my time.'

He stared at her, said nothing.

She smiled. 'Alas, they will approach from the north, whilst we approach from the south. Our journey ahead will be fraught indeed.'

'I admit I have been wondering,' Toc said. 'How, precisely, will we manage to cross a hostile, fanatic territory?'

'Simple, love, we shall carve our way through.'

Gods, if I stay with these people, I am a dead man.

Lady Envy was still smiling, her eyes on Tool. 'Like a white-hot knife through ice, we thrust to the heart . . . of a frozen, timeless soul.' Her voice rising slightly, she added, 'Or so we suspect, do we not, Onos T'oolan?'

The T'lan Imass stopped.

Baaljagg pulled away from beneath Toc's hand, padded forward. The dog Garath followed.

The Malazan spun upon hearing three sets of swords slide from scabbards.

'Oh,' Lady Envy said. 'Something's coming.'

Toc unslung his bow and planted its butt to string it as he scanned the horizon ahead. 'I don't see anything . . . but I'll take everyone's word for it.'

Moments later a K'Chain Che'Malle crested the ridge-line a hundred paces ahead, huge, slung forward and seeming to flow over the ground on two legs. Blades flashed at the ends of its arms.

Ay and dog flinched back.

Toc's recollection of such a creature – fraught with the pained memories of Trake's death – returned to him with a jolt that shortened his breath.

'K'ell Hunter,' Tool said. 'Lifeless.' He had not yet reached for his stone sword. The T'lan Imass pivoted, faced the three Seguleh. A frozen moment stretched between them, then Tool nodded.

Senu on Mok's right, Thurule on his left and both brothers a step ahead of the Third, the Seguleh padded forward to meet the K'Chain Che'Malle.

'A gamble,' Lady Envy murmured.

'The time has come,' Tool said, 'to gauge their worth, Lady. Here, at the border to the Domin. We must know our . . . knife's efficacy.'

Toc nocked an arrow. 'Something tells me I might as well throw twigs at it,' he muttered, recalling Trake's death.

'Wrong,' Tool said, 'yet there is no need to test the stone's power of your arrows.'

'Power, huh? Fine, but that's not the problem. I've only got one eye, Tool. I can't judge distances worth a damn. And that thing's *fast*.'

'Leave this one to the Seguleh,' the T'lan Imass said.

'As you say,' Toc replied, shrugging. His heart did not slow its hammering.

The K'Chain Che'Malle was blurred lightning as it plunged among the three brothers. The Seguleh were faster.

Senu and Thurule had already moved past the creature, throwing savage, unerring blows behind them without turning, sliding effortlessly like snakes to avoid the hunter's whipping tail.

Mok, standing directly in front of the creature, had not backed up a step.

The beast's huge arms flew past to either side of the Third – both severed at the shoulder joint by the flanking brothers in their single pass. Mok's swords darted upward, stabbed, cut, twisted, hooked then withdrew with the hunter's massive head balanced on the tips for the briefest of moments before the Third flung its blade-bending weight aside and leapt to the right, barely avoiding the decapitated body's forward pitch.

The K'Chain Che'Malle thundered as it struck the ground, legs kicking and tail thrashing. Then its movements ceased.

'Well,' Toc said after he'd regained his breath, 'that wasn't so hard. Those beasts look tougher than they are, obviously. Good thing, too. We'll just stroll into the Domin, now, right? Gawking at Bastion's wonder, then beyond—'

'You're babbling,' Lady Envy said. 'Very unattractive, Toc the Younger. Please stop, now.'

Mouth clamped shut, Toc managed a nod.

'Now, let us go and examine the K'Chain Che'Malle. I, for one, am curious.'

He watched her walk ahead, then followed at a stumble. As he passed Tool, he offered the T'lan Imass a sickly grin. 'I think you can relax, now, right?'

The deathless face turned to him. 'The Third's dismantling, Toc the Younger . . .'

'Yes?'

'I could not have done that. I have never seen such . . . skill.'

Toc paused, his eye narrowing. 'Tool, that was glorified dissection – are you not his match in speed?'

'Perhaps.'

'And could he have done that without his brothers slicing those arms off? What if the beast had attacked with its feet instead of its jaws? Tool, that K'Chain Che'Malle was trying for all three of them at once. Stupid. Arrogant.'

The T'lan Imass cocked his head. 'Arrogance. A vice of being undead, Toc the Younger.'

The Malazan's grin broadened. 'And yours has just been shaken, Tool?'

'An unfamiliar sensation.'

Toc shrugged, about to turn and rejoin Lady Envy.

The stone sword was in Tool's hands. 'I must challenge him.'

Grin falling away, Toc stepped closer. 'Hold on, friend – you don't—'

'I must challenge him. Now.'

'Why?'

'The First Sword of the T'lan Imass must be without equal, Aral Fayle.'

'Gods, not you too!'

The T'lan Imass set off towards the Seguleh.

'Wait! Tool—'

The First Sword glanced back. 'You share my shaken faith, mortal, despite your earlier words.'

'Damn it, Tool, now's not the time for this! Think! We need all of you – each in one piece. Intact—'

'Enough words, Aral Fayle.'

The brothers stood around the fallen K'Chain Che'Malle. Lady Envy had joined them and was now crouched, examining the creature's corpse.

Filled with dread, Toc matched Tool's steady, determined pace as they approached.

Senu was the first of the Seguleh to notice them. He slowly sheathed his swords, stepped back. A moment later Thurule did the same. Mok slowly faced the T'lan Imass.

'By the Abyss!' Lady Envy snapped, straightening, her expression darkening. 'Not now.' She waved a hand.

Mok collapsed.

Tool staggered to a halt. 'Awaken him, Lady,' he rasped.

'I shall not. Senu, you and Thurule, rig up a travois for your sleeping brother. You two can pull it.'

'Lady—'

'I'm not talking to you, T'lan Imass.' And to reinforce her announcement, she crossed her arms and turned her back on Tool.

After a long moment in which neither moved, the First Sword finally sheathed his blade. 'He cannot remain asleep for ever, Lady Envy,' he said. 'You do naught but prolong the inevitable.'

She made no reply.

Toc drew a deep breath. 'What a lovely woman,' he softly sighed.

She heard, and turned with a heart-stopping smile. 'Why, thank you!'

'That's not—' He stopped.

Her brow knitted. 'Excuse me?'

'Nothing.' *Gods, nothing!*

Fashioned of straps, leather webbing and two spear-shafts that Lady Envy conjured from somewhere, the travois carrying the Third was pulled by Senu and Thurule from rigged shoulder slings. The two brothers were clearly agitated by the turn of events but, as was evident to Toc – and doubtless the T'lan Imass too – there would be no challenging the Lady's will.

They ascended the ridge as the afternoon waned. Rain clouds approached from the north, obscuring the mountains beyond. The air grew cooler.

The border itself was marked by a series of cairns lining the ridge. Long-abandoned enclosures were visible here and there, the low unmortared stone walls hinting of more affluent times in the past. Flagstone byways crisscrossed the land ahead, overgrown with grasses. The hills gave way to a broad, shallow valley, treed at its base where a stream twisted its way northward. Three squat farmhouses were visible on the valley floor, and a cluster of structures positioned at the stream marked a hamlet at what had to be a ford. No livestock was in sight, nor were the chimneys streaming smoke, lending an eerie quality to the pastoral scene.

None the less, the transition from barren plain to green pastures and signs of human acitivity was something of a shock to Toc the Younger. He realized, with a dull and faint surge of unease, that he'd grown used to the solitude of the plain the Elin called Lamatath. Absence of people – those outside the group . . . *strangers* – had diminished what he now understood to be a constant tension in his life. *Perhaps in all our lives. Unfamiliar faces, gauging regard, every sense heightened in an effort to read the unknown. The natural efforts of society. Do we all possess a wish to remain unseen, unnoticed? Is the witnessing of our actions by others our greatest restraint?*

'You are looking thoughtful, darling,' Lady Envy murmured at his side.

He shrugged. 'We're not . . . unobtrusive, are we? This group of ours. Masked warriors and giant wolf and dog – and a T'lan Imass—'

Tool stopped and faced them. 'I shall make myself unseen, now.'

'When you fall to dust the way you do,' Toc asked, 'are you entering your Tellann warren?'

'No. I simply return to what I was meant to be, had not the Ritual taken place. It would be unwise to employ Tellann within this Domin, Toc the Younger. I shall, however, remain close, and vigilant.'

Toc grunted. 'I was used to having you around. In the flesh, I mean.' He scowled. 'As it were.'

The T'lan Imass shrugged, then vanished in a sluice of dust.

'Other solutions present themselves,' Lady Envy said, 'with respect to our canine companions. Observe.' She walked towards Baaljagg. 'You, pup, are far too . . . alarming in appearance . . . in your present form. Shall we make you smaller?'

The ay had not moved, and watched as she reached out a slim hand and rested a finger on its brow.

Between blinks, Baaljagg shifted from tall and gaunt to a size to match the dog, Garath. Smiling, Lady Envy glanced southward. 'Those yellow wolves are still following, so very curious, but it seems unlikely they will approach now that we are among humans. Alas, reducing the Seguleh to the size of children would achieve little in the way of anonymity, wouldn't you concur, Toc the Younger?'

The Malazan conjured in his mind an image of two masked, death-dealing 'children', and a moment later his imagination was in full retreat. 'Uh,' he managed, 'No. I mean, yes. Yes, I concur.'

'The hamlet yonder,' she continued, 'will prove a modest test as to how the locals react to the Seguleh. If further illusory adjustments to our party prove necessary, we can address them later. Have I covered all considerations, my dear?'

'Yes,' he reluctantly grumbled, 'I suppose.'

'The hamlet might have an inn of some sort.'

'I wouldn't count on it, Lady. These trader tracks haven't seen use in years.'

'How uncivilized! Shall we make our way down there in any case?'

The first drops of rain were spattering the stony trail when they reached the first of the hamlet's half-dozen squalid and ramshackle buildings. It had once been a travellers' inn, complete with stables and a low-walled compound for merchant carts, but was now unoccupied and partially dismantled, the wood and dressed stone of the kitchen wall scavenged, leaving the interior exposed to the elements. High grasses and herbs rose amidst the brick ovens.

Three small buildings lay just beyond the abandoned

inn. Smithy and tack stall, and a tithe-collector's office and residence. All lifeless. The only structure showing evidence of upkeep was on the other side of the shallow ford. High-walled – the stones revealing disparate provenance – and gated with wooden doors beneath an arch, all that was visible of the structure within was a pyramidal peak scaled in polished copper.

'I'd guess that to be a temple,' Toc muttered, standing in the centre of the hamlet's lone street, his eye narrowed on the building on the other side of the stream.

'Indeed,' Lady Envy replied. 'And those within are aware of us.'

He shot her a glance. 'How aware?'

She shrugged. 'We are strangers from Lamatath – a priest within has the power to quest, but he's easily led. You forget—' She smiled. 'I have had generations in which to perfect my innocuous persona.'

Innocuous? Hood's breath, woman, have you got that wrong!

'I already have the priest in hand, my dear, all un-suspecting, of course. Indeed, I believe if we ask they will grant us accommodation. Follow me.'

He stumbled after her. 'Accommodation? Have you lost your mind, Lady?'

'Hush, young man. I am feeling amicable at the moment – you wouldn't want to see me cross, would you?'

'No. Absolutely not. Still, Lady Envy, this is a risk we—'

'Nonsense! You must learn to have faith in me, Toc the Younger.' She reached out, curled an arm about his lower back and pulled him close. 'Walk with me, dearest. There, isn't this nice? The brushing contact of our hips, the sudden familiarity that sends the heart racing. The dampness of the rain, matching—'

'Yes, yes, Lady! Please, no more details, else my walking prove most awkward.'

She laughed. 'I believe I have finally succeeded in charm-ing you, my love. And now I wonder, upon what path shall I lead you? So many choices! How exciting. Tell me, do you think me cruel, Toc the Younger?'

He kept his gaze on the temple.

They stepped into the cool water of the stream, the flow swirling around their ankles but no higher.

'Yes,' he replied at length.

'I can be. In fact, I usually am. I suspected you always knew. I sympathize with your desire to resist, you know. What lies ahead, do you think?'

'I don't know. Well, here we are. Do we knock?'

Lady Envy sighed. 'I hear the patter of feet.'

The door on their left creaked open, revealing a naked, emaciated man of indeterminate age, pale-skinned, head and eyebrows shaved, his watery grey eyes fixed on Lady Envy.

'Welcome, mistress,' the man said. 'Please, enter. The Pannion Domin extends its hospitality' – his eyes flicked past her to take in the wolf and dog, then the Seguleh – 'to you and your companions.' He stepped back.

With an unreadable glance at Toc, Lady Envy followed the priest.

The compound's hot, moist air was rife with the stench of decay, and as soon as the Malazan strode from the shadow of the gate, he saw the source of the smell. A score of bodies lined the inside walls, large iron hooks jutting from beneath their breast bones, feet dangling an arm's length above the ground. The stone at their backs was stained yellow and deep red. Eyeless heads hung downward, strands of hair dripping with rainwater.

The priest, seeing where the attention of his guests had focused, surveyed the corpses with a faint smile. 'The villagers have been delivered. Once the labours of building this temple were completed, they were given their reward. They remain before us as reminders of our Lord's mercy.'

'A rather peculiar version of mercy,' Toc muttered, struggling against a wave of nausea.

'One you will come to understand in time, sir,' the priest

replied. 'Please. A meal is being prepared. Seerdomin Kahlt – the master of this temple – awaits you within the guest hall.'

'How kind,' Lady Envy said. 'An extraordinary construction, this temple of yours.'

Pulling his gaze from the murdered villagers, Toc studied the edifice rearing before them. The pyramidal shape continued down to ground level, the copper sheathing broken only by a dozen randomly placed skylights, each paned with slabs of thin rose quartzite. A narrow but high portal marked the entrance, framed by four massive cut-stones – a broad threshold underfoot, two tapering, flanking menhirs, and a single lintel stone overhead. The corridor beyond was three strides in length, revealing the breadth of the pyramid's foundations.

The air within, as they emerged into a wide and shallow chamber, proved hotter than in the compound, the light tinted pink and fractiously cast by the windows. A low table awaited them, crowded with footstuffs and lined by pillows on which to recline. Standing before another triangular doorway – this one directly opposite the entrance – stood a huge figure in arcane, black-wrought armour. A double-bladed, long-handled axe leaned on the door's frame to his left. The warrior was bare-headed, his pate shaved, and his angular beardless face revealed old scars along his jawline and down the length of his nose.

Hood's breath, I recognize those scars – a cheek-guarded, bridged helm makes those marks . . . when someone swings a mace flush against it, that is.

Frowning, Lady Envy hesitated, then turned to the priest. 'I believe you said the High Priest awaits us?'

The gaunt man smiled. 'And he does, mistress.' He bowed towards the warrior. 'This is Seerdomin Kahlt, the master of this temple. Seerdomin are the Gifted among the Pannion Seer's children. Warriors without parallel, yet learned as well. Now, to complete the introductions, will you grant me the honour of your names?'

391

'I am Lady Islah'Dracon,' Lady Envy said, eyes now on the Seerdomin. 'My companion is named Toc the Younger; my bodyguards Senu, Thurule, and the one presently sleeping is Mok. Do you wish the names of my pets as well?'

You just gave them, didn't you?

The priest shook his head. 'That will not be necessary. No respect is accorded mindless animals within the Domin. Provided you have them within control, they will, for the sake of hospitality, be tolerated. Thank you for the introductions, Lady. I shall now take my leave.' With another bow, he turned and hobbled towards a small side door.

Seerdomin Kahlt took a step forward, armour clanking. 'Seat yourselves,' he said, his voice soft and calm. 'It is not often that we are privileged with guests.'

Lady Envy raised an eyebrow. 'Not often?'

Kahlt smiled. 'Well, you are the first, in fact. The Pannion Domin is an insular land. Few visit, and rarely more than once. There are some, of course, who receive the wisdom and so take the faith, and these are welcomed as brothers and sisters. Great are the rewards when the faith is embraced.' His eyes glittered. 'It is my fervent hope that such gifting will come to you.'

Toc and Lady Envy settled onto the cushions. Baaljagg and Garath remained with the Seguleh, who stood just within the entrance.

Seerdomin Kahlt sat down opposite his guests. 'One of your servants is ill?' he asked. 'Shall I send for a healer, Lady?'

'Not necessary. Mok will recover in time. I am curious, Seerdomin. Why build a temple in such a paltry settlement? Particularly if you then execute all the inhabitants?'

'The inhabitants were rewarded, not executed,' Kahlt said, face darkening. 'We only execute criminals.'

'And the victims were satisfied with the distinction?'

'Perhaps you might enquire that of them yourselves, before too long, Lady.'

'Perhaps.'

'To answer your question. This temple is one of seventy such recent constructions, each commanding a traditional border crossing to and from the Domin. The Pannion Seer's borders are ones of spirit as well as geography. It falls to his most faithful to accept the responsibility of regulation and protection.'

'We are your guests, then, so that you may gauge our measure and judge us worthy of entering your empire, or unworthy.'

Kahlt shrugged, reaching for a wedge of some local fruit Toc did not recognize. 'Please, refresh yourselves. The wine is from Gredfallan, most agreeable. The slices of flesh are bhederin—'

Lady Envy leaned forward and daintily picked up a slice, which she then tossed towards the chamber's entrance. Garath stepped forward, sniffed the meat, then ate it. She smiled at the high priest. 'Thank you, we will.'

'Among our people,' Kahlt rasped, his hands twitching, 'what you have just done is a grave insult.'

'Among mine it's a matter of pragmatism.'

The Seerdomin bared his teeth in a cold smile. 'Trust and honour are valued traits in the Pannion Domin, Lady. The contrast with the culture you are from can be made no more obvious.'

'Indeed. Do you dare risk our corrupting influence?'

'You have no influence, Lady. Perhaps, however, *we* have.'

Toc poured himself some wine, wondering at what Envy was up to. They had walked into a hornets' nest and, smiling, she was plucking one man's wings.

Kahlt had regained his composure. 'Is it wise to mask your servants, Lady? The practice seems to run contrary to the needs of your unfortunate paranoia.'

'Ah, but they are more than simple servants, Seerdomin. They are, in fact, emissaries. Tell me, are you familiar with the Seguleh?'

Kahlt slowly leaned back, studying the silent warriors at

the entrance. 'The island people ... who slay all our monks. And have asked us to declare war upon them, and mount an invasion fleet. Arrogance reaps its own reward, as they shall discover. After all, it is one thing to murder unarmed priests ... Ten thousand Seerdomin shall enact vengeance upon the Seguleh. Very well,' he sighed, 'do these emissaries now come to beg forgiveness?'

'Oh no,' Lady Envy said. 'They come to—'

Toc's hand snapped out, closed on her arm. Surprised, she faced him. 'Lady,' he murmured, then turned to Kahlt. 'They have been sent to deliver a message to the Pannion Seer. In person.'

'That's certainly one way of putting it,' Envy remarked drily.

Withdrawing his hand, Toc sat back, waiting for his heart to slow its wild hammering.

'There are provisos to such an audience,' Kahlt said, eyes still on the Seguleh. 'Disarmed. Unmasked. Perhaps more – but that is not for me to decide.' His gaze flicked back to Lady Envy. 'How can these emissaries be your servants?'

'A woman's wiles,' she replied, flashing him a smile.

He visibly flinched.

Aye, I know what that's like. Your heart's just turned to water. Struggling not to prostrate yourself at her feet. Aye, plucked and now pinned and writhing ...

Kahlt cleared his throat. 'I shall now leave you to your repast. Sleeping chambers have been prepared. The monk who met you at the door will be your guide. Day's end is in a bell's time. Thank you for this most enlightening conversation.' He rose, collected his axe from the wall behind him, then exited through the inner door.

Toc grunted as the panel closed. 'Enlightening? Was that a joke?'

'Eat up, my love,' Envy said. 'Belly filled and content ... before we receive our reward.'

Toc choked on a mouthful of wine, coughed helplessly

for a time, then looked at her through a bleary eye. 'Reward?' he rasped.

'You and I, yes. I suspect the Seguleh will be given a proper escort or some such thing. Baaljagg and Garath will be butchered, of course. Here, try this, it's delicious. Before dawn, is my guess, the fire in our veins released to greet the sun's rise, or some such thing equally pathetic. Then again, we could embrace the faith – do you think we'll convince him? What kind of fruit is this? Tastes like a soldier's foot-wrap. I don't – he's made up his mind, you see.'

'And you helped him along, Lady.'

'Did I?' She paused, looked thoughtful for a moment, then reached for some bread. 'I can't imagine how. True, I was irritated. Have you ever noticed how language can be twisted to mask brutality? Ah, a thought! Look at the Seguleh – masked, yes, yet they speak true and plain, do they not? Is there something in that, do you think? Some hidden significance? Our malleable, fleshy visages are skilled at deceit – a far more subtle mask than what the brothers over there are wearing. More wine? Quite wonderful. Gredfallan? Never heard of it. The Seguleh reveal only their eyes, devoid of framing expression, yet portals to the soul none the less. Remarkable. I wonder who originated the custom, and why.'

'Lady, please,' Toc cut in. 'If they intend to kill us—'

'Intentions are unimportant, my dear. I taste clover in this honey. Lovely. By the way, the walls around us are mostly hollow, but not unoccupied. Would you be so kind as to deliver these plates of meat to my pups? Thank you, darling, you're sweet.'

'All right,' Toc growled. 'So now they know that we know. What now?'

'Well, I don't know about you, but I am dead tired. I do hope the beds are soft. Are the Pannions interested in such conveniences as plumbing, do you think?'

'Nobody's *interested* in plumbing, Lady Envy, but I'm sure they've worked something out.'

'Repast complete! Now where is our poor little monk?'

A side door opened and the man appeared.

'Extraordinary coincidence. Thank your master for the repast, cowed one, and please, lead the way.'

The monk bowed, gestured. 'Follow me, honoured guests. Alas, the beasts must remain outside, in the compound.'

'Of course.'

The man bowed again.

Lady Envy fluttered the fingers of one thin hand and Baaljagg and Garath loped outside.

'Well trained, Lady,' the monk murmured.

'You have no idea,' she replied.

The sleeping chambers ran the length of one wall, small square, low-ceilinged rooms, unfurnished except for narrow hide-mattressed cots and a lantern sitting on a shelf on one wall. A room at the far end of the hallway was provided for communal bathing, its floors tiled and sunken at gradating levels in the various pools, the water continually flowing and cool and clean.

Leaving the lady to her ablutions, Toc entered his sleeping chamber and set his pack down with a sigh. His nerves were already in tatters, and listening to Envy's melodic singing wasn't helping. He threw himself on the cot. *Sleep? Impossible. These bastards are whetting their knives right now, preparing our reward. We're about to embrace the faith, and its face is a death's head . . .*

His eye snapped open at a sudden, curdling scream. It was dark – the lanterns had either gone out or been removed. Toc realized he'd fallen asleep after all, and that had the stench of sorcery. The scream sounded again, ending in a dwindling gurgle.

Claws clicked down the hallway outside his room.

Covered in sweat yet shivering, Toc the Younger edged off the bed. He drew the broad-bladed obsidian dagger Tool had made for him, settled the hide-wrapped grip in his right hand, then unsheathed his own iron knife with his left.

Claws. Either there's Soletaken here . . . or Baaljagg and

Garath are paying a visit. He silently prayed it was the latter.

A crash of masonry made him jump, a wall tumbling into ruin somewhere close. Someone whimpered, then squealed as bones snapped. The sound of a body being dragged just outside his door had Toc crouching low, knives trembling.

Dark. What in Hood's name am I supposed to do? I can't see a damned thing!

The door splintered in its frame under the impact of some large body. As the report echoed, the door fell inward ... beneath the weight of a naked corpse faintly illuminated by low light coming from the hallway.

A massive head slid into view, eyes dully glowing.

Toc loosed a shuddering sigh. 'Baaljagg,' he whispered. 'You've grown since I last saw you.'

The ay, after the briefest pause of mutual recognition, lumbered past the doorway. Toc watched the full length of the beast's body slide by, then he followed.

The hallway was a shambles. Shattered stone, mangled cots and pieces of flesh everywhere. The walls were painted in splashes of blood and bile. *Gods, has this wolf been crashing through arm-length-thick stone walls? How?*

Head slung low, claws clacking, Baaljagg padded towards the bathing chamber. Toc moved lightly in the ay's wake.

Before they arrived a second four-legged shape emerged from a side passage beside the entrance, dark, mottled grey and black, and dwarfing Baaljagg. Coal-lit eyes set in a broad, blood-soaked head slowly fixed on Toc the Younger.

Garath?

The creature's shoulders were covered in white dust. It edged to one side to allow Baaljagg to pass.

'Garath,' Toc murmured as he followed, well within reach of those huge, dripping jaws. 'What was in those bhederin slices you ate, anyway?'

The gentle pet was gone this night, and in its place Garath had become a slayer of the highest, coldest order. Death capered in the huge hound's eyes.

The beast allowed Toc to pass, then swung round and slunk off back the way it had come.

A row of candles on the far wall lit the bathing chamber. Baaljagg, nose to the tiles, was skirting the pools. The trickling water was crimson and steaming. Through its murk Toc could see four corpses, all armoured, lying at the bottom of the pools. He could not be sure, but he thought that they had been boiled alive.

The Malazan pitched against a wall, and, in a series of racking heaves, lost the supper the Seerdomin had so kindly provided.

Distant crashing shook the floor beneath his feet. *Garath continuing his relentless hunt. Oh, you poor bastards, you invited the wrong guests into your temple . . .*

'Oh, there you are!'

Still sickened, he twisted round to see Lady Envy, dressed in her spotless white nightclothes, her raven hair tied up and pinned, standing at the doorway. 'That armour proved fatally heavy, alas,' she said regretfully, her eyes on the corpses in the pools, then brightened. 'Oh well! Come along, you two! Senu and Thurule should be finished with the Seerdomin warriors.'

'There's more than one?' Toc asked, bewildered.

'There were about twenty in all. Kahlt was their captain as well as being this temple's high priest. Warrior-priests – what an unfortunate combination. Back to your room, now, my dear. You must gather up your belongings. We're rendezvousing in the compound.'

She set off.

Stumbling in her wake, with Baaljagg trailing, Toc drew a deep, shuddering breath. 'Has Tool shown up for this?' he asked.

'I've not seen him. He wasn't required in any case. We had matters in hand.'

'With me snoring like a fool!'

'Baaljagg watched out on your behalf, my love. You were weary, were you not? Ah, here we are. Gather your accoutrements. Garath intends to destroy this temple—'

'Yes,' Toc snapped. 'About Garath—'

'You don't wake up well at all, do you, young man? Surely we can discuss all this later?'

'Fine,' he growled, entering his room. 'We will indeed.'

The inner chambers of the temple thundering into dust, Toc stood in the compound, watching the two Seguleh dismounting the corpses of the villagers and replacing them with the freshly butchered bodies of the Seerdomin warriors. Kahlt, bearing a single thrust wound through the heart, was among them.

'He fought with fierce determination,' Lady Envy murmured at Toc's side. 'His axe was everywhere, yet it seemed that Thurule barely moved. Unseen parries. Then he languidly reached out, and stabbed the Seerdomin captain straight through the heart. A wondrous display, Toc the Younger.'

'No doubt,' he muttered. 'So tell me, does the Seer know about us, now?'

'Oh yes, and the destruction of this temple will pain him greatly.'

'He'll send a Hood-damned army down on us.'

'Assuming he can spare one from his northern endeavours, that seems likely. Certainly he will feel the need to respond in some manner, if only to slow our progress.'

'I might as well turn back here and now,' Toc said.

She raised an eyebrow. 'You lack confidence?'

'Lady, I'm no Seguleh. I'm not an ay on the edge of ascendancy. I'm not a T'lan Imass. I'm not a dog that can stare eye-to-*level*-eye with a Hound of Shadow! And I'm *not* a witch who can boil men alive with a snap of her fingers!'

'A witch! Now I am offended!' She advanced on him, arms crossed, eyes flaring. 'A witch! And have you *ever* seen me snap my fingers? By the Abyss, what an inelegant notion!'

He took an involuntary step back. 'A figure of speech—'

'Oh, be quiet!' She took his face in her hands, pulled him inexorably closer. Her full lips parted slightly.

Toc tried to pull away, but his muscles seemed to be dissolving around his bones.

She stopped suddenly, frowned. 'No, perhaps not. I prefer you . . . free.' The frown shifted to a scowl. 'Most of the time, in any case, though you have tried my patience this morning.'

She released him, studied his face for a moment longer, then smiled and turned away. 'I need to get changed, I think. Senu! When you're done, find me my wardrobe!'

Toc slowly shook himself. He was trembling, chilled in the wake of a sure, instinctive knowledge of what that kiss would have done. *And poets write of the chains of love. Hah! What they write figuratively she embodies literally. If desire could have a goddess* . . .

A swirl of dust, and Tool rose from the ground beside him. The T'lan Imass turned his head, stared over at Mok's recumbent form near the outer gate, then said. 'K'ell Hunters are converging on us.' It seemed the T'lan Imass was about to say something more, then simply vanished once again.

'See?' Lady Envy called out to the Malazan. 'Now aren't you glad that I insisted you get some sleep?'

They came to a crossroads marked by two menhirs, leaning and half buried on a low rise between the two cobbled roads. Arcane hieroglyphs had been carved into their faces, the pictographs weathered and faint.

Lady Envy stood before them, chin propped on one hand as she studied the glyphs. 'How curious. The root of this language is Imari. Genostelian, I suspect.'

Toc rubbed sweaty dust from his brow. 'What do they say? Let me guess. "All who come here shall be torn in two, flayed alive, beheaded and badly beaten."'

She glanced back at him, a brow raised. 'The one to the right indicates the road to Kel Tor. The one to the left,

Bastion. None the less remarkable, for all the mundanity of the messages. Clearly, the Pannion Domin was once a Genostel colony – the Genostelians were distant seafarers, my dear. Alas, their glory waned centuries ago. A measure of their height is evinced by what we see before us, for the Genostel archipelago is halfway across the world from here.'

Grunting, Toc squinted up the heaved road that led to Bastion. 'Well, maybe their cities survived, but by all accounts the Pannions were once hill peoples. Herders. Barbaric. Rivals of the Daru and Gadrobi tribes. Your colony was conquered, Lady Envy.'

'It's always the way, isn't it? A civilization flowers, then a horde of grunting savages with close-set eyes show up and step on it. Malazan Empire take note.'

' "Never ignore the barbarians," ' Toc muttered. 'Emperor Kellanved's words.'

'Surprisingly wise. What happened to him?'

'He was murdered by a woman with close-set eyes . . . but she was from civilized stock. Napan . . . if you can call Napans civilized. From the heart of the empire, in any case.'

'Baaljagg looks restless, my dear. We should resume our journey, what with all these undead two-legged lizards on their way.'

'Tool said the nearest ones were still days distant. How far is it to Bastion?'

'We should arrive by dusk tomorrow night, assuming the distance indicated on these milestones remains accurate.'

They set off down the road, the Seguleh trailing with the travois. The cobbles underfoot, though worn deep in places, were now mostly clothed in grasses. There had been few if any travellers this season, and Toc saw no-one on the road as the day wound on. Old carcasses of cattle and sheep in the pastures to either side showed evidence of predation by wolves. No shepherds to tend the flocks, and among all domesticated livestock only goats and horses could survive a return to the wild.

401

As they paused for a mid-afternoon rest on the outskirts of yet another abandoned hamlet – this one without a temple – Toc checked his weapons one more time, then hissed in frustration and glared at Lady Envy who was sitting across from him. 'This doesn't make sense. The Domin's expanding. Voraciously. Armies need food. So do cities. If the countryside's home to nothing but ghosts, who in Hood's name is supplying them?'

Lady Envy shrugged. 'I am not the one to ask, my love. Questions of matériel and economics leave me deathly bored. Perhaps the answers to your irrelevant concerns will be found in Bastion.'

'Irrelevant?'

'Well, yes. The Domin is expanding. It has armies, and cities. These are facts. Details are for academics, Toc the Younger. Shouldn't you be concerning yourself with more salient matters, such as your survival?'

He stared at her, then slowly blinked. 'Lady Envy, I am already as good as dead. So why think about it?'

'Absurd! I value you too highly to see you simply cut down. You must learn to trust me, darling.'

He looked away. 'Details, Lady, reveal hidden truths. Know your enemy – that's a basic tenet. What you know you can use.' He hesitated, then continued. 'Details can lead one to trust, as well, when it comes to the motives and interests of those who would be allies.'

'Ah, I see. And what is it you wish to know?'

He met her eyes. 'What are you doing here?'

'Why, Toc the Younger, have you forgotten? Your T'lan Imass companion has said that the secrets of the Morn Rent can only be found within the Domin.'

'A convenience, Lady,' he growled. 'You're busy manipulating. All of us. Me, the Seguleh, even Tool himself.' He gestured. 'Garath, your *pup*. He could be a Hound of Shadow—'

'He *could* be indeed,' she smiled. 'I believe, however, that he is reluctant.'

402

'What does that mean?'

'You are very easily exasperated, my dear. If you're a leaf trembling on a wide, deep river, relax and ride the current. It's always worked for me, I assure you. As for manipulation, do you truly believe I have the power to pull and prod a T'lan Imass? The Seguleh are, uhm, unique – we travel in step, after all, thus the notion of coercion does not arise.'

'Not yet, maybe. But it will, Lady.'

She shrugged. 'Finally, I have no control over Garath, or Baaljagg. Of that I assure you.'

He bared his teeth. 'Leaving just me.'

She reached out, rested a slim hand lightly on his arm. 'In that, darling, I am simply a woman.'

He shook her hand off. 'There's sorcery in your charms, Lady Envy. Don't try and tell me otherwise.'

'Sorcery? Well, yes, you could call it that, I suppose. Mystery as well, yes? Wonder, and excitement. Hope and possibilities. Desire, darling, is a most alluring magic. And, my love, it is one to which I am not immune . . .'

She leaned closer, her eyes half closed. 'I will not force my kiss upon you, Toc the Younger. Don't you see? The choice must be yours, else you shall indeed be enslaved. What do you say?'

'Time to get going,' he said, rising. 'Obviously, I won't be hearing any honest answers from you.'

'I have just given them!' she retorted, also standing.

'Enough,' he said, collecting his gear. 'I've stopped playing, Lady Envy. Take the game elsewhere.'

'Oh, how I dislike you when you're like this!'

'Sulk away,' he muttered, setting off down the road.

'I shall lose my temper, young man! Do you hear me?'

He stopped, glanced back. 'We've got a few leagues' worth of daylight left.'

'Oh!' She stamped her foot. 'You're just like Rake!'

Toc's lone eye slowly widened, then he grinned. 'Take a few deep breaths, lass.'

'He *always* said that, too! Oh, this is infuriating!

It's all happening again! What is wrong with all of you?'

He laughed, not harshly, but with genuine warmth. 'Come along, Envy. I'll bore you with a detailed recounting of my youth – it'll pass the time. I was born on a ship, you know, and it was more than a few days before Toc the Elder stepped forward to acknowledge his fatherhood – my mother was Captain Cartheron Crust's sister, you see, and Crust had a temper . . .'

The lands lying just beyond Bastion's walls were devastated. Farmsteads were blackened, smouldering heaps; to either side of the road the ground itself had been torn into, ripped open like wounds in flesh. Within sight of the small city's squat walls, the remnants of massive bonfires dotted the landscape like round barrows dusted with white ash. No-one walked the wasteland.

Smoke hung over Bastion's block-like, tiered buildings. Above the grey wreaths rode the white flags of seagulls, their faint cries the only sound to reach Toc and Lady Envy as the group approached the city's inland gates. The stench of fire masked the smell of the lake on the other side of the city, the air's breath hot and gritty.

The gates were ajar. As they neared, Toc caught a glimpse of movement beyond the archway, as of a figure swiftly passing, dark and silent. His nerves danced. 'What has happened here?' he wondered aloud.

'Very unpleasant,' Lady Envy agreed.

They strode beneath the shadow of the arch, and the air was suddenly sickly sweet with the smell of burning flesh. Toc hissed through his teeth.

Baaljagg and Garath – both returned to modest proportions – trotted forward, heads slung low.

'I believe the question of sustenance has a grim answer indeed,' Lady Envy said.

Toc nodded. 'They're eating their own dead. I don't think it's a good idea to enter this city.'

She turned to him. 'Are you not curious?'

404

'Curious, aye, but not suicidal.'

'Fear not. Let us take a closer look.'

'Envy . . .'

Her eyes hardened. 'If the inhabitants are foolish enough to threaten us, they shall know my wrath. And Garath's as well. If you think this is ruination now, your judgement will receive a lesson in perspective, my dear. Come.'

'Yes, ma'am.'

'Familiarity breeds facetiousness, I see. How regrettable.'

The two Seguleh and their unconscious master trailing three paces behind them, Toc and Lady Envy strode into the square.

Split human long bones were piled against the inner walls, some calcined by heat, others red and raw. The buildings facing onto the square were blackened, doorways and windows gaping. The bones of various animals – dogs, mules, horses and oxen – lay about, gnawed and split.

Three men who were obviously priests awaited them in the centre of the square, clean-shaven, gaunt and pale in their colourless robes. One took a step forward as Toc and Envy approached.

'Strangers, welcome. An acolyte saw you on the road, and we three have hastened to greet you. You have chosen an auspicious day to visit glorious Bastion; alas, this day also places your lives in great peril. We shall endeavour to guide you, and thus improve the likelihood of your surviving the Embrasure's violent . . . afterbirth. If you will follow us . . .' He gestured towards a side street. 'At the mouth of Iltara Avenue, we shall have removed ourselves from the exodus's path, yet remain able to witness the miracle.'

'Ideal,' Lady Envy said. 'We thank you, holy ones.'

The walk to the mouth of the side street was no more than fifty paces, yet in that time the city's silence was replaced by a growing murmur, a dry susurration approaching from Bastion's heart. Upon arriving, Baaljagg and Garath returned to flank Lady Envy. Senu and Thurule set the travois down against the wall of a corner building, then faced the square once more, hands on their weapons.

'The will of the Faith has embraced the citizens of Bastion,' the priest said. 'It arrives like a fever . . . a fever that only death can abate. Yet it must be remembered that the Embrasure was first felt here in Bastion itself, fourteen years ago. The Seer had returned from the Mountain, speaking the Words of Truth, and the power of those words rippled outward . . .' The priest's voice broke with some kind of emotion wrought by his own words. He bowed his head, his entire body trembling.

Another priest continued for him. 'The Faith flowered here first. A caravan from Elingarth was encamped beyond the walls. The foreigners were rewarded in a single night. And the First Child of the Dead Seed was gifted to the mortal world nine months later. That child has now come of age, an event that has triggered a renewed burgeoning of the Faith – a second Embrasure has occurred, under the command of the First Child, Anaster. You shall see him now – his mother at his side – leading his newfound Tenescowri. A war awaits them far to the north – the faithless city of Capustan must be rewarded.'

'Holy ones,' Lady Envy said, raising her voice to be heard over the growing roar of chanting voices, 'please forgive my ignorance. A Child of the Dead Seed – what precisely is that?'

'The moment of reward among the male unbelievers, mistress, is often marked by an involuntary spilling of life-seed . . . and continues after life has fled. At this moment, with a corpse beneath her, a woman may ride and so take within her a dead man's seed. The children that are thus born are the holiest of the Seer's kin. Anaster is the first to reach his age.'

'That is,' Lady Envy said, 'extraordinary . . .'

Toc saw her face sickly pale for the first time in his memory.

'The Seer's gift, mistress. A Child of the Dead Seed bears the visible truth of death's kiss of life – proof of the Reward itself. We know that foreigners fear death. The Faithful do not.'

Toc cleared his throat, leaned close to the priest. 'Once these Tenescowri leave Bastion . . . is there anyone else still breathing in the city?'

'Embrasure is absolute, sir.'

'In other words, those who did not succumb to the fever have been . . . rewarded.'

'Indeed.'

'And then eaten.'

'The Tenescowri have needs.'

Conversation ended then as the leading edge of a mass of humanity poured from the main avenue and began spreading to fill the square. A young man was in the lead, the only person mounted, his horse an aged roan draught animal with a bowed spine and botfly sores on its neck. As the youth rode forward, his head whipped suddenly to where Toc and the others stood. He stabbed a long, thin arm in their direction and shrieked.

The cry was wordless, yet it was understood by his followers. Hundreds of faces swung to look upon the strangers, then surged towards them.

'Oh,' Lady Envy said.

The second priest flinched back. 'Alas, our protection is insufficient. Prepare for your reward, strangers!' And with that, the three acolytes fled.

Lady Envy raised her hands, and was suddenly flanked by two huge beasts. Both flowed in a blur to greet the mob. Suddenly, blood and bodies spilled onto the flagstones.

The Seguleh pushed past Toc. Senu stopped at Envy's side. 'Awaken our brother!' he shouted.

'Agreed,' she said. 'No doubt Tool is about to appear as well, but I suspect they will find themselves too busy to contest each other.'

Leather straps snapped as Mok seemed to fling himself upright, weapons already in his hands.

And here I am, all but forgotten. Toc reached a decision.

407

'Have fun, all of you,' he said, backing up the side street.

As the ay and the hound chewed through the screaming mass, Lady Envy spun, eyes wide. 'What? Where are you going?'

'I've embraced the Faith,' he called out. 'This mob's heading straight for the Malazan Army – though it doesn't know it yet! And I'm going with it!'

'Toc, listen! We shall obliterate this pathetic army and that pale runt leading them! There is no need—'

'Don't wipe them out! Please, Envy. Carve your way clear, yes, but I need them.'

'But—'

'No time! I've decided. With Oponn's luck we'll meet again – go find your answers, Envy. I've got friends to find!'

'Wait—'

With a final wave, Toc whirled and ran down the street.

A concussive blast of sorcery threw him forward, but he did not turn. Envy was letting loose. *Hood knows, she might even have just lost her temper. Gods, leave some of them standing, lass . . .*

He swung right at the first intersection he came to, and found himself plunging into the midst of screaming peasants, pushing like him towards the city's main artery, where flowed the mass of the Faithful. He added his screams – wordless, the sounds that a mute man might make – and clawed with mindless zeal.

Like a leaf on a wide, deep river . . .

CHAPTER TEN

Mother Dark begat three children,
the First, Tiste Andii, were her dearest,
dwellers of the land before Light.
Then were birthed in pain the Second, Tiste Lians,
the burning glory of Light itself,
and so the First denied their Mother,
in their fury, and so were cast out,
doomed children of Mother Dark.
She then gave rise, in her mercy, to the Third,
spawn of the war between Dark and Light,
the Tiste Edur, and there was shadow
upon their souls.

Kilmanar's Fables
Sebun Imanan

The hand slapped him hard, the shock quickly fading even as he struggled to comprehend its significance, leaving a tingling numbness that he was content to ride back into unconsciousness.

He was slapped a second time.

Gruntle pried open his eyes. 'Go away,' he mumbled, shutting them again.

'You're drunk,' Stonny Menackis snarled. 'And you stink. Gods, the blanket's soaked with vomit. That's it, he can rot for all I care. He's all yours, Buke. I'm heading back to the barracks.'

409

Gruntle listened to boots stamping away, across the creaking, uneven floorboards of his squalid room, listened to the door squeal open, then slam shut. He sighed, made to roll over and go back to sleep.

Cold, wet cloth slapped down on his face. 'Wipe yourself,' Buke said. 'I need you sober, friend.'

'No-one needs me sober,' Gruntle said, pulling the cloth away. 'Leave me be, Buke. You, of all people—'

'Aye, me of all people. Sit up, damn you.'

Hands gripped his shoulders, pulled him upright. Gruntle managed to grab Buke's wrists, but there was no strength in his arms and he could only manage a few feeble tugs. Pain rocked through his head, swarmed behind his closed eyes. He leaned forward and was sick, fermented bile pouring out through mouth and nostrils onto the floor between his scuffed boots.

The heaves subsided. His head was suddenly clearer. Spitting out the last dregs of vomit, he scowled. 'I'm not asking, you bastard. You got no right—'

'Shut up.'

Grumbling, he sank his head into his hands. 'How many days?'

'Six. You've missed your chance, Gruntle.'

'Chance? What are you talking about?'

'It's too late. The Septarch and his Pannion army have crossed the river. The investiture has begun. Rumour is, the blockhouses in the killing fields beyond the walls will be attacked before the day's done. They won't hold. That's one big army out there. Veterans who've laid more than one siege – and every one successful—'

'Enough. You're telling me too much. I can't think.'

'You won't, you mean. Harllo's dead, Gruntle. Time to sober up and grieve.'

'You should talk, Buke.'

'I've done my grieving, friend. Long ago.'

'Like Hood you have.'

'You misunderstand me. You always have. I have grieved,

410

and that's faded away. Gone. Now . . . well, now there's nothing. A vast, unlit cavern. Ashes. But you're not like me – maybe you think you are, but you're not.'

Gruntle reached out, groped for the wet cloth he'd let fall to the floor. Buke collected it and pushed it into his hand. Pressing it against his pounding brow, Gruntle groaned. 'A pointless, senseless death.'

'They're all pointless and senseless, friend. Until the living carve meaning out of them. What are *you* going to carve, Gruntle, out of Harllo's death? Take my advice, an empty cave offers no comfort.'

'I ain't looking for comfort.'

'You'd better. No other goal is worthwhile, and I should know. Harllo was my friend as well. From the way those Grey Swords who found us described it, you were down, and he did what a friend's supposed to do – he defended you. Stood over you and took the blows. And was killed. But he did what he wanted – he saved your hide. And is this his reward, Gruntle? You want to look his ghost in the eye and tell him it wasn't worth it?'

'He should never have done it.'

'That's not the point, is it?'

Silence filled the room. Gruntle scrubbed his bristled face, then slowly lifted bleary eyes to Buke.

The old man had tears tracking down the lines of his weathered cheeks. Caught by surprise, he turned away. 'Stonny's in a mood to kill you herself,' he muttered, walking over to unlatch the lone window's shutters. He opened them. Sunlight flooded the room. 'She lost one friend, and maybe now another.'

'She lost two out there, Buke. That Barghast lad . . .'

'Aye, true enough. We ain't seen much of Hetan and Cafal since arriving. They're tight with the Grey Swords – something's brewing there, I think. Stonny might know more about it – she's staying at the barracks as well.'

'And you?'

'Still in the employ of Bauchelain and Korbal Broach.'

411

'You Hood-damned fool.'

Wiping his face, Buke turned from the window, managed a tight grin. 'Welcome back.'

'Go to the Abyss, bastard.'

They made their way down the single flight of sagging steps to street level, Gruntle leaning heavily on his gaunt companion whilst the blood roared in his head and waves of nausea clenched his empty stomach.

His previous memories of the city had fragmented, and stained as they were by shock, then pint after pint of ale, he looked around in momentary bewilderment. 'Which district is this?' he asked.

'Backside of Old Daru, Temple District,' Buke said. 'One street north and you hit opulence and gardened temples. You found the quarter's only rotten alley and its only foul tenement, Gruntle.'

'Been there before, I guess,' he muttered, squinting at the nearby buildings. 'Some other excuse back then, can't remember what.'

'Excuses are easy enough to come by. I well recall that.'

'Aye, they are and no doubt you do.' He glanced down at the sorry state of his clothes. 'I need a bath – where are my weapons?'

'Stonny took care of them. And most of your coin as well. You're paid up – no debts – so you can put your back to all that.'

'And walk.'

'And walk. I'll join you, to the barracks, at least—'

'In case I get lost,' Gruntle said wryly.

Buke nodded.

'Well, it's a few bells yet before the shakes.'

'Aye. The Destriant might help with that, if you ask kindly.'

They turned south, skirting the battered tenement block, and approached the wide avenues between the high-walled, circular Camps. Few citizens were in the streets, and those that were moved furtively, as if skating a thin patina of panic. A city surrounded, awaiting the first drawing of blood.

Gruntle spat into a gutter. 'What are your masters up to, Buke?'

'They have taken possession of a recently abandoned estate. Settled in.'

The sudden tension in Buke's voice raised the hairs on Gruntle's neck. 'Go on.'

'That's why I . . . went to you. Partly. A Gidrath Watch found the first body last night, not a hundred paces from our estate. Disembowelled. Organs . . . missing.'

'Inform the prince, Buke. Make no hesitation – a cancer at the heart of a besieged city . . .'

'I cannot.' He stopped and gripped Gruntle's arm. 'We must not. You haven't seen what they can do when their backs are against a wall—'

'They need to be driven out, Buke. Let the Pannions embrace their company, with pleasure. Just cut yourself loose, first. And maybe that old manservant, Reese, too.'

'We can't.'

'Yes you can—'

Buke's grip tightened painfully. 'No,' he hissed, 'we *can't!*'

Scowling, Gruntle glanced up the avenue, trying to think.

'They'll start knocking down walls, Gruntle. Outer walls. They'll wipe out hundreds of soldiers – unleash demons, raise the corpses and fling them back in our faces. They'll level Capustan for the Pannions. But there's more to it than all that. Consider another possibility. If it's the *Pannions* who get them annoyed . . .'

'They'll let loose on them,' Gruntle sighed, nodding. 'Aye. In the meantime, however, the murder victims start piling up. Look around, Buke, these people are close enough to panic. What do you think it will take to push 'em over the edge? How many more victims? The Camps are kin-bound communities – every neighbourhood is knit together by blood and marriage. This is a fine line to walk . . .'

'I can't do it alone,' Buke said.

'Do what?'

'Shadow Korbal Broach. When he goes out at night. If I can foul his hunting . . . yet remain unseen, undiscovered—'

'You've lost your mind!' Gruntle hissed. 'He's a Hood-damned sorceror, old man! He'll sniff you out the first time!'

'If I'm working alone, you're right . . .'

Gruntle studied the man at his side, searched the worn, lean face, the hard eyes above the grey, tangled beard. Old burn scars painted Buke's forearms, from when he clawed through coals and embers the morning after the fire in some frenzied, insane faith that he would find them . . . find his family alive somewhere in the rubble.

Buke's gaze dropped beneath that steady examination. 'I've no cunning, friend,' the old man said, releasing Gruntle's arm. 'I need someone to think of a way to do this. I need someone with the brains to outwit Korbal Broach—'

'Not Broach. Bauchelain.'

'Aye, only he's not the one going out at night. Bauchelain tolerates Korbal's . . . peculiar interests. Broach has the mind of a child – an unfettered, malign child. I know them, now, Gruntle. I know them.'

'How many other fools have tried to outwit Bauchelain, I wonder?'

'Cemeteries full, I'd guess.'

Gruntle slowly nodded. 'All to achieve what? Save a few lives . . . so that they can get slaughtered and devoured by the Tenescowri?'

'A more merciful demise even so, friend.'

'Hood take me, Buke. Let me think on this.'

'I'll come by this evening, then. At the barracks. Stonny—'

414

'Stonny can't know a damn thing about it. If she catches on, she'll go after Broach herself, and she won't be subtle—'

'And they'll kill her. Aye.'

'Gods, my head's about to explode.'

Buke grinned. 'What you need is a priest.'

'A priest?'

'A priest with the powers to heal. Come on, I know just the man.'

Shield Anvil Itkovian stood by the barracks gate, fully armoured and gauntleted, his helm's visor raised though the cheek-guards remained in place. The afternoon's first bell had tolled a hundred heartbeats ago. The others were late, but that was nothing new; nor was Itkovian's punctuality. He'd grown long accustomed to awaiting Brukhalian and Karnadas, and it seemed that the two Barghast who were to join them for the meeting held a similar disregard.

The Mask Council would greet them all seething from the apparent insult – and not for the first time.

The contempt is mutual, alas. Dialogue has degraded. No-one wins in such a situation. And poor Prince Jelarkan . . . positioned directly between two parties exchanging mutual loathing.

The Shield Anvil had spent the morning on Capustan's walls, surveying the measured settling of the Domin's besieging army. He judged that Septarch Kulpath had been given command of fully ten legions of Beklites, the red- and gold-clad, peak-helmed regular infantry that was the heart of the Domin's forces – half of the famed Hundred Thousand, then. Kulpath's Urdomen – elite heavy infantry – numbered at least eight thousand. When the breach occurred, it would be the Urdomen who pushed through into the city. In addition to these arrayed forces were various augmented divisions: Betaklites, medium infantry; at least three Betrullid Wings, light cavalry; as well as a division of Desandi – sappers and engineers – and Scalandi skirmishers. Perhaps eighty thousand soldiers in all.

Beyond the impressively organized camps of the Septarch's army, the landscape was a seething mass of humanity, reaching down to the banks of the river to the south, and to the cobbled beaches of the coast to the east – the Tenescowri, the peasant army, with their wild-haired Women of the Dead Seed and their shrieking feral offspring; the scavenging parties – hunters of the weak and old among their own kind, and, soon, among the hapless citizens of Capustan. A starving horde, and seeing them crumbled the professional detachment with which Itkovian had viewed Kulpath's legions. He had left the walls, shaken for the first time in his life.

There were a hundred thousand Tenescowri, with more arriving on overloaded barges with every bell, and Itkovian was staggered by the waves of their palpable hunger.

The prince's Capanthall soldiers manning the battlements were pale as corpses, silent and virtually motionless. Upon arriving on the walls, the Shield Anvil had been dismayed by their fear; by the time he made his descent, he shared it, a cold knife lodged in his chest. The companies of Gidrath in the outside redoubts were the fortunate ones – their deaths were imminent, and would come beneath the blades of professional soldiers. Capustan's fate, and the fate of those defending it, was likely to be far more horrifying.

The soft slither of coin armour announced the approach of the two Barghast warriors. Itkovian studied the woman in the lead. Hetan's face was smeared in ash, as was her brother Cafal's. The mourning visage would remain for as long as they chose, and the Shield Anvil suspected he would not live to see its removal. *Even sheathed in grey, there is a brutal beauty to this woman.*

'Where is the hill bear and his scrawny pup?' Hetan demanded.

'Fener's Mortal Sword and the Destriant have just emerged from the building behind you, Hetan.'

She bared her teeth. 'Good, let us go meet these bickering priests, then.'

416

'I still wonder why you have requested this audience, Hetan,' Itkovian said. 'If you are to announce the impending arrival of the entire clans of the Barghast to our aid, the Mask Council is not the place to do so. Efforts will begin immediately to manipulate you and your people, towards an endless and infectious mire of petty rivalries and battles of will. If you will not inform the Grey Swords, then I strongly urge you to speak with Prince Jelarkan—'

'You talk too much, wolf.'

Itkovian fell silent, his eyes narrowing.

'Your mouth will be too busy when I bed you,' she continued. 'I will insist.'

The Shield Anvil swung to face Brukhalian and Karnadas as they arrived. He saluted.

'There's some colour in your face, sir,' the Destriant observed. 'Which was not the case when you returned from the walls.'

Hetan barked a laugh. 'He is about to lie with a woman for the first time.'

Karnadas raised his brows at Itkovian. 'What of your vows, Shield Anvil?'

'My vows remain,' the soldier grated. 'The Barghast is mistaken.'

Brukhalian grunted. 'Besides, aren't you in mourning, Hetan?'

'To mourn is to feel a flower's slow death, hill bear. To bed a man is to recall the flower's bright glory.'

'You'll have to pluck another,' Karnadas said with a faint smile. 'The Shield Anvil has taken monastic vows, alas—'

'Then he mocks his god! The Barghast know of Fener, the Tusked One. There is fire in his blood!'

'The fire of battle—'

'Of lust, scrawny pup!'

'Enough,' Brukhalian rumbled. 'We walk to the Thrall, now. I have news to relate to you all and will need the time. Come.'

They strode through the barracks gate, swung left to

417

cross the concourse that skirted the city's south wall. Capustan's open spaces – an accidental feature of the self-contained Camps – had needed little in their conversion into killing grounds. Strongpoints had been constructed at various approaches, of stone and wood and soaked bales of hay. When the walls were breached the enemy would pour into the concourses and enter an enfilade. Prince Jelarkan had emptied half his treasury for arrows, bows, ballistae, mangonels and other weapons of slaughter. The network of defences imposed a web on the city, in keeping with Brukhalian's plan of measured, organized contraction.

Yield not a single cobble until it is ankle deep in Pannion blood.

The few brightly clothed citizens in sight moved from the path of the Grey Swords and the ash-faced, barbaric Barghast.

Brukhalian spoke. 'The Destriant and I have held counsel with the Kron T'lan Imass. Bek Okhan informs us that their offer of alliance is in answer to the K'Chain Che'Malle. They will not fight mortal humans. He further informs us that the K'ell Hunters have gathered half a league to the north, perhaps eighty in all. From this I surmise that they will represent Septarch Kulpath's opening gambit – an assault on the north gate. The appearance of such formidable creatures will strike terror in our defenders. The gate will be shattered, the Hunters will enter the city, and the slaughter will begin. Kulpath will then send his Urdomen forward, against the other gates. By dusk Capustan will have fallen.' He paused, as if chewing his words, then resumed. 'No doubt the Septarch is confident. Fortunately for us, the K'ell Hunters will never reach the north gate, for fourteen thousand T'lan Imass and however many T'lan Ay with them will rise to block their path. Bek Okhan assures us the denial will be absolute, and final.'

'Assuming the validity of his assertion,' Itkovian allowed as they approached the Old Daru district, 'Septarch Kulpath will need to adjust his plan.'

'And in circumstances of great confusion,' Karnadas said.

Brukhalian nodded. 'It falls to us to predict his adjustment.'

'He won't know that the T'lan Imass are interested only in the K'Chain Che'Malle,' the Shield Anvil said. 'At least not immediately.'

'And that limitation may prove temporary,' the Destriant said. 'Once this Gathering takes place, the T'lan Imass may find themselves directed to a new purpose.'

'What more have we learned of the summoner?'

'She accompanies Brood's army.'

'How far away?'

'Six weeks.'

Hetan snorted. 'They are slow.'

'They are a small army,' Brukhalian growled. 'And cautious. I find no fault in the pace they have chosen. The Septarch intends to take Capustan in a single day, but he well knows that the longest he can safely take to conclude the siege is six weeks. Once he fails in his first effort, he will step back and reconsider. Probably at length.'

'We cannot hold for six weeks,' Itkovian murmured, his eyes reaching over the row of temples lining Old Daru's front street and fixing on the high walls of the ancient keep that was now the Thrall.

'We must, sir,' Brukhalian replied. 'Shield Anvil, your counsel, please. Kulpath's campaign at Setta – there were no K'Chain Che'Malle to hasten that siege. Its duration?'

'Three weeks,' Itkovian immediately replied. 'Setta is a larger city, sir, and the defenders were unified and well organized. They stretched to three weeks a siege that should only have required a week at most. Sir, Capustan is smaller, with fewer defenders – and disputatious defenders at that. Further, the Tenescowri has doubled its size since Setta. Finally, the Beklites and Urdomen have been honed by a hard-fought contest. Six weeks, sir? Impossible.'

'We must make the impossible possible, Shield Anvil.'

Itkovian's jaw clenched. He said nothing.

Within sight of the Thrall's high gates, Brukhalian stopped and faced the Barghast. 'You have heard us, Hetan. Should the clans of the White Face grasp the spear of war, how many warriors will march? How soon could they arrive?'

The woman bared her teeth. 'The clans have never united to wage war, but if they did, the warriors of the White Face would number seventy thousand.' Her smile broadened, cold and defiant. 'They will not do so now. No march. No relief. For you, no hope.'

'The Domin will set hungry eyes upon your people next, Hetan,' Itkovian said.

She shrugged.

'What then,' Brukhalian rumbled, 'is the purpose of this audience with the Mask Council?'

'When I give answer, it will be to the priests.'

Itkovian spoke. 'I was given to understand that you had travelled south to discover the nature of the K'Chain Che'Malle.'

'There was no cause to elaborate on our mission, wolf. We have completed one task set before us by the shoulder-men of the clans. Now, we must complete the second task. Will you now present us to the fools, or must we continue on alone?'

The Council Hall was a massive chamber, domed with a semicircle of wooden tiers facing the grand entrance. The dome's ceiling had once glittered with gold leaf, of which only a few patches remained. The bas-relief images the gold had once lit were now faded and mostly shapeless, hinting of a procession of human figures in ceremonial garb. The floor was laid with bright, geometric tiles, forming no discernible pattern around a central disc of polished granite, and much worn.

Torches high on the stone walls flickered yellow light and exhaled tendrils of black smoke that drifted in the chamber's currents. Standing motionless to either side of the entrance and before each of the fourteen doors arrayed behind the tiers were Gidrath guards, visored and in full scaled armour.

The fourteen priests of the Mask Council sat in a row on the highest of the three tiers, sombre in their robes and silent behind the carved, hinged masks of their gods. The representations were varied but singularly ghastly, caricatured in their malleable expressions, though at the moment every one of them was fixed in neutral regard.

Brukhalian's boots echoed as he strode to halt in the centre of the chamber, standing on the single huge millstone appropriately called the Navel. 'Mask Council,' he intoned, 'may I present to you Hetan and Cafal, Barghast emissaries of the White Face. The Grey Swords have honoured the request for this introduction. Now that it is complete, we shall depart this session.' He stepped back.

Rath'Dessembrae raised a slim hand. 'One moment, please, Mortal Sword,' she said. 'Whilst we know nothing of the nature of the Barghast's intentions, we ask that you remain in attendance, for there are matters that must be discussed at the conclusion of the audience.'

Brukhalian bowed his head. 'Then we must convey our distance from the Barghast and their unknown petition.'

'Of course,' the masked woman murmured, the sorrowful visage of her god's face shifting into a slight smile.

Itkovian watched Brukhalian return to where he and Karnadas stood just within the entrance.

Hetan and her brother strode to take position on the millstone. She studied the priests, then lifted her head and called out, 'The White Face is in mourning!'

A hand thumped down on the railing. Rath'D'rek was on his feet, the Worm of Autumn's goddess face twisted into a scowl. 'Again? By the Abyss, you deliver your tribe's claims *at this time*? The same opening words! The same idiotic assertion! The answer was no the first time, no the second time, no every time! This audience is closed!'

'*It is not!*'

'You dare address us in such a tone—'

'I do, you fart-fouled runt!'

Eyes wide, Itkovian stared at Hetan, then at the Council.

The Barghast woman spread out her arms. 'Attend my words! Ignore them at your peril!'

Her brother had begun a soft chant. The air swirled around the two savage warriors.

On all sides, the Gidrath guards reached for their weapons.

Itkovian stumbled as Karnadas pushed past him, robes flowing behind the priest in his haste. 'A moment, please!' he cried. 'Holy brothers and sisters! Would you see your loyal guards slain? Would you see the Thrall itself destroyed, with all of you killed in the process? Look carefully upon the sorcery you see before you, I beg you! No simple shaman's magic – *look!* The Barghast spirits have assembled. Brothers and sisters, *the Barghast Spirits are here, in this room!*'

Silence, save for Cafal's low chant.

Brukhalian drew close to Itkovian. 'Shield Anvil,' he muttered, 'know you anything, sir, of what we see before us?'

'The possibility had not even occurred to me,' Itkovian murmured. 'An old petition, this one. I did not think—'

'What is it they request?'

He slowly shook his head. 'Recognition, sir. The earth beneath this city is Barghast land, or so they assert. Reading the accounts of previous audiences, they have been dismissed with a boot to the backside, more or less. Mortal Sword, I did not imagine—'

'Listen, now, sir. The woman has leave to speak.'

The brothers and sisters had heeded the Destriant's words, were now once again seated, displaying an array of furious expressions. Had not the moment been so tense, Itkovian would have grinned at the obvious . . . consternation of the gods.

'Acceptable,' Hetan grated, narrow gaze studying the

priests and priestesses. 'What has been a request is now a demand. I shall now list your past arguments for denying our petition, and repeat once again our replies. Perhaps this time you will choose to see reason when you vote. If not, I shall force the issue.'

Rath'Hood barked a laugh, leaned forward. 'Force the issue? Dear lass, this city and all within it are perhaps no more than a few bells from annihilation. Yet you threaten us with force? Are you truly the foolish little girl you seem?'

Hetan's grin was savage. 'Your past arguments. The earliest Daru records of this settlement insist the land was unoccupied. Save for ancient buildings long abandoned that were clearly not Barghast in origin. The few records that the herder camps possessed reinforced this notion. The Barghast lived to the north, upon the slopes of the hills and within the Range itself. Aye, shouldermen made pilgrimages to this land, but such journeys were infrequent and of brief duration. Agreed thus far? Good. To these arguments we have in the past made simple reply. Barghast do not live upon holy ground – the dwelling place of the bones of their ancestors. Do *you* live in your own cemeteries? You do not. Nor do we. The first Capan tribes found naught but the barrows of Barghast dead. They levelled them and with the Daru raised a city on our sacred land.

'This affront cannot be undone. The past is immutable, and we are not so foolish as to insist otherwise. No, our request was simple. Formal recognition of our ownership, and right to make pilgrimage.

'You denied the request, again and again. Priests, our patience is at an end.'

Rath'Shadowthrone crowed his laughter. He threw up his hands. 'Indeed! Excellent! Very well! Brothers and sisters, let us grant the Barghast all they wish! Delicious irony, to freely give all that we are about to lose! Will the Pannions honour it?' His mask shifted into a sneer. 'I think not.'

Hetan shook her head. 'I said our patience has ended,

beetle-under-rock. Our past requests no longer obtain. This city will fall. The Pannions will offer no welcome. The desire of Barghast pilgrims none the less must be answered. Thus.' She crossed her arms.

The silence stretched.

Then Rath'Queen of Dreams gasped.

Hetan faced her squarely. 'Ah, you know the truth of it!'

With a visage of thoughtful regard belied by the flustered alarm evinced by her posture and gestures, the priestess cleared her throat. 'Not all among us. A few. Very few.' Her head turned, surveyed her brothers and sisters. Rath'Burn was the first to react, her breath hissing through the slitted mouth of her mask.

After a moment, Rath'Hood grunted. 'I see. An extraordinary solution indeed—'

'Obvious!' Rath'Shadowthrone snapped, jerking in his seat. 'No secret knowledge required! None the less, we must consider the matter! What is lost by relinquishment? What is gained by denial?'

'No,' Hetan said. 'Denial shall not force our hand into defending this land. Humbrall Taur, my father, rightly guessed the twist of your thoughts. If it must be, we shall accept our loss. However, my brother and I will kill everyone in this chamber before we leave here today, should you choose to deny us. Can you accept *your* loss?'

No-one spoke for a long moment, then Rath'Queen of Dreams coughed again. 'Hetan, may I ask you a question?'

The grey-faced woman nodded.

'How will you effect the expediting of . . . of what you seek?'

'What secret do you withhold?' Rath'Oponn shrieked. 'You and Rath'Hood and Rath'Burn! What are you all going on about! The rest of us must know!'

'Use that kernel of a brain,' Rath'Shadowthrone sneered. 'What do pilgrims go to honour and revere?'

'Uh . . . relics? Icons?'

Rath'Shadowthrone mimed a tutor's patient,

424

condescending nod. 'Very good, brother. So, how do you put an end to the pilgrimage?'

Rath'Oponn stared, his mask blank.

'You *move* the relics, you idiot!' Rath'Shadowthrone screamed.

'But wait!' Rath'Beru said. 'Doesn't that assume their location is known? Weren't all the mounds flattened? By the Abyss, how many estates and Camp hearthhomes have some battered Barghast urn up on a shelf? Are we to set out and search every house in the city?'

'We care nothing for vessels,' Hetan rumbled.

'*That's* precisely the secret!' Rath'Shadowthrone chimed to Rath'Beru, head wagging from side to side. 'Our two sisters and one brother know where the bones lie!' He faced Rath'Queen of Dreams. 'Don't you, dear? Some fool or wise spark gathered them all those centuries back and deposited them in one place – and that place still remains, doesn't it? Put that nauseating coyness to bed and out with the goods, woman!'

'You are so crass,' the priestess hissed.

Itkovian stopped listening as the bickering continued. His gaze was on Hetan, his attention sharpened. He wished he could see her eyes, if only to confirm what he now suspected.

She was trembling. So slight, the Shield Anvil doubted anyone else noticed. Trembling . . . *and I think I know why.*

Movement caught his eye. Karnadas was backing away, edging towards Brukhalian's side once again. The Destriant's gaze seemed to be fixed on the brothers and sisters on the council, in particular upon the silent, slight figure of Rath'Fener, seated on the far right. The set of Karnadas's back and shoulders – and his deliberate avoidance of focusing on Hetan – told Itkovian that the Destriant had come to the same revelation – a revelation that had the Shield Anvil's heart thumping.

The Grey Swords were not part of this. Indeed, they were neutral observers, but Itkovian could not help adding his silent will to Hetan's cause.

425

The Destriant withdrew to Brukhalian's side, casually glanced over and met Itkovian's eyes.

The Shield Anvil responded with the faintest of nods.

Karnadas's eyes widened, then he sighed.

Aye. The Barghast gambit. Generations of pilgrims . . . long before the coming of the Capan and Daru, long before the settlement was born. Barghast do not normally honour their dead in such a manner. No, the bones hidden here – somewhere – are not simply the bones of some dead warchief or shoulder-man. These bones belong to someone . . . profoundly important. Valued so highly that the sons and daughters of countless generations journeyed to their legendary resting place. Thus, one significant truth . . . which leads to the next one.

Hetan trembles. The Barghast spirits . . . tremble. They have been lost – made blind by the desecration. For so long . . . lost. Those holiest of remains . . . and the Barghast themselves were never certain – never certain that they were here, in this earth in this place, were never certain that they existed at all.

The mortal remains of their spirit-gods.

And Hetan is about to find them. Humbrall Taur's long-held suspicion . . . Humbrall Taur's audacious – no, outrageous – gambit. 'Find me the bones of the Founding Families, daughter Hetan.'

The White Face clans knew that the Domin would come for them, once Capustan fell. There would, in truth, be war. Yet the clans had never before been unified – the ancient blood-feuds and rivalries ever gnawed from within. Humbrall Taur needed those ancient holy remains. To raise as a standard. To knit the clans together – all feuds forgotten.

But Hetan is too late. Even if she wins, here, now, she is too late. Take the mortal remains, dear, by all means – but how will you get them out of Capustan? How will you get through rank upon rank of Pannion soldiers?

Rath'Queen of Dreams's voice cut through his thoughts. 'Very well. Hetan, daughter of Humbrall Taur, we accede to your request. We return to you the mortal remains of your ancestors.' She slowly rose and gestured to her Gidrath captain. The soldier stepped close and she began whispering instructions. After a moment the man nodded and exited through the door behind him. The masked woman turned once again to the Barghast. 'Some effort will be required in . . . reaching the resting place. With your permission, we would like to speak with Mortal Sword Brukhalian in the meantime, on matters pertaining to the defence of this city.'

Hetan scowled, then shrugged. 'As you wish. But our patience is short.'

The Queen of Dreams mask shifted into a smile. 'You shall be able to witness the extrication yourself, Hetan.'

The Barghast woman stepped back from the Navel.

'Approach, Mortal Sword,' Rath'Hood rumbled. 'Sword sheathed, this time.'

Itkovian watched his commander stride forward, wondering at the high priest's admonition, and at Brukhalian's answering cold smile.

Rath'Shadowthrone leaned forward. 'Know, Mortal Sword, that the Mask Council finally acknowledges what was obvious to you and me from the very start – the inevitable destruction of Capustan.'

'You are mistaken,' Brukhalian replied, his deep voice reverberating in the hall. 'There is nothing inevitable about this impending siege, provided we each hold to a unified defence—'

'The outlying redoubts shall be held,' Rath'Beru snapped, 'for as long as is possible.'

'They will be slaughtered, you blinkered fool!' Rath'Shadowthrone shrieked. 'Hundreds of lives thrown away! Lives we can ill afford to lose!'

'Enough!' Rath'Queen of Dreams shouted. 'This is not the issue we are meant to discuss. Mortal Sword, the return of the Shield Anvil's troop was witnessed by many. Specifically, the appearance of . . . large wolves. Reputedly somewhat . . . worse for wear. These creatures have not been seen since—'

427

An inner door opened to a line of unarmoured Gidrath soldiers, each carrying picks, who strode across the broad floor before fanning out at one end, where they set to examining the tiles along the edge.

Brukhalian cleared his throat. 'This is a subject, Rath'Queen of Dreams, that involves Prince Jelarkan—'

Only momentarily distracted by the arrival of the workers, the high priestess faced Brukhalian again. 'We have already had discourse with the prince on the subject. He was reluctant with his knowledge, and seemed intent on winning concessions from the Council in exchange for information. We will not participate in such crass bargaining, Mortal Sword. We wish to know the nature and the significance of these beasts, and you will provide us with answers.'

'Alas, in the absence of our employer,' Brukhalian said, 'we cannot comply. Should the prince instruct us otherwise . . .'

The workers began tapping their picks against the edge of the floor. Fragments of ceramic tile pattered like hail around their feet. Itkovian watched Hetan draw a step closer to the men. Cafal's chant had fallen to a whisper, a susurration beneath every other sound in the chamber, and his eyes were now fixed, glittering, on the Gidraths' efforts.

The bones lie beneath us. Gathered here, in the chambered heart of the Thrall – how long ago, I wonder?

Rath'Shadowthrone snorted at Brukhalian's words. 'Really, now. This avails us nothing. Someone call for the prince. Shield Anvil, there were two mages among those merchants you saved – were those undead wolves their pets, perhaps? We understand that the mages have taken up residence here in the Daru Quarter. While another of that merchant party has done the same; indeed, has purchased a small house and has petitioned the Council for Rights to Renovation. What an odd lot! A hundred thousand cannibals outside our walls, and these strangers are all buying property! With undead wolves for pets as well! What say you, Itkovian, to all this?'

The Shield Anvil shrugged. 'Your reasoning has a certain logic, Rath'Shadowthrone. As for the mages' and merchants' actions, I cannot, alas, account for their optimism. Perhaps you would be better advised to enquire of them directly.'

'So I shall, Shield Anvil, so I shall.'

The tiles proved to be fixed to larger, rectangular slabs of stone. The workers had managed to pry one loose and were dragging it to one side, revealing trusses of pitch-stained wooden beams. The trusses formed a gridwork, suspended above a subterranean chamber from which musty, turgid air flowed. Once the first slab was free, the removal process quickened in pace.

'I think,' Rath'Hood said, 'we should postpone our discussion with the Mortal Sword, for it seems that the chamber will soon lose its floor in answer to Hetan's demands. When that particular discussion resumes, Prince Jelarkan will attend, in order that he may hold the Mortal Sword's hand in the face of our questioning. In the meantime, we are witness to a historic unveiling which is swiftly acquiring our collective attention. So be it.'

'Gods,' Rath'Shadowthrone muttered, 'you do prattle on, Deathmask. Even so, let us heed your advice. Quickly, you damned soldiers, away with the floor! Let us see these mouldy bones!'

Itkovian edged closer to stand at Hetan's side. 'Well played,' he murmured.

Tension made her breath shallow, and she clearly did not trust herself to make reply.

More slabs were dragged clear. Pole-lanterns were found and readied, but thus far, darkness continued to swallow all that lay beneath the floor.

Cafal came to Itkovian's other side, his chant ended. 'They are here,' he rumbled. 'Crowding us.'

The Shield Anvil nodded in understanding. *The spirits,*

drawn through into our world by the chant. Arrived. Avid with yearning. I feel them indeed . . .

A vast pit had been opened, its sides ragged but geometric, perhaps seven paces across and almost as wide, reaching out to the central millstone which itself seemed to be standing atop a stone column. The Rath' priests and priestesses of the Council had risen from their places and were now edging down for a closer look. One figure separated himself from the others and approached the trio of Grey Swords.

Brukhalian and Itkovian bowed when Rath'Fener arrived. The man's tusked, furred mask was expressionless, the human eyes flatly regarding Karnadas. 'I have quested,' he said in a quiet, soft tone, 'to the very hooves of our Lord. I fasted for four days, slipped through the reeds and found myself on the blood-soaked shore of the Tusked One's own realm. When last, sir, did you make such a journey?'

The Destriant smiled. 'And what did you learn when there, Rath'Fener?'

'The Tiger of Summer is dead. His flesh rots on a plain far to the south of here. Slain by minions of the Pannion Seer. Yet, look upon Rath'Trake – he is possessed of a renewed vigour, nay, a silent joy.'

'It would seem, then,' Karnadas said after a moment, 'the tale of Trake is not yet done.'

Rath'Fener hissed, 'Is this a true gambit to godhood? There is but *one* lord of war!'

'Perhaps we'd be wise to look to our own, sir,' the Destriant murmured.

The masked priest snorted, then whirled away and stalked off.

Itkovian watched him for a moment, then leaned towards Karnadas. 'Are you immune to shock and dismay, sir? Did you know of this news?'

'Trake's death?' The Destriant's brows slowly rose, his eyes still on Rath'Fener. 'Oh yes. My colleague travelled far to arrive at Fener's cloven hooves. While I, sir, have never

430

left that place.' Karnadas turned to Brukhalian. 'Mortal Sword, the time has surely come to unmask this pompous shrew and his claims to pre-eminence—'

'No,' Brukhalian rumbled.

'He reeks of desperation, sir. We cannot trust such a creature among our flock—'

Brukhalian faced Karnadas. 'And the consequences of such an act, sir? Would you take your place among the Mask Council?'

'There would be value in that—'

'This city is not our home, Karnadas. Becoming snared in its web risks far too much. My answer remains no.'

'Very well.'

The pole-lanterns had been ignited, had begun a collectively cautious descent in the hands of Gidrath guards. All attention was suddenly fixed on what was revealed below.

The subterranean chamber's earthen floor was less than a man's height beneath the crossbeams. Filling the space between the two levels was the wooden prow of an open, seafaring craft, twisted with age and perhaps the one-time weight of soil and rocks, black-pitched and artfully carved. From where Itkovian stood he could see a web-like span of branches reaching out to an outrigger.

Three workers lowered themselves into the chamber, lanterns in hand. The Shield Anvil moved closer. The craft had been carved from a single tree, its entire length – more than ten paces – now flattened and corkscrewed in its resting place. Alongside it, Itkovian could now make out another craft, identical with the first, then another. The entire hidden floor of the Thrall's Council Chamber was crowded with boats. He had not known what to expect, but it was certainly not this. *The Barghast are not seafarers . . . not any more. Gods below, these craft must be thousands of years old.*

'Tens of thousands,' the Destriant whispered at his side. 'Even the sorcery that preserves them has begun to fail.'

Hetan dropped down to land lithely beside the first craft. Itkovian could see that she too was surprised, reaching out tentatively close to but not touching the gunnel, where her hand hovered in trembling uncertainty.

One of the guards moved his lantern pole directly over the boat.

Voices gasped.

Bodies filled the craft, stacked haphazardly, each one wrapped in what looked to be red-stained sailcloth, each limb separately entwined, the rough-woven cloth covering each corpse from head to toe. There appeared to be no desiccation beneath the wrapping.

Rath'Queen of Dreams spoke, 'The early writings of our Council describe the finding of such dugout canoes . . . in most of the barrows razed during the building of Capustan. Each held but a few bodies such as these you see here, and most of the canoes disintegrated in the effort of removing them. However, some measure of respect for the dead was honoured – those corpses not inadvertently destroyed in the excavations were gathered, and reinterred within the surviving craft. There are,' she continued, her words cutting through the silence, 'nine canoes beneath us, and over sixty bodies. It was the belief of scholars at that time that these barrows were not Barghast – I think you can see why that conclusion was reached. You may also note that the bodies are larger – almost Toblakai in stature – supporting the notion that they weren't Barghast. Although, it must be granted, there are most certainly Toblakai traits among Hetan and her people. My own belief is that the Toblakai, the Barghast and the Trell are all from the same stock, with the Barghast having more human blood than the other two. I have little evidence to support my belief, apart from simple observation of physical characteristics and ways of living.'

'These are our Founding Spirits,' Hetan said. 'The truth screams within me. The truth closes about my heart with iron fingers.'

432

'They find their power,' Cafal rumbled from the edge of the pit.

Karnadas nodded and said quietly, 'They do indeed. Joy and pain . . . exaltation tempered by the sorrow for the ones still lost. Shield Anvil, we are witnessing the birth of gods.'

Itkovian walked over to Cafal, laid a hand on the man's shoulder. 'Sir, how will you take these remains from the city? The Pannions view every god but their own as avowed enemies. They will seek to destroy all that you have found.'

The Barghast fixed his small, hard eyes on the Shield Anvil. 'We have no answer, wolf. Not yet. But we do not fear. Not now, and not ever again.'

Itkovian slowly nodded. 'It is well,' he said with fullest understanding, 'when you find yourself in the embrace of your god.'

Cafal bared his teeth. 'Gods, wolf. We have many. The first Barghast to come to this land, the very first.'

'Your ancestors have ascended.'

'They have. Who now dares challenge our pride?'

That remains to be seen, alas.

'You've an apology to make,' Stonny Menackis said as she stepped out of the practice circle and reached for a cloth to wipe the sweat from her face.

Gruntle sighed. 'Aye, I'm sorry, lass—'

'Not to me, you idiot. No point in apologizing for who you are and always will be, is there?' She paused to examine the narrow blade of her rapier, scowled at a nick near the inside edge a hand's span from the tip, and glanced back at the Grey Swords recruit who was still in the circle and awaiting a new opponent. 'Damn woman's green, but a fast learner. Your apology, oaf, should be made to Master Keruli—'

'Not my master any longer.'

'He saved our skins, Gruntle, including *your* worthless hide.'

Crossing his arms, Gruntle raised a brow. 'Oh, and how

433

did he manage that? Blacking out at the first rush – funny, I didn't see any lightning and conflagration from his Elder God, his nasty Lord—'

'We *all* went down, you fool. We were done for. But that priest plucked our souls away – as far as those K'Chain Che'Malle could sense, we were *dead*. Don't you remember dreaming? Dreaming! Pulled right into that Elder God's own warren. I recall every detail—'

'I guess I was too busy dying for real,' Gruntle snapped.

'Yes, you were, and Keruli saved you from that, too. Ungracious pig. One moment I was getting tossed around by a K'Chain Che'Malle, the next I woke up . . . somewhere else . . . with a huge ghost wolf standing over me. And I knew – knew instantly, Gruntle, that nothing was getting past that wolf. It was standing guard . . . over *me*.'

'Some kind of servant of the Elder God?'

'No, he doesn't have any servants. What he has is *friends*. I don't know about you, but knowing that – realizing it as I did there with that giant wolf – well, a god that finds friends instead of mindless worshippers . . . dammit, I'm his, Gruntle, body and soul. And I'll fight for him, because I know he'll fight for me. Horrible Elder Gods, bah! I'll take him over those snarling bickering fools with their temples and coffers and rituals any day.'

Gruntle stared at her, disbelieving. 'I must still be hallucinating,' he muttered.

'Never mind me,' Stonny said, sliding her rapier into its scabbard. 'Keruli and his Elder God saved your life, Gruntle. So we're now going to him, and you're going to apologize and if you're smart you're going to pledge to stand with him, in all that's to come—'

'Like Hood I am. Oh, sure, I'll say sorry and all that, but I don't want anything to do with any gods, Elder or otherwise, and that includes their priests—'

'I knew you weren't smart but I had to offer anyway. Let's go, then. Where's Buke disappeared to?'

'Not sure. He was just, uh, delivering me.'

'The Elder God saved him, too. And Mancy. Hood knows those two necromancers didn't give a damn whether they lived or died. If he's smart, he'll quit that contract.'

'Well, none of us are as smart as you, Stonny.'

'Don't I know it.'

They left the compound. Gruntle was still feeling the effects of the last few days, but with a belly full of food instead of wine and ale and the momentary but efficacious attention of the Grey Sword priest, Karnadas, he found his walk steadier and the pain behind his eyes had faded to a dull ache. He had to lengthen his stride to keep up with Stonny's habitual march. Even as her beauty attracted attention, her relentless pace and dark glare ensured a clear path through any crowd, and Capustan's few, cowed citizens scurried quicker than most to get out of her way.

They skirted the cemetery, the upright clay coffin-boles passing on their left. Another necropolis lay just ahead, evincing the Daru style of crypts and urns that Gruntle knew well from Darujhistan, and Stonny angled their route slightly to its left, taking the narrow, uneven passageway between the necropolis's low-walled grounds and the outer edge of the Tura'l Concourse. Twenty paces ahead was a smaller square, which they traversed before reaching the eastern edge of the Temple District.

Gruntle had had enough of stumbling in Stonny's wake like a dog in tow. 'Listen,' he growled, 'I just came from this quarter. If Keruli's camped nearby why didn't you just come to get me and save me the walk?'

'I did come to get you, but you stank like a pauper-tavern's piss pit. Is that how you wanted to show yourself to Master Keruli? You needed cleaning up, and food, and I wasn't going to baby you through all that.'

Gruntle subsided, muttering under his breath. *Gods, I wish the world was full of passive, mewling women.* He thought about that a moment longer, then scowled. *On second thoughts, what a nightmare that'd be. It's the job of a man to fan the spark into flames, not quench it . . .*

435

'Get that dreamy look off your face,' Stonny snapped. 'We're here.'

Blinking, Gruntle sighed, then stared at the small, dilapidated building before them – plain, pitted stone blocks, covered here and there by old plaster; a flat, beamed roof, the ancient wood sagging; and a doorway that he and Stonny would have to crouch to pass through. 'This is it? Hood's breath, this is pathetic.'

'He's a modest man,' Stonny drawled, hands on hips. 'His Elder God's not one for pomp and ceremony. Anyway, with its recent history, it went cheap.'

'History?'

Stonny frowned. 'Takes spilled blood to sanctify the Elder God's holy ground. A whole family committed suicide in this house, less than a week past. Keruli was . . .'

'Delighted?'

'Tempered delight. He grieved for the untimely deaths, of course—'

'Of course.'

'Then he put in a bid.'

'Naturally.'

'Anyway, it's now a temple—'

Gruntle swung to her. 'Hold on, now. I'm not buying into any faith when I enter, am I?'

She smirked. 'Whatever you say.'

'I mean, I'm not. Understand me? And Keruli had better understand, too. And his hoary old god! Not a single genuflection, not even a nod to the altar, and if that's not acceptable then I'm staying out here.'

'Relax, no-one's expecting anything of you, Gruntle. Why would they?'

He ignored the mocking challenge in her eyes. 'Fine, so lead the way, woman.'

'I always do.' She strode to the door and pulled it open. 'Local security measures – you can't kick these doors in, they all open outward, and they're built bigger than the inside frame. Smart, eh? The Grey Swords are expecting a

436

house by house scrap once the walls fall – those Pannions are going to find the going messy.'

'The defence of Capustan assumes the loss of the walls? Hardly optimistic. We're all in a death trap, and Keruli's dream-escape trick won't help us much when the Tenescowri are roasting our bodies for the main course, will it?'

'You're a miserable ox, aren't you?'

'The price for being clear-eyed, Stonny.'

She ducked as she entered the building, waving for Gruntle to follow. He hesitated, then, still scowling, stepped through.

A small reception chamber greeted them, bare-walled, clay-tiled, with a few lantern niches set in the walls and a row of iron pegs unadorned by clothing. Another doorway was opposite, a long leather apron providing the barrier. The air smelled of lye soap, with a faint undercurrent of bile.

Stonny unclasped her cloak and hung it on a hook. 'The wife crawled out of the main room to die here,' she said. 'Dragging her entrails the whole way. Raised the suspicion that her suicide wasn't voluntary. Either that or she changed her mind.'

'Maybe a goat's milk hawker knocked on the door,' Gruntle suggested, 'and she was trying to cancel her order.'

Stonny studied him for a moment, as if considering, then she shrugged. 'Seems a bit elaborate, as an explanation, but who knows? Could be.' She swung about and entered the inner doorway in a swish of leather.

Sighing, Gruntle followed.

The main chamber ran the full width of the house; a series of alcoves – storage rooms and cell-like bedrooms – divided up the back wall, a central arched walkway bisecting it to lead into the courtyard garden beyond. Benches and trunks crowded one corner of the chamber. A central firepit and humped clay bread-oven was directly before them, radiating heat. The air was rich with the smell of baking bread.

437

Master Keruli sat cross-legged on the tiled floor to the left of the firepit, head bowed, his pate glistening with beads of sweat.

Stonny edged forward and dropped to one knee. 'Master?'

The priest looked up, his round face creasing in a smile. 'I have wiped clean their slates,' he said. 'They now dwell at peace. Their souls have fashioned a worthy dream-world. I can hear the children laughing.'

'Your god is merciful,' Stonny murmured.

Rolling his eyes, Gruntle strode over to the trunks. 'Thanks for saving my life, Keruli,' he growled. 'Sorry I was so miserable about it. Looks like your supplies survived, that's good. Well, I'll be on my way now—'

'A moment please, Captain.'

Gruntle turned.

'I have something,' the priest said, 'for your friend, Buke. An . . . aid . . . for his endeavours.'

'Oh?' Gruntle avoided Stonny's searching stare.

'There, in that second trunk, yes, the small, iron one. Yes, open it. Do you see? Upon the dark grey bolt of felt.'

'The little clay bird?'

'Yes. Please instruct him to crush it into powder, then mix with cooled water that has been boiled for at least a hundred heartbeats. Once mixed, Buke must drink it – all of it.'

'You want him to drink muddy water?'

'The clay will ease the pains in his stomach, and there are other benefits as well, which he will discover in due time.'

Gruntle hesitated. 'Buke isn't a trusting man, Keruli.'

'Tell him that his quarry will elude him otherwise. With ease. Tell him, also, that to achieve what he desires, he must accept allies. You both must. I share your concerns on this matter. Additional allies will find him, in time.'

'Very well,' Gruntle said, shrugging. He collected the small clay object and dropped it into his belt-pouch.

'What are you two talking about?' Stonny asked quietly.

Gruntle tensed at that gentle tone, as it usually preceded an explosion of temper, but Keruli simply broadened his smile. 'A private matter, dear Stonny. Now, I have instructions for you – please be patient. Captain Gruntle, there are no debts between us now. Go in peace.'

'Right. Thanks,' he added gruffly. 'I'll make my own way out, then.'

'We'll talk later, Gruntle,' Stonny said. 'Won't we?'

You'll have to find me first. 'Of course, lass.'

A few moments later he stood outside, feeling strangely weighed down, by nothing less than an old man's kind, forgiving nature. He stood for a while, unmoving, watching the locals hurrying past. *Like ants in a kicked nest. And the next kick is going to be a killer . . .*

Stonny watched Gruntle leave, then turned to Keruli. 'You said you had instructions for me?'

'Our friend the captain has a difficult path ahead.'

Stonny scowled. 'Gruntle doesn't walk difficult paths. First sniff of trouble and he's off the opposite way.'

'Sometimes there is no choice.'

'And what am I supposed to do about it?'

'His time is coming. Soon. I ask only that you stay close to him.'

Her scowl deepened. 'That depends on him. He has a talent for not being found.'

Keruli turned back to tend the oven. 'I'd rather think,' he murmured, 'that his talent is about to fail him.'

Torchlight and diffuse sunlight bathed the array of dugout canoes and their wrapped corpses. The entire pit had been exposed, gutting most of the Thrall's floor – the granite pillar with its millstone cap standing alone in the very centre – to reveal the crafts, crushed and cluttered like the harvest of an ancient hurricane.

Hetan knelt, head bowed, before the first dugout. She had not moved in some time.

Itkovian had descended to conduct his own close examination of the remains, and now moved with careful steps among the wreckage, Cafal following in silence. The Shield Anvil's attention was drawn to the carving on the prows; while no two sets were identical, there was a continuity in the themes depicted – scenes of battle at sea, the Barghast clearly recognizable in their long, low dugouts, struggling with a singular enemy, a tall, lithe species with angular faces and large, almond-shaped eyes, in high-walled ships.

As he crouched to study one such panel, Cafal murmured behind him, 'T'isten'ur.'

Itkovian glanced back. 'Sir?'

'The enemies of our Founding Spirits. T'isten'ur, the Grey-Skinned. Demons in the oldest tales who collected heads, yet kept the victims living . . . heads that remained watchful, bodies that worked ceaselessly. T'isten'ur: demons who dwelt in shadows. The Founding Spirits fought them on the Blue Wastes . . .' He fell silent, brow knitting, then continued, 'The Blue Wastes. We had no understanding of such a place. The shouldermen believed it was our Birth Realm. But now . . . it was the sea, the oceans.'

'The Barghast Birth Realm in truth, then.'

'Aye. The Founding Spirits drove the T'isten'ur from the Blue Wastes, drove the demons back into their underworld, the Forest of Shadows – a realm said to lie far to the southeast . . .'

'Another continent, perhaps.'

'Perhaps.'

'You are discovering the truth behind your oldest legends, Cafal. In my home of Elingarth, far to the south of here, there are stories of a distant continent in the direction you have indicated. A land, sir, of giant firs and redwoods and spruce – a forest unbroken, its feet hidden in shadows and peopled with deadly wraiths.

'As Shield Anvil,' Itkovian resumed after a moment,

returning his attention once more to the carvings, 'I am as much a scholar as a warrior. T'isten'ur – a name with curious echoes. Tiste Andii, the Dwellers in Darkness. And, more rarely mentioned, and then in naught but fearful whispers, their shadow-kin, the Tiste Edur. Grey-skinned, believed extinct – and thankfully so, for it is a name sheathed in dread. T'isten'ur, the first glottal stop implies past tense, yes? Tlan, now T'lan – your language is kin to that of the Imass. Close kin. Tell me, do you understand Moranth?'

Cafal grunted. 'The Moranth speak the language of the Barghast shouldermen – the holy tongue – the language that rose from the pit of darkness from whence all thought and all words first came. The Moranth claim kinship with the Barghast – they call us their Fallen Kin. But it is they who have fallen, not us. They who have found a shadowed forest in which to live. They who have embraced the alchemies of the T'isten'ur. They who made peace with the demons long ago, exchanging secrets, before retreating into their mountain fastnesses and hiding for ever behind their insect masks. Ask no more of the Moranth, wolf. They are fallen and unrepentant. No more.'

'Very well, Cafal.' Itkovian slowly straightened. 'But the past refuses to remain buried – as you see here. The past hides restless truths, too, unpleasant truths as well as joyous ones. Once the effort of unveiling has begun . . . Sir, there is no going back.'

'I have reached that understanding,' the Barghast warrior growled. 'As my father warned us – in success, we shall find seeds of despair.'

'I should like to meet Humbrall Taur someday,' Itkovian murmured.

'My father can crush a man's chest in his embrace. He can wield hook-swords in both hands and slay ten warriors in a span of heartbeats. Yet what the clans fear most in their warleader is his intelligence. Of his ten children, Hetan is most like him in that wit.'

441

'She affects a blunt forthrightness.'

Cafal grunted. 'As does our father. I warn you now, Shield Anvil, she has lowered her lance in your direction and sighted along its length. You shall not escape. She will bed you despite all your vows, and then you shall belong to her.'

'You are mistaken, Cafal.'

The Barghast bared his filed teeth, said nothing.

You too have your father's wit, Cafal, as you deftly turn me away from the ancient secrets of the Barghast with yet another bold assault on my honour.

A dozen paces behind them, Hetan rose and faced the ring of priests and priestesses lining the edge of the floor. 'You may return the slabs of stone. The removal of the Founding Spirits' remains must wait—'

Rath'Shadowthrone snorted. 'Until when? Until the Pannions have completed razing the city? Why not call upon your father and have him bring down the clans of the Barghast? Have him break the siege, and then you and your kin can cart away these bones in peace and with our blessing!'

'No. Fight your own war.'

'The Pannions shall devour you once we're gone!' Rath' Shadowthrone shrieked. 'You are fools! You, your father! Your clans! All fools!'

Hetan grinned. 'Is it panic I see on your god's face?'

The priest hunched suddenly, rasped, 'Shadowthrone never panics.'

'Then it must be the mortal man behind the façade,' Hetan concluded with a triumphant sneer.

Hissing, Rath'Shadowthrone wheeled and pushed through his comrades, his sandals flapping as he hurried from the chamber.

Hetan clambered up from the pit. 'I am done here. Cafal! We return to the barracks!'

Brukhalian reached down to help Itkovian climb from the pit, and as the Shield Anvil straightened the Mortal

442

Sword pulled him close. 'Escort these two,' he murmured. 'They've something planned for the removal of—'

'Perhaps,' Itkovian interjected, 'but frankly, sir, I don't see how.'

'Think on it, then, sir,' Brukhalian commanded.

'I shall.'

'Through *any* means, Shield Anvil.'

Still standing close, Itkovian met the man's dark eyes. 'Sir, my vows—'

'I am Fener's Mortal Sword, sir. This demand for knowledge comes not from me, but from the Tusked One himself. Shield Anvil, it is a demand born of fear. Our god, sir, *is filled with fear*. Do you understand?'

'No,' Itkovian snapped. 'I do not. But I have heard your command, sir. So be it.'

Brukhalian released the Shield Anvil's arm, turned slightly to face Karnadas, who stood, pale and still, beside them. 'Contact Quick Ben, sir, by whatever means—'

'I am not sure I can,' the Destriant replied, 'but I shall try, sir.'

'This siege,' Brukhalian growled, eyes clouding with some inner vision, 'is a bloodied flower, and before this day is done it shall unfold before us. And in grasping the stalk, we shall discover its thorns—'

The three men turned at the approach of a Rath' priest. Calm, sleepy eyes were visible behind the striped, feline mask. 'Gentlemen,' the man said, 'a battle awaits us.'

'Indeed,' Brukhalian said drily. 'We were unaware of that.'

'Our lords of war will find themselves in its fierce midst. The Boar. The Tiger. An ascendant in peril, and a spirit about to awaken to true godhood. Do you not wonder, gentlemen, whose war this truly is? Who is it who would dare cross blades with our Lords? But there is something that is even more curious in all this – whose hidden face lies behind this fated ascension of Trake? What, indeed, would be the value of *two* gods of war? *Two* Lords of Summer?'

'That,' the Destriant drawled, 'is not a singular title, sir. We have never contested Trake's sharing it.'

'You have not succeeded in hiding your alarm at my words, Karnadas, but I shall let it pass. One final question, however. When, I wonder, will you depose Rath'Fener, as is your right as Fener's Destriant – a title no-one has rightfully held for a thousand years . . . except for you, of course and, in aside, why has Fener seen the need to revive that loftiest of positions now?' After a moment, he shrugged. 'Ah, well, never mind that. Rath'Fener is no ally of yours, nor your god's – you must know that. He senses the threat you present to him, and will do all he can to break you and your company. Should you ever require assistance, seek me out.'

'Yet you claim you and your Lord as our rivals, Rath'Trake,' Brukhalian growled.

The mask hinged into a fierce smile. 'It only seems that way, right now, Mortal Sword. I shall take my leave of you, for the moment. Farewell, friends.'

A long moment of silence passed whilst the three Grey Swords watched the Rath' priest stride away, then Brukhalian shook himself. 'Be on your way, Shield Anvil. Destriant, I would have a few more words with you . . .'

Shaken, Itkovian swung about and set off after the two Barghast warriors. *The earth has shifted beneath our feet. Unbalanced, moments from drawing blood, and peril now besets us from all sides. Tusked One, deliver us from uncertainty. I beg you. Now is not the time . . .*

CHAPTER ELEVEN

The Malazan military's vaunted ability to adapt to
whatever style of warfare the opposition offered
was in fact superficial. Behind the illusion of
malleability there remained a hard certainty in the
supremacy of the Imperial way. Contributing to
that illusion of flexibility was the sheer resiliency
of the Malazan military structure, and a
foundation bolstered by profound knowledge, and
insightful analysis, of disparate and numerous
styles of warfare.

Abstract (Part XXVII, Book VII, Vol. IX)
on Temul's thirteen-page treatise, 'Malazan Warfare'
Enet Obar (the Lifeless)

Spindle's hairshirt had caught fire. Eyes watering and
coughing at the foul stench, Picker watched the
scrawny mage rolling back and forth on the dusty
ground beside the firepit. Smoke snaked from smouldering
hair, curses rode sparks up into the night air. Since everyone else was too busy laughing, the corporal reached over
to collect a water skin, which she wedged between her
knees. Unstoppering the spout and pressing her thighs
together, she tracked Spindle with the lone stream of water
until she heard hissing sounds.

'All right all right!' the mage shrieked, smudged hands
waving about. 'Stop! I'm drowning!'

Convulsed in his own fits, Hedge had rolled perilously close to the flames. Picker stretched out one booted foot and kicked the sapper. 'Everyone calm down,' she snapped. 'Before the whole squad gets burnt crispy. Hood's breath!'

In the gloom at her side, Blend spoke. 'We're dying of boredom, Corporal, that's the problem.'

'If boredom was fatal there wouldn't be a soldier alive on this whole world, Blend. Feeble excuse. The problem's simple: starting with the sergeant writhing around over there, the whole Oponn-cursed squad is insane.'

'Except for you, of course—'

'You kissing my dung-stained boots, lass? Wrong move. I'm crazier than the rest of you. If I wasn't, I'd have run off long ago. Gods, look at these idiots. Got a mage wearing his dead mother's hair and every time he opens his warren we get attacked by snarling ground squirrels. Got a sapper with permanent flashburns whose bladder must be a warren unto itself since I ain't seen him wander off once and it's three days running now at this camp. Got a Napan woman being stalked by a rogue bhederin bull that's either blind or sees more than we do when he looks at her. And then there's a healer who went and got himself so badly sunburned he's running a fever.'

'Don't bother mentioning Antsy,' Blend murmured. 'The sergeant would top anyone's list as a wall-eyed lunatic—'

'I wasn't done. Got a woman who likes sneaking up on her friends. And finally,' she added in a low growl, 'dear old Antsy. Nerves of cold iron, that one. Convinced the gods themselves have snatched Quick Ben and it's all Antsy's own fault. Somehow.' Picker reached up and slipped a finger under the torcs on her arm, her scowl deepening. 'As if the gods care a whit about Quick Ben, never mind the sergeant himself. As if they take note of any of us no matter what we do.'

'Treach's torcs bothering you, Corporal?'

'Careful, Blend,' Picker murmured. 'I ain't in the mood.'

Sodden and miserable, Spindle was climbing to his feet.

'Evil spark!' he hissed. 'Finger-flicked like a burning booger – there's malevolent spirits lurkin' about, mark my words.'

'Mark 'em!' Picker snorted. 'I'll carve 'em in your gravestone, Spindle, and that's a Hood-blown promise!'

'Gods, what a stink!' Hedge swore. 'I doubt even a grease-smeared Barghast will come near you! I say we should vote – the whole squad, I mean. Vote to tear that disgusting shirt off of Spindle's pimply back and bury it somewhere – ideally under a few tons of rubble. What say you, Sergeant? Hey, Antsy?'

'Shhh!' the sergeant hissed from where he sat at the very edge of the firelight, staring out into the darkness. 'Something's out there!'

'If it's another angry squirrel—' Picker began.

'I ain't done nothing!' Spindle growled. 'And nobody's gonna bury my shirt, not while I'm still breathing, anyway. So forget it, sapper. Besides, we don't vote on nothing in this squad. Hood knows what Whiskeyjack let you idiots do back in the Ninth, but you ain't in the Ninth any more, are ya?'

'Be quiet!' Antsy snarled. 'Someone's out there! Snuffling around!'

A huge shape loomed into view directly in front of the sergeant, who let out a yelp and leapt back, almost stumbling into the fire in his gibbering retreat.

'It's that bhederin bull!' Hedge shouted. 'Hey, Detoran! Your date's arrived – ow! Gods, what did you just hit me with, woman? A mace? A Hood-cursed – your fist? Liar! Antsy, this soldier almost broke my head! Can't take a joke – ow! Ow!'

'Leave off him,' Picker ordered. 'Someone shoo that beast away—'

'This I gotta see,' Blend chortled. 'Two thousand pounds of horns, hooves and cock—'

'Enough of that,' Picker said. 'There's delicate ears present, lass. Look, you got Detoran all blushing in between punching Hedge senseless.'

'I'd say the high colour was exertion, Corporal. The sapper's got some good dodging tactics – oh, well, all right, so he missed slipping that one. Ouch.'

'Ease up, Detoran!' Picker bellowed. 'He ain't seeing straight any more as it is and you'd better start hoping it ain't permanent damage you done there!'

'Aye,' Spindle added. 'The lad's got cussers in that bag of his and if he can't throw straight . . .'

That was enough to make Detoran drop her fists and step back. Hedge reeled about drunkenly then sat with a heavy thump, blood streaming from his broken nose. 'Can't take a joke,' he mumbled through puffed lips. A moment later he keeled over.

'Terrific,' Picker muttered. 'If he ain't come to in the morning and we gotta march, guess who's pulling the travois, Detoran?'

The large woman scowled and turned away to find her bedroll.

'Who's injured?' a high voice piped up.

The soldiers looked up to see Mallet, wrapped in a blanket, totter into the firelight. 'I heard punching.'

'The boiled crayfish is awake,' Spindle observed. 'Guess you won't nap on any more sunward hillsides, eh, Healer?'

'It's Hedge,' Picker said. 'Rubbed Detoran's fur the wrong way. Slumped by the fire – see him?'

Nodding, Mallet hobbled to the sapper's side. 'Alarming image you conjured there, Corporal.' He crouched, began examining Hedge. 'Hood's breath! Busted nose, fractured jaw . . . and concussed, too – the man's done a quiet puke.' He glared over at Picker. 'Didn't anybody think to stop this little argument?'

With a soft grunt, the bhederin bull wheeled away and thumped off into the darkness.

Mallet's head snapped around. 'What by Fener's hoof was *that*?'

'Hedge's rival,' Blend murmured. 'Probably saw enough to take his chances elsewhere.'

Sighing, Picker leaned back, watching Mallet tend to the unconscious sapper. *Squad's not gelling too good. Antsy ain't no Whiskeyjack, Spindle ain't Quick Ben, and I ain't no Corporal Kalam neither. If there was a best of the best among the Bridgeburners, it was the Ninth. Mind you, Detoran could stand toe to toe with Trotts . . .*

'That wizard had better show up soon,' Blend murmured after a time.

Picker nodded in the darkness, then said, 'Might be the captain and the rest are with the White Faces already. Might be Quick Ben and us'll come too late to make any difference in the outcome—'

'We won't make any difference anyway,' Blend said. 'What you mean is we'll be too late to see the spectacle.'

'Could be a good thing, that.'

'You're starting to sound like Antsy.'

'Yeah, well, things ain't looking too good,' Picker said under her breath. 'The company's best mage has disappeared. Add that to a green nobleborn captain and Whiskeyjack gone and what do you know – we ain't the company we once was.'

'Not since Pale, that's for sure.'

Visions of the chaos and horror in the tunnels the day of the Enfilade returned to the corporal and she grimaced. 'Betrayed by our own. That's the worst thing there is, Blend. I can take falling to enemy swords, or magefire, or even demons tearing me limb from limb. But to have one of your own flash the knife when your back's turned . . .' She spat into the fire.

'It broke us,' Blend said.

Picker nodded again.

'Maybe,' the woman at her side continued, 'Trotts losing his contest with the White Faces and us getting executed one and all might be a good thing. Barghast allies or not, I ain't looking forward to this war.'

Picker stared into the flames. 'You're thinking of what might happen when we next step into battle.'

'We're brittle, Corporal. Riven with cracks . . .'

'Got no-one to trust, that's the problem. Got nothing to fight for.'

'There's Dujek, to answer both of those,' Blend said.

'Aye, our renegade Fist . . .'

Blend softly snorted.

Picker glanced over at her friend, frowned. 'What?'

'He ain't no renegade,' Blend said in a low voice. 'We're only cut loose 'cause of Brood and the Tiste Andii, 'cause we couldn't have managed the parley otherwise. Ain't you wondered, Corporal, who that new standard-bearer of Onearm's is?'

'What's his name? Arantal? Artanthos. Huh. He showed up—'

'About a day after the outlawry proclamation.'

'So? Who do you think he is, Blend?'

'A top-ranking Claw, is my wager. Here at the command of the Empress.'

'You got proof of that?'

'No.'

Picker swung her scowl back to the fire. 'Now who's jumping at shadows?'

'We're no renegades,' Blend asserted. 'We're doing the Empire's bidding, Corporal, no matter how it looks. Whiskeyjack knows, too. And maybe so does that healer over there, and Quick Ben—'

'You mean the Ninth.'

'Aye.'

Her scowl deepening, Picker rose, strode to Mallet's side and crouched down. 'How's the sapper, Healer?' she asked quietly.

'Not as bad as it first looked,' Mallet conceded. 'Mild concussion. A good thing – I'm having trouble drawing on my Denul warren.'

'Trouble? What kind of trouble?'

'Not sure. It's gone . . . foul. Somehow. Infected . . . by something. Spindle's got the same problem with

450

his warren. Might be what's delaying Quick Ben.'

Picker grunted. 'Could've mentioned this at the start, Mallet.'

'Too busy recovering from my *sunburn*, Corporal.'

Her eyes narrowed. 'If not sun scorching you, then what happened?'

'Whatever's poisoned my warren can cross over. Or so I found.'

'Mallet,' Picker said after a moment, 'there's a rumour going around, says we maybe ain't as outlawed as Dujek and Whiskeyjack are making out. Maybe the Empress nodded her head in our direction, in fact.'

In the firelight the healer's round face was blank as he shrugged. 'That's a new one to me, Corporal. Sounds like something Antsy would think up.'

'No, but he'll love it when he hears it.'

Mallet's small eyes settled on Picker's face. 'Now why would you do that?'

Picker raised her brows. 'Why would I tell Antsy? The answer should be obvious, Healer. I love watching him panic. Besides,' she shrugged, 'it's just an empty rumour, right?' She straightened. 'Make sure the sapper's ready to march tomorrow.'

'We going somewhere, Corporal?'

'In case the mage shows up.'

'Right. I'll do what I can.'

Hands clawing rotted, stained energy, Quick Ben dragged himself from his warren. Gagging, spitting the bitter, sicky taste from his mouth, the mage staggered forward a few paces, until the clear night air flowed into his lungs and he halted, waiting for his thoughts to clear.

The last half-day had been spent in a desperate, seemingly endless struggle to extricate himself from Hood's realm, yet he knew it to be the least poisoned among all the warrens he commonly used. The others would have killed him. The realization left him feeling bereft – a mage

451

stripped of his power, his vast command of his own discipline made meaningless, impotent.

The sharp, cool air of the steppes flowed over him, plucking the sweat from his trembling limbs. Stars glittered overhead. A thousand paces to the north, beyond the scrub-brush and grassy humps, rose a line of hills. Dull yellow firelight bathed the base of the nearest hill.

Quick Ben sighed. He'd been unable to establish sorcerous contact with anyone since beginning his journey. *Paran's left me a squad . . . better than I could have hoped for. I wonder how many days we've lost. I was supposed to be Trotts's back-up, in case things went wrong . . .*

He shook himself and strode forward, still fighting the remnants of the enervating influence of Hood's infected warren. *This is the Crippled God's assault, a war against the warrens themselves. Sorcery was the sword that struck him down. Now he seeks to destroy that weapon, and so leave his enemies unarmed. Helpless.*

The wizard drew his ash-stained cloak about him as he walked. *No, not entirely helpless. We've our wits. More, we can sniff out a feint – at least I can, anyway. And this is a feint – the whole Pannion Domin and its infectious influence. Somehow, the Chained One's found a way to open the floodgates of the Warren of Chaos. A conduit, perhaps the Pannion Seer himself entirely unaware that he is being used, that he's no more than a pawn thrown forward in an opening gambit. A gambit designed to test the will, the efficacy, of his foe . . . We need to take the pawn down. Fast. Decisively.*

He approached the squad's firelight, heard the low mutter of voices, and felt he was coming home.

A thousand skulls on poles danced along the ridge, their burning braids of oil-soaked grass creating manes of flame above the bleached death-grimaces. Voices rose and fell in a wavering, droning song. Closer to where Paran stood, young warriors contested with short hook-bladed knives, the occasional spatter of blood sizzling as it sprayed into the

452

clan's hearth-ring – rivalries took precedence over all else, it seemed.

Barghast women moved among the Bridgeburner squads, pulling soldiers of both sexes towards the hide tents of the encampment. The captain had thought to prohibit such amorous contact, but had then dismissed the notion as both unworkable and unwise. *Come tomorrow or the day after, we might all be dead.*

The clans of the White Face had gathered. Tents and yurts of the Senan, Gilk, Ahkrata and Barahn tribes – as well as many others – covered the valley floor. Paran judged that a hundred thousand Barghast had heeded Humbrall Taur's call to counsel. But not just counsel. *They've come to answer Trotts's challenge. He is the last of his own clan, and tattooed on his scarred body is the history of his tribe, a tale five hundred generations long. He comes claiming kinship, blood-ties knotted at the very beginning . . . and more, though no-one's explaining precisely what else is involved. Taciturn bastards. There are too many secrets at work here . . .*

A Nith'rithal warrior loosed a wet shriek as a rival clan's warrior opened his throat with a hook-knife. Voices bellowed, cursed. The stricken warrior writhed on the ground before the hearth-fire, life spilling out in a glimmering pool that spread out beneath him. His slayer strutted circles to wild cheers.

Amidst hisses from those Barghast near by, Twist came to the captain's side, the Black Moranth ignoring the curses.

'You're not too popular,' Paran observed. 'I didn't know the Moranth hunted this far east.'

'We do not,' Twist replied, his voice thin and flat behind his chitinous helm. 'The enmity is ancient, born of memories, not experience. The memories are false.'

'Are they now. I'd suggest you make no effort at informing them of your opinion.'

'Indeed, there is no point, Captain. I am curious, this warrior, Trotts – is he uniquely skilled as a fighter?'

Paran grimaced. 'He's come through a lot of nasty

scrapes. He can hold his own, I suppose. To be honest, I have never seen him fight.'

'And those among the Bridgeburners who have?'

'Disparaging, of course. They disparage everything, however, so I don't think that's a reliable opinion. We will see soon enough.'

'Humbrall Taur has selected his champion,' Twist said. 'One of his sons.'

The captain squinted through the darkness at the Black Moranth. 'Where did you hear this? Do you understand the Barghast language?'

'It is related to our own. The news of the selection is upon everyone's lips. Humbrall's youngest son, as yet unnamed, still two moons before his Death Night – his passage into adulthood. Born with blades in his hands. Undefeated in duel, even when facing seasoned warriors. Dark-hearted, without mercy . . . the descriptions continue, but I tire of repeating them. We shall see this formidable youth soon enough. All else is naught but wasted breath.'

'I still don't understand the need for the duel in the first place,' Paran said. 'Trotts doesn't need to make any claim – the history is writ plain on his skin. Why should there be any doubt as to its veracity? He's Barghast through and through – you just have to look at him.'

'He makes claim to leadership, Captain. His tribe's history sets his lineage as that of the First Founders. His blood is purer than the blood of these clans, and so he must make challenge to affirm his status.'

Paran grimaced. His gut was clenched in knots. A sour taste had come to his mouth and no amount of ale or wine would take it away. When he slept visions haunted his dreams – the chill cavern beneath the Finnest House, the carved stone flagstones with their ancient, depthless images from the Deck of Dragons. Even now, should he close his eyes and let his will fall away, he would feel himself falling into the Hold of the Beasts – the home of the T'lan Imass and its vacant, antlered throne – with a physical presence, tactile and rich with senses, as if he had bodily travelled to that place. *And to that time . . . unless that time is now, and the throne remains, waiting . . . waiting for a new occupant. Did it seem that way for the Emperor? When he found himself before the Throne of Shadow? Power, domination over the dread Hounds, all but a single step away?*

'You are not well, Captain.'

Paran glanced over at Twist. Reflected firelight glimmered on the Moranth's midnight armour, played like the illusion of eyes across the planes of his helm. The only proof that a flesh and blood man was beneath that chitinous shell was the mangled hand that dangled lifeless from his right arm. *Withered and crushed by the necromantic grasp of a Rhivi spirit . . . that entire arm hangs dead. Slow, but inevitable, the lifelessness will continue its climb . . . to shoulder, then into his chest. In a year this man will be dead – he'd need a god's healing touch to save him, and how likely is that?* 'I've an unsettled stomach,' the captain replied.

'You deceive by understatement,' Twist said. Then he shrugged. 'As you wish. I will pry no further.'

'I need you to do something,' Paran said after a moment, his eyes narrowed on yet another duel before the hearth-ring. 'Unless you and your quorl are too weary—'

'We are rested enough,' the Black Moranth said. 'Request, and it shall be done.'

The captain drew a deep breath, then sighed and nodded. 'Good. I thank you.'

A bruise of colour showed on the eastern horizon, spreading through the clefts in the ridge of hills just south of the Barghast Mountains. Red-eyed and shivering in the chill, Paran drew his quilted cloak tighter as he surveyed the first stirrings in the massive, smoke-wreathed encampment filling the valley. He was able to pick out various clans by the barbaric standards rising above the seemingly haphazard layout of tents – Whiskeyjack's briefing had been thorough – and held most of his attention on those that the commander had cited as being potential trouble-makers.

To one side of the Challenge Clearing, where Trotts and Humbrall Taur's champion would fight in a short while, was the thousand-strong camp of the Ahkrata. Distinguished by their characteristic nose-plugs, lone braids and multi-toned armour fashioned from Moranth victims – including Green, Black, Red and, here and there, Gold Clans – they were the smallest contingent, having travelled farthest, yet reputedly the meanest. Avowed enemies of the Ilgres Clan – who now fought for Brood – they could prove difficult in the fashioning of an alliance.

Humbrall Taur's closest rival was the warchief Maral Eb, whose own Barahn Clan had arrived in strength – over ten thousand weapon-bearers, painted in red ochre and wearing bronze brigandine armour, their hair spiked and bristling with porcupine quills. There was the risk that Maral might contest Humbrall's position if an opportunity arose, and the night just past had seen over fifty duels between the Barahn and Humbrall Taur's own Senan warriors. Such a challenge could trigger an all-out war between the clans.

Perhaps the strangest group of warriors Paran had seen was the Gilk. Their hair was cut in stiff, narrow wedges and they wore armour assembled from the plates of some kind of tortoise. Distinctively short and stout for Barghast, they looked to the captain to be a match for any heavy infantry they might face.

Scores of minor tribes contributed to the confused mix that made up the White Face nation. Mutually antagonistic and with longstanding feuds and rivalries, it was a wonder that Humbrall Taur had managed to draw them all together, and more or less keep the peace for four days and counting.

And today is the crux. Even if Trotts wins the duel, full acceptance is not guaranteed. Bloody eruptions could follow. And if he loses . . . Paran pulled his thoughts away from that possibility.

456

A voice wailed to greet the dawn, and suddenly the camps were alive with silent, rising figures. The muted clank of weapons and armour followed, amidst the barking of dogs and nasal bellowing of geese. As if the Challenge Clearing drew an invisible breath, warriors began converging towards it.

Paran glanced over to see his Bridgeburners slowly gathering themselves, like quarry pricked alert by a hunter's horn. Thirty-odd Malazans – the captain knew they were determined to put up a fight if things went wrong; knew as well that the struggle would be shortlived. He scanned the lightening sky, eyes narrowing to the southwest in the hopes that he would see a dark speck – Twist and his quorl, fast approaching – but there was nothing to mar the silver-blue vastness.

A deeper silence among the Barghast alerted Paran. He turned to see Humbrall Taur striding through the press to take position in the centre of the clearing. This was the closest the captain had come to the man since their arrival. The warrior was huge, bestial, bedecked in the withered, hair-matted skins of deboned human heads. His hauberk of overlapping coins glittered in the morning light: the horde of ancient, unknown money that the Senan stumbled across some time in the past must have been huge, for every warrior in the tribe wore such armour. *There must have been shiploads of the damned things. That, or an entire temple filled to its ceiling.*

The warchief wasted no time with words. He unslung the spiked mace at his hip and raised it skyward, slowly turning full circle. All eyes held on him, the elite warriors from all the tribes ringing the clearing, the rest massed behind them, all the way to the valley's slopes.

Humbrall Taur paused as a witless dog trotted across the expanse. A well-flung stone sent it scampering with a yelp. The warchief growled something under his breath, then gestured with his weapon.

Paran watched Trotts emerge from the crowd. The

tattooed Barghast wore the standard issue Malazan armour for marines: studded boiled leather with iron bands over the shoulders and hips. His half-helm had been collected from a dead officer among the soldiers of Aren, in Seven Cities. Bridge-guard and cheek-plates bore a filigreed design of inlaid silver. A chain camail protected the sides and back of his neck. A round shield was strapped to his left forearm, the hand protected by a spiked, iron-banded cestus. A straight, blunt-tipped broadsword was in his right hand.

His arrival elicited low growls from the gathered Barghast, which Trotts answered with a hard grin, revealing blue-stained, filed teeth.

Humbrall Taur eyed him for a moment, as if disapproving of Trotts's choice of Malazan weapons over those of the Barghast, then he swung in the opposite direction and gestured once more with the mace.

His youngest son emerged from the circle.

Paran had not known what to expect, but the sight of this scrawny, grinning youth – wearing only leathers, with a single short hook-knife in his right hand – did not match any of the images he had fashioned. *What is this? Some kind of twisted insult? Does Taur want to ensure his own defeat? At the cost of his youngest son's life?*

The warriors on all sides began thumping their feet on the hard earth, raising a rhythmic drumbeat that echoed its way across the valley.

The unnamed youth sauntered into the Circle to stand opposite Trotts, five paces between them. Eyeing the Bridgeburner from head to toe, the boy's smile broadened.

'Captain,' a voice hissed beside Paran.

He turned. 'Corporal Aimless, isn't it? What can I do for you? And be quick.'

The lean, stooped soldier's habitually dour expression was even bleaker than usual. 'We were just wondering, sir . . . If this scrap goes bad, I mean, well, me and a few others, we been hoarding some Moranth munitions.

Cussers too, sir, we got five of those at hand. We could open something of a path – see that knoll over there, a good place, we figured, to withdraw to and hold up. Those steep sides—'

'Stow it, Corporal,' Paran growled under his breath. 'My orders haven't changed. Everyone sits tight.'

'Sure he's a runt, sir, but what if—'

'You heard me, soldier.'

Aimless bobbed his head. 'Yes, sir. It's just that, uh, some – nine, maybe ten – well, they're muttering about maybe doing whatever they please and to Hood with you . . . sir.'

Paran pulled his gaze away from the two motionless warriors in the Circle and met the corporal's watery eyes. 'And you are their spokesman, Aimless?'

'No! Not me, sir! I ain't got no opinion, I never did. Never do, in fact, Captain. No, not me. I'm just here telling you what's going on among the squads right now, that's all.'

'And there they all are, watching you and me having this conversation, which is how they wanted it. You're the mouth, Corporal, whether you like it or not. This is one instance where I probably *should* kill the messenger, if only to rid myself of his stupidity.'

Aimless's dour expression clouded. 'I wouldn't try that, sir,' he said slowly. 'The last captain that drew his sword on me I broke his neck.'

Paran raised an eyebrow. *Beru fend me, I underestimate even the true idiots in this company.* 'Try showing some restraint this time, Corporal,' he said. 'Go back and tell your comrades to hold tight until I give the signal. Tell them there's no way we're going down without a fight, but trying a break-out when the Barghast most expect it will see us die fast.'

'You want me to say all that, sir?'

'In your own words, if you like.'

Aimless sighed. 'That's easy, then. I'll go now, Captain.'

'You do that, Corporal.'

Returning his attention to the Circle, Paran saw that

Humbrall Taur had moved to stand directly between the two contestants. If he addressed them it was brief and under his breath, for he then stepped back, once more raising the mace overhead. The thumping dance of the massed warriors ceased. Trotts swung his shield to the ready, dropping his left leg back and positioning his sword in a tight guard position. The youth's sloppy stance did not change, the knife held loosely at his side.

Humbrall Taur reached one edge of the ring. He waved the mace one final time over his head, then lowered it.

The duel had begun.

Trotts stepped back, crouching low with the shield rim just under his eyes. The blunt tip of his broadsword edged outward as he half extended his arm.

The youth pivoted to face him, the knife in his hand making slight bobbing, snake-head motions. At some unseen shift in weight from Trotts he danced lithely to the left, blade wavering in a haphazard, desultory defence, but the big Bridgeburner did not come forward. Ten paces still remained between them.

Every move the lad makes tells Trotts more, fills out the tactical map. What the boy reacts to, what makes him hesitate, tauten, withdraw. Every shift in weight, the play over the ground and the balls of his feet . . . and Trotts has yet to move.

The youth edged closer, approaching at an angle that Trotts matched only with his shield. Another step. The Bridgeburner's sword slid out to the side. The lad skittered back, then he neared again, sharpening the angle.

Like a stolid infantryman, Trotts swung round to replant his feet – and the Barghast attacked.

A snort gusted from Paran as the Bridgeburner's heavy-footedness vanished. Negating his own advantage in height, Trotts met the lashing assault from low behind his shield, surging forward unexpectedly into the lad's high-bladed attack. Hook-knife glanced without strength off Trotts's helm, then the heavy round shield hammered into the boy's chest, throwing him back.

The youth struck the ground, skidding, raising a cloud of dust as he tumbled and rolled.

A fool would have pursued, only to find the lad's knife slashing through the sunlit cloud – but Trotts simply settled back behind his shield. The youth emerged from the swirling dust, face powdered, knife wavering. His smile remained.

Not a style the lad's used to. Trotts could well be standing front-line in a phalanx, shoulder to shield with hard-eyed Malazan infantry. More than one barbaric horde has been deflowered and cut to pieces against that deadly human wall. These White Faces have never experienced an Imperial engagement.

The lithe Barghast began a swift, darting dance, circling Trotts, edging in then back out, playing with the bright sunlight and flashes on weapon and armour, kicking up clouds of dust. In answer, the Bridgeburner simply pivoted into one of four facings – he had become his own square – and waited, again and again seeming to hold a position too long before shifting, each time stamping the methodical steps of the Malazan infantry drill like a thick-skulled recruit. He ignored every feint, would not be pulled forward by the lad's moments of imbalance and awkwardness – which were themselves illusory.

The ring of warriors had begun shouting their frustration. This was not a duel as they knew duels. Trotts would not play the lad's game. *He is now a soldier of the Empire, and that is the addendum to his tale.*

The youth launched another attack, his blade blurring in a wild skein of feints, then slashing low, seeking the Bridgeburner's right knee – the hinge in the armour's joint. Shield came down, driving the knife away. Broadsword slashed horizontally for the boy's head. He ducked lower, hook-blade dropping down to slash ineffectually across the toe-cap of Trotts's boot. The Bridgeburner snapped his shield into the boy's face.

The youth reeled, blood spraying from his nose. Yet his

knife rose unerringly, skirting the rim of the shield as if following a hissing guide to dig deep into the armour's joint hinge of Trotts's left arm, the hook biting, then tearing through ligaments and veins.

The Malazan chopped down with his broadsword, severing the lad's knife-hand at the wrist.

Blood poured from the two warriors, yet the close-in engagement was not yet complete. Paran watched in amazement as the youth's left hand shot up, stiff-fingered, beneath the chin-guard of Trotts's helmet. A strange popping sound came from Trotts's throat. Shield-arm falling senseless in a welter of blood, knees buckling, the Bridgeburner sank to the ground.

Trotts's final gesture was a lightning-quick sweep of his broadsword across the lad's stomach. Sleek flesh parted and the youth looked down in time to see his intestines tumble into view in a gush of fluids. He convulsed around them, pitched to the ground.

Trotts lay before the dying boy, clawing frantically at his throat, legs kicking.

The captain lurched forward, but one of his Bridgeburners was quicker – Mulch, a minor healer from the Eleventh Squad, raced into the Circle to Trotts's side. A small flickblade flashed in the soldier's hand as he straddled the writhing warrior and pushed his head back to expose the throat.

What in Hood's name—

There was pandemonium on all sides. The Circle was dissolving as Barghast warriors surged forward, weapons out yet clearly confused as to what they should do with them. Paran's head snapped round, to see his Bridgeburners contracting within a ring of shrieking, belligerent savages.

Gods, it's all coming down.

A horn cut through the cacophony. Faces turned. Senan warriors were reasserting the sanctity of the Circle, bellowing as they pushed the other tribesmen and women back.

Humbrall Taur had once more raised high his mace, a silent yet inescapable demand for order.

Voices rose from the Barghast surrounding the company of Bridgeburners, and the captain saw Moranth munitions held high in the hands of his soldiers. The Barghast were recoiling, drawing lances back to throw.

'Bridgeburners!' Paran shouted, striding towards them. 'Put those damned things away! Now!'

The horn sounded a second time.

Faces turned. The deadly grenados disappeared once more beneath rain-capes and cloaks.

'Stand at ease!' Paran growled as he reached them. In a lower voice, he snapped, 'Hold fast, you damned fools! Nobody counted on a Hood-damned *draw*! Keep your wits. Corporal Aimless, go to Mulch and find out what in Fener's name he did with that flickblade – and get the bad news on Trotts – I know, I know, he looked done for. But so's the lad. Who knows, maybe it's a question of who dies first—'

'Captain,' one of the sergeants cut in. 'They were gonna have at us, sir, that's all. We wasn't planning on nothing – we was waitin' for your signal, sir.'

'Glad to hear it. Now keep your eyes open, but stay calm, while I go confer with Humbrall Taur.' Paran swung round and headed towards the Circle.

The Barghast warchief's face was grey, his gaze returning again and again to the small figure now ominously motionless on the stained ground a dozen paces away. A half-dozen minor chiefs clustered around Humbrall, each shouting to make himself heard above his rival. Taur was ignoring them one and all.

Paran pushed through the crowd. A glance to his right showed Aimless crouched down beside Mulch. The healer had a hand pressed tight against the wound in Trotts's left arm and seemed to be whispering under his breath, his eyes closed. Slight movement from Trotts revealed that the Bridgeburner still lived. And, the captain realized, he had

463

ceased his thrashing around. Somehow, Mulch had given him a means of drawing breath. Paran shook his head in disbelief. Crush a man's throat and he dies. *Unless there's a High Denul healer nearby . . . and Mulch isn't, he's a cutter with a handful of cantrips at his disposal – the man's pulled off a miracle . . .*

'Malazan!' Humbrall Taur's small, flat eyes were fixed on Paran. He gestured. 'We must speak, you and I.' He switched from Daru to bellow at the warriors crowding him. They withdrew, scowling, casting venomous glares towards the captain.

A moment later Paran and the Barghast warchief stood face to face. Humbrall Taur studied him for a moment, then said, 'Your warriors think little of you. Soft blood, they say.'

Paran shrugged. 'They're soldiers. I'm their new officer.'

'They are disobedient. You should kill one or two of them, then the others will respect you.'

'It's my task to keep them alive, not kill them, Warchief.'

Humbrall Taur's eyes narrowed. 'Your Barghast fought in the style of you foreigners. He did not fight as kin to us. Twenty-three duels, my unnamed son. Without loss, without so much as a wound. I have lost one of my blood, a great warrior.'

'Trotts lives still,' Paran said.

'He should be dead. Crush a man's throat and the convulsions take him. He should not have been able to swing his sword. My son sacrificed a hand to kill him.'

'A valiant effort, Warchief.'

'In vain, it seems. Do you claim that Trotts will survive his wounds?'

'I don't know. I need to confer with my healer.'

'The spirits are silent, Malazan,' Humbrall Taur said after a moment. 'They wait. As must we.'

'Your council of chiefs might not agree with you,' Paran observed.

Taur scowled. 'That is a matter for the Barghast. Return to your company, Malazan. Keep them alive . . . if you can.'

'Does our fate rest on Trotts's surviving, Warchief?'

The huge warrior bared his teeth. 'Not entirely. I am done with you, now.' He turned his back on the captain. The other chiefs closed in once again.

Paran pulled away, fighting a resurgence of pain in his stomach, and strode to where Trotts lay. Eyes on the Barghast warrior, he crouched down beside the healer, Mulch. There was a hole between Trotts's collar bones, home to a hollow bone tube that whistled softly as he breathed. The rest of his throat was crumpled, a mass of green and blue bruising. The Barghast's eyes were open, aware and filled with pain.

Mulch glanced over. 'I've healed the vessels and tendons in his arm,' he said quietly. 'He won't lose it, I think. It'll be weaker, though, unless Mallet gets here soon.'

Paran pointed at the bone tube. 'What in Hood's name is that, healer?'

'It ain't easy playing with warrens right now, sir. Besides, I ain't good enough to fix anything like that anyway. It's a cutter's trick, learned it from Bullit when I was in the 6th Army – he was always figuring ways of doing things without magic, since he could never find his warren when things got hot.'

'Looks . . . temporary.'

'Aye, Captain. We need Mallet. Soon.'

'That was fast work, Mulch,' Paran said, straightening. 'Well done.'

'Thanks, sir.'

'Corporal Aimless.'

'Captain?'

'Get some soldiers down here. I don't want any Barghast getting too close to Trotts. When Mulch gives the word, move him back to our camp.'

'Aye, sir.'

Paran watched the soldier hurry off, then he faced south and scanned the sky. 'Hood's breath!' he muttered with plaintive relief.

Mulch rose. 'You sent Twist to find 'em, didn't you, sir? Look, he's got a passenger. Probably Quick Ben, though . . .'

Paran slowly smiled, squinting at the distant black speck above the ridgeline. 'Not if Twist followed my orders, Healer.'

Mulch looked over. 'Mallet. Fener's hoof, that was a good play, Captain.'

Paran met the healer's gaze. 'Nobody dies on this mission, Mulch.'

The old veteran slowly nodded, then knelt once again to tend to Trotts.

Picker studied Quick Ben as they trudged up yet another grass-backed hillside. 'You want us to get someone to carry you, Mage?'

Quick Ben wiped the sweat from his brow, shook his head. 'No, it's getting better. The Barghast spirits are thick here, and getting thicker. They're resisting the infection. I'll be all right, Corporal.'

'If you say so, only you're looking pretty rough to me.' *And ain't that an understatement.*

'Hood's warren is never a fun place.'

'That's bad news, Mage. What have we all got to look forward to, then?'

Quick Ben said nothing.

Picker scowled. 'That bad, huh? Well, that's just great. Wait till Antsy hears.'

The wizard managed a smile. 'You tell him news only to see him squirm, don't you?'

'Sure. The squad needs its entertainment, right?'

The summit revealed yet another set of small cairns, scattered here and there on its weathered expanse. Tiny, long-legged grey birds hopped from their path as the soldiers marched on. Few words were wasted – the heat was oppressive, with half a day of sunlight remaining. Buzzing flies kept pace.

The squad had seen no-one since Twist's visit at dawn.

466

They knew the duel had taken place by now, but had no idea of its outcome. *Hood, we could walk in to our own execution.* Spindle and Quick Ben were next to useless, unable and unwilling to test the taste of their warrens, pallid and shaky and uncommunicative. Hedge's jaw was too swollen for him to manage anything more than grunts, but the looks he cast at Detoran's back as she walked point hinted at plans of murderous vengeance. Blend was scouting somewhere ahead, or behind – *or maybe in my Hood-damned shadow* – she glanced over her shoulder to check, but the woman wasn't there. Antsy, taking up the rear, kept up a private conversation with himself, his ceaseless mumbling a steady accompaniment to the droning flies.

The landscape showed no life beyond the grasses cloaking the hills and the stunted trees occasionally visible in the valleys where seasonal streams hoarded water beneath the soil. The sky was cloudless, not a bird in sight to mar the blue vastness. Far to the north and east rose the white peaks of the Barghast Range, jagged in their youth and forbidding.

By Twist's estimate, the Barghast gathering was in a valley four leagues to the north. They'd arrive before sunset, if all went well.

Striding at her side, Quick Ben voiced a soft grunt, and the corporal turned in time to see a score of dirt-smeared hands closing around the wizard's legs. The earth seemed to foam beneath Quick Ben's boots, then he was being dragged down, stained, bony fingers clutching, tugging, gnarled forearms reaching upward to wrap themselves about the wizard's struggling form.

'Quick!' Picker bellowed, flinging herself towards him. He reached for her, a look a dumb amazement on his face as the soil heaved around his waist. Pounding footsteps and shouts closed in. Picker's hand clamped on the wizard's wrist.

The earth surged to his chest. The hands reappeared to grasp Quick Ben's right arm and drag it down.

Her eyes met his, then he shook his head. 'Let me go, Corporal—'

'Are you mad—'

'Now, before you get my arm torn off—' His right shoulder was yanked beneath the soil.

Spindle appeared, flinging himself forward to wrap an arm around Quick Ben's neck.

'Let him go!' Picker yelled, releasing the wizard's wrist.

Spindle stared up at her. 'What?'

'Let him go, damn you!'

The squad mage unlocked his arm and rolled away, cursing.

Antsy burst among them, his short-handled shovel already in his hands as Quick Ben's head vanished beneath the earth. Dirt began flying.

'Ease off there, Sergeant,' Picker snapped. 'You'll end up taking off the top of his damned head!'

The sergeant stared at her, then leapt back as if standing on coals. 'Hood!' He raised his shovel and squinted at the blade. 'I don't see no blood! Anybody see any blood! Or – gods! – hair! Is that hair? Oh, Queen of Dreams—'

'That ain't hair,' Spindle growled, pulling the shovel from Antsy's hands. 'That's roots, you idiot! They got 'im. They got Quick Ben.'

'Who has?' Picker demanded.

'Barghast spirits. A whole horde of 'em! We was ambushed!'

'What about you, then?' the corporal asked.

'I ain't dangerous enough, I guess. At least' – his head snapped as he looked around – 'I hope not. I gotta get off this damned barrow, that's what I gotta do!'

Picker watched him scamper away. 'Hedge, keep an eye on him, will you?'

The swollen-faced sapper nodded, trudged off after Spindle.

'What do we do now?' Antsy hissed, his moustache twitching.

468

'We wait a bell or two, then if the wizard ain't managed to claw his way back out, we go on.'

The sergeant's blue eyes widened. 'We leave him?' he whispered.

'It's either that or we level this damned hill. And we wouldn't find him anyway – he's been pulled into their warren. It's here but it ain't here, if you know what I mean. Maybe when Spindle finds his nerve he can do some probing.'

'I knew that Quick Ben wasn't nothing but trouble,' Antsy muttered. 'Can't count on mages for nothing. You're right, what's the point of waiting around? They're damned useless anyway. Let's pack up and get going.'

'It won't hurt to wait a little while,' Picker said.

'Yeah, probably a good idea.'

She shot him a glance, then looked away with a sigh. 'Could do with something to eat. Might want to fix us something special, Sergeant.'

'I got dried dates and breadfruit, and some smoked leeches from that market south side in Pale.'

She winced. 'Sounds good.'

'I'll get right on it.'

He hurried off.

Gods, Antsy, you're losing it fast. And what about me? Mention dates and leeches and my mouth's salivating . . .

The high-prowed canoes lay rotting in the swamp, the ropes strung between them and nearby cedar boles bearded in moss. Dozens of the craft were visible. Humped bundles of supplies lay on low rises, swathed in thick mould, sprouting toadstools and mushrooms. The light was pallid, faintly yellow. Quick Ben, dripping with slime, dragged himself upright, spitting foul water from his mouth as he slowly straightened to look around.

His attackers were nowhere in sight. Insects flitted through the air in a desultory absence of haste. Frogs croaked and the sound of dripping water was constant. A

469

faint smell of salt was in the air. *I'm in a long-dead warren, decayed by the loss of mortal memory. The living Barghast know nothing of this place, yet it is where their dead go – assuming they make it this far.* 'All right,' he said, his voice strangely muted by the turgid, heavy air, 'I'm here. What do you want?'

Movement in the mists alerted him. Figures appeared, closing in tentatively, knee-deep in the swirling black water. The wizard's eyes narrowed. These creatures were not the Barghast he knew from the mortal realm. Squatter, wider, robustly boned, they were a mix of Imass and Toblakai. *Gods, how old is this place?* Hooded brow-ridges hid small, glittering eyes in darkness. Black leather strips stitched their way down gaunt cheeks, reaching past hairless jawlines where they were tied around small longbones that ran parallel to the jaw. Black hair hung in rough braids, parted down the middle. The men and women closing in around Quick Ben were one and all dressed in close-fitting sealskins decorated with bone, antler and shell. Long, thin-bladed knives hung at their hips. A few of the males carried barbed spears that seemed made entirely of bone.

A smaller figure skittered onto a rotted cedar stump directly in front of Quick Ben, a man-shaped bundle of sticks and string with an acorn head.

The wizard nodded. 'Talamandas. I thought you were returning to the White Faces.'

'And so I did, Mage, thanks solely to your cleverness.'

'You've an odd way of showing your gratitude, Old One.' Quick Ben looked around. 'Where are we?'

'The First Landing. Here wait the warriors who did not survive the journey's end. Our fleet was vast, Mage, yet when the voyage was done, fully half of the canoes held only corpses. We had crossed an ocean in ceaseless battle.'

'And where do the Barghast dead go now?'

'Nowhere, and everywhere. They are lost. Wizard, your challenger has slain Humbrall Taur's champion. The spirits

470

have drawn breath and hold it still, for the man may yet die.'

Quick Ben flinched. He was silent for a moment, then he said, 'And if he does?'

'Your soldiers will die. Humbrall Taur has no choice. He will face civil war. The spirits themselves will lose their unity. You would be too great a distraction, a source of greater divisiveness. But this is not why I have had you brought here.' The small sticksnare gestured at the figures standing silent behind him. 'These are the warriors. The army. Yet . . . our warchiefs are not among us. The Founding Spirits were lost long ago. Mage, a child of Humbrall Taur has found them. Found them!'

'But there's a problem.'

Talamandas seemed to slump. 'There is. They are trapped . . . within the city of Capustan.'

The implications of that slowly edged into place in the wizard's mind. 'Does Humbrall Taur know?'

'He does not. I was driven away by his shouldermen. The most ancient of spirits are not welcome. Only the young ones are allowed to be present, for they have little power. Their gift is comfort, and comfort has come to mean a great deal among the Barghast. It was not always so. You see before you a pantheon divided, and the vast schism between us is time – and the loss of memory. We are as strangers to our children; they will not listen to our wisdom and they fear our potential power.'

'Was it Humbrall Taur's hope that his child would find these Founding Spirits?'

'He embraces a grave risk, yet he knows the White Face clans are vulnerable. The young spirits are too weak to resist the Pannion Domin. They will be enslaved or destroyed. When comfort is torn away, all that will be revealed is a weakness of faith, an absence of strength. The clans will be crushed by the Domin's armies. Humbrall Taur reaches for power, yet he gropes blindly.'

'And when I tell him that the ancient spirits have been found . . . will he believe me?'

'You are our only hope. You must convince him.'

'I freed you from the wards,' Quick Ben said.

'What do you ask in return?'

'Trotts needs to survive his wounds. He must be recognized as champion, so that he can legitimately take his place among the council of chiefs. We need a position of strength, Talamandas.'

'I cannot return to the tribes, Wizard. I will only be driven away once again.'

'Can you channel your power through a mortal?'

The sticksnare slowly cocked his head.

'We've a Denul healer, but like me, he's having trouble making use of his warren – the Pannion's poison—'

'To be gifted with our power,' Talamandas said, 'he must be led to this warren, to this place.'

'Well,' Quick Ben said, 'why don't we figure out a way to achieve that?'

Talamandas slowly turned to survey his spirit kin. After a moment he faced the wizard once again. 'Agreed.'

A rogue javelin arced up towards Twist as the Black Moranth and his passenger began their descent. The quorl darted to one side, then quickly dropped towards the Circle. Laughter and cursing voices rose from the gathered warriors, but no further gestures were made.

Paran cast one last scan over the squad standing guard around Trotts and Mulch, then jogged to where Twist and a blistered Mallet were dismounting amidst challenges and threatening weapons.

'Clear them a path, damn you!' the captain bellowed, thrusting a Senan tribesman aside as he pushed closer. The man righted himself with a growl, then showed his filed teeth in a challenge. Paran ignored it. Five jostling strides later, he reached Twist and Mallet.

The healer's eyes were wide with alarm. 'Captain—'

'Aye, it's heating up, Mallet. Come with me. Twist, you might want to get the Abyss out of here—'

472

'Agreed. I shall return to Sergeant Antsy's squad. What has happened?'

'Trotts won the fight, but we might lose the war. Get going, before you get skewered.'

'Yes, Captain.'

Taking the healer by one arm, Paran swung about and began pushing through the crowd. 'Trotts needs you,' he said as they walked. 'It's bad. A crushed throat—'

'Then how in Hood's name is he still alive?'

'Mulch opened a hole above his lungs and the bastard's breathing through that.'

Mallet frowned, then slowly nodded. 'Clever. But Captain, I may not be much use to you, or Trotts—'

Paran's head snapped around. 'You'd better be. If he dies, so do we.'

'My warren—'

'Never mind the excuses, just heal the man, damn you!'

'Yes, sir, but just so you know, it'll probably kill me.'

'Fener's balls!'

'It's a good exchange, sir. I can see that. Don't worry, I'll heal Trotts – you'll all get out of this, and that's what matters right now.'

Paran stopped. He closed his eyes, fighting the sudden waves of pain from his stomach. Through clenched teeth, he said, 'As you say, Mallet.'

'Aimless is waving us over—'

'Aye, go on, then, Healer.'

'Yes, sir.'

Mallet disengaged his arm and headed over to the squad. Paran forced open his eyes.

Look at the bastard. Not a falter in his step. Not a blink at his fate. Who – what are these soldiers?

Mallet pushed Mulch aside, knelt next to Trotts, met the warrior's hard eyes and reached out a hand.

'Mallet!' Mulch hissed. 'Your warren—'

473

'Shut up,' Mallet said, eyes closing as his fingers touched the collapsed, mangled throat.

He opened his warren, and his mind shrieked as virulent power rushed into him. He felt his flesh swelling, splitting, heard the blood spurt and Mulch's shocked cry. Then the physical world vanished within a thrashing sea of pain.

Find the path, dammit! The mending way, the vein of order – gods! Stay sane, Healer. Hold on . . .

But he felt his sanity being torn away, devoured. His sense of self was being shredded to pieces before his mind's eye, and he could do nothing. He drew on that core of health within his own soul, drew on its power, felt it pour through his fingertips to the ravaged cartilage of Trotts's throat. But the core began to dissolve . . .

Hands grasped him, tore at him – a new assault. His spirit struggled, tried to pull away. Screams engulfed him from all sides, as of countless souls being destroyed. Hands fell away from his limbs, were replaced by new ones. He was being dragged, his mind yielding to the savage determination of those grasping, clawing hands.

Sudden calm. Mallet found himself kneeling in a fetid pool, shrouded in silence. Then a murmuring arose all around him. He looked up.

Take from us, a thousand voices whispered in susurrating unison. *Take our power. Return to your place, and use all that we give to you. But hurry – the path we have laid is a costly one – so costly . . .*

Mallet opened himself to the power swirling around him. He had no choice, he was helpless before its demand. His limbs, his body, felt like wet clay, moulded anew. From the bones outward, his tattered soul was being reassembled.

He lurched upright, swung round, and began walking. A lumpy, yielding ground was underfoot. He did not look down, simply pushed on. The Denul warren was all around him now, savage and deadly, yet held back from him. Unable to reclaim his soul, the poison howled.

Mallet could feel his fingers once more, still pressed

474

against the broken throat of his friend, yet within his mind he still walked. Step by step, inexorably pushed onward. *This is the journey to my flesh. Who has done this for me? Why?*

The warren began to dim around him. He was almost home. Mallet looked down, to see what he knew he would see. He walked a carpet of corpses – his path through the poisoned horror of his warren. Costly – so costly . . .

The healer's eyes blinked open. Bruised skin beneath his fingers, yet no more than that. He blinked sweat away, met Trotts's gaze.

Two paths, it seems. One for me, and one for you, friend.

The Barghast weakly lifted his right arm. Mallet clasped it with an iron grip. 'You're back,' the healer whispered, 'you shark-toothed bastard.'

'Who?' Trotts croaked, the skin around his eyes tightening at the effort. 'Who paid?'

Mallet shook his head. 'I don't know. Not me.'

The Barghast's eyes flicked down to the split and bleeding flesh of the healer's arms.

Mallet shook his head again. 'Not me, Trotts.'

Paran could not move, dared not approach closer. All he could see was a huddle of soldiers around where Trotts lay and Mallet knelt. *Gods forgive me, I ordered that healer to kill himself. If this is the true face of command, then it is a skull's grin. I want none of it. No more, Paran, you cannot steel yourself to this life, to these choices. Who are you to balance lives? To gauge worth, to measure flesh by the pound? No, this is a nightmare. I'm done with it.*

Mulch staggered into view, swung to the captain. The man's face was white, his eyes wide. He stumbled over.

No, tell me nothing. Go away, damn you. 'Let's hear it, Healer.'

'It's – it's all right, Captain. Trotts will make it—'

'And Mallet?'

'Superficial wounds – I'll take care of those, sir. He lives – don't ask me how—'

475

'Leave me, Mulch.'

'Sir?'

'Go. Back to Mallet. Get out of my sight.'

Paran swung his back to the man, listened to him scurrying away. The captain shut his eyes, waiting for the agony of his gut to resume, to rise once again like a fist of fire. But all was quiescent within him. He wiped at his eyes, drew a deep breath. *No-one dies. We're all getting out of here. Better tell Humbrall Taur. Trotts has won his claim . . . and damn the rest of you to Hood!*

Fifteen paces away, Mulch and Aimless crouched, watching their captain's back straighten, watching as Paran adjusted his sword belt, watching as he strode towards Humbrall Taur's command tent.

'He's a hard bastard,' the healer muttered.

'Cold as a Jaghut winter,' Aimless said, face twisting. 'Mallet looked a dead man there for a time.'

'For a time, he damn near was.'

The two men were silent for a while, then Mulch leaned to one side and spat. 'Captain might make it after all,' he said.

'Aye,' Aimless said. 'He might.'

'Hey!' one of the soldiers nearby shouted. 'Look at that ridge! Ain't that Detoran? And there's Spindle – they're carrying somebody between 'em!'

'Probably Quick Ben,' Mulch said, straightening. 'Played too long in his warrens. Idiot.'

'Mages,' Aimless sneered. 'Who needs the lazy bastards anyway?'

'Mages, huh? And what about healers, Corporal?'

The man's long face suddenly lengthened even more as his jaw dropped. 'Uh, healers are good, Mulch. Damned good. I meant wizards and sorcerors and the like—'

'Stow it before you say something real stupid, Aimless. Well, we're all here, now. Wonder what these White Faces will do to us?'

'Trotts won!'

'So?'

The corporal's jaw dropped a second time.

Woodsmoke filled Humbrall Taur's hide tent. The huge warchief stood alone, his back to the round hearth, silhouetted by the fire's light. 'What have you to tell me?' he rumbled as Paran let the hide flap drop behind him.

'Trotts lives. He asserts his claim to leadership.'

'Yet he has no tribe—'

'He has a tribe, Warchief. Thirty-eight Bridgeburners. He showed you that, in the style he chose for the duel.'

'I know what he showed us—'

'Yet who understood?'

'I did, and that is all that matters.'

There was silence. Paran studied the tent and its meagre scatter of contents, seeking clues as to the nature of the warrior who stood before him. The floor was covered in bhederin hides. A half-dozen spears lay to one side, one of them splintered. A lone wooden chest carved from a single tree trunk, big enough to hold a three-deep stack of stretched-out corpses, dominated the far wall. The lid was thrown back, revealing on its underside a huge, massively complex locking mechanism. An unruly tumble of blankets ran parallel to the chest where Taur evidently slept. Coins, stitched into the hide walls, glittered dully on all sides, and on the conical ceiling more coins hung like tassels – these ones blackened by years of smoke.

'You have lost your command, Captain.'

Paran blinked, met the warchief's dark eyes. 'That is a relief,' he said.

'Never admit your unwillingness to rule, Malazan. What you fear in yourself will cloud your judgement of all that your successor does. Your fear will blind you to his wisdom and stupidity both. Trotts has never been a commander – I saw that in his eyes when he first stepped forward from your ranks. You must watch him, now. With clear vision.' The man turned and walked to the chest. 'I have mead. Drink with me.'

Gods, my stomach . . . 'Thank you, Warchief.'

Humbrall Taur withdrew from the chest a clay jug and two wooden mugs. He unstoppered the jug, sniffed tentatively, then nodded and poured. 'We shall wait another day,' he said. 'Then I shall address the clans. Trotts will have leave to speak, he has earned his place among the chiefs. But I tell you this now, Captain.' He handed Paran a mug. 'We shall not march on Capustan. We owe those people nothing. Each year we lose more of our youths to that city, to their way of life. Their traders come among us with nothing of value, bold with claims and offers, and would strip my people naked if they could.'

Paran took a sip of the heady mead, felt it burn down his throat. 'Capustan is not your true enemy, Warchief—'

'The Pannion Domin will wage war on us. I know this, Malazan. They will take Capustan and use it to marshal their armies on our very borders. Then they will march.'

'If you understand all that, then why—'

'Twenty-seven tribes, Captain Paran.' Humbrall Taur drained his mug, then wiped his mouth. 'Of those, only eight chiefs will stand with me. Not enough. I need them all. Tell me, your new chief. Can he sway minds with his words?'

Paran grimaced. 'I don't know. He rarely uses them. Then again, up until now, he's had little need. We shall see tomorrow, I suppose.'

'Your Bridgeburners are still in danger.'

The captain stiffened, studied the thick honey wine in his mug. 'Why?' he asked after a moment.

'The Barahn, the Gilk, the Ahkrata – these clans are united against you. Even now, they spread tales of duplicity. Your healers are necromancers – they are conducting a ritual of resurrection to bring Trotts back to life. The White Faces have no love of Malazans. You are allied with the Moranth. You conquered the north – how soon will you

478

turn your hungry gaze on us? You are the plains bear at our side, urging us to lock talons with the southern tiger. A hunter always knows the mind of a tiger, but never the mind of a plains bear.'

'So it seems our fate still hangs in the balance,' Paran said.

'Come the morrow,' Humbrall Taur said.

The captain drained his mug and set it down on the edge of the chest. Spot-fires were growing in his stomach. Behind the cloying mead numbing his tongue, he could taste blood. 'I must attend to my soldiers,' he said.

'Give them this night, Captain.'

Paran nodded, then made his way out of the tent.

Ten paces away, Picker and Blend stood waiting for him. The captain scowled as the two women hurried over. 'More good news, I take it,' he growled under his breath.

'Captain.'

'What is it, Corporal?'

Picker blinked. 'Well, uh, we've made it. I thought I should report—'

'Where's Antsy?'

'He ain't feeling too good, sir.'

'Something he ate?'

Blend grinned. 'That's a good one. Something he ate.'

'Captain,' Picker interjected hastily, shooting Blend a warning glare. 'We lost Quick Ben for a while, then got him back, only he ain't woken up. Spindle figures it's some kind of shock. He was pulled into a Barghast warren—'

Paran started. 'He was what? Take me to him. Blend, get Mallet and join us, double-time! Well, Picker? Why are you just standing there? Lead on.'

'Yes, sir.'

The Seventh squad had dropped their gear in the Bridgeburner encampment. Detoran and Hedge were unfolding tents, watched morosely by a pale, shivering Antsy. Spindle sat beside Quick Ben, fingers combing absently through his tattered hairshirt as he frowned down at the unconscious wizard. The Black Moranth, Twist, stood nearby. Soldiers from other squads sat in their respective groups, watchful of the newcomers and coming no closer.

Paran followed the corporal to Spindle and Quick Ben. The captain glanced at the other squads. 'What's with them?' he wondered aloud.

Picker grunted. 'See Hedge's swollen face? Detoran's in a temper, sir. We're all thinking she's got a crush on the poor sapper.'

'And she showed her affection by beating him up?'

'She's a rough sort, sir.'

The captain sighed, guiding Spindle to one side as he crouched to study Quick Ben. 'Tell me what happened, Spin. Picker said a Barghast warren.'

'Aye, sir. Mind you, I'm just guessing. We was crossing a barrow—'

'Oh, that was smart,' Paran snapped.

The mage ducked. 'Aye, well, it wasn't the first one we crossed and all the others were sleepy enough. Anyway, the spirits reached up and snatched Quick, dragged him outa sight. We waited a while. Then they spat him back out, like this. Captain, the warrens have gone sour. Nasty sour. Quick said it was the Pannion, only not really the Pannion, but the hidden power behind it. Said we was all in trouble.'

Footsteps approached and Paran turned to see Mallet and Blend approach. Behind them walked Trotts. A few ragged, sardonic cheers rose to greet him from the other squads, followed by a loud raspberry. Trotts bared his teeth and changed direction. A figure bolted like a rabbit. The Barghast's grin broadened.

'Get back here, Trotts,' Paran ordered. 'We need to talk.'

Shrugging, the huge warrior swung round and resumed his approach.

Mallet leaned heavily on Paran's shoulder as he knelt down. 'Sorry, Captain,' he gasped. 'I ain't feeling right.'

'I won't ask you to use your warren again, Healer,' Paran

said. 'But I need Quick Ben awake. Any suggestions?'

Mallet squinted down at the wizard. 'I didn't say I was weakened, sir, only that I ain't feeling right. I got help healing Trotts. Spirits, I think now. Maybe Barghast. They put me back together, somehow, someway, and Hood knows I needed putting back together. Anyway, it's like I got someone else's legs, someone else's arms . . .' He reached out and laid a hand against Quick Ben's brow, then grunted. 'He's on his way back. It's protective sorcery that's keeping him asleep.'

'Can you speed things up?'

'Sure.' The healer slapped the wizard.

Quick Ben's eyes snapped open. 'Ow. You bastard, Mallet.'

'Stop complaining, Quick. Captain wants to talk to you.'

The wizard's dark eyes swivelled to take in Paran, then, looming over the captain's shoulder, Trotts. Quick Ben grinned. 'You all owe me.'

'Ignore that,' Mallet said to Paran. 'The man's always saying that. Gods, what an ego. If Whiskeyjack was here he'd clout you on the head, Wizard, and I'm tempted to stand in for him on that.'

'Don't even think it.' Quick Ben slowly sat up. 'What's the situation here?'

'Our heads are still on the chopping block,' Paran said in a low voice. 'We haven't many friends here, and our enemies are getting bolder. Humbrall Taur's command is shaky and he knows it. Trotts killing his favoured son hasn't helped. Even so, the warchief's on our side. More or less. He may not care one whit for Capustan, but he knows the threat the Pannion Domin represents.'

'He doesn't care about Capustan, huh?' Quick Ben smiled. 'I can change that attitude. Mallet, you got company in that body of yours?'

The healer blinked. 'What?'

'Feeling strange, are you?'

'Well—'

'So he says,' Paran cut in. 'What do you know about it?'

'Only everything. Captain, we've got to go to Humbrall Taur. The three – no, the four of us – you too, Trotts. Hood, let's bring Twist, too – he knows a lot more than he's let on, and maybe I can't see that grin, Moranth, but I know it's there. Spindle, that hairshirt reeks. Go away before I throw up.'

'Some gratitude for protecting your hide,' Spindle muttered, edging back.

Paran straightened and swung his gaze back to Humbrall Taur's tent. 'Fine, here we go again.'

Sunset approached, spreading a gloom across the valley. The Barghast had resumed their wild dancing and vicious duels with an almost febrile intensity. Thirty paces away from Humbrall Taur's tent, sitting amidst discarded armour, Picker scowled. 'They're still in there, the bastards. Leaving us to do a whole lot of nothing, except watch these savages mutilate each other. I don't think we should be thinking it's all over, Blend.'

The dark-eyed woman at her side frowned. 'Want me to hunt Antsy down?'

'Why bother? Hear those grunts? That's our sergeant taking that Barahn maiden for a ride. He'll be back in a moment or two, looking pleased—'

'And the lass trailing a step behind—'

'With a confused look on her face—'

'"That's it?"'

'She blinked and missed it.'

They shared a short, nasty laugh. Then Picker sobered again. 'We could be dead tomorrow no matter what Quick Ben says to Taur. That's still the captain's thinking, so he leaves us to our fun this night . . .'

'"Hooded comes the dawn . . ."'

'Aye.'

'Trotts did what he had to do in that scrap,' Blend observed. 'It should have been as simple as that.'

'Well, I'd have been happier if it'd been Detoran from the start. There wouldn't have been no near draw or whatever. She would have done that brat good. From what I've heard, our tattooed Barghast just stood back and let the weasel come to him. Detoran would've just stepped forward and brained the lad at the feather's drop—'

'Wasn't no feather drop, just a mace.'

'Whatever. Anyway, Trotts ain't got her meanness.'

'No-one has, and I've just noticed, she hasn't come back from dragging that Gilk warrior off into the bushes.'

'Compensation for Hedge running and hiding. Poor lad – the Gilk, that is. He's probably dead by now.'

'Let's hope she notices.'

The two women fell silent. The duels down by the fire were coming fast and with a ferocity that had begun drawing more and more Barghast onlookers. Picker grunted, watching another warrior go down with a rival's knife in his throat. *If this keeps up, they'll have to start building a new barrow tomorrow. Then again, they might do that anyway – a barrow for the Bridgeburners.* She looked around, picking out solitary Bridgeburners among the crowds of natives. Discipline had crumbled. That fast surge of hope at the news that Trotts would live had sunk just as fast with the rumour that the Barghast might kill them all anyway – out of spite.

'The air feels . . . strange,' Blend said.

Aye . . . as if the night itself was aflame . . . as if we're in the heart of an unseen firestorm. The torcs on Picker's arms were hot and slowly getting hotter. *I'm about due for another dousing in that water barrel – shortlived relief, but at least it's something.*

'Remember that night in Blackdog?' Blend continued in a low voice. 'That retreat . . .'

Stumbling onto a Rhivi Burn Ground . . . malign spirits rising up out of the ashes . . . 'Aye, Blend, I remember well enough.' *And if that wing of Black Moranth hadn't spied us and come down to pull us up . . .*

483

'Feels the same, Picker. We've got spirits loosed.'

'Not the big ones – these are ancestors we've got gathering. If it was the big ones our hair'd be standing on end.'

'True. So where *are* they? Where are the nastiest of the Barghast spirits?'

'Somewhere else, obviously. With Oponn's luck, they won't show up tomorrow.'

'You'd think they would. You'd think they'd not want to miss something like this.'

'Try thinking pleasant thoughts for a change, Blend. Hood's breath!'

'I was just wondering,' the woman shrugged. 'Anyway,' she continued, rising, 'I think I'm going to wander for a while. See what I can pick up.'

'You understand Barghast?'

'No, but sometimes the most telling communication doesn't use words.'

'You're as bad as the rest, Blend. Likely our last night among the living, and off you go.'

'But that's the whole point, isn't it?'

Picker watched her friend slip away into the shadows. *Damned woman . . . got me sitting here more miserable than before. How do I know where the serious Barghast spirits are? Maybe they're just waiting behind some hill. Ready to jump out tomorrow morning and scare us all shitless. And how do I know what that Barghast warchief's going to decide tomorrow? A pat on the head or a knife across the throat?*

Spindle pushed through the crowd and approached. The stench of burned hair hung around him like a second cloak and his expression was grim. He crouched down before her. 'It's going bad, Corporal.'

'That's a change,' she snapped. 'What is?'

'Half our soldiers are drunk and the rest are well on their way. Paran and his cronies disappearing into that tent and not coming out ain't been taken as a good sign. We won't be in any shape to do a damned thing come the dawn.'

Picker glanced over to Humbrall Taur's tent. The

484

silhouetted figures within had not moved in some time. After a moment she nodded to herself. 'All right, Spin. Stop worrying about it. Go have some fun.'

The man gaped. 'Fun?'

'Yeah, remember? Relaxation, pleasure, a sense of well-being. Go on, she's out there somewhere and you won't be around nine months from now either. Of course, you might have a better chance if you took off that hairshirt – for this night at least—'

'I can't do that! What will Mother think?'

Picker studied the mage's fraught, horrified expression. 'Spindle,' she said slowly, 'your mother's dead. She ain't here, she ain't watching over you. You can misbehave, Spindle. Honest.'

The mage ducked down as if an invisible hand had just clouted him and for a moment Picker thought she saw an impression of knuckles bloom on the man's pate, then he scampered away, muttering and shaking his head.

Gods . . . maybe all our ancestors are here! Picker glared about. Come near me, Da, and I'll slit your Hood-damned throat, just like I did the first time . . .

Grainy-eyed with exhaustion, Paran stepped clear of the tent entrance. The sky was grey, faintly luminescent. Mist and woodsmoke hung motionless in the valley. A pack of dogs loping along one ridge was the only movement he could see.

And yet they're awake. All here. The real battle is done, and now, here before me – I can almost see them – stand the dark godlings of the Barghast, facing the dawn . . . for the first time in thousands of years, facing the mortal dawn . . .

A figure joined him. Paran glanced over. 'Well?'

'The Barghast Elder Spirits have left Mallet,' Quick Ben said. 'The healer sleeps. Can you feel them, Captain? The spirits? All the barriers have been shattered, the Old Ones have joined with their younger spirit kin. The forgotten warren is forgotten no more.'

'All very well,' Paran muttered, 'but we've still a city to liberate. What happens if Taur raises the standard of war and his rivals deny him?'

'They won't. They can't. Every shoulderman among the White Faces will awaken to the change, to the burgeoning. They'll feel that power, and know it for what it is. More, the spirits will make it known that their masters – the true gods of the Barghast – are trapped in Capustan. The Founding Spirits are awake. The time has come to free them.'

The captain studied the wizard at his side for a moment, then asked, 'Did you know the Moranth were kin to the Barghast?'

'More or less. Taur may not like it – and the tribes will howl – but if the spirits themselves have embraced Twist and his people . . .'

Paran sighed. *I need to sleep. But I can't.* 'I'd better gather the Bridgeburners.'

'Trotts's new tribe,' Quick Ben said, grinning.

'Then why can I hear his snores?'

'He's new to responsibility, Captain. You'll have to teach him.'

Teach him what? How to live beneath the burden of command? That's something I can't manage myself. I need only look into Whiskeyjack's face to understand that no-one can – no-one who has a heart, anyway. We learn to achieve but one thing: the ability to hide our thoughts, to mask our feelings, to bury our humanity deep in our souls. And that can't be taught, only shown.

'Go rouse the bastard,' Paran growled.

'Yes, sir.'

486

CHAPTER TWELVE

In the Mountain's Heart she waited,
dreaming of peace, so deeply curled
around her grief, when he found her,
the man's search was done,
and he took upon himself her every scar
for power's embrace is a love
that wounds.

Rise of the Domin
Scintalla of Bastion (1129–1164)

The mountain fastness of outlook, its back to the lake, was the colour of water-thinned blood in the sunset. Condors wheeled around it, twice the mass of Great Ravens, their collared necks crooked as they studied the humans seething around the base of the fortress amidst a grounded starscape of campfires.

The one-eyed Tenescowri who had once been a scout in Onearm's Host followed their curving flight with deep concentration, as if godly messages could be read in the condors' sweeping patterns against the deepening sky. He had been truly embraced, agreed those who knew him by sight. Felled mute by the Domin's vastness since that day in Bastion, three weeks past. There had been a savage hunger in his lone eye from the very beginning, an ancient fire that whispered ever louder of wolves padding the darkness. It was said that Anaster himself, First among the Children of the Dead Seed, had noted the man, had indeed drawn him closer during the long march, until the one-eyed Tenescowri had been given a horse, and rode with Anaster's lieutenants at the vanguard of the human tide.

Of course, Anaster's company of lieutenants changed faces with brutal regularity.

The shapeless, starving army now waited at the feet of the Pannion Seer. At dawn he would appear upon a balcony of Outlook's central tower, and raise his hands in holy benediction. The bestial howl that would rise to greet his blessing would shatter a lesser man, but the Seer, ancient as he was, was no ordinary man. He was the embodiment of Pannion, the god, the only god.

When Anaster led the Tenescowri army north, to the river, then beyond, to Capustan, he would carry within him the power that was the Seer. And the enemy that had gathered to oppose them would be raped, devoured, obliterated from the earth. There was no doubt in the minds of the hundred thousand. Only certainty, a razor-sharp sword of iron held in the grip of ceaseless, desperate hunger.

The one-eyed man continued staring at the condors as the light faded. Perhaps, some whispered, he was in communion with the Seer himself, and his gaze was not on the wheeling birds, but on the fortress of Outlook itself.

This was as close to the truth as the peasants would come. Indeed, Toc the Younger was studying that towering fastness, an antiquated monastery warped misshapen by military accretions: battlements and enfilading walls, vast gatehouses and sheer-walled trenches. The efforts continued, the masons and engineers clearly intent on working through the night beneath towering braziers of dancing flames.

Oh, hurry with this latest frenzy of improvements. Feel what you feel, old man. It's a new emotion to you, but one the rest of us know very well. It's called fear. The seven K'ell Hunters you sent south yesterday, the ones that passed us on the road . . . they won't be coming back. And that magefire you see lighting the southern sky at night . . . it's coming closer. Inexorable. The reason's simple enough – you've angered dear Lady Envy. She's not nice when she's angry. Did you visit the carnage in Bastion? Did you send your favourite Urdomen there to return with a detailed report? Did the news turn your legs to water? It should have. The wolf and the dog, huge and silent, ripping through the press of humanity. The T'lan Imass, his sword a rust-hued blur as it sliced through your vaunted elites. And the Seguleh, oh, the Seguleh. The punitive army of three, come to answer your arrogance . . .

The pain in Toc's stomach had dulled; the knot of hunger had tightened, shrunk, become an almost senseless core of need, a need that had itself starved. His ribs were sharp and distinct beneath stretched skin. Fluids were swelling his belly. His joints ached interminably, and he'd felt his teeth loosening in their sockets. The only taste he knew these days was the occasional scrap, and the malty bitterness of his own saliva, washed away every now and then by stale, wine-tinted water from the casks on the wagons or a rare flagon of ale reserved for the First Child's favoured few.

Toc's fellow lieutenants – and indeed Anaster himself – were well enough fed. They welcomed the endless corpses the march had claimed and continued to claim. Their boiling cauldrons were ever full. The rewards of power.

The metaphor made real – I can see my old cynical teachers nodding at that. Here, among the Tenescowri, there is no obfuscating the brutal truth. Our rulers devour us. They always have. How could I ever have believed otherwise? I was a soldier, once. I was the violent assertion of someone else's will.

He had changed, not a difficult truth to recognize in himself. His soul torn by the horrors he saw all around him, the sheer amorality born of hunger and fanaticism, he had been reshaped, twisted almost beyond recognition into something new. The eradication of faith – faith in anything, especially the essential goodness of his kind – had left him cold, hardened and feral.

Yet he would not eat human flesh. *Better to devour myself from within, to take my own muscles away, layer by layer, and digest all that I was. This is the last remaining task before me, and it has begun.* None the less, he was coming to realize a deeper truth: his resolve was crumbling. *No, stay away from that thought.*

He had no idea what Anaster had seen in him. Toc played the mute, he was the defier of gifted flesh, he offered to the world nothing but his presence, the sharpness of his lone eye – seeing all that could be seen – and yet the First had descried him, somehow, from the multitudes, had dragged him forth and granted him a lieutenancy.

But I command no-one. Tactics, strategies, the endless difficulties of managing an army even as anarchistic as this one – I attend Anaster's meetings in silence. I am asked for no opinions. I make no reports. What is it he wants of me?

Suspicions still swirled dark and deep beneath the numbed surface. He wondered if Anaster somehow knew who he was. Was he about to be delivered into the hands of the Seer? It was possible – in what the world had become, anything was possible. Anything and everything. Reality itself had surrendered its rules – the living conceived by the dead, the savage love in the eyes of the women as they mounted a dying prisoner, the flaring hope that they would take within them the corpse's last seed as it fled – as if the dying body itself sought one last chance to escape the finality of oblivion – even as the soul drowned in darkness. *Love, not lust. These women have given their hearts to the moment of death. Should the seed take root . . .*

Anaster was the eldest of the first generation. A pale, gangly youth with yellow-stained eyes and lank, black hair, leading the vast army from atop his draught horse. His face was a thing of inhuman beauty, as if no soul resided behind the perfect mask. Women and men of all ages came to him, begging his gentle touch, but he denied them all. Only his mother would he let come close; to stroke his hair, rest a sun-darkened, wrinkled hand on his shoulder.

Toc feared her more than anyone else, more than Anaster and his random cruelty, more than the Seer. Something demonic lit her eyes from within. She had been the first to mount a dying man, screaming the Night Vows of a married couple's first night, then wailing in the manner of a village widow when the man died beneath her. A tale oft repeated. A multitude of witnesses. Other women of the Tenescowri flocked to her. Perhaps it was her act of power over helpless men; perhaps it was her brazen theft of their involuntarily spilled seed; perhaps the madness simply spread from one to the next.

On their march from Bastion, the army had come upon a village that had defied the Embrace. Toc had watched as Anaster released his mother and her followers, watched as they took men and young boys alike, their knives driving mortal blows, swarming over the bodies in a manner that the foulest beast could not match. And the thoughts he had felt then were now carved deep in his soul. *They were human once, these women. They lived in villages and towns no different from this one. They were wives and mothers, tending their homes and yard animals. They danced, and they wept, they were pious and respectful in propitiating the old gods. They lived normal lives.*

There was a poison within the Pannion Seer and whatever god spoke through him. A poison that seemed born of familial memories. Memories powerful enough to dismember those most ancient of bonds. *A child betrayed, perhaps. A child led by the hand . . . into terror and pain. This is how it feels – all that I see around me. Anaster's mother, reshaped malign, rack-born to a nightmarish role. A mother not a mother, a wife not a wife, a woman not a woman.*

Shouts rose to announce the appearance of a group of riders, emerging from the ramp gate of Outlook's outer wall. Toc swung his head, studied the visitors as they rode closer through the deepening gloom. Armoured. An Urdo commander, flanked by a pair of Seerdomin, the troop of Urdomen three abreast and seven deep riding in their wake.

Behind the troop, a K'ell Hunter.

A gesture from Anaster drew his lieutenants towards the low hill he had chosen as his headquarters, Toc the Younger among them.

The white of the First's eyes was the colour of honey, his pupils a murky, slate grey. Torchlight illuminated his alabaster-hued face, made his full lips strangely red. He'd remounted and now sat bareback on the huge, weary horse, slumped as he studied his chosen officers. 'News comes,' he rasped.

Toc had never heard him speak louder. Perhaps the lad could not, born with a defect of the throat or tongue. Perhaps he'd never found the need.

'The Seer and I have spoken within our minds, and now I know more than even the courtiers within Outlook's holy walls. Septarch Ultentha of Coral has been called to the Seer, leading to much speculation.'

'What news,' one of the lieutenants asked, 'from the north border, Glorious First?'

'The investment is nearly complete. I fear, my children, that we will come too late to partake of the siege.'

Breaths hissed on all sides.

I fear our hunger will not end. This was the true meaning of Anaster's words.

'It's said that Kaimerlor, a large village to the east, has refused the Embrace,' another officer said. 'Perhaps, Glorious First—'

'No,' Anaster grated. 'Beyond Capustan await the Barghast. In their hundreds of thousands, it is said. Divided amongst themselves. Weak of faith. We shall find all we need, my children.'

We'll not make it. Toc knew this for a certainty, as did the others. There was silence.

Anaster's eyes were on the approaching soldiers. 'The Seer,' he said, 'has prepared for us a gift in the meantime. He recognizes our need for sustenance. It seems,' he continued relentlessly, 'that the citizens of Coral have been found ... wanting. This is the truth behind the speculation. We need only cross the calm waters of Ortnal Cut to fill our bellies, and the Urdo who now comes will deliver to us the news that launches await us – sufficient to carry us all.'

'Then,' a lieutenant growled, 'we shall feast.'

Anaster smiled.

Feast. Hood take me, please ... Toc could feel the desire rising within him, a palpable demand that he realized would defeat him, shatter his defences. A *feast – gods, how I hunger!*

'I am not done with news,' the First said after a moment. 'The Urdo has a second mission.' The youth's sickly eyes fell on Toc the Younger. 'The Seer requests the presence of the Defier, he of the lone eye – an eye that, night by night, has slowly changed on our journey from Bastion, though I imagine that he knows it not. The Defier shall be the Seer's guest. The Defier, with his wolf's eye that so gleams in the dark. He will have no need for those extraordinary stone weapons – I shall personally keep them safe.'

Toc's obsidian-tipped arrows and the dagger were quickly removed, handed up to Anaster.

The soldiers arrived.

Toc strode to them, fell to his knees before the Urdo's horse.

'He is honoured,' Anaster said. 'Take him.'

And Toc's gratitude was real, a flood of relief rushing through his thinned veins. He would not see Coral's walls, would not see the citizens in their tens of thousands torn to pieces, would not see the rapes, would not see himself among the crowds, rushing to the flesh that was their righteous reward ...

The workers swarmed over the nascent battlements of the approach, dust- and dirt-smeared figures lit demonic in the firelight. Stumbling in the wake of the Urdo's warhorse, Toc studied their frenzied efforts with jaded detachment.

Stone, earth and wood were meagre obstacles to Lady Envy's sorcery, which he'd seen unleashed at Bastion. As in legends of old, hers was a power that rolled in broad waves, stripping the life from all it swept over, devouring rank upon rank, street by street, leaving bodies piled in their hundreds. She was, he reminded himself with something like fierce pride, the daughter of Draconus – an Elder God.

The Pannion Seer had thrown sorcerors in her path, he'd heard since, yet they fared little better. She shrugged aside their efforts, decimated their powers, then left them to Garath or Baaljagg. K'Chain Che'Malle sought to reach her, only to wither beneath an onslaught of sorcery. The dog that was Garath made sport of those that eluded Lady Envy, usually working alone but sometimes in tandem with Baaljagg. Both were quicker than the undead hunters, it was said, and far smarter. Three pitched battles had occurred, in which legions of Pannion Betaklites, supported by the mounted Betakullid and by Scalandi skirmishers, as well as the Domin equivalent of Mage Cadres, had engaged their handful of enemies as they would an opposing army. From these battles arose the whispered tales of the T'lan Imass – a creature of which the Pannions had no knowledge and had come to call Stonesword – and the Seguleh, two in the first two battles, but a third appearing for the last one. Stonesword would hold one flank, the Seguleh the opposite flank. Lady Envy stood at the centre, whilst Garath and Baaljagg flowed like ragged capes of darkness wheresoever they pleased.

Three engagements, three broken armies, thousands dead, the rest attempting to flee but always caught by Lady Envy's relentless wrath.

As terrible as the Pannion, my sweet-faced friend. As terrible . . . and as terrifying. Tool and the Seguleh honour the retreat of those who oppose them; they are content to claim the field and no more than that. Even the wolf and the dog cut short their pursuit. But not Envy. An unwise tactic – now that the enemy knows that retreat is impossible, they will stand and fight. The

494

*Seguleh do not escape wounds; nor do Garath and Baaljagg.
Even Tool has been buried beneath enraged swordsmen, though
he simply dissolves into dust and reappears elsewhere. One
charge of lancers came to within a dozen paces of Lady Envy
herself. The next well-flung javelin . . .*

He had no regrets about leaving them. He would not
have survived their company.

As they approached the outer gate fortification, Toc saw
Seerdomin among the battlements, hulking and silent.
Formidable as squads numbering a half-dozen, here they
were scores. *They might do more than slow the Seguleh. They
might stop them in their tracks. This is the Seer's final line of
defence . . .*

A single ramp led up to Outlook's inner gate, steep and
sheer-sided. Human bones littered the trenches to either
side. They ascended. One hundred paces later, they passed
beneath the gate's arch. The Urdo detached his troop to
stable their horses, then dismounted. Flanked by
Seerdomin, Toc watched the K'ell Hunter thump through
the gateway, bladed arms hanging low. It swung lifeless eyes
on the Malazan for a moment, then padded off down an
unlit roofed corridor running parallel to the wall.

The Urdo raised the visor of his helm. 'Defier, to your
left is the entrance to the Seer's tower. He awaits you
within. Go.'

Perhaps not a prisoner. Perhaps no more than a curiosity.
Toc bowed to the officer, then stumbled wearily to the
gaping doorway. *More likely the Seer knows he has nothing to
fear from me. I'm already in Hood's shadow. Not much longer,
now.*

A high-vaulted chamber occupied the tower's entire
main floor, the ceiling a chaotic inverted maze of
buttresses, spans, arches and false arches. Reaching down
from the centre to hover a hand's width above the floor was
a skeletal circular staircase of bronze that swung in a slow,
creaking circle. Lit by a single brazier near the wall opposite
the entrance, the chamber was shrouded in gloom, though

Toc had no difficulty discerning the unadorned stone blocks that were the walls, and the complete absence of furniture that left echoes dancing all around him as he crossed the flagstoned floor, scuffing through shallow puddles.

He set a hand on the staircase's lowest railing. The massive, depending structure pulled him inexorably to one side as it continued its rotation, causing him to stagger. Grimacing, he pulled himself onto the first step. *The bastard's at the top, I'd wager, in a swaying room. My heart's likely to give out halfway up. He'll sit up there, waiting for an audience that will never happen. Now there's a Hood-grinning joke for you.* He began climbing.

Forty-two steps brought him to the next level. Toc sank down onto the cold bronze of the landing, his limbs on fire, the world wavering drunken and sickly before him. He rested sweat-slick hands on the gritty, pebbled surface of the metal sheet, blinking as he attempted to focus.

The room surrounding him was unlit, yet his lone eye could discern every detail, the open racks crowded with instruments of torture, the low beds of stained wood, the bundle of dark, stiff rags against one wall, and, covering those walls like a mad artisan's tapestries, the skins of humans. Complete down to the fingertips and nails, stretched out into a ghastly, oversized approximation of the human form, the faces flattened with only the rough stone of the wall showing where the eyes had once been. Nostrils and mouths sewn shut, hair pulled to one side and loosely knotted.

Waves of revulsion swept through Toc, shuddering, debilitating waves. He wanted to scream, to release horror's pressure, but could only gasp. Trembling, he pulled himself upright, stared up the spiralling steps, began dragging himself higher once more.

Chambers marched by, scenes that swam with grainy uncertainty, as he climbed the seemingly endless stairs. Time was lost to him. The tower, now creaking and groaning on all sides – pitching in the wind – had become

496

the ascent of his entire life, what he had been born to, a mortal's solitary task. Cold metal, stone, faintly lit rooms rising then falling like the passage of weak suns, the traverse of aeons, civilizations born, then dying, and all that lay between was naught but the illusion of glory.

Fevered, his mind leapt off precipices, one after another, tumbling ever deeper into the well of madness even as his body clawed upward, step by step. *Dear Hood, come find me. I beg you. Take me from this god's diseased feet, end this shameful debasement – when I face him at last, I will be nothing—*

'The stairs have ended,' an ancient, high-pitched and quavering voice called to him. 'Lift your head, I would look upon this alarming countenance of yours. You have no strength? Allow me.'

A will seeped into Toc's flesh, a stranger's vigour imbuing health and strength in each muscle. None the less, its taste was foul, insipid. Toc moaned, struggled against it, but defiance failed him. Breath steadying, heart slowing, he lifted his head. He was kneeling on the last platform of hammered bronze.

Sitting hunched and twisted on a wooden chair was the wrinkled carcass of an old man, his eyes lit flaring as if their surface was no more than the thin film of two paper lanterns, stained and torn. The Pannion Seer was a corpse, yet a creature dwelt within the husk, animating it, a creature visible to Toc as a ghostly, vaguely man-shaped exhalation of power.

'Ah, now I see,' the voice said, though the mouth did not move. 'Indeed, that is not a human's eye. A wolf's in truth. Extraordinary. It is said you do not speak. Will you do so now?'

'If you wish,' Toc said, his voice rough with disuse, a shock to his own ears.

'I am pleased. I so tire of listening to myself. Your accent is unfamiliar to me. You are most certainly not a citizen of Bastion.'

'Malazan.'

The corpse creaked as it leaned forward, the eyes flaring brighter. 'Indeed. A child of that distant, formidable empire. Yet you have come from the south, whereas my spies inform me that your kin's army marches from Pale. How, then, did you become so lost?'

'I know nothing of that army, Seer,' Toc said. 'I am now a Tenescowri, and that is all that matters.'

'A bold claim. What is your name?'

'Toc the Younger.'

'Let us leave the matter of the Malazan army for a moment, shall we? The south has, until recently, been a place devoid of threat to my nation. But that has changed. I find myself irritated by a new, stubborn threat. These . . . Seguleh . . . and a disturbing, if mercifully small, collection of allies. Are these your friends, then, Toc the Younger?'

'I am without friends, Seer.'

'Not even your fellow Tenescowri? What of Anaster, the First Child who shall one day lead an entire army of Children of the Dead Seed? He noted you as . . . unique. And what of me? Am I not your Lord? Was it not I who embraced you?'

'I cannot be certain,' Toc said dully, 'which of you it was who embraced me.'

Entity and corpse both flinched back at his words, a blurring of shapes that hurt Toc's eye. *Two beings, the living hiding behind the dead.* Power waxed until it seemed the ancient's body would simply disintegrate. The limbs twitched spasmodically. After a moment, the furious emanation diminished, and the body fell still once more. 'More than a wolf's eye, that you should see so clearly what no-one else has been able to descry. Oh, sorcerors have looked upon me, brimming with their vaunted warrens, and seen nothing awry. My deception knew no challenge. Yet you . . .'

Toc shrugged. 'I see what I see.'

'With which eye?'

498

He shrugged again. To that, he had no answer.

'But we were speaking of friends, Toc the Younger. Within my holy embrace, a mortal does not feel alone. Anaster, I see now, was deceived.'

'I did not say I felt alone, Seer. I said I am without friends. Among the Tenescowri, I am one with your holy will. Yet, consider the woman who walks at my side, or the weary child whom I carry, or the men all around me . . . should they die, I will devour them. There can be no friendship in such company, Seer. There is only potential food.'

'Yet you would not eat.'

Toc said nothing.

The Seer leaned forward once again. '*You would now, wouldn't you?*'

And so madness steals upon me like the warmest cloak. 'If I am to live.'

'And is living important to you, Toc the Younger?'

'I do not know, Seer.'

'Let us see then, shall we?' A withered arm lifted. Sorcery rippled the air before Toc. A small table took form in front of the Malazan, heaped with steaming chunks of boiled meat. 'Here, then,' the Seer said, 'is the sustenance you require. Sweet flesh; it is an acquired taste, or so I am told. Ah, I see the hunger flare in your wolf's eye. There is indeed a beast within you – what does it care of its meal's provenance? None the less, I caution you to proceed slowly, lest your shrunken stomach reject all that you feed it.'

With a soft moan, Toc stumbled to his knees before the table, hands reaching out. His teeth ached as he began chewing, adding his own blood to the meat's juices. He swallowed, felt his gut clench around the morsel. He forced himself to stop, to wait.

The Seer rose from the chair, walked stiffly to a window. 'I have learned,' the ancient creature said, 'that mortal armies are insufficient to the task of defeating this threat that approaches from the south. Accordingly, I have withdrawn my forces, and will now dismiss the enemy with my own hand.' The Seer swung about and studied Toc. 'It is said wolves avoid human flesh, given the choice. Do not believe me without mercy, Toc the Younger. The meat before you is venison.'

I know, you bastard. It seems I've more than a wolf's eye – I've its sense of smell as well. He picked up another chunk. 'It no longer matters, Seer.'

'I am pleased. Do you feel strength returning to your body? I have taken the liberty of healing you – slowly, so as to diminish the trauma of the spirit. I like you, Toc the Younger. Though few know it, I can be the kindliest of masters.' The old man faced the window once more.

Toc continued eating, feeling the life flow back into him, his lone eye fixed on the Seer, narrrowing at the power that had begun building around the old man's animated corpse. *Cold, that sorcery. The smell of ice on the wind – here are memories, ancient memories – whose?*

The room blurred, dissolved before his vision. Baaljagg . . . A steady padding forward, an eye that swung to the left to see Lady Envy striding a dozen paces away. Beyond her loped Garath, massive, flanks crisscrossed in scars that still leaked seething, virulent blood – the blood of chaos. To Garath's left walked Tool. Swords had carved a new map on the T'lan Imass's body, splintering bones, splitting withered skin and muscle – Toc had never before seen a T'lan Imass so badly damaged. It seemed impossible that Tool could stand, much less walk.

Baaljagg's head did not turn to survey the Seguleh marching on his right, yet Toc knew that they were there, Mok included. The ay, like Toc himself, was gripped in memories sprung to life by the scent on that new, chill wind coming down from the north – memories that drew their twinned attention to Tool.

The T'lan Imass had lifted his head, steps slowing until he came to a halt. The others followed suit. Lady Envy turned to Tool.

'What sorcery is this, T'lan Imass?'

'You know as well as I, Lady,' Tool rasped in reply, still scenting the air. 'Unexpected, a deepening of the confusion surrounding the entity known as the Pannion Seer.'

'An unimaginable alliance, yet it would appear . . .'

'It would appear,' Tool agreed.

Baaljagg's eyes returned to the north, gauging the preternatural glow building on the jagged horizon, a glow that began flowing down between the mountains, filling the valleys, spreading outward. The wind rose to a howl, gelid and bitter.

Memories resurrected . . . this is Jaghut sorcery—

'Can you defeat it, Tool?' Lady Envy asked.

The T'lan Imass turned to her. 'I am clanless. Weakened. Lady, unless you can negate it, we shall have to cross as best we can, and it will build all the while, striving to deny us.'

The Lady's expression was troubled. Her frown deepened as she studied the emanation to the north. 'K'Chain Che'Malle . . . and Jaghut together. Is there precedence for such an alliance?'

'There is not,' Tool said.

Sleet swept down on the small group, swiftly turning into hail. Toc felt the stinging impacts through Baaljagg's hide as the animal hunched lower. A moment later they began moving once more, leaning against the blistering wind.

Before them, the mountains thickened with a mantle of green-veined white . . .

Toc blinked. He was in the tower, crouched before the meat-laden table. The Seer's back was to him, suffused with Jaghut sorcery – the creature within the old man's carcass was now entirely visible, thin, tall, hairless, tinted green. But no, there's more – grey roots roped down from the body's legs, chaotic power, plunging down through the stone floor, twisting with something like pain or ecstacy. The Jaghut draws on another sorcery, something older, far more deadly than Omtose Phellack.

The Seer turned. 'I am . . . disappointed, Toc the Younger. Did you think you could reach out to your wolf

501

kin without my knowing it? So, the one within you readies for its rebirth.'

The one within me?

'Alas,' the Seer went on, 'the Beast Throne is vacant – neither you nor that beast god can match my strength. Even so, had I remained ignorant, you might well have succeeded in assassinating me. *You lied!*'

This last accusation came as a shriek, and Toc saw, not an old man, but a child standing before him.

'Liar! Liar! And for that you shall suffer!' The Seer gestured wildly.

Pain clenched Toc the Younger, wrapped iron bands around his body, his limbs, lifted him into the air. Bones snapped. The Malazan screamed.

'Break! Yes, break into pieces! But I won't kill you, no, not yet, not for a long, *long* time! Oh, look at you writhe, but what do you know of true pain, mortal? Nothing. I will show you, Toc the Younger. I will teach you—' He gestured again.

Toc found himself hovering in absolute darkness. The agony clutching him did not cease, yet drew no tighter. His gasps echoed dully in heavy, stale air. *He – he sent me away. My god sent me away . . . and now I'm truly alone. Alone . . .*

Something moved nearby, something huge, hard skin rasping against stone. A mewling sound reached Toc's ears, growing louder, closer.

With a shriek, leathery arms wrapped around the Malazan, pulled him into a suffocating, desperate embrace. Pinned against a flabby, pebble-skinned bosom, Toc found himself in the company of a score or more corpses, in various stages of decomposition – all within the yearning hug of giant, reptilian arms.

Broken ribs ground and tore in Toc's chest. His skin was slippery with blood, yet whatever healing sorcery the Seer had gifted to him persisted, slowly mending, knitting, only to have the bones break yet again within the savage embrace of the creature who now held him.

The Seer's voice filled his skull. *I tired of the others . . . but you I shall keep alive. You are worthy to take my place in that sweet, motherly hug. Oh, she is mad. Mindless with insanity, yet the sparks of need reside within her. Such need. Beware, or it will devour you, as it did me – until I grew so foul that she spat me back out. Need, when it overwhelms, becomes poison, Toc the Younger. The great corrupter of love, and so it shall corrupt you. Your flesh. Your mind. Can you feel it? It has begun. Dear Malazan, can you feel it?*

He had no breath with which to scream, yet the arms holding him felt his shudder, and squeezed tighter.

Soft whimpers filled the chamber, the twin voices of Toc and his captor.

CHAPTER THIRTEEN

Onearm's Host, in that time, was perhaps the finest
army the Malazan Empire had yet to produce, even
given the decimation of the Bridgeburners at the
Siege of Pale. Drawn from disparate regiments
that included companies from Seven Cities, Falar,
and Malaz Island, these ten thousand soldiers were,
by roll, four thousand nine hundred and twelve women,
the remaining men; one thousand two hundred and
sixty-seven under the recorded age of twenty-five years,
seven hundred and twenty-one over the age of thirty-five
years; the remaining in between.

Remarkable indeed. More so when one considers
this: among its soldiers could be found veterans of the
Wickan Wars (see Coltaine's Rebellion), the Aren
Uprising (on both sides), and Blackdog Forest and
Mott Wood.

How does one measure such an army? By their
deeds; and that which awaited them in the Pannion
Domin would make of Onearm's Host a legend carved
in stone.

> *East of Saltoan*, a History of the Pannion Wars
> Gouridd Palah

Midges swarmed the tall-grass prairie, the grainy
black clouds tumbling over the faded, wavering
green. Oxen bellowed and moaned in their yokes,

their eyes covered with clusters of the frenzied insects. The Mhybe watched her Rhivi kin move among the beasts, their hands laden with grease mixed with the crushed seeds of lemon grass, which they smeared around the eyes, ears, nose and mouth. The unguent had served the bhederin well for as long as the huge bison had been under the care of the Rhivi; a slighter thinner version was used by the Rhivi themselves. Most of Brood's soldiers had taken to the pungent yet effective defence as well, whilst the Tiste Andii had proved evidently unpalatable to the biting insects. What had drawn the midges this time was the rank upon rank of unprotected Malazan soldiers.

Yet another march across this Hood-forsaken continent for that weary army of foreigners, these strangers who had been, for so many years, unwelcome, detested, feared. Our new allies, their surcoats dyed grey, their colourless standards proclaiming an unknown loyalty. They follow one man, and ask nothing of justification, or cause.

She drew the rough weave of her hood over her head as the slanting sun broke through the clouds gathered to the southwest. Her back was to the march; she sat in the bed of a Rhivi wagon, eyes on the trailing baggage train and the companies of Malazan soldiers flanking it.

Does Brood command such loyalty? He was the warlord who delivered the first defeat to the Malazan army. Our lands were being invaded. Our cause was clear, and we fought for the commander who could match the enemy. And even now, we face a new threat to our homeland, and Brood has chosen to lead us. Still, should he command us into the Abyss – would we follow? And now, knowing what I know, would I?

Her thoughts travelled from the warlord to Anomander Rake and the Tiste Andii. All strangers to Genabackis, yet they fought in its defence, in the name of its people's liberty. Rake's rule over his Tiste Andii was absolute. *Aye, they would stride unblinking into the Abyss. The fools.*

And now, marching at their sides, the Malazans. Dujek Onearm. Whiskeyjack. And ten thousand unwavering souls. What made such men and women so intractable in their sense of honour?

She had come to fear their courage. Within the husk of her body, there was a broken spirit. Dishonoured by its own cowardice, bereft of dignity, a mother no longer. Lost, even, to the Rhivi. *I am no more than food to the child. I have seen her, from a distance now and no closer – she is taller, she has filled out, her hips, her breasts, her face. This Tattersail was no gazelle. She devours me, this new woman, with her sleepy eyes, her full, broad mouth, her swaying, sultry walk—*

A horseman rode to the wagon's rear, his armour clanking, his dusty cloak flapping as he slowed his charger. The visor on his burnished helm was raised, revealing a greyshot beard, trimmed close, beneath hard eyes.

'Will you send me away as well, Mhybe?' he growled, his horse slowing to a walk to keep pace.

'Mhybe? That woman is dead,' she replied. 'You may leave here, Whiskeyjack.'

She watched him pull the tanned leather gloves from his wide, scarred hands, studied those hands as they finally came to a rest on the saddlehorn. *There is a mason's brutality about them, yet they are endearing none the less. Any woman still alive would desire their touch . . .*

'An end to the foolishness, Mhybe. We've need of your counsel. Korlat tells me you are racked with dreams. You cry out against a threat that approaches us, something vast and deadly. Woman, your terror is palpable – even now, I see that my words have rekindled it in your eyes. Describe your visions, Mhybe.'

Struggling against a painfully hammering heart, she barked a rough, broken laugh. 'You are all fools. Would you seek to challenge my enemy? My deadly, unopposable foe? Will you draw that sword of yours and stand in my stead?'

Whiskeyjack scowled. 'If that would help.'

'There is no need. What comes for me in my dreams comes for us all. Oh, perhaps we soften its terrible visage, the darkness of a cowl, a vague human shape, even a skull's grin which only momentarily shocks yet remains, none the less, deeply familiar – almost comforting. And we build temples to blunt the passage into its eternal domain. We fashion gates, raise barrows—'

'Your enemy is death?' Whiskeyjack glanced away, then met her eyes again. 'This is nonsense, Mhybe. You and I are both too old to fear death.'

'Face to face with Hood!' she snapped. 'That is how you see it – you fool! He is the mask behind which hides something beyond your ability to comprehend. *I have seen it!* I *know* what awaits me!'

'Then you no longer yearn for it—'

'I was mistaken, back then. I believed in my tribe's spirit-world. I have *sensed* the ghosts of my ancestors. But they are but memories made manifest, a sense of self desperately holding itself together by strength of its own will and naught else. Fail in that will, and all is lost. For ever.'

'Is oblivion so terrible, Mhybe?'

She leaned forward, gripping the wagon's sides with fingers that clawed, nails that dug into the weathered wood. 'What lies beyond is *not* oblivion, you ignorant man! No, imagine a place crowded with fragmented memories – memories of pain, of despair – all those emotions that carve deepest upon our souls.' She fell back, weakened, and slowly sighed, her eyes closing. 'Love drifts like ashes, Whiskeyjack. Even identity is gone. Instead, all that is left of you is doomed to an eternity of pain and terror – a succession of fragments from everyone – every *thing* – that has ever lived. In my dreams . . . I stand upon the brink. There is no strength in me – my will has already shown itself weak, wanting. When I die . . . I see what awaits me, I see what hungers for me, for my memories, for my pain.' She opened her eyes, met his gaze. 'It is the true Abyss, Whiskeyjack. Beyond all the legends and stories, it is the *true* Abyss. And it lives unto itself, consumed by rapacious hunger.'

'Dreams can be naught but an imagination's fashioning

of its own fears, Mhybe,' the Malazan said. 'You are pro-jecting a just punishment for what you perceive as your life's failure.'

Her eyes narrowed on him. 'Get out of my sight,' she growled, turning away, drawing her hood tighter about her head, cutting off the outside world – all that lay beyond the warped, stained planks of the wagon's bed. *Begone, Whiskeyjack, with your sword-thrust words, the cold, im-pervious armour of your ignorance. You cannot answer all that I have seen with a simple, brutal statement. I am not a stone for your rough hands. The knots within me defy your chisel.*

Your sword-thrust words shall not cut to my heart.

I dare not accept your wisdom. I dare—

Whiskeyjack. You bastard.

The commander rode at a gentle canter through the dust until he reached the vanguard of the Malazan army. Here, he found Dujek, flanked by Korlat on one side and the Daru, Kruppe, on the other, the latter tottering uneasily on a mule, hands waving about at the swarming midges.

'A plague on these pernicious gnats! Kruppe despairs!'

'The wind will pick up soon enough,' Dujek growled. 'We're approaching hills.'

Korlat drew closer alongside Whiskeyjack. 'How does she fare, Commander?'

He grimaced. 'No better. Her spirit is as twisted and shrunken as her body. She has fashioned a vision of death that has her fleeing it in terror.'

'Tat— Silverfox feels abandoned by her mother. This leads to bitterness. She no longer welcomes our company.'

'Her too? This is turning into a contest of wills, I think. Isolation is the last thing she needs, Korlat.'

'In that she is like her mother, as you have just intimated.'

He let out a long sigh, shifted in his saddle. His thoughts began to drift; he was weary, his leg aching and stiff. Sleep had been eluding him. They had heard virtually nothing of the fate of Paran and the Bridgeburners. The warrens had become impassable. Nor were they certain if the siege of Capustan was under way, or of the city's fate. Whiskeyjack had begun to regret sending the Black Moranth away. Dujek and Brood's armies were marching into the unknown; even the Great Raven Crone and her kin had not been seen for over a week.

It's these damned warrens and the sickness now filling them . . .

'They're late,' Dujek muttered.

'And no more than that, Kruppe assures one and all. Recall the last delivery. Almost dusk, it was. Three horses left on the lead wagon, the others killed and cut from the traces. Four shareholders gone, their souls and earnings scattered to the infernal winds. And the merchant herself! Near death, she was. The warning was clear, my friends – the warrens have been compromised. And as we march ever closer to the Domin, the foulment grows ever more . . . uh, foul.'

'Yet you insist they'll make it through again.'

'Kruppe does, High Fist! The Trygalle Trade Guild honours its contracts. They are not to be underestimated. 'Tis the day of their delivery of supplies. Said supplies shall therefore be delivered. And, assuming Kruppe's request has been honoured, among those supplies will be crates of the finest insect repellent ever created by the formidable alchemists of Darujhistan!'

Whiskeyjack leaned towards Korlat. 'Where in the line does she walk?' he asked quietly.

'At the very rear, Commander—'

'And is anyone watching her?'

The Tiste Andii woman glanced over and frowned. 'Is there need?'

'How in Hood's name should I know?' he snapped. A moment later he scowled. 'Your pardon, Korlat. I shall seek her out myself.' He swung his mount around, nudged it into a canter.

'Tempers grow short,' Kruppe murmured as the commander rode away. 'But not as short as Kruppe, for whom all nasty words whiz impactless over his head, and are thus lost in the ether. And those darts aimed lower, ah, they but bounce from Kruppe's ample equanimity—'

'Fat, you mean,' Dujek said, wiping dust from his brow then leaning over to spit onto the ground.

'Ahem, Kruppe, equably cushioned, blithely smiles at the High Fist's jibe. It is the forthright bluntness of soldiers that one must bathe in whilst on the march leagues from civilization. Antidote to the snipes of gutter rats, a refreshing balm to droll, sardonic nobles – why prick with a needle when one can use a hammer, eh? Kruppe breathes deep – but not so deep as to cough from the dust-laden stench of nature – such simple converse. The intellect must needs shift with alacrity from the intricate and delicate steps of the court dance to the tribal thumping of boots in grunting cadence—'

'Hood take us,' Korlat muttered to the High Fist, 'you got under his skin after all.'

Dujek's answering grin was an expression of perfect satisfaction.

Whiskeyjack angled his horse well to one side of the columns, then drew rein to await the rearguard. There were Rhivi everywhere in sight, moving singly or in small groups, their long spears balanced on their shoulders. Brown-skinned beneath the sun, they strode with light steps, seemingly immune to the heat and the leagues passing under their feet. The bhederin herd was being driven parallel to the armies, a third of a league to the north. The intervening gap revealed a steady stream of Rhivi, returning from the herd or setting off towards it. The occasional wagon joined the to-and-fro, unladen on its way north, burdened with carcasses on the way back.

The rearguard came within sight, flanked by outriders, the Malazan companies in sufficient strength to blunt a surprise attack long enough for the main force to swing round and come to their relief. The commander lifted the water-bladder from his saddle and filled his mouth, eyes narrowed as he studied the disposition of his soldiers.

Satisfied, he urged his mount into a walk, squinting into the trailing clouds of dust at the rearguard's tail-end.

She walked in that cloud as if seeking obscurity, her stride so like Tattersail's that Whiskeyjack felt a shiver dance up his spine. Twenty paces behind her marched a pair of Malazan soldiers, crossbows slung over their shoulders, helms on and visors lowered.

The commander waited until the trio had passed, then guided his horse into their wake. Within moments he was alongside the two marines.

The soldiers glanced up. Neither saluted, following standard procedure for battlefields. The woman closest to Whiskeyjack offered a curt nod. 'Commander. Here to fill your quota of eating dust, are ya?'

'And how did you two earn the privilege?'

'We volunteered, sir,' the other woman said. 'That's Tattersail up there. Yeah, we know, she calls herself Silverfox now, but we ain't fooled. She's our Cadre Mage, all right.'

'So you've elected to guard her back.'

'Aye. Fair exchange, sir. Always.'

'And are the two of you enough?'

The first woman grinned beneath her half-visor. 'We're Hood-damned killers, me and my sister, sir. Two quarrels every seventy heartbeats, both of us. And when time's run out for that, why, then, we switch to longswords, one for each hand. And when they're all busted, it's pig-stickers—'

'And,' the other growled, 'when we're outa iron we use our teeth, sir.'

'How many brothers did you two grow up with?'

'Seven, only they all ran away as soon as they was able. So did Da, but Mother was better off without 'im and that wasn't just bluster when she said so, neither.'

Whiskeyjack edged closer, rolling up his left sleeve. He leaned down and showed the two marines his forearm. 'See those scars – no, these ones here.'

'A nice even bite,' the nearest woman observed. 'Pretty small, though.'

'She was five, the little banshee. I was sixteen. The first fight I ever lost.'

'Did the lass grow up to be a soldier, Commander?'

He straightened, lowering his sleeve. 'Hood, no. When she was twelve, she set off to marry a king. Or so she claimed. That was the last any of us ever saw or heard of her.'

'I'd bet she did just that, sir,' the first woman said. 'If she was anything like you.'

'Now I'm choking on more than just dust, soldier. Carry on.'

Whiskeyjack trotted ahead until he reached Silverfox.

'They'll die for you now,' she said as soon as he came alongside. 'I know,' she continued, 'you don't do it on purpose. There's nothing calculated when you're being human, old friend. That's what makes you so deadly.'

'No wonder you're walking here on your own,' he replied.

Her smile was sardonic. 'We're very much alike, you know. All we need do is cup our hands and ten thousand souls rush in to fill them. And every now and then one of us recognizes that fact, and the sudden, overwhelming pressure hardens us a little more deep down inside. And what was soft gets a little smaller, a little weaker.'

'Not weaker, Silverfox. Rather, more concentrated, more selective. That you feel the burden at all is proof that it remains alive and well.'

'There is a difference, now that I think on it,' she said. 'For you, ten thousand souls. For me, a hundred thousand.'

He shrugged.

She was about to continue, but a sharp crack filled the air behind them. They spun to see a savage parting in their wake, a thousand paces away, from which poured a crimson

512

river. The two marines backpedalled as the torrent tumbled towards them.

The high grasses blackened, wavered, then sank down on all sides. Distant shouts rose from the Rhivi who had seen the conflagration.

The Trygalle wagon that emerged from the fissure burned with black fire. The horses themselves were engulfed, their screams shrill and horrible as they plunged madly onto the flooded plain. The beasts were devoured in moments, leaving the wagon to roll forward of its own momentum in the spreading red stream. One front wheel collapsed. The huge contrivance pitched, pivoted, burnt bodies falling from its flanks, then careened onto its side in an explosion of ebon flames.

The second wagon that emerged was licked by the same sorcerous fire, though not yet out of control. A nimbus of protective magic surrounded the eight horses in the train, fraying even as they thundered into the clear, splashing through the river of blood that continued to spread out from the portal. The driver, standing like a mad apparition with his cloak streaming black fire, bellowed a warning to the two marines before leaning hard to one side and sawing the traces. The horses swerved, pulling the huge wagon onto two wheels a moment before it came crunching back down. A guardsman who had been clinging to its side was thrown by the impact, landing with a turgid splash in the spreading river. A red-sheathed arm rose above the tide, then sank back down and out of sight.

The horses and wagon missed the two marines by a dozen paces, slowing as they cleared the river, its fires dying.

A third wagon appeared, followed by another, and another. The vehicle that then emerged was the size of a house, rolling on scores of iron-spoked wheels, caged by shimmering sorcery. Over thirty dray horses pulled it, but, Whiskeyjack guessed, even that many of the powerful beasts would be insufficient if not for the visible magic carrying much of the enormous wagon's weight.

Behind it the portal closed abruptly in a spray of blood.

The commander glanced down to see his horse's legs ankle-deep in the now-slowing flow. He glanced over at Silverfox. She stood motionless, looking down at the liquid as it lapped against her bared shins. 'This blood,' she said slowly, almost disbelieving, 'is his.'

'Who?'

She looked up, her expression one of dismay. 'An Elder God's. A – a *friend's*. This is what is filling the warrens. He has been wounded. Somehow. Wounded . . . perhaps fatally – gods! The warrens!'

With a curse, Whiskeyjack collected his reins and kicked his horse into a splashing canter towards the giant wagon.

Massive gouges had been ripped from its ornate sides. Blackened smears showed where guards had once clung. Smoke drifted above the entire train. Figures had begun emerging, staggering as if blind, moaning as if their souls had been torn from their bodies. He saw guards fall to their knees in the sludgy blood, weeping or simply bowing in shuddering silence.

The side door nearest Whiskeyjack opened as he rode up.

A woman climbed weakly into view, was helped down the steps. She pushed her companions away once her boots sank into the crimson, grass-matted mud and found purchase.

The commander dismounted.

The merchant bowed her head, her red-rimmed eyes holding steady as she drew herself straight. 'Please forgive the delay, sir,' she said in a voice that rasped with exhaustion.

'I take it you will find an alternate route back to Darujhistan,' Whiskeyjack said, eyeing the wagon behind her.

'We shall decide once we assess the damage.' She faced the dustcloud to the east. 'Has your army encamped for the night?'

'No doubt the order's been given.'

'Good. We're in no condition to chase you.'

'I've noticed.'

Three guards – shareholders – approached from one of the lead wagons, struggling beneath the weight of a huge, bestial arm, torn at the shoulder and still dripping blood. Three taloned fingers and two opposable thumbs twitched and waved a hand's breath away from the face of one of the guards. All three men were grinning.

'We figured it was still there, Haradas! Lost the other three, though. Still, ain't it a beauty?'

The merchant, Haradas, briefly closed her eyes and sighed. 'The attack came early on,' she explained to Whiskeyjack. 'A score of demons, probably as lost and frightened as we were.'

'And why should they attack you?'

'Wasn't an attack, sir,' one of the guards said. 'They just wanted a ride outa that nightmare. We would've obliged, too, only they was too heavy—'

'And they didn't sign a waiver neither,' another guard pointed out. 'We even offered a stake—'

'Enough, gentlemen,' Haradas said. 'Take that thing away.'

But the three men had come too close to the lead wheel of the huge wagon. As soon as the demonic hand made contact with the rim it closed with a snap around it. The three guards leapt back, leaving the arm hanging from the wheel.

'Oh, that's just terrific!' Haradas snapped. 'And whenever will we get *that* off?'

'When the fingers wear through, I guess,' a guard replied, frowning at the arm. 'Gonna be a lumpy ride for a while, dear. Sorry about that.'

A troop of riders approached from the army's train.

'Your escort's arrived,' Whiskeyjack noted. 'We will ask for a detailed report of the journey, mistress – I suggest you stand down until this evening, and leave the details of distribution to your second.'

She nodded. 'Good idea.'

The commander searched for Silverfox. She had resumed her march, the two marines trailing. The blood of the god had stained the marines' boots and the Rhivi's legs.

Across the plain, for two hundred or more paces, the earth looked like a red matted, tattered blanket, plucked and torn into dissolving disarray.

As ever, Kallor's thoughts were dark.

Ashes and dust. The fools prattle on and on in the command tent, a vast waste of time. Death flows through the warrens – what matter? Order ever succumbs to chaos, broken unto itself by the very strictures it imposes. The world will do better without mages. I for one will not rue the demise of sorcery.

The lone candle, streaked with the crushed fragments of a rare sea-worm, gusted thick, heavy smoke, filling the tent. Shadows crawled beneath the drifting plumes. Flickering yellow light glinted off ancient, oft-mended armour.

Seated on the ornate, ironwood throne, Kallor breathed deep of the invigorating fumes. *Alchemy is not magic. The arcana of the natural world holds far more wonders than any wizard could conjure in a thousand lifetimes. These Century Candles, for one, are well named. Upon my life, yet another layer seeps into my flesh and bone – I can feel it with each breath. A good thing, too. Who would want to live for ever in a body too frail to move? Another hundred years, gained in the passage of a single night, in the depth of this one reach of columned wax. And I have scores more . . .*

No matter the stretch of decades and centuries, no matter the interminable boredom of inactivity that was so much a part of living, there were moments . . . *moments when I must act, explosively, with certainty. And all that seemed nothing before was in truth preparation. There are creatures that hunt without moving; when they become perfectly still, perfectly motionless, they are at their most dangerous. I am as such a creature. I have always been so, yet all who know me are . . . gone. Ashes and dust. The children who now surround* me with their gibbering worries are blind to the hunter in their midst. Blind . . .

Pale hands gripping the arms of the throne, he sat unmoving, stalking the landscape of his own memories, dragging them forth like corpses pulled from the ground, drawing their visages close for a moment before casting them away and moving on.

Eight mighty wizards, hands linked, voices rising in unison. Desperate for power. Seeking it from a distant, unknown realm. Unsuspecting, curious, the strange god in that strange place edged closer, then the trap was sprung. Down he came, torn to pieces yet remaining alive. Brought down, shattering a continent, obliterating warrens. Himself broken, damaged, crippled . . .

Eight mighty wizards, who sought to oppose me and so loosed a nightmare that rises once more, millennia later. Fools. Now, they are dust and ashes . . .

Three gods, assailing my realm. Too many insults delivered by my hand. My existence had gone beyond irritation, and so they banded together to crush me once and for all. In their ignorance, they assumed I would play by their rules. Either fight, or yield my realm. My, weren't they surprised, striding into my empire, only to find . . . nothing left alive. Nothing but charred bones and lifeless ash.

They could not comprehend – nor did they ever – that I would yield nothing. Rather than surrender all I had fashioned, I destroyed it. That is the privilege of the creator – to give, then to take away. I shall never forget the world's death cry – for it was the voice of my triumph . . .

And one of you remains, pursuing me once more. Oh, I know it is you, K'rul. But, instead of me, you have found another enemy, and he is killing you. Slowly, deliciously. You have returned to this realm, only to die, as I said you would. And did you know? Your sister has succumbed to my ancient curse as well. So little left of her, will she ever recover? Not if I can help it.

A faint smile spread across his withered, pallid face.

His eyes narrowed as a portal began to take shape before him. Miasmic power swirled from it. A figure emerged, tall, gaunt, a face shattered – massive cuts gaping red, the shards of broken bone glimmering in the candlelight. The portal closed behind the Jaghut, who stood relaxed, eyes flickering pools of darkness.

'I convey greetings from the Crippled God,' the Jaghut said, 'to you, Kallor' – he paused to survey the tent's interior – 'and your vast empire.'

'You tempt me,' Kallor rasped, 'to add to your . . . facial distress, Gethol. My empire may be gone, but I shall not yield this throne. You, of all people, should recognize that I am not yet done in my ambitions, and I am a patient man.'

Gethol grunted a laugh. 'Ah, dear Kallor. You are to me the exception to the rule that patience is a virtue.'

'I can destroy you, Jaghut, no matter who you call master these days. I can complete what your capable punisher began. Do you doubt me?'

'Most certainly not,' Gethol replied easily. 'I've seen you wield that two-handed sword of yours.'

'Then withdraw your verbal knives and tell me what you do here.'

'Apologies for disrupting your . . . concentration. I shall now explain. I am Herald to the Crippled God – aye, a new House has come to the Deck of Dragons. The House of Chains. The first renditions have been fashioned. And soon every Reader of the Deck will be seeking their likenesses.'

Kallor snorted. 'And you expect this gambit to work? That House shall be assailed. Obliterated.'

'Oh, the battle is well under way, old man. You cannot be blind to that, nor to the fact that *we are winning.*'

Kallor's eyes thinned to slits. 'The poisoning of the warrens? The Crippled God is a fool. What point in destroying the power he requires to assert his claim? Without the warrens, the Deck of Dragons is nothing.'

'The appellation "poison" is erroneous, Kallor. Rather,

consider the infection one of enforcing a certain . . . alteration . . . to the warrens. Aye, those who resist it view it as a deadly manifestation, a "poison" indeed. But only because its primary effect is to make the warrens impassable to them. Servants of the Crippled God, however, will find themselves able to travel freely in the paths.'

'I am servant to no-one,' Kallor growled.

'The position of High King is vacant within the Crippled God's House of Chains.'

Kallor shrugged. 'None the less requiring that I stain my knees before the Chained One.'

'No such gestures are demanded of the High King. The House of Chains exists beyond the Crippled God's influence – is that not obvious? He is *chained*, after all. Trapped in a lifeless fragment of a long-dead warren. Bound to the flesh of the Sleeping Goddess – aye, that has proved his singular means of efficacy, but it is limited. Understand, Kallor, that the Crippled God now casts the House of Chains into the world, indeed, abandons it to its fate. Survival depends on those who come to the titles it contains. Some of those the Chained One can influence – though never directly – whilst others, such as that of King of High House Chains, must be freely assumed.'

'If so,' Kallor rumbled after a long moment, 'why are you not the King?'

Gethol bowed his head. 'You honour me, sir,' he said drily. 'I am, however, content to be Herald—'

'Under the delusion that the messenger is ever spared, no matter what the message? You were never as smart as your brother, were you? Somewhere, Gothos must be laughing.'

'Gothos never laughs. But, given that I know where he languishes, I do. Often. Now, should I remain here much longer awaiting your answer, my presence may well be detected. There are Tiste Andii nearby—'

'Very near. Not to mention Caladan Brood. Lucky for you Anomander Rake has left – returned to Moon's Spawn, wherever it is—'

'Its location must be discovered, revealed to the Crippled God.'

The grey-haired warrior raised an eyebrow. 'A task for the King?'

'Does betrayal sting your sense of honour, Kallor?'

'If you call it a sudden reversal of strategy, the sting fades. What I require, in exchange, is an opportunity, arranged howsoever the Crippled God pleases.'

'What is the nature of this opportunity, High King?'

Kallor smiled, then his expression hardened. 'The woman Silverfox . . . a moment of vulnerability, that is all I ask.'

Gethol slowly bowed. 'I am your Herald, sire, and shall convey your desires to the Crippled God.'

'Tell me,' Kallor said, 'before you go. Does this throne suit the House of Chains, Gethol?'

The Jaghut studied the battered, iron-coloured wood, noted the cracks in its frame. 'It most certainly does, sire.'

'Begone, then.'

The Herald bowed once more, the portal opening behind him. A moment later he stepped back, and was gone.

Smoke from the candle swirled in the wake of the vanishing portal. Kallor drew a deep breath. Adding years and years of renewed vigour. He sat motionless . . . *a hunter on the edge of ambush. Suitably explosive. Suitably deadly.*

Whiskeyjack stepped out of the command tent, stood gazing up at the sweep of stars overhead. It had been a long time since he'd felt so weary.

He heard movement behind him, then a soft, long-fingered hand settled on his shoulder, the touch sending waves through him. 'It would be nice,' Korlat murmured, 'to hear good news for a change.'

He grunted.

'I see the worry in your eyes, Whiskeyjack. It's a long list, isn't it? Your Bridgeburners, Silverfox, her mother, and now

520

this assault on the warrens. We are marching blind. So much rests on unknowns. Does Capustan still hold, or has the city fallen? And what of Trotts? And Paran? Quick Ben?'

'I am aware of that list, Korlat,' he rumbled.

'Sorry. I share them, that is all.'

He glanced at her. 'Forgive me, but why? This is not your war – gods below, it's not even your world! Why are you yielding to its needs?' He sighed loudly and shook his head, returning his gaze to the nightsky. 'That's a question we asked often, early in the campaigns. I remember, in Blackdog Forest, stumbling over a half-dozen of your kin. A Moranth cusser had taken them out. A squad of regulars was busy looting the bodies. They were cursing – not finding anything of worth. A few knotted strips of coloured cloth, a stream-polished pebble, plain weapons – the kind you could pick up in any market in any city.' He was silent for a moment, then he continued, 'And I remember wondering – what was the story of their lives? Their dreams, their aspirations? Would their kin miss them? The Mhybe once mentioned that the Rhivi took on the task of burying the Tiste Andii fallen . . . well, we did the same, there in that wood. We sent the regulars packing with boots to the backside. We buried your dead, Korlat. Consigned their souls in the Malazan way . . .'

Her eyes were depthless as she studied him. 'Why?' she asked quietly.

Whiskeyjack frowned. 'Why did we bury them? Hood's breath! We honour our enemies – no matter who they might be. But the Tiste Andii most of all. They accepted prisoners. Treated those that were wounded. They even accepted withdrawal – not once were we pursued after hightailing it from an unwinnable scrap.'

'And did not the Bridgeburners return the favour, time and again, Commander? And indeed, before long, so did the rest of Dujek Onearm's soldiers.'

'Most campaigns get nastier the longer they drag on,'

Whiskeyjack mused, 'but not that one. It got more . . . civilized. Unspoken protocols . . .'

'Much of that was undone when you took Pale.'

He nodded. 'More than you know.'

Her hand was still on his shoulder. 'Come with me back to my tent, Whiskeyjack.'

His brows rose, then he smiled and said in a dry tone, 'Not a night to be alone—'

'Don't be a fool!' she snapped. 'I did not ask for company – I asked for you. Not a faceless need that must be answered, and anyone will do. Not that. Am I understood?'

'Not entirely.'

'I wish us to become lovers, Whiskeyjack. Beginning tonight. I wish to awaken in your arms. I would know if you have feelings for me.'

He was silent for a long moment, then he said, 'I'd be a fool not to, Korlat, but I had also considered it even more foolish to attempt any advance. I assumed you were mated to another Tiste Andii – a union no doubt centuries long—'

'And what would be the point of such a union?'

He frowned, startled. 'Well, uh, companionship? Children?'

'Children arrive. Rarely, as much a product of boredom as anything else. Tiste Andii do not find companionship among their own kind. That died out long ago, Whiskeyjack. Yet even rarer is the occasion of a Tiste Andii emerging from the darkness, into the mortal world, seeking a reprieve from . . . from—'

He set a finger to her lips. 'No more. I am honoured to accept you, Korlat. More than you will ever realize, and I will seek to be worthy of your gift.'

She shook her head, eyes dropping. 'It is a scant gift. Seek my heart and you may be disappointed in what you find.'

The Malazan stepped back and reached for his belt-pouch. He untied it, upended the small leather sack into one cupped hand. A few coins fell out, then a small, bedraggled, multicoloured knot of cloth strips, followed by a lone dark, smooth pebble. 'I'd thought,' he said slowly, eyes on the objects in his hand, 'that one day I might have the opportunity to return what was clearly of value to those fallen Tiste Andii. All that was found in that search . . . I realized – even then – that I could do naught but honour them.'

Korlat closed her hand over his, trapping the objects within their joined clasp. She led him down the first row of tents.

The Mhybe dreamed. She found herself clinging to the edge of a precipice, white-knuckled hands gripping gnarled roots, the susurration of trickling dirt dusting her face as she strained to hold on.

Below waited the Abyss, racked with the storm of dismembered memories, streamers of pain, fear, rage, jealousy and dark desires. That storm wanted her, was reaching up for her, and she was helpless to defend herself.

Her arms were weakening.

A shrieking wind wrapped around her legs, yanked, snatched her away, and she was falling, adding her own scream to the cacophony. The winds tossed her this way and that, twisting, tumbling—

Something hard and vicious struck her hip, glanced away. Air buffeted her hard. Then the hard intrusion was back – talons closing around her waist, scaled, cold as death. A sharp tug snapped her head back, and she was no longer falling, but rising, carried higher and higher.

The storm's roar faded below her, then dwindled away to one side.

The Mhybe twisted her head, looked up.

An undead dragon loomed above her, impossibly huge. Desiccated, dried flaps of skin trailing from its limbs, its almost translucent wings thundering, the creature was bearing her away.

She turned to study what lay below.

A featureless plain stretched out beneath her, dun

brown. Long cracks in the earth were visible, filled with dully glowing ice. She saw a darker patch, ragged at its edges, flow over a hillside. *A herd. I have walked that land before. Here, in my dreams . . . there were footprints . . .*

The dragon banked suddenly, crooked its wings, and began a swift spiral earthward.

She found herself wailing – was shocked to realize that it was not terror she was feeling, but exhilaration. *Spirits above, this is what it is to fly! Ah, now I know envy in truth!*

The land rushed up to meet her. Moments before what would have been a fatal impact, the dragon's wings snapped wide, caught the air, then, the leg directly above curling upward to join its twin, the creature glided silently an arm's length above the loamy ground. Forward momentum abated. The leg lowered, the talons releasing her.

She landed with barely a thump, rolled onto her back, then sat up to watch the enormous dragon rising once more, wings thundering.

The Mhybe looked down and saw a youthful body – her own. She cried out at the cruelty of this dream. Cried out again, curling tight on the cool, damp earth.

Oh, why did you save me! Why? Only to awaken – spirits below – to awaken—

'She was passing through.' A soft voice – a stranger's voice, in the language of the Rhivi – spoke in her mind.

The Mhybe's head snapped up. She looked around. 'Who speaks? Where are you?'

'We're here. When you are ready to see us, you shall. Your daughter has a will to match yours, it seems. To have so commanded the greatest of the Bonecasters – true, she comes in answer to the child's summons. The Gathering. Making the detour a minor one. None the less . . . we are impressed.'

'My daughter?'

'She still stings from harsh words – we can feel that. Indeed, it is how we have come to dwell here. That small, round man hides obsidian edges beneath his surfeit of flesh.

Who would have thought? "*She has given to you all she has,
Silverfox. The time has come for you to gift in answer, lass.
Kruppe is not alone in refusing to abandon her to her fate.*" Ah,
he opened her eyes, then, swept away her obsessing with
her selves, and she only a child at the time, but she heeded
his words – though in truth he spoke only within her
dreams at that time. Heeded. Yes indeed.

'So,' the voice continued, 'will you see us now?'

She stared down at her smooth hands, her young arms,
and screamed. 'Stop torturing me with this dream! Stop!
Oh, stop—'

Her eyes opened to the musty darkness of her tent.
Aches and twinges prodded her thinned bones, her
shrunken muscles. Weeping, the Mhybe pulled her ancient
body into a tight ball. 'Gods,' she whispered, 'how I hate
you. *How I hate you!*'

BOOK THREE

CAPUSTAN

The Last Mortal Sword of Fener's Reve was Fanald of Cawn Vor, who was killed in the Chaining. The last Boar-cloaked Destriant was Ipshank of Korelri, who vanished during the Last Flight of Manask on the Stratem Icefields. Another waited to claim that title, but was cast out from the temple before it came to him, and that man's name has been stricken from all records. It is known, however, that he was from Unta; that he had begun his days as a cutpurse living on its foul streets, and that his casting out from the temple was marked by the singular punishment of Fener's Reve . . .

Temple Lives
Birrin Thund

CHAPTER FOURTEEN

If you can, dear friends, do not live through a siege.

Ubilast (the Legless)

The inn commanding the southeast corner of old Daru Street held no more than half a dozen patrons, most of them visitors to the city who, like Gruntle, were now trapped. The Pannion armies surrounding Capustan's walls had done nothing for five days and counting. There had been clouds of dust from beyond the ridgeline to the north, the caravan captain had heard, signalling . . . something. But that had been days ago and nothing had come of it.

What Septarch Kulpath was waiting for, no-one knew, though there was plenty of speculation. More barges carrying Tenescowri had been seen crossing the river, until it seemed that half the empire's population had joined the peasant army. 'With numbers like that,' someone had said a bell earlier, 'there'll be barely a mouthful of Capan citizen each.' Gruntle had been virtually alone in appreciating the jest.

He sat at a table near the entrance, his back to the rough-plastered, double-beamed door-frame, the door itself on his right, the low-ceilinged main room before him. A mouse was working its way along the earthen floor beneath the tables, scampering from shadow to shadow, slipping between the shoes or boots of whatever patron its path intersected.

Gruntle watched its progress with low-lidded eyes. There was still plenty of food to be found in the kitchen – or so its nose was telling it. That bounty, Gruntle well knew, would not last if the siege drew out.

His gaze flicked up to the smoke-stained main truss spanning the room, where the inn's cat slept, limbs dangling from the crossbeam. The feline hunted only in its dreams, for the moment at least.

The mouse reached the foot-bar of the counter, waddled parallel to it towards the kitchen entrance.

Gruntle took another mouthful of watered wine – more water than wine after almost a week's stranglehold on the city by the Pannions. The six other patrons were each sitting alone at a table or leaning up against the counter. Words were exchanged among them every now and then, a few desultory comments, usually answered by little more than a grunt.

Over the course of a day and night, the inn was peopled by two types, or so Gruntle had observed. The ones before him now virtually lived in the common room, nursing their wine and ale. Strangers to Capustan and seemingly friendless, they'd achieved a kind of community none the less, characterized by a vast ability to do nothing together for long periods of time. Come the night the other type would begin to assemble. Loud, boisterous, drawing the street whores inside with their coins which they tumbled onto the tabletops with no thought of tomorrow. Theirs was a desperate energy, a bluff hail to Hood. *We're yours, you scything bastard*, they seemed to say. *But not till the dawn!*

They'd churn like a foaming sea around the immovable, indifferent rocks that were the silent, friendless patrons.

The sea and the rocks. The sea celebrates in the face of Hood as soon as he looms close. The rocks have stared the bastard in the eye for so long they're past budging, much less celebrating. The sea laughs uproariously at its own jokes. The rocks grind out a terse line that can silence an entire room. A Capan mouthful . . .

530

Next time, I'll keep my tongue to myself.

The cat rose on the crossbeam, stretching, its banded black stripes rippling across its dun fur. Cocked its head downward, ears pricking.

The mouse was at the edge of the kitchen entrance, frozen.

Gruntle hissed under his breath.

The cat looked his way.

The mouse darted into the kitchen and out of sight.

With a loud creak, the inn door swung inward. Buke stepped inside, crossed Gruntle's view then sank down into the chair beside him.

'You're predictable enough,' the old man muttered, gesturing for two of the same when he caught the barkeep's eye.

'Aye,' Gruntle replied. 'I'm a rock.'

'A rock, huh? More like a fat iguana clinging to one. And when the big wave comes—'

'Whatever. You've found me, Buke. Now what?'

'Just wanted to thank you for all the help, Gruntle.'

'Was that subtle irony, old man? A little honing—'

'Actually, I was almost serious. That muddy water you made me drink – Keruli's concoction – it's done wonders.' His narrow face revealed a slightly secretive smile. 'Wonders . . .'

'Glad to hear you're all better. Any more earth-shattering news? If not . . .'

Buke leaned back as the barkeep delivered the two tankards, then said after the man shambled away, 'I've met with the elders of the Camps. At first they wanted to go straight to the prince—'

'But then they came to their senses.'

'With a little prodding.'

'So now you've got all the help you need in keeping that insane eunuch from playing doorman to Hood's gate. Good. Can't have panic in the streets, what with a quarter-million Pannions laying siege to the city.'

Buke's eyes thinned on Gruntle. 'Thought you'd appreciate the calm.'

'Now that's much better.'

'I still need your help.'

'Can't see how, Buke. Unless you want me to kick down the door and separate Korbal Broach's head from his shoulders. In which case you'll need to keep Bauchelain distracted. Set him on fire or something. I only need a moment. Of course, timing's everything. Once the walls have been breached, say, and there's Tenescowri mobbing the streets. That way we can all go hand in hand to Hood singing a merry tune.'

Buke smiled behind his tankard. 'That'll do,' he said, then drank.

Gruntle drained his own cup, reached for the new one. 'You know where to find me,' he said after a moment.

'Until the wave comes.'

The cat leapt down from the crossbeam, pounced forward, trapping a cockroach between its paws. It began playing.

'All right,' the caravan captain growled after a moment, 'what else do you want to say?'

Buke shrugged offhandedly. 'I hear Stonny has volunteered. Latest rumours have it the Pannions are finally ready for the first assault – any time now.'

'The first? Likely they'll only need the one. As for being ready, they've been ready for days, Buke. If Stonny wants to throw away her life defending the indefensible, that's her business.'

'What's the alternative? The Pannions won't take prisoners, Gruntle. We'll all have to fight, sooner or later.'

That's what you think.

'Unless,' Buke continued after a moment as he raised his tankard, 'you plan on switching sides. Finding faith as a matter of expedience—'

'What other way is there?'

The old man's eyes sharpened. 'You'd fill your belly with

human flesh, Gruntle? Just to survive? You'd do that, would you?'

'Meat is meat,' Gruntle replied, his eyes on the cat. A soft crunch announced that it had finished playing.

'Well,' Buke said, rising, 'I didn't think you were capable of shocking me. I guess I thought I knew you—'

'You thought.'

'So this is the man Harllo gave his life for.'

Gruntle slowly raised his head. Whatever Buke saw in his eyes made him step back. 'Which Camp are you working with right now?' the caravan captain calmly asked.

'Uldan,' the old man whispered.

'I'll look in on you, then. In the meantime, Buke, get out of my sight.'

The shadows had retreated across most of the compound, leaving Hetan and her brother, Cafal, in full sunlight. The two Barghast were squatting on a worn, faded rug, heads bowed. Sweat – blackened with ash – dripped from them both. Between them was a broad, shallow brazier, perched on three hand-high iron legs and filled with smouldering coals.

Soldiers and court messengers flowed around them on all sides.

Shield Anvil Itkovian studied the siblings from where he stood near the headquarters entrance. He had not known the Barghast as a people enamoured of meditation, yet Hetan and Cafal had done little else, it seemed, since their return from the Thrall. Fasting, uncommunicative, inconveniently encamped in the centre of the barracks compound, they had made of themselves an unapproachable island.

Theirs is not a mortal calm. They travel among the spirits. Brukhalian demands that I find a way through – by any means. Does Hetan possess yet one more secret? An avenue of escape, for her, her brother, and for the bones of the Founding Spirits? An unknown weakness in our defence? A flaw in the Pannion investiture?

533

Itkovian sighed. He had tried before, without success. He would now try once again. As he prepared to step forward, he sensed a presence at his side and turned, to find Prince Jelarkan.

The young man's face was etched deep with exhaustion. His long-fingered, elegant hands trembled despite being knitted together just above his robe's belt. His gaze was fixed on the swirling activity in the compound as he said, 'I must know, Shield Anvil, what Brukhalian intends. He holds what you soldiers call a shaved knuckle in the hole – that much is clear. And so I have come, once again, seeking audience with the man in my employ.' He made no effort to hide the sardonic bitterness of that statement. 'To no avail. The Mortal Sword has no time for me. No time for the Prince of Capustan.'

'Sir,' Itkovian said, 'you may ask your questions of me, and I shall do all I can to answer you.'

The young Capan swung to the Shield Anvil. 'Brukhalian has given you leave to speak?'

'He has.'

'Very well. The Kron T'lan Imass and their undead wolves. They have destroyed the Septarch's K'Chain demons.'

'They have.'

'Yet the Pannion Domin has more. Hundreds more.'

'Yes.'

'Then why do the T'lan Imass not march into the empire? An assault into the Seer's territory may well achieve the withdrawal of Kulpath's besieging forces. The Seer would have no choice but to pull them back across the river.'

'Were the T'lan Imass a mortal army, the choice would indeed be obvious, and consequently beneficial to our own needs,' Itkovian replied. 'Alas, Kron and his undead kin are bound by unearthly demands, of which we know virtually nothing. We have been told of a gathering, a silent summoning for purposes unknown. This, for the moment, takes precedence over all else. Kron and the T'lan Ay destroyed the Septarch's K'Chain Che'Malle because their presence was deemed a direct threat to the gathering.'

'Why? That explanation is insufficient, Shield Anvil.'

'I do not disagree with your assessment, sir. There does appear to be another reason – for Kron's reluctance to march southward. A mystery concerning the Seer himself. It seems the word "Pannion" is Jaghut. The Jaghut were the mortal enemies of the T'lan Imass, as you may know. It is my personal belief that Kron awaits the arrival of . . . allies. Other T'lan Imass, come to this impending gathering.'

'You are suggesting that Kron is intimidated by the Pannion Seer—'

'Aye, in his belief that the Seer is Jaghut.'

The prince was silent for a long moment, then he shook his head. 'Even should the T'lan Imass decide to march upon the Pannion Domin, the decision will come too late for us.'

'That seems likely.'

'Very well. Now, another question. Why is this gathering occurring *here*?'

Itkovian hesitated, then slowly nodded to himself. 'Prince Jelarkan, the one who has summoned the T'lan Imass is approaching Capustan . . . in the company of an army.'

'An army?'

'An army marching to wage war against the Pannion Domin; indeed, with the additional aim of relieving the siege here at Capustan.'

'*What?*'

'Sir, they are five weeks away.'

'We cannot hold—'

'This truth is known, Prince.'

'And does this summoner command that army?'

'No. Command is shared between two men. Caladan Brood and Dujek Onearm.'

'Dujek – *High Fist Onearm?* The Malazan? Lords below, Itkovian! How long have you known this?'

The Shield Anvil cleared his throat. 'Preliminary contact was established some time ago, Prince. Through sorcerous avenues. These have since grown impassable—'

'Yes, yes, I know that well enough. Continue, damn you.'

'The presence of the summoner among their company was news only recently told us – by a Bonecaster of the Kron T'lan Imass—'

'The army, Itkovian! Tell me more of this army!'

'Dujek and his legions have been outlawed by Empress Laseen. They are now acting independently. His complement numbers perhaps ten thousand. Caladan Brood has under his command a number of small mercenary companies, three Barghast clans, the Rhivi nation and the Tiste Andii – a total number of combatants of thirty thousand.'

Prince Jelarkan's eyes were wide. Itkovian watched the information breach the man's inner defences, watched as the host of hopes flowered then withered in swift succession.

'On the surface,' the Shield Anvil said quietly, 'all that I have told you seems of vital import. Yet, as I see you now comprehend, it is in truth all meaningless. Five weeks, Prince. Leave them to their vengeance, if you will, for that is all they might manage. And even then, given their limited numbers—'

'Are these Brukhalian's conclusions, or yours?'

'Both, I regret to say.'

'You fools,' the young man grated. 'You Hood-damned fools.'

'Sire, we cannot withstand the Pannions for five weeks.'

'I know that, damn you! The question now is: why do we even try?'

Itkovian frowned. 'Sir, such was the contract. The defence of the city—'

'Idiot – what do I care about your damned contract?

536

You've already concluded you will fail in any case! My concern is for the lives of my people. This army comes from the west? It must. Marching beside the river—'

'We cannot break out, Prince. We would be annihilated.'

'We concentrate everything to the west. A sudden sortie, that flows into an exodus. Shield Anvil—'

'We will be slaughtered,' Itkovian cut in. 'Sire, we have considered this. It *will not work*. The Septarch's wings of horsemen will surround us, grind us to a halt. Then the Beklites and Tenescowri will arrive. We will have yielded a defensible position for an indefensible one. It would all be over within the span of a single bell.'

Prince Jelarkan stared at the Shield Anvil with undisguised contempt and, indeed, hatred. 'Inform Brukhalian of the following,' he rasped. 'In the future, it is not the task of the Grey Swords to do the prince's thinking for him. It is not their task to decide what he needs to know and what he doesn't. The prince is to be informed of all matters, regardless of how you judge their relevance. Is this understood, Shield Anvil?'

'I shall convey your words precisely, sire.'

'I must presume,' the prince continued, 'that the Mask Council knows even less than I did a bell ago.'

'That would be an accurate assumption. Sire, their interests—'

'Save me from any more of your learned opinions, Itkovian. Good day.'

Itkovian watched the prince stalk away, towards the compound's exit, his gait too stiff to be regal. *Yet noble in its own way. You have my regret, dear prince, though I would not presume to voice it. I am the will of the Mortal Sword. My own desires are irrelevant.* He pushed away the surge of bitter anger that rose beneath these thoughts, returned his gaze to the two Barghast still seated on the rug.

The trance had broken. Hetan and Cafal were now leaning close to the brazier, where white smoke rose in twisting coils into the sunlit air.

Startled, it was a moment before Itkovian stepped forward.

As he approached, he saw that an object had been placed on the brazier's coals. Red-tinged on its edges, flat and milky white in the centre. A fresh scapula, too light to be from a bhederin, yet thinner and longer than a human's. A deer's shoulder blade, perhaps, or an antelope's. The Barghast had begun a divination, employing the object that gave meaning to the tribal name of their shamans.

More than just warriors, then. I should have guessed. Cafal's chant in the Thrall. He is a shoulderman; and Hetan is his female counterpart.

He stopped just beyond the edge of the rug, slightly to Cafal's left. The shoulder blade had begun to show cracks. Fat bubbled up along the thick edges of the bone, sizzled and flared like a ring of fire.

The simplest divination was the interpretation of the cracks as a map, a means of finding wild herds for the tribe's hunters. In this instance, Itkovian well knew, the sorcery under way was far more complex, the cracks more than simply a map of the physical world. The Shield Anvil stayed silent, tried to catch the mumbled conversation between Hetan and her brother.

They were speaking Barghast, a language of which Itkovian had but passing knowledge. Even stranger, it seemed the conversation was three-way, the siblings cocking their heads or nodding at replies only they could hear.

The scapula was a maze of cracks now, the bone showing blue, beige and calcined white. Before too long it would begin to crumble, as the creature's spirit surrendered to the overwhelming power flowing through its dwindling lifeforce.

The eerie conversation ended. As Cafal fell back into a trance, Hetan sat back, looked up and met Itkovian's eyes. 'Ah, wolf, I am pleased by the sight of you. There have been changes to the world. Surprising changes.'

'And are these changes pleasing to you, Hetan?'

She smiled. 'Would it give you pleasure if they were?'

Do I step over this precipice? 'That possibility exists.'

The woman laughed, slowly climbed to her feet. She winced as she stretched her limbs. 'Spirits take me, my bones ache. My muscles cry out for caring hands.'

'There are limbering exercises—'

'Don't I know it, wolf. Will you join me in such endeavours?'

'What news do you have, Hetan?'

She grinned, hands on her hips. 'By the Abyss,' she drawled, 'you are clumsy. Yield to me and learn all my secrets, is that the task set before you? It is a game you should be wary of playing. Especially with me.'

'Perhaps you are right,' he said, drawing himself up and turning away.

'Hold, man!' Hetan laughed. 'You flee like a rabbit? And I called you wolf? I should change that name.'

'That is your choice,' he replied over a shoulder as he set off.

Her laugh rang out behind him once more. 'Ah, now this is a game worth playing! Go on, then, dear rabbit! My elusive quarry, ha!'

Itkovian re-entered the headquarters, walked down the hallway skirting the outer wall until he came to the tower entrance. His armour shifted and clanked as he made his way up the steep stone stairs. He tried to drive out images of Hetan, her laughing face and bright, dancing eyes, the runnels of sweat tracking her brow through the layer of ash, the way she stood, back arched, chest thrown out in deliberate, provocative invitation. He resented the rebirth of long-buried desires now plaguing him. His vows were crumbling, his every prayer to Fener meeting with naught but silence, as if his god was indifferent to the sacrifices Itkovian had made in his name.

And perhaps that is the final, most devastating truth. The gods care nothing for ascetic impositions on mortal behaviour. Care nothing for rules of conduct, for the twisted morals of temple priests and monks. Perhaps indeed they laugh at the chains we wrap around ourselves – our endless, insatiable need to find flaws within the demands of life. Or perhaps they do not laugh, but rage at us. Perhaps our denial of life's celebration is our greatest insult to those whom we worship and serve.

He reached the arms room at the top of the circular stairs, nodded distractedly at the two soldiers stationed there, then made his way up the ladder to the roof platform.

The Destriant was already there. Karnadas studied Itkovian as the Shield Anvil joined him. 'Yours, sir, is a troubled mien.'

'Aye, I do not deny it. I have had discourse with Prince Jelarkan, which closed with his displeasure. Subsequently, I spoke with Hetan. Destriant, my faith is assailed.'

'You question your vows.'

'I do, sir. I admit to doubting their veracity.'

'Has it been your belief, Shield Anvil, that your rules of conduct existed to appease Fener?'

Itkovian frowned as he leaned on the merlon and stared out at the smoke-wreathed enemy camps. 'Well, yes—'

'Then you have lived under a misapprehension, sir.'

'Explain, please.'

'Very well. You found a need to chain yourself, a need to enforce upon your own soul the strictures as defined by your vows. In other words, Itkovian, your vows were born of a dialogue with yourself – not with Fener. The chains are your own, as is the possession of the keys with which to unlock them when they are no longer required.'

'No longer required?'

'Aye. When all that is encompassed by living ceases to threaten your faith.'

'You suggest, then, that my crisis is not with my faith, but with my vows. That I have blurred the distinction.'

'I do, Shield Anvil.'

'Destriant,' Itkovian said, eyes still on the Pannion encampments, 'your words invite a carnal flood.'

The High Priest burst out laughing. 'And with it a

540

dramatic collapse of your dour disposition, one hopes!'

Itkovian's mouth twitched. 'Now you speak of miracles, sir.'

'I would hope—'

'Hold.' The Shield Anvil raised a gauntleted hand. 'There is movement among the Beklites.'

Karnadas joined him, suddenly sober.

'And there,' Itkovian pointed, 'Urdomen. Scalandi to their flanks. Seerdomin moving to positions of command.'

'They will assail the redoubts first,' the Destriant predicted. 'The Mask Council's vaunted Gidrath in their strongholds. That may earn us more time—'

'Find me my messenger corps, sir. Alert the officers. And a word to the prince.'

'Aye, Shield Anvil. Will you stay here?'

Itkovian nodded. 'A worthy vantage point. Go, then, sir.'

Beklite troops were massing in a ring around the Gidrath stronghold out on the killing ground. Spearpoints glittered in the sunlight.

Now alone, Itkovian's eyes narrowed as he studied the preparations. 'Ah, well, it has begun.'

The streets of Capustan were silent, virtually empty beneath a cloudless sky, as Gruntle made his way down Calmanark Alley. He came to the curved wall of the self-contained Camp known as Ulden, kicked through the rubbish cluttering a stairwell leading down below street level and hammered a fist on the solid door cut into the wall's foundations.

After a moment it creaked open.

Gruntle stepped through into a narrow corridor, its floor a sharply angled ramp leading back up to ground level twenty paces ahead, where bright sunlight showed, revealing a central, circular courtyard.

Buke shut the massive door behind him, struggled beneath the weight of the bar as he lowered it back into the slots. The gaunt, grey-haired man then faced Gruntle. 'That was quick. Well?'

'What do you think?' the caravan captain growled. 'There's been movement. The Pannions are marshalling. Messengers riding this way and that—'

'Which wall were you on?'

'North, just this side of Lektar House, as if it makes any difference. And you? I forgot to ask earlier. Did the bastard go hunting the streets last night?'

'No. I told you, the Camps are helping. I think he's still trying to figure out why he came up empty the night before last – it's got him rattled, enough for Bauchelain to notice.'

'Not good news. He'll start probing, Buke.'

'Aye. I said there'd be risks, didn't I?'

Aye, trying to keep an insane murderer from finding victims – without his noticing – with a siege about to begin . . . Abyss take you, Buke, what you're trying to drag me into. Gruntle glanced up the ramp. 'Help, you said. How are your new friends taking this?'

The old man shrugged. 'Korbal Broach prefers healthy organs when collecting for his experiments. It's their children at risk.'

'Less so if they'd been left ignorant.'

'They know that.'

'Did you say children?'

'Aye, we've got at least four of the little watchers on the house at all times. Homeless urchins – there's plenty enough of the real kind for them to blend in. They're keeping their eyes on the sky, too—' He stopped abruptly, and a strangely furtive look came into his eyes.

The man, Gruntle realized, had a secret. 'On the sky? What for?'

'Uh, in case Korbal Broach tries the rooftops.'

In a city of widely spaced domes?

'The point I was trying to make,' Buke continued, 'is that there's eyes on the house. Luckily, Bauchelain's still holed up in the cellar, which he's turned into some kind of laboratory. He never leaves. And Korbal sleeps during the day. Gruntle, what I said earlier—'

Gruntle cut him off with a sharply raised hand. 'Listen,' he said.

The two men stood unmoving.

Distant thunder beneath their feet, a slowly rising roar from beyond the city's walls.

Buke, suddenly pale, cursed and asked, 'Where's Stonny? And don't try telling me you don't know.'

'Port Road Gate. Five squads of Grey Swords, a company of Gidrath, a dozen or so Lestari Guard—'

'It's loudest there—'

Scowling, he grunted. 'She figured it'd start with that gate. Stupid woman.'

Buke stepped close and gripped his arm. 'Then why,' he hissed, 'in Hood's name are you still standing here? The assault's begun, and Stonny's got herself right in the middle of it!'

Gruntle pulled free. 'Sing me the Abyss, old man. The woman's all grown up, you know – I told her – *I told you!* This isn't my war!'

'Won't stop the Tenescowri from lopping off your head for the pot!'

Sneering, Gruntle pushed Buke clear of the door. He gripped the weighted bar in his right hand and in a single surge lifted it clear of the slots and let it drop with a clang that echoed up the corridor. He pulled the door open, ducking to step through onto the stairwell.

The sound of the assault was a thunderous roar once he reached street level and emerged to stand in the alley. Amidst the muted clangour of weapons were screams, bellows, and that indefinable, stuttering shiver that came from thousands of armoured bodies in motion – outside the walls, along the battlements, on either side of the gate – which he knew would be groaning beneath repeated impacts from battering rams.

At long last, the siege had unsheathed its sharp iron. The waiting was over.

And they won't hold those walls. Nor the gates. This will be over by dusk. He thought about getting drunk, was comforted by the familiar track of that thought.

Movement from above caught his attention. He looked up to see, arcing in from the west, half a hundred balls of fire, ripping paths through the sky. Flames exploded within sight and beyond as the missiles struck buildings and streets with hammering concussions.

He turned to see a second wave, coming in from the north, one of them growing larger than the others. Still larger, a raging sun, flying directly towards him.

With a curse, Gruntle flung himself back down the stairwell.

The tarry mass struck the street, bounced in a storm of fire, and struck the curved wall of the Camp not ten paces to one side of the stairwell.

The stone core punched through the wall, drawing its flames after it.

Rubble showered the burning street.

Bruised, half deafened, Gruntle scrambled free of the stairwell. Screams sounded from within the Uldan Camp. Smoke was billowing from the hole. *Damned things are firetraps.* He turned as the door at the bottom of the stairwell banged open. Buke appeared, dragging an unconscious woman into the clear.

'How bad?' Gruntle shouted.

Buke glanced up. 'You still here? We're fine. Fire's almost out. Get out of here – go run and hide or something.'

'Good idea,' he growled.

Smoke cloaked the sky, rising in black columns from the entire east side of Capustan, spreading a pall as the wind carried it westward. Flames were visible in the Daru quarter, among the temples and tenements. Judging that the area safest from the burning missiles would be close to the walls, Gruntle set off east down the street. *It's only coincidence that Stonny's ahead, at Port Road Gate. She made her choices.*

It ain't our fight, dammit. If I'd wanted to be a soldier I'd have joined some Hood-damned army. Abyss take them all—

Another wave from the distant catapults clawed paths through the smoke. He picked up his pace, but the balls of fire were already past him, descending into the city's heart and landing with a staccato drum-roll. *They keep that up and I'm liable to get mad.* Figures ran through the smoke ahead. The sound of clashing weapons was louder, susurrating like waves flaying a pebble beach. *Fine. I'll just find the gate and pull the lass out. Won't take long. Hood knows, I'll beat her unconscious if she objects. We're going to find a way out of here, and that's that.*

He approached the back of the row of market stalls facing Inside Port Street. The alleys between the ramshackle stalls were narrow and knee-deep in refuse. The street beyond was invisible behind a wall of smoke. Kicking his way through the rubbish, Gruntle arrived at the street. The gate was to his left, barely visible. The massive doors were shattered, the passageway and threshold heaped with bodies. The block towers flanking the aperture, their blackened sides bearing white scars made by glancing arrows, quarrels and ballista bolts, were both issuing smoke from their arrow-slits. Screams and the clash of swords echoed from within them. Along the wall platforms to either side, soldiers in the garb of the Grey Swords were pushing their way into the top floors of the block towers.

Thumping boots approached from Gruntle's right. A half-dozen Grey Sword squads emerged from the smoke, the front two ranks with swords and shields, the rear two with cocked crossbows. They crossed in front of the caravan captain and took position behind the pile of bodies at the gateway.

A wayward wind swept the smoke from the street's length to Gruntle's right, revealing more bodies – Capanthall, Lestari, and Pannion Betaklites, continuing down the street to a barricaded intersection sixty paces

545

distant, where there was yet another mound of slain soldiers.

Gruntle jogged towards the troop of Grey Swords. Seeing no obvious officer, he elected the crossbow-woman nearest him. 'What's the situation here, soldier?'

She glanced at him, her face a flat, expressionless mask covered in soot, and he was surprised to realize she was Capan. 'We're clearing out the towers up top. The sortie should be back soon – we'll let them through then hold the gateway.'

He stared at her. *Sortie? Gods, they've lost their minds!* 'Hold, you said.' He glanced at the arched passage. 'For how long?'

She shrugged. 'Sappers are on their way with work crews. There'll be a new gate in a bell or two.'

'How many breaches? What's been lost?'

'I wouldn't know, citizen.'

'Cease your chatter over there,' a male voice called out. 'And get that civilian out of here—'

'Movement ahead, sir!' another soldier shouted.

Crossbows were readied over the shoulders of the crouching swordsmen.

Someone called from outside the passageway, 'Lestari Troop – hold your fire! We're coming in!'

There was no relaxing evident among the Grey Swords. A moment later the first elements of the sortie trundled into view. Cut and battered and bearing wounded, the heavily armoured foot-soldiers began shouting for the Grey Swords to clear a path.

The waiting squads split to form a corridor.

Every Lestari among the first thirty who passed through was encumbered by a wounded comrade. From beyond the gateway the sound of fighting drew Gruntle's attention. It was getting closer. There was a rearguard, protecting those bearing the wounded, and the pressure on them was building.

'Counterattack!' someone bellowed. 'Scalandi skirmishers—'

A horn moaned from high atop the wall to the right of the southside block tower.

The roar was growing from the killing field beyond the gateway. The cobbles beneath Gruntle's boots trembled. *Scalandi. They engage in legions of no less than five thousand—*

Ranks of Grey Swords were assembling further down Inside Port Street, swordsmen, crossbowmen, and Capanthall archers, forming a fall-back line. An even larger company was gathering beyond them, along with ballistae, trebuchets and hurlers – the latter with their buckets of scalding gravel steaming like cauldrons.

The rearguard stumbled into the passage. Javelins sliced among them, glancing off armour and shield, only one finding its mark, sending a soldier wheeling with the barbed shaft through his neck. The first of the Pannion Scalandi appeared, lithe, leather-shirted and leather-helmed, wielding spears and scavenged swords, a few with wicker shields, pushing against the yielding line of Lestari heavy infantry, dying one after another, yet still more came on, voicing a keening warcry.

'Break! Break!'

The bellowed command had an instant effect, as the Lestari rearguard suddenly disengaged, spun round and bolted down the corridor, leaving their fallen behind – to be claimed by the Scalandi, dragged back, vanishing from sight. Then the skirmishers boiled down the passageway.

The first line of Grey Swords re-formed in the wake of the Lestari. Crossbows snapped. Scores of Scalandi fell, their writhing bodies fouling the efforts of those behind them. Gruntle watched as the Grey Swords calmly reloaded.

A few from the front line of skirmishers reached the mercenary swordsmen, and were summarily cut down.

A second wave, clawing past their fallen kin, surged towards the line.

They withered beneath another flight of quarrels. The passageway was filling with bodies. The next mob of

547

Scalandi to appear were unarmed. Whilst the Grey Swords loaded their crossbows once more, the skirmishers began dragging their dead and dying kin back through the passageway.

The door to the left-side block tower slammed open, startling Gruntle. He spun, hands reaching for his Gadrobi cutlasses, to see a half-dozen Capanthall stumbling into view, coughing, blood-smeared. Among them: Stonny Menackis.

Her rapier was snapped a hand's length down from the tip; the rest of the weapon, down to and including the bell-hilt and its projecting quillons, was thick with human gore, as was her gloved hand and vambraced forearm. Something slick and ropy hung skewered on the thin blade of the main gauche in her other hand, dripping brown sludge. Her expensive leather armour was in tatters, one crossing slash having penetrated deep enough to cut through the padded shirt underneath. Leather and shirt had fallen away to reveal her right breast, the soft, white skin bearing bruises left behind by someone's hand.

She did not see him at first. Her gaze was fixed on the gateway, where the last of the corpses had been cleared, and yet another wave of Scalandi was pouring through. The front ranks fell to the quarrels, as before, but the surviving attackers rushed on, a frenzied, shrieking mob.

The four-deep line of Grey Swords split once more, wheeled and ran, each half sprinting for the nearest alley to either side of Port Street, where Capanthall archers stood, waiting for a cleared line of sight on the Scalandi pursuers.

Stonny barked a command to her few comrades, and the small troop backed away, parallel to the wall. She then saw Gruntle.

Their eyes locked.

'Get over here, you ox!' she hissed.

Gruntle jogged up to them. 'Hood's balls, woman, what—'

'What do you think? They boiled over us, through the

gate, up the towers, over the damned walls.' Her head snapped back, as if she had just taken an invisible blow. A flat calm settled over her eyes. 'It was room by room. One on one. A Seerdomin found me—' Another jolt ran through her. 'But the bastard left me alive. So I hunted him down. Come on, let's move!' She snapped her main gauche back at Gruntle as they hurried on, spraying his chest and face with bile and watery shit. 'I carved him inside out, and damn if he didn't beg.' She spat. 'Didn't work for me – why should it have for him? What a fool. A pathetic, whimpering . . .'

Hurrying in her wake, it was a moment before Gruntle understood what she was saying. *Oh, Stonny . . .*

Her steps slowed suddenly, her face turning white. She twisted round, met his eyes with a look of horror. 'This was supposed to be a fight. A war. That bastard—' She leaned against the wall. '*Gods!*'

The others continued on, too dazed to notice, or perhaps too numb to care.

Gruntle moved to her side. 'Carved him from the inside out, did you?' he asked softly, not daring to reach out and touch her.

Stonny nodded, her eyes squeezed shut, her breath coming in harsh, pained gasps.

'Did you save any of him for me, lass?'

She shook her head.

'That's too bad. Then again, one Seerdomin's as good as another.'

Stonny stepped forward, pressing her face into his shoulder. He wrapped his arms around her. 'Let's get out of this fight, lass,' he murmured. 'I got a clean room, with a basin in it and a stove and a jug of water. A room, close enough to the north wall for it to be safe. It's at the end of a hallway. Only one way in. I'll stand outside the door, Stonny, for as long as you need. No-one gets past. That's a promise.' He felt her nod. He reached down to lift her up.

'I can walk.'

'But do you *want* to, lass? That's the question.'

After a long moment, she shook her head.

Gruntle lifted her easily. 'Nap if you've mind to,' he said. 'You're safe enough.'

He set off, skirting the wall, the woman curling up in his arms, her face pressed hard against his tunic, the rough cloth growing wetter there.

Behind them, the Scalandi were dying by the hundreds, the Grey Swords and Capanthall delivering dread slaughter.

He wanted to be there with them. In the front line. Taking life after life.

One Seerdomin was not enough. A thousand would not be enough.

Not now.

He felt himself grow cold, as if the blood within him was now something else, flowing a bitter course along his veins, reaching out to fill his muscles with a strange, unyielding strength. He had never before felt such a thing, but he was beyond thinking about it. There were no words for this.

Nor, he would soon discover, were there words to describe what he would become, what he would do.

The slaughter of the K'Chain Che'Malle by the Kron T'lan Imass and the undead ay had thrown the Septarch and his forces into disarray, as Brukhalian had predicted. The confusion and the immobility it engendered had added days to Shield Anvil Itkovian's preparations for the siege to come. But now, the time for preparing had ended, and Itkovian was left with the command of the city's defences.

There would be no T'lan Imass, no T'lan Ay, to come to their rescue. *And no relieving army to arrive with the last grain of the hourglass.* Capustan was on its own.

And so it shall be. Fear, anguish and despair.

From his position atop the highest tower on the Barracks Wall, after Destriant Karnadas had left and the stream of messengers began its frenzied flow, he had watched the first concerted movement of enemy troops to the east and southeast, the rumbling appearance of siege weapons. Beklites and the more heavily armoured Betaklites marshalling opposite Port Gate, with a mass of Scalandi behind and to either side of them. Knots of Seerdomin shock troops, scurrying bands of Desandi – sappers – positioning still more siege weapons. And, waiting in enormous, sprawling encampments along the river and the coast, the seething mass of the Tenescowri.

He had watched the assault on the outside fortification of the Gidrath's East Watch redoubt, already isolated and surrounded by the enemy; had seen the narrow door battered down, the Beklites pushing into the passageway, three steps, two steps, one, then a standstill, and moments later, a step back, then another, bodies being pulled clear. Still more bodies. The Gidrath – the elite guards of the Mask Council – had revealed their discipline and determination. They expelled the intruders, raised yet another barricade in place of the door.

The Beklites outside had milled for a time, then they renewed their assault.

The battle continued through the afternoon, yet each time that Itkovian pulled his attention away from other events he saw that the Gidrath still held. Taking enemy lives by the score. *Twisting that thorn in the Septarch's midst.*

Finally, near dusk, siege weapons were wheeled about. Huge boulders were hurled against the fortress's walls. The pounding concussions continued as the last of daylight fell away.

Beyond this minor drama, the assault against the city's walls had begun on all sides. The north attack proved a feint, poorly executed and so quickly recognized as insignificant. Messengers relayed to the Shield Anvil that a similar cursory engagement was under way at the west wall.

The true assaults were delivered upon the south and east walls, concentrated at the gates. Itkovian, positioned directly between them, was able to directly oversee the

551

defence on both sides. He was visible to the enemy, and more than one missile had been fired in his direction, only a few coming close. This was the first day. Range and accuracy would improve in the days to come. Before long, he might have to yield his vantage point; in the meantime, he would let his presence mock the attackers.

As the Beklites and Betaklites rushed the walls, the ladder-bearing Desandi among them, Itkovian gave the command for counterfire from the walls and block towers. The ensuing slaughter was horrific. The attackers had not bothered with turtles or other forms of cover, and so died in appalling droves.

Yet such were their numbers that the gates were reached, battering rams deployed, and breaches effected. The Pannions, however, after pushing through the passageways, found themselves in open concourses that became killing grounds as Grey Swords and Capanthall archers launched a withering crossfire from behind barricades blocking side streets, intersections and alley mouths.

The Shield Anvil's strategy of layered defence was proving murderously efficient. Subsequent counterattacks had been so effective as to permit sorties beyond the gates, a vicious pursuit of fleeing Pannions. And, this day at least, none of the companies he'd sent out had gone too far. Discipline had held among the Capanthall, the Lestari and the Coralessian companies.

The first day was over, and it belonged to Capustan's defenders.

Itkovian stood on trembling legs, the coastal breeze building to dry the sweat from his face, sending cool tendrils through the half-visor's grille to brush his smoke-reddened eyes. As darkness closed around him, he listened to the rocks pounding the East Watch redoubt, and turned for the first time in hours to view the city.

Entire blocks were aflame, the fires reaching into the night sky, lighting the underbelly of a turgid canopy of solid smoke. *I knew what I would see. Why then does it shock me?*

Drive the blood from my veins? Suddenly weak, he leaned against the merlon behind him, one hand pressed against the rough stone.

A voice spoke from the shadows of the tower's doorway. 'You need rest, sir.'

Itkovian closed his eyes. 'Destriant, you speak the truth.'

'But there will be no rest,' Karnadas resumed. 'The other half of the attacking force is assembling. We can expect assaults through the night.'

'I know, sir.'

'Brukhalian—'

'Aye, it must be done. Come forward, then.'

'Such efforts are increasingly difficult,' Karnadas murmured as he strode up to stand before the Shield Anvil. He laid a hand against Itkovian's chest. 'The illness of the warrens threatens me,' he continued. 'Soon it will be all I can do to fend against it.'

The weariness drained from the Shield Anvil, vigour returning to his limbs. He sighed. 'I thank you, sir.'

'The Mortal Sword has just been called to the Thrall to give account of the first day's battle. And no, we were not fortunate enough to hear of the Thrall's destruction beneath a few hundred balls of fire. It stands intact. However, given those that it now houses, we would no longer wish such a fiery end.'

Itkovian pulled his gaze from the streets, studied the Destriant's red-lit face. 'Your meaning, sir?'

'The Barghast, Hetan and Cafal, have taken up residence in the Main Hall.'

'Ah, I see.'

'Before he left, Brukhalian asked me to enquire of your efforts to discover the means by which the bones of the Founding Spirits will be spared the coming conflagration.'

'I have failed, sir. Nor does it seem likely that I will have opportunity to renew my efforts in that direction.'

'That is understandable, sir. I will convey to the Mortal Sword your words, if not your obvious relief.'

553

'Thank you.'

The Destriant strode to look out upon the east killing field. 'Gods below, do the Gidrath still hold the redoubt?'

'Uncertain,' Itkovian murmured as he joined the man. 'At the very least, the bombardment has not ceased. There may be little but rubble there now – it's too dark to make out, but I believe I heard a wall collapse half a bell ago.'

'The legions are marshalling once more, Shield Anvil.'

'I need more messengers, sir. My last troop—'

'Aye, exhausted,' Karnadas said. 'I shall take my leave and do as you ask, sir.'

Itkovian listened to the man make his way down the ladder, but held his gaze on the enemy positions to the east and south. Hooded lanterns flashed here and there among what appeared to be troops arrayed in squares, the figures jostling and shifting behind wicker shields. Smaller companies of Scalandi skirmishers emerged, moving cautiously forward.

Bootsteps behind the Shield Anvil announced the arrival of the messengers. Without turning, Itkovian said, 'Inform the captains of the archers and trebuchets that the Pannions are about to renew their assault. Soldiers to the walls and battlements. Gate companies assembled, full complement, including sappers.'

A score of fiery balls rose skyward from behind the massed ranks of the Pannions. The missiles arced, their sizzling roar audible as they passed high over Itkovian's head. Explosions lit the city, shook the bronze-sheathed floorboards beneath his feet. The Shield Anvil faced his cadre of messengers. 'Go.'

Karnadas rode his horse at a canter across Tura'l Concourse. The huge arch fifty paces to his left had just taken a hit on one corner of the pedestal, spraying broken masonry and burning pitch onto the cobbles and onto the rooftops of the scatter of tenements beside it. Flames billowed, and the Destriant saw figures pouring from the building. Somewhere to the north, at the very edge of the Temple District, another tenement block was engulfed in fire.

He reached the far side of the concourse, not slackening his mount's pace as he rode up Shadows Street – the Temple of Shadow on his left, the Temple of the Queen of Dreams on his right – then angled his horse again to the left as they reached Daru Spear – the district's main avenue. Ahead loomed the dark stones of the Thrall, the ancient keep towering over the lower structures of the Daru tenements.

Three squads of Gidrath commanded the gate, fully armoured and with weapons drawn. Recognizing the Destriant, they waved him through.

He dismounted in the courtyard, leaving his horse to a stabler, then made his way to the Great Hall, where he knew he would find Brukhalian.

As he strode down the main aisle towards the double doors he saw that another man was ahead. Robed, hooded, he was without the usual escort provided strangers to the Thrall, yet he approached the entrance with a graceful assurance. Karnadas wondered how he had managed to get past the Gidrath, then his eyes widened as the stranger gestured with one hand and the huge doors swung open before him.

Voices raised in argument drifted out from the Great Hall, quickly falling silent as the stranger entered.

Karnadas increased his pace, and arrived in time to catch the end of a Rath' priest's expostulation.

'—this instant!'

The Destriant slipped through the entrance in the stranger's wake. He saw the Mortal Sword standing near the centre millstone, now turned to regard the newcomer. The Barghast, Hetan and Cafal, were sitting on their rug a few paces to Brukhalian's right. The priests and priestesses of the Mask Council were one and all leaning forward in their seats – their masks conveying caricatures of extreme

555

displeasure – with the exception of Rath'Hood who was standing, the wooden skull visage of his mask arched with outrage.

The stranger, hands clasped within the folds of his dun-coloured robe's sleeves, seemed unperturbed by the hostile welcome.

From where the Destriant stood, he could not see the man's face, but he saw the hood shift as the stranger scanned the masked assembly.

'Will you ignore my command?' Rath'Hood asked, visibly bridling his tone. The priest glared about. 'Where are our Gidrath? Why in the gods' names haven't they heard our summons?'

'Alas,' the stranger murmured in Daru, 'they have for the moment heeded the call of their dreams. Thus, we avoid any unnecessary interruptions.' The man turned to Brukhalian, allowing Karnadas – who now stood at the Mortal Sword's side – to see his face for the first time. Round, strangely unlined, unmemorable barring the expression of calm equanimity. *Ah, the merchant retrieved by Itkovian. His name . . . Keruli.* The man's pale eyes fixed on Brukhalian. 'My apologies to the commander of the Grey Swords, but I fear I must make address to the Mask Council. If he would be so kind as to temporarily yield the floor?'

The Mortal Sword tilted his head. 'By all means, sir.'

'We do not agree to this!' Rath'Shadowthrone hissed.

The stranger's eyes hardened as he swung his attention on the priest. 'You, unfortunately, have no choice. I look upon you all, and find the representation woefully inadequate.'

Karnadas choked back a laugh, and recovered in time to meet Brukhalian's raised eyebrow with an expression of innocent enquiry.

'By the Abyss,' Rath'Burn said, 'who are you to make such judgement?'

'I need make no claim as to my true name, Priestess, only to the title I now demand.'

556

'Title?'

'Rath'K'rul. I have come to take my place among the Mask Council, and to tell you this: there is one among you who will betray us all.'

She sat on the flatboard bed, long hair in disarray, hanging down her face. Gruntle reached out and slowly combed the tresses back.

Stonny's sigh was ragged. 'This is stupid. Things happen. There's no rules to battle. I was an idiot, trying to take on a Seerdomin with naught but a rapier – he'd batted it aside with a laugh.' She looked up. 'Don't stay with me, Gruntle. I can see what's there in your eyes. Go.' She glanced around the room. 'I just need to get . . . to get cleaned up. I don't want you here, not outside the door, either. If you took that position, Gruntle, you'd never leave it. Go. You're the best fighter I have ever seen. Kill some Pannions – Hood take me, kill them all.'

'Are you sure—'

Her laugh was harsh. 'Don't even try.'

He grunted, began checking his armour's straps and fittings. Adjusted the padding beneath. Dropped the visor on his helm. Loosened the heavy cutlasses in their scabbards.

Stonny watched him in silence.

Finally, he was ready. 'All right. Take your time, lass. There'll be plenty left whenever you're done here.'

'Aye, there will.'

Gruntle faced the door.

'Do some damage.'

He nodded. 'I will.'

The Beklites and Scalandi reached the east wall in their thousands. In the face of withering arrow fire, ladders were raised, figures swarmed upward, poured over the battlements. The East Gate was taken yet again, the enemy surging down the passageway to spill out onto the square of New East Market.

To the south, the city's Main Gate fell to a concerted barrage of catapult fire. A legion of Betaklites swept into Jelarkan Concourse. A well-aimed ball of burning pitch struck the Capanthall West Barracks – the building rose in a conflagration that lit the entire city a lurid red.

Shock troops of Urdomen and Seerdomin breached North Gate and entered the nearest Daru streets after destroying Nildar Camp and slaying everyone within it. The enemy was within the city on every side.

The battle, Itkovian concluded, was not going well.

With each report that a messenger delivered, the Shield Anvil issued commands in a soft, calm voice. 'Fourth Wing to the Ninth Barricade, between East Inside and Ne'ror towers. Resupply the Capanthall in the two towers ... Seventh Wing to West Inside tower and wall. I need a report on the status of Jehbar Tower. There were five hundred Capanthall in the West Barracks – likely they've been routed ... Fifth and Third Manes into the streets around Tular Concourse to rally the Capanthall ... First, Seventh and Sixth Manes doubletime to North Temple District – block and strike until North Gate is retaken ... Fourth, Second and Eighth Manes to New East Market. Once the East Gate is recovered, I want Wings One, Three and Five to sortie. Their rally point is the East Watch redoubt – I want the siege engines assailing it neutralized, then any Gidrath survivors retrieved. Have the Trimaster report to me ...'

In between commands and the coming and going of messengers, Itkovian watched the engagement at New East Market – what he could see of it in the glare of fires through seething clouds of smoke. The Scalandi were pushing hard to break the barricades preventing them from reaching the prince's palace. Boulders had been hammering the palace's outer walls incessantly, all to no effect – the thin, glistening stone walls did not so much as tremble. Burning pitch roared itself to extinction yet achieved nothing more than black stains marring the unknown stone's surface. The palace would have to be taken the hard way, step by step, every room, every level, and the Pannions were eager to begin the task.

The Grey Sword Trimaster commanding the First, Third and Fifth Wings arrived on the parapet. He was one of the Shield Anvil's oldest officers, lean and tall, grey-bearded to hide countless scars. 'My assignment has been conveyed to me, Shield Anvil.'

So why have I sent for you? I see the question in your eyes, sir. You do not require any stirring words to cleave you to what could be a suicidal mission. 'It will be unexpected,' Itkovian said.

The man's eyes narrowed, then he nodded. 'Aye, sir, it will. With all the breaches the enemy's front lines have lost their cohesion. Chaos claims all, this night. We shall destroy the siege engines as ordered. We shall retrieve the survivors in the redoubt.'

Aye, old friend. I am the one who needs stirring words. 'Keep your eyes open, sir. I would know the positioning of the Pannion forces to the rear. Specifically, the Tenescowri.'

'Understood, sir.'

A messenger arrived, stumbling as he cleared the ladder. 'Shield Anvil!' she gasped.

'Your report, sir,' Itkovian said.

'From the Trimaster of the First, Seventh and Sixth Manes, sir.'

North Gate. He looked to the north. Most of the Daru tenements there were burning. 'Proceed.'

'The Trimaster reports that he has encountered the shocktroops of Urdomen and Seerdomin. They're all dead, sir.'

'Dead?'

The young woman nodded, paused to wipe ash-smeared sweat from her brow. Her helm, Itkovian noted, was too large. 'A citizen rallied the remnants of the Capanthall Guard, as well as other civilians and some caravan guards. Sir, they engaged the Urdomen and Seerdomin in a succession of street battles – and drove them back. The Trimaster now controls North Gate, to which his company of sappers are effecting repairs.'

'And this impromptu militia and its commander?'

'Only a few wounded were there to greet the Trimaster, sir. The, uh, militia has set off westward, in pursuit of an Urdomen company that sought to storm Lektar House.'

'Messenger, send the First Wing to their aid. Upon delivering my command, take some rest, sir.'

'Yes, Shield Anvil.'

'That is not the helmet you were issued with, is it, sir?'

Abashed, she shook her head. 'I, uh, lost it, Shield Anvil.'

'Have the quartermaster find you one that fits.'

'Yes, sir.'

'Go.'

The two veterans watched the young woman depart.

'Careless,' the Trimaster murmured, 'losing her helm.'

'Indeed.'

'Clever, finding another one.'

The Shield Anvil smiled.

'I shall take my leave now, sir.'

'Fener go with you, Trimaster.'

Karnadas drew a long, quiet breath, the hairs of his neck rising at the sudden, heavy silence in the Great Hall. *Betrayal?* His eyes were drawn to one priest in particular. Rath'K'rul's words were fuel to suspicions the Destriant already held, and the bias led him to mistrust his own conclusions. He held his tongue, but his gaze remained fixed on Rath'Fener.

The boar mask was without expression, yet the man stood as if he had just taken a blow.

'The age of K'rul,' Rath'Shadowthrone hissed, 'is long past.'

'He has returned,' the robed man replied. 'A fact that

560

should give every one of you a certain measure of relief. It is K'rul's blood, after all, that has been poisoned. The battle now begun shall spare no-one, including the gods whom you serve. If you doubt my words, take your inner journeys – hear the truth from your gods. Aye, the words might well be reluctant, indeed, resentful. But they will be spoken none the less.'

'Your suggestion,' Rath'Queen of Dreams said, 'cannot be achieved in haste.'

'I am amenable to reconvening,' Rath'K'rul said with a slight bow. 'Be warned, however, we've little time.'

'You spoke of betrayal—'

'Aye, Rath'Queen of Dreams, I did.'

'You wound us with divisiveness.'

The robed man cocked his head. 'Those who know your own conscience to be clear, brothers and sisters, will thereby be united. The one who cannot make that claim, will likely be dealt with by his god.'

'*His?*'

Rath'K'rul shrugged.

Brukhalian cleared his throat in the subsequent silence. 'With the leave of the Mask Council, I shall now depart. My Shield Anvil has need of me.'

'Of course,' Rath'Hood said. 'Indeed, from the sounds beyond the Thrall, it would appear that the walls are breached and the enemy is within.'

And Hood stalks Capustan's streets. Ambivalence, sufficient to cool your tone.

The Mortal Sword smiled. 'It was our expectation from the very beginning, Rath'Hood, that the walls and gates would be taken. Periodically.' He swung to Karnadas. 'Join me, please. I require the latest information.'

The Destriant nodded.

Hetan suddenly rose, eyes flashing as she glared at Rath'K'rul. 'Sleeping Man, is your god's offer true? Will he in truth aid us?'

'He will. Which of you volunteers?'

561

The Barghast woman, eyes wide, jerked her head towards her brother.

The robed man smiled.

Rath'Shadowthrone seemed to spit out his words, 'What now? What now? *What now?*'

Karnadas turned to study Cafal, was shocked to see the man still seated cross-legged, with his head bowed in slumber.

'To all here,' Rath'K'rul said in a low voice, 'awaken him not, if you value your lives.'

An even dozen Capanthall remained of the sixty-odd followers Gruntle had led westward from North Gate, and only one Lestari guardsman, a short-legged, long-armed sergeant who had stepped into the role of second-in-command without a word.

Lestari House was one of the few well-fortified private residences in Capustan, the home of Kalan D'Arle, a merchant family with links to the Council in Darujhistan as well as the now fallen noble house of the same name in Lestari itself. The solid stone structure abutted the north wall and its flat roof had become a strongpoint and rallying position for the wall's defenders.

At street level, the grand entrance consisted of a thick bronze door set in a stone frame, the hinges recessed. A broad pediment overhung the entrance, held up by twin marble columns, its ceiling crowded with the carved heads of demons, their mouths open and now dripping with the last of the boiling water that had gushed down on the screaming Scalandi who had been hammering on the door.

Gruntle and his troop, still reeling from a savage clash with fifteen Urdomen that had seen most of the militia chopped to pieces – before Gruntle had personally cut down the last two Pannions – had come upon the Scalandi mob from behind.

The engagement was swift and brutal. Only the Lestari sergeant revealed any mercy when he slit the throats of those Scalandi who had been badly scalded by the boiling water. The cessation of their shrieks brought sudden silence to the scene.

Gruntle crouched beside a body and used its tunic to clean the blades of his cutlasses. The muscles of his arms and shoulders were leaden, trembling.

The night's breeze had strengthened, smelling of salt, sweeping the smoke inland. Enough fires still raged on all sides to drive back the darkness.

'Look at that, will you?'

The caravan captain glanced over at the Lestari sergeant, then followed the man's gaze.

The Thrall loomed to the southeast, only a few streets away. The entire keep was faintly glowing.

'What do you figure?' the grizzled soldier muttered.

Sorcery of some kind.

'I'd guess that's ritual magic,' the sergeant went on. 'Probably protective. Hood knows, we could do with some of that ourselves. We're cut to pieces, sir – I ain't got much left and as for the rest . . .' Eyeing the dozen battered, bleeding Capanthall crouched or kneeling, or leaning against the house's walls, he shook his head. 'They're done for.'

Sounds of fighting neared from the southwest.

The scraping of armour from the roof of Lestari House drew Gruntle's attention. A half-dozen Capanthall regulars were looking down on them. 'Nicely done, whoever you all are!' one shouted.

'What can you see up there?' the sergeant called up.

'We've retaken the North Gate! Grey Swords, damn near a thousand of them. The Pannions are reeling!'

'Grey Swords,' the Lestari muttered under his breath. He glared across at Gruntle. '*We* was the ones who retook that gate—'

'But we're not holding it, are we?' Gruntle growled, straightening. He faced his meagre troop. 'Look alive, you spineless Capans. We ain't finished.'

Dull, disbelieving eyes fixed on him.

'Sounds like the West Gate's down. Sounds like our defenders are back-pedalling. Meaning they've lost their officers, or their officers ain't worth shit. Sergeant, you're now a lieutenant. The rest of you, you're sergeants. We've got some scared soldiers to rally. Let's move, doubletime – don't want you all stiffening up.' Glaring at them, Gruntle rolled his shoulders, clashed his cutlasses. 'Follow me.'

He jogged down the street, towards West Gate. After a moment, the others fell in step.

Two bells before dawn. To the north and to the west, the roar of battle was diminishing. Itkovian's counterattacks had reclaimed the gates and walls there; the fight was out of the attackers on those sides, for the rest of this night at least.

Brukhalian had returned from the Thrall, Karnadas in tow, a bell earlier. The Mortal Sword had assembled the six hundred recruits the Shield Anvil had been holding in reserve, along with two Manes and two Wings, and set off towards the Jelarkan Concourse, where it was rumoured over a thousand Beklites had pushed their way in, threatening to overwhelm the inner defences.

The situation around the West Gate was even more dire. Three of Itkovian's messengers had not returned after being sent that way. The West Barracks was a massive fist of raging fire, revealing in lurid flashes the rubble that was the West Gate itself. This breach, should it prove able to reach through to the west side of Jelarkan Concourse, could see the fall of half the city.

The Shield Anvil paced with frustration. He was out of reserve forces. For a while there, it looked as if the Capanthall and Grey Sword detachments assigned to the West Gate had simply ceased to exist, the wound gushing into a flood. Then, inexplicably, resolve had stiffened. The flood had encountered a human wall, and though it rose, it had yet to pour over.

The fate of Capustan lay with those defenders, now. And Itkovian could only watch, as all hung in the balance.

Karnadas was below, in the barracks compound. Exhausting his Denul warren, struggling against whatever sorcerous infection plagued it, yet still managing to effect healing of wounded Grey Swords. Something had happened in the Thrall, was happening even now – the entire keep was glowing, a colourless penumbra. Itkovian wanted to ask the Destriant about it, but the opportunity had yet to arise.

Boots on the ladder. The Shield Anvil swung about.

The messenger who emerged was horribly burned along one side of his face, the red, blistered skin covering his jaw and upward, forming a ridge beneath the rim on his helm. His eye on that side was puckered, wrinkled and dark as a raisin.

He climbed clear of the ladder, and Itkovian saw Karnadas behind him.

The Destriant spoke first, halfway out of the hatch. 'He insisted he give his report to you first, sir. I can do nothing for the eye, but the pain—'

'In a moment,' Itkovian snapped. 'Messenger, make your report.'

'Apologies,' the young man gasped, 'for taking so long.'

The Shield Anvil's eyes widened. 'You humble me, sir. It has been a bell and more since I sent you to the West Gate.'

'The Pannions had reached through to Tular Camp, Shield Anvil. Senar Camp had fallen – its inhabitants slaughtered. Everyone. Children – sir – I am sorry, but the horror remains with me . . .'

'Go on.'

'Jehbar Tower was surrounded, its defenders besieged. Such was the situation upon my arrival, sir. Our soldiers were scattered, fighting in clumps, many of them surrounded. We were being cut down, everywhere I looked.' He paused, drew a ragged breath, then continued, 'Such was the situation upon my arrival. As I prepared to return to you with said news, I was . . . absconded—'

'You were *what*?'

'Apologies, sir. I can think of no other word. A foreigner appeared, with but half a score of Capan followers, a militia of sorts, sir. And a Lestari sergeant. The man took charge – of everyone, myself included. Shield Anvil, I argued—'

'Clearly this man was persuasive. Resume your tale, sir.'

'The foreigner had his own soldiers break down the door into Tular Camp. He demanded that its inhabitants come out and fight. For their children—'

'And he convinced them?'

'Sir, he held in his arms what was left of a child from Senar Camp. The enemy, sir – the Pannions – someone had begun to *eat* that child—'

Karnadas moved up behind the young man, hands settling on his shoulders.

'He convinced them,' Itkovian said.

The messenger nodded. 'The foreigner – he then . . . he then took what was left of the child's tunic, and has made of it a standard. I saw it myself. Sir, I ceased arguing, then – I'm sorry—'

'I understand you, sir.'

'There was no shortage of weapons. The Tular Capanthall armed themselves – four, five hundred came out. Men and women. The foreigner had sent out his own followers, and they began returning. With them, surviving bands of Capanthall soldiery, a few Gidrath, Coralessian, and Grey Swords, sir. The Trimaster had been killed, you see—'

'The foreigner rallied them,' Itkovian cut in. 'Then what?'

'We marched to the relief of Jehbar Tower, sir. Shield Anvil, behind that horrible banner, we delivered slaughter.'

'The condition of the tower?'

'Ruined, sir. Alas. There were but twenty survivors among the Capanthall defending it. They are now with the foreigner. I, uh, I returned to my responsibilities then, sir, and was given leave to report to you—'

'Generous of this stranger. What was the disposition of this militia at that time?'

'They were about to sortie through the rubble of West Gate, sir—'

'*What?*'

'A Beklite company was coming up to reinforce the attackers inside the city. But those attackers were all dead. The foreigner planned on surprising them with that fact.'

'Twin Tusks, who *is* this man?'

'I know not his name, sir. He wields two cutlasses. Fights like a . . . like a *boar*, sir, with those two cutlasses . . .'

Itkovian stared at the young man for a long moment, seeing the pain diminishing as the Destriant continued gripping his shoulders, seeing the blisters shrink, the welt fading, new skin closing around the ruined eye. The Shield Anvil swung about in a clank of armour, faced west. The fire of the West Barracks reached its crimson light only so far. Beyond, darkness ruled. He shifted his attention to the Jelarkan Concourse. No further breaches were evident, as far as he could determine. The Mortal Sword had matters well in hand, as Itkovian knew would be the case.

'Less than a bell,' Karnadas murmured, 'before dawn. Shield Anvil, the city holds.'

Itkovian nodded.

More boots on the ladder. They all turned as another messenger arrived.

'Shield Anvil, from the third sortie to East Watch redoubt. The surviving Gidrath have been recovered, sir. Movement to the southeast was discerned. The Trimaster sent a scout. Shield Anvil, the Tenescowri are on the move.'

Itkovian nodded. *They will arrive with the dawn. Three hundred thousand, maybe more.* 'Destriant, open the tunnels. Begin with the inner Camps, sir. Every citizen below. Take charge of the barracks Manes and Wings and whoever else you come across to effect swift directions and control of the entranceways.'

Karnadas's lined face twisted into a wry smile. 'Shield Anvil, it is my duty to remind you that the Mask Council has yet to approve the construction of said tunnels.'

Itkovian nodded again, 'Fortunately for the people of Capustan we proceeded without awaiting that approval.' Then he frowned. 'It seems the Mask Council has found its own means of self-defence.'

'Not them, sir. Hetan and Cafal. And a new priest, indeed, the very "merchant" whom you rescued out on the plain.'

The Shield Anvil slowly blinked. 'Did he not have a caravan guard – a large man with a pair of cutlasses belted to his hips?' *Cutlasses? More like Fener's own tusks.*

The Destriant hissed. 'I believe you are right, sir. In fact, only yesterday I spared a moment to heal him.'

'He was wounded?'

'Hungover, Shield Anvil. Very.'

'I see. Carry on, sir.' Itkovian looked to his two messengers. 'Word must be sent to the Mortal Sword . . . and to this foreigner . . .'

The Beklite's wicker shield exploded from the man's arm to Gruntle's backhand swing. The notched, gore-smeared cutlass in the caravan guard's other hand chopped straight down, through helm, then skull. Brain and blood sprayed down over his gauntlet. The Beklite fell to one side, limbs jerking.

Gruntle spun, whipping the ragged mess from his blade. A dozen paces behind him, looming above the feral ranks of his followers, was the Child's Standard, a torn, brightly dyed yellow tunic now splashed with a red that was drying to deep magenta.

The Beklite company had been crushed. Gruntle's victim had been the last. The caravan captain and his militia were forty paces outside what was left of the West

Gate, on the wide main avenue of what had been a shanty town. The structures were gone, their wooden walls and slate roofs dismantled and taken away. Patches of stained earthen floors and the scatter of broken pottery were all that remained. Two hundred paces further west ran the pickets of the besiegers, swarming in the dawn's growing light.

Gruntle could see half a thousand Betaklites marshalling along its edge, flanked by companies of Urdomen and Betrullid light cavalry. Beyond them, a vast veil of dust was rising, lit gold by the slanting sun.

The lieutenant had dropped to one knee beside Gruntle, struggling to regain control of his breathing. 'Time's – time's come – to – withdraw, sir.'

Scowling, the caravan captain swung to survey his militia. *Fifty, sixty still standing. What did I start with last night? About the same. Is that right? Gods, can that be right?* 'Where are our sergeants?'

'They're there, most of them, anyway. You want me to call them forward, sir?'

No, yes, I want to see their faces. I can't remember their faces. 'Have them assemble the squads.'

'Sir, if that cavalry rushes us—'

'They won't. They're masking.'

'Masking what?'

'Tenescowri. Why throw more veteran soldiers at us only to see them killed? Those bastards need a rest in any case. No, it's time for the starving horde.'

'Beru fend,' the lieutenant whispered.

'Don't worry,' Gruntle replied, 'they die easy.'

'We need to rest – we're sliced to pieces, sir. I'm too old for a suicide stand.'

'Then what in Hood's name are you doing in Capustan? Never mind. Let's see the squads. I want armour stripped from these bodies. Leathers only, and helms and gauntlets. I want my sixty to look like soldiers.'

'Sir—'

'*Then* we withdraw. Understood? Best be quick about it, too.'

Gruntle led his battered company back towards Capustan. There was activity amidst the ruin of West Gate. The plain grey cloaks of the Grey Swords dominated the crowd, though others – masons and ragtag crews of labourers – were present as well. The frenzied activity slowed as heads turned. Conversations fell away.

Gruntle's scowl deepened. He hated undue attention. *What are we, ghosts?*

Eyes were pulled to the Child's Standard.

A figure strode forward to meet them, an officer of the mercenaries. 'Welcome back,' the woman said with a grave nod. Her face was caked with dust, runnels of sweat tracking down from under her helm. 'We've got some weaponsmiths set up outside Tular Camp. I imagine your Tusks need sharpening—'

'Cutlasses.'

'As you say, sir. The Shield Anvil – no, we all would know your name—'

But Gruntle had already stepped past her. 'Sharpeners. Good idea. Lieutenant, you think we all need to get our tusks sharpened?'

The Grey Swords officer spun round. 'Sir, the reference is not to be taken lightly.'

He continued on. Over his shoulder, he said, 'Fine, let's call them tiger-claws, why don't we? Looks to me you've got a gate to rebuild. Best get to it, lass. Them Tenescowri want breakfast, and we're it.'

He heard her hiss in what might have been angry frustration.

Moments later, the workers resumed their efforts.

The weaponsmiths had set up their grindstone wheels in the street. Beyond them, in the direction of the Jelarkan Concourse, the sounds of battle continued. Gruntle waved his soldiers forward. 'Line up all of you. I want those blades so sharp you can shave with them.'

The lieutenant snorted. 'Most of your troop's women, sir.'

'Whatever.'

A rider was driving his horse hard down the street. He reined in with a clatter of hooves, dismounted and paused to adjust his armoured gauntlets before striding to Gruntle.

'Are you Keruli's caravan captain?' he asked, face hidden behind a full-visored helm.

'Was. What do you want, mercenary?'

'Compliments from the Shield Anvil, sir.' The voice was hard, deep. 'The Tenescowri are massing—'

'I know.'

'It is the Shield Anvil's belief that their main assault will be from the east, for it is there that the First Child of the Dead Seed has assembled his vanguard.'

'Fine, what of it?'

The messenger was silent for a moment, then he continued. 'Sir, Capustan's citizens are being removed—'

'Removed where?'

'The Grey Swords have constructed tunnels beneath the city, sir. Below are amassed sufficient supplies to support twenty thousand citizens—'

'For how long?'

'Two weeks, perhaps three. The tunnels are extensive. In many cases, old empty barrows were opened as well, as storage repositories – there were more of those than anyone had anticipated. The entranceways are well hidden, and defensible.'

Two weeks. Pointless. 'Well, that takes care of the non-combatants. What about us fighters?'

The messenger's eyes grew veiled between the black-iron bars of the visor. 'We fight. Street by street, building by building. Room by room, sir. The Shield Anvil enquires of you, which section of the city do you wish to assume? And is there anything you require? Arrows, food . . .'

'We've no archers, but food and watered wine, aye.

Which section?' Gruntle surveyed his troop. 'More like *which building*. There's a tenement just off Old Daru Street, the one with the black-stone foundations. We'll start at North Gate, then fall back to there.'

'Very good. Supplies will be delivered to that tenement house, sir.'

'Oh, there's a woman in one of the rooms on the upper floor – if your evacuation of citizens involved a house-by-house search—'

'The evacuation was voluntary, sir.'

'She wouldn't have agreed to it.'

'Then she remains where she is.'

Gruntle nodded.

The lieutenant came to the captain's side. 'Your cutlasses – time to hone your tiger-claws, sir.'

'Aye.' Turning away, Gruntle did not notice the messenger's head jerk back at the Lestari lieutenant's words.

Through the dark cage of his visor, Shield Anvil Itkovian studied the hulking caravan captain who now strode towards a swordsmith, the short-legged Lestari trailing a step behind. The blood-stained cutlasses were out, the wide, notched, tip-heavy blades the colour of smoky flames.

He had come to meet this man for himself, to take his fullest measure and fashion a face to accompany the man's extraordinary talents.

Itkovian already regretted the decision. He muttered a soft, lengthy curse at his own impetuosity. *Fights like a boar? Gods, no, this man is a big, plains-hunting cat. He has bulk, aye, but it passes unnoticed behind a deadly grace. Fener save us all, the Tiger of Summer's ghost walks in this man's shadow.*

Returning to his horse, Itkovian drew himself up into the saddle. He gathered the reins. Swinging his mount round, he tilted his head back and stared at the morning sun. *The truth of this has burst like fire in my heart. On this, our last day, I have met this unnamed man, this servant of Treach, the Tiger of Summer . . . Treach ascending.*

572

And Fener? The brutal boar whose savage cunning rides my soul – what of my lord?

Fener . . . descending. On this, our last day.

A susurrating roar rose in the distance, from all sides. The Tenescowri were on the move.

'Twin Tusks guard us,' Itkovian rasped, driving his heels into the horse's flanks. The animal surged forward, sparks raining as its hooves struck the cobbles.

Grey-faced with exhaustion, Buke made his way towards the necromancers' estate. It was a large edifice, commanding a long, low hill that looked too regular to be natural, surrounded by a high wall with mock guard towers at the corners. A grand entrance faced onto Kilsban Way, set back from the street itself with a ramped approach. The gate was a miniature version of the Thrall's, vertically raised and lowered by countersunk centre-holed millstones.

A fireball had struck the gate, blasting it into ruin. The flames had raged for a time, blackening the stone frame and cracking it, but somehow the structure remained upright.

As the old caravan guard limped his way up the ramp towards it, he was startled by the sudden exit of a tall, gaunt, black-robed man. Stumbling, half hopping like a huge ebon-winged vulture, the man spun round to glare at Buke. His face twisted. 'I am second only to Rath'Shadowthrone himself! Do you not know me? Do *they* not know me? I am Marble! Also known as the Malefic! Feared among all the cowering citizens of Capustan! A sorceror of powers unimagined! Yet *they* . . .' He sputtered with fury. 'A boot to the backside, no less! I will have my revenge, this I swear!'

'Ill-advised, priest,' Buke said, not unkindly. 'My employers—'

'Are arrogant scum!'

'That may be, but they're not ones to irritate, sir.'

'*Irritate?* When my master hears of this – this – *insult* delivered to his most valued servant, then, oh then shall the shadows flow!' With a final snarl, the priest stamped down the walkway, black robe skirling dramatically in his wake.

Buke paused for a long moment, watching until the man named Marble disappeared around a corner.

The sound of fighting was on all sides, but getting no closer. Hours earlier, in the deep of the night when Buke had been helping people from the Camps and from Daru District's tenements make their way to the Grey Swords' places of mustering – from which they would be led to the hidden tunnel entrances – the Pannions had reached all the way to the street Buke had just walked. Somehow, Capustan's motley collection of defenders had managed to drive them back. Bodies from both sides littered Kilsban Way.

Buke pushed himself into motion once more, passing beneath the scorched lintel of the entrance with a firm conviction that he would never again leave Bauchelain and Korbal Broach's estate. Even as his steps slowed to a sudden surge of self-preservation, he saw it was too late.

Bauchelain stood in the courtyard. 'Ah, my erstwhile employee. We'd wondered where you'd gone.'

Buke ducked his head. 'My apologies, sir. I'd delivered the tax exemption writ to the Daru civic authorities as requested—'

'Excellent, and was our argument well received?'

The old guard winced. 'The event of siege, alas, offers no relief from property taxes, master. The monies are due. Fortunately, with the evacuation, there is no-one at Daru House to await their arrival.'

'Yes, the evacuation. Tunnels. Very clever. We declined the offer, of course.'

'Of course.' Buke could no longer hold his gaze on the cobbles before him, and found his head turning, lifting slightly to take in the half-score Urdomen bodies lying bloodless, faces mottled black beneath their visors, on all sides.

574

'A precipitous rush of these misguided soldiers,' Bauchelain murmured. 'Korbal was delighted, and makes preparations to recruit them.'

'Recruit them, master? Oh, yes sir. Recruit them.'

The necromancer cocked his head. 'Odd, dear Emancipor Reese uttered those very words, in an identical tone, not half a bell ago.'

'Indeed, master.'

The two regarded each other for a brief span, then Bauchelain stroked his beard and turned away. 'The Tenescowri are coming, did you know? Among them, Children of the Dead Seed. Extraordinary, these children. A dying man's seed . . . Hmm. It's said that the eldest among them now commands the entire peasant horde. I look forward to meeting him.'

'Master? Uh, how, I mean—'

Bauchelain smiled. 'Korbal is most eager to conduct a thorough examination of this child named Anaster. What flavour is his biology? Even I wonder at this.'

The fallen Urdomen lurched, twitched as one, hands clawing towards dropped weapons, helmed heads lifting.

Buke stared in horror.

'Ah, you now have guards to command, Buke. I suggest you have them position themselves at the entrance. And perhaps one to each of the four corner towers. Tireless defenders, the best kind, yes?'

Emancipor Reese, clutching his mangy cat tight against his chest, stumbled out from the main house.

Bauchelain and Buke watched as the old man rushed towards one of the now standing Urdomen. Reese came up to the hulking warrior, reached out and tugged frantically at the undead's chain collar and the jerkin beneath it. The old man's hand reached down beneath both layers, down, down.

Emancipor started gibbering. He pulled his hand clear, staggered back. 'But – but—' His lined, pebbled face swung to Bauchelain. 'That . . . that man, Korbal – he has – he said – I saw! *He has their hearts!* He's sewn them together, a bloody, throbbing mass on the kitchen table! But—' He spun and thumped the Urdomen on the chest. 'No wound!'

Bauchelain raised one thin eyebrow. 'Ah, well, with you and friend Buke here interfering with Korbal Broach's normal nightly activities, my colleague was forced to modify his habits, his modus operandi, if you will. Now, you see, my friends, he has no need to leave his room in order to satisfy his needs of acquisition. None the less, it should be said, please desist in your misguided efforts.' The necromancer's flat grey eyes fixed on Buke. 'And as for the priest Keruli's peculiar sorcery now residing within you, unveil it not, dear servant. We dislike company when in our Soletaken forms.'

Buke's legs came close to giving out beneath him.

'Emancipor,' Bauchelain murmured, 'do lend your shoulder to our guard.'

The old man stepped close. His eyes were so wide that Buke could see white all around them. Sweat beaded his wrinkled face. 'I told you it was madness!' he hissed. 'What did Keruli do to you? Damn you, Buke—'

'Shut up, Mancy,' Buke growled. 'You *knew* they were Soletaken. Yet you said nothing – but Keruli knew as well.'

Bauchelain strode towards the main house, humming under his breath.

Buke twisted and gripped Emancipor's tunic. 'I can *follow* them now! Keruli's gift. I can follow those two anywhere!'

'They'll kill you. They'll swat you down, Buke. You Hood-damned idiot—'

Buke managed a sickly grin. 'Hood-damned? Oh yes, Mancy, we're all that. Aren't we just. Hood-damned, aye.'

A distant, terrible roar interrupted them, a sound that shivered through the city, swept in from all sides.

Emancipor paled. 'The Tenescowri . . .'

But Buke's attention had been drawn to the main building's square tower, to the open shutters of the top, third floor's room. Where two rooks now perched. 'Oh yes,' he muttered, baring his teeth, 'I see you. You're going after him, aren't you? That first child of the Dead Seed. Anaster. You're going after him.'

The rooks dropped from the ledge, wings spreading, swooped low over the compound, then, with heavy, audible flaps, lifted themselves clear of the compound wall. Flying southeast.

Buke pushed Reese away. 'I can follow them! Oh yes. Keruli's sweet gift . . .' *My own Soletaken form, the shape of wings, the air sliding over and beneath me. Gods, the freedom! What I will . . . finds form*—He felt his body veering, sweet warmth filling his limbs, the spice of his skin's breath as it assumed a cloak of feathers. His body dwindling, changing shape. Heavy bones thinning, becoming lighter.

Keruli's sweet gift, more than he ever imagined. Flight! Away from what I was! From all that I had been! Burdens, vanishing! Oh, I can follow those two dread creatures, those winged nightmares. I can follow, and where they strain and lumber on the unseen currents in the sky, I twist, dart, race like lightning!

Standing in the courtyard, Emancipor Reese watched through watering eyes Buke's transformation. A blurring of the man, a drawing inward, the air filling with pungent spice. He watched as the sparrowhawk that had been Buke shot upward in a cavorting climbing spiral.

'Aye,' he muttered. 'You can fly circles around them. But, dear Buke, when they decide to swat you down, it won't be a duel on the wing. It'll be sorcery. Those plodding rooks have no need for speed, no need for agility – and those gifts will avail you nothing when the time comes. Buke . . . you poor fool . . .'

High above Capustan, the sparrowhawk circled. The two rooks, Bauchelain and Korbal Broach, were far below yet perfectly visible to the raptor's eyes. Flapping ponderously through wreaths of smoke, southeast, past the East Gate . . .

The city still burned in places, thrusting columns of black smoke skyward. The sparrowhawk studied the siege from a point of view that the world's generals would die for. Wheeling, circling, watching.

The Tenescowri ringed the city in a thick, seething band. A third of a million, maybe more. Such a mass of people as Buke had never seen before. And the band had begun to constrict. A strangely colourless, writhing noose, drawing ever closer to the city's feeble, crumbled walls and what seemed but a handful of defenders.

There would be no stopping this assault. An army measured not by bravery, but by something far deadlier, something unopposable: hunger. An army that could not afford to break, that saw only wasting death in retreat.

Capustan was about to be devoured.

The Pannion Seer is a monster in truth. A tyranny of need. And this will spread. Defeat him? You would have to kill every man, woman and child on this world who are bowed to hunger, everyone who faces starvation's grisly grin. It has begun here, on Genabackis, but that is simply the heart. This tide will spread. It will infect every city, on every continent, it will devour empires and nations from within.

I see you now, Seer. From this height. I understand what you are, and what you will become. We are lost. We are all truly lost.

His thoughts were scattered by a virulent bloom of sorcery to the east. A knot of familiar magic swirled around a small section of the Tenescowri army. Black waves shot through with sickly purple streamed outward, cut down screaming peasants by the hundreds. Grey-streaming sorcery answered.

The sparrowhawk's eyes saw the twin corbies now, there, in the midst of the magical storm. Demons burst from torn portals on the plain, tore mayhem through the shrieking, flinching ranks. Sorcery lashed back, swarmed over the creatures.

The two rooks swept down, converged on a figure sitting on a bucking roan horse. Waves of magic collided with a midnight flash, the concussion a thunder that reached up to where Buke circled.

578

The sparrowhawk's beak opened, loosing a piercing cry. The rooks had peeled away. Sorcery hammered them, battered them as they flapped in hasty retreat.

The figure on the stamping horse was untouched. Surrounded by heaps of bodies, into which fellow Tenescowri now plunged. To feed.

Buke screamed another triumphant cry, dipped his wings, plummeted earthward.

He reached the estate's courtyard well ahead of Bauchelain and Korbal Broach, spiralling, slowing, wings buffeting the air. To hover the briefest of moments, before sembling, returning to his human form.

Emancipor Reese was nowhere to be seen. The undead Urdomen still stood in the positions where they had first arisen.

Feeling heavy and awkward in his body, Buke turned to study them. 'Six of you to the gate – you' – he pointed – 'and the ones directly behind you. And you, to the northwest tower.' He continued directing the silent warriors, placing them as Bauchelain had suggested. As he barked the last order, twin shadows tracked weaving paths across the cobbles. The rooks landed in the courtyard. Their feathers were in tatters. Smoke rose from one of them.

Buke watched the sembling, smiled at seeing, first Korbal Broach – his armour in shreds, rank tendrils of smoke wreathed around him – then Bauchelain, his pale face bruised along one side of his long jaw, blood crusting his moustache and staining his silver beard.

Korbal Broach reached up to the collar of his cloak, his pudgy, soft hands trembling, fumbling at the clasp. The black leather fell to the ground. He began stamping on it to kill the last of its smouldering patches.

Brushing dust from his arms, Bauchelain glanced over at Buke. 'Patient of you, to await our return.'

Wiping the smile from his lips, Buke shrugged. 'You didn't get him. What happened?'

'It seems,' the necromancer muttered, 'we must needs refine our tactics.'

The instinct of self-preservation vanished, then, as Buke softly laughed.

Bauchelain froze. One eyebrow arched. Then he sighed. 'Yes, well. Good day to you, too, Buke.'

Buke watched him head inside.

Korbal Broach continued stomping on his cloak long after the smouldering patches had been extinguished.

CHAPTER FIFTEEN

In my dreams I come face to face
with myriad reflections of myself,
all unknown and passing strange.
They speak unending
in languages not my own
and walk with companions
I have never met, in places
my steps have never gone.

In my dreams I walk worlds
where forests crowd my knees
and half the sky is walled ice.
Dun herds flow like mud,
vast floods tusked and horned
surging over the plain,
and lo, they are my memories,
the migrations of my soul.

In the Time before Night
D'arayans of the Rhivi

Whiskeyjack rose in the saddle as his horse leapt over the spiny ridge of outcroppings cresting the hill. Hooves thumped as the creature resumed its gallop, crossing the mesa's flat top, then slowing as the Malazan tautened the reins and settled back in the saddle. At a diminishing canter, he approached the summit's far side, then drew up at its edge.

A rumpled, boulder-strewn slope led down into a broad, dry riverbed. At its base two 2nd Army scouts sat on their horses, backs to Whiskeyjack. Before them, a dozen Rhivi were moving on foot through what seemed to be a field of bones.

Huge bones.

Clicking his mount into motion, Whiskeyjack slowly worked it down onto the ancient slide. His eyes held on the scatter of bones. Massive iron blades glinted there, as well as crumpled, oddly shaped armour and helmets. He saw long, reptilian jaws, rows of jagged teeth. Clinging to some of the shattered skeletons, the remnants of grey skin.

Clearing the scree, Whiskeyjack rode up to the nearest scout.

The man saluted. 'Sir. The Rhivi are jabbering away – can't quite follow what they're talking about. Looks to have been about ten of the demons. Whatever tore into them was nasty. Might be the Rhivi have gleaned more, since they're crawling around among the corpses.'

Nodding, Whiskeyjack dismounted. 'Keep an eye out,' he said, though he knew the scouts were doing just that, but feeling the need to say something. The killing field exuded an air of dread, old yet new, and – even more alarming – it held the peculiar tension that immediately followed a battle. *Thick silence, swirling as if not yet settled by the sounds of violence, as if somehow still trembling, still - shivering . . .*

He approached the Rhivi and the sprawl of bones.

The tribal scouts were indeed jabbering.

'Dead wolves . . .'

'Twice tracks, the touches heavy yet light, wider than my hand. Big.'

'Big dead wolves.'

'No blood, agreed? Barrow stench.'

'Black stone dust. Sharp.'

'Glittering beneath forearms – the skin . . .'

'Black glass fragments.'

'Obsidian. Far south . . .'

'Southwest. Or far north, beyond Laederon Plateau.'

'No, I see no red or brown. Laederon obsidian has wood-coloured veins. This is Morn.'

'If of this world . . .'

'The demons are *here*, are they not? Of this world. *In* this world.'

'Barrow stench.'

'Yet in the air, ice stench, tundra wind, the smell of frozen peat.'

'The wake of the wolves, the killers—'

Whiskeyjack growled, 'Rhivi scouts, attend to me, please.'

Heads lifted, faces turned. Silence.

'I will hear your report, now. Which of you commands this troop?'

Looks were exchanged, then one shrugged. 'I can speak this Daru you use. Better than the others. So, for this that you ask, me.'

'Very well. Proceed.'

The young Rhivi swept back the braided strands of his grease-laden hair, then waved expansively at the bones around them. 'Undead demons. Armoured, with swords instead of hands. Coming from the southeast, more east than south.' He made an exaggerated frown. 'Damaged. Pursued. Hunted. Fleeing. Driven like bhederin, this way and that, loping, silent followers four-legged and patient—'

'Big undead wolves,' Whiskeyjack cut in.

'Twice as big as the native wolves of this plain. Yes.' Then his expression cleared as if with revelation. 'They are like the ghost-runners of our legends. When the eldest shouldermen or women dream their farthest dreams, the wolves are seen. Never close, always running, all ghostly except the one who leads, who seems as flesh and has eyes of life. To see them is great fortune, glad tiding, for there is joy in their running.'

'Only they're no longer running just in the dreams of your witches and warlocks,' Whiskeyjack said. 'And this run was far deadlier.'

'Hunting. I said these wolves are *like* those in the dreams. I did not say they were those in the dreams.' His expression went blank, his eyes the eyes of a cold killer. 'Hunting. Driving their quarry, down to this, their trap. Then they destroyed them. A battle of undead. The demons are from barrows far to the south. The wolves are from the dust in the north winds of winter.'

'Thank you,' Whiskeyjack said. The Rhivi manner of narrative – the dramatic performance – had well conveyed the events this valley had witnessed.

More riders were approaching from the main column, and he turned to watch them.

Three. Korlat, Silverfox, and the Daru, Kruppe, the latter bobbing and weaving on his mule as it raced with stiff, short-legged urgency in the wake of the two horse-riding women. His cries of alarm echoed in the narrow valley.

'Yes.'

The commander swung round, eyes narrowing on the Rhivi scoutleader who, along with all his kin, was now studying the three riders. 'Excuse me?'

The Rhivi shrugged, expressionless, and said nothing.

The scree of boulders had forced the newcomers to slow, except for Kruppe who was thrown forward then back on his saddle as the mule pitched headlong down the slope. Somehow the beast kept its footing, plummeting past a startled Korlat and a laughing Silverfox, then, reaching the flat, slowing its wild charge and trotting up to where Whiskeyjack stood, its head lifted proudly, ears up and forward-facing.

Kruppe, on the other hand, remained hugging the animal's neck, eyes squeezed shut, face crimson and streaming sweat. 'Terror!' he moaned. 'Battle of wills, Kruppe has met his match in this brainless, delusional beast! Aye, he is defeated! Oh, spare me . . .'

584

The mule halted.

'You can climb off, now,' Whiskeyjack said.

Kruppe opened his eyes, looked around, then slowly sat straight. He shakily withdrew a handkerchief. 'Naturally. Having given the creature its head, Kruppe now reacquires the facility of his own.' Pausing a moment to pat his brow and daub his face, he then wormed off the saddle and settled to the ground with a loud sigh. 'Ah, here come Kruppe's lazy dust-eaters. Delighted you could make it, dear ladies! A fine afternoon for a trot, yes?'

Silverfox had stopped laughing, her veiled eyes now on the scattered bones.

Hood take me, that fur cloak becomes her indeed. Mentally shaking himself, Whiskeyjack glanced up to meet Korlat's steady, faintly ironic gaze. *But oh, she pales beside this Tiste Andii. Dammit, old man, think not of the nights past. Do not embrace this wonder so tightly you crush the life from it.*

'The scouts,' he said to both women, 'have come upon a scene of battle—'

'K'Chain Che'Malle,' Korlat nodded, eyeing the bones. 'K'ell Hunters, fortunately undead rather than enlivened flesh. Likely not as fast as they would have been. Still, to have been torn apart in such fashion—'

'T'lan Ay,' Silverfox said. 'They are why I have come.'

Whiskeyjack studied her. 'What do you mean?'

She shrugged. 'To see for myself, Commander. We are all drawing close. You to your besieged city, and I to the destiny to which I was born. Convergence, the plague of this world. Even so,' she added as she swung down from the saddle and strode among the bones, 'there are gifts. Dearest of such gifts . . . the T'lan Ay.' She paused, the wind caressing the fox fur on her shoulders, then whispered the name once more. 'T'lan Ay.'

'Kruppe shivers when she so names them, ah . . . gods bless this grim beauty in its barrenland tableau, from which starry dreams so dimmed with time are as rainbow rivers in the sky!' He paused, blinked at the others. 'Sweet sleep, in

585

which hidden poetry resides, the flow of the disconnected, so smooth as to seem entwined. Yes?'

'I'm not the man,' Whiskeyjack growled, 'to appreciate your abstractions, Kruppe, alas.'

'Of course, blunt soldier, as you say! But wait, does Kruppe see in your eyes a certain ... charge? The air veritably crackles with imminence – do you deny your sensitivity to that, Malazan? No, say nothing, the truth resides in your hard gaze and your gauntleted hand where it edges closer to the grip of your sword.'

Whiskeyjack could not deny the hairs rising on the back of his neck. He looked around, saw a similar alertness among the Rhivi, and in the pair of Malazan scouts who were scanning the hill-lines on all sides.

'What comes?' Korlat whispered.

'The gift,' Kruppe murmured with a beatific smile as he rested his eyes upon Silverfox.

Whiskeyjack followed the Daru's gaze.

To see the woman, so much like Tattersail, standing with her back to them, arms raised high.

Dust began swirling, rising in eddies on all sides.

The T'lan Ay took form, in the basin, on the slopes and the crests of the surrounding hills.

In their thousands ...

Grey dust into grey, matted fur, black shoulders, throats the hue of rain clouds, thick tails silver and black-tipped; while others were brown, the colour of rotted, powdered wood, faded to tan at throat and belly. Wolves, tall, gaunt, their eyes shadowed pits. Huge, long heads were turned, one and all, to Silverfox.

She glanced over a shoulder, her heavy-lidded eyes fixing on Whiskeyjack. She smiled. 'My escort.'

The commander, struck silent, stared at her. *So like Tattersail. Yet not. Escort, she says, but I see more – and her look tells me she is aware ... so very aware, now.*

Escort ... and bodyguard. Silverfox may no longer require us. And, now that her need for our protection has passed, she is free to do . . . whatever she pleases . . .

A cold wind seemed to rattle through Whiskeyjack's mind. *Gods, what if Kallor was right all along? What if we've all missed our chance?* With a soft grunt, he shook off the unworthy thoughts. *No, we have shown our faith in her, when it mattered most – when she was at her weakest. Tattersail would not forget that . . .*

So like . . . yet not. Nightchill, dismembered by betrayal. Is it Tayschrenn her remnant soul hates? Or the Malazan Empire and every son and daughter of its blood? Or the one she had been called upon to battle: Anomander Rake, and by extension Caladan Brood? The Rhivi, the Barghast . . . does she seek vengeance against them?

Kruppe cleared his throat. 'And a lovely escort they are, my dear lass. Alarming to your enemies, reassuring to your loyal friends! We are charmed, for we can see that you are as well, so very deeply charmed by these silent, motionless T'lan Ay. Such well-behaved pups, Kruppe is impressed beyond words, beyond gestures, beyond suitable response entire!'

'If only,' Korlat murmured, 'that were the case.' She faced Whiskeyjack, her expression closed and professional. 'Commander, I will take my leave now to report to our leaders—'

'Korlat,' Silverfox interrupted, 'forgive me for not asking earlier, but when did you last look upon my mother?'

'This morning,' the Tiste Andii replied. 'She can no longer walk, and this has been her condition for almost a week now. She weakens by the day, Silverfox. Perhaps if you were to come and see her . . .'

'There is no need for that,' the fur-cloaked woman said. 'Who attends her at this moment?'

'Councillor Coll and the Daru man, Murillio.'

'Kruppe's most loyal friends, Kruppe assures you all. She is safe enough.'

'Circumstances,' Silverfox said, her expression tight, 'are about to grow . . . tense.'

587

And what has it been till now, woman? Kallor haunts your shadow like a vulture – I'm surprised he let you get away just now . . . unless he's lurking about on the other side of the nearest hill . . .

'Do you ask something of me, Silverfox?' Korlat enquired.

She visibly gathered herself. 'Aye, some of your kin, to guard my mother.'

The Tiste Andii frowned. 'It would seem, with your new guardians in such number, that you have some to spare—'

'She would not let their approach her, I'm afraid. She has . . . nightmares. I am sorry, but I must ensure my T'lan Ay are kept out of her sight, and senses. She may look frail and seem powerless, but there is that within her that is capable of driving the T'lan Ay away. Will you do as I ask?'

'Of course, Silverfox.'

The woman nodded, attention shifting once more back to Whiskeyjack as Korlat wheeled her mount and rode back up the slope. She studied him in silence for a moment, then looked to Kruppe. 'Well, Daru? Are you satisfied thus far?'

'I am, dearest one.' Not Kruppe's usual tone, but spoken low, measured.

Satisfied. With what?

'Will she hold on, do you think?'

Kruppe shrugged. 'We shall see, yes? Kruppe has faith.'

'Enough for both of us?'

The Daru smiled. 'Naturally.'

Silverfox sighed. 'Very well. I lean heavily on you in this, you know.'

'Kruppe's legs are as pillars of stone. Your touch is so light as to pass unnoticed by worthy self. My dear, the sound of additional riders urges upon you a decision – what will you permit to be seen by those who now approach?'

'Nothing untoward,' the woman replied. She raised her arms again.

The T'lan Ay returned to the dust from which they had arisen.

With a soft grunt, Whiskeyjack strode back to his horse. There were too many mysteries roiling through the company of the two armies, secrets that seemed to hold promises of explosive revelation. *Probably violent ones at that.* He felt uneasy. *I wish Quick Ben was here . . . Hood knows, I wish I knew what was happening with him, and Paran and the Bridgeburners. Did they succeed? Or are they all now dead, their skulls surmounting poles around the Barghast camps?*

A substantial part of the column's vanguard reached the hill's crest, where they halted in a ragged line.

Whiskeyjack swung himself into the saddle and made his way towards the group.

Kallor, riding a gaunt, grey horse, had deliberately drawn rein apart from the others. His faded grey cloak was tight about his broad, armoured shoulders. Shadows deepened the lines of his ancient, weathered face. Long strands of his grey hair drifted to one side in the wind.

Whiskeyjack's gaze held on the man a moment longer, gauging, then shifted to the others lining the ridge. Brood and Dujek were side by side. On the warlord's right was the outrider, Hurlochel; on the Malazan's left, the standard-bearer, Artanthos. The Trygalle Trade Guild's merchant-mage, Haradas, was also present, and, of course, Korlat.

None were speaking as Whiskeyjack's horse reached the crest. Then Dujek nodded and growled, 'Korlat's described what the scouts found. Anything else to add?'

Whiskeyjack glanced at the Tiste Andii, but her expression was closed. He shook his head. 'No, High Fist. Korlat and her kin seem to know more about these K'Chain Che'Malle than the rest of us – what lies below are a jumble of shattered bones, some weapons and armour. I could not have identified them myself. The Rhivi scouts believe they were undead—'

'Fortunate for us all,' muttered Kallor. 'I am not so ignorant of these creatures as the rest of you, barring Korlat. Further, I am feeling unusually . . . loquacious. Thus.

Remnants of the K'Chain Che'Malle civilization can be found on virtually every continent on this world. Indeed, in the place of my old empire, Jacuruku, their strange mechanisms filled pits and holes in the earth – whenever my people had to cut below the surface, they discovered such constructs. More, barrows were found. Scholars conducted careful examination of their contents. Do you wish to hear an account of their conclusions or am I boring you?'

'Go on,' Caladan drawled.

'Very well. Perhaps there is more wisdom present here than I had previously credited. The beasts appear to be reptilian, capable of breeding their own kind to specific talents. Those the Tiste Andii called K'ell Hunters, for example, were born as warriors. Undead versions are in the valley below, yes? They had no hands, but swords in their stead, somehow melded to the very bones of their forearms. The K'Chain Che'Malle were matriarchal, matrilineal. As a population of bees have their queen, so too these beasts. She is the breeder, the mother of every child. And within this Matron resided the sorcerous capacity of her entire family. Power to beggar the gods of today. Power to keep the Elder Gods from coming to this world, and were it not for the self-destruction of the K'Chain Che'Malle, they would rule unchallenged to this day.'

'Self-destruction,' Korlat said, a sharpness in her eyes as she studied Kallor. 'An interesting detail. Can you explain?'

'Of course. Among the records found, once the language was deciphered – and that effort alone is worthy of lengthy monologue, but seeing how you all shift about in your saddles like impatient children, I'll spare the telling. Among the records found, then, it was learned that the Matrons, each commanding the equivalent of a modern city, had gathered to meld their disparate ambitions. What they sought, beyond the vast power they already possessed, is not entirely clear. Then again, what need there be for reasons when ambition rules? Suffice to say, an ancient breed was . . . resurrected, returned from extinction by the

590

Matrons; a more primitive version of the K'Chain Che'Malle themselves. For lack of a better name, my scholars at the time called them Short-Tails.'

Whiskeyjack, his eyes on Korlat, was the only one to see her stiffen at that. Behind him, he could hear Silverfox and Kruppe making their way back up the slope.

'For the singular reason,' Kallor went on in his dry monotone, 'that they physically deviated from the other K'Chain Che'Malle in having short, stubby tails rather than the normal, long, tapered ones. This made them not as swift – more upright, suited to whatever world and civilization they had originally belonged to. Alas, these new children were not as tractable as the Matrons were conditioned to expect among their brood – more explicitly, the Short-Tails would not surrender or merge their magical talents with their mothers'. The result was a civil war, and the sorceries unleashed were apocalyptic. To gauge something of the desperation among the Matrons, one need only travel south on this continent, to a place called Morn.'

'The Rent,' Korlat murmured, nodding.

Kallor's smile was wintry. 'She sought to harness the power of a gate itself, but not simply a common warren's gate. Oh no, she elected to open the portal that led to the Realm of Chaos. Such hubris, to think she could control – could assert *order* – upon such a thing.' He paused, as if reconsidering his own words, then laughed. 'Oh, a bitter lesson or two in that tale, don't you think?'

Caladan Brood grunted. 'Let's bring this back to the present, shall we? In the valley below, undead K'ell Hunters. The question to address is: what are they doing here?'

'They are being used.'

Everyone's eyes fixed on Silverfox, who stood before her horse, reins in hand.

'I like not the sound of that,' Dujek growled.

'Used,' Silverfox repeated, 'by the Pannion Seer.'

'Impossible,' Kallor snapped. 'Only a K'Chain Che'Malle Matron could command a Ke'll Hunter – even when *undead*.'

'Then it would appear,' Korlat said, 'that we have more than one enemy.'

'The Pannion Seer has an ally?' Dujek leaned on his saddle and spat. 'There's not been even so much as a hint—'

'None the less,' Silverfox cut in. 'Proof lies before us, in the valley below.'

'A Matron cannot breed more of her kind without the seed of living males,' Kallor said. 'Therefore, with each K'ell Hunter destroyed, there is one less for us to deal with.'

Brood turned at that, eyes thinning to slits. 'Easily swallowed, this revelation.'

Kallor shrugged.

'There is also before us,' the warlord continued, 'another truth. Regarding the destruction of the K'ell Hunters, someone is doing it for us, it seems.'

Silence; then, slowly, attention focused on Silverfox.

She smiled. 'I did say, some time ago, that you would all need help.'

Kallor snarled. 'T'lan Imass! So tell us, bitch, why would they concern themselves with K'Chain Che'Malle? Are not the *Jaghut* their avowed enemies? Why task your undead followers with a new one? *Why have you and the T'lan Imass joined this war, woman?*'

'We have joined nothing,' she replied, her eyes heavy-lidded, standing as Tattersail would stand, hands clasped and resting on the folds of her belly, her body solid yet curvaceous beneath her deerhide tunic.

Ah, I know that look. Sleight of hand. Careful, now . . .

'Do you deny, then,' Brood began slowly, his expression clouded, uncertain, 'that your T'lan Imass were responsible for destroying these K'ell Hunters?'

'Have none of you ever wondered,' Silverfox said, looking at each of them, 'why the T'lan Imass warred with the Jaghut?'

'Perhaps an explanation,' Dujek said, 'will assist us in

592

understanding.'

Silverfox gave a sharp nod. 'When the first Imass emerged, they were forced to live in the shadow of the Jaghut. Tolerated, ignored, but only in small, manageable numbers. Pushed to the poorest of lands. Then Tyrants arose among the Jaghut, who found pleasure in enslaving them, in forcing upon them a nightmarish existence – that successive generations were born into and so knew of no other life, knew nothing of freedom itself.

'The lesson was hard, not easily swallowed, for the truth was this: there were intelligent beings in the world who exploited the virtues of others, their compassion, their love, their faith in kin. Exploited, and mocked. How many Imass tribes discovered that their gods were in fact Jaghut Tyrants? Hidden behind friendly masks. Tyrants, who manipulated them with the weapon of faith.

'The rebellion was inevitable, and it was devastating for the Imass. Weaker, uncertain even of what it was they sought, or what freedom would show them should they find it . . . But we would not relent. We could not.'

Kallor sneered. 'There were never more than but a handful of Tyrants among the Jaghut, woman.'

'A handful was too many, and aye, we found allies among the Jaghut – those for whom the activities of the Tyrants were reprehensible. But we now carried scars. Scars born of mistrust, of betrayal. We could trust only in our own kind. In the name of our generations to come, all Jaghut would have to die. None could be left, to produce more children, to permit among those children the rise of new Tyrants.'

'And how,' Korlat asked, 'does this relate to the K'Chain Che'Malle?'

'Before the Jaghut ruled this world, the K'Chain Che'Malle ruled. The first Jaghut were to the K'Chain Che'Malle as the first Imass were to the Jaghut.' She paused, her heavy gaze moving among them all. 'In each species is born the seeds of domination. Our wars with the Jaghut destroyed us, as a living people, as a vibrant, evolving culture. That was the price *we* paid, to ensure the freedom *you* now possess. Our eternal sacrifice.' She fell silent once more, then continued in a harder tone, 'So, now, I ask you – all of you, who have taken upon yourselves the task of waging war against a tyrannical, all-devouring empire, of possibly sacrificing your own lives to the benefit of peoples who know nothing of you, of lands you have never and will never set foot upon – I ask you, what is there about us, about the T'lan Imass, that still escapes your understanding? Destroy the Pannion Domin. It must be done. For me, for my T'lan Imass, awaits the task of destroying the threat hiding *behind* the Pannion Seer, the threat that is the K'Chain Che'Malle.'

She slowly studied their faces. 'A Matron lives. Flesh and blood. Should she find a male of her kind, a flesh and blood male ... the tyranny of the Jaghut will be as nothing to that of the K'Chain Che'Malle. This, then, will be *our* sacrifice.'

Only the wind filled the silence following her words.

Then Caladan Brood turned to Kallor. 'And you find in this woman an abomination?'

'She lies,' he rasped in reply. 'This entire war is meaningless. Nothing more than a feint.'

'A feint?' Dujek repeated in disbelief. 'By whom?'

Kallor snapped his mouth shut, made no reply.

The Trygalle Trade Guild merchant-mage, Haradas, cleared her throat. 'There may be some truth in that. Not that the woman Silverfox is lying – I believe she speaks true, as far as she is willing to tell us. No, I meant the feint. Consider the infection of the warrens. Granted, its focus seems to emanate from the Pannion Domin, and granted, as well, that the poison's taint is that of the Warren of Chaos. Granted all of that, one must then ask: why would a K'Chain Che'Malle Matron, who is the repository of a vast wellspring of sorcery, seek to destroy the very conduits of her power? If she was present when Morn was destroyed – when the Rent was created – why would she then try to

594

harness chaos *again*? Ambitious, perhaps, but a fool? That is hard to countenance.'

Even as the import of her words sank in to Whiskeyjack, there came to him another realization. *There is another enemy indeed, and from the looks on most of the faces around me – barring Dujek and, no doubt, my own – the revelation is not as surprising as it should be. True, we'd caught a hint, but we'd failed to make the connection. Brood, Korlat, Kallor – gods, even Kruppe and Artanthos! Remind me to avoid every damn one of them the next time I join a game of bones!* He jerked his gaze back to Silverfox, was met with that sleepy, knowing regard.

No, that won't work again. 'Silverfox,' he growled. 'You spin a tale to sting sympathy from our hearts, yet it seems that your effort was misdirected, and so you end up undermining all you sought to achieve. If there is a deeper threat, a *third* hand, deftly manipulating both us and the Pannion Seer ... will you and your T'lan Imass then focus your attention on that hand?'

'No.'

'Why?'

He was surprised as her steady gaze wavered, then fell away. Her voice came out in a raw whisper. 'Because, Whiskeyjack, you ask too much of us.'

No-one spoke.

Dread swept through Whiskeyjack. He swung about, locked gazes with Dujek, saw in the old man's face a mirror to his own growing horror. *Gods below, we are heading to our deaths. An unseen enemy – but one we've known about for a long time, one we knew was coming, sooner or later, one that – by the Abyss – makes the T'lan Imass recoil . . .*

'Such palpable distraughtness!' Kruppe cried. 'Distraughtness? Is there such a word? If not, then among Kruppe's countless talents we must add linguistic invention! My friends! Attend! Hark! Listen! Take heart, one and all, in the knowledge that Kruppe has placed himself, feet square and ample girth firm, in the path of said

– yet unmentioned – formidable enemy of all existence! Sleep calm at night in this knowledge. Slumber as babes in your mother's arms, as each of you once did – even Kallor, though the image shocks and dismays—'

'Dammit!' Caladan Brood roared, 'what in Hood's name are you talking about, little man? You claim to stand in the path of the *Crippled God*? By the Abyss, you are mad! If you do not,' he continued in a low tone as he swung down from his horse, 'give instant proof of your efficacy' – he strode towards Kruppe, one hand reaching for the wrapped handle of his hammer – 'I will not predict the extremity of my temper.'

'I wouldn't do that, Brood,' Silverfox murmured.

The warlord twisted to face her, teeth bared. 'You now extend your protection to this arrogant, fat toad?'

Her eyes widened and she looked to the Daru. 'Kruppe, do you make such a request?'

'Absurd! No offence, dear, in that expostulation, Kruppe sweetly assures you!'

Whiskeyjack stared, disbelieving, as the round little man in his food- and drink-stained clothes drew himself up as straight as he was able and fixed small, glittering eyes on Caladan Brood. 'Threaten Kruppe of Darujhistan, will you? Demand an explanation, do you? Fondling that hammer, are you? Baring those fa—'

'Silence!' the warlord bellowed, struggling to control his anger.

Gods below, what is Kruppe up to?

'Kruppe defies all threats! Kruppe sneers at whatever demonstration bristling warlord would attempt—'

The hammer was suddenly in Brood's hands, a smudged blur as it swung through the air, a downward arc, to strike the earth almost at Kruppe's feet.

The detonation threw horses down, sent Whiskeyjack and the others flying. A thunderous concussion cracked the air. The ground seemed to leap up to meet the Malazan commander, the impact like a fist when he struck, rolled, then tumbled his way down the boulder-strewn slope.

Above him, horses were screaming. A wind, hot, shrieking, shot dust and earth skyward.

The scree of boulders was moving beneath Whiskeyjack, flowing, sliding down into the valley at an ever quickening pace with a rumbling, growing roar. Rocks clanged against his armour, rapped into the helm on his head, leaving him stunned. He caught a flashing glimpse, through a jagged tear in the dustcloud, of the line of hills on the other side the valley. Impossibly, they were rising, fast, the bedrock splitting the grassy hide, loosing gouts of dust, rock-shards and smoke. Then the swarming dust swallowed the world around him. Boulders bounced over him, tumbling. Others struck him solid, painful blows that left him gasping, coughing, choking as he rolled.

Even now, the ground continued to heave beneath the sliding scree. Distant detonations shook the air, trembled through Whiskeyjack's battered bones.

He came to a rest, half buried in gravel and rocks. Blinking, eyes burning, he saw before him the Rhivi scouts – dodging, leaping from the path of bounding boulders as if in some bizarre, deadly game. Beyond, black, steaming bedrock towered, the spine of a new mountain range, still growing, still rising, lifting and tilting the floor of the valley where the Malazan now lay. The sky behind it churned iron-grey with steam and smoke.

Hood take me ... poor Kruppe... Groaning, Whiskeyjack twisted round as far as he could. He was covered in scrapes, could feel the tender birth of huge bruises beneath his dented, torn armour, but his bones were, amazingly, intact. He strained his watering eyes to the hilltop behind him.

The scree was gone, leaving a gaping, raw cliff-face. Most of the mesa's summit was simply no longer there, obliterated, leaving a small, flat-topped island ... where Whiskeyjack now saw figures moving, rising. Horses scrambling upright. Faintly, came the brazen complaint of a mule.

To the north, cutting a path down along the side of a distant valley, then through distant hills, a narrow, steaming crack was visible, a fissure in the earth that seemed depthless.

Whiskeyjack painfully pulled himself clear of the rubble, slowly straightened.

He saw Caladan Brood, hammer hanging down from his hands, motionless . . . and standing before the warlord, on an island of his own, was Kruppe. Brushing dust from his clothes. The crack that had been born where the hammer had struck the earth, parted neatly around the short, fat Daru, joining again just behind him.

Whiskeyjack struggled to hold back a laugh, knowing how desperate, how jarring it would sound. *So, we have seen Brood's fury. And Kruppe, that preposterous little man, has stood it down. Well, if proof was ever needed that the Daru was not as he appeared to be . . .* He then frowned. *A demonstration indeed – directed towards whom, I wonder?*

A cry of dismay cut through his thoughts.

Korlat. She faced north, her posture somehow contracted, drawn in on itself.

The fissure, Whiskeyjack now saw – all amusement gone – was filling with blood.

Fouled blood, rotten blood. Beru fend, the Sleeping Goddess . . . Burn sleeps the sleep of the dying, the poisoned. And this, he realized, was the day's final, most terrible revelation. *Diseased . . . the hidden hand of the Crippled God . . .*

The Mhybe's eyes snapped open. The wagon rocked and pitched. Thunder shook the ground. The shouts of Rhivi were on all sides, a wailing chorus of alarm and consternation. Her bones and muscles protested as she was thrown about in the cataclysm, but she would not cry out. She wanted only to hide.

The rumbling faded, replaced by the distant lowing of the bhederin and, closer by, the soft footpads of her kin as they rushed past the wagon. The herd was close to panic, and a stampede was imminent.

Bringing ruin to us all. Yet that would be a mercy. An end to the pain, to my nightmares . . .

In her dreams she was young once more, but those dreams held no joy. Strangers walked the tundra landscape where she invariably found herself. They approached. She fled. Darting like a snow hare. Running, always running.

Strangers. She did not know what they wanted, but they were seeking her – that much was clear. Tracking her, like hunters their quarry. To sleep was to awaken exhausted, limbs trembling, chest heaving with agonized breaths.

She had been saved from the Abyss, from those countless tattered souls lost in eternal, desperate hunger. Saved, by a dragon. *To what end? Leaving me in a place where I am hunted, pursued without surcease?*

Time passed, punctuated by the herders' calming words to the frightened bhederin. There would be no stampede after all. Rumbles still trembled through the earth, in diminishing ripples that grew ever farther apart.

The Mhybe moaned softly to herself as the wagon rocked once more, this time to the arrival of the two Daru, Coll and Murillio.

'You've awakened,' the councillor noted. 'It's no surprise.'

'Leave me be,' she said, drawing the hides around her shivering body and curling away from the two men. *It's so cold . . .*

'Any idea what's happened up ahead?' Murillio asked Coll.

'Seems Brood lost his temper.'

'Gods! With whom? Kallor? That bastard deserves—'

'Not Kallor, friend,' Coll growled. 'Make another guess – shouldn't take you long.'

Murillio groaned. 'Kruppe.'

'Hood knows he's stretched the patience of all of us at one time or another . . . only none of us was capable of splitting apart half the world and throwing new mountains skyward.'

'Did the little runt get himself killed? I can't believe—'

'Word is, he's come out unscathed. Typically. Complaining of the dust. No-one else was injured, either, though the warlord himself almost got his head kicked in by an angry mule.'

'Kruppe's mule? The one that sleeps when it walks?'

'Aye, the very one.'

Sleeps. Dreams of being a horse, no doubt. Magnificent, tall, fierce . . .

'That beast is a strange one, indeed. Never seen a mule so . . . so watchful. Of everything. Queen of Dreams, that's the oddest looking range of mountains I've ever seen!'

'Aye, Murillio, it *does* look bigger than it really is. Twists the eye. A broken spine, like something you'd see at the very horizon, yet there it is, not half a league from us. Doesn't bear thinking about, if you ask me . . .'

Nothing bears thinking about. Not mountains, not mules, not Brood's temper. Souls crowd my daughter, there, within her. Two women, and a Thelomen named Skullcrusher. Two women and a man whom I've never met . . . yet I carried that child within me. I, a Rhivi, young, in the bloom of my life, drawn into a dream then the dream made real. Yet where, within my daughter, am I? Where is the blood, the heart, of the Rhivi?

She has nothing of me, nothing at all. Naught but a vessel in truth – that is all I was – a vessel to hold then birth into the world a stranger.

She has no reason to see me, to visit, to take my hand and offer me comfort. My purpose is done, over. And here I lie, a discarded thing. Forgotten. A mhybe.

A hand settled gently on her shoulder.

Murillio spoke. 'I think she sleeps once more.'

'For the best,' Coll murmured.

'I remember my own youth,' the Daru went on in a quiet, introspective tone.

'I remember your own youth, too, Murillio.'

'Wild and wasteful—'

'A different widow every night, as I recall.'

'I was a lodestone indeed, and, you know, it was all so effortless—'

'We'd noticed.'

The man sighed. 'But no longer. I've aged, paid the price for my younger days—'

'Nights, you mean.'

'Whatever. New rivals have arrived. Young bloods. Marak of Paxto, tall and lithe and turning heads wherever he saunters. The smug bastard. Then there's Perryl of M'necrae—'

'Oh, really, Murillio, spare me all this.'

'The point is, it was all a stretch of years. Full years. Pleasurable ones. And, for all that I'm on the wane, at least I can look back and recall my days – all right, my *nights* – of glory. But here, with this poor woman . . .'

'Aye, I hear you. Ever notice those copper ornaments she's wearing – there, you can see the pair on her wrist. Kruppe's gifts, from Darujhistan.'

'What about them?'

'Well, as I was saying. Ever noticed them? It's a strange thing. They get brighter, shinier, when she's sleeping.'

'Do they?'

'I'd swear it on a stack of Kruppe's handkerchiefs.'

'How odd.'

'They're kind of dull right now, though . . .'

There was silence from the two men crouched above her. After a long moment the hand resting on her shoulder squeezed slightly.

'Ah, my dear,' Murillio whispered, 'would that I could take back my words . . .'

Why? They were truth. Words from your heart, and it is a generous one for all your irresponsible youth. You've given voice to my curse. That changes nothing. Am I to be pitied? Only when I'm asleep, it seems. To my face, you say nothing, and consider your silence a kindness. But it mocks me, for it arrives as indifference.

And this silence of mine? To these two kind men looking down on me right now? Which of my countless flaws does this reveal?

Your pity, it seems, is no match for my own.

Her thoughts trailed away, then. The treeless, ochre wasteland of her dreamworld appeared. And she within it.

She began running.

Dujek flung his gauntlets against the tent wall as he entered, his face dark with fury.

Whiskeyjack unstoppered the jug of ale and filled the two goblets waiting on the small camp table before him. Both men were smeared in sweaty dust.

'What madness is this?' the High Fist rasped, pausing only long enough to snatch up one of the goblets before beginning to pace.

Whiskeyjack stretched his battered legs out, the chair creaking beneath him. He swallowed a long draught of ale, sighed and said, 'Which madness are you referring to, Dujek?'

'Aye, the list is getting damned long. The Crippled God! The ugliest legends belong to that broken bastard—'

'Fisher Kel Tath's poem on the Chaining—'

'I'm not one for reading poetry, but Hood knows, I've heard bits of it spoken by tavern bards and the like. Fener's balls, this isn't the war I signed on to fight.'

Whiskeyjack's eyes narrowed on the High Fist. 'Then don't.'

Dujek stopped pacing, faced his second. 'Go on,' he said after a moment.

'Brood already knew,' he replied with a shrug that made him wince. *As did Korlat.* 'With him, you could reasonably include Anomander Rake. And Kallor – though I liked not the avid glint in that man's eye. So, two ascendants and one would-be ascendant. The Crippled God is too powerful for people like you and me to deal with, High Fist. Leave it to them, and to the gods. Both Rake and Brood were there at the Chaining, after all.'

'Meaning it's their mess.'

'Bluntly, yes it is.'

'For which we're all paying, and might well pay the ultimate price before too long. I'll not see my army used as fodder in that particular game, Whiskeyjack. We were marching to crush the Pannion Domin, a mortal empire – as far as we could determine.'

'Manipulation seems to be going on on both sides, Dujek.'

'And I am to be comforted by that?' The High Fist's glare was fierce. He held it on his second for another moment, then quaffed his ale. He thrust the empty goblet out.

Whiskeyjack refilled it. 'We're hardly ones to complain of manipulation,' he rumbled, 'are we, friend?'

Dujek paused, then grunted.

Indeed. Calm yourself, High Fist. Think clear thoughts. 'Besides,' Whiskeyjack continued, 'I have faith.'

'In what?' his commander snapped. 'In whom? Pray, tell me!'

'In a certain short, corpulent, odious little man—'

'Kruppe! Have you lost your mind?'

Whiskeyjack smiled. 'Old friend, look upon your own seething anger. Your rage at this sense of being manipulated. Used. Possibly deceived. Now consider how an ascendant like Caladan Brood would feel, upon the realization that *he* is being manipulated? Enough to shatter the control of his temper? Enough to see him unlimber his hammer and seek to obliterate that smug, pompous puppet-master.'

Dujek stood unmoving for a long time, then a grin curved his lips. 'In other words, *he* took Krupp seriously . . .'

'Darujhistan,' Whiskeyjack said. 'Our grand failure. Through it all, I had the sense that someone, somewhere, was orchestrating the whole damned thing. Not Anomander Rake. Not the Cabal. Not Vorcan and her assassins. Someone else. Someone so cleverly hidden, so appallingly ... capable ... that we were helpless, utterly helpless.

'And then, at the parley, we all discover who was responsible for Tattersail's rebirth. As Silverfox, a child of a Rhivi woman, the seed planted and the birth managed within an unknown warren. The drawing together of threads – Nightchill, Bellurdan, Tattersail herself. And, it now appears, an Elder God, returned to the mortal realm. And, finally and most remarkably, the T'lan Imass. So, Tattersail, Nightchill and Bellurdan – all of the Malazan Empire – reborn to a Rhivi woman, of *Brood's* army ... with a parley looming, the potential of a grand alliance ... how Hood-damned convenient that a child should so bridge the camps—'

'Barring Kallor,' Dujek pointed out.

Whiskeyjack slowly nodded. 'And Kallor's just been reminded of Brood's power – hopefully sufficiently to keep him in line.'

'Is that what all that was about?'

'Maybe. He demanded a demonstration, did he not? What Kruppe manipulates is circumstance. Somehow. I don't feel we are fated to dance as he wills. There is an Elder God behind the Daru, but even there, I think it's more an alliance of ... mutual benefit, almost between equals. A partnership, if you will. Now, I'll grant you, all this is speculation on my part, but I'll tell you this: I have been manipulated before, as have you. But this time it feels different. Less inimical. Dujek, I sense compassion this time.'

'An alliance of equals,' the High Fist muttered, then he shook his head. 'What, then, does that make this Kruppe? Is he some god in disguise? A wizard of magnitude, an archmage?'

Whiskeyjack shrugged. 'My best guess. Kruppe is a mortal man. But gifted with an intelligence that is singular in its prowess. And I mean that most literally. Singular,

Dujek. If an Elder God was suddenly flung back into this realm, would he not seek out as his first ally the greatest of minds?'

Dujek's face revealed disbelieving wonder. 'But, Whiskeyjack . . . *Kruppe?*'

'Kruppe. Who gave us the Trygalle Trade Guild, the only traders capable of supplying us on the route we chose to march. Kruppe, who brought to the Mhybe the surviving possessions of the First Rhivi, for her to wear and so diminish the pain she feels, and those ornaments are, I suspect, yet to fully flower. Kruppe, the only one Silverfox will speak with, now that Paran is gone. And, finally, Kruppe, who has set himself in the Crippled God's path.'

'If just a mortal, then how did he survive Brood's wrath?'

'Well, I expect his ally the Elder God would not wish to see the Daru killed. I'd guess there was intervention, then. What else could it have been?'

Dujek emptied his goblet. 'Damn,' he sighed. 'All right. We ignore, as best we can, the Crippled God. We remain focused on the Pannion Domin. Still, my friend, I mislike it. I can't help but be nervous in that we are not actively engaged in considering this new enemy . . .'

'I don't think we are, High Fist.'

Dujek's glance was sharp, searching, then his face twisted. 'Quick Ben.'

Whiskeyjack slowly nodded. 'I think so. I'm not certain – Hood, I don't even know if he's still alive, but knowing Quick, he is. Very much alive. And, given his agitation the last time I saw him, he's without illusions, and anything but ignorant.'

'And he's all we've got? To outwit the Crippled God?'

'High Fist, if Kruppe is this world's foremost genius, then Quick Ben's but a step behind him. A very short step.'

They heard shouts outside the tent, then booted feet. A moment later the standard-bearer Artanthos pulled aside the flap and entered. 'Sirs, a lone Moranth has been spotted. Flying in from the northeast. It's Twist.'

Whiskeyjack rose, grunting at the cascade of aches and twinges the motion triggered. 'Queen of Dreams, we're about to receive some news.'

'Let's hope it's cheering news,' Dujek growled. 'I could do with some.'

Her face was pressed against the lichen-skinned stones, the roughness fading as her sweat soaked the ragged plant. Heart pounding, breaths coming in gasps, she lay whimpering, too tired to keep running, too tired to even so much as raise her head.

The tundra of her dreams had revealed new enemies. Not the band of strangers pursuing her this time.

This time, she had been found by wolves. Huge, gaunt creatures, bigger than any she had ever seen in her waking life. They had loped into view on a ridge marking the skyline to the north. Eight long-legged, shoulder-hunched beasts, their fur sharing the muted shades of the landscape. The one in the lead had turned, as if catching her scent on the dry, cold wind.

And the chase had begun.

At first the Mhybe had revelled in the fleetness of her young, lithe legs. Swift as an antelope – faster than anything a mortal human could achieve – she had fled across the barren land.

The wolves kept pace, tireless, the pack ranging out to the sides, one occasionally sprinting, darting in from one side or the other, forcing her to turn.

Again and again, when she sought to remain between hills, on level land, the creatures somehow managed to drive her upslope. And she began to tire.

The pressure never relented. Into her thoughts, amidst the burgeoning pain in her legs, the fire in her chest and the dry, sharp agony of her throat, came the horrifying realization that escape was impossible. That she was going to die. Pulled down like any other animal doomed to become a victim of the wolves' hunger.

For them, she knew, the sea of her mind, whipped now to a frenzied storm of panic and despair, meant nothing. They were hunters, and what resided within the soul of their quarry had no relevance. As with the antelope, the bhederin calf, the ranag, grace and wonder, promise and potential – reduced one and all to meat.

Life's final lesson, the only truthful one buried beneath a layered skein of delusions.

Sooner or later, she now understood, we are all naught but food. Wolves or worms, the end abrupt or lingering, it mattered not in the least.

Whimpering, half blind, she staggered up yet another hillside. They were closer. She could hear their paws crunching through wind-dried lichen and moss. To her right, to her left, closing, edging slightly ahead.

Crying out, the Mhybe stumbled, fell face first onto the rocky summit. She closed her eyes, waited for the first explosion of pain as teeth ripped into her flesh.

The wolves circled. She listened to them. Circled, then began spiralling in, closer, closer.

A hot breath gusted against the back of her neck.

The Mhybe screamed.

And awoke. Above her, a fading blue sky, a passing hawk. Haze of dust from the herd, drifting. In the air, distant voices and, much closer, the ragged, rattling sound of her own breathing.

The wagon had stopped moving. The army was settling in for the night.

She lay huddled, motionless beneath the furs and hides. A pair of voices were murmuring nearby. She smelled the smoke of a dung cookfire, smelled a herbal, meaty broth – sage, a hint of goat. A third voice arrived, was greeted by the first two – all strangely indistinct, beyond her ability to identify. *And not worth the effort. My watchers. My jailers.*

The wagon creaked. Someone crouched beside her. 'Sleep should not leave you so exhausted.'

'No, Korlat, it should not. Please, now, let me end this myself—'

'No. Here, Coll has made a stew.'

'I've no teeth left with which to chew.'

'Just slivers of meat, easily swallowed. Mostly broth.'

'I'm not hungry.'

'Nevertheless. Shall I help you sit up?'

'Hood take you, Korlat. You and the rest. Every one of you.'

'Here, I will help you.'

'Your good intentions are killing me. No, not killing. That's just it, isn't it—' She grunted, feebly trying to twist away from Korlat's hands as the Tiste Andii lifted her effortlessly into a sitting position. 'Torturing me. Your mercy. Which is anything but. No, look not at my face, Korlat.' She drew her hood tighter. 'Lest I grow avid for the pity in your eyes. Where is this bowl? I will eat. Leave me.'

'I will sit with you, Mhybe,' Korlat replied. 'There are two bowls, after all.'

The Rhivi woman stared down at her own wrinkled, pocked, skeletal hands, then at the bowl clutched between them, the watery broth with its slivers of wine-stained meat. 'See this? The butcher of the goat. The slayer. Did he or she pause at the desperate cries of the animal? Look into its pleading eyes? Hesitate with the knife? In my dreams, I am as that goat. This is what you curse me to.'

'The slaughterer of the goat was Rhivi,' Korlat said after a moment. 'You and I know that ritual well, Mhybe. Propitiation. Calling upon the merciful spirit whose embrace is necessity. You and I both know how that spirit comes upon the goat, or indeed any such creature whose body shall feed your people, whose skin shall clothe you. And so the beast does not cry out, does not plead. I have witnessed . . . and wondered, for it is indeed a remarkable thing. Unique to the Rhivi, not in its intent, but in its obvious efficacy. It is as if the ritual's arriving spirit shows the beast a better future – something beyond the life it's known to that point—'

'Lies,' the Mhybe murmured. 'The spirit deceives the poor creature. To make the slaying easier.'

Korlat fell silent.

The Mhybe raised the bowl to her lips.

'Perhaps, even then,' the Tiste Andii resumed, 'the deception is a gift . . . of mercy.'

'There is no such thing,' the Mhybe snapped. 'Words to comfort the killer and his kin and naught else. Dead is dead, as the Bridgeburners are wont to say. Those soldiers know the truth of it. Children of the Malazan Empire hold no illusions. They are not easily charmed.'

'You seem to know much of them.'

'Two marines come to visit occasionally. They've taken it upon themselves to guard my daughter. And to tell me of her, since no-one else has a mind to, and I cherish them for that.'

'I did not know this . . .'

'It alarms you? Have terrible secrets been revealed to me? Will you now put a stop to it?'

A hand closed on her shoulder. 'I wish you would at least look upon my face, Mhybe. No, I will do no such thing. Nor am I aware of any dire secrets being kept from you. Indeed, I now wish to seek out these two marines, to thank them.'

'Leave them be, Korlat. They do not ask for thanks. They are simple soldiers, two women of the Empire. Through them, I know that Kruppe visits Silverfox regularly. He's taken on the role of kindly uncle, perhaps. Such a strange man, endearing despite the terrible curse he has laid upon me.'

'Curse? Oh. Mhybe, of all that I have seen of Kruppe, I can tell you, he is not one to curse anyone. I do not believe he ever imagined what the rebirthing of Tattersail would mean to you.'

'So very true, that. I understand it well, you see. He was called upon by the Elder God – who either chose to become involved or was so already. An abomination had been created, as Kallor has called it, and it was an abomination in fact. The withered corpse of Nightchill, Tattersail's soul trapped within it, the apparition webbed by T'lan Imass sorcery. A nightmare creation. The Elder God sought to save it, somehow, in some form, and for that it seemed he needed Kruppe. Thus. The Daru did all he could, believing it to be a mercy. But make no mistake, now, Korlat. Kruppe and his Elder God have decided to *make use* of the child they fashioned. Opportunistic or deliberate from the start? Does it matter? And lo, Kruppe now walks with Silverfox. Do they conspire? Am I blind . . .'

'Conspire? To what end, Mhybe?'

'You don't know? I find that hard to believe.'

'Clearly, you have concluded we are all conspiring . . . against you.'

'Aren't you?' With all the strength she could muster, the Mhybe flung the bowl away, heard it splash, bounce off something, heard a shout of surprise from Murillio, who – it seemed – had the misfortune to be in its path of flight. 'Guard me!' she hissed. 'Feed me! Watch me so I don't take my own life! And this is not a conspiracy? And my daughter – *my own daughter* – does she visit? No! When have I last seen her face? *When?* I can barely remember the time!'

The hand tightened on her shoulder. Korlat's voice, when she spoke, was low yet taut. 'I hear you, my friend. I shall get to the bottom of this. I shall discover the truth, and then I shall tell you. This I promise, Mhybe.'

'Then tell me, what has happened? Earlier today. I felt . . . something. An event. Coll and Murillio spoke of a scene between Kruppe and Brood. Tell me, where was Silverfox in all this?'

'She was there,' Korlat replied. 'She joined me as I rode forward in answer to Whiskeyjack's summons. I will be honest, Mhybe. Something indeed did occur, before the clash between Brood and Kruppe. Your daughter has found . . . protectors, but she will not extend that protection to you – for some reason she believes you are in danger, now. I do not know the source.'

Yet I do. Oh, Korlat, your friendship for me has blinded you.

610

I am in danger indeed. From myself. 'Protectors. Who? What?'

Korlat drew a deep breath, let it out slowly. 'Silverfox asked that I say nothing to you of them. I could not understand why, yet I acquiesced. I realize now that to do so was wrong. Wrong to you, Mhybe. A conspiracy, and I shall not be party to it. Your daughter's protectors were wolves. Ancient, giant beasts—'

Terror ripped through the Mhybe. Snarling, she flung a hand at Korlat's face, felt her nails tear through skin. 'My hunters!' she screamed as the Tiste Andii flinched away. 'They want to kill me! My daughter—' *My daughter! Plaguing my dreams! Spirits below, she wants to kill me!*

Coll and Murillio had leapt onto the wagon, were shouting in alarm even as Korlat hissed at them to calm down, but the Mhybe ceased hearing them, ceased seeing anything of the world surrounding her at that moment. She continued thrashing, nails clawing the air, betrayal searing through her chest, turning her heart into ashes. *My daughter! My daughter!*

And my voice, it whimpers.

And my eyes, they plead.

And that knife is in her hands, and in her gaze there is naught but cold, cold intent.

Whiskeyjack's half-smile vanished when he turned upon Korlat's arrival, to see that her eyes were as white hot iron, to see as she stalked through the tent's entrance four parallel slashes on her right cheek, wet with blood that had run down to the line of her jaw and now dripped onto the rushes covering the floor.

The Malazan almost stepped back as the Tiste Andii strode towards him. 'Korlat, what has happened?'

'Hear my words, lover,' the woman grated in an icy voice. 'Whatever secrets you have withheld from me – about Tattersail reborn, about those damned T'lan Ay, about what you've instructed those two marines guarding

611

the child to say to the Mhybe – you will tell me. Now.'

He felt himself grow cold, felt his face twitch at the full thrust of her fury. 'Instructions?' he asked quietly. 'I have given them no instructions. Not even to guard Silverfox. What they've done has been their own decision. What they might have said, that it should lead to this – well, I shall accept responsibility for that, for I am their commander. And I assure you, if punishment is required—'

'Stop. A moment, please.' Something had settled within her, and now she trembled.

Whiskeyjack thought to take her in his arms, but held back. She needed comfort, he sensed, but his instincts told him she was not yet ready to receive it. He glanced around, found a relatively clean hand-cloth, soaked it in a basin, then held it out to her.

She had watched in silence, the shade of her eyes deepening to slate grey, but she made no effort to accept the cloth.

He slowly lowered his hand.

'Why,' Korlat asked, 'did Silverfox insist that her mother not learn of the T'lan Ay?'

'I have no idea, Korlat, beyond the explanation she voiced. At the time, I thought you knew.'

'You thought I knew.'

He nodded.

'You thought that I had been keeping from you . . . a secret. Something to do with Silverfox and her mother . . .'

Whiskeyjack shrugged.

'Were you planning to confront me?'

'No.'

Her eyes widened on him. Silence stretched, then, 'For Hood's sake, clean my wounds.'

Relieved, he stepped closer and began, with the gentlest of touches, to daub her cuts. 'Who struck you?' he asked quietly.

'The Mhybe. I think I have just made a dreadful mistake,

612

for all my good intentions . . .'

'That's often the case,' he murmured, 'with good intentions.'

Korlat's gaze narrowed searchingly. 'Pragmatic Malazans. Clear-eyed indeed. Why do we keep thinking of you as just soldiers? Brood, Rake, Kallor . . . myself, we all look upon you and Dujek and your army as something . . . ancillary. A sword we hope to grasp in our hands when the need arrives. It seems now that we're all fools. In fact, not one of us has come to realize the truth of how things now stand.'

He frowned. 'And how do they now stand?'

'You have become our backbone. Somehow, you are what gives us our strength, holds us together. Oh, I know you possess secrets, Whiskeyjack—'

He smiled wryly. 'Not as many as you seem to think. I will tell you the biggest one. It's this. We feel outmatched. By you – by Rake, by Caladan Brood, by Kallor. By the Tiste Andii army and that of the Rhivi and the Barghast. Hood, even that mob of mercenaries accompanying you makes us nervous. We don't have your power. We're just an army. Our best wizard isn't even ranked. He's a squad mage, and right now he's very far away and, I suspect, feeling like a fly in a web. So, come the battles, we know we'll be the spear's head, and it's going to cost us dear. As for the Seer himself, and whatever hides behind him, well, we're now hoping you'll deal with that. Same goes for the Crippled God. You're right, Korlat, we're just soldiers. Tired ones, at that. If we're this combined army's backbone, then Hood help us, it's a bowed, brittle one.'

She reached up and laid her hand over his, pressed it against her cheek. Their eyes locked. 'Bowed and brittle? I think not.'

Whiskeyjack shook his head. 'I'm not being modest, Korlat. I speak the truth, though I fear you're not prepared to hear it.'

'Silverfox is manipulating her mother,' the Tiste Andii said after a moment. 'Somehow. Possibly even being responsible for the old woman's terrible nightmares.'

'I find that hard to countenance—'

'Not something Tattersail would do, right? But what of this Nightchill? Or the Thelomen? You knew them, Whiskeyjack. Better than any of us, at least. Is it possible that one of them – or both – are responsible for this?'

He said nothing while he completed wiping clean the wounds on her cheek. 'This will require a healer's touch, Korlat, lest infection—'

'Whiskeyjack.'

He sighed, stepped back. 'Nightchill, I fear, might well harbour feelings of betrayal. Her targets for vengeance could be chosen indiscriminately. Same for Bellurdan Skullcrusher. Both were betrayed, after all. If you are right, about what's happening to the Mhybe – that they're doing something to her – then I still think that Tattersail would be resisting them.'

'What if she's already lost the struggle?'

'I've seen no sign of—'

Korlat's eyes flashed and she jabbed a finger against his chest. 'Meaning your two marines have reported no sign of it!'

He grimaced. 'They are volunteers none the less, Korlat. Given the alarming extent of our ignorance in these matters, it pays to be watchful. Those two marines chose to guard Silverfox because they see in her Tattersail. Not just physically, but in the woman's personality as well. If anything had gone awry, they would've noticed it, and they would've come to me. Fast.'

Korlat lowered her hand. She sighed. 'And here I've come storming in to tear your head from your shoulders. Damn you, Whiskeyjack, how did I come to deserve you? And, the Abyss take me, why are you still here? After all my accusations . . .'

'A few hours ago, Dujek made a similar entrance.' He grinned. 'It's just been that kind of day, I suppose. Now, we should call for a healer—'

'In a moment.' She studied him. 'Whiskeyjack. You've

614

truly no idea of how rare a man you are, do you?'

'Rare?' His grin broadened. 'Of course I know. There's only one of me, thank Hood.'

'That's not what I meant.'

He moved closer and drew an arm about her waist. 'Time to find a healer, woman. I've got simple needs, and we're wasting time.'

'A soldier's reply,' she said. 'I'm not fooled, you know.'

Unseen by her, he closed his eyes. *Oh, but you are, Korlat. If you'd known the full extent of my fear . . . that I might lose you . . .*

Arms waving expansively, Kruppe, Eel of Darujhistan, occasional fence and thief, Defier of Caladan Brood the Warlord, ambled his way down the main avenue of tents towards the supply wagons. He had just come from the cook tent of the Mott Irregulars, and in each hand was a Nathi black-cake, dripping with syrup. A few paces in his wake, his mule kept pace, nose stretched out to those two cakes, ears pricked forward.

The second bell since midnight had just tolled through the camps, stirring the distant herds of bhederin to a mournful lowing, which faded as the beasts slipped back into slumber. As he reached the edge of the wagons – arranged rectangularly to form a wheeled fort – he noted two Malazan marines, cloaks wrapped about their bodies, sitting before a small dung-fire.

Kruppe altered his course and approached. 'Gentle friends,' he softly called. ''Tis late and no doubt your pretty selves are due for some sweetness.'

The two women glanced up. 'Huh,' one of them grunted. 'It's that fat Daru.'

'And his mule, hovering there in the shadows.'

'Unique indeed is Kruppe! Behold!' He thrust forward the dripping cakes. 'For you, darlings.'

'So which should we eat, the cakes or your hands?'

The other drew her knife at her companion's words. 'A

615

couple of quick cuts and we can choose for ourselves, right?'

Kruppe stepped back. 'Queen of Dreams! Hard-bitten and distinctly unfeminine! Guardians of fair Silverfox, yes? Reassuring truth. Heart of Tattersail, shining so bright from the child-now-woman—'

'Aye, we seen you before plenty enough. Chatting with the lass. She's the sorceress, all right. Plain to see for them of us who knew her.'

'Extraordinary disconnectiveness, this exchange. Kruppe is delighted—'

'We getting them syrup cakes or what?'

'Naturally, though the flash of that blade still blinds generous Kruppe.'

'Y'ain't got no sense of humour, have ya? Join us, if you dare.'

The Daru smiled and strode forward. 'Nathi black-cakes, my dears.'

'We recognize 'em. The Mott Irregulars used to throw them at us when they ran out of arrows.'

'Jaybar got one full in the face, as I recall.'

'That he did, then he stumbled and when he came up he was like the forest floor with eyes.'

'Dreadful sap, deadly weapon,' Kruppe agreed, once more offering the cakes to the two marines.

They took them.

'Courageous task, protection of the Rhivi lass.'

'She ain't no Rhivi lass. She's Tattersail. That fur and the hides are just for show.'

'Ah, then you have spoken with her.'

'Not much and we don't need to. These cakes go down better without all the twigs and leaves, don't they just.'

Kruppe blinked, then slowly nodded. 'No doubt. Vast responsibility, being the eyes of your commander regarding said lass.'

Both women paused in their chewing. They exchanged a glance, then one of them swallowed and said, 'Who, Dujek?

If we're his eyes then he's blind as a mole.'

'Ah, Kruppe meant Whiskeyjack, of course.'

'Whiskeyjack ain't blind and he don't need us to see for him, either.'

'None the less,' the Daru smiled, 'he no doubt is greatly comforted by your self-appointed task and reports and such. Were Kruppe Whiskeyjack, he knows he would.'

'Would what?'

'Why, be comforted, of course.'

Both women grunted, then one snorted and said, 'That's a good one. If you were Whiskeyjack. Hah.'

'A figure of speech—'

'Ain't no such thing, fatty. You trying to walk in Whiskeyjack's footsteps? Trying to see through his eyes? Hah.'

'I'll say,' the other woman agreed. 'Hah.'

'And so you did,' Kruppe noted.

'Did what?'

'Agree.'

'Damned right. Whiskeyjack should've been Emperor, when the old one got knocked off. Not Laseen. But she knew who her rival was, didn't she just. That's why she stripped him of rank, turned him into a Hood-damned sergeant and sent him away, far away.'

'An ambitious man, this Whiskeyjack, then.'

'Not in the least, Daru. And that's the whole point. Would've made a good Emperor, I said. Not wanting the job is the best and only qualification worth considering.'

'A curious assertion, dear.'

'I ain't.'

'Pardon, you ain't what?'

'Curious. Listen, the Malazan Empire would be a far different thing if Whiskeyjack had taken the throne all those years ago. If he'd done what we all wanted him to do and grabbed Laseen by the scruff of the neck and sent her through a tower window.'

'And was he capable of such a remarkable feat?'

The two marines looked confused. One turned to her companion. 'Seen him out of his boots?'

The other shook her head. 'No. Still, they *might* be remarkable. Why not?'

'Then it'd be a boot to the backside, but I said by the scruff of the neck.'

'Well, feet that could do that would be remarkable, wouldn't they?'

'You got a point, friend.'

'Ahem,' Kruppe interrupted. 'A remarkable *feat*, dears. As in achievement.'

'Oh.'

'Oh yeah, right. Got it. So you're asking could he have done it if he'd a mind to? Sure. Not good to cross Whiskeyjack, and if that's not enough, he's got wits.'

'So, why then, Kruppe asks in wonder, did he not do so at the time?'

'Because he's a soldier, you idiot. Laseen's taking the throne was messy enough. The whole empire was shaky. People start stabbing and jumping into a blood-wet throne and sometimes it don't stop, sometimes it's like dominoes, right? One after another after another, and the whole thing falls apart. He was the one we all looked to, right? Waiting to see how he'd take it, Laseen and all that. And when he just saluted and said, "Yes, Empress," well, things just settled back down.'

'He was giving her a chance, you see.'

'Of course. And do you lasses now believe he made a mistake?'

The women shrugged in unison. 'Don't matter, now,' one said. 'We're here and here's here and that's that.'

'So be it and so be it,' Kruppe said, rising with a sigh. 'Wondrous conversation. Kruppe thanks you and will now take his leave.'

'Right. Thanks for the cakes.'

'Kruppe's pleasure. Good night, dears.'

He ambled off, back towards the supply wagons.

618

As he disappeared into the gloom the two marines said nothing for a time, busy as they were licking the sap from their fingers.

Then one sighed.

The other followed suit.

'Well?'

'Ah, that was damned easy.'

'Think so?'

'Sure. He came expecting to find two brains and found barely one.'

'Still, it might've babbled too much.'

'That's the nature of half-brains, love. T'do otherwise would've made him suspicious.'

'What do you figure he and Tattersail talk about, anyway?'

'The old woman, is my guess.'

'I'd figured the same.'

'They got something in the works.'

'My suspicions exactly.'

'And Tattersail's in charge.'

'So she is.'

'Which is good enough for me.'

'Same here. You know, that black-cake wasn't quite the same without the twigs and leaves.'

'That's odd, I was just thinking the same thing . . .'

Within the wheeled fort, Kruppe approached another campfire. The two men huddled around it looked up as he arrived.

'What's with your hands?' Murillio asked.

'All that Kruppe touches sticks to him, my friend.'

'Well,' Coll rumbled, 'we've known that for years.'

'And what's with that damned mule?' Murillio enquired.

'The beast haunts me in truth, but never mind that. Kruppe has had an interesting discourse with two marines. And he is pleased to inform that the lass Silverfox is in

619

capable hands indeed.'

'Sticky as yours?'

'They are now, dear Murillio, they are now.'

'What you say is fine enough,' Coll said, 'but is it any help to us? There's an old woman sleeping in yon wagon whose broken heart is the least of her pains and it's bad enough to break the strongest man, let alone a frail ancient.'

'Kruppe is pleased to assure you that matters of vast mercy are in progress. Momentary appearances are to be discounted.'

'Then why not tell her that?' Coll growled, nodding towards the Mhybe's wagon.

'Ah, but she is not yet ready to receive such truths, alas. This is a journey of the spirit. She must begin it within herself. Kruppe and Silverfox can only do so much, despite our apparent omnipotence.'

'Omnipotence, is it?' Coll shook his head. 'Yesterday, and I'd laugh at that claim. So you faced down Caladan Brood, did you? I'm interested in precisely how you managed that, you damned toad.'

Kruppe's brows rose. 'Dear boon companion Coll! Your lack of faith crushes frail Kruppe to his very toes which are themselves wriggling in anguish!'

'For Hood's sake don't show us,' Murillio said. 'You've been wearing those slippers for as long as I've known you, Kruppe. Poleil herself would balk at what might lurk likely between them.'

'And well she should! To answer Coll with succinct precision, Kruppe proclaims that anger – nay, rage – has no efficacy against one such as himself, for whom the world is as a pearl nestled within the slimy confines of his honed and muscled brain. Uh, perhaps the allusion falters with second thought ... and worse with third. Kruppe tries again! For whom, it was said, the world is naught but a plumaged dream of colours and wonders unimagined, where even time itself has lost meaning, speaking of which,

620

it's very late, yes? Sleep beckons, the stream of calm transubstantiation that metamorphoses oblivion into reparation and rejuvenation, and that alone is wonder enough for one and all to close this fitful night!' He fluttered his hands in a final wave and walked off. After a moment, the mule trotted in his wake.

The two men stared after them.

'Would that Brood's hammer connected with that oily pate,' Coll rumbled after a moment.

'It'd likely slip,' Murillio said.

'Aye, true enough.'

'Mussels and brains and cheesy toes, by the Abyss, I think I'm going to be sick.'

High above the camp, Crone crooked her weary, leaden wings and spiralled down towards the warlord's tent. Despite her exhaustion, shivers of excitement and curiosity ran through her. The fissure to the north of the encampment still bled Burn's fouled blood. The Great Raven had felt that detonation when still over the Vision Mountains far to the southeast, and had instantly known it for what it was.

Caladan Brood's anger.

Kiss of the hammer, and with it an explosive reshaping of the natural world. She could see despite the darkness, and the sharply defined spine of a basaltic mountain range loomed where no mountains belonged, here at the heart of the Catlin plain. And the sorcery emanating from the blood of the Sleeping Goddess – it, too, Crone recognized.

The touch of the Crippled God. Within Burn's veins, a transformation was taking place. The Fallen One was making her blood his own. *And that is a taste I know well, for it was as mother's milk to me, so very long ago. To me, and to my kin.*

Changes had come to the world below, and Crone revelled in changes. Her soul and that of her kin had been stirred once more to acute wakefulness. She never felt more alive.

Slipping beneath the warm thermals, she descended, bobbing on pockets of cool air – echoes of the traumatic disturbance that had churned through the atmosphere at the eruption of Brood's fury – then sliding down to land with a soft thump on the earth before the warlord's tent.

No lights showed within.

Faintly cackling, Crone hopped beneath the halfhitched entrance flap.

'Not a word,' Brood rumbled from the darkness, 'about my temper's snapped leash.'

The Great Raven cocked her head towards the cot. The warlord was seated on its edge, head in his hands. 'As you wish,' Crone murmured.

'Make your report.'

'I shall. First, from Anomander Rake. He has succeeded. Moon's Spawn has passed unseen and now ... *hides*. My children are ranging far over the lands of the Pannion Seer. Warlord, not just their eyes have witnessed the truth of all that lies below. I myself have seen—'

'Save those details for later. Moon's Spawn is in place. Good. Did you fly to Capustan as I requested?'

'I did, grave one. And was witness to the first day and first night of battle.'

'Your assessment, Crone?'

'The city will not hold, Warlord. Through no fault of the defenders. What opposes them is too vast.'

Brood grunted. 'Perhaps we should have reconsidered Dujek's disposition of the Black Moranth—'

'Ah, they too are emplaced, precisely where Onearm wanted them to be.' Crone hesitated, turning first one eye then the other towards Caladan Brood. 'One unusual detail must be uttered now, Warlord. Will you hear it?'

'Very well.'

'The Seer wages a war to the south.'

Brood's head snapped up.

'Aye,' Crone nodded. 'My children have seen Domin

622

armies, routed and retreating north. To Outlook itself. The Seer has unleashed formidable sorceries against the unknown enemy. Rivers of ice, walls of ice. Blistering cold, winds and storms – it has been a long time since we have witnessed said particular warren unveiled.'

'Omtose Phellack. The warren of the Jaghut.'

'Even so. Warlord, you seem less surprised by that than I had anticipated.'

'Of a war to the south, I am indeed surprised, Crone.' He rose, drawing a fur blanket about his shoulders, and began pacing. 'Of Omtose Phellack . . . no, I am not surprised.'

'Thus. The Seer is not as he seems.'

'Evidently not. Rake and I had suspicions . . .'

'Well,' Crone snapped, 'had I known them I would have more closely examined the situation at Outlook. Your recalcitrance wounds us all.'

'We'd no proof, Crone. Besides, we value your feathered hide too highly to risk your close approach to an unknown enemy's fastness. It is done. Tell me, does the Seer remain in Outlook?'

'My kin were unable to determine that. There are condors in the area, and they did not appreciate our presence.'

'Why should mundane birds cause you trouble?'

'Not entirely mundane. Aye, mortal birds are little more than feathered lizards, but these particular condors were more lizard than most.'

'The Seer's own eyes?'

'Possibly.'

'That could prove troublesome.'

Crone shrugged with her wings half crooked. 'Have you some slivers of meat? I hunger.'

'There's leftover goat from supper in the refuse pit behind the tent.'

'What? You would have me eat from a *refuse pit*?'

'You're a damned raven, Crone, why not?'

'Outrage! But if that's all there is . . .'

'It is.'

Clucking to contain her fury, Crone hopped towards the tent's back wall. 'Take me as an example in the future,' she murmured as she began edging her way under the fabric.

'What do you mean?' Brood asked behind her.

She ducked her head back inside, opened her beak in a silent laugh, then replied, 'Did *I* lose my temper?'

Growling, he stepped towards her.

The Great Raven squawked and fled.

CHAPTER SIXTEEN

The First Child of the Dead Seed
dreams of a father's dying breath
and hears in eternal refrain
the scream trapped in his lungs –
Dare you step behind his eyes
even for a moment?

The First Child of the Dead Seed
leads an army of sorrow
down hunger's bone-picked road
where a mother dances and sings –
Dare you walk in his steps
and dearly hold her hand?

The First Child of the Dead Seed
is sheathed in the clutter of failed armour
defending him from the moment of birth
through years of dire schooling –
Do not dare judge him hard
lest you wear his skin.

Silba of the Shattered Heart
K'alass

The Tenescowri rose like an inexorable flood against every wall of the city. Rose, then swept over, a mass of humanity driven mad by hunger.

625

Gate barricades buckled to the pressure, then gave way.

And Capustan drowned.

Four hundred paces from the barracks, Itkovian wheeled his blood-spattered mount. Figures reached up from below, clawed along the horse's armoured limbs. The beast, in cold fury, stamped down repeatedly, crushing bones, caving in chests and heads.

Three Manes of Grey Swords surrounded the Shield Anvil where they had been cut off from the barracks atop the gentle hill that was the cemetery of pillars. Most of those upright coffins had been toppled, shattering to spill their mouldy, cloth-wrapped contents, now jumbled among their cousins in death.

Itkovian could see the barracks gate, against which bodies were piled high – high enough to climb, which is what scores of Tenescowri were doing, clambering up towards the flanking revetments only to be met by the serrated blades of long-handled pikes. Pikes that killed, that wounded peasants who made no effort to defend themselves, that whipped back and forth trailing banners of blood and gore.

Itkovian had never witnessed such a horrifying sight. For all his battles, for all the terrors of combat and all that a soldier could not help but see, the vision before him swept all else from his mind.

As peasants fell back, tumbled their way down the slope of corpses, women leapt at the men among them, tore at their clothing, pinned them in place with straddled legs and, amidst blood, amidst shrieks and clawing fingers, they raped them.

Along the edges of the dead and dying, others fed on their kin.

Twin nightmares. The Shield Anvil was unable to decide which of the two shook him the most. His blood flowed glacial cold in his veins, and he knew, with dread verging on panic, that the assault had but just begun.

Another wave surged to close with the hapless band of

Grey Swords in the cemetery. To all sides, the wide avenues and streets were packed solid with frenzied Tenescowri. All eyes were fixed on Itkovian and his soldiers. Hands reached out towards them, no matter what the distance, and hungrily clawed the air.

Locking shields, the Grey Swords reformed their tattered square surrounding the Shield Anvil. It would be swallowed, Itkovian well knew, as it had been only moments earlier, yet, if his silent soldiers could do as they had done once before, the square would rise again from the sea of bodies, cutting its way clear, flinging the enemy back, clambering atop a newly made hill of flesh and bone. And, if Itkovian could remain on his horse, he would sweep his sword down on all sides, killing all who came within his reach – and those whom he wounded would then die beneath his mount's iron-clad hooves.

He had never before delivered such slaughter, and it sickened him, filled his heart with an overwhelming hatred – for the Seer. To have done such a thing to his own people. And for Septarch Kulpath, for his bloodless cruelty in sending these hapless peasants into the maw of a desperate army.

Even more galling, the tactic looked likely to succeed. *Yet at a cost beyond comprehension.*

With a roar, the Tenescowri attacked.

The first to reach the bristling square were cut to pieces. Reeling, shrieking, they were pulled back by their comrades, into a devouring midst that was even more vicious than the enemy they'd faced when in the front line. Others pushed ahead, to suffer an identical fate. Yet still more came, climbing the backs of the ones before them, now, whilst others clambered over their own shoulders. For the briefest of moments, Itkovian stared at a three-tiered wall of savage humanity, then it collapsed inward, burying the Grey Swords.

The square buckled beneath the weight. Weapons were snagged. Shields were pulled down, helms ripped from heads, and everywhere the Shield Anvil looked, there was blood.

Figures scrambled over the heaving surface. Cleavers and hatchets and knives swung down in passing, but Itkovian was their final target, as he knew he would be. The Shield Anvil readied his broadsword and shield. A slight shift in the pressure of his legs began turning his mount into a ceaseless spin. The beast's head tossed, then ducked low to defend its throat. The armour covering its brow, neck and chest was already smeared and dented. Hooves stamped, eager to find living flesh.

The first peasant came within range. Itkovian swung his sword, watched a head spin away from its body, watched as the body shivered and twitched before crumpling. His horse lashed out its hind hooves, connecting with crunching thumps, then the animal righted itself and reared, iron-shod front hooves kicking and clawing, dragging a screaming woman down. Another Tenescowri leapt to grab one of the horse's front legs. Itkovian leaned forward and drove his sword against the man's lower back, cutting deep enough to sever his spine.

His horse spun, the leg flinging the corpse away. Head snapped forward, teeth cracking down on a peasant's hair-matted pate, punching through bone to pull back with a mouthful of hair and skull.

Hands clawed against Itkovian's thigh on his shield side. He twisted, swung down across his mount's withers. The blade chopped through muscle and clavicle. Blood and meat reeled away.

His horse kicked again. Bit and stamped and whirled, but hands and pressure and weight were on all sides now. Itkovian's sword flashed, whipped blindly yet never failed to find a target. Someone climbed up onto the horse's rump behind him. He arched his back, gauntleted hand swinging up over his own head, point driving downward behind him. He felt the edge slice its way through skin and flesh, skitter along ribs, then punch down into lower belly.

628

A flood of bile and blood slicked the back of his saddle. The figure slid away.

He snapped a command and the horse ducked its head. Itkovian swung his weapon in a sweeping, horizontal slash. Cutting, glancing contact stuttered its entire path. His mount pivoted and the Shield Anvil reversed the slash. Spun again, and Itkovian whipped the sword again.

Man and beast turned in a full circle in this fashion, a circle delivering dreadful wounds. Through the blistering heat beneath his visored helm, Itkovian gained a fragmented collection of the scene on all sides.

There would be no rising from his Grey Swords. Not this time. Indeed, he could not see a single familiar surcoat. The Tenescowri closed on the Shield Anvil from all sides, a man's height's worth of bodies under their feet. And somewhere beneath that heaving surface, were Itkovian's soldiers. Buried alive, buried dying, buried dead.

He and his horse were all that remained, the focus of hundreds upon hundreds of avid, desperate eyes.

Captured pikes were being passed forward to those peasants nearest him. In moments, those long-handled weapons would begin jabbing in on all sides. Against this, neither Itkovian's nor his horse's armour would be sufficient.

Twin Tusks, I am yours. To this, the last moment.

'Break!'

His warhorse was waiting for that command. The beast surged forward. Hooves, chest and shoulders battered through the press. Itkovian carved his blade down on both sides. Figures reeled, parted, disappeared beneath the churning hooves. Pikes slashed out at him, skittered along armour and shield. The ones to his right he batted aside with his sword.

Something punched into the small of his back, snapping the links of his chain, twisting and gouging through leather and felt padding. Agony lanced through Itkovian as the jagged point drove through skin and grated against his lowest rib close to the spine.

629

At the same moment his horse screamed as it stumbled onto the point of another pike, the iron head plunging deep into the right side of its chest. The animal lurched to the left, staggering, head dipping, jaws snapping at the shaft.

Someone leapt onto Itkovian's shield, swung over it a woodsman's hatchet. The wedged blade buried itself deep between his left shoulder and neck, where it jammed.

The Shield Anvil jabbed the point of his sword into the peasant's face. The blade carved into one cheek, exited out through the other. Itkovian twisted the blade, his own visored face inches from his victim's as his sword destroyed her youthful visage. Gurgling, she toppled back.

He could feel the weight of the pike, its head still buried in his back, heard it clatter along his horse's rump-armour as the beast slewed and pitched.

A fishmonger's knife found the unprotected underside of his left knee, searing up into the joint. Itkovian chopped weakly down with the lower edge of his shield, barely sufficient to push the attacker away. The thin blade snapped, the six inches remaining in his knee grinding and slicing through tendon and cartilage. Blood filled the space between his calf and the felt padding sheathing it.

The Shield Anvil felt no pain. Brutal clarity commanded his thoughts. His god was with him, now, at this final moment. With him, and with the brave, indomitable warhorse beneath him.

The beast's sideways lurch ceased as the animal – pike plucked free – righted itself despite the blood that now gushed down its chest. The animal leapt forward, crushing bodies under it, kicked and clawed and clambered its way towards what seemed – impossibly to Itkovian's eyes – a cleared avenue, a place where only motionless bodies awaited.

The Shield Anvil, comprehending at last what he was seeing, renewed his efforts. The enemy was melting away, on all sides. Screams and the clash of iron echoed wildly in Itkovian's helmet.

A moment later and the horse stumbled clear, hooves lashing out as it reared – not in rage this time, but in triumph.

Pain arrived as Itkovian sagged onto the animal's armoured neck. Pain like nothing he had known before. The pike remained embedded in his back, the broken knife-blade in the heart of his left knee, the hatchet buried in the shattered remains of his collar bone. Jaws clenched, he managed to quell his mount's pitching about, succeeded in pivoting the animal round, to face, once more, the cemetery.

Disbelieving, he saw his Grey Swords carving their way free of the bodies that had buried them, rising as if from a barrow of corpses, silent as ghosts, their movements jerky as if they were clawing their way awake after a horrifying nightmare. Only a dozen were visible, yet that was twelve more than the Shield Anvil had thought possible.

Boots thumped up to Itkovian. Blinking gritty sweat from his eyes, he tried to focus on the figures closing in around him.

Grey Swords. Battered and stained surcoats, the young, pale faces of Capan recruits.

Then, on a horse to match Itkovian's own, the Mortal Sword. Brukhalian, black-armoured, his black hair a wild, blood-matted mane, Fener's holy sword in one huge, gauntleted hand.

He'd raised his visor. Dark eyes were fixed on the Shield Anvil.

'Apologies, sir,' Brukhalian rumbled as he drew rein beside him. 'For our tardiness.'

Behind the Mortal Sword, Itkovian now saw Karnadas, hurrying forward. His face, drawn and pale as a corpse's, was nevertheless beautiful to the Shield Anvil's eyes.

'Destriant!' he gasped, weaving on his saddle. 'My horse, sir . . . my soldiers . . .'

'Fener is with me, sir,' Karnadas replied in a trembling voice. 'And so shall I answer you.'

631

The world darkened then. Itkovian felt the sudden tug of hands beneath him, as if he had fallen into their embrace. Pondering that, his thoughts drifted – *my horse . . . my soldiers* – then closed into oblivion.

They battered down the flimsy shutters, pushed in through the rooms above the ground floor. They slithered through the tunnel of packed bodies that had once been stairwells. Gruntle's iron fangs were blunt, nicked and gouged. They had become ragged clubs in his hands. He commanded the main hallway and was slowly, methodic-ally creating barricades of cooling flesh and broken bone.

No weariness weighed down his arms or dulled his acuity. His breathing remained steady, only slightly deeper than usual. His forearms showed a strange pattern of blood stains, barbed and striped, the blood blackening and seem-ing to seep into his skin. He was indifferent to it.

There were Seerdomin, scattered here and there within the human tide of Tenescowri. Probably pulled along with-out volition. Gruntle cut down peasants in order to close with them. It was his only desire. To close with them. To kill them. The rest was chaff, irritating, getting in the way. Impediments to what he wanted.

Had he seen his own face, he would barely recognize it. Blackened stripes spread away from his eyes and bearded cheeks. Tawny amber streaked the beard itself. His eyes were the colour of sun-withered prairie grass.

His militia was a hundred strong now, silent figures who were as extensions of his will. Unquestioning, looking upon him with awe. Their faces shone when he settled his gaze on them. He did not wonder at that, either, did not realize that the illumination he saw was reflected, that they but mirrored the pale, yet strangely tropical emanation of his eyes.

Gruntle was satisfied. He was answering all that had been visited upon Stonny – she now fought alongside his second-in-command, that small, wiry Lestari soldier,

632

holding the tenement block's rear stairwell. They'd met but once since withdrawing to this building hours earlier. And it had shaken him, jarred him in a deep place within himself, and it was as if he had been shocked awake – as if all this time his soul had been hunkered down within him, hidden, silent, whilst an unknown, implacable force now ruled his limbs, rode the blood that pumped through him. She was broken still, the bravado torn away to reveal a human visage, painfully vulnerable, profoundly wounded in its heart.

The recognition had triggered a resurgence of cold desire within Gruntle. She was the debt he had only begun to pay. And whatever had rattled her upon their meeting once more, well, no doubt she had somehow comprehended his desire's bared fangs and unsheathed claws. A reasonable reaction, only troubling insofar as it deserved to be.

The decrepit, ancient Daru tenement now housed a storm of death, whipping winds of rage, terror and agony twisting and churning through every hallway, in every room no matter how small. It flowed vicious and without surcease. It matched, in every detail, the world of Gruntle's mind, the world within the confines of his skull.

There existed no contradictions between the reality of the outer world and that of his inner landscape. This truth beggared comprehension. It could only be grasped instinctively, a visceral understanding glimpsed by less than a handful of Gruntle's followers, the Lestari lieutenant among them.

He knew he had entered a place devoid of sanity. Knew, somehow, that he and the rest of the militia now existed more within the mind of Gruntle than they did in the real world. They fought with skills they had never before possessed. They did not tire. They did not shout, scream, or even so much as bark commands or rallying cries. There was no need for rallying cries – no-one broke, no-one was routed. Those that died fell where they had stood, silent as automatons.

Hallways were chest deep in bodies on the ground floor. Some rooms could not even be entered. Blood ran through these presses like a crimson river running beneath the surface of the land, seeping amidst hidden gravel lenses, pockets of sand, buried boulders – seeped, here in this dread building, around bone and meat and armour and boots and sandals and weapons and helms. Reeking like a sewer, thick as the flow in a surgeon's trench.

The attackers finally staggered back, withdrew down almost-blocked stairwells, clawed out of the windows. Thousands more waited outside, but the retreat clogged the approaches. A moment of peace settled within the building.

Light-headed and weaving as he clambered his way up the main hallway, the Lestari lieutenant found Gruntle. His master's striped arms glistened, the blades of his cutlasses were yellowed white – fangs in truth, now – and he swung a savagely feline visage to the Lestari.

'We surrender this floor, now,' Gruntle said, shaking the blood from his blades.

The hacked remains of Seerdomin surrounded the caravan captain. Armoured warriors literally chopped to pieces.

The lieutenant nodded. 'We're out of room to manoeuvre.'

Gruntle shrugged his massive shoulders. 'We've two more floors above us. Then the roof.'

Their eyes locked for a long moment, and the lieutenant was both chilled and warmed by what he saw within the vertical slits of Gruntle's pupils. *A man to fear . . . a man to follow . . . a man to love.* 'You are Trake's Mortal Sword,' he said.

The huge Daru frowned. 'Stonny Menackis.'

'She bears but minor injuries, Captain, and has moved up to the next landing.'

'Good.'

Weighed down with sacks of food and drink, the militia was converging, the command to do so unspoken, as it had been unspoken every time the gathering occurred. More than twenty had fallen in this last engagement, the Lestari saw. *We lose this many with each floor. By the time we reach the roof there'll be but a score of us. Well, that should be more than enough, to hold a single trapdoor. Hold it until the Abyss of Final Night.*

The silent followers were collecting serviceable weapons, scraps of armour – mostly from the Seerdomin. The Lestari watched with dull eyes a Capan woman pick up a gauntleted hand, severed raggedly at the wrist by one of Gruntle's cutlasses, and calmly pull the hand from the scaled glove, which she then donned.

Gruntle stepped over bodies on his way to the stairwell.

It was time to retreat to the next level, time to take command of the outer-lying rooms with their feebly shuttered windows, and the back stairs and the central stairs. *Time to jam yet more souls down Hood's clogged, choking throat.*

At the stairs, Gruntle clashed his cutlasses.

Outside, a resurging tide of noise . . .

Brukhalian sat astride his huge, lathered warhorse, watching as the Destriant's cutters dragged a barely breathing Itkovian into a nearby building that would serve, for the next bell or two, as a triage. Karnadas himself, drawing once more on his fevered Warren of Denul, had quelled the flow of blood from the chest of the Shield Anvil's horse.

The surviving Grey Swords at the cemetery were being helped clear by the Mortal Sword's own companies. There were wounds to be tended to there as well, but those that were fatal had already proved so. Corpses were being pulled away in a frantic search for more survivors.

The cutters carrying Itkovian now faced the task of removing buried iron from the Shield Anvil, weapons that had, by virtue of remaining embedded, in all likelihood saved the man's life. And Karnadas would be on hand for that surgery, to quench the blood that would gush from each wound as the iron was drawn free.

Brukhalian's flat, hard eyes followed the Destriant as the old man stumbled after his cutters. Karnadas had gone too far, pulled too much from his warren, too much and too often. His body had begun its irreversible surrender. Bruises marked the joints of his arms, the elbows, the wrists, the fingers. Within him, his veins and arteries were becoming as cheesecloth, and the seepage of blood into muscle and cavity would only grow more profound. Denul's flow was disintegrating all that it flowed through – the body of the priest himself.

He would be, Brukhalian knew, dead before dawn.

Yet, before then, Itkovian would be healed, brutally mended without regard to the mental trauma that accompanied all wounds. The Shield Anvil would assume command once again, but not as the man he had been.

The Mortal Sword was a hard man. The fate of his friends was a knowledge bereft of emotion. It was as it had to be.

He straightened on his saddle, scanned the area to gauge the situation. The attack upon the barracks had been repelled. The Tenescowri had broken on all sides, and none still standing remained within sight. This was not the case elsewhere, Brukhalian well knew. The Grey Swords had been virtually obliterated as an organized army. No doubt pockets of resistance remained, but they would be few and far between. To all intents and purposes, Capustan had fallen.

A mounted messenger approached from the northwest, horse leaping the mounds of bodies littering the avenue, slowing as it neared the Mortal Sword's companies.

Brukhalian gestured with his blade and the young Capan woman reined in before him.

'Sir!' she gasped. 'I bring word from Rath'Fener! A message, passed on to me by an acolyte!'

'Let us hear it, then, sir.'

'The Thrall is assailed! Rath'Fener invokes the Reve's Eighth Command. You are to ride with all in your company

636

to his aid. Rath'Fener kneels before the hooves – you are to be the Twin Tusks of his and Fener's shadow!'

Brukhalian's eyes narrowed. 'Sir, this acolyte managed to leave the Thrall in order to convey his priest's holy invocation. Given the protective sorcery around the building, how was this managed?'

The young woman shook her head. 'I do not know, sir.'

'And your path across the city, to arrive here, was it contested?'

'None living stood before me, sir.'

'Can you explain that?'

'No, sir, I cannot. Fener's fortune, perhaps . . .'

Brukhalian studied her a moment longer. 'Recruit, will you join us in our deliverance?'

She blinked, then slowly nodded. 'I would be honoured, Mortal Sword.'

His reply was a gruff, sorrowful whisper that only deepened her evident bewilderment, 'As would I, sir.' Brukhalian lowered the visor, swung to his followers. 'Eleventh Mane to remain with the Destriant and his cutters!' he commanded. 'Remaining companies, we march to the Thrall! Rath'Fener has invoked the Reve, and to this we must answer!' He then dismounted and handed the reins of his warhorse to the messenger. 'My mind has changed,' he rumbled. 'You are to remain here, sir, to guard my destrier. Also, to inform the Shield Anvil of my disposition once he awakens.'

'Your disposition, sir?'

'You will know it soon, recruit.' The Mortal Sword faced his troops once more. They stood in ranks, waiting, silent. Four hundred Grey Swords, perhaps the last left alive. 'Sirs,' Brukhalian asked them, 'are you in full readiness?'

A veteran officer grated, 'Ready to try, Mortal Sword.'

'Your meaning?' the commander asked.

'We are to cross half the city, sir. We shall not make it.'

'You assume our path to the Thrall will be contested, Nilbanas. Yes?'

The old soldier frowned, said nothing.

Brukhalian reached for his shield, which had waited at his side in the hands of an aide. 'I shall lead us,' he said. 'Do you follow?'

Every soldier nodded, and the Mortal Sword saw in those half-visored faces the emergence of an awareness, a knowledge to which he had already arrived. There would be no return from the journey to come. Some currents, he knew, could not be fought.

Readying the large bronze-plated shield on his left arm, adjusting his grip on his holy sword, Brukhalian strode forward. His Grey Swords fell in behind him. He chose the most direct route, not slowing even as he set across open, corpse-strewn squares.

The murmuring rumble of humanity was on all sides. Isolated sounds of battle, the collapse of burning buildings and the roar of unchecked fires, streets knee-deep in bodies – scenes of Hood's infernal pit rolled past them as they marched, as of two unfurling tapestries woven by a mad, soul-tortured artisan.

Yet their journey was uncontested.

As they neared the aura-sheathed Thrall, the veteran increased his pace to come alongside Brukhalian. 'I heard the messenger's words, sir—'

'Of that I am aware, Nilbanas.'

'It cannot be really from Rath'Fener—'

'But it is, sir.'

'Then the priest betrays us!'

'Yes, old friend, he betrays us.'

'He has desecrated Fener's most secret Reve! By the Tusks, sir—'

'The words of the Reve are greater than he is, Nilbanas. They are Fener's own.'

'Yet he has twisted them malign, sir! We should not abide!'

'Rath'Fener's crime shall be answered, but not by us.'

'At the cost of our lives?'

'Without our deaths, sir, there would be no crime. Thus, no punishment to match.'

'Mortal Sword—'

'We are done, my friend. Now, in this manner, we choose the meaning of our deaths.'

'But . . . but what does he gain? Betraying his own god—'

'No doubt,' Brukhalian said with a private, grim smile, 'his own life. For a time. Should the Thrall's protective sorcery be sundered, should the Council of Masks be taken, he will be spared the horrors that await his fellow priests. He judges this a worthwhile exchange.'

The veteran was shaking his head. 'And so Fener allows his own words to assume the weight of betrayal. How noble his Bestial Mien when he finally corners Rath'Fener?'

'Our god shall not be the one to deliver the punishment, Nilbanas. You are right, he could not do so in fullest conscience, for this is a betrayal that wounds him deeply, leaves him weakened and vulnerable to fatal consequence, sir.'

'Then,' the man almost sobbed, 'then who shall be our vengeful hand, Brukhalian?'

If anything, the Mortal Sword's smile grew grimmer. 'Even now, the Shield Anvil no doubt regains consciousness. And is moments from hearing the messenger's report. Moments from true comprehension. Nilbanas, our vengeful hand shall be Itkovian's. What is your countenance now, old friend?'

The soldier was silent for another half-dozen paces. Before them was the open concourse before the gate to the Thrall. 'I am calmed, sir,' he said, his voice deep and satisfied. 'I am calmed.'

Brukhalian cracked his sword against his shield. Black fire lit the blade, sizzled and crackled. 'They surround the concourse before us. Shall we enter?'

'Aye, sir, with great joy.'

The Mortal Sword and his four hundred followers strode into the clearing, not hesitating as the streets and alley mouths on all sides swiftly filled with Septarch Kulpath's crack troops, his Urdomen, Seerdomin and Betaklites, including the avenue they had just quitted. Archers appeared on the rooftops, and the hundreds of Seerdomin lying before the Thrall's gate, feigning death, now rose, readying weapons.

At Brukhalian's side, Nilbanas snorted. 'Pathetic.'

The Mortal Sword grunted a laugh that was heard by all. 'The Septarch deems himself clever, sir.'

'And us stupid with honour.'

'Aye, we are that indeed, are we not, old friend?'

Nilbanas raised his sword and roared triumphantly. Blade whirling over his head, he spun in place his dance of delighted defiance. The Grey Swords locked shields, ends curling to enclose the Mortal Sword as they readied their last stand in the centre of the concourse.

The veteran remained outside it, still spinning, still roaring, sword high in the air.

Five thousand Pannions and the Septarch himself looked on, in wonder, disbelieving, profoundly alarmed by the man's wild, bestial stamping on the cobbles. Then, with a silent snarl, Kulpath shook himself and raised one gauntleted hand.

He jerked it down.

The air of the concourse blackened as fifteen hundred bows whispered as one.

Eyes snapping open, Itkovian heard that whisper. He saw, with a vision filling his awareness, to the exclusion of all else, as the barbed heads plunged into the shielded turtle that was the Grey Swords. Shafts slipped through here and there. Soldiers reeled, fell, folded in on themselves.

Nilbanas, pierced through by a hundred arrows or more, whipped round one last time in a haze of blood droplets, then collapsed.

In roaring masses, the Pannion foot soldiers surged into the concourse. Crashed against the locked shields of the surviving Grey Swords even as they struggled to close the gaps in their ranks. The square was shattered, ripped apart. Battle turned to slaughter.

Still standing, the Mortal Sword's whirling blade raged with black fire. Studded with arrow shafts, he stood like a giant amidst feral children.

And fought on.

Pikes drove into him from all sides, lifted him off his feet. Sword arm swinging down, he chopped through the shafts, landed amidst writhing bodies.

Itkovian saw as a double-bladed axe separated Brukhalian's left arm from his body, at the shoulder, where blood poured unchecked as the severed, shield-laden arm fell away, frenziedly contracting at the elbow as would an insect's dismembered limb.

The huge man folded to his right.

More pikes jabbed, ripping into his torso.

The grip on the sword did not falter. The burning blade continued to spread its devouring flame outward, incinerating as it went. Screams filled the air.

Urdomen closed in with their short, heavy blades. Began chopping.

The Mortal Sword's intestines, snagged on a sword tip, unravelled like a snake from his gut. Another axe crashed down on Brukhalian's head, splitting the heavy black-iron helm, then the skull, then the man's face.

The burning sword exploded in a dark flash, the shards cutting down yet more Pannions.

The corpse that was Fener's Mortal Sword tottered upright a moment longer, riven through, almost headless, then slowly settled to its knees, back hunching, a scarecrow impaled by a dozen pikes, countless arrows.

Kneeling, now motionless, in the deepening shadow of the Thrall, as the Pannions slowly withdrew on all sides – their battle-rage gone and something silent and dreadful in its stead – staring at the hacked thing that had been Brukhalian . . . and at the tall, barely substantial apparition that took form directly before the Mortal Sword. A figure shrouded in black, hooded, hands hidden within the tattered folds of broad sleeves.

Hood. King of High House Death . . . come to greet this man's soul. In person.

Why?

A moment later and the Lord of Death was gone. Yet no-one moved.

It began to rain. Hard.

Kneeling, watery blood staining the black armour, making the chain's iron links gleam crimson.

Another set of eyes was sharing Itkovian's inner vision, eyes that he knew well. And in the Shield Anvil's mind there came a cold satisfaction, and in his mind he addressed the other witness and knew, without doubt, that his words were heard.

I have you, Rath'Fener.

You are mine, betrayer.

Mine.

The sparrowhawk twisted through the wind-whipped rain clouds, felt the drops like nails as they battered its wings, its splayed tail. Lurid flames glimmered in the city below amidst the grey, blackening buildings.

The day was drawing to a close, but the horror did not relent. Buke's mind was numb with all that he had witnessed, and the distance afforded him by his Soletaken form was no release. These eyes were too sharp, too sharp by far.

He banked hard directly over the estate that was home to Bauchelain and Korbal Broach. The gate was a mass of bodies. The mostly ornamental corner towers and the walk-ways along the compound's walls were occupied by silent sentinels, dark and motionless in the rain.

Korbal Broach's army of animated corpses had grown. Hundreds of Tenescowri had breached the gate and poured into the compound earlier. Bauchelain had greeted them with waves of deadly sorcery – magic that blackened their flesh, cracked it, then made it curl away in strips from their bones. Long after they were dead, the spell continued its relentless work, until the cobbles were ankle-deep in charred dust.

Two more attempts had been made, each more desperate than the last. Assailed by sorcery and the implacable savagery of the undead warriors, the Tenescowri had finally reeled back, fleeing in terror. A company of Beklites fared no better later in the afternoon. Now, as dusk swept in behind the rain, the streets surrounding the estate held only the dead.

On wearying wings, Buke climbed higher once more, following the Daru District's main avenue westward.

Gutted tenement buildings, smoke billowing from rubble, the fitful lick of flames. Seething mobs of Tenescowri, huge bonfires where spitted human flesh roasted. Roving squads and companies of Scalandi, Beklites and Betaklites, Urdomen and Seerdomin.

Bewildered, enraged, wondering where Capustan's citizens have gone. Oh, you have the city, now, yet you feel cheated none the less.

His acute vision was failing with the fading light. To the southeast, hazy with rain and smoke, rose the prince's palace towers. Dark, seemingly inviolate. Perhaps its inhabitants held out still. Or perhaps it was, once more, a lifeless edifice home only to ghosts. Returned to the comfort of silence, such as it had known for centuries before the coming of the Capan and Daru.

Turning his head back, Buke caught glimpse of a single tenement building just off to his left. Fires surrounded it, but it seemed the squat structure defied the flames. In the glow of the banked bonfires, he saw red-limned, naked corpses. Filling the surrounding streets and alleys.

No, that must be a mistake. My eyes deceive. Those dead are lying on rubble. They must be. Gods, the tenement's ground level isn't even visible. Buried. Rubble. There cannot be

643

naught but bodies, not piled that high . . . oh . . . depthless Abyss!

The building was where Gruntle had taken a room.

And, assailed by flames, it would not burn.

And there, lit on all sides from below, the walls *wept*.

Not water, but blood.

Buke wheeled closer, and the closer he flew, the more horrified he became. He could see windows, shutterless, on the first visible floor. Packed with bodies. The same on the next floor, and on the one above that, directly beneath the roof.

The entire building was, he realized, virtually solid. A mass of flesh and bone, seeping from the windows tears of blood and bile. A giant mausoleum, a monument to this day.

He saw figures on the roof. A dozen, huddled here and there beneath makeshift awnings and lean-to shelters. And one, standing apart, head bowed as if studying the horror in the street below. Tall, hulking. Broad, sloping shoulders. Strangely barbed in shadows. A cutlass hung heavy in each gauntleted hand, stripped and gleaming like bone.

A dozen paces behind him a standard had been raised, held upright by bundles that might be food packs, such as the Grey Swords issued. Sodden, yellow stained with dark bars of blood, a child's tunic.

Buke drew still closer, then swung away. He was not ready. Not for Gruntle. Not for the man as he was now, as he had become. A terrible transformation . . . *one more victim of this siege*.

As are we all.

Blinking, Itkovian struggled to make sense of his surroundings. A low, damp-blighted ceiling, the smell of raw meat. Yellow lantern light, the weight of a rough woollen blanket on his chest. He was lying on a narrow cot, and someone was holding his hand.

He slowly turned his head, wincing at the lash of pain

644

the motion elicited from his neck. *Healed, yet not healed. The mending . . . incomplete . . .*

Karnadas was at his side, collapsed onto his haunches, folded and motionless, the pale, wrinkled pate of his bowed head level with Itkovian's eyes.

The hand gripping his was all bone and deathly dry skin, icy cold.

The Shield Anvil squeezed it slightly.

The Destriant's face, as he lifted it into view, was skeletal, the skin mottled with deep bruises originating from the joints of his jaw; his red-webbed eyes sunken within charcoal-black pits.

'Ah,' the old man rasped, 'I have failed you, sir . . .'

'You have not.'

'Your wounds—'

'The flesh is sealed – I can feel as much. My neck, my back, my knee. There is naught but a tenderness, sir. Easily managed.' He slowly sat up, keeping his expression calm despite the agony that ripped through him. Flexing his knee left him bathed in sweat, suddenly chilled and light-headed. He did not alter his firm grip on the Destriant's hand. 'Your gift ever humbles me, sir.'

Karnadas settled his head on Itkovian's thigh. 'I am done, my friend,' he whispered.

'I know,' the Shield Anvil replied. 'But I am not.'

The Destriant's head moved in a nod but he did not look up.

Itkovian glanced around. Four other cots, each bearing a soldier. Rough blankets had been drawn up over their faces. Two of the priest's cutters sat on the blood-gummed floor, their backs to a wall, their eyes closed in the sleep of the exhausted. Near the small room's door stood a Grey Sword messenger, Capan by her features beneath the rim of her helmet. He had seen a younger version of her, among the recruits . . . perhaps a sister. 'How long have I been unconscious? Do I hear rain?'

Karnadas made no answer. Neither surgeon stirred

awake. After a moment, the messenger cleared her throat. 'Sir, it is less than a bell before midnight. The rain came with the dusk.'

With the dusk, and with a man's death. The hand holding his slackened in increments. 'How many soldiers here, sir? How many do I still command?'

She flinched. 'There are one hundred and thirty-seven in all, sir. Of these, ninety-six recruits. Of the Manes who stood with you at the cemetery, eleven soldiers survive.'

'Our barracks?'

'Fallen, sir. The structure burns.'

'Jelarkan's Palace?'

She shook her head. 'No word, sir.'

Itkovian slowly disengaged his hand from Karnadas's limp grip and looked down upon the motionless figure. He stroked the wisps of the man's hair. Moments passed, then the Shield Anvil broke the silence. 'Find us an orderly, sir. The Destriant is dead.'

Her eyes widened on him.

'He joins our Mortal Sword, Brukhalian. It is done.'

Following these words, Itkovian settled his boots onto the floor, almost blacking out at the pain in his ruined knee. He drew a deep, shaky breath, slowly straightened. 'Do any armourers remain?'

'An apprentice, sir,' she replied after a moment, her tone brittle as burned leather.

'I shall need a brace for my knee, sir. Anything he or she can fashion.'

'Yes, sir,' she whispered. 'Shield Anvil—'

He paused in his search for his surcoat, glanced over. The woman had gone deathly white.

'I – I voice the Reve's Thirteenth Law. I request . . . rightful punishment.' She was trembling.

'Punishment, sir? What was your crime?'

'I delivered the message. From Rath'Fener's acolyte.' She reeled at her own words, armour clunking as her back came up against the door. 'Fener forgive me! I sent the Mortal Sword to his death!'

Itkovian's eyes thinned as he studied her. 'You are the recruit who accompanied me and my wings on the last excursion onto the plain. My apologies, sir, for not recognizing you earlier. I should have anticipated the intervening ... experience, writ so clearly upon your face. I deny your voicing the Reve, soldier. Now, find us that orderly, and the apprentice.'

'But sir—'

'Brukhalian was not deceived. Do you understand? Moreover, your presence here evinces your innocence in the matter. Had you been party to the betrayal, you would have ridden with him at his command. And would have been dealt with accordingly. Now go. We cannot wait here much longer.'

Ignoring the tears now streaking her mud-spattered face, the Shield Anvil slowly made his way to a heap of discarded armour. A moment later she swung about, opened the door and fled out into the hallway.

Itkovian paused in his hobbling. He glanced over at the sleeping cutters. 'I am the bearer of Fener's grief,' he intoned in a whisper. 'I am my vow incarnate. This, and in all that follows. We are not yet done here. I am not yet done. Behold, I yield to nothing.' He straightened, expressionless once more. His pain retreated. Soon, it would be irrelevant.

One hundred and thirty-seven armoured faces looked upon the Shield Anvil. Through the streaming rain, he in turn surveyed them as they stood in their ranks on the dark street. Two warhorses remained; his own – chest wound a red welt but fire undimmed in the eyes – and Brukhalian's black destrier. The messenger held both sets of reins.

Strips from a banded cuirass had been lashed to either side of Itkovian's damaged knee, providing sufficient flex for him to ride and walk while offering vital support when he stood. The rents in his chain surcoat had been mended with copper wire; the weight of the sleeve was noticeable only on his left arm – there was little strength in it, and the skin between his neck and shoulder felt stretched and hot over the incompletely knitted tissue beneath. Straps had been rigged that would hold his arm at an angle when it bore his shield.

'Grey Swords.' The Shield Anvil addressed them. 'We have work before us. Our captain and her sergeants have formed you into squads. We march to the palace of the prince. The journey is not far. It appears that the enemy is chiefly massed around the Thrall. Should we happen to encounter roving bands, however, they will probably be small, and most likely Tenescowri and thus ill armed and untrained. March, therefore, in readiness.' Itkovian faced his lone captain, who had only days earlier been the master-sergeant responsible for the training of the Capan recruits. 'Sir, array the squads.'

The woman nodded.

Itkovian strode to his horse. A makeshift mounting block had been prepared, easing the transition into the saddle. Accepting the reins from the messenger, the Shield Anvil looked down upon her. 'The captain will walk with her soldiers, sir,' he said. 'The Mortal Sword's horse should be ridden. She is yours, recruit. She will know your capacity by your seat, and respond in accordance to ensure your safety. It will not avail you to defy her in this.'

Blinking, the young woman slowly nodded.

'Mount up, then, sir, and ride at my side.'

The ramp leading to Jelarkan's Palace's narrow, arched gateway was unoccupied, swept clean. The gates themselves had been shattered. Faint torchlight glimmered from the antechamber immediately beyond. Not a single soldier stood on the walls or revetments. Apart from the drumming rain, there was naught but silence to greet Itkovian and his Grey Swords.

Point squads had scouted to the gate's threshold, confirming that the enemy was nowhere to be seen. Nor, it seemed, were there any surviving defenders. Or bodies.

Smoke and hissing mist filled the spaces between stone, sheets of rain the night sky overhead. All sounds of fighting in other sections were gone.

Brukhalian had asked for six weeks. Itkovian had given him less than three days. The truth of that gnawed within him, as if a broken blade or arrowhead still remained in his body – missed by the cutters – buried in his gut, wrapping its pain around his heart.

But I am not yet done.

He held to those words. Back straight, teeth gritted. A gesture with one gauntleted hand sent the first scouts through the gateway. They were gone for some time, then a single runner returned, padding down the ramp to where Itkovian waited.

'Sir,' the woman reported, 'there are Tenescowri within. In the main hall, we believe. Sounds of feasting and revelry.'

'And are the approaches guarded?' the Shield Anvil asked.

'The three that we have found are not, sir.'

There were four entrances to Jelarkan's main hall. The double doors facing the gate on the other side of the antechamber, two flanking portals in the chamber itself that led to guest and guard rooms, and a narrow, curtain-shielded passage directly behind the prince's throne. 'Very well. Captain, position one squad to each of the two side entrances. Quietly. Six squads here at the gate. The remaining five are with me.'

The Shield Anvil carefully dismounted, landing mostly on his undamaged leg. He reeled none the less at the jolt that shot up his spine. The messenger had followed suit and now stepped to his side. Slowing his breathing, he glanced at her. 'Get me my shield,' he grated.

Another soldier assisted her in strapping the bronze

shield to Itkovian's arm, drawing the supporting sling over his shoulder.

The Shield Anvil lowered the visor on his helm, then slid his sword from its scabbard while the captain issued commands to the five squads arrayed around them.

'Those with crossbows to the second line, stay low and keep your weapons cocked but lower still. Front line overlapping shields, swords on guard. All visors down. Sir,' the captain addressed Itkovian, 'we are ready.'

He nodded, said to the recruit, 'You are to be on my left. Now, forward at my pace.'

He strode slowly up the rain-slick ramp.

Fifty-three silent soldiers followed.

Into the antechamber, the squarish, high-ceilinged room lit by a single wavering torch set in a bracket on the right-hand wall. The two squads assigned to the chamber split to either side as the Shield Anvil led his troop towards the broad hallway where waited the main hall's double doors. The patter of shed rain accompanied them.

Ahead, muted through the thick, oak doors, was the sound of voices. Laughter tinged with hysteria. The crackle of burning wood.

Itkovian did not pause upon reaching the entrance, using shield and mailed fist to thrust open the twin doors. As he stepped through, the squads behind him spread out to take command of his end of the long, vaulted chamber.

Faces snapped round. Gaunt figures in rags lurched up from the chairs on either side of the long table. Utensils clattered and bones thumped to the floor. A wild-haired woman shrieked, scrabbled madly towards the young man seated in Jelarkan's throne.

'Gentle Mother,' the man rasped, reaching out a shiny, grease-stained hand to her, yet holding his yellow-tinged eyes on Itkovian all the while, 'be calmed.'

She grasped that hand in both of hers, fell to her knees whimpering.

'These are naught but guests, Mother. Come too late, alas, to partake of the . . . royal feast.'

Someone screamed a laugh.

On the centre of the table was a huge silver plate, on which had been made a fire from snapped chair legs and picture frames – mostly charcoal now. Spitted above it was the remains of a skinned human torso, no longer being turned, underside blackening. Severed at the knees, the two thighs bound as one by copper wire. Arms pulled off at the shoulders, though they too had once been tied. Head left on, split and charred.

Knives had sliced off the flesh in places all over the body. Thighs, buttocks, chest, back, face. But this, Itkovian knew, had not been a feast born of hunger. These Tenescowri in this room looked better fed than any other he had yet seen. No, here, this night, had been a celebration.

To the left of the throne, half in shadow, was an X-shaped cross made from two pikes. On it was stretched Prince Jelarkan's skin.

'The dear prince was dead before we began cooking,' the young man on the throne said. 'We are not consciously cruel, after all. You are not Brukhalian, for Brukhalian is dead. You must be Itkovian, the so-called Shield Anvil of Fener.'

Seerdomin appeared from behind the throne, pale-armoured and helmed, fur-backed, their faces hidden by grilled face-baskets, heavy battleaxes in their gauntleted hands. Four, eight, a dozen. Twenty. And still more filed out.

The man on the throne smiled. 'Your soldiers look . . . tired. Unequal to this particular task. Do you know me, Itkovian? I am Anaster, First Child of the Dead Seed. Tell me, where are the people of this city? What have you done with them? Oh, let me guess. They cower in tunnels beneath the streets. Guarded by a handful of surviving Gidrath, a company or two of your Grey Swords, some of the prince's Capan Guard. I imagine Prince Arard hides below as well. A shame, that. We have wanted him a long time. Well, the search for the hidden entrances continues. They shall be found. Capustan shall be cleansed, Shield Anvil, though, alas, you will not live to see that glorious day.'

Itkovian studied the young man, and saw what he had not expected to see. 'First Child,' he said. 'There is despair within you. I will take it from you, sir, and with it your burdens.'

Anaster jolted as if he had been physically struck. He drew his knees up, climbed onto the seat of the throne, face twitching. A hand closed on the strange obsidian dagger in his belt, then flinched away as if the stone was hot.

His mother screamed, clawed up her son's outstretched arm. Snarling, he pulled himself free. She sank down to the floor, curled up.

'I am not your father,' Itkovian continued, 'but I shall be *as* him. Unleash your flood, First Child.'

The young man stared, lips peeling back to bare his teeth. 'Who – what are you?' he hissed.

The captain stepped forward. 'We forgive your ignorance, sir,' she said. 'He is the Shield Anvil. Fener knows grief, so much grief that it is beyond his capacity to withstand it. And so he chooses a human heart. Armoured. A mortal soul, to assume the sorrow of the world. The Shield Anvil.

'These days and nights have witnessed vast sorrow, profound shame – all of which, we see now, is writ as plain knowledge in your eyes. You cannot deceive yourself, sir, can you?'

'You never could,' Itkovian said. 'Give me your despair, First Child. I am ready to receive it.'

Anaster's wail rang through the main hall. He clambered still further up the throne's high back, arms wrapping around himself.

All eyes held on him.

No-one moved.

Chest heaving, the First Child stared at Itkovian. Then he shook his head. 'No,' he whispered, 'you shall not have my – my despair.'

The captain hissed. 'This is a gift! First Child—'

'*Not!*'

Itkovian seemed to sag. Sword-point wavering, lowering. The recruit moved close to support the Shield Anvil.

'You cannot have it! You cannot have it!'

The captain's eyes were wide as she turned to Itkovian. 'Sir, I am unable to countenance this—'

The Shield Anvil shook his head, slowly straightened once more. 'No, I understand. The First Child – within him there is naught but despair. Without it . . .'

He is as nothing.

'I want them all killed!' Anaster shrieked brokenly. 'Seerdomin! Kill them all!'

Forty Seerdomin surged forward to either side of the table.

The captain snapped a command. The front line behind her dropped in unison to one knee. The second line raised into view their crossbows. Twenty-four quarrels crossed the room. Not one missed.

From the flanking guest-room entrances, more quarrels flashed.

The front line behind Itkovian rose and readied their weapons.

Only six Seerdomin remained standing. Figures both writhing and motionless covered the floor.

The Tenescowri at the table were fleeing towards the portal behind the throne.

Anaster himself was the first to reach it, his mother a step behind him.

The Seerdomin charged Itkovian.

I am not yet done.

His blade flashed. A helmed head leapt from its shoulders. A backhand slash snapped chain links and opened wide another Seerdomin's belly.

Crossbows sounded once more.

And the Grey Swords stood unopposed.

The Shield Anvil lowered his weapon. 'Captain,' he said after a moment. 'Retrieve the prince's body. Have the skin taken down. We shall return Prince Jelarkan to his throne, to his rightful place. And this room, we shall now hold. For a time. In the name of the prince.'

'The First Child—'

Itkovian faced her. 'We will meet him again. I am his only salvation, sir, and I shall not fail him.'

'You are the Shield Anvil,' she intoned.

'I am the Shield Anvil.' *I am Fener's grief. I am the world's grief. And I will hold. I will hold it all, for we are not yet done.*

CHAPTER SEVENTEEN

What the soul can house, flesh cannot fathom.

The Reve of Fener
Imarak, First Destriant

Hot, fevered, the pebbled skin moved like a damp rock-filled sack. The Matron's body exuded an acrid oil. It had permeated Toc the Younger's ragged clothes. He slid between folds of flesh as the huge, bloated K'Chain Che'Malle shifted about on the gritty floor, massive arms wrapped around him in a fierce embrace.

Darkness commanded the cave. The glimmers of light he saw were born within his mind. Illusions that might have been memories. Torn, fragmented scenes, of yellow-grassed low hills beneath warm sunlight. Figures, caught at the very edge of his vision. Some wore masks. One was naught but dead skin stretched over robust bone. Another was . . . beauty. Perfection. He believed in none of them. Their faces were the faces of his madness, looming ever closer, hovering at his shoulder.

When sleep took him he dreamed of wolves. Hunting, not to feed, but to deliver . . . something else; he knew not what. The quarry wandered alone, the quarry fled when it saw him. Brothers and sisters at his side, he pursued. Relentless, leagues passing effortlessly beneath his paws. The small, frightened creature could not elude them. He and his kin drew nearer, exhausting it against the slopes of hills, until finally it faltered, then collapsed. They surrounded it.

As they closed in, to deliver . . . what was to be delivered . . . the quarry vanished.

Shock, then despair.

He and his kin would circle the spot where she'd lain. Heads lifted skyward, mournful howls issuing from their throats. Howling without surcease. Until Toc the Younger blinked awake, in the embrace of the Matron, the turgid air of the cave seeming to dance with the fading echoes of his howls. The creature would tighten her hold, then. Whimpering, prodding the back of his neck with a fanged snout, her breath like sugared milk.

The cycles of his life. Sleep, then wakefulness punctuated by hallucinations. Smeared scenes of figures in golden sunlight, delusions of being a babe in his mother's arms, suckling at her breast – the Matron possessed no breasts, so he knew these to be delusions, yet was sustained by them none the less – and times when he began voiding his bladder and bowels, and she held him out when he did this, so he fouled only himself. She would then lick him clean, a gesture that stripped him of his last shreds of dignity.

Her embrace broke bones. The more he screamed with the pain, the tighter she held him. He had learned to suffer in silence. His bones knitted with preternatural swiftness. Sometimes unevenly. He knew himself to be malformed – his chest, his hips, the blades of his shoulders.

Then there came the visitations. A ghostly face, sheathed in the wrinkled visage of an old man, the hint of gleaming tusks, took form within his mind. Yellowed eyes that shone with glee fixed on his own.

Familiar, those overlapping faces, but Toc was unable to take his recognition any further.

The visitor would speak to him.

They are trapped, my friend. All but the T'lan Imass, who fears solitude. Why else would he not leave his companions?

656

Swallowed in ice. Helpless. Frozen. The Seguleh – no need to fear them. Never was. I but played. And the woman! My rimed beauteous statue! Wolf and dog have vanished. Fled. Aye, the kin, brother of your eyes . . . fled. Tail between legs, hee hee!

And again.

Your Malazan army is too late! Too late to save Capustan! The city is mine. Your fellow soldiers are still a week away, my friend. We shall await them. We shall greet them as we greet all enemies.

I will bring you the head of the Malazan general. I will bring you his cooked flesh, and we shall dine together, you and I, once more.

How much blood can one world shed? Have you ever wondered, Toc the Younger? Shall we see? Let us see, then. You and I, and dear Mother here – oh, is that horror I see in her eyes? Some sanity still resides in her rotted brain, it seems. How unfortunate . . . for her.

And now, after a long absence, he returned once more. The false skin of the old man was taut against the unhuman visage. The tusks were visible as if through a transparent sheath. The eyes burned, but not, this time, with glee.

Deceit! They are not mortal beasts! How dare they assail my defences! Here, at the very gates! And now the T'lan Imass has vanished – I can find him nowhere! Does he come as well?

So be it. They shall not find you. We journey, the three of us. North, far beyond their reach. I have prepared another . . . nest for you two.

The inconvenience . . .

But Toc no longer heard him. His mind had been snatched away. He saw brittle white sunlight, a painful glare shimmering from ice-clad mountains and valleys buried in rivers of snow. In the sky, wheeling condors. And then, far more immediate, there was smoke, wooden structures shattered, stone walls tumbled. Figures running, screaming. Crimson spattering the snow, filling the milky puddles of a gravel road.

The point of view – eyes that saw through a red haze –

shifted, swung to one side. A mottled black and grey hound kept pace, shoulders at eye level to the armoured figures it was tearing into with blurred savagery. The creature was driving towards a second set of gates, an arched portal at the base of a towering fortress. None could stand before it, none could slow its momentum.

Grey dust swirled from the hound's shoulders. Swirled. Spun, twisted into arms, legs gripping the creature's flanks, a bone-helmed head, torn fur a ragged wing behind it. Raised high, a rippled sword the colour of old blood.

His bones are well, his flesh is not. My flesh is well, my bones are not. Are we brothers?

Hound and rider – nightmare vision – struck the huge, iron-banded gates.

Wood exploded. In the archway's gloom, terror plunged among a reeling knot of Seerdomin.

Loping towards the breached portal, Toc rode his wolf's vision, saw into the shadows, where huge, reptilian shapes stepped into view to either side of the hound and its undead rider.

The K'ell Hunters raised their broad blades.

Snarling, the wolf sprinted. His focus was the gate, every detail there sharp as broken glass whilst all that lay to either side blurred. A shift of weight brought him to the Ke'll Hunter closing from the hound and rider's left.

The creature pivoted, sword slashing to intercept his charge.

The wolf ducked beneath it, then surged upward, jaws wide. Leathery throat filled his mouth. His canines sank deep into lifeless flesh. Jaw muscles bunched. Bone cracked, then crumbled as the wolf inexorably closed its vice-grip, even as the momentum of his charge drove the K'ell Hunter back onto its tail, crashing against a wall that shuddered with the impact. Upper and lower canines met. Jagged molars ground together, slicing through wood-like tendon and dry muscle.

The wolf was severing the head from the body.

The K'Chain Che'Malle shook beneath him, spasmed. A flailing blade sliced into the wolf's right haunch.

Toc and beast flinched at the pain, yet did not relent.

The ornately helmed head fell back, away, thumped as it struck the slush-covered cobbles.

Snarling, lifeless shreds snagged on his teeth, the wolf spun round.

The hound crouched, spine hunched, in a corner of the archway. Blood poured from it. Alone, to battle its wounds.

The undead swordsman— *my brother* – was on his leather-wrapped feet now, his flint sword trading blows with the other K'ell Hunter's twin blades. At speeds unimaginable. Chunks of the K'Chain Che'Malle flew. A sword-bound forearm spun end over end to land near the flinching hound.

The K'ell Hunter lurched back in the face of the onslaught. Shin-bones snapped with a brittle report. The huge creature fell over, spraying slush out to all sides.

The undead warrior clambered onto it, systematically swinging his sword to dismember the K'Chain Che'Malle. It was a task swiftly completed.

The wolf approached the wounded hound. The animal snapped a warning to stay away—

Toc was suddenly blind, ripped away from the wolf's vision.

Bitter winds tore at him, but the Matron held him tight. On the move. Swiftly. They travelled a warren, a path of riven ice. They were, he realized, fleeing Outlook, fleeing the fortress that had just been breached.

By Baaljagg. And Garath and Tool. Garath – those wounds—

'Silence!' a voice shrieked.

The Seer was with them, leading the way through Omtose Phellack.

The gift of clarity remained in Toc's mind. His laugh was a ragged gurgle.

'*Shut up!*'

The entire warren shook to distant thunder, the sound of vast ice ... cracking, exploding in a conflagration of sorcery.

Lady Envy. With us once more—

The Seer screamed.

Reptilian arms clenched Toc. Bones cracked, splintered. Pain shoved him over a precipice. *My kin, my brothers—* He blacked out.

The night sky to the south was lit red. Though over a league distant, from the slope of the sparsely wooded hill, Capustan's death was plain to see, drawing the witnesses to silence apart from the rustle of armour and weapons, and the squelch of boots and moccasins in mud.

Leaves dripped a steady susurration. The soaked humus filled the warm air with its fecundity. Somewhere nearby a man coughed.

Captain Paran drew a dagger and began scraping the mud from his boots. He had known what to expect at this moment – his first sight of the city. Humbrall Taur's scouts had brought word back earlier in the day. The siege was over. The Grey Swords might well have demanded an emperor's ransom for their services, but fire-charred, tooth-gnawed bones could not collect it. Even so, knowing what to expect did little to diminish the pathos of a dying city.

Had those Grey Swords been Crimson Guard, the scene before Paran might well be different. With the lone exception of Prince K'azz D'Avore's Company of the Avowed, mercenaries were less than worthless as far as the captain was concerned. Tough talk and little else.

Let's hope those children of Humbrall Taur have fared better. It did not seem likely. Pockets of resistance perhaps remained. Small knots of cornered soldiers, knowing mercy was out of the question, would fight to the last. In alleys, in houses, in rooms. Capustan's death-throes would be protracted. *Then again, if these damned Barghast can actually manage a doubletime – instead of this squabbling saunter*

660

– we might be able to adjust that particular fate's conclusion.

Paran turned at the arrival of his new commander, Trotts.

The huge Barghast's eyes glittered as he studied the burning city. 'The rains have done little to dim the flames,' he rumbled, scowling.

'Perhaps it's not as bad as it looks,' Paran said. 'I can make out maybe five major fires. It could be worse – I've heard tales of firestorms . . .'

'Aye. We saw one from afar, in Seven Cities, once.'

'What's Humbrall Taur had to say, Warchief? Do we pick up our pace or do we just stand here?'

Trotts bared his filed teeth. 'He will send the Barahn and the Ahkrata clans southeast. They are tasked with taking the landings and the floating bridges and barges. His own Senan and the Gilk will strike towards Capustan. The remaining clans will seize the Septarch's main supply camp, which lies between the landings and the city.'

'That's all very well, but if we keep dawdling—'

'Hetan and Cafal, Taur's children, are alive and not at risk. So the shouldermen insist. The bones are being protected, by strange sorceries. Strange, yet profoundly powerful. There is—'

'Damn you, Trotts! People are dying down there! People are being *devoured*!'

The Barghast's grin broadened. 'Thus, I have been given leave . . . to lead my clan at a pace of my own choosing. Captain, are you eager to be first among the White Faces into Capustan?'

Paran growled under his breath. He felt a need to draw his sword, felt a need to deliver vengeance, to finally – after all this time – strike a blow against the Pannion Domin. Quick Ben, in those moments when he was lucid and not raving with fever, had made it clear that the Domin held dire secrets, and a malevolence stained its heart. The fact of the Tenescowri was proof enough of that to the captain's mind.

661

But there was more to his need. He lived with pain. His stomach raged with spotfires. He had thrown up acidic bile and blood – revealing that truth to no-one. The pain bound him within himself, and those bindings were getting tighter.

And another truth, one I keep pushing away. She's haunting me. Seeking my thoughts. But I'm not ready for her. Not yet, not with my stomach aflame . . .

It was no doubt madness – a delusion – but Paran believed that the pain would relent – all would be well once more – as soon as he delivered to the world the violence trapped within him. Folly or not, he clung to that belief. *Only then will these pressures relent. Only then.*

He was not ready to fail.

'Call up the Bridgeburners, then,' Paran muttered. 'We can be at the north gate inside of a bell.'

Trotts grunted. 'All thirty-odd of us.'

'Well, damn if we can't shame these Barghast into some haste—'

'This is your hope?'

Paran glanced over at the man. 'Hood take us all, Trotts, you were the one who asked Taur to grant you leave. Do you expect the thirty-seven of us to retake Capustan all on our own? With an unconscious mage in tow?'

The Barghast, eyes thinned to slits as he studied the city ahead, rolled his shoulders and said, 'We leave Quick Ben behind. As for retaking the city, I mean to try.'

After a long moment, the captain grinned. 'Glad to hear it.'

The march of the White Face Barghast had been slow, torturous. Early on, during the southward journey across the high plains, sudden duels brought the clans to a halt a half-dozen times a day. These were, finally, diminishing, and Humbrall Taur's decision to assign entire clans to specific tasks in the upcoming battle would effectively remove the opportunity in the days to come. For all that

662

every warchief had bowed to the single cause – the liberation of their gods – longstanding enmities persisted.

Trotts's new role as warchief of the Bridgeburners had proved something of a relief for Paran. He'd hated the responsibility of command. The pressure that was the well-being of every soldier under him had been a growing burden. As second-in-command, that pressure had diminished, if only slightly – but it was, for now, enough. Less pleasant was the fact that Paran had lost his role as representative of the Bridgeburners. Trotts had taken on the task of attending the war councils, leaving the captain out of the picture.

In the strictest sense, Paran remained in command of the Bridgeburners. But the company had become a tribe, insofar as Humbrall Taur and the Barghast were concerned, and tribes elected warchiefs, and that role belonged to Trotts.

The tree-studded hills behind them, the company of Bridgeburners moved down to the muddy verges of a seasonal stream that wound its way towards the city. Smoke from Capustan's fires obscured the stars overhead, and the rain of the past few days had softened the ground underfoot, lending it a spongy silence. Armour and weapons had been strapped tight; the Bridgeburners padded forward through the darkness without a sound.

Paran was three paces behind Trotts, who still held to his old role in Whiskeyjack's squad – that of taking point. Not the ideal position for the commander, but one that complemented the Barghast role of warchief. The captain was not happy with it. Worse, it showed Trotts's stubborn side all too clearly. A lack of adaptability that was disturbing in a leader.

An invisible presence seemed to settle on his shoulder, the touch of a distant, familiar mind. Paran grimaced. His link with Silverfox was growing stronger. This was the third time she had reached out to him this week. A faint brush of awareness, like the touching of fingers, tip to tip. He wondered if that made her able to see what he saw, wondered if she was reading his thoughts. Given all that he held within himself, Paran was beginning to instinctively recoil from her contact. His secrets were his own. She had no right to plunder them, if that was what she was doing. Even tactical necessity could not justify that to his mind. His frown deepened as her presence lingered. *If it is her. What if—*

Ahead, Trotts stopped, settling into a crouch, one hand raised. He gestured twice.

Paran and the soldier immediately behind him moved to join the Barghast warrior.

They had reached the Pannions' north pickets. The encampment was a shambles, bereft of organization, sloppily prepared and seriously undermanned. Litter cluttered the trodden paths between trenches, pits, and the ragged sprawl of makeshift tents. The air was redolent with poorly placed latrines.

The three men studied the scene for a moment longer, then withdrew to rejoin the others. The squad sergeants slipped forward. A huddle was formed.

Spindle, who had been the soldier accompanying Paran, was the first to speak. 'Medium infantry on station,' he whispered. 'Two small companies by the pair of standards—'

'Two hundred,' Trotts agreed. 'More in the tents. Sick and wounded.'

'Mostly sick, I'd say,' Spindle replied. 'Dysentery, I'd guess, by the smell. These Pannion officers ain't worth dung. Them sick ones won't be in the fighting no matter what we do. Guess everyone else is in the city.'

'The gates beyond,' Trotts growled.

Paran nodded. 'Lots of bodies before it. A thousand corpses, maybe more. No barricades at the gates themselves, nor could I see any guard. The overconfidence of victors.'

'We gotta punch through them medium infantry,' Sergeant Antsy muttered. 'Spindle, how are you and the rest of the sappers for Moranth munitions?'

The small man grinned. 'Found your nerve again, eh, Antsy?'

The sergeant scowled. 'This is fightin', ain't it? Now answer my question, soldier.'

'We got plenty. Wish we had a few of them lobbers Fiddler makes, though.'

Paran blinked, then recalled the oversized crossbows Fiddler and Hedge used to extend the range of cussers. 'Doesn't Hedge have one?' he asked.

'He broke it, the idiot. No, we'll prime some cussers but that'll be just for sowing. Sharpers, tonight. Burners would make too much light – let the enemy see how few of us there really are. Sharpers. I'll gather the lads and lasses.'

'I thought you were a mage,' Paran muttered as the man turned towards the waiting squads.

Spindle glanced back. 'I am, Captain. And I'm a sapper, too. Deadly combination, eh?'

'Deadly for us,' Antsy retorted. 'That and your damned hairshirt—'

'Hey, the burnt patches are growing back – see?'

'Get to it,' Trotts growled.

Spindle started tagging off squad sappers.

'So we just punch right through,' Paran said. 'With the sharpers that should be no problem, but then the ones on the outside flanks will sweep in behind us—'

Spindle rejoined them in time to grunt and say, 'That's why we'll sow cussers, Captain. Two drops on the wax. Ten heartbeats. The word's "run", and when we shout it that's what you'd better do, and fast. If you're less than thirty paces away when they go up, you're diced liver.'

'You ready?' Trotts asked Spindle.

'Aye. Nine of us, so expect just under thirty paces wide, the path we carve.'

'Weapons out,' the Barghast said. Then he reached out and gripped Spindle's hairshirt and dragged him close. Trotts grinned. 'No mistakes.'

665

'No mistakes,' the man agreed, eyes widening as Trotts clacked his sharpened teeth inches from his face.

A moment later, Spindle and his eight fellow sappers were moving towards the enemy lines, hooded and shapeless in their rain-capes.

The presence brushed Paran's awareness once again. He did all he could in his mind to push it away. The acid in his stomach swirled, murmuring a promise of pain. He drew a deep breath to steady himself. *If swords clash . . . it will be my first. After all this time, my first battle . . .*

The enemy medium infantry were huddled in groups, twenty or more to each of a row of hearths on the encampment's only high ground – what used to be a cart track running parallel to the city wall. Paran judged that a path thirty paces wide would take out most of three groups.

Leaving well over a hundred Pannions capable of responding. If there were any capable officers among them, this could get ugly. *Then again, if there were any capable officers there the squads wouldn't be clumped up the way they are . . .*

The sappers had gone to ground. The captain could no longer see them. Shifting his grip on his sword, he checked back over a shoulder to scan the rest of the Bridgeburners. Picker was at the forefront, a painful expression on her face. He was about to ask her what was wrong when detonations cracked through the night. The captain spun round.

Bodies writhed in the firelight of the now scattered hearths.

Trotts loosed a quavering warcry.

The Bridgeburners sprinted forward.

More sharpers exploded, out to the sides now, dropping the mobbed, confused soldiers around adjacent hearths.

Paran saw the dark forms of the sappers, converging directly ahead, squatting down amidst dead and dying Pannions.

Crossbows thunked in the hands of the dozen or so Bridgeburners who carried them.

Screams rang.

Trotts leading the way, the Bridgeburners reached the charnel path, passed around the crouching sappers who were one and all readying the larger cussers. Two drops of acid to the wax plug sealing the hole in the clay grenado.

A chorus of muted hisses.

'*Run!*'

Paran cursed. Ten heartbeats suddenly seemed no time at all. Cussers were the largest of the Moranth munitions. A single one could make the intersection of four streets virtually impassable. The captain ran.

His heart almost seized in his chest as he fixed his eyes on the gate directly ahead. The thousand corpses were stirring. *Oh damn. Not dead at all. Sleeping. The bastards were sleeping!*

'Down down down!'

The word was Malazan, the voice was Hedge's.

Paran hesitated only long enough to see Spindle, Hedge and the other sappers arrive among them ... to throw cussers. Forward. Into the massing ranks of Tenescowri between them and the gates. Then they dived flat.

'Oh, Hood!' The captain threw himself down, slid across gritty mud, releasing his grip on his sword and clamping both hands to his ears.

The ground punched the breath from his lungs, threw his legs into the air. He thumped back down in the mud. On his back. He had time to begin his roll before the cussers directly ahead exploded. The impact sent him tumbling. Bloody shreds rained down on him.

A large object thumped beside Paran's head. He blinked his eyes open. To see a man's hips – just the hips, the concavity where intestines belonged yawning black and wet. Thighs were gone, taken at the joints. The captain stared.

His ears were ringing. He felt blood trickling from his nose. His chest ached. Distant screaming wailed through the night.

A hand closed on his rain-cape, tugged him upright.

667

Mallet. The healer leaned close to press the captain's sword into his hands, then shouted words Paran barely heard. 'Come on! They're all getting the Hood out of here!' A shove sent the captain stumbling forward.

His eyes saw, but his mind failed in registering the devastation to either side of the path they now ran down towards the north gate. He felt himself shutting down inside, even as he slipped and staggered through the human ruin . . . shutting down as he had once before, years ago, on a road in Itko Kan.

The hand of vengeance stayed cold only so long. Any soul possessing a shred of humanity could not help but see the reality behind cruel deliverance, no matter how justified it might have at first seemed. Faces blank in death. Bodies twisted in postures no-one unbroken could achieve. Destroyed lives. Vengeance yielded a mirror to every atrocity, where notions of right and wrong blurred and lost all relevance.

He saw, to the right and left, fleeing figures. A few sharpers cracked, hastening the rout.

The Bridgeburners had announced themselves to the enemy.

We are their match, the captain realized as he ran, *in calculated brutality. But this is a war of nerves where no-one wins.*

The unchallenged darkness of the gate swallowed Paran and his fellow Bridgeburners. Boots skidded as the soldiers halted their mad sprint. Dropping into crouches. Reloading crossbows. Not a word spoken.

Trotts reached a hand out and dragged Hedge close. The Barghast shook the man hard for a moment, then made to throw him down. A squeal from Spindle stopped him. Hedge, after all, carried a leather sack half full of munitions.

His face still a mass of bruises from Detoran's fond touch, Hedge cursed. 'Ain't no choice, you big ape!'

Paran could hear the words. An improvement. He wasn't sure who he sided with on this one, but the truth of it was, it no longer mattered. 'Trotts!' he snapped. 'What now? If we wait here—'

The Barghast grunted. 'Into the city, low and quiet.'

'Which direction?' Antsy asked.

'We head to the Thrall—'

'Fine, and what's that?'

'The glowing keep, you thick-skulled idiot.'

They edged forward, out from beneath the archway's gloom, onto the concourse immediately beyond. Their steps slowed as flickering firelight revealed the nightmare before them.

There had been vast slaughter, and then there had been a feast. The cobbles were ankle-deep in bones, some charred, others red and raw with bits of tendon and flesh still clinging to them. And fully two-thirds of the dead, the captain judged from what he could see of uniforms and clothing, belonged to the invaders.

'Gods,' Paran muttered, 'the Pannions paid dearly.' *I think I should revise my estimation of the Grey Swords.*

Spindle nodded. 'Even so, numbers will tell.'

'A day or two earlier . . .' Mallet said.

No-one bothered finishing the thought. There was no need.

'What's your problem, Picker?' Antsy demanded.

'Nothing!' the woman snapped. 'It's nothing.'

'Is that the Thrall, then?' Hedge asked. 'That glowing dome? There, through the smoke—'

'Let's go,' Trotts said.

The Bridgeburners ranging out cautiously in the Barghast's wake, they set forth, across the grisly concourse, to a main avenue that seemed to lead directly towards the strangely illumined structure. The style of the houses and tenement blocks to either side – those that were still standing – was distinctly Daru to Paran's eyes. The rest of the city, he saw from fragmented glimpses down side alleys and avenues where fires still burned – was completely different. Vaguely alien. And, everywhere, bodies.

Further down the street, piles of still-fleshed corpses rose like the slope of a hill.

The Bridgeburners said nothing as they neared that slope. The truth before them was difficult to comprehend. On this street alone, there were at least ten thousand bodies. Maybe more. Sodden, already swollen, the flesh pale around gaping, blood-drained wounds. Concentrated mounds around building entrances, alley mouths, an estate's gate, the stepped approaches to gutted temples. Faces and sightless eyes reflected flames, making expressions seem to writhe in mocking illusion of animation, of life.

To continue on the street, the Bridgeburners would have to climb that slope.

Trotts did not hesitate.

Word arrived from the small company's rearguard. Tenescowri had entered through the gate, were keeping pace like silent ghosts behind them. A few hundred, no more than that. Poorly armed. No trouble. Trotts simply shrugged at the news.

They scrambled their way up the soft, flesh-laden ramp.

Do not look down. Do not think of what is underfoot. Think only of the defenders, who must have fought on. Think of courage almost inhuman, defying mortal limits. Of these Grey Swords – those motionless, uniformed corpses in those doorways, crowding the alley mouths. Fighting on, and on. Yielding nothing. Cut to pieces where they stood.

These soldiers humble us all. A lesson . . . for the Bridgeburners around me. This brittle, heart-broken company. We've come to a war devoid of mercy.

The ramp had been *fashioned*. There was an intention to its construction. It was an approach. To what?

It ended in a tumbled heap, at a level less than a man's height below the roof of a tenement block. Opposite the building there had been another just like it, but fire had reduced it to smouldering rubble.

Trotts stopped at the ramp's very edge. The rest followed

suit, crouching down, looking around, trying to comprehend the meaning of all that they saw. The ragged end revealed the truth: there was no underlying structure to this ghastly construct. It was indeed solid bodies.

'A siege ramp,' Spindle finally said in a quiet, almost diffident tone. 'They wanted to get to somebody—'

'Us,' a low voice rumbled from above them.

Crossbows snapped up.

Paran looked to the tenement building's roof. A dozen figures lined its edge. Distant firelight lit them.

'They brought ladders,' the voice continued, now speaking Daru. 'We beat them anyway.'

These warriors were not Grey Swords. They were armoured, but it was a ragtag collection of accoutrements. One and all, their faces and exposed skin were daubed in streaks and barbs. Like human tigers.

'I like the paint,' Hedge called up, also in Daru. 'Scared the crap out of me, that's for sure.'

The spokesman, tall and hulking, bone-white black-barbed cutlasses in his mailed hands, cocked his head. 'It's not paint, Malazan.'

Silence.

Then the man gestured with a blade. 'Come up, if you like.'

Ladders appeared from the rooftop, slid down its edge.

Trotts hesitated. Paran stepped close. 'I think we should. There's something about that man and his followers—'

The Barghast snorted. 'Really?' He waved the Bridgeburners to the ladders.

Paran watched the ascent, deciding he would be the last to go. He saw Picker hanging back. 'Problem, Corporal?'

She flinched, massaging her right arm.

'You're in pain,' the captain said, moving to her side, studying her pinched face. 'Did you take a wound? Let's go to Mallet.'

'He can't help me, Captain. Never mind about it.'

I know precisely how you feel. 'Climb, then.'

671

As if approaching gallows, the corporal made her way to the nearest ladder.

Paran glanced back down the ramp. Spectral figures moved in the gloom at its far base. Well out of any kind of missile range. Unwilling, perhaps, to ascend the slope. The captain wasn't surprised at that.

Fighting twinges, he began climbing.

The tenement's flat roof had the look of a small shanty-town. Tarps and tents, hearths smouldering on overturned shields. Food packs, caskets of water and wine. A row of blanket-wrapped figures – the fallen, seven in all. Paran could see others in some of the tents, most likely wounded.

A standard had been raised near the roof's trapdoor, the yellow flag nothing more than a dark-streaked child's tunic.

The warriors stood silent, watchful as Trotts sent squads out to each corner of the roof, where they checked on whatever lay both below and opposite the building.

Their spokesman turned suddenly, a fluid, frighteningly graceful motion, and faced Corporal Picker. 'You have something for me,' he rumbled.

Her eyes widened. 'What?'

He sheathed one of his cutlasses and stepped up to her.

Paran and the others nearby watched as the man reached out to Picker's right arm. He gripped her chain-sleeved bicep. A muted clatter sounded.

Picker gasped.

After a moment she dropped her sword to clunk on the tarred rooftop, and began stripping off her chain surcoat with quick, jerky motions. In a flood of relief, she spoke. 'Beru's blessing! I don't know who in Hood's name you are, sir, but they've been *killing* me. Getting tighter and tighter. Gods, the pain! He said they'd never come off. He said they'd be on me for good. Even Quick Ben said that – can't make a deal with Treach. The Tiger of Summer's mad, insane—'

'Dead,' the Daru cut in.

Half out of her surcoat, Picker froze. 'What?' she whispered. 'Dead? Treach is dead?'

'The Tiger of Summer has ascended, woman. Treach – Trake – now strides with the gods. I will have them now, and I thank you for delivering them to my hand.'

She pulled her right arm clear of the chain sleeve. Three ivory arm-torcs clattered down to her hand. 'Here! Yes, please! Glad to oblige—'

'Hood take your tongue, Picker,' Antsy snapped. 'You're embarrassing us! Just give him the damned things!'

The corporal stared about. 'Blend! Where in the Abyss you hiding, woman?'

'Here,' a voice murmured beside Paran.

Startled, he stepped back. *Damn her!*

'Hah!' Picker crowed. 'You hear me, Blend? *Hah!* '

The squads were converging once more.

The Daru rolled up a tattered sleeve. The striped pattern covered the large, well-defined muscles of his arm. He slid the three torcs up past the elbow. The ivory clicked. Something flashed amber in the darkness beneath the rim of his helmet.

Paran studied the man. *A beast resides within him, an ancient spirit, reawakened.* Power swirled around the Daru, but the captain sensed that it was born as much from a natural air of command as from the beast hiding within him – for that beast preferred solitude. Its massive strength had, somehow, been almost subsumed by that quality of leadership. *Together, a formidable union. There's no mistaking, this one's important. Something's about to happen here, and my presence is no accident.* 'I am Captain Paran, of Onearm's Host.'

'Took your time, didn't you, Malazan?'

Paran blinked. 'We did the best we could, sir. In any case, your relief this night and tomorrow will come from the White Face clans.'

'Hetan and Cafal's father, Humbrall Taur. Good. Time's come to turn the tide.'

'Turn the tide?' Antsy sputtered. 'Looks like you didn't need no help to turn the tide, man!'

'Trotts,' Hedge called out. 'I ain't happy about what's underfoot. There's cracks. This whole roof is nothing but cracks.'

'Same for the walls,' another sapper noted. 'All sides.'

'This building is filled with bodies,' said a small warrior in Lestari armour beside the Daru. 'They're swelling, I guess.'

His eyes still on the big Daru, Paran asked, 'Do you have a name?'

'Gruntle.'

'Are you some kind of sect, or something? Temple warriors?'

Gruntle slowly faced him, his expression mostly hidden beneath the helm's visor. 'No. We are nothing. No-one. This is for a woman. And now she's dying—'

'Which tent?' Mallet interrupted in his high, thin voice.

'The Warren of Denul is poisoned—'

'You feel that, do you, Gruntle? Curious.' The healer waited, then asked again, 'Which tent?'

Gruntle's Lestari companion pointed. 'There. She was stuck through bad. Blood in the lungs. She might already be . . .' He fell silent.

Paran followed Mallet to the tattered shelter.

The woman lying within was pale, her young face drawn and taut. Frothy blood painted her lips.

And here, there's more.

The captain watched the healer settle to his knees beside her, reach out his hands.

'Hold it,' Paran growled. 'The last time damn near killed you—'

'Not my gift, Captain. Got Barghast spirits crowding me with this one, sir. Again. Don't know why. Someone's taken a personal interest, maybe. It may be too late anyway. We'll see . . . all right?'

After a moment, Paran nodded.

Mallet laid his hands on the unconscious woman, closed his eyes. A dozen heartbeats passed. 'Aai,' he finally whispered. 'Layers here. Wounded flesh . . . wounded spirit. I shall need to mend both. So . . . will you help me?'

The captain realized the question was not being asked of him, and so made no reply.

Mallet, eyes still closed, sighed. 'You will sacrifice so many for this woman?' He paused, eyes still closed, then frowned. 'I can't see these threads you speak of. Not her, nor Gruntle, nor the man at my side—'

At your side? Me? Threads? Gods, why don't you just leave me alone?

'—but I'll take your word for it. Shall we begin?'

Moments passed, the healer motionless above the woman. Then she stirred on her pallet, softly moaned.

The tent was torn from around them, guidewires snapping. Paran's head jerked up in surprise. To see Gruntle, chest heaving, standing above them.

'What?' the Daru gasped. 'What—' He staggered back a step, was brought up by Trotts's firm hands on his shoulders.

'No such thing,' the Barghast growled, 'as too late.'

Approaching, Antsy grinned. 'Hello, Capustan. The Bridgeburners have arrived.'

The sounds of fighting from the north and the east accompanied the dawn. The White Face clans had finally engaged the enemy. Picker and the others would later learn of the sudden and bloody pitched battle that occurred at the landings on the coast and on the shore of Catlin River. The Barahn and Ahkrata clans had collided with newly arrived regiments of Betaklites and Betrullid cavalry. The commander there had elected to counterattack rather than hold poorly prepared defensive positions, and before long the Barghast were the ones digging in, harried on all sides.

The Barahn were the first to break. Witnessing the ensuing slaughter of their kin had solidified the resolve of the Ahkrata, and they held until midday, when Taur detached the Gilk from the drive into the city and sent the turtle-shell-armoured warriors to their aid. A plains clan whetted on interminable wars against mounted enemies, the Gilk locked horns with the Betrullid and became the fulcrum for a renewed offensive by the Ahkrata, shattering the Betaklites and seizing the pontoon bridges and barges. The last of the Pannion medium infantry were driven into the river's shallows, where the water turned red. Surviving elements of the Betrullid disengaged from the Gilk and retreated north along the coast to the marshlands – a fatal error, as their horses foundered in the salty mud. The Gilk pursued to resume a mauling that would not end until nightfall. Septarch Kulpath's reinforcements had been annihilated.

Humbrall Taur's push into the city triggered a panicked rout. Units of Seerdomin, Urdomen, Beklite, Scalandi and Betaklite were caught up and driven apart by the tens of thousands of Tenescowri fleeing before the Barghast hook-swords and lances. The main avenues became heaving masses of humanity, a swirling flood pushing westward, pouring through the breaches on that side, out onto the plain.

Taur did not relent in his clans' vigorous pursuit, driving the Pannions ever westward.

Crouched on the rooftop, Picker looked down on the screaming, panic-stricken mob below. The tide had torn into the ramp, cutting swathes through it, each one a narrow gully winding between walls of cold flesh. Every path was choked with figures, whilst others scrambled over-top, at times less than a long pike's reach from the Malazan's position.

Despite the horror she was witnessing below, she felt as if a vast burden had been lifted from her. The damned torcs no longer gripped her arm. The closer they had come to the city, the tighter and hotter they had grown – burns still ringed her upper arm and a deep ache still lingered in the bones. There were questions surrounding all that, but she was not yet prepared to mull on them.

From a few streets to the east came the now familiar sound of slaughter, the discordant battle-chants of the Barghast a rumbling undercurrent. A Pannion rearguard of sorts had formed, ragged elements of Beklite, Urdomen and Seerdomin joining ranks in an effort to blunt the White Face advance. The rearguard was fast disintegrating, overwhelmed by numbers.

There would be no leaving the rooftop until the routed enemy had passed, despite Hedge's moans about foundation cracks and the like. Picker was well pleased with that. The Bridgeburners were in the city; it'd been hairy outside the wall and north gate, but apart from that things had gone easy – easier than she'd expected. Moranth munitions had a way of evening out the odds, if not swinging them all the way round.

Not a single clash of blades yet. Good. We ain't as tough as we used to be, never mind Antsy's bravado.

She wondered how far away Dujek and Brood were. Captain Paran had sent Twist to make contact with them as soon as it was clear that Humbrall Taur had unified his tribes and was ready to announce the command to march south to Capustan. With Quick Ben out of the action, and Spindle too scared to test his warrens, there was no way of knowing whether the Black Moranth had made it.

Who knows what's happened to them. Tales among the Barghast of undead demonic reptiles on the plains . . . and those fouled warrens – who's to say that poison isn't some nasty's road? Spindle says the warrens are sick. What if they've just been taken over? Could be they're being used right now. Someone could have come through and hit them hard. There might be thirty thousand corpses rotting on the plain right now. We might be all that's left of Onearm's Host.

The Barghast did not seem interested in committing to the war beyond the liberation of Capustan. They wanted the bones of their gods. They were about to get them, and once that happened they'd probably head back home.

And if we're then on our own . . . what will Paran decide? That damned noble looks deathly. The man's sick. His thoughts ride nails of pain, and that ain't good. Ain't good at all.

Boots crunched beside her as someone stepped to the roof's edge. She looked up, to see the red-haired woman Mallet had brought back from almost-dead. A rapier snapped a third of the way down the blade was in her right hand. Her leather armour was in tatters, old blood staining countless rents. There was a brittleness to her expression, as well as something of . . . wonder.

Picker straightened. The screams from below were deafening. She moved closer and said, 'Won't be much longer, now. You can see the front ranks of the Barghast from here.' She pointed.

The woman nodded, then said, 'My name is Stonny Menackis.'

'Corporal Picker.'

'I've been talking with Blend.'

'That's a surprise. She ain't the talkative type.'

'She was telling me about the torcs.'

'Was she now? Huh.'

Stonny shrugged, hesitated, then asked, 'Are you . . . are you sworn to Trake or something? Lots of soldiers are, I gather. The Tiger of Summer, Lord of Battle—'

'No,' Picker growled. 'I'm not. I just figured they were charms – those torcs.'

'So you didn't know that you had been chosen to deliver them. To . . . to Gruntle . . .'

The corporal glanced over at the woman. 'That's what's got you kind of confused, is it? Your friend Gruntle. You never would've figured him for what . . . for whatever he's now become.'

Stonny grimaced. 'Anyone but him, to be honest. The man's a cynical bastard, prone to drunkenness. Oh, he's smart, as far as men go. But now, when I look at him . . .'

'You ain't recognizing what you see.'

'It's not just those strange markings. It's his eyes. They're

678

a cat's eyes, now, a damned tiger's. Just as cold, just as inhuman.'

'He says he fought for you, lass.'

'I was his excuse, you mean.'

'Can't say as I'd argue there was a difference.'

'But there is, Corporal.'

'If you say so. Anyway, the truth's right there in front of you. In this damned cryptorium of a building. Hood take us, it's there in Gruntle's followers – he ain't the only one all dappled, is he? The man stood between the Pannions and you, and that was a solid enough thing to pull in all the others. Did Treach shape all this? I guess maybe he did, and I guess I played a part in that, too, with me showing up with those torcs on my arm. But now I'm quit of the whole thing and that suits me fine.' *And I ain't going to think on it no more.*

Stonny was shaking her head. 'I won't kneel to Trake. By the Abyss, I've gone and found myself before the altar of another god – I've already made my choice, and Trake isn't it.'

'Huh. Maybe, then, *your* god found the whole thing with Gruntle and all that somehow useful. Humans ain't the only ones who spin and play with webs, right? We ain't the only ones who sometimes walk in step, or even work together to achieve something of mutual benefit – without explaining a damned thing to the rest of us. I ain't envying you, Stonny Menackis. It's deadly attention, when it's a god's. But it happens . . .' Picker fell silent.

Walk in step. Her eyes narrowed. *And keeping the rest of us in the dark.*

She swung about, searched the group around the tents until she spied Paran. The corporal raised her voice, 'Hey, Captain!'

He looked up.

And how about you, Captain? Keeping secrets, maybe? Here's a hunch for you. 'Any word from Silverfox?' she asked.

The Bridgeburners nearby all fixed their attention on the nobleborn officer.

Paran recoiled as if he had been struck. One hand went to his stomach as a spasm of pain took him. Jaws bunching, he managed to lift his head and meet Picker's eyes. 'She's alive,' he grated.

Thought so. You'd been too easy with this by far, Captain. Meaning, you have been keeping things from us. A bad decision. The last time us Bridgeburners was kept in the dark, that dark swallowed damn near every one of us. 'How close? How far away, Captain?'

She could see the effect of her words, yet a part of her was angry, enough to harden herself. Officers always held out. It was the one thing the Bridgeburners had learned to despise the most when it came to their commanders. Ignorance was fatal.

Paran slowly forced himself straight. He drew a deep breath, then another as he visibly clamped down on the pain. 'Humbrall Taur is driving the Pannions into their laps, Corporal. Dujek and Brood are maybe three leagues away—'

Sputtering, Antsy asked, 'And do they know what's coming down on them?'

'Aye, Sergeant.'

'How?'

Good question. Just how tight is this contact between you and Tattersail-reborn? And why ain't you told us? We're your soldiers. Expected to fight for you. So it's a damned good question.

Paran scowled at Antsy, but made no reply.

The sergeant wasn't about to let go, now that he'd taken the matter from Picker's hands and was speaking for all the Bridgeburners. 'So here we damn near got our heads lopped off by the White Faces, damn near got roasted by Tenescowri, and all the while thinking we might be alone. Completely alone. Not knowing if the alliance has held or if Dujek and Brood have ripped each other apart and there's nothing but

680

rotting bones to the west. And yet, you knew. So, if you was dead . . . right now, sir . . .'

We'd know nothing, not a damned thing.

'If I was dead, we wouldn't be having this conversation,' Paran replied. 'So why don't we just pretend, Sergeant?'

'Maybe we don't pretend at all,' Antsy growled, one hand reaching for his sword.

From nearby, where he had been crouching near the roof's edge, Gruntle slowly turned, then straightened.

Now wait a minute. 'Sergeant!' Picker snapped. 'You think Tattersail will turn a smile on you the next time she sees you? If you go ahead and do what you're thinking of doing?'

'Quiet, Corporal,' Paran ordered, eyes on Antsy. 'Let's get it over with. Here, I'll make it even easier.' The captain turned his back to the sergeant, waited.

So sick he wants it ended. Shit. And worse . . . all this, in front of an audience.

'Don't even think it, Antsy,' Mallet warned. 'None of this is as it seems—'

Picker turned on the healer. 'Well, now we're getting somewhere! You was jawing enough with Whiskeyjack before we left, Mallet. You and Quick Ben. Out with it! We got a captain hurting so bad he wants us to kill him and ain't nobody's telling us a damned thing – what in Hood's name is going on?'

The healer grimaced. 'Aye, Silverfox is reaching out to the captain – but he's been pushing her away – so there hasn't been some kind of endless exchange of information going on. He knows she's alive, as he says, and I guess he can make out something of just how far away she is, but it goes no further than that. Damn you, Picker. You think you and the rest of us Bridgeburners have been singled out for yet another betrayal, just because Paran's not talking to you? *He's not talking to anyone!* And if you had as many holes burned through your guts as he does, you'd be pretty damned tight-lipped yourself! Now, all of you, just cut it!

681

Look to yourselves and if that's shame you see it's damned well been earned!'

Picker fixed her gaze on the captain's back. The man had not moved. Would not face his company. Could not – not now. Mallet had a way of turning things right over. Paran was a sick man, *and sick people don't think right. Gods, I had torcs biting my arm and I was losing it fast. Oh, ain't I just stepped in a pile of dung. Swearing someone else's to blame all the while, too. I guess Pale's burns are a far way from healing. Damn. Hood's heel on my rotted soul, please. Down and twist hard.*

Paran barely heard the shouted exchanges behind him. He felt assailed by the pressure of Silverfox's presence, leading to a dark desire to be crushed lifeless beneath it – if such a thing was possible – rather than yield.

A sword between his shoulder-blades – *no god to intervene this time.* Or a final, torrential gush of blood into his stomach as its walls finally gave way – a painful option, but none the less as final as any other. Or a leap down into the mob below, to get torn apart, trampled underfoot. Futility whispering of freedom.

She was close indeed, as if she strode a bridge of bones stretching from her to where he now stood. No, not her. Her power, that was so much more than just Tattersail. Making its relentless desire to break through his defences much deadlier of purpose than a lover's simple affection; much more, even, than would be born of strategic necessity. *Unless Dujek and Brood and their armies are under assault . . . and they're not. Gods, I don't know how I know, but I do. With certainty. This – this isn't Tattersail at all. It's Nightchill. Bellurdan. One or both. What do they want?*

He was suddenly rocked by an image, triggering an almost audible snap within his mind. Away. Towards. Dry flagstones within a dark cavern, the deeply carved lines of a card of the Deck, stone-etched, the image seeming to writhe as if alive.

Obelisk. One of the Unaligned, a leaning monolith . . .

now of green stone. Jade. Towering above wind-whipped waves – no, dunes of sand. Figures, in the monolith's shadow. Three, three in all. Ragged, broken, dying.

Then, beyond the strange scene, the sky *tore*.

And the furred hoof of a god stepped onto mortal ground. Terror.

Savagely pulled into the world – *oh, you didn't choose that, did you? Someone pulled you down, and now . . .*

Fener was as good as dead. A god trapped in the mortal realm was like a babe on an altar. All that was required was a knife and a wilful hand.

As good as dead.

Bleak knowledge flowered like deadly nightshade in his mind. But he wanted none of it. Choices were being demanded of him, by forces ancient beyond imagining. The Deck of Dragons . . . Elder Gods were playing it . . . and now sought to play him.

And this is to be the role of the Master of the Deck, if that is what I've become? A possessor of fatal knowledge and, now, a Hood-damned mitigator? I see what you're telling me to do. One god falls, push another into its place? Mortals sworn to one, swear them now to another? Abyss below, are we to be shoved – flicked – around like pebbles on a board?

Rage and indignation fanned white hot in Paran's mind. Obliterating his pain. He felt himself mentally wheel round, to face that incessant, alien presence that had so hounded him. Felt himself open like an explosion.

All right, you wanted my attention. You've got it. Listen, and listen well, Nightchill – whoever – whatever you really are. Maybe there have been Masters of the Deck before, long ago, whom you could pluck and pull to do your bidding. Hood knows, maybe you're the one – you and your Elder friends – who selected me this time round. But if so, oh, you've made a mistake. A bad one.

I've been a god's puppet once before. But I cut those strings, and if you want details, then go ask Oponn. I walked into a cursed sword to do it, and I swear, I'll do it again – with far less

683

mercy in my heart – if I get so much as a whiff of manipulation from you.

He sensed cold amusement in reply, and the bestial blood within Paran responded. Raised hackles. Teeth bared. A deep, deadly growl.

Sudden alarm.

Aye, the truth of it. I won't be collared, Nightchill. And I tell you this, now, and you'd do well to take heed of these words. I'm taking a step forward. Between you and every mortal like me. I don't know what that man Gruntle had to lose, to arrive where you wanted him, but I sense the wounds in him – Abyss take you, is pain your only means of making us achieve what you want? It seems so. Know this, then: until you can find another means, until you can show me another way – something other than pain and grief – I'll fight you.

We have our lives. All of us, and they're not for you to play with. Not Picker's life, not Gruntle's or Stonny's.

You've opened this path, Nightchill. Connecting us. Fine. Good. Give me cause, and I'll come down it. Riding the blood of a Hound of Shadow – do you know, I think, if I wanted to, I could call the others with it. All of them.

Because I understand something, now. Come to a realization, and one I know to be truth. In the sword Dragnipur . . . two Hounds of Shadow returned to the Warren of Darkness. Returned, Nightchill. Do you grasp my meaning? They were going home.

And I can call them back, without doubt. Two souls of untamed Dark. Grateful souls, beloved spawn of destruction—

A reply came, then, a woman's voice unknown to Paran. 'You have no idea what you threaten, mortal. My brother's sword hides far more secrets than you can contemplate.'

He smiled. *Worse than that, Nightchill. The hand now wielding Dragnipur belongs to Darkness. Anomander Rake, the son of the mother. The pathway has never been so straight, so direct or so short, has it? Should I tell him what has happened within his own weapon—*

'Should Rake learn that you found a way into Dragnipur and

that you freed the two Hounds he had slain . . . he would kill you, mortal.'

He might. He's already had a few chances to do so, and just reasons besides. Yet he stayed his hand. I don't think you understand the Lord of Moon's Spawn as well as you think you do. There is nothing predictable in Anomander Rake – perhaps that is what frightens you so.

'Pursue not this course.'

I will do whatever I have to, Nightchill, to cut your strings. In your eyes, we mortals are weak. And you use our weakness to justify manipulating us.

'The struggle we face is far vaster – far deadlier – than you realize.'

Explain it. All of it. Show me this vast threat of yours.

'To save your sanity, we must not, Ganoes Paran.'

Patronizing bitch.

He sensed her anger flare at that. *'You say our only means of using you is through the deliverance of pain. To that we have but one answer: appearances deceive.'*

Keeping us ignorant is your notion of mercy?

'Bluntly worded, but in essence, you are correct, Ganoes Paran.'

A Master of the Deck cannot be left ignorant, Nightchill. If I am to accept this role and its responsibilities – whatever they might be and Hood knows, I don't yet know them – but if I am, then I need to know. Everything.

'In time—'

He sneered.

'In time, I said. Grant us this small mercy, mortal. The struggle before us is no different from a military campaign – incremental engagements, localized contests. But the field of battle is no less than existence itself. Small victories are each in themselves vital contributions to the pandemic war we have chosen to undertake—'

Who is 'we'?

'The surviving Elder Gods . . . and others somewhat less cognizant of their role.'

K'rul? The one responsible for Tattersail's rebirth?

'Yes. My brother.'

Your brother. But not the brother who forged Dragnipur.

'Not him. At the moment, Draconus can do naught but act indirectly, for he is chained within the very sword he created. Slain by his own blade, at the hand of Anomander Rake.'

Paran felt the cold steel of suspicion slide into him. *Indirectly, you said.*

'A moment of opportunity, Ganoes Paran. Unexpected. The arrival of a soul within Dragnipur that was not chained. The exchange of a few words that signified far more than you ever realized. As did the breach into the Warren of Darkness, the barrier of souls broken, so very briefly. But enough—'

Wait. Paran needed silence to think, fast and hard. When he'd been within Dragnipur, walking alongside the chained souls dragging their unimaginable burden, he had indeed spoken with one such prisoner. *Abyss below, that had been Draconus.* Yet he could recall nothing of the words exchanged between them.

The chains led into the Warren of Darkness, the knot beneath the groaning wagon. Thus, Darkness held those souls, one and all, held them fast.

I need to go back. Into the sword. I need to ask—

'Jen'isand Rul. Aye, Draconus, the one you spoke with within Dragnipur – my other brother – made use of you, Ganoes Paran. Does that truth seem brutal to you? Is it beyond understanding? Like the others within the sword, my brother faces . . . eternity. He sought to outwit a curse, yet he never imagined that doing so would take so long. He is changed, mortal. His legendary cruelty has been . . . blunted. Wisdom earned a thousand times over. More, we need him.'

You want me to free Draconus from Rake's sword.

'Yes.'

To then have him go after Rake himself in an effort to reclaim the weapon he forged. Nightchill, I would rather Rake than Draconus—

'There will be no such battle, Ganoes Paran.'

Why not?

'To free Draconus, the sword must be shattered.'

The cold steel between his ribs now twisted. *And that would free . . . everyone else. Everything else. Sorry, woman, I won't do it—*

'If there is a way to prevent that woeful release of mad, malign spirits – whose numbers are indeed beyond legion and too horrifying to contemplate – then only one man will know it.'

Draconus himself.

'Yes. Think on this, Ganoes Paran. Do not rush – there is still time.'

Glad to hear it.

'We are not as cruel as you think.'

Vengeance hasn't blackened your heart, Nightchill? Excuse my scepticism.

'Oh, I seek vengeance, mortal, but not against the minor players who acted out my betrayal, for that betrayal was fore-told. An ancient curse. The one who voiced that curse is the sole focus of my desire for vengeance.'

I'm surprised he or she's still around.

There was a cold smile in her words. 'Such was our curse against him.'

I'm beginning to think you all deserve each other.

There was a pause, then she said, 'Perhaps we do, Ganoes Paran.'

What have you done with Tattersail?

'Nothing. Her attentions are presently elsewhere.'

So I was flattering myself, thinking otherwise. Dammit, Paran, you're still a fool.

'We shall not harm her, mortal. Even were we able, which we are not. There is honour within her. And integrity. Rare qualities, for one so powerful. Thus, we have faith—'

A gloved hand on his shoulder startled Paran awake. He blinked, looked around. The roof. *I'm back.*

'Captain?'

He met Mallet's concerned gaze. 'What?'

'Sorry, sir, it seemed we'd lost you there . . . for a moment.'

He grimaced, wanting to deny it to the man's face, but unable to do so. 'How long?'

'A dozen heartbeats, sir.'

'Is that all? Good. We have to get moving. To the Thrall.'

'Sir?'

I'm between them and us, now, Mallet. But there's more of 'us' than you realize. Damn, I wish I could explain this. Without sounding like a pompous bastard. Not replying to the healer's question, he swung round and found Trotts. 'Warchief. The Thrall beckons.'

'Aye, Captain.'

The Bridgeburners were one and all avoiding his gaze. Paran wondered why. Wondered what he'd missed. Mentally shrugging, he strode over to Gruntle. 'You're coming with us,' he said.

'I know.'

Yes, you would at that. Fine, let's get this done.

The palace tower rose like a spear, wreathed in banners of ghostly smoke. The dark, colourless stone dulled the bright sunlight bathing it. Three hundred and thirty-nine winding steps led up the tower's interior, to emerge onto an open platform with a peaked roof of copper tiles that showed no sign of verdigris. The wind howled between the columns holding the roof and the smooth stone platform, yet the tower did not sway.

Itkovian stood looking east, the wind whipping against his face. His body felt bloodless, strangely hot beneath the tattered armour. He knew that exhaustion was finally taking its toll. Flesh and bone had its limits. The defence of the dead prince in his Great Hall had been brutal and artless. Hallways and entrances had become abattoirs. The stench of slaughter remained like a new layer beneath his skin – even the wind could not strip it away.

The battles at the coast and the landings were drawing to a grim close, a lone surviving scout had reported. The Betrullid had been broken, fleeing north along the coast, where the Shield Anvil well knew their horses would become mired in the salt marsh. The pursuing Barghast would make short work of them.

The besiegers' camps had been shattered, as if a tornado had ripped through them. A few hundred Barghast – old women and men and children – wandered through the carnage, gathering the spoils amidst squalling seagulls.

The East Watch redoubt, now a pile of rubble, barely rose above the carpet of bodies. Smoke drifted from it as if from a dying pyre.

Itkovian had watched the Barghast clans push into the city, had seen the Pannion retreat become a rout in the streets below. The fighting had swiftly swept past the palace. A Seerdomin officer had managed to rally a rear-guard in Jelarkan's Concourse, and that battle still raged on. But for the Pannions it was a withdrawing engagement. They were buying time for the exodus through what was left of the south and west gates.

A few White Face scouts had ventured into the palace grounds, close enough to discern that defenders remained, but no official contact had been established.

The recruit, Velbara, stood at Itkovian's side, a recruit no longer. Her training in weapons had been one of desperation. She'd not missed the foremost lesson – that of staying alive – that was the guiding force behind every skill she thereafter acquired in the heat of battle. As with all the other Capan newcomers to the company – who now made up most of the survivors under the Shield Anvil's command – she had earned her place as a soldier of the Grey Swords.

Itkovian broke a long silence. 'We yield the Great Hall, now.'

'Yes, sir.'

'The honour of the prince has been reasserted. We must needs depart – there is unfinished business at the Thrall.'

689

'Can we even yet reach it, sir? We shall need to find a Barghast warchief.'

'We shall not be mistaken for the enemy, sir. Enough of our brothers and sisters lie dead in the city to make our colours well known. Also, given the pursuit has, apart from the concourse, driven the Pannions west onto the plain, we shall likely find our path unopposed.'

'Yes, sir.'

Itkovian fixed his attention one last time on the destroyed redoubt in the killing field to the east. Two Gidrath soldiers in the Great Hall below were from that foolhardy but noble defence, and one of them bore recent wounds that would most likely prove fatal. The other, a bull of a man who had knelt before Rath'Hood, seemed no longer able to sleep. In the four days and nights since re-taking the Great Hall, he had but paced during his rest periods, oblivious of his surroundings. Pacing, muttering under his breath, his eyes darkly feverish in their intensity. He and his dying companion were, Itkovian suspected, the last Gidrath still alive outside the Thrall itself.

A Gidrath sworn to Hood, yet he follows my command without hesitation. Simple expedience, one might reasonably conclude. Notions of rivalry dispensed with in the face of the present extremity. Yet . . . I find myself mistrusting my own explanations.

Despite his exhaustion, the Shield Anvil had sensed a growing perturbation. Something had happened. Somewhere. And as if in response he'd felt his blood seem to drain from him, emptying his veins, hollowing his heart, vanishing through a wound he'd yet to find. Leaving him to feel . . . incomplete.

As if I had surrendered my faith. But I have not. 'The void of lost faith is filled with your swollen self.' Words from a long-dead Destriant. One does not yield, one replaces. Faith with doubt, scepticism, denial. I have yielded nothing. I have no horde of words crowding my inner defences. Indeed, I am diminished into silence. Emptied . . . as if awaiting renewal . . .

He shook himself. 'This wind screams too loud in my

ears,' he said, eyes still on the East Watch redoubt. 'Come, sir, we go below.'

One hundred and twelve soldiers remained in fighting condition, though not one was free of wounds. Seventeen Grey Swords lay dead or slowly dying along one wall. The air reeked of sweat, urine and rotting meat. The Great Hall's entranceways were framed in blackening blood, scraped clean on the tiles for firm footing. The long-gone architect who had given shape to the chamber would have been appalled at what it had become. Its noble beauty now housed a nightmare scene.

On the throne, his skin roughly sewn back onto his half-devoured form, sat Prince Jelarkan, eyeless, teeth exposed in a grin that grew wider as the lips lost their moisture and shrank away on all sides. Death's broadening smile, a precise, poetic horror. Worthy to hold court in what the Great Hall had become. A young prince who had loved his people, now joined to their fate.

It was time to leave. Itkovian stood near the main entrance, studying what was left of his Grey Swords. They in turn faced him, motionless, stone-eyed. To the left, two Capan recruits held the reins of the two remaining warhorses. The lone Gidrath – his companion had died moments earlier – paced with head sunk low, shoulders hunched, back and forth along the wall behind the ranked mercenaries. A battered longsword was held in each hand, the one on the left bent by a wild swing that had struck a marble column two nights past.

The Shield Anvil thought to address his soldiers, if only to honour decorum, but now, as he stood scanning their faces, he realized that he had no words left within him: none to dress what mutually bound them together; none capable of matching the strangely cold pride he felt at that moment. Finally, he drew his sword, tested the straps holding his shield-arm in place, then turned to the main entranceway.

The hallway beyond had been cleared of corpses, creating an avenue between the stacked bodies to the outer doors.

Itkovian strode down the ghastly aisle, stepped between the leaning, battered doors, and out into sunlight.

Following their many assaults, the Pannions had pulled their fallen comrades away from the broad, shallow steps of the approach, had used the courtyard to haphazardly pile the bodies – including those still living, who then either expired from wounds or from suffocation.

Itkovian paused at the top of the steps. The sounds of fighting persisted from the direction of Jelarkan's Concourse, but that was all he heard. Silence shrouded the scene before him, a silence so discordant in what had been a lively palace forecourt, in what had been a thriving city, that Itkovian was deeply shaken for the first time since the siege began.

Dear Fener, find for me the victory in this.

He descended the steps, the stone soft and gummy under his boots. His company followed, not a word spoken.

They strode through the shattered gate, began picking their way through the corpses on the ramp, then in the street beyond. Uncontested by the living, this would nevertheless prove a long journey. Nor would it be a journey without battle. Assailing them now were what their eyes saw, what their noses smelled, and what they could feel underfoot.

A battle that made shields and armour useless, that made flailing swords futile. A soul hardened beyond humanity was the only defence, and for Itkovian that price was too high. *I am the Shield Anvil. I surrender to what lies before me. Thicker than smoke, the grief unleashed and now lost, churning this lifeless air. A city has been killed. Even the survivors huddling in the tunnels below – Fener take me, better they never emerge . . . to see this.*

Their route took them between the cemeteries. Itkovian studied the place where he and his soldiers had made a

692

stand. It looked no different from anywhere else his eye scanned. The dead lay in heaps. As Brukhalian had promised, not one pavestone had gone uncontested. This small city had done all it could. Pannion victory might well have been inevitable, but thresholds nevertheless existed, transforming inexorable momentum into a curse.

And now the White Face clans of the Barghast had announced their own inevitability. What the Pannions had delivered had been in turn delivered upon them. *We are all pushed into a world of madness, yet it must now fall to each of us to pull back from this Abyss, to drag ourselves free of the descending spiral. From horror, grief must be fashioned, and from grief, compassion.*

As the company entered a choked avenue at the edge of the Daru district, a score of Barghast emerged from an alley mouth directly ahead. Bloodied hook-swords in hands, white-painted faces spattered red. The foremost among them grinned at the Shield Anvil.

'Defenders!' he barked in harshly-accented Capan. 'How sits this gift of liberation?'

Itkovian ignored the question, 'You have kin at the Thrall, sir. Even now I see the protective glow fading.'

'We shall see the bones of our gods, aye,' the warrior said, nodding. His small, dark eyes scanned the Grey Swords. 'You lead a tribe of women.'

'Capan women,' Itkovian said. 'This city's most resilient resource, though it fell to us to discover that. They are Grey Swords, now, sir, and for that we are strengthened.'

'We've seen your brothers and sisters everywhere,' the Barghast warrior growled. 'Had they been our enemies, we would be glad they are dead.'

'And as allies?' the Shield Anvil asked.

The Barghast fighters one and all made a gesture, back of sword-hand to brow, the briefest brush of leather to skin, then the spokesman said, 'The loss fills the shadows we cast. Know this, soldier, the enemy you left to us was brittle.'

Itkovian shrugged. 'The Pannions' faith knows not worship, only necessity. Their strength is a shallow thing, sir. Will you accompany us to the Thrall?'

'At your sides, soldiers. In your shadow lies honour.'

Most of the structures in the Daru district had burned, collapsing in places to fill the streets with blackened rubble. As the Grey Swords and Barghast wound their way through the least cluttered paths, Itkovian's eyes were drawn to one building still standing, off to their right. A tenement, its walls were strangely bowed. Banked fires had been built against the side facing him, scorching the stones, but the assault of flame had failed for some reason. Every arched window Itkovian could see looked to have been barricaded.

At his side, the Barghast spokesman growled, 'Your kind crowd your barrows.'

The Shield Anvil glanced at the man. 'Sir?'

The warrior nodded towards the smoke-hazed tenement and went on with his commentary, 'Easier, aye, than digging and lining a pit outside the city, then the lines passing buckets of earth. You like a clear view from the walls, it seems. But *we* do not live among our dead in the manner of your people . . .'

Itkovian turned back to study the tenement, now slightly to the rear on the right. His eyes narrowed. *The barricades blocking the windows. Once more, flesh and bone. Twin Tusks, who would build such a necropolis? Surely, it cannot be the consequence of defence?*

'We wandered close,' the warrior at his side said. 'The walls give off their own heat. Jellied liquid bleeds between the cracks.' He made another gesture, this one shuddering, hilt of his hook-sword clattering against the coin-wrought armour covering his torso. 'By the bones, soldier, we fled.'

'Is that tenement the only one so . . . filled?'

'We've seen no other, though we did pass one estate that still held – enlivened corpses stood guard at the gate and on the walls. The air stank of sorcery, an emanation foul with necromancy. I tell you this, soldier, we shall be glad to quit this city.'

Itkovian was silent. He felt rent inside. The Reve of Fener voiced the truth of war. It spoke true of the cruelty that humanity was capable of unleashing upon its own kind. War was played like a game by those who led others; played in an illusory arena of calm reason, but such lies could not survive reality, and reality seemed to have no limits. The Reve held a plea for restraint, and insisted the glory to be found was not to be a blind one, rather a glory born of solemn, clear-eyed regard. Within limitless reality resided the promise of redemption.

That regard was failing Itkovian now. He was recoiling like a caged animal cruelly prodded on all sides. Escape was denied to him, yet that denial was self-imposed, a thing born of his conscious will, given shape by the words of his vow. He must assume this burden, no matter the cost. The fires of vengeance had undergone a transformation within him. He would be, at the last, the redemption – for the souls of the fallen in this city.

Redemption. For everyone else, but not for himself. For that, he could only look to his god. *But, dear Fener, what has happened? Where are you? I kneel in place, awaiting your touch, yet you are nowhere to be found. Your realm . . . it feels . . . empty.*

Where, now, can I go?

Aye, I am not yet done. I accept this. And when I am? Who awaits me? Who shall embrace me? A shiver ran through him. *Who shall embrace me?*

The Shield Anvil pushed the question away, struggled to renew his resolve. He had, after all, no choice. He would be Fener's grief. And his Lord's hand of justice. Not welcome responsibilities, and he sensed the toll they were about to exact.

They neared the plaza before the Thrall. Other Barghast were visible, joining in the convergence. The distant sounds of battle in Jelarkan Concourse, which had accompanied them through most of the afternoon, now fell silent. The enemy had been driven from the city.

Itkovian did not think the Barghast would pursue. They had achieved what they had come here to do. The Pannion threat to the bones of their gods had been removed.

Probably, if Septarch Kulpath still lived, he would reform his tattered forces, reassert discipline and prepare for his next move. Either a counterattack, or a westward withdrawal. There were risks to both. He might have insufficient force to retake the city. And his army, having lost possession of their camps and supply routes, would soon suffer from lack of supplies. It was not an enviable position. Capustan, a small, inconsequential city on the east coast of Central Genabackis, had become a many-sided curse. And the lives lost here signified but the beginning of the war to come.

They emerged onto the plaza.

The place where Brukhalian had fallen lay directly ahead, but all the bodies had been removed – taken, no doubt, by the retreating Pannions. Flesh for yet another royal feast. *It doesn't matter. Hood came for him. In person. Was that a sign of honour, or petty gloating on the god's part?*

The Shield Anvil's gaze held on that stained stretch of flagstones for a moment longer, then swung to the Thrall's main gate.

The glow was gone. In the shadows beneath the gate's arch, figures had appeared.

Every approach to the plaza had filled with Barghast, but they ventured no further.

Itkovian turned back to his company. His eyes found his captain – who had been the master-sergeant in charge of training the recruits – then Velbara. He studied their tattered, stained armour, their lined, drawn faces. 'The three of us, sirs, to the centre of the plaza.'

The two women nodded.

The three strode onto the concourse. Thousands of eyes fixed on them, followed by a rumbling murmur, then a rhythmic, muted clashing of blade on blade.

Another party emerged, from the right. Soldiers, wearing uniforms Itkovian did not recognize, and, in their company, figures displaying barbed, feline tattooing. Leading the latter group, a man Itkovian had seen before. The Shield Anvil's steps slowed.

Gruntle. The name was a hammerblow to his chest. Brutal certainty forced his next thoughts. *The Mortal Sword of Trake, Tiger of Summer. The First Hero is ascended.*

We . . . we are replaced.

Steeling himself, Itkovian resumed his pace, then halted in the centre of the expanse.

A single soldier in the foreign uniform had moved up alongside Gruntle. He closed a hand around the big Daru's striped arm and barked something back to the others, who all stopped, while the man and Gruntle continued on, directly towards Itkovian.

A commotion from the Thrall's gate caught their attention. Priests and priestesses of the Mask Council were emerging, holding a struggling comrade among them as they hastened forward. In the lead, Rath'Trake. A step behind, the Daru merchant, Keruli.

The soldier and Gruntle reached Itkovian first.

Beneath the Daru's helm, Gruntle's tiger eyes studied the Shield Anvil. 'Itkovian of the Grey Swords,' he rumbled, 'it is done.'

Itkovian had no need to ask for elaboration. The truth was a knife in his heart.

'No, it isn't,' the foreign soldier snapped. 'I greet you, Shield Anvil. I am Captain Paran, of the Bridgeburners. Onearm's Host.'

'He is more than that,' Gruntle muttered. 'What he claims now—'

'Is nothing I do willingly,' Paran finished. 'Shield Anvil. Fener has been torn from his realm. He strides a distant land. You – your company – you have lost your god.'

And so it is known to all. 'We are aware of this, sir.'

'Gruntle says that your place, your role, is done. The

697

Grey Swords must step aside, for a new god of war has gained pre-eminence. But that doesn't have to be. A path for you has been prepared . . .' Paran's gaze went past Itkovian. He raised his voice. 'Welcome, Humbrall Taur. Your children no doubt await within the Thrall.'

The Shield Anvil glanced back over his shoulder to see, standing ten paces behind him, a huge Barghast warchief in coin-threaded armour.

'They can wait a while longer,' Humbrall Taur growled. 'I would witness this.'

Paran grimaced. 'Nosy bastard—'

'Aye.'

The Malazan returned his attention to Itkovian and made to speak, but the Shield Anvil interrupted him: 'A moment, sir.' He stepped past the two men.

Rath'Fener jerked and twisted in the grip of his fellow priests. His mask was awry, wisps of grey hair pulled free of the leather strapping. 'Shield Anvil!' he cried upon seeing Itkovian's approach. 'In the name of Fener—'

'In *his* name, aye, sir,' Itkovian cut in. 'To my side, Captain Norul. The Reve's law is invoked.'

'Sir,' the grizzled woman replied, stepping forward.

'You can't!' Rath'Fener screamed. 'For this, only the Mortal Sword can invoke the Reve!'

Itkovian stood motionless.

The priest managed to pull one arm forward to jab a finger at the Shield Anvil. 'My rank is as Destriant! Unless you've one to make claim to that title?'

'Destriant Karnadas is dead.'

'That man was no Destriant, Shield Anvil! An Aspirant, perhaps, but my rank was and remains pre-eminent. Thus, only a Mortal Sword can invoke the Reve against me, and this you know.'

Gruntle snorted. 'Itkovian, Paran here told me there was a betrayal. Your priest sold Brukhalian's life to the Pannions. Not only disgusting, but ill-advised. So.' He paused. 'Will any Mortal Sword do? If so, I invoke the

Reve.' He bared his teeth at Rath'Fener. 'Punish the bastard.'

We are replaced. The Lord of Battle is transformed indeed.

'He cannot!' Rath'Fener shrieked.

'A bold claim,' Itkovian said to the masked priest. 'In order to deny this man's right to the title, sir, you must call upon our god. In your defence. Do so, sir, and you shall walk from here a free man.'

The eyes within the mask went wide. 'You know that is impossible, Itkovian!'

'Then your defence is over, sir. The Reve is invoked. I am become Fener's hand of justice.'

Rath'Trake, who had been standing nearby in watchful silence, now spoke, 'There is no need for any of this, Shield Anvil. Your god's absence changes ... everything. Surely, you understand the implications of the traditional form of punishment. A simple execution – not the Reve's law—'

'Is denied this man,' Itkovian said. 'Captain Norul.'

She strode to Rath'Fener, reached out and plucked him from the hold of the priests and priestesses. He seemed like a rag doll in her large, scarred hands as she swung him round and threw him belly down on the flagstones. She then straddled him, stretching his arms out forward yet side by side. The man shrieked with sudden comprehension.

Itkovian drew his sword. Smoke drifted from the blade. 'The Reve,' he said, standing over Rath'Fener's out-stretched arms. 'Betrayal, to trade Brukhalian's life for your own. Betrayal, the foulest crime to the Reve's law, to Fener himself. Punishment is invoked, in accordance with the Boar of Summer's judgement.' He was silent for a moment, then he said, 'Pray, sir, that Fener finds what we send to him.'

'But he won't!' Rath'Trake cried. 'Don't you understand? His realm – your god no longer waits within it!'

'He knows,' Paran said. 'This is what happens when it gets personal, and believe me, I'd rather have had no part in this.'

Rath'Trake swung to the captain. 'And *who* are you, soldier?'

'Today. Right now. I am the Master of the Deck, priest. And it seems I am here to negotiate . . . on you and your god's behalf. Alas,' he added wryly, 'the Shield Anvil is proving admirably . . . recalcitrant . . .'

Itkovian barely heard the exchange. Eyes holding on the priest pinned to the ground before him, he said, 'Our Lord is . . . gone. Indeed. So . . . best pray, Rath'Fener, that a creature of mercy now looks kindly upon you.'

Rath'Trake whirled back to the Shield Anvil at those words, 'By the Abyss, Itkovian – there is *no* crime so foul to match what you're about to do! His soul will be torn apart! Where *they* will go, there *are* no creatures of mercy! Itkovian—'

'Silence, sir. This judgement is mine, and the Reve's.'

The victim shrieked.

And Itkovian swung down the sword. Blade's edge cracked onto the flagstones. Twin gouts of blood shot out from the stumps of Rath'Fener's wrists. The hands . . . were nowhere to be seen.

Itkovian jammed the flat of his blade against the stumps. Flesh sizzled. Rath'Fener's screams ceased abruptly as unconsciousness took him. Captain Norul moved away from the man, left him lying on the flagstones.

Paran began speaking. 'Shield Anvil, hear me. Please. Fener is gone – he strides the mortal realm. Thus, he *cannot* bless *you*. With what you take upon yourself . . . there is nowhere for it to go, no way to ease the burden.'

'I am equally aware of what you say, sir.' Itkovian still stared down at Rath'Fener, who was stirring to consciousness once more. 'Such knowledge is worthless.'

'There's another way, Shield Anvil.'

He turned at that, eyes narrowing.

Paran went on, 'A choice has been . . . fashioned. In this I am but a messenger—'

Rath'Trake stepped up to Itkovian. 'We shall welcome

700

you, sir. You and your followers. The Tiger of Summer has need for you, a Shield Anvil, and so offers his embrace—'

'No.'

The eyes within the mask narrowed.

'Itkovian,' Paran said, 'this was foreseen . . . the path prepared for . . . by Elder powers, once more awake and active in this world. I am here to tell you what they would have you do—'

'No. I am sworn to Fener. If need be, I shall share his fate.'

'This is an offer of salvation – *not* a betrayal!' Rath'Trake cried.

'Isn't it? No more words, sirs.' On the ground below, Rath'Fener had regained awareness. Itkovian studied the man. 'I am not yet done,' he whispered.

Rath'Fener's body jerked, a throat-tearing scream erupting from him, his arms snapping as if yanked by invisible, unhuman hands. Dark tattoos appeared on the man's skin, but not those belonging to Fener – for the god had not been the one to claim Rath'Fener's severed hands. Writhing, alien script swarmed his flesh as the unknown claimant made its mark, claimed possession of the man's mortal soul. Words that darkened like burns.

Blisters rose, then broke, spurting thick, yellow liquid.

Screams of unbearable, unimaginable pain filled the plaza, the body on the flagstones spasming as muscle and fat dissolved beneath the skin, then boiled, breaking through.

Yet the man did not die.

Itkovian sheathed his sword.

The Malazan was the first to comprehend. His hand snapped forward, closed on the Shield Anvil's arm. 'By the Abyss, do not—'

'Captain Norul.'

Face white beneath the rim of her helm, the woman settled a hand on the grip of her sword. 'Captain Paran,' she said in a taut, brittle voice, 'withdraw your touch.'

He swung on her. 'Aye, even you recoil at what he plans—'

'Nevertheless, sir. Release him or I will kill you.'

The Malazan's eyes glittered strangely at that threat, but Itkovian could spare no thought for the young captain. He had a responsibility. Rath'Fener had been punished enough. His pain must end.

And who shall save me?

Paran relinquished his grip.

Itkovian bent down to the writhing, barely recognizable shape on the flagstones. 'Rath'Fener, hear me. Yes, I come. Will you accept my embrace?'

For all the envy and malice within the tortured priest, all that led to the betrayal, not just of Brukhalian – the Mortal Sword – but of Fener himself, some small measure of mercy remained in the man's soul. Mercy, and comprehension. His body jerked away, limbs skidding as he sought to crawl from Itkovian's shadow.

The Shield Anvil nodded, then gathered the suppurating figure into his arms and rose.

I see you recoil, and know it for your final gesture. One that is atonement. To this, I cannot but answer in kind, Rath'Fener. Thus. I assume your pain, sir. No, do not fight this gift. I free your soul to Hood, to death's solace—

Paran and the others saw naught but the Shield Anvil standing motionless, Rath'Fener in his arms. The rendered, blood-streaked priest continued to struggle for a moment longer, then he seemed to collapse inward, his screams falling into silence.

The man's life unfolded in Itkovian's mind. Before him, the priest's path to betrayal. He saw a young acolyte, pure of heart, cruelly schooled not in piety and faith, but in the cynical lessons of secular power struggles. Rule and administration was a viper's nest, a ceaseless contest among small and petty minds with illusory rewards. A life within the cold halls of the Thrall that had hollowed out the priest's soul. The self filled the new cavern of lost faith, beset by fears and jealousies, to which malevolent acts were the only answer. The need for preservation made every virtue a commodity, to be traded away.

Itkovian understood him, could see each step taken that led, inevitably, to the betrayal, the trading of lives as agreed between the priest and the agents of the Pannion Domin. And within that, Rath'Fener's knowledge that he had in so doing wrapped a viper about himself whose kiss was deadly. He was dead either way, but he had gone too far from his faith, too far to ever imagine he might one day return to it.

I comprehend you, now, Rath'Fener, but comprehension is not synonymous with absolution. The justice that is your punishment does not waver. Thus, you were made to know pain.

Aye, Fener should have been awaiting you; our god should have accepted your severed hands, so that he might look upon you following your death, that he might voice the words prepared for you and you alone – the words on your skin. The final atonement to your crimes. This is as it should have been, sir.

But Fener is gone.

And what holds you now has . . . other desires.

I now deny it the possession of you—

Rath'Fener's soul shrieked, seeking to pull away once more. Carving words through the tumult: *Itkovian! You must not! Leave me with this, I beg you. Not for your soul – I never meant – please, Itkovian—*

The Shield Anvil tightened his spiritual embrace, breaking the last barriers. *No-one is to be denied their grief, sir, not even you.*

But barriers, once lowered, could not choose what would pass through.

The storm that hit Itkovian overwhelmed him. Pain so intense as to become an abstract force, a living entity that was itself a thing filled with panic and terror. He opened himself to it, let its screams fill him.

On a field of battle, after the last heart has stilled, pain remains. Locked in soil, in stone, bridging the air from each place to every other, a web of memory, trembling to a silent song. But for Itkovian, his vow denied the gift of silence. He could hear that song. It filled him entire. And he was its counterpoint. Its answer.

I have you now, Rath'Fener. You are found, and so I . . . answer.

Suddenly, beyond the pain, a mutual awareness – an alien presence. Immense power. Not malign, yet profoundly . . . different. From that presence: storm-tossed confusion, anguish. Seeking to make of the unexpected gift of a mortal's two hands . . . something of beauty. Yet that man's flesh could not contain that gift.

Horror within the storm. Horror . . . and grief.

Ah, even gods weep. Commend yourself, then, to my spirit. I will have your pain as well, sir.

The alien presence recoiled, but it was too late. Itkovian's embrace offered its immeasurable gift—

—and was engulfed. He felt his soul dissolving, tearing apart – *too vast!*

There was, beneath the cold faces of gods, warmth. Yet it was sorrow in darkness, for it was not the gods themselves who were unfathomable. It was mortals. As for the gods – they simply paid.

We – we are the rack upon which they are stretched.

Then the sensation was gone, fleeing him as the alien god succeeded in extracting itself, leaving Itkovian with but fading echoes of a distant world's grief – a world with its own atrocities, layer upon layer through a long, tortured history. Fading . . . then gone.

Leaving him with heart-rending knowledge.

A small mercy. He was buckling beneath Rath'Fener's pain and the growing onslaught of Capustan's appalling death as his embrace was forced ever wider. The clamouring souls on all sides, not one life's history unworthy of notice, of acknowledgement. Not one he would turn away. Souls in the tens of thousands, lifetimes of pain, loss, love and sorrow, each leading to – each riding memories of its own agonized death. Iron and fire and smoke and falling stone. Dust and airlessness. Memories of piteous, pointless ends to thousands and thousands of lives.

I must atone. I must give answer. To every death. Every death.

He was lost within the storm, his embrace incapable of closing around the sheer immensity of anguish assailing him. Yet he struggled on. The gift of peace. The stripping away of pain's trauma, to free the souls to find their way . . . to the feet of countless gods, or Hood's own realm, or, indeed, to the Abyss itself. Necessary journeys, to free souls trapped in their own tortured deaths.

I am the . . . the Shield Anvil. This is for me . . . to hold . . . hold on. Reach – gods! Redeem them, sir! It is your task. The heart of your vows – you are the walker among the dead in the field of battle, you are the bringer of peace, the redeemer of the fallen. You are the mender of broken lives. Without you, death is senseless, and the denial of meaning is the world's greatest crime to its own children. Hold, Itkovian . . . hold fast—

But he had no god against which to set his back, no solid, intractable presence awaiting him to answer his own need. And he was but one mortal soul . . .

Yet, I must not surrender. Gods, hear me! I may not be yours. But your fallen children, they are mine. Witness, then, what lies behind my cold face. Witness!

In the plaza, amidst a dreadful silence, Paran and the others watched as Itkovian slowly settled to his knees. A rotting, lifeless corpse was slumped in his arms. The lone, kneeling figure seemed – to the captain's eyes – to encompass the exhaustion of the world, an image that burned into his mind, and one that he knew would never leave him.

Of the struggles – the wars – still being waged within the Shield Anvil, little showed. After a long moment, Itkovian reached up with one hand and unstrapped his helm, lifting it clear to reveal the sweat-stained leather under-helm. The long, dripping hair plastered against his brow and neck shrouded his face as he knelt with head bowed, the corpse in his arms crumbling to pale ash. The Shield Anvil was motionless.

The uneven rise and fall of his frame slowed.

Stuttered.

Then ceased.

Captain Paran, his heart hammering loud in his chest, darted close, grasped Itkovian's shoulders and shook the man. 'No, damn you! This isn't what I've come here to see! Wake up, you bastard!'

—peace – I have you now? My gift – ah, this burden—

The Shield Anvil's head jerked back. Drew a sobbing breath.

Settling . . . such weight! Why? Gods – you all watched. You witnessed with your immortal eyes. Yet you did not step forward. You denied my cry for help. Why?

Crouching, the Malazan moved round to face Itkovian. 'Mallet!' he shouted over a shoulder.

As the healer ran forward, Itkovian, his eyes finding Paran, slowly raised a hand. Swallowing his dismay, he managed to find words. 'I know not how,' he rasped, 'but you have returned me . . .'

Paran's grin was forced. 'You are the Shield Anvil.'

'Aye,' Itkovian whispered. *And Fener forgive me, what you have done is no mercy . . .* 'I am the Shield Anvil.'

'I can feel it in the air,' Paran said, eyes searching Itkovian's. 'It's . . . it's been *cleansed*.'

Aye.

And I am not yet done.

Gruntle stood watching as the Malazan and his healer spoke with the Grey Sword commander. The fog of his thoughts – which had been closed around him for what he now realized was days – had begun to thin. Details now assailed him, and the evidence of the changes within himself left him alarmed.

706

His eyes saw . . . differently. Unhuman acuity. Motion – no matter how slight or peripheral – caught his attention, filled his awareness. Judged inconsequential or defined as threat, prey or unknown: instinctive decisions yet no longer buried deep, now lurking just beneath the surface of his mind.

He could feel his every muscle, every tendon and bone, could concentrate on each one to the exclusion of all the others, achieving a spatial sensitivity that made control absolute. He could walk a forest floor in absolute silence, if he so wished. He could freeze, shielding even the breath he drew, and become perfectly motionless.

But the changes he felt were far more profound than these physical manifestations. The violence residing within him was that of a killer. Cold and implacable, devoid of compassion or ambiguity.

And this realization terrified him.

The Tiger of Summer's Mortal Sword. Yes, Trake, I feel you. I know what you have made of me. Dammit, you could've at least asked.

He looked upon his followers, knowing them to be precisely that. Followers, his very own Sworn. An appalling truth. Among them, Stonny Menackis – *no, she isn't Trake's. She's chosen Keruli's Elder God. Good. If she was ever to kneel before me we wouldn't be thinking religious thoughts . . . and how likely is that? Ah, lass . . .*

Sensing his gaze, she looked at him.

Gruntle winked.

Her brows rose, and he understood her alarm, making him even more amused – his only answer to his terror at the brutal murderer hiding within him.

She hesitated, then approached. 'Gruntle?'

'Aye. I feel like I've just woken up.'

'Yeah, well, the hangover shows, believe me.'

'What's been going on?'

'You don't know?'

'I think I do, but I'm not entirely sure . . . of myself, of my own memories. We defended our tenement, and it was uglier than what's between Hood's toes. You were wounded. Dying. That Malazan soldier there healed you. And there's Itkovian – the priest in his arms has just turned to dust – gods, he must've needed a bath—'

'Beru fend us all, it really is you, Gruntle. I'd thought you were lost to m— to us for good.'

'I think a part of me is, lass. Lost to us all.'

'Since when were you the worshipping type?'

'That's the joke on Trake. I'm not. He's made a terrible choice. Show me an altar and I'm more likely to piss on it than kiss it.'

'You might *have* to kiss it, so I'd suggest you reverse the gestures.'

'Ha ha.' He shook himself, rolling his shoulders, and sighed.

Stonny recoiled slightly at the motion. 'Uh, that was too cat-like for me – your muscles rippled under that barbed skin.'

'And it felt damned good. Rippled? You should be considering new . . . possibilities, lass.'

'Keep dreaming, oaf.'

The banter was brittle, and they both sensed it.

Stonny was silent for a moment, then the breath hissed between her teeth. 'Buke. I guess he's gone—'

'No, he's alive. Circling overhead right now, in fact. That sparrowhawk – Keruli's gift to help the man keep an eye on Korbal Broach. He's Soletaken, now.'

Stonny was glaring skyward, hands on her hips. 'Well, that's just great!' She swung a venomous look upon Keruli – who was standing well off to one side, hands within sleeves, unnoticed, watching all in silence. 'Everybody gets blessed but me! Where's the justice in that?'

'Well, you're already blessed with incomparable beauty, Stonny—'

'Another word and I'll cut your tail off, I swear it.'

'I haven't got a tail.'

'Precisely.' She faced him. 'Now listen, we've got some-thing to work out. Something tells me that for both of us, heading back to Darujhistan isn't likely – at least not for the next while, anyway. So, now what? Are we about to part ways, you miserable old man?'

'No rush on all that, lass. Let's see how things settle—'

'Excuse me.'

Both turned at the voice, to find that Rath'Trake had joined them.

Gruntle scowled at the masked priest. 'What?'

'I believe we have matters to discuss, you and I, Mortal Sword.'

'You believe what you like,' the Daru replied. 'I've already made it plain to the Whiskered One that I'm a bad choice—'

Rath'Trake seemed to choke. 'The Whiskered One?' he sputtered in indignation.

Stonny laughed, and clouted the priest on the shoulder. 'He's a reverent bastard, ain't he just?'

'I don't kneel to anyone,' Gruntle growled. 'And that includes gods. And if scrubbing would do it, I'd get these stripes off my hide right now.'

The priest rubbed his bruised shoulder, the eyes within the feline mask glaring at Stonny. At Gruntle's words he faced the Daru again. 'These are not matters open to debate, Mortal Sword. You are what you are—'

'I'm a caravan guard captain, and damned good at it. When I'm sober, that is.'

'You are the master of war in the name of the Lord of Summer—'

'We'll call that a hobby.'

'A – a what!?'

They heard laughter. Captain Paran, still crouching beside Itkovian, was looking their way, and had clearly heard the conversation. The Malazan grinned at Rath'Trake. 'It never goes how you think it should, does it, priest? That's the glory of us humans, and your new god had

709

best make peace with that, and soon. Gruntle, keep playing by your own rules.'

'I hadn't planned otherwise, Captain,' Gruntle replied. 'How fares the Shield Anvil?'

Itkovian glanced over. 'I am well, sir.'

'Now that's a lie,' Stonny said.

'None the less,' the Shield Anvil said, accepting Mallet's shoulder as he slowly straightened.

Gruntle looked down at the two white cutlasses in his hands. 'Hood take me,' he muttered, 'but these have turned damned ugly.' He forced the blades into their scarred, tattered sheaths.

'They are not to leave your hands until this war is done,' Rath'Trake snapped.

'Another word from you, priest,' Gruntle said, 'and you'll be done.'

No-one else had ventured onto the plaza. Corporal Picker stood with the other Bridgeburners at the alley mouth, trying to determine what was going on. Conversations surrounded her, as the soldiers conjectured in time-honoured fashion, guessing at the meaning of the gestures and muted exchanges they witnessed among the dignitaries.

Picker glared about. 'Blend, where are you?'

'Here,' she replied at the corporal's shoulder.

'Why don't you sidle out there and find out what's happening?'

She shrugged. 'I'd get noticed.'

'Really?'

'Besides, I don't need to. It's plain to me what's happened.'

'Really?'

Blend made a wry face. 'You lose your brain when you gave up those torcs, Corporal? Never seen you so consistently wide-eyed before.'

'Really,' Picker repeated, this time in a dangerous drawl. 'Keep it up and you'll regret it, soldier.'

'An explanation? All right. Here's what I think I've been seeing. The Grey Swords had some personal business to clear up, which they've done, only it damn near ripped that commander to pieces. But Mallet, drawing on Hood-knows whose powers, has lent some strength – though I think it was the captain's hand that brought the man back from the dead – and no, I never knew Paran had it in him, and if we've been thinking lately that he was more than just a willow-spined nobleborn officer, we've just seen proof of our suspicions. But I don't think that's necessarily a bad thing for us – he won't stick a sword in our backs, Corporal. He might step in front of one heading our way, in fact. As for Gruntle, well, I think he's just shaken himself awake – and that masked priest of Trake's ain't happy about it – but no-one else gives a damn, because sometimes a smile is precisely what we all need.'

Picker's reply was a grunt.

'And finally, after watching all that,' Blend continued, 'it's time for Humbrall Taur and his Barghast . . .'

Humbrall Taur had raised his axe high, and had begun walking towards the Thrall's gate. Warchiefs and shoulder-men and women emerged from the gathered tribes, crossing the plaza in the giant warrior's wake.

Trotts pushed his way through the knot of Bridgeburners and joined them.

Staring at his back, Picker snorted.

'He goes to meet his gods,' Blend murmured. 'Give him that, Corporal.'

'Let's hope he stays with them,' she replied. 'Hood knows, he don't know how to command—'

'But Captain Paran does,' Blend said.

She glanced at her companion, then shrugged. 'I suppose he does at that.'

'Might be worth cornering Antsy,' Blend continued in a low tone, 'and anyone else who's been talking through their cracks of late . . .'

'Cornering, aye. Then beating them senseless. Sound

plan, Blend. Find us Detoran. Seems we got personal business, too, to clear up.'

'Well. Guess your brain's working after all.'

Picker's only reply was another grunt.

Blend slipped back into the crowd.

Personal business. I like the sound of that. We'll straighten 'em up for ya, Captain. Hood knows, it's the least I can do . . .

Circling high overhead, the sparrowhawk's sharp eyes missed nothing. The day was drawing to a close, shadows lengthening. Banks of dust on the plain to the west revealed the retreating Pannions – still being driven ever westward by elements of Humbrall Taur's Barahn clan.

In the city itself, still more thousands of Barghast moved through the streets. Clearing away dead, whilst tribes worked to excavate vast pits beyond the north wall, which had begun filling as commandeered wagons began filing out from Capustan. The long, soul-numbing task of cleansing the city had begun.

Directly below, the plaza's expanse was now threaded with figures, Barghast moving in procession from streets and alley mouths, following Humbrall Taur as the warchief approached the Thrall's gate. The sparrowhawk that had once been Buke heard no sound but the wind, lending the scene below a solemn, ethereal quality.

None the less, the raptor drew no closer. Distance was all that kept it sane, was all that had been keeping it sane since the dawn.

From here, far above Capustan, vast dramas of death and desperation were diminished, almost into abstraction. Tides of motion, the blurring of colours, the sheer muddiness of humanity – all diminished, the futility reduced to something strangely manageable.

Burned-out buildings. The tragic end of innocents. Wives, mothers, children. Desperation, horror and grief, the storms of destroyed lives—

No closer.

Wives, mothers, children. Burned-out buildings.

No closer.

Ever again.

The sparrowhawk caught an updraught, swept skyward, eyes now on the livening stars as night swallowed the world below.

There was pain in the gifts of the Elder Gods.

But sometimes, there was mercy.

CHAPTER EIGHTEEN

The birth of Barghast gods rang like a hammer on the anvil of the pantheon. Primordial in their aspect, these ascended spirits emerged from the Hold of the Beast, that most ancient of realms from the long-lost Elder Deck. Possessors of secrets and mysteries born in the bestial shadow of humanity, theirs was a power wreathed in antiquity.

Indeed, the other gods must have felt the tremor of their rising, rearing their heads in alarm and consternation. One of their own, after all, had just been abandoned in the mortal realm, whilst a First Hero assumed the warrior mantle in his place. More, the Fallen One had returned to the game in dire malice, corrupting the warrens to announce his deadly desire for vengeance and, it must be said in clear-eyed retrospect, domination.

Burn's sleep was fevered. Human civilization floundered in countless lands, drowning in the mire of spilled blood. These were dark times, and it was a darkness that seemed made for the dawn of the Barghast gods . . .

In the Wake of Dreams
Imrygyn Tallobant the Younger

The wizard's eyes opened.

To see, squatting atop a backpack directly in front of him, a small figure of wrapped sticks and knotted twine, its head an acorn, that now cocked slightly to one side.

'Awake. Yes. A mind once more sound.'

Quick Ben grimaced. 'Talamandas. For a moment there, I thought I was reliving a particularly unpleasant nightmare.'

'By your ravings these past few days and nights, Ben Adaephon Delat, you've lived through more than a few unpleasant nightmares, yes?'

Light rain was pattering on the tent's sloped walls. The wizard pushed the furs from his body and slowly sat up. He found he was wearing little more than his thin wool under-garments: leather armour and quilted tunic had been removed. He was sweat-chilled, the grubby, coarse wool damp. 'Ravings?'

The sticksnare's laugh was soft. 'Oh yes. And I listened, I listened indeed. So, you know the cause of the illness besetting the Sleeping Goddess. You would set yourself in the Crippled God's path, match his wits if not his power, and defeat all he seeks. Mortal, yours is a surpassing conceit . . . which I cannot but applaud.'

Quick Ben sighed, scanning the tumbled contents of the tent. 'Mockingly, no doubt. Where are the rest of my clothes?'

'I do not mock you, Wizard. Indeed, I am humbled by the depth of your . . . integrity. To find such, in a common soldier, one serving a malevolent, spiteful Empress who sits on a blood-stained throne, ruling an empire of murderers—'

'Now hold on, you misbegotten puppet—'

Talamandas laughed. 'Oh, but it has always been so, has it not? Within the rotting corpse hide diamonds! Pure of heart and stalwart with honour, yet besieged within their own house by the foulest of masters. And when the historians are done, the ink drying, may the house shine and sparkle even as it burns!'

'You've lost me, runt,' Quick Ben muttered. 'How long have I been . . . out?'

'Long enough. With the city retaken, the Thrall yielding the bones of our Founders, and the Pannions driven into the maw of Brood and your Malazan kin, well, you have missed most of the fun. For the moment, in any case. The tale's far from done, after all.'

The wizard found his quilted tunic. 'All of that,' he muttered as he pulled the heavy garment on, 'would have been nice to witness, but given my present lack of efficacy—'

'Ah, as to that . . .'

Quick Ben glanced at the sticksnare. 'Go on.'

'You would best the Crippled God, yet you find yourself unable to use the powers you possess. How, then, will you manage?'

He reached for his leggings. 'I'll think of something, eventually. Of course, you think you have an answer for me, don't you?'

'I do.'

'Well, let's hear it, then.'

'My gods are awakened, Wizard. Nose in the air, gleaning the scent of things, given to troubled thought and dour contemplation. You, Ben Adaephon Delat, pursue a worthy course. Sufficiently bold to snare their regard. Leading to certain conclusions. Sacrifices must be made. To your cause. Into the warrens, a necessary step. Thus, the need to supply you with . . . suitable armour. So that you may be fended from the Crippled God's poisons.'

Quick Ben massaged his brow. 'Talamandas, if you and your gods have sewn together some kind of impervious cloak or baldric or something, just say so. Please.'

'Nothing so . . . bland, Wizard. No, your flesh itself must be immune to infection. Your mind must be implacable to fevers and other similar plagues. You must be imbued with protective powers that by nature defy all that the Crippled God attempts when he seeks to thwart you.'

716

'Talamandas, what you describe is impossible.'

'Precisely.' The sticksnare untangled itself and rose. 'Thus. Before you, stands the worthy sacrifice. Twigs and twine do not sicken. A soul that has known death cannot be made fevered. The protective powers binding me are ancient and vast, the highest of sorceries to trap me within myself—'

'Yet you were taken. Once before. Torn from your barrow—'

'By necromancers, rot their foul hearts. There shall be no repetition. My gods have seen to that, with the power of their own blood. I shall accompany you, Ben Adaephon Delat. Into the warrens. I am your shield. Use me. Take me where you will.'

Quick Ben's dark eyes narrowed as he studied the stick-snare. 'I don't walk straight paths, Talamandas. And no matter how little sense my actions may make to you, I won't waste time with explanations.'

'My gods have given their trust in you, mortal.'

'Why?'

'Because they like you.'

'Hood's breath! What *have* I been raving about?'

'I cannot in truth tell you why they trust you, Wizard, only that they do. Such matters are not for me to question. In your fevered state, you revealed the way your mind works – you wove a net, a web, yet even I could not discern all the links, the connecting threads. Your grasp of causality surpasses my intellect, Ben Adaephon Delat. Perhaps my gods caught a glimmer of your design. Perhaps no more than a hint, triggering an instinctive suspicion that in you, mortal, the Crippled God will meet his match.'

Quick Ben climbed to his feet and strode to where his leather armour and Bridgeburner colours waited in a heap near the tent flap. 'That's the plan, anyway. All right, Talamandas, we've a deal. I admit, I was at a loss as to how to proceed without my warrens.' He paused, turned to the sticksnare once more. 'Maybe you can answer me a few

717

questions. Someone else is in this game. Seems to be shaping its own opposition to the Fallen One. Do you know who or what that might be?'

Talamandas shrugged. 'Elder Gods, Wizard. My Barghast gods conclude their actions have been reactionary by and large—'

'Reactionary?'

'Aye, a kind of fighting withdrawal. They seem incapable of changing the future, only preparing for it.'

'That's damned fatalistic of them.'

'Their perennial flaw, Wizard.'

Quick Ben shrugged himself into his armour. 'Mind you,' he muttered, 'it's not really their battle. Except for maybe K'rul . . .'

Talamandas leapt to the floor and scrambled to stand directly in front of the wizard. 'What did you say? K'rul? What do you know of *him*?'

Quick Ben raised an eyebrow. 'Well, he made the warrens, after all. We swim his immortal blood – we mages, and everyone else who employs the pathways of sorcery, including the gods. Yours, too, I imagine.'

The sticksnare hopped about, twig fingers clutching at the yellowed grass bound to its acorn head. 'No-one knows all that! No-one! You – you – how can you – aagh! The web! The web of your infernal brain!'

'K'rul is in worse shape even than Burn, given the nature of the Crippled God's assault,' Quick Ben said. 'So, if I felt helpless, imagine how *he* must feel. Makes that fatalism a little more understandable, don't you think? And if that's not enough, all the last surviving Elder Gods have lived under a host of nasty curses for a long, long time. Haven't they? Given those circumstances, who wouldn't be feeling a little fatalistic?'

'Bastard mortal! Warp and weft! Deadly snare! Out with it, damn you!'

Quick Ben shrugged. 'Your Barghast gods aren't ready to go it alone. Not by throwing all their weight behind me, in

718

any case. Not a chance, Talamandas – they're still babes in the woods. Now, the Elder Gods have been on the defensive – tried to go it alone, I imagine. Legendary hubris, with that lot. But that wasn't working, so they've gone looking for allies.

'Thus . . . who was at work refashioning you into something capable of shielding me in the warrens? Hood, for one, I'd imagine. Layers of death protecting your soul. And your own Barghast gods, of course. Cutting those binding spells that constrained your own power. And Fener's thrown you a bone, or Treach, or whoever's on that particular roost right now – you can hit back if something comes at you. And I'd guess the Queen of Dreams has stepped in, a bridge between you and the Sleeping Goddess, to turn you into a lone and likely formidable crusader against the poison in her flesh, and in K'rul's veins. So, you're all ready to go, but where? How? And that's where I come in. How am I doing so far, Talamandas?'

'We are relying upon you, Ben Adaephon Delat,' the sticksnare growled.

'To do what?'

'Whatever it is you're planning to do!' Talamandas shrieked. 'And it had better work!'

After a long moment, Quick Ben grinned down at the creature.

But said nothing.

The sticksnare scrambled after Quick Ben when he left the tent. The mage paused to look around. What he had thought to be rain had been, in fact, water dripping from the leaves of a broad, verdant oak, its branches hanging over the tent. It was late afternoon, the sky clear overhead.

A Barghast encampment was sprawled out on all sides. Wicker and hide dwellings rose from the forest floor along the base of a lightly treed slope directly behind the wizard, whilst before him – to the south – were the dun-coloured humps of rounded tipis. The different styles reflected at least two distinct tribes. The mud-churned pathways crisscrossing the encampment were crowded with warriors, many wounded or bearing fallen kin.

'Where,' Quick Ben asked Talamandas, 'are my fellow Bridgeburners?'

'First into Capustan, Wizard, and still there. At the Thrall, likely.'

'Did they get into any fighting?'

'Only at the north gate – breaking through the siege line. Swiftly done. There are none wounded, Ben Adaephon Delat. Making your tribe unique, yes?'

'So I see,' Quick Ben murmured, watching the warriors filing into the camp. 'Not much duelling of late, I take it.'

The sticksnare grunted. 'True enough. Our gods have spoken to our shamans, who have in turn conveyed to the clan warriors a ... chastisement. It would appear that the White Faces are not yet done with these Pannions – or with your war, Wizard.'

Quick Ben glanced down. 'You'll be marching south with us, Talamandas?'

'We shall. It is not enough blunting the sword – we must sever the hand wielding it.'

'I need to contact my allies ... in the army to the west. Should I attempt a warren?'

'I am ready.'

'Good. Let's find somewhere private.'

Two leagues to the west of Capustan, in the shadows edging down a broad slope, the massed ranks of Malazan heavy infantry locked shields and advanced. Marines armed with crossbows ranged ahead, firing quarrels into the milling line of Betaklites less than thirty paces distant.

Whiskeyjack watched through the slits of his helm's visor from where he had reined in at the hill's crest, his horse tossing its head at the smell of blood. Aides and messengers gathered around him.

Dujek's flank attack on the Septarch's regiment of archers had virtually eliminated the whizzing flight of arrows from the valley side opposite. Whiskeyjack's heavy infantry had drawn their fire, which had provided Onearm's heavy cavalry the time needed to mount a charge along the north slope. Had the Pannion archers the discipline – and competent commanders – they would have had time to wheel in formation and loose at least three flights at the charging cavalry, perhaps sufficient to beat off the attack. Instead, they had milled in confusion upon seeing the horsewarriors closing on their right flank, then had disintegrated into a rout. Pursuit and wholesale slaughter followed.

The marines slipped back through aisles in the advancing heavy infantry. They would reappear on each wing, resuming their crossbow-fire against the enemy line's edges. Before then, however, four thousand silent, scale-armoured and shield-bearing veterans closed with the Betaklites. Javelins preceded their charge when but a dozen paces remained, the long-headed, barbed spears cutting into the Pannion line – a tactic peculiar to Onearm's Host – then thrusting swords snapped from scabbards. And the Malazans surged forward.

The Betaklite line crumpled.

Whiskeyjack's heavy infantry reformed into individual four-squad wedges, each one independently driving deeper into the Pannion ranks once the battle was fully joined.

The details before the commander were precise in following the Malazan doctrine of set battles, as devised by Dassem Ultor decades past. Shield-locked lines and squares worked best in defending engagements. When delivering chaos into massed enemy ranks in an assault, however, it was found that smaller, tighter units worked best. A successful advance that drove the enemy back often lost its momentum, and, indeed, its contact with the retreating foes, amidst a corpse-cluttered ground and the need to maintain closed ranks. Almost a thousand four-squad wedges, of thirty-five to forty soldiers each, on the other hand, actually delayed the moment of rout. Flight was more difficult, communication problematic, and lines of sight to fellow soldiers often broken – none knew what the others were doing, and in the face of that uncertainty, they often hesitated before fleeing – a fatal option. There was another choice, of course, and that was to fight, but it took a very special army to be capable of maintaining such discipline and adaptability in those circumstances, and in those instances the Malazan forces would hold their shield-locked formation.

These Betaklites possessed none of these qualities. Within fifty heartbeats, the division was shattered. Entire companies, finding themselves surrounded by the silent, deadly Malazans, flung their weapons down.

This part of the battle, Whiskeyjack concluded, was finished.

A Saltoan messenger rode up to Whiskeyjack's side. 'Sir! Word from the warlord!'

Whiskeyjack nodded.

'The Ilgres Barghast and their Rhivi skirmishers have broken the Seerdomin and Urdomen. There was a Mage Cadre active in the engagement, at least at the start, but the Tiste Andii nullified them. Brood owns the field on the south flank.'

'Very good,' Whiskeyjack grunted. 'Anything else?'

'Sir, a well-aimed slingstone from a Rhivi gave Septarch Kulpath a third eye – killed the bastard outright. We are in possession of his army's standard, sir.'

'Inform the warlord that the Betaklites, Beklites, Scalandi and Desandi companies have been defeated. We command the centre and north. Enquire of the warlord as to our next move – my scouts inform me that upwards of two hundred thousand Tenescowri are encamped half a league to the east. Rather mauled by all accounts, yet potentially a nuisance. At the same time – and on this Dujek and I are agreed – an unmitigated slaughter of these peasants would not sit well with us.'

'I will convey your words, Commander.' The messenger

saluted, swung his horse round, and rode southward.

A slash of darkness opened before Whiskeyjack, startling his horse and those of the riders nearest him. Snorting, stamping, the beast came close to rearing until a low growl from Whiskeyjack calmed it. His retinue managed the same.

Korlat emerged from her warren. Her black armour glittered with blood-spray, but he saw no obvious wounds. None the less . . .

'Are you injured?'

She shook her head. 'A hapless Pannion warlock. Whiskeyjack, I need you to come with me. Are you done here?'

He grimaced, ever loath to leave a battle – even one drawing to a quick, satisfying conclusion. 'I'll assume it's important – enough to have you risk your warren – so the answer is yes. Do we go far?'

'To Dujek's command tent.'

'He's taken wounds?'

'No. All is well, you old worrier,' she said, cracking a smile. 'How long would you have me wait?'

'Well enough,' he growled. He turned to an officer sitting on a roan destrier nearby. 'Barack, you're in charge here.'

The young man's eyes widened. 'Sir, I'm a captain—'

'So here's your chance. Besides, I'm a sergeant – at least I would be if I was still drawing coin on the Empress's paylists. Besides again, you're the only officer present who doesn't have his or her own company to worry about.'

'But sir, I am Dujek's liaison to the Black Moranth—'

'And are they here?'

'Uh, no sir.'

'So, enough jawing and make sure things get wrapped up here, Barack.'

'Yes, sir.'

Whiskeyjack dismounted and handed the reins of his charger to an aide, then joined Korlat. He resisted an urge to draw her into his arms, and was disconcerted to see a glimmer of prescient knowledge in her eyes.

'Not in front of the troops, surely,' she murmured.

He growled. 'Lead me through, woman.'

Whiskeyjack had travelled a warren only a few times, but his memories of those fraught journeys did little to prepare him for Kurald Galain. Taking him by the hand, Korlat drew him into the ancient realm of Mother Dark, and though he could feel the sure grip of her fingers, he stepped into blindness.

No light. Gritty flagstones under his boots, the air perfectly motionless, scentless, with an ambient temperature that seemed no different from that of his skin.

He was pulled forward, his boots seeming to barely touch the floor.

A sudden streak of grey assaulted his eyes, and he heard Korlat hiss: 'We are assailed even here – the Crippled God's poison seeps deep, Whiskeyjack. This does not bode well.'

He cleared his throat. 'No doubt Anomander Rake has recognized the threat, and if so, do you know what he plans to do about it?'

'One thing at a time, dear lover. He is the Knight of Darkness, the Son. Mother Dark's own champion. Not one to shy from a confrontation.'

'I'd never have guessed,' he replied wryly. 'What's he waiting for, then?'

'We're a patient people, us Tiste Andii. The true measure of power lies in the wisdom to wait for the propitious moment. When it comes, and he judges it to be so, then Anomander Rake will respond.'

'Presumably the same holds for unleashing Moon's Spawn on the Pannion Domin.'

'Aye.'

And, somehow, Rake's managed to hide a floating fortress the size of a mountain . . . 'You've considerable faith in your Lord, haven't you?'

He felt her shrug through the hand clasped in his. 'There is sufficient precedent to disregard notions of

724

faith, when it comes to my Lord. I am comforted by certainty.'

'Glad to hear it. And are you comfortable with me, Korlat?'

'Devious man. The answer to every facet of that question is yes. Would you now have me ask in kind?'

'You shouldn't have to.'

'Tiste Andii or human, when it comes to males, they're all the same. Perhaps I shall force the words from you none the less.'

'You won't have to work hard. My answer's the same as yours.'

'Which is?'

'Why, the very word you used, of course.'

He grunted at the jab in his ribs. 'Enough of that. We've arrived.'

The portal opened to painful light – the interior of Dujek's command tent, shrouded in the gloom of late afternoon. They stepped within, the warren closing silently behind them.

'If all this was just to get me alone—'

'Gods, the ego!' She gestured with her free hand and a ghostly figure took form in front of Whiskeyjack. A familiar face – that smiled.

'What a charming sight,' the apparition said, eyeing them. 'Hood knows, I can't recall the last time I had a woman.'

'Watch your tongue, Quick Ben,' Whiskeyjack growled, disengaging his hand from Korlat's. 'It's been a while, and you look terrible.'

'Why, thanks a whole lot, Commander. I'll have you know I feel even worse. But I can traverse my warrens, now, more or less shielded from the Fallen One's poison. I bring news from Capustan – do you want it or not?'

Whiskeyjack grinned. 'Go ahead.'

'The White Faces hold the city.'

'We'd guessed that much, once Twist delivered the news

of your success with the Barghast, and once the Pannion army stumbled into our laps.'

'Fine. Well, assuming you've taken care of that army, I'll add just one more thing. The Barghast are marching with us. South. If you and Dujek found things tense dealing with Brood and Kallor and company – your pardon, Korlat – now you've got Humbrall Taur to deal with as well.'

Whiskeyjack grunted at that. 'What's he like, then?'

'Too clever by half, but at least he's united the clans, and he's clear-eyed on the mess he's heading into.'

'I'm glad one of us is. How fare Paran and the Bridgeburners?'

'Reportedly fine, though I haven't seen them in a while. They are at the Thrall – with Humbrall Taur and the survivors of the city's defenders.'

Whiskeyjack's brows rose. 'There are survivors?'

'Aye, so it seems. Non-combatants still cowering in tunnels. And some Grey Swords. Hard to believe, isn't it? Mind you, I doubt there's much fight left in them. From what I've heard about Capustan's streets . . .' Quick Ben shook his head. 'You'll have to see it to believe it. So will I, in fact, which is what I'm about to do. With your leave, that is.'

'With caution, I trust.'

The wizard smiled. 'No-one will see me unless I want them to, sir. When do you anticipate reaching Capustan?'

Whiskeyjack shrugged. 'We've the Tenescowri to deal with. That could get complicated.'

Quick Ben's dark eyes narrowed. 'You're not intending to parley with them, are you?'

'Why not? Better than slaughter, Wizard.'

'Whiskeyjack, the Barghast are returning with stories . . . of what happened in Capustan, of what the Tenescowri did to the defenders. They have a leader, those Tenescowri, a man named Anaster, the First Child of the Dead Seed. The latest rumour is he personally skinned Prince Jelarkan, then served him up as the main course of a banquet – in the prince's own throne room.'

The breath hissed from Korlat.

Grimacing, Whiskeyjack said, 'If such crimes can be laid with certainty at the feet of this Anaster – or of any Tenescowri – then Malazan military law will prevail.'

'Simple execution grants them a mercy not accorded their victims.'

'Then they will be fortunate that Onearm's Host captured them, and none other.'

Quick Ben still looked troubled. 'And Capustan's surviving citizens, the defenders and the priests of the Thrall – will they have no say in the disposition of the prisoners? Sir, troubled times might await us.'

'Thank you for the warning, Wizard.'

After a moment, Quick Ben shrugged, then sighed. 'See you in Capustan, Whiskeyjack.'

'Aye.'

The apparition faded.

Korlat turned to the commander. 'Malazan military law.'

He raised his brows. 'My sense of Caladan Brood is that he's not the vengeful type. Do you anticipate a clash?'

'I know what Kallor will advise.' A hint of tension was present in her tone.

'So do I, but I don't think the warlord's inclined to listen. Hood knows, he hasn't thus far.'

'We have not yet seen Capustan.'

He released a long breath, drew off his gauntlets. 'Horrors to answer in kind.'

'An unwritten law,' she said in a low voice. 'An ancient law.'

'I don't hold to it,' Whiskeyjack growled. 'We become no better, then. Even simple execution . . .' He faced her. 'Over two hundred thousand starving peasants. Will they stand about like sheep? Not likely. As prisoners? We couldn't feed them if we tried, nor have we sufficient soldiers to spare guarding them.'

Korlat's eyes were slowly widening. 'You are proposing we leave them, aren't you?'

She's leading up to something here. I've caught glimmers before, the whisper of a hidden wedge, poised to drive itself between us. 'Not all of them. We'll take their leaders. This Anaster, and his officers – assuming there are any. If the Tenescowri walked a path of atrocity, then the First Child led the way.' Whiskeyjack shook his head. 'But the real criminal awaits us within the Domin itself – the Seer – who would starve his followers into cannibalism, into madness. Who would destroy his own people. We'd be executing the victims – *his* victims.'

The Tiste Andii frowned. 'By that token, we should absolve the Pannion armies as well, Whiskeyjack.'

The Malazan's grey eyes hardened. 'Our enemy is the Seer. Dujek and I agree on this – we're not here to annihilate a nation. The armies that impede our march to the Seer, we will deal with. Efficiently. Retribution and revenge are distractions.'

'And what of liberation? The conquered cities—'

'Incidental, Korlat. I'm surprised at your confusion on this. Brood saw it the same as we did – at that first parley when tactics were discussed. We strike for the heart—'

'I believe you misunderstood, Whiskeyjack. For over a decade, the warlord has been waging a war of liberation – from the rapacious hunger of your Malazan Empire. Caladan Brood has now shifted his focus – a new enemy – but the same war. Brood is here to free the Pannions—'

'Hood's breath! You can't free a people *from themselves*!'

'He seeks to free them from the Seer's rule.'

'And who exalted the Seer to his present status?'

'Yet you speak of absolving the commonalty, even the soldiers of the Pannion armies, Whiskeyjack. And that is what is confusing me.'

Not entirely. 'We speak at cross-purposes here, Korlat. Neither I nor Dujek will willingly assume the role of judge and executioner – should we prove victorious. Nor are we here to put the pieces back together for the Pannions. That's for them to do. That responsibility will turn us into administrators, and to effectively administrate, we must *occupy*.'

She barked a harsh laugh. 'And is that not the Malazan way, Whiskeyjack?'

'This is not a Malazan war!'

'Isn't it? Are you sure?'

He studied her through slitted eyes. 'What do you mean? We're outlawed, woman. Onearm's Host is . . .' He fell silent, seeing a flatness come to Korlat's gaze, then realized – too late – that he had just failed a test. And with that failure had ended the trust that had grown between them. *Damn, I walked right into it. Wide-eyed stupid.*

She smiled then, and it was a smile of pain and regret. 'Dujek approaches. You might as well await him here.'

The Tiste Andii turned and strode from the tent.

Whiskeyjack stared after her, then, when she'd left, he flung his gauntlets on the map table and sat down on Dujek's cot. *Should I have told you, Korlat? The truth? That we've got a knife at our throats. And the hand holding it – on Empress Laseen's behalf – is right here in this very camp, and has been ever since the beginning.*

He heard a horse thump to a halt outside the tent. A few moments later Dujek Onearm entered, his armour sheathed in dust. 'Ah, wondered where you'd got to—'

'Brood knows,' Whiskeyjack cut in, his voice low and raw.

Dujek paused but a moment. 'He does, does he? What, precisely, has he worked out?'

'That we're not quite as outlawed as we've made out to be.'

'Any further?'

'Isn't that enough, Dujek?'

The High Fist strode over to the side table where waited a jug of ale. He unstoppered it and poured two tankards full. 'There are . . . mitigating circumstances—'

'Relevant only to us. You and I—'

'And our army—'

729

'Who believe their lives are forfeit in the Empire, Dujek. Made into victims once again – no, it's you and I and no-one else this time.'

Dujek drained his tankard, refilled it in silence. Then he said, 'Are you suggesting we spread our hand on the table for Brood and Korlat? In the hopes that they'll do something about our . . . predicament?'

'I don't know – not if we're hoping for absolution for having maintained this deceit all this time. That would be a motive that wouldn't sit well with me, even if patently untrue. Appearances—'

'Will make it seem precisely that, aye. "We've been lying to you from the very beginning to save our own necks. But now that you know, we'll tell you . . ." Gods, that's insulting even to me and I'm the one saying it. All right, the alliance is in trouble—'

A thud against the tent flap preceded the arrival of Artanthos. 'Your pardon, sirs,' the man said, flat eyes studying the two soldiers in turn before he continued, 'Brood has called for a counsel.'

Ah, standard-bearer, your timing is impeccable . . .

Whiskeyjack collected the tankard awaiting him and drained it, then turned to Dujek and nodded.

The High Fist sighed. 'Lead the way, Artanthos, we're right behind you.'

The encampment seemed extraordinarily quiet. The Mhybe had not realized how comforting the army's presence had been on the march. Now, only elders and children and a few hundred rearguard Malazan soldiers remained. She had no idea how the battle fared; either way, deaths would make themselves felt. Mourning among the Rhivi and Barghast, bereft voices rising into the darkness.

Victory is an illusion. In all things.

She fled in her dreams every night. Fled and was, eventually, caught, only to awaken. Sudden, as if torn away, her withered body shivering, aches filling her joints. An escape of sorts, yet in truth she left one nightmare for another.

An illusion. In all things.

This wagon bed had become her entire world, a kind of mock sanctuary that reappeared each and every time sleep ended. The rough woollen blankets and furs wrapped around her were a personal landscape, the bleak terrain of dun folds startlingly similar to what she had seen when in the dragon's grip, when the undead beast flew high over the tundra in her dream, yielding an echo of the freedom she had experienced then, an echo that was painfully sardonic.

To either side of her ran wooden slats. Their patterns of grain and knots had become intimate knowledge. Far to the north, she recalled, among the Nathii, the dead were buried in wood boxes. The custom had been born generations ago, arising from the more ancient practice of interring corpses in hollowed-out tree trunks. The boxes were then buried, for wood was born of earth and to earth it must return. A vessel of life now a vessel of death. The Mhybe imagined that, if a dead Nathii could see, moments before the lid was lowered and darkness swallowed all, that Nathii's vision would match hers.

Lying in the box, unable to move, awaiting the lid. A body past usefulness, awaiting the darkness.

But there would be no end. Not for her. They were keeping it away. Playing out their own delusions of mercy and compassion. The Daru who fed her, the Rhivi woman who cleaned and bathed her and combed the wispy remnants of her hair. Gestures of malice. Playing out, over and over, scenes of torture.

The Rhivi woman sat above her now, steadily pulling the horn comb through the Mhybe's hair, humming a child's song. A woman the Mhybe remembered from her other life. Old, she had seemed back then, a hapless woman who had been kicked in the head by a bhederin and so lived in a simple world.

I'd thought it simple. But that was just one more illusion. No,

731

*she lives amidst unknowns, amidst things she cannot com-
prehend. It is a world of terror. She sings to fend off the fear born
of her own ignorance. Given tasks to keep her busy.*

*Before I had come along for her, this woman had helped prepare
corpses. After all, the spirits worked through such childlike adults.
Through her, the spirits could come close to the fallen, and so
comfort them and guide them into the world of the ancestors.*

It could be nothing other than malice, the Mhybe concluded, to have set this woman upon her. Possibly, she was
not even aware that the subject of her attentions was still
alive. The woman met no-one's eyes, ever. Recognition had
fled with the kick of a bhederin's hoof.

The comb dragged back and forth, back and forth. The
humming continued its ceaseless round.

*Spirits below, I would rather even your terror of the unknown.
Rather that, than the knowledge of my daughter's betrayal – the
wolves she has set upon me, to pursue me in my dreams. The
wolves, which are her hunger. The hunger, which has already
devoured my youth and now seeks yet more. As if anything's left.
Am I to be naught but food for my daughter's burgeoning life? A final
meal, a mother reduced to nothing more than sustenance?*

*Ah, Silverfox, are you every daughter? Am I every mother?
There have been no rituals severing our lives – we have forgotten
the meaning behind the Rhivi ways, the true reasons for those
rituals. I ever yield. And you suckle in ceaseless demand. And
so we are trapped, pulled deeper and deeper, you and I.*

*To carry a child is to age in one's bones. To weary one's
blood. To stretch skin and flesh. Birthing splits a woman in two,
the division a thing of raw agony. Splitting young from old.
And the child needs, and the mother gives.*

*I have never weaned you, Silverfox. Indeed, you have never
left my womb. You, daughter, draw far more than just milk.*

*Spirits, please, grant me surcease. This cruel parody of
motherhood is too much to bear. Sever me from my daughter.
For her sake. My milk is become poison. I can feed naught but
spite, for there is nothing else within me. And I remain a young
woman in this aged body—*

732

The comb caught on a snarl, tugging her head back. The Mhybe hissed in pain, shot a glare up at the woman above her. Her heart suddenly lurched.

Their gazes were locked.

The woman, who looked at no-one, was looking at her.

I, a young woman in an old woman's body. She, a child in a woman's body—

Two prisons, in perfect reflection.

Eyes locked.

'Dear lass, you look weary. Settle here with magnanimous Kruppe and he will pour you some of this steaming herbal brew.'

'I will, thank you.'

Kruppe smiled, watching Silverfox slowly lower herself onto the ground and lean back against the spare saddle, the small hearth between them. The well-rounded curves of the woman were visible through the worn deer-leather tunic. 'So where are your friends?' she asked.

'Gambling. With the crew of the Trygalle Trade Guild. Kruppe, for some odd reason, has been barred from such games. An outrage.' The Daru handed her a tin cup. 'Mostly sage, alas. If you've a cough—'

'I haven't, but it's welcome anyway.'

'Kruppe, of course, never coughs.'

'And why is that?'

'Why, because he drinks sage tea.'

Her brown eyes slipped past his and settled on the wagon a dozen paces away. 'How does she fare?'

Kruppe's brows lifted. 'You might ask her, lass.'

'I can't. I can be nothing other than an abomination for my mother – her stolen youth, in the flesh. She despises me, with good reason, especially now that Korlat's told her about my T'lan Ay.'

'Kruppe wonders, do you now doubt the journey undertaken?'

Silverfox shook her head, sipped at the tea. 'It's too late for that. The problem persists – as you well know. Besides, our journey is done. Only hers remains.'

'You dissemble,' Kruppe murmured. 'Your journey is anything but done, Silverfox. But let us leave that subject for the moment, yes? Have you gleaned news of the dreadful battle?'

'It's over. The Pannion forces are no more. Barring a couple of hundred thousand poorly armed peasants. The White Faces have liberated Capustan – what's left of it, that is. The Bridgeburners are already in the city. More pressing: Brood has called a council – you might be interested in attending that.'

'Indeed, if only to bless the gathering with Kruppe's awesome wisdom. What of you – are you not also attending?'

Silverfox smiled. 'As you said earlier, Daru, my journey's not quite over.'

'Ah, yes. Kruppe wishes you well in that, lass. And dearly hopes he will see you again soon.'

The woman's eyes glanced once more at the wagon. 'You will, friend,' she replied, then drained her tea and rose with a soft sigh.

Kruppe saw her hesitate. 'Lass? Is something wrong?'

'Uh, I'm not sure.' Her expression was troubled. 'A part of me desires to accompany you to that council. A sudden urge, in fact.'

The Daru's small eyes narrowed. 'A part of you, Silverfox?'

'Aye, inviting the question: *which* part? Whose soul within me now twitches with suspicion? Who senses that sparks are about to fly in this alliance of ours? Gods, even worse, it's as if I know precisely *why* . . . but I don't.'

'Tattersail doesn't, yes? Leaving Nightchill and Bellurdan as potential candidates possessing prescient knowledge fraught with dire motivation. Uh, perhaps that can be said a simpler way—'

'Never mind, Kruppe.'

'You are torn, Silverfox, to put it bluntly. Consider this: will a minor delay in seeking your destiny unduly affect its outcome? Can you, in other words, spare the time to come with me to the warlord's command tent?'

She studied him. 'You've a hunch as well, don't you?'

'If a rift is imminent, lass, then your personage could prove essential, for you are the bridge indeed between these formidable camps.'

'I – I don't trust Nightchill, Kruppe.'

'Most mortals occasionally fail in trusting parts of themselves. Excepting Kruppe, of course, whose well-earned confidence is absolute. In any case, conflicting instincts are woven in our natures, excepting Kruppe, of—'

'Yes, yes. All right. Let's go.'

A slash of darkness opened in the canvas wall. The mild breath of Kurald Galain flowed into the command tent, dimming the lanterns. Anomander Rake strode through. The midnight rent closed silently behind him. The lanterns flared back into life.

Brood's wide, flat face twisted. 'You are late,' he growled. 'The Malazans are already on their way.'

Shrugging the black leather cape from his shoulders, the Lord of Moon's Spawn said, 'What of it? Or am I to adjudicate yet again?'

Her back to one side of the tent wall, Korlat cleared her throat. 'There have been . . . revelations, Lord. The alliance itself is in question.'

A dry snort came from Kallor, the last person present. 'In question? We've been lied to from the very start. A swift strike against Onearm's Host – before it's had a chance to recover from today's battles – is imperative.'

Korlat watched her master study his allies in silence.

After a long moment, Rake smiled. 'Dear Caladan, if by lying you are referring to the hidden hand of the Empress – the daggers poised behind the backs of Dujek Onearm and Whiskeyjack – well, it would seem that, should action be required – which I add I do not believe to be the case – our position should be one of intervention. On behalf of Dujek and Whiskeyjack, that is. Unless, of course' – his eyes flattened on Brood – 'you are no longer confident of their capabilities as commanders.' He slowly withdrew his gauntlets. 'Yet Crone's report to me of today's engagement was characterized by naught but grudging praise. The Malazans were professional, perfunctory and relentless. Precisely as we would have them.'

'It's not their fighting ability that is the problem,' Kallor rasped. 'This was to be a war of liberation—'

'Don't be a fool,' Rake muttered. 'Is there wine or ale? Who will join me in a drink?'

Brood grunted. 'Aye, pour me one, Rake. But let it be known, whilst Kallor has uttered foolish statements in the past, he did not do so now. Liberation. The Pannion Domin—'

'Is just another empire,' the Lord of Moon's Spawn drawled. 'And as such, its power represents a threat. Which we are intending to obliterate. Liberation of the commonalty may well result, but it cannot be our goal. Free an adder and it will still bite you, given the chance.'

'So we are to crush the Pannion Seer, only to have some High Fist of the Malazan Empire take his place?'

Rake handed the warlord a cup of wine. The Tiste Andii's eyes were veiled, almost sleepy as he studied Brood. 'The Domin is an empire that sows horror and oppression among its own people,' Rake said. 'None of us here would deny that. Thus, for ethical reasons alone, there was just cause for marching upon it.'

'Which is what we've been saying all along—'

'I heard you the first time, Kallor. Your penchant for repetition is wearisome. I have described but one . . . excuse. One *reason*. Yet it appears that you have all allowed that reason to overwhelm all others, whilst to my mind it is the *least* in importance.' He sipped his wine, then continued. 'However, let us stay with it for a moment. Horror and oppression, the face of the Pannion Domin. Consider, if you will, those cities and territories on Genabackis that are now under Malazan rule. Horror? No more so than mortals must daily face in their normal lives. Oppression? Every government requires laws, and from what I can tell Malazan laws are, if anything, among the least repressive of any empire I have known.

'Now. The Seer is removed, a High Fist and Malazan-style governance replaces it. The result? Peace, reparation, law, order.' He scanned the others, then slowly raised a single eyebrow. 'Fifteen years ago, Genabaris was a fetid sore on the northwest coast, and Nathilog even worse. And now, under Malazan rule? Rivals to Darujhistan herself. If you truly wish the best for the common citizens of Pannion, why do you not *welcome* the Empress?

'Instead, Dujek and Whiskeyjack are forced into an elaborate charade to win us as allies. They're soldiers, in case you've forgotten. Soldiers are given orders. If they don't like them, that's just too bad. If it means a false proclamation of outlawry – without letting every private in the army in on the secret and thereby eliminating the chance of it ever *remaining* a secret – then a good soldier grits his teeth and gets on with it.

'The truth is simple – to me at least. Brood, you and I, we have fought the Malazans as liberators in truth. Asking no coin, no land. Our motives aren't even clear to us – imagine how they must seem to the Empress? Inexplicable. We appear to be bound to lofty ideals, to nearly outrageous notions of self-sacrifice. We are her enemy, and I don't think *she even knows why.*'

'Sing me the Abyss,' Kallor sneered. 'In her Empire there would be no place for us – not one of us.'

'Does that surprise you?' Rake asked. 'We cannot be controlled. The truth laid bare is we fight for our own freedom. No borders for Moon's Spawn. No world-spanning peace that would make warlords and generals and mercenary companies obsolete. We fight against the imposition of order and the mailed fist that must hide behind it, because we're not the ones wielding that fist.'

'Nor would I ever wish to,' Brood growled.

'Precisely. So why begrudge the Empress possessing the desire and its attendant responsibilities?'

Korlat stared at her Lord. Stunned once again, thrown off-balance yet one more time. *The Draconian blood within him. He does not think as we do. Is it that blood? Or something else?* She had no answer, no true understanding of the man she followed. A sudden welling of pride filled her. *He is the Son of Darkness. A master worth swearing fealty to – perhaps the only one. For me. For the Tiste Andii.*

Caladan Brood let out a gusting sigh. 'Pour me another, damn you.'

'I shall set aside my disgust,' Kallor said, rising from his chair in a rustle of chain armour, 'and voice a subject only marginally related to what's been said thus far. Capustan has been cleansed. Before us, the river. South of that, three cities to march on. To do so in succession as a single army will slow us considerably. Setta, in particular, is not on our path to Coral. So, the army must divide in two, meeting again south of Lest and Setta, perhaps at Maurik, before striking for Coral. Now, the question: along what lines do we divide?'

'A reasonable subject,' Rake murmured, 'for discussion at this pending meeting.'

'And none other, aye,' Caladan Brood rumbled. 'Won't they be surprised?'

They will indeed. Regret seeped through Korlat's thoughts. *And more, I have done Whiskeyjack an injustice. I hope it is not too late to make reparations. It is not well for a Tiste Andii to judge in haste. My vision was clouded. Clouded? No, more like a storm. Of emotions, born of need and of love. Can you forgive me, Whiskeyjack?*

The tent flap was drawn back and the two Malazan commanders entered, trailed by the standard-bearer, Artanthos. Dujek's face was dark. 'Sorry we were delayed,'

738

he growled. 'I have just been informed that the Tenescowri are on the move. Straight for us.'

Korlat sought to meet Whiskeyjack's eyes, but the man was studying the warlord as he added, 'Expect another battle, at dawn. A messy one.'

'Leave that to me,' Anomander Rake drawled.

The voice pulled Whiskeyjack round in surprise. 'Lord, forgive me. I didn't see you. I'm afraid I was somewhat . . . preoccupied.'

Dujek asked, 'You are offering to set your Tiste Andii against the Tenescowri, Lord?'

'Hardly,' Rake replied. 'I mean to scare them witless. In person.'

No-one spoke for a moment, then Caladan Brood began rummaging in a trunk for more cups. 'We have another issue to discuss, High Fist,' he said.

'So I gather.'

The old man looked positively sick, while Whiskeyjack's colour was high.

The warlord poured more wine, then gestured at the cups he had filled. 'Help yourselves. Kallor has noted a pending problem in the disposition of our forces.'

Oh, the bastards are making fun of this. Enough. Korlat spoke, 'High Fist, to the south await three cities. Lest and Setta should be taken simultaneously, if possible, with a rejoining of our forces at Maurik, before continuing on to Coral. We would like to discuss with you how to divide the armies.'

Whiskeyjack's eyes found hers. She offered him a half-smile. He frowned in reply.

'I see,' Dujek said after a moment. He collected his cup and sat down on a camp chair. 'Well enough.' And, for the moment, said no more.

Whiskeyjack cleared his throat and spoke, 'The division, at least initially, seems fairly obvious. Onearm's Host south-west to Setta – which will close our lines of communication with our Black Moranth, who remain in place in the Vision

Mountains. The warlord and his forces straight south to Lest. Once we have taken Setta, we strike for the head-waters of the Maurik River, then follow the course south to Maurik itself. Possibly, you will have arrived there first, but that is not especially problematic.'

'Agreed,' Brood said.

'I said initially, alas,' Whiskeyjack continued.

The others turned to him.

The man shrugged. 'The White Face Barghast are join-ing the campaign. We also have to consider the surviving elements of Capustan's defenders – they might well desire to accompany us. Finally, there is the looming question of Silverfox, and her T'lan Imass.'

'If we allow the bitch and her T'lan Imass into this war,' Kallor snarled, 'we will have lost all hope of guiding it.'

Whiskeyjack studied the ancient warrior. 'Yours is a singular obsession, Kallor. It has twisted your mind—'

'And sentiment has twisted yours, soldier. Perhaps a day will come when you and I can test our respective resolve—'

'Enough,' Brood cut in. 'It seems, then, that this meeting must be adjourned. We can reconvene when all the relevant commanders are present.' The warlord turned to Rake. 'How fares Moon's Spawn?'

The Tiste Andii Lord shrugged. 'We will rendezvous at Coral as planned. It might be worth noting that the Seer has been under serious assault from the south, which he answers with Omtose Phellack sorcery. My Great Ravens have caught sight of his enemy, or at least some of them. A T'lan Imass, a she-wolf and a very large dog. Thus, the old battle: Omtose Phellack, ever retreating from Tellann. There might well be other players as well – lands to the south of Outlook have been completely shrouded in mists born of dying ice. The significance of all this is that the Seer has fled Outlook, and is heading by warren to Coral.'

There was silence as the implications of Rake's revel-ations slowly settled in the minds of those present.

Whiskeyjack was the first to speak. 'A lone T'lan Imass? A Bonecaster, then, to have sufficient power to single-handedly sunder a Jaghut's sorcery.'

'Having heard the summons made by Silverfox,' Dujek added. 'Yes, that's likely.'

'This T'lan Imass is a warrior,' Rake responded laconically. 'Wielding a two-handed flint sword. Bonecasters carry no weapons. Clearly, he has singular skill. The wolf is an ay, I believe, a creature thought long extinct. The hound rivals those of Shadow.'

'And they are driving the Seer into our laps,' Brood rumbled. 'It seems that Coral will not simply be the last city we can reach this campaigning season. We'll be facing the Seer himself.'

'Damn well ensuring that the battle will be fraught with sorcery,' Dujek muttered. 'Bloody terrific.'

'We've plenty of time to formulate our tactics,' Brood said after a moment. 'This meeting is adjourned.'

Thirty paces from the command tent, as darkness settled ever deeper on the camp, Silverfox slowed her steps.

Kruppe glanced at her. 'Ah, lass, you sense the storm's passing unbroken. As do I. Shall we pay a visit to formidable personages in any case?'

She hesitated, then shook her head. 'No, why precipitate a confrontation? I must now turn to my own . . . destiny. If you please, Kruppe, inform no-one of my departure. At least not for a while.'

'The Gathering is come.'

'It is,' she agreed. 'I sense the imminent convergence of the T'lan Imass, and would rather it occur somewhere beyond the sight of anyone else.'

'A private matter, of course. None the less, Silverfox, would you resent company? Kruppe is wise – wise enough to keep silent when silence is called for, and yet wiser still to speak when wise words are required. Wisdom, after all, is Kruppe's blood brother.'

She smiled down at him. 'You would witness the Second Gathering?'

'There is no better witness to all things wondrous than Kruppe of Darujhistan, lass. Why, the tales that could flow effortlessly from these rather oily lips, should you ever but prod with curiosity—'

'Forgive me if I refrain from doing so,' she replied. 'At least in the near future.'

'Lest you become distracted, of course. It is clear, is it not, that even Kruppe's mere presence generates wisdom in bounty.'

'Very clear. Very well. We'll have to find you a horse, since I plan to ride.'

'A horse? Horrors! Foul beasts. Nay, I hold to my trusty mule.'

'Tightly.'

'To the limits of my physical abilities, aye.' He turned at a clopping sound behind them. 'Ah, speak of the demon! And look, a moonstruck horse follows like a pup on a leash, and is it any wonder, when one looks upon my handsome, proud beast?'

Silverfox studied the saddled horse trailing the mule with narrowed eyes. 'Tell me, Kruppe, who else will be witness to the Gathering through you?'

'Through Kruppe? Why, naught but Kruppe himself! He swears!'

'Not the mule, surely?'

'Lass, the mule's capacity for sleep – in no matter what the circumstances – is boundless, unaffected and indeed, admirable. I assure you, none shall witness through its eyes!'

'Sleep, is it? No doubt, to dream. Very well, let us be on with it, Kruppe. I trust you're comfortable with a ride through the night?'

'Not in the least, but perseverance is Kruppe's closest cousin . . .'

* * *

'Walk with me.'

Pausing as he emerged from the tent entrance, Whiskeyjack looked left, to see Anomander Rake standing in the gloom. *Ah, not Korlat, then. Oh well . . .* 'Of course, Lord.'

The Son of Darkness led him through the tent rows, southward, out to the very edge of the encampment, then beyond. They ascended a ridge and came within sight of Catlin River. Starlight played on its swirling surface two hundred paces away.

Moths fluttered like flecks of snow fleeing the warm wind.

Neither man spoke for a long while.

Finally, Anomander Rake sighed, then asked, 'How fares the leg?'

'It aches,' Whiskeyjack answered truthfully. 'Especially after a full day in the saddle.'

'Brood is an accomplished healer. High Denul. He would not hesitate should you ask.'

'When there's time—'

'There has been plenty of that, as we both know. None the less, I share something of your stubbornness, so I'll not raise the subject again. Have you been contacted by Quick Ben?'

Whiskeyjack nodded. 'He's in Capustan. Or should be by now.'

'I am relieved. The assault on the warrens has made being a mage somewhat perilous. Even Kurald Galain has felt the poison's touch.'

'I know.'

Rake slowly turned to regard him. 'I had not expected to find in her such . . . renewal. A heart I'd believed closed for ever. To see it flowering so . . .'

Whiskeyjack shifted uneasily. 'I may have wounded it this evening.'

'Momentarily, perhaps. Your false outlawry is known.'

'Thus the meeting, or so we thought.'

743

'I pulled the thorn before you and the High Fist arrived.'

The Malazan studied the Tiste Andii in the gloom. 'I wasn't sure. The suspicion could find no root, however.'

'Because, to you, my position makes no sense.'

'Aye.'

Rake shrugged. 'I rarely see necessity as a burden.'

Whiskeyjack thought about that, then nodded. 'You still need us.'

'More than ever, perhaps. And not just your army. We need Quick Ben. We need Humbrall Taur and his White Face clans. We need your link to Silverfox and through her to the T'lan Imass. We need Captain Paran—'

'Ganoes Paran? Why?'

'He is the Master of the Deck of Dragons.'

'It's no secret, then.'

'It never was.'

'Do you know,' Whiskeyjack asked, 'what that role signifies? A genuine question, because, frankly, I don't and wish I damn well did.'

'The Crippled God has fashioned a new House and now seeks to join it to the Deck of Dragons. A sanction is required. A blessing, if you will. Or, conversely, a denial.'

Whiskeyjack grunted. 'What of the House of Shadow, then? Was there a Master of the Deck around who sanctioned its joining?'

'There was no need. The House of Shadow has always existed, more or less. Shadowthrone and Cotillion simply reawakened it.'

'And now, you want Paran – the Master of the Deck – to deny the Crippled God's House.'

'I believe he must. To grant the Fallen One legitimacy is to grant him power. We see what he is capable of in his present weakened state. The House of Chains is the foundation he will use to rebuild himself.'

'Yet, you and the gods took him down once before. The Chaining.'

'A costly endeavour, Whiskeyjack. One in which the

god Fener was vital. Tell me, among your soldiers, the Tusked One is a popular god – have you priests as well?'

'No. Fener's popular enough, being the Lord of Battle. Malazans are somewhat . . . relaxed when it comes to the pantheon. We tend to discourage organized cults within the military.'

'Fener is lost to us,' Rake said.

'Lost? What do you mean?'

'Torn from his realm, now striding the mortal earth.'

'How?'

There was a grim smile in Rake's tone as he explained. 'By a Malazan. A once-priest of Fener, a victim of the Reve.'

'Which means?'

'His hands were ritually severed. The power of the Reve then sends those hands to the hooves of Fener himself. The ritual must be the expression of purest justice, but this one wasn't. Rather, there was a perceived need to reduce the influence of Fener, and in particular that High Priest, by agents of the Empire – likely the Claw. You mentioned the discouraging of cults within the army. Perhaps that was a factor – my knowledge is not complete, alas. Certainly the High Priest's penchant for historical analysis was another – he had completed an investigation that concluded that the Empress Laseen in fact failed in her assassination of the Emperor and Dancer. Granted, she got the throne she so badly wanted, but neither Kellanved nor Dancer actually died. Instead, they ascended.'

'I can see why Surly's back would crawl at that revelation.'

'Surly?'

'The Empress Laseen. Surly was her old name.'

'In any case, those severed hands were as poison to Fener. He could not touch them, nor could he remove them from his realm. He burned the tattoos announcing his denial upon the high priest's skin, and so sealed the virulent power of the hands, at least for the time being. And that should

745

have been that. Eventually, the priest would die, and his spirit would come to Fener to retrieve what had been cruelly and wrongfully taken from him. That spirit would then become the weapon of Fener's wrath, his vengeance upon the priests of the fouled temple, and indeed upon the Claw and the Empress herself. A dark storm awaited the Malazan Empire, Whiskeyjack.'

'But something's happened.'

'Aye. The High Priest has, by design or chance, come into contact with the Warren of Chaos – an object, perhaps, forged within that warren. The protective seal around his severed hands was obliterated by that vast, uncontrolled surge of power. And, finding Fener, those hands . . . *pushed*.'

'Hood's breath,' Whiskeyjack muttered, his eyes on the glittering river.

'And now,' Rake continued, 'the Tiger of Summer ascends to take his place. But Treach is young, much weaker, his warren but a paltry thing, his followers far fewer in number than Fener's. All is in flux. No doubt the Crippled God is smiling.'

'Wait a moment,' Whiskeyjack objected. 'Treach has ascended? That's one huge coincidence.'

'Some fates were foreseen, or so it seems.'

'By whom?'

'The Elder Gods.'

'And why are they so interested in all this?'

'They were there when the Crippled God fell – was dragged – down to this earth. The Fall destroyed many of them, leaving but a few survivors. Whatever secrets surround the Fallen One – where he came from, the nature of his aspect, the ritual itself that captured him – K'rul and his kin possess them. That they have chosen to become directly involved, now that the Crippled God has resumed his war, has dire implications as to the seriousness of the threat.'

'Quite an understatement, Lord.' Whiskeyjack said nothing for a time, then he sighed. 'Leading us back to

Ganoes Paran and the House of Chains. All right, I understand why you want him to deny the Crippled God's gambit. I should warn you, however, Paran doesn't take orders well.'

'We must hope, then, that he sees which course is wisest. Will you advise him on our behalf?'

'I'll try.'

'Tell me, Whiskeyjack,' Rake said in a different tone, 'do you ever find the voice of a river unsettling?'

The Malazan frowned. 'To the contrary, I find it calming.'

'Ah. This, then, points to the essential difference between us.'

Between mortals and immortals? Beru fend . . . Anomander Rake, I know precisely what you need. 'I've a small cask of Gredfallan ale, Lord. I would like to retrieve it, now, if you don't mind waiting?'

'A sound plan, Whiskeyjack.'

And by dawn, may you find the voice grown calm.

The Malazan turned and made his way back to the encampment. As he approached the first row of tents, he paused and turned back to look at the distant figure, standing tall and motionless on the grassy ridge.

The sword Dragnipur, strapped crossways on Anomander Rake's back, hung like an elongated cross, surrounded in its own breath of preternatural darkness.

Alas, I don't think Gredfallan ale will be enough . . .

'And which warren will you choose for this?'

Quick Ben studied the sprawled bodies and the tumbled, blood-stained stones of the city wall. Spot-fires were visible through the gap, smoke blotting the night sky above dark, seemingly lifeless buildings. 'Rashan, I think,' he said.

'Shadow. I should have guessed.' Talamandas scrambled atop a heap of corpses then turned to look at the wizard. 'Shall we proceed?'

Quick Ben opened the warren, tightly leashed, and held

it close about him. The sorcery swallowed him in shadows. Talamandas snickered, then approached.

'I shall ride your shoulder for this, yes?'

'If you insist,' the wizard grumbled.

'You leave me little choice. To control a warren by tumbling it before you and sweeping it up behind you may well reveal your mastery, but I am left with little room to manoeuvre within it. Though why we need bother with warrens at all right now is beyond me.'

'I need the practice. Besides, I hate being noticed.' Quick Ben gestured. 'Climb aboard, then.'

The sticksnare clambered up the wizard's leg, set its feet of bound twine on his belt, then dragged itself up Quick Ben's tunic. The weight, as Talamandas settled on his left shoulder, was insubstantial. Twig fingers closed on his collar. 'I can handle a tumble or two,' the sticksnare said, 'but don't make a habit of it.'

Quick Ben moved forward, slipping through the gap in the wall. The firelight threw stark slashes through the shadows, randomly painting glimpses of the wizard's body. Deep shadow cutting through any firelit scene would have been noticeable. He concentrated on blending into what surrounded him.

Flame, smoke and ashes. Vague moans from collapsed buildings; a few streets away, the mourning chant of Barghast.

'The Pannions are all gone,' Talamandas whispered. 'Why the need to hide?'

'It's my nature. Caution keeps me alive, now be quiet.'

He entered a street lined by Daru estates. While other avenues evinced the efforts of the White Face tribes to clear away bodies, no such task had taken place here. Pannion soldiery lay dead in appalling numbers, heaped around one estate in particular, its blackened gatehouse a maw ringed in dried blood. A low wall ran to either side of the gate. Dark, motionless figures stood guard along it, apparently perched on some kind of walkway halfway up the other side.

Crouched at the foot of another building, sixty paces away, Quick Ben studied the scene. The bitter breath of sorcery still clung to the air. On his shoulder, Talamandas hissed in sudden recognition.

'The necromancers! The ones who tore me from my barrow!'

'I thought you had nothing to fear from them any more,' Quick Ben murmured.

'I don't, but that does nothing to diminish my hatred or disgust.'

'That's unfortunate, because I want to talk to them.'

'Why?'

'To take their measure, why else?'

'Idiocy, Wizard. Whatever they are, is nothing good.'

'And I am? Now let me think.'

'You'll never get past those undead guards.'

'When I say let me think, I mean shut up.'

Grumbling, shifting about on Quick Ben's shoulder, Talamandas reluctantly subsided.

'We'll need a different warren for this,' the wizard finally said. 'The choice is this: Hood's own, or Aral Gamelon—'

'Aral what? I've never heard—'

'Demonic. Most conjurors who summon demons are opening a path to Gamelon – though they probably don't know it, not by its true name, anyway. Granted, one can find demons in other warrens – the Aptorians of Shadow, for example. But the Korvalahrai and the Galayn, the Empire's favoured, are both of Gamelon. Anyway, if my instincts are accurate, there's both kinds of necromancy present in that estate – you did say there were two of them, didn't you?'

'Aye, and two kinds of madness.'

'Sounds interesting.'

'This is a whim! Have you learned nothing from your multiple souls, Wizard? Whims are deadly. Do something for no reason but curiosity and it closes like a wolf's jaws on your throat. And even if you manage to escape, it haunts you. For ever.'

'You talk too much, Sticksnare. I've made my decision. Time to move.' He folded the warren of Rashan about himself, then stepped forward.

'Ashes in the urn!' Talamandas hissed.

'Aye, Hood's own. Comforted by the familiarity? It's the safer choice, since Hood himself has blessed you, right?'

'I am not comforted.'

That wasn't too surprising, as Quick Ben studied the transformation around him. Death ran riot in this city. Souls crowded the streets, trapped in cycles of their own last moments of life. The air was filled with shrieks, wailing, the chop of weapons, the crushing collapse of stone and the suffocating smoke. Layered beneath this were countless other deaths – those that were set down, like successive snowfalls, on any place where humans gathered. Generation upon generation.

Yet, Quick Ben slowly realized, this conflagration was naught but echoes, the souls themselves ghostly. 'Gods below,' he murmured in sudden understanding. 'This is but memory – what the stones of the streets and buildings hold, memories of the air itself. The souls – they've all gone through Hood's Gate . . .'

Talamandas was motionless on his shoulder. 'You speak true, Wizard,' he muttered. 'What has happened here? Who has taken all these dead?'

'Taken, aye, under wing. They've been blessed, one and all, their pain ended. Is this the work of the Mask Council?'

The sticksnare spat, 'Those fools? Not likely.'

Quick Ben said nothing for a time, then he sighed. 'Capustan might recover, after all. I didn't think that was possible. Well, shall we walk with these ghosts?'

'Do we have to?'

Not replying, Quick Ben strode forward. The undead guards – Seerdomin and Urdomen – were dark smears, stains on Hood's own warren. But they were blind to his presence in the realm where the wizard now walked. Of the two necromancers residing within, one was now negated.

The only risk remaining was if the other one – the summoner – had released any demons to supplement the estate's defences.

Quick Ben strode through the gateway. The compound before him was clear of any bodies, though caked blood coated the flagstones here and there.

Twig fingers spasmed tight on his shoulder. 'I smell—'

The Sirinth demon had been squatting in front of the main house doors, draped in the lintel stone's shadow. It now grunted and heaved its bulk clear of the landing, coming into full view. Swathed in folds of toad-like skin, splay-limbed, with a wide, low head that was mostly jaws and fangs, the Sirinth massed more than a bhederin bull. In short bursts, however, it could be lightning fast.

A short burst was all it needed to reach Quick Ben and Talamandas.

The sticksnare shrieked.

Quick Ben lithely side-stepped, even as he unfolded yet another warren, this one layered over Hood's own. A backward stride took him into that warren, where heat flowed like liquid and dry amber light suffused the air.

The Sirinth wheeled, then dropped flat on its belly within Aral Gamelon.

Quick Ben edged further into the demonic warren.

Whining, the Sirinth sought to follow, only to be brought short by a now visible iron collar and chain, the chain leading back out – all the way, Quick Ben knew, to whatever binding circle the summoner had conjured when chaining this creature.

'Too bad, friend,' the wizard said as the demon squealed. 'Might I suggest a deal, Sirinth? I break the chain and you go find your loved ones. Peace between us.'

The creature went perfectly motionless. Folded lids slid back to reveal large, luminous eyes. In the mortal realm they'd just left, those eyes burned like fire. Here, within Aral Gamelon, they were almost docile.

Almost. Don't fool yourself, Quick. This thing could gobble you up in one bite. 'Well?'

The Sirinth slithered sideways, stretched its neck.

Sorcery glowed from the collar and chain, the iron crowded with carved glyphs.

'I'll need to take a closer look,' Quick Ben told the demon. 'Know that Hood's warren remains with us—'

'Not well enough!' Talamandas hissed. 'Those undead guards have seen us!'

'We've a few moments yet,' Quick Ben replied. 'If you shut up, that is. Sirinth, if you attack me when I come close, I'll reveal for you another chain about your neck – Hood's. Dead but not dead, trapped in the in-between. For ever. Understand me?'

The creature squealed again, but made no other move.

'Good enough.'

'You fool—'

Ignoring the sticksnare, Quick Ben stepped to the side of the huge demon. He knew that head could snap round, fast enough to be nothing more than a blur, the jaws opening to swallow head, shoulders – Talamandas included – and torso down to hips.

He studied the glyphs, then grunted. 'Accomplished indeed. The key, however, to breaking this chaining lies in unravelling but a single thread. The challenge is finding the right one—'

'Will you hurry! Those undead are converging! On us!'

'A moment, please.' Quick Ben leaned closer, squinting at the sigils. 'Curious,' he murmured, 'this is Korelri script. High Korelri, which hasn't been used in centuries. Well, easy enough then.' He reached out, muttering a few words, and scored one glyph with the nail of his thumb. 'Thus, changing its meaning—' Gripping the chain on either side of the marred sigil, Quick Ben gave a quick yank.

The chain snapped.

The Sirinth lunged forward, then spun, jaws wide.

Talamandas screamed.

Quick Ben was already in the air, through the warren's gate, back into Hood's own, where he dipped a shoulder as he struck the flagstones, rolling over then back onto his feet – with Talamandas still clinging to his tunic. The wizard then froze.

They were surrounded by dark, insubstantial figures, now motionless as their quarry was no longer visible.

Wisely, Talamandas said nothing. Still crouching, Quick Ben slowly, silently edged between two undead guards, then padded clear, approaching the double doors.

'Gods,' the sticksnare moaned in a whisper, 'why are we doing this?'

'Because it's fun.'

The doors were unlocked.

Quick Ben slipped inside and shut the door behind them, the soft click of the latch seeming over-loud in the alcove.

'So,' Talamandas breathed, 'which warren now?'

'Ah, do I sense you're getting into the spirit of the thing?'

'Bad word to choose, mortal.'

Smiling, Quick Ben closed Hood's own. *It should be clear why I'm doing this, Sticksnare. I've been without warrens for too long. I need the practice. More, I need to know just how efficacious you are. And so far, so good. The poison is held at bay, unable to close on me. I'm pleased.* He strode to the nearest wall, set both hands against the cool stone.

Talamandas chuckled. 'D'riss. The Path of Stone. Clever bastard.'

Quick Ben pushed the warren open, slid into the wall.

There was nothing easy in this. Stone could be traversed easily enough – its resistance no more than water – but mortar was less yielding, tugging at his passage like the strands of a particularly stubborn spider's web. Worse, the walls were thin, forcing him to edge along sideways.

He followed the wall's course from room to room,

working his way ever inward. Daru-style architecture was predictable and symmetrical. The main chamber of the ground floor would be central. Upper levels were more problematic, but more often than not the ground floor's main chamber was vaulted, pushing the upper rooms to the building's sides.

The rooms were visible to him, but just barely. Grainy, grey, the furniture smudged and indistinct. But living flesh positively glowed. *'Stone knows blood, but cannot hold it. Stone yearns for life, yet can only mimic it.'* The words were ancient ones, a mason and sculptor who'd lived centuries ago in Unta. Appropriate enough when on the Path of D'riss. When in the flesh of the Sleeping Goddess.

Slipping round a corner, Quick Ben caught his first sight of the main chamber.

A figure reclined on some kind of divan near the fireplace. He seemed to be reading a book. Another man stoked the fire's faintly pink, dull flames, muttering under his breath. Pacing back and forth on the mantel was a small creature, a crow or raven perhaps.

The man on the divan was speaking even as he flipped parchment pages in his book, his words made muted and brittle-sounding by the stone. 'When you're done there, Emancipor, return the guards to their positions on the wall. Having them standing in the courtyard all facing inward on nothing is suggestive of the ridiculous. Hardly a scene to inspire fear in potential intruders.'

'If you don't mind my saying so, master,' Emancipor said as he rose from before the hearth and wiped soot from his hands, 'if we've unwelcome company shouldn't we be doing something about it?'

'Much as I dislike losing my demons, dear servant, I do not assume that all visitors are malign. Dismissing my Sirinth was no doubt the only option available, and even then it must have been a risk-laden endeavour. The chain is but half of the geas, of course; the commands within the collar cannot so easily be defeated. Thus, some patience, now, until our guest decides to make formal his or her visit.'

Talamandas's acorn head touched Quick Ben's ear. 'Leave me here when you step through, Wizard. Treachery from this man is not just a likelihood, it's a damned certainty.'

Quick Ben shrugged. The sticksnare's weight left his shoulder.

Smiling, the wizard stepped from the warren, began brushing gritty dust from his tunic and rain-cape.

The seated man slowly closed his book without looking up. 'Some wine, Emancipor, for me and my guest.'

The servant spun to face Quick Ben. 'Hood's breath! Where did he come from?'

'The walls have ears, eyes and all the rest. Be on with your task, Emancipor.' The man finally lifted his head and met the wizard's gaze.

Now that's a lizard's regard. Well, I've never quailed from the like before, so why should I now? 'Wine would be wonderful,' Quick Ben said, matching the seated man's Daru.

'Something . . . flowery,' the necromancer added as the servant strode towards a side door.

The crow on the mantel had ceased its pacing and now studied the wizard with cocked head. After a moment, it resumed its back and forth ambling.

'Please, be seated. My name is Bauchelain.'

'Quick Ben.' The wizard walked to the plush chair opposite the necromancer and settled into it. He sighed.

'An interesting name. Aptly chosen, if I may so presume. To have dodged the Sirinth's attack – I assume it attacked once you'd released it?'

'Clever,' Quick Ben conceded, 'locking a hold-over spell in that collar, one last command to kill whomever frees it. I assume that doesn't include you, its summoner.'

'I never free my demons,' Bauchelain said.

'Never?'

'Every exception to a magical geas weakens it. I allow none.'

'Poor demons!'

Bauchelain shrugged. 'I hold no sympathy for mere tools. Do you weep for your dagger when it breaks in someone's back?'

'That depends on whether it killed the bastard or just made him mad.'

'Ah, but then you weep for yourself.'

'I was making a joke.'

Bauchelain raised a single, thin eyebrow.

The subsequent silence was broken by Emancipor's return, bearing a tray on which sat a dusty bottle and two crystal goblets.

'Not a glass for yourself?' the necromancer asked. 'Am I so unegalitarian, Emancipor?'

'Uh, I took a swig below, master.'

'You did?'

'T'see if it was flowery.'

'And was it?'

'Not sure. Maybe. What's flowery?'

'Hmm, we must resume your education, I think, of such finer things. Flowery is the opposite of . . . woody. Not bitter memory of sap, in other words, but something sweet, as of narcissus or skullcrown—'

'Those flowers are poisonous,' Quick Ben noted in faint alarm.

'But pretty and sweet in appearance, yes? I doubt any of us are in the habit of eating flowers, thus in analogy I sought visual cues for dear Emancipor.'

'Ah, I see.'

'Before you pour from that bottle, then, Emancipor. Was the aftertaste bitter or sweet?'

'Uh, it was kind of thick, master. Like iron.'

Bauchelain rose and grasped the bottle. He held it close, then sniffed the mouth. 'You idiot, this is blood from Korbal Broach's collection. Not that row, the one opposite. Take this back to the cellar.'

Emancipor's lined face had gone parchment-white. 'Blood? Whose?'

756

'Does it matter?'

As Emancipor gaped, Quick Ben cleared his throat and said, 'To your servant, I think the answer would be "yes, it does".'

The crow cackled from the mantelpiece, head bobbing.

The servant sagged on watery knees, the goblets on the tray clinking together.

Frowning, Bauchelain collected the bottle again and sniffed once more. 'Well,' he said, returning it to the tray, 'I'm not the one to ask, of course, but I think it's virgin's blood.'

Quick Ben had no choice but to enquire, 'How can you tell?'

Bauchelain regarded him with raised brows. 'Why, it's woody.'

To Hood with plans. Paran sat slouched on one of the lower benches in the Thrall's council chamber. The night outside seemed to have flowed into the vast, dusty room, dulling the torchlight along the walls. Before him, the floor had been gutted, revealing an array of dust-caked outrigger canoes. The wrapped corpses that had once filled them had been removed by the Barghast in solemn ceremony, but, to the captain's senses, the most important artefacts had been left behind. His eyes never left the seafaring canoes, as if they held truths that might prove overwhelming, if only he could glean them.

The pain in his stomach rode dwindling echoes. He thought he now understood the source of his illness. He was not a man who welcomed power, but it had been thrust upon him regardless. Nothing so clear or obvious as a sword, such as Dragnipur; nothing that he could wield, cutting through enemies like an avenging demon who knelt only before cold justice. Yet, power none the less. Sensitivity to unseen currents, knowledge of the inter-connectedness that bound all things and everyone to everyone else. Ganoes Paran, who despised authority, had been chosen as an adjudicator. A mitigator of power whose task was to assert a structure – the rules of the game – upon players who resented every challenge to their freedom to do as they pleased.

Worse than a Malazan magistrate in Unta. Holding fast to the law, whilst being pressured by every influence imaginable, from rival factions to the wishes of the Empress herself. Prod and pull, push and tug, turning even the easiest and most straight-forward of decisions into a nightmare.

No wonder my body recoils, seeks to reject what has been forced upon me.

He was alone in the Thrall's council chamber. The Bridgeburners had found the Gidrath barracks more to their style and were no doubt gambling and drinking them-selves blind with the half-hundred Gidrath who comprised the Thrall's Inner Guard; whilst the priests of the Mask Council had retired for the night.

And it seemed Trake's Mortal Sword, the man named Gruntle, had initiated a friendship with Humbrall Taur's daughter, Hetan, in a manner that Paran suspected might eventually result in kin ties with the White Face clan – the two had made their way into the heart of the Thrall, no doubt in search of somewhere private. Much to the disgust of the woman, Stonny Menackis.

Shield Anvil Itkovian had led his troop back to the barracks near Jelarkan's Palace, to effect repairs and, come the morrow, begin the task of retrieving the refugees hidden in the tunnels beneath the city. The resurrection of Capustan would likely prove torturous and anguished, and the captain did not envy the Grey Sword the task.

We, on the other hand, will have moved on. Itkovian will need to find, among the survivors, someone with royal blood – no matter how thinned – to set on that stained throne. The city's infrastructure is in ruins. Who will feed the survivors? How long before trade is re-established with cities like Saltoan and Darujhistan? Hood knows the Barghast don't owe the people of Capustan anything . . .

Peace had come to his stomach, finally. He drew a tentative breath, slowly sighed. *Power.* His thoughts had a way of slipping into mundane considerations – a means to procrastination, he well knew, and it was a struggle to return to the one issue he would have to deal with sooner or later. *A storm of plans, each one trying to make me into a fulcrum. I need only spread the fingers of one hand, and so encompass the entire Deck of Dragons. A truth I'd rather not recognize. But I feel those damned cards within me, like the barely articulated bones of a vast beast, so vast as to be unrecognizable in its entirety. A skeleton threatening to blow apart. Unless I can hold on, and that is the task forced upon me now. To hold it all together.*

Players in the game, wanting no others. Players outside the game and wanting in. Players to the forefront and ones behind, moving in the shadows. Players who play fair, players who cheat. Gods, where do I begin to unravel all of this?

He thought about Gruntle, Mortal Sword to the newly ascended Treach. In a way, the Tiger of Summer had always been there, silently padding in Fener's wake. If the tales were true, the First Hero had lost his way long ago, surrendered entirely to the bestial instincts of his Soletaken form. *Still, the sheer, overwhelming coincidence . . .* Paran had begun to suspect that the Elder Gods had not orchestrated matters to the degree Nightchill had implied; that opportunism and serendipity was as much responsible for the turn of events as anything else. *Otherwise, against the Elder Gods, none of us stand a chance, including the Crippled God. If it was all planned, then that plan would have had to involve Treach losing his way – thereby becoming a sleeper in the game, his threat to Fener deftly negated until the moment the First Hero was needed. And his death, too, would have had to have been arranged, the timing made precise, so that he would ascend at the right moment.*

And every event that led, ultimately, to Fener's extremity, his sudden, brutal vulnerability, would have had to have been known to the Elder Gods, down to the last detail.

Thus, unless we are all playing out roles that are pre-determined and so inevitable – thereby potentially knowable by such beings as the Elder Gods – unless that, then, what each and every one of us chooses to do, or not to do, can have profound consequences. Not just on our own lives, but on the world – the worlds, every realm in existence.

He recalled the writings of historians who had asserted precisely that. *The old soldier Duiker, for one, though he's long since fallen out of favour. Any scholar who accepts an Imperial robe is immediately suspect . . . for obvious reasons of compromised integrity and bias. Still, in his early days, he was a fierce proponent of individual efficacy.*

The curse of great minds. Arriving young to an idea, surviving the siege that invariably assails it, then, finally, standing guard on the ramparts long after the war's over, weapons dull in leaden hands . . . damn, I'm wandering yet again.

So, he was to be the fulcrum. A position demanding a sudden burgeoning of his ego, the unassailable belief in his own efficacy. *That's the last thing I'm capable of, alas. Plagued by uncertainty, scepticism, by all the flaws inherent in someone who's chronically without purpose. Who undermines every personal goal like a tree gnawing its own roots, if only to prove its grim opinion by toppling.*

Gods, talk about the wrong choice . . .

A scuffling sound alerted Paran to the presence of someone else in the chamber. Blinking, he scanned the gloom. A figure was among the canoes, hulking, armoured in tarnished coins.

The captain cleared his throat. 'Paying a last visit?'

The Barghast warrior straightened.

His face was familiar, but it was a moment before Paran recognized the young man. 'Cafal, isn't it? Brother to Hetan.'

'And you are the Malazan captain.'

'Ganoes Paran.'

'The One Who Blesses.'

Paran frowned. 'No, that title would better fit Itkovian, the Shield Anvil—'

760

Cafal shook his head. 'He but carries burdens. You are the One Who Blesses.'

'Are you suggesting that if anyone is capable of relieving Itkovian's . . . burden . . . then it's me? I need only . . . *bless* him?' *Adjudicator, I'd thought. Obviously more complicated than that. The power to bless? Beru fend.*

'Not for me to say,' Cafal growled, his eyes glittering in the torchlight. 'You can't bless someone who denies your right to do so.'

'A good point. No wonder most priests are miserable.'

Teeth glimmered in either a grin or something nastier.

Oh, I think I dislike this notion of blessing. But it makes sense. How else does a Master of the Deck conclude arbitration? Like an Untan magistrate indeed, only there's something of the religious in this – and that makes me uneasy. Mull on that later, Ganoes . . .

'I was sitting here,' Paran said, 'thinking – every now and then – that there is a secret within those decaying canoes.'

Cafal grunted.

'If I take that as agreement, would I be wrong?'

'No.'

Paran smiled. He'd learned that Barghast hated saying yes to anything, but an affirmative could be gleaned by guiding them into saying *no* to the opposite. 'Would you rather I leave?'

'No. Only cowards hoard secrets. Come closer, if you like, and witness at least one of the truths within these ancient craft.'

'Thank you,' Paran replied, slowly pushing himself upright. He collected a lantern and strode to the edge of the pit, then climbed down to stand on the mouldy earth beside Cafal.

The Barghast's right hand was resting on a carved prow.

Paran studied it. 'Battle scenes. On the sea.'

'Not the secret I would show you,' Cafal rumbled. 'The carvers possessed great skill. They hid the joins, and even the passing of centuries has done little to reveal their

761

subterfuge. See how this canoe looks to have been carved of a single tree? It was, but none the less the craft was constructed in pieces – can you discern that, Ganoes Paran?'

The captain crouched close. 'Barely,' he said after a while, 'but only because some of the pieces have warped away from the joins. These panels with the battle scenes, for example—'

'Aye, those ones. Now, witness the secret.' Cafal drew a wide-bladed hunting knife. He worked the point and edge between the carved panel and its underlying contact. Twisted.

The battle-scene gunnel sprang free at the prow end. Within, a long hollow was visible. Something gleamed dull within it. Returning the knife to his belt, Cafal reached into the cavity and withdrew the object.

A sword, its water-etched blade narrow, single-edged, and like liquid in the play of torchlight. The weapon was overlong, tip flaring at the last hand-span. A small diamond-shaped hilt of black iron protected the sinew-wrapped grip. The sword was unmarked by its centuries unoiled and unsheathed.

'There is sorcery within that.'

'No.' Cafal raised the weapon, closing both hands in an odd finger-locking grasp around the grip. 'In our people's youth, patience and skill were wedded in perfect union. The blades we made were without equal then, and remain so now.'

'Forgive me, Cafal, but the hook-blades and spears I've seen among your warriors hardly evince singular skill.'

Cafal bared his teeth. 'No need to forgive. Indeed, you tread too kindly with your words. The weapons our smiths forge these days are poorly made. We have lost the ancient knowledge.'

'I can't imagine a wholly mundane sword to survive unscathed such neglect, Cafal. Are you sure it has not been imbued with—'

'I am. The blend of metals defies time's assault. Among

762

them, metals that have yet to be rediscovered and now, with sorcery so prevalent, may never be.' He held the sword out to Paran. 'It looks unbalanced, yes? Top-heavy. Here.'

Paran accepted the weapon. It was as light as a dagger. 'Impossible,' he muttered. 'It must break—'

'Not easily, Captain. The flex seems stiff, yes? Thus you conclude it is brittle, but it is not. Examine the edge. There are no nicks, yet this particular sword has seen battle many, many times. The edge remains true and sharp. This sword does not need mothering.'

Handing it back, Paran turned his gaze upon the canoes. 'And these craft possess more of such weapons?'

'They do.'

'Who will use them? The warchiefs?'

'No. Children.'

'Children?'

'Carefully selected, to begin their training with these swords. Imagine swinging this blade, Captain. Your muscles are tuned to something far heavier. You will either over-swing or over-compensate. A hard blow could spring it from your hand. No, the true potential of these swords can only be found in hands that know no other weapon. And much of what those children learn, they must do so by themselves – after all, how can we teach what we do not know?'

'And what will be the purpose of these swords? Of those young warriors who will wield them?'

'You may find an answer one day, Ganoes Paran.'

Paran was silent for a time. 'I think,' he finally said, 'I have gleaned another secret.'

'And what is that?'

You will dismantle these canoes. Learn the art of making them. 'Will the land remain your home for much longer, Barghast?'

Cafal smiled. 'No.'

'Thus.'

'Thus. Captain, Humbrall Taur would ask something of

763

you. Would you hear his request from him, or may I voice it on his behalf?'

'Go ahead.'

'The Barghast would have their gods . . . blessed.'

'What? You don't need me for that—'

'That is true. We ask it none the less.'

'Well, let me think about it, Cafal. One of my problems is, I don't know how it's done. Do I just walk up to the bones and say "I bless you" or is something more complicated necessary?'

Cafal's heavy brows rose. 'You do not know?'

'No. You might want to call together all your shamans and discuss the matter.'

'Aye, we shall need to do just that. When we discover the ritual that is necessary, will you agree to it?'

'I said I'd think about it, Cafal.'

'Why do you hesitate?'

Because I'm a Hood-damned fulcrum and what I choose to do could – will – change everything. 'I intend no offence. But I'm a cautious bastard.'

'A man possessing power must act decisively, Ganoes Paran. Else it trickle away through his fingers.'

'When I decide to act, Cafal, it will be decisive. If that makes sense. One thing it won't be is precipitous, and if indeed I possess vast power then be glad for that.'

The Barghast warrior grunted. 'Perhaps your caution is wise, after all. I shall convey your words to my father.'

'So be it.'

'If you wish solitude now, find somewhere else. My kin are coming to retrieve the remaining weapons. This will be a busy night.'

'All right. I'll go for a walk.'

'Be careful, Ganoes Paran.'

The captain turned. 'Of what?'

'The Mask Council know who – what – you are, and they dislike it.'

'Why?'

764

Cafal grinned once more. 'Rivals do not sit well with the Mask Council. They have still not relented in acknowledgement of Keruli, who seeks to join their company. You – you might well be in a position to claim yourself as their master in all things. Eyes are darting within those masks, Captain.'

'Hood's breath,' Paran sighed. 'Who is Keruli, by the way?'

'K'rul's High Priest.'

'K'rul? The Elder God?'

'Expect Keruli to seek your blessing. On his god's behalf.'

Paran rubbed his brow, suddenly weary beyond belief. 'I've changed my mind,' he muttered. 'Never mind the walk.'

'What will you do?'

'Find a hole and crawl into it, Cafal.'

The warrior's laugh was harsh, and not quite as sympathetic as Paran would have liked.

Emancipor Reese had managed to find a more suitable bottle from the cellars and had filled the two goblets before hastily retreating from the room, his sickly pallor if anything even starker on his lined face.

Quick Ben was none the less tentative as he took his first sip. After a moment, he swallowed, then sighed.

Sitting across from him, Bauchelain half smiled. 'Excellent. Now, having made the effort to penetrate this estate's defences, you are here with some purpose in mind. Thus, you have my utmost attention.'

'Demonic summoning. It's the rarest and most difficult discipline among the necromantic arts.'

Bauchelain responded with a modest shrug.

'And the power it draws upon,' Quick Ben continued, 'while from Hood's own warren, is deeply tainted with Chaos. Striding both sides of that border between those warrens. As an aside, why do you think the summoning of demons is death-aspected?'

'The assertion of absolute control over a life-force, Quick Ben. The threat of annihilation is inherently death-aspected. Regarding your observation of the influence of the Warren of Chaos, do go on.'

'The warrens have been poisoned.'

'Ah. There are many flavours to chaotic power. That which assails the warrens has little to do with the elements of the Warren of Chaos with which I am involved.'

'So, your access to your warrens has not been affected.'

'I did not say that,' Bauchelain replied, pausing to drink some wine. 'The . . . infection . . . is an irritant, an unfortunate development that threatens to get worse. Perhaps, at some point in the future, I shall find need to retaliate upon whomever is responsible. My companion, Korbal Broach, has communicated to me his own growing concern – he works more directly through Hood's warren, and thus has felt the greater brunt.'

Quick Ben glanced over at the crow on the mantelpiece. 'Indeed. Well,' he added, returning his gaze to Bauchelain, 'as to that, I can tell you precisely who is responsible.'

'And why would you tell us, mage? Unless it be to elicit our help – I am assuming you are opposing this . . . poisoner. And are in search of potential allies.'

'Allies? Elicit your help? No, sir, you misunderstand me. I offer my information freely. Not only do I expect nothing in return, should you offer I will respectfully decline.'

'Curious. Is yours a power to rival the gods, then?'

'I don't recall referring to gods in this conversation, Bauchelain.'

'True enough; however, the entity responsible for poisoning all the warrens is without doubt a formidable individual – if not a god then an aspirant.'

'In any case,' Quick Ben said with a smile, 'I don't rival gods.'

'A wise decision.'

'But, sometimes, I beat them at their own game.'

Bauchelain studied the wizard, then slowly leaned back.

'I find myself appreciating your company, Quick Ben. I am not easily entertained, but you have indeed proved a worthy diversion this night, and for that I thank you.'

'You're quite welcome.'

'My companion, Korbal Broach, alas, would like to kill you.'

'Can't please everyone.'

'Very true. He dislikes being confused, you see, and you have confused him.'

'Best he remain perched on the mantelpiece,' Quick Ben quietly advised. 'I don't treat hecklers very well.'

Bauchelain raised a brow.

The shadow of wings spread suddenly vast to Quick Ben's left, as Korbal Broach dropped from his position and began sembling even as he descended.

The Malazan flung his left arm out, waves of layered sorcery sweeping across the intervening space, to strike the necromancer.

Half man, half bedraggled crow, Korbal Broach had not completed his sembling into human form. The waves of power had yet to blossom. The necromancer was lifted from his feet by the magical impact, caught in the crest of that sorcery. It struck the wall above the fireplace, carrying the oddly winged, semi-human figure with it, then detonated.

Painted plaster exploded in a cloud of dust. The wall shook, crumpling inward at the point where Korbal Broach hit – punching a hole through to whatever was on the other side. The last sight Quick Ben had of the man was that of his boots, before the roiling dust and twisting tendrils of power obscured the wall.

There was the sound of a heavy thump beyond, in what was probably a corridor, then the patter of plaster on the hearthstone was all that broke the silence.

Quick Ben slowly settled back into his chair.

'More wine?' Bauchelain asked.

'Please. Thank you. Apologies for the mess.'

'Think nothing of it. I have never before seen – what –

six, perhaps seven warrens all unleashed at once, all intricately bound together in such complementary fashion. You, sir, are an artist. Will Korbal Broach recover?'

'I am your guest, Bauchelain. It would be poor form to kill your companion. After all, strictly speaking I am *his* guest, as well.'

With the chimney thoroughly compromised, the room was slowly filling with smoke.

'True,' Bauchelain admitted. 'Although, I reluctantly point out, he sought to kill you.'

'No need for dismay,' the Malazan responded. 'I was not greatly inconvenienced.'

'And that is what I find most astonishing. There was no sign of chaotic poison in your sorcery, Quick Ben. You can imagine the plethora of questions I would like to ask.'

There was a groan from the corridor.

'And, I confess,' Bauchelain continued, 'that curiosity is a rather obsessive trait of mine, often resulting in regrettable violence to the one being questioned, particularly when he or she is not as forthcoming as I would like. Now, six, seven warrens—'

'Six.'

'Six warrens, then – all at once – your claim to finding little inconvenience in the effort strikes me as bravado. Therefore, I conclude that you are, shall we say it bluntly: *used up.*'

'You make it clear that my welcome is at an end,' Quick Ben said, sighing as he set down the goblet.

'Not necessarily. You need only tell me everything, and we can continue in this civil fashion.'

'I'm afraid that won't be possible,' the Malazan replied. 'None the less, I will inform you that the entity poisoning the warrens is the Crippled God. You will have to consider . . . retaliation . . . against him. Rather sooner than you might think.'

'Thank you. I'll not deny I am impressed by your mastery of six warrens, Quick Ben. In retrospect, you should have

768

held back on at least half of what you command.' The man made to rise.

'But, Bauchelain,' the wizard replied, 'I did.'

The divan, and the man on it, fared little better when struck by the power of a half-dozen bound warrens than had the wall and Korbal Broach moments earlier.

Quick Ben met Emancipor Reese in the smoky hallway leading to the estate's front doors. The servant had wrapped a cloth around the lower half of his face, his eyes streaming as he squinted at the wizard.

'Your masters require your attention, Emancipor.'

'They're alive?'

'Of course. Although smoke inhalation—'

The servant pushed past Quick Ben. 'What is *wrong* with all of you?' he barked.

'What do you mean?' the Malazan asked after him.

Emancipor half turned. 'Ain't it obvious? When you swat a wasp to the ground, you then use your heel, right? Otherwise, you're liable to get stung!'

'Are you encouraging me to kill your masters?'

'You're all Hood-damned idiots, that's what you are! Clean this up, Mancy! Scrub that down! Bury this in the garden! Pack those trunks – we're leaving in a hurry! It's my curse – *no-one kills them!* You think I like my job? Idiots! You think—'

The old man was still roaring as Quick Ben retreated outside.

Talamandas awaited him on the threshold. 'He's right, you know—'

'Quiet,' the wizard snapped.

In the courtyard beyond, the undead guards had all toppled from the walkway on the wall and lay sprawled on the flagstones, but movement was returning to them. Limbs wavered and twitched. *Like armoured beetles on their backs. We'd better get out of here. Because, now, I am all used up.*

'I'd almost moved to that wall you destroyed, you know.'

'That would have been very unfortunate,' Quick Ben replied. 'Climb aboard – we're leaving.'

'Finally, some wisdom!'

Bauchelain's eyes opened. Emancipor looked down on him.

'We're in the garden, master,' the servant said. 'I dragged you and Korbal out. Doused the fire, too. Got to go open all the windows now . . .'

'Very good, Emancipor,' the grey-bearded necromancer groaned after a moment. 'Emancipor,' he called when the servant made to move away.

'Master?'

'I confess . . . to a certain . . . confusion. Do we possess some chronic flaw, Emancipor?'

'Sir?'

'Underestima— oh, never mind, Emancipor. Be about your tasks, then.'

'Aye, master.'

'Oh, and you've earned a bonus for your efforts – what do you wish?'

The servant stared down at Bauchelain for a dozen heartbeats, then he shook his head. 'It's all right, master. Part of my job. And I'll be about it, now.'

The necromancer raised his head to watch the old man trudge back into the house. 'Such a modest man,' he breathed. He looked down the length of his tattered, bruised body, and raggedly sighed. 'What's left in my wardrobe, I wonder?'

Insofar as he could recall – and given recent events – not much.

Shrouded once more in shadow, Quick Ben made his way down the rubble-littered street. Most of the fires had either died down or been extinguished, and not one of the remaining structures showed any light behind shutters or from gaping windows. The stars commanded the night sky, though darkness ruled the city.

'Damned eerie,' Talamandas whispered.

The wizard softly grunted. 'That's rich, coming from someone who's spent generations in an urn in the middle of a barrow.'

'Wanderers like you have no appreciation of familiarity,' the sticksnare sniffed.

The dark mass of the Thrall blotted the skyline directly ahead. Faint torchlight from the square before the main gate cast the structure's angled stones in dulled relief. As they entered an avenue that led to the concourse they came upon the first knot of Barghast, surrounding a small fire built from broken furniture. Tarps slung between the buildings down the avenue's length made the passage beyond a kind of tunnel, strikingly similar to market streets in Seven Cities. Figures lay sleeping along the edges down the entire length. Various cookfires painted smoke-stained, mottled patterns of light on the undersides of the tarps. A good many Barghast warriors remained awake, watchful.

'Try wending unseen through that press, Wizard,' Talamandas murmured. 'We'll have to go round, assuming you still cling to your bizarre desire to slink like a mouse in a hut full of cats. In case you've forgotten, those are my kin—'

'Be quiet,' Quick Ben commanded under his breath. 'Consider this another test of our partnership – and the warrens.'

'We're going straight through?'

'We are.'

'Which warren? Not D'riss again, please – these cobbles—'

'No no, we'd end up soaked in old blood. We won't go under, Talamandas. We'll go over. Serc, the Path of the Sky.'

'Thought you'd exhausted yourself back at the estate.'

'I have. Mostly. We could sweat a bit on this one.'

'I don't sweat.'

'Let's test that, shall we?' The wizard unveiled the warren

of Serc. Little alteration was discernible in the scene around them. Then, slowly, as Quick Ben's eyes adjusted, he detected currents in the air, the layers of cold and warm flowing parallel to the ground, the spirals coiling skyward from between the tarps, the wake of passing figures, the heat-memory of stone and wood.

'Looks sickly,' the sticksnare muttered. 'You would swim those currents?'

'Why not? We're almost as insubstantial as the air we see before us. I can get us started, but the problem then is keeping me afloat. You're right – I've no reserves left. So, it's up to you, Talamandas.'

'Me? I know nothing of Serc.'

'I'm not asking you to learn, either. What I want is your power.'

'That wasn't part of the deal!'

'It is now.'

The sticksnare shifted and twitched on Quick Ben's shoulder. 'By drawing on my power, you weaken the protection I offer against the poison.'

'And we need to find that threshold, Talamandas. I need to know what I can pull from you in an emergency.'

'Just how nasty a situation are you anticipating when we finally challenge the Crippled God?' the sticksnare demanded. 'Those secret plans of yours – no wonder you're keeping them secret!'

'I could have sworn you said you were offering yourself up as a sacrifice to the cause – do you now balk?'

'At madness? Count on it, Wizard!'

Quick Ben smiled to himself. 'Relax, I'm not stoking a pyre for you. Nor have I any plans to challenge the Crippled God. Not directly. I've been face to face with him once, and once remains enough. Even so, I was serious about finding that threshold. Now, pull the cork, shaman, and let's see what we can manage.'

Hissing with fury, Talamandas growled reluctant assent.

Quick Ben rose from the ground, slipped forward on the nearest current sweeping down the length of the street. The flow was cool, dipping down beneath the tarps. A moment before reaching the downdraught, the wizard nudged himself upward, into a spiral of heat from one of the fires. They shot straight up.

'Dammit!' Quick Ben snapped as he spun and cavorted on the column of heat. Gritting his teeth, the wizard reached for the sticksnare's power – and found what he had suspected to be the truth all along.

Hood's. Through and through. Of the Barghast gods, barely a drop of salty piss. The damned newcomers are stretched far too thin. Wonder what's drawing on their energies? There's a card in the Deck, in the House of Death, that's been a role unfilled for a long, long time. The Magi. I think it's just found a face – one painted on a stupid acorn. Talamandas, you may have made a terrible mistake. And as for you, Barghast gods, here's some wisdom to heed in the future. Never hand your servants over to another god, because they're not likely to stay your servants for long. Instead, that god's likely to turn them into weapons . . . aimed directly at your backs.

Dear Barghast gods, you're in a world of predators, nastier by far than what was around in the past. Lucky for you I'm here.

He drew on that power, harshly.

The sticksnare writhed, twig fingers digging into the wizard's shoulder and neck.

In his mind, Quick Ben closed an implacable grip on the Lord of Death's power, and *pulled.*

Come to me, bastard. We're going to talk, you and I.

Within his clenched hand was the rough weave of cloth, stretching, bunching. The breath of Death flowed over the wizard, the presence undeniable, heavy with rage.

And, in the clutch of a mortal, entirely helpless.

Quick Ben grunted a laugh. 'So much for thresholds. You want to ally with me, Hood? All right, I'll give you fair consideration, despite the deception. But you're going to have to tell me what you're up to.'

'*Damned fool!*' Hood's voice was thunderous in the wizard's skull, launching waves of pain.

'Quieter,' Quick Ben gritted. 'Or I'll drag you through hide and all and Fener won't be the only god who's fair game.'

'*The House of Chains must be denied!*'

The wizard blinked, knocked sideways by Hood's statement. 'The House of Chains? It's the *poison* we're trying to excise, isn't it? Burn's fever – the infected warrens—'

'*The Master of the Deck must be convinced, mortal. The Crippled God's House is finding . . . adherents—*'

'Wait a moment. Adherents? Among the pantheon?'

'*Betrayal, aye. Poliel, Mistress of Pestilence, aspires to the role of Consort to the King in Chains. A Herald has been . . . recruited. An ancient warrior seeks to become Reaver; whilst the House has found, in a distant land, its Mortal Sword. Mowri now embraces the Three – Cripple, Leper and Fool – which are in place of Spinner, Mason and Soldier. Most disturbing of all, ancient power trembles around the last of the dread cards . . . mortal, the Master of the Deck must not remain blind to the threat.*'

Quick Ben scowled. 'Captain Paran's not the blinkered type, Hood. Indeed, he likely sees things clearer than even you – far more dispassionately, at least, and something tells me that cold reason is what will be needed come the time to decide. In any case, the House of Chains may be your problem, but the poison within the warrens is mine.' *That, and what it's doing to Burn.*

'*Misdirection, wizard – you are being led astray. You will find no answers, no solutions within the Pannion Domin, for the Seer is at the heart of an altogether different tale.*'

'I'd guessed as much, Hood. Even so, I plan on unravelling the bastard – and his power.'

'*Which will avail you nothing.*'

'That's what you think,' Quick Ben replied, grinning. 'I am going to call upon you again, Hood.'

'*And why should I answer? You've not heard a word I've—*'

774

'I have, but consider this, Lord. The Barghast gods may be young and inexperienced, but that won't last. Besides, young gods are dangerous gods. Scar them now and they'll not forget the one who delivered the wound. You've offered to help, so you'd better do just that, Hood.'

'*You dare threaten me—*'

'Now who's not listening? I am not threatening you, I am warning you. And not just about the Barghast gods, either. Treach has found a worthy Mortal Sword – can you not feel him? Here I am, a thousand paces or more away from him, with at least twenty walls of stone between us, and I can feel the man. He's wrapped in the pain of a death – someone close, whose soul you now hold. He's no friend of yours, Hood, this Mortal Sword.'

'*Do you not think I welcomed all that he has delivered? Treach promised me souls, and his human servant has provided them.*'

'In other words, the Tiger of Summer and the Barghast gods have followed through on their sides of the deal. Now, you'd better do the same, and that includes relinquishing Talamandas when the time comes. Hold to the spirit of the agreement, Hood ... unless you learned nothing from the mistakes you made with Dassem Ultor ...'

The wizard felt seething rage burgeon from the Lord of Death, yet the god remained silent.

'Aye,' Quick Ben growled, 'think on that. In the meantime, you're going to ease loose your power, sufficient to carry me over this crowd of Barghast, and into the plaza in front of the Thrall. Then you're going to withdraw, far enough to give Talamandas the freedom he's supposed to have. Hover behind his painted eyes, if you so desire, but no closer. Until I decide I need you once more.'

'*You will be mine one day, mortal—*'

'No doubt, Hood. In the meantime, let's just luxuriate in the anticipation, shall we?' With these words, the wizard released his grip on the god's cloak. The presence flinched back.

Power flowed steady, the currents of air drawing Quick Ben and the sticksnare clinging to his shoulder over the tops of the canopies.

Talamandas hissed. 'What has happened? I, uh, vanished for a moment.'

'Everything's fine,' the wizard murmured. 'Does the power feel true, Sticksnare?'

'Aye, it does. This, this I can use.'

'Glad to hear it. Now, guide us to the plaza.'

A thin gauze of old smoke dulled the stars overhead. Captain Paran sat on the wide steps of the Thrall's main entrance. Directly ahead, at the end of a wide avenue, stood the gatehouse. Visible through its open doorway, in the plaza beyond, firelight from Barghast camps gleamed through gathering mists.

The Malazan was exhausted, yet sleep would not come to him. His thoughts had wandered countless paths since he'd left Cafal's company two bells earlier. Barghast shoulder-men still worked in the chamber, dismantling the canoes, collecting ancient weapons. Outside that room and beyond that activity, the Thrall seemed virtually deserted, lifeless.

The empty halls and corridors led Paran inexorably to what he imagined his parents' estate in Unta might now look like, with his mother and father dead, Felisin chained to a line in some mining pit a thousand leagues away, and dear sister Tavore dwelling in a score opulent chambers in Laseen's palace.

A house alone with its memories, looted by servants and guards and the street's gutter rats. Did the Adjunct ever ride past? Did her thoughts turn to it in the course of her busy day?

She was not one to spare a moment to sentiment. Cold-eyed, hers was a brutal rationality, pragmatism with a thousand honed edges – to cut open anyone foolish enough to come close.

The Empress would be well pleased with her new Adjunct.

And what of you, Felisin? With your wide smile and dancing eyes? There is no modesty in the Otataral Mines, nothing to shield you from the worst of human nature. You'll have been taken under wing none the less, by some pimp or pit-thug.

A flower crushed underfoot.

Yet your sister has it in mind to retrieve you – that much I know of her. She might well have thrown in a guardian or two for the length of your sentence.

But she'll not be rescuing a child. Not any more. No smile, and something hard and deadly in those once-dancing eyes. You should have found another way, sister. Gods, you should have killed Felisin outright – that would have been a mercy.

And now, now I fear you will some day pay dearly . . .

Paran slowly shook his head. His was a family none would envy. *Torn apart by our own hands, no less. And now, we siblings, each launched on our separate fates.* The likelihood of those fates' one day converging never seemed so remote.

The worn steps before him were flecked with ash; as if the only survivor in this city was the stone itself. The darkness felt solemn, sorrowful. All the sounds that should have accompanied the night, in this place, were absent. *Hood feels close this night . . .*

One of the massive double doors behind him swung open. The captain glanced back over a shoulder, then nodded. 'Mortal Sword. You look well . . . rested.'

The huge man grimaced. 'I feel beaten to within a finger's breadth of life. That's a mean woman.'

'I've heard men say that of their women before, and always there's a pleased hint to the complaint. As I hear now.'

Gruntle frowned. 'Aye, you're right. Funny, that.'

'These stairs are wide. Have a seat if you like.'

'I would not disturb your solitude, Captain.'

'Please do, it's nothing I would regret abandoning. Too many dark thoughts creep in when I'm alone.'

The Mortal Sword moved forward and slowly settled down onto the step at Paran's side, his tattered armour – straps loose – rustling and clinking. He rested his forearms on his knees, the gauntleted hands dangling. 'I share the same curse, Captain.'

'Fortunate, then, that you found Hetan.'

The man grunted. 'Problem is, she's insatiable.'

'In other words, you're the one in search of solitude, which my presence has prevented.'

'So long as you don't claw my back, your company is welcome.'

Paran nodded. 'I'm not the catty type – uh, sorry.'

'No need. If Trake ain't got a sense of humour that's his problem. Then again, he must have, since he picked me as his Mortal Sword.'

Paran studied the man beside him. Behind the barbed tattoos was a face that had lived hard years. Weathered, roughly chiselled, with eyes that matched those of a tiger's now that the god's power was within his flesh and blood. None the less, there were laugh lines around those eyes. 'Seems to me Trake chose wisely . . .'

'Not if he expects piety, or demands vows. Hood knows, I don't even like fighting. I'm not a soldier and have no desire to be. How, then, am I supposed to serve the God of War?'

'Better you, I think, than some blood-lusting square-foot with a single eyebrow, Gruntle. Reluctance to unsheathe those swords and all they represent seems a good thing to me. The gods know it's rare enough at the moment.'

'Not sure about that. This whole city was reluctant. The priests, the Gidrath, even the Grey Swords. If there'd been any other way . . .' He shrugged. 'The same for me. If it wasn't for what happened to Harllo and Stonny, I'd be down in the tunnels right now, gibbering with the rest of them.'

'Stonny's your friend with the broken rapier, right? Who's Harllo?'

Gruntle turned his head away for a moment. 'Another victim, Captain.' Bitterness filled his tone. 'Just one more on the trail. So I hear that your Malazan army's just west of here, come to join this death-cursed war. Why?'

'A temporary aberration. We ran out of enemies.'

'Soldiers' humour. I never could understand it. Is fighting that important to you?'

'If you mean me, personally, then no, it isn't. But for men like Dujek Onearm and Whiskeyjack, it's the sum total of their lives. They're makers of history. Their gift is the power to command. What they do revises the scholar's maps. As for the soldiers who follow them, I'd say that most of them see it as a profession, a career, probably the only one they're any good at. They are the physical will of the commanders they serve, and so are their own makers of history, one soldier at a time.'

'And what happens if their commanders are suicidal fools?'

'It's a soldier's lot to complain about their officers. Every mud-crusted footman is an artist at second-guessing, master strategists after the fact. But the truth is, the Malazan Empire has a tradition of superb, competent commanders. Hard and fair, usually from the ranks, though I'll grant you my own noble class has made destructive inroads on that tradition. Had I myself followed a safer path, I might well be a Fist by now – not through competence, of course, or even experience. Connections would have sufficed. The Empress has finally recognized the rot, however, and has already acted upon it, though likely too late.'

'Then why in Hood's name would she have outlawed Dujek Onearm?'

Paran was silent for a moment, then he shrugged. 'Politics. Expedience can force even the hand of an Empress, I suppose.'

'Has the sound of a feint to me,' Gruntle muttered. 'You don't cut loose your best commander in a fit of pique.'

'You might be right. Alas, I'm not the one who can

779

either confirm or deny. There's some old wounds still festering between Laseen and Dujek, in any case.'

'Captain Paran, you speak too freely for your own good – not that I'm a liability, mind you. But you've an openness and an honesty that might earn you the gallows some day.'

'Here's some more, Mortal Sword. A new House has appeared, seeking membership in the Deck of Dragons. It belongs to the Crippled God. I can feel the pressure – the voice of countless gods, all demanding that I deny my sanction, since it seems that I am the one cursed with that responsibility. Do I bless the House of Chains, or not? The arguments against such a blessing are overwhelming, and I don't need any god whispering in my head to apprise me of that.'

'So, where is the problem, Captain?'

'It's simple. There's a lone voice crying out, deep within me, so buried as to be almost inaudible. A lone voice, Gruntle, demanding the very opposite. Demanding that I must sanction the House of Chains. I *must* bless the Crippled God's right to a place within the Deck of Dragons.'

'And whose voice cries out such madness?'

'I think it's mine.'

Gruntle was silent for a dozen heartbeats, yet Paran felt the man's unhuman eyes fixed on him. Eventually, the Mortal Sword looked away and shrugged. 'I don't know much about the Deck of Dragons. Used for divinations, yes? Not something I've ever pursued.'

'Nor I,' Paran admitted.

Gruntle barked a laugh, sharp and echoing, then he slowly nodded. 'And what did you say of me earlier? Better a man who hates war to serve the God of War than one who lusts for it. Thus, why not a man who knows nothing of the Deck of Dragons to adjudicate it rather than a life-long practitioner?'

'You may have something there. Not that it alleviates my sense of inadequacy.'

'Aye, just that.' He paused, then continued, 'I felt my god recoil at your words, Captain – your instincts on the Crippled God's House of Chains. But as I said before, I'm not a follower. So I guess I saw it different. If Trake wants to tremble on four watery legs that's his business.'

'Your lack of fear has me curious, Gruntle. You seem to see no risk in legitimizing the House of Chains. Why is that?'

The man shrugged his massive shoulders. 'But that's just it, isn't it. Legitimizing. Right now, the Crippled God's *outside* the whole damned game, meaning he's not bound by any rules whatsoever—'

Paran suddenly sat straight. 'You're right. Abyss take me, that's it. If I bless the House of Chains then the Crippled God becomes . . . *bound*—'

'Just another player, aye, jostling on the same board. Right now, he just keeps kicking it whenever he gets the chance. When he's on it, he won't have that privilege. Anyway, that's how it seems to me, Captain. So when you said you wanted to sanction the House, I thought: why the fuss? Sounds perfectly reasonable to me. The gods can be damned thick-witted on occasion – probably why they need us mortals to do the straight thinking when straight thinking's required. Listen to that lone voice, lad, that's my advice.'

'And it's good advice—'

'Maybe, or maybe not. I might end up being roasted over the eternal fires of the Abyss by Trake and all the other gods for having given it.'

'I'll have company, then,' Paran said, grinning.

'Good thing we both hate solitude.'

'That's a soldier's humour, Gruntle.'

'Is it? But I was being serious, Captain.'

'Oh.'

Gruntle glanced over. 'Got you.'

A sliding downdraught of cool air brought Quick Ben onto

the gritty flagstones of the plaza. A dozen paces ahead loomed the gatehouse. Beyond it, seated side by side on the Thrall's wide, low steps, were Captain Paran and the Mortal Sword.

'Just the two I wanted to talk with,' the wizard muttered, relinquishing the Warren of Serc.

'No more arguments, please,' Talamandas replied from his perch on Quick Ben's shoulder. 'Those are two powerful men—'

'Relax,' the wizard said. 'I'm not anticipating a confrontation.'

'Well, I'll make myself unseen, just in case.'

'Suit yourself.'

The sticksnare vanished, though the wizard could still feel his meagre weight, and the twig fingers gripping his cloak.

The two men looked up as Quick Ben approached.

Paran nodded a greeting. 'Last time I saw you, you were racked with fever. I'm glad to see you're better. Gruntle, this is Quick Ben, a soldier in the Bridgeburners.'

'A mage.'

'That, too.'

Gruntle studied Quick Ben for a moment, and Paran sensed a bestial presence shifting uneasily behind the man's amber, feline eyes. Then the Daru said, 'You smell of death and it's not to my liking.'

Quick Ben started. 'Indeed? I've been consorting with the wrong company lately. Unpalatable, agreed, but, alas, necessary.'

'Is it just that?'

'I hope so, Mortal Sword.'

A brutal threat glared for a moment in Gruntle's eyes, then, slowly, dimmed. He managed a shrug. 'It was a Bridgeburner who saved Stonny's life, so I'll keep my reins taut. At least until I see if it wears off.'

'Consider it,' Paran said to Quick Ben, 'an elaborate way of saying you need to bathe soon.'

'Well,' the wizard replied, eyes on the captain, 'humour from you makes for a change.'

'Plenty of changes,' Paran agreed, 'of late. If you're looking to rejoin the company they're in the Gidrath barracks.'

'Actually, I bring word from Whiskeyjack.'

Paran sat straighter. 'You've managed to contact him? Despite the poisoned warrens? Impressive, Wizard. Now you have my utmost attention. Has he new orders for me?'

'Another parley has been requested by Brood,' Quick Ben said. 'With *all* the commanders, including Gruntle here, and Humbrall Taur and whomever's left of the Grey Swords. Can you make the request known to the other principals here in Capustan?'

'Aye, I suppose so. Is that it?'

'If you've a report to make to Whiskeyjack, I can convey it.'

'No thank you. I'll save that for when we meet in person.'

Quick Ben scowled. *Be that way, then.* 'Regarding the rest, best we speak in private, Captain.'

Gruntle made to rise but Paran reached out and halted the motion.

'I can probably anticipate your questions right here and now, Quick Ben.'

'Maybe you can but I'd rather you didn't.'

'Too bad for you, then. I'll make it plain. I have not yet decided whether or not to sanction the House of Chains. In fact, I haven't decided anything about anything, and it might be some time before that changes. Don't bother trying to pressure me, either.'

Quick Ben raised both hands. 'Please, Captain. I have no intention of pressuring you, since I was the victim of such an effort only a short while ago, by Hood himself, and it's left me riled. When someone warns me to follow one course of action, my instinct is to do the very opposite. You're not the only one inclined to stir the manure.'

Gruntle barked a laugh. 'Such droll understatement!

Seems I've found perfect company this night. Do go on, Wizard.'

'Only one more thing to add,' Quick Ben continued, studying Paran. 'An observation. Might be a wrong one, but I don't think so. You got sick, Captain, not from resisting the power forced upon you, but from resisting yourself. Whatever your instincts are demanding, listen to them. Follow them, and Abyss take the rest. That's all.'

'Is that your advice,' Paran quietly asked, 'or Whiskeyjack's?'

Quick Ben shrugged. 'If he was here, he'd say no different, Captain.'

'You've known him a long time, haven't you?'

'Aye, I have.'

After a moment, Paran nodded. 'I'd just about reached the same conclusion myself, this night, with Gruntle's help, that is. Seems the three of us are about to make some very powerful beings very angry.'

'Let 'em squeal,' the Mortal Sword growled. 'Hood knows, we've done more than our share, while they sat back and laughed. Time's come to pull the gauntlet onto the other hand.'

Quick Ben sighed under his breath. *All right, Hood, so I didn't really try, but only because it was clear that Paran wasn't inclined to heed you. And maybe I see why, now that I think on it. So, for what it's worth, consider this advice: there will be a House of Chains. Accept it, and prepare for it. You've ample time . . . more or less.*

Oh, one more thing, Hood. You and your fellow gods have been calling out the rules uncontested for far too long. Step back, now, and see how us mortals fare . . . I think you're in for a surprise or two.

Wan, dirt-smeared, but alive. The survivors of Capustan emerged from the last pit mouth as the sky paled to the east, blanched dwellers from the city's roots, shying from the torchlight as they stumbled onto the concourse, where they milled, as if lost in the place they had once known as home.

Shield Anvil Itkovian sat once more astride his warhorse, even though any quick movement made him sway, head spinning with exhaustion and the pain of his wounds. His task now was to be visible, his sole purpose was his presence. Familiar, recognizable, reassuring.

Come the new day, the priests of the Mask Council would begin a procession through the city, to add their own reassurance – that authority remained, that someone was in control, that things – life – could now begin again. But here, in the still darkness – a time Itkovian had chosen to ease the shock of the surrounding ruination – with the priests sleeping soundly in the Thrall, the Grey Swords, numbering three hundred and nineteen in all when including those from the tunnels, were positioned at every tunnel mouth and at every place of convergence.

They were there to ensure martial law and impart a sombre order to the proceedings, but their greatest value, as Itkovian well knew, was psychological.

We are the defenders. And we still stand.

While grieving was darkness, victory and all it meant was a greying to match the dawn, a lessening of the oppression that was loss, and of the devastation that slowly revealed itself on all sides. There could be no easing of the conflict within each and every survivor – the brutal randomness of fate that plagued the spirit – but the Grey Swords made of themselves a simple, solid presence. They had become, in truth, the city's standard.

And we still stand.

Once this task was complete, the contract was, to Itkovian's mind, concluded. Law and order could be left to the Gidrath from the Thrall. The surviving Grey Swords would leave Capustan, likely never to return. The question now occupying the Shield Anvil concerned the company's future. From over seven thousand to three hundred and nineteen: this was a siege from which the Grey Swords might never recover. But even such horrific losses, if borne alone, were manageable. The expelling of Fener from his warren was another matter. An army sworn to a god bereft of its power was, as far as Itkovian was concerned, no different from any other band of mercenaries: a collection of misfits and a scattering of professional soldiers. A column of coins offered no reliable backbone; few were the existent companies that could rightly lay claim to honour and integrity; few would stand firm when flight was possible.

Recruiting to strength had become problematic. The Grey Swords needed sober, straight-backed individuals; ones capable of accepting discipline of the highest order; ones for whom a vow held meaning.

Twin Tusks, what I need is fanatics . . .

At the same time, such people had to be without ties, of any sort. An unlikely combination.

And, given such people could be found, to whom could they swear? Not Trake – that army's core already existed, centred around Gruntle.

There were two other war-aspected gods that Itkovian knew of; northern gods, rarely worshipped here in the midlands or to the south.

What did Hetan call me? She never likened me to a cat, or a bear. No. In her eyes, I was a wolf.

Very well, then . . .

He raised his head, scanned over the heads of the milling survivors in the concourse until he spied the other lone rider.

She was watching him.

Itkovian gestured her over.

It was a few moments before she could pick her horse through the press and reach his side. 'Sir?'

'Find the captain. We three have a task before us, sir.'

The woman saluted, swung her mount round.

He watched her ride onto a side street, then out of sight. There was a strong logic behind his decision, yet, for him, it felt hollow, as if he personally was to have no part to play in what was to come beyond the act of preparation – no subsequent role in what had to be. None the less, the survival of the Grey Swords took precedence over his own wishes; indeed, his own life. *It has to be this way. I can think of no other. A new Reve must be fashioned. Even in this, I am not yet done.*

Captain Norul had found a horse for herself. Her face was aged beneath the rim of her helm: sleep had been denied them all for too long. She said nothing as she and the recruit reined in beside the Shield Anvil.

'Follow me, sirs,' Itkovian said, wheeling his mount.

They rode through the city, the sky paling to cerulean blue overhead, and left through the north gate. Encamped on the hills a third of a league away were the Barghast, the yurts and tents sparsely patrolled by a modest rearguard. Smoke rose from countless fires as the camp's old men and women began the morning meal. Children already ran down the uneven aisles, quieter than their city counterparts, but no less energetic.

The three Grey Swords crossed the looted remains of the Pannion lines and rode directly for the nearest Barghast camp.

Itkovian was not surprised to see a half-dozen old women gathering to meet them at the camp's edge. *There is a current that carries us to this, and you witches have felt it as surely as have I, and thus the trueness is made known and plain.* The realization did little to diminish the bleakness of his resolution. *Consider it but one more burden, Shield Anvil, one for which you were made as you were for all the others.*

They drew rein before the Barghast elders.

No-one spoke for a long moment, then one old woman cackled and gestured. 'Come, then.'

Itkovian dismounted, his companions following suit. Children appeared to take the reins of the three horses and the beasts were led away.

787

The elders, led by the spokeswoman, set off down the camp's main path, to a large yurt at the far end. The entrance was flanked by two Barghast warriors. The old woman hissed at them and both men retreated.

Itkovian, the recruit and the captain followed the elders into the yurt's interior.

'Rare is the man who comes to this place,' the spokeswoman said as she hobbled to the other side of the central hearth and lowered herself onto a bundle of furs.

'I am honoured—'

'Don't be!' she replied with a cackle. 'You would have to beat a warrior senseless and drag him, and even then it's likely his brothers and friends would attack you before you reached the entrance. You, a young man, are among old women, and there is nothing in the world more perilous!'

'But look at him!' another woman cried. 'He has no fear!'

'The hearth of his soul is nothing but ashes,' a third sniffed.

'Even so,' the first woman retorted, 'with what he now seeks, he would promise a firestorm to a frozen forest. Togctha and Farand, the lovers lost to each other for eternity, the winter hearts that howl in the deep fastnesses of Laederon and beyond – we have all heard those mournful cries, in our dreams. Have we not? They come closer – only not from the north, oh no, not the north. And now, this man.' She leaned forward, lined face indistinct behind the hearth's smoke. 'This man . . .'

The last words were a sigh.

Itkovian drew a deep breath, then gestured to the recruit. 'The Mortal Sword—'

'No,' the old woman growled.

The Shield Anvil faltered. 'But—'

'No,' she repeated. 'He has been found. He exists. It is already done. Look at her hands, Wolf. There is too much caring in them. She shall be the Destriant.'

'Are you – are you certain of this?'

The old woman nodded towards the captain. 'And this

one,' she continued, ignoring Itkovian's question, 'she is to be what you were. She will accept the burden – you, Wolf, have shown her all she must know. The truth of that is in her eyes, and in the love she holds for you. She would be its answer, in kind, in blood. She shall be the Shield Anvil.'

The other elders were nodding agreement, their eyes glittering in the gloom above beaked noses – as if a murder of crows now faced Itkovian.

He slowly turned to Captain Norul. The veteran looked stricken.

She faced him. 'Sir, what—'

'For the Grey Swords,' Itkovian said, struggling to contain his own welling of pain and anguish. 'It must be done, sir,' he rasped. 'Togg, Lord of Winter, a god of war long forgotten, recalled among the Barghast as the wolf-spirit, Togctha. And his lost mate, the she-wolf, Fanderay. Farand in the Barghast tongue. Among our company, now, more women than men. A Reve must be proclaimed, kneeling before the wolf god and the wolf goddess. You are to be the Shield Anvil, sir. And you,' he said to the recruit – whose eyes were wide – 'are to be the Destriant. The Grey Swords are remade, sirs. The sanction is here, now, among these wise women.'

The captain stepped back, armour clanking. 'Sir, you are the Shield Anvil of the Grey Swords—'

'No. I am the Shield Anvil of Fener, and Fener, sir, is . . . gone.'

'The company is virtually destroyed, sir,' the veteran pointed out. 'Our recovery is unlikely. The matter of quality—'

'You will require *fanatics*, Captain. That cast of mind, of breeding and culture, is vital. You must search, sir, you must needs find such people. People with nothing left to their lives, with their faith dismantled. People who have been made . . . lost.'

Norul was shaking her head, but he could see growing comprehension in her grey eyes.

'Captain,' Itkovian continued inexorably, 'the Grey Swords shall march with the two foreign armies. South, to see the end of the Pannion Domin. And, at a time deemed propitious, you will recruit. You will find the people you seek, sir, among the Tenescowri.'

Fear not, I shall not abandon you yet, my friend. There is much you must learn.

And, it seems, no end to my purpose.

He saw the bleakness come to her, saw it, and struggled against the horror of what he had done. Some things should never be shared. *And that is my most terrible crime, for to the title – the burden that is Shield Anvil – I gave her no choice.*

I gave her no choice.

CHAPTER NINETEEN

There were dark surprises that day.

The Year of the Gathering
Koralb

'We are being followed.'

Silverfox turned in her saddle, eyes narrowing. She sighed. 'My two Malazan minders.' She hesitated, then added, 'I doubt we'll dissuade them.'

Kruppe smiled. 'Clearly, your preternaturally unseen departure from the camp was less than perfect in its sorcerous efficacy. More witnesses, then, to the forthcoming fell event. Are you shy of audiences, lass? Dreadful flaw, if so—'

'No, Kruppe, I am not.'

'Shall we await them?'

'Something tells me they prefer it this way – at a distance. We go on, Daru. We're almost there.'

Kruppe scanned the low grass-backed hills on all sides. The sun's morning light was sharp, stripping away the last of shadows in the broad, shallow basins. They were, barring the two Malazan soldiers a thousand paces behind them, entirely alone. 'A modest army, it seems,' he observed. 'Entrenched in gopher holes, no doubt.'

'Their gift, and curse,' Silverfox replied. 'As dust, in all things, the T'lan Imass.'

Even as she spoke – their mounts carrying them along at

a slow trot – shapes appeared on the flanking hills. Gaunt wolves, loping in silence. The T'lan Ay, at first only a score to either side, then in their hundreds.

Kruppe's mule brayed, ears snapping and head tossing. 'Be calmed, beast!' the Daru cried, startling the animal yet further.

Silverfox rode close and stilled the mule with a touch to its neck.

They approached a flat-topped hill between two ancient, long-dry river beds, the channels wide, their banks eroded to gentle slopes. Ascending to the summit, Silverfox reined in and dismounted.

Kruppe hastily followed suit.

The T'lan Ay remained circling at a distance. The wolves numbered in the thousands, now, strangely spectral amidst the dust lifted into the air by their restless padding.

Arriving behind Rhivi and Daru, and ignored by the T'lan Ay, the two marines walked their horses up the slope.

'It's going to be a hot one,' one commented.

'Plenty hot,' the other woman said.

'Good day to miss a scrap, too.'

'That it is. Wasn't much interested in fighting Tenescowri in any case. A starving army's a pathetic sight. Walking skeletons—'

'Curious image, that,' Kruppe said. 'All things considered.'

The two marines fell silent, studying him.

'Excuse my interrupting the small talk,' Silverfox said drily. 'If you would all take position behind me. Thank you, no, a little farther back. Say, five paces, at the very least. That will do. I'd prefer no interruptions, if you please, in what follows.'

Kruppe's gaze – and no doubt that of the women flanking him – had gone past her, to the lowlands surrounding the hill, where squat, fur-clad, desiccated warriors were rising from the ground in a sea of shimmering dust. A sudden, uncannily silent conjuration.

As dust, in all things . . .

But the dust had found shape.

Uneven ranks, the dull glimmer of flint weapons a rippling of grey, black and russet brown amidst the betel tones of withered, polished skin. Skull helms, a few horned or antlered, made of every slope and every basin a spread of bone, as of stained, misaligned cobbles on some vast plaza. There was no wind to stir the long, ragged hair that dangled beneath those skullcaps, and the sun's light could not dispel the shadow beneath helm and brow ridge that swallowed the pits of the eyes. But every gaze was fixed on Silverfox, a regard of vast weight.

Within the span of a dozen heartbeats, the plain to all sides had vanished. The T'lan Imass, in their tens of thousands, now stood in its place, silent, motionless.

The T'lan Ay were no longer visible, ranging beyond the periphery of the amassed legions. Guardians. Kin, Hood-forsworn.

Silverfox turned to face the T'lan Imass.

Silence.

Kruppe shivered. The air was pungent with undeath, the gelid exhalation of dying ice, filled with something like loss.

Despair. *Or perhaps, after this seeming eternity, only its ashes.*

There is, all about us, ancient knowledge – that cannot be denied. Yet Kruppe wonders, are there memories? True memories? Of enlivened flesh and the wind's caress, of the laughter of children? Memories of love?

When frozen between life and death, in the glacial in-between, what can exist of mortal feeling? Not even an echo. Only memories of ice, of ice and no more than that. Gods below . . . such sorrow . . .

Figures approached the slope before Silverfox. Weaponless, robed in furs from ancient, long-extinct beasts. Kruppe's eyes focused on one in particular, a broad-shouldered Bonecaster, wearing an antlered skullcap and the stained fur of an arctic fox. With a shock the Daru realized that he knew this apparition.

Ah, we meet again, Pran Chole. Forgive me, but my heart breaks at the sight of you – at what you have become.

The antlered Bonecaster was the first to address Silverfox. 'We are come,' he said, 'to the Second Gathering.'

'You have come,' Silverfox grated, 'in answer to my summons.'

The Bonecaster slowly tilted his head. 'What you are was created long ago, guided by the hand of an Elder God. Yet, at its heart, Imass. All that follows has run in your blood from the moment of your birth. The wait, Summoner, has been long. I am Pran Chole, of Kron T'lan Imass. I stood, with K'rul, to attend your birth.'

Silverfox's answering smile was bitter. 'Are you my father, then, Pran Chole? If so, this reunion has come far too late. For us both.'

Despair flooded Kruppe. This was old anger, held back overlong, now turning the air gelid and brittle. A dreadful exchange to mark the first words of the Second Gathering.

Pran Chole seemed to wilt at her words. His desiccated face dropped, as if the Bonecaster was overcome with shame.

No, Silverfox, how could you do this?

'Where you then went, daughter,' Pran Chole whispered, 'I could not follow.'

'True,' she snapped. 'After all, you had a *vow* awaiting you. A ritual. *The* ritual, the one that turned your hearts to ash. All for a war. But that is what war is all about, isn't it? Leaving. Leaving home. Your loved ones – indeed, the very capacity of love itself. You chose to abandon it all. You abandoned *everything*! You abandoned—' She cut her words off suddenly.

Kruppe closed his eyes for a brief moment, so that he might in his mind complete her sentence. *You abandoned . . . me.*

Pran Chole's head remained bowed. Finally, he raised it slightly. 'Summoner, what would you have us do?'

'We will get to that soon enough.'

Another Bonecaster stepped forward, then. The rotted fur of a large brown bear rode his shoulders and it seemed the beast itself had reared behind the shadowed eyes. 'I am Okral Lom,' he said in a voice like distant thunder. 'All the Bonecasters of Kron T'lan Imass now stand before you. Agkor Choom. Bendal Home, Ranag Ilm, and Brold Chood. Kron, as well, who was chosen as War Leader at the First Gathering. Unlike Pran Chole, we care nothing for your anger. We played no role in your creation, in your birth. None the less, you cling to a misapprehension, Summoner. Pran Chole can in no way be considered your father. He stands here, accepting the burden of your rage, for he is what he is. If you would call anyone your father, if you so require a face upon which hatred can focus, then you must forbear, for the one you seek is not among us.'

The blood had slowly drained from Silverfox's face, as if she'd not been prepared for such brutal condemnation flung back at her by this Bonecaster. 'N-not among you?'

'Your souls were forged in the Warren of Tellann, yet not in the distant past – the past in which Pran Chole lived – not at first, at any rate. Summoner, the unveiled warren of which I speak belonged to the First Sword, Onos T'oolan. Now clanless, he walks alone, and that solitude has twisted his power of Tellann—'

'Twisted? How?'

'By what he seeks, by what lies at the heart of his desires.'

Silverfox was shaking her head, as if striving to deny all that Okral Lom said. 'And what does he seek?'

The Bonecaster shrugged. 'Summoner, you will discover that soon enough, for Onos T'oolan has heard your call to the Second Gathering. He will, alas, be rather late.'

Kruppe watched as Silverfox slowly returned her gaze to Pran Chole, whose head was bowed once more.

In assuming the responsibility for her creation, this

*Bonecaster offered her a gift – a focus for her anger, a victim to
stand before its unleashing. I do remember you, Pran Chole,
there in my dream-world. Your face, the compassion in your
eyes. Would I the courage to ask: were you Imass once, in
truth, all like this?*

Another pair was emerging from the ranks. In the silence
that followed Okral Lom's words, the foremost one spoke.
'I am Ay Estos, of Logros T'lan Imass.' The furs of arctic
wolves hung from the Bonecaster, who was taller, leaner
than the others.

Silverfox's reply was almost distracted. 'I greet you, Ay
Estos. You are given leave to speak.'

The T'lan Imass bowed in acknowledgement, then said,
'Logros could but send two Bonecasters to this Gathering,
for the reason I would now tell you.' He paused, then, as
Silverfox made no reply to that, he continued. 'Logros
T'lan Imass hunts renegades – our own kin, who have
broken from the Vow. Crimes have been committed,
Summoner, which must be answered. I have come, then, on
behalf of the clans of Logros.'

Silverfox shook herself, visibly wrenching her gaze from
Pran Chole. She drew a deep breath, straightened. 'You
said,' she said tonelessly, 'that another Bonecaster of Logros
is present.'

The wolf-clad T'lan Imass stepped to one side. The
figure standing behind him was hugely boned, the skull
beneath the thin, withered flesh bestial. She wore a scaled,
leathery cloak of skin that hung down to the ground behind
her. Unadorned by a helm, the broad, flat skull revealed
only a few remaining patches of skin that each bore but a
few strands of long, white hair.

'Olar Ethil,' Ay Estos said. 'First among the Bonecasters.
Eleint, the First Soletaken. She has not journeyed with me,
for Logros set for her another task, which has taken her far
from the clans. Until this day, we among the Logros had
not seen Olar Ethil in many years. Eleint, will you speak of
success or failure in what you have sought?'

The First Bonecaster tilted her head, then addressed Silverfox. 'Summoner. As I neared this place, you commanded my dreams.'

'I did, though I knew not who you were. We can discuss that another time. Tell me of this task set for you by Logros.'

'Logros sent me in search of the remaining T'lan Imass armies, such as we knew from the First Gathering. The Ifayle, the Kerluhm, the Bentract and the Orshan.'

'And did you find them?' she asked.

'The four remaining clans of Bentract T'lan Imass are on Jacuruku, I believe, yet trapped within the Warren of Chaos. I searched there, Summoner, without success. Of the Orshan, the Ifayle and Kerluhm, I report my failure in discovering any sign. It follows that we must conclude they no longer exist.'

Silverfox was clearly shaken by Olar Ethil's words. 'So many . . .' she whispered, 'lost?' A moment later Kruppe saw her steel herself. 'Olar Ethil, what inspired Logros to despatch you to find the remaining armies?'

'Summoner, the First Throne found a worthy occupant. Logros was commanded so by the occupant.'

'An occupant? Who?'

'A mortal known then as Kellanved, Emperor of Malaz.'

Silverfox said nothing for a long moment, then, 'Of course. But he no longer occupies it, does he?'

'He no longer occupies it, Summoner, yet he has not yielded it.'

'What does that mean? Ah, because the Emperor didn't die, did he?'

Olar Ethil nodded. 'Kellanved did not die. He ascended, and has taken the Throne of Shadow. Had he died in truth, the First Throne would be unoccupied once more. He has not, so it is not. We are at an impasse.'

'And when this . . . event . . . occurred – the result was your ceasing to serve the Malazan Empire, leaving Laseen to manage on her own for the first, crucial years of her rule.'

'They were uncertain times, Summoner. Logros T'lan Imass was divided unto itself. The discovery of surviving Jaghut in the Jhag Odhan proved a timely, if short-lived, distraction. Clans among us have since returned to the Malazan Empire's service.'

'And was the schism responsible for the renegades the rest now pursue?'

Ah, her mind returns, sharply honed. This is fell information indeed. Renegades among the T'lan Imass . . .

'No, Summoner. The renegades have found another path, which as yet remains hidden from us. They have, on occasion, employed the Warren of Chaos in their flight.'

Chaos? I wonder, to whom do these renegade T'lan Imass now kneel? No, muse on it not. Still a distant threat, Kruppe suspects. All in its own time . . .

Silverfox asked, 'What Soletaken shape do you assume, Olar Ethil?'

'When I veer, I am as an undead twin to Tiam, who spawned all dragons.'

Nothing more was added. The thousands of T'lan Imass stood motionless, silent. A score heartbeats passed in Kruppe's chest. Finally, he cleared his throat and stepped closer to Silverfox. 'It appears, lass, that they await your command – whatever command that might be. A reasonable resolu—'

Silverfox swung to face him. 'Please,' she grated. 'No advice. This is my Gathering, Kruppe. Leave me to it.'

'Of course, my dear. Humblest apologies. Please do resume your hesitation.'

She made a sour face. 'Impudent bastard.'

Kruppe smiled.

Silverfox turned back to the awaiting T'lan Imass. 'Pran Chole, please forgive my earlier words.'

He raised his head. 'Summoner, it is I who must ask for forgiveness.'

'No. Okral Lom was right in condemning my anger. I feel

798

as if I have awaited this meeting for a thousand lifetimes – the expectation, the pressure . . .'

Kruppe cleared his throat. 'A thousand lifetimes, Silverfox? Scry more closely those who stand before you—'

'Thank you, that's enough, Kruppe. Believe me, I am quite capable of castigating myself without any help from you.'

'Of course,' the Daru murmured.

Silverfox settled her gaze on Pran Chole once more. 'I would ask of you and your kin a question.'

'We await, Summoner.'

'Are there any Jaghut left?'

'Of pure blood, we know of but one who remains in this realm. One, who hides not in the service of a god, or in service to the Houses of the Azath.'

'And he will be found at the heart of the Pannion Domin, won't he?'

'Yes.'

'Commanding K'Chain Che'Malle undead. How can that be?'

Kruppe noted the hesitation in Pran Chole as the Bonecaster replied. 'We do not know, Summoner.'

'And when he is destroyed, Pran Chole, what then?'

The Bonecaster seemed taken aback by the question. 'Summoner, this is your Gathering. You are flesh and blood – our flesh and blood, reborn. When the last Jaghut is slain—'

'A moment, if you please!' Kruppe said, edging another step forward. Silverfox hissed in exasperation but the Daru continued. 'Pran Chole, do you recall worthy Kruppe?'

'I do.'

'Worthy, clever Kruppe, yes? You said *you know of but one* Jaghut. No doubt accurate enough. None the less, saying such is not quite the same as saying there is but one left, is it? Thus, you are not certain, are you?'

Olar Ethil replied. 'Mortal, other Jaghut remain. Isolated. Hidden – they have learned to hide very well indeed. We believe they exist, but we cannot find them.'

'Yet you seek an official end to the war, do you not?'

A susurration of motion rippled through the undead ranks.

Silverfox wheeled on him. 'How did you know, damn you?'

Kruppe shrugged. 'Sorrow unsurpassed and unsurpassing. They in truth seek to become dust. Had they eyes, Kruppe would see the truth no plainer writ. The T'lan Imass wish oblivion.'

'Which I would only grant if all the Jaghut on this world had ceased to exist,' Silverfox said. 'For that is the burden laid upon me. My *intended* purpose. The threat of tyranny removed, finally, once and for all time. Only then could I grant the T'lan Imass the oblivion they seek – so the Ritual demands of me, for that is a linkage that cannot be broken.'

'You must make the pronouncement, Summoner,' Okral Lom said.

'Yes,' she replied, still glaring at Kruppe.

'Your words,' Pran Chole added, 'can shatter the Ritual's bindings.'

Her head snapped round. 'So easily? Yet—' She faced the Daru once more, and scowled. 'Kruppe, you force into the open an unpleasant truth—'

'Aye, Silverfox, but not the same truth as that which you seem to see. No, Kruppe has unveiled a deeper one, far more poignant.'

She crossed her arms. 'And that is?'

Kruppe studied the sea of undead figures, narrowed his gaze on the shadowed sockets of countless eyes. After a long moment, he sighed, and it was a sigh ragged with emotion. 'Ah, my dear, look again, please. It was a pathetic deceit, not worth condemnation. Understand, if you will, the very beginning. The First Gathering. There was but one enemy, then. One people, from whom tyrants emerged. But time passes, aye? And now, dominators and tyrants

800

abound on all sides – yet are they Jaghut? They are not. They are human, for the most part, yes?

'The truth in all its layers? Very well. Silverfox, the T'lan Imass have *won their war*. Should a new tyrant emerge from among the few hidden Jaghut, he or she will not find the world so simple to conquer as it once was. There are gods to oppose the effort; nay, there are mere ascendants! Men such as Anomander Rake, women such as Korlat – have you forgotten the fate of the last Jaghut Tyrant?

'The time has passed, Silverfox. For the Jaghut, and thus, for the T'lan Imass.' Kruppe rested a hand on her shoulder and looked up into her eyes. 'Summoner,' he whispered, 'these indomitable warriors are . . . *weary*. Weary beyond all comprehension. They have existed for hundreds of thousands of years, for one sole cause. And that cause is now . . . a farce. Pointless. Irrelevant. They want it to end, Silverfox. They tried to arrange it with Kellanved and the First Throne, but the effort failed. Thus, they gave shape to you, to what you would become. For this one task.

'Redeem them. Please.'

Pran Chole spoke, 'Summoner, we shall destroy the Jaghut who hides within this Pannion Domin. And then, we would ask for an end. It is as Kruppe has said. We have no reason to exist, thus we exist without honour, and it is destroying us. The renegades Logros T'lan Imass hunts are but the first. We shall lose more of our kin, or so we fear.'

Kruppe saw that Silverfox was trembling, but her words were tightly controlled as she addressed the antlered shaman. 'You create me as the first flesh and blood Bonecaster in almost three hundred thousand years. The first, and, it seems, the last.'

'Do as we ask, Summoner, and the remainder of your life is yours.'

'What life? I am neither Rhivi nor Malazan. I am not even truly human. It is what all of you do not grasp!' She jabbed a finger at Kruppe and the two marines to complete an all-encompassing gesture. 'None of you! Not even

Paran, who thinks – no, what he thinks I will deal with in my own time – it is not for any of you. T'lan Imass! I am your kin, damn you! *Your first child in three hundred thousand years! Am I to be abandoned again?'*

Kruppe stepped back. *Again? Oh, gods below—* 'Silverfox—'

'Silence!'

But there was no silence. Instead, a rustling and creaking whispered through the air, and Silverfox and Kruppe swung to the sound.

To see tens of thousands of T'lan Imass lowering themselves to their knees, heads bowing.

Olar Ethil was the last standing. She spoke. 'Summoner, we beg you to release us.' With those words, she too settled onto the ground.

The scene twisted a knife in Kruppe's very soul. Unable to speak, barely able to breathe, he simply stared out at the broken multitude in growing horror. And when Silverfox gave answer, the Daru's heart threatened to burst.

'No.'

In the distance, on all sides, the undead wolves began to howl.

'Hood's breath!' one of the marines swore.

Aye, theirs is a voice of such unearthly sorrow, it tears at the mortal mind. Oh, K'rul, what are we to do now?

'One assumes a lack of complexity in people whose lives are so short.'

Whiskeyjack grinned sourly. 'If that's meant to be an apology, you'll have to do better, Korlat.'

The Tiste Andii sighed, ran a hand through her long black hair in a very human gesture.

'Then again,' the Malazan continued, 'from you, woman, even a grunt will do.'

Her eyes flashed. 'Oh? And how am I to take *that?*'

'Try the way it was meant, lass. I've not enjoyed the last few days much, and I'd rather we were as before, so I will take what I can get. There, as simple as I can make it.'

She leaned in her saddle and laid a hand against his chain-clothed arm. 'Thank you. It seems I am the one needing things simple.'

'To that, my lips are sealed.'

'You are a wise man, Whiskeyjack.'

The plain before them, at a distance of two thousand paces and closing, swarmed with Tenescowri. There was no order to their ranks, barring the lone rider who rode before them, a thin, gaunt youth, astride a spine-bowed roan dray. Immediately behind the young man – whom Whiskeyjack assumed to be Anaster – ranged a dozen or so women. Wild-haired, loosing random shrieks, there was an aura of madness and dark horror about them.

'Women of the Dead Seed, presumably,' Korlat said, noting his gaze. 'There is sorcerous power there. They are the First Child's true bodyguard, I believe.'

Whiskeyjack twisted in his saddle to examine the Malazan legions formed up behind him fifty paces away. 'Where is Anomander Rake? This mob could charge at any moment.'

'They will not,' Korlat asserted. 'Those witches sense my Lord's nearness. They are made uneasy, and cry out caution to their chosen child.'

'But will he listen?'

'He had bett—'

A roaring sound shattered her words.

The Tenescowri were charging, a surging tide of fearless desperation. A wave of power from the Women of the Dead Seed psychically assailed Whiskeyjack, made his heart thunder with a strange panic.

Korlat hissed between her teeth. 'Resist the fear, my love!'

Snarling, Whiskeyjack drew his sword and wheeled his horse round to face his troops. The sorcerous assault of terror had reached them, battering at the lines. They rippled, but not a single soldier stepped back. A moment later, his Malazans steadied.

''Ware!' Korlat cried. 'My Lord arrives in his fullest power!'

The air seemed to descend on all sides, groaning beneath a vast, invisible weight. The sky darkened with a palpable dread.

Whiskeyjack's horse stumbled, legs buckling momentarily before the animal regained its balance. The beast screamed.

A cold, bitter wind whistled fiercely, flattening the grasses before the commander and Korlat, then it struck the charging mass of Tenescowri.

The Women of the Dead Seed were thrown back, staggering, stumbling, onto the ground where they writhed. Behind them, the front runners in the mob tried to stop and were overrun. Within a single heartbeat, the front ranks collapsed into chaos, figures seething over others, bodies trampled or pushed forward in a flailing of limbs.

The silver-maned black dragon swept low over Whiskeyjack's head, sailing forward on that gelid gale.

The lone figure of Anaster, astride his roan horse that had not even flinched, awaited him. The front line of the Tenescowri was a tumbling wall behind the First Child.

Anomander Rake descended on the youth.

Anaster straightened in his saddle and spread his arms wide.

Huge talons snapped down. Closed around the First Child and plucked him from the horse.

The dragon angled upward with its prize.

Then seemed to stagger in the air.

Korlat cried out. 'Gods, he is as poison!'

The dragon's leg whipped to one side, flinging Anaster away. The young man spun, cartwheeling like a tattered doll through the air. To plunge into the mob of Tenescowri on the far right, where he disappeared from view.

Righting himself, Anomander Rake lowered his wedge-shaped head as he closed on the peasant army. Fanged mouth opened.

Raw Kurald Galain issued from that maw. Roiling darkness that Whiskeyjack had seen before, long ago, outside the city of Pale. But then, it had been tightly controlled. And more recently, when led by Korlat through the warren itself; again, calmed. But now, the Elder Warren of Darkness was unleashed, wild.

So there's another way into the Warren of Kurald Galain – right down that dragon's throat.

A broad, flattened swathe swept through the Tenescowri. Bodies dissolving to nothing, leaving naught but ragged clothing. The dragon's flight was unswerving, cutting a path of annihilation that divided the army into two seething, recoiling halves.

The first pass completed, Anomander Rake lifted skyward, banked around for another.

It was not needed. The Tenescowri forces had broken, figures scattering in all directions. Here and there, Whiskeyjack saw, it turned on itself, like a hound biting its own wounds. Senseless murder, self-destruction, all that came of blind, unreasoning terror.

The dragon glided back over the writhing mobs, but did not unleash its warren a second time.

Then Whiskeyjack saw Anomander Rake's head turn.

The dragon dropped lower, a wide expanse clearing before it as the Tenescowri flung themselves away, leaving only a half-score of figures, lying prone but evincing motion none the less – slowly, agonizingly attempting to regain their feet.

The Women of the Dead Seed.

The dragon, flying now at a man's height over the ground, sembled, blurred as it closed on the witches, reformed into the Lord of Moon's Spawn – who strode towards the old women, hand reaching up to draw his sword.

'Korlat—'

'I am sorry, Whiskeyjack.'

'He's going to—'

'I know.'

Whiskeyjack stared in horror as Anomander Rake reached the first of the women, a scrawny, hunchbacked hag half the Tiste Andii's height, and swung Dragnipur.

Her head dropped to the ground at her feet on a stream of gore. The body managed an eerie side-step, as if dancing, then crumpled.

Anomander Rake walked to the next woman.

'No – this is not right—'

'Please—'

Ignoring Korlat's plea, Whiskeyjack spurred his horse forward, down the slope at a canter, then a gallop as they reached level ground.

Another woman was slain, then a third before the Malazan arrived, sawing his reins to bring his horse to a skidding halt directly in Rake's path.

The Lord of Moon's Spawn was forced to halt his stride. He looked up in surprise, then frowned.

'Stop this,' Whiskeyjack grated. He realized he still held his sword unsheathed, saw Rake's unhuman eyes casually note it before the Tiste Andii replied.

'To one side, my friend. What I do is a mercy—'

'No, it is a judgement, Anomander Rake. And,' he added, eyes on Dragnipur's black blade, 'a sentence.'

The Lord's answering smile was oddly wistful. 'If you would have it as you say, Whiskeyjack. None the less, I claim the right to judgement of these creatures.'

'I will not oppose that, Anomander Rake.'

'Ah, it is the . . . sentence, then.'

'It is.'

The Lord sheathed his sword. 'Then it must be by your hand, friend. And quickly, for they recover their powers.'

He flinched in his saddle. 'I am no executioner.'

'You'd best become one, or step aside. Now.'

Whiskeyjack wheeled his horse round. The seven remaining women were indeed regaining their senses, though he saw in the one nearest him a glaze of incomprehension lingering still in her aged, yellowed eyes.

Hood take me—

He kicked his mount into motion, readied his blade in time to drive its point into the nearest woman's chest.

Dry skin parted almost effortlessly. Bones snapped like twigs. The victim reeled back, fell.

Pushing his horse on, Whiskeyjack shook the blood from his sword, then, reaching the next woman, he swung crossways, opened wide her throat.

He forced a cold grip onto his thoughts, holding them still, concentrated on the mechanics of his actions. No errors. No pain-stretched flaws for his victims. Precise executions, one after another, instinctively guiding his horse, shifting his weight, readying his blade, thrusting or slashing as was required.

One, then another, then another.

Until, swinging his mount around, he saw that he was done. It was over.

His horse stamping as it continued circling, Whiskeyjack looked up.

To see Onearm's Host lining the ridge far to his left – the space between them littered with trampled bodies but otherwise open. Unobstructed.

His soldiers.

Lining the ridge. Silent.

To have witnessed this . . . Now, I am indeed damned. From this, no return. No matter what the words of explanation, of justification. No matter the crimes committed by my victims. I have slain. Not soldiers, not armed opponents, but creatures assailed by madness, stunned senseless, uncomprehending.

He turned, stared at Anomander Rake.

The Lord of Moon's Spawn returned the regard without expression.

This burden – you have taken it before, assumed it long ago, haven't you? This burden, that now assails my soul, it is what you live with – have lived with for centuries. The price for the sword on your back—

807

'You should have left it with me, friend,' the Tiste Andii said quietly. 'I might have insisted, but I would not cross blades with you. Thus,' he added with a sorrowful smile, 'the opening of my heart proves, once more, a curse. Claiming those I care for, by virtue of that very emotion. Would that I had learned my lesson long ago, do you not agree?'

'It seems,' Whiskeyjack managed, 'we have found something new to share.'

Anomander Rake's eyes narrowed. 'I would not have wished it.'

'I know.' He held hard on his control. 'I'm sorry I gave you no choice.'

They regarded each other.

'I believe Korlat's kin have captured this Anaster,' Rake said after a moment. 'Will you join me in attending to him?'

Whiskeyjack flinched.

'No, my friend,' Rake said. 'I yield judgement of him. Let us leave that to others, shall we?'

In proper military fashion, you mean. That rigid structure that so easily absolves personal responsibility. Of course. We've time for that, now, haven't we? 'Agreed, Lord. Lead on, if you please.'

With another faint, wistful smile, Anomander Rake strode past him.

Whiskeyjack sheathed his bloodied sword, and followed.

He stared at the Tiste Andii's broad back, at the weapon that hung from it. *Anomander Rake, how can you bear this burden? This burden that has so thoroughly broken my heart?*

But no, that is not what so tears at me.

Lord of Moon's Spawn, you asked me to step aside, and you called it a mercy. I misunderstood you. A mercy, not to the Women of the Dead Seed. But to me. Thus your sorrowed smile when I denied you.

Ah, my friend, I saw only your brutality – and that hurt you. Better, for us both, had you crossed blades with me.

808

For us both.

And I – I am not worth such friends. Old man, foolish gestures plague you. Be done with it. Make this your last war.

Make it your last.

Korlat waited with her Tiste Andii kin, surrounding the gaunt figure that was Anaster, First Child of the Dead Seed, at a place near where the youth had landed when thrown by Anomander Rake.

Whiskeyjack saw tears in his lover's eyes, and the sight of them triggered a painful wrench in his gut. He forced himself to look away. Although he needed her now, and perhaps she in turn needed him to share all that she clearly comprehended, it would have to wait. He resolved to take his lead from Anomander Rake, for whom control was both armour and, if demanded by circumstance, a weapon.

Riders were approaching from the Malazan position, as well as from Brood's. There would be witnesses to what followed – *and that I now curse such truths is true revelation of how far I have fallen. When, before, did I ever fear witnesses to what I did or said? Queen of Dreams, forgive me. I have found myself in a living nightmare, and the monster that stalks me is none other than myself.*

Reining his horse to a halt before the gathered Tiste Andii, Whiskeyjack was able to examine Anaster closely for the first time.

Disarmed, bruised and blood-smeared, his face turned away, he looked pitiful, weak and small.

But that is always the way with leaders who have been broken. Whether kings or commanders, defeat withers them—

And then he saw the youth's face. Something had gouged out one of his eyes, leaving a welter of deep red blood. The remaining eye lifted, fixed on Whiskeyjack. Intent, yet horrifyingly lifeless, a stare both cold and casual, curious yet vastly – fundamentally – indifferent. 'The slayer of my mother,' Anaster said in a lilting voice, cocking his head as he continued to study the Malazan.

Whiskeyjack's voice was hoarse. 'I am sorry for that, First Child.'

'I am not. She was insane. A prisoner of herself, possessed by her own demons. Not alone in that curse, we must presume.'

'Not any more,' Whiskeyjack answered.

'It is as a plague, is it not? Ever spreading. Devouring lives. That is why you will, ultimately, fail. All of you. You become what you destroy.'

The tone of Anomander Rake's response was shockingly vulgar. 'No more appropriate words could come from a cannibal. What, Anaster, do you think we should do with you? Be honest, now.'

The young man swung his singular gaze to the Lord of Moon's Spawn. Whatever self-possession he contained seemed to falter suddenly with that contact, for he reached up a tentative hand to hover before the bloodied eye-socket, and his pale face grew paler. 'Kill me,' he whispered.

Rake frowned. 'Korlat?'

'Aye, he lost control, then. His fear has a face. One that I have not seen before—'

Anaster turned on her. 'Shut up! You saw nothing!'

'There is darkness within you,' she replied in calm tones. 'Virulent cousin to Kurald Galain. A darkness of the soul. When you falter, child, we see what hides within it.'

'Liar!' he hissed.

'A soldier's face,' Anomander Rake said. He slowly faced westward. 'From the city. From Capustan.' He turned back to Anaster. 'He is still there, isn't he? It seems, mortal, that you have acquired a nemesis – one who promises something other than death, something far more terrible. Interesting.'

'You do not understand! He is Itkovian! Shield Anvil! He wishes my soul! Please, kill me!'

Dujek and Caladan Brood had arrived from the allied lines, as well as Kallor and Artanthos. They sat on their horses, watchful, silent.

'Perhaps we will,' the Lord of Moon's Spawn replied after

a moment. 'In time. For now, we will take you with us to Capustan—'

'*No! Please! Kill me now!*'

'I see no absolution in your particular madness, child,' Anomander Rake said. 'No cause for mercy. Not yet. Perhaps, upon meeting the one – Itkovian? – who so terrifies you, we will judge otherwise, and so grant you a swift end. As you are our prisoner, that is our right. You might be spared your nemesis after all.' He faced Brood and the others. 'Acceptable?'

'Aye,' Dujek growled, eyes on Whiskeyjack.

'Agreed,' Brood said.

Anaster made a desperate attempt to snatch a dagger from a Tiste Andii warrior beside him, which was effortlessly denied. The youth collapsed, then, weeping, down onto his knees, his thin frame racked by heaves.

'Best take him away,' Anomander Rake said, studying the broken figure. 'This is no act.'

That much was plain to everyone present.

Whiskeyjack nudged his horse to come alongside Dujek.

The old man nodded in greeting, then muttered, 'That was damned unfortunate.'

'It was.'

'From the distance, it looked—'

'It looked bad, High Fist, because it was.'

'Understand, Whiskeyjack, I comprehend your . . . your mercy. Rake's sword – but, dammit, could you not have waited?'

Explanations, sound justifications crowded Whiskeyjack's mind, but all he said was, 'No.'

'Executions demand procedures—'

'Then strip me of my rank, sir.'

Dujek winced, looked away. He sighed roughly. 'That's not what I meant, Whiskeyjack. I know well enough the significance of such procedures – the real reason for their existing in the first place. A sharing of necessary but brutal acts—'

811

'Diminishes the personal cost, aye,' Whiskeyjack answered in low tones. 'No doubt Anomander Rake could have easily managed those few souls added to his legendary list. But I took them instead. I *diminished his personal cost*. A paltry effort, granted, and one he asked me not to do. But it is done now. The issue is ended.'

'The issue is anything but,' Dujek grated. 'I am your friend—'

'No.' *We're not at risk of crossing blades, so there won't be any sharing of this one.* 'No,' he repeated. *Not this time.*

He could almost hear Dujek's teeth grinding.

Korlat joined them. 'A strange young man, the one known as Anaster.'

The two Malazans turned at her words.

'Does that surprise you?' Dujek asked.

She shrugged. 'There was much hidden within the darkness of his soul, High Fist. More than just a soldier's face. He could not bear leading his army. Could not bear to see the starvation, the loss and desperation. And so was resolved to send it to its death, to absolute annihilation. As an act of mercy, no less. To relieve the suffering.

'For himself, he committed crimes that could only be answered with death. Execution at the hands of those survivors among his victims. But not a simple death – he seeks something more. He seeks damnation as his sentence. An eternity of damnation. I cannot fathom such self-loathing.'

I can, for I feel as if I am tottering on the very edge of that steep slope myself. One more misstep . . . Whiskeyjack looked away, towards the Malazan legions massed on the distant ridge. The sun flashing from armour and weapons was blinding, making his eyes water.

Dujek moved his horse away, rejoining Artanthos, Brood and Kallor.

Leaving Whiskeyjack alone with Korlat.

She reached up, touched his gauntleted hand.

He could not meet her gaze, continued studying the motionless lines of his soldiers.

'My love,' she murmured. 'Those women – they were not defenceless. The power they drew on came from the Warren of Chaos itself. My Lord's initial attack was intended to destroy them; instead, it but left them momentarily stunned. They were *recovering*. And, in their awakened power, they would have unleashed devastation. Madness and death, for your army. This entire day could have been lost.'

He grimaced. 'I do not rail at necessity,' he said.

'It seems . . . you do.'

'War has its necessities, Korlat, and I have always understood that. Always known the cost. But, this day, by my own hand, I have realized something else. War is not a natural state. It is an imposition, and a damned unhealthy one. With its rules, we willingly yield our humanity. Speak not of just causes, worthy goals. We are takers of life. Servants of Hood, one and all.'

'The Women of the Dead Seed would have killed hundreds, perhaps thousands, Whiskeyjack—'

'And I have commanded the same, in my time, Korlat. What difference is there between us?'

'You are not afraid of the questions that follow such acts,' she said. 'Those that you willingly ask of yourself. Perhaps you see that as self-destructive ruthlessness, but I see it as courage – a courage that is extraordinary. A man less brave would have left my Lord to his unseemly task.'

'These are pointless words, Korlat. The army standing over there has witnessed its commander committing murder—'

Korlat's hissing retort shocked him. 'Do not dare underestimate them!'

'Underest—'

'I have come to know many of your soldiers, Whiskeyjack. They are not fools. Perhaps many of them – if not most – are unable to articulate their fullest

813

understanding, but they understand none the less. Do you not think that they – each in his or her own way – have faced the choice you faced this morning? The knife-point turn of their lives? And every one of them still feels the scar within them.'

'I see little—'

'Whiskeyjack, listen to me. They witnessed. They *saw*, in fullest knowing. Damn you, I know this for I felt the same. They hurt for you. With every brutal blow, they felt the old wounds within them resonate in sympathy. Commander, your shame is an insult. Discard it, or you will deliver unto your soldiers the deepest wound of all.'

He stared down at her. 'We're a short-lived people,' he said after a long moment. 'We lack such complexity in our lives.'

'Bastard. Remind me to never again apologize to you.'

He looked back once more at the Malazan legions. 'I still fear to face them at close range,' he muttered.

'The distance between you and them has already closed, Whiskeyjack. Your army will follow you into the Abyss, should you so command.'

'The most frightening thought uttered thus far today.'

She made no reply to that.

Aye, war's imposition – of extremities. Harsh, yet simple. It is no place for humanity, no place at all. 'Dujek was displeased,' he said.

'Dujek wants to keep his army alive.'

His head snapped round.

Her eyes regarded him, cool and gauging.

'I have no interest in usurping his authority—'

'You just did, Whiskeyjack. Laseen's fear of you be damned, the natural order has reasserted itself. She could handle Dujek. That's why she demoted you and put him in charge. Gods, you can be dense at times!'

He scowled. 'If I am such a threat to her, why didn't she—' He stopped, closed his mouth. *Oh, Hood. Pale. Darujhistan. It wasn't the Bridgeburners she wanted destroyed. It was me.*

'Guard your trust, my love,' Korlat said. 'It may be that your belief in honour is being used against you.'

He felt himself go cold inside.

Oh, Hood.

Hood's marble balls on an anvil . . .

Coll made his way down the gentle slope towards the Mhybe's wagon. Thirty paces to the right were the last of the Trygalle Trade Guild's carriages, a group of shareholders throwing bones on a tarp nearby. Messengers rode in the distance, coming from or returning to the main army's position a league to the southwest.

Murillio sat with his back to one of the Rhivi wagon's solid wood wheels, eyes closed.

They opened upon the councillor's arrival.

'How does she fare?' Coll asked, crouching down beside him.

'It is exhausting,' Murillio replied. 'To see her suffer those nightmares – they are endless. Tell me the news.'

'Well, Kruppe and Silverfox haven't been seen since yesterday; nor have those two marines Whiskeyjack had guarding the Mhybe's daughter. As for the battle . . .' Coll looked away, squinting southwestward. 'It was short-lived. Anomander Rake assumed his Soletaken form. A single pass dispersed the Tenescowri. Anaster was captured, and, uh, the mages in his service were . . . executed.'

'Sounds unpleasant,' Murillio commented.

'By all reports it was. In any case, the peasants are fleeing back to Capustan, where I doubt they will be much welcome. It's a sad fate indeed for those poor bastards.'

'She's been forgotten, hasn't she?'

Coll did not need to ask for elaboration. 'A hard thing to swallow, but aye, it does seem that way.'

'Outlived her usefulness, and so discarded.'

'I cling to a faith that this is a tale not yet done, Murillio.'

'We are the witnesses. Here to oversee the descent.

Naught else, Coll. Kruppe's assurances are nothing but wind. And you and I, we are prisoners of this unwelcome circumstance – as much as she is, as much as that addled Rhivi woman who comes by to comb her hair.'

Coll slowly swung to study his old friend. 'What do you suggest we do?' he asked.

Shrugging, Murillio growled, 'What do most prisoners do sooner or later?'

'They try to escape.'

'Aye.'

Coll said nothing for a long moment, then he sighed. 'And how do you propose we do that? Would you just leave her? Alone, untended—'

'Of course not. No, we take her with us.'

'Where?'

'I don't know! Anywhere! So long as it's away.'

'And how far will she need to go to escape those nightmares?'

'We need only find someone willing to help her, Coll. Someone who does not judge a life by expedience and potential usefulness.'

'This is an empty plain, Murillio.'

'I know.'

'Whereas, in Capustan . . .'

The younger man's eyes narrowed. 'By all accounts, it's little more than rubble.'

'There are survivors. Including priests.'

'Priests!' he snorted. 'Self-serving confidence artists, swindlers of the gullible, deceivers of—'

'Murillio, there are exceptions to that—'

'I've yet to see one.'

'Perhaps this time. My point is, if we're to escape this – with her – we've a better chance of finding help in Capustan than out here in this wasteland.'

'Saltoan—'

'Is a week or more away, longer with this wagon. Besides, the city is Hood's crusted navel incarnate. I wouldn't take Rallick Nom's axe-wielding mother to Saltoan.'

Murillio sighed. 'Rallick Nom.'

'What of him?'

'I wish he were here.'

'Why?'

'So he could kill someone. Anyone. The man's a wonder at simplifying matters.'

Coll grunted a laugh. '"Simplifying matters." Wait until I tell him that one. Hey, Rallick, you're not an assassin, you know, you're just a man who simplifies.'

'Well, it's a moot point in any case, since he disappeared.'

'He's not dead.'

'How do you know?'

'I just know. So, Murillio, do we wait until Capustan?'

'Agreed. And once there, we follow the example of Kruppe and Silverfox. We slip away. Vanish. Hood knows, I doubt anyone will notice, much less care.'

Coll hesitated, then said, 'Murillio, if we find someone – someone who can do something for the Mhybe – well, it's likely to be expensive.'

The man shrugged. 'I've been in debt before.'

'As have I. So long as it's understood that this will likely mean our financial ruin, and all that might be achieved is a kinder end to her life.'

'A worthwhile exchange, then.'

Coll did not ask for another affirmation of his friend's resolve. He knew Murillio too well for that. *Aye, it's naught but coin, isn't it? No matter the amount, a fair exchange to ease an old woman's suffering. One way or the other. For at least we will have cared – even if she never again awakens and thus knows nothing of what we do. Indeed, it is perhaps better that way. Cleaner. Simpler . . .*

The howl echoed as if from a vast cavern. Echoed, folded in on itself until the mourning call became a chorus. Bestial voices in countless numbers, voices that stripped away the sense of time itself, that made eternity into a single now.

The voices of winter.

Yet they came from the south, from the place where the tundra could go no further; where the trees were no longer ankle-high, but rose, still ragged, wind-torn and spindly, over her head, so that she could pass unseen – no longer towering above the landscape.

Kin answered that howl. The pursuing beasts, still on her trail, yet losing her now, as she slipped among the black spruce, the boggy ground sucking hungrily at her bare feet, the black-stained water swirling thick and turgid as she waded chill pools. Huge mosquitoes swarmed her, each easily twice the size of those she knew on the Rhivi Plain. Blackflies crawled in her hair, bit her scalp. Round leeches like black spots covered her limbs.

In her half-blind flight she had stumbled into a spatulate antler, jammed in the crotch of two trees at eye-level. The gouge a tine had made under her right cheek still trickled blood.

It is my death that approaches. That gives me strength. I draw from that final moment, and now they cannot catch me.

They cannot catch me.

The cavern lay directly ahead. She could not yet see it, and there was nothing in the landscape to suggest a geology natural to caves, but the echoing howl was closer.

The beast calls to me. A promise of death, I think, for it gives me this strength. It is my siren call—

Darkness drew down around her, and she knew she had arrived. The cavern was a shaping of a soul, a soul lost within itself.

The air was damp and cool. No insects buzzed or lit on her skin. The stone under the soles of her feet was dry.

She could see nothing, and the howl had fallen silent.

When she stepped forward she knew it was her mind that moved, her mind alone, leaving her body, questing out, seeking that chained beast.

'Who?'

The voice startled her. A man's voice, muffled, taut with pain.

'Who comes?'

She did not know how to answer, and simply spoke the first words that came into her head. 'It is I.'

'I?'

'A – a mother . . .'

The man's laugh grated harshly. 'Another game, then? You've no words, Mother. You've never had them. You've whimpers and cries, you've warning growls, you've a hundred thousand wordless sounds to describe your need – that is your voice and I know it well.'

'A mother.'

'Leave me. I am beyond taunting. I circle my own chain, here in my mind. This place is not for you. Perhaps, in finding it, you think you've defeated my last line of defence. You think you now know all of me. But you've no power here. Do you know, I imagine seeing my own face, as if in a mirror.

'But it's the wrong eye – the wrong eye staring back at me. And worse, it's not even human. It took me a long time to understand, but now I do.

'You and your kind played with winter. Omtose Phellack. But you never understood it. Not true winter, not the winter that is not sorcery, but born of the cooling earth, the dwindling sun, the shorter days and longer nights. The face I see before me, Seer, it is winter's face. A wolf's. A god's.'

'My child knows wolves,' *the Mhybe said.*

'He does indeed.'

'Not he. She. I have a daughter—'

'Confusing the rules defeats the game, Seer. Sloppy—'

'I am not who you think I am. I am – I am an old woman. Of the Rhivi. And my daughter wishes to see me dead. But not a simple passage, not for me. No. She's sent wolves after me. To rend my soul. They hunt my dreams – but here, I have escaped them. I've come here to escape.'

The man laughed again. 'The Seer has made this my prison. And I know it to be so. You are the lure of madness, of

819

strangers' voices in my head. I defy you. Had you known of my real mother, you might have succeeded, but your rape of my mind was ever incomplete. There is a god here, Seer, crouched before my secrets. Fangs bared. Not even your dear mother, who holds me so tight, dares challenge him. As for your Omtose Phellack – he would have confronted you at that warren's gate long ago. He would have denied it to you, Jaghut. To all of you. But he was lost. Lost. And know this, I am helping him. I am helping him to find himself. He's growing aware, Seer.'

'I do not understand you,' the Mhybe replied, faltering as despair slowly stole through her. This was not the place she had believed it to be. She had indeed fled to another person's prison, a place of personal madness. 'I came here for death—'

'You'll not find it, not in these leathery arms.'

'I am fleeing my daughter—'

'Flight is an illusion. Even Mother here comprehends that. She knows I am not her child, yet she cannot help herself. She even possesses memories, of a time when she was a true Matron, a mother to a real brood. Children who loved her, and other children – who betrayed her. And left her to suffer for eternity.

'She never anticipated an escape from that. Yet when she found herself free at last, it was to discover that her world had turned to dust. Her children were long dead, entombed in their barrows – for without a mother, they withered and died. She looked to you, then, Seer. Her adopted son. And showed you your power, so that she could use it. To recreate her world. She raised her dead children. She set them to rebuilding the city. But it was all false, the delusion could not deceive her, could only drive her mad.

'And that,' he continued, 'is when you usurped her. Thus, her child has made her a prisoner once more. There is no escaping the paths of our lives, it seems. A truth you're not prepared to face, Seer. Not yet.'

'My child has made me a prisoner as well,' the Mhybe whispered. 'Is this the curse of all mothers?'

820

'It is the curse of love.'

A faint howl rang through the dark air.

'Hear that?' the man asked. 'That is my mate. She's coming. I looked for so long. For so long. And now, she's coming.'

The voice had acquired a deeper timbre with these words. It seemed to be no longer the man's voice.

'And now,' the words continued, 'now, I answer.'

His howl tore through her, flung her mind back. Out of the cavern, out beyond the straggly forests, back onto the tundra's barren plain.

The Mhybe screamed.

Her wolves answered. Triumphantly.

They had found her once again.

A hand touched her cheek. 'Gods, that was blood-curdling.'

A familiar voice, but she could not yet place it.

Another man spoke, 'There is more to this than we comprehend, Murillio. Look at her cheek.'

'She has clawed herself—'

'She cannot lift her arms, friend. And look, the nails are clean. She did not inflict this wound on herself.'

'Then who did? I've been here all this time. Not even the old Rhivi woman has visited since I last looked upon her – and there was no wound then.'

'As I said, there is a mystery here . . .'

'Coll, I don't like this. Those nightmares – could they be real? Whatever pursues her in her dreams – are they able to physically damage her?'

'We see the evidence—'

'Aye, though I scarce believe my own eyes. Coll, this cannot go on.'

'Agreed, Murillio. First chance in Capustan . . .'

'The very first. Let's move the wagon to the very front of the line – the sooner we reach the streets the better.'

'As you say.'

821

CHAPTER TWENTY

It is a most ancient tale. Two gods from before the time
of men and women. Longing and love and loss, the beasts
doomed to wander through the centuries.

A tale of mores, told with the purpose of no resolution.
Its meaning, gentle readers, lies not in a soul-warming
conclusion, but in all that is unattainable in this world.

Who then could have imagined such closure?

Winter's Love
Silbaratha

The heart of the vast palace lay buried in the cliff.
Seas born to the east of the bay battered the cliff's
jagged hooves, lifting spray to darken the rockface.
Immediately beyond the broken shore's rough spars, the
waters of Coral Bay pitched into inky blackness, fathoms
deep. The city's harbour was little more than a narrow,
crooked cut on the lee side of the cliff, a depthless fissure
that opened a split nearly bisecting the city. It was a
harbour without docks. The sheer faces of the sides had
been carved into long piers, surmounted by causeways. At
high tide level, mooring rings had been driven into
the living stone. Broad sweeps of thick netting, twice the
height of an ocean trader's masts, spanned the entire
breadth of water from the harbour's mouth all the way to its
apex. Where no tethered anchor could touch the fjord's
bottom, and where the shores themselves offered no strand,

no shallows whatsoever, a ship's anchors were drawn upward. The cat-men, as they were called – that strange, almost tribal collection of workers who lived with their wives and children in shacks on the netting and whose sole profession was the winching of anchors and the tethering of sway-lines – had made of the task artistry in motion.

From the wide, sea-facing battlement of the palace, the sealskin-roofed huts and driftwood sheds of the cat-men were like a scattering of brown pebbles and beach detritus, snagged on netting that was thread-like with distance. No figures scampered between the structures. No smoke rose from the angled hood-chimneys. Had he an eagle's eye, Toc the Younger would have had no trouble seeing the salt-dried bodies tangled here and there in the netting; as it was, he could only take the Seerdomin's word for it that those small, bedraggled smudges were indeed corpses.

The trader ships no longer came to Coral. The cat-men had starved. Every man, every woman, every child. A legendary and unique people within the city had become extinct.

The observation had been delivered in a detached tone, but Toc sensed an undercurrent in the nameless warrior-priest's words. The huge man stood close, one hand gripping Toc's left arm above the elbow. To keep him from flinging himself from the cliff. To keep him standing upright. What had begun as one task had quickly become the other. This reprieve from the clutches of the Matron was but temporary. The Malazan's broken body had no strength left within it. Muscles had atrophied. Warped bones and seized joints gave him the flexibility of dry wood. His lungs were filled with fluid, making his drawn breath a wheeze, his exhalation a milky gurgle.

The Seer had wanted him to see. Coral. The palace fortress – often assailed, by Elingarth warships and pirate fleets, never taken. His vast cordon of mages, the thousand or more K'Chain Che'Malle K'ell Hunters, the elite legions of his main army. The defeats to the north meant little to him; indeed, he would yield Setta, Lest and Maurik; he would leave the invaders to their long, exhausting march – through scorched lands that offered no sustenance; where even the wells had been fouled. As for the enemies to the south, there was now a vast stretch of rough sea to impede their progress – a sea the Seer had filled with shattered mountains of ice. There were no boats to be found on the far shore in any case. A journey to the western end of Ortnal Cut would take months. True, the T'lan Imass could cross the water, as wave-borne dust. But it would have to fight the fierce currents the entire way, currents that plunged into the depths on cold streams, that swept in submerged rivers eastward, out into the ocean.

The Seer was well satisfied, said the nameless Seerdomin. Pleased enough to yield Toc this momentary mercy. Out from his Mother's arms.

The chill, salty wind whipped at his face, tugged at his ragged, long, dirty hair. His clothes were little more than crusted strips – the Seerdomin had given him his cloak, which Toc had wrapped about himself like a blanket. It had been this gesture that had hinted to the Malazan that the man at his side still possessed a shred of humanity.

The discovery had brought water to his eyes.

Clarity had been reborn within him, aided by the Seerdomin's detailed account of the battles to the south. Perhaps it was insanity's final, most convincing delusion, but Toc clung to it none the less. He stared southward across the wind-whipped seas. The mountainous shoreline on the far side was barely visible.

They had surely reached it by now. They might well be standing on the beach, staring bleakly towards him, and all that lay in between. Baaljagg would not be discouraged. A goddess hid within her, driving ever onward, ever onward, to find her mate.

The mate who hides within me. We'd travelled, side by side, all unknowing of the secrets within each other. Ah, such brutal irony . . .

And perhaps Tool would not be daunted. Time and distance meant nothing to the T'lan Imass. The same, no doubt, was true for the three Seguleh – they still had their singular message to deliver, after all. Their people's invitation to war.

But Lady Envy . . .

Mistress of adventure, seduced by serendipity – true, she was angry, now. That much was clear from the Seerdomin's reportage. Affronted was a better description, Toc corrected. Sufficient to see her temper flare, but that temper was not a driven thing. She was not one to smoulder, not one to kindle deep-bedded fires of vengeance. She existed for distraction, for wayward whims.

Lady Envy, and likely her wounded, hurting dog, Garath, would turn away now, at last. Tired of the hunt, they would not set to themselves the task of pursuit, not across this violent sea with its glowing, awash leviathans of jagged ice.

He told himself not to be disappointed, but a pang of sadness twisted within him at the thought. He missed her, not as a woman – not precisely, in any case. *No, the immortal face she presents, I think. Unburdened, a trickster's glint to her millennial regard. I teased her, once . . . danced around that nature . . . made her stamp her foot and frown. As only an immortal could do when the unlikely brunt of such mocking. I turned the knife. Gods, did I truly possess such audacity?*

Well, dear Lady, I humbly apologize, now. I am not the brave man I once was, if it was indeed bravery and not simple stupidity. Mocking's been taken from my nature. Never to return, and perhaps that's a good thing. Ah, I can see you nod most wholeheartedly at that. Mortals should not mock, for all the obvious reasons. Detachment belongs to gods, because only they can afford its price. So be it.

Thank you, Lady Envy. No recriminations will pursue you. It was well run.

'You should have seen Coral in its day, Malazan.'

'It was your home, wasn't it?'

'Aye. Though my home now is in the heart of my Seer.'

'Where the winds are even colder,' Toc muttered.

The Seerdomin was silent for a moment.

Toc was expecting a blow from a gauntleted fist, or a painful wrench from the hand gripping his frail arm. Either one would have been an appropriate response; either one would have elicited an approving nod from the Seer. Instead, the man said, 'This is a summer day, but not like the summer days I remember in my youth. Coral's wind was warm. Soft, caressing as a lover's breath. My father, he fished out beyond the cut. Up along the coast north of here. Vast, rich shoals. He'd be gone for a week or more with every season's run. We'd all go down to the causeway to watch the fleets return, to see our father's orange sail among the barques.'

Toc glanced up at the man, saw the smile, the glimmering echo of a child's joy in his eyes.

Saw them die once more.

'He came back the last time . . . to find that his family had embraced the Faith. His wife, to the Tenescowri. His sons, to the ranks, eldest begun schooling as Seerdomin. He did not throw his lines to me on that day – seeing my uniform. Seeing my mother – hearing her mindless shrieks. Seeing my brothers with spears in hand, my sisters naked and clinging to men thrice their age. No, he swung the boom, tacked onto the offshore breeze.

'I watched his sail until I could see it no more. It was my way, Malazan—'

'Of saying goodbye,' Toc whispered.

'Of saying good luck. Of saying . . . well done.'

Destroyer of lives. Seer, how could you have done this to your people?

A distant bell rang in the palace behind them.

The Seerdomin's grip tightened. 'The allotted time is done.'

'Back to my own embrace,' Toc said, his gaze straining to catch, one last time, the world before him. *Remember this, for you will not see it again, Toc the Younger.*

826

'Thank you for the use of your cloak,' he said.

'You are welcome, Malazan. These winds were once warm. Come, lean on me while we walk – your weight is as nothing.'

They slowly made their way towards the building. 'Easily borne, you mean.'

'I did not say that, Malazan. I did not say that.'

The gutted tenement seemed to shiver a moment before collapsing in a cloud of dust. The cobbles of the street trembled beneath Shield Anvil Itkovian's boots and thunder shook the air.

Hedge turned to him, grinning through the smears of soot. 'See? Easy.'

Itkovian answered the Bridgeburner with a nod, watched as Hedge rejoined his fellow sappers and they set off for the next unrecoverable building.

'At the very least,' Captain Norul said beside him as she brushed dust from her surcoat, 'there will be no shortage of material.'

The morning was hot, the sun bright. Life was returning to Capustan. People with scarves covering their faces crawled through the rubble of their homes. Bodies were still being retrieved as wreckage was cleared away, wrapped and thrown onto fly-swarmed wagons. The air of the street stank with decay, but it seemed that the horses they rode had long since grown used to it.

'We should proceed, sir,' the captain said.

They resumed their journey. Beyond the west gate were gathering the official representatives – the contingent that would set out to meet the approaching armies of Dujek Onearm and Caladan Brood. The parley was set to take place in three bells' time.

Itkovian had left the company's new Destriant in command. Tenescowri refugees were arriving from the plain by the hundreds. Those few who'd attempted to enter Capustan had been set upon by the survivors. Reports of peasants being torn apart by frenzied mobs had reached the Shield Anvil. In response he had sent the Grey Swords out to establish an internment camp outside the west wall. Food was scarce. Itkovian wondered how his new Destriant was managing. At the very least, shelters were being prepared for the hapless refugees.

Who will soon become recruits. Those who survive the next few weeks in any case. It's likely the Grey Swords' coffers will be emptied purchasing food and supplies from the Barghast. Fener grant – no, Togg grant that the investment will prove worthwhile.

He was not looking forward to the parley. Indeed, the truth was, he had no real business attending it. The captain at his side was now the commander of the Grey Swords. His role as her adviser was dubious; she was capable of representing the company's interests without any help from him.

They approached the west gate, which now resembled nothing more than a massive hole in the city's wall.

Leaning against one of the burnt-out, most fallen gate-towers, Gruntle watched them with a half-grin on his barbed face. Stonny Menackis paced nearby, apparently in a temper.

'Now there's only Humbrall Taur to wait for,' Gruntle said.

Itkovian frowned as he reined in. 'Where is the Mask Council's retinue?'

Stonny spat. 'They've gone ahead. Seems they want a private chat first.'

'Relax, lass,' Gruntle rumbled. 'Your friend Keruli's with them, right?'

'That's not the point! They *hid*. While you and the Grey Swords here kept them and their damned city alive!'

'None the less,' Itkovian said, 'with Prince Jelarkan dead and no heir apparent, they are Capustan's ruling body.'

'And they could damn well have waited!'

Captain Norul twisted in her saddle to look back up the avenue. 'Humbrall Taur's coming. Perhaps, if we rode fast enough, we could catch them.'

'Is it important?' Itkovian asked her.

'Sir, it is.'

He nodded. 'I concur.'

'Let's ready our horses, Stonny,' Gruntle said, pushing himself from the wall.

They set out across the plain, Humbrall Taur, Hetan and Cafal equally awkward on their borrowed mounts. The Barghast had been none too pleased by the Mask Council's attempted usurpation – old enmities and mistrust had flared to life once more. By all reports, the approaching armies were still a league, perhaps two, distant. Keruli, Rath'Hood, Rath'Burn and Rath'Shadowthrone were in a carriage, drawn by the three horses of the Gidrath that had not been butchered and eaten during the siege.

Itkovian recalled the last time he had ridden this road, recalled faces of soldiers now dead. Farakalian, Torun, Sidlis. Behind the formality imposed by the Reve, these had been his friends. *A truth I dared not approach. Not as Shield Anvil, not as a commander. But that has changed. They are my own grief, as difficult to bear as those tens of thousands of others.*

He pushed the thought away. Control was still necessary. He could afford no emotions.

They came within sight of the priests' carriage.

Stonny snarled in triumph. 'Won't they be delighted!'

'Ease on the gloating, lass,' Gruntle advised. 'We reach them now in all innocence—'

'Do you think me an idiot? Do you think me incapable of subtlety? I'll have you know—'

'All right, woman,' her companion growled. 'Forget I spoke—'

'I always do, Gruntle.'

The Gidrath driver drew the carriage to a halt as they rode up. A window shutter slid to one side and Rath' Shadowthrone's masked face appeared, the expression neutral. 'How fortunate! The rest of our honourable entourage!'

Itkovian sighed under his breath. *There was nothing subtle in that tone, alas.*

'Honourable?' Stonny queried, brows lifting, 'I'm surprised you recognize the concept, Priest.'

'Ah.' The mask swivelled to her. 'Master Keruli's wench. Shouldn't you be on your knees?'

'I'll give you a knee, runt – right between the—'

'Well now!' Gruntle said loudly. 'We're all here. I see outriders ahead. Shall we proceed?'

'We're early,' Rath'Shadowthrone snapped.

'Aye, and that's unfortunately unprofessional of us. Never mind. We can continue at the slowest pace possible, to give them time to prepare.'

'A wise course, in the circumstances,' Rath' Shadowthrone conceded. The mask's hinged lips twisted into a broad smile, then the head withdrew and the shutter slid back in place.

'I am going to cut that man into very small pieces,' Stonny said in a bright tone.

'We all appreciated your sense of subtlety, lass,' Gruntle muttered.

'And well you should, oaf.'

Itkovian stared at the woman, then at the caravan captain, wondering.

Corporal Picker sat on the dusty steps of what had once been a temple. Her back and shoulders ached from throwing chunks of masonry since dawn.

Blend must have been hovering nearby for she appeared with a waterskin. 'You look thirsty.'

Picker accepted it. 'Funny how you do your vanishing act whenever there's hard work to be done.'

'Well, I brought you water, didn't I?'

Picker scowled.

Across the street Captain Paran and Quick Ben were saddling horses, preparing to head out to the reunion with Onearm's Host and Brood's army. They'd been uncommonly cosy since meeting up once more, making Picker suspicious. Quick Ben's schemes were never pleasant.

'I'd rather we were all going,' she muttered.

'To the parley? Why? This way everyone else does the walking.'

'Easier to be lurking about, is it? Weighed down with a half-full waterskin. You'd be saying different if you'd been tossing rocks with the rest of us, Blend.'

The lean woman shrugged. 'I've been busy enough.'

'Doing what?'

'Gathering information.'

'Oh yeah. Whose whispering you been listening in on, then?'

'People. Us and them, here and there.'

'Them? Who's *them*?'

'Uhm, let's see. Barghast. Grey Swords. A couple of loose-lipped Gidrath from the Thrall. Three acolytes from the temple behind you—'

Picker flinched, swiftly rose to cast a nervous eye on the fire-scorched building behind her. 'Which god, Blend? No lies—'

'Why would I lie, Corporal? Shadowthrone.'

Picker grunted. 'Spyin' on the sneaks, was you? And what were they talking about?'

'Some bizarre plan of their master's. Vengeance against a couple of necromancers holed up in an estate just up the street.'

'The one with all the bodies out front and the smelly guards on the walls?'

'Presumably the same and none other.'

'All right, so let's hear the report on the rest of them.'

'The Barghast are crowing. Agents of the Mask Council are buying food to feed the citizens. The Grey Swords are buying food, too, to feed a fast-growing camp of Tenescowri refugees outside the city. The White Faces are getting rich.'

'Hold on, Blend. Did you say Tenescowri refugees? What

are the Grey Swords up to? Hood knows there's enough corpses lying around for those cannibals, why give 'em *real* food? Why feed the evil bastards at all?'

'Sound questions,' Blend agreed. 'Certainly, I admit my own curiosity was piqued.'

'No doubt you've come up with a theory, too.'

'I have assembled the puzzle, to be more precise. Disparate facts. Observances. Offhand comments believed to be uttered in private, overheard by none other than the faithful servant standing before you—'

'Oponn's quivering knees, woman, get on with it!'

'You never did appreciate a good gloat. All right. The Grey Swords were sworn to Fener. They weren't just a mercenary company, more like damned crusaders to the holy cause of war. And they took it seriously. Only something's happened. They've lost their god—'

'No doubt there's a tale there.'

'Indeed, but it's not relevant.'

'Meaning you don't know it.'

'Precisely. The point is, the company's surviving officers rode off to the Barghast camps, found a gaggle of tribal witches waiting for them, and together they all arranged a reconsecration.'

'You mean they switched gods. Oh no, don't tell me Treach—'

'No, not Treach. Treach already has his crusaders.'

'Oh, right. Must be Jhess, then. Mistress of Weaving. They're all taking up knitting, but fiercely—'

'Not quite. Togg. And Fanderay, the She-Wolf of Winter – Togg's long lost mate. Recall the story? You must have heard it when you were a child, assuming you were ever a child—'

'Careful, Blend.'

'Sorry. Anyway, the Grey Swords were virtually wiped out. They're looking for recruits.'

Picker's brows rose. 'The Tenescowri? Hood's breath!'

'Makes sense, actually.'

832

'Sure. If I needed an army I'd look first to people who eat each other when things get tough. Absolutely. In an instant.'

'Well, that's an unfortunate angle to take. It's more a question of finding people with no lives—'

'Losers, you mean.'

'Uh, yes. No ties, no loyalties. Ripe for arcane rituals of induction.'

Picker grunted again. 'Mad. Everyone's gone mad.'

'Speaking of which,' Blend murmured.

Captain Paran and Quick Ben rode up.

'Corporal Picker.'

'Aye, Captain?'

'Do you know where Spindle is right now?'

'No idea, sir.'

'I'd suggest you keep better track of your squad, then.'

'Well, he went off with Sergeant Antsy. Someone's come up from the tunnels, claiming to be Prince Arard – some dispossessed ruler from one of the cities south of the river. The man was demanding to speak with a representative of Onearm's Host and since we couldn't find you at the time . . .'

Paran cursed under his breath. 'Let me get this straight. Sergeant Antsy and Spindle elected themselves to be Onearm's Host's official representatives to take audience with a prince? Antsy? *Spindle?*'

Beside the captain, Quick Ben choked back a laugh, earning a glare from Paran.

'Detoran volunteered, too,' Picker added in an innocent tone. 'So it was the three of them, I think. Maybe a few others.'

'Mallet?'

She shook her head. 'He's with Hedge, sir. Tending to healing and whatever.'

'Captain,' Quick Ben interjected. 'We'd best start our journey. Antsy will stall as soon as he gets confused, and he usually gets confused immediately after the making of introductions. Detoran won't say a thing and likely none of the others will, either. Spindle might babble, but he's wearing a hairshirt. It should be all right.'

'Really? And shall I hold you to that, Wizard?'

Quick Ben's eyes widened.

'Never mind,' Paran growled, gathering his reins. 'Let's quit this city . . . before we find ourselves in a whole new war. Corporal Picker.'

'Sir?'

'Why are you just standing here on your own?'

She quickly glanced around. 'The bitch,' she whispered.

'Corporal?'

'Nothing. Sorry, sir. I was just resting.'

'When you're done resting, Corporal, go retrieve Antsy, Spindle and the others. Send Arard to the Thrall, with word that the real representatives of Onearm's Host will see him shortly, should he wish an audience.'

'Understood, Captain.'

'I hope so.'

She watched the two men ride off down the street, then spun around. 'Where are you, you coward?'

'Sir?' Blend queried, emerging from the shadows of the temple's entrance.

'You heard me.'

'I'd noted something inside this hovel, went to investigate—'

'Hovel? Shadowthrone's sacred abode, you mean.'

She was pleased to see Blend suddenly pale. 'Oh. I'd, uh, forgotten.'

'You panicked. Hee hee. Blend panicked. Smelled a scene about to happen and fled into the nearest building like a rabbit down a bolt-hole! Just wait until I tell the others—'

'An unseemly version,' Blend sniffed, 'malignly twisting a purely coincidental occurrence. They'll not believe you.'

'That's what you—'

'Oh oh.'

Blend vanished once again.

Startled, Picker looked round.

Two black-cloaked figures were coming down the street, making directly for the corporal.

'Dear soldier,' the taller, pointy-bearded one called out.

Her hackles rose at the imperious tone. 'What?'

A thin brow arched. 'Respect is accorded ourselves, woman. We demand no less. Now listen. We are in need of supplies to effect the resumption of our journey. We require food, clean water and plenty of it, and if you could direct us to a clothier . . .'

'At once. Here—' She stepped up to him and drove her gauntleted fist full into his face. The man's feet flew out from under him and he struck the cobbles with a meaty smack. Out cold.

Blend stepped up behind the other man and cracked him in the head with the pommel of her short sword. With a high-pitched grunt, he crumpled.

Closing fast behind them was an old man in ragged servant garb. He skidded to a halt five paces away and raised his hands. 'Don't hit me!' he shrieked.

Picker frowned. 'Now why would we do that? Are these two . . . yours?'

The manservant's expression was despondent. 'Aye,' he sighed, lowering his hands.

'Advise them,' Picker said, 'of proper forms of address. When they awaken.'

'Absolutely, sir.'

'We should get moving, Corporal,' Blend said, eyes on the two unconscious men.

'Yes. Yes, please!' the manservant begged.

Picker shrugged. 'I see no point in dawdling. Lead on, soldier.'

Paran and Quick Ben rode within a thousand paces of the Tenescowri encampment, which lay north of the road, on their right. Neither man spoke until they were well past, then the captain sighed. 'That looks to be trouble fast approaching.'

'Oh? Why?'

Paran shot his companion a startled glance, then returned his gaze to the road. 'The lust for vengeance against those peasants. The Capans might well swarm out through the gate and slaughter them, with the Mask Council's blessing.' *And why, Wizard, do I think I see something out of the corner of my eye? There, on your shoulder. Then, when I look more closely, it's gone.*

'That'd be a mistake for the Mask Council,' Quick Ben commented. 'The Grey Swords looked ready to defend their guests, if those pickets and trenches were any indication.'

'Aye, they're anticipating becoming very unpopular, with what they're now up to.'

'Recruiting. Then again, why not? That mercenary company paid a high price defending the city and its citizens.'

'The memory of their heroic efforts could vanish in an eye's wink, Wizard. There's only a few hundred Grey Swords left, besides. Should a few thousand Capans charge them—'

'I wouldn't worry, Captain. Even the Capans – no matter how enraged – would hesitate before crossing those soldiers. They're the ones who survived, after all. As I said, the Mask Council would be foolish to hold the grudge. We'll discover more at the parley, no doubt.'

'Assuming we're invited. Quick Ben, we'd do better with a private conversation with Whiskeyjack. I personally have very little to say to most of the others who will be present. I have a report to deliver, in any case.'

'Oh, I wasn't planning on speaking at the parley, Captain. Just listening.'

They had left the occupied areas behind and now rode down an empty road, the rolling plain stretching out on their right, the bluffs marking the river three hundred paces distant on their left.

'I see riders,' Quick Ben said. 'North.'

Paran squinted, then nodded. 'It's happened.'

'What has?'

'The Second Gathering.'

The wizard shot him a glance. 'The T'lan Imass? How do you know?'

Because she's stopped reaching out to me. Tattersail, Nightchill, Bellurdan – something's happened. Something . . . unexpected. And it's left them reeling. 'I just know, Wizard. Silverfox is the lead rider.'

'Your vision must be as a hawk's.'

Paran said nothing. *I don't need eyes. She's coming.*

'Captain, does Tattersail's soul still dominate within Silverfox?'

'I don't know,' he admitted. 'All I will say, however, is that whatever faith we held to that we could predict Silverfox's actions should now be dispensed with.'

'What has she become, then?'

'A Bonecaster in truth.'

They reined in to wait for the four riders. Kruppe's mule seemed to be competing for the lead position, the short-legged beast slipping between a frenzied trot and a canter, the round Daru wobbling and bouncing atop the saddle. Two Malazan marines rode behind Silverfox and Kruppe, looking relaxed.

'Would that I had seen,' Quick Ben murmured, 'what her companions had seen.'

Yet nothing went as planned. I can see that in her posture – the bridled anger, the diffidence – and, buried deep, pain. She's surprised them. Surprised, and defied. And the T'lan Imass have answered in an equally unexpected way. Even Kruppe looks off-balanced, and not just by that pitching mule.

Silverfox was staring at him as she drew rein, an expression that Paran could not define. *As I had sensed, she's thrown up a wall between us – gods, but she looks like Tattersail! A woman, now. No longer the child. And the illusion of years spanning our parting is complete – she's become guarded, a possessor of secrets that as a child she would not have hesitated to reveal. Hood's breath, every time we meet it seems I must readjust . . . everything.*

Quick Ben spoke, 'Well met. Silverfox, what—'

'No.'

'Excuse me?'

'No, Wizard. I have no explanations that I am prepared to voice. No questions that I will answer. Kruppe has already tried, too many times. My temper is short – do not test it.'

Guarded, and harder. Much, much harder.

After a moment, Quick Ben shrugged. 'Be that way, then.'

'I *am* that way,' she snapped. 'The anger you would face is Nightchill's, and the rest of us will do nothing to restrain it. I trust I am understood.'

Quick Ben simply grinned. Cold, challenging.

'Kind sirs!' Kruppe cried. 'By chance would you be riding to our fair armies? If so, we would accompany you, delighted and relieved to return to said martial bosom. Delighted indeed, with the formidable company of your-selves. Relieved, as Kruppe has said, by the welcoming destination so closely pending. Impatient, it must be admitted, for the resumption of the journey. Incorrigibly optimistic—'

'That will do, Kruppe,' Silverfox growled.

'Ahem, of course.'

If anything truly existed between us, it is now over. She has left Tattersail behind. She is indeed a Bonecaster, now. The realization triggered a weaker pang of loss than he had expected. *Perhaps we both have moved on. The pressure of what we have grown into, our hearts cannot overcome.*

So be it. No self-pity. Not this time. We've tasks before us.

Paran gathered his reins. 'As Kruppe has said. Let us resume – we're already late as it is.'

A large sheet of burlap had been raised over the hilltop to

shield the parley from the hot afternoon sun. Malazan soldiers ringed the hill in a protective cordon, crossbows cradled in their arms.

Eyes on the figures beneath the tarp, Itkovian halted his horse and dismounted a dozen paces from the guards. The Mask Council's carriage had also stopped, the side-doors swinging open to the four representatives of Capustan.

Hetan had clambered down from her horse with a relieved grunt and now came alongside Itkovian. She thumped his back. 'I've missed you, wolf!'

'The wolves may be all around me, sir,' Itkovian said, 'but I make no such claim for myself.'

'The tale's run through the clans,' Hetan said, nodding. 'Old women never shut up.'

'And young women?' he asked, still studying the figures on the hilltop.

'Now you dance on danger, dear man.'

'Forgive me if I offended.'

'I would forgive you a smile no matter its reason. Aye, not likely. If you've humour you hide it far too well. This is too bad.'

He regarded her. 'Too bad? Do you not mean tragic?'

Her eyes narrowed, then she hissed in frustration and set off up the slope.

Itkovian watched her for a moment, then shifted his attention to the priests who were now gathered beside the carriage. Rath'Shadowthrone was complaining.

'They would have us all winded! A gentler slope and we could have stayed in the carriage—'

'Sufficient horses and we might have done the same,' Rath'Hood sniffed. 'This is calculated to insult—'

'It is nothing of the sort, comrades,' Keruli murmured. 'Even now, swarms of biting insects begin their assault upon our fair selves. I suggest you cease complaining and accompany me to the summit and its saving wind.' With that, the small, round-faced man set off.

'We should insist – ow!'

The three scrambled after Keruli, deer-flies buzzing their heads.

Humbrall Taur laughed. 'They need have only smeared themselves in bhederin grease!'

Gruntle replied, 'They're slippery enough as it is, Warchief. Besides, it's a far more fitting introduction for our visitors – three masked priests stumbling and puffing and waving at phantoms circling their heads. At least Keruli's showing some dignity, and he's probably the only one among them with a brain worthy of the name.'

'Thank the gods!' Stonny cried.

Gruntle turned to her. 'What? Why?'

'Well, you've just used up your entire store of words, oaf. Meaning you'll be silent for the rest of the day!'

The huge man's grin was far more feral than he intended.

Itkovian watched the two Daru set off, followed by Humbrall Taur, Hetan and Cafal.

Captain Norul said, 'Sir?'

'Do not wait for me,' he replied. 'You now speak for the Grey Swords, sir.'

She sighed, strode forward.

Itkovian slowly scanned the landscape. Apart from the cordon encircling the base of the hill, the two foreign armies were nowhere to be seen. There would be no blustery display of strength to intimidate the city's representatives – a generous gesture that might well be lost on the priests; which was unfortunate indeed, since Rath'Hood, Rath'Burn and Rath'Shadowthrone were in serious need of humbling.

Fly-bitten and winded would have to do.

He cast an appraising glance at the Malazan guards. Their weapons, he noted, were superbly crafted, if a little worn. The repairs and mending on their armour had been done in the field – this was an army a long way from home, a long way from resupply annexes. Dark-skinned faces beneath battered helms studied him in return, expressionless, perhaps curious that he had remained here, with only a silent Gidrath carriage-driver for company.

I am garbed as an officer. Misleading details, now. He drew off his gauntlets, reached up and removed the brooch denoting his rank, let it drop to the ground. He pulled free the grey sash tied about his waist and threw it to one side. Finally, he unstrapped his visored helm.

The soldier closest to him stepped forward then.

Itkovian nodded. 'I am amenable to an exchange, sir.'

'It would hardly be fair,' the man replied in broken Daru.

'Forgive me if I disagree. The silver inlay and gold crest may well suggest an ornamental function to my war-helm, but I assure you, the bronze and iron banding are of the highest quality, as are the cheek-guards and the webbing. Its weight is but a fraction more than the one you presently bear.'

The soldier was silent for a long moment, then he slowly unstrapped his camailed helm. 'When you change your mind—'

'I shall not.'

'Yes. Only, I was saying, when you change your mind, seek me out and not a single harsh thought to the return. I am named Azra Jael. Eleventh squad, fifth cohort, the third company of marines in Onearm's Host.'

'I am Itkovian . . . once a soldier of the Grey Swords.'

They made the exchange.

Itkovian studied the helm in his hands. 'Solidly fashioned. I am pleased.'

'Aren steel, sir. Hasn't needed hammering out once, so the metal's sound. The camail's Napan, yet to see a sword-cut.'

'Excellent. I am enriched by the exchange and so humbled.'

The soldier said nothing.

Itkovian looked up to the summit. 'Would they be offended, do you think, if I approached? I'll not venture an opinion, of course, but I would hear—'

The soldier seemed to be struggling against some strong emotion, but he shook his head. 'They would be honoured by your presence, sir.'

Itkovian half smiled. 'I think not. Besides, I'd rather they did not notice, if truth be told.'

'Swing round the hill, then. Come up from behind, sir.'

'Good idea. Thank you, sir, I will. And thank you, as well, for this fine helm.'

The man simply nodded.

Itkovian strode through the cordon, the soldiers to either side stepping back a measured pace to let him pass, then saluting as he did so.

Misplaced courtesy, but appreciated none the less.

He made his way to the hill's opposite side. The position revealed to him the two encamped armies to the west. Neither one was large, but both had been professionally established, the Malazan forces marked by four distinct but connected fortlets created by mounded ridges and steep-sided ditches. Raised trackways linked them.

I am impressed by these foreigners. And I must now conclude that Brukhalian was right – could we have held, these would have proved more than a match to Septarch Kulpath's numerically superior forces. They would have broken the siege, if we but could have held . . .

He began the ascent, the Malazan helm tucked under his left arm.

The wind was fierce near the summit, driving the insects away. Reaching the crest, Itkovian paused. The sun-tarp on its poles was fifteen paces directly ahead. On this, the back-side of the formal meeting place, sat a row of water casks and ornate crates bearing the sigil of the Trygalle Trade Guild – well recognizable as the traders had first become established in Elingarth, Itkovian's homeland. Eyes resting on that sigil, he felt proud on their behalf for their evident success.

A large table had been set up beneath the tarp, but everyone stood beyond it, under the sun, as if the formalities of introductions were not yet complete.

Perhaps there has already been a disagreement. Probably the Mask Council, voicing their complaints.

Itkovian angled to his left and walked quietly forward, intending to take position in the leeside of the tarp, close to the water casks.

Instead, a Malazan officer noticed him and leaned towards another man. A short exchange followed, then the other man, also a commander of the Malazans, slowly turned to study Itkovian.

A moment later everyone else was doing the same.

Itkovian halted.

A large warrior, hammer strapped to his back, stepped forward. 'The man we have been waiting to meet. You are Itkovian, Shield Anvil of the Grey Swords. Defender of Capustan. I am Caladan Brood—'

'Your pardon, sir, but I am no longer Shield Anvil, and no longer a soldier of the Grey Swords.'

'So we have been told. None the less, please come forward.'

Itkovian did not move. He studied the array of faces fixed on him. 'You would unveil my shame, sir.'

The warrior frowned. 'Shame?'

'Indeed. You called me the defender of Capustan, and in that I must accept the mocking title, for I did not defend Capustan. The Mortal Sword Brukhalian commanded that I hold the city until your arrival. I failed.'

No-one spoke. A half-dozen heartbeats passed.

Then Brood said, 'No mockery was intended. And you failed only because you could not win. Do you understand me, sir?'

Itkovian shrugged. 'I comprehend your argument, Caladan Brood, but I see little value in debating semantics. I would, if you so permit, stand to one side of these proceedings. I shall venture no comments or opinions, I assure you.'

'Then the loss is ours,' the warrior growled.

Itkovian glanced at his captain and was shocked to see her weathered cheeks streaked with tears.

'Would you have us argue your value, Itkovian?' Brood asked, his frown deepening.

'No.'

'Yet you feel that you have no worth here at this gathering.'

'It may be that I am not yet done, sir, but such responsibilities that I must one day embrace are mine to bear, and thus must be borne alone. I lead no-one, and so have no role in those discussions that are to be undertaken here. I would only listen. It is true that you have no cause to be generous—'

'Please,' Caladan Brood cut in. 'Enough. You are welcome, Itkovian.'

'Thank you.'

As if in silent agreement the dignitaries ended their immobility and approached the large, wooden table. The priests of the Mask Council sat themselves down at one end. Humbrall Taur, Hetan and Cafal took positions behind the chairs closest to them, making it clear that they would stand during the proceedings. Gruntle and Stonny sat opposite each other near the middle, the Grey Swords' new Shield Anvil beside the latter. Caladan Brood and the two Malazan commanders – one of them, Itkovian now saw, one-armed – sat down at the end opposite the priests. A tall, grey-haired warrior in full-length chain stood two paces behind Brood, on his left. A Malazan standard-bearer hovered behind his commanders to the right.

Cups were filled from a jug of watered wine, yet even before the task had been completed for everyone present, Rath'Hood was speaking.

'A more civilized location for this historic gathering would have been at the Thrall, the palace from which the rulers of Capustan govern—'

'Now that the prince is dead, you mean,' Stonny drawled, her lip curling. 'The place has no floor, in case you forgot, Priest.'

'You could call that a structural metaphor, couldn't you?' Gruntle asked her.

'You might, being an idiot.'

Rath'Hood tried again. 'As I was saying—'

'You weren't saying, you were posturing.'

'This wine is surprisingly good,' Keruli murmured. 'Given that this is a martial gathering, the location seems appropriate. I, for one, have a question or two for the commanders of the foreign army.'

The one-armed commander grunted, then said, 'Ask them.'

'Thank you, High Fist, I will. First of all, someone is missing, true? Are there not Tiste Andii among you? And their legendary leader, Anomander Rake, Lord of Moon's Spawn, should he not be present? Indeed, one wonders at the disposition of Moon's Spawn itself – the tactical advantages of such an edifice—'

'Pause there, if you will,' Brood interrupted. 'Your questions assume . . . much. I do not think we've advanced to point of discussing tactics. As far as we are concerned, Capustan is but a temporary stop in our march; its liberation by the Barghast was a strategic necessity, but only the first of what will doubtless be many in this war. Do you now suggest, High Priest, that you wish to contribute to the campaign in some direct fashion? It would seem that your primary concern at the moment is the rebuilding of your city.'

Keruli smiled. 'Thus, questions are exchanged, but as yet, no answers.'

Brood frowned. 'Anomander Rake and the majority of his Tiste Andii have returned to Moon's Spawn. They – and it – shall have a role in this war, but there will be no further elaboration on that subject.'

'Just as well Rake isn't here,' Rath'Shadowthrone said, his mask fixed in a sneer. 'He's hopelessly unpredictable and outright murderous company.'

'To which your god can attest,' Keruli smiled, then

845

turned back to Brood. 'Sufficient answers to warrant the like in return. As you point out, the Mask Council's overriding concern is with the reparation of Capustan. None the less, my companions here are all – beyond impromptu governors – servants to their respective gods. No-one here can be entirely unaware of the tumultuous condition of the pantheon. You, Caladan Brood, carry Burn's hammer, after all, and continue to struggle with the responsibilities that entails. Whilst the Grey Swords, bereft of one god, have chosen to kneel before two others – a mated, if riven, pair. My once-caravan captain, Gruntle, is reborn as a new god's Mortal Sword. The Barghast gods have been rediscovered, and so represent an ancient horde of untested power and disposition. Indeed, in surveying those gathered here, the only truly unaspected agents at this table are High Fist Dujek and his second, Whiskeyjack. The Malazans.'

Itkovian saw the suddenly closed expression of the warlord, Caladan Brood, and wondered at the hammer's responsibilities that Keruli had so blithely mentioned.

The standing, grey-haired warrior broke the ensuing silence with a barking laugh. 'You conveniently forgot *yourself*, Priest. Of the Mask Council, yet unmasked. Indeed, unwelcome in their company, it seems. Your companions make their gods plain, but not you, and why is that?'

Keruli's smile was benign, unperturbed. 'Dear Kallor, how you've withered under your curse. Do you still cart that meaningless throne with you? Yes, I had guessed as much—'

'I thought it was you,' Kallor hissed. 'Such a paltry disguise—'

'Issues of physical manifestation have proved problematic.'

'You've lost your power.'

'Not entirely. It has . . . evolved, and so I am forced to adjust, and learn.'

The warrior reached for his sword. 'In other words, I could kill you now—'

846

'I am afraid not,' Keruli sighed. 'Only in your dreams, perhaps. But then, you no longer dream, do you, Kallor? The Abyss takes you into its embrace each night. Oblivion, your own personal nightmare.'

Without turning, Brood rumbled, 'Remove your hand from your weapon, Kallor. My patience with you has stretched to its limit.'

'This is no priest sitting before you, Warlord!' the warrior rasped. 'It is an Elder God! K'rul himself.'

'I had gathered as much,' Brood sighed.

For a half-dozen heartbeats no-one spoke, and Itkovian could almost hear the grating, jarring shift of power. An Elder God was among them. Seated, expression benign, at this table.

'A limited manifestation,' Keruli said, then, 'to be more precise.'

'It had better be,' Gruntle interjected, his feline eyes fixed squarely on him, 'given Harllo's fate.'

Sorrow flitted across the Elder God's smooth, round features. 'Profoundly so, at the time, I am afraid. I did all that I could, Gruntle. I regret that it proved insufficient.'

'So do I.'

'Well!' Rath'Shadowthrone snapped. 'You can hardly sit on the Mask Council, then, can you?'

The Malazan named Whiskeyjack burst out laughing, the sound startling everyone at the table.

Stonny twisted in her seat to the High Priest of Shadow. 'Does your god truly know how small your brain really is? What is the issue? Elder Gods don't know the secret handshake? His mask is too realistic?'

'He's immortal, you slut!'

'Kind of guarantees seniority,' Gruntle commented. 'Eventually . . .'

'Do not make light of this, eater of rats!'

'And if you dare throw that word again at Stonny, I will kill you,' the Daru said. 'As for making light, it is hard not to. We're all trying to swallow the implications of all this.

An Elder God has stepped into the fray . . . against what we'd thought to be a mortal empire – by the Abyss, what have we got ourselves into? But you, your first and solitary thought is fixated on membership in your paltry, over-inflated council. Shadowthrone must be cringing right now.'

'He's likely used to it,' Stonny grated, sneering at the High Priest, 'when it comes to this bag of slime.'

Rath'Shadowthrone gaped at her.

'Let's get back to the task before us,' Brood said. 'Your words are accepted, K'rul. The Pannion Domin concerns all of us. As gods and priests, no doubt you can find your own roles in countering whatever threats are manifesting against the pantheon and the warrens – though we both know that the source of those threats is not directly associated with the Pannion Seer. My point is, we are here to discuss the organization of the forces that will now march with us south of the river, into the heart of the Domin. Mundane considerations, but essential none the less.'

'Accepted,' K'rul replied. 'Provisionally,' he added.

'Why provisionally?'

'I anticipate a few masks coming off in these proceedings, Warlord.'

Humbrall Taur cleared his throat. 'The course is simple enough,' he growled. 'Cafal.'

His son nodded. 'A division of forces, lords. One to Setta, the other to Lest. Convergence at Maurik, then onward to Coral. The White Face Barghast shall march with Onearm's Host, for it was by their efforts that we are here and my father likes this man's sense of humour' – he gestured towards Whiskeyjack, whose brows rose – 'as do our gods. It is further advisable that the Grey Swords, now recruiting from the Tenescowri, be in the other army, for the White Faces will not abide said recruits.'

The company's new Shield Anvil spoke. 'Agreeable, assuming Caladan Brood and his disparate forces can stomach our presence.'

848

'Can you truly find anything worthwhile in such creatures?' Brood asked her.

'We are all worthwhile, sir, once we assume the burden of forgiveness and the effort of absolution.' She looked over then and met Itkovian's eyes.

And this is my lesson? he wondered. *Then why am I both proud and pained by her words? No, not her words, precisely. Her faith. A faith that, to my sorrow, I have lost. This is envy you feel, sir. Discard it.*

'We shall manage, then,' Caladan Brood said after a moment.

Dujek Onearm sighed and reached for his cup of wine. 'So resolved. Easier than you'd imagined, Brood, wouldn't you say?'

The warlord bared his teeth in a satisfied, if hard, grin. 'Aye. We're all riding the same track. Good.'

'Time to proceed, then,' Rath'Burn said, eyes on Caladan Brood, 'to other issues. You are the one who was gifted the hammer, the focus of Burn's power. To you was entrusted the task of awakening her at the time of her greatest need—'

The warlord's grin grew feral. 'And so destroy every civilization on this world, aye. No doubt you judge her need as sufficiently pressing, High Priestess.'

'And you dare not?' she snapped, leaning forward with both hands on the table. 'You have deceived her!'

'No. I have *constrained* her.'

His reply left her momentarily speechless.

'There's a rug-seller's shop,' Gruntle said, 'in Darujhistan. To cross its floor is to scale layer upon layer of woven artistry. Thus are the lessons of mortals laid down before the gods. Pity that they keep stumbling so – you'd think they'd have learned by now.'

Rath'Burn wheeled on him. 'Silence! You know nothing of this! If Brood does not act, Burn will die! And when she dies, so too does all life on this world! That is the choice, you fool! Topple a handful of corrupt civilizations or absolute annihilation – what would you choose?'

'Well, since you're asking—'

'I withdraw the question, for you are clearly as insane as the warlord here. Caladan Brood, you must yield the hammer. To me. Here and now. In the name of Burn, the Sleeping Goddess, I demand it.'

The warlord rose, unslung the weapon. 'Here, then.' He held it out in his right hand.

Rath'Burn's eyes blinked, then she shot upright, strode round the table.

She grasped the hammer's copper-wrapped handle in both hands.

Brood released it.

The weapon plunged earthward. The snaps of the woman's wrist bones cut through the air. Then she screamed, even as the hill trembled to the impact of the hammer's massive head. Cups bounced on the table, splashed red wine across its surface. Rath'Burn had fallen to her knees, no longer holding the weapon, her broken arms cradled on her lap.

'Artanthos,' Dujek said, his eyes on Brood – who looked down on the woman with a dispassionate regard – 'find us a healer. A good one.'

The soldier standing behind the High Fist headed off.

The warlord addressed the High Priestess. 'The difference between you and your goddess, woman, is faith. A simple thing, after all. You see only two options open to me. Indeed, so did the Sleeping Goddess, at first. She gave to me the weapon, and gave to me the freedom to choose. It has taken a long while for me to understand what else she gave to me. I have withheld acting, withheld making that choice, and thought myself a coward. Perhaps I still am, yet a small measure of wisdom has finally lodged itself in my head—'

'Burn's faith,' K'rul said. 'That you would find a third choice.'

'Aye. Her faith.'

Artanthos reappeared with another Malazan, but Brood

held out a hand to halt them. 'No, I will heal her myself. She was not to know, after all.'

'Too generous,' K'rul murmured. 'She abandoned her goddess long ago, Warlord.'

'No journey is too long,' Brood replied, lowering himself to kneel before Rath'Burn.

Itkovian had last seen High Denul unveiled by Destriant Karnadas, and that fraught with the infection poisoning the warrens. What he saw now was . . . clean, unaffected, and appallingly powerful.

K'rul rose suddenly, looked around.

Rath'Burn gasped.

The Elder God's odd actions drew Itkovian's attention, and he followed K'rul's gaze. To see that another group had arrived on the hilltop, standing at a distance to the right of the tarp. Captain Paran was the only one among the four newcomers that Itkovian recognized, and he was not the man at whom the Elder God was looking.

A dark-skinned, tall and lean man, faintly smiling, was watching the proceedings from the back of the group, focused, it seemed, on Brood. After a moment, some instinct made him glance at K'rul. The man answered the Elder God's rapt attention with a slight, strangely uneven shrug – as if some invisible weight burdened his left shoulder.

Itkovian heard K'rul sigh.

Rath'Burn and Caladan Brood rose together, then. Her bones had been knitted. No swelling or bruising marred her bared forearms. She stood as if in shock, leaning against the warlord.

'What is this?' Kallor demanded. 'That warren bore no sign of poison.'

'Indeed,' K'rul smiled. 'It seems the illness has been pushed back from this location. Temporary, yet sufficient. Perhaps this is another lesson in the powers of faith . . . which I shall endeavour to heed . . .'

Itkovian's eyes narrowed. *He speaks with two meanings.*

One, for us. A deeper second meaning, for that man standing over there.

A moment later the large, heavy-set woman standing beside Captain Paran approached the table.

Seeing her, Kallor backed off a step.

'Careless,' she drawled to the warlord, who spun at her words, 'dropping your hammer like that.'

'Silverfox. We'd wondered if we would see you again.'

'Yet you sent Korlat out to track me, Warlord.'

'Only to ascertain your whereabouts and direction of travel. It appears she got lost, for she has yet to return.'

'A temporary misdirection. My T'lan Ay now surround her and are guiding her back here. Unharmed.'

'I am relieved to hear that. By your words, I assume that the Second Gathering has taken place.'

'It has.'

Whiskeyjack had seen Captain Paran and was approaching him for a private word. The tall, dark-skinned man moved to join them.

'Tell us, then,' the warlord continued, 'has another army joined in the proceedings?'

'My T'lan Imass have tasks before them that will require a journey to the Pannion Domin. To your advantage, should there be more K'Chain Che'Malle K'ell Hunters, for we will deal with them.'

'Presumably, you've no intention of elaborating on these tasks that you mentioned.'

'Warlord, they are private matters, and have no bearing on you or your war.'

'Don't believe her,' Kallor growled. 'They want the Seer, for they know what he is – a Jaghut Tyrant.'

Silverfox faced Kallor. 'And should you capture the Pannion Seer, what would you do with him? He is insane, his mind twisted by the taint of the Warren of Chaos and the Crippled God's manipulations. Execution is the only option. Leave that to us, for we exist to kill Jaghut—'

'Not always,' Dujek interjected.

'What do you mean?'

'Did not one of your T'lan Imass accompany the Adjunct Lorn when she freed the Jaghut Tyrant south of Darujhistan?'

Silverfox looked troubled. 'The Clanless One. Yes. An event I do not as yet understand. None the less, that Tyrant was awakened from a cursed sleep, only to die in truth—'

A new voice spoke. 'Actually, while a little worse for wear, Raest was admirably animate the last time I saw him.'

Silverfox spun. 'Ganoes, what do you mean? The Tyrant was slain.'

The small, round man now standing beside Captain Paran drew a handkerchief from a sleeve and mopped his brow. 'Well, as to that . . . not quite, Kruppe reluctantly advises. Matters were somewhat confused, alas—'

'A House of the Azath took the Jaghut Tyrant,' K'rul explained. 'The Malazan plan, as I understand it, was to force Anomander Rake's hand – a confrontation that was intended to weaken him, if not see him slain outright. Raest never did come face to face with the Lord of Moon's Spawn, as it turned out—'

'I see little relevance in all this,' Silverfox cut in. 'If the Clanless One has indeed broken his vow, then he will have to answer to me.'

'My point was,' Dujek said, 'you make a claim that the T'lan Imass and what they do or don't do is separate from everyone and everything else. You insist on detachment, but, as a veteran of the Malazan campaigns, I tell you that what you assert is patently untrue.'

'Perhaps indeed the Logros T'lan Imass grew . . . confused. If so, such ambivalence is past. Unless, of course, you would challenge the authority that I was born to.'

No-one spoke in answer to that.

Silverfox nodded. 'Very well. You have been told of the position of the T'lan Imass. We will have this Jaghut Tyrant. Does anyone here wish to counter our claim?'

'From the implicit threats in your tone, woman,' Brood

grated, 'that would be a foolhardy position to take. I for one will not squabble and tug the Seer's limbs.' He swung to Dujek. 'High Fist?'

The one-armed soldier grimaced, then shook his head.

Itkovian's attention was drawn to the short, fat Daru, for some reason he could not have hoped to explain. A benign smile curved those full, slightly greasy lips.

This is a most fell gathering of powers here. Yet why do I believe that the very epicentre of efficacy lies with this strange little man? He holds even K'rul's regard, as would an admiring companion rest eyes upon a lifelong . . . prodigy of sorts, perhaps. A prodigy whose talents have come to overwhelm his master's. But there is no envy in that regard, nor even pride – which always whispers of possessiveness, after all. No, the emotion is far more subtle, and complex . . .

'We have matters of supply to discuss,' Caladan Brood finally said. The High Priestess still leaned on him. He now guided her back to her chair, with surprising gentleness, and spoke to her in low tones. She nodded in reply.

'The Barghast,' Cafal said, 'have come prepared. Your numbers are manageable.'

'And the price?' Dujek asked.

The young warrior grinned. 'You'll find it palatable . . . more or less.'

Silverfox strode away, as if she had said all she'd intended to say and had no interest in the mundane matters still needing discussion. Itkovian noted that Captain Paran, his dark-skinned companion and Whiskeyjack had already departed. Gruntle seemed to have begun dozing in his chair, oblivious of Stonny's scowl opposite him. Rath'Hood and Rath'Shadowthrone were slumped in their chairs, masks angled into morose expressions – leaving Itkovian to wonder at how much control the priests had over those lacquered, hinged contrivances.

The new Shield Anvil of the Grey Swords sat motionless, her gaze fixed on Itkovian with unveiled sorrow.

And . . . pity.

I am a distraction. Very well. He stepped back, turned about and made his way towards the back of the tarp.

He was surprised to find Paran, Whiskeyjack and the dark-skinned man waiting there. A tall, martial woman with midnight skin had joined them and now studied Itkovian with extraordinary, almond-shaped eyes the colour of sun-bleached grass.

Meeting that gaze, Itkovian almost staggered. *Fener's tusks, such sadness – an eternity of loss . . . empty existence—*

She broke the contact with a startled, then alarmed, expression.

Not for me. Not for my embrace. Not that. Some wounds can never be healed, some memories should never be re-awakened. Cast no light upon that darkness, sir. It is too much— He came then to another realization. Fener was gone, and with the god had vanished his protection. Itkovian was vulnerable as he had never been before. Vulnerable to the world's pain, to its grief.

'Itkovian, we were hoping,' Captain Paran said, 'that you'd come. This is my commander, Whiskeyjack. And Quick Ben, of the Bridgeburners. And the Tiste Andii is Korlat, second to Anomander Rake. We are pleased with your company, Itkovian. Will you join us?'

'I've a restless cask of Gredfallan ale in my tent,' Whiskeyjack said.

My vow— 'A welcome invitation, sirs. I accept. Thank you. Mistress,' he added to Korlat, 'my deepest apologies.'

'They are mine to make,' she replied. 'I was unguarded, and carelessly unmindful of all that you are.'

The three Malazans looked back and forth at the two of them, but none ventured a query or comment.

'Allow me,' Whiskeyjack finally said, setting off down the slope towards the Host's camp.

The Bridgeburner, Quick Ben, paced alongside Itkovian. 'Well, it seems Silverfox has surprised us all this day.'

'I do not know her, sir, and so can make no observation as to her disposition.'

'You sensed nothing from her?'

'I did not say that.'

The man flashed a white grin. 'True enough. You didn't.'

'She has done a terrible wrong, sir, yet upon her shoulders it weighs nothing.'

The breath hissed between Quick Ben's teeth. 'Nothing? Are you certain? Hood's breath, that's not good. Not good at all.'

'Nightchill,' Paran said behind them.

Quick Ben threw a glance over a shoulder. 'You think?'

'I know, Wizard. And, to make matters worse, Nightchill was – is – a whole lot more than what we'd thought. Not just a High Mage of the Empire. She's all hard edges – her mate Bellurdan was her balance, but of the Thelomen I sense nothing.'

'And Tattersail?'

'In the shadows. Observing, but without much interest, it seems.'

'A woman named Silverfox was the subject,' Itkovian murmured, 'yet you speak of three others.'

'Sorry. All reborn within Silverfox. It's a long story.'

He nodded. 'All perforce needing to live with one another, no matter how disparate their individual natures.'

'Aye,' Paran sighed. 'Not surprising that there'd be a war of wills—'

'There is no war within her,' Itkovian said.

'What?'

'They walk in agreement, sir. She is calm within.'

They reached level ground, approached the Malazan camp. Whiskeyjack and Korlat strode side by side and close, a half-dozen paces ahead.

'Now that,' Quick Ben muttered, 'is the most surprising revelation this day.'

'So far,' Paran pointed out. 'Something tells me we're not done yet.'

'Gentlemen!' a voice wheezed behind them. 'A moment please, whilst Kruppe's formidable yet sadly short legs propel self hastily into your company!'

The elaborate statement was sufficient to close the distance as the three men paused to permit Kruppe's breathless arrival, upon which they resumed their walk.

'Wind of fortune!' Kruppe panted. 'Carrying to Kruppe all your words—'

'How convenient,' Quick Ben wryly muttered. 'And no doubt you've a comment or ten to make on the subject of Silverfox.'

'Indeed! Kruppe was witness, after all, to said dreadful Gathering. Yet all alarm subsequent to said events has grown quiet within oneself, for truths have marched out from the darkness to prostrate themselves at Kruppe's slippered feet.'

'That conjures up an image of you stumbling and falling flat on your face, Daru,' the wizard commented.

'Carelessly constructed, Kruppe allows, yet none of you have ever seen Kruppe dance! And dance he can, with breathtaking artistry and grace – nay! He glides like an unbroken egg on a greased skillet. Stumble? Fall? Kruppe? Never!'

'You'd mentioned truths,' Paran reminded him.

'Ah yes! Truths, squirming like puppies around Kruppe, upon which he laid patting hand on each one and all in turn, as would any kindly master. The result? Kruppe advises that all is well within Silverfox! Be at ease. Be calmed. Be . . . lieve – uh . . .'

'Was that a stumble?'

'Nonsense. Even linguistic confusion has value.'

'Really? How so?'

'Uh, the matter is too subtle for mere words, alas. We must not stray too far from the subject at hand, or foot, which was the matter of truths—'

'Squirming like puppies.'

'Indeed, Captain. Like wolf puppies, to be more precise.'

857

The two Malazans stopped suddenly, followed a moment later by Itkovian, as Kruppe's dream-like, mesmerizing stream of words revealed sudden substance, as if swirling before a rock. *A rock . . . one of Kruppe's truths? These Malazans are used to this – or simply smarter than I.*

'Out with it,' Paran growled.

'Out with what, precisely, dear Captain? Kruppe revels in sly ambiguity, after all, and so hoards his secrets as must any respectable hoarder of secrets . . . must. Does the subject concern this honour-bound ex-mercenary who walks alongside us? Indirectly, yes. Or, rather, the company he has so recently departed. Indirectly, Kruppe utters once more. Two ancient gods, once mere spirits, the first to run with mortals – those T'lan Imass of flesh and blood of so long ago – the most ancient of companions. And their kin, who followed in kind, and run still with the T'lan Imass.

'Two wolf-gods, yes? Does anyone here not recall the bedtime story of their separation, their eternal search for one another? Of course, all of you do. Such a sorrowful story, the kind impressionable children never forget. But what drove them apart? How goes the tale? *Then one day horror visited the land. Horror from the dark sky. Descending to shatter the world. And so the lovers were thrown apart, never again to embrace.* And it goes on blah blah and so forth and forthwhich.

'Gentlemen, the horror was of course the Fallen One's fateful descent. And whatever healing was demanded of the surviving powers proved a difficult, burdensome task. The Elder Gods did what they could, but understand, they were themselves younger than the two wolf-gods, and, more significantly, they did not find ascendancy walking in step with humans – or those who would one day become humans, that is—'

'Stop, please!' Paran snapped.

'Kruppe cannot! To pause here would be to lose all that must be said! The dimmest of memories are all that remain, and even they are succumbing to the gathering gloom! Frail fragments come as fraught dreams, and the promise of reunion and rebirth are lost, unrecognized, the redemption promised wandering a tundra alone, howling with the wind – yet salvation is at hand! Disparate spirits are united in their resolve! A spirit of hard edges, to hold the others to their course despite all the pain that others must bear. Another spirit, to clasp hard the hurt of abandonment until it can find proper answer! And yet a third spirit, filled with love and compassion – if somewhat witless, granted – to so flavour the pending moment. And a fourth, possessing the power to achieve the necessary reparation of old wounds—'

'Fourth?' Quick Ben sputtered. 'Who's the fourth in Silverfox?'

'Why, the seed-child of a T'lan Imass Bonecaster, of course. Pran Chole's daughter, the one whose true name is indeed the one by which we all know her!'

Itkovian's gaze flicked past Kruppe, to see Korlat and Whiskeyjack twenty paces off, standing in front of a large tent, looking back at the group. No doubt curious, yet maintaining a respectful distance.

'Thus, Kruppe advises one and all,' the Daru resumed after a moment, his tone deeply satisfied, pudgy fingers lacing together to rest on his paunch, 'faith. Patience. Await what must be awaited.'

'And you call that an explanation?' Paran demanded, scowling.

'The very paradigm of explication, dear friends. Cogent, clear, if somewhat quaintly couched. Precision is a precise art. Poignancy is pre-eminent and precludes prevarication. Truths are no trivial thing, after all—'

Itkovian swung towards Whiskeyjack and Korlat and set off.

Paran called out, 'Itkovian?'

'I was reminded of that Gredfallan ale,' he replied over a shoulder. 'It has been years, yet I find the need suddenly overwhelming, sir.'

'I concur. Wait up.'

'Wait, indeed, you three! What of Kruppe's own prodigious thirst?'

'By all means,' Quick Ben replied, setting off in the wake of Itkovian and Paran, 'quaintly quench it – just do so somewhere else.'

'Oh ho! But is that not Whiskeyjack waving Kruppe hence? Generous, kindly soldier, is Whiskeyjack! A moment! Kruppe would catch up!'

The two marines sat on boulders that were part of an old tipi ring, fifteen paces from where Silverfox stood. Shadows were stretching as the day closed over the prairie.

'So,' one of them muttered, 'how long do you think?'

'I'd guess she's communing with them T'lan Imass. See the swirls of dust around her? Could be all night.'

'I'm hungry.'

'Yeah, well, I admit I've been eyeing your leather straps, darling.'

'Problem is, they've forgotten about us.'

'That's not the problem. It's maybe we ain't needed no more. She doesn't need bodyguards. Not dirt-nosed mortals like us, anyway. And we've already seen what we were supposed to see, meaning we're overdue on making a report.'

'We weren't supposed to report, love. Remember? Anyone wants news from us they come by for a conversation.'

'Right, only nobody's come by for a while now. Which was my point in the first place.'

'Doesn't mean we should up and walk away. Besides, here's somebody coming now . . .'

The other marine twisted in her seat. After a moment, she grunted. 'Nobody we're supposed to report to. Hood knows, I don't even recognize 'em.'

'Sure you do. One, anyway. That's the Trygalle trader-sorceress, Haradas.'

'The other's a soldier, I'd say. An Elin lass, nice sway to the hips—'

'Hard face, though.'

'Eyes fulla hurt. Could be one of them Grey Swords – saw her at the parley.'

'Yeah, well, they're coming our way.'

'So am I,' a voice spoke from a few paces to their left. The marines turned to see that Silverfox was joining them. 'This is a fell thing,' she murmured.

'Oh, what's that?' one of the marines asked her.

'A gathering of women.'

The soldier grunted. 'We ain't gonna gossip, are we?'

Silverfox smiled at the facetious tone. 'Among the Rhivi, it's the men who do all the gossiping. The women are too busy giving them things to gossip about.'

'Huh. That's a surprise. I would've thought there'd be all kind of ancient laws against adultery and such. Banishment, stoning, it's what tribes do, ain't it?'

'Not the Rhivi. Bedding the wrong husbands is great sport. For the women, that is. The men take it all too seriously, of course.'

'They take everything too seriously, if you ask me,' the marine muttered.

'Self-importance will do that,' Silverfox replied, nodding.

Haradas and her companion arrived. In their wake, still sixty paces distant, a Barghast was approaching as well.

The trader-sorceress bowed to Silverfox, then the two Malazans. 'Dusk is a magical time, is it not?'

'What would you ask?' Silverfox drawled.

'A question born of a thought, Bonecaster, that but recently came to me, hence my coming to you.'

'You've been around Kruppe too long, Haradas.'

'Perhaps. Issues of supply continue to plague these armies, as you well know. At the parley, the White Face Barghast offered to provide a fair portion of what will be required. Despite their confidence, I believe that they too will find their resources stretched before long—'

'You would enquire of Tellann,' Silverfox said.

861

'Ah, indeed, I would. The warren of the T'lan Imass must surely remain . . . uninfected, after all. Could our guild respectfully employ its path—'

'Uninfected. Yes, it so remains. None the less, there is within Tellann the potential for violence, for risk to your caravans.'

Haradas's brows rose. 'It is assailed?'

'In a fashion. The Throne of the Beast Hold is . . . contested. There are renegades among the T'lan Imass. The Vow is weakening.'

The sorceress sighed. 'I thank you for the warning, Bonecaster. Risk, of course, is factored in when it comes to the Trygalle Trade Guild. Thus, the usurious fees we charge for our services. Will you then permit us the use of Tellann?'

Silverfox shrugged. 'I see no reason why not. Have you the means to fashion a portal into our warren? If not, I can—'

'No need, Bonecaster,' Haradas said with a faint smile. 'We have long since found such means, yet in respect to the T'lan Imass, and given the accessibility of less . . . uncivilized . . . warrens, such portals were never employed.'

Silverfox studied the sorceress for a long moment. 'Remarkable. I can only conclude that the Trygalle Trade Guild is run by a cabal of High Mages, of singular prowess. Do you know that not even the Malazan Empire's most powerful, most knowledgeable mages were ever successful in penetrating the secrets of Tellann? I would like to meet your guild's founders one day.'

Haradas's smile broadened. 'I am sure they would be delighted and indeed honoured by your company, Bonecaster.'

'You are perhaps too generous on their behalf, Sorceress.'

'Not in the least, I assure you. I am pleased that the matter has been concluded so effortlessly—'

'We're a fell gathering indeed,' Silverfox murmured.

Haradas blinked, then recovered and continued, 'So that

I may now introduce you to the new Shield Anvil of the Grey Swords, Captain Norul.'

The soldier bowed. 'Bonecaster.' The woman hesitated, then her expression hardened with resolve. 'The Grey Swords are sworn to Togg, Wolf of Winter, and to Fanderay, She-Wolf of Winter.'

'Interesting choices,' Silverfox said. 'Lovers lost for all eternity, yet in your twice-sworn company, united in spirit. A bold and courageous gesture, Shield Anvil.'

'Bonecaster, Togg and Fanderay are no longer lost to each other. Each has finally caught the other's scent. Your manner seems to convey no knowledge of this, which confuses me, sir.'

Now it was Silverfox who frowned. 'Why should it? I've no particular interest in ancient wolf-gods . . .' Her words slowly trailed to silence.

The Shield Anvil spoke again, 'Bonecaster, Summoner of the Second Gathering of the T'lan Imass, I formally ask that you yield the T'lan Ay – the children of our gods.'

Silence.

Silverfox stared at the Grey Sword commander, eyes half lidded, her full, rounded face expressionless. Then a tremor crossed her features.

'You don't understand,' she finally whispered. 'I need them.'

The Shield Anvil cocked her head. 'Why?'

'F-for a . . . *gift*. A . . . repayment. I have sworn—'

'To whom?'

'To – to myself.'

'And how, sir, are the T'lan Ay involved in the fashioning of this gift? They have run with the T'lan Imass, it is true. But they are not to be *owned*. Not by the T'lan Imass. Not by you.'

'Yet they were joined in the Ritual of Tellann, the First Gathering—'

'They were . . . encompassed. In ignorance. Bound by loyalty and love to the flesh and blood Imass. As a result, they lost their souls. Sir, my gods are coming, and in their cries – which now visit me each night in my dreams – they demand . . . reparation.'

'I must deny you,' Silverfox said. 'Until Togg and Fanderay can come, physically and manifesting their power, to enforce their demand, I shall not yield the T'lan Ay.'

'You risk your life, Bonecaster—'

'Will the wolf-gods announce war against the T'lan Imass? Will they and the T'lan Ay come for our throats, Shield Anvil?'

'I do not know, sir. You will have to answer for the decisions you have made. But I fear for you, Bonecaster. Togg and Fanderay are ascended *beasts*. Their souls are unknowable to such as you and me. Who can predict what lies in the hearts of such creatures?'

'Where are they now?'

The Shield Anvil shrugged. 'South. We shall, it seems, all converge within the Pannion Domin.'

'Then I still have time.'

'The achievement of your gift, sir, could see you killed.'

'Always an even exchange,' Silverfox muttered, half to herself.

The marines exchanged a glance at those words, legendary in Onearm's Host.

The Barghast woman had arrived and was standing a few paces distant, sharp, dark eyes fixed intently on the exchange between the Shield Anvil and Silverfox. At the pause, she laughed low in her throat, drawing everyone's attention.

'Too bad there are no men worthy of this company,' she growled. 'Seeing you, I am reminded of this world's true heart of power. Malazan marines, a Shield Anvil of the Grey Swords, a witch and a sorceress. And now, to complete the tapestry, a daughter of the White Face Barghast . . . bringing food and wine.'

The two marines shot to their feet, grinning.

'And I would gossip!' Hetan shouted. 'Shield Anvil! Itkovian holds to vows no longer, true? I can bed him—'

'If you can catch him,' the Grey Sword replied, one brow arching.

'If he had fifty legs I could still catch him! Silverfox! What of Kruppe, hey?'

The Bonecaster blinked. 'What of him?'

'You're a big woman. You could trap him under you! Leave him squealing!'

'What a horrifying image.'

'I'll grant you he's round and small and slimy, but clever, yes? Clever heats the blood all on its own, does it not? I have heard that, while you may look like a woman, you remain as a child in the most important way. Stir yourself with desire, lass! You've been consorting with the undead and the withered for far too long! Grasp the spear with both hands, I always say!'

Silverfox slowly shook her head. 'You said you brought wine?'

Grin broadening, Hetan approached. 'Aye, two bladders as big as your breasts and no doubt just as sweet. Gather, formidable companions, and let us feast!'

Haradas smiled. 'A wonderful idea, thank you.'

The Shield Anvil hesitated. She glanced over at the marines, then began removing her battered helm. She sighed loudly. 'Let the wolves wait,' she said. 'I cannot hold to dread comportment in the manner of my predecessor—'

'Cannot?' Hetan challenged. 'Or *will* not?'

'Will not,' the woman corrected, pulling her helm free. Sweat-soaked, iron-streaked hair tumbled loose. 'May the Wolves forgive me.'

'One of them will,' the Barghast asserted, crouching to lay out the foodstuffs from her pack.

Coll drew the furs closer about the Mhybe's frail, shrunken form. There was movement behind the lids of her eyes, random and frantic. Her breath was a broken wheeze. The

Daru councillor looked down on her for a moment longer, then he straightened and slipped down from the edge of the wagon-bed.

Murillio stood nearby, tightening the straps of the water casks attached to the wagon's right side-rail. Old tents had been used to cover the packages of food they had purchased from a Barghast trader that morning, which had been affixed to the opposite side-rail, giving the Rhivi wagon a wide, bloated appearance.

The two men had also acquired a pair of horses, at exorbitant cost, from the Mott Irregulars, a strangely ineffectual-looking company of mercenaries attached to Caladan Brood's army that Coll had not even known were present. Mercenaries whose backwoods garb belied the martial profession, yet perfectly suited the company's name. The horses were barely broken, thick-limbed yet tall, a breed the Irregulars claimed was their own – bloodlines that included Nathi destriers, Mott carthorses and Genabarii drays, all drawn together to produce a large, sturdy, ill-tempered animal with a surprisingly wide back that made riding them a luxury.

'Provided they don't bite your hand off,' the buck-toothed Mottman had added, pulling lice from his long, stringy hair and popping them into his mouth as he talked.

Coll sighed, vaguely discomfited by the memory, and warily approached the two horses.

The two mounts could have been twins, both sorrel, their manes uncut and long, thick tails snagged with burrs and spar-grass seeds. The saddles were Malazan – old spoils of war, no doubt – the thick blankets beneath them Rhivi. The beasts eyed him.

One casually swung its hindquarters in the Daru's direction. He stopped, muttering a soft curse.

'Sweetroot,' Murillio said from beside the wagon. 'Bribe 'em. Here, we have some in the packs.'

'And reward their ill manners? No.' Coll circled at a distance. The horses had been tethered to a tent peg, allowing them to match his movement. Three steps closer and the Daru would get his head kicked in. He cursed in a slightly louder tone, then said, 'Murillio, lead the oxen up beside that peg – use the wagon to block them. And if this doesn't work, find me a mallet.'

Grinning, Murillio climbed up onto the seat and gathered the traces. Fifteen heartbeats later he halted the beasts just past the tent peg, the wagon effectively barring the horses from circling any further.

Coll hurried round until the wagon was between him and the mounts.

'So you'd rather a bite than a kick,' Murillio commented, watching his friend come up to the wagon, climb its side, then cross the bed – stepping over the Mhybe's unconscious form – and halt within an arm's reach of the horses.

They had pulled their tethers taut, backing as far as they could, tugging on the tent peg. A Rhivi wedge, the peg's design was intended to hold against even the fiercest prairie wind. Driven deep in the hard-packed earth, it did not budge.

Coll's leather-gauntleted hand snapped out, closed on one of the tethers. He tugged sharply down as he dropped from the wagon.

The animal stumbled towards him, snorting. Its comrade skittered back in alarm.

The Daru collected the reins from the saddle-horn, still gripping the tether in his other hand and holding the horse's head down, and edged to its shoulder. He planted a boot in the stirrup and swung himself into the saddle in a single motion.

The horse tried to duck out from under his weight, a sideways slew that thudded against its comrade – with Coll's leg trapped in between.

He grunted but held the reins firm.

'That'll be a nice bruise,' Murillio commented.

'Keep saying pleasant things why don't you?' Coll said through gritted teeth. 'Now come over and slip the tether.

Carefully, mind. There's a lone vulture above our heads, looking hopeful.'

His companion glanced skyward, scanned for a moment, then hissed. 'All right, so I was momentarily gullible – stop gloating.' He clambered over the seat-back.

Coll watched him drop lightly to the ground and warily approach the tent peg.

'On second thoughts, maybe you should have found me that mallet.'

'Too late now, friend,' Murillio said, pulling the knot free.

The horse plunged back a half-dozen steps, then planted its hind legs and reared.

To Murillio's eyes, Coll's backward somersault displayed almost poetic grace, artfully concluded by the big Daru's landing squarely on his feet, only to lunge straight back to avoid a vicious two-hoofed kick that, had it connected, would have shattered his chest. He landed four paces away with a thud.

The horse ran off, bucking with glee.

Coll lay unmoving for a moment, blinking at the sky.

'You all right?' Murillio asked.

'Get me a lasso. And some sweetroot.'

'I'd suggest a mallet instead,' Murillio replied, 'but since you know your mind, I won't.'

Distant horns sounded.

'Hood's breath,' Coll groaned. 'The march to Capustan's begun.' He slowly sat up. 'We were supposed to be up front for this.'

'We could always ride in the wagon, friend. Return the horses to the Mott Irregulars and get our money back.'

'That wagon's overloaded as it is.' Coll painfully regained his feet. 'Besides, he said no refunds.'

Murillio squinted at his companion. 'Did he now? And not even a stir of suspicion from you at that?'

'Quiet.'

'But—'

868

'Murillio, you want the truth? The man was so homely I felt sorry for him, all right? Now stop babbling and let's get on with this.'

'Coll! He was asking a prince's ransom for—'

'Enough,' he growled. 'That ransom's going to pay for the privilege of killing the damned beasts, or you – which do you prefer?'

'You can't kill them—'

'Then another word from you and it's this hillside under a pile of boulders for dear old Murillio of Darujhistan. Am I understood? Good. Now hand me that lasso and the sweet-root – we'll start with the one still here.'

'Wouldn't you rather run after—'

'Murillio,' Coll warned.

'Sorry. Make the boulders small, please.'

The miasmic clouds churned low over the heaving waves, waves that warred with each other amidst jagged mountains of ice, waves that spun and twisted even as they struck the battered shoreline, flinging spume skyward. The thunderous roar was shot through with grinding, cracking, and the ceaseless hiss of driving rain.

'Oh my,' Lady Envy murmured.

The three Seguleh crouched on the leeside of a large basaltic boulder, applying thick grease to their weapons. They were a sadly bedraggled trio, sodden with rain, smeared with mud, their armour in tatters. Minor wounds crisscrossed their arms, thighs and shoulders, the deeper ones roughly stitched with gut, the rows of knots black and gummed with old blood that streamed crimson in the rain.

Nearby, surmounting a jutting spar of basalt, stood Baaljagg. Matted, scabbed, her fur in tangled tufts around bare patches, a hand's length of broken spear shaft jutting from her right shoulder – three days it had been, yet the beast would not allow Envy close, nor the Seguleh – the giant wolf stared steadily northward with feverish, gleaming eyes.

869

Garath lay three paces behind her, shivering uncontrollably, wounds suppurating as if his body wept since he could not, massive and half mad, allowing no-one – not even the wolf – to come near.

Only Lady Envy remained, to all outward appearances, untouched by the horrendous war they had undertaken; untouched, even, by the driving rain. Her white telaba showed not a single stain. Her unbound black hair hung full and straight down to the small of her back. Her lips were painted a deep, vaguely menacing red. The kohl above her eyes contained the hues of dusk.

'Oh my,' she whispered yet again. 'How shall we follow Tool across . . . this? And why was he not a T'lan Elephant, or a T'lan Whale, so that he could carry us on his back, in sumptuous howdahs? With running hot water and ingenious plumbing.'

Mok appeared at her side, rain streaming from his enamel mask. 'I will face him yet,' he said.

'Oh really. And when did duelling Tool become more important than your mission to the Seer? How will the First or the Second react to such self-importance?'

'The First is the First and the Second is the Second,' Mok replied laconically.

Lady Envy rolled her eyes. 'How astute an observation.'

'The demands of the self have primacy, mistress. Always, else there would be no champions. There would be no hierarchy at all. The Seguleh would be ruled by mewling martyrs blindly trampling the helpless in their lust for the common good. Or we would be ruled by despots who would hide behind an army to every challenge, creating of brute force a righteous claim to honour. We know of other lands, mistress. We know much more than you think.'

She turned to study him. 'Goodness. And here I have been proceeding on the assumption that entertaining conversation was denied to me.'

'We are immune to your contempt, mistress.'

870

'Hardly, you've been smarting ever since I reawakened you. Smarting? Indeed, seething.'

'There are matters to be discussed,' Mok said.

'Are you sure? Would you by chance be referring to this tumultuous tempest barring our advance? Or perhaps to the fleeing remnants of the army that pursued us here? They'll not return, I assure you—'

'You have sent a plague among them.'

'What an outrageous accusation! It's been a miracle that disease has not struck them long ago, what with eating each other without even the civil application of cooking. Dear me, that you would so accuse—'

'Garath succumbs to that plague, mistress.'

'What? Nonsense! He is ailed by his wounds—'

'Wounds that the power of his spirit should have long since healed. The fever within the beast, that so fills the lungs, is the same as that which afflicts the Pannions.' He slowly turned to face her. 'Do something.'

'An outrage—'

'Mistress.'

'Oh, all right! But don't you see the delicious irony? Poleil, Queen of Disease, has allied herself with the Crippled God. A decision that deeply affronts me, I will have you know. How cunning of me to loot her warren and so beset her allies!'

'I doubt the victims appreciate the irony, mistress. Nor, I imagine, does Garath.'

'I'd much rather you'd stayed taciturn!'

'Heal him.'

'He'll not let me close!'

'Garath is no longer capable of standing, mistress. Where he now lies, he will not rise from, unless you heal him.'

'Oh, what a miserable man you are! If you're wrong and he tries to bite me, I will be very upset with you, Mok. I will lay waste to your loins. I will make your eyes crossed so that everyone who looks at you and your silly mask will not be able to help but laugh. And I will think of other things, too, I assure you.'

'Heal him.'

'Of course I will! Garath is my beloved companion, after all. Even if he once tried to pee on my robe – though I will acknowledge that since he was asleep at the time it was probably one of K'rul's pranks. All right, all right, stop interrupting me.'

She approached the huge hound.

His eyes were glazed, each breath a hacking contortion. Garath did not raise his head as she edged closer.

'Oh, dear, forgive my inattention, dearest pup. I'd thought only the wounds, and so had already begun to grieve. You are felled by an unseemly vapour? Unacceptable. Easily negated, in fact.' She reached out, fingers lightly resting on the hot, steaming hide. 'There—'

Garath swung his head, lips slowly peeling back.

Lady Envy scampered away. 'And that is how you thank me? I have healed you, dearest one!'

'You made him ill in the first place, mistress,' Mok said behind her.

'Be quiet, I'm not talking to you any more. Garath! Look at how your strength returns, even as we watch! See, you are standing! Oh, how wonderful! And – no, stay away, please. Unless you want a pat? Do you want a pat? If so, you must stop growling at once!'

Mok stepped between them, eyes on the bristling hound. 'Garath, we have need of her, even as we have need of you. There is no value in continuing this enmity.'

'He can't understand you!' Lady Envy said. 'He's a *dog*! An angry dog, in fact.'

The hulking creature turned away, padded slowly to where Baaljagg stood facing the storm. The wolf did not so much as glance at him.

Mok stepped forward. 'Baaljagg sees something, mistress.'

'What? Out there?'

872

They hurried up the pinnacle's slope.

The bergs of ice had captured a prize. Less than a thousand paces away, at the very edge of the small inlet before them, floated a structure. High-walled on two sides with what appeared to be a latticework of wicker, and surmounted by frost-rimed houses – three in all – it looked nothing more than a broken, torn-away piece of a port town or city. A narrow, crooked alley was indeed visible between the tall, warped houses. As the ice gripping the base of the structure twisted to some unseen current, the two opposites sides came into view, revealing the broken maw of wooden framework reaching beneath the street level, crowded with enormous balsa logs and what appeared to be massive inflated bladders, three of them punctured and flaccid.

'How decidedly peculiar,' Lady Envy said.

'Meckros,' Mok said.

'Excuse me?'

'The home of the Seguleh is an island, mistress. We are, on rare occasion, visited by the Meckros, who dwell in cities that ride the oceans. They endeavour to raid our coastline, ever forgetful of the unfortunate results of the previous raids. Their fierce zeal entertains those among the Lower Schools.'

'Well,' Lady Envy sniffed, 'I see no occupants in that . . . misplaced neighbourhood.'

'Nor do I, mistress. However, look at the ice immediately beyond the remnant. It has found an outward current and now seeks to join it.'

'Goodness, you can't be suggesting—'

Baaljagg gave clear answer to her unfinished question. The wolf spun, flashed past them, and hastened down to the wave-hammered rocks below. Moments later, they saw the huge wolf lunging from the thrashing water onto a broad raft of ice, then scampering across to the other side. Baaljagg then leapt outward, to land skidding on another floe.

'The method seems viable,' Mok said.

Garath plunged past them, following the wolf's route down to the shoreline.

'Oh!' Lady Envy cried, stamping a foot. 'Can't we ever *discuss* things?'

'I see a possible route forming, mistress, which might well permit us to avoid getting too wet—'

'Wet? Who's wet? Very well, call your brothers and lead the way.'

The journey across the pitching, heaving, often awash floes of ice proved frantic, perilous and exhausting. Upon reaching the rearing wall of wicker, they found no sign of Baaljagg or Garath, yet could follow their tracks on the snow-crusted raft, which seemed to be holding afloat most of the Meckros structure, round to the unwalled, broken side.

Within the chaotic framework of beams and struts, steeply angled, thick-planked ladders had been placed – no doubt originally built to assist in maintenance of the city's undercarriage. The frosted steps within sight all revealed deep gouging from the wolf's and the hound's passage upward.

Water streamed down the jumbled, web-like framework, revealing the sundered nature of the street and houses above.

Senu in the lead, followed by Thurule then Mok, with Lady Envy last, the travellers climbed slowly, cautiously upward.

They eventually emerged through a warehouse-sized trap door that opened onto the pitched, main floor of one of the houses. The chamber was crowded along three of its four walls with burlap-wrapped supplies. Huge barrels had tumbled, rolled, and were now gathered at one end. To its right were double doors, now shattered open, no doubt by Baaljagg and Garath, revealing a cobbled street beyond.

The air was bitter cold.

'It might be worthwhile,' Mok said to Lady Envy, 'to examine each of these houses, from level to level, to determine which is the most structurally sound and there-fore inhabitable. There seem to be considerable stores remaining which we can exploit.'

'Yes, yes,' Lady Envy said distractedly. 'I leave to you and your brothers such mundane necessities. The assumption that our journey has brought us to, however, rests in the untested belief that this contraption will perforce carry us north, across the entire breadth of Coral Bay, and hence to the city that is our goal. I, and I alone, it seems, must do the fretting on this particular issue.'

'As you like, mistress.'

'Watch yourself, Mok!' she snapped.

He tilted his masked head in silent apology.

'My servants forget themselves, it seems. Think on the capacity of my fullest irritation, you three. In the mean-time, I shall idle on the city's street, such as it is.' With that, she pivoted and strode languidly towards the doorway.

Baaljagg and Garath stood three paces beyond, the rain striking their broad backs hard enough to mist with spray. Both animals faced a lone figure, standing in the gloom of the opposite house's overhanging dormer.

For a moment, Lady Envy almost sighed, then the fact that she did not recognize the figure struck home. 'Oh! And here I was about to say: dear Tool, you waited for us after all! But lo, you are not him, are you?'

The T'lan Imass before them was shorter, squatter than Tool. Three black-iron broadswords of unfamiliar style impaled this undead warrior's broad, massive chest, two of them driven in from behind, the other from the T'lan Imass's left. Broken ribs jutted through black, salt-rimed skin. The leather strapping of all three sword handles hung in rotted, unravelled strips from the grips' wooden under-plates. Wispy remnants of old sorcery flowed fitfully along the pitted blades.

The warrior's features were extraordinarily heavy, the brow ridge a skinless shelf of bone, stained dark brown, the cheek bones swept out and high to frame flattened oval-shaped eye sockets. Cold-hammered copper fangs capped the undead's upper canines. The T'lan Imass did not wear a helm. Long hair, bleached white, dangled to either side of the broad, chinless face, weighted at the ends with shark teeth.

A most dreadful, appalling apparition, Lady Envy reflected. 'Have you a name, T'lan Imass?' she asked.

'I have heard the summons,' the warrior said in a voice that was distinctly feminine. 'It came from a place to match the direction I had already chosen. North. Not far, now. I shall attend the Second Gathering, and I shall address my Kin of the Ritual, and so tell them that I am Lanas Tog. Sent to bring word of the fates of the Ifayle T'lan Imass and of my own Kerluhm T'lan Imass.'

'How fascinating,' Lady Envy said. 'And their fates are?'

'I am the last of the Kerluhm. The Ifayle, who heeded our first summons, are all but destroyed. Those few that remain cannot extricate themselves from the conflict. I myself did not expect to survive the attempt. Yet I have.'

'A horrific conflict indeed,' Lady Envy quietly observed. 'Where does it occur?'

'The continent of Assail. Our losses: twenty-nine thousand eight hundred and fourteen Kerluhm. Twenty-two thousand two hundred Ifayle. Eight months of battle. We have lost this war.'

Lady Envy was silent for a long moment, then she said, 'It seems you've finally found a Jaghut Tyrant who is more than your match, Lanas Tog.'

The T'lan Imass cocked her head. 'Not Jaghut. Human.'

BOOK FOUR

MEMORIES OF ICE

First in, last out.

Motto of the Bridgeburners

CHAPTER TWENTY-ONE

> Your friend's face might prove the mask
> the daub found in subtle shift
> to alter the once familiar visage.
> Or the child who formed unseen
> in private darkness as you whiled oblivious
> to reveal cruel shock as a stone
> through a temple's pane.
> To these there is no armour on the soul.
> And upon the mask is writ the bold word,
> echoed in the child's eyes,
> a sudden stranger to all you have known.
> Such is betrayal.
>
> *Death Vigil of Sorulan*
> Minir Othal

Captain Paran reined in his horse near the smoke-blackened rubble of the East Watch redoubt. He twisted in his saddle for a last look at Capustan's battered walls. Jelarkan's Palace reared tall and dark against the bright blue sky. Streaks of black paint etched the tower like cracks, a symbol of the city's mourning for its lost prince. The next rain would see that paint washed away, leaving no sign. That structure, he had heard, never wore the mortal moment for very long.

The Bridgeburners were filing out through the East Gate.

879

First in, last out. They're always mindful of such gestures.

Sergeant Antsy was in the lead, with Corporal Picker a step behind. The two looked to be arguing, which was nothing new. Behind them, the soldiers of the other seven squads had lost all cohesion; the company marched in no particular order. The captain wondered at that. He'd met the other sergeants and corporals, of course. He knew the names of every surviving Bridgeburner and knew their faces as well. None the less, there was something strangely ephemeral about them. His eyes narrowed as he watched them walk the road, veiled in dust, like figures in a sun-bleached, threadbare tapestry. The march of armies, he reflected, was timeless.

Horse hooves sounded to his right and he swung to see Silverfox ride up to halt at his side.

'Better we'd stayed avoiding each other,' Paran said, returning his gaze to the soldiers on the road below.

'I'd not disagree,' she said after a moment. 'But something's happened.'

'I know.'

'No, you don't. What you no doubt refer to is not what I'm talking about, Captain. It's my mother – she's gone missing. Her and those two Daru who were caring for her. Somewhere in the city they turned their wagon, left the line. No-one seems to have seen a thing, though of course I cannot question an entire army—'

'What of your T'lan Imass? Could they not find them easily enough?'

She frowned, said nothing.

Paran glanced at her. 'They're not happy with you, are they?'

'That is not the problem. I have sent them and the T'lan Ay across the river.'

'We've reliable means of reconnoitring already, Silverfox—'

'Enough. I do not need to explain myself.'

'Yet you're asking for my help—'

'No. I am asking if you knew anything about it. Those Daru had to have had assistance.'

'Have you questioned Kruppe?'

'He's as startled and dismayed as I am, and I believe him.'

'Well,' Paran said, 'people have a habit of under-estimating Coll. He's quite capable of pulling this off all on his own.'

'You do not seem to realize the severity of what they've done. In kidnapping my mother—'

'Hold on, Silverfox. You left your mother to their care. Left? No, too calm a word. Abandoned her. And I have no doubt at all that Coll and Murillio took the charge seriously, with all the compassion for the Mhybe you do not seem to possess. Consider the situation from their point of view. They're taking care of her, day in and day out, watch-ing her wither. They see the Mhybe's daughter, but only from a distance. Ignoring her own mother. They decide that they have to find someone who is prepared to help the Mhybe. Or at the very least grant her a dignified end. Kidnapping is taking someone away from someone else. The Mhybe has been taken away, but from whom? No-one. No-one at all.'

Silverfox, her face pale, was slow to respond. When she did, it was in a rasp, 'You have no idea what lies between us, Ganoes.'

'And it seems you've no idea of how to forgive – not her, not yourself. Guilt has become a chasm—'

'That is rich indeed, coming from you.'

His smile was tight. 'I've done my climb down, Silverfox, and am now climbing up the other side. Things have changed for both of us.'

'So you have turned your back on your avowed feelings for me.'

'I love you still, but with your death I succumbed to a kind of infatuation. I convinced myself that what you and I had, so very briefly, was of far vaster and deeper import than it truly was. Of all the weapons we turn upon

881

ourselves, guilt is the sharpest, Silverfox. It can carve one's own past into unrecognizable shapes, false memories leading to beliefs that sow all kinds of obsessions.'

'Delighted to have you clear the air so, Ganoes. Has it not occurred to you that clinical examination of oneself is yet another obsession? What you dissect has to be dead first – that's the principle of dissection, after all.'

'So my tutor explained,' Paran replied, 'all those years ago. But you miss a more subtle truth. I can examine myself, my every feeling, until the Abyss swallows the world, yet come no closer to mastery of those emotions within me. For they are not static things; nor are they immune to the outside world – to what others say, or don't say. And so they are in constant flux.'

'Extraordinary,' she murmured. 'Captain Ganoes Paran, the young master of self-control, the tyrant unto himself. You have indeed changed. So much so that I no longer recognize you.'

He studied her face, searching for a hint of the feelings behind those words. But she had closed herself to him. 'Whereas,' he said slowly, 'I find you all too recognizable.'

'Would you call that ironic? You see me as a woman you once loved, while I see you as a man I never knew.'

'Too many tangled threads for irony, Silverfox.'

'Perhaps pathos, then.'

He looked away. 'We've wandered far from the subject. I am afraid I can tell you nothing of your mother's fate. Yet I am confident, none the less, that Coll and Murillio will do all they can for her.'

'Then you're an even bigger fool than they are, Ganoes. By stealing her, they have sealed her doom.'

'I didn't know you for the melodramatic type.'

'I am not—'

'She is an old woman, an old, *dying* woman. Abyss take me, leave her alone—'

'You are not listening!' Silverfox hissed. 'My mother is trapped in a nightmare – within her own mind, lost,

882

terrified. *Hunted!* I have stayed closer to her than any of you realized. Far closer!'

'Silverfox,' Paran said quietly, 'if she is within a nightmare, then her living has become a curse. The only true mercy is to see it ended, once and for all.'

'No! She is my mother, damn you! And I *will not abandon her!*'

She wheeled her horse, drove her heels into its flanks.

Paran watched her ride off. *Silverfox, what machinations have you wrapped around your mother? What is it you seek for her? Would you not tell us, please, so that we are made to understand that what we all see as betrayal is in fact something else?*

Is it something else?

And these machinations – whose? Not Tattersail, surely. No, this must be Nightchill. Oh, how you've closed yourself to me, now. When once you reached out, incessantly, relentlessly seeking to pry open my heart. It seems that what we shared, so long ago in Pale, is as nothing.

I begin to think, now, that it was far more important to me than it was to you. Tattersail . . . you were, after all, an older woman. You'd lived your share of loves and losses. On the other hand, I'd barely lived at all.

What was, then, is no more.

Flesh and blood Bonecaster, you've become colder than the T'lan Imass you now command.

I suppose, then, they have indeed found a worthy master.

Beru fend us all.

Of the thirty transport barges and floating bridges the Pannions had used to cross the Catlin River, only a third remained serviceable, the others having fallen prey to the overzealous White Face Barghast during the first day of battle. Companies from Caladan Brood's collection of mercenaries had begun efforts at salvaging the wrecks with the intention of cobbling together a few more; while a lone serviceable floating bridge and the ten surviving barges already rode the lines across the river's expanse, loaded with troops, mounts and supplies.

Itkovian watched them as he walked the shoreline. He'd left his horse on a nearby hillock where the grasses grew thick, and now wandered alone, with only the shift of pebbles underfoot and the soft rush of the river accompanying him. The wind was sweeping up the river's mouth, a salt-laden breath from the sea beyond, so the sounds of the barges behind him – the winches, the lowing of yoked cattle, the shouts of drivers – did not reach him.

Glancing up, he saw a figure on the beach ahead, seated cross-legged and facing the scene of the crossing. Wild-haired, wearing a stained collection of rags, the man was busy painting on wood-backed muslin. Itkovian paused, watching the artist's head bob up and down, the long-handled brush darting about in his hand, now hearing his mumbling conversation with himself.

Or, perhaps, not with himself. One of the skull-sized boulders near the artist moved suddenly, revealing itself to be a large, olive-green toad.

And it had just replied to the artist's tirade, in a low, rumbling voice.

Itkovian approached.

The toad saw him first and said something in a language Itkovian did not understand.

The artist looked up, scowled. 'Interruptions,' he snapped in Daru, 'are not welcome!'

'My apologies, sir—'

'Wait! You're the one named Itkovian! Defender of Capustan!'

'Failed defen—'

'Yes, yes, everyone's heard your words from the parley. Idiocy. When I paint you in the scene, I'll be sure to include the noble failure – in your stance, perhaps, in where your eyes rest, maybe. A certain twist to the shoulders, yes, I think I see it now. Precisely. Excellent.'

'You are Malazan?'

884

'Of course I'm Malazan! Does Brood give one whit for history? He does not. But the old Emperor! Oh yes, he did, he did indeed! Artists with every army! On every campaign! Artists of purest talent, sharp-eyed – yes, dare I admit it, *geniuses*. Such as Ormulogun of Li Heng!'

'I am afraid I've not heard that name – he was a great artist of the Malazan Empire?'

'Was? Is! I am Ormulogun of Li Heng, of course. Endlessly mimicked, never surpassed! Ormulogun seraith Gumble!'

'An impressive title—'

'It's not a title, you fool. Gumble is my critic.' With that he gestured at the toad, then said to it, 'Mark him well, Gumble, so that you note the brilliance of my coming rendition. He stands straight, does he not? Yet his bones may well be iron, their burden that of a hundred thousand foundation stones . . . or souls, to be more precise. And his features, yes? Look carefully, Gumble, and you will see the fullest measure of this man. And know this, though I capture all he is on the canvas recording the parley outside Capustan, know this . . . in that image you will see that Itkovian is not yet done.'

The soldier started.

Ormulogun grinned. 'Oh yes, warrior, I see all too well for your comfort, yes? Now Gumble, spew forth your commentary, for I know its tide is building! Come now!'

'You are mad,' the toad observed laconically. 'Forgive him, Shield Anvil, he softens his paint in his own mouth. It has poisoned his brain—'

'Poisoned, pickled, poached, yes, yes, I've heard every variation from you until I'm sick to my stomach!'

'Nausea is to be expected,' the toad said with a sleepy blink. 'Shield Anvil, I am no critic. Merely a humble observer who, when able, speaks on behalf of the tongue-tied multitudes otherwise known as the commonalty, or, more precisely, the rabble. An audience, understand, wholly incapable of self-realization or cogent articulation, and thus possessors of depressingly vulgar tastes when not apprised of what they *truly* like, if only they knew it. My meagre gift, therefore, lies in the communication of an aesthetic framework upon which most artists hang themselves.'

'Ha, slimy one! Ha! So very slimy! Here, have a fly!' Ormulogun plunged his paint-smeared fingers into a pouch at his side. He withdrew a deerfly and tossed it at the toad.

The still living but dewinged insect landed directly in front of Gumble, who lunged forward and devoured it in a pink flash. 'As I was saying—'

'A moment, if you please,' Itkovian interrupted.

'I will allow a moment,' the toad said, 'if possessing admirable brevity.'

'Thank you, sir. Ormulogun, you say it was the practice of the Emperor of Malaz to assign artists to his armies. Presumably to record historical moments. Yet is not Onearm's Host outlawed? For whom, then, do you paint?'

'A record of the outlawry is essential! Besides, I had little choice but to accompany the army. What would you have me do, paint sunsets on cobbles in Darujhistan for a living? I found myself on the wrong continent! As for the so-called community of artisans and patrons in the so-called city of Pale and their so-called *styles of expression*—'

'They hated you,' Gumble said.

'And I hated them! Tell me, did you see *anything* worthy of mention in Pale? Did you?'

'Well, there was one mosaic—'

'What?'

'Fortunately, the attributed artist was long dead, permitting my effusiveness in its praise.'

'You call that effusive? "It shows promise . . ." Isn't that what you said? You well know it's precisely what you said, as soon as that foppish host mentioned the artist was dead!'

'Actually,' Itkovian commented, 'rather droll, to say such a thing.'

'I am never droll,' the toad said.

'Though you do drool on occasion! Ha! Slimy one, yes? Ha!'

'Suck another lump of paint, will you? There, that quick-silvered white. Looks very tasty.'

'You just want me dead,' Ormulogun muttered, reaching for the small gummy piece of paint. 'So you can get effusive.'

'If you say so.'

'You're a leech, you know that? Following me around everywhere. A vulture.'

'Dear man,' Gumble sighed, 'I am a toad. While you are an artist. And for my fortune in the distinction, I daily thank every god that is and every god that ever was.'

Itkovian left them exchanging ever more elaborate insults, and continued on down the shoreline. He forgot to look at Ormulogun's canvas.

Once the armies were across the river, they would divide. The city of Lest lay directly south, four days' march, while the road to Setta angled west-southwest. Setta was at the very feet of the Vision Mountains, rising on the banks of the river from which it took its name. That same river continued on to the sea south of Lest, and would need to be crossed by both forces, eventually.

Itkovian would accompany the army that struck for Lest, which consisted of the Grey Swords, elements of Tiste Andii, the Rhivi, Ilgres Barghast, a regiment of cavalry from Saltoan, and a handful of lesser mercenary companies from North Genabackis. Caladan Brood remained in over-all command, with Kallor and Korlat as his seconds. The Grey Swords were attached in the manner of an allied force, with the Shield Anvil considered Brood's equal. This distinction did not apply to the other mercenary companies, for they were one and all contracted to the warlord. The Daru, Gruntle, and his motley followers were being viewed as wholly independent, welcome at the brief-ings but free to do as they pleased.

All in all, Itkovian concluded, the organization of the

command was confused, the hierarchies of rank ephemeral. *Not unlike our circumstances in Capustan, with the prince and the Mask Council ever muddying the waters. Perhaps this is a characteristic of the north and its independent city-states – before the Malazan invasion forced them into a confederacy of sorts, that is. And even then, it seemed, old rivalries and feuds perennially undermined the unification, to the invaders' advantage.*

The structure imposed by the Malazan High Fist upon those forces accompanying him was far clearer in its hierarchy. The imperial way was instantly recognizable to Itkovian, and indeed was similar to what he would have established, were he in Dujek Onearm's place. The High Fist commanded. His seconds were Whiskeyjack and Humbrall Taur – the latter displaying his wisdom by insisting upon Dujek's pre-eminence – as well as the commander of the Black Moranth, whom Itkovian had yet to meet. These three were considered equal in rank, yet distinct in their responsibilities.

Itkovian heard horse hooves and turned to see the Malazan second, Whiskeyjack, riding towards him along the strand. That he had paused to speak with the artist was evident in Ormulogun's hastily gathering up his supplies in the soldier's wake.

Whiskeyjack reined in. 'Good day to you, Itkovian.'

'And to you, sir. Is there something you wish of me?'

The bearded soldier shrugged, scanning the area. 'I am looking for Silverfox. Her, or the two marines who are supposed to be accompanying her.'

'Following her, you no doubt mean. They passed me earlier, first Silverfox, then the two soldiers. Riding east.'

'Did any of them speak with you?'

'No. They rode at some distance from me, so courtesies were not expected. Nor did I endeavour to hail them.'

The commander grimaced.

'Is something wrong, sir?'

'Quick Ben's been using his warrens to assist in the

crossing. Our forces are on the other side and are ready to march, since we've the longer road.'

'Indeed. Is Silverfox not of the Rhivi, however? Or do you simply wish to make formal your goodbye?'

His frown deepened. 'She's as much Malazan as Rhivi. I would ask her to choose whom to accompany.'

'Perhaps she has, sir.'

'Maybe not,' Whiskeyjack replied, eyes now fixed on something to the east.

Itkovian turned, but since he was on foot it was a moment longer before the two riders came into his line of sight. The marines, approaching at a steady canter.

They drew up before their commander.

'Where is she?' Whiskeyjack asked.

The marine on the right shrugged. 'We followed her to the coast. Above the tide-line was a row of lumpy hills surrounded by swampy ditches. She rode into one of the hills, Whiskeyjack—'

'Rode into the side of one of 'em,' the other elaborated. 'Vanished. Not a pause nor a stumble from her horse. We rode up to the spot but there was nothing there but grass, mud and rocks. We've lost her, which is, I guess, what she wanted.'

The commander was silent.

Itkovian had expected a heartfelt curse at the very least, and was impressed at the man's self-control.

'All right. Ride back with me. We're crossing to the other side.'

'We saw Gumble's pet on the way out.'

'I've already sent him and Ormulogun back. Theirs is the last wagon, and you well know Ormulogun's instructions regarding his collection.'

The marines nodded.

Itkovian asked, 'His collection? How many scenes has he painted since Pale?'

'Since Pale?' one of the marines grinned. 'There's over eight hundred stretches in that wagon. Ten, eleven years' worth. Dujek here, Dujek there, Dujek even where he wasn't but should have been. He's already done one of the siege of Capustan, with Dujek arriving in the nick of time, tall in his saddle and coming through the gate. There's one White Face Barghast crouching in the gate's shadow, looting a dead Pannion. And in the storm clouds over the scene you'll make out Laseen's face if you look carefully enough—'

'Enough,' Whiskeyjack growled. 'Your words give offence, soldier. The man before you is Itkovian.'

The marine's grin broadened but she said nothing.

'We know that, sir,' the other one said. 'Which is why my comrade here was teasing him. Itkovian, there's no such painting. Ormulogun is the Host's historian, since we ain't got any other, and he's charged on pain of death to keep things accurate, right down to the nosehairs.'

'Ride,' Whiskeyjack told them. 'I would a private word with Itkovian.'

'Aye, sir.'

The two marines departed.

'Apologies, Itkovian—'

'No need, sir. There is welcome relief to such irreverence. In fact, it pleases me that they would display such comfort.'

'Well, they're only like that with people they respect, though it's often taken as the opposite, which can lead to all sorts of trouble.'

'So I would imagine.'

'Well,' Whiskeyjack said gruffly, then surprised Itkovian by dismounting, stepping up to him and holding out his gauntleted hand. 'Among the soldiers of the Empire,' he said, 'where the worn gauntlet is for war and nothing other than war, to remain gauntleted when grasping the hand of another, in peace, is the rarest of gestures.'

'So it, too, is often misunderstood,' Itkovian said. 'I, sir, do not miscomprehend the significance, and so am honoured.' He grasped the commander's hand. 'You accord me far too much—'

'I do not, Itkovian. I only wish you were travelling with us, so that I could come to know you better.'

'Yet we will meet at Maurik, sir.'

Whiskeyjack nodded. 'Until then, Itkovian.'

They released their grips. The commander swung himself back into the saddle and gathered the reins. He hesitated, then said, 'Are all Elin like you, Itkovian?'

He shrugged. 'I am not unique.'

'Then 'ware the Empress the day her legions assail your homeland's borders.'

His brows rose. 'And come that day, will you be commanding those legions?'

Whiskeyjack grinned. 'Go well, sir.'

Itkovian watched the man ride away, down the strand, his horse's hooves kicking up green clumps of sand. He had a sudden, inexplicable conviction that they would never see each other again. After a moment, he shook his head to dispel the dread thought.

'Well, of course Kruppe will bless this company with his presence!'

'You misunderstood,' Quick Ben sighed. 'That was only a question, not an invitation.'

'Poor wizard is weary, yes? So many paths of sorcery to take the place of mundane barges plagued with leaky lack of integrity. None the less, Kruppe is impressed with your prowess – such a dance of warrens rarely if ever before witnessed by humble self. And each one pristine! As if to say *faugh!* to the foolish one in chains! Such a bold challenge! Such a—'

'Oh, be quiet! Please!' Quick Ben stood on the river's north shore. Mud covered his leggings to mid-thigh, the price for minimizing as much as possible the distance of the paths he had fashioned for the columns of troops, the wagons, the livestock and the spare mounts. He only awaited the last few stragglers who'd yet to arrive, Whiskeyjack included. To make his exhaustion even more unpleasant, the spirit of Talamandas whined unceasing complaint from his invisible perch on the wizard's left shoulder.

Too much power had been unveiled here. Sufficient to draw notice. Careless, claimed the sticksnare in a whisper. Suicidal, in fact. *The Crippled God cannot help but find us. Stupid bluster! And what of the Pannion Seer? A score of dread warrens all trembling to our passage! Proof of our singular efficacy against the infection! Will either of them simply sit back and do nothing in answer to what they have seen here?*

'Silence,' Quick Ben muttered.

Kruppe's wiry brows rose. 'One rude command was sufficient, Kruppe haughtily assures miserable wizard!'

'Not you. Never mind. I was thinking aloud.'

'Curious habit for a mage, yes? Dangerous.'

'You think so? How about some more loudly uttered thoughts, Daru? The display is deliberate. The unveiling of power here is precisely intended to kick the hornet nests. Both of them! Clumsily massive, an appalling absence of subtlety. Thunder to those who had been expecting the almost soundless padding of a mouse's feet and its whispering tail. Now, why would I do that, do you wonder?'

'Kruppe does not wonder at all, except, perhaps, at your insisting on explaining such admirable tactics of misdirection to these squalling seagulls.'

Quick Ben scowled down at the round little man. 'Really? I had no idea I was that obvious. Maybe I should reconsider.'

'Nonsense, Wizard! Hold to your unassailable self-confidence – aye, some might well call it megalomania, but not Kruppe, for he too is in possession of unassailable self-confidence, such as only mortals are capable of and then rightfully but a mere handful the world over. You've singular company, Kruppe assures you!'

Quick Ben grinned. 'Singular? And what about these seagulls?'

Kruppe waved a plump hand. 'Pah! Lest one should land

on your left shoulder, that is. Which would be another matter entirely, would it not?'

The wizard's dark eyes thinned suspiciously on the Daru at his side.

Kruppe blithely continued, 'In which case, poor ignorant bird would be witness to such potent plurality of cunning converse so as to reel confused if not mercifully constipated!'

Quick Ben blinked in startlement. 'What did you say?'

'Well sir, were we not suggesting the placement of corks? *Be quiet. Shut up.* Kruppe simply advised of an internal version with which seagull's ceaseless bleating complaint is silenced, indeed, stoppered up to the relief of one and all!'

Two hundred paces to their right another barge loaded with Brood's forces set out, the craft quickly drawing the lines down-current as it left the shore.

A pair of marines rode up to Quick Ben and Kruppe.

The wizard scowled at them. 'Where's Whiskeyjack?'

'On the way, Bridgeburner. Did the toad and his artist show up?'

'Just in time to take charge of their wagon, aye. They're on the other side.'

'Fancy work. We crossing the same way?'

'Well, I was thinking of dropping you halfway – when did you two last bathe?'

The women exchanged a glance, then one shrugged and said, 'Don't know. A month? Three? We've been busy.'

'And we'd rather not get wet, Wizard,' the other marine said. 'Our armour and the clothes under 'em might fall apart.'

'Kruppe asserts that would prove a sight never to be forgotten!'

'Bet your eyes'd fall out,' the soldier agreed. 'And if they didn't we'd have to help 'em along some.'

'At least our nails would be clean,' the other observed.

'Aai! Coarse women! Kruppe sought only to compliment!'

'You're the one needing a bath,' the marine said.

The Daru's expression displayed shock, then dismay. 'Outrageous notion. Sufficient layers of sweet scent applied over sufficient years, nay, decades, have resulted in a permanent and indeed impervious bouquet of gentlest fragrance.' He waved his plump, pale hands. 'A veritable aura about oneself to draw lovestruck butterflies—'

'Look like deerflies to me—'

'These are uncivil lands – yet do you see a single insect alight?'

'Well, there's a few drowned in your oily hair, now that you ask.'

'Precisely. Inimical foes one and all fall to the same fate.'

'Ah,' Quick Ben said, 'here comes Whiskeyjack. Finally. Thank the gods.'

Darkness swallowed the alley as dusk descended on the ruined city. A few oil lamps lit the major thoroughfares, and the occasional squad of Gidrath walked rounds carrying lanterns of their own.

Wrapped in a cloak hiding his full armour, Coll stood within an alcove and watched one such squad troop past at the alley's mouth, watched as the pool of yellow light slowly dwindled, until the night once more reclaimed the street.

He stepped out and gestured.

Murillio flicked the traces, startling the oxen into motion. The wagon creaked and rocked over the cracked, heat-blasted cobbles.

Coll strode in advance, out onto the street. It had been only partially cleared of rubble. Three gutted temples were within the range of his vision, showing no indication of having been reoccupied. No different from the four others they had found earlier that afternoon.

At the moment, the prospects were grim. It seemed the only surviving priests were those in the Thrall, and that was the last place they wanted to visit. Rumour was, political rivalries had reached a volatile state, now that the Mask Council was free of the presence of powerful allies; free, as well, of a royal presence who traditionally provided a levelling influence on their excesses. The future of Capustan was not a promising one.

Coll turned to the right – northeast – waving behind him as he made his way up the street. He heard Murillio's muted cursing as he slapped the traces down onto the backs of the two oxen. The animals were tired and hungry, the wagon behind them overburdened.

Hood take us, we might have made a terrible mistake . . .

He heard the flap of a bird's wings overhead, soft and momentary, and thought nothing of it.

Deep ruts had been worn into the cobbles from the passage of countless wagons, many of them of late heavily loaded down with broken stone, but their width did not match that of the Rhivi wagon – a thick-wheeled, plains vehicle built to contest high grasses and muddy sinkholes. Nor could Murillio manage to avoid the wagon's slipping into one of the ruts, for the oxen had a grooved path of their own on this side of the street. The result was a sharply canted, awkward progress, the yokes shifted into angles that were clearly uncomfortable for the oxen.

Behind him, Coll heard one low a complaint, which ended with a strange grunt and whip of the traces. He spun in time to see Murillio's body pitching from the seat, to strike the cobbles with a bone-cracking impact.

A huge figure, all in black, who seemed for the briefest moment to be winged, now stood atop the wagon.

Murillio lay in a motionless heap beside the front wheel.

Fear ripped through the Daru. 'What the—'

The figure gestured. Black sorcery bloomed from him, swept tumbling towards Coll.

Swearing, the Daru flung himself to the right, rolled clanking, metal snapping on stone, to collide with the first half-moon step of a temple.

But the magic flowed too wide to escape, swirling and

spinning its inky power to fill the street like a flash-flood.

Lying on his side, back jammed against the step, Coll could only throw up a forearm to cover his eyes as the sorcery loomed over him, then plunged down.

And vanished. Blinking, Coll grunted, dropped his arm in time to see a dark, armoured figure step directly over him from behind – from the direction of the temple's entrance.

His peripheral vision caught flanking longswords, one of them strangely bent, gliding past as the massive warrior reached the cobbles of the street.

The attacker perched on the wagon spoke in a high voice, the tone bemused. '*You* should be dead. I can feel the coldness of you. I can sense the fist of Hood, coiled there in your lifeless chest. He's kept you here. Wandering.'

Huh, this new arrival doesn't look very dead to me. His eyes scanned the shadows to the right of the wagon, seeking Murillio's motionless form.

'Not wandering,' the warrior rasped, still striding towards the figure. '*Hunting*.'

'Us? But we've taken so few from you! Less than a score in this city. Knight of Death, has your master not fed unto bursting of late? And I but sought the unconscious hag – she lies in the bed of this wagon. Hovering at the very edge of the chasm. Surely your master—'

'Not for you,' the warrior rumbled. 'Her spirit awaits. And those of her gathered kin. And the beasts whose hearts are empty. All await. Not for you.'

The air in the alley had grown bitter cold.

'Oh, all right, then,' the attacker sighed. 'What of this driver and his guard? I could use so many pieces of them—'

'No. Korbal Broach, hear the words of my master. You are to release the undead who guard your compound. You and the one named Bauchelain are to leave the city. This night.'

'We'd planned on a morning departure, Knight of Death – for you *are* the Knight, yes? High House Death stirs to wakefulness, I now sense. A morning departure, yes? To follow these fascinating armies southward—'

'This night, or I shall descend upon you, and claim your souls. Do you realize the fate my master has in store for you two?'

Coll watched as the bald, pallid-faced man atop the wagon raised his arms – which then blurred, broadened into midnight wings. He giggled. 'You will have to catch us first!' The blurring became a smear, then where the man had stood there was only a bedraggled crow, cawing sharply as it rose upward, wings thrumming, and was swallowed by darkness.

The warrior walked to where Murillio lay.

Coll drew a deep breath, seeking to slow his hammering heart, then climbed painfully to his feet. 'My thanks to you, sir,' he grunted, wincing at what in the morning would be fierce bruising on his right shoulder and hip. 'Does my companion live?'

The warrior, who Coll now saw was wearing the remnants of Gidrath armour, swung to face him. 'He lives. Korbal Broach requires that they be alive . . . for his work. At least at first. You are to come with me.'

'Ah, when you said hunting, that sorceror assumed it was him you were hunting. But it wasn't, was it?'

'They are an arrogant pair.'

Coll slowly nodded. He hesitated, then said, 'Forgive me if I am being rude, but I would know what you – what your Lord – would do with us? We've an elderly woman to care for—'

'You are to have my master's protection. Come, the Temple of Hood has been prepared for your residence.'

'Not sure how I should take that. The Mhybe needs help.'

'What the Mhybe needs, Coll of Darujhistan, is not for you to give.'

'Is it for Hood to give?'

'The woman's flesh and bone must be maintained. Fed, given water, cared for. That is your responsibility.'

'You did not answer.'

'Follow me. We have not far to go.'

'At the moment,' Coll said quietly, 'I am inclined otherwise.' He reached for his sword.

The Knight of Death cocked his head. 'Tell me, Coll of Darujhistan, do you sleep?'

The Daru frowned. 'Of course. What—'

'I did once, too. I must have, yes? But now, I do not. Instead, I pace. You see, I cannot remember sleep. I cannot remember what it was like.'

'I – I am sorry for that.'

'Thus, one who does not sleep . . . and, here in this wagon, one who will not awaken. I believe, Coll of Darujhistan, that we will have need of each other. Soon. This woman and I.'

'What kind of need?'

'I do not know. Come, we've not far.'

Coll slowly resheathed his sword. He could not have explained why he did so; none of his questions had been answered to his satisfaction, and the thought of entering Hood's protection chilled his skin. None the less, he nodded and said, 'A moment, if you will. I have to lift Murillio onto the bed.'

'Ah, yes. That is true. I would have done so but, alas, I find myself unable to release my swords from my own hands.' The warrior was silent a moment longer, then he said, 'Korbal Broach saw into me. His words have made my mind . . . troubled. Coll of Darujhistan, I think I am dead. Am I? Am I dead?'

'I don't know,' the Daru replied, 'but . . . I think so.'

'The dead, it is said, do not sleep.'

Coll well knew the saying, and knew that it had originally come from Hood's own temple. He knew, as well, the wry observation that closed the quote. ' "While the living do not live." Not that that makes much sense.'

'It does to me,' the warrior said. 'For I now know that I have lost what I did not know I once possessed.'

898

Coll's mind stumbled through that statement, then he sighed. 'I'd be a fool not to take your word for it . . . have you a name?'

'I believe so, but I have forgotten it.'

'Well,' Coll said as he crouched down over Murillio and gathered the man into his arms, 'Knight of Death won't do, I'm afraid.' He straightened, grunting at the weight in his arms. 'You were a Gidrath, yes? And a Capan – though I admit, with that bronze hue to your skin, you've more the colouring of—'

'No, I was not Gidrath. Not Capan. I am not, I think, from this continent at all. I do not know why I appeared here. Nor how. I have not been here long. This is as my master wills. Of my past, I recall but one thing.'

Coll carried Murillio to the back of the wagon and laid the man down. 'And what's that?'

'I once stood within fire.'

After a long moment, Coll sighed roughly. 'An unfortunate memory . . .'

'There was pain. Yet I held on. Fought on. Or so I believe. I was, I think, sworn to defend a child's life. But the child was no more. It may be . . . that I failed.'

'Well, we still need a name for you.'

'Perhaps one will come to you eventually, Coll of Darujhistan.'

'I promise it.'

'Or perhaps one day my memories will return in full, and with them my name.'

And if Hood has any mercy in him that day will never come, friend. For I think there was nothing easy in your life. Or in your death. And it seems he does possess mercy, for he's taken you far away from all that you once knew, for if I'm not mistaken, if only by your features and never mind that strange skin, you're Malazan.

Itkovian had crossed on the last barge, beneath a vast spread of spearpoint stars, in the company of Stonny

Menackis and Gruntle and his score of barbed followers, along with a hundred or so Rhivi – mostly elders and their dogs. The animals snapped and squabbled in the confines of the flat, shallow craft, then settled down for the journey's second half once they'd managed to fight their way to the gunnels and could look out over the river.

The dogs were the first off when the barge ground ashore on the south side, barking wildly as they splashed through the reeds, and Itkovian was glad for their departure. Only half listening to Gruntle and Stonny exchanging insults like a husband and wife who had known each other far too long, Itkovian readied his horse to await the laying down of planks, and watched with mild interest the Rhivi elders following in the wake of their dogs without heed to the shore's churned mud and matted reeds.

The low, worn-down hills on this side of the river still held a haze of dust and dung-smoke, draped like a mourner's veil over the army's score thousand or more tents. Apart from a few hundred Rhivi herders and the bhederin herd they were tasked to drive across come the dawn, the entire force of the invaders was now on Pannion territory.

No-one had contested the landing. The low hills to the south seemed devoid of life, revealing naught but the worn tracks left behind by Septarch Kulpath's besieging army.

Gruntle moved up alongside him. 'Something tells me we'll be marching through razed land all the way down to Coral.'

'That seems likely, sir. It is as I would have done, were I the Seer.'

'I sometimes wonder if Brood and Dujek realize that the army that besieged Capustan was but one among at least three of comparable size. And while Kulpath was a particularly effective Septarch, there are six others competent enough to cause us grief.'

Itkovian pulled his gaze from the encampment ahead to study the hulking warrior at his side. 'We must assume our enemy is preparing for us. Yet, within the Domin, the last grains of the bell-glass are even now trickling down.'

Treach's Mortal Sword grunted. 'You know something the rest of us don't?'

'Not specifically, sir. I have but drawn conclusions based on such details as I was able to observe when viewing Kulpath's army, and the Tenescowri.'

'Well, don't keep them to yourself.'

Itkovian returned his gaze to the south. After a moment he sighed. 'Cities and governments are but the flowering head of a plant whose stalk is the commonalty, and it is the commonalty whose roots are within the earth, drawing the necessary sustenance that maintains the flower. The Tenescowri, sir, is the Domin's surviving commonalty – people torn from their land, from their villages, their homes, their farms. All food production has ceased, and in its place has arisen the horror of cannibalism. The country-side before us is indeed razed, but not in answer to us. It has been a wasteland for some time, sir. Thus, while the flower still blazes its colour, it is in fact already dead.'

'Drying from a hook beneath the Crippled God's shelf?'

Itkovian shrugged. 'Caladan Brood and the High Fist have selected cities as their destinations. Lest, Setta, Maurik and Coral. Of these, I believe only the last still lives. None of the others would be able to feed a defending army; indeed, not even its own citizenry – if any still remain. The Seer has no choice but to concentrate his forces on the one city where he now resides, and his soldiers will have no choice but to assume the practices of the Tenescowri. I suspect that the Tenescowri were created for that eventual purpose – as food for the soldiers.'

Gruntle's expression was troubled. 'What you describe, Itkovian, is an empire that was never meant to sustain itself.'

'Unless it could continue to expand without surcease.'

'But even then, it would be alive only on its outer,

ever-advancing edges, spreading out from a dead core, a core that grew with it.'

Itkovian nodded. 'Aye, sir.'

'So, if Brood and Dujek are expecting battles at Setta, Lest and Maurik, they may be in for a surprise.'

'So I believe.'

'Those Malazans will end up doing a lot of pointless marching,' Gruntle observed, 'if you're right.'

'Perhaps there are other issues sufficient to justify the division of forces, Mortal Sword.'

'Not quite as united as they would have us believe?'

'There are powerful leaders gathered within that command, sir. It is perhaps miraculous that a serious clash of wills has not yet occurred.'

Gruntle said nothing for a time.

The broad wicker platforms were being anchored in place at the front of the barge, a company of mercenaries assembling the walkway with practised efficiency.

'Let us hope, then,' he finally rumbled, 'the siege at Coral is not a long one.'

'It will not be,' Itkovian asserted. 'I predict a single attack, intended to overwhelm. A combination of soldiery and sorcery. The massive sundering of defences is the intention of the warlord and the High Fist. Both are well aware of the risks inherent in any prolonged investment.'

'Sounds messy, Itkovian.'

Stonny Menackis came up behind them, leading her horse. 'Get moving, you two – you're holding us all up and this damned barge is settling. If I get any mud on these new clothes, I will kill whoever's to blame. Barbed or otherwise.'

Itkovian smiled. 'I'd intended complimenting you on your garb—'

'The wonders of the Trygalle. Made to order by my favourite tailor in Darujhistan.'

'You seem to favour green, sir.'

'Ever seen a jaelparda?'

Itkovian nodded. 'Such snakes are known in Elingarth.'

'Deadly kissers, jaelparda. This green is a perfect match, isn't it? It'd better be. It's what I paid for and it wasn't cheap. And this pale gold – you see? Lining the cloak? Ever looked at the underbelly of a white paralt?'

'The spider?'

'The death-tickler, aye. This is the colour.'

'I could not have mistaken it for otherwise,' Itkovian replied.

'Good, I'm glad someone here understands the subtle nuances of high civilization. Now move your damned horse or what you ain't used for far too long will get introduced to the toe of my shiny new boot.'

'Yes, sir.'

Corporal Picker watched Detoran drag Hedge towards her tent. The two passed in silence along the very edge of the firepit's light. Before they vanished once more into the gloom, Picker was witness to a comic pantomime as Hedge, the skin of his face stretched taut in a wild grimace, sought to bolt in an effort to escape Detoran. She responded by reaching up to grip the man's throat and shaking his head back and forth until his struggles ceased.

After they'd disappeared, Blend grunted. 'What night thankfully hides . . .'

'Not well enough, alas,' Picker muttered, poking at the fire with a splintered spear-shaft.

'Well, she'll probably be gagging him right now, then ripping off his—'

'All right all right, I take your point.'

'Poor Hedge.'

'Poor Hedge nothing, Blend. If it didn't get him going it wouldn't still be going on night after night.'

'Then again, we're soldiers one and all.'

'And what's that mean?'

'Means we know that following orders is the best way of staying alive.'

'So Hedge had better stand to attention if he wants to

keep breathing? Is that what you're saying? I'd have thought terror'd leave it limp and dangling.'

'Detoran used to be a master sergeant, remember. I once saw a recruit stay at attention for a bell and a half after the poor lad's heart had burst to one of her tirades. A bell and a half, Picker, standing there dead and cold—'

'Rubbish. I was there. It was about a tenth of a bell and you know it.'

'My point still stands, and I'd bet my whole column of back pay that Hedge's is doing the same.'

Picker stabbed at the fire. 'Funny, that,' she murmured after a while.

'What is?'

'Oh, what you were saying. Not the dead recruit, but Detoran having been a master sergeant. We've all been busted about, us Bridgeburners. Almost every damned one of us, starting right up top with Whiskeyjack himself. Mallet led a healer's cadre back when we had enough healers and the Emperor was in charge. And didn't Spindle captain a company of sappers once?'

'For three days, then one of 'em stumbled onto his own cusser—'

'And then they all went up, yeah. We were a thousand paces up the road and my ears rang for days.'

'That was the end of companies made up of sappers. Dassem broke 'em up after that, meaning that Spindle had no specialist corps to captain any more. So, Picker, what about it?'

'Nothing. Just that none of us is what we once was.'

'I've never been promoted.'

'Well, surprise! You've made a profession of not getting noticed!'

'Even so. And Antsy was born a sergeant—'

'And it's stunted his growth, aye. He's never been busted down, granted, but that's because he's the worst sergeant there ever was. Keeping him one punishes all of us, starting with Antsy himself. All I was saying was, we're all of us losers.'

'Oh, that's a welcome thought, Picker.'

'And who said every thought has to be a nice one? Nobody.'

'I would, only I didn't think of it.'

'Ha. Ha.'

The slow clump of horse hooves reached them. A moment later Captain Paran came into view, leading his horse by the reins.

'Been a long day, Captain,' Picker said. 'We got some tea if you'd like.'

Paran looped the reins over the saddle horn and approached. 'Last fire left among the Bridgeburners. Don't you two ever sleep?'

'We could ask the same of you, sir,' Picker replied. 'But we all already know that sleep's for weaklings, right?'

'Depends on how peaceful it is, I'd think.'

'Captain's right on that,' Blend said to Picker.

'Well,' the corporal sniffed, 'I'm peaceful enough when I sleep.'

Blend grunted. 'That's what you think.'

'We've had word,' Paran said, accepting the cup of steaming herbal brew from Picker, 'from the Black Moranth.'

'They reconnoitred Setta.'

'Aye. There's no-one there. Not breathing, anyway. The whole city's one big necropolis.'

'So why are we still marching there?' Picker asked. 'Unless we're not . . .'

'We are, Corporal.'

'What for?'

'We're marching to Setta because we're not marching to Lest.'

'Well,' Blend sighed, 'I'm glad that's been cleared up.'

Paran sipped his tea, then said, 'I have elected a second.'

'A second, sir?' Picker asked. 'Why?'

'Obvious reasons. In any case, I've chosen you, Picker. You're now a lieutenant. Whiskeyjack has given his blessing. In my absence you're to command the Bridgeburners—'

'No thanks, sir.'

'It's not up for discussion, Picker. Your lieutenancy is already inscribed in the rolls. Official, with Dujek's seal on it.'

Blend nudged her. 'Congratulations – oh, I suppose I should have saluted.'

'Shut up,' Picker growled. 'But you're right on one thing – don't ever bump me again, woman.'

'That's a hard order to follow . . . sir.'

Paran drained the last of his tea and straightened. 'I've only got one order for you, Lieutenant.'

She looked up at him. 'Captain?'

'The Bridgeburners,' Paran said, and his expression was suddenly severe. 'Keep them together, no matter what happens. Together, Lieutenant.'

'Uh, yes, sir.'

They watched Paran return to his horse and lead it away.

Neither woman said much for a while thereafter, then Blend sighed. 'Let's go to bed, Picker.'

'Aye.'

They stamped out the remnants of the fire. Darkness closing around them, Blend stepped closer and hooked her arm around Picker's.

'It's all down,' she murmured, 'to what the night hides . . .'

To Hood it is. It's all down to what the captain was saying behind what he said. That's what I need to figure out. Something tells me it's the end of sleeping peacefully for Lieutenant Picker . . .

They strode from the dying embers and were swallowed by darkness.

Moments later, no movement was visible, the stars casting their faint silver light down on the camp of the Bridgeburners. The oft-patched tents were colourless in the dull, spectral glow. A scene that was ghostly and strangely timeless. Revealing its own kind of peace.

Whiskeyjack entered Dujek's command tent. As expected, the High Fist was prepared for him. Hooded lantern on camp table, two tankards of ale and a block of Gadrobi goat cheese. Dujek himself sat in one of the chairs, head lowered in sleep.

'High Fist,' Whiskeyjack said as he removed his gauntlets, eyes on the ale and cheese.

The old commander grunted, sat straighter, blinking. 'Right.'

'We've lost her.'

'Too bad. You must be hungry, so I – oh, good. Keep filling your mouth and leave the talking to me, then.' He leaned forward and retrieved his tankard. 'Artanthos found Paran and delivered the orders. So, the captain will get the Bridgeburners ready – ready for what, they won't know and that's probably for the best. As for Paran himself, all right, Quick Ben convinced me. Too bad, that, though I'll be honest and say as far as I can see we'll miss the wizard more than we will that nobleborn lad—'

Holding up one hand to stop Dujek, Whiskeyjack washed down the last of the cheese with a mouthful of ale.

The High Fist sighed, waited.

'Dujek—'

'Comb the crumbs from your beard,' the High Fist growled, 'since I expect you'll want me to take you seriously.'

'A word on Paran. With the loss of Tatter— of Silverfox, I mean, the captain's value to us can't be overestimated. No, not just us. The Empire itself. Quick Ben's been adamant on this. Paran is the Master of the Deck. Within him is the power to reshape the world, High Fist.' He paused, mulling on his own words. 'Now, maybe there's no chance of Laseen ever regaining the man's favour, but at the very least she'd be wise to avoid making the relationship worse.'

Dujek's brows lifted. 'I'll so advise her the next time I see her.'

'All right. Sorry. No doubt the Empress is cognizant—'

'No doubt. As I was saying, however, it's the loss of Quick Ben that stings the most. From my own point of view, that is.'

'Well, sir, what the wizard has in mind . . . uh, I agree with him that the less Brood and company know of it the better. So long as the division of forces proceeds as planned, they'll have no reason but to believe that Quick Ben marches in step with the rest of us.'

'The wizard's madness—'

'High Fist, the wizard's madness has saved our skins more than once. Not just mine and the Bridgeburners', but yours as well—'

'I am well aware of that, Whiskeyjack. Forgive an old man his fears, please. It was Brood and Rake and the Tiste Andii – and the damned Elder Gods, as well – who were supposed to step into the Crippled God's path. They're the ones with countless warrens and frightening levels of potency – not us, not one mortal squad wizard and a young nobleborn captain who's already died once. Even if they don't mess things up, look at the enemies we'll acquire.'

'Assuming our present allies are so short-sighted as to fail to comprehend.'

'Whiskeyjack, we're the Malazans, remember? Nothing we do is ever supposed to reveal a hint of our long-term plans – mortal empires aren't supposed to think that far ahead. And we're damned good at following that principle, you and I. Hood take me, Laseen inverted the command structure for a reason, you know.'

'So the right people would be there at ground level when Shadowthrone and Cotillion made their move, aye.'

'Not just them, Whiskeyjack.'

'This should be made known to Quick Ben – to all of the Bridgeburners, in fact.'

'No. In any case, don't you think your wizard's figured things out yet?'

'If so, then why did he send Kalam after the Empress?'

'Because Kalam needs to be convinced in person, that's why. Face to face with the Empress. Quick Ben knew that.'

'Then I must be the only thick-witted one in this entire imperial game,' Whiskeyjack sighed.

'Maybe the only truly honourable one, at any rate. Look, we knew the Crippled God was getting ready to make a move. We knew the gods would make a mess of things. Granted, we didn't anticipate the Elder Gods getting involved, but that's neither here nor there, is it? The point was, we knew trouble was coming. From more than one direction – but how could we have guessed that what was going on in the Pannion Domin was in any way related to the efforts of the Crippled God?

'Even so, I don't think it was entirely chance that it was a couple of Bridgeburners who bumped into that agent of the Chained One – that sickly artisan from Darujhistan; nor that Quick Ben was there to confirm the arrival of the House of Chains. Laseen has always understood the value of tactical placement yielding results – Hood knows, she taught that to the Emperor, not the other way round. The Crippled God's pocket-warren wanders – it always has. That it wandered to the hills between Pale and Darujhistan was an opportunity the Crippled God could not pass up – if he was going to do anything, he had to act. And we caught him. Maybe not in a way we'd anticipated, but we caught him.'

'Well enough,' Whiskeyjack muttered.

'As for Paran, there's a certain logic there, as well. Tayschrenn was grooming Tattersail to the role of Mistress of the Deck, after all. And when that went wrong, well, there was a residual effect – straight to the man closest to her at the time. Not physically, but certainly spiritually. In all this, Whiskeyjack – if we look on things in retrospect – the only truly thick-witted player was Bellurdan Skullcrusher. We'll never know what happened between him and Tattersail on that plain, but by the Abyss it ranks as one of the worst foul-ups in imperial history. That the role of Master of the Deck fell to a Malazan and not to some Gadrobi herder who'd happened to be nearby, well, Oponn's luck played into our hands there, and that's about all we can say of that, I think.'

'Now I'm the one who's worried,' Whiskeyjack said. 'We've been too clever by far, leaving me wondering who's manipulating whom. We're playing shadowgames with the Lord of Shadow, rattling the chains of the Crippled God, and now buying Brood more time without him even knowing it, whilst at the same time defying the T'lan Imass, or at least intending to . . .'

'Opportunity, Whiskeyjack. Hesitation is fatal. When you find yourself in the middle of a wide, raging river, there's only one direction to swim in. It's up to us to keep Laseen's head above water – and through her, the Malazan Empire. If Brood swings his hammer in Burn's name – we drown, all of us. Law, order, peace – civilization, all gone.'

'So, to keep Brood from doing that, we sacrifice ourselves by challenging the Crippled God. Us, one damned weary army already decimated by one of Laseen's panics.'

'Best forgive her her panics, Whiskeyjack. Shows she's mortal, after all.'

'Virtually wiping out the Bridgeburners at Pale—'

'Was an accident and while you didn't know it at the time, you know it now. Tayschrenn ordered them to remain in the tunnels because he thought it was the safest place. The safest.'

'Seemed more like someone wanted us to be a collateral fatality,' Whiskeyjack said. *No, not us. Me. Damn you, Dujek, you lead me to suspect you knew more of that than I'd hoped. Beru fend, I hope I'm wrong . . .* 'And with what happened at Darujhistan—'

'What happened at Darujhistan was a mess. Miscommunication on all sides. It was too soon after the Siege of Pale – too soon for all of us.'

'So I wasn't the only one rattled, then.'

'At Pale? No. Hood take us, we all were. That battle

910

didn't go as planned. Tayschrenn really believed he could take down Moon's Spawn – and force Rake into the open. And had he not been left virtually on his own in the attack, things might well have turned out differently. From what I learned later, Tayschrenn didn't know at the time who Nightchill really was, but he knew she was closing in on Rake's sword. Her and Bellurdan, who she was using to do her research for her. It looked like a play for power, a private one, and Laseen wasn't prepared to permit that. And even then, Tayschrenn only hit her when she took out A'Karonys – the very High Mage who came to Tayschrenn with his suspicions about her. When I said Bellurdan killing Tattersail was the worst foul-up in Malazan history, that day at Pale runs a close second.'

'There have been more than a few lately . . .'

Dujek slowly nodded, his eyes glittering in the lantern light. 'All starting, I'd say, with the T'lan Imass slaughtering the citizens of Aren. But, as even with that one, each disaster yields its truths. Laseen didn't give that order, but someone did. Someone returned to sit down in that First Throne – and that someone was supposed to be dead – and he used the T'lan Imass to wreak vengeance on Laseen, to shake her grip on the Empire. Lo, the first hint that Emperor Kellanved wasn't quite as dead as we would have liked.'

'And still insane, aye. Dujek, I think we're heading for another disaster.'

'I hope you're wrong. In any case, I was the one who needed his confidence boosted tonight, not you.'

'Well, I guess that's the price of inverted commands . . .'

'For all that I've been saying, a new observation comes to me, Whiskeyjack, and it's not a pleasant one.'

'And that is?'

'I'm beginning to think we're not half as sure of what we're up to as we think we are.'

'Who's "we"?'

'The empire. Laseen. Tayschrenn. As for you and I, well,

we're the least of the players and what little we know isn't even close to what we need to know. We stepped up to the assault on Moon's Spawn at Pale knowing virtually nothing of what was really going on. And if I hadn't cornered Tayschrenn after, we still wouldn't.'

Whiskeyjack studied the dregs of ale in the tankard in his hands. 'Quick Ben's smart,' he murmured. 'I can't really say how much he's worked out. He can get pretty cagey at times.'

'He's still willing, surely?'

'Oh yes. And he's made it plain that he has acquired a powerful faith in Ganoes Paran. In this new Master of the Deck.'

'Does that strike you as odd, then?'

'A little. Paran has been used by a god. He's walked within the sword, Dragnipur. He has the blood of a Hound of Shadow in his veins. And none of us know what changes such things have wrought in him, or even what they portend. He's been anything but predictable, and he's almost impossible to manage – oh, he'll follow orders I give him, but I think if Laseen believes she can use him, she might be in for a surprise.'

'You like the man, don't you?'

'I admire him, Dujek. For his resilience, for his ability to examine himself with a courage that is ruthless, and, most of all, for his inherent humanity.'

'Sufficient to warrant faith, I'd say.'

Whiskeyjack grimaced. 'Stabbed by my own sword.'

'Better that than someone else's.'

'I'm thinking of retiring, Dujek. When this war is finished.'

'I'd guessed as much, friend.'

Whiskeyjack looked up. 'You think she'll let me?'

'I don't think we should give her the choice.'

'Shall I drown like Crust and Urko did? Shall I be seen to be slain then have my body vanish like Dassem did?'

'Assuming none of those really happened—'

912

'Dujek—'

'All right, but some doubt still remains, you have to admit.'

'I don't share it, and one day I'll track down Duiker and force the truth from him – if anyone knows, it's that cranky historian.'

'Has Quick Ben heard from Kalam yet?'

'He's not told me so if he has.'

'Where's your wizard right now?'

'I last saw him jawing with those Trygalle traders.'

'The man should be getting some sleep, with what's coming.'

Whiskeyjack set down the tankard and rose. 'So should we, old friend,' he said, wincing as he settled too much weight on his bad leg. 'When are the Black Moranth arriving?'

'Two nights hence.'

Whiskeyjack grunted, then swung towards the tent's exit. 'Good night, Dujek.'

'And to you, Whiskeyjack. Oh, one last thing.'

'Yes?'

'Tayschrenn. He's been wanting to apologize to you. For what happened to the Bridgeburners.'

'He knows where to find me, Dujek.'

'He wants a proper moment.'

'What's proper?'

'I'm not sure, but it hasn't happened yet.'

Whiskeyjack said nothing for a half-dozen heartbeats, then he reached for the tent flap. 'See you in the morning, Dujek.'

'Aye,' the High Fist replied.

As Whiskeyjack made his way towards his own tent he saw a tall, dark-robed figure standing before it.

He smiled as he approached. 'I'd missed you.'

'And I you,' Korlat responded.

'Brood's been keeping you busy. Come inside, it'll only be a moment before I get the lantern lit.'

He heard her sighing behind him as they entered the tent. 'I'd rather you didn't bother.'

'Well, you can see in the dark, but—'

She drew him round and settled against him, murmured, 'If there is to be a conversation, keep it short, please. What I desire is not answered by words.'

He closed his arms around her. 'I'd only wondered if you'd found Silverfox.'

'No. It seems she is able to travel paths I did not think still existed. Instead, two of her undead wolves arrived . . . to escort me home. They are . . . unusual.'

Whiskeyjack thought back to when he'd first seen the T'lan Ay, rising as dust from the yellow grasses, finding their bestial shapes until the hills on all sides were covered. 'I know. There's something strangely disproportionate about them—'

'Yes, you are right. They jar the eye. Too long limbs, too large shoulders, yet short-necked and wide-jawed. But there is more than just their physical appearance that I found . . . alarming.'

'More so than the T'lan Imass?'

She nodded. 'There is, within the T'lan Imass, an emptiness, as of a smoke-blackened cavity. But not with the T'lan Ay. Within these wolves . . . I see sorrow. Eternal sorrow . . .'

She shivered in his arms. Whiskeyjack said nothing. *You see in their eyes, dear lover, what I see in yours. And it is the reflection – the recognition – that has shaken you so.*

'At the camp's edge,' Korlat went on, 'they fell to dust. One moment trotting on either side, then . . . gone. I don't know why, but that disturbed me more than anything else.'

Because it is what awaits all of us. Even you, Korlat. 'This conversation was supposed to be short. It ends now. Come to bed, lass.'

She looked into his eyes. 'And after tonight?'

He grimaced. 'It may be a while, aye.'

'Crone has returned.'

'Has she now?'

Korlat nodded. She was about to say more, then hesitated, searching his eyes, and said nothing.

Setta, Lest, Maurik. The cities were empty. Yet the armies were dividing none the less. And neither would speak of why. Both sides of the alliance had things to hide, secrets to maintain, and the closer they got to Coral the more problematic it became maintaining those secrets.

Most of the Tiste Andii have vanished. Gone with Rake, probably to Moon's Spawn. But where is Moon's Spawn? And what in Hood's name are they planning? Will we arrive at Coral only to find the city already fallen, the Pannion Seer dead – his soul taken by Dragnipur – and that massive mountain hanging overhead?

The Black Moranth have searched for that damned floating rock . . . to no avail.

And then there are our secrets. We're sending Paran and the Bridgeburners ahead; Hood take us, we're doing a lot more than that.

This is an unwelcome play for power, now imminent – we all knew it was coming. Setta, Lest, Maurik. The subtle game is no longer subtle.

'My heart is yours, Korlat,' Whiskeyjack said to the woman in his arms. 'Nothing else matters to me. Nothing – no-one.'

'Please – do not apologize for what has not even happened yet. Don't talk about it at all.'

'I didn't think I was, lass.' *Liar. You were. In your own way. You were apologizing.*

She accepted the lie with a wry smile. 'Very well.'

Later, Whiskeyjack would think back on his words, and wish that they had been cleaner – devoid of hidden intent.

Eyes grainy from lack of sleep, Paran watched Quick Ben close his conversation with Haradas then leave the company of the Trygalle trader to rejoin the captain.

'The sappers will howl,' Paran said as the two of them

resumed their walk towards the Malazan encampment, newly established on the south shore of Catlin River.

Quick Ben shrugged. 'I'll take Hedge to one side for a word or two. After all, Fiddler's closer than a brother to him, and with the mess that Fid's got into he needs all the help he can get. The only issue is whether the Trygalle can deliver the package in time.'

'They're an extraordinary lot, those traders.'

'They're insane. Doing what they're doing. Sheer audacity is the only thing that keeps them alive.'

'I'd add a certain skill for travelling inimical warrens, Quick.'

'Let us hope it's sufficient,' the wizard responded.

'It wasn't just Moranth munitions, was it?'

'No. The situation in Seven Cities couldn't be more desperate. Anyway, I've done what I could. As to its effectiveness, we'll see.'

'You're a remarkable man, Quick Ben.'

'No, I'm not. Now, best keep all this as private an affair as possible. Hedge will keep his trap shut, and so will Whiskeyjack—'

'Gentlemen! Such a lovely evening!'

Both swung at the voice booming directly behind them. 'Kruppe!' Quick Ben hissed. 'You slippery—'

'Now now, Kruppe begs your indulgence. 'Twas mere happy accident that Kruppe heard your admirable words whilst almost stumbling ever so quietly on your heels, and indeed, now desires nothing else than to partake, ever so humbly, in courageous enterprise!'

'If you speak a word of this to anyone,' Quick Ben growled, 'I will slit your throat.'

The Daru withdrew his decrepit handkerchief and mopped his forehead, three quick dabs that seemed to leave the silk cloth sodden with sweat. 'Kruppe assures deadly wizard that silence is as Kruppe's closest mistress, lover unseen and unseeable, unsuspected and unmitigable. Whilst at the same time, Kruppe proclaims that the fair citizens of Darujhistan will hark to such a noble cause – Baruk himself so assures and would do so in person were he able. Alas, he has naught but this to offer.' With that Kruppe withdrew with a flourish a small glass ball from the handkerchief, then dropped it to the ground. It broke with a soft tinkle. Mists rose, gathered knee-high between the Daru and the two Malazans, and slowly assumed the form of a bhokaral.

'Aai,' Kruppe muttered, 'such ugly, indeed visually offensive, creatures.'

'Only because you resemble them all too closely,' Quick Ben pointed out, his eyes on the apparition.

The bhokaral twisted its neck to look up at the wizard, glittering black eyes in a black, grapefruit-sized head. The creature bared its needle teeth. 'Greet! Baruk! Master! Would! Help!'

'Sadly terse effort on dear, no doubt overworked Baruk's part,' Kruppe said. 'His best conjurations display linguistic grace, if not amiable fluidity, whilst this . . . thing, alas, evinces—'

'Quiet, Kruppe,' Quick Ben said. He spoke to the bhokaral. 'Uncharacteristic as it sounds, I would welcome Baruk's help, but I must wonder at the alchemist's interest. This is a rebellion in Seven Cities, after all. A Malazan matter.'

The bhokaral's head bobbed. 'Yes! Baruk! Master! Raraku! Azath! Great!' The head jumped up and down again.

'Great?' Paran echoed.

'Great! Danger! Azath! Icarium! More! Coltaine! Admire! Honour! Allies! Yes! Yes?'

'Something tells me this won't be easy,' Quick Ben muttered. 'All right, let's get down to details . . .'

Paran turned at the sound of an approaching rider. The figure appeared, indistinct in the starlight. The first detail the captain noted was the horse, a powerful destrier, proud and clearly short-tempered. The woman astride the animal

917

was by contrast unprepossessing, her armour plain and old, the face beneath the rim of the helm apparently undistinguished, middle-aged.

Her gaze flicked to Kruppe, the bhokaral and Quick Ben. Her expression unchanged, she said to Paran, 'Captain, I would a word with you in private, sir.'

'As you wish,' he replied, and led her off fifteen paces from the others. 'Private enough?'

'This will suffice,' the woman replied, reining in and dismounting. She stepped up to him. 'Sir, I am the Destriant of the Grey Swords. Your soldiers hold a prisoner and I have come to formally request that he be taken into our care.'

Paran blinked, then nodded. 'Ah, that would be Anaster, who once commanded the Tenescowri.'

'It would, sir. We are not yet done with him.'

'I see . . .' He hesitated.

'Has he recovered from his wounds?'

'The lost eye? He has been treated by our healers.'

'Perhaps,' the Destriant said, 'I should deliver my request to High Fist Dujek.'

'No, that won't be necessary. I can speak on behalf of the Malazans. In that capacity, however, it's incumbent that I ask a few questions first.'

'As you wish, sir. Proceed.'

'What do you intend to do with the prisoner?'

She frowned. 'Sir?'

'We do not countenance torture, no matter what his crime. If it is required, we would be forced to extend protection over Anaster, and so deny your request.'

She glanced away briefly, then fixed her level gaze on him once more, and Paran realized she was much younger than he had at first assumed. 'Torture, sir, is a relative term.'

'Is it?'

'Please, sir, permit me to continue.'

'Very well.'

'The man, Anaster, might well view what we seek for him as torture, but that is a fear born of ignorance. He will not be harmed. Indeed, my Shield Anvil seeks the very opposite for the unfortunate man.'

'She would take the pain from him.'

The Destriant nodded.

'That spiritual embrace – such as Itkovian did to Rath'Fener.'

'Even so, sir.'

Paran was silent a moment, then he said, 'The notion terrifies Anaster?'

'Yes.'

'Why?'

'Because he knows of nothing else within him. He has equated his entire identity with the pain of his soul. And so fears its end.'

Paran turned towards the Malazan camp. 'Follow me,' he said.

'Sir?' she asked behind him.

'He is yours, Destriant. With my blessing.'

She staggered then, against her horse, which grunted and sidestepped.

Paran spun. 'What—'

The woman righted herself, lifted a hand to her brow, then shook her head. 'I am sorry. There was . . . weight . . . to your use of that word.'

'My use – oh.'

Oh. Hood's breath, Ganoes – that was damned careless. 'And?' he reluctantly asked.

'And . . . I am not sure, sir. But I think you would be well advised to, uh, exercise caution in the future.'

'Aye, I think you're right. Are you recovered enough to continue?'

She nodded, collecting the reins of her horse.

Don't think about it, Ganoes Paran. Take it as a warning and nothing more. You did nothing to Anaster – you don't even know the man. A warning, and you'll damn well heed it . . .

CHAPTER TWENTY-TWO

Glass is sand and sand is glass!
The ant dancing blind as blind ants do
on the lip of the rim and the rim of the lip.

White in the night and grey in the day –
smiling spider she never smiles but smile she does
though the ant never sees, blind as it is –

and now was!

> *Tales to Scare Children*
> Malesen the Vindictive (b.?)

'**M**indless panic, alas, makes her twitch.'
The Seerdomin's voice above him said, 'I believe it has grown . . . excessive of late, Holy One.'

The Pannion Seer's reply was a shriek: 'Do you think I can't see that? Do you think I'm blind?'

'You are all wise and all knowing,' the Seerdomin officer rumbled. 'I was simply expressing my concern, Holy One. He can no longer walk, and his breath seems so laboured within that malformed chest.'

'*He*' . . . *crippled* . . . *crumpled ribs like skeleton hands closing tighter on lungs, ever tighter. Seerdomin. This is me you describe.*

But who am I?

I'd felt power once. Long ago.

There is a wolf.

A wolf. Trapped in this cage – my chest, these bones, yes, he cannot breathe. It hurts so to breathe.

The howls are gone. Silenced. The wolf cannot call . . . call . . .

To whom?

I'd rested my hand, once, on her furred shoulder. Near the neck. We'd not yet awakened, she and I. So close, travelling in step, yet not awakened . . . such tragic ignorance. Yet she'd gifted me her mortal visions, her only history – such as she knew it to be, whilst deep in her heart slept . . .

. . . slept my beloved.

'Holy One, your mother's embrace will kill him, should he be returned to it—'

'You dare order me?' the Seer hissed, and there was trembling in his voice.

'I do not command, Holy One. I state a fact.'

'Ultentha! Dearest Septarch, come forward! Yes, look upon this man at your Seerdomin's feet. What think you?'

'Holy One,' a new voice, softer, 'my most trusted servant speaks true. This man's bones are so mangled—'

'*I can see!*' the Seer screamed.

'Holy One,' the Septarch continued, 'relieve him from his horror.'

'No! I will not! He is mine! He is Mother's! She needs him – someone to hold – she needs him!'

'Her love is proving fatal,' the Seerdomin said.

'You both defy me? Shall I gather my Winged Ones? To send you to oblivion? To fight and squabble over what's left? Yes? Shall I?'

'As the Holy One wills.'

'Yes, Ultentha! Precisely! As *I* will!'

The Seerdomin spoke. 'Shall I return him to the Matron, then, Holy One?'

'Not yet. Leave him there. I am amused by the sight of him. Now, Ultentha, your report.'

'The trenches are completed, Holy One. The enemy will come across the flats to face the city wall. They'll not send scouts to the forested ridge on their right – I will stake my soul on that.'

'You have, Ultentha, you have. And what of those damned Great Ravens? If but one has seen . . .'

'Your Winged Ones have driven them off, Holy One. The skies have been cleared, and so the enemy's intelligence is thus thwarted. We shall permit them to establish their camps on the flats, then we shall rise from our hidden positions and descend upon their flank. This, in time with the assault of the Mage Cadres from the walls and the Winged Ones from the sky, as well as Septarch Inal's sortie from the gates – Holy One, victory will be ours.'

'I want Caladan Brood. I want his hammer, delivered into my hands. I want the Malazans annihilated. I want the Barghast gods grovelling at my feet. But most of all, I want the Grey Swords! Is that understood? I want that man, Itkovian – then I will have a replacement for my mother. Thus, hear me well, if you seek mercy for Toc the Younger, bring to me Itkovian. Alive.'

'It will be as you will, Holy One,' Septarch Ultentha said.

It will be as he wills. He is my god. What he wills, all that he wills. The wolf cannot breathe. The wolf is dying.

He – we are dying.

'And where is the enemy now, Ultentha?'

'They have indeed divided, two days past, since they crossed the river.'

'Yet are they not aware that the cities they march towards are dead?'

'So their Great Ravens must have reported, Holy One.'

'Then what are they up to?'

'We are unsure. Your Winged Ones dare not draw too close – their presence is yet to be noted, I believe, and best we keep it that way.'

'Agreed. Well, perhaps they imagine we have set traps – hidden troops, or some such thing – and fear a surprise attack from behind should they simply ignore the cities.'

'We are granted more time by their caution, Holy One.'

'They are fools, swollen with the victory at Capustan.'

'Indeed, Holy One. For which they will dearly pay.'

Everyone pays. No-one escapes. I thought I was safe. The wolf was a power unto himself, stretching awake. He was where I fled to.

But the wolf chose the wrong man, the wrong body. When he came down to take my eye – that flash of grey, burning, that I'd thought a stone – I'd been whole, young, sound.

But the Matron has me now. Old skin sloughing from her massive arms, the smell of abandoned snakepits. The twitch of her embrace – and bones break, break and break again. There has been so much pain, its thunder endless of late. I have felt her panic, as the Seer has said. This is what has taken my mind. This is what has destroyed me.

Better I had stayed destroyed. Better my memories never returned. Knowledge is no gift.

Cursed aware. Lying here on this cold floor, the softly surging waves of pain receding – I can no longer feel my legs. I smell salt. Dust and mould. There is weight on my left hand. It is pinned beneath me, and now grows numb.

I wish I could move.

'. . . salt the bodies. There's no shortage. Scurvy's taken so many of the Tenescowri, it's all our troops can do to gather the corpses, Holy One.'

'Mundane diseases will not take the soldiers, Ultentha. I have seen this in a dream. The mistress walked among the Tenescowri, and lo, their flesh swelled, their fingers and toes rotted and turned black, their teeth fell out in streams of red spit. But when she came upon my chosen warriors, I saw her smile. And she turned away.'

'Holy One,' the Seerdomin said, 'why would Poleil bless our cause?'

'I know not, nor do I care. Perhaps she has had her own

923

vision, of the glory of our triumph, or perhaps she simply begs favour. Our soldiers will be hale. And once the invaders are destroyed, we can begin our march once more, to new cities, new lands, and there grow fat on the spoils.'

The invaders . . . among them, my kin. I was Toc the Younger, a Malazan. And the Malazans are coming.

The laugh that came from his throat began softly, a liquid sound, then grew louder as it continued.

The conversation fell silent. The sound he made was the only one in the chamber.

The Seer's voice spoke from directly above him. 'And what amuses you so, Toc the Younger? Can you speak? Ah, haven't I asked that once before?'

Breath wheezing, Toc answered, 'I speak. But you do not hear me. You never hear me.'

'Indeed?'

'Onearm's Host, Seer. The deadliest army the Malazan Empire has ever produced. It's coming for you.'

'And I should quake?'

Toc laughed again. 'Do as you like. But your mother knows.'

'You think she fears your stupid soldiers? I forgive your ignorance, Toc the Younger. Dear Mother, it must be explained, has ancient . . . terrors. Moon's Spawn. But let me be more precise, so as to prevent your further misunderstanding. Moon's Spawn is now home to the Tiste Andii and their dreaded Lord, but they are as lizards in an abandoned temple. They dwell unaware of the magnificence surrounding them. Dear Mother cannot be reached by such details, alas. She is little more than instinct these days, the poor, mindless thing.

'The Jaghut remember Moon's Spawn. I alone am in possession of the relevant scrolls from Gothos's Folly that whisper of the K'Chain Nah'rhuk – the Short-Tails, misbegotten children of the Matrons – who fashioned mechanisms that bound sorcery in ways long lost, who built vast, floating fortresses from which they launched devastating attacks upon their long-tailed kin.

'Oh, they lost in the end. Were destroyed. And but one floating fortress remained, damaged, abandoned to the winds. Gothos believed it had drifted north, to collide with the ice of a Jaghut winter, and was so frozen, trapped for millennia. Until found by the Tiste Andii Lord.

'Do you comprehend, Toc the Younger? Anomander Rake knows nothing of Moon's Spawn's fullest powers – powers he has no means of accessing even were he to know of them. Dear Mother remembers, or at least some part of her does. Of course, she has nothing to fear. Moon's Spawn is not within two hundred leagues of here – my Winged Ones have searched for it, high overhead, through the warrens, everywhere. The only conclusion is that Moon's Spawn has fled, or failed at last – was it not almost destroyed over Pale? So you've told me.

'So you see, Toc the Younger, your Malazan army holds no terror for any of us, including dear Mother. Onearm's Host will be crushed in the assault on Coral. As will Brood and his Rhivi. Moreover, the White Faces will be shattered – they've not the discipline for this kind of war. I will have them all. And I will feed you bits of Dujek Onearm's flesh – you'd like some meat again, wouldn't you? Something that hasn't been . . . regurgitated. Yes?'

He said nothing, even as his stomach clenched in visceral greed.

The Seer crouched lower and touched a fingertip to Toc's temple. 'It's so easy breaking you. All your faiths. One by one. Almost too easy. The only salvation you can hope for is mine, Toc the Younger. You understand that now, don't you?'

'Yes,' he replied.

'Very good. Pray, then, that there is mercy in my soul. True, I've yet to find any myself, though I admit I've little searched. But perhaps it exists. Hold to that, my friend.'

'Yes.'

The Seer straightened. 'I hear my mother's cries. Take him back, Seerdomin.'

'As you command, Holy One.'

Strong arms gathered Toc the Younger, lifted him with ease from the cold floor.

He was carried from the room. In the hallway, the Seerdomin paused.

'Toc, listen to me, please. She's chained down below, and the reach does not encompass the entire room. Listen. I will set you down beyond her grasp. I will bring food, water, blankets – the Seer will pay little heed to her cries, for she is always crying these days. Nor will he probe towards her mind – there are matters of far greater import consuming him.'

'He will have you devoured, Seerdomin.'

'I was devoured long ago, Malazan.'

'I – I am sorry for that.'

The man holding him said nothing for a long moment, and when he spoke at last, his voice cracked. 'You . . . you offer compassion. Abyss take me, Toc, I am ever surpassed. Allow to me, please, my small efforts—'

'With gratitude, Seerdomin.'

'Thank you.'

He set off once more.

Toc spoke. 'Tell me, Seerdomin, does the ice still grip the sea?'

'Not for at least a league, Toc. Some unexpected twist of the currents has cleared the harbour. But the storms still rage over the bay, and the ice out there still thunders and churns like ten thousand demons at war. Can you not hear it?'

'No.'

'Aye, I'll grant you it's faint from here. From the keep's causeway, it is a veritable assault.'

'I – I remember the wind . . .'

'It no longer reaches us. Yet another wayward vagary, for which I am thankful.'

926

'In the Matron's cave,' Toc said, 'there is no wind.'

Wood splintered, a sickening sound that trembled through the entire Meckros fragment. Lady Envy paused in her climb towards the street's ragged, torn end. The slope had grown suddenly steeper, the frost slick on the cobbles underfoot. She hissed in frustration, then drew on a warren and floated to where Lanas Tog stood on the very edge.

The T'lan Imass did not so much as sway on her perilous perch. Wind ripped at her tattered skins and bone-white hair. The swords still impaling her glistened with rime.

Reaching her side, Lady Envy saw more clearly the source of the terrible, snapping sounds. A vast section of ice had collided with them, was grinding its way along the base in a foaming sluice of jetting water and spraying ice.

'Dear me,' Lady Envy muttered. 'It seems we are ever pushed westward.'

'Yet we drive towards land none the less,' Lanas Tog replied. 'And that is sufficient.'

'Twenty leagues from Coral by this course, and all of it wilderness, assuming my memories of the region's map are accurate. I was so weary of walking, alas. Have you seen our abode yet? Apart from the canting floor and alarming views through the windows, it is quite sumptuous. I cannot abide discomfort, you know.'

The T'lan Imass made no reply, continued staring northwestward.

'You're all alike,' Lady Envy sniffed. 'It took weeks to get Tool in a conversational mood.'

'You have mentioned the name earlier. Who is Tool?'

'Onos T'oolan, First Sword. The last time I saw him, he was even more bedraggled than you, dear, so there's hope for you yet.'

'Onos T'oolan. I saw him but once.'

'The First Gathering, no doubt.'

'Yes. He spoke against the ritual.'

'So of course you hate him.'

The T'lan Imass did not immediately reply. The structure shifted wildly beneath them, their end pitching down as the floe punched clear, then lifting upward once more. There was not even a waver to Lanas Tog's stance. She spoke. 'Hate him? No. Of course I disagreed. We all did, and so he acquiesced. It is a common belief.'

Lady Envy waited, then crossed her arms and asked, 'What is?'

'That truth is proved by weight of numbers. That what the many believe to be right, must be so. When I see Onos T'oolan once more, I will tell him: he was the one who was right.'

'I don't think he holds a grudge, Lanas Tog. I suppose, thinking on it, that makes him unique among the T'lan Imass, doesn't it?'

'He is the First Sword.'

'I have had yet another, equally frustrating conversation with Mok. I'd been wondering, you see, why he and his brothers have not challenged you to combat yet. Both Senu and Thurule have fought Tool – and lost. Mok was next. Turns out the Seguleh will not fight women, unless attacked. So, by way of warning, do not attack them.'

'I have no reason to, Lady Envy. Should I find one, however—'

'All right, I'll be more direct. Tool was hard-pressed by both Senu and Thurule. Against Mok, well, it was probably even. Are you a match to the First Sword, Lanas Tog? If you truly seek to reach the Second Gathering in one piece, to deliver your message, then show some restraint.'

Iron grated against bone as Lanas Tog shrugged.

Lady Envy sighed. 'Now, which is more depressing? Attempting civil conversation with you and the Seguleh, or staring into the suffering eyes of a wolf? I cannot even comment on Garath's mood, for the beast still seems upset with me.'

'The ay has awakened,' Lanas Tog said.

'I know, I know, and truly, my heart weeps on her behalf,

or at least on behalf of the miserable goddess residing within her. Then again, they *both* deserve a few tears, don't they? An eternity alone for the not-quite-mortal ay cannot have been fun, after all.'

The T'lan Imass turned her head. 'Who has granted the beast this edged gift?'

Lady Envy shrugged, smiling with delight at the opportunity to return such a gesture. 'A misguided sibling who'd thought he was being kind. All right, perhaps that was too simplistic an answer. My sibling had found the goddess, terribly damaged by the Fall, and needed a warm-blooded place to lay her spirit, so that it could heal. Serendipity. The ay's pack was dead, whilst she herself was too young to survive in normal circumstances. Worse yet, she was the last left on the entire continent.'

'Your sibling has a misplaced sense of mercy, Lady Envy.'

'I agree. We have something in common after all! How wonderful!'

A moment later, as she studied the T'lan Imass at her side, her effusiveness drained away. 'Oh,' she muttered, 'what a distressing truth that proved to be.'

Lanas Tog returned her gaze to the tumultuous panorama stretching away to the northwest. 'Most truths are,' she said.

'Well!' Lady Envy ran her hands through her hair. 'I think I'll head down and stare into a wolf's miserable eyes for a time! Just to improve my mood, you understand. You know, at least Tool had a sense of humour.'

'He is the First Sword.'

Muttering under her breath as she made her way back down the street, slippered feet barely brushing the icy cobbles, Lady Envy only paused when she reached the entrance to the house. 'Oh! That was quite funny! In an odd way. Well! How extraordinary!'

Crone hopped about in a fury. Brood stood watching the Great Raven. Off to one side was Korlat. Lingering a half-dozen paces away was Kallor. The army marched in wide ranks down the raised road to their left, whilst to their right, at a distance of two thousand paces, rumbled the herd of bhederin.

There were fewer of the beasts, Korlat noted. The crossing had claimed hundreds.

A shrill hiss from Crone recaptured her wandering attention.

The Great Raven had half spread her wings, halting directly in front of the warlord. 'You still do not grasp the gravity of this! Fool! Ox! Where is Anomander Rake? Tell me! I must speak with him – warn him—'

'Of what?' Brood asked. 'That a few hundred condors have chased you away?'

'Unknown sorcery hides within those abominable vultures! We are being deliberately kept away, you brainless thug!'

'From Coral and environs,' Kallor noted drily. 'We've just come in sight of Lest, Crone. One thing at a time.'

'Stupid! Do you think they're just sitting on their hands? They're *preparing*—'

'Of course they are,' Kallor drawled, sneering down at the Great Raven. 'What of it?'

'What's happened to Moon's Spawn? We know what Rake planned – has it succeeded? I cannot reach it! I cannot reach *him*! *Where is Moon's Spawn?*'

No-one spoke.

Crone's head darted down. 'You know less than I! Don't you? All this is bravado! We are lost!' The Great Raven wheeled to pin Korlat with her glittering, black eyes. 'Your Lord has failed, hasn't he? And taken three-quarters of the Tiste Andii with him! Will you be enough, Korlat? Will you—'

'Crone,' Brood rumbled. 'We'd asked for word on the Malazans, not a list of your fears.'

'The Malazans? They march! What else would they do? Endless wagons on the road, dust everywhere. Closing on

930

Setta, which is empty but for a handful of sun-withered corpses!'

Kallor grunted. 'They're making a swift passage of it, then. As if in a hurry. Warlord, there is deceit here.'

Brood scowled, crossed his arms. 'You heard the bird, Kallor. The Malazans *march*. Faster than we'd expected, true, but that is all.'

'You dissemble,' Kallor grated.

Ignoring him, Brood faced the Great Raven once more. 'Have your kin keep an eye on them. As for what's happening at Coral, we'll worry about that when we reach Maurik and reunite our forces. Finally, regarding your master, Anomander Rake, have faith, Crone.'

'Upon *faith* you hold to success? Madness! We must prepare for the worst!'

Korlat's attention drifted once more. It had been doing that a lot of late. She'd forgotten what love could do, as it threaded its roots through her entire soul, as it tugged and pulled at her thoughts, obsession ripening like seductive fruit. She felt only its life, thickening within her, claiming all she was.

Fears for her Lord and her kin seemed almost inconsequential. If truly demanded, she could attempt her warren, reach him via the paths of Kurald Galain. But there was no urgency within her to do any such thing. This war would find its own path.

Her wants were held, one and all, in the eyes of a man. A mortal, of angled, edged nobility. A man past his youth, a soul layered in scars – yet he had surrendered it to her.

Almost impossible to believe.

She recalled her first sight of him up close. She had been standing with the Mhybe and Silverfox, the child's hand in her own. He had ridden towards the place of parley at Dujek's side. A soldier whose name she had already known – as a feared enemy, whose tactical prowess had defied Brood time and again, despite the odds against the Malazan's poorly supplied, numerically weakened forces.

Even then, he had been as a lodestone to her eye.

And not just hers alone, she realized. Her Lord had called him friend. The rarity of such a thing still threatened to steal her breath. Anomander Rake, in all the time she had known him, had acknowledged but one friend, and that was Caladan Brood. And between those two men, thousands of years of shared experiences, an alliance never broken. Countless clashes, it was true, but not once a final, irretrievable sundering.

The key to that, Korlat well understood, lay in their maintaining a respectable distance from each other, punctuated by the occasional convergence.

It was, she believed, a relationship that would never be broken. And from it, after centuries, had been born a friendship.

Yet Rake had shared but a few evenings in Whiskeyjack's company. Conversations of an unknown nature had taken place between them. And it had been enough.

Something in each of them has made them kin in spirit. Yet even I cannot see it. Anomander Rake cannot be reached out to, cannot be so much as touched – not his true self. I have never known what lies behind my Lord's eyes. I have but sensed its vast capacity – but not the flavour of all that it contains.

But Whiskeyjack – my dear mortal lover – while I cannot see all that is within him, I can see the cost of containment. The bleeding, but not the wound. And I can see his strength – even the last time, when he was so weary . . .

Directly south, the old walls of Lest were visible. There was no sign that repairs had been made since the Pannion conquest. The air above the city was clear of smoke, empty of birds. The Rhivi scouts had reported that there was naught but a few charred bones littering the streets. There had been raised gardens once, for which Lest had been known, but the flow of water had ceased weeks past and fire had since swept through the city – even at this distance Korlat could see the dark stain of soot on the walls.

'Devastation!' moaned Crone. 'This is the tale before us!

All the way to Maurik. Whilst our alliance disintegrates before our eyes.'

'It does nothing of the sort,' rumbled Brood, his frown deepening.

'Oh? And where is Silverfox? What has happened to the Mhybe? Why do the Grey Swords and Trake's Legion march so far behind us? Why were the Malazans so eager to leave our sides? And now, Anomander Rake and Moon's Spawn have vanished! The Tiste Andii—'

'Are alive,' Korlat cut in, her own patience frayed at last.

Crone wheeled on her. 'Are you certain?'

Korlat nodded. *Yet . . . am I? No. Shall I then seek them out? No. We shall see what is to be seen at Coral. That is all.* Her gaze slowly swung westward. *And you, my dear lover, thief of all my thoughts, will you ever release me?*

Please. Do not. Ever.

Riding beside Gruntle, Itkovian watched the two Grey Sword outriders canter towards the Shield Anvil and Destriant.

'Where are they coming from?' Gruntle asked.

'Flanking rearguard,' Itkovian replied.

'With news to deliver, it seems.'

'So it appears, sir.'

'Well? Aren't you curious? They've both asked you to ride with them – if you'd said yes you'd be hearing that report right now, instead of slouching along with us riffraff. Hey, that's a thought – I could divide my legion into two companies, call one Riff and the other—'

'Oh, spare us!' Stonny snapped behind them.

Gruntle twisted in his saddle. 'How long have you been in our shadow, woman?'

'I'm never in your shadow, Gruntle. Not you, not Itkovian. Not any man. Besides, with the sun so low on our right, I'd have to be alongside you to be in your shadow, not that I would be, of course.'

'So instead,' the Mortal Sword grinned, 'you're the woman behind me.'

'And what's that supposed to mean, pig?'

'Just stating a fact, lass.'

'Really? Well, you were wrong. I was about to make my way over to the Grey Swords, only you two oafs were in the way.'

'Stonny, this ain't a road, it's a plain. How in Hood's name could we be in your way when you could ride your horse anywhere?'

'Oafs. Lazy pigs. *Someone* here has to be curious. That someone needs a brain, of course, which is why you'll both just trot along, wondering what those outriders are reporting, wondering and doing not a damned thing about it. Because you're both brainless. As for me—'

'As for you,' Itkovian said drily, 'you seem to be talking to us, sir. Indeed, engaged in a conversation—'

'Which has now ended!' she snapped, neck-reining her horse to the left, then launching it past them.

They watched her ride towards the other column.

After a moment, Gruntle shrugged, then said, 'Wonder what she'll hear.'

'As do I,' Itkovian replied.

They rode on, their pace steady if a little slow. Gruntle's legion marched in their wake, a rabble, clumped like sea-raiders wandering inland in search of a farmhouse to pillage. Itkovian had suggested, some time earlier, that some training might prove beneficial, to which Gruntle had grinned and said nothing.

Trake's Mortal Sword despised armies; indeed, despised anything even remotely connected to the notion of military practices. He was indifferent to discipline, and had but one officer – a Lestari soldier, fortunately – to manage his now eight-score followers: stony-eyed misfits that he'd laughingly called Trake's Legion.

Gruntle was, in every respect, Itkovian's opposite.

'Here she comes,' the Mortal Sword growled.

'She rides,' Itkovian observed, 'with much drama.'

934

'Aye. A fierceness not unique to sitting a saddle, from all that I've heard.'

Itkovian glanced at Gruntle. 'My apologies. I had assumed you and she—'

'A few times,' the man replied. 'When we were both drunk, alas. Her more drunk than me, I'll admit. Neither of us talk about it, generally. We stumbled onto the subject once and it turned into an argument about which of us was the more embarrassed – ah, lass! What news?'

She reined in hard, her horse's hooves kicking up dust. 'Why in Hood's name should I tell you?'

'Then why in Hood's name did you ride back to us?'

She scowled. 'I was simply returning to my position, oaf – and you, Itkovian, that had better not be a hint of a smile I see there. If it was, I'd have to kill you.'

'Most certainly not, sir.'

'Glad to hear it.'

'So?' Gruntle asked her.

'What?'

'The news, woman!'

'Oh, that. Wonderful news, of course, it's the only kind we hear these days, right? Pleasing revelations. Happy times—'

'Stonny.'

'Old friends, Gruntle! Trundling after us about a league back. Big, bone carriage, pulled by a train that ain't quite what it seems. Dragging a pair of flatbed wagons behind, too, loaded with junk – did I say junk? I meant loot, of course, including more than one sun-blackened corpse. And an old man on the driver's seat. With a mangy cat in his lap. Well, what do you know? Old friends, yes?'

Gruntle's expression had flattened, his eyes suddenly cold. 'No Buke?'

'Not even his horse. Either he's flown, or—'

The Mortal Sword wheeled his horse round and drove his heels into the beast's flanks.

Itkovian hesitated. He glanced at Stonny and was

935

surprised to see undisguised sympathy softening her face. Her green eyes found him. 'Catch up with him, will you?' she asked quietly.

He nodded, lowered the visor of his Malazan helm. The faintest shift in weight and a momentary brush of the reins against his horse's neck brought the animal about.

His mount was pleased with the opportunity to stretch its legs, and given its lighter burden was able to draw Itkovian alongside Gruntle with two-thirds of a league remaining. The Mortal Sword's horse was already labouring.

'Sir!' Itkovian called. 'Pace, sir! Else we'll be riding double on the return!'

Gruntle hissed a curse, made as if to urge his horse yet faster, then relented, straightening in the saddle, reins loose, as the beast's gallop slowed, fell into a canter.

'Fast trot now, sir,' Itkovian advised. 'We'll drop to a walk in a hundred paces so she can stretch her neck and open full her air passages.'

'Sorry, Itkovian,' Gruntle said a short while later. 'There's no heat to my temper these days, but that seems to make it all the deadlier, I'm afraid.'

'Trake would—'

'No, don't even try, friend. I've said it before. I don't give a damn what Trake wants or expects of me, and the rest of you had best stop seeing me that way. Mortal Sword – I hate titles. I didn't even like being called captain when I guarded caravans. I only used it so I could charge more.'

'Do you intend to attempt harm upon these travellers, sir?'

'You well know who they are.'

'I do.'

'I had a friend . . .'

'Aye, the one named Buke. I recall him. A man broken by sorrow. I once offered to take his burdens, but he refused me.'

Gruntle's head snapped round at that. 'You did? He did?'

Itkovian nodded. 'Perhaps I should have been more . . . direct.'

'You should have grabbed him by the throat and done it no matter what he wanted. That's what the new Shield Anvil's done to that one-eyed First Child of the Dead Seed, Anaster, isn't it? And now the man rides at her side—'

'Rides unknowing. He is naught but a shell, sir. There was naught else within him but pain. Its taking has stolen his knowledge of himself. Would you have had that as Buke's fate as well, sir?'

The man grimaced.

Less than a third of a league remained, assuming Stonny's claim was accurate, but the roll of the eroded beach ridges reduced the line of sight, and indeed it was the sound that the carriage made, a muted clanking riding the wind, that alerted the two men to its proximity.

They crested a ridge and had to rein in quickly to avoid colliding with the train of oxen.

Emancipor Reese was wearing a broad, smudged bandage, wrapped vertically about his head, not quite covering a swollen jaw and puffy right eye. The cat in his lap screamed at the sudden arrival of the two riders, then clawed its way up the servant's chest, over the left shoulder, and onto the roof of the ghastly carriage, where it vanished into a fold of K'Chain Che'Malle bone and skin. Reese himself jumped in his seat, almost toppling from his perch before recovering his balance.

'Bathtardth! Why you do tha? Hood'th b'eth!'

'Apologies, sir,' Itkovian said, 'for startling you so. You are injured—'

'In'ured? Tho. Tooth. B'oke ith. Olib pith.'

Itkovian frowned, glanced at Gruntle.

The Mortal Sword shrugged. 'Olive pit, maybe?'

'Aye!' Reese nodded vigorously, then winced at the motion. 'Wha you wanth?'

Gruntle drew a deep breath, then said, 'The truth, Reese. Where's Buke?'

The servant shrugged. 'Gone.'

'Did they—'

'Tho! Gone! Thlown!' He jerked his arms up and down. 'Thlap thlap! Unnerthan? Yeth?'

Gruntle sighed, glanced away, then slowly nodded. 'Well enough,' he said a moment later.

The carriage door opened and Bauchelain leaned out. 'Why have we stop— ah, the caravan captain . . . and the Grey Sword, I believe, but where, sir, is your uniform?'

'I see no need—'

'Never mind,' Bauchelain interrupted, climbing out, 'I wasn't really interested in your answer. Well, gentlemen, you have business to discuss, perhaps? Indulge my rudeness, if you will, I am weary and short of temper of late, alas. Indeed, before you utter another word, I advise you not to irritate me. The next unpleasant interruption is likely to see my temper snap entirely, and that would be a truly fell thing, I assure you. Now, what would you with us?'

'Nothing,' Gruntle said.

The necromancer's thin, black brows rose fractionally. 'Nothing?'

'I came to enquire of Buke.'

'Buke? Who – oh yes, him. Well, the next time you see him, tell him he is fired.'

'I'll do that.'

No-one spoke for a moment, then Itkovian cleared his throat. 'Sir,' he said to Bauchelain, 'your servant has broken a tooth and appears to be in considerable discomfort. Surely, with your arts . . .'

Bauchelain turned and looked up at Reese. 'Ah, that explains the head garb. I admit I'd been wondering . . . a newly acquired local fashion, perhaps? But no, as it turns out. Well, Reese, it seems I must once more ask Korbal Broach to make ready for surgery – this is the third such tooth to break, yes? More olives, no doubt. If you still persist in the belief that olive pits are deadly poison, why are you so careless when eating said fruit? Ah, never mind.'

938

'Tho thurgery, pleath! Tho! Pleath!'

'What are you babbling about, man? Be quiet! Wipe that drool away – it's unsightly. Do you think I cannot see your pain, servant? Tears have sprung from your eyes, and you are white – deathly white. And look at you shake so – not another moment must be wasted! Korbal Broach! Come out, if you will, with your black bag! Korbal!'

The wagon rocked slightly in answer.

Gruntle swung his horse round. Itkovian followed suit.

'Until later, then, gentlemen!' Bauchelain called out behind them. 'Rest assured I am grateful for your advising me of my servant's condition. As he is equally grateful, no doubt, and were he able to speak coherently I am sure he would tell you so.'

Gruntle lifted a hand in a brusque wave.

They set off to rejoin Trake's Legion.

Neither spoke for a time, until a soft rumbling from Gruntle drew Itkovian's attention. The Mortal Sword, he saw, was laughing.

'What amuses you so, sir?'

'You, Itkovian. I expect Reese will curse your concern for the rest of his days.'

'An odd expression of gratitude that would be. Will he not be healed?'

'Oh, yes, I am sure he will, Itkovian. But here's something for you to ponder on, if you will. Sometimes the cure is worse than the disease.'

'Can you explain that?'

'Ask Emancipor Reese, the next time you see him.'

'Very well, I will do just that, sir.'

The stench of smoke clung to the walls, and sufficient old stains blotting the rugs attested to the slaughter of acolytes down hallways and in anterooms and annexes throughout the temple.

Coll wondered if Hood had been pleased to have his own

children delivered unto him, within the god's own sanctified structure.

It appeared to be no easy thing to desecrate a place made sacred to death. The Daru could feel the breath of unabated power, cool and indifferent, as he sat on the stone bench outside the chamber of the sepulchre.

Murillio paced up and down the wide main hallway to his right, stepping into his line of sight then out again, over and over.

In the holy chamber beyond, the Knight of Death was preparing a place for the Mhybe. Three bells had passed since Hood's chosen servant had walked into the chamber of the sepulchre, the doors closing of their own accord behind him.

Coll waited until Murillio reappeared once more. 'He can't let go of those swords.'

Murillio paused, glanced over. 'So?'

'Well,' Coll rumbled, 'it might well take him three bells to make a bed.'

His friend's expression filled with suspicion. 'That was supposed to be funny?'

'Not entirely. I was thinking in pragmatic terms. I was trying to imagine the physical awkwardness of attempting to do anything with swords stuck to your hands. That's all.'

Murillio made to say something, changed his mind with a muttered oath, wheeled and resumed his pacing.

They had carried the Mhybe into the temple five days past, settling her into a room that had once belonged to a ranking priest. They had unloaded the wagon and stored their food and water in the cellars amidst the shards of hundreds of shattered jugs and the floor and the walls made sticky with wine, the air thick and cloying and rank as an innkeeper's apron.

Every meal since had tasted wine-soaked, reminding Coll of the almost two years he had wasted as a drunk, drowning in misery's dark waters as only a man in love with self-pity can. He would have liked to call the man he had been a stranger now, but the world had a way of spinning unnoticed, until what he'd thought he'd turned his back on suddenly faced him again.

Even worse, introspection – for him at least – was a funnel in sand, a spider waiting at the bottom. And Coll well knew he was quite capable of devouring himself.

Murillio strode into view again.

'The ant danced blind,' Coll said.

'What?'

'The old children's tale – remember it?'

'You've lost your mind, haven't you?'

'Not yet. At least I don't think so.'

'But that's just it, Coll. You wouldn't know, would you?'

He watched Murillio spin round once more, step past the wall's edge and out of sight. *The world spins about us unseen. The blind dance in circles. There's no escaping what you are, and all your dreams glittered white at night, but grey in the light of day. And both are equally deadly. Who was that damned poet? The Vindictive. An orphan, he'd claimed. Wrote a thousand stories to terrify children. Was stoned by a mob in Darujhistan, which he survived. I think – that was years ago. His tales live in the streets, now. Singsong chants to accompany the games of the young.*

Damned sinister, if you ask me.

He shook himself, seeking to clear his mind before stumbling into yet another pitfall of memory. Before she'd stolen his estate, before she'd destroyed him, Simtal had told him she carried his child. He wondered if that child had ever existed – Simtal fought with lies where others used knives. There'd been no announcement of any birth. Though of course the chance of his missing such an announcement was pretty much certain in those days that followed his fall. But his friends would have known. Would have told him, if not then, then now . . .

Murillio stepped into view.

'A moment there,' Coll growled.

'Now what? The beetle flipped on its back? The worm circling the hole?'

'A question, Murillio.'

'All right, if you insist.'

'Did you ever hear tell of a child born to Simtal?'

He watched his friend's face slowly close, the eyes narrowing. 'That is a question not to be asked in this temple, Coll.'

'I'm asking it none the less.'

'I do not think you're ready—'

'Not for you to judge and you should know better, Murillio. Dammit, I've been sitting on the Council for months! And I'm still not *ready*? What absurdity is—'

'All right all right! It's just this: there's only rumours.'

'Don't lie to me.'

'I'm not. There was a span of more than a few months – just after your, uh, demise – when she made no public appearance. Explained away as mourning, of course, though everyone knew—'

'Yes, I know what everyone knew. So she hid out for a time. Go on.'

'Well, we believed she was consolidating her position. Behind the scenes. Rallick was keeping an eye on her. At least I think he was. He'd know more.'

'And you two never discussed the details of what she was up to, what she looked like? Murillio—'

'Well, what would Rallick know of mothering?'

'When they're with child, their bellies swell and their breasts get bigger. I'm sure our assassin friend has seen one or two so-afflicted women on Darujhistan's streets – did he just think they were eating melons whole?'

'No need to be sarcastic, Coll. All I'm saying is, he wasn't sure.'

'What about the estate's servants? Any women who'd just given birth?'

'Rallick never mentioned—'

'My, what an observant assassin.'

'Fine!' Murillio snapped. 'Here's what I think! She had a child. She sent it away. Somewhere. She wouldn't have

942

abandoned it, because at some point she would have wanted to use it, as a verifiable heir, as marriage-bait, whatever. Simtal was lowborn; whatever contacts she had from her past were private ones – kept from everyone but those involved, including you, as you well know. I think she sent the child that way, somewhere no-one would think of looking.'

'Almost three, now,' Coll said, slowly leaning back to rest his head against the wall. He closed his eyes. 'Three years of age . . .'

'Maybe so. But at the time there wasn't any way of finding—'

'You'd have needed my blood. Then Baruk . . .'

'Right,' Murillio snapped, 'we'd just go and bleed you one night when you were passed-out drunk.'

'Why not?'

'Because, you ox, back then, there didn't seem much point!'

'Fair enough. But I've walked a straight line for months now, Murillio.'

'Then you do it, Coll. Go to Baruk.'

'I will. Now that I know.'

'Listen, friend, I've known a lot of drunks in my time. You look at four, five months being sober and think it's eternity. But me, I see a man still brushing the puke from his clothes. A man who could get knocked right back down. I wasn't going to push – it's too soon—'

'I hear you. I don't curse your decision, Murillio. You were right to be cautious. But what I see – what I see now, that is – is a reason. Finally, a real reason to hold myself up.'

'Coll, I hope you're not thinking you can just walk into whatever household your child's being raised in and take it away—'

'Why not? It's mine.'

'And there's a place waiting for it on your mantelpiece, right?'

'You think I can't raise a child?'

'I *know* you can't, Coll. But, if you do this right, you can pay to see it grow up well, with opportunities that it might not otherwise have.'

'A hidden benefactor. Huh. That would be . . . noble.'

'Be honest: it would be *convenient*, Coll. Not noble, not heroic.'

'And you call yourself a friend.'

'I do.'

Coll sighed. 'And so you should, though I don't know what I've done to deserve such friendship.'

'Since I don't want to depress you further, we'll discuss that subject some other time.'

The massive stone doors to the chamber of the sepulchre swung open.

Grunting, Coll rose from the bench.

The Knight of Death stepped into the hallway to stand directly before Murillio. 'Bring the woman,' the warrior said. 'The preparations are complete.'

Coll strode to the entrance and looked within. A large hole had been carved through the floor's solid stone in the centre of the chamber. Shattered stone rose in heaps banked against a side wall. Suddenly chilled, the Daru pushed past the Knight of Death. 'Hood's breath!' he exclaimed. 'That's a damned sarcophagus!'

'What?' Murillio cried, rushing to join Coll. He stared at the burial pit, then spun to the Knight. 'The Mhybe's not dead, you fool!'

The warrior's lifeless eyes fixed on Coll's companion. 'The preparations,' he said, 'are complete.'

Ankle-deep in dust, she stumbled across a wasteland. The tundra had disintegrated, and with it the hunters, the demonic pursuers who had been such unwelcome company for so long. The desolation surrounding her was, she realized, far worse. No grasses underfoot, no sweet cool wind. The hum of the blackflies was gone, those avid companions so eager to feed on her flesh – though her scalp still crawled as if some had survived the devastation.

944

And she was weakening, her youthful muscles failing in some undefinable way. Not weariness alone, but some kind of chronic dissolution. She was losing her substantiality, and that realization was the most terrifying of all.

The sky overhead was colourless, devoid of cloud or even sun, yet faintly illuminated by some unseen source. It seemed impossibly distant – to look upward for too long was to risk madness, mind railing at its inability to comprehend what the eyes were seeing.

So she held her gaze fixed directly ahead as she staggered on. There was nothing to mark the horizon in any direction. She might well be walking in circles for all she knew, though if so it was a vast circle, for she'd yet to cross her own path. She had no destination in mind for this journey of the spirit; nor the will to seek to fashion one in this deathly dreamscape, had she known how.

Her lungs ached, as if they too were losing their ability to function. Before long, she believed, she herself would begin to dissolve, this young body defeated in a way that was opposite to what she had feared for so long. She would not be torn to pieces by wolves. The wolves were gone. No, she knew now that nothing had been as it had seemed – it had all been something different, something secret, a riddle she'd yet to work out. And now it was too late. Oblivion had come for her.

The Abyss she had seen in her nightmares of so long ago had been a place of chaos, of frenzied feeding on souls, of miasmic memories detached and flung on storm winds. Perhaps those visions had been the products of her own mind, after all. The true Abyss was what she was now seeing, on all sides, in every direction—

Something broke the horizon's flat line, something monstrous and crouched, bestial, off to her right. It had not been there a moment ago.

Or perhaps it had. Perhaps this world itself was shrinking, and her few frail steps had unveiled what lay beyond the land's curvature.

She moaned in sudden terror, even as her steps shifted direction, drew her towards the apparition.

It grew visibly larger with every stride she took, swelled horribly until it claimed a third of the sky. Pink-streaked, raw bones, rising upward, a cage of ribs, each rib scarred, knotted with malignant growths, calcifications, porous nodes, cracks, twists and fissures. Between each bone, skin was stretched, enclosing whatever lay within. Blood vessels spanned the skin, pulsing like red lightning, flickering and dimming before her eyes.

For this, the storm of life was passing. For this, and for her as well.

'Are you mine?' she asked in a rasping voice as she stumbled to within twenty paces of the ghastly cage. 'Does my heart lie inside? Slowing with each beat? Are you me?'

Emotions suddenly assailed her – feelings that were not her own, but came from whatever lay within the cage. Anguish. Overwhelming pain.

She wanted to flee.

Yet it sensed her. It demanded that she stay.

That she come closer.

Close enough to reach out.

To touch.

The Mhybe screamed. *She was in a cloud of dust that clawed her eyes blind, on her knees suddenly, feeling as if she was being torn apart – her spirit, her every instinct for survival rearing up one last time. To resist the summons. To flee.*

But she could not move.

And then the force reached out. It began to pull.

And the land beneath her shifted, tilted. The dust slicked. The dust became as glass.

On her hands and knees, she looked up through streaming eyes, the scene dancing before her.

The ribs were ribs no longer. They were legs.

And skin was not skin. It had become a web.

And she was sliding.

946

CHAPTER TWENTY-THREE

Were the Black Moranth a loquacious people, the
history of Achievant Twist would be known. And were
it known, from what preceded first mention of him
following the alliance with the Malazan Empire;
his sojourn during the Genabackan Campaigns of
that same empire; and of his life within the Moranth
Hegemony itself – one cannot but suspect that
the tale would be worthy of more than one legend.

Lost Heroes
Badark of Nathii

The vision mountains loomed dark and massive,
blotting the stars to the west. Her back to the
vertical root wall of a toppled tree, Corporal Picker
drew her rain cloak tighter against the chill. On her left,
the distant walls of Setta formed a ragged black line on the
other side of the starlit river. The city had proved closer to
the mountains and to the river than the maps had
indicated, which had been a good thing.

Her gaze remained fixed on the path below, straining in
search of the first smudge of motion. At least the rain had
passed, though mist had begun to gather. She listened to
the drip of water from the pine boughs on all sides.

A boot squelched in mossy mud, then grated on granite.
Picker glanced over, nodded, then returned her attention
to the trail.

'Expect a while yet,' Captain Paran murmured. 'They've considerable ground to cover.'

'Aye,' Picker agreed. 'Only Blend runs a fast point, sir. She has eyes like a cat.'

'Let's hope she doesn't leave the others behind, then.'

'She won't.' *She'd better not.*

Paran slowly crouched at her side. 'I suppose we could have flown directly over the city and saved ourselves the trouble of checking it out on foot.'

'And if there'd been watchers they'd have seen us. No need to second guess yourself, Captain. We don't know what the Pannion Seer's got for eyes in this land, but we'd be fools to think we were entirely alone. We're already risking big with thinking we can travel at night and not be detected.'

'Quick Ben says it's the condors and nothing else, Lieutenant, and they only take to the sky during the day. So long as we keep under cover when the sun's out, we should be able to pull this off.'

Picker slowly nodded in the darkness. 'Spindle agrees. So do Bluepearl and Shank and Toes. Captain, with us and just us Bridgeburners frog-hopping with the Black Moranth, I'd have little concern. But since we're flying point on—'

'Shh – there, down below. Saw something.'

Blend was her usual admirable self, moving like a shadow, vanishing entirely for one, two, three heartbeats, then reappearing ten paces closer, zigzagging her way to where Picker and Paran waited.

Though neither officer had moved nor made a sound, Blend had somehow found them. Her teeth flashed white as she squatted down in front of them.

'Very impressive,' Paran muttered. 'Are you here to report or will you leave that to the man who's supposed to be doing that? Unless, of course, you've left Antsy and the rest stumbling lost half a league in your wake.'

The smile disappeared. 'Uh, no sir, they're about thirty paces back – can't you hear 'em? There, that was Spindle –

his hairshirt snagging on a branch. And those steps out front – that's Antsy, he's bandy-legged, walks like an ape. Those clunks? Hedge. The quietest one of the lot is Detoran, oddly enough.'

'You making this up, soldier?' Paran asked. 'Because I don't hear a thing.'

'No, sir,' Blend said innocently.

Picker wanted to reach out and cuff the woman. 'Go down and find them, Blend,' she growled. *If they're that loud they've lost the trail, you idiot. Not that they are. Not that they have. Paran stuck you right sharp and you don't like it. Fine.* 'Now.'

'Aye, Lieutenant.' Blend sighed.

They watched her slither and slide her way back down to the path, then vanish.

Paran grunted. 'She almost had me there.'

Picker glanced over. 'She thinks she's done just that.'

'That's right, she does.'

She said nothing, then grinned. *Damn, I think you're our captain now. Finally, we found a good one.*

'Here they come,' Paran observed.

They were a match to Blend, or close enough to make little difference. Flowing silent, weapons bound, armour muffled. They watched Antsy raise a hand, halt those following with a gesture, then inscribe a circle in the air with his index finger. The squads dispersed to the sides, each one seeking a place of cover. The patrol was done.

The sergeant made his way up to where Paran and Picker waited.

Before he arrived, Quick Ben slipped down to join the two officers. 'Captain,' he said under his breath, 'I've been talking with Twist's second.'

'And?'

'And the Moranth is worried, sir. About his commander – that killer infection's moved up past the shoulder. Twist only has a few weeks left, and he's living with a lot of pain right now – Hood knows how he stays in control.'

'All right,' Paran sighed. 'We'll resume conversation on that subject later. Let's hear Antsy now.'

'Right.'

The sergeant arrived, settled down in front of them. Picker handed him a flask and he took it, swallowed a half-dozen mouthfuls of wine, handed it back. Antsy cleared both nostrils with explosive snorts, then wiped his moustache and spent another few moments grooming and patting it down.

'If you start washing your armpits next,' Paran warned, 'I'll kill you. Once I get over the nausea, that is. So you've visited Setta – what did you see, Sergeant?'

'Uh, yes, sir, Captain. Setta. A ghost city, damned eerie. All those empty streets, empty buildings, feast-piles—'

'Feast what?'

'Feast-piles. In the squares. Big mounds of burnt bone and ash. Human. Feast-piles. Oh, and huge birds' nests on the city's four towers – Blend climbed close to one.'

'She did?'

'Well, closer, anyway. We'd noticed the guano on the tower sides when the sun's light was still clinging up high. Anyway, there's those mountain vultures bedded down in them.'

Quick Ben cursed. 'And Blend's sure she wasn't seen?'

'Absolutely, Wizard. You know Blend. We kept to blocking lines of sight just in case, which wasn't easy – those towers were well placed. But those birds had bedded down for real.'

'See any Great Ravens?' Quick Ben enquired.

The sergeant blinked. 'No. Why?'

'Nothing. But the rule holds – trust nothing in the sky, Antsy. Be sure everyone knows and remembers that, right?'

'Aye, as you say, Wizard.'

'Anything else?' Paran asked.

Antsy shrugged. 'No, not a thing. Setta's dead as dead gets. Maurik's probably the same.'

'Never mind Maurik,' Paran said. 'We're bypassing Maurik.'

He had Picker's fullest attention with that. 'Just us, Captain?'

'We're flying point all the way,' Quick Ben answered.

Antsy growled something under his breath.

'Speak clearly, Sergeant,' Paran ordered.

'Nothing, sir.'

'Let's have it, Antsy.'

'Well, just Hedge and Spindle and the other sappers, Captain. Been complaining about that missing crate of munitions – they were expecting to get resupplied, at Maurik. They'll squeal, sir.'

Picker saw Paran glance at Quick Ben.

The wizard scowled. 'I forgot to have a word with Hedge. Sorry. I'll get right on it.'

'The thing is,' Antsy said, 'we're undersupplied and that's the truth of it. If we run into trouble . . .'

'Really, Sergeant,' Picker muttered. 'When you've burned the bridges behind you, don't go starting a fire on the one in front of you. Tell those sappers to stiffen their spines. If we get into a situation where the fifteen or so available cussers and thirty or forty sharpers aren't enough, we're just one more feast-pile anyway.'

'Chat's over,' Paran announced. 'Quick, get the Moranth ready – we're making one more jump tonight. I want us within sight of the River Eryn come the dawn. Picker, check the cairns one more time, please. I don't want them obvious – we give ourselves away now and things'll get hot.'

'Aye, sir.'

'All right, let's move.'

He watched as his soldiers scrambled. A few moments later he sensed a presence and turned. The Black Moranth commander, Twist, had come to stand beside him.

'Captain Paran.'

'Yes?'

'I would know if you blessed the Barghast gods. In Capustan, or perhaps thereafter.'

Paran frowned. 'I was warned that they might ask, but no, I've not been approached.'

The black-armoured warrior was silent for a moment, then he said, 'Yet you acknowledge their place in the pantheon.'

'I don't see why not.'

'Is that a yes, Captain?'

'All right. Yes. Why? What's wrong?'

'Nothing is wrong. I will die soon, and I wish to know what will await my soul.'

'Have the Barghast shouldermen finally acknowledged that the Moranth share the same blood?'

'Their pronouncements one way or the other are without relevance.'

'Yet mine are?'

'You are the Master of the Deck.'

'What caused the schism, Twist? Between the Moranth and the Barghast?'

The achievant slowly raised his withered arm. 'Perhaps, in another realm, this arm is hale, whilst the rest of me is shrunken and lifeless. Perhaps,' he went on, 'it already feels the clasp, firm and strong, of a spirit. Who now but waits for my complete passage into that world.'

'An interesting way of viewing it.'

'Perspective, Captain. The Barghast would see us withered and lifeless. To be cut away.'

'While you see it the other way round?'

Twist shrugged. 'We do not fear change. We do not resist it. The Barghast must accept that growth is necessary, even if painful. They must learn what the Moranth learned long ago, when we did not draw our swords and instead spoke with the Tiste Edur – the grey-skinned wanderers of the seas. Spoke, to discover they were as lost as we were, as weary of war, as ready for peace.'

'Tiste Edur?'

'Children of the Shattered Warren. A fragment had been discovered, in the vast forest of Moranth that would

952

become our new homeland. Kurald Emurlahn, the true face of Shadow. There were so few Tiste Edur left, we chose to welcome them. The last of them are gone now, from Moranth Wood, long gone, but their legacy is what has made us as we are.'

'Achievant, it may take me a while to make sense of what you've just described. I have questions—'

Twist shrugged again. 'We did not slay the Tiste Edur. In Barghast eyes, that is our greatest crime. I wonder, however, if the Elder Spirits – now gods – see it in similar light.'

'They've had a long time to think,' Paran murmured. 'Sometimes, that's all that's needed. The heart of wisdom is tolerance. I think.'

'If so, Captain, then you must be proud.'

'Proud?'

The achievant slowly turned away as soft calls announced the troop was ready. 'I now return to Dujek Onearm.' He paused, then added, 'The Malazan Empire is a wise empire. I think that rare, and precious. And so I wish it – and you – well.'

Paran watched Twist stride away.

It was time to go.

Tolerant. Maybe. Keep that word in mind, Ganoes – there's a whisper that it will prove the fulcrum in what's to come . . .

Kruppe's mule carried him swiftly up the embankment, through a press of marching marines on the road – who scattered from its path – then down the other side and out onto the plain. Shouts and helpful advice followed him.

'Brainless beast! Blind, stubborn, braying creature of the Abyss! Stop, Kruppe cries! Stop! No, not that way—'

The mule charged a tilting path back round, fast-trotted smartly for the nearest clan of White Face Barghast.

A dozen savagely painted children raced out to meet them.

The mule baulked in sudden alarm, pitching Kruppe

forward onto its neck. The animal then wheeled, and slowed to a placid walk, tail switching its rump.

The Daru managed to right himself with a succession of grunts. 'Exercise is madness!' he exclaimed to the children who jogged up alongside. 'Witness these frightening urchins, already so musclebound as to laugh with stupid delight at Kruppe's woeful fate! The curse of vigour and strain has addled them. Dear Kruppe, forgive them as befits your admirable nature, your amiable equanimity, your effortlessly estimable ease among the company of those sadly lacking in years. Ah, you poor creatures, so short of leg yet self-deluded into expressions witlessly wise. You strut in step with this confounded mule, and so lay bare the tragic truth – your tribe is doomed, Kruppe pronounces! Doomed!'

'They understand not a word, Man of Lard!'

Kruppe twisted round to see Hetan and Cafal riding to join him. The woman was grinning.

'Not a word, Daru, and a good thing, too. Else they tear your heart from your chest at such damnations!'

'Damnations? Dear woman, Kruppe's deadly temper is to blame. His white hot rage that so endangers all around him! It is this beast, you see—'

'Not even worth eating,' Hetan noted. 'What think you, brother?'

'Too scrawny,' Cafal agreed.

'None the less, Kruppe pleads for forgiveness on behalf of his worthy self and the conversely worthless beast he rides. Forgive us, somewhat longer-legged spawn of Humbrall Taur, we beg you!'

'We've a question for you, Man of Lard.'

'You need only ask, and Kruppe shall answer. Shining with truth, his words smooth as oil to scent your un-blemished skin – there, just above the left breast, perhaps? Kruppe has in his possession—'

'No doubt,' Hetan interrupted. 'And were you to carry on this war would be over before I'd the chance to ask you the question. Now shut up, Daru, and listen. Look, if you will, upon the Malazan ranks on yonder road. The tent-covered wagons, the few foot-dragging companies who walk alongside them and between them, raising skyward clouds of dust—'

'Dear lass, you are one after Kruppe's own heart! Pray, resume this non-interrogative question, at length, wax your words into the thickest candle so that I may light an unquenchable flame of love in its honour.'

'I said *look*, Daru. Observe! Do you find nothing odd about our allies at present?'

'At present. Past and no doubt future, too, Kruppe asserts. Malazan mysteries, yes! Peculiar people, Kruppe proclaims. Discipline in said march approaching dishevelled dissolution, dust rising to be seen for leagues yet what is seen – well, naught but dust!'

'Just my point,' Hetan growled.

'And a sharp one it is.'

'So you'd noticed, then.'

'Noticed what, my dear? The sumptuous curves of yourself? How could Kruppe not notice such wondrous, if slightly barbaric, beauty? As a prairie flower—'

'—about to kill you,' Hetan said, grinning.

'A prairie flower, Kruppe observes, such as blooms on prickly cactus . . .'

''Ware the misstep, Man of Lard.'

'Kruppe's wares are without misstep, for he wears wariness well – uh . . .'

'This morning,' Hetan resumed after a moment, 'I watched one company of marines strike the tents of three companies, all through the Malazan camp. One for three, again and again.'

'Aye, one can count on the Malazans!'

Hetan rode closer, reached out and closed a hand on Kruppe's cloak collar. She half dragged him from his saddle, her smile broadening. 'Man of Lard,' she hissed, 'when I bed you – soon – this mule will need a travois to carry what's left of you. Dragging everyone along in your dance of words is a fine talent, but come tonight, I will pump the breath from your lungs. I will leave you speechless for days to come. And I will do all this to prove who is the master between us. Now, another utterance from you and I won't wait until tonight – I will give these children and everyone else a show that you, Daru, will never live down. Ah, I see by your bulging eyes that you understand. Good. Now, stop clenching that mule with your knees – the beast hates it. Settle in that saddle as if it was a horse, for it believes itself to be so. It notes how everyone else rides, notes how the horses carry their charges. Its eyes never rest – have you not noticed? This is the most alert beast this world has ever seen, and don't ask me why. There, my words are done. Until tonight, Man of Lard, when I will see you melt.' She released him.

Gasping, Kruppe dropped back onto the saddle. He opened his mouth to say something, then snapped it shut.

Cafal grunted. 'He learns fast, sister.'

She snorted. 'You all do, brother.'

The two rode away.

Staring after them, Kruppe removed his handkerchief from a sleeve and patted the sweat from his brow. 'Dear me. Dear, dearest me. You heard, mule? It is Kruppe who is doomed. *Doomed!*'

Whiskeyjack studied the two women standing before him, then said, 'Permission denied.'

'She ain't here, sir,' one of the marines reiterated. 'We got no-one to watch, right?'

'You will not rejoin your company, soldiers. You stay with me. Any other issues you wanted to discuss? No? Dismissed.'

The two marines exchanged a glance, then saluted and marched off.

'Sometimes,' Artanthos said from a half-dozen paces away, 'it comes back and sinks its teeth into you, doesn't it?'

Whiskeyjack eyed the man. 'What does?'

'Dassem Ultor's style of command. Soldiers given permission to think, to question, to argue . . .'

'Making us the best army this world has ever seen, Standard-Bearer.'

'None the less . . .'

'There is no "none the less". It is the *reason* why we're the best. And when time comes for the hard orders, you'll see the discipline – you may not have seen it here and now, but it's there, under the surface, and it's solid.'

'As you say,' Artanthos replied with a shrug.

Whiskeyjack resumed leading his horse to the kraal. The sun was already pulling the last of its lurid light below the horizon. On all sides, soldiers hurried to pitch tents and prepare cook fires. They were, he could see, a weary lot. Too many doubletime shifts through the day, then the added bell's worth of marching through dusk. He realized he'd need to tail that off over at least three days then add two more bells of stationary rest before reaching Coral, to give his infantry sufficient recovery time. An exhausted army was a defeated army.

A stabler collected Whiskeyjack's horse, and the commander set off towards Dujek's tent.

A squad of marines sat on their packs in front of the entrance, helms and armour on, still wearing the scarves that had covered their faces against the day's dust. None rose at Whiskeyjack's arrival.

'Carry on,' he growled sarcastically as he strode between the soldiers and entered the tent.

Within, Dujek was on his knees. He'd thrown a map down on the carpeted floor and was studying it by lantern-light, muttering under his breath.

'So,' Whiskeyjack said as he pulled a camp chair close and settled, 'the divided army . . . divides yet again.'

Dujek glanced up, his bushy brows knitting into a momentary frown before he resumed his perusal of the map. 'My bodyguard outside?'

'Aye.'

'They're a miserable lot at the best of times, and this isn't exactly best.'

Whiskeyjack stretched out his legs, wincing as old pain awoke once more in the left one. 'They're all Untan, aren't they? Haven't seen them around much of late.'

'You haven't seen them around because I told them to get scarce. Calling 'em miserable was being kind. They're not of the Host and as far as they're concerned they'll never be and, damn, I agree with 'em. Anyway, they wouldn't have saluted you even if we wasn't splitting into two commands. It's a struggle them saluting even me, and I'm the one they're sworn to protect.'

'We've got a tired army out there.'

'I know. With Oponn's luck the pace will return to sanity once we're the other side of Maurik. That's three days of loose reins and stretched necks to Coral – we've managed with less.'

'Managed to get mauled, you mean. That run to Mott damn near finished us, Dujek. We can't afford a repetition – there's a lot more to lose this time.'

The High Fist leaned back and began rolling up the map. 'Have faith, friend.'

Whiskeyjack glanced around, noted the cross-slung backpack resting against the centre pole, the old short-sword in its equally ancient scabbard draped over it. 'So soon?'

'You ain't been paying attention,' Dujek said. 'We've been peeling off without a hitch every night since the divide. Do the roll call, Whiskeyjack, you're six thousand short. Come the morning, you've got your command back – well, slightly under half of it, anyway. You should be dancing round the pole.'

'No, I should be the one flying out tonight, not you, Dujek. The risk—'

'Precisely,' the High Fist growled. 'The risk. You never seem to realize, but you're more important to this army

958

than I am. You always have been. To the soldiers, I'm just a one-armed ogre in a fancy uniform – they damned well see me as a pet.'

Whiskeyjack studied Dujek's battered, unadorned armour and grinned sourly.

'A figure of speech,' the High Fist said. 'Besides, it's as the Empress has commanded.'

'So you keep saying.'

'Whiskeyjack, Seven Cities is devouring itself. The Whirlwind has risen over blood-soaked sands. The Adjunct has a new army and it's on its way, but too late for the Malazan forces already there. I know you were talking retirement, but look at it from Laseen's point of view. She has two commanders left who know Seven Cities. And, before long, only one seasoned army – stuck here on Genabackis. If she has to risk one of us in the Pannion War, it has to be me.'

'She plans on sending the Host to Seven Cities? Hood take us, Dujek—'

'If the new Adjunct falls to Sha'ik, what choice does she have? More important, she wants you in command.'

Whiskeyjack slowly blinked. 'What about you?'

Dujek grimaced. 'I don't think she expects me to survive what's about to come. And if by some miracle I do, well, the campaign in Korel is a shambles . . .'

'You don't want Korel.'

'What I want doesn't matter, Whiskeyjack.'

'And Laseen would say the same of me, I gather. Dujek, as I said before, I intend to retire, to disappear if need be. I'm done. With all of this. Some log cabin in some frontier kingdom, a long way away from the Empire—'

'And a wife swinging a pot at your head. Marital, domestic bliss – you think Korlat will settle for that?'

Whiskeyjack smiled at High Fist's gentle mockery. 'It's her idea – not the pot-swinging – that's your particular nightmare, Dujek. But all the rest . . . all right, not a log cabin. More like a remote, wind-battered keep in

959

some mountain fastness. A place with a forbidding view—'

'Well,' Dujek drawled, 'you can still plant a small vegetable garden in the courtyard. Wage war against weeds. All right, that's our secret, then. Too bad for Laseen. Should I survive Coral, I'll be the one taking the Host back to Seven Cities. And should I not survive, well, I won't be in a position to care one whit about the Malazan Empire.'

'You'll scrape through, Dujek. You always do.'

'A weak effort, but I'll take it. So, share one last meal with me? The Moranth won't be here till after the midnight bell.'

It was an odd choice of words, and they hung heavy between the two old friends for a long moment.

'One last meal before I leave, I meant,' Dujek said with a faint smile. 'Until Coral.'

'I'd be delighted,' Whiskeyjack replied.

The wastes southwest of River Eryn stretched out beneath the stars, the sands rippled by inland winds born on the Dwelling Plain in the heart of the continent. Ahead, on the horizon's very edge, the Godswalk Mountains were visible, young and jagged, forming a barrier to the south that stretched sixty leagues. Its easternmost edge was swallowed by forests that continued unbroken all the way to Ortnal's Cut and Coral Bay, resuming on the other side of the water to surround the city of Coral itself.

The River Eryn became Ortnal's Cut twenty or more leagues from Coral Bay, the river's red water plunging into a deep chasm and reputedly turning oddly black and impenetrable. Coral Bay seemed to be but a continuation of that chasm.

The Cut was not yet visible to Paran, even from this height, yet he knew it was there. Scouts from the flight of Black Moranth now winging him and his Bridgeburners down the river's path had confirmed its nearness – sometimes the maps were wrong, after all. Fortunately, most of the Black Moranth had been positioned in the Vision

Mountains for months, making nightly sorties to study the lie of the land, to formulate the best approach to Coral in anticipation of this moment.

They would likely reach Eryn's mouth before dawn, assuming the stiff, steady winds rushing towards the Godswalk Mountains continued unabated, and the following night would see them skimming over the Cut's black waters, towards Coral itself.

And once there, we work out what the Seer's planned for us. Work it out and, if possible, dismantle it. And once that's done, it'll be time for me and Quick Ben—

Some unseen signal had the quorls plunging earthward, angling towards the river's western bank. Paran gripped hard the bony projections on the Black Moranth rider's armour, the wind whistling through his helm's visor to shriek in his ears. Gritting his teeth, Paran ducked his head low behind the warrior as the dark ground swiftly rose to meet them.

A snap of wings less than a man's height above the boulder-strewn shore slowed them abruptly, and then they were slipping silently along the strand. Paran twisted round to see the others in single file behind them. He tapped a finger against his rider's armour, leaned forward.

'What's happening?'

'There is carrion ahead,' the Black Moranth replied, the words strangely clicking – a sound the captain knew he would never get used to.

'You're hungry?'

The chitin-armoured warrior did not reply.

All right, so that was a little low.

The stench of whatever lay on the shore ahead reached Paran. 'Do we have to do this? Is it the quorls who need to feed? Have we time, Moranth?'

'Our scouts saw nothing the night last, Captain. Never before has this river yielded such a creature. Perhaps, that it has done so now is important. We shall investigate.'

Paran relented. 'Very well.'

The quorl beneath them angled to the right, up and over the grassy embankment, then settled on the level ground beyond it. The others followed suit.

Joints aching, Paran released the saddle-straps and cautiously dismounted.

Quick Ben limped to his side. 'Abyss take me,' he grumbled, 'much more of this and my legs will fall off.'

'Any idea what they've found?' the captain asked him.

'Only that it stinks.'

'Some dead beast, apparently.'

A half-dozen Black Moranth had gathered around the lead rider. Clicks and buzzes were exchanged among them in a rapid discussion, then the officer – whose quorl Paran had been riding – gestured for the captain and the wizard to approach.

'The creature,' the officer said, 'lies directly ahead. We would have you examine it as we shall. Speak freely, so that we might finally circle the truth and so know its hue. Come.'

Paran glanced at Quick Ben, who simply shrugged. 'Lead the way, then,' the captain said.

The corpse lay among boulders high on the strand, fifteen paces from the southward-rushing water. Limbs twisted, revealing broken bones – some of them jutting through torn flesh – the figure was naked, bloated with decomposition. The ground around it seethed with crayfish, clicking and scraping and, here and there, locked in titanic battle over possession of the feast – a detail Paran found amusing at first, then ineffably disturbing. His attention only momentarily drawn away from the body by the scavengers, he fixed his gaze once more on the figure.

Quick Ben spoke a soft question to the Moranth officer, who nodded. The wizard gestured and a muted glow rose from the boulders on all sides, illuminating the corpse.

Hood's breath. 'Is that a Tiste Andii?'

Quick Ben stepped closer, squatted, and was silent for a long moment, then he said, 'If he is, he's not one of

Anomander Rake's people . . . no, in fact, I don't think he's Tiste Andii at all.'

Paran frowned. 'He's damned tall, Wizard. And those facial features – such as we can see—'

'His skin's too pale, Captain.'

'Bleached by water and sun.'

'No. I've seen a few Tiste Andii bodies. In Blackdog Forest, and in the swamplands surrounding it. I've seen 'em in all sorts of conditions. Nothing like this. He's heat-swelled from the day, aye, and we have to assume he came from the river, but he's not water-logged. Captain, have you ever seen a victim of Serc sorcery?'

'The Path of the Sky? Not that I recall.'

'There's one spell, that bursts the victim from the inside out. Has to do with pressure, with violently altering it, even taking it away entirely. Or, as this looks like, increasing it outside the body a hundredfold. This man was killed by implosive pressure, as if he'd been hit by a mage using High Serc.'

'All right.'

'Not all right, Captain. All wrong, in fact.' Quick Ben looked up at the Moranth officer. 'Circle the truth, you said. OK. Talk.'

'Tiste Edur.'

The name – *oh, yes. Twist spoke of them. Some old war . . . a shattered warren—*

'Agreed. Though I've never seen one before.'

'He did not die here.'

'You're right, he didn't. And he didn't drown, either.'

The Moranth nodded. 'He did not drown. Nor was he killed by sorcery – for the smell is wrong.'

'Aye, no taint of magic. Keep circling.'

'The Blue Moranth, who ply the seas and sink nets into the deep trenches – their catch arrives upon the deck already dead. This effect concerns the nature of pressure.'

'I imagine it does.'

'This man was killed by the reverse. By appearing, suddenly, in a place of great pressure.'

'Aye.' Quick Ben sighed. He glanced out over the river. 'There's a trench, a crevasse, out there – you can see it by the current's upstream pull out in the middle. Ortnal's Cut reaches this far, unseen, cracking the river bed. That trench is deep.'

'Hold it,' Paran said. 'You're suggesting that this Tiste Edur appeared, suddenly, somewhere down in that underwater trench. The only way that could be true is if he'd opened a warren in order to get there – that's a seriously complicated means of suicide.'

'Only if he'd intended to do as he did,' Quick Ben replied. 'Only if he was the one who opened the warren in the first place. If you want to kill someone – nastily – you throw them, push them, trip them – whatever – into an inimical portal. I think this poor bastard was murdered.'

'By a High Mage of Serc?'

'More like a High Mage of Ruse – the Path of the Sea. Captain, the Malazan Empire is a seafaring empire, or at least its roots are seafaring. You won't find a true High Mage of Ruse in all the empire. It's the hardest warren to master.' Quick Ben turned to the Moranth. 'And among your Blue Moranth? Your Silver or Gold? Any High Mages of Ruse?'

The warrior shook his helmed head. 'Nor do our annals reveal any in our past.'

'And how far back do those annals go?' Quick Ben asked casually, returning his attention to the corpse.

'Seven tens.'

'Decades?'

'Centuries.'

'So,' the wizard said, straightening, 'a singular killer.'

'Then why,' Paran murmured, 'do I now believe that this man was killed by another Tiste Edur?'

The Moranth and Quick Ben turned to him, were silent.

Paran sighed. 'A hunch, I suppose. A gut whisper.'

'Captain,' the wizard said, 'don't forget what you've

964

become.' He fixed his attention once more on the corpse. 'Another Tiste Edur. All right, let's circle this one, too.'

'There is no objection,' the Moranth officer said, 'to the possibility.'

'The Tiste Edur are of Elder Shadow,' Quick Ben noted.

'Within the seas, shadows swim. Kurald Emurlahn. The Warren of the Tiste Edur, Elder Shadow, is broken, and has been lost to mortals.'

'Lost?' Quick Ben's brows rose. 'Never found, you mean. Meanas – where Shadowthrone and Cotillion and the Hounds dwell—'

'Is naught but a gateway,' the Moranth officer finished.

Paran grunted. 'If a shadow could cast a shadow, that shadow would be Meanas – is that what you two are saying? Shadowthrone rules the guardhouse?'

Quick Ben grinned. 'What a delicious image, Captain.'

'A disturbing one,' he muttered in reply. *The Hounds of Shadow – they are the guardians of the gate. Damn, that makes too much sense to be in error. But the warren is also shattered. Meaning, that gate might not lead anywhere. Or maybe it belongs to the largest fragment. Does Shadowthrone know the truth? That his mighty Throne of Shadows is . . . is what? A castellan's chair? A gatekeeper's perch? My oh my, as Kruppe would say.*

'Ah,' Quick Ben sighed, his grin fading, 'I think I see your point. The Tiste Edur are active once more, by what we've seen here. They're returning to the mortal world – perhaps they've re-awakened the true Throne of Shadow, and maybe they're about to pay their new gatekeeper a visit.'

'Another war in the pantheon – the Crippled God's chains are no doubt rattling with his laughter.' Paran rubbed at the bristle on his jaw. 'Excuse me – I need some privacy. Carry on here, if you like – I won't be long.' *I hope.*

He strode inland twenty paces, stood facing northwest, eyes on the distant stars. *All right, I've done this before, let's see if it works a second time . . .*

The transition was so swift, so effortless, that it left him reeling, stumbling across uneven flagstones in swirling, mote-filled darkness. Cursing, he righted himself. The carved images beneath his feet glowed faintly, cool and vaguely remote.

So, I'm here. As simple as that. Now, how do I find the image I'm looking for? Raest? You busy at the moment? What a question. If you were busy we'd all be in trouble, wouldn't we? Never mind. Stay where you are, wherever that is. This is for me to work out, after all.

Not in the Deck of Dragons – I don't want the gateway, after all, do I. Thus, the Elder Deck, the Deck of Holds . . .

The flagstone directly before him twisted into a new image, one he had not seen before, yet he instinctively recognized it as the one he sought. The carving was rough, worn, the deep grooves forming a chaotic web of shadows.

Paran felt himself being pulled forward, down, into the scene.

He appeared in a wide, low chamber. Unadorned, dressed stone formed the walls, water-stained and covered in lichen, mould and moss. High to his right and left were wide windows – horizontal slits – both crowded with a riot of creepers and vines that snaked down into the room, onto the floor and through a carpet of dead leaves.

The air smelled of the sea, and somewhere outside the chamber seagulls bickered above a crashing surf.

Paran's heart thudded loud in his chest. He had not expected this. *I'm not in another realm. This is mine.*

Seven paces ahead, on a raised dais, stood a throne. Carved from a single trunk of crimson wood, unplaned, broad strips of bark on its flanks, many of them split, had pulled away from the wood beneath. Shadows flowed in that bark, swam the deep grooves, spilling out to dart through the surrounding air before vanishing in the chamber's gloom.

The Throne of Shadow. Not in some hidden, long-forgotten realm. It's here, on – or rather in – my world . . . A small, tattered fragment of Kurald Galain.

*. . . and the Tiste Edur have come to find it. They're search-
ing, crossing the seas, seeking this place. How do I know this?*

He stepped forward. The shadows raced over the throne
in a frenzy. Another step. *You want to tell me something,
Throne, don't you?* He strode to the dais, reached out—

The shadows poured over him.

*Hound – not Hound! Blood and not blood! Master and
mortal!*

'Oh, be quiet! Tell me of this place.'

*The wandering isle! Wanders not! Flees! Yes! The Children
are corrupted, the souls of the Edur are poisoned! Storm of
madness – we elude! Protect us, Hound not Hound! Save us –
they come!*

'The wandering isle. This is Drift Avalii, isn't it? West of
Quon Tali. I thought there were supposed to be Tiste Andii
on this island—'

*Sworn to defend! Spawn of Anomander Rake – gone!
Leaving a blood trail, leading the Edur away with the spilling out
of their own lives – oh, where is Anomander Rake? They call for
him, they call and call! They beg for his help!*

'He's busy, I'm afraid.'

*Anomander Rake, Son of Darkness! The Edur have sworn to
destroy Mother Dark. You must warn him! Poisoned souls, led
by the one who has been slain a hundred times, oh, 'ware this
new Emperor of the Edur, this Tyrant of Pain, this Deliverer of
Midnight Tides!*

Paran pulled himself back with a mental wrench,
staggered a step further away, then another. He was
sheathed in sweat, trembling with the aftermath of such
visceral terror.

Barely conscious of his own intent, he whirled – the
chamber around him blurring, swallowed by darkness, then,
with a grinding shift, something deeper than darkness.

'Oh, Abyss . . .'

A rubble-strewn plain beneath a dead sky. In the
distance to his right, the groan of massive, wooden wheels,
the slither and snap of chains, countless plodding footfalls.

In the air, a pall of suffering that threatened to suffocate Paran where he stood.

Gritting his teeth, he swung towards the dreadful sounds, pushed himself forward.

Grainy shapes appeared ahead, coming directly for Paran. Leaning figures, stretched chains. Beyond them, a hundred or more paces distant, loomed the terrible wagon, massed with writhing bodies, clunking and shifting over stones, swallowed in a haze of mist.

Paran stumbled forward. 'Draconus!' he shouted. 'Where in Hood's name are you? Draconus!'

Faces lifted, then all but one—hooded and indistinct – lowered once more.

The captain slipped between victims of Dragnipur, closing on the one shadowed face still regarding him, stepping within reach of the mad, the numbed, the failing – not one of whom sought to impede him, or even acknowledged his presence. He moved as a ghost through the press.

'Greetings, mortal,' Draconus said. 'Walk with me, then.'

'I wanted Rake.'

'You found his sword, instead. For which I am not sorry.'

'Yes, I've spoken with Nightchill, Draconus – but don't press me on that subject. When I reach a decision, you'll be the first to know. I need to speak with Rake.'

'Aye,' the ancient warrior rumbled, 'you do. Explain to him this truth, mortal. He is too merciful, too merciful to wield Dragnipur. The situation is growing desperate.'

'What are you talking about?'

'Dragnipur needs to feed. Look around us, mortal. There are those who, at long last, fail in pulling this burden. They are carried to the wagon, then, and tossed onto it – you think this preferable? Too weak to move, they are soon buried by those like them. Buried, trapped for eternity. And the more the wagon bears, the greater its weight – the more difficult the burden for those of us still able to heave on these chains. Do you understand? Dragnipur needs to feed. We require . . . fresh legs. Tell Rake – he must draw the

968

sword. He must take souls. Powerful ones, preferably. And he must do so soon—'

'What will happen if the wagon stops, Draconus?'

The man who forged his own prison was silent for a long time. 'Project your vision, mortal, onto our trail. See for yourself, what pursues us.'

Pursues? He closed his eyes, yet the scene did not vanish – the wagon lumbered on, there in his mind, the multitudes passing by him like ghosts. Then the massive contrivance was past, its groans fading behind him. The ruts of its wheels flanked him, each one as wide as an imperial road. The earth was sodden with blood, bile and sweat, a foul mud that drew his boots down, swallowed them up to his ankles.

His gaze followed those tracks, back, to the horizon.

Where chaos raged. Filling the sky, a storm such as he had never seen before. Rapacious hunger poured from it. Frenzied anticipation.

Lost memories.

Power born from rendered souls.

Malice and desire, a presence almost self-aware, with hundreds of thousands of eyes all fixed on the wagon behind Paran.

So . . . so eager to feed . . .

He recoiled.

With a gasp, Paran found himself stumbling once more alongside Draconus. The residue of what he had witnessed clung to him, making his heart drum savagely in his chest. Another thirty steps passed before he was able to raise his head, to speak. 'Draconus,' he grated, 'you have made a very unpleasant sword.'

'Darkness has ever warred against Chaos, mortal. Ever retreated. And each time that Mother Dark relented – to the Coming of Light, to the Birth of Shadow – her power has diminished, the imbalance growing more profound. Such was the state of the realms around me in those early times. A growing imbalance. Until Chaos approached the

969

very Gate to Kurald Galain itself. A defence needed to be fashioned. Souls were . . . required . . .'

'Wait, please. I need to think—'

'Chaos hungers for the power in those souls – for what Dragnipur has claimed. To feed on such power will make it stronger – tenfold. A hundredfold. Sufficient to breach the Gate. Look to your mortal realm, Ganoes Paran. Devastating, civilization-destroying wars, civil wars, pogroms, wounded and dying gods – you and your kind progress at a perilous pace on the path forged by Chaos. Blinded by rage, lusting for vengeance, those darkest of desires—'

'Wait—'

'Where history means nothing. Lessons are forgotten. Memories – of humanity, of all that is *humane* – are lost. Without balance, Ganoes Paran—'

'*But you want me to shatter Dragnipur!*'

'Ah, now I understand your resistance to all that I say. Mortal, I have had time to think. To recognize the grave error I have made. I had believed, Ganoes Paran, in those early times, that only in Darkness could the power that is *order* be manifested. I sought to help Mother Dark – for it seemed she was incapable of helping herself. She would not answer, she would not even acknowledge her children. She had withdrawn, deep into her own realm, far from all of us, so far that we could not find her.'

'Draconus—'

'Hear me, please. Before the Houses, there were Holds. Before Holds, there was *wandering*. Your own words, yes? But you were both right and wrong. Not wandering, but migration. A seasonal round – predictable, cyclical. What seemed aimless, random, was in truth fixed, bound to its own laws. A truth – a power – I failed to recognize.'

'So the shattering of Dragnipur will release the Gate once more – to its migration.'

'To what gave it its own strength to resist Chaos, yes. Dragnipur has bound the Gate of Darkness to flight, for eternity – but should the souls chained to it diminish—'

'The flight slows down—'

'Fatally.'

'So, either Rake begins killing – taking souls – or Dragnipur must be destroyed.'

'The former is necessary – to buy us time – until the latter occurs. The sword must be shattered. The purpose of its very existence was misguided. Besides which, there is another truth I have but stumbled on – far too late for it to make any difference. At least to me.'

'And that is?'

'Just as Chaos possesses the capacity to act in its own defence, to indeed alter its own nature to its own advantage in its eternal war, so too can Order. It is not solely bound to Darkness. It understands, if you will, the value of balance.'

Paran felt an intuitive flash. 'The Houses of the Azath. The Deck of Dragons.'

The hooded head shifted slightly and Paran felt cold, unhuman eyes fixing upon him. 'Aye, Ganoes Paran.'

'The Houses take souls . . .'

'And bind them in place. Beyond the grasp of Chaos.'

'So it shouldn't matter, then, if Darkness succumbs.'

'Don't be a fool. Losses and gains accumulate, shift the tide, but not always in ways that redress the balance. We are in an *imbalance*, Ganoes Paran, that approaches a threshold. This war, which has seemed eternal to us trapped within it, may come to an end. What awaits us all, should that happen . . . well, mortal, you have felt its breath, there in our wake.'

'I need to speak with Rake.'

'Then find him. Assuming, of course, he still carries the sword.'

Easier said than done, it seems— 'Hold on – what do you mean by that? About still carrying the sword?'

'Just that, Ganoes Paran.'

But why wouldn't he be? What in Hood's name are you hinting at, Draconus? This is Anomander Rake we're talking about, damn it! If we were living in one of those bad fables with some dimwitted farmboy stumbling on a magical sword, well, then losing the weapon might be possible. But . . . Anomander Rake? Son of Darkness? Lord of Moon's Spawn?

A grunt from Draconus drew his attention. Directly in their path, tangled in chains gone slack, lay a huge, demonic figure. 'Byrys. I myself killed him, so long ago. I did not think . . .' He came up to the black-skinned creature, reached down and – to Paran's astonishment – heaved it over a shoulder. 'To the wagon,' Draconus said, 'my old nemesis . . .'

'Who summoned me,' the demon rumbled, 'to do battle with you?'

'Ever the same question, Byrys. I do not know. I have never known.'

'Who summoned me, Draconus, to die by the sword?'

'Someone long dead, no doubt.'

'Who summoned . . .'

As Draconus and the demon draped across his shoulders continued their pointless conversation, Paran felt himself drawing away, the words growing indistinct, the image dimming . . . until he stood once more on flagstones, far beneath the Finnest House.

'Anomander Rake. Knight of Dark, High House Dark . . .' His eyes strained to see the rise of the image he had summoned, out among the endless sprawl of etched flagstones.

But nothing came.

Feeling a sudden chill in the pit of his stomach, Paran mentally reached out, questing into High House Dark, seeking the place, the figure with his black sword trailing ethereal chains—

He had no comprehension of what rushed up to meet him, blinding, hammering into his skull – a flash—

—then oblivion.

He opened his eyes to dappled sunlight. Water traced cool

rivulets down his temples. A shadow slipped over him, then a familiar, round face with small, sharp eyes.

'Mallet,' Paran croaked.

'We were wondering if you'd ever return, Captain.' He held up a dripping cloth. 'You'd run a fever for a while there, sir, but I think it's broke—'

'Where?'

'Mouth of River Eryn. Ortnal's Cut. It's midday – Quick Ben had to go find you last night, Captain – the risk of getting caught out in the open before dawn – we just strapped you to your quorl and rode hard those winds.'

'Quick Ben,' Paran muttered. 'Get him here. Fast.'

'Easily done, sir.' Mallet leaned back, gestured to one side.

The wizard appeared. 'Captain. We've had four of those condors pass nearby since sunrise – if they're looking for us—'

Paran shook his head. 'Not us. Moon's Spawn.'

'You might be right – but that would mean they haven't sighted it yet, and that seems damned unlikely. How do you hide a floating mountain? More likely—'

'Anomander Rake.'

'What?'

Paran closed his eyes. 'I sought him out – through the Deck, the Knight of Dark. Wizard, I think we've lost him. And Moon's Spawn. We've lost the Tiste Andii, Quick Ben. *Anomander Rake is gone.*'

'Gruesome city! Ghastly! Ghoulish! Grimy! Kruppe regrets said witnessing of said settlement—'

'So you've said,' Whiskeyjack murmured.

'It bodes ill, those ill abodes. Cause for dread, such ghostly streets and such enormous vultures roosting and winging about ever so freely in yon sky over Kruppe's noble head. When, oh when will darkness come? When will merciful darkness fall, Kruppe reiterates, so that blessed blindness enwreathes proper selves, thus permitting

973

inspiration to flash and thus reveal the deceit of deceits, the sleightest of sleight of hands, the non-illusion of illusions, the—'

'Two days,' Hetan growled from Whiskeyjack's other side. 'I stole his voice . . . for two days – I had been expecting longer, since the man's heart damn near gave out.'

'Shut him up again,' Cafal said.

'Tonight, and with luck, he'll be in no shape to say a word until Maurik at the very least.'

'Dear lass has misunderstood Kruppe's uncharacteristic silence! He swears! Nay, he veritably begs, that you spare him pending thrash and oof, on the night to come, and every night to follow! He is too tender of spirit, too easily bruised, scratched, and bodily thrown about. Kruppe has never known the horror of cartwheels before, nor does he wish to ever experience said discombobulation of sorted self again. Thus, to explain extraordinary terseness, these two days of muted apparel so unstylishly clothing honourable Kruppe, worse indeed than a shroud of despond. To explain! Kruppe has, dear friends, been thinking.

'Thinking, aye! Such as he never thought to have before! Ever, nor never. Thoughts to shine with glory, so bright as to blind mortal ken, so palling as to pillage appalling fears to leave naught but purest courage, upon which one sails as on a raft into the mouth of paradise!'

Hetan sniffed. 'Those tumbles weren't cartwheels. They were flops. Very well, I will give you cartwheels in plenty tonight, slippery one!'

'Kruppe prays, oh how he prays, that darkness never falls! That from the depths the flash is but muted in a world vast with light and wonder! Hold back, merciful darkness! We must march on, brave Whiskeyjack! And on! Without pause, without surcease, without delay! Wear our feet to mere nubs, Kruppe pleads! Night, oh night! Beckoning fatal lures to weak self – the mule was there, after all, and look upon poor beast – exhausted by what its eyes could not help but witness! Exhausted unto near death by simple empathy!

974

'Oh, hear naught of Kruppe and his secret desires for self-destruction at hands of delicious woman! Hear naught! Hear naught until meaning itself disperses . . .'

Picker stared out on the black waters of Ortnal's Cut. Chunks of ice brunted the current, grinding and pushing their way upstream. To the southeast, Coral Bay was white as a winter field under the stars. The journey from Eryn Mouth had taken but half the night. From this point on, the Bridgeburners would travel on foot, staying under cover as they edged round the dark, forest-clad mountains, skirting the relatively level region between the Cut and the range.

She glanced down the slight slope to where Captain Paran sat with Quick Ben, Spindle, Shank, Toes and Bluepearl. A gathering of mages always made her nervous, especially when Spindle counted among them. Beneath the skin beneath the hairshirt, there scrabbled the soul of a sapper, half mad – as were the souls of all sappers. Spindle's magery was notoriously unpredictable, and more than once she had seen him unveiling his warren with one hand while throwing a Moranth munition with the other.

The three other Bridgeburner wizards weren't much to crow over. Bluepearl was a pigeon-toed Napan who shaved his head and pretended to airs of vast knowledge concerning the Warren of Ruse.

Shank had Seti blood, the importance of which he exaggerated by wearing countless charms and trinkets from the north Quon Tali tribe – even though the Seti themselves had long since ceased to exist except in name, so thoroughly had they been assimilated into Quon culture. Shank, however, wore as part of his uniform a strangely romanticized version of Seti plains garb, all of which had been made by a seamstress in the employ of a theatre company in Unta. Picker was unsure which warren Shank specialized in, since his rituals calling upon power usually took longer than the average battle.

Toes had earned his name by his habit of collecting toes among the enemy's dead – whether he'd been personally responsible for killing them or not. He had concocted some kind of drying powder with which he treated his trophies before sewing them onto his vest – the man smelled like a crypt in dry weather, like a pauper's pit before the lime when it rained. He claimed to be a necromancer, and that some disastrously botched ritual in the past had left him over-sensitive to ghosts – they followed him, he would assert, adding that by cutting off their mortal toes he took from the ghosts all sense of balance so that they fell down so often that he was able to leave them far behind.

Indeed, he looked a haunted man, but, as Blend had pointed out, who wouldn't be haunted with all those dead toes hanging from him?

The journey had been an exhausting one. Being strapped to the rear saddle of a quorl and shivering in the fiercely cold winds, as league after league passed beneath, had a way of leaving one enervated, stiff-limbed and leaden. The sodden nature of this mountainside forest didn't help. She was frozen down to her bones. There'd be rain and mist all morning – the warmth of the sun would not arrive until the afternoon.

Mallet moved to her side. 'Lieutenant,' he said.

She scowled at him. 'Any idea what they're talking about, Healer?'

Mallet glanced down at the mages. 'They're just worried, sir. About those condors. They've had close enough looks at them of late and there doesn't seem much doubt that those birds are anything but birds.'

'Well, we'd all guessed that.'

'Aye.' Mallet shrugged, added, 'And, I expect, Paran's news about Anomander Rake and Moon's Spawn hasn't left their minds at ease. If they've been lost, as the captain believes, taking Coral – and taking down the Pannion Seer – will be a lot uglier.'

'We might get slaughtered, you mean.'

976

'Well . . .'

Picker's attention slowly fixed on the healer. 'Out with it,' she growled.

'Just a hunch, Lieutenant.'

'Which is?'

'Quick Ben and the captain, sir. They've got something else planned, stewed up between them, that is. Or so I suspect. I've known Quick a long time, you see, up close. I've picked up a sense of how he works. We're here covertly, right? The lead elements for Dujek. But for those two it's a double-blind – there's another mission hiding under this one, and I don't think Onearm knows anything about it.'

Picker slowly blinked. 'And Whiskeyjack?'

Mallet grinned sourly. 'As to that, I can't say, sir.'

'Is it just you with these suspicions, Healer?'

'No. Whiskeyjack's squad. Hedge. Trotts – the damned Barghast is showing his sharp teeth a lot and when he does that it usually means he knows something's going on but doesn't know exactly what, only he won't let on with that last bit. If you gather my meaning.'

Picker nodded. She'd seen Trotts grinning almost every time she'd set eyes on the warrior the past few days. Unnerving, despite Mallet's explanation.

Blend appeared in front of them.

Picker's scowl deepened.

'Sorry, Lieutenant,' she said. 'Captain sniffed me out – not sure how, but he did. I didn't get much chance to listen in, I'm afraid. Anyway, I'm to tell you to get the squads ready.'

'Finally,' Picker muttered. 'I was about to freeze in place.'

'Even so,' Mallet said, 'but I'm already missing the Moranth – these woods are damned dark.'

'But empty, right?'

The healer shrugged. 'Seems so. It's the skies we've got to worry about, come the day.'

Picker straightened. 'Follow me, you two. Time to rouse the others . . .'

Brood's march to Maurik had become something of a race, the various elements of his army straggling out depending on whatever speed they could maintain – or, in the case of the Grey Swords and Gruntle's legion, what they chose to maintain. As a consequence, the forces were now stretched over almost a league of scorched farmland along the battered trader road leading south, with the Grey Swords, Trake's Legion and another ragtag force in effect forming a rearguard, by virtue of their leisurely pace.

Itkovian had chosen to remain in Gruntle's company. The big Daru and Stonny Menackis wove a succession of tales from their shared past that kept Itkovian entertained, as much from the clash of their disparate recollections as from the often outrageous events the two described.

It had been a long time since Itkovian had last allowed himself such pleasure. He had come to value highly their company, in particular their appalling irreverence.

On rare occasions, he rode up to the Grey Swords, spoke with the Shield Anvil and the Destriant, but the awkwardness soon forced him to leave – his old company had begun to heal, drawing into its weave the Tenescowri recruits, training conducted on the march and when the company halted at dusk. And, as the soldiers grew tighter, the more Itkovian felt himself to be an outsider – the more he missed the family he had known all his adult life.

At the same time, they were his legacy, and he allowed himself a measure of pride when looking upon them. The new Shield Anvil had assumed the title and all it demanded – and for the first time Itkovian understood how others must have seen him, when he'd held the Reve's title. Remote, uncompromising, entirely self-contained. A hard figure, promising brutal justice. Granted, he'd had both Brukhalian and Karnadas from whom he could draw support. But, for the new Shield Anvil, there was naught but the Destriant – a young Capan woman of few words who had herself been a recruit not too long ago. Itkovian well understood how alone the Shield Anvil must be feeling, yet he could think of no way to ease that burden. Every word of advice he gave came, after all, from a man who had – in his own mind at least – failed his god.

His return to Gruntle and Stonny, each time, held the bitter flavour of flight.

'You chew on things like no other man I've known,' Gruntle said.

Blinking, Itkovian glanced over at the Daru. 'Sir?'

'Well, not quite true, come to think of it. Buke . . .'

On Itkovian's other side, Stonny sniffed. 'Buke? Buke was a drunk.'

'More than that, you miserable woman,' Gruntle replied. 'He carried on his shoulders—'

'None of that,' Stonny warned.

To Itkovian's surprise, Gruntle fell abruptly silent. *Buke . . . ah, I recall. On his shoulders, the deaths of loved ones.* 'There is no need, Stonny Menackis, for such uncharacteristic sensitivity. I see how I appear, to you both, similar to Buke. I am curious: did your sad friend seek redemption in his life? While he may have refused me when I was Shield Anvil, he might well have drawn strength from some inner resolve.'

'Not a chance, Itkovian,' Stonny said. 'Buke drank to keep his torment at bay. He wasn't looking for redemption. He wanted death, plain and simple.'

'Not simple,' Gruntle objected. 'He wanted an honourable death, such as his family was denied – by that honour he would redeem them in exchange. I know, a twisted notion, but what went on in his mind is less a mystery to me than to most, I suspect.'

'Because you've thought the same,' Stonny snapped. 'Even though you didn't lose a family to some tenement fire. Even though the worst thing you've lost is maybe that harlot who married that merchant—'

'Stonny,' the Daru growled, 'I lost Harllo. I nearly lost you.'

The admission clearly left her speechless.

Ah, these two . . . 'The distinction,' Itkovian said, 'between myself and Buke lies in the notion of redemption. I accept torment, such as it is for me, and so acknowledge responsibility for all that I have and have not done. As Shield Anvil, my faith demanded that I relieve others of their pain. In the name of Fener, I was to bring peace to souls, and to do so without judgement. This I have done.'

'But your god's gone,' Stonny said. 'So who, in Hood's name, did you deliver those souls to?'

'Why, no-one, Stonny Menackis. I carry them still.'

Stonny was glaring across at Gruntle, who answered her with a despondent shrug. 'As I told you, lass,' he muttered.

She rounded on Itkovian. 'You damned fool! That new Shield Anvil – what about her? Won't she embrace your burden or whatever it is you do? Won't she take those souls – *she* has a god, damn her!' Stonny gathered her reins. 'If she thinks she can—'

Itkovian stayed her with a hand. 'No, sir. She has offered, as she must. But she is not ready for such a burden – it would kill her, destroy her soul – and that would wound her god, perhaps fatally so.'

Stonny pulled her arm away, but remained beside him. Her eyes were wide. 'And what, precisely, do you plan on doing with – with – all of those souls?'

'I must find a means, Stonny Menackis, of redeeming them. As my god would have done.'

'Madness! You're not a god! You're a damned mortal! You can't—'

'But I must. So, you see, I am like yet unlike your friend Buke. Forgive me, sirs, for "chewing" on such things. I know my answer awaits me – soon, I believe – and you are right, I would do better to simply exercise calm patience. I have held on this long, after all.'

'Be as you are, Itkovian,' Gruntle said. 'We talk too much, Stonny and I. That's all. Forgive us.'

'There is nothing to forgive, sir.'

'Why can't I have normal friends?' Stonny demanded.

'Ones without tiger stripes and cat eyes? Ones without a hundred thousand souls riding their backs? Here comes a rider from that other lagging company – maybe *he's* normal! Hood knows, he's dressed like a farmer and looks inbred enough to manage only simple sentences. A perfect man! Hey! You! No, what are you hesitating for? Come to us, then! Please!'

The lanky figure riding what seemed to be an odd breed of dray horse cautiously walked his mount forward. In terribly accented Daru, he called out, 'Hello, friends! Is this a bad time? It seems you argue—'

'Argue?' Stonny snorted. 'You've been living in the woods too long if you think that was an argument! Come closer, and how by the Abyss did you come by such a huge nose?'

The man wilted, hesitated.

'Stonny!' Gruntle admonished. He addressed the rider, 'This woman is rude and miserable to everyone, soldier.'

'I wasn't being rude!' she exclaimed. 'Big noses are like big hands, that's all . . .'

No-one spoke.

Slowly, the stranger's long, narrow face deepened to crimson.

'Welcome, sir,' Itkovian said. 'Regrets that we have not met before – especially since we all seem to have been left behind by Brood's vanguard, and the Rhivi and all the other companies.'

The man managed a nod. 'Yeah. We'd noticed. I am High Marshal Straw, of the Mott Irregulars.' His pale, watery eyes flicked to Gruntle. 'Nice tattoos. I've got one, too.' He rolled up a grimy sleeve, revealing a muddled, mis-shapen image on his dirt-smeared shoulder. 'Not sure what happened to it, but it was supposed to be a treefrog on a stump. Of course, treefrogs are hard to see, so it might be pretty good at that – that smudge – here – I think that's the treefrog. Could be a mushroom, though.' His smile reveal-ing enormous teeth, he rolled down his sleeve once more and settled back in his saddle. He suddenly frowned. 'Do you know where we're marching to? And why is everyone in such a hurry?'

'Uh . . .'

It seemed all Gruntle could manage, so Itkovian spoke up, 'Excellent questions, sir. We march to a city called Maurik, there to rejoin the Malazan army. From Maurik, we will proceed further south, to the city of Coral.'

Straw frowned. 'Will there be a battle at Maurik?'

'No, the city is abandoned. It is simply a convenient locale for the reunification.'

'And Coral?'

'There will likely be a battle there, yes.'

'Cities don't run away. So why are they all rushing?'

Itkovian sighed. 'A perspicacious enquiry, sir, one that leads to certain challenges to previously held assumptions for all concerned.'

'What?'

'Good question, he said,' Stonny drawled.

The Marshal nodded. 'That's why I asked it. I'm known for asking good questions.'

'We see that,' she replied levelly.

'Brood's in a hurry,' Gruntle said, 'because he wants to get to Maurik before the Malazans – who seem to be marching at a faster pace than we'd thought possible.'

'So?'

'Well, uh, the alliance has become rather . . . uncertain, of late.'

'They're Malazans – what did you expect?'

'To be honest,' Gruntle said, 'I don't think Brood knew what to expect. Are you saying you're not surprised by the recent schism?'

'Schism? Oh, right. No. Anyway, it's obvious why the Malazans are moving so fast.'

Itkovian leaned forward in his saddle. 'It is?'

Straw shrugged. 'We've some of our people there—'

'You have *spies* among the Malazans?' Gruntle demanded.

'Sure. We always do. It pays to know what they're up to, especially when we was fighting them. Just because we allied with them there was no reason not to keep watching.'

'So why are they marching so fast, Marshal Straw?'

'The Black Moranth, of course. Coming each night, taking whole companies away. There's only about four thousand Malazans left on the road, and half of them support. Dujek's gone, too. Whiskeyjack leads the march – they've come to Maurik River and are making barges.'

'Barges?'

'Sure. To float down the river, I guess. Not to cross, since there was a ford there anyway, and the barges are downriver of it besides.'

'And the river, of course,' Gruntle muttered, 'will take them straight to Maurik. In only a few days.'

Itkovian addressed the Marshal. 'Sir, have you made Caladan Brood aware of this information?'

'No.'

'Why not?'

Straw shrugged again. 'Well, me and the Bole brothers, we talked about that, some.'

'And?'

'We decided that Brood's kind of forgotten.'

'Forgotten, sir? Forgotten what?'

'About us. The Mott Irregulars. We think maybe he'd planned on leaving us behind. Up north. Blackdog Forest. There might have been some kind of order, back then, something about us staying while he went south. We're not sure. We can't remember.'

Gruntle cleared his throat. 'Have you considered informing the warlord of your presence?'

'Well, we don't want to make him mad. I think there *was* some kind of order, you see. Something like "go away", maybe.'

'Go away? Why would Brood say that to you?'

'Uh, that's just it. Not the warlord. Kallor. That's what

983

had us confused. We don't like Kallor. We usually ignore his orders. So, anyway, here we are. Who are you people?'

'I think, sir,' Itkovian said, 'you should send a rider to Brood – with your report on the Malazans.'

'Oh, we have people there, too, up in the vanguard. They'd been trying to reach the warlord, but Kallor kept turning them back.'

'Now, that's curious,' Gruntle murmured.

'Kallor says we shouldn't even be here. Says the warlord will be furious. So, we're not going close any more. We're thinking of turning round, in fact. We miss Mott Wood – there's no trees here. We like wood. All kinds – we've just reacquired this amazing table . . . no legs, though, they seemed to have snapped off.'

'For what it is worth,' Gruntle said, 'we'd rather you didn't leave the army, Marshal.'

The man's long face grew glum.

'There's trees!' Stonny suddenly exclaimed. 'South! A forest, around Coral!'

The High Marshal brightened. 'Really?'

'Indeed,' Itokovian said. 'Purportedly a forest of cedars, firs and spruce.'

'Oh, that's OK, then. I'll tell the others. They'll be happy again, and it's better when they're all happy. They've been blunting their weapons of late – a bad sign when they do that.'

'Blunting, sir?'

Straw nodded. 'Dull the edges, make nicks. That way, the damage they do is a lot messier. It's a bad sign when they get into that kind of mood. Very bad. Pretty soon they start dancing around the fire at night. Then that stops and when it stops you know it couldn't get worse, because that means the lads are ready to make war parties, head out in the night looking for something to kill. They been eyeing that big wagon on our trail . . .'

'Oh,' Gruntle said, 'don't do that – tell them not to do that, Marshal. Those people—'

'Necromancers, yeah. Dour. Very dour. We don't like necromancers, especially the Bole brothers don't like necromancers. They had one squatting on their land, you know, holed up in some old ruined tower in the swamp. Wraiths and spectres every night. So finally the Boles had to do something about it, and they went and rousted the squatter. It was messy, believe me – anyway, they strung up what was left of him at the Low Crossroads, just as a warning to others, you see.'

'These Bole brothers,' Itkovian said, 'sound to be a formidable pair.'

'Pair?' Straw's tangled brows rose. 'There's twenty-three of 'em. Not one of 'em shorter than me. And smart – some of 'em, anyway. Can't read, of course, but can count past ten and that's something, isn't it? Anyway, I got to go. Tell everyone about the trees down south. Goodbye.'

They watched the man ride off.

'He never did get an answer to his question,' Gruntle said after a while.

Itkovian glanced at him. 'Which was?'

'Who we are.'

'Don't be an idiot,' Stonny said, 'he knows precisely who we are.'

'You think that was an act?'

'High Marshal Straw! Abyss take me, of course it was! And he had you both, didn't he? Well, not me. I saw right through it. Instantly.'

'Do you think Brood should be informed, sir?' Itkovian asked her.

'About what?'

'Well, the Malazans, for one.'

'Does it make any difference? Brood will still reach Maurik first. So we wait two days instead of two weeks, what of it? Just means we get this whole mess over with that much sooner – Hood knows, maybe Dujek's already conquered Coral – and he can have it, as far as I'm concerned.'

'You've got a point,' Gruntle muttered.

Itkovian glanced away. *Perhaps she has. To what am I riding? What do I still seek from this world? I do not know. I care nothing for this Pannion Seer – he'll accept no embrace from me, after all, assuming the Malazans leave him breathing, which is itself unlikely.*

Is this why I lag so far behind those who will reshape the world? Indifferent, empty of concern? I seem to be done – why can I not accept that truth? My god is gone – my burden is my own. Perhaps there is no answer for me – is that what the new Shield Anvil sees when she looks upon me with such pity in her eyes?

Is the entirety of my life now behind me, save for the daily, senseless trudge of this body?

Perhaps I am done. Finally done . . .

'Cheer up, Itkovian,' Gruntle said, 'the war might be over before we get even close – wouldn't that be a wild whimper to close this tale, eh?'

'Rivers are for drinking from and drowning in,' Hetan grumbled, one arm wrapped about a barrel.

Whiskeyjack smiled. 'I thought your ancestors were seafarers,' he said.

'Who finally came to their senses and buried their damn canoes once and for all.'

'You are sounding uncharacteristically irreverent, Hetan.'

'I'm about to puke on your boots, old man, how else should I sound?'

'Ignore my daughter,' Humbrall Taur said, hide-wrapped feet thumping as he approached. 'She's been bested by a Daru.'

'Do not mention that slug!' Hetan hissed.

'You'll be pleased to know he's been on another barge these last three days whilst you suffered,' Whiskeyjack told her. 'Recovering.'

'He only left this one because I swore I'd kill him,' Hetan

muttered. 'He wasn't supposed to get besotted, the slimy worm! Spirits below, such an appetite!'

Humbrall Taur's laugh rumbled. 'I had never thought to witness such delicious—'

'Oh, be quiet, Father!'

The huge Barghast warchief winked at Whiskeyjack. 'I now look forward to actually meeting this man from Darujhistan.'

'Then I should forewarn you that appearances deceive,' Whiskeyjack said, 'particularly in the person of Kruppe.'

'Oh, I have seen him from afar, being dragged hither and thither by my daughter, at least in the beginning. And then of late I noted that the role of the master had reversed. Remarkable. Hetan is very much my wife's child, you see.'

'And where is your wife?'

'Almost far enough away back in the White Face Range to leave me breathing easily. Almost. Perhaps, by Coral . . .'

Whiskeyjack smiled, feeling once more his wonder at the gifts of friendship he had received of late.

The once-tamed shore of River Maurik swept past opposite him. Reeds surrounded fishing docks and mooring poles; old boats lay rotting and half buried in silts on the bank. Grasses grew high around fisher shacks further up the strand. The abandonment and all it signified darkened his mood momentarily.

'Even for me,' Humbrall Taur growled beside him, 'it is an unwelcome sight.'

Whiskeyjack sighed.

'We approach the city, yes?'

The Malazan nodded. 'Perhaps another day.'

Behind them, Hetan groaned in answer to that.

'Do you imagine that Brood knows?'

'I think so, at least in some part. We've got Mott Irregulars among the stablers and handlers . . .'

'Mott Irregulars – who or what is that, Commander?'

'Something vaguely resembling a mercenary company, Warchief. Woodcutters and farmers, for the most part.

Created by accident – by us Malazans, in fact. We'd just taken the city of Oraz and were marching west to Mott – which promptly surrendered with the exception of the outlanders in Mott Wood. Dujek didn't want a company of renegades preying on our supply lines with us pushing ever inland, so he sent the Bridgeburners into Mott Wood with the aim of hunting them down. A year and a half later and we were still there. The Irregulars were running circles around us. And the times they'd decided to stand and fight, it was as if some dark swamp god possessed them – they bloodied our noses more than once. Did the same to the Gold Moranth. Eventually, Dujek pulled us out, but by then the Mott Irregulars had been contacted by Brood. He drew them into his army. In any case,' he shrugged, 'they're a deceptive bunch, keep coming back like a bad infestation of gut-worms – which we've learned to live with.'

'So you know what your enemy knows of you,' Humbrall nodded.

'More or less.'

'You Malazans,' the Barghast said, shaking his head, 'play a complicated game.'

'Sometimes,' Whiskeyjack conceded. 'At other times, we're plain simple.'

'One day, your armies will march to the White Face Range.'

'I doubt it.'

'Why not?' Humbrall Taur demanded. 'Are we not worthy enough foes, Commander?'

'Too worthy, Warchief. No, the truth is this. We have treated with you, and the Malazan Empire takes such precedents seriously. You will be met with respect and offers to establish trade, borders and the like – if you so desire. If not, the envoys will depart and that will be the last you ever see of the Malazans, until such time as you decide otherwise.'

'Strange conquerors, you foreigners.'

'Aye, we are at that.'

'Why are you on Genabackis, Commander?'

'The Malazan Empire? We're here to unify, and through unification, grow rich. We're not selfish about getting rich, either.'

Humbrall Taur thumped his coin-threaded hauberk. 'And silver is all that interests you?'

'Well, there's more than one kind of wealth, Warchief.'

'Indeed?' The huge warrior's eyes had narrowed.

Whiskeyjack smiled. 'Meeting the White Face clans of the Barghast is one such reward. Diversity is worth celebrating, Humbrall Taur, for it is the birthplace of wisdom.'

'Your words?'

'No, the Imperial Historian, Duiker.'

'And he speaks for the Malazan Empire?'

'In the best of times.'

'And are these the best of times?'

Whiskeyjack met the warrior's dark eyes. 'Perhaps they are.'

'Will you two be quiet!' Hetan growled behind them. 'I am about to die.'

Humbrall Taur swung about to study his daughter where she crouched against the barrels of grain. 'A thought,' he rumbled.

'What?'

'Only that you might not be seasick, daughter.'

'Really! Then what—' Hetan's eyes went wide. 'Spirits below!'

Moments later, Whiskeyjack was forced to lean un-ceremoniously, feet first, over the barge's gunnel, the current tugging at his boots, the flowing water giving them a thorough cleansing.

A seastorm had struck Maurik some time since its desertion, toppling ornamental trees and heaping seaweed-tangled dunes of sand against building walls. The streets were buried beneath an unmarred, evenly rippled white carpet of sand, leaving no bodies or other detritus visible.

Korlat rode alone down the port city's main thoroughfare. Squat, sprawling warehouses were on her left, civic buildings, taverns, inns and trader shops on her right. Overhead, hauling ropes linked the upper floors of the warehouses to the flat rooftops of the trader shops, festooned now with seagrasses as if decorated for a maritime festival.

Apart from what came with the warm wind's steady sigh, there was no movement down the length of the street, nor in the alleys intersecting it. Windows and doorways gaped black and forlorn. The warehouses had been stripped bare, their wide sliding doors facing onto the street left open.

She approached the westernmost reaches of the city, the smell of the sea behind her giving way to a sweeter taint of freshwater decay from the river beyond the warehouses on her left.

Caladan Brood, Kallor and the others had elected to ride round Maurik, inland, on their way to the flats, Crone flying overhead for a time, before once more winging away. Korlat had never known the Matron Great Raven to be so rattled. If indeed the loss of contact meant that Anomander Rake and Moon's Spawn had been destroyed, then Crone had lost both her master and her murder's roost. Unpleasant notions, both. More than enough to crook the Great Raven's wings with despair as she continued on, south once more.

Korlat had decided to ride alone, taking a route longer than the others – through the city. There was no need for haste, after all, and anticipation had a way of drawing out any stationary wait – better, then, to lengthen the approach at a controlled pace. There was much to think about, after all. If her Lord was well, then she would have to stand before him and formally sever her service – ending a relationship that had existed for fourteen thousand years, or, rather, suspending it for a time. *For the remaining years of a mortal man's life.* And if some calamity had befallen

Anomander Rake, then Korlat would find herself the ranking commander to the dozen Tiste Andii who, like her, had remained with Brood's army. She would make that responsibility shortlived, for she had no wish to rule her kin. She would free them to decide their own fates.

Anomander Rake had unified these Tiste Andii by strength of personality – a quality Korlat well knew she did not share. The disparate causes in which he chose to engage himself and his people were, she had always assumed, each a reflection upon a single theme – but that theme and its nature had ever eluded Korlat. There were wars, there were struggles, enemies, allies, victories and losses. A procession through centuries that seemed random not just to her, but to her kin as well.

A sudden thought came to her, twisting like a dull knife in her chest. Perhaps Anomander Rake was equally lost. *Perhaps this endless succession of causes reflects his own search. I had all along assumed a simple goal – to give us a reason to exist, to take upon ourselves the nobility of others . . . others for whom the struggle meant something. Was that not the theme underlying all we have done? Why do I now doubt? Why do I now believe that, if a theme does indeed exist, it is something other?*

Something far less noble . . .

She attempted to shake off such thoughts, before they dragged her towards despair. *For despair is the nemesis of the Tiste Andii. How often have I seen my kin fall on the field of battle, and have known – deep in my soul – that my brothers and sisters did not die through an inability to defend themselves? They died, because they had chosen to die. Slain by their own despair.*

Our gravest threat.

Does Anomander Rake lead us away from despair – is that his only purpose, his only goal? Is his a theme of denial? If so, then, dear Mother Dark, he was right in seeking to confound our understanding, in seeking to keep us from ever realizing his singular, pathetic goal. And I – I should never have pursued these thoughts, should never have clawed my way to this conclusion.

Discovering my Lord's secret holds no reward. Curse of the Light, he has spent centuries evading my questions, discouraging my desire to come to know him, to pierce through his veil of mystery. And I have been hurt by it, I have lashed out at him more than once, and he has stood before my anger and frustration. Silent.

To choose not to share . . . what I had seen as arrogance, as patronizing behaviour of the worst sort – enough to leave me incensed . . . ah, Lord, you held to the hardest mercy.

And if despair assails us, it assails you a hundredfold . . .

She knew now she would not release her kin. Like Rake, she could not abandon them, and like Rake, she could voice no truth when they begged – or demanded – justification.

And so, should that moment come soon, I must needs find strength – the strength to lead – the strength to hide the truth from my kin.

Oh, Whiskeyjack, how will I be able to tell you this? Our desires were . . . simplistic. Foolishly romantic. The world holds no paradise for you and me, dear lover. Thus, all I can offer is that you join me, that you stay at my side. And I pray to Mother Dark, how I pray, that it will, for you, be enough . . .

The city's outskirts persisted along the river's edge in a straggly, ramshackle ribbon of fisher huts, smokeshacks and drying nets, storm-battered and rubbish-strewn. The settlement reached upriver to the very edge of the flats, and indeed a half-score shacks on stilts connected by raised causeways encroached upon the reedy sweep of mud itself.

Twin lines of poles on this side of the river marked out the wide underwater trench that had been excavated, leading to the edge of the flats, where broad, solid platforms had been built. River Maurik's mouth to the east was impassable to all but the most shallow-draughted craft, for its bed constantly shifted beneath the clash of tide and current, raising hidden bars of sand in the span of a few bells, then sweeping them away to create others elsewhere. Supplies brought downriver off-loaded west of the mouth – here at the flats.

The warlord, Kallor, Outrider Hurlochel and Korlat's second, Orfantal, stood on the platform, their horses tethered on the road at the platform's inland edge.

All four men faced upriver.

Korlat guided her horse onto the causeway linking the city and the platform. As she reached the slightly higher elevation of the raised road, she saw the first of the Malazan barges.

Sorcery had aided in their construction, she concluded. They were solid, sound craft, flat-bottomed and broad. Massive, untrimmed logs framed the hulls. Tarpaulins roofed at least half of each deck. She saw no fewer than twenty of them from her vantage point. *Even with sorcery, building these must have been a huge undertaking. Then again, to have completed them so quickly . . .*

Ah, is this what the Black Moranth were up to all this time? If so, then Dujek and Whiskeyjack had planned for this from the very beginning.

Great Ravens circled the flotilla, their shrieks audibly derisive.

Soldiers, Barghast and horses were visible on the lead barge. At the inland edge of the platform, Korlat reined in beside the greeting party's horses, dismounted. A Rhivi collected the reins. She nodded her thanks and strode the length of the platform to come alongside Caladan Brood.

The warlord's face revealed no expression, whilst Kallor's was twisted into an ugly sneer.

Orfantal moved to join Korlat, bowing his greeting. 'Sister,' he said in their native tongue, 'was the ride through Maurik pleasing?'

'How long have you been standing here, brother?'

'Perhaps a bell and a half.'

'Then I have no regrets.'

He smiled. 'A *silent* bell and a half at that. Almost long

993

enough to drive a Tiste Andii to distraction.'

'Liar. We can stand around in silence for weeks, as you well know, brother.'

'Ah, but that is without emotion, is it not? I know for myself, I simply listen to the wind, and so am not troubled.'

She glanced at him. *Without emotion? Now your lying is no jest.*

'And, I dare say,' Orfantal continued, 'the tension still rises.'

'You two,' Kallor growled, 'speak a language we can understand, if you must speak at all. There's been enough dissembling here to last a lifetime.'

Orfantal faced him and said in Daru, 'Not *your* lifetime, surely, Kallor?'

The ancient warrior bared his teeth in a silent snarl.

'That will do,' Brood rumbled. 'I'd rather the Malazans not see us bickering.'

Korlat could see Whiskeyjack now, standing near the broad, blunt bow of the lead barge. He was helmed, in full armour. Humbrall Taur stood beside him, his coin hauberk glittering. The Barghast was clearly enjoying the moment, standing tall and imperious, both hands resting on the heads of the throwing axes belted to his hips. The standard-bearer, Artanthos, hovered in the background, arms crossed, a half-smile on his lean face.

Soldiers were manning the sweeps, shouting to one another as they guided the craft between the poles. The manoeuvre was deftly done, as the huge barge slipped from the stronger currents and glided gently down the approach.

Korlat watched, her eyes on Whiskeyjack – who had in turn seen her – as the craft drew closer to the platform.

The crunch and grind as the barge came alongside the landing was muted. Soldiers with lines poured from the side onto the platform and made fast. Out on the river, the other barges were each pulling towards the shore to make their own landing along the muddy strand.

Hetan appeared between her father and Whiskeyjack

and pushed forward to leap onto the platform. There was no colour in her face and her legs almost buckled beneath her. Orfantal rushed forward to offer a supporting arm – which she batted away with a snarl before stumbling past them all towards the far end of the platform.

'Well thought,' Humbrall Taur boomed with a laugh. 'But if you value your life, Tiste Andii, leave the lass to her gravid misery. Warlord! Thank you for the formal greeting! We've hastened the day to Coral, yes?' The Barghast warchief stepped onto the platform, Whiskeyjack following.

'Unless there's another hundred barges upstream,' Brood growled, 'you've lost two-thirds of your forces. Now, how did that come to be?'

'Three clans came for the float, Warlord,' Humbrall Taur replied, grinning. 'The rest elected to walk. Our spirit gods were amused, yes? Though, I grant you, sourly so!'

'Well met, Warlord,' Whiskeyjack said. 'We'd not the watercraft to carry the entire force, alas. Thus, Dujek Onearm decided to split the army—'

'And where in Hood's name is he?' Kallor demanded. 'As if I need to ask,' he added.

Whiskeyjack shrugged. 'The Black Moranth are taking them—'

'To Coral, yes,' Kallor snapped. 'To what end, Malazan? To conquer the city in the name of your empire?'

'I doubt that is possible,' Whiskeyjack replied. 'But if it were, would you so dearly resent arriving at a pacified Coral, Kallor? If your bloodlust needs appeasing—'

'I never thirst for long, Malazan,' Kallor said, one gauntleted hand lifting towards the bastard sword strapped to his back.

'It seems,' Brood said, ignoring Kallor, 'that there have been considerable changes to what we had agreed was a sound plan. Indeed,' he continued, eyes shifting to the barge, 'that plan was clearly created with deceit in your mind, from the very start.'

'I disagree,' Whiskeyjack said. 'Just as you had Moon's

Spawn and whatever Rake intended to do with it as your own private plan, we concluded that we'd best fashion something similar. The precedent is yours, Warlord – so I do not think you are in a position to voice complaint.'

'Commander,' Brood grated, 'we had never intended Moon's Spawn to launch a pre-emptive strike on Coral in order to gain advantage over our presumed allies. The timing we have held to has been towards a combined effort.'

'And Dujek still agrees with you, Warlord. As do I. Tell me, has Crone managed to get close to Coral?'

'She attempts to do so yet again.'

'And she will likely be driven back once more. Meaning, we've no intelligence as to the preparations being made against us. If the Pannion Seer or his advisers have even a modicum of military acuity, they will have set up a trap for us – something we cannot help but march into by virtue of drawing within sight of Coral's walls. Warlord, our Black Moranth have delivered Captain Paran and the Bridgeburners to within ten leagues of the city, to make a covert approach and so discover what the Pannions have devised. But the Bridgeburners alone are not sufficient to counter those efforts, whatever they may be. Thus, Dujek leads six thousand of the Host, delivered by the Black Moranth, with the intention of destroying whatever the Pannions have planned.'

'And why in Hood's name should we believe you?' Kallor demanded. 'You've done nothing but lie – since the very beginning.'

Whiskeyjack shrugged once more. 'If six thousand Malazan soldiers are sufficient to take Coral and destroy the Pannion Domin, then we have seriously overestimated our enemy. I don't think we have. I think we're in for a fight, and whatever advantage we can achieve beforehand, we will likely need.'

'Commander,' Brood said, 'the Pannion forces are augmented by Mage Cadres, as well as these unnatural condors. How does Dujek hope to defend against them? Your army has no sorcerors to speak of.'

'Quick Ben's there, and he's found a means to access his warrens without interference. Secondly, they have the Black Moranth to challenge for control of the skies, and a respectable supply of munitions. But I will grant you, it might not be enough.'

'You might see more than half your army slaughtered, Commander.'

'It's possible, Warlord. Thus, if it is agreeable to you, we should now make all haste to Coral.'

'Indeed,' Kallor snarled. 'Perhaps we'd be better off to leave the Pannions to exhaust themselves destroying Dujek and his six thousand, and *then* we arrive. Warlord, hear me. The Malazans have fashioned their own potentially fatal situation, and now come begging that we relieve them of the cost. I say, let the bastards rot.'

Korlat sensed that Kallor's judgement reached through to Brood. She saw the warlord hesitate. 'A rather petty response,' she sniffed. 'Stained by emotion. Therefore, probably tactically suicidal on all our parts.'

Kallor wheeled. '*You*, woman, cannot pretend to objectivity! Of course you'd side with your lover!'

'If his position was untenable, I most certainly would *not*, Kallor. And there lies the difference between you and me.' She faced Caladan Brood. 'I now speak for the Tiste Andii accompanying your army, Warlord. I urge you to hasten our march to Coral, with the aim of relieving Dujek. Commander Whiskeyjack has arrived with sufficient barges to effect a swift crossing to the south shore. Five days of quickmarch will bring us within sight of Coral.'

'Or eight days at a normal pace,' Kallor said, 'ensuring that we arrive well rested. Is Onearm's Host so overrated that they cannot hold out an extra three days?'

'Trying a new tack?' Orfantal asked Kallor.

The grey warrior shrugged.

Brood's breath hissed between his teeth. 'He now speaks

with reasoned consideration, Tiste Andii. Five days, or eight. Exhausted, or rested and thus capable of engaging the enemy at once. Which of the two is more tactically sound?'

'It could mean the difference between joining a sound, efficacious force and finding naught but chopped up corpses,' Whiskeyjack said. He shook himself. 'Decide what you will, then. We will leave you the barges, of course, but my forces will cross first – we'll risk the exhaustion.' He swung about and gestured towards Artanthos who had remained on the barge. The standard-bearer nodded, reached down and collected a half-dozen signal flags, then set off towards the stern.

'You anticipated this,' Kallor hissed, 'didn't you?'

That you would win the day, yes, I think he did.

Whiskeyjack said nothing.

'And so, your forces reach Coral first, after all. Very clever, bastard. Very clever indeed.'

Korlat stepped up to Brood. 'Warlord, do you hold to your faith in the Tiste Andii?'

The huge man frowned. 'To you and your kin? Aye, of course I do.'

'Very well, then we will accompany Commander Whiskeyjack, Humbrall Taur and their forces. And so represent your interests. Orfantal and I are Soletaken – one of us can if need be bring swift word back to you, either of peril, or of betrayal. Further, our presence might well prove decisive should it be necessary to effect Dujek's withdrawal from an unwinnable engagement.'

Kallor laughed. 'The lovers rejoined, and we are asked to bow before false objectivity—'

Orfantal took a step towards Kallor. 'That was the last insult you will deliver to the Tiste Andii,' he said quietly.

'Stop!' bellowed Caladan Brood. 'Kallor, know this: I hold to my trust in the Tiste Andii. Nothing you can say will shake that faith, for it was earned centuries ago, a hundredfold, and not once betrayed. Your loyalty, on the other hand, I begin to doubt more and more . . .'

'Beware your fears, Warlord,' Kallor growled, 'lest you make them true.'

Brood's response was so low Korlat barely heard it. 'You now taunt me, Kallor?'

The warrior slowly paled. 'What would be the value of that?' he asked quietly, tonelessly.

'Indeed.'

Korlat turned to her brother. 'Call our kin, Orfantal. We shall accompany the commander and warchief.'

'As you say, sister.' The Tiste Andii pivoted, then paused and studied Kallor for a long moment, before saying, 'I think, old man, when all this is done . . .'

Kallor bared his teeth. 'You think what?'

'That I will come for you.'

Kallor held his smile in answer, but the strain of the effort was betrayed by a twitch along one lined cheek.

Orfantal set off towards the waiting horses.

Humbrall Taur's deep laugh broke the tense silence. 'And here we'd thought you'd be bickering when we arrived.'

Korlat faced the barge – and met Whiskeyjack's gaze. He managed a drawn smile, revealing to her the pressure he had been feeling. But it was what she saw in his eyes that quickened her heart. Love and relief, tenderness . . . and raw anticipation.

Mother Dark, but these mortals live!

Riding side by side at a gentle canter, Gruntle and Itkovian reached the causeway and approached the platform. The sky was paling to the east, the air cool and clear. A score of Rhivi herders were guiding the last of the first three hundred bhederin onto the railed ramp.

A few hundred paces behind the two men, the second three hundred were being driven towards the causeway. There were at least two thousand bhederin to follow, and it was clear to Gruntle and Itkovian that, if they wished to lead their companies across the river any time soon, they would have to cut in.

The Malazans had built well, each barge carrying broad, solid ramps that neatly joined bow to bow, while the sterns had been designed to fit flush once the backwash guards had been removed. The bridge they formed when linked was both flexible where required, and secure everywhere else, and it was surprisingly wide – capable of allowing two wagons to travel side by side.

Commander Whiskeyjack and his companies of the Host had crossed the river more than fifteen bells ago, followed by Humbrall Taur's three clans of Barghast. Gruntle knew that Itkovian had hoped to see and meet with both men once again, in particular Whiskeyjack, but by the time they'd come within sight of the river, Malazan and Barghast were both long gone.

Caladan Brood had encamped his forces for the night on this side of River Maurik, rousing his troops three bells before dawn. They had just completed their crossing. Gruntle wondered at the disparity of pace between the two allied armies.

They reined in among the Rhivi herders. A tall, awkward-looking man who was not Rhivi stood off to one side, watching the bhederin thump their way across the first barge to hoots and whistles from the drivers.

Gruntle dismounted and approached the lone man. 'Mott Irregulars?' he asked.

'High Marshal Sty,' the man replied with a lopsided, toothy grin. 'I'm glad you're here – I can't understand these little guys at all. I've been trying real hard, too. I guess they're speaking a different language.'

Gruntle glanced back at Itkovian, expressionless, then faced the High Marshal once more. 'So they are. Have you been standing here long?'

'Since last night. Lots of people have crossed. Lots. I watched them put the barges together. They were fast. The Malazans know wood, all right. Did you know Whiskeyjack was apprenticed as a mason, before he became a soldier?'

'No, I didn't. What has that got to do with carpentry, High Marshal?'

'Nothing. I was just saying.'

'Are you waiting for the rest of your company?' Gruntle asked.

'Not really, though I suppose they'll show up sooner or later. They'll come after the bhederin, of course, so they can collect the dung. These little guys do that, too. We've had a few fights over that, you know. Tussles. Good-natured, usually. Look at them, what they're doing – kicking all that dung into a pile and guarding it. If I get any closer, they'll pull knives.'

'Well, then I'd suggest you not get any closer, High Marshal.'

Sty grinned again. 'There'd be no fun, then. I ain't waiting here for nothing, you know.'

Itkovian dismounted and joined them.

Gruntle swung to the herders, spoke in passable Rhivi, 'Which of you is in charge here?'

A wiry old man looked up, stepped forward. 'Tell him to go away!' he snapped, stabbing a finger at High Marshal Sty.

'Sorry,' Gruntle replied with a shrug, 'I can't order him to do anything, I'm afraid. I'm here for my legion and the Grey Swords. We'd like to cross . . . before the rest of your herd—'

'No. Can't do that. No. You have to wait. Wait. The bhederin don't like to be split up. They get nervous. Unhappy. We need them calm on the crossing. You see that, don't you? No, you have to wait.'

'Well, how long do you think that will take?'

The Rhivi shrugged. 'It will be done when it is done.'

The second three hundred bhederin rumbled their way up the causeway. The herders moved to meet them.

Gruntle heard a meaty thud, then the Rhivi were all shouting, racing back. The Daru turned in time to see High

Marshal Sty, the front of his long shirt pulled up around a hefty pile of dung, run full tilt past, onto the ramp, then thump down the length of the barge.

A single Rhivi herder, who had clearly been left to guard the dung, lay sprawled beside the looted heap, unconscious, the red imprint of a large, bony fist on his jaw.

Gruntle grinned over at the old herder, who was jumping about, spitting with fury.

Itkovian moved up alongside him. 'Sir, did you see that?'

'No, alas, just the tail end.'

'That punch came out of nowhere – I did not even see him step close. The poor Rhivi dropped like a sack of . . . of—'

'Dung?'

After a long moment – so long that Gruntle thought it would never come – Itkovian smiled.

Rain clouds had rolled in from the sea, the rain driven on fierce winds, each drop striking iron helms, shields and leather rain-cloaks with enough force to shatter into mist. The abandoned farmland on all sides vanished behind a grey wall, the trader road churned to clinging mud beneath hooves, wagon wheels and boots.

Water sluicing down through his visor – which he had lowered in an only partially successful attempt to keep the rain from his eyes – Whiskeyjack struggled to make sense of the scene. A messenger had called him back from the vanguard, shouting barely heard words concerning a broken axle, the train halted in disarray, injured animals. At the moment, all he could make out was a mass of mud-covered soldiers scrambling, slipping, knotting ropes and shouting inaudibly to each other, and at least three wagons buried to their axles on what had once been the road but had since turned into a river of mud. Oxen were being pulled clear on the far side, the beasts bellowing.

He sat on his horse, watching. There was no point in cursing the fickle vagaries of nature, nor the failure of overburdened wagons, nor even the pace which they all laboured under. His marines were doing what needed to be done, despite the apparent chaos. The squall was likely to be shortlived, given the season, and the sun's thirst was fierce. None the less, he wondered which gods had conspired against him, for since the crossing not a single day of this frantic march had passed without incident – and not one of those incidents had yielded mercy to their desires.

It would be two more days, at the very least, before they reached Coral. Whiskeyjack had received no communication from Quick Ben since before Maurik, and the wizard, Paran and the Bridgeburners had been still half a night's travel from Coral's environs at that time. He was sure they had reached the city by now, was equally certain that Dujek and his companies were even now closing in for the rendezvous. If a battle was to come, it would be very soon.

Whiskeyjack swung his horse round, nudged the weary beast along the track's edge to return to the vanguard. Night was fast approaching, and they would have to stop, at least for a few bells. He would then have some precious time alone with Korlat – the rigours of this march had kept them apart far too often, and while he and Korlat held to the belief that her Lord, Anomander Rake, could not yet be counted out, she had assumed the role of commander among her Tiste Andii kin in all respects – cold, remote, focused exclusively on the disposition of her brothers and sisters.

They were, under her direction, exploring Kurald Galain, their Warren of Darkness, drawing upon its power in an effort to purge it of the Crippled God's infection. Whiskeyjack had seen, upon their short-lived, infrequent reappearances, the cost borne by Orfantal and the other Tiste Andii. But Korlat wanted Kurald Galain's power within reach – without fear of corruption – by the time battle was joined at Coral.

A change had come to her, he sensed. Some bleak resolve had hardened all that was within her. Perhaps it was the possible death of Anomander Rake that had forced such induration upon her spirit. Or, perhaps, it was their future paths they had so naively entwined without regard for the harsh demands of the real world. The past was ever restless, for them both.

Whiskeyjack, in his heart, was certain that Anomander Rake was not dead. Nor even lost. In the half-dozen late-night conversations he had shared with the Lord of Moon's Spawn, the Malazan had acquired a sense of the Tiste Andii: despite the alliances, including the long-term partnership with Caladan Brood, Anomander Rake was a man of solitude – an almost pathological independence. He was indifferent to the needs of others, for whatever re-assurance or confirmation they might expect or demand. *He said he would be there for the assault on Coral, and so he will.*

Through the grey murk ahead he could make out the vanguard, a knotted clump of mounted officers surrounding the fivesome of Humbrall Taur, Hetan, Cafal, Kruppe and Korlat on the road. Beyond them, he saw as he approached, the sky was lighter. They were about to fight their way clear of the squall, with Oponn's luck in time to halt and prepare a warm meal by sunset's warm glow before continuing on.

He was pushing his four thousand soldiers too hard. They were the finest he had ever commanded, yet he was demanding the impossible from them. Though the Malazan understood it, Caladan Brood's sudden loss of faith had shaken Whiskeyjack, more than he would admit to anyone, even Korlat. A fast march by the combined forces might well have given the Seer pause – seeing the arrival of legion upon legion would give any enemy commander incentive to withdraw from an ongoing engagement with Dujek. Exhausted or not, sometimes numbers alone proved sufficient intimidation. The Pannion resources were limited: the Seer would not risk persisting in battle beyond the city's walls if it endangered his main army.

The appearance of four thousand mud-coated, stumbling

soldiers was more likely to bring a smile to the Seer's lips. Whiskeyjack would have to make his few numbers count – the twelve Tiste Andii, the Ilgres Clan and Humbrall Taur's elite clans of the White Face would most likely prove crucial, though the combined Barghast support was less than two thousand.

We threw ourselves into the sprint too soon, too far from our prey. In our senseless haste, we've left fifty thousand White Face Barghast far behind. This decision may be a fatal one . . .

Feeling old beyond his years, burdened by flaws born of a spirit mired deep in exhaustion, Whiskeyjack rejoined the vanguard.

Water streamed down the full-length chain surcoat, left long grey hair plastered against it down the back and across the wide but gaunt shoulders. Dull grey helmet gleamed, reflecting the pewter sky with milky indistinction. He stood motionless, head lowered, at the base of a shallow basin, his horse waiting a dozen paces behind him.

Flat, lifeless eyes studied the saturated prairie ground through his great-helm's fixed, slitted visor. Unblinking, narrowed eyes. Watching the flow of muddy water slashed by the frenzied rain, tiny rivulets, broader sweeps, a ceaseless flow through minute channels, over exposed stone, between the knotted roots of tufted grasses.

The water wended southward.

And here, in this basin, carrying oddly-coloured silts in racing streams, it flowed uphill.

From dust . . . to mud. So you march with us after all. No, understand, I am pleased.

Kallor swung round, strode back to his horse.

He rode along his own trail, and, with dusk gathering quickly beneath the leaden clouds and driving rain, came at last to the encampment. There were no fires outside the rows of tents, and the glow of lanterns was dull through patchy canvas. The muddy aisles were crowded with Great Ravens, hunched and motionless under the deluge.

Reining in before Caladan Brood's command tent, Kallor dismounted and strode within.

The outrider, Hurlochel, stood just within the flap, present as Brood's messenger should such need arise. The young man was wan, half asleep at his station. Ignoring him, Kallor raised his visor and stepped past.

The warlord was uncharacteristically slumped in a camp chair, his hammer resting across his thighs. He had not bothered to clean the mud from his armour or boots. His strangely bestial eyes lifted, took in Kallor, then dropped once more. 'I have made a mistake,' he rumbled.

'I agree, Warlord.'

That earned Brood's sharpened attention. 'You must have misunderstood . . .'

'I have not. We should have joined Whiskeyjack. The annihilation of Onearm's Host – no matter how much that might please me personally – will be a tactical disaster for this campaign.'

'All very well, Kallor,' Brood rumbled, 'but there is little we can do about it, now.'

'This storm will pass, Warlord. You can increase our pace come the morning – we can perhaps shave off a day. I am here for another reason, however. One that is, conveniently, related to our change of heart.'

'Spit it out short and sweet, Kallor, or not at all.'

'I would ride to join Whiskeyjack and Korlat.'

'To what end? An apology?'

Kallor shrugged. 'If that would help. More directly, however, you seem to forget my . . . experience. For all that I seem to grate upon all of you, I have walked this land when the T'lan Imass were but children. I have commanded armies a hundred thousand strong. I have spread the fire of my wrath across entire continents, and sat alone upon tall thrones. Do you grasp the meaning of this?'

'Yes. You never learn, Kallor.'

'Clearly,' he snapped, 'you do not grasp the meaning. I know a field of battle better than any man alive, including

1006

you.'

'The Malazans seem to have done very well on this continent without your help. Besides, what makes you think Whiskeyjack or Dujek will heed your suggestions?'

'They are rational men, Warlord. You forget something else about me, as well, it seems. With my blade drawn, I have not faced defeat in a hundred thousand years.'

'Kallor, you choose your enemies well. Have you ever crossed weapons with Anomander Rake? Dassem Ultor? Graymane? The Seguleh First?'

He did not need to add: *with me?* 'I will face none of them in Coral,' Kallor growled. 'Just Seerdomin, Urdomen, Septarchs—'

'And perhaps a K'Chain Che'Malle or three?'

'I did not think any remained, Warlord.'

'Maybe. Maybe not. I am somewhat surprised, Kallor, by your sudden . . . zeal.'

The tall warrior shrugged. 'I would answer my own ill advice, that is all. Do you give me leave to join Whiskeyjack and Korlat?'

Brood studied him for a time, then he sighed and waved one mud-spattered, gauntleted hand. 'Go.'

Kallor spun and strode from the tent. Outside, he approached his horse.

A few miserable Great Ravens, huddled beneath a wagon, were the only witnesses to his sudden smile.

The floes abutting the rocky shoreline were all awash in darkly stained water. Lady Envy watched Baaljagg and Garath splash through it towards the forest-crowded strand. Sighing, she parted the veil on her warren, enough to permit her to cross without getting wet.

She had had more than enough of wild seas, black water, submerged mountains of ice and freezing rain, and was contemplating fashioning a suitably efficacious curse upon Nerruse and Beru both, the Lady for her failure to maintain reasonable order upon her waters, the Lord for his evidently senseless outrage at being so thoroughly exploited. Of course, such a curse might well weaken the pantheon yet further, and that would not be appreciated.

She sighed. 'So, I must forgo such pleasure . . . or at least suspend it for a time. Oh well.' Turning, she saw Senu, Thurule and Mok clambering down the near-vertical ice sheet that led down to the floe. Moments later, the Seguleh were sloshing their way to the shore.

Lanas Tog had vanished a short while past, to reappear beneath the trees directly opposite them.

Lady Envy stepped off the jagged, frost-rimed edge of the Meckros street, settled slowly towards the bridge of ice. She approached the strand's tumbled line of rocks where the others had gathered.

'Finally!' she said upon arriving, stepping gingerly onto sodden moss close to where Lanas Tog stood. Huge cedars marched into the gloom of the slope that climbed steep and rough up the mountainside behind the T'lan Imass. Brushing flecks of snow from her telaba, Lady Envy studied the unwelcoming forest for a moment, then fixed her attention on Lanas Tog.

Ice was slipping in long, narrow slivers from the swords impaling the T'lan Imass. White frost died in spreading patches on the undead creature's withered face.

'Oh dear, you're thawing.'

'I will scout ahead,' Lanas Tog said. 'People have passed along this shoreline recently. More than twenty, less than fifty, some heavily laden.'

'Indeed?' Lady Envy glanced around, saw no sign that anyone had walked where they now stood. 'Are you certain? Oh, never mind. I didn't ask that question. Well! In which direction were they walking?'

The T'lan Imass faced east. 'The same as us.'

'How curious! We will by chance catch up with them?'

'Unlikely, mistress. They are perhaps fours days ahead—'

'Four days! They have reached Coral, then!'

'Yes. Do you wish to rest, or shall we proceed?'

Lady Envy turned to examine the others. Baaljagg still carried a spearhead in her shoulder, though it seemed to be slowly making its way out, and the flow of blood had slowed considerably. She would have liked to have healed the ay's wound, but the beast would not let her come close enough. Garath looked hale, though a solid mass of old scars etched the hound's mottled hide. The three Seguleh had effected what repairs they could to their armour and weapons, and stood waiting, their masks freshly painted. 'Hmm, it seems there is to be no delay, no delay at all! Such eagerness, oh pity poor Coral!' She swung round suddenly. 'Lanas Tog, tell me, has Onos T'oolan passed this way as well?'

'I do not know, mistress. Those mortals who preceded us, however, were tracked by a predator. No doubt curious. I sense no lingering violence in this area, so the beast probably abandoned them once it fully gauged their strength.'

'A beast? What kind of beast, darling?'

The T'lan Imass shrugged. 'A large cat. A tiger, perhaps – forests such as these suit them, I believe.'

'Now, isn't that titillating? By all means, Lanas Tog, strike out on this fated trail – we shall follow upon your very heels!'

The trenches and tunnel entrances had been well disguised, beneath cedar branches and piles of moss, and without the preternatural skills of the mages the Bridgeburners might not have found them.

Paran made his way down what he had mentally labelled the command tunnel, passing racks of weapons – pikes, halberds, lances, longbows and bundles of arrows – and alcoves packed solid with food, water and other supplies, until he came to the large, fortified chamber which the Septarch had clearly intended to be his headquarters.

Quick Ben and his motley cadre of mages sat, squatted or sprawled in a rough half-circle near the far end, beyond the map table, looking like a pack of water-rats who'd just taken over a beaver's lodge.

The captain glanced down at the large painted hide pinned to the tabletop as he strode past, on which the Pannions had conveniently mapped out the entire maze of tunnels and entrenchments, the location of supplies and what kind, the approaches and retreats.

'All right,' Paran said as he joined the mages, 'what do you have?'

'Someone's got wise in Coral,' Quick Ben said, 'and realized that this place should have a company holed up here, as a guard – Trotts was keeping an eye on the city and watched them file out. They'll reach us in a bell.'

'A company,' Paran scowled. 'What's that in Pannion terms?'

'Four hundred Beklites, twenty Urdomen, four Seerdomin, one of them ranking and likely a sorceror.'

'And which approaches do you think they'll use?'

'The three stepped ones,' Spindle replied, reaching to scratch under his hairshirt. 'They go under trees all the way, lots of switchbacks, meaning the poor bastards will have a hard time rushing our positions once we let loose.'

Paran turned back to study the map. 'Assuming they're flexible, what will they choose as an alternative?'

'The main ramp,' Quick Ben said, rising to join the captain. He tapped a finger on the map. 'The one they'd planned on using for the downward march to launch the ambush. No cover for them, but if they can lock shields out front and turtle . . . well, there's only forty of us . . .'

'Munitions?'

The wizard looked back at Spindle, who made a sour face and said, 'We're short. Maybe if we use 'em right, we'll squash this company – but then the Seer will know what's up, and he'll send twenty thousand up this mountainside. If Dujek doesn't show soon, we'll have to pull out, Captain.'

'I know, Spindle, which is why I want you to set aside the cussers and burners – I want these tunnels rigged. If we have to scramble, we leave this strongpoint nothing but mud and ashes.'

The sapper gaped. 'Captain, without them cussers and burners, the Seer won't need to send anybody after this company – it'll take us clean out!'

'Assuming there's enough of them left to regroup and come up the main ramp. In other words, Spindle, pull the sappers together and cook up the messiest stew you can for those three hidden trails. If we can make it seem like the whole Malazan army's up here ... better yet, if we can make sure not one soldier in this company gets out alive, we'll have purchased the time we need. The less certain we leave the Seer the safer we'll be. So, close that mouth and find Hedge and the rest. Your moment of glory's arrived, Spindle – go.'

Muttering, the man scrambled out of the chamber.

Paran faced the others. 'A Seerdomin sorceror, you said. All right, he needs to drop fast once the fun starts. What do you have in mind, gentlemen?'

Shank grinned. 'My idea, Captain. It's classic, deadly – especially because it's so unexpected. I've already completed the ritual, left it primed – all Quick Ben needs to do is tell me when he's spotted the bastard.'

'What kind of ritual, Shank?'

'The ingenious kind, Captain – Bluepearl loaned me the spell, but I can't describe it, can't write it down and show you, neither. Words and meanings hang around in the air, you know, seep into suspicious minds and trigger gut instinct. There's nothing to blocking it if you know it's coming – it only works when you don't.'

Scowling, Paran turned to Quick Ben.

The wizard shrugged, 'Shank wouldn't cough himself to the front of the line if he wasn't sure of this, Captain. I'll sniff the Seerdomin out as he's asked. And I'll have a few back-ups in case it goes sour.'

Bluepearl added, 'Spindle will hold back on a sharper, Captain, with the mage's name on it.'

'Literally,' Toes threw in, 'and that makes all the difference, Spin being a wizard and all.'

'Yes? And how often has it made the difference in the past, Toes?'

'Well, uh, there's been a bad string of, uh, mitigating circumstances—'

'Abyss below,' Paran breathed. 'Quick Ben, if we don't knock that sorceror out we'll be feeding roots a drop at a time.'

'We know, Captain. Don't worry. We'll stamp him out before he sparks.'

Paran sighed. 'Toes, find me Picker – I want all these longbows trundled out and issued to everyone without a munition or spell in hand, twenty arrows each, and I want them to have pikes as well.'

'Aye, sir.' Toes climbed to his feet. He reached for one large, mummified toe strung around his neck and kissed it. Then he headed out.

Bluepearl spat onto the ground. 'I feel sick every time he does that.'

A bell and a half later, the captain lay alongside Quick Ben, looking down on the middle stepped trail, where the glint of helms and weapons appeared in the late afternoon's dull light.

The Pannions had not bothered to send scouts ahead, nor was their column preceded by a point. A degree of overconfidence that Paran hoped would prove fatal.

In the soft earth before Quick Ben, the wizard had set a half-dozen twigs, upright, in a rough line. Faint sorcery whispered between them that the captain's eyes could only register peripherally. Twenty paces behind the two men, Shank sat hunched over his modest, pebble-ringed circle of ritual; six twigs from the same branch that Quick Ben had used, jabbed into the moss before the squad mage, surrounding a bladder filled with water. Beads of condensation glistened from these twigs.

Paran heard Quick Ben's soft sigh. The wizard reached

out, hovered an index finger over the third twig, then tapped it.

Shank saw one of his twigs twitch. He grinned, whispered the last word of his ritual, releasing its power. The bladder shrivelled, suddenly empty.

Down on the trail, the Seerdomin sorceror, third in the line, buckled, water spraying from his mouth, lungs filled, clawing at his own chest.

Shank's eyes closed, his face runnelled in sweat as he swiftly added binding spells to the water that filled the Seerdomin's lungs, holding it down against their desperate, spasming efforts to expel the deadly fluid.

Soldiers shouted, gathered around the writhing mage.

Four sharpers sailed into their midst.

Multiple, snapping explosions, at least one of them triggering the row of sharpers buried along the length of the trail, these ones in turn triggering the crackers at the base of the flanking trees, which began toppling inward onto the milling soldiers.

Smoke, the screams of the wounded and dying, figures sprawled, pinned beneath trees and trapped by branches.

Paran saw Hedge and four other sappers, Spindle included, plunging down the slope to one side of the trail. Munitions flew from their hands.

The fallen trees – wood and branches liberally drenched in lantern oil – lit up in a conflagration as the first of the burners exploded. Within the span of a heartbeat, the trail and the entire company trapped upon it were in flames.

Abyss below, we're not a friendly bunch, are we?

Down at the bottom, well behind the last of the Pannions, Picker and her squads had emerged from cover, bows in hand, and were – Paran hoped – taking down those of the enemy who had managed to avoid the ambush and were attempting to flee.

At the moment, all the captain could hear were screams and the thunderous roar of the fire. The gloom of approaching night had been banished from the trail, and

Paran could feel the heat gusting against his face. He glanced over at Quick Ben.

The wizard's eyes were closed.

Faint movement on the man's shoulder caught the captain's attention – a tiny figure of sticks and twine – Paran blinked. It was gone, and he began to wonder if he'd seen anything at all . . . the wild flaring and ebb of firelight, the writhing shadows . . . *ah, I must be imagining things. Not enough sleep, the horror that is this dance of light, heightened senses – those damned screams . . .*

Were fading now, and the fire itself was losing its raging hunger, unable to reach very far into the rain-soaked forest beyond. Smoke wreathed the trail, drifted through the surrounding boles. Blackened bodies filled the path, plates of armour rainbow-burnished, leather curled and peeling, boots blistered and cracking open with terrible sizzling sounds.

If Hood has reserved a pit for his foulest servants, then the Moranth who made these munitions belong in it. And us, since we've used them. This was not battle. This was slaughter.

Mallet slid down to Paran's side. 'Captain! Moranth are dropping out of the sky on the entrenchments – Dujek's arrived, the first wave with him. Sir, our reinforcements are here.'

Quick Ben scraped a hand across his little row of twigs. 'Good. We'll need them.'

Aye, the Seer won't yield these entrenchments without a fight. 'Thank you, Healer. Return to the High Fist and inform him I will join him shortly.'

'Yes, sir.'

CHAPTER TWENTY-FOUR

Some tides move unseen. Priests and priestesses of the
twin cults of Togg and Fanderay had for so long presided
over but a handful of adherents in their respective temples,
and those temples were few and far between. A shortlived
expansion of the cults swept through the Malazan armies
early in Laseen's reign, but then seemed to wither of its
own accord. In retrospect, that flurry might be
interpreted as being only marginally premature,
anticipating by less than a decade the reawakening
that would bring the ancient cults to the fore. The first
evidence of that reawakening occurred on the very edges
of the Empire's borders [strictly speaking, not even close, *tr.*],
in the recently liberated city of Capustan, where the tide
revealed its power for all to see . . .

Cults of Resurrection
Korum T'bal (translated by Illys of Darujhistan)

T
he two masked figures, ancient and shrunken,
slowly hobbled towards the low, wide entrance of
Hood's temple. Coll had been seeing to the Mott
horses in the courtyard and now stood silent in the shadows
of the wall, watching as the figure closest to him – a woman
– raised a cane and rapped it sharply against the door.

Distant drums still sounded, indicating that the coron-
ation of Prince Arard was dragging on. Given that the

ceremony was under the guidance of the Mask Council, Coll was more than a little curious to see these two council members here, clearly intent on paying an un-official, private visit. He was also suspicious, since he'd assumed that no-one had known of the reoccupancy of Hood's temple.

He started at a low voice close beside him: 'What good will come of this, do you think?'

Another masked priest was standing in the shadows beside the Daru, strangely indistinct, hooded, gloved hands folded over the bulge of a pot-belly – though the rest of the man appeared to be stick-thin.

'Where did you come from?' Coll hissed, his heart thudding in his chest.

'I? I was here before you! This is *my* shadow, you fool! Look at that torchlight – where we stand should be bathed in it. Are all the nobles of Darujhistan as stupid as you?'

Coll grimaced. 'All right, shadow-priest, you've been spying – on what? What state secrets have you learned watching me groom these horses?'

'Only that they hate you, Daru. Every time your back was turned, they got ready to nip you – only you always seemed to step away at precisely the right moment—'

'Yes, I did, since I knew what they were intending. Each time.'

'Is this pride I hear? That you outwitted two horses?'

'Another remark like that, priest, and I will toss you over this wall.'

'You wouldn't dare – oh, all right, you would. Come no closer. I will be civil. I promise.'

Both turned at the sound of the temple doors squealing open.

'Aai!' Rath'Shadowthrone whispered. 'Who is that?'

'My friend, Murillio.'

'No, you idiot – the other one!'

'The one with the swords, you mean? Ah, well, he works for Hood.'

'And is Rath'Hood aware of this?'

'You're asking me?'

'Well, has he paid a visit?'

'No.'

'The brainless idiot!'

Coll grunted. 'Is that a quality all your acquaintances share?'

'So far,' Rath'Shadowthrone muttered.

'Those two,' Coll said, 'what kind of masks are they wearing under those cowls?'

'You mean, do I recognize them? Of course I do. The old man's Rath'Togg. The older woman's Rath'Fanderay. On the Council we use them as bookends – in all my years in the Thrall, I don't think I've heard either one say a word. Even more amusing, they're lovers who've never touched each other.'

'How does that work?'

'Use your imagination, Daru. Ho, they're being invited inside! What bubbles in this cauldron?'

'Cauldron? What cauldron?'

'Shut up.'

Coll smiled. 'Well, I'm having too much fun. Time to go inside.'

'I'm going with you.'

'No, you're not. I don't like spies.' With that, Coll's fist connected with the priest's jaw. The man dropped in a heap.

The shadows slowly dissolved to flickering torchlight.

Coll rubbed at his knuckles, then set off for the temple.

He closed the door behind him. Murillio, the warrior and the guests were nowhere to be seen. He strode to the entrance to the chamber of the sepulchre. One of the doors had been left slightly ajar. Coll nudged it open and stepped through.

Murillio sat close to where they had laid out a cot for the Mhybe – the burial pit remained empty, despite the undead warrior's constant instructions to place the old woman within it. The sword-wielding servant of Hood stood facing the two masked councillors, the pit between them. No-one was speaking.

Coll approached Murillio. 'What's happened?' he whispered.

'Nothing. Not a word, unless they're jabbering in their heads, but I doubt it.'

'So . . . they're all waiting, then.'

'So it seems. Abyss take us, they're worse than vultures . . .'

Coll studied his friend for a long moment, then said, 'Murillio, were you aware you're sitting on a corner of Hood's altar?'

The land beyond Coral's north wall was forested parkland, glades divided by stands of coppiced trees that had not been trimmed for at least three seasons. The trader road wound like a serpent through the parkland, straightening as it reached a two-hundred-pace-wide killing field, then rising in a narrow stone bridge over a steep, dry moat just before the wall. The gate was a massive construction, the track through barely the width of a wagon and overhung with abutments. The doors were sheeted bronze.

Lieutenant Picker blinked sweat from her eyes. She had brought Antsy and his squad as close as possible, lying flat along the edge of an overgrown woodcutter's path thirty or forty paces up the mountainside's east-facing flank. Coral's high walls were to their right, southeasterly; the killing field directly opposite and the parkland to their left. Packed ranks of Pannion Beklites had assembled in the killing field, were arranged to face the mountain – and the entrenchments now held by Dujek and six thousand of Onearm's Host.

The sergeant lying beside her grunted. 'There, coming through the gate. That's some kind of standard, and that clump of riders . . . sitting too tall . . .'

'A Septarch and his officers,' Picker agreed. 'So, Antsy, does your count match mine?'

'Twenty-five, thirty thousand,' the man muttered, tugging on his moustache.

'But we've the high ground—'

'Aye, only those trenches and tunnels weren't meant to be defended – they were hiding places. Too many straight lines, no cul-de-sacs, no funnels, no chance for an enfilade – and too many Hood-damned trees!'

'The sappers are—'

'They ain't got the time!'

'So it seems,' Picker agreed. 'Mind you, do you see any of those condors gathering to join in the assault?'

'No, but that don't mean—'

'What it means, Sergeant, is the Seer is holding them back. He knows we're not the main punch. We messed up his ambush and knocked out a company, and no doubt that's irritated him enough to send out, what, a third of his army? Maybe a cadre of mages to guard the Septarch? And if they find out we're a bear in a den, I doubt they'll push—'

'Unless the Seer decides that killing six thousand of the Host is worth a third of his army, Picker. If I was him—'

The lieutenant grimaced. 'Aye, me too.' *I'd annihilate us, stamp us out before the rest arrive.* 'Still, I don't think the Seer's that sharp – after all, what does he know of the Malazans? Distant tales of wars far to the north . . . an invasion that's bogged down. He'd have no reason to know what we're capable of.'

'Picker, you're fishing with a bare hook. The Seer knows we've somehow jumped onto his entrenchments. Knows we slipped past those condors without tickling a single beak. Knows we knocked flat an entire company using Moranth munitions. Knows we're sitting here, watching this army assemble, and we ain't running. Knows, too, we ain't got any support – not yet – and maybe, just maybe, we jumped in the slough before the shit's settled.'

Picker said nothing for a time. The Pannion legions had settled, officers dispersing to take positions at the head of

1019

each one. Drums rattled. Pikes lifted skyward. Then before each arrayed legion, sorcery began to play.

Oh . . . 'Where's Blend?'

'Here.'

'Hightail it back to Dujek—'

'Aye, Lieutenant. We're in it, now.'

Squatting on the lead embankment above the slope, Quick Ben slowly straightened. 'Spindle, Bluepearl, Toes, Shank, to me, if you will.'

The four mages scrambled to his side and all were babbling. 'A dozen sorcerors!' 'Drawing from the same warren!' 'And it's clean and ugly!' 'They're *weaving*, Quick!' 'Working togeth—'

'Be quiet, all of you!'

'We're all going to die!'

'Dammit, Toes, shut up!'

He glared until the four men settled, surveyed the bleak expressions for a moment, then grinned. 'Twelve of the bastards, right? And who is this, standing here before you? Quick Ben. Right? Ben Adaephon Delat. Now, if any of you has already filled his breeches, go change, then rejoin the companies you've been attached to – whatever gets through me is for you to handle. Any way you can.' Glancing over, he saw Dujek, Paran and Blend approaching, the latter looking winded and somewhat wild-eyed. 'All right, Cadre, dismissed.'

The mages scurried away.

Dujek was wearing his full armour – the first time Quick Ben had seen that in years. The wizard nodded in greeting.

Paran spoke, 'Quick Ben, Blend here's delivered some bad—'

'I know, Captain. I've split up my cadre, so we won't get taken out in a clump. I'll draw their attention to me, right here—'

'Hold on,' Dujek growled. 'That cadre ain't a cadre, and

worse: they know it. Secondly, you're not a combat mage. If we lose you early . . .'

The wizard shrugged. 'High Fist, I'm all you've got. I'll keep 'em busy for a while.'

Paran said, 'I'll assign the Bridgeburners to guard you – we've resupplied on munitions—'

'He's being generous,' Dujek cut in. 'Half a crate, and most of it close-in stuff. If the enemy gets near enough for them to have to use it, you're way too close to one stray arrow headed your way, Wizard. I'm not happy with this, not happy at all.'

'Can't say I am, either,' Quick Ben replied. He waited. He could hear the High Fist's molars grinding.

'Captain?' Dujek grunted.

'Aye, sir?'

'Are the cussers and crackers in place? Can we collapse this damned hillside?'

'Hedge says it's all rigged, High Fist. We can bury every tunnel and flatten every entrenchment.'

'So, we could just pull out and leave the Pannions to retake . . . a steaming mess of nothing.'

'We could, sir.'

'Meaning, we'll have travelled half the continent, only to retreat before our first engagement.'

'A temporary retreat, sir,' Paran pointed out.

'Or we can bloody their noses . . . maybe take out ten thousand Beklites, ten, twelve mages and a Septarch. At the possible cost of this army, including Quick Ben here. Gentlemen, is that a fair exchange?'

'That is for you to decide—' Paran began, but Dujek cut him off.

'No, Captain. It isn't. Not this time.'

Quick Ben met the High Fist's eyes. *I made a promise to Burn. The captain and I had . . . plans. To keep all of that, I say no right now. And we blow the entrenchments and scamper. But then again, I'm a soldier. A Bridgeburner. And the brutal truth is, tactically, it's more than a fair exchange. We make it for*

Whiskeyjack. For the siege to come. We save lives. He glanced at Paran, saw the same knowledge in the captain's eyes. The wizard turned back to Dujek. 'High Fist, it is a fair exchange.'

Dujek reached up and lowered his helm's visor. 'All right, let's get to work.'

Quick Ben watched the two men leave, then he sighed. 'What do you want, Blend?'

'Sir?'

'Don't you "sir" me, woman. Are you planning on rejoining your squad any time soon, or do you want a close look at my impending demise?'

'I thought I might . . . uh, give you a hand.'

He faced her, eyes narrowing. 'How?'

'Well . . .' She drew out a small stone from round her neck. 'I picked up this charm, a few years back.'

The wizard's brows rose. 'And what is it supposed to do, Blend?'

'Uh, makes me harder to focus on – seems to work pretty good.'

'And where did you come by it?'

'An old desert merchant, in Pan'potsun.'

Quick Ben smiled, 'Keep it, lass.'

'But—'

'If you weren't wearing it, you wouldn't be Blend any more, would you?'

'I suppose not. Only—'

'Return to your squad. And tell Picker to keep her lads and lasses tight and out of the scrap – you're to remain on that far flank, watching the city. If the condors suddenly show, get back to me as fast as possible.'

'Aye, sir.'

'Go on, then.'

She hurried off.

Well, damn me. The lass buys a worthless piece of stone from a Gral swindler and suddenly she's invisible. Raw but pure talent, right in her bones, and she doesn't even know it.

1022

Hidden beneath fronds and brush, Picker and her squad had a clear view of the Pannion legions, the front lines reaching the base of the treeless ramp that led to the entrenchments. Grey sorcery spun a wall of tangled webbing before the chanting Beklites. The Seerdomin commanders were wreathed in the magic, advancing now on foot ahead of their companies, marching upslope with an air of inexorability.

On a bank high above the Pannions, Quick Ben looked down, exposed and alone. Or so Blend had told her – the trees on her left blocked the view.

Suicide. The wizard was good, she knew, but good only because he kept his head low and did whatever he did behind backs, in the shadows, unseen. He wasn't Tattersail, wasn't Hairlock or Calot. In all the years she had known him, she had not once seen him openly unveil a warren and let loose. Not only wasn't it his style, it also wasn't, she suspected, within his capacity.

You unsheathed the wrong weapon for this fight, High Fist . . .

Sudden motion in the midst of the first Pannion square. Screams. Picker's eyes widened. Demons had appeared. Not one, but six – no, seven. *Eight.* Huge, towering, bestial, tearing through the massed ranks of soldiery. Blood sprayed. Limbs flew.

The Seerdomin mages wheeled.

'Damn,' Blend whispered at her side. 'They've swallowed it.'

Picker snapped a glare at the woman. 'What are you talking about?'

'They're illusions, Lieutenant. Can't you tell?'

No.

'It's all that uncertainty – they don't know what they're facing. Quick Ben's playing on their fears.'

'Blend! Wait! How in Hood's name can *you* tell?'

'Not sure, but I can.'

The Seerdomin unleashed waves of grey sorcery that broke up over the legion, sent snaking roots down towards the eight demons.

'That will have to knock them out,' Blend said. 'If Quick Ben ignored the attack, the Pannions will get suspicious – let's see how – oh!'

The magic darted like plummeting nests of adders, enwreathed the roaring demons. Their death-throes were frenzied, lashing, killing and maiming yet more soldiers on all sides. But die they did, one by one.

The first legion's formation was a shambles, torn bodies lying everywhere. Its onward climb had been shattered, and the reassertion of order was going to take a while.

'Amazing what happens when you believe.' Blend said after a time.

Picker shook her head. 'If wizards can do that, why don't we have illusionists in every damned squad?'

'It only works, Lieutenant, because of its rarity. Besides, it takes serious mastery to manage faking even a lone demon – how Quick Ben pulled off eight of 'em is—'

The Seerdomin mages counterattacked. A crackling, spinning wave rolled up the slope, chewing up the ground, exploding tree stumps.

'That's headed straight for him!' Blend hissed, one hand clutching Picker's shoulder, fingers digging in.

'Ow! Let go!'

A thunderous concussion shook the ground and air.

'Gods! He's been killed! Blasted! Annihilated – Beru fend us all!'

Picker stared at the wailing soldier at her side, then forced her eyes once more to the scene on the ramp.

Another Seerdomin wizard appeared from the legion's ranks, mounted on a huge dun charger. Sorcery danced over his armour, pale, dull, flickering on the double-bladed axe in his right hand.

'Oh,' Blend whispered. 'That's a sharp illusion.'

He rode to join one of his fellow mages.

Who turned.

The axe flew from the rider's hand, its wake sparkling with suspended ice. Changed shape, blackening, twisting, reaching out clawed, midnight limbs.

The victim screamed as the wraith struck him. Death-magic punched through the protective weave of chaotic sorcery like a spearpoint through chain armour, plunged into the man's chest.

The wraith reappeared even as the Seerdomin toppled – up through his helmed head in an explosion of iron, bone, blood and brains – clutching in its black, taloned hands the Seerdomin's soul – a thing that flared, radiating terror. The wraith, hunched over its prize, flew a zigzag path towards the forest. Vanished into the gloom.

The rider, after throwing the ghastly weapon, had driven his heels into his horse's flanks. The huge beast had veered, hooves pounding, to ride down a second Seerdomin in a flurry of stamping that, within moments, flung blood-soaked clumps of mud into the air.

Sorcery tumbled towards the rider.

Who drove his horse forward. A ragged tear parted before them, into which horse and rider vanished. The rent closed a moment before the chaotic magic arrived. The spinning sorcery thunderclapped, gouging a crater in the hillside.

Antsy thumped Picker's other shoulder. 'Look! Further down! The legions at the back!'

She twisted. To see soldiers breaking formation, spreading out to disappear in the wooded hillside on either side of the ramp. 'Damn, someone got smart.'

'Smart ain't all – they're going to stumble right onto us!'

Paran saw Quick Ben reappear on the bank, stumbling from a warren, smoke streaming from his scorched leather armour. Moments earlier, the captain had thought the man annihilated, as a crackling wave of chaotic magic had hammered into the ridge of mounded earth that the wizard had chosen as his position. Grey-tongued fires still burned in the chewed-up soil around Quick Ben.

'Captain!'

Paran turned to see a marine scrabbling up the entrenchment's incline towards him.

'Sir, we've had reports – the legions are coming up through the trees!'

'Does the High Fist know?'

'Yes sir! He's sending you another company to hold this line.'

'Very well, soldier. Go back to him and ask him to get the word passed through the ranks. I've got a squad down there somewhere – they'll be coming up ahead of the enemy, likely at a run.'

'Aye, sir.'

Paran watched the man hurry off. He then scanned his dug-in troops. They were hard to see – shadows played wildly over their positions, filled the pits and the trenches linking them. The captain's head snapped round to Quick Ben. The wizard was hunched down, almost invisible beneath swirling shadows.

The ground below the embankment writhed and churned. Rocks and boulders were pushing up through the mulch, grinding and snapping against each other, the water on their surfaces sizzling into steam that cloaked the building mass of stone.

Two warrens unveiled – no, must be three – those boulders are red hot.

Shadows slipped down the bank, flowed between and beneath the gathering boulders.

He's building a scree – one that the enemy won't notice . . . until it's too late.

Down among the trees Paran could now see movement, ragged lines of Pannions climbing towards them. No shield-lines, no turtles – the toll among the Beklites, once they closed to attack, would be fearful.

Damn, where in the Abyss is Picker and the squad, then?

1026

On the ramp, the first legion had reformed and were doggedly marching upward once more, three Seerdomin mages in the lead. Webs of sorcery wove protective cloaks about them.

In rapid succession, three waves of magic roared up the ramp. The first clambered towards Quick Ben, building as it drew near. The other two rolled straight at the lead trench – in front of which stood Captain Paran.

Paran wheeled. 'Everyone down!' he bellowed, then threw himself flat. There was little point, he well knew. Neither his shouted warning nor his lying low would make any difference. Twisting round through the damp mulch, he was able to watch the tumbling wave approach.

The first one, aimed at Quick Ben, should have struck by now, but there was no sound, no dreadful explosion—

—except far down the slope, shaking the ground, shivering through the trees. Distant screams.

He could not pull his gaze from the magic rushing up towards him.

In its path – only moments before it reached the captain and his soldiers – a flare of darkness, a rip through the air itself, slashing across the entire width of the ramp.

The sorcery plunged into the warren with a hissing whisper.

Another detonation, far below among the massed legions.

The second wave followed the first.

A moment later, as a third explosion echoed, the warren narrowed, then vanished.

Disbelieving, Paran twisted further until he could see Quick Ben.

The wizard had built a wall of heaving stone before him, and it began to move amidst the flowing shadows, leaning, shifting, pushing humus before it. Suddenly the shadows raced downslope, between the trees, in a confusing, overwhelming wave. A moment later, the boulders followed – an avalanche that thundered, took trees with it, pouring like liquid towards the ragged lines of soldiers climbing the slope.

If they saw what struck them, there was no time to so much as scream. The slide continued to grow, burying every sign of the Beklites on that flank, until it seemed to the Paran that the whole hillside was on the move, hundreds of trees slashing the air as they toppled.

Sharpers exploded on the opposite flank, drawing Paran's attention. The Beklites on that side had reached the entrenchment's bank. Following the deadly hail of sharpers, pikes rose above the trench's line, and the Malazans poured up the side to form a bristling line atop the bank. Among them, heavy-armoured marines with assault crossbows.

The Beklites struggled upward, died by the score.

Then, at almost point-blank range, sorcery lashed the Malazan line. Bodies exploded within the grey fire.

As the miasmic magic dwindled, Paran could see naught but mangled corpses on the bank. The Beklites swarmed upward. Overhead, a condor trailing grey flames climbed laboriously back into the sky.

A flight of thirty Black Moranth darted to meet it. A score loosed crossbow quarrels towards the huge bird. Grey lightning lashed out from the condor, incinerating the missiles. A writhing wave blighted the sky, swept through the Black Moranth. Armour and flesh exploded.

Quick Ben stumbled to Paran's side, frantically cleared the mulch away in front of the captain, until a patch of bare earth was revealed.

'What are you—'

'Draw that damned bird, Captain! With your finger – *draw a card!*'

'But I can't—'

'*Draw!*'

Paran dragged his gloved index finger through the damp earth, beginning with a rectangular outline. His hand shook as he attempted to sketch the basic lines of the condor.

'This is madness – it won't work – gods, I can't even draw!'

'Are you done? Is that it?'

'What in Hood's name do you want?'

'Fine!' the wizard snapped. He made a fist and thumped the image.

Overhead, the demonic condor had begun another dive.

Suddenly, its wings flapped wildly, as if it could find no air beneath them. The creature plummeted straight down.

Quick Ben leapt to his feet, dragging Paran upright with him. 'Come on! Pull out your damned sword, Captain!'

They sprinted along the bank, the wizard leading them to where the condor had landed just beyond the overrun trench.

Moments later, they were running through steaming shards of armour and smouldering flesh – all that was left of the company of Malazans. The first wave of Beklites had fought their way to the second trench and were locked in fierce battle with Dujek's heavy infantry. To Paran and Quick Ben's right, downslope, the second wave was less than thirty paces away.

'Another Seerdomin!' Quick Ben screamed, dragging Paran to the ground.

Sorcery leapt from the second line of Beklites, ripped straight for the two men.

Quick Ben twisted onto his side, cursing. 'Hold on, Captain!'

A warren opened around them.

And they were suddenly under water, armour pulling them down into darkness.

Grey light streaked wild and savage directly above, a thundering concussion visibly descending towards the two men.

Water exploded on all sides, hard roots cracking against Paran's ribs. Coughing, gasping, he clawed at mud.

A hand closed round a strap of his harness, began dragging him across the sodden forest floor. 'Where's your damned sword?'

Paran managed to pull his legs under him, stumbled upright. 'Sword? You bastard! I was drowning!'

'Damn!' the wizard swore. 'You'd better hope that bird's still stunned.'

A murderous glance revealed Quick Ben's sorry state – blood streamed from the man's ears, nose and mouth. His leather armour had split along every seam. Paran looked down to see that his own banded armour was similarly mangled. He wiped at his mouth – his gauntlet came away smeared red.

'I've still got my pig-sticker.'

'Pull it out, I think we're close . . .'

Ahead, between the trees, broken branches littered the floor. Smoke drifted from the ground.

Then Paran saw it – Quick Ben's warning grip on the captain's arm indicated that the wizard, too, had detected the black mass in the shadows off to one side, a mass that glistened as it moved.

The flash of a pale grey neck, the glimmer of a hooked beak. Tendrils of sorcery, dancing, building.

Paran hesitated no longer, rushing past the wizard, knife sliding from its scabbard.

The creature was huge, its body the size of a female bhederin, the neck rising from hunched shoulders like a snake. Black, slimy head with nightmare eyes swinging towards him.

Something whipped past Paran from behind – a wraith, clawed hands reaching for the condor.

The creature hissed, recoiling, then the head snapped out.

Sorcery flashed.

The wraith was gone.

Paran twisted away from the condor's head. Drove the sticker's long blade down, deep into its back. He felt the blade deflect from the spine and cursed.

A shrill scream, a flash of black motion, and Paran found himself engulfed in black, oily, smothering feathers.

Hooked beak scored lashing pain along his temple, ripping down to take his ear – he felt the grisly snip, the spray of hot blood down onto his neck.

Awareness fragmented to an explosion of bestial rage, rising within him—

Ten paces away, on his knees – too battered to do more than simply watch – Quick Ben stared, disbelieving, as the two figures thrashed in battle. Paran was almost invisible within a writhing, shadow-woven Hound. *Not a Soletaken – not a veering. These are two creatures – man and beast – woven together . . . somehow. And the power behind it – it's Shadow. Kurald Emurlahn.*

The Hound's massive jaws and finger-long canines ripped into the condor, chewing a path up the creature's shoulders towards the neck. The demon, in turn, tore again and again into the beast – its flanks ribboned and spurting all too real blood.

The earth shook beneath the two beasts. A wing shot up to hammer into a tree. Bone and wood snapped as one. The condor screamed.

The tree's broken base – knee-high – punched out and then down, pinning the flailing wing, then grinding through the limb as it toppled back, away from the two contestants, crashing in a storm of branches and bark.

Hound's jaws closed on condor's neck.

Vertebrae crunched.

The creature's head flopped back to thud onto the churned forest floor.

The shadows of the triumphant Hound flickered – then the beast vanished.

Paran rolled from the dead bird's body.

Quick Ben could barely see the man beneath the shredded flesh and blood. The wizard's eyes widened as the ghastly figure slowly climbed to its feet. The skin along his right temple hung down, away from the bone. Half the ear on that side was gone, cut in a curved line that streamed blood.

Paran lifted his head, met the wizard's gaze. 'What happened?'

Quick Ben pushed himself to his feet. 'Come with me, Captain. We're taking a warren to a healer.'

'A healer?' Paran asked. 'Why?'

The wizard looked into the captain's eyes and saw no sign of awareness at all. 'All right.' Quick Ben took Paran's arm. 'Here we go . . .'

Picker pushed her way through the boughs until she came within sight of the forest floor below. No-one in sight. Muddy tracks were all that remained of the Beklites who had passed beneath them half a bell past. She could hear fighting upslope, along the embankment and perhaps beyond.

The explosions of sorcery that had struck the legions at the base of the ramp had not continued – a cause for worry. They'd had a worse scare with the avalanche, but its path had missed them by a hundred paces or more. *As if Quick Ben had known where we were. Somehow. Even more incredible, that damned wizard also managed to control the descent of a third of the mountainside. Maybe if a dozen High Mages had showed up to give him a hand, I might believe it.*

Or a god . . .

With that chilling thought, she began to make her way down the tree.

There had been condors in the sky earlier, and at least one had attacked the Malazan defences. Briefly. Where the others had gone, she had no idea.

Not here, thank Hood . . .

She dropped the last man's height to land on the ground in a jangle and clank of armour.

'That was subtle.'

Picker spun. 'Damn you, Blend—'

'Shh . . . uh, sir.'

'Do you know where the others are?'

'More or less. Want me to collect them?'

'That would be useful.'

'Then what?'

Damned if I know, woman. 'Just get them, Blend.'

'Aye, sir.'

Paran awoke to the stench of vomit, which he realized, from the stale taste in his mouth, was his own. Groaning, he rolled onto his side. It was dark. Muted voices conversed nearby. He sensed, but could not quite see, that others lay in the trench he'd found himself in.

Other . . . casualties . . .

Someone approached, a wide, burly shape.

Paran reached up to his temple, winced as his fingertips touched knotted gut. He tentatively traced the wound's length, down to a mass of damp bandages covering his ear.

'Captain?'

'That you, Mallet?'

'Aye, sir. We only just made it back.'

'Picker?'

'The squad's still breathing, sir. Had a couple of scrapes on the way up, but nothing to slow us much.'

'Why's it so dark?'

'No torches, sir. No lanterns. Dujek's order – we're assembling.'

Assembling. No, ask that later. 'Is Quick Ben still breathing? The last I remember, we were closing in on a downed condor . . .'

'Aye, though from what I hear, it was you plucking the goose, Captain. He brought you here and the cutters put you back together . . . more or less. Mostly superficial, you'll be glad to hear – I've come to make your face pretty again.'

Paran slowly sat up. 'There's plenty of soldiers around me who need your healing touch more than I do, Mallet.'

'True enough, sir, only Dujek said—'

'I'll carry my scars, Healer. See what you can do with these wounded. Now, where will I find the High Fist and Quick Ben?'

'Headquarters, Captain. That big chamber—'

'I know it.' Paran rose, stood for a moment until the spinning nausea passed. 'Now, a more important question – where am I?'

'Main trench, sir. Head left, straight down.'

'Thanks.'

The captain slowly threaded through the rows of wounded marines. The fight, he saw, had been bad – but not as bad as it might have been.

Dujek's Untan bodyguard commanded the tunnel's entrance. By their kit, they'd yet to draw blades. Their officer waved the captain past without a word.

Thirty paces later, Paran reached the chamber.

High Fist Dujek, Quick Ben and Lieutenant Picker were seated at the map table, a small lantern hanging from the wood-beamed ceiling above them. All three turned in their chairs as the captain entered.

Dujek scowled. 'Didn't Mallet find you?'

'He did, High Fist. I am fine.'

'You'll be seamed with scars, lad.'

Paran shrugged. 'So, what has happened? The Beklites don't like fighting at night?'

'They've withdrawn,' Dujek replied. 'And before you ask, no, it wasn't because we were too hard – they could've pushed, and if they had we'd be doubletiming through the woods right now – those few of us still able to draw breath, that is. Only one of those condors came after us, as well. We've been sitting here, Captain, trying to figure out why we got off so easy.'

'Any possible answers to that, sir?'

'Only one. We think Whiskeyjack and Brood are closing fast. The Seer doesn't want his forces tangled up with us when they arrive. He also doesn't want to risk any more of his damned condors.'

'One was more than enough,' Quick Ben muttered.

The wizard's exhaustion left the man looking aged, almost bent as he leaned on the table with both arms, bleary, red-webbed eyes fixed on the table's scarred surface.

Numbed by the sight, Paran pulled his gaze away, back to the High Fist. 'Mallet said we were assembling, sir. Since Lieutenant Picker is here, I assume you have something in mind for the Bridgeburners.'

'We do. We were just waiting for you, Captain.'

Paran nodded, said nothing.

'These trenches are indefensible,' Dujek growled. 'We're too exposed up here. Two or three more of those condors will finish us – and the Black Moranth. And I won't risk sending any more Moranth messengers back to Whiskeyjack – the Seer's birds cut the last ones down before they'd gone a tenth of a league from the mountainside. This close to Coral, it seems they're willing to fly at night. Nor is Quick Ben in any shape to try to magically contact Whiskeyjack. So, we're not waiting.'

We're going into Coral. From the night sky, straight down into the damned streets. 'Understood, High Fist. And the Bridgeburners are the first in, sir?'

'First in . . .' Dujek slowly nodded.

And last out.

'You're to strike straight for that keep. Knock a hole in the wall of its compound. The Black Moranth will take you in as close as they can.'

'Sir,' Paran said, 'if Brood and Whiskeyjack aren't as close as you think . . .'

Dujek shrugged. 'As I said earlier, Captain, this ain't the place to be waiting for one or the other. We're all going in – my first wave will be half a bell behind you.'

This could drop us into a viper's nest . . . 'The lieutenant and I had better ready the squads, then.'

'Aye. You'll have Quick Ben with you, and the mages – his cadre – are back with their respective squads. Hedge and the rest of the sappers have six cussers between them, ten crackers and twenty sharpers – you're to breach that wall, then pull back to us. Don't go after the Seer yourselves, understood?'

'Understood, High Fist.'

'All right, you three, get going.'

Dawn still almost two bells away, the mists drifted grey and low through the parkland north of Coral, reaching tendrils out onto the plain beyond.

Korlat rode to where Whiskeyjack had halted beneath the tree-lined crest that marked the beginning of the coppiced parkland, and drew rein alongside him.

The Malazan wasted no time, 'What did he say?'

'All rather peculiar, Whiskeyjack. Formal apologies from himself and from Brood. He humbly offers both his sword and his, as he called it, tactical prowess. I admit, it leaves me . . . uneasy.'

Whiskeyjack shrugged. 'I'd welcome any advice Kallor might provide.'

He noted but chose to ignore Korlat's wry disbelief at this statement.

After a moment, the Malazan continued, 'Follow me.' He nudged his horse forward, down the wide trader road as it wound between groves and across gently humped glades.

Their horses stumbled often, heads drooping as they trotted through the dark. A short while later they approached another ridge, this one cleared of trees. Beyond it, rising slowly as they drew nearer, was the city of Coral, climbing in tiers revealed by dull reflections of torchlight from the streets. The dark mass of the keep was an indistinct presence hunched above the last visible tier.

They reached the ridge and halted.

Korlat studied the lie of the land before them. The killing ground before the city's wall was a sixth of a league across, a single stone bridge spanning a ditch close to the wall. Half a league to the west loomed a forested mountain, the flank facing them wreathed in mist or smoke.

'Aye,' Whiskeyjack said, following her gaze, 'that's where the flashes of sorcery came from. It's where I would have positioned an army to break the siege, were I the Seer.'

'And Dujek has fouled their plans.'

'He's there, I suspect. Likely driven back or surrounded – that magic we saw lighting the sky was mostly Pannion. Quick Ben must have been overwhelmed. I think Dujek's taken a beating, Korlat. We need to draw the Seer's attention away from that mountain, buy the High Fist time to regroup.'

She faced him, was silent for a moment, then said, 'Your soldiers are dead on their feet, Whiskeyjack.' *As you are, my love.*

'None the less, I will have us lining this ridge come the dawn, the Ilgres Clan on our left, Taur and his White Faces on our right.' He glanced at her. 'I admit the thought of the other . . . form you can assume still leaves me, uh, alarmed. None the less, if you and Orfantal could take to the sky . . .'

'My brother and I have already discussed it, Whiskeyjack. He would fly to Dujek. Perhaps his presence will give the Seer's condors pause.'

'More likely draw them like a lodestone, Korlat. With the two of you together, guarding each other . . .'

'Even alone, we are not easily driven off. No, Dujek's need is greater. I shall take my Soletaken form and guard your forces. Orfantal will strike for the mountain. At the very least, he will be able to determine the disposition of the High Fist and his army.'

She saw the muscles of his jaw bunching beneath the beard. Finally, he sighed and said, 'I fear for you, Korlat – you will be alone above us.'

'With, among your soldiers, my remaining kin – mages all, my love – I shall not be as alone as you imagine.'

Whiskeyjack gathered his reins. 'Have you sensed anything at all of your Lord?'

She shook her head.

'Does that trouble you? No, you've no need to answer that.'

True, it seems there is little I can disguise from you.

'We'd best get back,' Whiskeyjack continued.

Both swung their mounts round.

Had their conversation continued for another half-dozen heartbeats, Korlat – with her preternatural vision – would have seen the first flight of Black Moranth rise from the mountain's forested slope, forty in all, and, flying low, wing hard and fast for the city.

A half-dozen heartbeats, within which Oponn's coin spun . . .

A single, lazy turn . . .

From Lady to Lord.

Less than a man's height beneath them, the city's wall blurred past. Once past it, the Moranth swept their quorls still lower, slipped into an avenue between buildings, flying below the roof-lines. A sharp turn at an intersection directed the flight towards the keep.

Paran, struggling to ignore the fierce burning itch of the stitches threading the side of his face, risked a glance down. Feast-piles were visible in the street, many of them still glowing dull red and sheathed in smoke. The occasional torch mounted on building walls revealed cobbles cluttered with refuse. The city slept beneath them, it seemed – he saw not a single guard or soldier.

The captain returned his attention to the keep. Its outer wall was high, well fortified – if anything, stronger than the one enclosing the city. The main structure beyond it was as much raw rock as worked stone. The keep had been carved into a mountainside.

Monstrous gargoyles lined the ragged roof's edge, black and hunched, barely visible as darker blots against the night sky.

Then Paran saw one move.

Condors. Oh, we're in the Abyss now . . . He thumped on the Moranth's shoulder, jabbed a gloved finger down to the street below. The officer nodded.

As one, the quorls carrying the Bridgeburners darted

down, skimmed a dozen paces at waist-height over the street, then settled with a single tilt of wings.

Soldiers scrambled from the saddles, seeking shadows.

The Moranth and their quorls leapt skyward once more, wheeling for the return flight.

Crouched in a dark alley mouth, Paran waited for the squads to gather around him. Quick Ben was first to his side.

'The keep's roof—'

'I saw,' Paran growled. 'Any ideas, Wizard?'

Antsy spoke up, 'How 'bout finding a cellar and hiding, Captain?'

Quick Ben glared at the sergeant, then looked around. 'Where's Hedge?'

The sapper pushed forward, waddling beneath bulging leather sacks.

'Did you see the damned sparrows?' the wizard asked him, making a strange half-shrugging motion with his left shoulder.

'Aye. We need sharpshooters atop the wall. I got twelve quarrels with sharpers instead of points. We do it right and we can take out that many—'

'Raining bird-meat,' Spindle cut in. 'Burning feathers.'

'Is that worse than burning hairshirt, Spin?'

'Quiet,' Paran snapped. 'All right, get hooks on the wall and line our brilliant crossbow experts to the top. Hedge, find the right place to set the cusser-bundle and crackers, and do it fast – we've got to time this right. I want those birds knocked from their perches, not in the air. Dujek's first wave is probably already on the way, so let's move.'

The captain waved Picker to point. They headed towards the keep wall.

Reaching the street's edge opposite, Picker raised a hand and crouched low. Everyone froze.

Paran moved up to just behind her. She leaned back. 'Urdomen guards,' she whispered. 'The gate's twenty paces to the left, well lit—'

'The guards are well lit?'

'Aye.'

'Idiots!'

'Aye, but I'm wondering . . .'

'What?'

'We switch back and head right, come up again, we'll be at a corner of the wall. Hedge likes corners . . .'

'So we leave the guards where they are.'

'Aye, Captain. Hood knows, in that light, they won't see a damned thing. And we'll be far enough away for the sound the hooks make if they make any not to reach 'em.'

'You hope.'

'They're all wearing great-helms, sir.'

'All right, take us round, Lieutenant.'

'A moment, sir. Blend?'

'Here.'

'Stay here. Keep an eye on those guards.'

'Aye, sir.'

Picker nodded to Paran and headed back down the street. The squads wheeled and followed.

It seemed to the captain as he padded along that he was the only one making a sound – and far too much sound at that. The thirty-odd soldiers around him were ghostly silent. They moved from shadow to shadow without pause.

A sixth of a bell later, Picker once more approached the street facing the compound wall. Directly ahead was a squared corner tower, surmounted by a massive battlement. The squads closed in behind the lieutenant.

Paran heard the sappers whispering with glee upon seeing the tower.

'Won't that come down pretty—'

'Like a potato on a spindly stick—'

'Brace the crackers, right? Drive the forces in at an angle to meet an arm's reach inside the cornerstone—'

'You tellin' Granda where's the pretty hole, Runter? Shut up and leave it to me and Spin, right?'

'I was just sayin', Hedge—'

Paran cut in, 'Enough, all of you. Crossbows up top before any of you do anything else.'

'Aye, sir,' Hedge agreed. 'Ready the hooks, dearies. You with the crossbows, line up and get your sharper-quarrels – hey, no cutting in, show some manners, woman!'

Paran drew Quick Ben to one side a few paces behind the others. 'Twelve explosive quarrels, Wizard,' he muttered under his breath. 'There's at least thirty condors.'

'You don't think Dujek's attack inside the city walls will draw 'em away?'

'Sure, long enough for them to annihilate that first wave, leave a few of their own circling to greet the second wave, while the rest come back to take care of us.'

'You've something in mind, Captain?'

'A second diversion, one to pull the rest of the condors away from both Dujek and the Bridgeburners. Quick, can you take us through a warren to that roof?'

'Us, sir?'

'You and I, yes. And Antsy, Spindle, Detoran, Mallet and Trotts.'

'I can do that, Captain, but I'm just about used up—'

'Just get us there, Wizard. Where's Spin?' Paran looked back at the others, nodded when he found the man. 'Wait here.' The captain hurried to where Spindle crouched with the other sappers, reached out and dragged him from the huddle. 'Hedge, you'll have to do without this man.'

Hedge grinned. 'What a relief, Captain.'

'Hey!'

'Quiet, Spindle.' Paran pulled him to where Quick Ben waited.

'What have you got in mind?' the wizard asked as soon as they arrived.

'In a moment. Quick, those condors – what precisely are they?'

'Not sure, sir.'

'Not what I want to hear, Wizard. Try again.'

'All right, I think they once were real condors – smaller,

normal sized, that is. Then the Seer somehow figured out a way of stuffing the birds—'

'Stuffing the birds, ha!' Spindle snickered.

Quick Ben reached out and cuffed the man. 'Don't interrupt again, Spin. Demons, Captain. Possession. Chaos-aspected, which is why their bodies can't quite hold it all.'

'So, demon and bird both.'

'One the master over the other, of course.'

'Of course. Now, which one does the flying?'

'Well, the condor . . .' Quick Ben's eyes narrowed. He glanced at Spindle, then grinned. 'Well, hey, maybe . . .'

'What are you two going on about?'

'You hoarding any munitions, Spindle?' Paran asked.

'Six sharpers.'

'Good, in case this goes wrong.'

They turned at a hissed command from Picker to see a half-dozen soldiers sprinting across the street to pull up at the base of the compound wall. Hooks and ropes were readied.

'Damn, I didn't realize how high that wall was – how are they—'

'Look again, sir,' Quick Ben said. 'Toes is with them.'

'So?'

'Watch, sir.'

The squad mage had opened his warren. Paran tried to recall the man's speciality, was answered by the smoky appearance of a dozen ghosts who drifted close around Toes. Paran softly grunted, 'If those are the ones who keep falling over . . .'

'No, these are local spirits, Captain. People fall from walls all the time, and since this one is more than a few hundred years old, well, the numbers pile up. Anyway, most ghosts are somewhat . . . single-minded. The last they remember, they were on the wall, patrolling, standing guard, whatever. So, they want to get back up there . . .'

Paran watched the spirits, six of them now somehow

carrying hooks, slither up the wall. The other six had closed ghostly hands on Toes and were lifting him to follow. The squad mage did not look happy, legs flailing.

'I thought the warrens were poisoned.'

Quick Ben shrugged. 'Hood's hit back hard, Captain. He's cleared a space . . .'

Paran frowned, but said nothing.

Reaching the top of the wall, Toes took charge once more, retrieving and placing each hook since it was clear that the spirits were either incapable of such precision with physical objects, or disinclined. The mage had to struggle with a couple of them to get the roped hooks from their hands. Eventually, he had all the hooks positioned. Ropes uncoiled, snaked down to the soldiers waiting below.

The first six crossbow-equipped soldiers began climbing.

Paran cast an anxious glance up at the row of condors surmounting the main building. None stirred. 'Thank Hood they sleep deep.'

'Aye, building power for what's to come. Far into their chaotic warren.'

Paran turned round and studied the dark sky to the northwest. Nothing. Then again, it wasn't likely that he'd be able to see them in any case. They'd be coming in low, just as his flight had done.

The second six soldiers with crossbows strapped to their backs crossed the street and set hands to ropes.

'Wizard, ready that warren . . .'

'It's ready, Captain.'

Picker was suddenly waving madly in Paran's direction. Hissing a curse, the captain rushed to join her. The remaining squads had pulled far back from the street.

'Captain! Lean out, sir, and check down at the gate.'

Paran did so.

There was activity there. The gates had opened, and out were filing, one after another, huge reptilian warriors – K'Chain Che'Malle – *so that's what the damned things look like.*

Hood's breath. Five . . . ten . . . fifteen . . . still more, marching out into the city – towards the north wall.

And Dujek's about to land in their laps . . .

He settled back, met Picker's eyes. 'Lieutenant, we've got to divert those damned things.'

She rubbed at her face, glanced back at the remaining squads. 'They're supposed to be pretty fast, those undead lizards, but with all these alleys and streets . . .' She faced Paran once more, gave a swift nod. 'We've a few sharpers in hand – we'll give 'em good reason to come after us.'

'Just make sure you stay ahead, Lieutenant. If you can, keep everyone together.'

'Sir, that's not likely – we'll have to scatter, I expect, just to keep the things confused.'

'All right, but try anyway.'

'And you, Captain?'

'Quick and Antsy's squad – we're headed onto the keep's roof. We'll be trying our own diversion with the rest of those condors. You've got the Bridgeburners now, Lieutenant.'

'Aye, Captain. So, who do you figure will die first, you or us?'

'That's too close to call.'

She grinned. 'Half my back pay, Captain, we'll be a step behind you. Pay up at Hood's Gate.'

'You're on, Lieutenant. Now, leave Hedge and his sappers to blowing that tower, gather up Blend and the rest of you get going.'

'Aye, sir.'

Paran made to move away, but Picker reached out and touched his arm.

'Captain?'

'What?'

'Well, uh, those knives at your back? They've been turned the other way for some time. Just wanted you to know.'

Paran glanced away. 'Thank you, Lieutenant.'

Quick Ben had pulled together Antsy and his squad, minus Hedge and Blend. As soon as Paran joined them, the wizard nodded and said, 'Say when, Captain.'

Paran glanced over at the compound wall. The ropes hung slack. No-one was in sight along the top. 'How long since you last saw them?'

The wizard shrugged. 'I expect they're in position now, sir. Hedge looks about ready.'

Paran's eyes dropped to see the team of sappers gathered in a tight, nervously shifting pack at the tower's base. 'That was fast.'

'Hedge is lightning when he's scared witless, sir. We'd better—'

'Yes. Open your warren.' He glanced over at Antsy. The sergeant, Detoran, Trotts and Mallet had dropped the visors on their helms. Weapons were out. Spindle crouched nearby, a sharper clutched in his right hand. 'Hold it, Quick – did you tell Spin what—'

'Aye, sir, and he's working on it just fine.'

Spindle managed a weak grin.

'All right. Let's go.'

The portal flashed open, bled darkness into the street. Paran's eyes widened. *Kurald Galain. What*—

'Follow me!' Quick Ben hissed, darting into the warren.

The squad plunged forward, was swallowed. Paran flung himself into their wake.

The transition was almost instantaneous. The captain stumbled across slick tiles – they were on the keep's roof, thirty paces behind the row of condors—

A dozen of the huge, demonic creatures suddenly exploded, spraying blood and flesh to spatter across the roof. The others jerked awake as one. Loosing piercing cries, they spread vast wings and launched themselves upward.

Spindle had already unleashed his warren, and its effect was instantaneous.

The condors shrilled with terror, wings thundering in

panic, heads twisting on spasming necks as the mortal beast within each body – gripped with blind fear engendered by Spindle's twisted talent – warred with demon for command.

Crossbow quarrels shot up from along the compound wall, thudded into the flailing creatures.

The entire keep shuddered. Paran spun to see the compound tower to his left suddenly topple, the enormous battlement pitching towards the street. Smoke billowed. Shouts followed as the Bridgeburners lining the top of the wall scrambled towards the ropes.

Sharpers echoed from the streets to the east – Picker and her remaining Bridgeburners had just surprised the column of K'Chain Che'Malle – and the pursuit was on.

Quick Ben pulled Paran close. 'The demons are winning the struggle!'

The condors were slowly gaining height, drawing ever further from the influence of Spindle's warren. If they felt any discomfort for being studded with quarrels, they showed no sign of it. Sorcery crackled around them.

'They'll come round for us, Captain,' Quick Ben predicted.

'Better us than Dujek. Now, can we keep them occupied for a time, Wizard?'

'Most of 'em, aye.'

'How?'

'Well, to start, we can run to the south side of this building.'

Run? That's it? 'Let's move, then.'

Outside the city's west wall, close to the shoreline's broken, jagged edge, a lazy swirl of dust rose from the ground, took form.

Tool slowly settled the flint sword into its shoulder-hook, his depthless gaze ignoring the abandoned shacks to either side and fixing on the massive stone barrier before him.

Dust on the wind could rise and sweep high over this wall. Dust could run in streams through the rubble fill beneath the foundation stones. The T'lan Imass could make his arrival unknown.

But the Pannion Seer had taken Aral Fayle. Toc the Younger. A mortal man . . . who had called Tool *friend*.

He strode forward, hide-wrapped feet kicking through scattered bones.

The time had come for the First Sword of the T'lan Imass to announce himself.

The second wave, bearing another thousand soldiers, plunged down to fill the streets directly behind Dujek's position, even as explosions lit the skyline to the south – along the keep's roof-line, then directly beneath it, the latter a deeper sound, rumbling through the ground to rattle the cobbles – a sound the High Fist recognized. The breach had been made.

'Time to push forward,' he barked to his officers. 'Take your commands – we drive for the keep.'

Dujek raised his visor. The air above was filled with the whispering flutter of quorl wings. The second wave of carriers were climbing back into the night sky, even as a third approached from the north – moments from delivering another thousand marines.

Sharpers echoed from the city to the east. Dujek paused to wonder at that – then the sky ignited, a grey, rolling wave, sweeping towards the third flight.

The High Fist watched, silent, as between two beats of his cold heart a thousand Black Moranth, their quorls, and five companies of Onearm's Host disintegrated in grey flames.

Behind the wave, sailing black and deadly, flew three condors.

The Moranth of the second wave, who had climbed high before intending to turn about and race north, reappeared, above the three condors, diving en masse towards the creatures.

A fourth flight of carriers approaching from the north-west had captured the birds' attention.

Rider and quorl descended on the unsuspecting condors, in successive, suicidal attacks. Black-armoured warriors drove lances deep into feathered bodies. Quorls twisted their triangular heads, chitinous jaws tearing strips of flesh, even as the collisions shattered their frail bodies and frailer wings.

Hundreds of quorls died, their riders falling with them to strike roofs and streets, lying broken and unmoving.

The three condors followed, dying as they fell.

Dujek had no time to think of the horrific price his Moranth had paid for that momentary victory. The fourth wing dropped down into the streets, soldiers flinging themselves from the saddles and scrambling for cover.

The High Fist beckoned for a messenger.

'New orders to the officers – the companies are to take buildings – defensible ones. The keep will have to wait – I want roofs over us—'

Another message-bearer appeared. 'High Fist!'

'What?'

'The Pannion legions are assembling, sir – every street in a line from the north gate right up to the keep.'

'And we hold the west third of the city. They're coming to drive us out. All right.' He faced the first messenger and said, 'Let the officers know so they can adjust their defence—'

But the second message-bearer wasn't finished. 'High Fist, sir – sorry. There's K'Chain Che'Malle with those legions.'

Then where is Silverfox and her damned T'lan Imass? 'They could be dragons for all it matters,' he growled after a moment. 'Go,' he said to the first messenger. The soldier saluted and left. The High Fist glared at the other message-bearer, then said, 'Find Twist and inform him we'll need a pass of his heavies – east of our position – just one, though. Tell him that they probably won't make it back, so he'd better hold a wing in reserve.' Dujek raised his visor and studied the sky overhead. Dawn was arriving – the fifth and sixth wings had delivered their troops and were distant specks racing back towards the mountain. *That's it, then, we're all in Coral. And if we don't get help soon we'll never leave.* 'That's all.' He nodded to the soldier.

The condors circled above the rooftop, crying out to each other, dipping and diving then, wings thudding the air, lifting back towards the paling sky.

Paran stared up, disbelieving. 'They must be able to see us!' he hissed.

They crouched against a low wall beyond which was a parapet overlooking the harbour and Coral Bay, and the darkness that had swallowed them was fast fading.

'They can't see us,' Quick Ben muttered at his side, 'because I'm keeping them from seeing us. But they know we're here . . . somewhere.'

And that's why they're hanging around. Fine. Good. That means they're not busy annihilating Dujek's army.

The keep shook beneath them, rattling tiles. 'Hood's breath, what was that?'

The wizard at his side scowled. 'Not sure. That didn't sound like munitions . . . but I'd say the compound wall's been breached again.'

Again? By whom? The detonation had come from the harbour side, east. A billowing cloud of dust slowly lifted into view.

Paran cautiously lifted his head until he could see past the low wall.

Out over the bay, seagulls were screaming. The sea beyond, which seemed to be solid ice, was rumbling. Spouts exploded skyward along that south horizon. A storm was building out there. *Let's hope it comes here – we could do with the confusion.*

'Get your head down!' Quick Ben hissed.

'Sorry.'

'I'm having enough trouble as it is, Captain – we need to stay tight – stop kicking, Detoran – what? Oh. Captain, look north, sir! High up!'

Paran twisted round.

A wing of Moranth – no more than specks – were sailing over the city, east to west.

Six condors were climbing to meet them – but they had a long way to go.

Smaller specks dropped from the Moranth, down onto the east half of the city.

Their descent seemed to take for ever, then the first one struck the roof of a building. The explosion shattered the roof and upper floor. All at once, detonations trembled as cusser after cusser struck.

Sorcery swept from the six condors, raced up towards the distant Moranth.

Bombs expended, the wing scattered. None the less, more than a score did not escape the sorcerous wave.

Smoke and dust shrouded the east side of Coral.

Above the captain and the squad, the remaining condors screamed with rage.

'That worked, more or less,' Quick Ben whispered. 'Those streets were likely packed solid with Pannion soldiers.'

'Not to mention,' Paran gritted, 'the rest of the Bridgeburners.'

'They'd have withdrawn by now.'

Paran heard the effort in the wizard's hopeful tone.

A cusser had struck the street fifty paces behind Picker and her decimated squads, less than ten paces behind the K'Chain Che'Malle K'ell Hunter that had been closing on them. The undead creature was obliterated by the blast, its mass absorbing most of the lethal, flailing rain of shattered cobbles.

Fragments of withered skin, flesh and splinters of bone pattered down almost within reach of the Bridgeburners.

Picker raised a hand to call the soldiers to a halt. She was not alone in needing to catch her breath, to wait until her hammering heart slowed somewhat.

'That makes a damned change,' Blend gasped at the lieutenant's side.

Picker did not bother replying, but she could not help but agree with Blend's bitter comment. As Paran had instructed, they had indeed drawn the attention of at least some of the K'Chain Che'Malle.

And had paid for it.

Her last count had sixteen Bridgeburners capable of combat and six wounded, of whom three were at Hood's Gate. The K'Chain Che'Malle were more than fast, they were lightning. And relentless. Sharpers did little more than irritate them.

In any case, the munitions were gone. Picker had turned her soldiers back on one of the K'ell Hunters, to gauge their chances in a close-in fight. She would not do that again. They'd been lucky to disengage at all. Seeing friends on all sides cut into pieces where they stood was an image that would haunt her all her remaining days – *days? I haven't got days. I'll be surprised if we live out this bell.*

'Hood take us, another one!'

The lieutenant wheeled at the shout.

Another Hunter had appeared from a side alley, claws scraping on cobbles, head hunched low, blades out.

Less than fifteen paces away, head swinging to face them.

All right . . . heartbeats, then.

'Scatter!'

Even as the Bridgeburners began to bolt, a wall close to the K'Chain Che'Malle exploded onto the street. Another Hunter arrived within the dust and bricks that tumbled out, this one a chopped-up ruin, head swinging wildly – connected to neck by a thin strip of tendon – missing one arm, a leg ending in a stump at the ankle. The creature fell, pounded onto the cobbles, ribs snapping, and did not move.

The Bridgeburners froze in place.

As did the first K'Chain Che'Malle. Then it hissed and swung to face the ragged hole in the building's wall.

Through the dust stepped a T'lan Imass. Desiccated flesh torn, hanging in strips, the gleam of bone visible everywhere, a skull-helmed head that had once held horns. The flint sword in its hands was so notched it appeared denticulated.

Ignoring the Malazans, it turned to the other K'Chain Che'Malle.

The Hunter hissed and attacked.

Picker's eyes could not fully register the speed of the exchange of blows. All at once, it seemed, the K'Chain Che'Malle was toppling, a leg severed clean above what passed for a knee. A sword clanged on the cobbles as a dismembered arm fell. The T'lan Imass had stepped back, and now moved forward once more, an overhead chop that shattered bone down through shoulder, chest, then hip, bursting free to strike the cobbles in a spray of sparks.

The K'ell Hunter collapsed.

The lone T'lan Imass turned to face the keep, and began walking.

Picker and the others watched the warrior stride past them, continue on up the street.

'Hood's breath!' Blend muttered.

'Come on!' Picker snapped.

'Where?' Corporal Aimless demanded.

'After him,' she replied, setting off. 'Looks like the safest place to be is in that thing's shadow.'

'But it's heading for the keep!'

'Then so are we!'

Crusted in mud, boots dragging, Whiskeyjack's army slowly moved forward to form a line facing the killing field, and the city beyond it. Far to either flank were the Barghast, Ilgres Clan on one side, White Faces on the other.

Korlat left her horse with the others behind the line and strode to the low hill immediately to the west of the trader road, where stood Whiskeyjack, Kallor and the standard-bearer, Artanthos.

They had witnessed, one and all, the aerial battles over Coral, the slaughter of the Black Moranth and at least one wing carrying troops of Onearm's Host. They had watched the bombardment, but not a single soldier on the ridge had cheered. There could be no disguising the brutal truth: Dujek was trapped in Coral, his army was being slaughtered, and Whiskeyjack and his exhausted force could do little about it.

Condors had been seen following the Black Moranth flying back to the mountain entrenchments – but there they would meet Orfantal. In his Soletaken form, her brother was second only to Rake himself. Korlat envied him his chance for immediate vengeance.

She approached her companions, preparing her mind for the veering into her draconic form. The power that came with the transition had always frightened her, for it was a cold, hard manifestation, unhuman and inhuman both. This time, however, she would welcome it.

Reaching the crest, she saw what the others were seeing. The north gate had opened across from them. K'Chain Che'Malle were emerging, spreading out to form a line. Eight hundred, perhaps more.

Weapons were readied among the Malazans. When Whiskeyjack gave the order, they would march down to meet that undead line of slayers.

And die. Eight hundred less K'Chain Che'Malle in Coral. Eight hundred K'Chain Che'Malle . . . occupied for a time. Does Dujek even know? Brood is still half a day behind us. The Grey Swords two bells, perhaps more – I'd not expected that news from Kallor – but they will have ridden too hard, too long.

And Gruntle and his legion – they seem to have vanished entirely. Have we lost our shock-troops? Abyss knows, that Daru had no love of battle . . .

Does Dujek comprehend what we do to purchase for him this day?

Eight hundred K'Chain Che'Malle on the plain. How many

remain in the city? How many now carve deadly paths through the High Fist's companies?

The twenty or so condors left over the city were one and all circling the keep itself, a measure, perhaps, of the Seer's confidence, that he would see no need for their participation in what was to come.

The thought brought a bitter taste to her mouth.

Whiskeyjack turned as she arrived, nodded in greeting. 'Did you find Kruppe? I trust he has chosen a safe place.'

'With Hetan,' Korlat replied. 'Demanding white paint for his face.'

Whiskeyjack could not quite manage a smile.

'My Tiste Andii will precede your soldiers when they advance,' Korlat said after a moment. 'We will see how these undead fare against Kurald Galain.'

Kallor's expression hinted at a smirk, 'Your warren is still beset, Korlat. You would require a full unveiling – by all your kin, not just the ones here – to achieve a cleansing. Your brothers and sisters are about to be slaughtered.'

Her eyes narrowed. *A full unveiling. Kallor, you know far too much of us.* 'I appreciate your tactical acumen,' she replied drily.

She saw Whiskeyjack glance back at Artanthos, who stood fifteen paces from the others, wrapped against the morning chill in a fur-lined cloak. The man was paying no attention to the others, his gaze fixed on the plain below, a slight frown slowly marring his unlined brow.

Two marines approached on horseback from the east, riding hard in front of the Malazan line.

Whiskeyjack's two marines . . .

Labouring, coughing froth, the horses galloped up the slope. The two women reined in. 'Commander!' one shouted.

The other added, 'We found her!' Then she pointed.

Emerging from the ranks to the east . . . Silverfox.

The sound of thousands of voices crying out in surprise alerted Korlat – she turned to see the killing field before the

K'Chain Che'Malle vanish in a sudden haze of dust, thinning quickly to reveal rank upon rank of T'lan Imass.

Silverfox approached. She seemed to have chosen Artanthos as her destination, her eyes half lidded, her round, heavy face expressionless.

A roar from Whiskeyjack's army rose into the morning air.

'Yes . . .' rasped Kallor beside her.

Korlat pulled her gaze from Silverfox, curious enough at Kallor's tone to draw her attention.

In time to see the rough-edged blade flashing at her head.

Pain exploded. A moment of confusion, when all was strangely still, then the ground hammered her side. Heat flared down her face, lancing down from her forehead. She blinked, wondered at her own body, which had begun thrashing.

Warren—

—chaotic—

Kallor—

A blurred scene before her eyes, her point of view from the ground.

Skull – broken – dying—

Her vision cleared, every line and edge of what she saw too sharp, sharp like knife-blades, slicing her soul to ribbons. Kallor, with a delighted roar, charged towards Silverfox, chain armour flowing like a cloak. Grey-veined magic danced on the ground around the warrior.

The Rhivi woman stopped, mouth opening, terror filling her eyes. She screamed something—

—something—

'*T'lan Ay. Defend me!*'

Yet she remained alone—

Kallor closed, sword gripped in both gauntleted hands, closed, raising the weapon high.

Then Whiskeyjack stood in his path, longsword lashing up to clang against Kallor's weapon. A sudden, fierce exchange, sparks flashing. Kallor leapt back, bellowing his frustration, and his heel caught—

Whiskeyjack saw his moment. Sword thrusting out, a duellist's lunge, fully extending, weight pounding down on the lead leg—

Which buckled.

She saw the sliver of bone rip up through the man's leather-clad thigh.

Saw the pain on her lover's face, the sudden recognition—

As Kallor's huge sword punched into his chest. Slid between ribs. Ripped through heart and lungs in a diagonal, inward-slicing thrust.

Whiskeyjack died on that blade – life dropping back from the eyes that met Korlat's, back, away, then gone.

Kallor dragged his weapon free.

He reeled suddenly, impaled by two crossbow quarrels. Chaotic magic snaked up around the offending missiles, disintegrating them. Blood spurted. Unmindful, Kallor readied his sword once more, as the two marines closed in tandem.

The women were superb, fighting as one.

But the man they fought—

A mortal scream – the marine on the right stumbled in a welter of blood, reaching down to gather uncoiling, tumbling intestines, then sinking earthward. Her helmed head left her shoulders before her knees touched ground.

The other woman rushed Kallor, sword thrusting high for the warrior's face.

A side-step, a downward chop, severing the arm—

But the marine had already surrendered it, and her left hand, gripping a pig-sticker, was unimpeded as it punched through the chainlinks covering Kallor's stomach.

The edge of Kallor's sword carved up through the marine's throat. She spun in a red spray, toppled.

Gasping, the ancient warrior reeled back,

1056

yellow-streaked blood spurting from the hole in his stomach. 'Chained One!' he screamed. 'Heal me!'

Hot – a warren—

—not chaotic – where?

A wave of knotted gold hammered into Kallor, swallowed him in frenzied fire. He shrieked, thrown off his feet, battered as the magic pursued, ripping into him, blood threading the air as he sprawled to the ground.

A second wave rolled towards the man, coruscating with sunfire—

The warren that opened around Kallor was a miasmic stain, a sickly tear – that swept around him—

—to vanish, taking Kallor with it.

The golden sorcery flickered, dissipated.

No – such control. Who?

Korlat's body no longer spasmed. It was now numb and cool, strangely remote. Blood was filling one eye. She had to keep blinking to clear it. She was lying on the ground, she finally realized. Kallor had struck her—

Someone knelt by her side, a soft, warm hand settling on her cheek.

Korlat struggled to focus.

'It's me, Silverfox. Help is coming—'

The Tiste Andii tried to lift a hand, to manage some kind of gesture towards Whiskeyjack, but the desire remained within her mind, racing in circles, and she knew by the faint feel of damp grasses under her palm that her hand did not heed her call.

'Korlat! Look at me. Please. Brood is coming – and I see a black dragon approaching from the west – Orfantal? The warlord possesses High Denul, Korlat. You must hold on—'

A shadow over her face. Silverfox glancing up, features twisting into something bitter. 'Tell me,' she said to the newcomer, 'the sorcery that accompanied Kallor's betrayal: was it truly so efficacious as to leave you stunned for so long? Or did you hold back? Calculating your moment, observing the consequences of your inaction – after all, you've done it before, Tayschrenn, haven't you?'

Tayschrenn?

But the ragged, pain-racked voice that replied was that of Artanthos, the standard-bearer. 'Silverfox. Please. I would not—'

'Wouldn't you?'

'No. Whiskeyjack – he's—'

'I know,' Silverfox snapped.

A poorly mended leg . . . never the right time – Brood could have—

He's dead. Oh, my love, no . . .

Blurred figures were on all sides now. Malazan soldiers. Barghast. Someone began keening with grief.

The man she had known as Artanthos leaned over her. Sorcery had split the flesh of his face – the touch of chaos, she recognized. A fiercer touch than what she could have survived. She knew, then, in her soul, that the High Mage had willed no delay to his response. That he'd managed anything at all was . . . extraordinary. She met his eyes, saw the layers of pain that still racked through the man.

'Sil . . .'

'Korlat?'

'Woman,' the Tiste Andii said, the word slurred but audible, 'this man . . .'

'Yes? He is Tayschrenn, Korlat. The part of me that is Nightchill has known for a long time. I was coming to conf—'

'. . . thank him.'

'What?'

'For . . . your . . . life. Thank him, woman . . .' She held still to Tayschrenn's eyes. Dark grey, like Whiskeyjack's. 'Kallor – he surprised us all . . .'

The man winced, then slowly nodded. 'I am sorry, Korlat. I should have seen—'

'Yes. Me, too. And Brood.'

She could feel horse hooves drumming the earth

1058

beneath her, the vibration rising up to settle into her bones.

A dirge. Drums, a lost sound. Horses, driven hard . . . knowing nothing of the reason, yet on they come. Closer. Mindless, yet filled with the urgency of incomprehensible masters.

But death has already ridden across this hilltop.

Knowing nothing of reason.

My love.

He is yours, now, Hood . . . do you smile?

My love is . . . yours . . .

Brave and magnificent as it was, Itkovian's mount was faltering. With dawn still two bells away, Gruntle had roused him with uncharacteristic curtness. 'Something's gone wrong,' he'd growled. 'We must ride for Coral, friend.'

The Grey Swords had not stopped for the night – Itkovian had watched them for as long as he could, until the night's gloom took them from his vision. The Shield Anvil had elected to ride to Whiskeyjack's support. He had thought himself indifferent to the decision, and to what their departure signified, yet bleakness filled his heart, and the sleep that eventually came to him was troubled. After Gruntle's rough awakening, he sought to reflect upon the source of his restlessness, but it eluded him.

Saddling his horse, Itkovian had paid little attention to Gruntle and his legion, and only when he swung himself up onto his mount and gathered the reins did he note that the Daru and his followers waited – on foot.

Itkovian had frowned at Gruntle. 'Mortal Sword, what do you intend?'

The large man grimaced, then said, 'For this journey, swiftness is required. For this journey,' he repeated, glancing at a fiercely scowling Stonny Menackis, 'Trake risks the heart of his power.'

'Not my god!' Stonny snapped.

Gruntle offered her a sad smile, 'No, alas. You will have to join Itkovian, and simply ride. We'll not wait for you,

1059

but perhaps you will keep up with us . . . for a while.'

Itkovian had not understood any of this. 'Sir,' he said to Gruntle, 'will you travel by warren?'

'No. Well, not quite. Maybe, how do I know? I just know – somehow – that my legion is capable of . . . well, of something different. Something . . . *fast*.'

Itkovian had glanced at Stonny, then shrugged. 'Both Stonny Menackis and I are blessed with exceptional horses. We shall endeavour to keep pace.'

'Good.'

'Mortal Sword.'

'What is it, Itkovian?'

'What lies ahead, sir, that troubles you so?'

'I'm not sure, friend, but I'm feeling sick to my stomach. I believe we are about to be betrayed.'

Itkovian had said nothing to that for a long moment, then, 'Sir, if one regards recent events with an unclouded eye, then one might observe that the betrayal has already occurred.'

Gruntle had simply shrugged, turning to his followers. 'Stay tight, you damned misfits. Anyone straggles at the start and you'll be left behind.'

Stonny moved over to Itkovian's side, leading her horse. 'Do you know,' Itkovian asked her, 'what is about to occur?'

'Probably nothing,' she snapped, swinging up into her saddle. 'Gruntle must've bumped his head—'

She got no further, as before them Gruntle and his legion seemed to blur, to meld together in an indistinct flicker of barbed stripes, a single form, massive, low to the ground – that suddenly flowed forward, cat-like, and was gone in the night.

'Beru fend!' Stonny hissed. 'After it!' she cried, driving heels to her horse's flanks.

And so they had ridden, hard.

They passed by Brood's encampment, had noted that it was rousing, even though dawn was still a bell away, with considerable haste.

They witnessed, without a word exchanged between them, the flash and flare of sorcery in the sky to the southwest.

Occasionally, through the darkness, they caught a glimpse of the huge creature they pursued, the dull flicker of yellow, black-slashed, moving as if through impossibly high grasses, as if beneath jungle fronds, webbed in shadows, a fluid hint of motion, deadly in its speed and in its silence.

Then the sky began to lighten, and the horizon to the south was revealed, stands of trees, the trader road wending between them.

Still the striped beast defied the eye, evaded sharp detection as it reached the parkland's hills.

Lathered, mouths coughing foam, the horses thundered on, hooves pounding heavy and ragged. Neither animal would ever recover from this ordeal, Itkovian knew. Indeed, their deaths waited only for the journey's end.

Brave and magnificent, and he wondered if the sacrifice was worth it.

They rode the track between coppiced stands, the path gently rising towards what Itkovian judged to be an escarpment of some kind.

Then, directly ahead, wagons. A few figures, turning to watch them approach.

If they had seen the creature, they showed no sign – no alarms had been raised, all seemed calm.

Itkovian and Stonny rode past the Malazan rearguard.

The crackle of sorcery – close.

Soldiers lined the ridge before them, an army assembled, facing south – now breaking into disorganized motion. Dismay struck Itkovian with palpable force, a flood of raw pain, of immeasurable loss.

He reeled in his saddle, forced himself upright once more. Urgency thundered through him, now, sudden, overwhelming.

Stonny was shouting, angling her stumbling horse to the

right, leaving the road, approaching a hilltop where stood the Malazan standard, drooped in the windless air. Itkovian followed, but slower, drawing back. His soul was drowning in cold horror.

His horse surrendered its gallop, staggered, head thrusting out. Canter to a weaving, loose walk, then halting, slowly drawing square-footed twenty paces from the hill's base.

Then dying.

Numbed, Itkovian slipped his boots from the stirrups, drew an aching leg over the beast's rump, then dropped down to the ground.

On the hill to his right, he saw Stonny, stumbling free from her horse – the slope had defeated it – and clambering upward. Gruntle and his troop had arrived, human once again, crowding the hill, yet seemingly doing nothing.

Itkovian turned his gaze away, began walking along one side of the road, which had straightened for the final, downhill approach to the killing field, and the city beyond.

Cold horror.

His god was gone. His god could not deflect it as it had once done, months ago, on a plain west of Capustan.

Loss and sorrow, such as he had never felt before.

The truth. Which I have known. Within me. Hidden, now revealed. I am not yet done.

Not yet done.

He walked, seeing nothing of the soldiers to his left and right, stepping clear of the uneven line, leaving behind the army that now stood, weapons lowered, broken before the battle had even begun – broken by a man's death.

Itkovian was oblivious. He reached the slope, continued on.

Down.

Down to where the T'lan Imass waited in ranks before eight hundred K'Chain Che'Malle.

The T'lan Imass, who, as one, slowly turned round.

Warrens flared on the hilltop.

Bellowing, Gruntle ordered his followers to take position on the south slope. He stood, motionless after so long, still trembling from the god's power. The promise of murder filled him, impassive yet certain, a predator's intent that he had felt once before, in a city far to the north.

His vision was too sharp, every motion tugging at his attention. He realized he had his cutlasses in his hands.

He watched Orfantal stride from a warren, Brood appearing behind him. He saw Stonny Menackis, looking down on three corpses. Then the warlord was pushing past her, sparing but a single glance at the bodies on his way to where a fourth body lay – closer to where Gruntle stood. A Tiste Andii woman. Two figures crouched beside her, flesh rent, one whose soul still writhed in the grip of savage, chaotic sorcery. The other ... Silverfox, round face streaked with tears.

He saw Kruppe, flanked by Hetan and Cafal. The Daru was pale, glassy-eyed, and seemed moments from unconsciousness. Strange, that, for it was not grief that so assailed the Daru. He saw Hetan suddenly reach for him even as he collapsed.

But the man Gruntle was looking for was nowhere to be seen.

He strode to the south crest to observe the positioning of his legion. They were readying weapons. Assembling below them were the Grey Swords, clearly preparing to advance on the city—

—a city shrouded in smoke, lit with the flash of sorcery, of munitions, a city ripping itself apart—

Gruntle's hunting gaze found the man.

Itkovian.

Walking towards the T'lan Imass.

A sharp cry sounded from the hilltop behind Gruntle, and he turned to see Silverfox straightening from Korlat's side, wheeling round—

But the tens of thousands of T'lan Imass faced Itkovian now.

Gruntle watched his friend's steps slow, then stop when he was twenty paces from the undead warriors.

Silverfox screamed in comprehension, began running—

Aye, Summoner. You were about to send them against the K'Chain Che'Malle. Gruntle did not need to stand within hearing range to know what Itkovian said, then, to the silent T'lan Imass.

You are in pain. I would embrace you now . . .

He felt his god's horror, burgeoning to overwhelm his own—

As the T'lan Imass made reply.

Falling to their knees. Heads bowing.

Ah, Summoner . . .

And, now, it was far too late.

CHAPTER TWENTY-FIVE

There can be no true rendition of betrayal, for the
moment hides within itself, sudden, delivering such
comprehension that one would surrender his or her
own soul to deny all that has come to pass. There
can be no true rendition of betrayal, but of that day,
Ormulogun's portrayal is the closest to what was true
that any mortal could hope to achieve . . .

N'aruhl's Commentary on Ormulogun's
Slaying of Whiskeyjack

Footsteps in the hallway announced yet another guest
– Coll had no idea if invited or not – and he pulled
his gaze away from the two ancient Rath' councillors
kneeling before the burial pit, to see a robed figure appear
in the doorway. Unmasked, face strangely indistinct.

The Knight of Death swung in a crackle of armour to
face the newcomer. 'K'rul,' he grated, 'my Lord welcomes
you to his sacred abode.'

*K'rul? Isn't there an old temple in Darujhistan – the one with
the belfry – K'rul's Belfry. Some kind of elder . . .* Coll glanced
over, met Murillio's eyes, saw the same slow realization writ
plain on his friend's features. *An Elder God has entered this
chamber. Stands a half-dozen paces away. Beru fend us all!
Another blood-hungry bastard from antiquity—*

K'rul strode towards the Mhybe.

Coll, hand settling on the grip of his sword, fear rising to lodge in his throat, stepped into the Elder God's path. 'Hold,' he growled. His heart pounded as he locked gazes with K'rul, seeing in those eyes . . . nothing. Nothing at all. 'If you're planning on opening her throat on that altar, well, Elder God or not, I won't make it easy for you.'

Rath'Togg's toothless mouth dropped open in a gasp on the other side of the pit.

The Knight of Death made a sound that might have been laughter, then said in a voice that was no longer his own, 'Mortals are nothing if not audacious.'

Murillio moved up to stand at Coll's side, raising a trembling hand to close on the hilt of his rapier.

K'rul glanced at the undead champion and smiled. 'Their most admirable gift, Hood.'

'Until it turns belligerent, perhaps. Then, it is best answered by annihilation.'

'Your answer, yes.' The Elder God faced Coll. 'I have no desire to harm the Mhybe. Indeed, I am here for her . . . salvation.'

'Well then,' snapped Murillio, 'maybe you can explain why there's a burial pit in here!'

'That shall become clear in time . . . I hope. Know this: something has happened. Far to the south. Something . . . unexpected. The consequences are unknown – to us all. None the less, the time has come for the Mhybe—'

'And what does that mean, precisely?' Coll demanded.

'Now,' the Elder God replied, moving past him to kneel before the Mhybe, 'she must dream for real.'

They were gone. Gone from her soul, and with their departure – with what Itkovian had done, was doing – all that she had hoped to achieve had been torn down, left in ruins.

Silverfox stood motionless, cold with shock.

Kallor's brutal attack had revealed yet another truth – the T'lan Ay had abandoned her. A loss that twisted a knife blade into her soul.

Once more, betrayal, the dark-hearted slayer of faith. Nightchill's ancient legacy. Tattersail and Bellurdan Skullcrusher both – killed by the machinations of Tayschrenn, the hand of the Empress. *And now ... Whiskeyjack. The two marines, my twin shadows for so long. Murdered.*

Beyond the kneeling T'lan Imass waited the K'Chain Che'Malle undead. The huge creatures made no move towards the T'lan Imass – yet. *They need only wade into the ranks, blades chopping down, and begin destroying. My children are beyond resistance. Beyond caring. Oh, Itkovian, you noble fool.*

And this mortal army – she saw the Grey Swords down below, readying lassos, lances and shields – preparing to charge the K'Chain Che'Malle. Dujek's army was being destroyed within the city – the north gate had to be breached. She saw Gruntle, Trake's Mortal Sword, leading his motley legion down to join the Grey Swords. She saw officers riding before the wavering line of Malazans, rallying the heartbroken soldiers. She saw Artanthos – Tayschrenn – preparing to unleash his warren. Caladan Brood knelt beside Korlat, High Denul sorcery enwreathing the Tiste Andii woman. Orfantal stood behind the warlord – she felt the dragon in his blood, icy hunger, eager to return.

All for naught. The Seer and his demonic condors ... and the K'Chain Che'Malle ... will kill them all.

She had no choice. She would have to begin. Defy the despair, begin all that she had set in motion so long ago. Without hope, she would take the first step on the path.

Silverfox opened the Warren of Tellann.

Vanished within.

A mother's love abides.

But I was never meant to be a mother. I wasn't ready. I was unprepared to give so much of myself. A self I had only begun to unveil.

The Mhybe could have turned away. At the very beginning. She could have defied Kruppe, defied the Elder God, the Imass – what were these lost souls to her? Malazans, one and all. The enemy. Dire in the ways of magic. All with the blood of Rhivi staining their hands.

Children were meant to be gifts. The physical manifestation of love between a man and a woman. And for that love, all manner of sacrifice could be borne.

Is it enough that the child issued from my flesh? Arrived in this world in the way of all children? Is the simple pain of birth the wellspring of love? Everyone else believed so. They took the bond of mother and child as given, a natural consequence of the birth itself.

They should not have done that.

My child was not innocent.

Conceived out of pity, not love; conceived with dread purpose – to take command of the T'lan Imass, to draw them into yet another war – to betray them.

And now, the Mhybe was trapped. Lost in a dreamworld too vast to comprehend, where forces were colliding, demanding that she act, that she do . . . *something.*

Ancient gods, bestial spirits, a man imprisoned in pain, in a broken, twisted body. This cage of ribs before me – is it his? The one I spoke with, so long ago? The one writhing so in a mother's embrace? Are we as kin, he and I? Both trapped in ravaged bodies, both doomed to slide ever deeper into this torment of pain?

The beast waits for me – the man waits for me. We must reach out to each other. To touch, to give proof to both of us that we are not alone.

Is this what awaits us?

The cage of ribs, the prison, must be broken from the outside.

Daughter, you may have forsaken me. But this man, this brother of mine, him I shall not forsake.

She could not be entirely sure, but she believed that she started crawling once more.

The beast howled in her mind, a voice raw with agony.

She would have to free it, if she could. Such was pity's demand.

Not love.

Ah, now I see . . .

Thus.

He would embrace them. He would take their pain. In this world, where all had been taken from him, where he walked without purpose, burdened with the lives and deaths of tens of thousands of mortal souls – unable to grant them peace, unable – unwilling – to simply cast them off, he was not yet done.

He would embrace them. These T'lan Imass, who had twisted all the powers of the Warren of Tellann into a ritual that devoured their souls. A ritual that had left them – in the eyes of all others – as little more than husks, animated by a purpose they had set outside themselves, yet were chained to – for eternity.

Husks, yet . . . anything but.

And that was a truth Itkovian had not expected, had no way to prepare for.

Insharak Ulan, who was born third to Inal Thoom and Sultha A'rad of the Nashar Clan that would come to be Kron's own, in the spring of the Year of Blighted Moss, below the Land of Raw Copper, and I remember—

I remember—

A snow hare, trembling, no more than a dusk-shadow's length from my reach, my child's arm and hand stretching. Streaks in the white, the promise of summer. Trembling hand, trembling hare, born together in the snows just past. Reaching out. Lives touching – small-heart-patter, slow-drum-hunger my chest's answer to the world's hidden music – I remember—

Kalas Agkor – my arms wrapped about little Jala, little sister, hot with fever but the fire grew too hot, and so, in my arms, her flesh cooled to dawn-stone, mother keening – Jala was the ember now lifeless, and from that day, in mother's eyes, I became naught but its bed of ash—

Ulthan Arlad herd-tracks in the snow, tufts of moult, ay on the flanks, we were hungry in that year yet held to the trail, old as it was—

Karas Av riding Bonecaster Thal's son in the Valley of Deep Moss, beneath the sun we were breaking the ancient law – I was breaking the ancient law, I, mate to Ibinahl Chode, made the boy a man before his circle was knotted—

—in the Year of the Broken Antler, we found wolf cubs—

—I dreamed I said no to the Ritual, I dreamed I strode to Onos T'oolan's side—

—a face streaming tears – my tears—

—Chode, who watched my mate lead the boy into the valley, and knew the child would be remade into a man – knew that he was in the gentlest of hands—

—the grasslands were burning—

—ranag in the Horned Circle—

—I loved her so—

Voices, a flood, memories – these warriors had not lost them. They had known them as living things – within their own dead bodies.

Known them.

For almost three hundred thousand years.

—friend to Onrack of the Logros, I last saw him kneeling amidst the corpses of his clan. All slain in the street, yet the Soletaken were finally broken. Ah, at such a cost—

—oh, heart laid at his feet, dear Legana Breed. So clever, sharpest of wit, oh how he made me laugh—

—our eyes met, Maenas Lot and I, even as the Ritual began its demand, and we saw the fear in each other's eyes – our love, our dreams of more children, to fill the spaces of those we had lost out on the ice, our lives of mingled shadows – our love, that must now be surrendered—

—I, Cannig Tol, watched as my hunters hurled their spears. She fell without making a sound, the last of her kind on this continent, and had I a heart, it would have burst, then. There was no justice in this war. We'd left our gods behind, and knelt only before an altar of brutality. Truth. And

I, Cannig Tol, shall not turn away from truth—

Itkovian's mind reeled back, sought to fend off the diluvial tide, to fight himself clear of his own soul's answering cry of sorrow, the torrent of truths shattering his heart, the secrets of the T'lan Imass – *no, the Ritual – how – Fener's Tusks, how could you have done that to yourselves?*

And she has denied you. She has denied you all—

He could not escape – he had embraced their pain, and the flood of memories was destroying him. Too many, too fiercely *felt* – relived, every moment relived by these lost creatures – he was drowning.

He had promised them release, yet he knew now he would fail. There was no end, no way he could encompass this yearning gift, this desperate, begging desire.

He was alone—

— am Pran Chole, you must hear me, mortal!

Alone. Fading . . .

Hear me, mortal! There is a place – I can lead you! You must carry all we give you – not far, not long – carry us, mortal! There is a place!

Fading . . .

Mortal! For the Grey Swords – you must do this! Hold on – succeed – and you will gift them. I can lead you!

For the Grey Swords . . .

Itkovian reached out—

—and a hand, solid, warm, clasped his forearm—

The ground crawled beneath her. Lichens – green-stalked and green-cupped, the cups filled with red; another kind, white as bone, intricate as coral; and beneath these, grey shark-skin on the mostly buried stones – an entire world, here, a hand's width from the ground.

Her slow, inexorable passage destroyed it all, scraped a swathe through the lichens' brittle architecture. She wanted to weep.

Ahead, close now, the cage of bone and stained skin, the creature within it a shapeless, massive shadow.

Which still called to her, still exerted its terrible demand.

To reach.

To touch the ghastly barrier.

The Mhybe suddenly froze in place, a vast, invisible weight pinning her to the ground.

Something was happening.

The earth beneath her twisting, flashes through the gathering oblivion, the air suddenly hot. A rumble of thunder—

Drawing up her legs, pushing with one arm, she managed to roll onto her back. Breath rasping in shallow lungs, she stared—

The hand held firm. Itkovian began to comprehend. Behind the memories awaited the pain, awaited all that he come to embrace. Beyond the memories, absolution was his answering gift – could he but survive . . .

The hand was leading him. Through a mindscape. Yet he strode across it as would a giant, the land distant below him.

Mortal, shed these memories. Free them to soak the earth in the season's gift. Down to the earth, mortal – through you, they can return life to a dying, desolate land.

Please. You must comprehend. Memories belong in the soil, in stone, in wind. They are the land's unseen meaning, such that touches the souls of all who would look – truly look – upon it. Touches, in faintest whisper, old, almost shapeless echoes – to which a mortal life adds its own.

Feed this dreamscape, mortal.

And know this. We kneel before you. Silenced in our hearts by what you offer to us, by what you offer of yourself.

You are Itkovian, and you would embrace the T'lan Imass.

Shed these memories – weep for us, mortal—

Heaving, churning cloud where before there had been naught but a formless, colourless, impossibly distant dome – the cloud spreading, tumbling out to fill the entire sky, drawing dark curtains across bruised rainbows. Lightning, crimson-stained, flickered from horizon to horizon.

She watched the falling, watched the descent – rain, no, hail—

It struck. Drumming roar on the ground, the sound filling her ears – sweeping closer—

To pummel her.

She screamed, throwing up her hands.

Each impact was explosive, something more than simply frozen rain.

Lives. Ancient, long forgotten lives.

And memories—

All raining down.

The pain was unbearable—

Then cessation, a shadow slipping over her, close, a figure, hunched beneath the trammelling thud of hail. A warm, soft hand on her brow, a voice—

'Not much further, dear lass. This storm – unexpected—' the voice broke, gasping as the deluge intensified, 'yet . . . wonderful. But you must not stop now. Here, Kruppe will help you . . .'

Shielding as much of her from the barrage as he could, he began dragging her forward, closer . . .

Silverfox wandered. Lost, half blinded by the tears that streamed without surcease. What she had begun as a child, on a long forgotten barrow outside the city of Pale – what she had begun so long ago – now seemed pathetic.

She had denied the T'lan Imass.

Denied the T'lan Ay.

But only for a time – or so had been her intent. A brief time, in which she would work to fashion the world that awaited them. The spirits that she had gathered, spirits who would serve that ancient people, become their gods – she had meant them to bring healing to the T'lan Imass, to their long-bereft souls.

A world where her mother was young once more.

A dreamworld, gift of K'rul. Gift of the Daru, Kruppe.

Gift of love, in answer to all she had taken from her mother.

But the T'lan Ay had turned away, were silent to her desperate call – and now Whiskeyjack was dead. Two marines, two women whose solid presence she had come to depend on – more than they could ever have realized. Two marines, killed defending her.

Whiskeyjack. All that was Tattersail keened with inconsolable grief. She had turned from him as well. Yet he had stepped into Kallor's path.

He had done that, for he remained the man he had always been.

And now, lost too were the T'lan Imass. The man, Itkovian, the mortal, Shield Anvil without a god, who had taken into himself the slain thousands of Capustan – he had opened his arms—

You cannot embrace the pain of the T'lan Imass. Were your god still with you, he would have refused your thought. You cannot. They are too much. And you, you are but one man – alone – you cannot take their burden. It is impossible.

Heart-breakingly brave.

But impossible.

Ah, Itkovian . . .

Courage had defeated her, but not her own – which had never been strong – no, the courage of those around her. On all sides – Coll and Murillio, with their misguided honour, who had stolen her mother and were no doubt guarding her even now, as she slowly died. Whiskeyjack and the two marines. Itkovian. And even Tayschrenn, who had torn himself – badly – unleashing his warren to drive Kallor away. Such extraordinary, tragically misguided courage—

I am Nightchill, Elder Goddess. I am Bellurdan, Thelomen Skullcrusher. I am Tattersail, who was once mortal. And I am Silverfox, flesh and blood Bonecaster, Summoner of the T'lan.

And I have been defeated.

By mortals—

The sky heaved over her – she looked up. Eyes widening in disbelief—

1074

The wolf thrashed, battered against the bone bars of its cage – its cage . . . *my ribs. Trapped. Dying—*

And that is a pain I share.

His chest was on fire, blossoms of intense agony lashing into him as if arriving from somewhere outside, a storm, blistering the skin covering his ribs—

—yet it grew no stronger, indeed, seemed to fade, as if with each wounding something was imparted to him, a gift—

Gift? This pain? How – what is it? What comes to me?

Old, so very old. Bittersweet, lost moments of wonder, of joy, of grief – a storm of memories, not his – so many, arriving like ice, then melting in the flare of impact – he felt his flesh grow numb beneath the unceasing deluge—

—was suddenly tugged away—

Blinking in the darkness, his lone eye as blind as the other one – the one he had lost at Pale. Something was pounding at his ears, a sound, then. Shrieking, the floor and walls shaking, chains snapping, dust raining from the low ceiling. *I am not alone in here. Who? What?*

Claws gouged the flagstones near his head, frantic and yearning.

Reaching. It wants me. What does? What am I to it?

The concussions were growing closer. And now voices, desperate bellowing coming from the other side of walls . . . down a corridor, perhaps. Clash of weapons, screams and gurgles, clatter of armour – pieces dancing on the floor.

Toc shifted his head – and saw something in the darkness. Huge, straining as it shrieked without pause. Massive, taloned hands stretched imploringly – reaching out—

For me.

Grey light flashed in the cavern, revealing in an instant the monstrous, fat-layered reptile chained opposite Toc, its eyes lit with terror. The stone that was within reach of the creature was gouged with countless scars, on all sides, a hatch-marked nightmare of madness, triggering horror within the Malazan ... for it was a nightmare he recognized within himself.

She – she is my soul—

The Seer stood before him, moving in desperate, jerky motions – the old man's body, that the Jaghut had occupied for so long, was falling to pieces – and muttering a singsong chant as, ignoring Toc, he edged ever closer to the Matron, to Mother.

The enormous beast cringed, claws scraping as it pushed itself against the wall. Its shrieks did not pause, resounding through the cavern.

The Seer held something in his hands, pallid, smooth and oblong – an egg, not from a bird. A lizard's egg, latticed in grey magic.

Magic that waxed with every word of the Seer's song.

Toc watched as something exploded from the Matron's body, a coruscation of power that sought to flee upward—

—but was, instead, snared by the web of sorcery; snared, then drawn into the egg in the Seer's hands.

The Matron's shrieking suddenly ceased. The creature settled back with a mindless whimper.

In the numbing silence within the cavern, Toc could now hear more clearly the sounds of battle in the corridor beyond. Close, and closing.

The Seer, clutching the Finnest, spun to stare down at Toc. The Jaghut's smile split the corpse's desiccated lips. 'We shall return,' he whispered.

The sorcery blossomed once more, then, as heavy chains clattered freely to the floor, darkness returned.

And Toc knew that he was alone within the cavern. The Seer had taken Mother's power, and then he had taken her as well.

The wolf thrashed in his chest, launching spikes of pain along his broken, malformed limbs. It yearned to loose its howl, its call to lover and to kin. Yet it could not draw breath—

—*cannot draw breath. It dies. The hail, these savage gifts,*

1076

they mean nothing. With me, the god's fatal choice, we die—

The sounds of fighting had stopped. Toc heard iron bars snap, one after another, heard metal clang on the flagstones.

Then someone was crouching down beside him. A hand that was little more than rough bone and tendon settled on Toc's forehead.

The Malazan could not see. There was no light. But the hand was cool, its weight gentle.

'Hood? Have you come for us, then?' The words were clearly spoken in his mind, but came out incomprehensibly – and he realized that his tongue was gone.

'Ah, my friend,' the figure replied in a rasp. 'It is I, Onos T'oolan, once of the Tarad Clan, of the Logros T'lan Imass, but now kin to Aral Fayle, to Toc the Younger.'

Kin.

Withered arms gathered him up.

'We are leaving now, young brother.'

Leaving?

Picker eyed the breach. The bravado that had been behind her proclamation that they would follow the T'lan Imass into the keep had not survived a sudden return to caution once they came within sight of the fortress. It was under assault, and whatever enemy had stormed into the keep had kicked hard the hornet nest.

K'Chain Che'Malle were thundering back through the compound gate. Sorcerous detonations shook the entire structure. Urdomen and Beklites raced along the top of the walls. Twisting spirals of grey lightning writhed skyward from the south roof, linking the score of condors wheeling overhead. Beyond it, filling the sky above the harbour, was an enormous storm-cloud, flashes burgeoning from its heaving depths.

The lieutenant glanced back at her paltry squads. They'd lost the three badly wounded soldiers, as she had expected. Not one of the Bridgeburners crouching in the smoke-hazed street had been spared – she saw far too much blood on the soot-smeared uniforms behind her.

To the northwest, the sounds of battle continued, drawing no closer. Picker knew that Dujek would have sought to reach the keep, if at all possible. From what she could hear, however, he was being pushed back, street by street.

The gambit had failed.

Leaving us on our own.

'K'Chain Che'Malle!' a soldier hissed from the back. 'Coming up behind us!'

'Well, that settles it, then,' Picker muttered. 'Doubletime to Hedge's breach!'

The Bridgeburners sprinted across the rubble-littered street.

Blend was the first to complete her scramble over the tower's wreckage. Immediately beyond was a shattered building – three walls and half of the roof remaining. Within lay dusty darkness, and what might be a doorway far to the left of the room's far wall.

Two steps behind Blend, Picker leapt clear of the tumbled stone blocks to land skidding on the room's floor – colliding with a cursing, backpedalling Blend.

Feet tangling, the two women fell.

'Damn it, Blend—'

'Guards—'

A third voice cut in. 'Picker! Lieutenant!'

As her Bridgeburners gathered behind her, Picker sat up to see Hedge, Bluepearl and seven additional Bridgeburners – the ones who had taken crossbows to the top of the wall and had survived the consequences – emerge from the shadows.

'We tried getting back to you—'

'Never mind, Hedge,' Picker said, clambering to her feet. 'You played it right, soldier, trust me—'

Hedge was holding a cusser in one hand, which he raised with a grin. 'Held one back—'

'Did a T'lan Imass come through here?'

1078

'Aye, a beat-up bastard, looked neither left nor right – just walked right past us – deeper into the keep—'

A Bridgeburner to the rear shouted, 'We got that K'Chain Che'Malle coming up behind us!'

'Through the door back there!' Hedge squealed. 'Clear the way, idiots! I've been waiting for this—'

Picker began shoving her soldiers towards the back wall.

The sapper scrambled back towards the breach.

The following events were a tumble in Picker's mind—

Blend gripped her arm and bodily threw her towards the doorway, where her soldiers were plunging through into whatever lay beyond. Picker swore, but Blend's hands were suddenly on her back, pushing her face first through the portal. Picker twisted with a snarl, and saw over Blend's shoulder—

The K'Chain Che'Malle seemed to flow as it raced over the rubble, blades lifting.

Hedge looked up – to find himself four paces away from the charging reptile.

Picker heard him grunt, a muted, momentary sound—

The sapper threw the cusser straight down.

The K'Chain Che'Malle was already swinging – two huge blades descending—

The explosion beat them clean.

Blend and Picker were thrown through the doorway. The lieutenant's head snapped back to the thudding, staccato impact of flying stones against her helm and the lowered visor and cheek-guards. Those that made it past lanced fire into her face, filled her nose and mouth with blood.

Deafened, she reeled back through clouds of dust and smoke.

Voices were screaming – issuing from what seemed very far away then swiftly closing to surround her.

Stones falling – a cross-beam of tarred wood, raging with flames, sweeping down, ending with a solid thud and crunch of bones – a death-groan amidst the chaos, so close to Picker that she wondered if it wasn't her own.

Hands gripped her once again, pulled her round, propelled her down what seemed to be a corridor.

A tunnel of smoke and dust – no air – the pounding of boots, blind collisions, curses – darkness – that suddenly dissipated.

Picker stumbled into the midst of her soldiers, spitting blood, coughing. Around them, a room littered with dead Beklites, another door, opposite, that looked to have been shattered with a single punch. A lone lantern swung wildly from a hook above them.

'Look!' someone grunted. 'A dog's been chewing on the lieutenant's chin!'

Not even a jest – simply the absurd madness of battle. Shaking her head to a spatter of blood, Picker spat again and surveyed her troops through stinging, streaming eyes.

'Blend?' The name came out mangled but understandable.

Silence.

'Bucklund – back into the corridor! Find her!'

The Twelfth Squad's sergeant was back a moment later, dragging a blood-drenched body through the doorway. 'She's breathing – Hood knows how! Her back's full of stones and shards!'

Picker dropped to her knees beside her friend. 'You damned idiot,' she mumbled.

'We should've had Mallet with us,' Bucklund grumbled beside her.

Aye, not the only mistake in this fouled-up game.

'Oh!' a woman's voice cried. 'You are not Pannions!'

Weapons swung to the doorway.

A woman in a blindingly white telaba stood there, her long black hair shimmering, impossibly clean, perfectly combed. Veiled, stunningly beautiful eyes studied them. 'Have you, by any chance, seen three masked warriors? They should have passed this way, looking for the throne room, assuming there is one, that is. You might have heard some fighting—'

'No,' Bucklund growled. 'I mean, yes, we've heard fighting. Everywhere, ma'am. That is—'

'Shut up,' Picker sighed. 'No,' she said to the woman, 'we ain't seen no three masked warriors—'

'What of a T'lan Imass?'

'As a matter of fact, yeah—'

'Excellent! Tell me, does she still have all those swords impaling her? I can't imagine she'd leave—'

'What swords?' Picker demanded. 'Besides, it was male. I think.'

'It was,' another soldier piped up, then reddened as her comrades swung to her with broad grins.

'A male T'lan Imass?' The white-robed woman raised a finger to her full lips, then smiled, 'Why, that would be Tool! Excellent!' The smile vanished. 'Unless, of course, Mok finds him . . .'

'Who are you?' Picker demanded.

'You know, dear, it's growing increasingly difficult to understand what you are saying through all that blood and such. I believe you're Malazans, yes? Unwitting allies, but you are all so terribly injured. I have an idea, a wonderful idea – as are all my ideas, of course. Wonderful, that is. We are here, you see, to effect the rescue of one Toc the Younger, a soldier of—'

'Toc the Younger?' Picker repeated. 'Toc? But he's—'

'A prisoner of the Seer, alas. A distressing fact, and I dislike being distressed. It irritates me. Immeasurably. Now, as I was saying, I have an idea. Assist me in this rescue, and I will heal those of you who need healing – which seems to be all of you.'

Picker gestured down at Blend. 'Deal. Start with her.'

As the woman stepped into the room, Bucklund shouted and scrabbled back from the doorway.

Picker looked up. A massive wolf stood in the hallway beyond, eyes gleaming through the dust-shrouded gloom.

The woman glanced back. 'Oh, not to worry. That is Baaljagg. Garath has wandered off, I believe. Busy killing

Pannions, I expect. He seems to have acquired a taste for Seerdomin . . . now, this poor woman – well, we'll have you right in no time, dear . . .'

'What in Hood's name is happening over there?'

On the other side of the low wall, a flight of stairs gave access to the parapet overlooking the harbour and the bay beyond – or, rather, so Paran concluded, since nothing else made sense. In any case, some kind of approach was being contested, and from the screams, whatever was on its way to the flat rooftop was wreaking havoc on the defenders.

Beside Paran, Quick Ben raised his head a fraction. 'I don't know and I'm not popping up for a look, either,' he said in answer to the captain's question, 'but let's hope it proves a worthwhile diversion. I can't keep us here much longer, without those condors finding us.'

'Something's keeping them busy,' Spindle asserted, 'and you know it, Quick. If one of them took the time to look hard – we'd be feeding the chicks in its nest by now.'

'You're right.'

'Then what in Hood's name are we still doing here?'

Good question. Paran twisted round, looked back along the roof to the north. There was a trapdoor there.

'We're still here,' Quick Ben grated, 'because this is where we need to be—'

'Hold it,' Paran growled, reaching up to wipe what he thought was sweat from his eyes, though the smear on his hand was red – the stitches on his temple had pulled loose. 'Not quite true, Quick. It's where you and I need to be. Mallet, if there's anything left of the Bridgeburners, they need you right now.'

'Aye, Captain, and knowing that's been eating me up inside.'

'All right. Listen, then. The fiery Abyss has broken loose down in this keep under us. We've no idea who's doing the fighting, but we do know one thing – they're no friends of the Pannions. So, Mallet, take Spindle and the rest – that trapdoor back there looks flimsy enough to break open if it's locked.'

'Aye, Captain. Only, how do we get there without being seen?'

'Spindle's right about those condors – they're busy with something else, and looking more agitated with every beat of the heart. It's a short sprint, Healer. But if you're not willing to risk it—'

Mallet glanced at Spindle, then at Detoran and Trotts. Finally, at Antsy. The sergeant nodded. Mallet sighed. 'Aye, sir, we'll give it a go.'

Paran glanced at Quick Ben. 'Any objections, Wizard?'

'No, Captain. At the very least . . .' He fell silent.

At the very least, they've a better chance of getting out alive. I hear you, Quick. 'OK, Mallet, make your run when you're ready.'

'Push and pull, Captain.'

'And to you, Healer.'

With a grunted command, the squad scrambled for the trapdoor.

Dujek dragged the wounded soldier through the doorway, and only then noticed that the man's legs had been left behind, and the trail of blood leading back to the limbs thinned to virtually nothing by the time it reached the threshold. He let the body drop, sagged against the frame.

The K'Chain Che'Malle had cut through the company in the span of a dozen heartbeats, and though the Hunter had lost an arm, it had not slowed as it thumped westward – in search of another company of hapless Malazans.

Dujek's elite bodyguard of Untan heavy infantry lay in a chopped ruin in front of the building into which they had pushed the High Fist. As sworn, they'd given their lives in his defence. At the moment, however, Dujek would rather they'd failed – or, better yet, fled.

Locked in battle since dawn with Beklites, Urdomen and Seerdomin, Onearm's Host had more than held its own.

And when the first dozen or so K'Chain Che'Malle appeared, Moranth munitions – cussers and burners – destroyed the undead K'ell Hunters. The same fate befell the second wave. By the time the third arrived, the cussers were gone, and soldiers died by the score. The fifth and sixth waves were met only with swords, and battle became slaughter.

Dujek had no idea how many remained among the five thousand Malazans who had been delivered into the city. He did not think a cohesive defence still existed. The battle had become a hunt, plain and simple. A cleansing by the K'Chain Che'Malle of pockets of Malazan resistance.

Until recently, he could still hear sounds of battle – of collapsing walls and perhaps sorcery – from the keep, though perhaps, he now reflected, he had been wrong in that – the storm-cloud that filled the sky to the south was itself thundering, arcs of lightning splitting the sky to lance at the thrashing seas below. Its rage now overwhelmed all other sounds.

A scrabble of boots behind him. Dujek swung about, shortsword in hand.

'High Fist!'

'Which company, soldier?'

'Eleventh, sir,' the woman gasped. 'Captain Hareb sent a squad to look for you, High Fist. I'm what's left.'

'Does Hareb still hold?'

'Aye, sir. We're collecting souvenirs – pieces of K'Chain Che'Malle.'

'And how in Hood's name are you managing that?'

'Twist, sir, he led a final flight in with the last of the munitions – mostly sharpers and crackers, High Fist – but the sappers are rigging buildings along our retreat, dropping tons of brick and stone on the damned lizards – your pardon, sir – on the Hunters.'

'Where is Hareb's company right now, soldier?'

'Not far, High Fist. Follow me.'

Hareb, that Seven Cities nobleborn with the permanent sneer. Gods, I could kiss the man.

Moving to the head of his legion, Gruntle watched the Shield Anvil of the Grey Swords approach. The woman reined in even as he arrived.

'I greet you, sir,' she said, only the lower half of her face visible beneath the helm's broad, flaring cheek-guards. 'We are about to advance upon the enemy – would you flank us?'

The Daru grimaced. 'No, Shield Anvil.'

She hesitated, then gave a brusque nod and gathered up her reins. 'As you wish, sir. No dishonour in refusing a suicidal engagement.'

'You misunderstand,' Gruntle interrupted her. 'My legion leads, you follow in our wake – as close as you can. We'll drive across that stone bridge and head straight for the gate. Granted, it looks damned solid, but we might still batter it down.'

'We are seeking to relieve Dujek Onearm, agreed, Mortal Sword?'

'Aye.' *And we both know we will fail.*

They turned at the sound of horns, the sudden staccato of Malazan drums.

The standard-bearer – sorcery swirling from the man like flecks of gold – seemed to have taken command, calling together the company officers. Along the line, shields were readied, locked overlapping. Pikes, twice the height of a man, wavered like wind-tugged reeds above the ranks of soldiery – an uncharacteristic unsteadiness that Gruntle found disturbing.

Artanthos had despatched a rider who rode towards the Daru and the Shield Anvil at a gallop.

The Malazan reined in. 'Sirs! The High Mage Tayschrenn would know your intentions!'

Gruntle bared his teeth. 'Tayschrenn, is it? Let's hear his, first.'

1085

'Dujek, sirs. These K'Chain Che'Malle must be broken, the gate breached, an assault on the defenders—'

'And what of the High Mage himself?' the Shield Anvil enquired.

'They're mages on the walls, sir. Tayschrenn will endeavour to deny their involvement. Orfantal and his Tiste Andii will seek to assist us in our attack upon the K'Chain Che'Malle, as will the shouldermen of the White Faces.'

'Inform the High Mage,' the Shield Anvil said, 'that Trake's Legion will initiate the charge, supported by my company.'

The soldier saluted and rode back towards the Malazan line.

Gruntle turned to study his followers. He wondered again at the effect that the Lord of Summer's gift had had upon these grim-faced Capans. *Like D'ivers . . . only in reverse. From many, to one – and such power!* They had crossed the land swift as a flowing shadow. Gruntle had found himself looking out upon the world with a tiger's eyes – no, not simply a tiger, a creature immortal, boundless in strength, a mass of muscle and bone within which was the Legion. *His* Legion. A will, fused, terrifyingly focused.

And now they would become that beast once again. This time, to enter battle.

His god seemed to possess a particular hatred for these K'Chain Che'Malle, as if Treach had a score to settle. The cold killer was giving way to bloodlust – a realization that left Gruntle vaguely troubled.

His gaze flicked to the hilltop – to see Caladan Brood, Korlat slowly straightening beside him. Distance was irrelevant – she was covered in blood, and he could feel the sickly pain that flowed and ebbed, then flowed again within her.

Brood's warren suffers, and if that's the case, then so too must . . . He swung round, back to where Artanthos – High Mage Tayschrenn – stood before the Malazan companies. *Ah, I see the price he pays . . .* 'Shield Anvil.'

'Sir?'

''Ware the mages on the city wall.'

'We await you, sir.'

Gruntle nodded.

A moment later, the Mortal Sword and his Legion were one, bones and muscle merging, identities – entire lives – swept under a deluge of cold, animal rage.

A tawny swirl, surging, flowing forward.

Ahead, K'Chain Che'Malle raised weapons. And stood their ground.

Again. We have done this before – no, not us. Our Lord. Tearing dead flesh . . . the spray of blood . . . blood . . . oh, Hood—

Kurald Galain, the darkness within the soul, flowing outward, filling her limbs, sweeping round to swallow her feelings – the comfort of oblivion. Korlat stood, her back to the three lifeless figures on the hilltop that still lay where they fell. Stood, silent, the power of her warren – flickering, dimming to surges of pain – reaching out, seeking her kin.

Caladan Brood, hammer unlimbered in his hands, was beside her. He was speaking, his rumbling voice as distant as thunder on the sea's horizon. 'Late afternoon. No earlier. It will be over long before then . . . one way or another. Korlat, please listen to me. You must seek your Lord – that storm-cloud, does Moon's Spawn hide within it? He said he would come. At the precise moment. He said he would strike . . .'

Korlat no longer heard him.

Orfantal was veering, there before the now marching Malazan forces, black, blossoming outward, wings spreading, sinuous neck lifting – a thudding pulsation of sorcery and the dragon was in the air, climbing—

Condors winged out from the keep, a dozen of the demonic creatures, each linked by a writhing chain of chaotic magic.

On the plain below, the beast that was the Mortal Sword and Trake's Legion seemed to flow in and out of her vision, blurred, deadly motion – and struck the line of K'Chain Che'Malle.

Sorcery stained the air around the impact in blood-spattered sheets as within the savage maelstrom blades flashed. A K'ell Hunter reeled away and toppled, its bones shattered. The huge tiger twisted from side to side as swords descended, tore into its flanks. Where each blade struck, human figures fell away from the beast, limbs severed, torsos cut through, heads crushed.

Sorcery was building along the top of the city wall.

Korlat saw Artanthos – Tayschrenn – step forward then, to answer it.

A golden wave appeared suddenly behind the K'Chain Che'Malle, rose for a moment, building, then tumbled forward. The ground it rolled over on its way to the wall burned with fierce zeal, then the wave lifted, climbed towards the Pannion mages.

This – this is what was launched against Moon's Spawn. This is what my Lord struggled against. Alone, in the face of such power—

The ground trembled beneath her boots as the wave crashed into the top of the wall to the west of the gate. Blinding – *this is High Telas, the Warren of Fire – child of Tellann—*

Chaotic magic exploded from the conflagration like shrapnel. The raging fire then dispersed.

The top third of the city wall, from near the gate and westward for at least forty paces, was simply gone. And with it, at least a dozen Pannion mages.

On the killing field, Trake's Legion was now surrounded by K'Chain Che'Malle, who were a match for the enormous beast's lightning speed. K'ell Hunters were falling, but the tiger was being, literally, cut to pieces.

The Grey Swords, all mounted, were attempting to open an avenue for it on the other side. Long, strangely barbed lances were being driven into Hunters from behind, fouling their steps as they wheeled to lash out at the enemy harrying them. Lassos spun in the air, snapped tight around necks, limbs—

A grey wave of sorcery raced out from the mages on the wall east of the gate, swept over the heads of those battling on the killing field, clambered through the air like some multilimbed beast – to strike Artanthos.

Coruscating fire met the assault, and both sorceries seemed to devour each other. When they vanished, Artanthos was on his knees. Soldiers ran towards him from the Malazan lines.

He is done. Too soon—

'Korlat!'

The bellow shook her. Blinking, she turned to Brood. 'What?'

'Call your Lord, Korlat! *Call him!*'

Call? I cannot. Could not – dare not.

'Korlat! Look to that damned storm-cloud!'

She twisted her head. Beyond the city, rising skyward in a churning, towering column, the storm-cloud was tearing itself apart even as it rose – rose, shreds spinning away, sunlight shafting through—

Moon's Spawn . . . not within – the cloud hid nothing. Nothing but senseless, empty violence. Dissipating.

Call him? Despair ripped through her. She heard her own dull reply, 'Anomander Rake is no more, Warlord.' *He is dead. He must be—*

'Then help your damned brother, woman! He is assailed—'

She looked up, saw Orfantal high above, harried by specks. Sorcery lanced at the black dragon like darts.

Brother . . . Korlat looked back down, at the Malazan ranks that had now closed with the K'Chain Che'Malle. Darkness shrouded them – Kurald Galain's whisper. *A whisper . . . and no more than a whisper—*

'Korlat!'

'Move away from me, Warlord. I shall now veer . . . and join my brother.'

'When you two are done with those condors, will you—'

She turned away from the killing field. 'This battle is lost, Caladan Brood. I fly to save Orfantal.' Without awaiting a reply, she strode down the slope, unfolding the power within her as she did so. Draconian blood, cold as ice in her veins, a promise of murder. Brutal, unwavering hunger.

Wings, into the sky.

Wedge-shaped head tilted, fixed on the condors circling her brother. Her talons twitched, then stretched in anticipation.

Caladan Brood stood on the very edge of the slope, the hammer in his hands. K'Chain Che'Malle had pulled away from the assault upon Trake's Legion – the giant tiger was dying, surrounded on all sides by flashing blades – and were now wading through the Malazan press, slaying soldiers by the score. Others pursued the Grey Swords, whose ranks had been scattered by the far too quick Hunters.

Barghast had closed from both flanks, to add their spilled blood to the slaughter.

Slowly, the warlord swung about and surveyed the hilltop behind him. Three bodies. Four Malazan soldiers who had carried an unconscious Kruppe to the summit and were now laying the Daru down.

Brood's eyes held on Kruppe, wondering at the man's sudden, inexplicable collapse, then he turned.

The T'lan Imass, in their tens of thousands, still kneeled, motionless, before Itkovian, who had himself sunk down, a mortal reflection of them. Whatever was happening there had taken them all far away, to a place from which it seemed there would be no return – not, in any case, until it was far too late.

No choice.

Burn . . . forgive me . . . .

Caladan Brood faced the city once more. Eyes on the

masses warring on the killing field below, the warlord slowly raised his hammer—

—then froze.

They came to yet another hallway filled with the dead and dying. Picker scowled. 'Mistress, how many in this Seguleh army you told us about?'

'Three, my dear. Clearly, we are on the right path—'

'The right path for what, Lady Envy?'

The woman turned. 'Hmm, an interesting point. The Seguleh are no doubt eagerly lobbying for an audience with the Seer, but who's to say the Seer has Toc the Younger with him? Indeed, is it not more likely that our friend lies in chains somewhere far below?'

Blend spoke from beside Picker. 'There looks to be a landing of some sort at the far end. Could be stairs . . .'

'Sharp-eyed,' Lady Envy murmured in appreciation. 'Baaljagg, dear pup, will you lead the way?'

The huge wolf slipped past noiselessly, somehow managing to stay silent even as it clambered over the bodies down the length of the corridor. At the far end, it halted, swung its long-snouted head back, eyes like smouldering coals.

'Ah, the all-clear,' Lady Envy sighed, softly clapping her hands. 'Come along, then, you grim-faced Malazans.'

As they approached, Blend plucked at Picker's sleeve. 'Lieutenant,' she whispered, 'there's fighting up ahead . . .'

They reached the landing. Dead Urdomen lay heaped, their bodies sprawled on steps that led upward. A second flight of stone stairs, leading down, showed only the flow of thickening blood from the landing.

Blend edged forward to crouch before the descending steps. 'There's tracks here in the blood,' she said, 'three sets . . . the first one, uh, bony, followed by someone in moccasins – a woman, I'd say—'

'In moccasins?' Lady Envy wondered, brows lifting. 'How peculiar. The bony ones are likely to be either Tool or

Lanas Tog. Now who might be following either of them? Such mystery! And the last set?'

Blend shrugged. 'Worn boots. A man's.'

The sound of fighting that Blend had detected earlier was audible to everyone now – from somewhere up the flight of stairs, distant, possibly at the uppermost floor, which was at least a half-dozen levels above them.

Baaljagg had limped to stand beside Blend. The wolf lowered its head, nose testing the footprints leading down.

A moment later the animal was a grey flash, racing downward and out of sight.

'Well!' Lady Envy said. 'The issue seems decided, wouldn't you say? The ailing pup has a certain . . . feeling for Toc the Younger. An affinity, to be more precise.'

'Your pardon,' Picker snapped, 'but what in Hood's name are you going on about?' *One more cryptic statement from this lady and I'll brain her.*

'That was rude. None the less, I will acknowledge that the matter is a secret but not one of my own, so I shall freely speak of it.'

'Oh good,' one of the soldiers behind Picker muttered, 'gossip.'

Lady Envy wheeled. 'Who said that?'

No-one spoke.

'I *abhor* gossip, I will have you all know. Now, shall I tell you the tale of two ancient gods, who each in turn found mortal flesh – or, rather, somewhat mortal flesh in the case of Baaljagg, but all too mortal flesh in the case of dear Toc the Younger?'

Picker stared at the woman, and was about to speak when one of her soldiers cursed loud and with feeling – and blades clashed—

—shouts—

A score Urdomen had just arrived from behind the squads, and the hallway was suddenly filled with vicious, close-in fighting.

Picker snapped out a hand and caught Blend's

blood-stiffened cloak, pulled. As the lieutenant dragged free her sword, she hissed: 'Head down the stairs, lass! We'll follow once we clear this up.' She shoved Blend towards the stairs, then spun.

'Will this take long?' Lady Envy asked, her voice somehow cutting through the tumult to echo in Picker's ears as she pushed into the press. The Urdomen were better armoured, fresher, and had had surprise on their side. Picker saw Bucklund reel, half his head cut away. 'No,' she grated, as two more Bridgeburners crumpled, 'it won't . . .'

Detoran had moved to point as the four Bridgeburners headed down the corridor. Mallet strode five paces behind the big Napan woman, Spindle trotting at his heels, followed by Antsy, with Trotts a dozen paces back as rearguard. Thus far, they'd found naught but bodies – Pannion bodies – cut down one and all by blades.

'Someone's a holy terror,' Spindle muttered behind the healer.

They could hear fighting, but the echoes were bouncing, making it difficult to determine the direction.

Detoran drew up and raised a hand, then waved Mallet forward.

'Stairs ahead,' she grunted. 'Going down.'

'Clear,' the healer observed.

'For now.'

Antsy joined them. 'What's the hold-up? We gotta keep moving.'

'We know, Sergeant,' Mallet said, then he swung back to the Napan. 'It'll have to do. Lead us down, Detoran.'

More corpses littered the stone steps, the blood making purchase uncertain.

They descended past two landings unchallenged. Halfway down the next flight, at a switchback in the stairs, Mallet heard the Napan grunt, and weapons suddenly rang.

A wordless shout from behind twisted into a Barghast warcry.

'Dammit!' Mallet snapped. Fighting above and below – they were in trouble. 'Spin, back up Antsy and Trotts! I'll lend Det a hand!'

'Aye, sir!'

The healer plunged down a half-dozen steps to the bend. Detoran had already pushed her attackers back to a landing. The healer saw, beyond the Napan, at least six Seerdomin, heavy, short-handled double-bladed axes in their gauntleted hands. Detoran, a shortsword in her left hand, broadsword in her right, had just cut down the warrior in front of her. Without hesitating, she stepped over the dying Seerdomin, reaching the landing.

The Seerdomin rushed her.

There was no way to get past the Napan. Swearing, Mallet sheathed his shortsword and unlimbered his crossbow. A quarrel already rested in the slot, held in place by a loop of leather that the healer now pulled clear. Ignoring the bellows and singing iron, he hooked the clawfoot over the braided string and cinched it back.

Up beyond the bend in the staircase, Trotts had begun chanting, broken only by an ominous shriek from Antsy. Fresh blood thinned with bile was streaming down the steps.

Mallet moved back to find a clear shot over Detoran.

The Napan had thrust her shortsword up into a Seerdomin's head from below. The blade jammed between the mandibles. Instead of pulling, Detoran pushed, sending the victim and weapon flying back to foul the two warriors beyond. With the broadsword in her right hand extended, she was keeping another Seerdomin at bay. He was swinging his shorter weapons at the blade in an effort to bat it aside so he could close, but Detoran made her heavy blade dance and weave as if it was a duellist's rapier.

Mallet's attention fixed on the two recovering Seerdomin. A third warrior was pulling the fallen Seerdomin away. The healer snapped the crossbow up and depressed the trigger. The weapon bucked in his hands.

One of the recovering Seerdomin shrieked, a quarrel buried to its leather fins in his chest. He sagged back.

A tumbling body knocked Mallet from his feet as he was about to reload. Cursing, the healer fell back against a side wall and made to kick the corpse away with his boots as he fumbled for a quarrel, then he saw that it was Antsy. Not yet dead, though his chest was sheathed in blood. From the sounds above, Trotts was pushing his way back up the stairs.

He twisted round at a shout from Detoran. She had lunged with her broadsword, breaking her timing to dip her blade round a desperate parry, then sliding the edge up and under the Seerdomin's helm, ripping open the side of the man's neck – even as his other axe slashed a wild arc, straight for Detoran's head.

The Napan threw her left shoulder into its path.

Chain snapped, blood sprayed. The axe-blade cut clear, carrying with it most of the muscle of Detoran's shoulder.

She reeled. Then, blood spurting, righted herself and rushed the remaining two Seerdomin.

The nearest one threw one of his axes.

The Napan chopped it aside then swung a backhand slash that the man barely managed to block. Detoran closed, dropping her sword and jamming her fingers into the helm's eye-slit. The momentum of her rush carried her round the man, twisting his head to follow.

Mallet heard an audible pop of vertebrae, even as he finished loading his crossbow. He raised it—

The last Seerdomin's axes flashed.

Detoran's right arm, stretched out with the fingers still snagged in the visor, was severed halfway between shoulder and elbow.

The second axe drove deep between her shoulder-blades, throwing her forward to slap face first against the landing's wall.

The Seerdomin moved forward to tug the second axe free.

Mallet's quarrel vanished into the man's right arm-pit.

1095

He buckled, then collapsed in a clatter of armour.

The healer, setting another quarrel into the slot, clambered to where Detoran still leaned, upright, face first against the wall. The rush of blood from her wounds had slowed to turgid streams.

He did not need to reach out to touch the Napan to know that she was dead.

Boots thumped on the stairs and the healer swung round to see Spindle stumbling onto the landing. He'd taken a blow against his pot-helm, snapping the brow-band and its rivets on one side. Blood painted that side of his face. His eyes were wild.

'A score of 'em up there, Mallet! Trotts is holding them off—'

'The damned idiot!' The healer finished loading his cross-bow and scrambled to the stairs, pausing briefly to examine Antsy. 'Find yourself a new helm, Spin, then follow!'

'What about Antsy?'

'He'll live a while longer. Hurry, damn you!'

The staircase was crowded with fresh bodies, all the way up to the next landing.

Mallet arrived in time to find himself caught in a descending rush – Seerdomin and, in their midst, a snarling Trotts, tumbling in a thrashing wall of flesh straight down onto the healer. A blade – the Barghast's – plunged through Mallet's shoulder, then whipped back out as they one and all fell onto the hard stone steps. Axe-blades, daggers, gauntlets, helms and greaves made the human avalanche a vicious shock of pain that did not end even when they were brought to a flailing halt at the bend in the stairwell.

Trotts was the first one to extricate himself, stabbing down with his shortsword, kicking and stamping with his boots. Cursing, Mallet dragged himself clear of the Barghast's frenzy, fire lancing from the wound in his shoulder.

Moments later, there was only the sound of gasping breaths in the stairwell.

The healer twisted round, found a wall at his back, and slowly pushed himself upright – to glare up at Trotts. 'You stabbed me, you bastard!'

Even as he said it, his words fell away as he looked at the Barghast. The huge warrior had taken more wounds than Mallet had thought possible. He had been chopped to pieces. Yet he did not even so much as waver as he grinned down at the healer. 'Stabbed you, did I? Good.'

Mallet grimaced. 'I see your point, you blue-toothed cattle-dog. Why should you get all the fun?'

'Aye. Where's Antsy and Det and Spin?'

'Landing below. Det's dead. We'll have to carry Antsy. From the sound, Spin's still looking for a new helm.'

'They'll all be too big,' Trotts growled. 'We need to find the kitchen – a cup.'

Mallet pushed himself from the wall. 'Good idea. Let's get going, then.'

'I'll take point, now – cooks are dangerous.'

The Barghast, streaming blood, moved past the healer.

'Trotts.'

He paused. 'Aye?'

'Spin said a score.'

'Aye.'

'All dead?'

'Maybe half. The rest ran away.'

'You scared them off, did you?'

'Spin's hairshirt, is my guess. Come on, Healer.'

Toc's head lolled, the scene rising and falling as the T'lan Imass carried him down the torchlit corridor. Occasionally, Tool stepped over a body or two.

My brother. He called me that.

I have no brother.

Only a mother.

And a god. Seer, where are you? Will you not come for me, now? The wolf dies. You have won. Free me, Lord of All. Free me to walk through Hood's Gate.

They reached an arched doorway, the door lying shattered on this side. Wood still nailed to bronze bands shifted unsteadily underfoot as Tool crossed it. A large, domed chamber, twenty paces across, was before them. It had once been filled with strange mechanisms – machines used by torturers – but these had all been smashed into ruin, flung to the sides to lean like broken-boned beasts against the walls.

Victims of rage . . . was this Tool's work? This undead, emotionless . . . thing?

A sudden clang of blades from the arched doorway opposite.

The T'lan Imass stopped. 'I shall have to set you down, now.'

Down. Yes. It's time.

Toc twisted his head as Tool slowly lowered him to the flagstones. A figure stood in the doorway on the other side of the chamber. Masked, white enamel, twin-scarred. A sword in each hand. *Oh, I know you, do I not?*

The figure said nothing and simply waited until Tool had stepped away from Toc. The battered T'lan Imass drew the two-handed flint sword from his shoulder sling, then spoke, 'Mok, Third among the Seguleh, when you are done with me, would you take Toc the Younger from this place?'

Lying on his side, Toc watched as the masked warrior tilted his head in acknowledgement. *Mok, you damned fool. You are about to kill my friend . . . my brother.*

Blurred motion, two warriors closing too fast for Toc's lone eye to follow. Iron sang with stone. Sparks shooting through the gloom to light the broken instruments of torture surrounding them, in racing flashes of revelation – shadows dancing in the wood and metal tangle, and, to Toc, it was as if all the accumulated pain that these mechanisms had absorbed in their lifetimes was suddenly freed.

By the sparks.

By the two warriors . . . and all that sheathed their hidden souls.

Freed, writhing, dancing, spider-bitten – *mad, frantic in answer . . .*

In answer . . .

Somewhere within him – as the battle continued on, the masked warrior driving the T'lan Imass back, back – the wolf stirred.

Trapped. In this bent but unbroken mechanism, this torturing cage of bone . . . He saw, close, the shattered frame of . . . something. A beam, massive, its end capped in black, bruised bronze. Where bits were smeared – flesh, flesh and hair.

Cage.

Toc the Younger drew his mangled legs under him, planted a pustuled, malformed elbow on the flagstones, felt flesh tear as he twisted round, pivoted, dragged his legs up to kneel – then, hands, frozen into fists, pushing down on the stone. Lifting, tilting back to settle weight on hips that ground and seemed to crumble beneath tendon and thin muscle.

He set his hands down once more, drew the knobbed things that had once been his feet under him, knees lifting.

Balance . . . now. And will.

Trembling, slick with sweat beneath the tattered remnants of his shapeless tunic, Toc slowly rose upright. His head spun, blackness threatening, but he held on.

Kruppe gasped, lifting her, pulling at her arm. 'You must touch, lass. This world – it was made for you – do you understand? A gift – there are things that must be freed.'

Freed.

Yes, she understood that word. She longed for it, worshipped it, knelt, head bowed, before its altar. Freed. Yes, that made sense.

Like these memories of ice, raining, raining down upon us.

Freed . . . to feed the earth—

—deliverance, of meaning, of emotion, history's gift – the land underfoot, the layers, so many layers—

To feed the earth.
What place is this?
'Reach, dearest Mhybe, Kruppe begs you! Touch—'
She raised a trembling hand—

Upright.

To see Tool reeling beneath blows, the flint sword fending slower with each flashing blade that reached for him.

Upright. A step. *One step. Will do.*

The cage, the wolf stirring, the wolf seeking to draw breath – unable—

He lurched towards the beam and its upthrust, bronze-capped end.

One step, then toppling.

Forward, lifting his arms high – clear – the beam's end seeming to rise to meet him. Meet his chest – the ribs – bones shattering in an explosion of pain—

To touch—

The cage!
Broken!
Freed!
The wolf drew breath.
And howled.

The hammer held high in Brood's hands, trembling, iron shaking—

As a god's howl ripped the air, a howl climbing, a call—
Answered.

On the killing field, T'lan Ay rising from the ground, the beasts blurring forward in a silent, grey wave, cutting through K'Chain Che'Malle – tearing the undead reptiles down, rending – the giant, armoured reptiles buckling before the onslaught.

Other K'ell Hunters wheeling, racing for the gate – wolves pursuing.

1100

Far overhead, condors breaking away from their deadly dance with two black dragons, speeding back towards the keep, Korlat and Orfantal following, and behind them, tens of thousands of Great Ravens—

—and above the keep, something was happening—

Holding the Mhybe, now unconscious, in his arms, Kruppe staggered back as Togg tore itself free of the shattered cage, the god's howl blistering the air.

The deluge of hail ceased. Abrupt. The sky darkened.

A pressure, a force, ancient and bestial. Growing.

Togg, huge, one-eyed, white, silver-tipped fur – howling –

The wolf-god, emerging with the force of heaving stone, his cry seeming to span the sky.

A cry that was answered.

On all sides.

Paran ducked even lower to a sudden descent of gloom, cold, a weight overwhelming the captain.

Beside him, Quick Ben groaned, then hissed. 'This is it, friend. Kurald Galain. I can use this – get us over this wall – we have to see—'

See what? Gods, I'm being crushed!

The pressure dimmed suddenly. Hands gripped his harness, dragged him up, metal scraping, leather catching, up and over the low wall to thump down on the other side.

The darkness continued its preternatural fall, dulling the sun to a grey, fitfully wavering disc.

Condors overhead, screaming—

—and in those screams, raw terror—

Paran twisted round, looked upon the scene on the parapet. Thirty paces away, on the far edge, crouching, was a figure the captain knew instinctively to be the Seer. Human flesh and skin had sloughed away, revealing a Jaghut, naked, surrounded in misty clouds of ice crystals. Clutched in the Seer's hands, an egg the size of a cusser. At his side, huge and misshapen, a K'Chain Che'Malle – *no.*

The Matron. What flowed from her left Paran horrified and filled with pity. She was mindless, her soul stripped, filled with a pain he knew she could not even feel – the only mercy that remained.

Two heavily armoured K'ell Hunters had been guarding their mother, but were now moving forward, weapons rising, thumping across the roof as, at a stairwell fifteen paces to Paran's left, two figures appeared. Masked, painted from head to toe in blood, each wielding two swords, clambering free of a passageway strewn with the bodies of Urdomen and Seerdomin.

'Hood take us!' Quick Ben swore. 'Those are Seguleh!'

But Paran's attention had already left them, was oblivious of the battle as the K'ell Hunters closed with the Seguleh. The storm-cloud that had towered overhead for so long was still climbing, shredding apart, almost lost in darkness. Something, he realized with a chill, was coming.

'Captain! Follow me!'

Quick Ben was edging along the low wall, following its curve towards the harbourside.

Paran scrambled after the wizard. They halted where they had a full view of the harbour and the bay.

Far out in the bay, the horizon's line of ice was exploding all along its length, in white, spewing clouds.

The waters of the harbour had grown glass-smooth beneath the dark, now motionless air. The web of ropes spanning it – with its shacks and dangling lines and withered corpses – suddenly trembled.

'In Hood's name what's—'

'Shh! Oh, Abyss! Watch!'

And he did.

The glass-smooth waters of the harbour . . . shivered . . . swelled . . . bulged.

Then, impossibly, fled on all sides.

Black, enormous – *something* – rising from the depths.

Seas thrashed, a ring of foam racing outward. A sudden

push of cold wind hammered the parapet, made the structure sway, then tremble.

Rock, ragged, scarred – *a Hood-damned mountain!* – rising from the harbour, lifting the vast net with it.

And the mountain grew larger, rose higher, darkness bleeding from it in radiating waves.

'They've unveiled Kurald Galain!' Quick Ben shouted through the roaring wind. '*All* of them!'

Paran stared.

Moon's Spawn.

Rising.

Rake hid it –

—oh, Abyss below, did Rake hide it!

Rising, water descending down its battered sides in tumbling falls, into mist that flowed as the edifice climbed ever higher.

The Cut. Ortnal's Cut – that chasm—

'Look!' Quick Ben hissed. 'Those cracks . . .'

And now he saw the cost of Rake's gambit. Huge fissures scarred the face of Moon's Spawn, fissures from which water still poured in undiminished volume.

Rising.

Two-thirds now clear of the churned seas.

Slowly spinning, bringing into view, high on one side, a ledge—

Where stood a lone figure.

Memories . . . gone. In their wake, tens of thousands of souls. Silent.

'To me, then, I will take your pain, now.'

'*You are mortal.*'

'I am mortal.'

'*You cannot carry our pain.*'

'I can.'

'*You cannot deliver it—*'

'I shall.'

'*Itkovian—*'

1103

'Your pain, T'lan Imass. Now.'

It rose before him, a wave of immeasurable height, rose, towering, then plunged towards him.

And they saw, one and all.

They saw Itkovian's welcoming smile.

Moon's Spawn rose, shrouded in darkness, beyond the city. Caladan Brood stared. Cascading clouds of mist, streams of water falling, fading. Dragons, now, wheeling outward, black, one crimson, waves of Kurald Galain, lashing out, incinerating the demonic condors.

Moon's Spawn, leaning – a massive chunk of midnight stone sloughing from one side, rocking the entire edifice – leaning, sliding, forward, towards the keep—

On the killing field below, scattered remnants of soldiers – Malazan, Barghast, Grey Swords, Gruntle and the handful of followers that were all that remained of his legion – had one and all crossed the stone bridge and were converging on the shattered north gate. Unimpeded. The wall east of the gate was empty of mages, of anyone – stripped clean.

Fires lit the city beyond the wall. The sky was filling with Black Moranth, Great Ravens – Kurald Galain spreading out, down, onto Coral—

A true unveiling. All of the Tiste Andii, joined in ritual magic – the world has never known this – in all the millennia since their arrival – never known this. Burn's heart, what will come of this unveiling?

He continued staring, overcome with a vast, soul-numbing helplessness.

The power flowed towards Korlat. Her eyes flashed as she and her brother swept on the cold, familiar currents of Kurald Galain, towards Moon's Spawn.

Oh, it was dying – she could see that. Dying, but not yet completed its dreadful, deadly task.

She watched it moving, drawing closer to the keep's parapet – to where, she could now see, stood the Seer – the

Jaghut, clutching the Matron's Finnest, staring upward, frozen, as the black, towering mountain inexorably approached.

Darkness, come to this world. To this place, this city.

Darkness, that would never dissipate.

Coral. Black, black Coral . . .

It took no more than a half-dozen heartbeats before Lady Envy realized – as she watched the Bridgeburners crumble before the Urdomen attack – that she had misunderstood Picker's last comment. Not confidence, not even bravado. Rather, a comment rife with fatalism, no doubt typical of these soldiers, but entirely new to Lady Envy.

As comprehension struck her, she acted. A small gesture with one hand.

Sufficient to rupture the flesh of the Urdomen warriors.

They crumpled en masse.

But the damage had already been done.

Two Bridgeburners remained standing, and both bore wounds.

She watched as they began checking their fallen comrades, finally gathering around one, pulling him clear. Only one among those fallen, then, who still breathed.

Heavy boots down the hallway, fast approaching.

Lady Envy scowled, raised her hand again—

'Wait!' Picker screamed. 'That's Mallet! Spin! Over here, you bastards!'

Behind the first two who had appeared – Mallet and Spin, she presumed – staggered two more soldiers in the garb of the Bridgeburners. All were terribly wounded – the Barghast in particular, whose armour was nothing more than fragments and whose body was a mass of cuts and gaping holes. Even as she watched, he staggered, sank to his knees, teeth bared in a smeared grin.

And died.

'Mallet!'

The large man in the lead spun round, reeled at the

sudden motion – and Lady Envy noted that he had taken a sword thrust that had gone right through him, just below the right shoulder. He stumbled back towards the Barghast.

'It is too late for him, I am afraid,' Lady Envy called out. 'And you, Healer – Mallet – you are done with your warren and you know it. Gather to me, then, and I shall oblige. As for you, Picker, a more honest answer to my question earlier would have resulted in a far less horrible episode.'

Wiping blood from her eyes, Picker simply stared.

'Ah, well,' Lady Envy sighed, 'perhaps it is best that you have no recollection of that sardonic quip. Come forward all of you – oh!'

She swung about suddenly, as sorcery descended – Kurald Galain – overwhelming in its power.

'Down those stairs!' she cried. 'We must work clear of this! Quickly!'

Four dragging one, the surviving Bridgeburners followed Lady Envy.

Splinters of bone struck the wall. Tool staggered back, crashing against the stone, sword falling from his hands, ringing on the flagstones.

Mok raised both weapons—

—and flew to one side, through the air, spinning, weapons sailing from his hands – to collide with a wall, then slide in a heap among shattered wood and metal.

Tool raised his head.

A huge black panther, lips peeled back in a silent snarl, slowly padded towards the unconscious Seguleh.

'No, sister.'

The Soletaken hesitated, then glanced back.

'No. Leave him.'

The panther swung round, sembled.

Yet the rage remained in Kilava's eyes as she strode towards Tool. 'You were defeated! You! The First Sword!'

Tool slowly lowered himself to collect his notched sword. 'Aye.'

1106

'He is a mortal man!'

'Go to the Abyss, Kilava.' He straightened, back scraping as he continued leaning against the wall.

'Let me kill him. Now. Then once more you shall have no worthy challenger.'

'Oh, sister,' Tool sighed. 'Do you not realize? Our time – it has passed. We must relinquish our place in this world. Mok – that man you so casually struck from behind – he is the Third. The Second and the First are his masters with swords. Do you understand me, Kilava? Leave him . . . leave them all.'

He slowly turned until he could see Toc the Younger.

The body, speared through on a shaft of wood, did not move.

'The ancient wolf-god is free,' Kilava said, following his gaze. 'Can you not hear it?'

'No. I cannot.'

'That howl now fills another realm, the sound of birth. A realm . . . brought into existence by the Summoner. As for what now gives it life, something else, something else *entire*.'

A scrape from the doorway.

Both swung their heads.

Another T'lan Imass stood beneath the arch. Impaled with swords, cold-hammered copper sheathing canines. 'Where is she?'

Tool tilted his head. 'Who do you seek, kin?'

'You are Onos T'oolan.' The attention then shifted to Kilava. 'And you are his sister, the One who Defied—'

Kilava's lip curled in contempt. 'And so I remain.'

'Onos T'oolan, First Sword, where is the Summoner?'

'I do not know. Who are you?'

'Lanas Tog. I must find the Summoner.'

Tool pushed himself from the wall. 'Then we shall seek her together, Lanas Tog.'

'Fools,' Kilava spat.

The patter of claws behind Lanas Tog – she wheeled, then backed away.

Baaljagg limped into the chamber. Ignoring everyone but Toc the Younger, the wolf approached the body, whimpered.

'He is free,' Tool said to Baaljagg. 'Your mate.'

'She is not deaf to that howl,' Kilava muttered. 'Togg has passed into the Warren of Tellann. Then . . . to a place beyond. Brother, take that path, since you are so determined to find the Summoner. They converge, one and all.'

'Come with us.'

Kilava turned away. 'No.'

'Sister. Come with us.'

She spun, face dark. 'No! I've come for the Seer. Do you understand me? I've come—'

Tool's gaze fell to Toc's broken corpse. 'For redemption. Yes. I understand. Find him, then.'

'I shall! Now that I've saved you, I am free to do as I please.'

Tool nodded. 'And when you are done, sister, seek me out once more.'

'And why should I?'

'Kilava. Blood-kin. Seek me out.'

She was silent for a long moment, then she gave a curt nod.

Lanas Tog strode to Tool's side. 'Lead me, then, First Sword.'

The two T'lan Imass fell to dust, then that, too, vanished.

Kilava was alone in the chamber.

Barring an unconscious Seguleh.

And an ay now lying beside a corpse.

She hesitated, took a step towards Mok's inert form, then sighed, wheeled about and approached Baaljagg.

'You grieve for this mortal,' she whispered, reaching down to rest her hand on the beast's lowered head. 'For him, you hold back on what you so long for – your reunion with your lost mate. Was this man truly worthy of such loyalty? No, answer not – that is plain enough in your eyes.

'And so I will tell you something, Baaljagg, that you clearly fail to realize. This mortal's soul – it rides Togg's own – and your mate would deliver it, but not to Hood's Gate. Go, then, pursue that trail. Here, I shall open the way.'

She straightened, gestured.

The Warren of Tellann opened. The chamber's musty air was swept away. A sweet smell of wet tundra, acrid mosses and softened lichen flowed in on a soft, warm breeze.

The ay bound through the portal.

Kilava closed it after the beast.

Then walked from the chamber.

A moment later, Blend stepped from the shadows. She strode to where Mok lay amidst broken wood and twisted metal, looked down on the unconscious figure. *Oh, that mask. So . . . tempting—*

Startled shouts from the corridor behind her, the sound of soldiers scattering, then heartfelt curses.

'—a damned panther!'

'Kilava,' Lady Envy replied. 'I have crossed paths with her before. Rude, indeed, to push us all aside in such contemptuous fashion.'

Blend turned as the troop arrived.

Lady Envy paused, veiled eyes flicking from Mok to Toc the Younger. 'Oh,' she said in a low voice, 'my dear lad . . . Would that you had remained in our company.'

Picker. Mallet. Spindle. Antsy. Bluepearl.

Blend closed her eyes.

'Well, that settles it, then,' Lady Envy said. 'We return to the keep's roof. Swiftly, before Kilava robs me of my vengeance against the Seer.'

'You can return to the roof,' Picker growled. 'We're leaving.'

Leaving, oh, my love . . .

Lady Envy crossed her arms. 'I exhaust myself healing you ungracious soldiers, and this is your answer? I want *company*!'

1109

Mallet and Spindle moved to retrieve Toc's body.

Picker slumped against a wall, studied Lady Envy with red-shot eyes. 'Our thanks for the healing,' she muttered. 'But we need to rejoin Onearm's Host.'

'And what if still more Pannion soldiers are lurking about?'

'Then we join our slain brothers and sisters. What of it?'

'Oh, you're all the same!'

With that, and a flurry of white robes, Lady Envy stormed from the chamber.

Blend drew closer to Picker, quietly said, 'There's a hint of fresh air . . . coming from the doorway beyond.'

The lieutenant nodded. 'Lead on.'

Canted to one side, shrouded in black mist, the ruptured basalt groaning like a living thing, Moon's Spawn drew ever closer to the keep's parapet.

Beneath the vast, overwhelming weight of Kurald Galain, the Seer crouched in his madness, head tilted to stare up at the edifice, the Finnest cradled with desperate possessiveness in his arms. Off to one side, the Matron seemed to be trying to claw her way through the tiles beneath her. The pressure was unrelenting.

The two Seguleh had not reached the rooftop unscathed, and the K'ell Hunters were proving more than their match. Both masked warriors had been driven back over the low ringwall, leaving trails of blood. Even so, Paran had never before seen such a display of skill. The swords were a blur, seemingly everywhere at once, and the K'ell Hunters were being hacked to shreds even as they pressed on. The captain had thought to help the two strangers, but had concluded that he'd prove more a hindrance.

Paran glanced back at the sky to the north.

Dragons, diving towards the city, waves of power lashing down to thunder in the streets, against buildings, darkness billowing.

Great Ravens, wheeling, voicing triumphant cries.

'Uh, it's not going to clear . . .'

The captain frowned at Quick Ben's strange statement. *Clear? What's not* – he snapped his head round, back to Moon's Spawn. *Oh.*

The base of the floating mountain was directly opposite, sliding ever closer. *So close* – towering, filling the sky.

'I thought Rake would at least come down in person for this,' the wizard went on. 'Instead, he's elected something . . . uh, less subtle.'

Like obliterating this entire keep and everyone in it. 'Quick Ben—'

'Aye, we'd better make our move.'

A huge black panther flowed from the stairwell, paused, lambent eyes taking in the scene on the rooftop, then fixing on the Seer.

Quick Ben was suddenly on his feet. 'No!' he shouted to the beast. 'Wait!'

The panther's huge head swung to the wizard, eyes blazing, lips peeling back.

'I don't think it wants to wait.'

Tail lashing, the panther drew a step closer to the cowering Seer – whose back was to them all—

'*Damn!*' Quick Ben hissed. 'Time's now, Talamandas!'

Who?

Moon's Spawn struck the parapet roof's wall with a grinding, grating crunch. The inexorable wall of stone ploughed forward—

The Matron screamed—

Wet, streaming basalt pinned the K'Chain Che'Malle where she lay, then seemed to gather her in. Blood sprayed, bones snapped, Moon's Spawn's apex edging across the rooftop, leaving in its wake chewed tiles and smears of blood and flesh.

The Seer shrieked, back-pedalled – directly towards the panther, which suddenly coiled—

Moon's Spawn sank suddenly, dropping a man's height, punching through the roof.

Tiles dipped beneath Paran, bricks buckling on all sides – the world swayed.

Quick Ben struck. Sorcery tumbling out, hammering into the panther's flank – sending it flying, claws skittering—

'Follow me!' the wizard screamed, lunging forward.

Paran, struggling to maintain his balance, reached and grasped the wizard's rain-cape, was pulled along. *So it's now – to cheat them all. Gods forgive us.*

The Seer spun to them – 'What?'

'Talamandas!' Quick Ben roared as they closed with the Seer, the wizard throwing himself onto the Jaghut—

Warren opening round them—

—and away.

Portal closing – then flaring as the panther plunged through it in pursuit.

Moon's Spawn settled further, and the parapet burst apart, bricks snapping out to all sides. The two Seguleh darted back from the K'ell Hunters, leapt the low wall behind which Paran and Quick Ben had hidden, and raced for the far end of the roof. Behind them, where the Seer had crouched, a massive chunk of basalt split away from the apex in a gush of saltwater, plunged down to bury the two K'ell Hunters, down, through floor after floor, into the bowels of the keep.

Gruntle staggered, shoulder striking a wall, leaving a red stain as he slowly slid to a crouch. Before him, bent over in exhaustion or pain, kneeling, or standing, blank-faced and ashen, were eight Capan women. Three little more than children, two others with grey in their tangled, sweat-matted hair, their weapons hanging from trembling hands. All he had left.

His Lestari officer was gone, dead, what was left of his body somewhere out in the killing field beyond the wall.

Gruntle lowered his swords, leaned his head back against the dusty stone facing, and closed his eyes.

He could hear fighting to the west. The Grey Swords had ridden in that direction, searching for Dujek. The Black Moranth had returned to the sky above the westernmost third of the city, and seemed to be concentrated in one particular area, plunging in small groups down into streets as if participating in a desperate defence. The snap of sharpers echoed.

Closer at hand, directly opposite Gruntle and what was left of his legion, a cusser had struck a large tenement. The building was moments from collapsing, raging with flames. Bodies of Pannion soldiers lay amidst rubble in the street.

And, slowly tearing its way through the keep, Moon's Spawn, bleeding its darkness out into the city, the path of its destruction a chorus of demolition.

His eyes remained closed.

Boots kicked through broken masonry, then one nudged Gruntle's thigh.

'Lazy pig!'

The Mortal Sword sighed. 'Stonny—'

'This fight ain't over.'

He opened his eyes, stared up at her. 'It is. Coral's fallen – ha, no, it's *falling*. And isn't the victory sweet. Where have you been?'

The dusty, sweat-streaked woman shrugged, glanced down at the rapier in her hand. 'Here and there. Did what I could, which wasn't much. The Mott Irregulars are here, did you know that? How in Hood's name did they manage that? Damn if they weren't there, inside the gate, when me and the Grey Swords showed up – and we thought we were first.'

'Stonny—'

The preternatural darkness deepened suddenly.

Moon's Spawn had drawn clear of the keep in a final toppling of walls: Still canted, still raining water and chunks of black rock, it drifted closer, a few men's heights above the city's buildings, filling the sky – now almost above them.

On the high ledge, no-one remained visible. Great Ravens were swinging close to the Moon's sides, then wheeling away again with loud, echoing shrieks.

'Abyss take us,' Stonny whispered, 'that thing looks like it could fall at any moment. Just drop. Straight down – or in pieces. It's finished, Gruntle. Finished.'

He could not disagree. The edifice looked ready to break apart.

Salty rain soaked his upturned face, mist from the mountain looming directly overhead. It was, all at once, as dark as an overcast night, and if not for the reflection from the fires spotting the city, Moon's Spawn would have been virtually invisible. *Gods, I wish it was.*

The sound of fighting to the west fell away, strangely sudden.

They heard horse hooves pounding the cobbles. A moment later, riding into the glare of the burning buildings opposite, the Destriant of the Grey Swords.

She saw them, slowed her canter and swung her warhorse round to approach, then halt.

'We have found the High Fist, sirs. He lives, as well as at least eight hundred of his soldiers. The city is taken. I return, now, to our staging area beyond the killing field. Will you accompany me, sirs? There will be a gathering . . .'

Of survivors. He looked around once more. The T'lan Ay were gone. Without those undead wolves, the K'Chain Che'Malle would have killed everyone outside the city. *Perhaps they, too, are gathering around that hill. And what of Itkovian? That damned fool. Does he still kneel before the T'lan Imass? Does he still live?* Gruntle sighed, slowly pushed himself upright. His gaze fell once more on his few remaining followers. *All this, just to get fifty paces inside the gate.* 'Aye, Destriant, we'll follow.'

Wings spread wide, flowing across power-ridden air, Korlat sailed in a slow bank around Moon's Spawn. Blood-matted feathers and bits of flesh still clung to her claws. At the end, the demonic condors had died easily – proof enough that the Seer had either fled or had been killed. Perhaps her Lord had descended, had drawn Dragnipur to take the Jaghut's soul. She would discover the truth soon enough.

Head twisting, she glanced at her brother flying beside her, guarding her flank. Orfantal bore wounds, yet did not waver, his power and will still formidable weapons should any surprises rise up to challenge them.

None did.

Their path took them out towards the sea, east of Coral, and within sight of the ocean. Late afternoon's light still commanded the distance.

And she saw, half a league from shore, four ships of war, sails out, flying the colours of the Malazan Imperial Navy as they skirted the periphery of dying ice floes.

Artanthos – Tayschrenn . . . oh, the plans within plans, the games of deceit and misdirection . . .

Our history, my lost love, our history destroyed us all.

Swinging around yet further, until they approached Coral once more, angling down and away from Moon's Spawn's slow path as it continued drifting northward. Below, the shattered gate. Figures, torchlight.

Her eyes found Caladan Brood, soldiers of the Grey Swords, Barghast and others.

Orfantal spoke within her mind. '*Go down, sister. I will guard the skies. I, our Soletaken kin, and Silanah. Look, Crone descends. Join her.*'

I would guard you, Brother—

'*The enemy is destroyed, Korlat. What you would guard, staying with me, is the heart within you. You would fend it from pain. From loss. Sister, he deserves more. Go down, now. To grieve is the gift of the living – a gift so many of our kin have long lost. Do not retreat. Descend, Korlat, to the mortal realm.*'

Korlat crooked her wings, spiralled earthward. *Brother, thank you.*

She sembled as she landed in the modest concourse onto which the north gate opened. Her arrival had forced soldiers to scatter, if only momentarily. Tiste Andii once more, suddenly weak from the wound that Brood had managed to heal but superficially, she stumbled slightly as she made her way to where the Warlord waited just inside the gate. Crone had reported something to him and now rose once more into the darkness.

She had never seen Brood look so . . . defeated. The notion of victory seemed . . . irrevelant, in the face of such personal loss. *For us all.*

As she drew nearer, a man walked up to the warlord. Lean, slope-shouldered, his long, pale hair a tangled mess that sat strangely high on his head.

Korlat watched the man salute, heard him say, 'High Marshal Stump, sir. Mott Irregulars. About that order—'

'What order?' Brood snapped.

The man's smile revealed long, white teeth. 'Never mind. We were there, you see—'

'Where?'

'Uh, this side of the wall, east of the gate, sir, and there was mages up top. The Bole brothers didn't like that, so they roughed them up some. Ain't none breathing any more. Anyway, what do you want us to do now?'

Caladan Brood stared at the man, expressionless, then he shook his head. 'I have not a clue, High Marshal Stump.'

The man from Mott nodded. 'Well, we could put out some fires.'

'Go to it, then.'

'Yes sir.'

Korlat, who had held back during the exchange, now stepped forward as the High Marshal ambled off.

Brood was staring after the man.

'Warlord?'

'We'd left them behind, I'd thought,' he muttered. 'But then . . . they were in the city. They were on the other side of the K'Chain Che'Malle – through the gate or over the wall, taking out mages. Now, how did they . . .'

1116

'Warlord, there are Malazan ships. Approaching.'

Brood slowly nodded. 'So Artanthos informed me, before he travelled by warren to the deck of the command ship. There is an imperial delegation aboard, an ambassador, a legate, a governor—'

'All three?'

'No, just one. Lots of titles, depending on the negotiations to follow.'

Korlat drew a deep breath. *Hold back on the pain, on the loss – just a short while longer.* 'With Onearm's Host so badly . . . damaged . . . the Malazans won't be bargaining from a position of strength.'

Brood's eyes narrowed on her. 'Korlat,' he said softly, 'as far as I am concerned, the Malazans have earned all they might ask for. If they want it, Coral is theirs.'

Korlat sighed. 'Warlord, the unveiling of Kurald Galain . . . is a permanent manifestation. The city now lies as much within the Tiste Andii warren as within this world.'

'Aye, meaning the negotiations are properly between Rake and the Malazans. Not me. Tell me, will your Lord claim Coral? Moon's Spawn . . .'

There was no need to continue. The city within the mountain of rock still held, trapped in its deepest chambers, massive volumes of water, weight that could not be withstood for much longer. Moon's Spawn was dying. It would, she knew, have to be abandoned. *A place, our home for so long. Will I grieve? I know not.*

'I have not spoken with Anomander Rake, Warlord. I cannot anticipate his disposition.' She turned away, began walking towards the gate.

Brood called after her.

Not yet.

She continued on, beneath the gate's arch, her eyes fixing on the hilltop beyond the shattered corpses carpeting the killing field. *Where I will find him. All that is left. His face, gift of memories, now grown cold. I saw the life flee his eyes. That moment of death, of dying. Withdrawing, away from those eyes, withdrawing, back and away. Leaving, leaving me.*

Her steps slowed, the pain of loss threatening to overwhelm her.

Dear Mother Dark, do you look down upon me, now? Do you see me, your child? Do you smile, to see me so broken? I have, after all, repeated your fatal errors of old. Yielding my heart, succumbing to the foolish dream – Light's dance, you longed for that embrace, didn't you?

And were betrayed.

You left us, Mother . . . to eternal silence.

Yet . . .

Mother Dark, with this unveiling, I feel you close. Was it grief that sent you away, sent you so far from your children? When, in our deadly, young way – our appalling insensitivity – we cursed you. Added another layer to your pain.

These steps . . . you walked them once.

How can you help but smile?

Rain struck her brow, stung the ragged, open gash of her wound. She halted, looked up, to see Moon's Spawn directly overhead . . . weeping down upon her . . .

. . . and upon the field of corpses surrounding her, and, beyond and to the right, upon thousands of kneeling T'lan Imass. The dead, the abandoned, a wash of deepening colours, as if in the rain the scene, so softly saturated, was growing more solid, more real. No longer the faded tableau of a Tiste Andii's regard. *Life, drawn short, to sharpen every detail, flush every colour, to make every moment an ache.*

And she could hold back no longer. *Whiskeyjack. My love.*

Moments later, her own tears joined the salt-laden water running down her face.

In the gate's gloom, Caladan Brood stared out, across the stone bridge, over the mangled plain to where Korlat stood halfway to the hill, surrounded by corpses and shattered K'Chain Che'Malle. Watched as her head tilted back, face slowly lifting to the grey shroud of the rain. The black mountain, fissures widening, groans issuing from the dying edifice, seemed to pause directly over her. A heart, once of stone, made mortal once more.

This image – what he now saw – he knew, with bleak certainty, would never leave him.

Silverfox had walked for what seemed a long time, heedless of direction, insensate to all that surrounded her, until distant movement caught her attention. She now stood on the barren tundra, beneath solid white overcast, and watched the approach of the Rhivi spirits.

A small band, pitifully small, less than forty individuals, insignificant in the distance, almost swallowed by the immense landscape, the sky, this damp air with its unforgiving chill that had settled into her bones like the blood of failure.

Events had occurred. Elsewhere in this nascent realm. She could sense that much – the hail, deluge of memories, born from she knew not where. And though they had struck her with the same indiscriminate randomness as they struck the ground on all sides, she had felt but the faintest hint of all that they had contained.

If a gift, then a bitter one.

If a curse, then so too is life itself a curse. For there were lives within that frozen rain. Entire lives, sent down to strike the flesh of this world, to seep down, to thaw the soil with its fecundity.

But it has nothing to do with me.

None of this. All that I sought to fashion . . . destroyed. This dreamworld was itself a memory. Ghostworld of Tellann, remembrance of my own world, from long, long ago. Remembrances, taken from the Bonecaster who was there in my refashioning, taken from the Rhivi spirits, the First Clan, taken from K'rul, from Kruppe. Taken from the slumbering land itself – Burn's own flesh.

I myself . . . possessed nothing. I simply stole.

To fashion a world for my mother, a world where she could be young once more, where she could live out a normal life, growing old through the normal span of seasons.

All that I stole from her, I would give back.

Bitterness filled Silverfox. It had begun with that first barrow, outside Pale. This belief in the righteousness, the efficacy, of theft. Justified by the worthiest of ends.

But ownership bereft of propriety was a lie. All that she hoarded was in turn stripped of value. Memories, dreams, lives.

Gone to dust.

The hapless band of Rhivi spirits drew closer, cautiously, hesitating.

Yes. I understand. What demands will I make of you now? How many more empty promises will I voice? I had a people for you, a people who had long since lost their own gods, their own spirits to whom they had once avowed allegiance, were less than the dust they could make of themselves. A people.

For you.

Lost.

What a lesson for four bound souls – no matchmaker, we four.

She did not know what to tell them – these modest, timid spirits.

'Bonecaster, we greet you.'

Silverfox blinked her eyes clear. 'Elder Spirit. I have—'

'Have you seen?'

She saw then, in all their faces, a kind of wonder. And frowned in reply.

'Bonecaster,' the foremost Rhivi continued, 'we have found something. Not far from here – do you know of what we speak?'

She shook her head.

'There are thrones, Bonecaster. Two thrones. In a long hut of bones and hide.'

Thrones? 'What – why? Why should there be thrones in this realm? Who—?'

The elder shrugged, then offered her a soft smile. 'They await, Bonecaster. We can feel the truth of

1120

that. Soon. Soon, will come this warren's true masters.'

'True masters!' Anger flared in Silverfox. 'This realm – it was for *you*! Who dares seek to usurp—'

'No,' the spirit's quiet denial cut through her, swept the breath from her lungs. 'Not for us. Bonecaster, we are not powerful enough to command such a world as this. It has grown too vast, too powerful. Do not fear – we do not wish to leave, and we will endeavour to treat with the new masters. I believe they will permit us to remain. Perhaps indeed we will find ourselves pleased to serve them.'

'No!' *No! Not how it was supposed to be!*

'Bonecaster, there is no need for such strong feelings within you. The shaping continues. The fulfilment of your desires is still possible – perhaps not in the manner you originally intended . . .'

She no longer heard him. Despair was sundering her soul. *As I stole . . . so it has been stolen from me. There is no injustice here, no crime. Accept the truth.*

Nightchill's strength of will.

Tattersail's empathy.

Bellurdan's loyalty.

A Rhivi child's wonder.

None were enough. None could of themselves – or together – absolve what has been done, the choices made, the denials voiced.

Leave them. Leave them to this, to all of this, and all that is to come. Silverfox turned away. 'Find her, then. Go.'

'Will you not walk with us? Your gift to her—'

'Go.'

My gift to her. My gift to you. They are all as one. Grand failures, defeats born from the flaws within me. I will not stand witness to my own shame – I cannot. I have not the courage for that.

I'm sorry.

She walked away.

Brief flower. Seed to stalk to deadly blossom, all in the span of a single day. Bright-burning poison, destroying all who came too close.

An abomination.

The Rhivi spirits – a small band, men, women, children and elders, wearing hides and furs, their round faces burnished by sun and wind – watched Silverfox leave them. The elder who had spoken with her did not move until she slipped out of sight beneath the rim of a worn beach ridge, then he ran the back of four spread fingers across his eyes in a gesture of sad departing, and said, 'Build a fire. Prepare the ranag's shoulder blade. We have walked this land enough to see the map within.'

'Once more,' an old woman sighed.

The elder shrugged. 'The Bonecaster commanded that we find her mother.'

'She will simply flee us again. As she did the ay. Like a hare—'

'None the less. The Bonecaster has commanded. We shall lay the blade upon the flames. We shall see the map find its shape.'

'And why should it be true this time?'

The elder slowly lowered himself to press a hand down on the soft mosses. 'Why? Open your senses, doubting one. This land . . .' he smiled, 'now lives.'

Running.

Free!

Riding the soul of a god, within the muscles of a fierce, ancient beast. Riding a soul—

— suddenly singing with joy. Mosses and lichen beneath the paws, spray of old rain water to streak the leg-fur. Smell of rich, fertile life – a world—

Running. Pain already a fading memory, vague recollections of a cage of bone, growing pressure, ever more shallow breaths.

Throwing head back, loosing a thunderous howl that trembled the sky.

Distant answers.

Which drew closer.

Shapes, grey, brown and black flashes of movement on the tundra, streaming over ridges, sweeping down into shallow valleys, broad moraines. Ay. Kin. The children of Baaljagg – of Fanderay – ghost memories that were the souls of the T'lan Ay. Baaljagg had not released them, had held to them, within herself, within her dreams – in an ageless world into which an Elder God had breathed eternal life.

Ay.

Their god had challenged the heavens with his bestial voice, and now they came to him.

And . . . another.

Togg slowed, head lifting – the ay all around him now, clan after clan, long-legged tundra wolves, swirling—

She was here. She had come.

She had found him.

Running. Coming nearer. Shoulder to shoulder with Baaljagg, with the ay who had carried her wounded, lost soul for so long. Baaljagg, coming to rejoin her kin – the kin of her dreams.

Emotions. Beyond measure—

Then, Fanderay was padding at his side.

Their beast-minds touched. A moment. Nothing else. Nothing more was needed.

Together, shoulders brushing—

Two ancient wolves. God and goddess.

He looked upon them, without knowing who he, himself, was; nor even where he might be, that he might so witness this reunion. Looked, and, for these two, knew nothing but gentle joy.

Running.

Ahead awaited their thrones.

The Mhybe's head snapped up, her body stiffening, writhing in an attempt to break his grip. Small as he was, his strength defeated her.

'Wolves, lass. We've nothing to fear.'

Nothing to fear. Lies. They have hunted me. Again and again. Pursuing me across this empty land. And now, listen, they come once more. And this Daru who drags me, he has not even so much as a knife.

'Something ahead,' Kruppe gasped, shifting his awkward embrace as he staggered under her weight. 'Easier,' he panted, 'when you were but a hag! Now, but you found the will, you could throw me down – nay! You could carry *me*!'

Will. Need I only find the will? To break from this grip? To flee?

Flee where?

'Lass, hear Kruppe's words! He begs you! This – this world – Kruppe's dream no longer! Do you understand? It must pass from me. It must be passed on!'

They were stumbling up a gentle slope.

Wolves howled behind them, fast approaching.

Leave me.

'Dearest Mhybe, so aptly named! You are the vessel in truth, now! Within you – take this dream from me. Allow it to fill your spirit. Kruppe must pass it on to you – do you understand?'

Will.

She twisted suddenly, threw an elbow into Kruppe's stomach. He gasped, doubled over. She pulled herself free as he fell, leapt to her feet—

Behind them, tens of thousands of wolves. Charging towards her. And, leading them, two gigantic beasts that radiated blinding power.

The Mhybe cried out, spun.

A shallow depression before her. A long, low hut of arched bones, hides, bound with hemp rope, the entrance yawning wide.

And, standing in a clump before the hut, a band of Rhivi.

The Mhybe staggered towards them.

Wolves were suddenly all around, flowing in a wild,

chaotic circle around the hut. Ignoring the Rhivi. Ignoring her.

Groaning, Kruppe levered himself, after a couple of tries, to his feet. Weaving, he joined her. She stared at him without comprehension.

He drew a faded handkerchief from his sleeve and daubed the sweat from his brow. 'Any lower with that elbow, dear . . .'

'What? What is happening?'

Kruppe paused, looked around. 'They are within, then.'

'Who?'

'Why, Togg and Fanderay, of course. Come to claim the Beast Throne. Or, in this case, *Thrones*. Not that, should we enter the hut, we will see two wolves perched on chairs, of course. Presence alone asserts possession, no doubt. Kruppe's imagination tempts other, shall we say, prosaic images, but best avoid those, yes? Now, lass, permit Kruppe to edge back. Those who approach you now – well, this is the passing of a dream, from one to the other, and into the background noble Kruppe must now go.'

She swung round.

A Rhivi elder faced her, face creasing in a sad smile. 'We asked her to come with us,' he said.

The Mhybe frowned. 'Asked who?'

'Your daughter. This world – it is for you. Indeed, it exists within you. With this world, your daughter asks for forgiveness.'

'S-she made this—'

'There were many participants, each and all driven by the injustice that befell you. There was . . . desperation, the day your daughter was . . . created. The one known as Kruppe. The Elder God, K'rul. The one named Pran Chole. And yourself. And, when she gathered us within her, ourselves as well. Silverfox sought to answer yet more – the tragedy that are the T'lan Imass and the T'lan Ay. It may be,' he added, one hand making a faint gesture of bereavement, 'that what her heart sought has proved too vast—'

1125

'Where is she? Where is my daughter?'

The elder shook his head. 'Despair has taken her. Away.'

The Mhybe fell silent. *I was hunted. You were hunting me. And the ay.* She looked down, slowly raised her youthful limbs. *Is this real, then?* She slowly turned about, looked across to meet Kruppe's eyes.

The Daru smiled.

The old woman . . .

'Will I awaken?'

Kruppe shook his head. 'That woman now sleeps eternal, lass. Warded, guarded. Your daughter spoke with Hood. Reached an agreement, yes? She believes, having lost the T'lan Imass, that she has broken it. Yet, one cannot but think that there are facets to this . . . resolution. Kruppe remains confident.'

An agreement. Freedom for the T'lan Imass. An end. Their souls . . . delivered to Hood.

Spirits below – she has lost them? Lost the T'lan Imass? 'Hood will not abide—'

'Ah, but won't he? Whyever not, dear? If the Lord of Death is without patience, then Kruppe can dance on Coll's pointy head! Which he most assuredly cannot. You shall *not* return to that ancient body.'

The Mhybe glanced back at the Rhivi spirits. 'Will I age here? Will I eventually . . .'

The elder shrugged. 'I do not know, but I suspect not. You are the vessel. The Mhybe.'

The Mhybe . . . Oh, Silverfox. Daughter. Why are you not here? Why can I not look now into your eyes. The begging for forgiveness goes both ways. She drew a deep breath, tasted the sweet life filling the cool, moist air. *So easily, then, to take this world into myself.* She removed the first copper bracelet, held it out to the Rhivi. 'This is yours, I believe.'

The elder smiled. 'Did its power serve you well?'

She nodded. 'Without measure . . .'

A presence filled her mind. *'Mhybe.'*

Togg, a rumbling power, the will of winter itself.

1126

'We reside within this realm, realm of the Beast Thrones, but you are its mistress. There is one within me. A mortal spirit. Cherished spirit. I would release him. We would release him. From this realm. Do you give us—'

Yes. Release him.

Benediction. Godless, he could not give it. Not in its truest form.

But he had not comprehended the vast capacity within him, within a mortal soul, to take within itself the suffering of tens of thousands, the multitudes who had lived with loss and pain for almost three hundred thousand years.

He saw faces, countless faces. Desiccated, eyes nothing more than shadowed pits. Dry, torn skin. He saw bone glimmering from between layers of root-like tendons and muscles. He saw hands, chipped, splintered, empty now – yet the ghost of swords lingered there still.

He was on his knees, looking out upon their ranks, and it was raining, a wavering deluge accompanied by reverberating groans, splintering cracks filling the darkness above.

He looked upon them, and they were motionless, heads bowed.

Yet he could see their faces. Each face. Every face.

I have your pain.

Heads slowly lifted.

He sensed them, sensed the sudden lightness permeating them. *I have done all I am able to do. Yes, it was not enough, I know. Yet. I have taken your suffering—*

'You have taken our suffering, mortal.'

Into myself—

'We do not understand how.'

And so I will now leave you—

'We do not understand . . . why.'

For all that my flesh cannot encompass—

'We cannot answer the gift you have given.'

I will take with me.

'Please, mortal—'

1127

Somehow.

'The reason. Please. That you would so bless us—'

I am the . . .

'Mortal?'

Your pardon, sirs. You wish to know of me. I am . . . a mortal, as you say. A man, born three decades ago in the city of Erin. My family name, before I surrendered it to Fener's Reve, was Otanthalian. My father was a hard, just man. My mother smiled but once in all the years I knew her. The moment when I departed. Still, it is the smile I remember. I think now that my father embraced in order to possess. That she was a prisoner. I think, now, that her smile answered my escape. I think now that in my leaving, I took something of her with me. Something worthy of being set free.

Fener's Reve. In the Reve . . . I wonder, did I simply find for myself another prison?

'She is free within you, mortal.'

That would be . . . a good thing.

'We would not lie to you, Itkovian Otanthalian. She is free. And smiles still. You have told us what you were. But we still do not understand – your . . . generosity. Your compassion. And so we ask again. Why have you done this for us?'

Sirs, you speak of compassion. I understand something, now, of compassion. Would you hear?

'Speak on, mortal.'

We humans do not understand compassion. In each moment of our lives, we betray it. Aye, we know of its worth, yet in knowing we then attach to it a value, we guard the giving of it, believing it must be earned. T'lan Imass. Compassion is priceless in the truest sense of the word. It must be given freely. In abundance.

'We do not understand, but we will consider long your words.'

There is always more to do, it seems.

'You do not answer our question—'

No.

'Why?'

1128

Beneath the rain, as darkness gathered, with every face raised to him, Itkovian closed himself about all that he held within him, closed himself, then fell back.

Back.

Because. I was the Shield Anvil. But now . . .

I am done.

And beneath the Moon's torrential rain, he died.

On the vast, reborn tundra with its sweet breath of spring, Silverfox looked up.

Standing before her were two T'lan Imass. One speared through with swords. The other so badly battered that it could barely stand.

Beyond them, silent, motionless, the T'lan Ay.

Silverfox made to turn away.

'No. You shall not.'

Silverfox glared back at the battered warrior who'd spoken. 'You dare torment me?' she hissed.

The T'lan Imass seemed to rock in the face of her vehemence, then steadied. 'I am Onos T'oolan, First Sword. You are the Summoner. You shall listen to me.'

Silverfox said nothing for a long moment, then she nodded. 'Very well. Speak.'

'Free the T'lan Ay.'

'They have denied me—'

'They are here before you, now. They have come. Their spirits await them. They would be mortal once more, in this world that you have created. Mortal, no longer lost within dreams, Summoner. Mortal. Gift them. Now.'

Gift them . . . 'And this is what they wish?'

'Yes. Reach to them, and you will know the truth of that.'

No, no more pain. She raised her arms, drew on the power of Tellann, closed her eyes – *for too long have they known chains. For too long have these creatures known the burden of loyalty—*

—and released them of the Ritual. An effort demanding

1129

so little of herself, she was left feeling appalled. *So easy, then, to release. To make free once more.*

She opened her eyes. The undead wolves were gone.

Not into oblivion, however. Their souls had been reunited, she knew, with flesh and bone. Extinct no longer. Not here, within this realm and its wolf gods. She was a Bonecaster, after all. Such gifts were hers to give. *No, they are not gifts. They are what I was fashioned to do, after all. My purpose. My sole purpose.*

Onos T'oolan's bones creaked as he slowly looked around, scanning the now empty barrens surrounding them. His shoulders seemed to slump. 'Summoner. Thank you. The ancient wrong is righted.'

Silverfox studied the First Sword. 'What else do you wish of me?'

'She who stands beside me is Lanas Tog. She will lead you back to the T'lan Imass. Words must be exchanged.'

'Very well.'

Onos T'oolan made no move.

Silverfox frowned. 'What are we waiting for, then?'

He was motionless a moment longer, then he reached up and slowly drew his flint sword. 'For me,' he rasped, raising the sword—

— then releasing it, to fall to the ground at his feet.

She frowned down at the weapon, wondering at the significance of the gesture – from the warrior who was called the First Sword.

Slowly, as comprehension filled her, her eyes widened.

What, after all, I was fashioned to do . . .

'The time has come.'

Coll started. He had been dozing. 'What? What time?'

Murillio rushed over to the Mhybe.

The Knight of Death continued, 'She is ready for interment. My Lord has avowed his eternal protection.'

The Elder God, K'rul, was studying the huge, undead

1130

warrior. 'I remain bemused. No – astonished. Since when has Hood become a generous god?'

The Knight slowly faced K'rul. 'My Lord is ever generous.'

'She's still alive,' Murillio pronounced, straightening to place himself between the Mhybe and the Knight of Death. 'The time has *not* come.'

'This is not a burial,' K'rul said to him. 'The Mhybe now sleeps, and will sleep for ever more. She sleeps, to dream. And within her dream, Murillio, lives an entire world.'

'Like Burn?' Coll asked.

The Elder God smiled in answer.

'Wait a moment!' Murillio snapped. 'Just how many sleeping old women are there?'

'She must be laid to rest,' the Knight of Death pronounced.

Coll stepped forward, settled a hand on Murillio's shoulder. 'Come on, let's make sure she's comfortable down there – furs, blankets . . .'

Murillio seemed to shiver under Coll's hand. 'After all this?' He wiped at his eyes. 'We just . . . leave her? Here, in a tomb?'

'Help me with the bedding, my friend,' Coll said.

'There is no need,' the Knight said. 'She will feel nothing.'

'That's not the point,' Coll sighed. He was about to say something more, then he saw that Rath'Fanderay and Rath'Togg had both removed their masks. Pallid, wrinkled faces, eyes closed, streaming with tears. 'What's wrong with them?' he demanded.

'Their gods have finally found each other, Coll. Within the Mhybe's realm, home now to the Beast Thrones. You do not witness sorrow, but joy.'

After a moment, Coll grunted. 'Let's get to work, Murillio. Then we can go home.'

'I still want to know about these old women dreaming up worlds like this!'

The warren flared, the three figures emerging from it spilling onto dusty grey earth in a tangle.

Paran rolled clear of Quick Ben and the Seer as sorcery roiled around the two grappling men. As the captain drew his sword, he heard the Jaghut shriek. Black webs raced, wrapped tight about the thrashing Seer.

Gasping, Quick Ben kicked himself away, the Finnest in his hands.

Crouched on the Jaghut's chest was a tiny figure of twigs and knotted grasses, cackling with glee.

'Who in Hood's name—'

A massive black shape exploded from the portal with a hissing snarl. Paran cried out, wheeled, sword swinging in a desperate horizontal slash.

Which bit muscle then bone.

Something – a paw – hammered Paran's chest, throwing him from his feet.

'Stop – you damned cat!'

Quick Ben's frantic shout was punctuated by a sorcerous detonation that made the panther scream in pain.

'On your feet, Paran!' the wizard gasped. 'I've nothing left.'

On my feet? Gods, I feel broken into a thousand pieces, and the man wants me on my feet. Somehow, he pushed himself upright, tottering as he faced the beast once more.

It crouched six paces away, tail thrashing, coal-lit eyes fixed on his own. It bared its fangs in a silent snarl.

From somewhere within the captain emerged an answering growl. Deeper than a human throat could manage. A brutal strength flowed into him, stealing from him all awareness of his own body – except that now, he realized, he was – somehow – on eye-level with the gigantic panther.

He heard Quick Ben's ragged whisper behind him: '*Abyss below!*'

The cat, ears laid back flat, was clearly hesitating.

What in Hood's name is it seeing?

'Bonecaster!' Quick Ben snapped. 'Hold. Look around you – see where we are! We're not your enemies – we seek what you seek. Here. Right now.'

The panther drew back another step, and Paran saw it tensing for a charge.

'Vengeance is not enough!' the wizard cried.

The cat flinched. A moment later, Paran saw its muscles relax, then the entire beast blurred, changed shape – and a small, dark, heavy-boned woman stood before them. On her right shoulder was a deep gash, the blood freely flowing down to paint her arm, dripping from her fingertips to the dusty ground. Black, extraordinarily beautiful eyes regarded him.

Paran slowly sighed, felt something subside within him – and he could sense his own body once more, limbs trembling, sword-grip slick in his hand.

'Who are you?' she asked.

The captain shrugged.

Her gaze dismissed him, lifted past him. 'Morn,' she said.

Paran slowly turned.

He felt the rent like a physical blow against his heart. A welt in the air, almost within reach of the ragged roof of an abandoned tower. A wound, bleeding pain – *such pain . . . an eternity – gods below, there is a soul within it. A child. Trapped. Sealing the wound. I remember that child – the child of my dreams . . .*

Quick Ben had regained his feet, stood looking down on the magically imprisoned Seer, the sticksnare crouched on the man's chest.

The Jaghut, unhuman eyes filled with terror, stared back up at him.

The wizard smiled. 'You and I, Seer. We are going to come to an arrangement.' He still held the Finnest and now slowly raised it. 'The Matron's power . . . resides within this egg. Correct? A power unable to sense itself, yet alive none the less. Torn from the body that once housed it, presumably it feels no pain. It simply exists, here in this Finnest, for anyone to use it. Anyone at all.'

'No,' the Jaghut rasped, eyes widening with fear. 'The Finnest is aspected to me. To me alone. You foolish—'

'Enough of the insults, Seer. Do you want to hear my proposal? Or will Paran and I simply step back and leave you to this Bonecaster's tender talons?'

The dark-haired woman approached them. 'What do you plan, Wizard?'

Quick Ben glanced back at her. 'An arrangement, Bonecaster, where everyone wins.'

She sneered. 'No-one wins. Ever. Leave him to me now.'

'The T'lan Vow is that important to you? I think not. You are flesh and blood—you did not participate in that ritual.'

'I am not bound to any vow,' she replied. 'I act now for my brother.'

'Your brother?' Paran asked, sheathing his sword and joining them.

'Onos T'oolan. Who knew a mortal, and called him kin.'

'I imagine such an honour is . . . rare,' Paran acknowledged, 'but what has that to do with the Seer?'

She looked down at the bound Jaghut. 'To answer the death of Toc the Younger, brother to Onos T'oolan, I must kill you, Seer.'

Paran stared, disbelieving the name he had just heard.

The Jaghut's response was a grim unsheathing of his lower tusks. Then he said, 'You should have killed us the first time. Yes, I remember you. Your *lies*.'

'Toc the Younger?' Quick Ben asked. 'From Onearm's Host? But—'

'He was lost,' Paran said. 'Thrown into a chaotic warren by Hairlock.'

The wizard was scowling. 'To land in the Seer's lap? That hardly seems—'

'He appeared here,' the woman cut in. 'At Morn. The Seer interrupted his journey north to rejoin his people, a journey that, for a time, he shared with Onos T'oolan. The Seer tortured the mortal, destroyed him.'

'Toc's dead?' Paran asked, his mind feeling rocked in every direction.

'I saw his body, yes. And now, I will deliver unto this Jaghut pain to match.'

'Have you not already done so?' the Jaghut hissed.

The Bonecaster's face tightened.

'Wait,' Quick Ben said, looking now to both her and Paran. 'Listen to me. Please. I knew Toc as well, and I grieve for the loss. But it changes nothing, not here, not now.' He turned once more back to the Seer. 'She is still in there, you know.'

The Jaghut flinched, eyes widening.

'Didn't you understand that? The Matron could only take one. You.'

'No—'

'Your sister is still there. Her soul seals that wound. It's the way warrens heal themselves, to keep from bleeding into each other. The first time, it was the Matron – the K'Chain Che'Malle. Time's come, Seer, to send her back. Hood knows what that Finnest will do – once you release it, once you send it into that rent—'

The Jaghut managed a ghastly smile. 'To free my sister? To what? You fool. You blind, stupid fool. Ask the Bonecaster – how long would we survive in this world? The T'lan Imass will hunt us in earnest now. I free my sister, to what? A short life, filled with flight – I remember, mortal. *I remember!* Running. Never enough sleep. Mother, carrying us, slipping in the mud—' He shifted his head a fraction, 'And oh how I remember *you*, Bonecaster! You sent us into that wound – you—'

'I was mistaken,' the woman said. 'I thought – I believed – it was a portal into Omtose Phellack.'

'Liar! You may be flesh and blood, but in your hatred for the Jaghut you are no different from your undead kin. No, you'd discovered a more horrible fate for us.'

'No. I believed I was saving you.'

'And you never knew the truth? You never realized?'

1135

Paran watched the woman's expression close, her eyes flattening. 'I saw no way of undoing what I had done.'

'Coward!' the Jaghut shrieked.

'Enough of all this,' Quick Ben cut in. 'We can fix it now. Return the Matron to the wound, Seer. Retrieve your sister.'

'Why? Why should I? To see us both cut down by the T'lan Imass?'

'He is right,' the woman said. 'Even so, Jaghut, better that than an eternity of pain, such as your sister is now suffering.'

'I need only wait. One day,' the Seer hissed, 'some fool will come upon this site, will probe, will reach into the portal—'

'And will make the exchange? Freeing your sister.'

'Yes! Beyond the sight or knowledge of the T'lan Imass! Beyond—'

'A small child,' Quick Ben said. 'Alone. In a wasteland. I have a better idea.'

The Jaghut bared his teeth in a silent snarl.

The wizard slowly crouched down beside the Seer. 'Omtose Phellack. Your warren is under siege, isn't it? The T'lan Imass long ago breached it. And now, whenever it is unveiled, they know about it. They know where, and they come . . .'

The Jaghut simply glared.

Quick Ben sighed. 'The thing is, Seer, I have found a place for it. A place that can remain . . . hidden. Beyond the ability of the T'lan Imass to detect. Omtose Phellack can survive, Seer, in its fullest power. Survive, and *heal*.'

'Lies.'

The sticksnare on his chest spoke, 'Listen to this wizard, Jaghut. He offers a mercy you do not deserve.'

Paran cleared his throat, said, 'Seer. Were you aware that you have been manipulated? Your power – it wasn't Omtose Phellack, was it?'

'I used,' the Jaghut grated, 'what I could find.'

1136

'The Warren of Chaos, yes. Wherein is trapped a wounded god. The Chained One, a creature of immense power, a creature in pain, who seeks only the destruction of this world, of every warren – including Omtose Phellack. He is indifferent to your desires, Seer, and he has been *using* you. Worse, the venom of his soul – he's been speaking . . . through you. Thriving on pain and suffering . . . *through* you. Since when were Jaghut interested only in destruction? Not even the Tyrants ruled with such cruelty as you have. Tell me, Seer, do you still feel as twisted inside? Do you still delight in thoughts of delivering pain?'

The Jaghut was silent for a long moment.

Gods, Quick Ben, I hope you're right. I hope the madness of this Seer was not his own. That it's now gone – torn away—

'I feel,' the Jaghut rasped, '*empty*. Still, why should I believe you?'

Paran studied the Jaghut, then said, 'Release him, Quick.'

'Now, wait—'

'Let him go. You can't negotiate with a prisoner and expect him to believe a thing you're saying. Seer, the place Quick Ben has in mind – no-one – *no-one* – will be able to manipulate you there. And perhaps more importantly, you will possess the opportunity to make the Chained One pay for his temerity. And, finally, you will have a sister – still a child – who will need to heal. Seer, she will need *you*.'

'You hold too much to this Jaghut's still retaining a shred of honour, integrity and the capacity for compassion,' the Bonecaster pronounced. 'With all that he has done – whether by his will or not – he will twist that child, as he himself has been twisted.'

Paran shrugged. 'Fortunate for that child, then, that she and her brother will not be entirely alone.'

The Seer's eyes narrowed. 'Not alone?'

'Free him, Quick Ben.'

The wizard sighed, then spoke to the sticksnare crouching on the Jaghut's chest. 'Let him go, Talamandas.'

'We'll likely regret it,' it replied, then clambered off. The sorcerous web flickered, then vanished.

The Seer scrambled to his feet. Then hesitated, eyes on the Finnest in Quick Ben's hands.

'This other place,' he finally whispered, looking to Paran, 'is it far?'

The Jaghut child, a girl of but a handful of years, wandered from the wounded warren as if lost, her small hands folded together on her lap in a manner she must have learned from her long-dead mother. A small detail, but it granted her a heart-breaking dignity that started tears in Paran's eyes.

'What will she remember?' Kilava whispered.

'Hopefully, nothing,' Quick Ben replied. 'Talamandas and I will, uh, work on that.'

A soft sound from the Seer drew Paran's attention. The Jaghut stood, trembling, unhuman eyes fixed on the approaching child – who had now seen them, yet was clearly seeking someone else, her steps slowing.

'Go to her,' Paran told the Seer.

'She remembers . . . a *brother*—'

'So now she finds an uncle.'

Still he hesitated. 'We Jaghut are not . . . not known for compassion among our blood-tied, our kin—'

Paran grimaced. 'And we humans are? You're not the only one who finds such things a struggle. There's much you have to repair, Pannion, starting with what is within yourself, with what you've done. In that, let the child – your sister – be your guide. Go, damn you – you need each other.'

He staggered forward, then hesitated once more and swung back to meet Paran's eyes. 'Human, what I have done – to your friend, to Toc the Younger – I now regret.' His gaze shifted to Kilava. 'You said you have kin, Bonecaster. A brother.'

She shook her head, as if anticipating his question. 'He is T'lan Imass. Of the Ritual.'

1138

'It seems, then, that, like me, you have a great distance to travel.'

She cocked her head. 'Travel?'

'This path to redemption, Bonecaster. Know that I cannot forgive you. Not yet.'

'Nor I you.'

He nodded. 'We both have learning ahead of us.' With that, he turned once more. Back straightening, he strode to his sister.

She knew her own kind, and had not yet been shorn of her love, her need, for kin. And, before Pannion began lifting his hands towards her, she opened her arms to him.

The vast cavern's rippled, curved walls streamed watery mud. Paran stared up at the nearest diamond-studded giant with its massive arms raised to the ceiling. It seemed to be dissolving before his eyes. The infection in Burn's flesh was all too apparent as inflamed streaks, radiating away from a place almost directly above them.

The giant was not alone – the entire length of the cavern, in each direction for as far as the eye could see, revealed more of the huge, childlike servants. If they were aware of the arrival of newcomers, they showed no sign.

'She sleeps,' Kilava murmured, 'to dream.'

Quick Ben shot her a look, but said nothing. The wizard seemed to be waiting for something.

Paran glanced down at the sticksnare, Talamandas. 'You were Barghast once, weren't you?'

'I still am, Master of the Deck. My newborn gods are within me.'

Actually, there's more of Hood's presence within you than your Barghast gods. But the captain simply nodded. 'You were the reason why Quick Ben could use his warrens.'

'Aye, but I am much more than that.'

'No doubt.'

'Here she comes,' Quick Ben announced with relief.

Paran turned to see a figure approaching down the long,

winding tunnel. Ancient, wrapped in rags, hobbling on two canes.

'Welcome!' Quick Ben called out. 'I wasn't sure—'

'The young lack faith, and you, Desert Snake, are no exception!' She leaned on a single cane and fumbled in the folds of her cloak for a moment, then withdrew a small stone. 'You left me this, yes? Your summons was heard, Wizard. Now, where are these fell Jaghut? Ah – and a Bonecaster Soletaken, too. My, such extraordinary company – what a tale it must be, that has seen you all brought together! No, don't tell it to me, I'm not *that* interested.' She halted in front of the Seer and studied the child in his arms for a moment before lifting her sharp gaze. 'I'm an old woman,' she hissed. 'Chosen by the Sleeping Goddess, to assist you in the care of your sister. But first, you must unveil your warren. With cold, you shall fight this infection. With cold, you shall slow the dissolution, harden this legion of servants. Omtose Phellack, Jaghut. Free it. Here. Burn will now embrace you.'

Paran grimaced. 'That's a poor choice of words.'

The ancient witch cackled. 'But words he will understand, yes?'

'Not unless you plan on killing him.'

'Don't be pedantic, soldier. Jaghut, your warren.'

The Seer nodded, unveiled Omtose Phellack.

The air was suddenly bitter cold, rime and frost misting the air.

Quick Ben was grinning. 'Chilly enough for you, witch?'

She cackled again. 'I knew you were no fool, Desert Snake.'

'Truth to tell, I'll have to thank Picker for giving me the idea. The night I crossed paths with the Crippled God. That, and your hints about the cold.'

The witch twisted to glare at Kilava. 'Bonecaster,' she snapped. 'Heed my words well – this warren is not to be assailed by you or your kin. You are to tell no-one of this, the final manifestation of Omtose Phellack.'

'I understand you, Witch. I begin, here, my own path to redemption, it seems. I have defied my own kin enough times to suffer few pangs doing so once more.' She turned to Quick Ben. 'And now, Wizard, I would leave. Will you guide us from this place?'

'No, better the Master of the Deck lead us out – that way, there'll be no trail.'

Paran blinked. 'Me?'

'Fashion a card, Captain. In your mind.'

'A card? Of what?'

The wizard shrugged. 'Think of something.'

Soldiers had drawn the three bodies to one side, covered them with standard-issue rain-capes. Gruntle saw Korlat standing near them, her back to him.

The Daru stood near the side closest to the trader road, beyond which, he could see, lay Itkovian. Motionless, forlorn in the distance.

The T'lan Imass were gone.

The surviving Grey Swords were slowly approaching Itkovian, on foot with the exception of one-eyed Anaster, who sat on his dray horse, seemingly unaffected by anything, including the massive floating mountain that loomed over the north ridge, throwing a deep shroud upon the parkland forest.

On the hilltop, facing the dark city, stood Caladan Brood, flanked by Humbrall Taur on his right, Hetan and Cafal on his left.

Gruntle could see, emerging in a ragged line from the north gate, Dujek's surviving army. There were so few left. Rhivi wagons were being driven into Coral, their beds cleared for the coming burden of bodies. Dusk was less than a bell away – the night ahead would be a long one.

A troop of Malazan officers, led by Dujek, had reached the base of the hill. Among them, a Seerdomin representing the now surrendered forces of the Domin.

Gruntle moved closer to where Brood and the Barghast waited.

The High Fist had heard the news – Gruntle could see it in his slumped shoulders, the way he repeatedly drew his lone hand down the length of his aged face, the spirit of the man so plainly, unutterably broken.

A warren opened to Brood's right. Emerging from it were a half-dozen Malazans, led by Artanthos. Bright, unsullied uniforms beneath grave expressions.

'Mortal Sword?'

Gruntle turned at the voice. One of the older women in his legion stood before him. 'Yes?'

'We would raise the Child's Standard, Mortal Sword.'

'Not here.'

'Sir?'

Gruntle pointed down to the killing field. 'There, among our fallen.'

'Sir, that is within the darkness.'

He nodded. 'So it is. Raise it there.'

'Aye, sir.'

'And no more of the titles or honorifics. The name's Gruntle. I'm a caravan guard, temporarily unemployed.'

'Sir, you are the Mortal Sword of Trake.'

His eyes narrowed on her.

Her gaze flicked away, down to the killing field. 'A title purchased in blood, sir.'

Gruntle winced, looked away, and was silent for a long moment. Then he nodded. 'All right. But I'm not a soldier. I hate war. I hate killing.' *And I never want to see another battlefield ever again.*

To that, she simply shrugged and set off to rejoin her meagre squad.

Gruntle returned his attention to the gathering of dignitaries.

Artanthos – Tayschrenn – was making introductions. Ambassador Aragan – a tall, battle-scarred man who seemed to be suffering from a headache – here to speak on behalf of Empress Laseen, regarding the governance of Black Coral. A handful of hangers-on.

Brood replied that the formal negotiations would have to await the arrival of Anomander Rake, who was expected shortly.

Gruntle's gaze returned to Dujek, who had just arrived with his officers. The High Fist's eyes were fixed on Korlat at the far end, and on the three covered bodies lying in the grasses. The rain still falling, the stench of burning heavy in the air, a shroud descending.

Aye, this day ends in ashes and rain.

In ashes and rain.

Running, memory's echo of glory and joy. He rode the sensation, the flight from pain, from prisons of bone, from massive arms damp and scaled, from a place without wind, without light, without warmth.

From chilled meat. Pale, boiled. Black, charred. From numbed, misshapen fingers pushing the morsels into a mouth that, as he chewed, filled with his own blood. From hard, cold stone with its patina of human grease.

Flesh fouled, the stench of smeared excrement—

Running—

An explosion of pain, swallowed in a sudden rush. Blood in veins. Breath drawn ragged – yet deep, deep into healthy lungs.

He opened his lone eye.

Toc looked around. He sat on a broad-backed horse. Grey-clad soldiers surrounded him, studying him from beneath war-worn helms.

I – I am . . . whole.

Hale.

I—

An armoured woman stepped forward. 'Would you leave your god, now, sir?'

My god? Dead flesh clothing, hard Jaghut soul – no, not a god. The Seer. Fear-clutched. Betrayal-scarred.

My god?

Running. Freed. The beast.

The wolf.

Togg.

My namesake . . .

'He has delivered you, sir, yet would make no demands. We know that your soul has run with the wolf-gods. But you are once more in the mortal realm. The body you now find yourself in was blessed. It is now yours. Still, sir, you must choose. Would you leave your gods?'

Toc studied his own arms, the muscles of his thighs. Long-fingered hands. He reached up, probed his face. A fresh scar, taking the same eye. No matter. He'd grown used to that. A young body – younger than he had been.

He looked down at the woman, then at the ring of soldiers. 'No,' he said.

The soldiers lowered themselves to one knee, heads bowing. The woman smiled. 'Your company welcomes you, Mortal Sword of Togg and Fanderay.'

Mortal Sword.

Then, I shall run once more . . .

In the Warren of Tellann, Lanas Tog led Silverfox to the edge of a broad valley. Filling it, the gathered clans of the T'lan Imass. Standing, motionless—

Yet different.

Unburdened?

Pain and regret filled her. *I have failed you all . . . in so many ways . . .*

Pran Chole strode forward. The undead Bonecaster tilted his head in greeting. 'Summoner.'

Silverfox realized she was trembling. 'Can you forgive me, Pran Chole?'

'Forgive? There is nothing to forgive, Summoner.'

'I'd never intended to deny your wish for very long – only until, until . . .'

1144

'We understand. You need not weep. Not for us, nor for yourself.'

'I – I will free you now, as I have done the T'lan Ay – I will end your Vow, Pran Chole, to free you . . . through Hood's Gate, as you wished.'

'No, Summoner.'

She stared, shocked silent.

'We have heard Lanas Tog, the warrior at your side. There are kin, Summoner, who are being destroyed on a continent far to the south. They cannot escape their war. We would travel there. We would save our brothers and sisters.

'Summoner, once this task is completed, we will return to you. Seeking the oblivion that awaits us.'

'Pran Chole . . .' Her voice broke. 'You would remain in your torment . . .'

'We must save our kin, Summoner, if we are so able. Within the Vow, our power remains. It will be needed.'

She slowly drew herself up, stilled her grief, her trembling. 'Then I will join you, Pran Chole. We. Nightchill, Tattersail, Bellurdan, and Silverfox.'

The Bonecaster was silent for a long moment, then he said, 'We are honoured, Summoner.'

Silverfox hesitated, then said, 'You are . . . changed. What has Itkovian done?'

A sea of bone-helmed heads bowed at mention of that name, and seeing that stole the breath from her lungs. *By the Abyss, what has that man done?*

Pran Chole was long in replying. 'Cast your eyes about you, Summoner. At the life now in this realm. Reach out and sense the power, here in the earth.'

She frowned. 'I do not understand. This realm is now home to the Beast Thrones. There are Rhivi spirits here . . . two wolf-gods . . .'

Pran Chole nodded. 'And more. You have, perhaps unwitting, created a realm where the Vow of Tellann unravels. T'lan Ay . . . now mortal once more – that gesture was easier than you had expected, was it not? Summoner, Itkovian freed our souls and found, in this realm you created, a place. For us.'

'You have been . . . *redeemed*!'

'Redeemed? No, Summoner. Only you are capable of that. The T'lan Imass have been awakened. Our memories – they live once more, in the earth beneath our feet. And they are what we will return to, the day you release us. Bonecaster – we expected nothing but oblivion, upon that release. We could not have imagined that an alternative was possible.'

'And now?' she whispered.

Pran Chole cocked his head. 'It surpasses us . . . what one mortal man so willingly embraced.' He swung about to make his way back down to the ranks, then paused and looked back at her. 'Summoner.'

'Yes.'

'One task awaits us . . . before we begin the long journey . . .'

Picker sat on a smoke-stained foundation stone, eyes dulled with exhaustion, and watched the Rhivi move through the rubble, seeking still more bodies. There were Pannion soldiers about, unarmed – seemingly the only citizens left in the city were either dead or gnawed down to little more than bones.

The Bridgeburners who had died within the keep had already left on a wagon – Picker and her meagre squad had retrieved most of them on the way out, even as the structure began to come down around them. A handful of other bodies had been found and recovered through sorcery, by the Tiste Andii, some of whom still lingered in the area, as if awaiting something, or someone. The only two no-one had yet found were Quick Ben and Paran, and Picker suspected it was because they weren't there.

Torches lit the area, feeble in their battling the un-natural darkness that shrouded the city. The air stank of smoke and mortar dust. Distant cries of pain rose every now and then, like haunting memories.

We were brittle. Destroyed months ago, outside Pale, it's just taken this long for the few of us left to realize it. Hedge, Trotts, Detoran. Corpses who kept saluting—

Blend spoke beside her. 'I told the Rhivi on our wagon to wait inside the north gate.'

Our wagon. The wagon carrying the dead Bridgeburners.

First in.

Last out.

For the last time.

A flash of light from the keep's rubble, a warren opening, through which figures emerged. A scarred hound – a cattle-dog, it looked like – followed by Lady Envy, and two Seguleh dragging a third masked warrior between them.

'Well,' Blend murmured, 'that about does it, doesn't it?'

Picker was unsure what Blend meant, did not pursue it.

Lady Envy had seen them. 'Lieutenant dear! What a relief to see you well. Could you believe the audacity of that white-haired, sword-stuffed—'

'Would you be referring to me?' a deep voice asked.

Through the gloom stepped Anomander Rake. 'Had I known you were within the keep, Lady Envy, I would have brought Moon's Spawn all the way down.'

'Oh, what a thing to say!'

'What are you doing here?' the Son of Darkness growled.

'Oh, this and that, my love. And aren't you looking very martial this afternoon – it's still afternoon, isn't it? Hard to tell here.'

'Oh,' Blend whispered, 'there's history between those two.'

'Really,' Picker quietly drawled, 'and how could you tell?' *Damned lady – not a scuff on that telaba. Now there's a different world from mine. Yet there we stood, side by side, in that hallway.*

Anomander Rake was eyeing the woman standing before him. 'What do you want, Envy?'

'Why, I have travelled half a continent, you ungrateful man, to deliver to you words of most vital import.'

'Let's hear them, then.'

Lady Envy blinked, looked around. 'Here, my love? Wouldn't you rather somewhere more . . . private?'

'No. I have things to do. Out with it.'

She crossed her arms. 'Then I will, though the gods know why I bother bravely retaining this generous mood of mine—'

'Envy.'

'Very well. Hear me, then, Wielder of Dragnipur. My dear father, Draconus, plots to escape the chains within the sword. How do I know? Blood whispers, Anomander.'

The Lord of Moon's Spawn grunted. 'I am surprised he's taken this long. Well, what of it?'

Envy's eyes went wide. 'Is this bravado madness? In case you've forgotten, we worked damned hard to slay him the *first* time!'

Picker glanced over at Blend, saw the woman standing slack-jawed as she stared at Rake and Envy.

'I don't recall you doing much,' Anomander Rake was saying, 'at the time. You stood by and watched the battle—'

'Precisely! And what do you think my father thought of *that?*'

The Lord of Moon's Spawn shrugged. 'He knew enough not to ask for your help, Envy. In any case, I heed your warning, but there is scant little I can do about it, at least until Draconus actually manages to free himself.'

The woman's dark eyes narrowed. 'Tell me, my dear, what – if anything – do you know of the Master of the Deck?'

Rake's brows rose. 'Ganoes Paran? The mortal who walked within Dragnipur? The one who sent the two Hounds of Shadow into Kurlad Galain's gate?'

Envy stamped her foot. 'You are insufferable!'

The Tiste Andii Lord turned away. 'We've spoken enough, Envy.'

'They will seek a way to break the sword!'

'Aye, they might.'

'Your very life totters on the whim of a mortal man!'

Anomander Rake paused, glanced back at her. 'I'd best step careful, then, hadn't I?' A moment later, he continued on, into the loose crowd of Tiste Andii.

Hissing in exasperation, Envy set off in pursuit.

Blend slowly faced Picker. 'Ganoes Paran? The captain?'

'Mull on it some other time,' Picker replied. 'Either way, in the end, it's nothing to do with us.' She slowly straightened. 'Gather 'em up, Blend. We're for the north gate.'

'Aye, sir. Shouldn't take long.'

'I'll be at the arch.'

'Lieutenant? Picker?'

'What?'

'You did what you could.'

'Wasn't good enough, was it?' Without waiting for a reply, Picker set off. Tiste Andii parted to either side to let her pass. She neared the blackened arch.

'A moment.'

Picker turned to see Anomander Rake approach.

Picker's eyes involuntarily shied from the Tiste Andii's hard, unhuman gaze.

'I would walk with you,' he said.

Unsettled by the attention, she glanced back at Lady Envy, who was now busy examining the unconscious Seguleh warrior. *You're a brave woman, Lady – you didn't even flinch.*

The Son of Darkness must have followed her gaze, for he sighed. 'I've no interest in resuming that particular conversation, Lieutenant. And should she decide to awaken that Seguleh – and given her present mood she just might – well, I'm not inclined to resume that old argument, either. I assume you and your squad are marching to the command position north of the city.'

Were we? I hadn't thought that far. She nodded.

'May I join you, then?'

Gods below! Picker drew a deep breath, then said, 'We're not pleasant company at the moment, Lord.'

'No indeed. Yet you are *worthy* company.'

She met his eyes at that, wondering.

He grimaced, then said, 'I regret my late arrival. Nor was I aware that there were Malazan soldiers within the keep.'

'It wouldn't have mattered, Lord,' Picker said, managing a shrug. 'From what I've heard, Dujek's companies weren't spared any for not being in the keep.'

Anomander Rake glanced away for a moment, eyes tightening. 'A sad conclusion to the alliance.'

The remaining Bridgeburners had drawn close, listening in silence. Picker was suddenly aware of them, of the words they had heard in this exchange, and the things left unsaid. 'That alliance,' she said, 'was solid as far as we were concerned.' *We. Us. The ones now standing before* you.

Perhaps he understood. 'Then I would walk with my allies, Lieutenant, one more time.'

'We would be honoured, sir.'

'To the command position north of the city.'

'Aye, sir.'

The Lord of the Tiste Andii sighed. 'There is a fallen soldier to whom I would . . . pay my respects . . .'

Aye, the saddest news we've heard yet this day. 'As will we all, Lord.'

Rake stayed at her side as she walked, the five surviving soldiers of the Bridgeburners falling in behind them.

She came to his side, her eyes, like his, on the figures gathering on the hilltop around them. 'Do you know what I wish?'

Gruntle shook his head. 'No, Stonny, what do you wish?'

'That Harllo was here.'

'Aye.'

'I'd settle for just his body, though. He belongs here, with

1150

these other fallen. Not under a small pile of stones in the middle of nowhere.'

Harllo, were you the first death in this war? Did our ragged troop represent the first allies to join the cause?

'Do you remember the bridge?' Stonny asked. 'All busted down, Harllo fishing from the foundation stones. We saw Moon's Spawn, didn't we? South horizon, drifting east. And now, here we are, in that damn thing's shadow.'

Caladan Brood and Dujek were approaching Korlat, who had remained standing over the three covered bodies. Two steps behind them, Tayschrenn, the sorcerous patina of youth gone from him.

There was an unnatural hush in the dark air, through which their voices easily carried.

Dujek had stepped past Korlat to kneel before the three fallen Malazans. 'Who was here?' he grated, hand reaching up to rub at his own face. 'Who saw what happened?'

'Myself,' Korlat replied without inflection. 'And Tayschrenn. The moment Silverfox appeared, Kallor struck the two of us down first, ensuring that we would be incapable of reacting. I do not think he anticipated that Whiskeyjack and the two marines would step into his path. They delayed him long enough for Tayschrenn to recover. Kallor was forced to flee to his new master – the Crippled God.'

'Whiskeyjack crossed swords with Kallor?' Dujek drew the rain-cape away from Whiskeyjack's body, silently studied his friend. 'This shattered leg – was it responsible ...'

Gruntle saw Korlat – who still stood behind Dujek – hesitate, then she said, 'No, High Fist. It broke after the mortal blow.'

After a long moment, Dujek shook his head. 'We kept telling him to have it properly healed. "Later," he'd say. Always "later". Are you certain, Korlat? That it broke after?'

'Yes, High Fist.'

Dujek frowned, eyes fixed on the dead soldier before him. 'Whiskeyjack was a superb swordsman . . . used to spar with Dassem Ultor and it'd take a while for Dassem to get past his guard.' He glanced back over his shoulder, at Korlat, then at Tayschrenn. 'And with the two marines on his flanks . . . how long, High Mage, until you recovered?'

Tayschrenn grimaced, shot Korlat a glance, then said, 'Only moments, Dujek. Moments . . . too late.'

'High Fist,' Korlat said, 'Kallor's prowess with the blade . . . he is a formidable warrior.'

Gruntle could see the frown on Dujek's face deepening.

Stonny muttered under her breath, 'This doesn't sound right. That broken leg must've come first.'

He reached out and gripped her arm, then shook his head. *No, Korlat must have a reason for this. This . . . deceit.*

Stonny's eyes narrowed, but she fell silent.

With a rough sigh, Dujek straightened. 'I have lost a friend,' he said.

For some reason, the raw simplicity of that statement struck through to Gruntle's heart. He felt an answering stab of pain, of grief, within him.

Harllo . . . my friend.

Itkovian . . .

Gruntle turned away, blinking rapidly.

Anomander Rake had arrived, the Great Raven Crone flapping desultorily from his path. Beside the Son of Darkness, Picker. Gruntle saw other Bridgeburners behind them: Blend, Mallet, Antsy, Spindle, Bluepearl. Armour in tatters, old blood crusting them, and all the life gone from their eyes.

On the slopes, now, were gathered the survivors of Onearm's Host. Gruntle judged less than a thousand. Beyond them, Barghast and Rhivi, Tiste Andii and the rest of Brood's army. Silent, standing to honour the fallen.

The healer, Mallet, strode straight to where Whiskeyjack's body lay.

Gruntle saw the healer's eyes study the wounds, saw the

1152

truth strike home. The large man staggered back a step, arms wrapping around himself, and seemed to inwardly collapse. Dujek closed on him in time to take his weight, ease him into a sitting position on the ground.

Some wounds never heal, and that man has just taken such a wounding. Would that Dujek had left Whiskeyjack hidden beneath the rain-cape . . .

Anomander Rake was at Korlat's side. He said nothing for a long time, then he turned away. 'Korlat, how will you answer this?'

She replied tonelessly, 'Orfantal makes ready, Lord. We will hunt Kallor down, my brother and I.'

Rake nodded. 'When you do, leave him alive. He has earned Dragnipur.'

'We shall, Lord.'

The Son of Darkness then faced the others. 'High Fist Dujek. High Mage Tayschrenn. Moon's Spawn is dying, and so has been abandoned by my people. It shall be sent eastward, over the ocean – the power within it is failing, and so it will soon settle beneath the waves. I ask that these three fallen Malazans – slain by a betrayer delivered here by myself and Caladan Brood – these three Malazans, be interred in Moon's Spawn. It is, I believe, a worthy sarcophagus.'

No-one spoke.

Rake then looked at Picker. 'And I ask that the dead among the Bridgeburners be interred there, as well.'

'Is there room for *all* our fallen?' Picker asked.

'Alas, no. Most of the chambers within are flooded.'

Picker drew a deep breath, then glanced at Dujek.

The High Fist seemed incapable of making a decision. 'Has anyone seen Captain Paran?'

No-one replied.

'Very well. As to the disposition of the fallen Bridgeburners, the decision is yours, Lieutenant Picker.'

'They were always curious about what was inside Moon's Spawn,' she said, managing a wry grin. 'I think that would please them.'

1153

In the supply camp haphazardly assembled in the parkland north of the killing field, at one edge, the seven hundred and twenty-two Mott Irregulars were slowly gathering, each one carrying burlap sacks stuffed with loot taken from the city.

Leaning against a tree was a massive table, flipped over to reveal the painted underside. The legs had snapped off some time in the past, but that had simply made it easier to transport.

The painted image had been glowing for some time before anyone noticed, and a substantial crowd had gathered to stare at it by the time the warren within the image opened, and out stepped Paran and Quick Ben, followed by a short, robustly muscled woman with black hair.

All three were sheathed in frost, which began to fade immediately as the warren closed behind them.

One of the Mott Irregulars stepped forward. 'Greetings. I am High Marshal Jib Bole, and something's confusing me.'

Paran, still shivering from Omtose Phellack's brutally cold air, stared at the man for a moment, then shrugged. 'And what's that, High Marshal?'

Jib Bole scratched his head. 'Well, that's a table, not a door . . .'

A short while later, as Paran and Quick Ben made their way through the dusk towards the killing field, the wizard softly laughed.

The captain glanced over at him. 'What?'

'Backwoods humour, Paran. Comes with talking with the scariest mages we've ever faced.'

'Mages?'

'Well, maybe that's the wrong name for them. Warlocks might be better. Swamp-snuffling warlocks. With bits of bark in their hair. Get them into a forest and you won't find them unless they want you to. Those Bole brothers, they're the worst of the lot, though I've heard that there's a lone sister among them who you wouldn't want to meet, ever.'

Paran shook his head.

Kilava had departed their company immediately after their arrival. She had offered the two men a simple word of thanks, which Paran sensed was in itself an extraordinary lowering of her guard, then had slipped into the gloom of the forest.

The captain and the wizard reached the trader track and could see it straightening and climbing towards the ridge that faced the killing field and the city beyond. Moon's Spawn hung almost directly above them, shedding misty rain. A few fires still lit Coral, but it seemed that the darkness that was Kurald Galain was somehow smothering them.

He could not push the recent events from his mind. He was unused to being the hand of ... *redemption*. The deliverance of the Jaghut child from the wounded portal of Morn had left him numb.

So long ago, now ... outside Pale. I'd felt her, felt this child, trapped in her eternal pain, unable to comprehend what she had done to deserve what was happening to her. She had thought she was going to find her mother – so Kilava had told her. She had been holding her brother's hand—

And then it had all been torn away.

Suddenly alone.

Knowing only pain.

For thousands of years.

Quick Ben and Talamandas had done something to the child, had worked their sorcery to take from her all memory of what had happened. Paran had sensed Hood's direct involvement in that – only a god could manage such a thing, not a simple blocking of memories, but an absolute taking away, a cleansing of the slate.

Thus. The child had lost her brother. Had found an uncle instead.

But not a kindly one. The Seer carries his own wounds, after all ...

And now Burn's realm had found new denizens. Was now home to an ancient warren.

'Memories,' Quick Ben had said, 'of ice. There is heat within this chaotic poison – heat enough to destroy these servants. I needed to find a way to slow the infection, to weaken the poison.

'I'd warned the Crippled God, you know. Told him I was stepping into his path. We've knocked him back, you know . . .'

Paran smiled to himself at the recollection. The ego of gods was as nothing to Quick Ben's. Even so, the wizard had earned the right to some fierce satisfaction, hadn't he? They had stolen the Seer from under Anomander Rake's nose. They had seen an ancient wrong righted, and were fortunate enough to have Kilava present, to partake of the redemption. They had removed the threat of the Seer from this continent. And, finally, through the preservation of Omtose Phellack, they had slowed the Crippled God's infection to a turgid crawl.

And we gave a child her life back.

'Captain,' Quick Ben murmured, a hand reaching up to touch his shoulder.

Ahead, beyond the last of the trees, a mass of figures, covering the slopes of a broad, flat-topped hill. Torches like wavering stars.

'I don't like the feel of this,' the wizard muttered.

When the darkness dissipated, the bodies were gone, those on the hilltop and those on the bed of the wagon that Picker and her soldiers had guided onto the side of the road below. There had been nothing elaborate to the interment. The disposition of the fallen within the massive, floating edifice was left to the Tiste Andii, to Anomander Rake himself.

Gruntle turned and looked up to study Moon's Spawn. Leaning drunkenly, it drifted seaward, blotting the brightening stars that had begun painting the land silver. The night's natural darkness would soon swallow it whole.

As Moon's Spawn drew its shadow after it, there was

revealed, on the ridge on the other side of the trader road, a small gathering of soldiers, positioned in a half-circle around a modest bier and a pile of stones.

It was a moment before Gruntle understood what he was seeing. He reached out and drew Stonny closer to him. 'Come on,' he whispered.

She did not protest as he led her from the hill, down the slope, through silent, ghostly ranks that parted to let them pass. Over the road, across the shallow ditch, then onto the slope leading to the ridge.

Where the remaining hundred or so Grey Swords stood to honour the man who had once been Fener's Shield Anvil.

Someone was following at a distance behind Gruntle and Stonny, but neither turned to see who it was.

They reached the small gathering.

Uniforms had been scrubbed clean, weapons polished. Gruntle saw, in the midst of the mostly Capan women and gaunt Tenescowri recruits, Anaster, still astride his horse. The Mortal Sword's feline eyes thinned on the strange, one-eyed young man. *No, he is not as he was. No longer . . . empty. What has he become, that he now feels like my . . . rival?*

The Destriant stood closest to the still form on the bier, and seemed to be studying Itkovian's death-pale face. On the other side of the bier a shallow pit had been excavated, earth heaped on one side, boulders on the other. A modest grave awaited Itkovian. Finally, the Capan woman turned.

'We mark the death of this man, whose spirit travels to no god. He has walked through Hood's Gate, and that is all. Through. To stand alone. He will not relinquish his burden, for he remains in death as he was in life. Itkovian, Shield Anvil of Fener's Reve. Remember him.'

As she made to gesture for the interment to begin, someone stepped round Gruntle and Stonny, and approached the Destriant.

A Malazan soldier, holding a cloth-wrapped object under

one arm. In halting Daru, he said, 'Please, Destriant, I seek to honour Itkovian . . .'

'As you wish.'

'I would do . . . something else, as well.'

She cocked her head. 'Sir?'

The Malazan removed the cloth to reveal Itkovian's helm. 'I – I did not wish to take advantage of him. Yet – he insisted that he fared better in the exchange. Untrue, Destriant. You can see that. Anyone can. See the helm he wears – it was mine. I would take it back. He should be wearing his own. This one . . .'

The Destriant swung round, looked down at the body once more, said nothing for a long moment, then she shook her head. 'No. Sir, Itkovian would refuse your request. Your gift pleased him, sir. None the less, if you have now decided that the helmet you gave to him is indeed of greater value, then he would not hesitate in returning it to . . .' She was turning as she spoke, and, her gaze travelling to the now weeping soldier, then past to something beyond them all, her words trailed away to silence.

Gruntle saw the young woman's eyes slowly widen.

The Grey Swords' Shield Anvil suddenly pivoted in a soft clatter of armour, then, a moment later, the other soldiers followed suit.

As did Gruntle and Stonny.

The lone Malazan had been but the first. Beneath the silver starlight, every surviving soldier of Dujek's Host had marched to position themselves at the base of the ridge's slope, forming ranks. Flanked by Tiste Andii, Rhivi, Barghast, Black Moranth – a vast sweep of figures, standing silent—

—and then Gruntle's scan continued eastward, down to the killing field, and there, once more, were the T'lan Imass, and they too were coming forward.

Silverfox stood off to the far side, watching.

The Grey Swords, stunned into silence, slowly parted as the first of the T'lan Imass reached the ridge.

A Bonecaster came first, holding in one hand a battered seashell hanging from a leather thong. The undead creature halted and said to the Destriant, 'For the gift this mortal has given us, we shall each offer one in turn. Together, they shall become his barrow, and it shall be unassailable. If you refuse us this, we will defy you.'

The Destriant shook her head. 'No, sir,' she whispered. 'There will be no refusal.'

The Bonecaster walked up to Itkovian, laid the shell down on the man's chest.

Gruntle sighed. *Ah, Itkovian, it seems you have made yet more friends.*

The solemn procession of modest gifts – at times nothing more than a polished stone, carefully set down on the growing pile covering the body – continued through the night, the stars completing their great wheel in the sky until fading at last to dawn's light.

When the Malazan soldier added Itkovian's helmet to the barrow, a second wave began, as soldier after soldier ascended the slope to leave the man a gift. Sigils, diadems, rings, daggers.

Through it all, Gruntle and Stonny stood to one side, watching. As did the Grey Swords.

With the last soldiers leaving the hill, Gruntle stirred. He stared at the massive, glittering barrow, seeing the faint emanation of Tellann sorcery that would keep it intact – every object in its place, immovable – then reached up with his left hand. A soft click, and the torcs fell free.

Sorry, Treach. Learn to live with the loss.

We do.

The gloom remained, suffusing the entire city of Coral, as the sun edged clear over the seas to the east. Paran stood with Quick Ben. They had both watched the procession, but had not moved from their position on the hill. They had watched Dujek join the silent line of gift-givers, one soldier honouring another.

1159

The captain felt diminished by his inability to follow suit. In his mind, the death of Whiskeyjack had left him too broken to move. He and Quick Ben had arrived too late, had been unable to stand with the others in formal acknowledgement – Paran had not believed that so simple a ritual possessed such importance within himself. He had attended funerals before – even as a child in Unta, there had been solemn processions where he walked with his sisters, his mother and father, to eventually stand before a crypt in the necropolis, as some elder statesman's wrapped corpse was delivered into the hands of his ancestors. Ceremonies through which he had fidgeted, feeling nothing of grief for a man he had never met. Funerals had seemed pointless. Hood had already taken the soul, after all. Weeping before an empty body had seemed a waste of time.

His mother, his father. He had not been there for either funeral, had believed himself sufficiently comforted by the knowledge that Tavore would have ensured noble ceremony, proper respect.

Here, the soldiers had kept ceremony to a minimum. Simply standing at attention, motionless, each alone with their thoughts, their feelings. Yet bound together none the less. The binding that was shared grief.

And he and Quick Ben had missed it, had come too late. Whiskeyjack's body was gone. And Ganoes Paran was bereft, his heart a vast cavern, dark, echoing with emotions he would not, could not show.

He and the wizard, silent, stared at Moon's Spawn as it drifted ever farther eastward, out over the sea, now a third of a league distant. It rode low in the air, and some time soon – perhaps a month from now – it would touch the waves, somewhere in the ocean, and then, as water rushed once more into the fissures, filling the chambers within, Moon's Spawn would sink. Down, beneath the insensate seas . . .

No-one approached them.

Finally, the wizard turned. 'Captain.'

'What is it, Quick Ben?'

'Moon's Spawn. Draw it.'

Paran frowned, then his breath caught. He hesitated, then crouched down, hand reaching to wipe smooth a small span of earth. With his index finger he etched a round-cornered rectangle, then, within it, a rough but recognizable outline. He studied his work for a moment, then looked up at Quick Ben and nodded.

The wizard took a handful of Paran's cloak in one hand, said, 'Lead us through.'

Right. Now how do I do that? Study the card, Paran – no, that alone will land us on its damned surface, a short but no doubt thoroughly fatal fall to the waves below. A chamber, Picker said. Rake's throne room. Think darkness. Kurald Galain, a place unlit, silent, a place with cloth-wrapped corpses . . .

Eyes closed, Paran stepped forward, dragging Quick Ben with him.

His boot landed on stone.

He opened his eyes, saw nothing but inky blackness, but the air smelled . . . different. He moved forward another step, heard Quick Ben's sigh behind him. The wizard muttered something and a fitful globe of light appeared above them.

A high-ceilinged chamber, perhaps twenty paces wide and more than forty paces long. They had arrived at what seemed the formal entrance – behind them, beyond an arched threshold, was a hallway. Ahead, at the far end of the chamber, a raised dais.

The huge, high-backed chair that had once commanded that dais had been pushed to one side, two of its legs on a lower step, the throne leaning. On the centre of the dais three black-wood sarcophagi now resided.

Along the length of the approach, to either side, were additional sarcophagi, upright, on which black-webbed sorcery played.

Quick Ben hissed softly through his teeth. ''Ware the looter who penetrates this place.'

Paran studied the sorcery's soft dance over the unadorned sarcophagi. 'Wards?' he asked.

'That, and a lot more, Captain. But we need not be worried. The Bridgeburners are within these ones flanking the approach. Oh, and one Black Moranth.' He pointed to a sarcophagus that, to Paran's eyes, looked no different from all the others. 'Twist. The poison in his arm took him a bell before the first wave of Dujek's companies.' Quick Ben slowly walked towards another sarcophagus. 'In here . . . what was left of Hedge. Not much. The bastard blew himself up with a cusser.' The wizard stopped to stand before the coffin. 'Picker described it well, Hedge. And I will tell Fiddler. Next time I see him.' He was silent a moment longer, then he turned to Paran with a grin. 'I can picture him, his soul, crouching at the base of Hood's Gate, driving a cracker between the stones . . .'

Paran smiled, but it was a struggle. He set off towards the dais. The wizard followed.

Quick Ben spoke names in a soft voice as they proceeded. 'Shank . . . Toes . . . Detoran . . . Aimless . . . Runter . . . Mulch . . . Bucklund . . . Story . . . Liss . . . Dasalle . . . Trotts – uh, I would've thought the Barghast . . . no, I suppose not. He was as much a Bridgeburner as the rest of us. Behind that lid, Paran, he's still grinning . . .'

As they walked, Quick Ben spoke aloud every name of those they passed. Thirty-odd Bridgeburners, Paran's fallen command.

They reached the dais.

And could go no further. Sorcery commanded the entire platform, a softly coruscating web of Kurald Galain.

'Rake's own hand,' the wizard murmured. 'These . . . spells. He worked alone.'

Paran nodded. He had heard the same from Picker, but he understood Quick Ben's need to talk, to fill the chamber with his echoing voice.

'It was his leg, you know. Gave out at the wrong moment. Probably a lunge . . . meaning he had Kallor. Had him dead. He would never have extended himself so fully otherwise. That damned leg. Shattered in that garden in Darujhistan. A marble pillar, toppling . . . and Whiskeyjack was just standing in the wrong place at the wrong time.

'From then . . . to this.'

And now, Picker and the others are watching Mallet. Every moment, someone's hovering close. The healer might try to fall on his knife at any time . . . given the chance. Ah, Mallet, he kept pushing you away. 'Another time, I've too much on my mind right now. Nothing more than a dull ache. When this is done, we'll get to it, then.' It wasn't your fault, Mallet. Soldiers die.

He watched Quick Ben remove a small pebble from his pouch and lay it on the floor in front of the dais. 'I may want to visit later,' he said, offering Paran a faint, sad smile. 'Me and Kalam . . .'

Oh, Wizard . . .

Paran lifted his gaze to the three sarcophagi. He did not know which one held whom. For some reason, that didn't matter much. Whiskeyjack and two marines – *they were there for Tattersail, at the last.*

Always an even exchange, sorceress.

'I am ready to leave them, now, Captain.'

Paran nodded.

They turned and slowly retraced their steps.

Reaching the arched entrance, they stopped.

Quick Ben glanced into the hallway. 'They left everything, you know.'

'What? Who?'

'Rake. The Tiste Andii. Left their possessions. Everything.'

'Why would they do that? They are to settle in Black Coral, aren't they? The city's been stripped clean . . .'

Quick Ben shrugged. 'Tiste Andii,' he said, in a tone that silently added: *we'll never know.*

A vague portal took shape before them.

The wizard grunted. 'You've certainly a particular style with these things, Captain.'

Yes, the style of awkward ignorance. 'Step through, Wizard.'

He watched Quick Ben vanish within the portal. Then Paran turned, one last time, to look upon the chamber. The globe of light was fast dimming.

Whiskeyjack, for all that you have taught me, I thank you. Bridgeburners, I wish I could have done better by you. Especially at the end. At the very least, I could have died with you.

All right, it's probably far too late. But I bless you, one and all.

With that, he turned back, stepped through the portal.

In the silent chamber, the light faded, the globe flickering, then finally vanishing.

But a new glow had come to the chamber. Faint, seeming to dance with the black web on the sarcophagi.

A dance of mystery.

The carriage of bone clattered its way down the trader road, Emancipor flicking the traces across the broad, midnight backs of the oxen.

Gruntle, halfway across the road, stopped, waited.

The manservant scowled, reluctantly halted the carriage. He thumped one fist on the wall behind him, the reptilian skin reverberating like a war drum.

A door opened and Bauchelain climbed out, followed by Korbal Broach.

Bauchelain strode to stand opposite Gruntle, but his flat grey eyes were focused on the dark city beyond. 'Extraordinary,' he breathed. 'This – this is a place I could call home.'

Gruntle's laugh was harsh. 'You think so? There are Tiste Andii there, now. More, it is now a part of the Malazan Empire. Do you believe that either will tolerate your friend's hobbies?'

'He's right,' Korbal Broach whined from beside the carriage. 'I won't have any fun there.'

Bauchelain smiled. 'Ah, but Korbal, think of all the fresh corpses. And look to this field below. K'Chain Che'Malle, already conveniently dismembered – manageable portions, if you will. Enough material, dear colleague, to build an entire estate.'

Gruntle watched Korbal Broach suddenly smile.

Gods, spare me the sight of that – never again, please.

'Now, barbed Captain,' Bauchelain said, 'kindly remove yourself from our path. But first, if you would be so kind, a question for you.'

'What?'

'I have but recently received a note. Terrible penmanship, and worse, written on bark. It would seem that a certain Jib Bole and his brothers wish to pay me a visit. Are you, by any chance, knowledgeable of these good sirs? If so, perhaps some advice on the proper etiquette of hosting them . . .'

Gruntle smiled. 'Wear your best, Bauchelain.'

'Ah. Thank you, Captain. And now, if you would . . .'

With a wave, Gruntle resumed crossing the road.

The Grey Swords had established a temporary encampment fifty paces east of the massive, glittering barrow that had already acquired the name of Itkovian's Gift. Ragged bands of Tenescowri, emaciated and sickly, had emerged from Black Coral, and from the woodlands, and were all congregating around the camp. Word of Anaster's . . . rebirth had spread, and with it the promise of salvation.

Recruitment. Those Tenescowri could never go back to what they had once been. They, too, need to be reborn. The stranger within Anaster – this new Mortal Sword of Togg and Fanderay – has much to do . . .

Time had come for Gruntle to take the man's measure. *He'll likely prove a better Mortal Sword than I am. Likely smug, sanctimonious up there on that damned ugly horse. Aye, I'm ready to hate the bastard, I admit it.*

1165

Gruntle approached Anaster, who was guiding his horse through the decrepit camp of Tenescowri. Stick-limbed figures were reaching up on all sides, touching him, his horse. Trailing a half-dozen paces behind walked the Destriant, and Gruntle could feel healing sorcery swirling out from her – the embrace of the Wolf's Reve had begun.

Anaster finally rode clear of the camp. His lone eye noted Gruntle and the man reined in, waited for the Daru.

He spoke before Gruntle had a chance to do the same, 'You're Gruntle, Trake's Mortal Sword. The Destriant has told me about you. I'm glad you've come.' Anaster glanced back at the Tenescowri, who hung back, within their encampment, as if its edge was some kind of invisible, impassable barrier, then the young man dismounted. 'The Shield Anvil insisted I remain visible,' he grunted, wincing as he stretched his legs. 'Much more of this and I'll start walking like a Wickan.'

'You said you are glad that I've come,' Gruntle rumbled. 'Why?'

'Well, you're a Mortal Sword, right? They're calling me one, too. I guess, uh, well. What does that mean, anyway?'

'You don't know?'

'No. Do you?'

Gruntle said nothing for a long moment, then he grinned. 'Not really.'

The tension left Anaster in a heartfelt sigh. He stepped close. 'Listen. Before this – uh, before I arrived in this body, I was a scout in the Malazan army. And as far as I was concerned, temples were where poor people paid to keep the priests' wine cellars well stocked. I don't want followers. That Destriant back there, the Shield Anvil – gods, what a hard woman! They're piling expectations on me – I'm feeling like that man Itkovian is feeling right now, not that he's feeling anything, I suppose. Hood, just mentioning his name breaks my heart and I never even knew him.'

'I did, Anaster. Relax, lad – about everything. Did you think I *asked* to be Trake's Mortal Sword? I was a caravan guard, and a miserable one and I was happy with it—'

'You were happy being miserable?'

'Damned right I was.'

Anaster suddenly smiled. 'I stumbled on a small cask of ale – it's back in the camp of the Grey Swords. We should go for a walk, Gruntle.'

'Under the trees, aye. I'll find Stonny – a friend. You'll like her, I think.'

'A woman? I like her already. I'll get the ale, meet you back here.'

'A sound plan, Anaster. Oh, and don't tell the Destriant or the Shield Anvil—'

'I won't, even if they torture me . . .' His voice fell away, and Gruntle saw the young man grow paler than usual. Then he shook his head. 'See you soon, friend.'

'Aye.' *Friend . . . Yes, I think so.*

He watched Anaster swing back onto the horse – the man he had been knew how to ride.

No, not the man he had been. The man he is. Gruntle watched him riding away for a moment longer, then turned back to find Stonny.

Steam or smoke still drifted from the four Trygalle Trade Guild carriages waiting at the base of the hill. Quick Ben had gone ahead to speak with the train's master – an opulently dressed, overweight man whose bone-deep exhaustion was discernible from fifty paces away.

Paran, waiting with the Bridgeburners for Dujek on the crest of the hill, watched the wizard and the Trygalle mage engaging in a lengthy conversation the result of which seemed to leave Quick Ben bemused. The Daru, Kruppe, then joined them, and the discussion resumed once more. Heatedly.

'What's all that about?' Picker wondered beside the captain.

Paran shook his head. 'I have no idea, Lieutenant.'

'Sir.'

Something in her tone brought him round. 'Yes?'

'You shouldn't have left me in command – I messed it up, bad, sir.'

He saw the raw pain in her eyes, continued to meet them despite a sudden desire to look away. 'Not you, Lieutenant. The command was mine, after all. I abandoned all of you.'

She shook her head. 'Quick's told us what you two did, Captain. You went where you had to, sir. It was well played. It'd seemed to us that there was no victory to be found, in any of this, but now we know that's not true – and that means more than you might realize.'

'Lieutenant, you walked out of that keep with survivors. No-one could have done better.'

'I agree,' a new voice growled.

Dujek's appearance shocked both soldiers to silence. The man seemed to have aged ten years in the span of a single day and night. He was bent, the hand of his lone arm trembling. 'Lieutenant, call the Bridgeburners over. I would speak to you all.'

Picker turned and gestured the five soldiers closer.

'Good,' the High Fist grunted. 'Now, hear me. There's half a wagon of back pay being loaded onto one of those Trygalle carriages below. Back pay for the company known as the Bridgeburners. Full complement. Enough to buy each of you an estate and a life of well-earned idyll. The Trygalle will take you to Darujhistan – I don't recommend you head back to the Empire. As far as Tayschrenn and Fist Aragan and I are concerned, not one Bridgeburner walked out of that keep. No, say not a single word, soldiers – Whiskeyjack wanted this for you. Hood, he wanted it for himself, too. Respect that.

'Besides, you've one more mission, and it takes you to Darujhistan. The Trygalle has delivered someone. He's presently in the care of the High Alchemist, Baruk. The man's not well – he needs you, I think. Malazans. Soldiers. Do what you can for him when you're there, and when you

1168

decide that you can't do anything more, then walk away.'

Dujek paused, eyed them, then nodded and said, 'That's all, Bridgeburners. The Trygalle are waiting for you. Captain, remain a moment – I would a private word with you. Oh, Picker, send High Mage Quick Ben up here, will you?'

Picker blinked. 'High Mage?'

Dujek grimaced. 'That bastard can't hide any longer. Tayschrenn's insisted.'

'Yes, sir.'

Paran watched the small troop head down the hill.

Dujek drew a palsied hand across his face, turned away. 'Walk with me, Paran.'

Paran did. 'That was well done, sir.'

'No, it wasn't, Ganoes, but it was all I could do. I don't want the last of the Bridgeburners to die on some field of battle, or in some nameless city that's fighting hard to stay free. I'm taking what's left of my Host to Seven Cities, to reinforce Adjunct Tavore's retributive army. You are welcome—'

'No, sir. I'd rather not.'

Dujek nodded, as if he had expected that. 'There's a dozen or so columns for you, near the carriages below. Go with your company, then, with my blessing. I'll have you counted among the casualties.'

'Thank you, High Fist. I don't think I was ever cut out to be a soldier.'

'Not another word of that, Captain. Think what you like about yourself, but we will continue seeing you as you are – a noble man.'

'Noble—'

'Not that kind of noble, Ganoes. This is the kind that's earned, the only kind that means anything. Because, in this day and age, it's damned rare.'

'Well, sir, there I'll respectfully disagree with you. If there's but one experience I will carry with me of my time in this campaign, High Fist, it is that of being humbled, again and again, by those around me.'

'Go join your fellow Bridgeburners, Ganoes Paran.'

'Yes, sir. Goodbye, High Fist.'

'Goodbye.'

As Paran made his way down the slope, he stumbled momentarily, then righted himself. *My fellow Bridgeburners, he said . . . well, the achievement is shortlived, but even so.*

I made it.

Ignoring the grim-faced soldiers on all sides, Toc – Anaster – reined in beside the small tent the Grey Swords had given him. *Aye, I remember Anaster, and this may be his body, but that's all.* He slipped from the saddle and entered it.

He hunted until he found the cask, hid it within a leather sack and slung that over a shoulder, then hurried back outside.

As he drew himself into the saddle once more, a man stepped up to him.

Toc frowned down at him. This was no Tenescowri, nor a Grey Sword. If anything, he looked, from his faded, tattered leathers and furs, to be Barghast.

Covered in scars – more scars of battle than Toc had ever seen on a single person before. Despite this, there was a comfort, there in his face – a gentleman's face, no more than twenty years of age, the features pronounced, heavy-boned, framed in long black hair devoid of any fetishes or braids. His eyes were a soft brown as he looked up at Toc.

Toc had never met this man before. 'Hello. Is there something you wish?' he asked, impatient to be away.

The man shook his head. 'I only sought to look upon you, to see that you were well.'

He believes me to be Anaster. A friend of old, perhaps – not one of his lieutenants, though – I would have remembered this one. Well, I'll not disappoint him. 'Thank you. I am.'

'This pleases me.' The man smiled, reached up and laid a hand on Toc's leg. 'I will go, now, brother. Know that I hold you in my memory.' Still smiling, he turned and strode away, passing through the midst of curious Grey Swords, heading north towards the forest.

Toc stared after him. *Something . . . something about that walk . . .*

'Mortal Sword—'

The Shield Anvil was approaching.

Toc gathered the reins. 'Not now,' he called out. 'Later.' He swung his horse round. 'All right, you wretched hag, let's see how you gallop, shall we?' He drove his heels into the beast's flanks.

His sister awaited him at the edge of the forest. 'You are done?' she asked him.

'I am.'

They continued on, under the trees. 'I have missed you, brother.'

'And I you.'

'You have no sword . . .'

'Indeed, I have not. Do you think I will need one?'

She leaned close to him. 'Now more than before, I would think.'

'Perhaps you are right. We must needs find a quarry.'

'The Barghast Range. A flint the colour of blood – I will invest it, of course, to prevent its shattering.'

'As you did once before, sister.'

'Long ago.'

'Aye, so very long ago.'

Under the impassive gaze of the two brothers, Lady Envy relinquished the sorcery that kept Mok from returning to consciousness. She watched as the Third slowly regained awareness, the eyes within the mask dulled with pain. 'There, now,' she murmured. 'You *have* suffered of late, haven't you?'

Mok struggled to sit upright, his gaze hardening upon finding his brothers.

Lady Envy straightened and glanced over at Senu and

1171

Thurule with an appraising eye. After a moment, she sighed. 'Indeed, they are a sight. They suffered in your absence, Third. Then again,' she noted brightly, 'you've not fared much better! I must inform you, Mok, that your mask has cracked.'

The Seguleh reached up, probed tentatively, finding then following the hairline fissure running two-thirds of the length on the left side.

Lady Envy continued, 'In fact, I reluctantly admit, none of our façades has survived ... unfractured. If you can imagine it, Anomander Rake – the Seventh – has unceremoniously banished us from the city.'

Mok climbed unsteadily to his feet, looked around.

'Yes,' Lady Envy said, 'we find ourselves in the very same forest we spent days trudging through. Your punitive exercise is concluded, perhaps satisfactorily, perhaps not. The Pannion Domin is no more, alas. Time's come, my three grim servants, to begin the journey home.'

Mok examined his weapons, then faced her. 'No. We shall demand an audience with the Seventh—'

'Oh, you foolish man! He'll not see you! Worse, you'll have to carve your way through a few hundred Tiste Andii to get to him – and no, they won't cross blades with you. They will simply annihilate you with sorcery. They're a perfunctory people, the Children of Mother Dark. Now, I have decided to escort the three of you home. Isn't that generous of me?'

Mok regarded her, the silence stretching.

Lady Envy offered him a sweet smile.

On their long journey north, the White Face Barghast broke up into clans, then family bands, ranging far and wide as was their wont. Hetan walked with Cafal, lagging behind their father and his closest followers and angling some distance eastward.

The sun was warm on their heads and shoulders, the air

fresh with the gentle surf brushing the shore two hundred paces to their right.

It was midday when she and her brother spotted the two travellers ahead. Close kin, Hetan judged as they drew nearer. Neither one particularly tall, but robust, both black-haired, walking very slowly side by side closer to the coastline.

They looked to be Barghast, but of a tribe or clan unknown to either Hetan or Cafal. A short while later they came alongside the two strangers.

Hetan's eyes focused on the man, studied the extra-ordinary scars crisscrossing his flesh. 'We greet you, strangers!' she called out.

Both turned, clearly surprised that they had company.

Hetan now looked upon the man's face. That the woman beside him was his sister could be no more obvious.

Good. 'You!' she called to the man, 'what is your name?'

The man's smile made her heart catch. 'Onos Toolan.'

Hetan strode closer, offering a wink to the dark-haired woman, then settling her eyes once more on the man called Onos Toolan. 'I see more than you imagine,' she said in a low voice.

The young warrior cocked his head. 'You do?'

'Aye, and what I see tells me you've not bedded a woman in a long time.'

The man's eyes widened – *oh, such lovely eyes, a lover's eyes* – 'Indeed,' he said, his smile broadening.

Oh yes, my lover's eyes . . .

1173

EPILOGUE

Paran shoved the door open. Shouldering his heavy, gold-filled pack, he stepped into the antechamber beyond.

'Raest! Where are you?'

The armour-clad Jaghut emerged from somewhere to halt before Paran, said nothing.

'That's right,' Paran muttered, 'I've decided to take up residence here.'

Raest's voice was a cold rasp, 'You have.'

'Aye. Three weeks in that damned inn was enough, believe me. So, here I am, courage worked up, ready to settle into the dreaded, infamous Finnest House – and I see your skills as housekeeper leave much to be desired.'

'These two bodies on the threshold – what will you do with them?'

Paran shrugged. 'I haven't decided yet. Something, I suppose. But, for now, I want to drop this gold off – so I can sleep easy for a change. They're opening the place up tonight, you know . . .'

The giant warrior replied, 'No, Master of the Deck, I do not.'

'Never mind. I said I'd go. Hood knows, I doubt anybody else in this city will, except maybe Kruppe, Coll and Murillio.'

'Go where, Master of the Deck?'

'Ganoes, please. Or Paran. Where, you ask? Picker's new tavern, that's where.'

'I know nothing of—'

'I know you don't, that's why I'm telling—'

'—nor do I care, Ganoes Paran, Master of the Deck.'

'Well, your loss, Raest. As I was saying, Picker's new tavern. Her and her partner's, that is. They've spent half their pay on this insane project.'

'Insane?'

'Yes – you don't know the meaning of insane?'

'I know it all too well, Ganoes Paran, Master of the Deck.'

Paran was brought up short by that. He studied the helmed face, seeing only shadows behind the visor's slots. A faint shiver ran through the Malazan. 'Uh, yes. In any case, they purchased the K'rul Temple, belfry and all. Made it into a—'

'A tavern.'

'A temple everyone in the city calls haunted.'

'I imagine,' Raest said, turning away, 'it came cheap, all things considered . . .'

Paran stared after the armoured Jaghut. 'See you later,' he called.

Faintly came the reply, 'If you insist . . .'

Emerging from the battered gateway onto the street, Paran almost stumbled over a decrepit, hooded figure sitting awkwardly on the edge of the gutter. A grimy hand lifted from the rags towards the Malazan.

'Kind sir! A coin, please! A single coin!'

'Luckily for you, I can spare more than one, old man.' Paran reached for the leather purse tucked into his belt. He drew out a handful of silvers.

The beggar grunted, dragged himself closer, his legs trailing like dead weights. 'A man of wealth! Listen to me. I have need of a partner, generous sir! I have gold. Councils! Hidden in a cache on the slopes of the Tahlyn Hills! A fortune, sir! We must needs only mount an expedition – it's not far.'

Paran dropped the coins into the old man's hands. 'Buried treasure, friend? No doubt.'

'Sir, the sum is vast, and I would gladly part with half of it – the repayment to your investment will be ten times at the very least.'

'I've no need for more riches.' Paran smiled. He stepped away from the beggar, then paused and added, 'By the way, you probably shouldn't linger overlong at this particular gate. The House does not welcome strangers.'

The old man seemed to shrink in on himself. His head twisted to one side. 'No,' he muttered from beneath his ragged hood, 'not *this* House.' Then he softly cackled. 'But I know one that does . . .'

Shrugging at the beggar's obscure words, Paran turned once more and set off.

Behind him, the beggar broke into a wretched cough.

Picker could not pull her eyes from the man. He sat hunched over, on a chair that had yet to find a table, still clutching in his hands the small rag of tattered cloth on which something had been written. The alchemist had done all he could to return life to what had been a mostly destroyed, desiccated body, and Baruk's talents had been stretched to their limits – there was no doubt of that.

She knew of him, of course. They all did. They all knew, as well, where he had come from.

He spoke not a word. Had not since the resurrection. No physical flaw kept him from finding his voice, Baruk had insisted.

The Imperial Historian had fallen silent. No-one knew why.

She sighed.

The grand opening of K'rul's Bar was a disaster. Tables waited, empty, forlorn in the massive main chamber. Paran,

1176

Spindle, Blend, Antsy, Mallet and Bluepearl sat at the one nearest the blazing hearth, barely managing a word among them. Nearby was the only other occupied table, at which sat Kruppe, Murillio and Coll.

And that's it. Gods, we're finished. We should never have listened to Antsy . . .

The front door swung open.

Picker looked over hopefully. But it was only Baruk.

The High Alchemist paused within the antechamber, then slowly made his way forward to where the other Daru sat.

'Dearest friend of honourable Kruppe! Baruk, stalwart champion of Darujhistan, could you ask for better company this night? Here, yes, at this very table! Kruppe was astonishing his companions – and indeed, these grim-faced ex-soldiers next to us – with his extraordinary account of Kruppe and this tavern's namesake, conspiring to fashion a new world.'

'Is the tale done, then?' Baruk asked as he approached.

'Just, but Kruppe would be delighted to—'

'Excellent. I'll hear it some other time, I suppose.' The High Alchemist glanced over at Duiker, but the Imperial Historian had not so much as even looked up. Head still bowed, eyes fixed on the cloth in his hands. Baruk sighed. 'Picker, have you mulled wine?'

'Aye, sir,' she said. 'Behind you, beside the hearth.'

Antsy reached for the clay jug, rose to pour Baruk a cup.

'All right,' Picker said in a loud voice, walking over. 'So, this is it. Fine. The fire's warm enough, we've drunk enough, and I for one am ready for some stories to be told – no, not you, Kruppe. We've heard yours. Now, Baruk here, and Coll and Murillio for that matter, might be interested in the tale of the final taking of Coral.'

Coll slowly leaned forward. 'So, you'll finally talk, will you? It's about time, Picker.'

'Not me,' she replied. 'Not to start, anyway. Captain?

Refill your cup, sir, and weave us a tale.'

The man grimaced, then shook his head. 'I'd like to, Picker.'

'Too close,' Spindle grumbled, nodding and turning away.

'Hood's breath, what a miserable bunch!'

'Sure,' Spindle snapped, 'a story to break our hearts all over again! What's the value in that?'

A rough, broken voice replied, 'There is value.'

Everyone fell silent, turned to Duiker.

The Imperial Historian had looked up, was studying them with dark eyes. 'Value. Yes. I think, much value. But not yours, soldiers. Not yet. Too soon for you. Too soon.'

'Perhaps,' Baruk murmured, 'perhaps you are right in that. We ask too much—'

'Of them. Yes.' The old man looked down once more at the cloth in his hands.

The silence stretched.

Duiker made no move.

Picker began to turn back to her companions – when the man began speaking. 'Very well, permit me, if you will, on this night. To break your hearts once more. This is the story of the Chain of Dogs. Of Coltaine of the Crow Clan, newly come Fist to the 7th Army . . .'

This ends the Third Tale of the
Malazan Book of the Fallen

GLOSSARY

Pannion Domin Terminology:

Pannion Seer: the political and spiritual leader of the Domin
Septarch: ruler of one of seven districts in Domin (also commands armies)
Urdo: commander of elite heavy infantry (Urdomen)
Urdomen: elite heavy infantry, fanatical followers of the Seer
Seerdomin: fanatical bodyguard and assassin sect of the Domin
Betaklites: medium infantry
Beklites: regular infantry (also known as the Hundred Thousand)
Betrullid: light cavalry
Betakullid: medium cavalry
Scalandi: skirmishers
Desandi: sappers
Tenescowri: the peasant army

In Capustan:

The Grey Swords: a mercenary cult hired to defend against the Pannion Domin
The Mask Council: High Priests of the Fourteen Ascendants represented in Capustan
The Gidrath: soldiers serving the fourteen temples
The Capanthall: Capustan's city garrison, under command of

Prince Jelarkan

The Coralessian Company: followers of exiled Prince Arard of Coral

Lestari Guard: refugee Palace Guard from the city of Lest

Capan: name for distinct self-contained neighbourhoods and people in Capustan

Daru Quarter: old town at centre of Capustan

The Thrall: old Daru keep now home to the Mask Council

The Fourteen Ascendants of Capustan's Mask Council:

Fener/Tennerock
Trake/Treach
D'rek
Hood
Burn
Togg
Beru
Mowri
Oponn
Soliel and Poliel
Queen of Dreams
Fanderay
Dessembrae
Shadowthrone

Peoples and Places

The Rhivi: pastoral nomadic society in central plains of Genabackis

The Barghast: a warrior caste tribe found on various continents:

Ilgres Clan

White Face Clan (including: Senan, Gilk, Ahkrata, Barahn, Nith'rithal)

T'lan Imass (the Armies of the Diaspora):
  Logros, Guardians of the First Throne
  Kron, First to the Gathering
  Betrule (lost)
  Ifayle (lost)
  Bentract (lost)
  Orshayn (lost)
  Kerluhm (lost)
Tiste Andii: an Elder Race
Jaghut: an Elder Race
K'Chain Che'Malle: one of the Four Founding Races, presumed extinct
Moranth: a highly regimented culture, centred in Cloud Forest
Daru: a cultural and linguistic group on Genabackis
Capan: a citizen of Capustan
Domin/Pannion: name for a new empire on Genabackis
Lestari: a citizen of Lest
Coralessian: a citizen of Coral
Morn: a ruined, haunted place on the southwest coast of Genabackis
Coral: a city in the Pannion Domin
Lest: a city in the Pannion Domin
Capustan: a city on the north side of the Catlin River
Darujhistan: last Free City on Genabackis
Lamatath Plain: plains to south of Darujhistan
Jhagra Til: T'lan Imass name for now-extinct inland sea

The world of sorcery

The Warrens (the Paths – those Warrens accessible to humans)

Denul: the Path of Healing
D'riss: The Path of Stone
Hood's Path: the Path of Death
Meanas: The Path of Shadow and Illusion
Ruse: the Path of the Sea

Rasham: The Path of Darkness
Serc: the Path of the Sky
Tennes: the Path of the Land
Thyr: the Path of Light

The Elder Warrens

Kurald Galain: the Tiste Andii Warren of Darkness
Kurald Emurlahn: the Tiste Edur Warren
Tellann: the T'lan Imass Warren
Omtose Phellack: the Jaghut Warren
Starvald Demelain: the Tiam Warren, the First Warren

The Deck of Dragons – The Fatid (and associated Ascendants)

High House Life
King
Queen (Queen of Dreams)
Champion
Priest
Herald
Soldier
Weaver
Mason
Virgin

High House Death
King (Hood)
Queen
Knight (once Dassem Ultor)
Magi
Herald
Soldier
Spinner
Mason
Virgin